I0784605

Clarence Mulford

Hopalong Cassidy & His Wild West Adventures – 7 Westerns in One Edition

OK Publishing 2021

Clarence Mulford

Hopalong Cassidy & His Wild West Adventures – 7 Westerns in One Edition

The Original Books Behind the Famous Movies Hero

Published by
MUSAICUM
Books

- Advanced Digital Solutions & High-Quality book Formatting -

musaicumbooks@okpublishing.info

2021 OK Publishing

ISBN 978-80-272-7634-9

Contents

Bar-20 — 17

Chapter I. Buckskin — 18

Chapter II. The Rashness of Shorty — 21

Chapter III. The Argument — 22

Chapter IV. The Vagrant Sioux — 27

Chapter V. The Law of the Range — 31

Chapter VI. Trials of the Convalescent — 37

Chapter VII. The Open Door — 39

Chapter VIII. Hopalong Keeps His Word — 43

Chapter IX. The Advent of McAllister — 49

Chapter. X. Peace Hath its Victories — 55

Chapter XI. Holding the Claim — 59

Chapter XII. The Hospitality of Travennes — 68

Chapter XIII. Travennes' Discomfiture — 71

Chapter XIV. The Tale of a Cigarette — 73

Chapter XV. The Penalty — 77

Chapter XVI. Rustlers on the Range — 80

Chapter XVII. Mr. Trendley Assumes Added Importance — 83

Chapter XVIII. The Search Begins — 85

Chapter XIX. Hopalong's Decision — 87

Chapter XX. A Problem Solved — 89

Chapter XXI. The Call — 92

Chapter XXII. The Showdown — 94

Chapter XXIII. Mr. Cassidy Meets a Woman — 97

Chapter XXIV. The Strategy of Mr. Peters — 100

Chapter XXV. Mr. Ewalt Draws Cards — 103

The Coming of Cassidy and Others — 111

Preface — 112

I. The Coming of Cassidy — 113

II. The Weasel — 118

III. Jimmy Price — 129

IV. Jimmy Visits Sharpsville — 136

V. The Luck of Fools — 142

VI. Hopalong's Hop — 150

VII. "Dealing the Odd" — 156

VIII. The Norther 161

IX. The Drive 167

X. The Hold-Up 174

XI. Sammy Finds a Friend 183

XII. Sammy Knows the Game 190

XIII. His Code 197

XIV. Sammy Hunts a Job 205

XV. When Johnny Sloped 211

Hopalong Cassidy 221

Chapter I. Antonio's Scheme 222

Chapter II. Mary Meeker Rides North 225

Chapter III. The Roundup 229

Chapter IV. In West Arroyo 235

Chapter V. Hopalong Asserts Himself 238

Chapter VI. Meeker is Told 241

Chapter VII. Hopalong Meets Meeker 243

Chapter VIII. On the Edge of the Desert 246

Chapter IX. On the Peak 250

Chapter X. Buck Visits Meeker 252

Chapter XI. Three is a Crowd 255

Chapter XII. Hobble Burns and Sleepers 259

Chapter XIII. Hopalong Grows Suspicious 261

Chapter XIV. The Compromise 262

Chapter XV. Antonio Meets Friends 266

Chapter XVI. The Feint 269

Chapter XVII. Pete is Tricked 271

Chapter XVIII. The Line House Re-captured 275

Chapter XIX. Antonio Leaves the H2 279

Chapter XX. What the Dam Told 284

Chapter XXI. Hopalong Rides South 289

Chapter XXII. Lucas Visits the Peak 294

Chapter XXIII. Hopalong and Red Go Scouting 297

Chapter XXIV. Red's Discomfiture 300

Chapter XXV. Antonio's Revenge 305

Chapter XXVI. Frisco Visits Eagle 310

Chapter XXVII. Shaw has Visitors 312

Chapter XXVIII. Nevada Joins Shaw 314

Chapter XXIX. Surrounded 316

Chapter XXX. Up the Wall 321

Chapter XXXI. Fortune Snickers at Doc 325

Chapter XXXII. Nature Takes a Hand 327

Chapter XXXIII. Doc Trails 332

Chapter XXXIV. Discoveries 335

Chapter XXXV. Johnny Takes the Hut 338

Chapter XXXVI. The Last Night 340

Chapter XXXVII. Their Last Fight 343

Chapter XXXVIII. A Disagreeable Task 345

Chapter XXXIX. Thirst 347

Chapter XL. Changes 348

Chapter XLI. Hopalong's Reward 349

Bar-20 Days 353

Chapter I. On a Strange Range 354

Chapter II. The Rebound 358

Chapter III. Dick Martin Starts Something 363

Chapter IV. Johnny Arrives 366

Chapter V. The Ghost of the San Miguel 370

Chapter VI. Hopalong Loses a Horse 373

Chapter VII. Mr. Cassidy Cogitates 378

Chapter VIII. Red Brings Trouble 381

Chapter IX. Mr. Holden Drops In 386

Chapter X. Buck Takes a Hand 391

Chapter XI. Hopalong Nurses a Grouch 394

Chapter XII. A Friend in Need 397

Chapter XIII. Mr. Townsend, Marshal 402

Chapter XIV. The Stranger's Plan 405

Chapter XV. Johnny Learns Something 411

Chapter XVI. The End of the Trail 414

Chapter XVII. Edwards' Ultimatum 418

Chapter XVIII. Harlan Strikes 422

Chapter XIX. The Bar-20 Returns 425

Chapter XX. Barb Wire 426

Chapter XXI. The Fence 430

Chapter XXII. Mr. Boggs is Disgusted 435

Chapter XXIII. Tex Ewalt Hunts Trouble 439

Chapter XXIV. The Master 445

Buck Peters, Ranchman 449

Chapter I. Tex Returns 450

Chapter II. H. Whitby Booth is Shown How 459

Chapter III. Buck Makes Friends 464

Chapter IV. The Foreman of the Double Y 472

Chapter V. "Comin' Thirty" has Notions 477

Chapter VI. An Honest Man and a Rogue 480

Chapter VII. The French Rose 483

Chapter VIII. Tex Joins the Enemy 486

Chapter IX. Any Means to an End 490

Chapter X. Introducing a Parasite 496

Chapter XI. The Man Outside 498

Chapter XII. A Hidden Enemy 501

Chapter XIII. Punctuation as a Fine Art 506

Chapter XIV. Fighting the Itch 509

Chapter XV. The Slaughter of the Innocents 514

Chapter XVI. The Master Mind 521

Chapter XVII. Hopalong's Night Ride 523

Chapter XVIII. Karl to the Rescue 528

Chapter XIX. The Weak Link 533

Chapter XX. Misplaced Confidence 536

Chapter XXI. Pickles Tries to Talk 540

Chapter XXII. "A Ministering Angel" 541

Chapter XXIII. Hopalong's Move 549

Chapter XXIV. The Rebellion of Cock Murray 553

Chapter XXV. Mary Receives Company 554

Chapter XXVI. Hunters and Hunted 558

Chapter XXVII. Points of the Compass 567

Chapter XXVIII. The Heart of a Rose 573

The Bar-20 Three 575

Chapter I. "Put a 'T' in it" 576

Chapter II. Well-known Strangers 581

Chapter III. A Question of Identity 585

Chapter IV. A Journey Continued 593

Chapter V. What the Storm Hid 599

Chapter VI. The Writing on the Wall ... 605

Chapter VII. The Third Man ... 608

Chapter VIII. Notes Compared ... 613

Chapter IX. Ways of Serving Notice ... 617

Chapter X. Twice in the Same Place ... 621

Chapter XI. A Job Well Done ... 624

Chapter XII. Friends on the Outside ... 630

Chapter XIII. Out and Away ... 634

Chapter XIV. The Staked Plain ... 640

Chapter XV. Discoveries ... 647

Chapter XVI. A Vigil Rewarded ... 656

Chapter XVII. A Well-Planned Raid ... 663

Chapter XVIII. The Trail-Boss Tries His Way ... 667

Chapter XIX. A Desert Secret ... 670

Chapter XX. The Redoubt Falls ... 676

Chapter XXI. All Wrapped Up ... 679

Chapter XXII. The Bonfire ... 687

Chapter XXXIII. Surprise Valley ... 692

Chapter XXIV. Squared Up All Around ... 699

Tex ... 705

Chapter I. The Trail Calls ... 706

Chapter II. Refreshed Memories ... 711

Chapter III. Tempted Anew ... 716

Chapter IV. A Crowded Day ... 720

Chapter V. A Trimmer Trimmed ... 729

Chapter VI. Friendly Interest ... 736

Chapter VII. Weights and Measures ... 741

Chapter VIII. After Dark ... 746

Chapter IX. A Pleasant Excursion ... 751

Chapter X. Speed and Guile ... 761

Chapter XI. Empty Honors ... 765

Chapter XII. Closer Friendships ... 770

Chapter XIII. Outcheating Cheaters ... 777

Chapter XIV. Tact and Courage ... 782

Chapter XV. A Good Samaritan ... 786

Chapter XVI. Buffalo Creek in the Spotlight ... 789

Chapter XVII. The Rush ... 793

Chapter XVIII. "Here Lies the Road to Rome!" 797

Chapter XIX. A Lecture Wasted 802

Chapter XX. Plans Awry 806

Chapter XXI. An Equal Guilt 810

Chapter XXII. The False Trail and the True 815

Footnotes 821

Bar-20

Chapter I
Buckskin

The town lay sprawled over half a square mile of alkali plain, its main Street depressing in its width, for those who were responsible for its inception had worked with a generosity born of the knowledge that they had at their immediate and unchallenged disposal the broad lands of Texas and New Mexico on which to assemble a grand total of twenty buildings, four of which were of wood. As this material was scarce, and had to be brought from where the waters of the Gulf lapped against the flat coast, the last-mentioned buildings were a matter of local pride, as indicating the progressiveness of their owners.

These creations of hammer and saw were of one story, crude and unpainted; their cheap weather sheathing, warped and shrunken by the pitiless sun, curled back on itself and allowed unrestricted entrance to alkali dust and air. The other shacks were of adobe, and reposed in that magnificent squalor dear to their owners, Indians and Mexicans.

It was an incident of the Cattle Trail, that most unique and stupendous of all modern migrations, and its founders must have been inspired with a malicious desire to perpetrate a crime against geography, or else they reveled in a perverse cussedness, for within a mile on every side lay broad prairies, and two miles to the east flowed the indolent waters of the Rio Pecos itself. The distance separating the town from the river was excusable, for at certain seasons of the year the placid stream swelled mightily and swept down in a broad expanse of turbulent, yellow flood.

Buckskin was a town of one hundred inhabitants, located in the valley of the Rio Pecos fifty miles south of the Texas-New Mexico line. The census claimed two hundred, but it was a well-known fact that it was exaggerated. One instance of this is shown by the name of Tom Flynn. Those who once knew Tom Flynn, alias Johnny Redmond, alias Bill Sweeney, alias Chuck Mullen, by all four names, could find them in the census list. Furthermore, he had been shot and killed in the March of the year preceding the census, and now occupied a grave in the young but flourishing cemetery. Perry's Bend, twenty miles up the river, was cognizant of this and other facts, and, laughing in open derision at the padded list, claimed to be the better town in all ways, including marksmanship.

One year before this tale opens, Buck Peters, an example for the more recent Billy the Kid, had paid Perry's Bend a short but busy visit. He had ridden in at the north end of Main Street and out at the south. As he came in he was fired at by a group of ugly cowboys from a ranch known as the C 80. He was hit twice, but he unlimbered his artillery, and before his horse had carried him, half dead, out on the prairie, he had killed one of the group. Several citizens had joined the cowboys and added their bullets against Buck. The deceased had been the best bartender in the country, and the rage of the suffering citizens can well be imagined. They swore vengeance on Buck, his ranch, and his stamping ground.

The difference between Buck and Billy the Kid is that the former never shot a man who was not trying to shoot him, or who had not been warned by some action against Buck that would call for it. He minded his own business, never picked a quarrel, and was quiet and pacific up to a certain point. After that had been passed he became like a raging cyclone in a tenement house, and storm-cellars were much in demand.

"Fanning" is the name of a certain style of gun play not unknown among the bad men of the West. While Buck was not a bad man, he had to rub elbows with them frequently, and he believed that the sauce for the goose was the sauce for the gander. So be bad removed the trigger of his revolver and worked the hammer with the thumb of the "gun hand" or the heel of the unencumbered hand. The speed thus acquired was greater than that of the more modern double-action weapon. Six shots in a few seconds was his average speed when that number was required, and when it is thoroughly understood that at least some of them found their intended bullets it is not difficult to realize that fanning was an operation of danger when Buck was doing it.

He was a good rider, as all cowboys are, and was not afraid of anything that lived. At one time he and his chums, Red Connors and Hopalong Cassidy, had successfully routed a band of fifteen Apaches who wanted their scalps. Of these, twelve never hunted scalps again, nor anything else on this earth, and the other three returned to their tribe with the report that three evil Spirits had chased them with "wheel guns" (cannons).

So now, since his visit to Perry's Bend, the rivalry of the two towns had turned to hatred and an alert and eager readiness to increase the inhabitants of each other's graveyard. A state of war existed, which for a time resulted in nothing worse than acrimonious suggestions. But the time came when the score was settled to the satisfaction of one side, at least.

Four ranches were also concerned in the trouble. Buckskin was surrounded by two, the Bar 20 and the Three Triangle. Perry's Bend was the common point for the C 80 and the Double Arrow. Each of the two ranch contingents accepted the feud as a matter of course, and as a matter of course took sides with their respective towns. As no better class of fighters ever lived, the trouble assumed Homeric proportions and insured a danger zone well worth watching.

Bar-20's northern line was C 80's southern one, and Skinny Thompson took his turn at outriding one morning after the season's round-up. He was to follow the boundary and turn back stray cattle. When he had covered the greater part of his journey he saw Shorty Jones riding toward him on a course parallel to his own and about long revolver range away. Shorty and he had "crossed trails" the year before and the best of feelings did not exist between them.

Shorty stopped and stared at Skinny, who did likewise at Shorty. Shorty turned his mount around and applied the spurs, thereby causing his indignant horse to raise both heels at Skinny. The latter took it all in gravely and, as Shorty faced him again, placed his left thumb to his nose, wiggling his fingers suggestively. Shorty took no apparent notice of this but began to shout:

"Yu wants to keep yore busted-down cows on yore own side. They was all over us day afore yisterday. I'm goin' to salt any more what comes over, and don't yu fergit it, neither."

Thompson wigwagged with his fingers again and shouted in reply: "Yu c'n salt all yu wants to, but if I ketch yu adoin' it yu won't have to work no more. An' I kin say right here thet they's more C 80 cows over here than they's Bar-20's over there."

Shorty reached for his revolver and yelled, "Yore a liar!"

Among the cowboys in particular and the Westerners in general at that time, the three suicidal terms, unless one was an expert in drawing quick and shooting straight with one movement, were the words "liar," "coward," and "thief." Any man who was called one of these in earnest, and he was the judge, was expected to shoot if he could and save his life, for the words were seldom used without a gun coming with them. The movement of Shorty's hand toward his belt before the appellation reached him was enough for Skinny, who let go at long range-and missed.

The two reports were as one. Both urged their horses nearer and fired again. This time Skinny's sombrero gave a sharp jerk and a hole appeared in the crown. The third shot of Skinny's sent the horse of the other to its knees and then over on its side. Shorty very promptly crawled behind it and, as he did so, Skinny began a wide circle, firing at intervals as Shorty's smoke cleared away.

Shorty had the best position for defense, as he was in a shallow coule, but he knew that he could not leave it until his opponent had either grown tired of the affair or had used up his ammunition. Skinny knew it, too. Skinny also knew that he could get back to the ranch house and lay in a supply of food and ammunition and return before Shorty could cover the twelve miles he had to go on foot.

Finally Thompson began to head for home. He had carried the matter as far as he could without it being murder. Too much time had elapsed now, and, besides, it was before breakfast and he was hungry. He would go away and settle the score at some time when they would be on equal terms.

He rode along the line for a mile and chanced to look back. Two C 80 punchers were riding after him, and as they saw him turn and discover them they fired at him and yelled. He rode on for some distance and cautiously drew his rifle out of its long holster at his right leg. Suddenly he turned around in the saddle and fired twice. One of his pursuers fell forward on the neck of his horse, and his comrade turned to help him. Thompson wig-wagged again and rode on, reaching the ranch as the others were finishing their breakfast.

At the table Red Connors remarked that the tardy one had a hole in his sombrero, and asked its owner how and where he had received it.

"Had a argument with C 80 out'n th' line."

"Go 'way! Ventilate enny?"

"One."

"Good boy, sonny! Hey, Hopalong, Skinny perforated C 80 this mawnin'!"

Hopalong Cassidy was struggling with a mouthful of beef. He turned his eyes toward Red without ceasing, and grinning as well as he could under the circumstances managed to grunt out "Gu —," which was as near to "Good" as the beef would allow.

Lanky Smith now chimed in as he repeatedly stuck his knife into a reluctant boiled potato, "How'd yu do it, Skinny?"

"Bet he sneaked up on him," joshed Buck Peters; "did yu ask his pardin, Skinny?"

"Ask nuthin'," remarked Red, "he jest nachurly walks up to C 80 an' sez, 'Kin I have the pleasure of ventilatin' yu?' an' C So he sez, 'If yu do it easy like,' sez he. Didn't he, Thompson?"

"They'll be some ventilatin' under th' table if yu fellows don't lemme alone; I'm hungry," complained Skinny.

"Say, Hopalong, I bets yu I kin clean up C 80 all by my lonesome," announced Buck, winking at Red.

"Yah! Yu onct tried to clean up the Bend, Buckie, an' if Pete an' Billy hadn't afound yu when they come by Eagle Pass that night yu wouldn't be here eatin' beef by th' pound," glancing at the hard-working Hopalong. "It was plum lucky fer yu that they was acourtin' that time, wasn't it, Hopalong?" suddenly asked Red. Hopalong nearly strangled in his efforts to speak. He gave it up and nodded his head.

"Why can't yu git it straight, Connors? I wasn't doin' no courtin', it was Pete. I runned into him on th' other side o' th' pass. I'd look fine acourtin', wouldn't I?" asked the downtrodden Williams.

Pete Wilson skillfully flipped a potato into that worthy's coffee, spilling the beverage of the questionable name over a large expanse of blue flannel shirt. "Yu's all right, yu are. Why, when I meets yu, yu was lost in th' arms of yore ladylove. All I could see was yore feet. Go an' git tangled up with a two hundred and forty pound half-breed squaw an' then try to lay it onter me! When I proposed drownin' yore troubles over at Cowan's, yu went an' got mad over what yu called th' insinooation. An' yu shore didn't look any too blamed fine, neither."

"All th' same," volunteered Thompson, who had taken the edge from his appetite, "we better go over an' pay C 80 a call. I don't like what Shorty said about saltin' our cattle. He'll shore do it, unless I camps on th' line, which same I hain't hankerin' after."

"Oh, he wouldn't stop th' cows that way, Skinny; he was only afoolin'," exclaimed Connors meekly.

"Foolin' yore gran'mother! That there bunch'll do anything if we wasn't lookin'," hotly replied Skinny.

"That's shore nuff gospel, Thomp. They's sore fer mor'n one thing. They got aplenty when Buck went on th' warpath, an they's hankerin' to git square," remarked Johnny Nelson, stealing the pie, a rare treat, of his neighbor when that unfortunate individual was not looking. He had it halfway to his mouth when its former owner, Jimmy Price, a boy of eighteen, turned his head and saw it going.

"Hi-yi! Yu clay-bank coyote, drap thet pie! Did yu ever see such a son-of-a-gun fer pie?" he plaintively asked Red Connors, as he grabbed a mighty handful of apples and crust. "Pie'll kill yu some day, yu bob-tailed jack! I had an uncle that died onct. He et too much pie an' he went an' turned green, an so'll yu if yu don't let it alone."

"Yu ought'r seed th' pie Johnny had down in Eagle Flat," murmured Lanky Smith reminiscently. "She had feet that'd stop a stampede. Johnny was shore loco about her. Swore she was the finest blossom that ever growed." Here he choked and tears of laughter coursed down his weather-beaten face as he pictured her. "She was a dainty Mexican, about fifteen han's high an' about sixteen han's around. Johnny used to chalk off when he hugged her, usen't yu, Johnny? One night when he had got purty well around on th' second lap he run inter a feller jest startin' out on his fust. They hain't caught that Mexican yet."

Nelson was pelted with everything in sight. He slowly wiped off the pie crust and bread and potatoes. "Anybody'd think I was a busted grub wagon," he grumbled. When he had fished the last piece of beef out of his ear he went out and offered to stand treat. As the round-up was over, they slid into their saddles and raced for Cowan's saloon at Buckskin.

Chapter II
The Rashness of Shorty

Buckskin was very hot; in fact it was never anything else. Few people were on the streets and the town was quiet. Over in the Houston hotel a crowd of cowboys was lounging in the barroom. They were very quiet —a condition as rare as it was ominous. Their mounts, twelve in all, were switching flies from their quivering skins in the corral at the rear. Eight of these had a large C 80 branded on their flanks; the other four, a Double Arrow.

In the barroom a slim, wiry man was looking out of the dirty window up the street at Cowan's saloon. Shorty was complaining, "They shore oughter be here now. They rounded up last week." The man nearest assured him that they would come. The man at the window turned and said, "They's yer now."

In front of Cowan's a crowd of nine happy-go-lucky, daredevil riders were sliding from their saddles. They threw their reins over the heads of their mounts and filed in to the bar. Laughter issued from the open door and the clink of glasses could be heard. They stood in picturesque groups, strong, self-reliant, humorous, virile. Their expensive sombreros were pushed far back on their heads and their hairy chaps were covered with the alkali dust from their ride.

Cowan, bottle in hand, pushed out several more glasses. He kicked a dog from under his feet and looked at Buck. "Rounded up yet?" he inquired.

"Shore, day afore yesterday," came the reply. The rest were busy removing the dust from their throats, and gradually drifted into groups of two or three. One of these groups strolled over to the solitary card table, and found Jimmy Price resting in a cheap chair, his legs on the table.

"I wisht yu'd extricate yore delicate feet from off'n this hyar table, James," humbly requested Lanky Smith, morally backed up by those with him.

"Ya-as, they shore is delicate, Mr. Smith," responded Jimmy without moving.

"We wants to play draw, Jimmy," explained Pete.

"Yore shore welcome to play if yu wants to. Didn't I tell yu when yu growed that mustache that yu didn't have to ask me any more?" queried the placid James, paternally.

"Call 'em off, sonny. Pete sez he kin clean me out. Anyhow, yu kin have the fust deal," compromised Lanky.

"I'm shore sorry fer Pete if he cayn't. Yu don't reckon I has to have fust deal to beat yu fellers, do yu? Go way an' lemme alone; I never seed such a bunch fer buttin' in as yu fellers."

Billy Williams returned to the bar. Then he walked along it until he was behind the recalcitrant possessor of the table. While his aggrieved friends shuffled their feet uneasily to cover his approach, he tiptoed up behind Jimmy and, with a nod, grasped that indignant individual firmly by the neck while the others grabbed his feet. They carried him, twisting and bucking, to the middle of the street and deposited him in the dust, returning to the now vacant table.

Jimmy rested quietly for a few seconds and then slowly arose, dusting the alkali from him.

"Th' wall-eyed piruts," he muttered, and then scratched his head for a way to "play hunk." As he gazed sorrowfully at the saloon he heard a snicker from behind him. He, thinking it was one of his late tormentors, paid no attention to it. Then a cynical, biting laugh stung him. He wheeled, to see Shorty leaning against a tree, a sneering leer on his flushed face. Shorty's right hand was suspended above his holster, hooked to his belt by the thumb —a favorite position of his when expecting trouble.

"One of yore reg'lar habits?" he drawled.

Jimmy began to dust himself in silence, but his lips were compressed to a thin white line.

"Does they hurt yu?" pursued the onlooker.

Jimmy looked up. "I heard tell that they make glue outen cayuses, sometimes," he remarked.

Shorty's eyes flashed. The loss of the horse had been rankling in his heart all day.

"Does they git yu frequent?" he asked. His voice sounded hard.

"Oh, 'bout as frequent as yu lose a cayuse, I reckon," replied Jimmy hotly.

Shorty's hand streaked to his holster and Jimmy followed his lead. Jimmy's Colt was caught. He had bucked too much. As he fell Shorty ran for the Houston House.

Pistol shots were common, for they were the universal method of expressing emotions. The poker players grinned, thinking their victim was letting off his indignation. Lanky sized up his hand and remarked half audibly, "He's a shore good kid."

The bartender, fearing for his new beveled, gilt-framed mirror, gave a hasty glance out the window. He turned around, made change and remarked to Buck, "Yore kid, Jimmy, is plugged." Several of the more credulous craned their necks to see, Buck being the first. "Judas!" he shouted, and ran out to where Jimmy lay coughing, his toes twitching. The saloon was deserted and a crowd of angry cowboys surrounded their chum-aboy. Buck had seen Shorty enter the door of the Houston House and he swore. "Chase them C 80 and Arrow cayuses behind the saloon, Pete, an' git under cover."

Jimmy was choking and he coughed up blood. "He's shore-got me. My-gun stuck," he added apologetically. He tried to sit up, but was not able and he looked surprised. "It's purty-damn hot-out here," he suggested. Johnny and Billy carried him in the saloon and placed him by the table, in the chair he had previously vacated. As they stood up he fell across the table and died.

Billy placed the dead boy's sombrero on his head and laid the refractory six-shooter on the table. "I wonder who th' dirty killer was." He looked at the slim figure and started to go out, followed by Johnny. As he reached the threshold a bullet zipped past him and thudded into the frame of the door. He backed away and looked surprised. "That's Shorty's shootin' —he allus misses 'bout that much." He looked out and saw Buck standing behind the live oak that Shorty had leaned against, firing at the hotel. Turning around he made for the rear, remarking to Johnny that "they's in th' Houston." Johnny looked at the quiet figure in the chair and swore softly. He followed Billy. Cowan, closing the door and taking a buffalo gun from under the bar, went out also and slammed the rear door forcibly.

Chapter III
The Argument

Up the street two hundred yards from the Houston House Skinny and Pete lay hidden behind a bowlder. Three hundred yards on the other side of the hotel Johnny and Billy were stretched out in an arroyo. Buck was lying down now, and Hopalong, from his position in the barn belonging to the hotel, was methodically dropping the horses of the besieged, a job he hated as much as he hated poison. The corral was their death trap. Red and Lanky were emitting clouds of smoke from behind the store, immediately across the street from the barroom. A buffalo gun roared down by the plaza and several Sharps cracked a protest from different points. The town had awakened and the shots were dropping steadily.

Strange noises filled the air. They grew in tone and volume and then dwindled away to nothing. The hum of the buffalo gun and the sobbing pi-in-in-ing of the Winchesters were liberally mixed with the sharp whines of the revolvers.

There were no windows in the hotel now. Raw furrows in the bleached wood showed yellow, and splinters mysteriously sprang from the casings. The panels of the door were producing cracks and the cheap door handle flew many ways at once. An empty whisky keg on the stoop boomed out mournfully at intervals and finally rolled down the steps with a rumbling protest. Wisps of smoke slowly climbed up the walls and seemed to be waving defiance to the curling wisps in the open.

Pete raised his shoulder to refill the magazine of his smoking rifle and dropped the cartridges all over his lap. He looked sheepishly at Skinny and began to load with his other hand.

"Yore plum loco, yu are. Don't yu reckon they kin hit a blue shirt at two hundred?" Skinny cynically inquired. "Got one that time," he announced a second later.

"I wonder who's got th' buffalo," grunted Pete. "Mus' be Cowan," he replied to his own question and settled himself to use his left hand.

"Don't yu git Shorty; he's my meat," suggested Skinny.

"Yu better tell Buck-he ain't got no love fer Shorty," replied Pete, aiming carefully.

The panic in the corral ceased and Hopalong was now sending his regrets against the panels of the rear door. He had cut his last initial in the near panel and was starting a wobbly "H" in its neighbor. He was in a good position. There were no windows in the rear wall, and as the door was a very dangerous place he was not fired at.

He began to get tired of this one-sided business and crawled up on the window ledge, dangling his feet on the outside. He occasionally sent a bullet at a different part of the door, but amused himself by annoying Buck.

"Plenty hot down there?" he pleasantly inquired, and as he received no answer he tried again. "Better save some of them cartridges fer some other time, Buck."

Buck was sending 45-70's into the shattered window with a precision that presaged evil to any of the defenders who were rash enough to try to gain the other end of the room.

Hopalong bit off a chew of tobacco and drowned a green fly that was crawling up the side of the barn. The yellow liquid streaked downward a short distance and was eagerly sucked up by the warped boards.

A spurt of smoke leaped from the battered door and the bored Hopalong promptly tumbled back inside. He felt of his arm, and then, delighted at the notice taken of his artistic efforts, shot several times from a crack on his right. "This yer's shore gittin' like home," he gravely remarked to the splinter that whizzed past his head. He shot again at the door and it sagged outward, accompanied by the thud of a falling body. "Pies like mother used to make," he announced to the loft as he slipped the magazine full of .45-70's. "An' pills like popper used to take," he continued when he had lowered the level of the water in his flask.

He rolled a cigarette and tossed the match into the air, extinguishing it by a shot from his Colt.

"Got any cigarettes, Hoppy?" said a voice from below.

"Shore," replied the joyous puncher, recognizing Pete; "how'd yu git here?"

"Like a cow. Busy?"

"None whatever. Comin' up?"

"Nope. Skinny wants a smoke too."

Hopalong handed tobacco and papers down the hole. "So long."

"So long," replied the daring Pete, who risked death twice for a smoke.

The hot afternoon dragged along and about three o'clock Buck held up an empty cartridge belt to the gaze of the curious Hopalong. That observant worthy nodded and threw a double handful of cartridges, one by one, to the patient and unrelenting Buck, who filled his gun and piled the few remaining ones up at his side. "Th' lives of mice and men gang aft all wrong," he remarked at random.

"Th' son-of-a-gun's talkin' Shakespeare," marveled Hopalong. "Satiate any, Buck?" he asked as that worthy settled down to await his chance.

"Two," he replied, "Shorty an' another. Plenty damn hot down here," he complained. A spurt of alkali dust stung his face, but the hand that made it never made another. "Three," he called. "How many, Hoppy?"

"One. That's four. Wonder if th' others got any?"

"Pete said Skinny got one," replied the intent Buck.

"Th' son-of-a-gun, he never said nothin' about it, an' me a fillin' his ornery paws with smokin'." Hopalong was indignant.

"Bet yu ten we don't git 'em afore dark," he announced.

"Got yu. Go yu ten more I gits another," promptly responded Buck.

"That's a shore cinch. Make her twenty."

"She is."

"Yu'll have to square it with Skinny, he shore wanted Shorty plum' bad," Hopalong informed the unerring marksman.

"Why didn't he say suthin' about it? Anyhow, Jimmy was my bunkie."

Hopalong's cigarette disintegrated and the board at his left received a hole. He promptly disappeared and Buck laughed. He sat up in the loft and angrily spat the soaked paper out from between his lips.

"All that trouble fer nothin', th' white-eyed coyote," he muttered. Then he crawled around to one side and fired at the center of his "C." Another shot hurtled at him and his left arm fell to his side. "That's funny-wonder where th' damn pirut is?" He looked out cautiously and saw a cloud of smoke over a knothole which was situated close up under the eaves of the barroom; and it was being agitated. Some one was blowing at it to make it disappear. He aimed very carefully at the knot and fired. He heard a sound between a curse and a squawk and was not molested any further from that point.

"I knowed he'd git hurt," he explained to the bandage, torn from the edge of his kerchief, which he carefully bound around his last wound.

Down in the arroyo Johnny was complaining.

"This yer's a no good bunk," he plaintively remarked.

"It shore ain't —but it's th' best we kin find," apologized Billy.

"That's th' sixth that feller sent up there. He's a damn poor shot," observed Johnny; "must be Shorty."

"Shorty kin shoot plum' good-tain't him," contradicted Billy.

"Yas-with a six-shooter. He's off'n his feed with a rifle," explained Johnny.

"Yu wants to stay down from up there, yu ijit," warned Billy as the disgusted Johnny crawled up the bank. He slid down again with a welt on his neck.

"That's somebody else now. He oughter a done better'n that," he said.

Billy had fired as Johnny started to slide and he smoothed his aggrieved chum. "He could onct, yu means."

"Did yu git him?" asked the anxious Johnny, rubbing his welt. "Plum' center," responded the business-like Billy. "Go up agin, mebby I kin git another," he suggested tentatively.

"Mebby you kin go to blazes. I ain't no gallery," grinned the now exuberant owner of the welt.

"Who's got the buffalo?" he inquired as the great gun roared.

"Mus' be Cowan. He's shore all right. Sounds like a bloomin' cannon," replied Billy. "Lemme alone with yore fool questions, I'm busy," he complained as his talkative partner started to ask another. "Go an' git me some water—I'm alkalied. An' git some .45's, mine's purty near gone."

Johnny crawled down the arroyo and reappeared at Hopalong's barn.

As he entered the door a handful of empty shells fell on his hat and dropped to the floor. He shook his head and remarked, "That mus' be that fool Hopalong."

"Yore shore right. How's business?" inquired the festive Cassidy.

"Purty fair. Billy's got one. How many's gone?"

"Buck's got three, I got two and Skinny's got one. That's six, an' Billy is seven. They's five more," he replied.

"How'd yu know?" queried Johnny as he filled his flask at the horse trough.

"Because they's twelve cayuses behind the hotel. That's why."

"They might git away on 'em," suggested the practical Johnny.

"Can't. They's all cashed in."

"Yu said that they's five left," ejaculated the puzzled water carrier.

"Yah; yore a smart cuss, ain't yu?"

Johnny grinned and then said, "Got any smokin'?" Hopalong looked grieved. "I ain't no store. Why don't yu git generous and buy some?"

He partially filled Johnny's hand, and as he put the sadly depleted bag away he inquired, "Got any papers?"

"Nope."

"Got any matches?" he asked cynically.

"Nope."

"Kin yu smoke 'em?" he yelled, indignantly.

"Shore nuff," placidly replied the unruffled Johnny. "Billy wants some .45-70's."

Hopalong gasped. "Don't he want my gun, too?"

"Nope. Got a better one. Hurry up, he'll git mad." Hopalong was a very methodical person. He was the only one of his crowd to carry a second cartridge strap. It hung over his right shoulder and rested on his left hip. His waist belt held thirty cartridges for the revolvers. He extracted twenty from that part of the shoulder strap hardest to get at, the back, by simply pulling it over his shoulder and plucking out the bullets as they came into reach.

"That's all yu kin have. I'm Buck's ammernition jackass," he explained. "Bet yu ten we gits 'em afore dark" —he was hedging.

"Any fool knows that. I'll take yu if yu bets th' other way," responded Johnny, grinning. He knew Hopalong's weak spot.

"Yore on," promptly responded Hopalong, who would bet on anything.

"Well, so long," said Johnny as he crawled away.

"Hey, yu, Johnny!" called out Hopalong, "don't yu go an' tell anybody I got any pills left. I ain't no ars'nal."

Johnny replied by elevating one foot and waving it. Then he disappeared.

Behind the store, the most precarious position among the besiegers, Red Connors and Lanky Smith were ensconced and commanded a view of the entire length of the barroom. They could see the dark mass they knew to be the rear door and derived a great amount of amusement from the spots of light which were appearing in it.

They watched the "C" (reversed to them) appear and be completed. When the wobbly "H" grew to completion they laughed heartily. Then the hardwood bar had been dragged across the field of vision and up to the front windows, and they could only see the indiscriminate holes which appeared in the upper panels at frequent intervals.

Every time they fired they had to expose a part of themselves to a return shot, with the result that Lanky's forearm was seared its entire length. Red had been more fortunate and only had a bruised ear.

They laboriously rolled several large rocks out in the open, pushing them beyond the shelter of the store with their rifles. When they had crawled behind them they each had another wound. From their new position they could see Hopalong sitting in his window. He promptly waved his sombrero and grinned.

They were the most experienced fighters of all except Buck, and were saving their shots. When they did shoot they always had some portion of a man's body to aim at, and the damage they inflicted was considerable. They said nothing, being older than the rest and more taciturn, and they were not reckless. Although Hopalong's antics made them laugh, they grumbled at his recklessness and were not tempted to emulate him. It was noticeable, too, that they shoved their rifles out simultaneously and, although both were aiming, only one fired. Lanky's gun cracked so close to the enemy's that the whirr of the bullet over Red's head was merged in the crack of his partner's reply.

When Hopalong saw the rocks roll out from behind the store he grew very curious. Then he saw a flash, followed instantly by another from the second rifle. He saw several of these follow shots and could sit in silence no longer. He waved his hat to attract attention and then shouted, "How many?" A shot was sent straight up in the air and he notified Buck that there were only four left.

The fire of these four grew less rapid-they were saving their ammunition. A pot shot at Hopalong sent that gentleman's rifle hurtling to the ground. Another tore through his hat, removing a neat amount of skin and hair and giving him a lifelong part. He fell back inside and proceeded to shoot fast and straight with his revolvers, his head burning as though on fire. When he had vented the dangerous pressure of his anger he went below and tried to fish the rifle in with a long stick. It was obdurate, so he sent three more shots into the door, and, receiving no reply, ran out around the corner of his shelter and grasped the weapon. When half way back he sank to the ground. Before another shot could be fired at him with any judgment a ripping, spitting rifle was being frantically worked from the barn. The bullets tore the door into seams and gaps; the lowest panel, the one having the "H" in it, fell inward in chunks. Johnny had returned for another smoke.

Hopalong, still grasping the rifle, rolled rapidly around the corner of the barn. He endeavored to stand, but could not. Johnny, hearing rapid and fluent swearing, came out.

"Where'd they git yu?" he asked.

"In th' off leg. Hurts like blazes. Did yu git him?"

"Nope. I jest come fer another cig; got any left?"

"Up above. Yore gall is shore apallin'. Help me in, yu two-laigged jackass."

"Shore. We'll shore pay our 'tentions to that door. She'll go purty soon-she's as full of holes as th' Bad Lan's," replied Johnny. "Git aholt an' hop along, Hopalong."

He helped the swearing Hopalong inside, and then the lead they pumped into the wrecked door was scandalous. Another panel fell in and Hopalong's "C" was destroyed. A wide crack appeared in the one above it and grew rapidly. Its mate began to gape and finally both were driven in. The increase in the light caused by these openings allowed Red and Lanky to secure better aim and soon the fire of the defenders died out.

Johnny dropped his rifle and, drawing his six-shooter, ran out and dashed for the dilapidated door, while Hopalong covered that opening with a fusilade.

As Johnny's shoulder sent the framework flying inward he narrowly missed sudden death. As it was he staggered to the side, out of range, and dropped full length to the ground, flat on his face. Hopalong's rifle cracked incessantly, but to no avail. The man who had fired the shot was dead. Buck got him immediately after he had shot Johnny.

Calling to Skinny and Red to cover him, Buck sprinted to where Johnny lay gasping. The bullet had struck his shoulder. Buck, Colt in hand, leaped through the door, but met with no resistance. He signaled to Hopalong, who yelled, "They's none left."

The trees and rocks and gullies and buildings yielded men who soon crowded around the hotel. A young doctor, lately graduated, appeared. It was his first case, but he eased Johnny. Then he went over to Hopalong, who was now raving, and attended to him. The others were patched up as well as possible and the struggling young physician had his pockets crammed full of gold and silver coins.

The scene of the wrecked barroom was indescribable. Holes, furrows, shattered glass and bottles, the liquor oozing down the walls of the shelves and running over the floor; the ruined furniture, a wrecked bar, seared and shattered and covered with blood; bodies as they had been piled in the corners; ropes, shells, hats; and liquor everywhere, over everything, met the gaze of those who had caused the chaos.

Perry's Bend had failed to wipe out the score.

Chapter IV
The Vagrant Sioux

Buckskin gradually readjusted itself to the conditions which had existed before its sudden leap into the limelight as a town which did things. The soiree at the Houston House had drifted into the past, and was now substantially established as an epoch in the history of the town. Exuberant joy gave way to dignity and deprecation, and to solid satisfaction; and the conversations across the bar brought forth parallels of the affair to be judged impartially-and the impartial judgment was, unanimously, that while there had undoubtedly been good fights before Perry's Bend had disturbed the local quiet, they were not quite up to the new standard of strenuous hospitality. Finally the heat blistered everything back into the old state, and the shadows continued to be in demand.

One afternoon, a month after the reception of the honorable delegation from Perry's Bend, the town of Buckskin seemed desolated, and the earth and the buildings thereon were as huge furnaces radiating a visible heat, but when the blazing sun had begun to settle in the west it awoke with a clamor which might have been laid to the efforts of a zealous Satan. At this time it became the Mecca of two score or more joyous cowboys from the neighboring ranches, who livened things as those knights of the saddle could.

In the scant but heavy shadow of Cowan's saloon sat a picturesque figure from whom came guttural, resonant rumblings which mingled in a spirit of loneliness with the fretful sighs of a flea-tormented dog. Both dog and master were vagrants, and they were tolerated because it was a matter of supreme indifference as to who came or how long they stayed as long as the ethics and the unwritten law of the cow country were inviolate. And the breaking of these caused no unnecessary anxiety, for justice was both speedy and sure.

When the outcast Sioux and his yellow dog had drifted into town some few months before they had caused neither expostulation nor inquiry, as the cardinal virtue of that whole broad land was to ask a man no questions which might prove embarrassing to all concerned; judgment was of observation, not of history, and a man's past would reveal itself through actions. It mattered little whether he was an embezzler or the wild chip from some prosperous eastern block, as men came to the range to forget and to lose touch with the pampered East; and the range absorbed them as its own.

A man was only a man as his skin contained the qualities necessary; and the illiterate who could ride and shoot and live to himself was far more esteemed than the educated who could not do those things. The more a man depends upon himself and the closer is his contact to a quick judgment the more laconic and even-poised he becomes. And the knowledge that he is himself a judge tends to create caution and judgment. He has no court to uphold his honor and to offer him protection, so he must be quick to protect himself and to maintain his own standing. His nature saved him, or it executed; and the range absolved him of all unpaid penalties of a careless past.

He became a man born again and he took up his burden, the exactions of a new environment, and he lived as long as those exactions gave him the right to live. He must tolerate no restrictions of his natural rights, and he must not restrict; for the one would proclaim him a coward, the other a bully; and both received short shrifts in that land of the self-protected. The basic law of nature is the survival of the fittest.

So, when the wanderers found their level in Buckskin they were not even asked by what name men knew them. Not caring to hear a name which might not harmonize with their idea of the fitness of things, the cowboys of the Bar-20 had, with a freedom born of excellent livers and fearless temperaments, bestowed names befitting their sense of humor and adaptability. The official title of the Sioux was By-and-by; the dog was known as Fleas. Never had names more clearly described the objects to be represented, for they were excellent examples of cowboy discernment and aptitude.

In their eyes By-and-by was a man. He could feel and he could resent insults. They did not class him as one of themselves, because he did not have energy enough to demand and justify such classification. With them he had a right to enjoy his life as he saw fit so long as he did not trespass on or restrict the rights of others. They were not analytic in temperament, neither were they moralists. He was not a menace to society, because society had superb defenses. So they vaguely recognized his many poor qualities and clearly saw his few good ones. He could shoot, when permitted, with the best; no horse, however refractory, had ever been known to throw him; he was an adept at following the trails left by rustlers, and that was an asset; he became of value to the community; he was an economic factor.

His ability to consume liquor with indifferent effects raised him another notch in their estimation. He was not always talking when some one else wished to-another count. There remained about him that stoical indifference to the petty; that observant nonchalance of the Indian; and there was a suggestion, faint, it was true, of a dignity common to chieftains. He was a log of grave deference which tossed on their sea of mischievous hilarity.

He wore a pair of corduroy trousers, known to the care-free as "pants," which were held together by numerous patches of what had once been brilliantly colored calico. A pair of suspenders, torn into two separate straps, made a belt for himself and a collar for his dog. The trousers had probably been secured during a fit of absent-mindedness on his part when their former owner had not been looking. Tucked at intervals in the top of the corduroys (the exceptions making convenient shelves for alkali dust) was what at one time had been a stiff-bosomed shirt. This was open down the front and back, the weight of the trousers on the belt holding it firmly on the square shoulders of the wearer, thus precluding the necessity of collar buttons. A pair of moccasins, beautifully worked with wampum, protected his feet from the onslaughts of cacti and the inquisitive and pugnacious sand flies; and lying across his lap was a repeating Winchester rifle, not dangerous because it was empty, a condition due to the wisdom of the citizens in forbidding any one to sell, trade or give to him those tubes of concentrated trouble, because he could get drunk.

The two were contented and happy. They had no cares nor duties, and their pleasures were simple and easily secured, as they consisted of sleep and a proneness to avoid moving. Like the untrammeled coyote, their bed was where sleep overtook them; their food, what the night wrapped in a sense of security, or the generosity of the cowboys of the Bar-20. No tub-ridden Diogenes ever knew so little of responsibility or as much unadulterated content. There is a penalty even to civilization and ambition.

When the sun had cast its shadows beyond By-and-by's feet the air became charged with noise; shouts, shots and the rolling thunder of madly pounding hoofs echoed flatly throughout the town. By-and-by yawned, stretched and leaned back, reveling in the semi-conscious ecstasy of the knowledge that he did not have to immediately get up. Fleas opened one eye and cocked an ear in inquiry, and then rolled over on his back, squirmed and sighed contentedly and long. The outfit of the Bar-20 had come to town.

The noise came rapidly nearer and increased in volume as the riders turned the corner and drew rein suddenly, causing their mounts to slide on their haunches in ankle-deep dust.

"Hullo, old Buck-with-th'-pants, how's yore liver?"

"Come up an irrigate, old tank!"

"Chase th' flea ranch an' trail along!"

These were a few of the salutations discernible among the medley of playful yells, the safety valves of supercharged good-nature.

"Skr-e-e!" yelled Hopalong Cassidy, letting off a fusillade of shots in the vicinity of Fleas, who rapidly retreated around the corner, where he wagged his tail in eager expectation. He was not disappointed, for a cow pony tore around in pursuit and Hopalong leaned over and scratched the yellow back, thumping it heartily, and, tossing a chunk of beef into the open jaws of the delighted dog, departed as he had come. The advent of the outfit meant a square meal, and the dog knew it.

In Cowan's, lined up against the bar, the others were earnestly and assiduously endeavoring, with a promise of success, to get By-and-by drunk, which endeavors coincided perfectly with By-and-by's idea of the fitness of things. The fellowship and the liquor combined to thaw out his reserve and to loosen his tongue. After gazing with an air of injured surprise at the genial loosening of his knees he gravely handed his rifle with an exaggerated sweep of his arm, to the cowboy nearest him, and wrapped his arms around the recipient to insure his balance. The rifle was passed from hand to hand until it came to Buck Peters, who gravely presented it to its owner as a new gun.

By-and-by threw out his stomach in an endeavor to keep his head in line with his heels, and grasping the weapon with both hands turned to Cowan, to whom he gave it.

"Yu hab this un. Me got two. Me keep new un, mebby so." Then he loosened his belt and drank long and deep.

A shadow darkened the doorway and Hopalong limped in. Spying By-and-by pushing the bottle into his mouth, while Red Connors propped him, he grinned and took out five silver dollars, which he jingled under By-and-by's eyes, causing that worthy to lay aside the liquor and erratically grab for the tantalizing fortune.

"Not yet, sabe?" said Hopalong, changing the position of the money. "If yu wants to corral this here herd of simoleons yu has to ride a cayuse what Red bet me yu can't ride. Yu has got to grow on that there saddle and stayed growed for five whole minutes by Buck's ticker. I ain't a-goin' to tell yu he's any saw-horse, for yu'd know better, as yu reckons Red wouldn't bet on no losin' proposition if he knowed better, which same he don't. Yu straddles that four-laigged cloudburst an' yu gets these, sabe? I ain't seen th' cayuse yet that yu couldn't freeze to, an' I'm backin' my opinions with my moral support an' one month's pay."

By-and-by's eyes began to glitter as the meaning of the words sifted through his befuddled mind. Ride a horse-five dollars-ride a five-dollars horse-horses ride dollars-then he straightened up and began to speak in an incoherent jumble of Sioux and bad English. He, the mighty rider of the Sioux; he, the bravest warrior and the greatest hunter; could he ride a horse for five dollars? Well, he rather thought he could. Grasping Red by the shoulder, he tacked for the door and narrowly missed hitting the bottom step first, landing, as it happened, in the soft dust with Red's leg around his neck. Somewhat sobered by the jar, he stood up and apologized to the crowd for Red getting in the way, declaring that Red was a "Heap good un," and that he didn't mean to do it.

The outfit of the Bar-20 was, perhaps, the most famous of all from Canada to the Rio Grande. The foreman, Buck Peters, controlled a crowd of men (who had all the instincts of boys) that had shown no quarter to many rustlers, and who, while always carefree and easy-going (even fighting with great good humor and carelessness), had established the reputation of being the most reckless gang of daredevil gun-fighters that ever pounded leather. Crooked gaming houses, from El Paso to Cheyenne and from Phoenix to Leavenworth, unanimously and enthusiastically damned them from their boots to their sombreros, and the sheriffs and marshals of many localities had received from their hands most timely assistance-and some trouble. Wiry, indomitable, boyish and generous, they were splendid examples of virile manhood; and, surrounded as they were with great dangers and a unique civilization, they should not, in justice, be judged by opinions born of the commonplace.

They were real cowboys, which means, public opinion to the contrary notwithstanding, that they were not lawless, nor drunken, shooting bullies who held life cheaply, as their kin has been unjustly pictured; but while these men were naturally peaceable they had to continually rub elbows with men who were not. Gamblers, criminals, bullies and the riffraff that fled from the protected East had drifted among them in great numbers, and it was this class that caused the trouble.

The hardworking "cow-punchers" lived according to the law of the land, and they obeyed that greatest of all laws, that of self-preservation. Their fun was boisterous, but they paid for all the damage they inflicted; their work was one continual hardship, and the reaction of one extreme swings far toward the limit of its antithesis. Go back to the Apple if you would trace the beginning of self-preservation and the need.

Buck Peters was a man of mild appearance, somewhat slow of speech and correspondingly quick of action, who never became flurried. His was the master hand that controlled, and his Colts enjoyed the reputation of never missing when a hit could have been expected with reason. Many floods, stampedes and blizzards had assailed his nerves, but he yet could pour a glass of liquor, held at arm's length, through a knothole in the floor without wetting the wood.

Next in age came Lanky Smith, a small, undersized man of retiring disposition. Then came Skinny Thompson, six feet four on his bared soles, and true to his name; Hopalong described him as "th' shadow of a chalk mark." Pete Wilson, the slow-witted and very taciturn, and Billy Williams, the wavering pessimist, were of ordinary height and appearance. Red Connors, with hair that shamed the name, was the possessor of a temper which was as dry as tinder; his greatest weakness was his regard for the rifle as a means of preserving peace. Johnny Nelson was the protege, and he could do no wrong.

The last, Hopalong Cassidy, was a combination of irresponsibility, humor, good nature, love of fighting, and nonchalance when face to face with danger. His most prominent attribute was that of always getting into trouble without any intention of so doing; in fact, he was much aggrieved and surprised when it came. It seemed as though when any "bad man" desired to add to his reputation he invariably selected Hopalong as the means (a fact due, perhaps, to the perversity of things in general). Bad men became scarce soon after Hopalong became a fixture in any locality. He had been crippled some years before in a successful attempt to prevent the assassination of a friend, Sheriff Harris, of Albuquerque, and he still possessed a limp.

When Red had relieved his feelings and had dug the alkali out of his ears and eyes, he led the Sioux to the rear of the saloon, where a "pinto" was busily engaged in endeavoring to pitch a saddle from his back, employing the intervals in trying to see how much of the picket rope he could wrap around his legs.

When By-and-by saw what he was expected to ride he felt somewhat relieved, for the pony did not appear to have more than the ordinary amount of cussedness. He waved his hand, and Johnny and Red bandaged the animal's eyes, which quieted him at once, and then they untangled the rope from around his legs and saw that the cinches were secure. Motioning to By-and-by that all was ready, they jerked the bandage off as the Indian settled himself in the saddle.

Had By-and-by been really sober he would have taken the conceit out of that pony in chunks, and as it was he experienced no great difficulty in holding his seat; but in his addled state of mind he grasped the end of the cinch strap in such a way that when the pony jumped forward in its last desperate effort the buckle slipped and the cinch became unfastened; and By-and-by, still seated in the saddle, flew head foremost into the horse trough, where he spilled much water.

As this happened Cowan turned the corner, and when he saw the wasted water (which he had to carry, bucketful at a time, from the wells a good quarter of a mile away) his anger blazed forth, and yelling, he ran for the drenched Sioux, who was just crawling out of his bath. When the unfortunate saw the irate man bearing down on him he sputtered in rage and fear, and, turning, he ran down the street, with Cowan thundering flatfootedly behind on a fat man's gallop, to the hysterical cheers of the delighted outfit, who saw in it nothing but a good joke.

When Cowan returned from his hopeless task, blowing and wheezing, he heard sundry remarks, sotto voce, which were not calculated to increase his opinion of his physical condition.

"Seems to me," remarked the irrepressible Hopalong, "that one of those cayuses has got th' heaves."

"It shore sounds like it," acquiesced Johnny, red in the face from holding in his laughter, "an' say, somebody interferes."

"All knock-kneed animals do, yu heathen," supplied Red.

"Hey, yu, let up on that and have a drink on th' house," invited Cowan. "If I gits that durn war whoop I'll make yu think there's been a cyclone. I'll see how long that bum hangs around this here burg, I will."

Red's eyes narrowed and his temper got the upper hand. "He ain't no bum when yu gives him rotgut at a quarter of a dollar a glass, is he? Any time that 'bum' gits razzled out for nothin' more'n this, why, I goes too; an' I ain't sayin' nothin' about goin' peaceable-like, neither."

"I knowed somethin' like this 'ud happen," dolefully sang out Billy Williams, strong on the side of his pessimism.

"For th' Lord's sake, have you broke out?" asked Red, disgustedly. "I'm goin' to hit the trail-but just keep this afore yore mind: if By-and-by gits in any accidents or ain't in sight when I comes to town again, this here climate'll be a heep sight hotter'n it is now. No hard feelings, sabe? It's just a casual bit of advice. Come on, fellows, let's amble —I'm hungry."

As they raced across the plain toward the ranch a pair of beady eyes, snapping with a drunken rage, watched them from an arroyo; and when Cowan entered the saloon the next morning he could not find By-and-by's rifle, which he had placed behind the bar. He also missed a handful of cartridges from the box near the cash drawer; and had he looked closely at his bottled whisky he would have noticed a loss there. A horse was missing from a Mexican's corral and there were rumors that several Indians had been seen far out on the plain.

Chapter V
The Law of the Range

"Phew! I'm shore hungry," said Hopalong, as he and Red dismounted at the ranch the next morning for breakfast. "Wonder what's good for it?"

"They's three things that's good for famine," said Red, leading the way to the bunk house. "Yu can pull in yore belt, yu can drink, an yu can eat. Yore getting as bad as Johnny-but he's young yet."

The others met their entrance with a volley of good-humored banter, some of which was so personal and evoked such responses that it sounded like the preliminary skirmish to a fight. But under all was that soft accent, that drawl of humorous appreciation and eyes twinkling in suppressed merriment. Here they were thoroughly at home and the spirit of comradeship manifested itself in many subtle ways; the wit became more daring and sharp, Billy lost some of his pessimism, and the alertness disappeared from their manner.

Skinny left off romping with Red and yawned. "I wish that cook'ud wake up an' git breakfast. He's the cussedest hombre I ever saw-he kin go to sleep standin' up an' not know it. Johnny's th' boy that worries him-th' kid comes in an' whoops things up till he's gorged himself."

"Johnny's got th' most appallin' feel for grub of anybody I knows," added Red. "I wonder what's keepin' him-he's usually hangin' around here bawlin' for his grub like a spoiled calf, long afore cookie's got th' fire goin'."

"Mebby he rustled some grub out with him —I saw him tip-toein' out of th' gallery this mornin' when I come back for my cigs," remarked Hopalong, glancing at Billy.

Billy groaned and made for the gallery. Emerging half a minute later he blurted out his tale of woe: "Every time I blows myself an' don't drink it all in town some slab-sided maverick freezes to it. It's gone," he added, dismally.

"Too bad, Billy-but what is it?" asked Skinny.

"What is it? Wha'd yu think it was, you emaciated match? Jewelry? Cayuses? It's whisky-two simoleons' worth. Some-thin's allus wrong. This here whole yearth's wrong, just like that cross-eyed sky pilot said over to —"

"Will yu let up?" Yelled Red, throwing a sombrero at the grumbling unfortunate. "Yu ask Buck where yore tanglefoot is.

"I'd shore look nice askin' th' boss if he'd rustled my whisky, wouldn't I? An' would yu mind throwin' somebody else's hat? I paid twenty wheels for that eight years ago, and I don't want it mussed none."

"Gee, yore easy! Why, Ah Sing, over at Albuquerque, gives them away every time yu gits yore shirt washed," gravely interposed Hopalong as he went out to cuss the cook.

"Well, what'd yu think of that?" Exclaimed Billy in an injured tone.

"Oh, yu needn't be hikin' for Albuquerque-WasheeWashee'ud charge yu double for washin' yore shirt. Yu ought to fall in di' river some day-then he might talk business," called Hopalong over his shoulder as he heaved an old boot into the gallery. "Hey, yu hibernatin' son of morphine, if yu don't git them flapjacks in here pretty sudden-like I'll scatter yu all over di' landscape, sabe? Yu just wait till Johnny comes!"

"Wonder where th' kid is?" asked Lanky, rolling a cigarette. "Off somewhere lookin' at di' sun through di' bottom of my bottle," grumbled Billy.

Hopalong started to go out, but halted on the sill and looked steadily off toward the northwest. "That's funny. Hey, fellows, here comes Buck an' Johnny ridin' double-on a walk, too!" he exclaimed. "Wonder what th' —thunder! Red, Buck's carryun' him! Somethin's busted!" he yelled, as he dashed for his pony and made for the newcomers.

"I told yu he was hittin' my bottle," pertly remarked Billy, as he followed the rest outside.

"Did yu ever see Johnny drunk? Did yu ever see him drink more'n two glasses? Shut yore wailin' face-they's somethin' worse'n that in this here," said Red, his temper rising. "Hopalong an' me took yore cheap liquor-it's under Pete's bunk," he added.

The trio approached on a walk and Johnny, delirious and covered with blood, was carried into the bunk house. Buck waited until all had assembled again and then, his face dark with anger, spoke sharply and without the usual drawl: "Skragged from behind, blast them! Get some grub an' water an' be quick. We'll see who the gent with th' grudge is."

At this point the expostulations of the indignant cook, who, not understanding the cause, regarded the invasion of china shop bulls as sacrilegious, came to his ears. Striding quickly to the door, he grabbed the pan the Mexican was about to throw and, turning the now frightened man around, thundered, "Keep quiet an' get 'em some grub."

When rifles and ammunition had been secured they mounted and followed him at a hard gallop along the back trail. No words were spoken, for none were necessary. All knew that they would not return until they had found the man for whom they were looking, even if the chase led to Canada. They did not ask Buck for any of the particulars, for the foreman was not in the humor to talk, and all, save Hopalong, whose curiosity was always on edge, recognized only two facts and cared for nothing else: Johnny had been ambushed and they were going to get the one who was responsible.

They did not even conjecture as to who it might be, because the trail would lead them to the man himself, and it mattered nothing who or what he was-there was only one course to take with an assassin. So they said nothing, but rode on with squared jaws and set lips, the seven ponies breast to breast in a close arc.

Soon they came to an arroyo which they took at a leap. As they approached it they saw signs in the dust which told them that a body had lain there huddled up; and there were brown spots on the baked alkali. The trail they followed was now single, Buck having ridden along the bank of the arroyo when hunting for Johnny, for whom he had orders. This trail was very irregular, as if the horse had wandered at will. Suddenly they came upon five tracks, all pointing one way, and four of these turned abruptly and disappeared in the northwest. Half a mile beyond the point of separation was a chaparral, which was an important factor to them.

Each man knew just what had taken place as if he had been an eyewitness, for the trail was plain. The assassins had waited in the chaparral for Johnny to pass, probably having seen him riding that way. When he had passed and his back had been turned to them they had fired and wounded him severely at the first volley, for Johnny was of the stuff that fights back and his revolvers had showed full chambers and clean barrels when Red had examined them in the bunk house. Then they had given chase for a short distance and, from some inexplicable motive, probably fear, they had turned and ridden off without knowing how bad he was hit. It was this trail that led to the northwest, and it was this trail that they followed without pausing.

When they had covered fifty miles they sighted the Cross Bar O ranch where they hoped to secure fresh mounts. As they rode up to the ranch house the owner, Bud Wallace, came around the corner and saw them.

"Hullo, boys! What deviltry are yu up to now?" he asked. Buck leaped from his mount, followed by the others, and shoved his sombrero back on his head as he started to remove the saddle.

"We're trailin' a bunch of murderers. They ambushed Johnny an' blame near killed him. I stopped here to get fresh cayuses."

"Yu did right!" replied Wallace heartily. Then raising his voice he shouted to some of his men who were near the corral to bring up the seven best horses they could rope. Then he told the cook to bring out plenty of food and drink.

"I got four punchers what ain't doin' nothin' but eat," he suggested.

"Much obliged, Wallace, but there's only four of 'em, an' we'd rather get 'em ourselves-Johnny'ud feel better," replied Buck, throwing his saddle on the horse that was led up to him.

"How's yore cartridges-got plenty?" Persisted Wallace.

"Two hundred apiece," responded Buck, springing into his saddle and riding off. "So long," he called.

"So long, an' plug blazes out of them," shouted Wallace as the dust swept over him.

At five in the afternoon they forded the Black River at a point where it crossed the state line from New Mexico, and at dusk camped at the base of the Guadalupe Mountains. At daybreak they took up the chase, grim and merciless, and shortly afterward they passed the smoldering remains of a camp fire, showing that the pursued had been in a great hurry, for it should have been put out and masked. At noon they left the mountains to the rear and sighted the Barred Horeshoe, which they approached.

The owner of the ranch saw them coming, and from their appearance surmised that something was wrong.

"What is it?" He shouted. "Rustlers?"

"Nope. Murderers. I wants to swap cayuses quick," answered Buck.

"There they are. Th' boys just brought 'em in. Anything else I can let yu have?"

"Nope," shouted Buck as they galloped off.

"Somebody's goin' to get plugged full of holes," murmured the ranch owner as he watched them kicking up the dust in huge clouds.

After they had forded a tributary of the Rio Penasco near the Sacramento Mountains and had surmounted the opposite bank, Hopalong spurred his horse to the top of a hummock and swept the plain with Pete's field glasses, which he had borrowed for the occasion, and returned to the rest, who had kept on without slacking the pace. As he took up his former position he grunted, "War-whoops," and unslung his rifle, an example followed by the others.

The ponies were now running at top speed, and as they shot over a rise their riders saw their quarry a mile and a half in advance. One of the Indians looked back and discharged his rifle in defiance, and it now became a race worthy of the name-Death fled from Death. The fresher mounts of the cowboys steadily cut down the distance and, as the rifles of the pursuers began to speak, the hard-pressed Indians made for the smaller of two knolls, the plain leading to the larger one being too heavily strewn with bowlders to permit speed.

As the fugitives settled down behind the rocks which fringed the edge of their elevation a shot from one of them disabled Billy's arm, but had no other effect than to increase the score to be settled. The pursuers rode behind a rise and dismounted, from where, leaving their mounts protected, they scattered out to surround the knoll.

Hopalong, true to his curiosity, finally turned up on the highest point of the other knoll, a spur of the range in the west, for he always wanted to see all he could. Skinny, due to his fighting instinct, settled one hundred yards to the north and on the same spur. Buck lay hidden behind an enormous bowlder eight hundred yards to the northeast of Skinny, and the same distance southeast of Buck was Red Connors, who was crawling up the bed of an arroyo. Billy, nursing his arm, lay in front of the horses, and Pete, from his position between Billy and Hopalong, was crawling from rock to rock in an endeavor to get near enough to use his Colts, his favorite and most effective weapons. Intermittent puffs of smoke arising from a point between Skinny and Buck showed where Lanky Smith was improving each shining hour.

There had been no directions given, each man choosing his own position, yet each was of strategic worth. Billy protected the horses, Hopalong and Skinny swept the knoll with a plunging fire, and Lanky and Buck lay in the course the besieged would most likely take if they tried a dash. Off to the east Red barred them from creeping down the arroyo, and from where Pete was he could creep up to within sixty yards if he chose the right rocks. The ranges varied from four hundred yards for Buck to sixty for Pete, and the others averaged close to three hundred, which allowed very good shooting on both sides.

Hopalong and Skinny gradually moved nearer to each other for companionship, and as the former raised his head to see what the others were doing he received a graze on the ear.

"Wow!" he yelled, rubbing the tingling member.

Two puffs of smoke floated up from the knoll, and Skinny swore.

"Where'd he get yu, Fat?" asked Hopalong.

"G'wan, don't get funny, son," replied Skinny.

Jets of smoke arose from the north and east, where Buck and Red were stationed, and Pete was half way to the knoll. So far he hadn't been hit as he dodged in and out, and, emboldened by his luck, he made a run of five yards and his sombrero was shot from his head. Another dash and his empty holster was ripped from its support. As he crouched behind a rock he heard a yell from Hopalong, and saw that interested individual waving his sombrero to cheer him on. An angry pang! from the knoll caused that enthusiastic rooter to drop for safety.

"Locoed son-of-a-gun," complained Pete. "He'll shore git potted." Then he glanced at Billy, who was the center of several successive spurts of dust.

"How's business, Billy?" he called pleasantly.

"Oh, they'll git me yet," responded the pessimist. "Yu needn't git anxious. If that off buck wasn't so green he'd 'a' had me long ago."

"Ya-hoo! Pete! Oh, Pete!" called Hopalong, sticking his head out at one side and grinning as the wondering object of his hail craned his neck to see what the matter was.

"Huh?" grunted Pete, and then remembering the distance he shouted, "What's th' matter?"

"Got any cigarettes?" asked Hopalong.

"Yu poor sheep!" said Pete, and turning back to work he drove a .45 into a yellow moccasin.

Hopalong began to itch and he saw that he was near an ant hill. Then the cactus at his right boomed out mournfully and a hole appeared in it. He fired at the smoke and a yell informed him that he had made a hit. "Go 'way!" he complained as a green fly buzzed past his nose. Then he scratched each leg with the foot of the other and squirmed incessantly, kicking out with both feet at once. A warning metallic whir-r-r! on his left caused to yank them in again, and turning his head quickly he the pleasure of lopping off the head of a rattlesnake with his Colt's.

"Glad yu wasn't a copperhead," he exclaimed. "Somebody had ought 'a' shot that fool Noah. Blast the ants!" He drowned with a jet of tobacco juice a Gila monster that was staring at him and took a savage delight in its frantic efforts to bury itself.

Soon he heard Skinny swear and he sung out: "What's the matter, Skinny? Git plugged again?"

"Naw, bugs-ain't they mean?" Plaintively asked his friend. "They ain't none over here. What kind of bugs?"

"Sufferin' Moses, I ain't no bugologist! All kinds!"

But Hopalong got it at last. He had found tobacco and rolled a cigarette, and in reaching for a match exposed his shoulder to a shot that broke his collar bone. Skinny's rifle cracked in reply and the offending brave rolled out from behind a rock. From the fuss emanating from Hopalong's direction Skinny knew that his neighbor had been hit.

"Don't yu care, Hoppy. I got th' cuss," he said consolingly. "Where'd he git yu?" he asked.

"In di' heart, yu pie-faced nuisance. Come over here an' corral this cussed bandage an' gimme some water," snapped the injured man.

Skinny wormed his way through the thorny chaparral and bound up the shoulder. "Anything else?" he asked.

"Yes. Shoot that bunch of warts an' blow that tobacco-eyed Gila to Cheyenne. This here's worse than the time we cleaned out th' C 80 outfit!" Then he kicked the dead toad and swore at the sun.

"Close yore yap; yore worse than a kid! Anybody'd think yu never got plugged afore," said Skinny indignantly.

"I can cuss all I wants," replied Hopalong, proving his assertion as he grabbed his gun and fired at the dead Indian. A bullet whined above his head and Skinny fired at the smoke. He peeped out and saw that his friends were getting nearer to the knoll.

"They's closin' in now. We'll soon be gittin' home," he reported.

Hopalong looked out in time to see Buck make a dash for a bowlder that lay ten yards in front of him, which he reached in safety. Lanky also ran in and Pete added five more yards to his advance. Buck made another dash, but leaped into the air, and, coming down as if from an intentional high jump, staggered and stumbled for a few paces and then fell flat, rolling over and over toward the shelter of a split rock, where he lay quiet. A leering red face peered over the rocks on the knoll, but the whoop of exultation was cut short, for Red's rifle cracked and the warrior rolled down the steep bank, where another shot from the same gun settled him beyond question.

Hopalong choked and, turning his face away, angrily dashed his knuckles into his eyes. "Blast 'em! Blast 'em! They've got Buck! They've got Buck, blast 'em! They've got Buck, Skinny! Good old Buck! They've got him! Jimmy's gone, Johnny's plugged, and now Buck's gone! Come on!" he sobbed in a frenzy of vengeance. "Come on, Skinny! We'll tear their cussed hides into a deeper red than they are now! Oh, blast it, I can't see-where's my gun?" He groped for the rifle and fought Skinny when the latter, red-eyed but cool, endeavored to restrain him. "Lemme go, curse yu! Don't yu know they got Buck? Lemme go!"

"Down! Red's got di' skunk. Yu can't do nothin' —they'd drop yu afore yu took five steps. Red's got him, I tell yu! Do yu want me to lick yu? We'll pay 'em back with interest if yu'll keep yore head!" exclaimed Skinny, throwing the crazed man heavily.

Musical tones, rising and falling in weird octaves, whining pityingly, diabolically, sobbing in a fascinating monotone and slobbering in ragged chords, calling as they swept over the plain, always calling and exhorting, they mingled in barbaric discord with the defiant barks of the six-shooters and the inquiring cracks of the Winchesters. High up in the air several specks sailed and drifted, more coming up rapidly from all directions. Buzzards know well where food can be found.

As Hopalong leaned back against a rock he was hit in the thigh by a ricochet that tore its way out, whirling like a circular saw, a span above where it entered. The wound was very nasty, being ripped twice the size made by an ordinary shot, and it bled profusely. Skinny crawled over and attended to it, making a tourniquet of his neckerchief and clumsily bandaging it with a strip torn from his shirt.

"Yore shore lucky, yu are," he grumbled as he made his way back to his post, where he vented his rancor by emptying the semi-depleted magazine of his Winchester at the knoll.

Hopalong began to sing and shout and he talked of Jimmy and his childhood, interspersing the broken narrative with choice selections as sung in the music halls of Leavenworth and Abilene. He wound up by yelling and struggling, and Skinny had his hands full in holding him.

"Hopalong! Cassidy! Come out of that! Keep quiet-yu'll shore git plugged if yu don't stop that plungin'. For gosh sake, did yu hear that?" A bullet viciously hissed between them and flattened out on a near-by rock; others cut their way through the chaparral to the sound of falling twigs, and Skinny threw himself on the struggling man and strapped Hopalong with his belt to the base of a honey mesquite that grew at his side.

"Hold still, now, and let that bandage alone. Yu allus goes off di' range when yu gets plugged," he complained. He cut down a cactus and poured the sap over the wounded man's face, causing him to gurgle and look around. His eyes had a sane look now and Skinny slid off his chest.

"Git that-belt loose; I ain't —no cow," brokenly blazed out the picketed Hopalong. Skinny did so, handed the irate man his Colts and returned to his own post, from where he fired twice, reporting the shots.

"I'm tryin' to get him on th' glance' first one went high an' th' other fell flat," he explained.

Hopalong listened eagerly, for this was shooting that he could appreciate. "Lemme see," he commanded. Skinny dragged him over to a crack and settled down for another try.

"Where is he, Skinny?" Asked Hopalong.

"Behind that second big one. No, over on this here side. See that smooth granite? If I can get her there on th' right spot he'll shore know it." He aimed carefully and fired.

Through Pete's glasses Hopalong saw a leaden splotch appear on the rock and he notified the marksman that he was shooting high. "Put her on that bump closer down," he suggested. Skinny did so and another yell reached their ears.

"That's a dandy. Yore shore all right, yu old cuss," complimented Hopalong, elated at the success of the experiment.

Skinny fired again and a brown arm flopped out into sight. Another shot struck it and it jerked as though it were lifeless.

"He's cashed. See how she jumped? Like a rope," remarked Skinny with a grin. The arm lay quiet.

Pete had gained his last cover and was all eyes and Colts. Lanky was also very close in and was intently watching one particular rock. Several shots echoed from the far side of the knoll and they knew that Red was all right. Billy was covering a cluster of rocks that protruded above the others and, as they looked, his rifle rang out and the last defender leaped down and disappeared in the chaparral. He wore yellow trousers and an old boiled shirt.

"By an'-by, by all that's bad!" yelled Hopalong. "Th' measly coyote! An' me a-fillin' his ornery hide with liquor. Well, they'll have to find him all over again now," he complained, astounded by the revelation. He fired into the chaparral to express his pugnacious disgust and scared out a huge tarantula, which alighted on Skinny's chaps, crawling rapidly toward the unconscious man's neck. Hopalong's face hardened and he slowly covered the insect and fired, driving it into the sand, torn and lifeless. The bullet touched the leathern garment and Skinny remonstrated, knowing that Hopalong was in no condition for fancy shooting.

"Huh!" exclaimed Hopalong. "That was a tarantula what I plugged. He was headin' for yore neck," he explained, watching the chaparral with apprehension.

"Go 'way, was it? Bully for yu!" exclaimed Skinny, tarantulas being placed at par with rattlesnakes, and he considered that he had been saved from a horrible death. "Thought yu said they wasn't no bugs over here," he added in an aggrieved tone.

"They wasn't none. Yu brought 'em. I only had th' main show-Gilas, rattlers an' toads," he replied, and then added, "Ain't it cussed hot up here?"

"She is. Yu won't have no cinch ridin' home with that leg. Yu better take my cayuse-he's busted more'n yourn," responded Skinny.

"Yore cayuse is at th' Cross Bar O, yu wall-eyed pirute."

"Shore 'nuff. Funny how a feller forgets sometimes. Lemme alone now, they's goin' to git By-an'-by. Pete an' Lanky has just went in after him."

That was what had occurred. The two impatient punchers, had grown tired of waiting, and risked what might easily have been death in order to hasten matters. The others kept up a rapid fire, directed at the far end of the chaparral on the knoll, in order to mask the movements of their venturesome friends, intending also to drive By-and-by toward them so that he would be the one to get picked off as he advanced.

Several shots rang out in quick succession on the knoll and the chaparral became agitated. Several more shots sounded from the depth of the thicket and a mounted Indian dashed out of the northern edge and headed in Buck's direction. His course would take him close to Buck, whom he had seen fall, and would let him escape at a point midway between Red and Skinny, as Lanky was on the knoll and the range was very far to allow effective shooting by these two.

Red saw him leave the chaparral and in his haste to reload jammed the cartridge, and By-and-by swept on toward temporary safety, with Red dancing in a paroxysm of rage, swelling his vocabulary with words he had forgotten existed.

By-and-by, rising to his full height in the saddle, turned and wiggled his fingers at the frenzied Red and made several other signs that the cowboy was in the humor to appreciate to the fullest extent. Then he turned and shook his rifle at the marksmen on the larger knoll, whose best shots kicked up the dust fully fifty yards too short. The pony was sweeping toward the reservation and friends only fifteen miles away, and By-and-by knew that once among the mountains he would be on equal footing at least with his enemies.

As he passed the rock behind which Buck lay sprawled on his face he uttered a piercing whoop of triumph and leaned forward on his pony's neck. Twenty leaps farther and the spiteful crack of a rifle echoed from where the foreman was painfully supporting himself on his elbows. The pony swept on in a spurt of nerve-racking speed, but alone. By-and-by shrieked again and crashed heavily to the ground, where he rolled inertly and then lay still. Men like Buck are dangerous until their hearts have ceased to beat.

Chapter VI
Trials of the Convalescent

The days at the ranch passed in irritating idleness for those who had obstructed the flight of hostile lead, and worse than any of the patients was Hopalong, who fretted and fumed at his helplessness, which retarded his recovery. But at last the day came when he was fit for the saddle again, and he gave notice of his joy in whoops and forthwith announced that he was entitled to a holiday; and Buck had not the heart to refuse him.

So he started forth in his quest of peace and pleasure, but instead had found only trouble and had been forced to leave his card at almost every place he had visited.

There was that affair in Red Hot Gulch, Colorado, where, under pressure, he had invested sundry pieces of lead in the persons of several obstreperous citizens and then had paced the zealous and excitable sheriff to the state line.

He next was noticed in Cheyenne, where his deformity was vividly dwelt upon, to the extent of six words, by one Tarantula Charley, the aforesaid Charley not being able to proceed to greater length on account of heart failure. As Charley had been a ubiquitous nuisance, those present availed themselves of the opportunity offered by Hopalong to indulge in a free drink.

Laramie was his next stopping place, and shortly after his arrival he was requested to sing and dance by a local terror, who informed all present that he was the only seventeen-buttoned rattlesnake in the cow country. Hopalong, hurt and indignant at being treated like a common tenderfoot, promptly knocked the terror down. After he had irrigated several square feet of parched throats belonging to the audience he again took up his journey and spent a day at Denver, where he managed to avoid any further trouble.

Santa Fe loomed up before him several days later and he entered it shortly before noon. At this time the old Spanish city was a bundle of high-strung nerves, and certain parts of it were calculated to furnish any and all kinds of excitement except revival meetings and church fairs. Hopalong straddled a lively nerve before he had been in the city an hour. Two local bad men,

Slim Travennes and Tex Ewalt, desiring to establish the fact that they were roaring prairie fires, attempted to consume the placid and innocent stranger as he limped across the plaza in search of a game of draw poker at the Black Hills Emporium, with the result that they needed repairs, to the chagrin and disgust of their immediate acquaintances, who endeavored to drown their mortification and sorrow in rapid but somewhat wild gun play, and soon remembered that they had pressing engagements elsewhere.

Hopalong reloaded his guns and proceeded to the Emporium, where he found a game all prepared for him in every sense of the word. On the third deal he objected to the way in which the dealer manipulated the cards, and when the smoke cleared away he was the only occupant of the room, except a dog belonging to the bartender that had intercepted a stray bullet.

Hunting up the owner of the hound, he apologized for being the indirect cause of the animal's death, deposited a sum of Mexican dollars in that gentleman's palm and went on his way to Alameda, which he entered shortly after dark, and where an insult, simmering in its uncalled-for venom, met him as he limped across the floor of the local dispensary on his way to the bar. There was no time for verbal argument and precedent had established the manner of his reply, and his repartee was as quick as light and most effective. Having resented the epithets he gave his attention to the occupants of the room.

Smoke drifted over the table in an agitated cloud and dribbled lazily upward from the muzzle of his six-shooter, while he looked searchingly at those around him. Strained and eager faces peered at his opponent, who was sliding slowly forward in his chair, and for the length of a minute no sound but the guarded breathing of the onlookers could be heard. This was broken by a nervous cough from the rear of the room, and the faces assumed their ordinary nonchalant expressions, their rugged lines heavily shadowed in the light of the flickering oil lamps, while the shuffling of cards and the clink of silver became audible. Hopalong Cassidy had objected to insulting remarks about his affliction.

Hopalong was very sensitive about his crippled leg and was always prompt to resent any scorn or curiosity directed at it, especially when emanating from strangers. A young man of twenty-three years, when surrounded by nearly perfect specimens of physical manhood, is apt to be painfully self-conscious of any such defect, and it reacted on his nature at times, even though he was well-known for his happy-go-lucky disposition and playfulness. He consoled himself with the knowledge that what he lost in symmetry was more than balanced by the celerity and certainty of his gun hand, which was right or left, or both, as the occasion demanded.

Several hours later, as his luck was vacillating, he felt a heavy hand on his shoulder, and was overjoyed at seeing Buck and Red, the latter grinning as only Red could grin, and he withdrew from the game to enjoy his good fortune.

While Hopalong had been wandering over the country the two friends had been hunting for him and had traced him successfully, that being due to the trail he had blazed with his six-shooters. This they had accomplished without harm to themselves, as those of whom they inquired thought that they must want Hopalong "bad," and cheerfully gave the information required.

They had started out more for the purpose of accompanying him for pleasure, but that had changed to an urgent necessity in the following manner:

While on the way from Denver to Santa Fe they had met Pete Willis of the Three Triangle, a ranch that adjoined their own, and they paused to pass the compliments of the season.

"Purty far from th' grub wagon, Pie," remarked Buck.

"Oh, I'm only goin' to Denver," responded Pie.

"Purty hot," suggested Red.

"She shore is. Seen anybody yu knows?" Pie asked.

"One or two-Billy of th' Star Crescent an' Panhandle Lukins," answered Buck.

"That so? Panhandle's goin' to punch for us next year. I'll hunt him up. I heard down south of Albuquerque that Thirsty Jones an' his brothers are lookin' for trouble," offered Pie.

"Yah! They ain't lookin' for no trouble-they just goes around blowin' off. Trouble? Why, they don't know what she is," remarked Red contemptuously.

"Well, they's been dodgin' th' sheriff purty lively lately, an' if that ain't trouble I don't know what is," said Pie.

"It shore is, an' hard to dodge," acquiesced Buck.

"Well, I has to amble. Is Panhandle in Denver? Yes? I calculates as how me an' him'll buck th' tiger for a whirl-he's shore lucky. Well, so long," said Pie as he moved on.

"So long," responded the two.

"Hey, wait a minute," yelled Pie after he had ridden a hundred yards. "If yu sees Hopalong yu might tell him that th' Joneses are goin' to hunt him up when they gits to Albuquerque. They's shore sore on him. 'Tain't none of my funeral, only they ain't always a-carin' how they goes after a feller. So long," and soon he was a cloud of dust on the horizon.

"Trouble!" snorted Red; "well, between dodgin' Harris an' huntin' Hopalong I reckons they'll shore find her." Then to himself he murmured, "Funny how everythin' comes his way."

"That's gospel shore enough, but, as Pie said, they ain't a whole lot particular as how they deal th' cards. We better get a move on an' find that ornery little cuss," replied Buck.

"O. K., only I ain't losin' no sleep about Hoppy. His gun's too lively for me to do any worryin'," asserted Red.

"They'll get lynched some time, shore," declared Buck.

"Not if they find Hoppy," grimly replied Red.

They tore through Santa Fe, only stopping long enough to wet their throats, and after several hours of hard riding entered Alameda, where they found Hopalong in the manner narrated.

After some time the three left the room and headed for Albuquerque, twelve miles to the south. At ten o'clock they dismounted before the Nugget and Rope, an unpainted wooden building supposed to be a clever combination of barroom, dance and gambling hall and hotel. The cleverness lay in the man who could find the hotel part.

Chapter VII
The Open Door

The proprietor of the Nugget and Rope, a German named Baum, not being troubled with police rules, kept the door wide open for the purpose of inviting trade, a proceeding not to the liking of his patrons for obvious reasons. Probably not one man in ten was fortunate enough to have no one "looking for him," and the lighted interior assured good hunting to any one in the dark street. He was continually opening the door, which every newcomer promptly and forcibly slammed shut. When he saw men walk across the room for the express purpose of slamming it he began to cherish the idea that there was a conspiracy on foot to anger him and thus force him to bring about his own death.

After the door had been slammed three times in one evening by one man, the last slam being so forcible as to shake two bottles from the shelf and to crack the door itself, he became positive that his suspicions were correct, and so was very careful to smile and take it as a joke. Finally, wearied by his vain efforts to keep it open and fearing for the door, he hit upon a scheme, the brilliancy of which inflated his chest and gave him the appearance of a prize-winning bantam. When his patrons strolled in that night there was no door to slam, as it lay behind the bar.

When Buck and Red entered, closely followed by Hopalong, they elbowed their way to the rear of the room, where they could see before being seen. As yet they had said nothing to Hopalong about Pie's warning and were debating in their minds whether they should do so or not, when Hopalong interrupted their thoughts by laughing. They looked up and he nodded toward the front, where they saw that anxious eyes from all parts of the room were focused on the open door. Then they noticed that it had been removed.

The air of semi-hostile, semi-anxious inquiry of the patrons and the smile of satisfaction covering the face of Baum appealed to them as the most ludicrous sight their eyes had seen for months, and they leaned back and roared with laughter, thus calling forth sundry looks of disapproval from the innocent causes of their merriment. But they were too well known in Albuquerque to allow the disapproval to approach a serious end, and finally, as the humorous side of the situation dawned on the crowd, they joined in the laugh and all went merrily.

At the psychologic moment some one shouted for a dance and the suggestion met with uproarious approval. At that moment Harris, the sheriff, came in and volunteered to supply the necessary music if the crowd would pay the fine against a straying fiddler he had corraled the day before. A hat was quickly passed and a sum was realized which would pay several fines to come and Harris departed for the music.

A chair was placed on the bar for the musician and, to the tune of "Old Dan Tucker" and an assortment of similar airs, the board floor shook and trembled. It was a comical sight and Hopalong, the only wallflower besides Baum and the sheriff, laughed until he became weak. Cow punchers play as they work, hard and earnestly, and there was plenty of action. Sombreros flapped like huge wings and the baggy chaps looked like small, distorted balloons.

The Virginia reel was a marvel of supple, exaggerated grace and the quadrille looked like a free-for-all for unbroken colts. The honor of prompter was conferred upon the sheriff, and he gravely called the changes as they were usually called in that section of the country:

> "Oh, th' ladies trail in
> An' th' gents trail out,
> An' all stampede down th' middle.
> If yu ain't got th' tin
> Yu can dance an' shout,
> But yu must keep up with th' fiddle."

As the dance waxed faster and the dancers grew hotter Hopalong, feeling lonesome because he wouldn't face ridicule, even if it was not expressed, went over and stood by the sheriff. He and Harris were good friends, for he had received the wound that crippled him in saving the sheriff from assassination. Harris killed the man who had fired that shot, and from this episode on the burning desert grew a friendship that was as strong as their own natures.

Harris was very well liked by the majority and feared by the rest, for he was a square man and the best sheriff the county had ever known. Quiet and unassuming, small of stature and with a kind word for every one, he was a universal favorite among the better class of citizens. Quick as a flash and unerring in his shooting, he was a nightmare to the "bad men." No profane word had ever been known to leave his lips, and he was the possessor of a widespread reputation for generosity. His face was naturally frank and open; but when his eyes narrowed with determination it became blank and cold. When he saw his young friend sidle over to him he smiled and nodded a hearty welcome.

"They's shore cuttin' her loose," remarked Hopalong.

"First two pairs forward an' back! —they shore is," responded the prompter.

"Who's th' gent playin' lady to Buck?" Queried Hopalong.

"Forward again an' ladies change! —Billy Jordan."

Hopalong watched the couple until they swung around and then he laughed silently. "Buck's got too many feet," he seriously remarked to his friend.

"Swing th' girl yu loves th' best! —he ain't lonesome, look at that —"

Two shots rang out in quick succession and Harris stumbled, wheeled and pitched forward on his face as Hopalong's sombrero spun across his body. For a second there was an intense silence, heavy, strained and sickening. Then a roar broke forth and the crowd of frenzied merry-makers, headed by Hopalong, poured out into the street and spread out to search the town. As daylight dawned the searchers began to straggle back with the same report of failure. Buck and Red met on the street near the door and each looked questioningly at the other. Each shook his head and looked around, their fingers toying absentmindedly at their belts. Finally Buck cleared his throat and remarked casually,

"Mebby he's following 'em."

Red nodded and they went over toward their horses. As they were hesitating which route to take, Billy Jordan came up.

"Mebby yu'd like to see yore pardner-he's out by Buzzard's Spring. We'll take care of him," jerking his thumb over his shoulder toward the saloon where Harris's body lay. "And we'll all git th' others later. They cain't git away for long."

Buck and Red nodded and headed for Buzzard's Spring. As they neared the water hole they saw Hopalong sitting on a rock, his head resting in one hand while the other hung loosely from his knee. He did not notice them when they arrived, and with a ready tact they sat quietly on their horses and looked in every direction except toward him. The sun became a ball of molten fire and the sand flies annoyed them incessantly, but still they sat and waited, silent and apologetic.

Hopalong finally arose, reached for his sombrero, and, finding it gone, swore long and earnestly at the scene its loss brought before him. He walked over to his horse and, leaping into the saddle, turned and faced his friends. "Yu old sons-of-guns," he said. They looked sheepish and nodded negatively in answer to the look of inquiry in his eyes. "They ain't got 'em yet," remarked Red slowly. Hopalong straightened up, his eyes narrowed and his face became hard and resolute as he led the way back toward the town.

Buck rode up beside him and, wiping his face with his shirt sleeve, began to speak to Red. "We might look up th' Joneses, Red. They had been dodgin' th' sheriff purty lively lately, an' they was huntin' Hopalong. Ever since we had to kill their brother in Buckskin they has been yappin' as how they was goin' to wipe us out. Hopalong an' Harris was standin' clost together an' they tried for both. They shot twice, one for Harris an' one for Hopalong, an' what more do yu want?"

"It shore looks thataway, Buck," replied Red, biting into a huge plug of tobacco which he produced from his chaps. "Anyhow, they wouldn't be no loss if they didn't. Member what Pie said?"

Hopalong looked straight ahead, and when he spoke the words sounded as though he had bitten them off: "Yore right, Buck, but I gits first try at Thirsty. He's my meat an' I'll plug th' fellow what says he ain't. Damn him!"

The others replied by applying their spurs, and in a short time they dismounted before the Nugget and Rope. Thirsty wouldn't have a chance to not care how he dealt the cards.

Buck and Red moved quickly through the crowd, speaking fast and earnestly. When they returned to where they had left their friend they saw him half a block away and they followed slowly, one on either side of the street. There would be no bullets in his back if they knew what they were about, and they usually did.

As Hopalong neared the corner, Thirsty and his two brothers turned it and saw him. Thirsty said something in a low voice, and the other two walked across the street and disappeared behind the store. When assured that they were secure, Thirsty walked up to a huge boulder on the side of the street farthest from the store and turned and faced his enemy, who approached rapidly until about five paces away, when he slowed up and finally stopped.

For a number of seconds they sized each other up, Hopalong quiet and deliberate with a deadly hatred; Thirsty pale and furtive with a sensation hitherto unknown to him. It was Right meeting Wrong, and Wrong lost confidence. Often had Thirsty Jones looked death in the face and laughed, but there was something in Hopalong's eyes that made his flesh creep.

He glanced quickly past his foe and took in the scene with one flash of his eyes. There was the crowd, eager, expectant, scowling. There were Buck and Red, each lounging against a boulder, Buck on his right, Red on his left. Before him stood the only man he had ever feared.

Hopalong shifted his feet and Thirsty, coming to himself with a start, smiled. His nerve had been shaken, but he was master of himself once more.

"Well!" he snarled, scowling.

Hopalong made no response, but stared him in the eyes.

Thirsty expected action, and the deadly quiet of his enemy oppressed him. He stared in turn, but the insistent searching of his opponent's eyes scorched him and he shifted his gaze to Hopalong's neck.

"Well!" he repeated uneasily.

"Did yu have a nice time at th' dance last night?" Asked Hopalong, still searching the face before him.

"Was there a dance? I was over in Alameda," replied Thirsty shortly.

"Ya-as, there was a dance, an' yu can shoot purty durn far if yu was in Alameda," responded Hopalong, his voice low and monotonous.

Thirsty shifted his feet and glanced around. Buck and Red were still lounging against their bowlders and apparently were not paying any attention to the proceedings. His fickle nerve came back again, for he knew he would receive fair play. So he faced Hopalong once more and regarded him with a cynical smile.

"Yu seems to worry a whole lot about me. Is it because yu has a tender feelin', or because it's none of yore blame business?" He asked aggressively.

Hopalong paled with sudden anger, but controlled himself.

"It's because yu murdered Harris," he replied.

"Shoo! An' how does yu figger it out?" Asked Thirsty, jauntily.

"He was huntin' yu hard an' yu thought yu'd stop it, so yu came in to lay for him. When yu saw me an' him together yu saw di' chance to wipe out another score. That's how I figger it out," replied Hopalong quietly.

"Yore a reg'lar 'tective, ain't yu?" Thirsty asked ironically.

"I've got common sense," responded Hopalong.

"Yu has? Yu better tell th' rest that, too," replied Thirsty.

"I know yu shot Harris, an' yu can't get out of it by makin' funny remarks. Anyhow, yu won't be much loss, an' th' stage company'll feel better, too."

"Shoo! An' suppose I did shoot him, I done a good job, didn't I?"

"Yu did the worst job yu could do, yu highway robber," softly said Hopalong, at the same time moving nearer. "Harris knew yu stopped th' stage last month, an' that's why yu've been dodgin' him."

"Yore a liar!" shouted Thirsty, reaching for his gun.

The movement was fatal, for before he could draw, the Colt in Hopalong's holster leaped out and flashed from its owner's hip and Thirsty fell sideways, face down in the dust of the street.

Hopalong started toward the fallen man, but as he did so a shot rang out from behind the store and he pitched forward, stumbled and rolled behind the bowlder. As he stumbled his left hand streaked to his hip, and when he fell he had a gun in each hand.

As he disappeared from sight Goodeye and Bill Jones stepped from behind the store and started to run away. Not able to resist the temptation to look again, they stopped and turned and Bill laughed.

"Easy as sin," he said.

"Run, yu fool-Red an' Buck'll be here. Want to git plugged?" shouted Goodeye angrily.

They turned and started for a group of ponies twenty yards away, and as they leaped into the saddles two shots were fired from the street. As the reports died away Buck and Red turned the corner of the store, Colts in hand, and, checking their rush as they saw the saddles emptied, they turned toward the street and saw Hopalong, with blood oozing from an abrasion on his cheek, sitting up cross-legged, with each hand holding a gun, from which came thin wisps of smoke.

"Th' son-of-a-gun!" cried Buck, proud and delighted.

"Th' son-of-a-gun!" echoed Red, grinning.

Chapter VIII
Hopalong Keeps His Word

The waters of the Rio Grande slid placidly toward the Gulf, the hot sun branding the sleepy waters with streaks of molten fire. To the north arose from the gray sandy plain the Quitman Mountains, and beyond them lay Bass Ca on. From the latter emerged a solitary figure astride a broncho, and as he ascended the topmost rise he glanced below him at the placid stream and beyond it into Mexico. As he sat quietly in his saddle he smiled and laughed gently to himself. The trail he had just followed had been replete with trouble which had suited the state of his mind and he now felt humorous, having cleaned up a pressing debt with his six-shooter. Surely there ought to be a mild sort of excitement in the land he faced, something picturesque and out of the ordinary. This was to be the finishing touch to his trip, and he had left his two companions at Albuquerque in order that he might have to himself all that he could find.

Not many miles to the south of him lay the town which had been the rendezvous of Tamale Jose, whose weakness had been a liking for other people's cattle. Well he remembered his first man hunt: the discovery of the theft, the trail and pursuit and-the ending. He was scarcely eighteen years of age when that event took place, and the wisdom he had absorbed then had stood him in good stead many times since. He had even now a touch of pride at the recollection how, when his older companions had failed to get Tamale Jose, he with his undeveloped strategy had gained that end. The fight would never be forgotten, as it was his first, and no sight of wounds would ever affect him as did those of Red Connors as he lay huddled up in the dark corner of that old adobe hut.

He came to himself and laughed again as he thought of Carmencita, the first girl he had ever known-and the last. With a boy's impetuosity he had wooed her in a manner far different from that of the peons who sang beneath her window and talked to her mother. He had boldly scaled the wall and did his courting in her house, trusting to luck and to his own ability to avoid being seen. No hidden meaning lay in his words; he spoke from his heart and with no concealment. And he remembered the treachery that had forced him, fighting, to the camp of his outfit; and when he had returned with his friends she had disappeared.

To this day he hated that mud-walled convent and those sisters who so easily forgot how to talk. The fragrance of the old days wrapped themselves around him, and although he had ceased to pine for his black-eyed Carmencita-well, it would be nice if he chanced to see her again. Spurring his mount into an easy canter he swept down to and across the river, fording it where he had crossed it when pursuing Tamale Jose.

The town lay indolent under the Mexican night, and the strumming of guitars and the tinkle of spurs and tiny bells softly echoed from several houses. The convent of St. Maria lay indistinct in its heavy shadows and the little church farther up the dusty street showed dim lights in its stained windows. Off to the north became audible the rhythmic beat of a horse and soon a cowboy swept past the convent with a mocking bow.

He clattered across the stone-paved plaza and threw his mount back on its haunches as he stopped before a house. Glancing around and determining to find out a few facts as soon as possible, he rode up to the low door and pounded upon it with the butt of his Colt. After waiting for possibly half a minute and receiving no response he hammered a tune upon it with two Colts and had the satisfaction of seeing half a score of heads protrude from the windows in the nearby houses.

"If I could scare up another gun I might get th' whole blamed town up," he grumbled whimsically, and fell on the door with another tune.

"Who is it?" came from within. The voice was distinctly feminine and Hopalong winked to himself in congratulation.

"Me," he replied, twirling his fingers from his nose at the curious, forgetting that the darkness hid his actions from sight.

"Yes, I know; but who is 'me'?" Came from the house.

"Ain't I a fool!" he complained to himself, and raising his voice he replied coaxingly, "Open th' door a bit an' see. Are yu Carmencita?"

"O-o-o! but you must tell me who it is first."

"Mr. Cassidy," he replied, flushing at the 'mister,' "an' I wants to see Carmencita."

"Carmencita who?" teasingly came from behind the door. Hopalong scratched his head. "Gee, yu've roped me —I suppose she has got another handle. Oh, yu know-she used to live here about seven years back. She had great big black eyes, pretty cheeks an' a mouth that 'ud stampede anybody. Don't yu know now? She was about so high," holding out his hands in the darkness.

The door opened a trifle on a chain and Hopalong peered eagerly forward.

"Ah, it is you, the brave Americano! You must go away quick or you will meet with harm. Manuel is awfully jealous and he will kill you! Go at once, please!"

Hopalong pulled at the half-hearted down upon his lip and laughed softly. Then he slid the guns back in their holsters and felt for his sombrero.

"Manuel wants to see me first, Star Eyes."

"No! no!" she replied, stamping upon the floor vehemently. "You must go now-at once!"

"I'd shore look nice hittin' th' trail because Manuel Somebody wants to get hurt, wouldn't I? Don't yu remember how I used to shinny up this here wall an' skin th' cat gettin' through that hole up there what yu said was a window? Ah, come on an' open th' door —I'd shore like to see yu again!" pleaded the irrepressible.

"No! no! Go away. Oh, won't you please go away!"

Hopalong sighed audibly and turned his horse. As he did so he heard the door open and a sigh reached his ears. He wheeled like a flash and found the door closed again on its chain. A laugh of delight came from behind it.

"Come out, please! —just for a minute," he begged, wishing that he was brave enough to smash the door to splinters and grab her.

"If I do, will you go away?" Asked the girl. "Oh, what will Manuel say if he comes? And all those people, they'll tell him!"

"Hey, yu!" shouted Hopalong, brandishing his Colts at the protruding heads. "Git scarce! I'll shore plug th' last one in!" Then he laughed at the sudden vanishing.

The door slowly opened and Carmencita, fat and drowsy, wobbled out to him. Hopalong's feelings were interfering with his breathing as he surveyed her. "Oh, yu shore are mistaken, Mrs. Carmencita. I wants to see yore daughter!"

"Ah, you have forgotten the little Carmencita who used to look for you. Like all the men, you have forgotten," she cooed reproachfully. Then her fear predominated again and she cried, "Oh, if my husband should see me now!"

Hopalong mastered his astonishment and bowed. He had a desire to ride madly into the Rio Grande and collect his senses.

"Yu are right-this is too dangerous —I'll amble on some," he replied hastily. Under his breath he prayed that the outfit would never learn of this. He turned his horse and rode slowly up the street as the door closed.

Rounding the corner he heard a soft footfall, and swerving in his saddle he turned and struck with all his might in the face of a man who leaped at him, at the same time grasping the uplifted wrist with his other hand. A curse and the tinkle of thin steel on the pavement accompanied the fall of his opponent. Bending down from his saddle he picked up the weapon and the next minute the enraged assassin was staring into the unwavering and, to him, growing muzzle of a Colt's .45.

"Yu shore had a bum teacher. Don't yu know better'n to push it in? An' me a cowpuncher, too! I'm most grieved at yore conduct-it shows you don't appreciate cow-wrastlers. This is safer," he remarked, throwing the stiletto through the air and into a door, where it rang out angrily and quivered. "I don't know as I wants to ventilate yu; we mostly poisons coyotes up my way," he added. Then a thought struck him. "Yu must be that dear Manuel I've been hearin' so much about?"

A snarl was the only reply and Hopalong grinned.

"Yu shore ain't got no call to go loco that way, none whatever. I don't want yore Carmencita. I only called to say hulloo," responded Hopalong, his sympathies being aroused for the wounded man before him from his vivid recollection of the woman who had opened the door.

"Yah!" snarled Manuel. "You wants to poison my little bird. You with your fair hair and your cursed swagger!"

The six-shooter tentatively expanded and stopped six inches from the Mexican's nose. "Yu wants to ride easy, hombre. I ain't no angel, but I don't poison no woman; an' don't yu amble off with th' idea in yore head that she wants to be poisoned. Why, she near stuck a knife in me!" he lied.

The Mexican's face brightened somewhat, but it would take more than that to wipe out the insult of the blow. The horse became restless, and when Hopalong had effectively quieted it he spoke again.

"Did yu ever hear of Tamale Jose?"

"Yes."

"Well, I'm th' fellow that stopped him in th' 'dobe hut by th' arroyo. I'm tellin' yu this so yu won't do nothin' rash an' leave Carmencita a widow. Sabe?"

The hate on the Mexican's face redoubled and he took a short step forward, but stopped when the muzzle of the Colt kissed his nose. He was the brother of Tamale Jose. As he backed away from the cool touch of the weapon he thought out swiftly his revenge. Some of his brother's old companions were at that moment drinking mescal in a saloon down the street, and they would be glad to see this Americano die. He glanced past his house at the saloon and Hopalong misconstrued his thoughts.

"Shore, go home. I'll just circulate around some for exercise. No hard feelings, only yu better throw it next time," he said as he backed away and rode off. Manuel went down the street and then ran into the saloon, where he caused an uproar.

Hopalong rode to the end of the plaza and tried to sing, but it was a dismal failure. Then he felt thirsty and wondered why he hadn't thought of it before. Turning his horse and seeing the saloon he rode up to it and in, lying flat on the animal's neck to avoid being swept off by the door frame. His entrance scared white some half a dozen loungers, who immediately sprang up in a decidedly hostile manner. Hopalong's Colts peeped over the ears of his horse and he backed into a corner near the bar.

"One, two, three-now, altogether, breathe! Yu acts like yu never saw a real puncher afore. All th' same," he remarked, nodding at several of the crowd, "I've seen yu afore. Yu are th' gents with th' hot-foot get-a-way that vamoosed when we got Tamale."

Curses were flung at him and only the humorous mood he was in saved trouble. One, bolder than the rest, spoke up: "The senor will not see any 'hot-foot get-a-way,' as he calls it, now! The senor was not wise to go so far away from his friends!'"

Hopalong looked at the speaker and a quizzical grin slowly spread over his face. "They'll shore feel glad when I tells them yu was askin' for 'em. But didn't yu see too much of 'em once, or was yu poundin' leather in the other direction? Yu don't want to worry none about me-an' if yu don't get yore hands closter to yore neck they'll be heck to pay! There, that's more like home," he remarked, nodding assurance.

Reaching over he grasped a bottle and poured out a drink, his Colt slipping from his hand and dangling from his wrist by a thong. As the weapon started to fall several of the audience involuntarily moved as if to pick it up. Hopalong noticed this and paused with the glass half way to his lips. "Don't bother yoreselves none; I can git it again," he said, tossing off the liquor.

"Wow! Holy smoke!" he yelled. "This ain't drink! Sufferin' coyotes, nobody can accuse yu of sellin' liquor! Did yu make this all by yoreself?" He asked incredulously of the proprietor, who didn't know whether to run or to pray. Then he noticed that the crowd was spreading out and his Colts again became the center of interest.

"Yu with th' lovely face, sit down!" he ordered as the person addressed was gliding toward the door. "I ain't a-goin' to let yu pot me from th' street. Th' first man who tries to get scarce will stop somethin' hot. An' yu all better sit down," he suggested, sweeping them with his guns. One man, more obdurate than the rest, was slow in complying and Hopalong sent a bullet through the top of his high sombrero, which had a most gratifying effect.

"You'll regret this!" hissed a man in the rear, and a murmur of assent arose. Some one stirred slightly in searching for a weapon and immediately a blazing Colt froze him into a statue.

"Yu shore looks funny; eeny, meeny, miny, mo," counted off the daring horseman; "move a bit an' off yu go," he finished. Then his face broke out in another grin as he thought of more enjoyment.

"That there gent on th' left," he said, pointing out with a gun the man he meant. "Yu sing us a song. Sing a nice little song."

As the object of his remarks remained mute he let his thumb ostentatiously slide back with the hammer of the gun under it. "Sing! Quick!" The man sang.

As Hopalong leaned forward to say something a stiletto flashed past his neck and crashed into the bottle beside him. The echo of the crash was merged into a report as Hopalong fired from his waist. Then he backed out into the Street and, wheeling, galloped across the plaza and again faced the saloon. A flash split the darkness and a bullet hummed over his head and thudded into an adobe wall at his back. Another shot and he replied, aiming at the flash.

From down the Street came the sound of a window opening and he promptly caused it to close again. Several more windows opened and hastily closed, and he rode slowly toward the far end of the plaza. As he faced the saloon once more he heard a command to throw up his hands and saw the glint of a gun, held by a man who wore the insignia of sheriff. Hopalong complied, but as his hands went up two spurts of fire shot forth and the sheriff dropped his weapon, reeled and sat down. Hopalong rode over to him and swinging down, picked up the gun and looked the officer over.

"Shoo, yu'll be all right soon-yore only plugged in th' arms," he remarked as he glanced up the street. Shadowy forms were gliding from cover to cover and he immediately caused consternation among them by his accuracy. "Ain't it sad?" He complained to the wounded man. "I never starts out but what somebody makes me shoot 'em. Came down here to see a girl an' find she's married. Then when I moves on peaceable-like her husband makes me hit him. Then I wants a drink an' he goes an' fans a knife at me, an' me just teachin' him how! Then yu has to come along an' make more trouble".

"Now look at them fools over there," he said, pointing at a dark shadow some fifty paces off. "They're pattin' their backs because I don't see 'em, an' if I hurts them they'll git mad. Guess I'll make 'em dust along," he added, shooting into the spot. A howl went up and two men ran away at top speed.

The sheriff nodded his sympathy and spoke. "I reckons you had better give up. You can't get away. Every house, every corner and shadow holds a man. You are a brave man, but, as you say, unfortunate. Better help me up and come with me-they'll tear you to pieces."

"Shore I'll help yu up —I ain't got no grudge against nobody. But my friends know where I am an' they'll come down here an' raise a ruction if I don't show up. So, if it's all th' same to you, I'll be ambling right along," he said as he helped the sheriff to his feet.

"Have you any objections to telling me your name?" Asked the sheriff as he looked himself over.

"None whatever," answered Hopalong heartily. "I'm Hopalong Cassidy of th' Bar 20, Texas."

"You don't surprise me —I've heard of you," replied the sheriff wearily. "You are the man who killed Tamale Jose, whom I hunted for unceasingly. I found him when you had left and I got the reward. Come again some time and I'll divide with you; two hundred and fifty dollars," he added craftily.

"I shore will, but I don't want no money," replied Hopalong as he turned away. "Adios, senor," he called back.

"Adios," replied the sheriff as he kicked a nearby door for assistance.

The cow-pony tied itself up in knots as it pounded down the street toward the trail, and although he was fired on he swung into the dusty trail with a song on his lips. Several hours later he stood dripping wet on the American side of the Rio Grande and shouted advice to a score of Mexican cavalrymen on the opposite bank. Then he slowly picked his way toward El Paso for a game at Faro Dan's.

The sheriff sat in his easy chair one night some three weeks later, gravely engaged in rolling a cigarette. His arms were practically well, the wounds being in the fleshy parts. He was a philosopher and was disposed to take things easy, which accounted for his being in his official position for fifteen years. A gentleman at the core, he was well educated and had visited a goodly portion of the world. A book of Horace lay open on his knees and on the table at his side lay a shining new revolver, Hopalong having carried off his former weapon. He read aloud several lines and in reaching for a light for his cigarette noticed the new six-shooter. His mind leaped from Horace to Hopalong, and he smiled grimly at the latter's promise to call.

Glancing up, his eyes fell on a poster which conveyed the information in Spanish and in English that there was offered

```
+ — — — — — — — — — — — — — — — — — — —+
        | | FIVE HUNDRED PESOS | |
REWARD

For Hopalong Cassidy, of the Ranch

| | Known as the Bar-20, Texas, U. S. A. | |

+ — — — — — — — — — — — — — — — — — — —+
```

and which gave a good description of that gentleman.

Sighing for the five hundred, he again took up his book and was lost in its pages when he heard a knock, rather low and timid. Wearily laying aside his reading, he strode to the door, expecting to hear a lengthy complaint from one of his townsmen. As he threw the door wide open the light streamed out and lighted up a revolver and behind it the beaming face of a cowboy, who grinned.

"Well, I'll be damned!" ejaculated the sheriff, starting back in amazement.

"Don't say that, sheriff; you've got lots of time to reform," replied a humorous voice. "How's th' wings?"

"Almost well: you were considerate," responded the sheriff. "Let's go in-somebody might see me out here an' get into trouble," suggested the visitor, placing his foot on the sill.

"Certainly-pardon my discourtesy," said the sheriff. "You see, I wasn't expecting you to-night," he explained, thinking of the elaborate preparations that he would have gone to if he had thought the irrepressible would call.

"Well, I was down this way, an' seeing as how I had promised to drop in I just natchurally dropped," replied Hopalong as he took the chair proffered by his host.

After talking awhile on everything and nothing the sheriff coughed and looked uneasily at his guest.

"Mr. Cassidy, I am sorry you called, for I like men of your energy and courage and I very much dislike to arrest you," remarked the sheriff. "Of course you understand that you are under arrest," he added with anxiety.

"Who, me?" Asked Hopalong with a rising inflection.

"Most assuredly," breathed the sheriff.

"Why, this is the first time I ever heard anything about it," replied the astonished cow-puncher. "I'm an American-don't that make any difference?"

"Not in this case, I'm afraid. You see, it's for manslaughter."

"Well, don't that beat th' devil, now?" Said Hopalong. He felt sorry that a citizen of the glorious United States should be prey for troublesome sheriffs, but he was sure that his duty to Texas called upon him never to submit to arrest at the hands of a Mexican. Remembering the Alamo, and still behind his Colt, he reached over and took up the shining weapon from the table and snapped it open on his knee. After placing the cartridges in his pocket he tossed the gun over on the bed and, reaching inside his shirt, drew out another and threw it after the first.

"That's yore gun; I forgot to leave it," he said, apologetically. "Anyhow yu needs two," he added.

Then he glanced around the room, noticed the poster and walked over and read it. A full swift sweep of his gloved hand tore it from its fastenings and crammed it under his belt. The glimmer of anger in his eyes gave way as he realized that his head was worth a definite price, and he smiled at what the boys would say when he showed it to them. Planting his feet far apart and placing his arms akimbo he faced his host in grim defiance.

"Got any more of these?" He inquired, placing his hand on the poster under his belt.

"Several," replied the sheriff.

"Trot 'em out," ordered Hopalong shortly.

The sheriff sighed, stretched and went over to a shelf, from which he took a bundle of the articles in question. Turning slowly he looked at the puncher and handed them to him.

"I reckons they's all over this here town," remarked Hopalong.

"They are, and you may never see Texas again."

"So? Well, yu tell yore most particular friends that the job is worth five thousand, and that it will take so many to do it that when th' mazuma is divided up it won't buy a meal. There's only one man in this country tonight that can earn that money, an' that's me," said the puncher. "An' I don't need it," he added, smiling.

"But you are my prisoner-you are under arrest," enlightened the sheriff, rolling another cigarette. The sheriff spoke as if asking a question. Never before had five hundred dollars been so close at hand and yet so unobtainable. It was like having a check-book but no bank account.

"I'm shore sorry to treat yu mean," remarked Hopalong, "but I was paid a month in advance an' I'll have to go back an' earn it."

"You can-if you say that you will return," replied the sheriff tentatively. The sheriff meant what he said and for the moment had forgotten that he was powerless and was not the one to make terms.

Hopalong was amazed and for a time his ideas of Mexicans staggered under the blow. Then he smiled sympathetically as he realized that he faced a white man.

"Never like to promise nothin'," he replied. "I might get plugged, or something might happen that wouldn't let me." Then his face lighted up as a thought came to him. "Say, I'll cut di' cards with yu to see if I comes back or not."

The sheriff leaned back and gazed at the cool youngster before him. A smile of satisfaction, partly at the self-reliance of his guest and partly at the novelty of his situation, spread over his face. He reached for a pack of Mexican cards and laughed. "Man! You're a cool one —I'll do it. What do you call?"

"Red," answered Hopalong.

The sheriff slowly raised his hand and revealed the ace of hearts. Hopalong leaned back and laughed, at the same time taking from his pocket the six extracted cartridges. Arising and going over to the bed he slipped them in the chambers of the new gun and then placed the loaded weapon at the sheriff's elbow.

"Well, I reckon I'll amble, sheriff," he said as he opened the door. "If yu ever sifts up my way drop in an' see me-th' boys'll give yu a good time."

"Thanks; I will be glad to," replied the sheriff. "You'll take your pitcher to the well once too often some day, my friend. This courtesy," glancing at the restored revolver, "might have cost you dearly."

"Shoo! I did that once an' th' feller tried to use it," replied the cowboy as he backed through the door. "Some people are awfully careless," he added. "So long—"

"So long," replied the sheriff, wondering what sort of a man he had been entertaining.

The door closed softly and soon after a joyous whoop floated in from the Street. The sheriff toyed with the new gun and listened to the low caress of a distant guitar.

"Well, don't that beat all?" He ejaculated.

Chapter IX
The Advent of McAllister

The blazing sun shone pitilessly on an arid plain which was spotted with dust-gray clumps of mesquite and thorny chaparral. Basking in the burning sand and alkali lay several Gila monsters, which raised their heads and hissed with wide-open jaws as several faint, whip-like reports echoed flatly over the desolate plain, showing that even they had learned that danger was associated with such sounds.

Off to the north there became visible a cloud of dust and at intervals something swayed in it, something that rose and fell and then became hidden again. Out of that cloud came sharp, splitting sounds, which were faintly responded to by another and larger cloud in its rear. As it came nearer and finally swept past, the Gilas, to their terror, saw a madly pounding horse, and it carried a man. The latter turned in his saddle and raised a gun to his shoulder and the thunder that issued from it caused the creeping audience to throw up their tails in sudden panic and bury themselves out of sight in the sand.

The horse was only a broncho, its sides covered with hideous yellow spots, and on its near flank was a peculiar scar, the brand. Foam flecked from its crimsoned jaws and found a resting place on its sides and on the hairy chaps of its rider. Sweat rolled and streamed from its heaving flanks and was greedily sucked up by the drought-cursed alkali. Close to the rider's knee a bloody furrow ran forward and one of the broncho's ears was torn and limp. The broncho was doing its best-it could run at that pace until it dropped dead. Every ounce of strength it possessed was put forth to bring those hind hoofs well in front of the forward ones and to send them pushing the sand behind in streaming clouds. The horse had done this same thing many times-when would its master learn sense?

The man was typical in appearance with many of that broad land. Lithe, sinewy and bronzed by hard riding and hot suns, he sat in his Cheyenne saddle like a centaur, all his weight on the heavy, leather-guarded stirrups, his body rising in one magnificent straight line. A bleached moustache hid the thin lips, and a gray sombrero threw a heavy shadow across his eyes. Around his neck and over his open, blue flannel shirt lay loosely a knotted silk kerchief, and on his thighs a pair of open-flapped holsters swung uneasily with their ivory handled burdens. He turned abruptly, raised his gun to his shoulder and fired, then he laughed recklessly and patted his mount, which responded to the confident caress by lying flatter to the earth in a spurt of heart-breaking speed.

"I'll show 'em who they're trailin'. This is th' second time I've started for Muddy Wells, an' I'm goin' to git there, too, for all th' Apaches out of Hades!"

To the south another cloud of dust rapidly approached and the rider scanned it closely, for it was directly in his path. As he watched it he saw something wave and it was a sombrero!

Shortly afterward a real cowboy yell reached his ears. He grinned and slid another cartridge in the greasy, smoking barrel of the Sharp's and fired again at the cloud in his rear. Some few minutes later a whooping, bunched crowd of madly riding cowboys thundered past him and he was recognized.

"Hullo, Frenchy!" yelled the nearest one. "Comin' back?"

"Come on, McAllister!" shouted another; "we'll give 'em blazes!" In response the straining broncho suddenly stiffened, bunched and slid on its haunches, wheeled and retraced its course. The rear cloud suddenly scattered into many smaller ones and all swept off to the east. The rescuing band overtook them and, several hours later, when seated around a table in Tom Lee's saloon, Muddy Wells, a count was taken of them, which was pleasing in its facts.

"We was huntin' coyotes when we saw yu," said a smiling puncher who was known as Salvation Carroll chiefly because he wasn't.

"Yep! They've been stalkin' Tom's chickens," supplied Waffles, the champion poker player of the outfit. Tom Lee's chickens could whip anything of their kind for miles around and were reverenced accordingly.

"Sho! Is that so?" Asked Frenchy with mild incredulity, such a state of affairs being deplorable.

"She shore is!" answered Tex Le Blanc, and then, as an afterthought, he added, "Where'd yu hit th' War-whoops?"

"'Bout four hours back. This here's th' second time I've headed for this place-last time they chased me to Las Cruces."

"That so?" Asked Bigfoot Baker, a giant. "Ain't they allus interferin', now? Anyhow, they're better'n coyotes."

"They was purty well heeled," suggested Tex, glancing at a bunch of repeating Winchesters of late model which lay stacked in a corner. "Charley here said he thought they was from th' way yore cayuse looked, didn't yu, Charley?" Charley nodded and filled his pipe.

"'Pears like a feller can't amble around much nowadays without havin' to fight," grumbled Lefty Allen, who usually went out of his way hunting up trouble.

"We're goin' to th' Hills as soon as our cookie turns up," volunteered Tenspot Davis, looking inquiringly at Frenchy. "Heard any more news?"

"Nope. Same old story-lots of gold. Shucks, I've bit on so many of them rumors that they don't feaze me no more. One man who don't know nothin' about prospectin' goes an' stumbles over a fortune an' those who know it from A to Izzard goes 'round pullin' in their belts."

"We don't pull in no belts-we knows just where to look, don't we, Tenspot?" Remarked Tex, looking very wise.

"Ya-as we do," answered Tenspot, "if yu hasn't dreamed about it, we do."

"Yu wait; I wasn't dreamin', none whatever," assured Tex.

"I saw it!"

"Ya-as, I saw it too onct," replied Frenchy with sarcasm. "Went and lugged fifty pound of it all th' way to th' assay office-took me two days! an' that there four-eyed cuss looks at it and snickers. Then he takes me by di' arm an' leads me to th' window. 'See that pile, my friend? That's all like yourn,' sez he. 'It's worth about one simoleon a ton at th' coast. They use it for ballast.'"

"Aw! But this what I saw was gold!" exploded Tex.

"So was mine, for a while!" laughed Frenchy, nodding to the bartender for another round.

"Well, we're tired of punchin' cows! Ride sixteen hours a day, year in an' year out, an' what do we get? Fifty a month an' no chance to spend it, an' grub that'd make a coyote sniffle! I'm for a vacation, an' if I goes broke, why, I'll punch again!" asserted Waffles, the foreman, thus revealing the real purpose of the trip.

"What'd yore boss say?" Asked Frenchy.

"Whoop! What didn't he say! Honest, I never thought he had it in him. It was fine. He cussed an hour frontways an' then trailed back on a dead gallop, with us a-laughin' fit to bust.

Then he rustles for his gun an' we rustles for town," answered Waffles, laughing at his remembrance of it.

As Frenchy was about to reply his sombrero was snatched from his head and disappeared. If he "got mad" he was to be regarded as not sufficiently well acquainted for banter and he was at once in hot water; if he took it good-naturedly he was one of the crowd in spirit; but in either case he didn't get his hat without begging or fighting for it. This was a recognized custom among the O-Bar-O outfit and was not intended as an insult.

Frenchy grabbed at the empty air and arose. Punching Lefty playfully in the ribs he passed his hands behind that person's back. Not finding the lost head-gear he laughed and, tripping Lefty up, fell with him and, reaching up on the table for his glass, poured the contents down Lefty's back and arose.

"Yu son-of-a-gun!" indignantly wailed that unfortunate. "Gee, it feels funny," he added, grinning as he pulled the wet shirt away from his spine.

"Well, I've got to be amblin'," said Frenchy, totally ignoring the loss of his hat. "Goin' down to Buckskin," he offered, and then asked, "When's yore cook comin'?"

"Day after to-morrow, if he don't get loaded," replied Tex.

"Who is he?"

"A one-eyed Mexican-Quiensabe Antonio."

"I used to know him. He's a heck of a cook. Dished up th' grub one season when I was punchin' for th' Tin-Cup up in Montana," replied Frenchy.

"Oh, he kin cook now, all right." replied Waffles.

"That's about all he can cook. Useter wash his knives in th' coffee pot an' blow on di' tins. I chased him a mile one night for leavin' sand in th' skillet. Yu can have him —I don't envy yu none whatever.

"He don't sand no skillet when little Tenspot's around," assured that person, slapping his holster. "Does he, Lefty?"

"If he does, yu oughter be lynched," consoled Lefty.

"Well, so long," remarked Frenchy, riding off to a small store, where he bought a cheap sombrero.

Frenchy was a jack-of-all-trades, having been cow-puncher, prospector, proprietor of a "hotel" in Albuquerque, foreman of a ranch, sheriff, and at one time had played angel to a venturesome but poor show troupe. Beside his versatility he was well known as the man who took the stage through the Sioux country when no one else volunteered. He could shoot with the best, but his one pride was the brand of poker he handed out. Furthermore, he had never been known to take an unjust advantage over any man and, on the contrary, had frequently voluntarily handicapped himself to make the event more interesting. But he must not be classed as being hampered with self-restraint.

His reasons for making this trip were two-fold: he wished to see Buck Peters, the foreman of the Bar-20 outfit, as he and Buck had punched cows together twenty years before and were firm friends; the other was that he wished to get square with Hopalong Cassidy, who had decisively cleaned him out the year before at poker. Hopalong played either in great good luck or the contrary, while Frenchy played an even, consistent game and usually left off richer than when he began, and this decisive defeat bothered him more than he would admit, even to himself.

The round-up season was at hand and the Bar-20 was short of ropers, the rumors of fresh gold discoveries in the Black Hills having drawn all the more restless men north. The outfit also had a slight touch of the gold fever, and only their peculiar loyalty to the ranch and the assurance of the foreman that when the work was over he would accompany them, kept them from joining the rush of those who desired sudden and much wealth as the necessary preliminary of painting some cow town in all the "bang up" style such an event would call for. Therefore they had been given orders to secure the required assistance, and they intended to do so, and were prepared to kidnap, if necessary, for the glamour of wealth and the hilarity of the vacation made the hours falter in their speed.

As Frenchy leaned back in his chair in Cowan's saloon, Buckskin, early the next morning, planning to get revenge on Hopalong and then to recover his sombrero, he heard a medley of yells and whoops and soon the door flew open before the strenuous and concentrated entry of a mass of twisting and kicking arms and legs, which magically found their respective owners and reverted to the established order of things.

When the alkali dust had thinned he saw seven cow-punchers sitting on the prostrate form of another, who was earnestly engaged in trying to push Johnny Nelson's head out in the street with one foot as he voiced his lucid opinion of things in general and the seven in particular. After Red Connors had been stabbed in the back several times by the victim's energetic elbow he ran out of the room and presently returned with a pleased expression and a sombrero full of water, his finger plugging an old bullet hole in the crown.

"Is he any better, Buck?" Anxiously inquired the man with the reservoir.

"About a dollar's worth," replied the foreman. "Jest put a little right here," he drawled as he pulled back the collar of the unfortunate's shirt.

"Ow! wow! WOW!" wailed the recipient, heaving and straining. The unengaged leg was suddenly wrested loose, and as it shot up and out Billy Williams, with his pessimism aroused to a blue-ribbon pitch, sat down forcibly in an adjacent part of the room, from where he lectured between gasps on the follies of mankind and the attributes of army mules.

Red tiptoed around the squirming bunch, looking for an opening, his pleased expression now having added a grin.

"Seems to be gittin' violent-like," he soliloquized, as he aimed a stream at Hopalong's ear, which showed for a second as Pete Wilson strove for a half-nelson, and he managed to include Johnny and Pete in his effort.

Several minutes later, when the storm had subsided, the woeful crowd enthusiastically urged Hopalong to the bar, where he "bought."

"Of all th' ornery outfits I ever saw —" began the man at the table, grinning from ear to ear at the spectacle he had just witnessed.

"Why, hullo, Frenchy! Glad to see yu, yu old son-of-a-gun! What's th' news from th' Hills?" Shouted Hopalong.

"Rather locoed, an' there's a locoed gang that's headin' that way. Goin' up?" he asked.

"Shore, after round-up. Seen any punchers trailin' around loose?"

"Ya-as," drawled Frenchy, delving into the possibilities suddenly opened to him and determining to utilize to the fullest extent the opportunity that had come to him unsought. "There's nine over to Muddy Wells that yu might git if yu wants them bad enough. They've got a sombrero of mine," he added deprecatingly.

"Nine! Twisted Jerusalem, Buck! Nine whole cow-punchers a-pinin' for work," he shouted, but then added thoughtfully, "Mebby they's engaged," it being one of the courtesies of the land not to take another man's help.

"Nope. They've stampeded for th' Hills an' left their boss all alone," replied Frenchy, well knowing that such desertion would not, in the minds of the Bar-20 men, add any merits to the case of the distant outfit.

"Th' sons-of-guns," said Hopalong, "let's go an' get 'em," he suggested, turning to Buck, who nodded a smiling assent.

"Oh, what's the hurry?" Asked Frenchy, seeing his projected game slipping away into the uncertain future and happy in the thought that he would be avenged on the O-Bar-O outfit.

"They'll be there till to-morrow noon-they's waitin' for their cookie, who's goin' with them."

"A cook! A cook! Oh, joy, a cook!" exulted Johnny, not for one instant doubting Buck's ability to capture the whole outfit and seeing a whirl of excitement in the effort.

"Anybody we knows?" Inquired Skinny Thompson.

"Shore. Tenspot Davis, Waffles, Salvation Carroll, Bigfoot Baker, Charley Lane, Lefty Allen, Kid Morris, Curley Tate an' Tex Le Blanc," responded Frenchy.

"Umm-m. Might as well rope a blizzard," grumbled Billy. "Might as well try to git th' Seventh Cavalry. We'll have a pious time corralling that bunch. Them's th' fellows that hit that bunch of inquirin' Crow braves that time up in th' Bad Lands an' then said by-bye to th' Ninth."

"Aw, shut up! They's only two that's very much, an' Buck an' Hopalong can sing 'em to sleep," interposed Johnny, afraid that the expedition would fall through.

"How about Curley and Tex?" Pugnaciously asked Billy.

"Huh, jest because they buffaloed yu over to Las Vegas yu needn't think they's dangerous. Salvation an' Tenspot are only ones who can shoot," stoutly maintained Johnny.

"Here yu, get mum," ordered Buck to the pair. "When this outfit goes after anything it generally gets it. All in favor of kidnappin' that outfit signify di' same by kickin' Billy," whereupon Bill swore.

"Do yu want yore hat?" Asked Buck, turning to Frenchy.

"I shore do," answered that individual.

"If yu helps us at th' round-up we'll get it for yu. Fifty a month an' grub," offered the foreman.

"O.K." replied Frenchy, anxious to even matters.

Buck looked at his watch. "Seven o'clock-we ought to get there by five if we relays at th' Barred-Horseshoe. Come on."

"How are we goin' to git them?" Asked Billy.

"Yu leave that to me, son. Hopalong an' Frenchy'll tend to that part of it," replied Buck, making for his horse and swinging into the saddle, an example which was followed by the others, including Frenchy.

As they swung off Buck noticed the condition of Frenchy's mount and halted. "Yu take that cayuse back an' get Cowan's," he ordered.

"That cayuse is good for Cheyenne-she eats work, an' besides I wants my own," laughed Frenchy.

"Yu must had a reg'lar picnic from th' looks of that crease," volunteered Hopalong, whose curiosity was mastering him. "Shoo! I had a little argument with some feather dusters-th' O-Bar-O crowd cleaned them up."

"That so?" Asked Buck.

"Yep! They sorter got into th' habit of chasin' me to Las Cruces an' forgot to stop."

"How many'd yu get?" Asked Lanky Smith.

"Twelve. Two got away. I got two before th' crowd showed up-that makes fo'teen."

"Now th' cavalry'll be huntin' yu," croaked Billy.

"Hunt nothin'! They was in war-paint-think I was a target? —Think I was goin' to call off their shots for 'em?"

They relayed at the Barred-Horseshoe and went on their way at the same pace. Shortly after leaving the last-named ranch Buck turned to Frenchy and asked, "Any of that outfit think they can play poker?"

"Shore. Waffles."

"Does th' reverend Mr. Waffles think so very hard?"

"He shore does."

"Do th' rest of them mavericks think so too?"

"They'd bet their shirts on him."

At this juncture all were startled by a sudden eruption from Billy. "Haw! Haw! Haw!" he roared as the drift of Buck's intentions struck him. "Haw! Haw! Haw!"

"Here, yu long-winded coyote," yelled Red, banging him over the head with his quirt, "If yu don't 'Haw! Haw!' away from my ear I'll make it a Wow! Wow! What d'yu mean? Think I am a echo cliff? Yu slabsided doodle-bug, yu!"

"G'way, yu crimson topknot, think my head's a hunk of quartz? Fer a plugged peso I'd strew yu all over th' scenery!" shouted Billy, feigning anger and rubbing his head.

"There ain't no scenery around here," interposed Lanky. "This here be-utiful prospect is a sublime conception of th' devil."

"Easy, boy! Them highfalutin' words'il give yu a cramp some day. Yu talk like a newly-made sergeant," remarked Skinny.

"He learned them words from the sky-pilot over at El Paso," volunteered Hopalong, winking at Red. "He used to amble down th' aisle afore the lights was lit so's he could get a front seat. That was all hunky for a while, but every time he'd go out to irrigate, that female organ-wrastler would seem to call th' music off for his special benefit. So in a month he'd sneak in an' freeze to a chair by th' door, an' after a while he'd shy like blazes every time he got within eye range of th' church."

"Shore. But do yu know what made him get religion all of a sudden? He used to hang around on di' outside after th' joint let out an' trail along behind di' music-slinger, lookin' like he didn't know what to do with his hands. Then when he got woozy one time she up an' told him that she had got a nice long letter from her hubby. Then Mr. Lanky hit th' trail for Santa Fe so hard that there wasn't hardly none of it left. I didn't see him for a whole month," supplied Red innocently.

"Yore shore funny, ain't yu?" sarcastically grunted Lanky. "Why, I can tell things on yu that'd make yu stand treat for a year."

"I wouldn't sneak off to Santa Fe an' cheat yu out of them. Yu ought to be ashamed of yoreself."

"Yah!" snorted the aggrieved little man. "I had business over to Santa Fe!"

"Shore," endorsed Hopalong. "We've all had business over to Santa Fe. Why, about eight years ago I had business —"

"Choke up," interposed Red. "About eight years ago yu was washin' pans for cookie, an' askin' me for cartridges. Buck used to larrup yu about four times a day eight years ago."

To their roars of laughter Hopalong dropped to the rear, where, red-faced and quiet, he bent his thoughts on how to get square.

"We'll have a pleasant time corralling that gang," began Billy for the third time.

"For heaven's sake get off that trail!" replied Lanky. "We aint goin' to hold 'em up. Deplomacy's th' game."

Billy looked dubious and said nothing. If he hadn't proven that he was as nervy as any man in the outfit they might have taken more stock in his grumbling.

"What's the latest from Abilene way?" Asked Buck of Frenchy.

"Nothin' much 'cept th' barb-wire ruction," replied the recruit.

"What's that?" Asked Red, glancing apprehensively back at Hopalong.

"Why, th' settlers put up barb-wire fence so's the cattle wouldn't get on their farms. That would a been all right, for there wasn't much of it. But some Britishers who own a couple of big ranches out there got smart all of a sudden an' strung wire all along their lines. Punchers crossin' th' country would run plumb into a fence an' would have to ride a day an' a half, mebbe, afore they found th' corner. Well, naturally, when a man has been used to ridin' where he blame pleases an' as straight as he pleases he ain't goin' to chase along a five-foot fence to Trisco when he wants to get to Waco. So th' punchers got to totin' wire-snips, an' when they runs up agin a fence they cuts down half a mile or so. Sometimes they'd tie their ropes to a strand an' pull off a couple of miles an' then go back after th' rest. Th' ranch bosses sent out men to watch th' fences an' told 'em to shoot any festive puncher that monkeyed with th' hardware. Well, yu know what happens when a puncher gets shot at."

"When fences grow in Texas there'll be th' devil to pay," said Buck. He hated to think that some day the freedom of the range would be annulled, for he knew that it would be the first blow against the cowboys' occupation. When a man's cattle couldn't spread out all over the land he wouldn't have to keep so many men. Farms would spring up and the sun of the free-and-easy cowboy would slowly set.

"I reckons th' cutters are classed th' same as rustlers," remarked Red with a gleam of temper.

"By th' owners, but not by th' punchers; an' it's th' punchers that count," replied Frenchy.

"Well, we'll give them a fight," interposed Hopalong, riding up. "When it gets so I can't go where I please I'll start on th' warpath. I won't buck the cavalry, but I'll keep it busy huntin' for me an' I'll have time to 'tend to th' wire-fence men, too. Why, we'll be told we can't tote our guns!"

"They're sayin' that now," replied Frenchy. "Up in Buffalo, Smith, who's now marshal, makes yu leave 'em with th' bartenders."

"I'd like to see any two-laigged cuss get my guns If I didn't want him to!" began Hopalong, indignant at the idea.

"Easy, son," cautioned Buck. "Yu would do what th' rest did because yu are a square man. I'm about as hard-headed a puncher as ever straddled leather an' I've had to use my guns purty considerable, but I reckons if any decent marshal asked me to cache them in a decent way, why, I'd do it. An' let me brand somethin' on yore mind —I've heard of Smith of Buffalo, an' he's mighty nifty with his hands. He don't stand off an' tell yu to unload yore lead-ranch, but he ambles up close an' taps yu on yore shirt; if yu makes a gunplay he naturally knocks yu clean across th' room an' unloads yu afore yu gets yore senses back. He weighs about a hundred an' eighty an' he's shore got sand to burn."

"Yah! When I makes a gun play she plays! I'd look nice in Abilene or Paso or Albuquerque without my guns, wouldn't I? Just because I totes them in plain sight I've got to hand 'em over to some liquor-wrastler? I reckons not! Some hip-pocket skunk would plug me afore I could wink. I'd shore look nice loping around a keno layout without my guns, in th' same town with some cuss huntin' me, wouldn't I? A whole lot of good a marshal would a done Jimmy, an' didn't Harris get his from a cur in th' dark?" shouted Hopalong, angered by the prospect.

"We're talkin' about Buffalo, where everybody has to hang up their guns," replied Buck. "An' there's th' law —"

"To blazes with th' law!" whooped Hopalong in Red's ear as he unfastened the cinch of Red's saddle and at the same time stabbing that unfortunate's mount with his spurs, thereby causing a hasty separation of the two. When Red had picked himself up and things had quieted down again the subject was changed, and several hours later they rode into Muddy Wells, a town with a little more excuse for its existence than Buckskin. The wells were in an arid valley west of Guadaloupe Pass, and were not only muddy but more or less alkaline.

Chapter. X
Peace Hath its Victories

As they neared the central group of buildings they heard a hilarious and assertive song which sprang from the door and windows of the main saloon. It was in jig time, rollicking and boisterous, but the words had evidently been improvised for the occasion, as they clashed immediately with those which sprang to the minds of the outfit, although they could not be clearly distinguished. As they approached nearer and finally dismounted, however, the words became recognizable and the visitors were at once placed in harmony with the air of jovial recklessness by the roaring of the verses and the stamping of the time.

> Oh we're red-hot cow-punchers playin' on our luck,
> An' there ain't a proposition that we won't buck:
> From sunrise to sunset we've ridden on the range,
> But now we're oft for a howlin' change.

> CHORUS
> Laugh a little, sing a little, all th' day;

Play a little, drink a little-we can pay;
Ride a little, dig a little an' rich we'll grow.
Oh, we're that bunch from th' O-Bar-O!
Oh, there was a little tenderfoot an' he had a little gun,

An' th' gun an' him went a-trailin' up some fun.
They ambles up to Santa Fe' to find a quiet game,
An' now they're planted with some more of th' same!

As Hopalong, followed by the others, pushed open the door and entered he took up the chorus with all the power of Texan lungs and even Billy joined in. The sight that met their eyes was typical of the men and the mood and the place. Leaning along the walls, lounging on the table and straddling chairs with their forearms crossed on the backs were nine cowboys, ranging from old twenty to young fifty in years, and all were shouting the song and keeping time with their hands and feet.

In the center of the room was a large man dancing a fair buck-and-wing to the time so uproariously set by his companions. Hatless, neck-kerchief loose, holsters flapping, chaps rippling out and close, spurs clinking and perspiration streaming from his tanned face, danced Bigfoot Baker as though his life depended on speed and noise. Bottles shook and the air was fogged with smoke and dust. Suddenly, his belt slipping and letting his chaps fall around his ankles, he tripped and sat down heavily. Gasping for breath, he held out his hand and received a huge plug of tobacco, for Bigfoot had won a contest.

Shouts of greeting were hurled at the newcomers and many questions were fired at them regarding "th' latest from th' Hills." Waffles made a rush for Hopalong, but fell over Big-foot's feet and all three were piled up in a heap. All were beaming with good nature, for they were as so many school boys playing truant. Prosaic cow-punching was relegated to the rear and they looked eagerly forward to their several missions. Frenchy told of the barb-wire fence war and of the new regulations of "Smith of Buffalo" regarding cow-punchers' guns, and from the caustic remarks explosively given it was plain to be seen what a wire fence could expect, should one be met with, and there were many imaginary Smiths put hors de combat.

Kid Morris, after vainly trying to slip a blue-bottle fly inside of Hopalong's shirt, gave it up and slammed his hand on Hopalong's back instead, crying: "Well, I'll be doggoned if here ain't Hopalong! How's th' missus an' th' deacon an' all th' folks to hum? I hears yu an' Frenchy's reg'lar poker fiends!"

"Oh, we plays onct in a while, but we don't want none of yore dust. Yu'll shore need it all afore th' Hills get through with yu," laughingly replied Hopalong.

"Oh, yore shore kind! But I was a sort of reckonin' that we needs some more. Perfesser P. D. Q. Waffles is our poker man an' he shore can clean out anything I ever saw. Mebbe yu fellers feel reckless-like an' would like to make a pool," he cried, addressing the outfit of the Bar-20, "an' back yore boss of th' full house agin ourn?"

Red turned slowly around and took a full minute in which to size the Kid up. Then he snorted and turned his back again.

The Kid stared at him in outraged dignity. "Well, what say!" he softly murmured. Then he leaped forward and walloped Red on the back. "Hey, yore royal highness!" he shouted. "Yu-yu-yu-oh, hang it-yu! Yu slab-sided, ring-boned, saddle-galled shade of a coyote, do yu think I'm only meanderin' in th' misty vales of-of—"

Suggestions intruded from various sources. "Hades?" offered Hopalong. "Cheyenne?" Murmured Johnny. "Misty mistiness of misty?" tentatively supplied Waffles.

Red turned around again. "Better come up an' have somethin'," he sympathetically invited, wiping away an imaginary tear.

"An' he's so young!" sobbed Frenchy.

"An' so fair!" wailed Tex.

"An' so ornery!" howled Lefty, throwing his arms around the discomfited youngster. Other arms went around him, and out of the sobbing mob could be heard earnest and heart-felt cussing, interspersed with imperative commands, which were gradually obeyed.

The Kid straightened up his wearing apparel. "Come on, yu locoed —"

"Angels?" Queried Charley Lane, interrupting him. "Sweet things?" breathed Hopalong in hopeful expectancy.

"Oh, blast it!" yelled the Kid as he ran out into the street to escape the persecution.

"Good Kid, all right," remarked Waffles. "He'll go around an' lick some Mexican an' come back sweet as honey."

"Did somebody say poker?" Asked Bigfoot, digressing from the Kid.

"Oh, yu fellows don't want no poker. Of course yu don't. Poker's mighty uncertain," replied Red.

"Yah!" exclaimed Tex Le Blanc, pushing forward. "I'll just bet yu to a standstill that Waffles an' Salvation'll round up all th' festive simoleons yu can get together! An' I'll throw in Frenchy's hat as an inducement."

"Well, if yore shore set on it make her a pool," replied Red, "an' th' winners divide with their outfit. Here's a starter," he added, tossing a buckskin bag on the table. "Come on, pile 'em up."

The crowd divided as the players seated themselves at the table, the O-Bar-O crowd grouping themselves behind their representatives; the Bar-20 behind theirs. A deck of cards was brought and the game was on.

Red, true to his nature, leaned back in a corner, where, hands on hips, he awaited any hostile demonstration on the part of the O-Bar-O; then, suddenly remembering, he looked half ashamed of his warlike position and became a peaceful citizen again. Buck leaned with his broad back against the bar, talking over his shoulder to the bartender, but watching Tenspot Davis, who was assiduously engaged in juggling a handful of Mexican dollars.

Up by the door Bigfoot Baker, elated at winning the buck-and-wing contest, was endeavoring to learn a new step, while his late rival was drowning his defeat at Buck's elbow. Lefty Allen was softly singing a Mexican love song, humming when the words would not come. At the table could be heard low-spoken card terms and good-natured banter, interspersed with the clink of gold and silver and the soft pat-pat of the onlookers' feet unconsciously keeping time to Lefty's song. Notwithstanding the grim assertiveness of belts full of .45's and the peeping handles of long-barreled Colts, set off with picturesque chaps, sombreros and tinkling spurs, the scene was one of peaceful content and good-fellowship.

"Ugh!" grunted Johnny, walking over to Red and informing that person that he, Red, was a worm-eaten prune and that for half a wink he, Johnny, would prove it. Red grabbed him by the seat of his corduroys and the collar of his shirt and helped him outside, where they strolled about, taking pot shots at whatever their fancy suggested.

Down the street in a cloud of dust rumbled the Las Cruces-El Paso stage and the two punchers went up to meet it. Raw furrows showed in the woodwork, one mule was missing and the driver and guard wore fresh bandages. A tired tenderfoot leaped out with a sigh of relief and hunted for his baggage, which he found to be generously perforated. Swearing at the God-forsaken land where a man had to fight highwaymen and Indians inside of half a day he grumblingly lugged his valise toward a forbidding-looking shack which was called a hotel.

The driver released his teams and then turned to Red. "Hullo, old hoss, how's th' gang?" he asked genially. "We've had a heck of a time this yere trip," he went on without waiting for Red to reply. "Five miles out of Las Cruces we stood off a son-of-a-gun that wanted th' dude's wealth. Then just this side of the San Andre foothills we runs into a bunch of young bucks who turned us off this yere way an' gave us a runnin' fight purty near all th' way. I'm a whole lot farther from Paso now than I was when I started, an seem as I lost a jack I'll be some time gittin' there. Yu don't happen to sabe a jack I can borrow, do yu?"

"I don't know about no jack, but I'll rope yu a bronch," offered Red, winking at Johnny.

"I'll pull her myself before I'll put dynamite in di' traces," replied the driver. "Yu fellers might amble back a ways with me–them buddin' warriors'll be layin' for me."

"We shore will," responded Johnny eagerly. "There's nine of us now an' there'll be nine more an' a cook to-morrow, mebby."

"Gosh, yu grows some," replied the guard. "Eighteen'll be a plenty for them glory hunters."

"We won't be able to," contradicted Red, "for things are peculiar."

At this moment the conversation was interrupted by the tenderfoot, who sported a new and cheap sombrero and also a belt and holster complete.

"Will you gentlemen join me?" He asked, turning to Red and nodding at the saloon. "I am very dry and much averse to drinking alone."

"Why, shore," responded Red heartily, wishing to put the stranger at ease.

The game was running about even as they entered and Lefty Allen was singing "The Insult," the rich tenor softening the harshness of the surroundings.

> I've swum th' Colorado where she's almost lost to view, I've braced
> th' Jaro layouts in Cheyenne;
> I've fought for muddy water with a howlin' bunch of Sioux, An'
> swallowed hot tamales, an' cayenne.
> I've rid a pitchin' broncho 'till th' sky was underneath, I've
>
> tackled every desert in th' land;
> I've sampled XXXX whiskey 'till I couldn't hardly see, An' dallied
> with th' quicksands of the Grande.
> I've argued with th' marshals of a half-a-dozen burgs, I've been
>
> dragged free an' fancy by a cow;
> I've had three years' campaignin' with th' fightin', bitin' Ninth,
> An' never lost my temper 'till right now.
> I've had the yaller fever an I've been shot full of holes, I've
>
> grabbed an army mule plumb by its tail;
> I've never been so snortin', really highfalutin' mad As when y'u up
> an' hands me ginger ale!

Hopalong laughed joyously at a remark made by Waffles and the stranger glanced quickly at him. His merry, boyish face, underlined by a jaw showing great firmness and set with an expression of aggressive self-reliance, impressed the stranger and he remarked to Red, who lounged lazily near him, that he was surprised to see such a face on so young a man and he asked who the player was.

"Oh, his name's Hopalong Cassidy," answered Red. "He's di' cuss that raised that ruction down in Mexico last spring. Rode his cayuse in a saloon and played with the loungers and had to shoot one before he got out. When he did get out he had to fight a whole bunch of Mexicans an' even potted their marshal, who had di' drop on him. Then he returned and visited the marshal about a month later, took his gun away from him an' then cut th' cards to see if he was a prisoner or not. He's a shore funny cuss."

The tenderfoot gasped his amazement. "Are you not fooling with me?" He asked.

"Tell him yu came after that five hundred dollars reward and see," answered Red goodnaturedly.

"Holy smoke!" shouted Waffles as Hopalong won his sixth consecutive pot. "Did yu ever see such luck?" Frenchy grinned and some time later raked in his third. Salvation then staked his last cent against Hopalong's flush and dropped out.

Tenspot flipped to Waffles the money he had been juggling and Lefty searched his clothes for wealth. Buck, still leaning against the bar, grinned and winked at Johnny, who was pouring hair-raising tales into the receptive ears of the stranger. Thereupon Johnny confided to his newly found acquaintance the facts about the game, nearly causing that person to explode with delight.

Waffles pushed back his chair, stood up and stretched. At the finish of a yawn he grinned at his late adversary. "I'm all in, yu old son-of-a-gun. Yu shore can play draw. I'm goin' to try yu again some time. I was beat fair an' square an' I ain't got no kick comin', none whatever," he remarked, as he shook hands with Hopalong.

"Oh, we're that gang from th' O-Bar-O," hummed the Kid as he sauntered in. One cheek was slightly swollen and his clothes shed dust at every step. "Who wins?" he inquired, not having heard Waffles.

"They did, blast it!" exploded Bigfoot.

One of the Kid's peculiarities was revealed in the unreasoning and hasty conclusions he arrived at. From no desire to imply unfairness, but rather because of his bitterness against failure of any kind and his loyalty to Waffles, came his next words:

"Mebby they skinned yu."

Like a flash Waffles sprang before him, his hand held up, palm out. "He don't mean nothin'—he's only a ignorant kid!" he cried.

Buck smiled and wrested the Colt from Johnny's ever-ready hand. "Here's another," he said. Red laughed softly and rolled Johnny on the floor. "Yu jackass," he whispered, "don't yu know better'n to make a gun-play when we needs them all?"

"What are we goin' to do?" Asked Tex, glancing at the bulging pockets of Hopalong's chaps.

"We're goin' to punch cows again, that's what we're to do," answered Bigfoot dismally.

"An' whose are we goin' to punch? We can't go back to the old man," grumbled Tex.

Salvation looked askance at Buck and then at the others. "Mebby," he began, "Mebby we kin git a job on th' Bar-20." Then turning to Buck again he bluntly asked, "Are yu short of punchers?"

"Well, I might use some," answered the foreman, hesitating. "But I ain't got only one cook, an' — —"

"We'll git yu th' cook all O.K.," interrupted Charley Lane vehemently. "Hi, yu cook!" he shouted, "amble in here an' git a rustle on!"

There was no reply, and after waiting for a minute he and Waffles went into the rear room, from which there immediately issued great chunks of profanity and noise. They returned looking pugnacious and disgusted, with a wildly fighting man who was more full of liquor than was the bottle which he belligerently waved.

"This here animated distillery what yu sees is our cook," said Waffles. "We eats his grub, nobody else. If he gits drunk that's our funeral; but he won't get drunk! If yu wants us to punch for yu say so an' we does; if yu don't, we don't."

"Well," replied Buck thoughtfully, "mebby I can use yu." Then with a burst of recklessness he added, "Yes, if I lose my job! But yu might sober that Mexican up if yu let him fall in th' horse trough."

As the procession wended its way on its mission of wet charity, carrying the cook in any manner at all, Frenchy waved his long lost sombrero at Buck, who stood in the door, and shouted, "Yu old son-of-a-gun, I'm proud to know yu!"

Buck smiled and snapped his watch shut "Time to amble," he said.

Chapter XI
Holding the Claim

"Oh, we're that gang from th' O-Bar-O," hummed Waffles, sinking the branding-iron in the flank of a calf. The scene was one of great activity and hilarity. Several fires were burning near the huge corral and in them half a dozen irons were getting hot. Three calves were being held down for the brand of the "Bar-20" and two more were being dragged up on their sides by the ropes of the cowboys, the proud cow-ponies showing off their accomplishments at the expense of the calves' feelings. In the corral the dust arose in steady clouds as calf after calf was "cut out" by the ropers and dragged out to get "tagged." Angry cows fought valiantly for their terrorized offspring, but always to no avail, for the hated rope of some perspiring and dust-grimed rider sent them crashing to earth. Over the plain were herds of cattle and groups of madly riding cowboys, and two cook wagons were stalled a short distance from the corral. The round-up of the Bar-20 was taking place, and each of the two outfits tried to outdo the other and each individual strove for a prize. The man who cut out and dragged to the fire the most calves in three days could leave for the Black Hills at the expiration of that time, the rest to follow as soon as they could.

In this contest Hopalong Cassidy led his nearest rival, Red Connors, both of whom were Bar-20 men, by twenty cut-outs, and there remained but half an hour more in which to compete. As Red disappeared into the sea of tossing horns Hopalong dashed out with a whoop.

"Hi, yu trellis-built rack of bones, come along there! Whoop!" he yelled, turning the prisoner over to the squad by the fire.

"Chalk up this here insignificant wart of cross-eyed perversity: an' how many?" He called as he galloped back to the corral.

"One ninety-eight," announced Buck, blowing the sand from the tally sheet. "That's shore goin' some," he remarked to himself.

When the calf sprang up it was filled with terror, rage and pain, and charged at Billy from the rear as that pessimistic soul was leaning over and poking his finger at a somber horned-toad. "Wow!" he yelled as his feet took huge steps up in the air, each one strictly on its own course. "Woof!" he grunted in the hot sand as he arose on his hands and knees and spat alkali.

"What's s'matter?" He asked dazedly of Johnny Nelson. "Ain't it funny!" he yelled sarcastically as he beheld Johnny holding his sides with laughter. "Ain't it funny!" he repeated belligerently. "Of course that four-laigged, knock-kneed, wobblin' son-of-a-Piute had to cut me out. They wasn't nobody in sight but Billy! Why didn't yu say he was comin'? Think I can see four ways to once? Why didn't —" At this point Red cantered up with a calf, and by a quick maneuver, drew the taut rope against the rear of Billy's knees, causing that unfortunate to sit down heavily. As he arose choking with broken-winded profanity Red dragged the animal to the fire, and Billy forgot his grievances in the press of labor.

"How many, Buck?" Asked Red.

"One-eighty."

"How does she stand?"

"Yore eighteen to th' bad," replied the foreman. "Th' son-of-a-gun!" marveled Red, riding off.

Another whoop interrupted them, and Billy quit watching out of the corner eye for pugnacious calves as he prepared for Hopalong.

"Hey, Buck, this here cuss was with a Barred-Horseshoe cow," he announced as he turned it over to the branding man. Buck made a tally in a separate column and released the animal. "Hullo, Red! Workin'?" Asked Hopalong of his rival.

"Some, yu little cuss," answered Red with all the good nature in the world. Hopalong was his particular "side partner," and he could lose to him with the best of feelings.

"Yu looks so nice an' cool, an' clean, I didn't know," responded Hopalong, eyeing a streak of sweat and dust which ran from Red's eyes to his chin and then on down his neck.

"What yu been doin'? Plowin' with yore nose?" Returned Red, smiling blandly at his friend's appearance.

"Yah!" snorted Hopalong, wheeling toward the corral. "Come on, yu pie-eatin' doodle-bug; I'll beat yu to th' gate!"

The two ponies sent showers of sand all over Billy, who eyed them in pugnacious disgust. "Of all th' locoed imps that ever made life miserable fer a man, them's th' worst! Is there any piece of fool nonsense they hain't harnessed me with?" He beseeched of Buck. "Is there anything they hain't done to me? They hides my liquor; they stuffs th' sweat band of my hat with rope; they ties up my pants; they puts water in. My boots an' toads in my bunk-ain't they never goin' to get sane?"

"Oh, they're only kids-they can't help it," offered Buck. "Didn't they hobble my cayuse when I was on him an' near bust my neck?"

Hopalong interrupted the conversation by driving up another calf, and Buck, glancing at his watch, declared the contest at an end.

"Yu wins," he remarked to the newcomer. "An' now yu get scarce or Billy will shore straddle yore nerves. He said as how he was goin' to get square on yu to-night."

"I didn't, neither, Hoppy!" earnestly contradicted Billy, who bad visions of a night spent in torment as a reprisal for such a threat. "Honest I didn't, did I, Johnny?" He asked appealingly.

"Yu shore did," lied Johnny, winking at Red, who had just ridden up.

"I don't know what yore talkin' about, but yu shore did," replied Red.

"If yu did," grinned Hopalong, "I'll shore make yu hard to find. Come on, fellows," he said; "grub's ready. Where's Frenchy?"

"Over chewin' th' rag with Waffles about his hat-he's lost it again," answered Red. "He needs a guardian fer that bonnet. Th' Kid an' Salvation has jammed it in th' corral fence an' Waffles has to stand fer it."

"Let's put it in th' grub wagon an see him cuss cookie," suggested Hopalong.

"Shore," indorsed Johnny; Cookie'll feed him bum grub for a week to get square."

Hopalong and Johnny ambled over to the corral and after some trouble located the missing sombrero, which they carried to the grub wagon and hid in the flour barrel. Then they went over by the excited owner and dropped a few remarks about how strange the cook was acting and how he was watching Frenchy.

Frenchy jumped at the bait and tore over to the wagon, where he and the cook spent some time in mutual recrimination. Hopalong nosed around and finally dug up the hat, white as new-fallen snow.

"Here's a hat-found it in th' dough barrel," he announced, handing it over to Frenchy, who received it in open-mouthed stupefaction.

"Yu pie-makin' pirate! Yu didn't know where my lid was, did yu! Yu cross-eyed lump of hypocrisy!" yelled Frenchy, dusting off the flour with one full-armed swing on the cook's face, driving it into that unfortunate's nose and eyes and mouth. "Yu white-washed Chink, yu-rub yore face with water an' yu've got pancakes."

"Hey! What you doin'!" yelled the cook, kicking the spot where he had last seen Frenchy. "Don't yu know better'n that!"

"Yu live close to yoreself or I'll throw yu so high th' sun'll duck," replied Frenchy, a smile illuminating his face.

"Hey, cookie," remarked Hopalong confidentially, "I know who put up this joke on yu. Yu ask Billy who hid th' hat," suggested the tease. "Here he comes now-see how queer he looks."

"Th' mournful Piute," ejaculated the cook. "I'll shore make him wish he'd kept on his own trail. I'll flavor his slush [coffee] with year-old dish-rags!"

At this juncture Billy ambled up, keeping his weather eye peeled for trouble. "Who's a dish-rag?" He queried. The cook mumbled something about crazy hens not knowing when to quit cackling and climbed up in his wagon. And that night Billy swore off drinking coffee.

When the dawn of the next day broke, Hopalong was riding toward the Black Hills, leaving Billy to untie himself as best he might.

The trip was uneventful and several weeks later he entered Red Dog, a rambling shanty town, one of those western mushrooms that sprang up in a night. He took up his stand at the Miner's

Rest, and finally secured six claims at the cost of nine hundred hard-earned dollars, a fund subscribed by the outfits, as it was to be a partnership affair.

He rode out to a staked-off piece of hillside and surveyed his purchase, which consisted of a patch of ground, six holes, six piles of dirt and a log hut. The holes showed that the claims bad been tried and found wanting.

He dumped his pack of tools and provisions, which he had bought on the way up, and lugged them into the cabin. After satisfying his curiosity he went outside and sat down for a smoke, figuring up in his mind how much gold he could carry on a horse. Then, as he realized that he could get a pack mule to carry the surplus, he became aware of a strange presence near at hand and looked up into the muzzle of a Sharp's rifle. He grasped the situation in a flash and calmly blew several heavy smoke rings around the frowning barrel.

"Well?" He asked slowly.

"Nice day, stranger," replied the man with the rifle, "but don't yu reckon yu've made a mistake?"

Hopalong glanced at the number burned on a near-by stake and carelessly blew another smoke ring. He was waiting for the gun to waver.

"No, I reckons not," he answered. "Why?"

"Well, I'll jest tell yu since yu asks. This yere claim's mine an' I'm a reg'lar terror, I am. That's why; an' seein' as it is, yu better amble some."

Hopalong glanced down the street and saw an interested group watching him, which only added to his rage for being in such a position. Then he started to say something, faltered and stared with horror at a point several feet behind his opponent. The "terror" sprang to one side in response to Hop-along's expression, as if fearing that a snake or some such danger threatened him. As he alighted in his new position he fell forward and Hopalong slid a smoking Colt in its holster.

Several men left the distant group and ran toward the claim. Hopalong reached his arm inside the door and brought forth his rifle, with which he covered their advance.

"Anything yu want?" he shouted savagely.

The men stopped and two of them started to sidle in front of two others, but Hopalong was not there for the purpose of permitting a move that would screen any gun play and he stopped the game with a warning shout. Then the two held up their hands and advanced.

"We wants to git Dan," called out one of them, nodding at the prostrate figure.

"Come ahead," replied Hopalong, substituting a Colt for the rifle.

They carried their badly wounded and insensible burden back to those whom they had left, and several curses were hurled at the cowboy, who only smiled grimly and entered the hut to place things ready for a siege, should one come. He had one hundred rounds of ammunition and provisions enough for two weeks, with the assurance of reinforcements long before that time would expire. He cut several rough loopholes and laid out his weapons for quick handling. He knew that he could stop any advance during the day and planned only for night attacks. How long he could go without sleep did not bother him, because he gave it no thought, as he was accustomed to short naps and could awaken at will or at the slightest sound.

As dusk merged into dark he crept forth and collected several handfuls of dry twigs, which he scattered around the hut, as the cracking of these would warn him of an approach. Then he went in and went to sleep.

He awoke at daylight after a good night's rest, and feasted on canned beans and peaches. Then he tossed the cans out of the door and shoved his hat out. Receiving no response he walked out and surveyed the town at his feet. A sheepish grin spread over his face as he realized that there was no danger. Several red-shirted men passed by him on their way to town, and one, a grizzled veteran of many gold camps, stopped and sauntered up to him.

"Mornin'," said Hopalong.

"Mornin'," replied the stranger. "I thought I'd drop in an' say that I saw that gun-play of yourn yesterday. Yu ain't got no reason to look fer a rush. This camp is half white men an' half bullies, an' th' white men won't stand fer no play like that. Them fellers that jest passed are neighbors of yourn, an' they won't lay abed if yu needs them. But yu wants to look out fer th' joints in th' town. Guess this business is out of yore line," he finished as he sized Hopalong up.

"She shore is, but I'm here to stay. Got tired of punchin' an' reckoned I'd get rich." Here he smiled and glanced at the hole. "How're yu makin' out?" He asked.

"'Bout five dollars a day apiece, but that ain't nothin' when grub's so high. Got reckless th' other day an' had a egg at fifty cents."

Hopalong whistled and glanced at the empty cans at his feet. "Any marshal in this burg?"

"Yep. But he's one of th' gang. No good, an' drunk half th' time an' half drunk th' rest. Better come down an' have something," invited the miner.

"I'd shore like to, but I can't let no gang get in that door," replied the puncher.

"Oh, that's all right; I'll call my pardner down to keep house till yu gits back. He can hold her all right. Hey, Jake!" he called to a man who was some hundred paces distant; "Come down here an' keep house till we gits back, will yu?"

The man lumbered down to them and took possession as Hopalong and his newly found friend started for the town.

They entered the "Miner's Rest" and Hopalong fixed the room in his mind with one swift glance. Three men-and they looked like the crowd he had stopped before-were playing poker at a table near the window. Hopalong leaned with his back to the bar and talked, with the players always in sight.

Soon the door opened and a bewhiskered, heavy-set man tramped in, and walking up to Hopalong, looked him over.

"Huh," he sneered, "Yu are th' gent with th' festive guns that plugged Dan, ain't yu?"

Hopalong looked at him in the eyes and quietly replied:

"An' who th' deuce are yu?"

The stranger's eyes blazed and his face wrinkled with rage as he aggressively shoved his jaw close to Hopalong's face.

"Yu runt, I'm a better man than yu even if yu do wear hair pants," referring to Hopalong's chaps. "Yu cow-wrastlers make me tired, an' I'm goin' to show yu that this town is too good for you. Yu can say it right now that yu are a ornery, game-leg —"

Hopalong smashed his insulter squarely between the eyes with all the power of his sinewy body behind the blow, knocking him in a heap under the table. Then he quickly glanced at the card players and saw a hostile movement. His gun was out in a flash and he covered the trio as he walked up to them. Never in all his life had he felt such a desire to kill. His eyes were diamond points of accumulated fury, and those whom he faced quailed before him.

"Yu scum! Draw, please draw! Pull yore guns an' gimme my chance! Three to one, an' I'll lay my guns here," he said, placing them on the bar and removing his hands. "'Nearer My God to Thee' is purty appropriate fer yu just now! Yu seem to be a-scared of yore own guns. Git down on yore dirty knees an' say good an' loud that yu eats dirt! Shout out that yu are too currish to live with decent men," he said, even-toned and distinct, his voice vibrant with passion as he took up his Colts. "Get down!" he repeated, shoving the weapons forward and pulling back the hammers.

The trio glanced at each other, and all three dropped to their knees and repeated in venomous hatred the words Hopalong said for them.

"Now git! An' if I sees yu when I leaves I'll send yu after yore friend. I'll shoot on sight now. Git!" He escorted them to the door and kicked the last one out.

His miner friend still leaned against the bar and looked his approval.

"Well done, youngster! But yu wants to look out-that man," pointing to the now groping victim of Hopalong's blow, "is th' marshal of this town. He or his pals will get yu if yu don't watch th' corners."

Hopalong walked over to the marshal, jerked him to his feet and slammed him against the bar. Then he tore the cheap badge from its place and threw it on the floor. Reaching down, he drew the marshal's revolver from its holster and shoved it in its owner's hand.

"Yore th' marshal of this place an' it's too good for me, but yore gain' to pick up that tin lie," pointing at the badge, "an' yore goin' to do it right now. Then yore gain' to get kicked out of that door, an' if yu stops runnin' while I can see yu I'll fill yu so full of holes yu'll catch cold. Yore a sumptious marshal, yu are! Yore th' snortingest ki-yi that ever stuck its tail atween its laigs, yu are. Yu pop-eyed wall flower, yu wants to peep to yoreself or some papoose'll slide yu over th' Divide so fast yu won't have time to grease yore pants. Pick up that license-tag an' let me see you perculate so lively that yore back'll look like a ten-cent piece in five seconds. Flit!"

The marshal, dazed and bewildered, stooped and fumbled for the badge. Then he stood up and glanced at the gun in his hand and at the eager man before him. He slid the weapon in his belt and drew his hand across his fast-closing eyes. Cursing streaks of profanity, he staggered to the door and landed in a heap in the street from the force of Hopalong's kick. Struggling to his feet, he ran unsteadily down the block and disappeared around a corner.

The bartender, cool and unperturbed, pushed out three glasses on his treat: "I've seen yu afore, up in Cheyenne —'member? How's yore friend Red?" He asked as he filled the glasses with the best the house afforded.

"Well, shore 'nuff! Glad to see yu, Jimmy! What yu doin' away off here?" Asked Hopalong, beginning to feel at home.

"Oh, jest filterin' round like. I'm awful glad to see yu-this yere wart of a town needs siftin' out. It was only last week I was wishin' one of yore bunch 'ud show up-that ornament yu jest buffaloed shore raised th' devil in here, an' I wished I had somebody to prospect his anatomy for a lead mine. But he's got a tough gang circulating with him. Ever hear of Dutch Shannon or Blinky Neary? They's with him."

"Dutch Shannon? Nope," he replied.

"Bad eggs, an' not a-carin' how they gits square. Th' feller yu' salted yesterday was a bosom friend of th' marshal's, an' he passed in his chips last night."

"So?"

"Yep. Bought a bottle of ready-made nerve an' went to his own funeral. Aristotle Smith was lookin' fer him up in Cheyenne last year. Aristotle said he'd give a century fer five minutes' palaver with him, but he shied th' town an' didn't come back. Yu know Aristotle, don't yu? He's th' geezer that made fame up to Poison Knob three years ago. He used to go to town ridin' astride a log on th' lumber flume. Made four miles in six minutes with th' promise of a ruction when he stopped. Once when he was loaded he tried to ride back th' same way he came, an' th' first thing he knowed he was three miles farther from his supper an' a-slippin' down that valley like he wanted to go somewhere. He swum out at Potter's Dam an' it took him a day to walk back. But he didn't make that play again, because he was frequently sober, an' when he wasn't he'd only stand off an' swear at th' slide."

"That's Aristotle, all hunk. He's th' chap that used to play checkers with Deacon Rawlins. They used empty an' loaded shells for men, an' when they got a king they'd lay one on its side. Sometimes they'd jar th' board an' they'd all be kings an' then they'd have a cussin' match," replied Hopalong, once more restored to good humor.

"Why," responded Jimmy, "he counted his wealth over twice by mistake an' shore raised a howl when he went to blow it-thought he's been robbed, an' laid behind th' houses fer a week lookin' fer th' feller that done it."

"I've heard of that cuss-he shore was th' limit. What become of him?" Asked the miner.

"He ambled up to Laramie an' stuck his head in th' window of that joint by th' plaza an' hollered 'Fire,' an' they did. He was shore a good feller, all th' same," answered the bartender. Hopalong laughed and started for the door. Turning around he looked at his miner friend and asked: "Comin' along? I'm goin' back now."

"Nope. Reckon I'll hit th' tiger a whirl. I'll stop in when I passes."

"All right. So long," replied Hopalong, slipping out of the door and watching for trouble. There was no opposition shown him, and he arrived at his claim to find Jake in a heated argument with another of the gang.

"Here he comes now," he said as Hopalong walked up. "Tell him what yu said to me."

"I said yu made a mistake," said the other, turning to the cowboy in a half apologetic manner.

"An' what else?" Insisted Jake.

"Why, ain't that all?" Asked the claim-jumper's friend in feigned surprise, wishing that he had kept quiet.

"Well I reckons it is if yu can't back up yore words," responded Jake in open contempt.

Hopalong grabbed the intruder by the collar of his shirt and hauled him off the claim. "Yu keep off this, understand? I just kicked yore marshal out in th' street, an' I'll pay yu th' next call. If yu rambles in range of my guns yu'll shore get in th' way of a slug. Yu an' yore gang wants to browse on th' far side of th' range or yu'll miss a sunrise some mornin'. Scoot!"

Hopalong turned to his companion and smiled. "What'd he say?" He asked genially.

"Oh, he jest shot off his mouth a little. They's all no good. I've collided with lots of them all over this country. They can't face a good man an' keep their nerve. What'd yu say to th' marshal?"

"I told him what he was an' threw him outen th' street," replied Hopalong. "In about two weeks we'll have a new marshal an' he'll shore be a dandy."

"Yes? Why don't yu take th' job yoreself? We're with yu."

"Better man comin'. Ever hear of Buck Peters or Red Connors of th' Bar-20, Texas?"

"Buck Peters? Seems to me I have. Did he punch fer th' Tin-Cup up in Montana, 'bout twenty years back?"

"Shore! Him and Frenchy McAllister punched all over that country an' they used to paint Cheyenne, too," replied Hopalong, eagerly.

"I knows him, then. I used to know Frenchy, too. Are they comin' up here?"

"Yes," responded Hopalong, struggling with another can while waiting for the fire to catch up. "Better have some grub with me-don't like to eat alone," invited the cowboy, the reaction of his late rage swinging him to the other extreme.

When their tobacco had got well started at the close of the meal and content had taken possession of them Hopalong laughed quietly and finally spoke:

"Did yu ever know Aristotle Smith when yu was up in Montana?"

"Did I! Well, me an' Aristotle prospected all through that country till he got so locoed I had to watch him fer fear he'd blow us both up. He greased th' fryin' pan with dynamite one night, an' we shore had to eat jerked meat an' canned stuff all th' rest of that trip. What made yu ask? Is he comin' up too?"

"No, I reckons not. Jimmy, th' bartender, said that he cashed in up at Laramie. Wasn't he th' cuss that built that boat out there on th' Arizona desert because he was scared that a flood might come? Th' sun shore warped that punt till it wasn't even good for a hencoop."

"Nope. That was Sister-Annie Tompkins. He was purty near as bad as Aristotle, though. He roped a puma up on th' Sacramentos, an' didn't punch no more fer three weeks. Well, here comes my pardner an' I reckons I'll amble right along. If yu needs any referee or a side pardner in any ruction yu has only got to warble up my way. So long."

The next ten days passed quietly, and on the afternoon of the eleventh Hopalong's miner friend paid him a visit.

"Jake recommends yore peaches," he laughed as he shook Hopalong's hand. "He says yu boosted another of that crowd. That bein' so I thought I would drop in an' say that they're comin' after yu to-night, shore. Just heard of it from yore friend Jimmy. Yu can count on us when th' rush comes. But why didn't yu say yu was a pard of Buck Peters'? Me an' him used to shoot up Laramie together. From what yore friend James says, yu can handle this gang by yore lonesome, but if yu needs any encouragement yu make some sign an' we'll help th' event along some. They's eight of us that'll be waitin' up to get th' returns an' we're shore goin' to be in range."

"Gee, it's nice to run across a friend of Buck's! Ain't he a son-of-a-gun?" Asked Hopalong, delighted at the news. Then, without waiting for a reply, he went on: "Yore shore square, all right, an' I hates to refuse yore offer, but I got eighteen friends comin' up an' they ought to get here by tomorrow. Yu tell Jimmy to head them this way when they shows up an' I'll have th' claim for them. There ain't no use of yu fellers gettin' mixed up in this. Th' bunch that's comin' can clean out any gang this side of sunup, an' I expects they'll shore be anxious to begin when they finds me eatin' peaches an' wastin' my time shootin' bums. Yu pass th' word along to yore friends, an' tell them to lay low an' see th' Arory Boerallis hit this town with its tail up. Tell Jimmy to do it up good when he speaks about me holdin' th' claim —I likes to see Buck an' Red fight when they're good an' mad."

The miner laughed and slapped Hopalong on the shoulder. "Yore all right, youngster! Yore just like Buck was at yore age. Say now, I reckons he wasn't a reg'lar terror on wheels! Why, I've seen him do more foolish things than any man I knows of, an' I calculate that if Buck pals with yu there ain't no water in yore sand. My name's Tom Halloway," he suggested.

"An' mine's Hopalong Cassidy," was the reply. "I've heard Buck speak of yu."

"Has yu? Well, don't it beat all how little this world is? Somebody allus turnin' up that knows somebody yu knows. I'll just amble along, Mr. Cassidy, an' don't yu be none bashful about callin' if yu needs me. Any pal of Buck's is my friend. Well, so long," said the visitor as he strode off. Then he stopped and turned around. "Hey, mister!" he called. "They are goin' to roll a fire barrel down agin yu from behind," indicating by an outstretched arm the point from where it would start. "If it burns yu out I'm goin' to take a band from up there," pointing to a cluster of rocks well to the rear of where the crowd would work from, "an' I don't care whether yu likes it or not," he added to himself.

Hopalong scratched his head and then laughed. Taking up a pick and shovel, he went out behind the cabin and dug a trench parallel with and about twenty paces away from the rear wall. Heaping the excavated dirt up on the near side of the cut, he stepped back and surveyed his labor with open satisfaction. "Roll yore fire barrel an' be dogged," he muttered. "Mebby she won't make a bully light for pot shots, though," he added, grinning at the execution he would do.

Taking up his tools, he went up to the place from where the gang would roll the barrel, and made half a dozen mounds of twigs, being careful to make them very flimsy. Then he covered them with earth and packed them gently. The mounds looked very tempting from the view-point of a marksman in search of earth-works, and appeared capable of stopping any rifle ball that could be fired against them. Hopalong looked them over critically and stepped back.

"I'd like to see th' look on th' face of th' son-of-a-gun that uses them for cover-won't he be surprised" and he grinned gleefully as he pictured his shots boring through them. Then he placed in the center of each a chip or a pebble or something that he thought would show up well in the firelight.

Returning to the cabin, he banked it up well with dirt and gravel, and tossed a few shovelfuls up on the roof as a safety valve to his exuberance. When he entered the door he had another idea, and fell to work scooping out a shallow cellar, deep enough to shelter him when lying at full length. Then he stuck his head out of the window and grinned at the false covers with their prominent bull's-eyes.

"When that prize-winnin' gang of ossified idiots runs up agin' these fortifications they shore will be disgusted. I'll bet four dollars an' seven cents they'll think their medicine-man's no good. I hopes that puff-eyed marshal will pick out that hump with th' chip on it," and he hugged himself in anticipation.

He then cut down a sapling and fastened it to the roof and on it he tied his neckerchief, which fluttered valiantly and with defiance in the light breeze. "I shore hopes they appreciates that," he remarked whimsically, as he went inside the hut and closed the door.

The early part of the evening passed in peace, and Hopalong, tired of watching in vain, wished for action. Midnight came, and it was not until half an hour before dawn that he was attacked. Then a noise sent him to a loophole, where he fired two shots at skulking figures some distance off. A fusillade of bullets replied; one of them ripped through the door at a weak spot and drilled a hole in a can of the everlasting peaches. Hopalong set the can in the frying pan and then flitted from loophole to loophole, shooting quick and straight. Several curses told him that he had not missed, and he scooped up a finger of peach juice. Shots thudded into the walls of his fort in an unceasing stream, and, as it grew lighter, several whizzed through the loopholes. He kept close to the earth and waited for the rush, and when it came sent it back, minus two of its members.

As he reloaded his Colts a bullet passed through his shirt sleeve and he promptly nailed the marksman. He looked out of a crack in the rear wall and saw the top of an adjoining hill crowned with spectators, all of whom were armed. Some time later he repulsed another attack and heard a faint cheer from his friends on the hill. Then he saw a barrel, blazing from end to end, roll out from the place he had so carefully covered with mounds. It gathered speed and bounded over the rough ground, flashed between two rocks and leaped into the trench, where it crackled and roared in vain.

"Now," said Hopalong, blazing at the mounds as fast as he could fire his rifle, "we'll just see what yu thinks of yore nice little covers."

Yells of consternation and pain rang out in a swelling chorus, and legs and arms jerked and flopped, one man, in his astonishment at the shot that tore open his cheek, sitting up in plain sight of the marksman. Roars of rage floated up from the main body of the besiegers, and the discomfited remnant of barrel-rollers broke for real cover.

Then he stopped another rush from the front, made upon the supposition that he was thinking only of the second detachment. A hearty cheer arose from Tom Halloway and his friends, ensconced in their rocky position, and it was taken up by those on the hill, who danced and yelled their delight at the battle, to them more humorous than otherwise.

This recognition of his prowess from men of the caliber of his audience made him feel good, and he grinned: "Gee, I'll bet Halloway an' his friends is shore itchin' to get in this," he murmured, firing at a head that was shown for an instant. "Wonder what Red'll say when Jimmy tells him-bet he'll plow dust like a cyclone," and Hopalong laughed, picturing to himself the satiation of Red's anger. "Old red-headed son-of-a-gun," murmured the cowboy affectionately, "he shore can fight."

As he squinted over the sights of his rifle his eye caught sight of a moving body of men as they cantered over the flats about two miles away. In his eagerness he forgot to shoot and carefully counted them. "Nine," he grumbled. "Wonder what's th' matter?" Fearing that they were not his friends. Then a second body numbering eight cantered into sight and followed the first.

"Whoop! There's th' Red-head!" he shouted, dancing in his joy. "Now," he shouted at the peach can joyously, "yu wait about thirty minutes an' yu'll shore reckon Hades has busted loose!"

He grabbed up his Colts, which he kept loaded for repelling rushes, and recklessly emptied them into the bushes and between the rocks and trees, searching every likely place for a human target. Then he slipped his rifle in a loophole and waited for good shots, having worked off the dangerous pressure of his exuberance.

Soon he heard a yell from the direction of the "Miner's Rest," and fell to jamming cartridges into his revolvers so that he could sally out and join in the fray by the side of Red.

The thunder of madly pounding hoofs rolled up the trail, and soon a horse and rider shot around the corner and headed for the copse. Three more raced close behind and then a bunch of six, followed by the rest, spread out and searched for trouble.

Red, a Colt in each hand and hatless, stood up in his stirrups and sent shot after shot into the fleeing mob, which he could not follow on account of the nature of the ground. Buck wheeled and dashed down the trail again with Red a close second, the others packed in a solid mass and after them. At the first level stretch the newcomers swept down and hit their enemies, going through them like a knife through cheese. Hopalong danced up and down with rage when he could not find his horse, and had to stand and yell, a spectator.

The fight drifted in among the buildings, where it became a series of isolated duels, and soon Hopalong saw panic-stricken horses carrying their riders out of the other side of the town. Then he went gunning for the man who had rustled his horse. He was unsuccessful and returned to his peaches.

Soon the riders came up, and when they saw Hopalong shove a peach into his powder-grimed mouth they yelled their delight.

"Yu old maverick! Eatin' peaches like yu was afraid we'd git some!" shouted Red indignantly, leaping down and running up to his pal as though to thrash him.

Hopalong grinned pleasantly and fired a peach against Red's eye. "I was savin' that one for yu, Reddie," he remarked, as he avoided Buck's playful kick. "Yu fellers git to work an' dig up some wealth —I'm hungry." Then he turned to Buck: "Yore th' marshal of this town, an' any son-of-a-gun what don't like it had better write. Oh, yes, here comes Tom Halloway —'member him?"

Buck turned and faced the miner and his hand went out with a jerk.

"Well, I'll be locoed if I didn't punch with yu on th' Tin-Cup!" he said.

"Yu shore did an' yu was purty devilish, but that there Cassidy of yourn beats anything I ever seen."

"He's a good kid," replied Buck, glancing to where Red and Hopalong were quarreling as to who had eaten the most pie in a contest held some years before.

Johnny, nosing around, came upon the perforated and partially scattered piles of earth and twigs, and vented his disgust of them by kicking them to pieces. "Hey! Hoppy! Oh, Hoppy!" he called, "what are these things?"

Hopalong jammed Red's hat over that person's eyes and replied: "Oh, them's some loaded dice I fixed for them."

"Yu son-of-a-gun!" sputtered Red, as he wrestled with his friend in the exuberance of his pride. "Yu son-of-a-gun! Yu shore ought to be ashamed to treat 'em that way!"

"Shore," replied Hopalong. "But I ain't!"

Chapter XII
The Hospitality of Travennes

Mr. Buck Peters rode into Alkaline one bright September morning and sought refreshment at the Emporium. Mr. Peters had just finished some business for his employer and felt the satisfaction that comes with the knowledge of work well done. He expected to remain in Alkaline for several days, where he was to be joined by two of his friends and punchers, Mr. Hopalong Cassidy and Mr. Red Connors, both of whom were at Cactus Springs, seventy miles to the east. Mr. Cassidy and his friend had just finished a nocturnal tour of Santa Fe and felt somewhat peevish and dull in consequence, not to mention the sadness occasioned by the expenditure of the greater part of their combined capital on such foolishness as faro, roulette and wet-goods.

Mr. Peters and his friends had sought wealth in the Black Hills, where they had enthusiastically disfigured the earth in the fond expectation of uncovering vast stores of virgin gold. Their hopes were of an optimistic brand and had existed until the last canister of cornmeal flour had been emptied by Mr. Cassidy's burro, which waited not upon it's master's pleasure nor upon the ethics of the case. When Mr. Cassidy had returned from exercising the animal and himself over two miles of rocky hillside in the vain endeavor to give it his opinion of burros and sundry chastisements, he was requested, as owner of the beast, to give his counsel as to the best way of securing eighteen breakfasts. Remembering that the animal was headed north when he last saw it and that it was too old to eat, anyway, he suggested a plan which had worked successfully at other times for other ends, namely, poker. Mr. McAllister, an expert at the great American game, volunteered his service in accordance with the spirit of the occasion and, half an hour later, he and Mr. Cassidy drifted into Pell's poker parlors, which were located in the rear of a Chinese laundry, where they gathered unto themselves the wherewithal for the required breakfasts. An hour spent in the card room of the "Hurrah" convinced its proprietor that they had wasted their talents for the past six weeks in digging for gold. The proof of this permitted the departure of the outfits with their customary elan.

At Santa Fe the various individuals had gone their respective ways, to reassemble at the ranch in the near future, and for several days they had been drifting south in groups of twos and threes and, like chaff upon a stream, had eddied into Alkaline, where Mr. Peters had found them arduously engaged in postponing the final journey. After he had gladdened their hearts and soothed their throats by making several pithy remarks to the bartender, with whom he established their credit, he cautioned them against letting any one harm them and, smiling at the humor of his warning, left abruptly.

Cactus Springs was burdened with a zealous and initiative organization known as vigilantes, whose duty it was to extend the courtesies of the land to cattle thieves and the like. This organization boasted of the name of Travennes' Terrors and of a muster roll of twenty. There was also a boast that no one had ever escaped them which, if true, was in many cases unfortunate. Mr. Slim Travennes, with whom Mr. Cassidy had participated in an extemporaneous exchange of Colt's courtesies in Santa Fe the year before, was the head of the organization and was also chairman of the committee on arrivals, and the two gentlemen of the Bar-20 had not been in town an hour before he knew of it.

Being anxious to show the strangers every attention and having a keen recollection of the brand of gun-play commanded by Mr. Cassidy, he planned a smoother method of procedure and one calculated to permit him to enjoy the pleasures of a good old age. Mr. Travennes knew that horse thieves were regarded as social enemies, that the necessary proof of their guilt was the finding of stolen animals in their possession, that death was the penalty and that every man, whether directly concerned or not, regarded, himself as judge, jury and executioner.

He had several acquaintances who were bound to him by his knowledge of crimes they had committed and would could not refuse his slightest wish. Even if they had been free agents they were not above causing the death of an innocent man. Mr. Travennes, feeling very self-satisfied at his cleverness, arranged to have the proof placed where it would do the most harm and intended to take care of the rest by himself.

Mr. Connors, feeling much refreshed and very hungry, arose at daylight the next morning, and dressing quickly, started off to feed and water the horses. After having several tilts with the landlord about the bucket he took his departure toward the corral at the rear. Peering through the gate, he could hardly believe his eyes. He climbed over it and inspected the animals at close range, and found that those which he and his friend had ridden for the last two months were not to be seen, but in their places were two better animals, which concerned him greatly. Being fair and square himself, he could not understand the change and sought enlightenment of his more imaginative and suspicious friend.

"Hey, Hopalong!" he called, "come out here an' see what th' blazes has happened!"

Mr. Cassidy stuck his auburn head out of the wounded shutter and complacently surveyed his companion. Then he saw the horses and looked hard.

"Quit yore foolin', yu old cuss," he remarked pleasantly, as he groped around behind him with his feet, searching for his boots. "Anybody would think yu was a little boy with yore fool jokes. Ain't yu ever goin' to grow up?"

"They've got our bronch," replied Mr. Connors in an injured tone. "Honest, I ain't kiddin' yu," he added for the sake of peace.

"Who has?" Came from the window, followed immediately by, "Yu've got my boots!"

"I ain't —they're under th' bunk," contradicted and explained Mr. Connors. Then, turning to the matter in his mind he replied, "I don't know who's got them. If I did do yu think I'd be holdin' hands with myself?"

"Nobody'd accuse yu of anything like that," came from the window, accompanied by an overdone snicker.

Mr. Connors flushed under his accumulated tan as he remembered the varied pleasures of Santa Fe, and he regarded the bronchos in anything but a pleasant state of mind.

Mr. Cassidy slid through the window and approached his friend, looking as serious as he could.

"Any tracks?" He inquired, as he glanced quickly over the ground to see for himself.

"Not after that wind we had last night. They might have growed there for all I can see," growled Mr. Connors.

"I reckon we better hold a pow-wow with th' foreman of this shack an' find out what he knows," suggested Mr. Cassidy. "This looks too good to be a swap."

Mr. Connors looked his disgust at the idea and then a light broke in upon him. "Mebby they was hard pushed an' wanted fresh cayuses," he said. "A whole lot of people get hard pushed in this country. Anyhow, we'll prospect th' boss."

They found the proprietor in his stocking feet, getting the breakfast, and Mr. Cassidy regarded the preparations with open approval. He counted the tin plates and found only three, and, thinking that there would be more plates if there were others to feed, glanced into the landlord's room. Not finding signs of other guests, on whom to lay the blame for the loss of his horse, he began to ask questions.

"Much trade?" He inquired solicitously.

"Yep," replied the landlord.

Mr. Cassidy looked at the three tins and wondered if there had ever been any more with which to supply his trade. "Been out this morning?" he pursued.

"Nope."

"Talks purty nigh as much as Buck," thought Mr. Cassidy, and then said aloud, "Anybody else here?"

"Nope."

Mr. Cassidy lapsed into a painful and disgusted silence and his friend tried his hand.

"Who owns a mosaic bronch, Chinee flag on th' near side, Skillet brand?" asked Mr. Connors.

"Quien sabe?"

"Gosh, he can nearly keep still in two lingoes," thought Mr. Cassidy.

"Who owns a bob-tailed pinto, saddle-galled, cast in th' near eye, Star Diamond brand, white stockin' on th' off front prop, with a habit of scratchin' itself every other minute?" went on Mr. Connors.

"Slim Travennes," replied the proprietor, flopping a flapjack. Mr. Cassidy reflectively scratched the back of his hand and looked innocent, but his mind was working overtime.

"Who's Slim Travennes?" Asked Mr. Connors, never having heard of that person, owing to the reticence of his friend.

"Captain of th' vigilantes."

"What does he look like on th' general run?" Blandly inquired Mr. Cassidy, wishing to verify his suspicions. He thought of the trouble he had with Mr. Travennes up in Santa Fe and of the reputation that gentleman possessed. Then the fact that Mr. Travennes was the leader of the local vigilantes came to his assistance and he was sure that the captain had a hand in the change. All these points existed in misty groups in his mind, but the next remark of the landlord caused them to rush together and reveal the plot.

"Good," said the landlord, flopping another flapjack, "and a warnin' to hoss thieves."

"Ahem," coughed Mr. Cassidy and then continued, "is he a tall, lanky, yaller-headed son-of-a-gun, with a big nose an' lots of ears?"

"Mebby so," answered the host.

"Urn, slopping over into bad Sioux," thought Mr. Cassidy, and then said aloud, "How long has he hung around this here layout?" At the same time passing a warning glance at his companion.

The landlord straightened up. "Look here, stranger, if yu hankers after his pedigree so all-fired hard yu had best pump him."

"I told yu this here feller wasn't a man what would give away all he knowed," lied Mr. Connors, turning to his friend and indicating the host. "He ain't got time for that. Anybody can see that he is a powerful busy man. An' then he ain't no child."

Mr. Cassidy thought that the landlord could tell all he knew in about five minutes and then not break any speed records for conversation, but he looked properly awed and impressed. "Well, yu needn't go an' get mad about it! I didn't know, did I?"

"Who's gettin' mad?" Pugnaciously asked Mr. Connors. After his injured feelings had been soothed by Mr. Cassidy's sullen silence he again turned to the landlord.

"What did this Travennes look like when yu saw him last?" Coaxed Mr. Connors.

"Th' same as he does now, as yu can see by lookin' out of th' window. That's him down th' street," enlightened the host, thawing to the pleasant Mr. Connors.

Mr. Cassidy adopted the suggestion and frowned. Mr. Travennes and two companions were walking toward the corral and Mr. Cassidy once again slid out of the window, his friend going by the door.

Chapter XIII
Travennes' Discomfiture

When Mr. Travennes looked over the corral fence he was much chagrined to see a man and a Colt both paying strict attention to his nose.

"Mornin', Duke," said the man with the gun. "Lose anything?"

Mr. Travennes looked back at his friends and saw Mr. Connors sitting on a rock holding two guns. Mr. Travennes' right and left wings were the targets and they pitted their frowns against Mr. Connors' smile.

"Not that I knows of," replied Mr. Travennes, shifting his feet uneasily.

"Find anything?" Came from Mr. Cassidy as he sidled out of the gate.

"Nope," replied the captain of the Terrors, eying the Colt. "Are yu in the habit of payin' early mornin' calls to this here corral?" persisted Mr. Cassidy, playing with the gun.

"Ya-as. That's my business —I'm th' captain of the vigilantes."

"That's too bad," sympathized Mr. Cassidy, moving forward a step.

Mr. Travennes looked put out and backed off. "What yu mean, stickin' me up this-away?" He asked indignantly.

"Yu needn't go an' get mad," responded Mr. Cassidy. "Just business. Yore cayuse an' another shore climbed this corral fence last night an' ate up our bronchs, an' I just nachurly want to know about it."

Mr. Travennes looked his surprise and incredulity and craned his neck to see for himself. When he saw his horse peacefully scratching itself he swore and looked angrily up the street. Mr. Connors, behind the shack, was hidden to the view of those on the street, and when two men ran up at a signal from Mr. Travennes, intending to insert themselves in the misunderstanding, they were promptly lined up with the first two by the man on the rock.

"Sit down," invited Mr. Connors, pushing a chunk of air out of the way with his guns. The last two felt a desire to talk and to argue the case on its merits, but refrained as the black holes in Mr. Connors' guns hinted at eruption. "Every time yu opens yore mouths yu gets closer to th' Great Divide," enlightened that person, and they were childlike in their belief.

Mr. Travennes acted as though he would like to scratch his thigh where his Colt's chafed him, but postponed the event and listened to Mr. Cassidy, who was asking questions.

"Where's our cayuses, General?"

Mr. Travennes replied that he didn't know. He was worried, for he feared that his captor didn't have a secure hold on the hammer of the ubiquitous Colt's.

"Where's my cayuse?" Persisted Mr. Cassidy.

"I don't know, but I wants to ask yu how yu got mine," replied Mr. Travennes.

"Yu tell me how mine got out an' I'll tell yu how yourn got in," countered Mr. Cassidy.

Mr. Connors added another to his collection before the captain replied.

"Out in this country people get in trouble when they're found with other folks' cayuses," Mr. Travennes suggested.

Mr. Cassidy looked interested and replied: "Yu shore ought to borrow some experience, an' there's lots floating around. More than one man has smoked in a powder mill, an' th' number of them planted who looked in th' muzzle of a empty gun is scandalous. If my remarks don't perculate right smart I'll explain."

Mr. Travennes looked down the street again, saw number five added to the line-up, and coughed up chunks of broken profanity, grieving his host by his lack of courtesy.

"Time," announced Mr. Cassidy, interrupting the round. "I wants them cayuses an' I wants 'em right now. Yu an' me will amble off an' get 'em. I won't bore yu with tellin' yu what'll happen if yu gets skittish. Slope along an' don't be scared; I'm with yu," assured Mr. Cassidy as he looked over at Mr. Connors, whose ascetic soul pined for the flapjacks of which his olfactories caught intermittent whiffs.

"Well, Red, I reckons yu has got plenty of room out here for all yu may corral; anyhow there ain't a whole lot more. My friend Slim an' I are shore going to have a devil of a time if we can t find them cussed bronchs. Whew, them flapjacks smell like a plain trail to payday. Just think of th' nice maple juice we used to get up to Cheyenne on them frosty mornings."

"Get out of here an' lemme alone! 'What do yu allus want to go an' make a feller unhappy for? Can't yu keep still about grub when yu knows I ain't had my morning's feed yet?" Asked Mr. Connors, much aggrieved.

"Well, I'll be back directly an' I'll have them cayuses or a scalp. Yu tend to business an' watch th' herd. That shorthorn yearling at th' end of th' line" —pointing to a young man who looked capable of taking risks —"he looks like he might take a chance an' gamble with yu," remarked Mr. Cassidy, placing Mr. Travennes in front of him and pushing back his own sombrero. "Don't put too much maple juice on them flapjacks, Red," he warned as he poked his captive in the back of the neck as a hint to get along. Fortunately Mr. Connors' closing remarks are lost to history.

Observing that Mr. Travennes headed south on the quest, Mr. Cassidy reasoned that the missing bronchos ought to be somewhere in the north, and he postponed the southern trip until such time when they would have more leisure at their disposal. Mr. Travennes showed a strong inclination to shy at this arrangement, but quieted down under persuasion, and they started off toward where Mr. Cassidy firmly believed the North Pole and the cayuses to be.

"Yu has got quite a metropolis here," pleasantly remarked Mr. Cassidy as under his direction they made for a distant corral. "I can see four different types of architecture, two of 'em on one residence," he continued as they passed a wood and adobe hut. "No doubt the railroad will put a branch down here some day an' then yu can hire their old cars for yore public buildings. Then when yu gets a post-office yu will shore make Chicago hustle some to keep her end up. Let's assay that hollow for horse-hide; it looks promisin'."

The hollow was investigated but showed nothing other than cactus and baked alkali. The corral came next, and there too was emptiness. For an hour the search was unavailing, but at the end of that time Mr. Cassidy began to notice signs of nervousness on the part of his guest, which grew less as they proceeded. Then Mr. Cassidy retraced their steps to the place where the nervousness first developed and tried another way and once more returned to the starting point.

"Yu seems to hanker for this fool exercise," quoth Mr. Trayennes with much sarcasm. "If yu reckons I'm fond of this locoed ramblin' yu shore needs enlightenment."

"Sometimes I do get these fits," confessed Mr. Cassidy, "an' when I do I'm dead sore on objections. Let's peek in that there hut," he suggested.

"Huh; yore ideas of cayuses are mighty peculiar. Why don't you look for 'em up on those cactuses or behind that mesquite? I wouldn't be a heap surprised if they was roostin' on th' roof. They are mighty knowing animals, cayuses. I once saw one that could figger like a schoolmarm," remarked Mr. Travennes, beginning sarcastically and toning it down as he proceeded, out of respect for his companion's gun.

"Well, they might be in th' shack," replied Mr. Cassidy. "Cayuses know so much that it takes a month to unlearn them. I wouldn't like to bet they ain't in that hut, though."

Mr. Travennes snickered in a manner decidedly uncomplimentary and began to whistle, softly at first. The gentleman from the Bar-20 noticed that his companion was a musician; that when he came to a strong part he increased the tones until they bid to be heard at several hundred yards. When Mr. Travennes had reached a most passionate part in "Juanita" and was expanding his lungs to do it justice he was rudely stopped by the insistent pressure of his guard's Colt's on the most ticklish part of his ear.

"I shore wish yu wouldn't strain yoreself thataway," said Mr. Cassidy, thinking that Mr. Travennes might be endeavoring to call assistance. "I went an' promised my mother on her deathbed that I wouldn't let nobody whistle out loud like that, an' th' opery is hereby stopped. Besides, somebody might hear them mournful tones an' think that something is th' matter, which it ain't."

Mr. Travennes substituted heartfelt cursing, all of which was heavily accented.

As they approached the hut Mr. Cassidy again tickled his prisoner and insisted that he be very quiet, as his cayuse was very sensitive to noise and it might be there. Mr. Cassidy still thought Mr. Travennes might have friends in the hut and wouldn't for the world disturb them, as he would present a splendid target as he approached the building.

Chapter XIV
The Tale of a Cigarette

The open door revealed three men asleep on the earthen floor, two of whom were Mexicans. Mr. Cassidy then for the first time felt called upon to relieve his companion of the Colt's which so sorely itched that gentleman's thigh and then disarmed the sleeping guards.

"One man an' a half," murmured Mr. Cassidy, it being in his creed that it took four Mexicans to make one Texan.

In the far corner of the room were two bronchos, one of which tried in vain to kick Mr. Cassidy, not realizing that he was ten feet away. The noise awakened the sleepers, who sat up and then sprang to their feet, their hands instinctively streaking to their thighs for the weapons which peeked contentedly from the bosom of Mr. Cassidy's open shirt. One of the Mexicans made a lightning-like grab for the back of his neck for the knife which lay along his spine and was shot in the front of his neck for his trouble. The shot spoiled his aim, as the knife flashed past Mr. Cassidy's arm, wide by two feet, and thudded into the door frame, where it hummed angrily.

"The only man who could do that right was th' man who invented it, Mr. Bowie, of Texas," explained Mr. Cassidy to the other Mexican. Then he glanced at the broncho, that was squealing in rage and fear at the shot, which sounded like a cannon in the small room, and laughed.

"That's my cayuse, all right, an' he wasn't up no cactus nor roostin' on th' roof, neither. He's th' most affectionate beast I ever saw. It took me nigh onto six months afore I could ride him without fighting him to a standstill," said Mr. Cassidy to his guest. Then he turned to the horse and looked it over. "Come here! What d'yu mean, acting thataway? Yu ragged end of nothin' wobbling in space! Yu wall-eyed, ornery, locoed guide to Hades! Yu won't be so frisky when yu've made them seventy hot miles between here an' Alkaline in five hours," he promised, as he made his way toward the animal.

Mr. Travennes walked over to the opposite wall and took down a pouch of tobacco which hung from a peg. He did this in a manner suggesting ownership, and after he had deftly rolled a cigarette with one hand he put the pouch in his pocket and, lighting up, inhaled deeply and with much satisfaction. Mr. Cassidy turned around and glanced the group over, wondering if the tobacco had been left in the hut on a former call.

"Did yu find yore makings?" He asked, with a note of congratulations in his voice.

"Yep. Want one?" Asked Mr. Travennes.

Mr. Cassidy ignored the offer and turned to the guard whom he had found asleep.

"Is that his tobacco?" He asked, and the guard, anxious to make everything run smoothly, told the truth and answered:

"Shore. He left it here last night," whereupon Mr. Travennes swore and Mr. Cassidy smiled grimly.

"Then yu knows how yore cayuse got in an' how mine got out," said the latter. "I wish yu would explain," he added, fondling his Colts.

Mr. Travennes frowned and remained silent.

"I can tell yu, anyhow," continued Mr. Cassidy, still smiling, but his eyes and jaw belied the smile. "Yu took them cayuses out because yu wanted yourn to be found in their places. Yu remembered Santa Fe an' it rankled in yu. Not being man enough to notify me that yu'd shoot on sight an' being afraid my friends would get yu if yu plugged me on th' sly, yu tried to make out that me an' Red rustled yore cayuses. That meant a lynching with me an' Red in th' places of honor. Yu never saw Red afore, but yu didn't care if he went with me. Yu don't deserve fair play, but I'm going to give it to yu because I don't want anybody to say that any of th' Bar-20 ever murdered a man, not even a skunk like yu. My friends have treated me too square for that. Yu can take this gun an yu can do one of three things with it, which are: walk out in th' open a hundred paces an' then turn an walk toward me-after you face me yu can set it a-going whenever yu want to; the second is, put it under yore hat an' I'll put mine an' th' others back by the cayuses. Then we'll toss up an' th' lucky man gets it to use as he wants. Th' third is, shoot yourself."

Mr. Cassidy punctuated the close of his ultimatum by handing the weapon, muzzle first, and, because the other might be an adept at "twirling," he kept its recipient covered during the operation. Then, placing his second Colt's with the captured weapons, he threw them through the door, being very careful not to lose the drop on his now armed prisoner.

Mr. Travennes looked around and wiped the sweat from his forehead, and being an observant gentleman, took the proffered weapon and walked to the east, directly toward the sun, which at this time was halfway to the meridian. The glare of its straight rays and those reflected from the shining sand would, in a measure, bother Mr. Cassidy and interfere with the accuracy of his aim, and he was always thankful for small favors.

Mr. Travennes was the possessor of accurate knowledge regarding the lay of the land, and the thought came to him that there was a small but deep hole out toward the east and that it was about the required distance away. This had been dug by a man who had labored all day in the burning sun to make an oven so that he could cook mesquite root in the manner he had seen the Apaches cook it. Mr. Travennes blessed hobbies, specific and general, stumbled thoughtlessly and disappeared from sight as the surprised Mr. Cassidy started forward to offer his assistance.

Upon emphatic notification from the man in the hole that his help was not needed, Mr. Cassidy wheeled around and in great haste covered the distance separating him from the hut, whereupon Mr. Travennes swore in self-congratulation and regret. Mr. Cassidy's shots barked a cactus which leaned near Mr. Travennes' head and flecked several clouds of alkali near that person's nose, causing him to sneeze, duck, and grin.

"It's his own gun," grumbled Mr. Cassidy as a bullet passed through his sombrero, having in mind the fact that his opponent had a whole belt full of .44's. If it had been Mr. Cassidy's gun that had been handed over he would have enjoyed the joke on Mr. Travennes, who would have had five cartridges between himself and the promised eternity, as he would have been unable to use the .44's in Mr. Cassidy's .45, while the latter would have gladly consented to the change, having as he did an extra .45. Never before had Mr. Cassidy looked with reproach upon his .45 caliber Colt's, and he sighed as he used it to notify Mr. Travennes that arbitration was not to be considered, which that person indorsed, said indorsement passing so close to Mr. Cassidy's ear that he felt the breeze made by it.

"He's been practicin' since I plugged him up in Santa Fe," thought Mr. Cassidy, as he retired around the hut to formulate a plan of campaign.

Mr. Travennes sang "Hi-le, hi-lo," and other selections, principally others, and wondered how Mr. Cassidy could hoist him out. The slack of his belt informed him that he was in the middle of a fast, and suggested starvation as the derrick that his honorable and disgusted adversary might employ.

Mr. Cassidy, while figuring out his method of procedure, absent-mindedly jabbed a finger in his eye, and the ensuing tears floated an idea to him. He had always had great respect for ricochet shots since his friend Skinny Thompson had proved their worth on the hides of Sioux. If he could disturb the sand and convey several grains of it to Mr. Travennes' eyes the game would be much simplified. While planning for the proposed excavation, a la Colt's, he noticed several stones lying near at hand, and a new and better scheme presented itself for his consideration. If Mr. Travennes could be persuaded to get out of-well, it was worth trying.

Mr. Cassidy lined up his gloomy collection and tersely ordered them to turn their backs to him and to stay in that position, the suggestion being that if they looked around they wouldn't be able to dodge quickly enough. He then slipped bits of his lariat over their wrists and ankles, tying wrists to ankles and each man to his neighbor. That finished to his satisfaction, he dragged them in the hut to save them from the burning rays of the sun.

Having performed this act of kindness, he crept along the hot sand, taking advantage of every bit of cover afforded, and at last he reached a point within a hundred feet of the besieged. During the trip Mr. Travennes sang to his heart's content, some of the words being improvised for the occasion and were not calculated to increase Mr. Cassidy's respect for his own wisdom if he should hear them. Mr. Cassidy heard, however, and several fragments so forcibly intruded on his peace of mind that he determined to put on the last verse himself and to suit himself.

Suddenly Mr. Travennes poked his head up and glanced at the hut. He was down again so quickly that there was no chance for a shot at him and he believed that his enemy was still sojourning in the rear of the building, which caused him to fear that he was expected to live on nothing as long as he could and then give himself up. Just to show his defiance he stretched himself out on his back and sang with all his might, his sombrero over his face to keep the glare of the sun out of his eyes.

He was interrupted, however, forgot to finish a verse as he had intended, and jumped to one side as a stone bounced off his leg. Looking up, he saw another missile curve into his patch of sky and swiftly bear down on him. He avoided it by a hair's breadth and wondered what had happened. Then what Mr. Travennes thought was a balloon, being unsophisticated in matters pertaining to aerial navigation, swooped down upon him and smote him on the shoulder and also bounced off.

Mr. Travennes hastily laid music aside and took up elocution as he dodged another stone and wished that the mesquite-loving crank had put on a roof. In evading the projectile he let his sombrero appear on a level with the desert, and the hum of a bullet as it passed through his head-gear and into the opposite wall made him wish that there had been constructed a cellar, also.

"Hi-le, hi-lo" intruded upon his ear, as Mr. Cassidy got rid of the surplus of his heart's joy. Another stone the size of a man's foot shaved Mr. Travennes' ear and he hugged the side of the hole nearest his enemy.

"Hibernate, blank yu!" derisively shouted the human catapult as he released a chunk of sandstone the size of a quail. "Draw in yore laigs an' buck," was his God-speed to the missile.

"Hey, yu!" indignantly yowled Mr. Travennes from his defective storm cellar. "Don't yu know any better'n to heave things thataway?"

"Hi-le, hi-lo," sang Mr. Cassidy, as another stone soared aloft in the direction of the complainant. Then he stood erect and awaited results with a Colt's in his hand leveled at the rim of the hole. A hat waved and an excited voice bit off chunks of expostulation and asked for an armistice. Then two hands shot up and Mr. Travennes, sore and disgusted and desperate, popped his head up an blinked at Mr. Cassidy's gun.

"Yu was fillin' th' hole up," remarked Mr. Travennes in an accusing tone, hiding the real reason for his evacuation. "In a little while I'd a been th' top of a pile instead of th' bottom of a hole," he announced, crawling out and rubbing his head.

Mr. Cassidy grinned and ordered his prisoner to one side while be secured the weapon which lay in the hole. Having obtained it as quickly as possible be slid it in his open shirt and clambered out again.

"Yu remind me of a feller I used to know," remarked Mr. Travennes, as he led the way to the hut, trying not to limp. "Only he throwed dynamite. That was th' way he cleared off chaparral-blowed it off. He got so used to heaving away everything he lit that he spoiled three pipes in two days."

Mr. Cassidy laughed at the fiction and then became grave as he pictured Mr. Connors sitting on the rock and facing down a line of men, any one of whom was capable of his destruction if given the interval of a second.

When they arrived at the hut Mr. Cassidy observed that the prisoners had moved considerably. There was a cleanly swepttrail four yards long where they had dragged themselves, and they sat in the end nearer the guns. Mr. Cassidy smiled and fired close to the Mexican's ear, who lost in one frightened jump a little of what he had so laboriously gained.

"Yu'll wear out yore pants," said Mr. Cassidy, and then added grimly, "an' my patience."

Mr. Travennes smiled and thought of the man who so ably seconded Mr. Cassidy's efforts and who was probably shot by this time. The outfit of the Bar-20 was so well known throughout the land that he was aware the name of the other was Red Connors. An unreasoning streak of sarcasm swept over him and he could not resist the opportunity to get in a stab at his captor.

"Mebby yore pard has wore out somebody's patience, too," said Mr. Travennes, suggestively and with venom.

His captor wheeled toward him, his face white with passion, and Mr. Travennes shrank back and regretted the words.

"I ain't shootin' dogs this here trip," said Mr. Cassidy, trembling with scorn and anger, "so yu can pull yourself together. I'll give yu another chance, but yu wants to hope almighty hard that Red is O. K. If he ain't, I'll blow yu so many ways at once that if yu sprouts yu'll make a good acre of weeds. If he is all right yu'd better vamoose this range, for there won't be no hole for yu to crawl into next time. What friends yu have left will have to tote yu off an' plant yu," he finished with emphasis. He drove the horses outside, and, after severing the bonds on his prisoners, lined them up.

"Yu," he began, indicating all but Mr. Travennes, "yu amble right smart toward Canada," pointing to the north. "Keep a-going till yu gets far enough away so a Colt won't find yu." Here he grinned with delight as he saw his Sharp's rifle in its sheath on his saddle and, drawing it forth, he put away his Colts and glanced at the trio, who were already industriously plodding northward. "Hey!" he shouted, and when they sullenly turned to see what new idea he had found he gleefully waved his rifle at them and warned them further: "This is a Sharp's an' it's good for half a mile, so don't stop none too soon."

Having sent them directly away from their friends so they could not have him "potted" on the way back, he mounted his broncho and indicated to Mr. Travennes that he, too, was to ride, watching that that person did not make use of the Winchester which Mr. Connors was foolish enough to carry around on his saddle. Winchesters were Mr. Cassidy's pet aversion and Mr. Connors' most prized possession, this difference of opinion having upon many occasions caused hasty words between them. Mr. Connors, being better with his Winchester than Mr. Cassidy was with his Sharp's, had frequently proved that his choice was the wiser, but Mr. Cassidy was loyal to the Sharp's and refused to be convinced. Now, however, the Winchester became pregnant with possibilities and, therefore, Mr. Travennes rode a few yards to the left and in advance, where the rifle was in plain sight, hanging as it did on the right of Mr. Connors' saddle, which Mr. Travennes graced so well.

The journey back to town was made in good time and when they came to the buildings Mr. Cassidy dismounted and bade his companion do likewise, there being too many corners that a fleeing rider could take advantage of. Mr. Travennes felt of his bumps and did so, wishing hard things about Mr. Cassidy.

Chapter XV
The Penalty

While Mr. Travennes had been entertained in the manner narrated, Mr. Connors had passed the time by relating stale jokes to the uproarious laughter of his extremely bored audience, who had heard the aged efforts many times since they had first seen the light of day, and most of whom earnestly longed for a drink. The landlord, hearing the hilarity, had taken advantage of the opportunity offered to see a free show. Not being able to see what the occasion was for the mirth, he had pulled on his boots and made his way to the show with a flapjack in the skillets which, in his haste, he had forgotten to put down. He felt sure that he would be entertained, and he was not disappointed. He rounded the corner and was enthusiastically welcomed by the hungry Mr. Connors, whose ubiquitous guns coaxed from the skillet its dyspeptic wad.

"Th' saints be praised!" ejaculated Mr. Connors as a matter of form, not having a very clear idea of just what saints were, but he knew what flapjacks were and greedily overcame the heroic resistance of the one provided by chance and his own guns. As he rolled his eyes in ecstatic content the very man Mr. Cassidy had warned him against suddenly arose and in great haste disappeared around the corner of the corral, from which point of vantage he vented his displeasure at the treatment he had received by wasting six shots at the mortified Mr. Connors.

"Steady!" sang out that gentleman as the line-up wavered. "He's a precedent to hell for yu fellers! Don't yu get ambitious, none whatever." Then he wondered how long it would take the fugitive to secure a rifle and return to release the others by drilling him at long range.

His thoughts were interrupted by the vision of a red head that climbed into view over a rise a short distance off and he grinned his delight as Mr. Cassidy loomed up, jaunty and triumphant. Mr. Cassidy was executing calisthenics with a Colt in the rear of Mr. Travennes' neck and was leading the horses.

Mr. Connors waved the skillet and his friend grinned his congratulations at what the token signified.

"I see yu got some more," said Mr. Cassidy, as he went down the line-up from the rear and collected nineteen weapons of various makes and conditions, this number being explained by the fact that all but one of the prisoners wore two. Then he added the five that had kicked against his ribs ever since he had left the hut, and carefully threaded the end of his lariat through the trigger guards.

"Looks like we stuck up a government supply mule, Red," he remarked, as he fastened the whole collection to his saddle. "Fourteen colts, six Merwin-Hulbert's, three Prescott, an' one puzzle," he added, examining the puzzle. "Made in Germany, it says, and it shore looks like it. It's got little pins stickin' out of th' cylinder, like you had to swat it with a hammer or a rock, or somethin' to make it go off. Must be damn dangerous, to most anybody around. Looks more like a cactus than a six-shooter-gosh, it's a ten-shooter! I allus said them Dutchmen was bloody-minded cusses. Think of bein' able to shoot yoreself ten times before th' blame thing stops!" Then looking at the line-up for the owner of the weapon, he laughed at the woeful countenances displayed. "Did they sidle in by companies or squads?" He asked.

"By twos, mostly. Then they parade-rested an' got discharged from duty. I had eleven, but one got homesick, or disgusted, or something, an' deserted. It was that cussed flapjack," confessed and explained Mr. Connors.

"What!" said Mr. Cassidy in a loud voice. "Got away! Well, we'll have to make our get-away plumb sudden or we'll never go."

At this instant the escaped man again began his bombardment from the corner of the corral and Mr. Cassidy paused, indignant at the fusillade which tore up the dust at his feet. He looked reproachfully at Mr. Connors and then circled out on the plain until he caught a glimpse of a fleeing cow-puncher, whose back rapidly grew smaller in the fast-increasing distance.

"That's yore friend, Red," said Mr. Cassidy as he returned from his reconnaissance. "He's that short-horn yearling. Mebby he'll come back again," he added hopefully. "Anyhow, we've got to move. He'll collect reinforcements an' mebby they all won't shoot like him. Get up on yore Clarinda an' hold th' fort for me," he ordered, pushing the farther horse over to his friend. Mr. Connors proved that an agile man can mount a restless horse and not lose the drop, and backed off three hundred yards, deftly substituting his Winchester for the Colts. Then Mr. Cassidy likewise mounted with his attention riveted elsewhere and backed off to the side of his companion.

The bombardment commenced again from the corral, but this time Mr. Connors' rifle slid around in his lap and exploded twice. The bellicose gentleman of the corral yelled in pain and surprise and vanished.

"Purty good for a Winchester," said Mr. Cassidy in doubtful congratulation.

"That's why I got him," snapped Mr. Connors in brief reply, and then he laughed. "Is them th' vigilantes what never let a man get away?" He scornfully asked, backing down the street and patting his Winchester.

"Well, Red, they wasn't all there. They was only twelve all told," excused Mr. Cassidy. "An' then we was two," he explained, as he wished the collection of six-shooters was on Mr. Connors' horse so they wouldn't bark his shin.

"An we still are," corrected Mr. Connors, as they wheeled and galloped for Alkaline.

As the sun sank low on the horizon Mr. Peters finished ordering provisions at the general store, the only one Alkaline boasted, and sauntered to the saloon where he had left his men. He found diem a few dollars richer, as they had borrowed ten dollars from the bartender on their reputations as poker players and had used the money to stake Mr. McAllister in a game against the local poker champion.

"Has Hopalong an' Red showed up yet?" Asked Mr. Peters, frowning at the delay already caused.

"Nope," replied Johnny Nelson, as he paused from tormenting Billy Williams.

At that minute the doorway was darkened and Mr. Cassidy and Mr. Connors entered and called for refreshments. Mr. Cassidy dropped a huge bundle of six-shooters on the floor, making caustic remarks regarding their utility.

"What's th' matter?" Inquired Mr. Peters of Mr. Cassidy. "Yu looks mad an' anxious. An' where in blazes did yu corral them guns?"

Mr. Cassidy drank deep and then reported with much heat what had occurred at Cactus Springs and added that he wanted to go back and wipe out the town, said desire being luridly endorsed by Mr. Connors.

"Why, shore," said Mr. Peters, "we'll all go. Such doings must be stopped instanter." Then he turned to the assembled outfits and asked for a vote, which was unanimous for war.

Shortly afterward eighteen angry cowpunchers rode to the east, two red-haired gentlemen well in front and urging speed. It was 8 P.M. when they left Alkaline, and the cool of the night was so delightful that the feeling of ease which came upon them made them lax and they lost three hours in straying from the dim trail. At eight o'clock the next morning they came in sight of their destination and separated into two squads, Mr. Cassidy leading the northern division and Mr. Connors the one which circled to the south. The intention was to attack from two directions, thus taking the town from front and rear.

Cactus Springs lay gasping in the excessive heat and the vigilantes who had toed Mr. Connors' line the day before were lounging in the shade of the "Palace" saloon, telling what they would do if they ever faced the same man again. Half a dozen sympathizers offered gratuitous condolence and advice and all were positive that they knew where Mr. Cassidy and Mr. Connors would go when they died.

The rolling thunder of madly pounding hoofs disturbed their post-mortem and they arose in a body to flee from half their number, who, guns in hands, charged down upon them through clouds of sickly white smoke. Travennes' Terrors were minus many weapons and they could not be expected to give a glorious account of themselves. Windows rattled and fell in and doors and walls gave off peculiar sounds as they grew full of holes. Above the riot rattled the incessant crack of Colt's and Winchester, emphasized at close intervals by the assertive roar of buffalo guns. Off to the south came another rumble of hoofs and Mr. Connors, leading the second squad, —arrived to participate in the payment of the debt.

Smoke spurted from windows and other points of vantage and hung wavering in the heated air. The shattering of woodwork told of heavy slugs finding their rest, and the whines that grew and diminished in the air sang the course of .45s.

While the fight raged hottest Mr. Nelson sprang from his horse and ran to the "Palace," where he collected and piled a heap of tinder like wood, and soon the building burst out in flames, which, spreading, swept the town from end to end.

Mr. Cassidy fired slowly and seemed to be waiting for something. Mr. Connors laid aside his hot Winchester and devoted his attention to his Colts. A spurt of flame and smoke leaped from the window of a 'dobe hut and Mr. Connors sat down, firing as he went. A howl from the window informed him that he had made a hit, and Mr. Cassidy ran out and dragged him to the shelter of a near-by bowlder and asked how much he was hurt.

"Not much-in the calf," grunted Mr. Connors. "He was a bad shot-must have been the cuss that got away yesterday," speculated the injured man as he slowly arose to his feet. Mr. Cassidy dissented from force of habit and returned to his station. Mr. Travennes, who was sleeping late that morning, coughed and fought for air in his sleep, awakened in smoke, rubbed his eyes to make sure and, scorning trousers and shirt, ran clad in his red woolen undergarments to the corral, where he mounted his scared horse and rode for the desert and safety.

Mr. Cassidy, swearing at the marksmanship of a man who fired at his head and perforated his sombrero, saw a crimson rider sweep down upon him, said rider being heralded by a blazing .44.

"Gosh!" ejaculated Mr. Cassidy, scarcely believing his eyes. "Oh, it's my friend Slim going to hades," he remarked to himself in audible and relieved explanation. Mr. Cassidy's Colts cracked a protest and then he joined Mr. Peters and the others and with them fought his way out of the flame-swept town of Cactus Springs.

An hour later Mr. Connors glanced behind him at the smoke silhouetted on the horizon and pushed his way to where Mr. Cassidy rode in silence. Mr. Connors grinned at his friend of the red hair, who responded in the same manner.

"Did yu see Slim?" Casually inquired Mr. Connors, looking off to the south.

Mr. Cassidy sat upright in his saddle and felt of his Colts. "Yes," he replied, "I saw him."

Mr. Connors thereupon galloped on in silence.

Chapter XVI

Rustlers on the Range

The affair at Cactus Springs had more effect on the life at the Bar-20 than was realized by the foreman. News travels rapidly, and certain men, whose attributes were not of the sweetest, heard of it and swore vengeance, for Slim Travennes had many friends, and the result of his passing began to show itself. Outlaws have as their strongest defense the fear which they inspire, and little time was lost in making reprisals, and these caused Buck Peters to ride into Buckskin one bright October morning and then out the other side of the town. Coming to himself with a start he looked around shamefacedly and retraced his course. He was very much troubled, for, as foreman of the Bar-20, he had many responsibilities, and when things ceased to go aright he was expected not only to find the cause of the evil, but also the remedy. That was what he was paid seventy dollars a month for and that was what he had been endeavoring to do. As yet, however, he had only accomplished what the meanest cook's assistant had done. He knew the cause of his present woes to be rustlers (cattle thieves), and that was all.

Riding down the wide, quiet street, he stopped and dismounted before the ever-open door of a ramshackle, one-story frame building. Tossing the reins over the flattened ears of his vicious pinto he strode into the building and leaned easily against the bar, where he drummed with his fingers and sank into a reverie.

A shining bald pate, bowed over an open box, turned around and revealed a florid face, set with two small, twinkling blue eyes, as the proprietor, wiping his hands on his trousers, made his way to Buck's end of the bar.

"Mornin', Buck. How's things?"

The foreman, lost in his reverie, continued to stare out the door.

"Mornin'," repeated the man behind the bar. "How's things?"

"Oh!" ejaculated the foreman, smiling, "purty cussed."

"Anything flew?"

"Th' C-80 lost another herd last night."

His companion swore and placed a bottle at the foreman's elbow, but the latter shook his head. "Not this mornin' —I'll try one of them vile cigars, however."

"Them cigars are th' very best that —" began the proprietor, executing the order.

"Oh, heck!" exclaimed Buck with weary disgust. "Yu don't have to palaver none: I shore knows all that by heart."

"Them cigars —" repeated the proprietor.

"Yas, yas; them cigars —I know all about them cigars. Yu gets them for twenty dollars a thousand an' hypnotizes us into payin' yu a hundred," replied the foreman, biting off the end 'of his weed. Then he stared moodily and frowned. "I wonder why it is?" He asked. "We punchers like good stuff an' we pays good prices with good money. What do we get? Why, cabbage leaves an' leather for our smokin' an' alcohol an' extract for our drink. Now, up in Kansas City we goes to a sumptious layout, pays less an' gets bang-up stuff. If yu smelled one of them K. C. cigars yu'd shore have to ask what it was, an' as for the liquor, why, yu'd think St. Peter asked yu to have one with him. It's shore wrong somewhere."

"They have more trade in K. C.," suggested the proprietor.

"An' help, an' taxes, an' a license, an' rent, an' brass, cut glass, mahogany an' French mirrors," countered the foreman.

"They have more trade," reiterated the man with the cigars.

"Forty men spend thirty dollars apiece with yu every month." The proprietor busied himself under the bar. "Yu'll feel better to-morrow. Anyway, what do yu care, yu won't lose yore job," he said, emerging.

Buck looked at him and frowned, holding back the words which formed in anger. What was the use, he thought, when every man judged the world in his own way.

"Have yu seen any of th' boys?" He asked, smiling again.

"Nary a boy. Who do yu reckon's doin' all this rustlin'?"

"I'm reckonin', not shoutin'," responded the foreman.

The proprietor looked out the window and grinned: "Here comes one of yourn now."

The newcomer stopped his horse in a cloud of dust, playfully kicked the animal in the ribs and entered, dusting the alkali from him with a huge sombrero. Then he straightened up and sniffed: "What's burnin'?" he asked, simulating alarm. Then he noticed the cigar between the teeth of his foreman and grinned: "Gee, but yore a brave man, Buck."

"Hullo, Hopalong," said the foreman. "Want a smoke?" Waving his hand toward the box on the bar.

Mr. Hopalong Cassidy side-stepped and began to roll a cigarette: "Shore, but I'll burn my own —I know what it is."

"What was yu doin' to my cayuse afore yu come in?" Asked Buck.

"Nothin'," replied the newcomer. "That was mine what I kicked in th' corrugations."

"How is it yore ridin' the calico?" Asked the foreman. "I thought yu was dead stuck on that piebald."

"That piebald's a goat; he's beein livin' off my pants lately," responded Hopalong. "Every time I looks th' other way he ambles over and takes a bite at me. Yu just wait 'til this rustler business is roped, an' branded, an' yu'll see me eddicate that blessed scrapheap into eatin' grass again." He swiped Billy's shirt th' other day-took it right off th' corral wall, where Billy's left it to dry. Then, seeing Buck raise his eyebrows, he explained: "Shore, he washed it again. That makes three times since last fall."

The proprietor laughed and pushed out the ever-ready bottle, but Hopalong shoved it aside and told the reason: "Ever since I was up to K. C. I've been spoiled. I'm drinkin' water an' slush."

"For Pete's sake, has any more of yu fellers been up to K. C.?" queried the proprietor in alarm.

"Shore: Red an' Billy was up there, too." responded Hopalong. "Red's got a few remarks to shout to yu about yore pain-killer. Yu better send for some decent stuff afore he comes to town," he warned.

Buck swung away from the bar and looked at his dead cigar. Then he turned to Hopalong. "What did you find?" He asked.

"Same old story: nice wide trail up to th' Staked Plain-then nothin'.'"

"It shore beats me," soliloquized the foreman. "It shore beats me."

"Think it was Tamale Jose's old gang?" Asked Hopalong.

"If it was they took th' wrong trail home-that ain't th' way to Mexico."

Hopalong tossed aside his half-smoked cigarette. "Well, come on home; what's th' use stewin' over it? It'll come out all O.K. in th' wash." Then he laughed: "There won't be no piebald waitin' for it."

Evading Buck's playful blow he led the way to the door, and soon they were a cloud of dust on the plain. The proprietor, despairing of customers under the circumstances, absent-mindedly wiped oil on the bar, and sought his chair for a nap, grumbling about the way his trade had fallen off, for there were few customers, and those who did call were heavy with loss of sleep, and with anxiety, and only paused long enough to toss off their drink. On the ranges there were occurrences which tried men's souls.

For several weeks cattle had been disappearing from the ranges and the losses had long since passed the magnitude of those suffered when Tamale Jose and his men had crossed the Rio Grande and repeatedly levied heavy toll on the sleek herds of the Pecos Valley. Tamale Jose had raided once too often, and prosperity and plenty had followed on the ranches and the losses had been forgotten until the fall round-ups clearly showed that rustlers were again at work.

Despite the ingenuity of the ranch owners and the unceasing vigilance and night rides of the cow-punchers, the losses steadily increased until there was promised a shortage which would permit no drive to the western terminals of the railroad that year. For two weeks the banks of the Rio Grande had been patrolled and sharp-eyed men searched daily for trails leading southward, for it was not strange to think that the old raiders were again at work, notwithstanding the fact that they had paid dearly for their former depredations.

The patrols failed to discover anything out of the ordinary and the searchers found no trails. Then it was that the owners and foremen of the four central ranches met in Cowan's saloon and sat closeted together for all of one hot afternoon.

The conference resulted in riders being dispatched from all the ranches represented, and one of the couriers, Mr. Red Connors, rode north, his destination being far-away Montana. All the ranches within a radius of a hundred miles received letters and blanks and one week later the Pecos Valley Cattle-Thief Elimination Association was organized and working, with Buck as Chief Ranger.

One of the outcomes of Buck's appointment was a sudden and marked immigration into the affected territory. Mr. Connors returned from Montana with Mr. Frenchy McAllister, the foreman of the Tin-Cup, who was accompanied by six of his best and most trusted men. Mr. McAllister and party were followed by Mr. You-bet Somes, foreman of the Two-X-Two of Arizona, and five of his punchers, and later on the same day Mr. Pie Willis, accompanied by Mr. Billy Jordan and his two brothers, arrived from the Panhandle. The O-Bar-O, situated close to the town of Muddy Wells, increased its payroll by the addition of nine men, each of whom bore the written recommendation of the foreman of the Bar-20. The C-80, Double Arrow and the Three Triangle also received heavy reinforcements, and even Carter, owner of the Barred Horseshoe, far removed from the zone of the depredations, increased his outfits by half their regular strength.

Buck believed that if a thing was worth doing at all that it was worth doing very well, and his acquaintances were numerous and loyal. The collection of individuals that responded to the call were noteworthy examples of "gun-play" and their aggregate value was at par with twice their numbers in cavalry.

Each ranch had one large ranch-house and numerous line-houses scattered along the boundaries. These latter, while intended as camps for the outriders, had been erected in the days, none too remote, when Apaches, Arrapahoes, and even Cheyennes raided southward, and they had been constructed with the idea of defense paramount. Upon more than one occasion a solitary line-rider had retreated within their adobe walls and had successfully resisted all the cunning and ferocity of a score of paint-bedaubed warriors and, when his outfit had rescued him, emerged none the worse for his ordeal.

On the Bar-20, Buck placed these houses in condition to withstand seige. Twin barrels of water stood in opposite corners, provisions were stored on the hanging shelves and the bunks once again reveled in untidiness. Spare rifles, in pattern ranging from long-range Sharp's and buffalo guns to repeating rifles, leaned against the walls, and unbroken boxes of cartridges were piled above the bunks. Instead of the lonesome outrider, he placed four men to each house, two of whom were to remain at home and hold the house while their companions rode side by side on their multi-mile beat.

There were six of these houses and, instead of returning each night to the same line-house, the outriders kept on and made the circuit, thus keeping every one well informed and breaking the monotony. These measures were expected to cause the rustling operations to cease at once, but the effect was to shift the losses to the Double Arrow, the line-houses of which boasted only one puncher each. Unreasonable economy usually defeats its object.

The Double Arrow was restricted on the north by the Staked Plain, which in itself was considered a superb defense. The White Sand Hills formed its eastern boundary and were thought to be second only to the northern protection. The only reason that could be given for the hitherto comparative immunity from the attacks of the rustlers was that its cattle clung to the southern confines where there were numerous springs, thus making imperative the crossing of its territory to gain the herds.

It was in line-house No. 3, most remote of all, that Johnny Redmond fought his last fight and was found face down in the half ruined house with a hole in the back of his head, which proved that one man was incapable of watching all the loop holes in four walls at once. There must have been some casualties on the other side, for Johnny was reputed to be very painstaking in his "gunplay," and the empty shells which lay scattered on the floor did not stand for as many ciphers, of that his foreman was positive.

He was buried the day he was found, and the news of his death ran quickly from ranch to ranch and made more than one careless puncher arise and pace the floor in anger. More men came to the Double Arrow and its sentries were doubled. The depredations continued, however, and one night a week later Frank Swift reeled into the ranch-house and fell exhausted across the supper table. Rolling hoof-beats echoed flatly and died away on the plain, but the men who pursued them returned empty handed. The wounds of the unfortunate were roughly dressed and in his delirium he recounted the fight. His companion was found literally shot to pieces twenty paces from the door. One wall was found blown in, and this episode, when coupled with the use of dynamite, was more than could be tolerated.

When Buck had been informed of this he called to him Hopalong Cassidy, Red Connors and Frenchy McAllister, and the next day the three men rode north and the contingents of the ranches represented in the Association were divided into two squads, one of which was to remain at home and guard the ranches; the other, to sleep fully dressed and armed and never to stray far from their ranch-houses and horses. These latter would be called upon to ride swiftly and far when the word came.

Chapter XVII
Mr. Trendley Assumes Added Importance

That the rustlers were working under a well organized system was evident. That they were directed by a master of the game was ceaselessly beaten into the consciousness of the Association by the diversity, dash and success of their raids. No one, save the three men whom they had destroyed, had ever seen them. But, like Tamale Jose, they had raided once too often.

Mr. Trendley, more familiarly known to men as "Slippery," was the possessor of a biased conscience, if any at all. Tall, gaunt and weather-beaten and with coal-black eyes set deep beneath hairless eyebrows, he was sinister and forbidding. Into his forty-five years of existence he had crowded a century of experience, and unsavory rumors about him existed in all parts of the great West. From Canada to Mexico and from Sacramento to Westport his name stood for brigandage. His operations had been conducted with such consummate cleverness that in all the accusations there was lacking proof.

Only once had he erred, and then in the spirit of pure deviltry and in the days of youthful folly, and his mistake was a written note. He was even thought by some to have been concerned in the Mountain Meadow Massacre; others thought him to have been the leader of the band of outlaws that had plundered along the Santa Fe Trail in the late '60's. In Montana and Wyoming he was held responsible for the outrages of the band that had descended from the Hole-in-the-Wall territory and for over a hundred miles carried murder and theft that shamed as being weak the most assiduous efforts of zealous Cheyennes. It was in this last raid that he had made the mistake and it was in this raid that Frenchy McAllister had lost his wife.

When Frenchy had first been approached by Buck as to his going in search of the rustlers he had asked to go alone. This had been denied by the foreman of the Bar-20 because the men whom he had selected to accompany the scout were of such caliber that their presence could not possibly form a hindrance. Besides being his most trusted friends they were regarded by him as being the two best exponents of "gun-play" that the West afforded. Each was a specialist: Hopalong, expert beyond belief with his Colt's six-shooters, was only approached by Red, whose Winchester was renowned for its accuracy. The three made a perfect combination, as the rashness of the two younger men would be under the controlling influence of a man who could retain his coolness of mind under all circumstances.

When Buck and Frenchy looked into each other's eyes there sprang into the mind of each the same name-Slippery Trendley. Both had spent the greater part of a year in fruitless search for that person, the foreman of the Tin-Cup in vengeance for the murder of his wife, the blasting of his prospects and the loss of his herds; Buck, out of sympathy for his friend and also because they had been partners in the Double Y. Now that the years had passed and the long-sought-for opportunity was believed to be at hand, there was promised either a cessation of the outrages or that Buck would never again see his friends.

When the three mounted and came to him for final instructions Buck forced himself to be almost repellent in order to be capable of coherent speech. Hopalong glanced sharply at him and then understood, Red was all attention and eagerness and remarked nothing but the words.

"Have yu ever heard of Slippery Trendley?" Harshly inquired the foreman.

They nodded, and on the faces of the younger men a glint of hatred showed itself, but Frenchy wore his poker countenance.

Buck continued: "Th' reason I asked yu was because I don't want yu to think yore goin' on no picnic. I ain't shore it's him, but I've had some hopeful information. Besides, he is th' only man I knows of who's capable of th' plays that have been made. It's hardly necessary for me to tell yu to sleep with one eye open and never to get away from yore guns. Now I'm goin' to tell yu th' hardest part: yu are goin' to search th' Staked Plain from one end to th' other, an' that's what no white man's ever done to my knowledge.

"Now, listen to this an' don't forget it. Twenty miles north from Last Stand Rock is a spring; ten miles south of that bend in Hell Arroyo is another. If yu gets lost within two days from th' time yu enters th' Plain, put yore left hand on a cactus sometime between sun-up an' noon, move around until yu are over its shadow an' then ride straight ahead-that's south. If you goes loco beyond Last Stand Rock, follow th' shadows made before noon-that's th' quickest way to th' Pecos. Yu all knows what to do in a sand-storm, so I won't bore you with that. Repeat all I've told yu," he ordered and they complied.

"I'm tellin' yu this," continued the foreman, indicating the two auxiliaries, "because yu might get separated from Frenchy. Now I suggests that yu look around near the' Devils Rocks: I've heard that there are several water holes among them, an' besides, they might be turned into fair corrals. Mind yu, I know what I've said sounds damned idiotic for anybody that has had as much experience with th' Staked Plain as I have, but I've had every other place searched for miles around. Th' men of all th' ranches have been scoutin' an' th' Plain is th' only place left. Them rustlers has got to be found if we have to dig to hell for them. They've taken th' pot so many times that they reckons they owns it, an' we've got to at least make a bluff at drawin' cards. Mebby they're at th' bottom of th' Pecos," here he smiled faintly, "but wherever they are, we've got to find them. I want to holler 'Keno.'

"If you finds where they hangs out come away instanter," here his face hardened and his eyes narrowed, "for it'll take more than yu three to deal with them th' way I'm a-hankerin' for. Come right back to th' Double Arrow, send me word by one of their punchers an' get all the rest you can afore I gets there. It'll take me a day to get th' men together an' to reach yu. I'm goin' to use smoke signals to call th' other ranches, so there won't be no time lost. Carry all th' water yu can pack when yu leaves th' Double Arrow an' don't depend none on cactus juice. Yu better take a pack horse to carry it, an' yore grub-yu can shoot it if yu have to hit th' trail real hard."

The three riders felt of their accouterments, said "So long," and cantered off for the pack horse and extra ammunition. Then they rode toward the Double Arrow, stopping at Cowan's long enough to spend some money, and reached the Double Arrow at nightfall. Early the next morning they passed the last line-house and, with the profane well-wishes of its occupants ringing in their ears, passed onto one of Nature's worst blunders-the Staked Plain.

Chapter XVIII

The Search Begins

As the sun arose it revealed three punchers riding away from civilization. On all sides, stretching to the evil-appearing horizon, lay vast blotches of dirty-white and faded yellow alkali and sand. Occasionally a dwarfed mesquite raised its prickly leaves and rustled mournfully. With the exception of the riders and an occasional Gila monster, no life was discernible. Cacti of all shapes and sizes reared aloft their forbidding spines or spread out along the sand. All was dead, ghastly; all was oppressive, startlingly repellent in its sinister promise; all was the vastness of desolation.

Hopalong knew this portion of the desert for ten miles inward-he had rescued straying cattle along its southern rim-but once beyond that limit they would have to trust to chance and their own abilities. There were water holes on this skillet, but nine out of ten were death traps, reeking with mineral poisons, colored and alkaline. The two mentioned by Buck could not be depended on, for they came and went, and more than one luckless wanderer had depended on them to allay his thirst, and had died for his trust.

So the scouts rode on in silence, noting the half-buried skeletons of cattle which were strewn plentifully on all sides. Nearly three per cent, of the cattle belonging to the Double Arrow yearly found death on this tableland, and the herds of that ranch numbered many thousand heads. It was this which made the Double Arrow the poorest of the ranches, and it was this which allowed insufficient sentries in its line-houses. The skeletons were not all of cattle, for at rare intervals lay the sand-worn frames of men.

On the morning of the second day the oppression increased with the wind and Red heaved a sigh of restlessness. The sand began to skip across the plain, in grains at first and hardly noticeable. Hopalong turned in his saddle and regarded the desert with apprehension. As he looked he saw that where grains had shifted handfuls were now moving. His mount evinced signs of uneasiness and was hard to control.

A gust of wind, stronger than the others, pricked his face and grains of sand rolled down his neck. The leather of his saddle emitted strange noises as if a fairy tattoo was being beaten upon it and he raised his hand and pointed off toward the east. The others looked and saw what had appeared to be a fog rise out of the desert and intervene between them and the sun. As far as eye could reach small whirlwinds formed and broke and one swept down and covered them with stinging sand. The day became darkened and their horses whinnied in terror and the clumps of mesquite twisted and turned to the gusts.

Each man knew what was to come upon them and they dismounted, hobbled their horses and threw them bodily to the earth, wrapping a blanket around the head of each. A rustling as of paper rubbing together became noticeable and they threw themselves flat upon the earth, their heads wrapped in their coats and buried in the necks of their mounts. For an hour they endured the tortures of hell and then, when the storm had passed, raised their heads and cursed Creation. Their bodies burned as though they had been shot with fine needles and their clothes were meshes where once was tough cloth. Even their shoes were perforated and the throat of each ached with thirst.

Hopalong fumbled at the canteen resting on his hip and gargled his mouth and throat, washing down the sand which wouldn't come up. His friends did likewise and then looked around. After some time had elapsed the loss of their pack horse was noticed and they swore again. Hopalong took the lead in getting his horse ready for service and then rode around in a circle half a mile in diameter, but returned empty handed. The horse was gone and with it went their main supply of food and drink.

Frenchy scowled at the shadow of a cactus and slowly rode toward the northeast, followed closely by his friends. His hand reached for his depleted canteen, but refrained-water was to be saved until the last minute.

"I'm goin' to build a shack out here an' live in it, I am!" exploded Hopalong in withering irony as he dug the sand out of his ears and also from his sixshooter. "I just nachurally dotes on this, I do!"

The others were too miserable to even grunt and he neatly severed the head of a Gila monster from its scaly body as it opened it venomous jaws in rage at this invasion of its territory. "Lovely place!" he sneered.

"You better save them cartridges, Hoppy," interposed Red as his companion fired again, feeling that he must say something.

"An' what for?" blazed his friend. "To plug sand storms? Anybody what we find on this God-forsaken lay-out won't have to be shot-they will commit suicide an' think it's fun! Tell yu what, if them rustlers hangs out on this sand range they're better men than I reckons they are. Anybody what hides up here shore earns all he steals." Hopalong grumbled from force of habit and because no one else would. His companions understood this and paid no attention to him, which increased his disgust.

"What are we up here for?" He asked, belligerently. "Why, because them Double Arrow idiots can't even watch a desert! We have to do their work for them an' they hangs around home an' gets slaughtered! Yes, sir!" he shouted, "they can't even take care of themselves when they're in line-houses what are forts. Why, that time we cleaned out them an' th' C-80 over at Buckskin they couldn't help runnin' into singin' lead!"

"Yes," drawled Red, whose recollection of that fight was vivid. "Yas, an' why?" He asked, and then replied to his own question. "Because yu sat up in a barn behind them, Buck played his gun on th' side window, Pete an' Skinny lay behind a rock to one side of Buck, me an' Lanky was across th' Street in front of them, an' Billy an' Johnny was in th' arroyo on th' other side. Cowan laid on his stummick on th' roof of his place with a buffalo gun, an' the whole blamed town was agin them. There wasn't five seconds passed that lead wasn't rippin' through th' walls of their shack. Th' Houston House wasn't made for no fort, an' besides, they wasn't like th' gang that's punchin' now. That's why."

Hopalong became cheerful again, for here was a chance to differ from his friend. The two loved each other the better the more they squabbled.

"Yas!" responded Hopalong with sarcasm. "Yas!" he reiterated, drawling it out. "Yu was in front of them, an' with what? Why, an' old, white-haired, interfering Winchester, that's what! Me an' my Sharp's —"

"Yu and yore Sharp's!" exploded Red, whose dislike for that rifle was very pronounced. "Yu and yore Sharp's."

"Me an' my Sharp's, as I was palaverin' before bein' interrupted," continued Hopalong, "did more damage in five min —"

"Says yu!" snapped Red with heat. "All yu an yore Sharp's could do was to cut yore initials in th' back door of their shack, an' — —"

"Did more damage in five minutes," continued Hopalong, "than all th' blasted Winchesters in th' whole damned town. Why —"

"An' then they was cut blamed poor. Every time that cannon of yourn exploded I shore thought th' —"

"Why, Cowan an' his buffalo did more damage (Cowan was reputed to be a very poor shot) than yu an —"

"I thought th' artillery was comin' into th' disturbance. I could see yore red head —"

"MY red head!" exclaimed Hopalong, sizing up the crimson warlock of his companion. "MY red head!" he repeated, and then turned to Frenchy: "Hey, Frenchy, who's got th' reddest hair, me or Red?"

Frenchy slowly turned in his saddle and gravely scrutinized them. Being strictly impartial and truthful, he gave up the effort of differentiating and smiled. "Why, if the tops of yore heads were poked through two holes in a board an' I didn't know which was which, I'd shore make a mistake if I tried to name 'em"

But Red had the last word. "Anyhow, you didn't have a Sharp's in that fight-you had a .45-70 Winchester, just like mine!"

Thereupon the discussion was directed at the judge, and the forenoon passed very pleasantly, Frenchy even smiling in his misery.

Chapter XIX
Hopalong's Decision

Shortly after noon, Hopalong, who had ridden with his head bowed low in meditation, looked up and slapped his thigh. Then he looked at Red and grinned.

"Look ahere, Red," he began, "there ain't no rustlers with their headquarters on this God-forsaken sand heap, an' there never was. They have to have water an' lots of it, too, an' th' nearest of any account is th' Pecos, or some of them streams over in th' Panhandle. Th' Panhandle is th' best place. There are lots of streams an' lakes over there an' they're right in a good grass country. Why, an' army could hide over there an' never be found unless it was hunted for blamed good. Then, again, it's close to the railroad. Up north aways is th' south branch of th' Santa Fe Trail an' it's far enough away not to bother anybody in th' middle Panhandle. Then there's Fort Worth purty near, an' other trails. Didn't Buck say he had all th' rest of th' country searched? He meant th' Pecos Valley an th' Davis Mountains country. All th' rustlers would have to do if they were in th' Panhandle would be to cross th' Canadian an th' Cimarron an' hit th' trail for th' railroad. Good fords, good grass an' water all th' way, cattle fat when they are delivered an plenty of room. Th' more I thinks about it th' more I cottons to the Panhandle."

"Well, it shore does sound good," replied Red, reflectively.

"Do yu mean th' Cunningham Lake region or farther north?"

"Just th' other side of this blasted desert: anywhere where there's water," responded Hopalong, enthusiastically. "I've been doin' some hot reckonin' for th' last two hours an' this is th' way it looks to me: they drives th' cows up on this skillet for a ways, then turns east an' hits th' trail for home an' water. They can get around th' ca on near Thatcher's Lake by a swing of th' north. I tell yu that's th' only way out'n this. Who could tell where they turned with th' wind raisin' th' deuce with the trail? Didn't we follow a trail for a ways, an' then what? Why, there wasn't none to follow. We can ride north 'till we walk behind ourselves an' never get a peek at them. I am in favor of headin' for th' Sulphur Spring Creek district. We can spend a couple of weeks, if we has to, an' prospect that whole region without havin' to cut our' water down to a smell an' a taste an live on jerked beef. If we investigates that country we'll find something else than sand storms, poisoned water holes an' blisters."

"Ain't th' Panhandle full of nesters (farmers)?" Inquired Red, doubtfully.

"Along th' Canadian an' th' edges, yas; in th' middle, no," explained Hopalong. "They hang close together on account of th' war-whoops, an' they like th' trails purty well because of there allus bein' somebody passin'."

"Buck ought to send some of th' Panhandle boys up there," suggested Red. "There's Pie Willis an' th' Jordans-they knows th' Panhandle like yu knows poker."

Frenchy had paid no apparent attention to the conversation up to this point, but now he declared himself. "Yu heard what Buck said, didn't yu?" He asked. "We were told to search th' Staked Plains from one end to th' other an' I'm goin' to do it if I can hold out long enough. I ain't goin' to palaver with yu because what yu say can't be denied as far as wisdom is concerned. Yu may have hit it plumb center, but I knows what I was ordered to do, an' yu can't get me to go over there if you shouts all night. When Buck says anything, she goes. He wants to know where th' cards are stacked an' why he can't holler 'Keno,' an' I'm goin' to find out if I can. Yu can go to Patagonia if yu wants to, but yu go alone as far as I am concerned."

"Well, it's better if yu don't go with us," replied Hopalong, taking it for granted that Red would accompany him. "Yu can prospect this end of th' game an' we'll be takin' care of th' other. It's two chances now where we only had one afore."

"Yu go east an' I'll hunt around as ordered," responded Frenchy.

"East nothin'," replied Hopalong. "Yu don't get me to wallow in hot alkali an' lose time ridin' in ankle-deep sand when I can hit th' south trail, skirt th' White Sand Hills an' be in God's country again. I ain't goin' to wrastle with no ca on this here trip, none whatever. I'm goin' to travel in style, get to Big Spring by ridin' two miles to where I could only make one on this stove. Then I'll head north along Sulpher Spring Creek an' have water an' grass all th' way, barrin' a few stretches. While you are bein' fricasseed I'll be streakin' through cottonwood groves an' ridin' in the creek."

"Yu'll have to go alone, then," said Red, resolutely. "Frenchy ain't a-goin' to die of lonesome-ness on this desert if I knows what I'm about, an' I reckon I do, some. Me an' him'll follow out what Buck said, hunt around for a while an' then Frenchy can go back to th' ranch to tell Buck what's up an' I'll take th' trail yu are a-scared of an' meet yu at th' east end of Cunningham Lake three days from now."

"Yu better come with me," coaxed Hopalong, not liking what his friend had said about being afraid of the trail past the ca on and wishing to have some one with whom to talk on his trip. "I'm goin' to have a nice long swim to-morrow night," he added, trying bribery.

"An' I'm goin' to try to keep from hittin' my blisters," responded Red. "I don't want to go swimmin' in no creek full of moccasins —I'd rather sleep with rattlers or copperheads. Every time I sees a cotton-mouth I feels like I had just sit down on one.

"I'll flip a coin to see whether yu comes or not," proposed Hopalong.

"If yu wants to gamble so bad I'll flip yu to see who draws our pay next month, but not for what you said," responded Red, choking down the desire to try his luck.

Hopalong grinned and turned toward the south. "If I sees Buck afore yu do, I'll tell him yu an' Frenchy are growin' watermelons up near Last Stand Rock an' are waitin' for rain. Well, so long," he said.

"Yu tell Buck we're obeyin' orders!" shouted Red, sorry that he was not going with his bunkie.

Frenchy and Red rode on in silence, the latter feeling strangely lonesome, for he and the departed man had seldom been separated when journeys like this were to be taken. And when in search of pleasure they were nearly always together. Frenchy, while being very friendly with Hopalong, a friendship that would have placed them side by side against any odds, was not accustomed to his company and did not notice his absence.

Red looked off toward the south for the tenth time and for the tenth time thought that his friend might return. "He's a son-of-a-gun," he soliloquized.

His companion looked up: "He shore is, an' he's right about this rustler business, too. But we'll look around for a day or so an' then yu raise dust for th' Lake. I'll go back to th' ranch an' get things primed, so there'll be no time lost when we get th' word."

"I'm sorry I went an' said what I did about me takin' th' trail he was a-scared of," confessed Red, after a pause. "Why, he ain't a-scared of nothin'."

"He got back at yu about them watermelons, so what's th' difference?" Asked Frenchy. "He don't owe yu nothin'."

An hour later they searched the Devil's Rocks, but found no rustlers. Filling their canteens at a tiny spring and allowing their mounts to drink the remainder of the water, they turned toward Hell Arroyo, which they reached at nightfall. Here, also, their search availed them nothing and they paused in indecision. Then Frenchy turned toward his companion and advised him to ride toward the Lake in the night when it was comparatively cool.

Red considered and then decided that the advice was good. He rolled a cigarette, wheeled and faced the east and spurred forward: "So long," he called.

"So long," replied Frenchy, who turned toward the south and departed for the ranch.

The foreman of the Bar-20 was cleaning his rifle when he heard the hoof-beats of a galloping horse and he ran around the corner of the house to meet the newcomer, whom he thought to be a courier from the Double Arrow. Frenchy dismounted and explained why he returned alone.

Buck listened to the report and then, noting the fire which gleamed in his friend's eyes, nodded his approval to the course. "I reckon it's Trendley, Frenchy —I've heard a few things since yu left. An' yu can bet that if Hopalong an' Red have gone for him he'll be found. I expect action any time now, so we'll light th' signal fire." Then he hesitated; "Yu light it-yu've been waiting a long time for this."

The balls of smoke which rolled upward were replied to by other balls at different points on the plain, and the Bar-20 prepared to feed the numbers of hungry punchers who would arrive within the next twenty-four hours.

Two hours had not passed when eleven men rode up from the Three Triangle, followed eight hours later by ten from the O-Bar-O. The outfits of the Star Circle and the Barred Horseshoe, eighteen in all, came next and had scarcely dismounted when those of the C-80 and the Double Arrow, fretting at the delay, rode up. With the sixteen from the Bar-20 the force numbered seventy-five resolute and pugnacious cowpunchers, all aching to wipe out the indignities suffered.

Chapter XX
A Problem Solved

Hopalong worried his way out of the desert on a straight line, thus cutting in half the distance he had traveled when going into it. He camped that night on the sand and early the next morning took up his journey. It was noon when he began to notice familiar sights, and an hour later he passed within a mile of line-house No. 3, Double Arrow. Half an hour later he espied a cow-puncher riding like mad. Thinking that an investigation would not be out of place, he rode after the rider and overtook him, when that person paused and retraced his course.

"Hullo, Hopalong!" shouted the puncher and he came near enough to recognize his pursuer. "Thought yu was farmin' up on th' Staked Plain?"

"Hullo, Pie," replied Hopalong, recognizing Pie Willis. "What was yu chasin' so hard?"

"Coyote-damn 'em, but can't they go some? They're gettin' so thick we'll shore have to try strichnine an' thin 'em out."

"I thought anybody that had been raised in th' Panhandle would know better'n to chase greased lightnin'," rebuked Hopalong. "Yu has got about as much show catchin' one of them as a tenderfoot has of bustin' an outlawed cayuse."

"Shore; I know it," responded Pie, grinning. "But it's fun seem' them hunt th' horizon. What are yu doin' down here an' where are yore pardners?"

Thereupon Hopalong enlightened his inquisitive companion as to what had occurred and as to his reasons for riding south.

Pie immediately became enthusiastic and announced his intention of accompanying Hopalong on his quest, which intention struck that gentleman as highly proper and wise. Then Pie hastily turned and played at chasing coyotes in the direction of the line-house, where he announced that his absence would be accounted for by the fact that he and Hopalong were going on a journey of investigation into the Panhandle. Billy Jordan who shared with Pie the accommodations of the house, objected and showed, very clearly, why he was eminently better qualified to take up the proposed labors than his companions. The suggestions were fast getting tangled up with the remarks, when Pie, grabbing a chunk of jerked beef, leaped into his saddle and absolutely refused to heed the calls of his former companion and return. He rode to where Hopalong was awaiting him as if he was afraid he wasn't going to live long enough to get there. Confiding to his companion that Billy was a "locoed sage hen," he led the way along the base of the White Sand Hills and asked many questions. Then they turned toward the east and galloped hard.

It had been Hopalong's intention to carry out what he had told Red and to go to Big Spring first and thence north along Sulphur Spring Creek, but to this his guide strongly dissented. There was a short cut, or several of them for that matter, was Pie's contention, and any one of them would save a day's hard riding. Hopalong made no objection to allowing his companion to lead the way over any trail he saw fit, for he knew that Pie had been born and brought up in the Panhandle, the Cunningham Lake district having been his back yard, as it were. So they followed the short cut having the most water and grass, and pounded out a lively tattoo as they raced over the stretches of sand which seemed to slide beneath them.

"What do yu know about this here business?" Inquired Pie, as they raced past a chaparral and onto the edge of a grassy plain.

"Nothin' more'n yu do, only Buck said he thought Slippery Trendley is at th' bottom of it."

"What!" ejaculated Pie in surprise. "Him!"

"Yore on. An' between yu an' me an' th' Devil, I wouldn't be a heap surprised if Deacon Rankin is with him, neither."

Pie whistled: "Are him an' th' Deacon pals?"

"Shore," replied Hopalong, buttoning up his vest and rolling a cigarette. "Didn't they allus hang out together! One watched that th' other didn't get plugged from behind. It was a sort of yu-scratch-my-back-an'-I'll-scratch-yourn arrangement."

"Well, if they still hangs out together, I know where to hunt for our cows," responded Pie. "Th' Deacon used to range along th' headwaters of th' Colorado-it ain't far from Cunningham Lake. Thunderation!" he shouted, "I knows th' very ground they're on —I can take yu to th' very shack!" Then to himself he muttered: "An' that doodlebug Billy Jordan thinkin' he knowed more about th' Panhandle than me!"

Hopalong showed his elation in an appropriate manner and his companion drank deeply from the proffered flask; Thereupon they treated their mounts to liberal doses of strap-oil and covered the ground with great speed.

They camped early, for Hopalong was almost worn out from the exertions of the past few days and the loss of sleep he had sustained. Pie, too excited to sleep and having had unbroken rest for a long period, volunteered to keep guard, and his companion eagerly consented.

Early the next morning they broke camp and the evening of the same day found them fording Sulphur Spring Creek, and their quarry lay only an hour beyond, according to Pie. Then they forded one of the streams which form the headwaters of the Colorado, and two hours later they dismounted in a cottonwood grove. Picketing their horses, they carefully made their way through the timber, which was heavily grown with brush, and, after half an hour's maneuvering, came within sight of the further edge.

Dropping down on all fours, they crawled to the last line of brush and looked out over an extensive bottoms. At their feet lay a small river, and in a clearing on the farther side was a rough camp, consisting of about a dozen leanto shacks and log cabins in the main collection, and a few scattered cabins along the edge. A huge fire was blazing before the main collection of huts, and to the rear of these was an indistinct black mass, which they knew to be the corral.

At a rude table before the fire more than a score of men were eating supper and others could be heard moving about and talking at different points in the background. While the two scouts were learning the lay of the land, they saw Mr. Trendley and Deacon Rankin walk out of the cabin most distant from the fire, and the latter limped. Then they saw two men lying on rude cots, and they wore bandages. Evidently Johnny Redmond had scored in his fight.

The odor of burning cowhide came from the corral, accompanied by the squeals of cattle, and informed them that brands were being blotted out. Hopalong longed to charge down and do some blotting out of another kind, but a heavy hand was placed on his shoulder and he silently wormed his way after Pie as that person led the way back to the horses. Mounting, they picked their way out of the grove and rode over the plain at a walk. When far enough away to insure that the noise made by their horses would not reach the ears of those in the camp they cantered toward the ford they had taken on the way up.

After emerging from the waters of the last forded stream, Pie raised his hand and pointed off toward the northwest, telling his companion to take that course to reach Cunningham Lake. He himself would ride south, taking, for the saving of time, a yet shorter trail to the Double Arrow, from where he would ride to Buck. He and the others would meet Hopalong and Red at the split rock they had noticed on their way up.

Hopalong shook hands with his guide and watched him disappear into the night. He imagined he could still catch whiffs of burning cowhide and again the picture of the camp came to his mind. Glancing again at the point where Pie had disappeared, he stuffed his sombrero under a strap on his saddle and slowly rode toward the lake. A coyote slunk past him on a time-destroying lope and an owl hooted at the foolishness of men. He camped at the base of a cottonwood and at daylight took up his journey after a scanty breakfast from his saddle-bags.

Shortly before noon he came in sight of the lake and looked for his friend. He had just ridden around a clump of cotton-woods when he was hit on the back with something large and soft. Turning in his saddle, with his Colts ready, he saw Red sitting on a stump, a huge grin extending over his features. He replaced the weapon, said something about fools and dismounted, kicking aside the bundle of grass his friend had thrown.

"Yore shore easy," remarked Red, tossing aside his cold cigarette. "Suppose I was Trendley, where would yu be now?"

"Diggin' a hole to put yu in," pleasantly replied Hopalong. "If I didn't know he wasn't around this part of the country I wouldn't a rode as I did."

The man on the stump laughed and rolled a fresh cigarette. Lighting it, he inquired where Mr. Trendley was, intimating by his words that the rustler had not been found.

"About thirty miles to th' southeast," responded the other. "He's figurin' up how much dust he'll have when he gets our cows on th' market. Deacon Rankin is with him, too."

"Th' deuce!" exclaimed Red, in profound astonishment.

"Yore right," replied his companion. Then he explained all the arrangements and told of the camp.

Red was for riding to the rendezvous at once, but his friend thought otherwise and proposed a swim, which met with approval. After enjoying themselves in the lake they dressed and rode along the trail Hopalong had made in coming for his companion, it being the intention of the former to learn more thoroughly the lay of the land immediately surrounding the camp. Red was pleased with this, and while they rode he narrated all that had taken place since the separation on the Plain, adding that he had found the trail left by the rustlers after they had quitted the desert and that he had followed it for the last two hours of his journey. It was well beaten and an eighth of a mile wide.

At dark they came within sight of the grove and picketed their horses at the place used by Pie and Hopalong. Then they moved forward and the same sight greeted their eyes that had been seen the night before. Keeping well within the edge of the grove and looking carefully for sentries, they went entirely around the camp and picked out several places which would be of strategic value later on. They noticed that the cabin used by Slippery Trendley was a hundred paces from the main collection of huts and that the woods came to within a tenth part of that distance of its door. It was heavily built, had no windows and faced the wrong direction.

Moving on, they discovered the storehouse of the enemy, another tempting place. It was just possible, if a siege became necessary, for several of the attacking force to slip up to it and either destroy it by fire or take it and hold it against all comers. This suggested a look at the enemy's water supply, which was the river. A hundred paces separated it from the nearest cabin and any rustler who could cross that zone under the fire of the besiegers would be welcome to his drink.

It was very evident that the rustlers had no thought of defense, thinking, perhaps, that they were immune from attack with such a well covered trail between them and their foes. Hopalong mentally accused them of harboring suicidal inclinations and returned with his companion to the horses. They mounted and sat quietly for a while, and then rode slowly away and at dawn reached the split rock, where they awaited the arrival of their friends, one sleeping while the other kept guard. Then they drew a rough map of the camp, using the sand for paper, and laid out the plan of attack.

As the evening of the next day came on they saw Pie, followed by many punchers, ride over a rise a mile to the south and they rode out to meet him.

When the force arrived at the camp of the two scouts they were shown the plan prepared for them. Buck made a few changes in the disposition of the men and then each member was shown where he was to go and was told why. Weapons were put in a high state of efficiency, canteens were refilled and haversacks were somewhat depleted. Then the newcomers turned in and slept while Hopalong and Red kept guard.

Chapter XXI
The Call

At three o'clock the next morning a long line of men slowly filed into the cottonwood grove, being silently swallowed up by the dark. Dismounting, they left their horses in the care of three of their number and disappeared into the brush. Ten minutes later forty of the force were distributed along the edge of the grove fringing on the bank of the river and twenty more minutes gave ample time for a detachment of twenty to cross the stream and find concealment in the edge of the woods which ran from the river to where the corral made an effective barrier on the south.

Eight crept down on the western side of the camp and worked their way close to Mr. Trendley's cabin door, and the seven who followed this detachment continued and took up their positions at the rear of the corral, where, it was hoped, some of the rustlers would endeavor to escape into the woods by working their way through the cattle in the corral and then scaling the stockade wall. These seven were from the Three Triangle and the Double Arrow, and they were positive that any such attempt would not be a success from the view-point of the rustlers.

Two of those who awaited the pleasure of Mr. Trendley crept forward, and a rope swished through the air and settled over the stump which lay most convenient on the other side of the cabin door. Then the slack moved toward the woods, raised from the ground as it grew taut and, with the stump for its axis, swung toward the door, where it rubbed gently against the rough logs. It was made of braided horsehair, was half an inch in diameter and was stretched eight inches above the ground.

As it touched the door, Lanky Smith, Hopalong and Red stepped out of the shelter of the woods and took up their positions behind the cabin, Lanky behind the northeast corner where he would be permitted to swing his right arm. In his gloved right hand he held the carefully arranged coils of a fifty-foot lariat, and should the chief of the rustlers escape tripping he would have to avoid the cast of the best roper in the southwest.

The two others took the northwest corner and one of them leaned slightly forward and gently twitched the tripping-rope. The man at the other end felt the signal and whispered to a companion, who quietly disappeared in the direction of the river and shortly afterward the mournful cry of a whip-poor-will dirged out on the early morning air. It had hardly died away when the quiet was broken by one terrific crash of rifles, and the two camp guards asleep at the fire awoke in another world.

Mr. Trendley, sleeping unusually well for the unjust, leaped from his bed to the middle of the floor and alighted on his feet and wide awake. Fearing that a plot was being consummated to deprive him of his leadership, he grasped the Winchester which leaned at the head of his bed and, tearing open the door, crashed headlong to the earth. As he touched the ground, two shadows sped out from the shelter of the cabin wall and pounced upon him. Men who can rope, throw and tie a wild steer in thirty seconds flat do not waste time in trussing operations, and before a minute had elapsed he was being carried into the woods, bound and helpless. Lanky sighed, threw the rope over one shoulder and departed after his friends.

When Mr. Trendley came to his senses he found himself bound to a tree in the grove near the horses. A man sat on a stump not far from him, three others were seated around a small fire some distance to the north, and four others, one of whom carried a rope, made their way into the brush. He strained at his bonds, decided that the effort was useless and watched the man on the stump, who struck a match and lit a pipe. The prisoner watched the light flicker up and go out and there was left in his mind a picture that he could never forget. The face which had been so cruelly, so grotesquely revealed was that of Frenchy McAllister, and across his knees lay a heavy caliber Winchester. A curse escaped from the lips of the outlaw; the man on the stump spat at a firefly and smiled.

From the south came the crack of rifles, incessant and sharp. The reports rolled from one end of the clearing to the other and seemed to sweep in waves from the center of the line to the ends. Faintly in the infrequent lulls in the firing came an occasional report from the rear of the corral, where some desperate rustler paid for his venture.

Buck went along the line and spoke to the riflemen, and after some time had passed and the light had become stronger, he collected the men into groups of five and six. Taking one group and watching it closely, it could be seen that there was a world of meaning in this maneuver. One man started firing at a particular window in an opposite hut and then laid aside his empty gun and waited. When the muzzle of his enemy's gun came into sight and lowered until it had nearly gained its sight level, the rifles of the remainder of the group crashed out in a volley and usually one of the bullets, at least, found its intended billet. This volley firing became universal among the besiegers and the effect was marked.

Two men sprinted from the edge of the woods near Mr. Trendley's cabin and gained the shelter of the storehouse, which soon broke out in flames. The burning brands fell over the main collection of huts, where there was much confusion and swearing. The early hour at which the attack had been delivered at first led the besieged to believe that it was an Indian affair, but this impression was soon corrected by the volley firing, which turned hope into despair. It was no great matter to fight Indians, that they had done many times and found more or less enjoyment in it; but there was a vast difference between brave and puncher, and the chances of their salvation became very small. They surmised that it was the work of the cow-men on whom they had preyed and that vengeful punchers lay hidden behind that death-fringe of green willow and hazel.

Red, assisted by his inseparable companion, Hopalong, laboriously climbed up among the branches of a black walnut and hooked one leg over a convenient limb. Then he lowered his rope and drew up the Winchester which his accommodating friend fastened to it. Settling himself in a comfortable position and sheltering his body somewhat by the tree, he shaded his eyes by a hand and peered into the windows of the distant cabins.

"How is she, Red?" Anxiously inquired the man on the ground.

"Bully: want to come up?"

"Nope. I'm goin' to catch yu when yu lets go," replied Hopalong with a grin.

"Which same I ain't goin' to," responded the man in the tree.

He swung his rifle out over a forked limb and let it settle in the crotch. Then he slew his head around until he gained the bead he wished. Five minutes passed before he caught sight of his man and then he fired. Jerking out the empty shell he smiled and called out to his friend: "One."

Hopalong grinned and went off to tell Buck to put all the men in trees.

Night came on and still the firing continued. Then an explosion shook the woods. The storehouse had blown up and a sky full of burning timber fell on the cabins and soon three were half consumed, their occupants dropping as they gained the open air. One hundred paces makes fine pot-shooting, as Deacon Rankin discovered when evacuation was the choice necessary to avoid cremation. He never moved after he touched the ground and Red called out: "Two," not knowing that his companion had departed.

The morning of the next day found a wearied and hopeless garrison, and shortly before noon a soiled white shirt was flung from a window in the nearest cabin. Buck ran along the line and ordered the firing to cease and caused to be raised an answering flag of truce. A full minute passed and then the door slowly opened and a leg protruded, more slowly followed by the rest of the man, and Cheyenne Charley strode out to the bank of the river and sat down. His example was followed by several others and then an unexpected event occurred. Those in the cabins who preferred to die fighting, angered at this desertion, opened fire on their former comrades, who barely escaped by rolling down the slightly inclined bank into the river. Red fired again and laughed to himself. Then the fugitives swam down the river and landed under the guns of the last squad. They were taken to the rear and, after being bound, were placed under a guard. There were seven in the party and they looked worn out.

When the huts were burning the fiercest the uproar in the corral arose to such a pitch as to drown all other sounds. There were left within its walls a few hundred cattle whose brands had not yet been blotted out, and these, maddened to frenzy by the shooting and the flames, tore from one end of the enclosure to the other, crashing against the alternate walls with a noise which could be heard far out on the plain. Scores were trampled to death on each charge and finally the uproar subsided in sheer want of cattle left with energy enough to continue. When the corral was investigated the next day there were found the bodies of four rustlers, but recognition was impossible.

Several of the defenders were housed in cabins having windows in the rear walls, which the occupants considered fortunate. This opinion was revised, however, after several had endeavored to escape by these openings. The first thing that occurred when a man put his head out was the hum of a bullet, and in two cases the experimenters lost all need of escape.

The volley firing had the desired effect, and at dusk there remained only one cabin from which came opposition. Such a fire was concentrated on it that before an hour had passed the door fell in and the firing ceased. There was a rush from the side, and the Barred Horseshoe men who swarmed through the cabins emerged without firing a shot. The organization that had stirred up the Pecos Valley ranches had ceased to exist.

Chapter XXII
The Showdown

A fire burned briskly in front of Mr. Trendley's cabin that night and several punchers sat around it occupied in various ways. Two men leaned against the wall and sang softly of the joys of the trail and the range. One of them, Lefty Allen, of the O-Bar-O, sang in his sweet tenor, and other men gradually strolled up and seated themselves on the ground, where the fitful gleam of responsive pipes and cigarettes showed like fireflies. The songs followed one after another, first a lover's plea in soft Spanish and then a rollicking tale of the cow-towns and men. Supper had long since been enjoyed and all felt that life was, indeed, well worth living.

A shadow loomed against the cabin wall and a procession slowly made its way toward the open door. The leader, Hopalong, disappeared within and was followed by Mr. Trendley, bound and hobbled and tied to Red, the rear being brought up by Frenchy, whose rifle lolled easily in the crotch of his elbow. The singing went on uninterrupted and the hum of voices between the selections remained unchanged. Buck left the crowd around the fire and went into the cabin, where his voice was heard assenting to something. Hopalong emerged and took a seat at the fire, sending two punchers to take his place. He was joined by Frenchy and Red, the former very quiet.

In the center of a distant group were seven men who were not armed. Their belts, half full of cartridges, supported empty holsters. They sat and talked to the men around them, swapping notes and experiences, and in several instances found former friends and acquaintances. These men were not bound and were apparently members of Buck's force. Then one of them broke down, but quickly regained his nerve and proposed a game of cards. A fire was started and several games were immediately in progress. These seven men were to die at daybreak.

As the night grew older man after man rolled himself in his blanket and lay down where he sat, sinking off to sleep with a swiftness that bespoke tired muscles and weariness. All through the night, however, there were twelve men on guard, of whom three were in the cabin.

At daybreak a shot from one of the guards awakened every man within hearing, and soon they romped and scampered down to the river's edge to indulge in the luxury of a morning plunge. After an hour's horseplay they trooped back to the cabin and soon had breakfast out of the way.

Waffles, foreman of the O-Bar-O, and You-bet Somes strolled over to the seven unfortunates who had just completed a choking breakfast and nodded a hearty "Good morning." Then others came up and finally all moved off toward the river. Crossing it, they disappeared into the grove and all sounds of their advance grew into silence.

Mr. Trendley, escorted outside for the air, saw the procession as it became lost to sight in the brush. He sneered and asked for a smoke, which was granted. Then his guards were changed and the men began to straggle back from the grove.

Mr. Trendley, with his back to the cabin, scowled defiantly at the crowd that hemmed him in. The coolest, most damnable murderer in the West was not now going to beg for mercy. When he had taken up crime as a means of livelihood he had decided that if the price to be paid for his course was death, he would pay like a man. He glanced at the cottonwood grove, wherein were many ghastly secrets, and smiled. His hairless eyebrows looked like livid scars and his lips quivered in scorn and anger.

As he sneered at Buck there was a movement in the crowd before him and a pathway opened for Frenchy, who stepped forward slowly and deliberately, as if on his way to some bar for a drink. There was something different about the man who had searched the Staked Plain with Hopalong and Red: he was not the same puncher who had arrived from Montana three weeks before. There was lacking a certain air of carelessness and he chilled his friends, who looked upon him as if they had never really known him. He walked up to Mr. Trendley and gazed deeply into the evil eyes.

Twenty years before, Frenchy McAllister had changed his identity from a happy-go-lucky, devil-may-care cow-puncher and became a machine. The grief that had torn his soul was not of the kind which seeks its outlet in tears and wailing; it had turned and struck inward, and now his deliberate ferocity was icy and devilish. Only a glint in his eyes told of exultation, and his words were sharp and incisive; one could well imagine one heard the click of his teeth as they bit off the consonants: every letter was clear-cut, every syllable startling in its clearness.

"Twenty years and two months ago to-day," he began, "you arrived at the ranchhouse of the Double Y, up near the Montana-Wyoming line. Everything was quiet, except, perhaps, a woman's voice, singing. You entered, and before you left you pinned a note to that woman's dress. I found it, and it is due."

The air of carelessness disappeared from the members of the crowd and the silence became oppressive. Most of those present knew parts of Frenchy's story, and all were in hearty accord with anything he might do. He reached within his vest and brought forth a deerskin bag. Opening it, he drew out a package of oiled silk and from that he took a paper. Carefully replacing the silk and the bag, he slowly unfolded the sheet in his hand and handed it to Buck, whose face hardened. Two decades had passed since the foreman of the Bar-20 had seen that precious sheet, but the scene of its finding would never fade from his memory. He stood as if carved from stone, with a look on his face that made the crowd shift uneasily and glance at Trendley.

Frenchy turned to the rustler and regarded him evilly. "You are the hellish brute that wrote that note," pointing to the paper in the hand of his friend. Then, turning again, he spoke: "Buck, read that paper."

The foreman cleared his throat and read distinctly:

"McAllister: Yore wife is too blame good to live.

TRENDLEY."

There was a shuffling sound, but Buck and Frenchy, silently backed up by Hopalong and Red, intervened, and the crowd fell back, where it surged in indecision.

"Gentlemen," said Frenchy, "I want you to vote on whether any man here has more right to do with Slippery Trendley as he sees fit than myself. Any one who thinks so, or that he should be treated like the others, step forward. Majority rules."

There was no advance and he spoke again: "Is there any one here who objects to this man dying?"

Hopalong and Red awkwardly bumped their knuckles against their guns and there was no response.

The prisoner was bound with cowhide to the wall of the cabin and four men sat near and facing him. The noonday meal was eaten in silence, and the punchers rode off to see about rounding up the cattle that grazed over the plain as far as eye could see. Supper-time came and passed, and busy men rode away in all directions. Others came and relieved the guards, and at midnight another squad took up the vigil.

Day broke and the thunder of hoofs as the punchers rounded up the cattle became very noticeable. One herd swept past toward the south, guarded and guided by fifteen men. Two hours later and another followed, taking a slightly different trail so as to avoid the close-cropped grass left by the first. At irregular intervals during the day other herds swept by, until six had passed and denuded the plain of cattle.

Buck, perspiring and dusty, accompanied by Hopalong and Red, rode up to where the guards smoked and joked. Frenchy came out of the cabin and smiled at his friends. Swinging in his left hand was a newly filled Colt's .45, which was recognized by his friends as the one found in the cabin and it bore a rough "T" gouged in the butt.

Buck looked around and cleared his throat: "We've got th' cows on th' home trail, Frenchy," he suggested.

"Yas?" Inquired Frenchy. "Are there many?"

"Yas," replied Buck, waving his hand at the guards, ordering them to follow their friends. "It's a good deal for us: we've done right smart this hand. An' it's a good thing we've got so many punchers: we got a lot of cattle to drive."

"About five times th' size of th' herd that blamed near made angels out'en me an' yu," responded Frenchy with a smile.

"I hope almighty hard that we don't have no stampedes on this here drive. If th' last herds go wild they'll pick up th' others, an' then there'll be th' devil to pay."

Frenchy smiled again and shot a glance at where Mr. Trendley was bound to the cabin wall.

Buck looked steadily southward for some time and then flecked a foam-sud from the flank of his horse. "We are goin' south along th' Creek until we gets to Big Spring, where we'll turn right smart to th' west. We won't be able to average more'n twelve miles a day, 'though I'm goin' to drive them hard. How's yore grub?"

"Grub to burn."

"Got yore rope?" Asked the foreman of the Bar-20, speaking as if the question had no especial meaning.

Frenchy smiled: "Yes."

Hopalong absent-mindedly jabbed his spurs into his mount with the result that when the storm had subsided the spell was broken and he said "So long," and rode south, followed by Buck and Red. As they swept out of sight behind a grove Red turned in his saddle and waved his hat. Buck discussed with assiduity the prospects of a rainfall and was very cheerful about the recovery of the stolen cattle. Red could see a tall, broad-shouldered man standing with his feet spread far apart, swinging a Colt's .45, and Hopalong swore at everything under the sun. Dust arose in streaming clouds far to the south and they spurred forward to overtake the outfits.

Buck Peters, riding over the starlit plain, in his desire to reach the first herd, which slept somewhere to the west of him under the care of Waffles, thought of the events of the past few weeks and gradually became lost in the memories of twenty years before, which crowded up before his mind like the notes of a half-forgotten song. His nature, tempered by two decades of a harsh existence, softened as he lived again the years that had passed and as he thought of the things which had been. He was so completely lost in his reverie that he failed to hear the muffled hoofbeats of a horse that steadily gained upon him, and when Frenchy McAllister placed a friendly hand on his shoulder he started as if from a deep sleep.

The two looked at each other and their hands met. The question which sprang into Buck's eyes found a silent answer in those of his friend. They rode on side by side through the clear night and together drifted back to the days of the Double Y.

After an hour had passed, the foreman of the Bar-20 turned to his companion and then hesitated:

"Did, did-was he a cur?"

Frenchy looked off toward the south and, after an interval, replied: "Yas." Then, as an after thought, he added, "Yu see, he never reckoned it would be that way."

Buck nodded, although he did not fully understand, and the subject was forever closed.

Chapter XXIII
Mr. Cassidy Meets a Woman

The work of separating the cattle into herds of the different brands was not a big contract, and with so many men it took but a comparatively short time, and in two days all signs of the rustlers had faded. It was then that good news went the rounds and the men looked forward to a week of pleasure, which was all the sharper accentuated by the grim mercilessness of the expedition into the Panhandle. Here was a chance for unlimited hilarity and a whole week in which to give strict attention to celebrating the recent victory.

So one day Mr. Hopalong Cassidy rode rapidly over the plain, thinking about the joys and excitement promised by the carnival to be held at Muddy Wells. With that rivalry so common to Western towns the inhabitants maintained that the carnival was to break all records, this because it was to be held in their town. Perry's Bend and Buckskin had each promoted a similar affair, and if this year's festivities were to be an improvement on those which had gone before, they would most certainly be worth riding miles to see. Perry's Bend had been unfortunate m being the first to hold a carnival, inasmuch as it only set a mark to be improved upon, and Buckskin had taken advantage of this and had added a brass band, and now in turn was to be eclipsed.

The events slated were numerous and varied, the most important being those which dealt directly with the everyday occupations of the inhabitants of that section of the country. Broncho busting, steer-roping and tying, rifle and revolver shooting, trick riding and fancy roping made up the main features of the programme and were to be set off by horse and foot racing and other county fair necessities. Altogether, the proud citizens of the town looked forward with keen anticipation to the coming excitements, and were prone to swagger a bit and to rub their hands in condescending egoism, while the crowded gambling halls and saloons, and the three-card-monte men on the street corners enriched themselves at the cost of venturesome know-it-ails.

Hopalong was firmly convinced that his day of hard riding was well worth while, for the Bar-20 was to be represented in strength. Probably a clearer insight into his idea of a carnival can be gained by his definition, grouchily expressed to Red Connors on the day following the last affair: "Raise cain, go broke, wake up an' begin punching cows all over again." But that was the day after and the day after is always filled with remorse.

Hopalong and Red, having twice in succession won the revolver and rifle competitions, re-spectively, hoped to make it 'Three straight.' Lanky Smith, the Bar-20 rope expert, had taken first prize in the only contest he had entered. Skinny Thompson had lost and drawn with Lefty Allen, of the O-Bar-O, in the broncho-busting event, but as Skinny had improved greatly in the interval, his friends confidently expected him to "yank first place" for the honor of his ranch. These expectations were backed with all the available Bar-20 money, and, if they were not re-alized, something in the nature of a calamity would swoop down upon and wrap that ranch in gloom. Since the O-Bar-O was aggressively optimistic the betting was at even money, hats and guns, and the losers would begin life anew so far as earthly possessions were concerned. No other competitors were considered in this event, as Skinny and Lefty had so far outclassed all others that the honor was believed to lie between these two.

Hopalong, blissfully figuring out the chances of the different contestants, galloped around a clump of mesquite only fifteen miles from Muddy Wells and stiffened in his saddle, for twenty rods ahead of him on the trail was a woman. As she heard him approach she turned and waited for him to overtake her, and when she smiled he raised his sombrero and bowed.

"Will you please tell me where I am?" She asked.

"Yu are fifteen miles southeast of Muddy Wells," he replied.

"But which is southeast?"

"Right behind yu," he answered. "Th' town lies right ahead."

"Are you going there?" She asked.

"Yes, ma'am."

"Then you will not care if I ride with you?" She asked. "I am a trifle frightened."

"Why, I'd be some pleased if yu do, 'though there ain't nothing out here to be afraid of now."

"I had no intention of getting lost," she assured him, "but I dismounted to pick flowers and cactus leaves and after a while I had no conception of where I was."

"How is it yu are out here?" He asked. "Yu shouldn't get so far from town."

"Why, papa is an invalid and doesn't like to leave his room, and the town is so dull, although the carnival is waking it up somewhat. Having nothing to do I procured a horse and determined to explore the country. Why, this is like Stanley and Livingstone, isn't it? You rescued the explorer!" And she laughed heartily. He wondered who in thunder Stanley and Livingstone were, but said nothing.

"I like the West, it is so big and free," she continued. "But it is very monotonous at times, especially when compared with New York. Papa swears dreadfully at the hotel and declares that the food will drive him insane, but I notice that he eats much more heartily than he did when in the city. And the service! —it is awful. But when one leaves the town behind it is splendid, and I can appreciate it because I had such a hard season in the city last winter-so many balls, parties and theaters that I simply wore myself out."

"I never hankered much for them things," Hopalong replied. "An' I don't like th' towns much, either. Once or twice a year I gets as far as Kansas City, but I soon tires of it an' hits th' back trail. Yu see, I don't like a fence country —I wants lots of room an' air."

She regarded him intently: "I know that you will think me very forward."

He smiled and slowly replied: "I think yu are all O. K."

"There do not appear to be many women in this country," she suggested.

"No, there ain't many," he replied, thinking of the kind to be found in all of the cow-towns. "They don't seem to hanker for this kind of life-they wants parties an' lots of dancin' an' them kind of things. I reckon there ain't a whole lot to tempt em to come.

"You evidently regard women as being very frivolous," she replied.

"Well, I'm speakin' from there not being any out here," he responded, "although I don't know much about them, to tell th' truth. Them what are out here can't be counted." Then he flushed and looked away.

She ignored the remark and placed her hand to her hair:

"Goodness! My hair must look terrible!"

He turned and looked: "Yore hair is pretty —I allus did like brown hair."

She laughed and put back the straggling locks: "It is terrible! Just look at it! Isn't it awful?"

"Why, no: I reckons not," he replied critically. "It looks sort of free an' easy thataway."

"Well, it's no matter, it cannot be helped," she laughed. "Let's race!" she cried and was off like a shot.

He humored her until he saw that her mount was getting unmanageable, when he quietly overtook her and closed her pony's nostrils with his hand, the operation having a most gratifying effect.

"Joe hadn't oughter let yu had this cayuse," he said.

"Why, how do you know of whom I procured it?" She asked. "By th' brand: it's a O-Bar-O, canceled, with J. H. over it. He buys all of his cayuses from th' O-Bar-O."

She found out his name, and, after an interval of silence, she turned to him with eyes full of inquiry: "What is that thorny shrub just ahead?" She asked.

"That's mesquite," he replied eagerly.

"Tell me all about it," she commanded.

"Why, there ain't much to tell," he replied, "only it's a valuable tree out here. Th' Apaches use it a whole lot of ways. They get honey from th' blossoms an' glue an' gum, an' they use th' bark for tannin' hide. Th' dried pods an' leaves are used to feed their cattle, an' th' wood makes corrals to keep 'em in. They use th' wood for making other things, too, an' it is of two colors. Th' sap makes a dye what won't wash out, an' th' beans make a bread what won't sour or get hard. Then it makes a barrier that shore is a dandy-coyotes an' men can't get through it, an' it protects a whole lot of birds an' things. Th' snakes hate it like poison, for th' thorns get under their scales an' whoops things up for 'em. It keeps th' sand from shiftin', too. Down South where there is plenty of water, it often grows forty feet high, but up here it squats close to th' ground so it can save th' moisture. In th' night th' temperature sometimes falls thirty degrees, an' that helps it, too."

"How can it live without water?" She asked.

"It gets all th' water it wants," he replied, smiling. "Th' tap roots go straight down 'til they find it, sometimes fifty feet. That's why it don't shrivel up in th' sun. Then there are a lot of little roots right under it an' they protects th' tap roots. Th' shade it gives is th' coolest out here, for th' leaves turn with th' wind an' lets th' breeze through-they're hung on little stems."

"How splendid!" she exclaimed. "Oh! Look there!" she cried, pointing ahead of them. A chaparral cock strutted from its decapitated enemy, a rattlesnake, and disappeared in the chaparral.

Hopalong laughed: "Mr. Scissors-bill Road-runner has great fun with snakes. He runs along th' sand-an' he can run, too-an' sees a snake takin' a siesta. Snip! goes his bill an' th' snake slides over th' Divide. Our fighting friend may stop some coyote's appetite before morning, though, unless he stays where he is."

Just then a gray wolf blundered in sight a few rods ahead of them, and Hopalong fired instantly. His companion shrunk from him and looked at him reproachfully.

"Why did you do that!" she demanded.

"Why, because they costs us big money every year," he replied. "There's a bounty on them because they pull down calves, an' sometimes full grown cows. I'm shore wonderin' why he got so close-they're usually just out of range, where they stays."

"Promise me that you will shoot no more while I am with you.

"Why, shore: I didn't think yu'd care," he replied. "Yu are like that sky-pilot over to Las Cruces-he preached agin killin' things, which is all right for him, who didn't have no cows."

"Do you go to the missions?" She asked.

He replied that he did, sometimes, but forgot to add that it was usually for the purpose of hilarity, for he regarded sky-pilots with humorous toleration.

"Tell me all about yourself-what you do for enjoyment and all about your work," she requested.

He explained in minute detail the art of punching cows, and told her more of the West in half an hour than she could have learned from a year's experience. She showed such keen interest in his words that it was a pleasure to talk to her, and he monopolized the conversation until the town intruded its sprawling collection of unpainted shacks and adobe huts in their field of vision.

Chapter XXIV

The Strategy of Mr. Peters

Hopalong and his companion rode into Muddy Wells at noon, and Red Connors, who leaned with Buck Peters against the side of Tom Lee's saloon, gasped his astonishment. Buck looked twice to be sure, and then muttered incredulously: "What th' heck!" Red repeated the phrase and retreated within the saloon, while Buck stood his ground, having had much experience with women, inasmuch as he had narrowly escaped marrying. He thought that he might as well get all the information possible, and waited for an introduction. It was in vain, however, for the two rode past without noticing him.

Buck watched them turn the corner and then called for Red to come out, but that person, fearing an ordeal, made no reply and the foreman went in after him. The timorous one was corraling bracers at the bar and nearly swallowed down the wrong channel when Buck placed a heavy hand on his broad shoulder.

"G'way!" remarked Red. "I don't want no introduction, none whatever," he asserted. "G'way!" he repeated, backing off suspiciously.

"Better wait 'til yu are asked," suggested Buck. "Better wait 'til yu sees th' rope afore yu duck." Then he laughed: "Yu bashful fellers make me plumb disgusted. Why, I've seen yu face a bunch of guns an never turn a hair, an' here yore all in because yu fear yu'll have to stand around an' hide yore hands. She won't bite yu. Anyway, from what I saw, Hopalong is due to be her grub-he never saw me at all, th' chump."

"He shore didn't see me, none," replied Red with distinct relief. "Are they gone?"

"Shore," answered Buck. "An' if they wasn't they wouldn't see us, not if we stood in front of them an' yelled. She's a hummer-stands two hands under him an' is a whole lot prettier than that picture Cowan has got over his bar. There's nothing th' matter with his eyesight, but he's plumb locoed, all th' same. He'll go an' get stuck on her an' then she'll hit th' trail for home an' mamma, an' he won't be worth his feed for a year." Then he paused in consternation: "Thunder, Red: he's got to shoot to-morrow!"

"Well, suppose he has?" Responded Red. "I don't reckon she'll stampede his gun-play none."

"Yu don't reckon, eh?" Queried Buck with much irony. "No, an' that's what's th' matter with yu. Why, do yu expect to see him to-morrow? Yu won't if I knows him an' I reckon I do. Nope, he'll be follerin' her all around."

"He's got sand to burn," remarked Red in awe. "Wonder how he got to know her?"

"Yu can gamble she did th' introducing part-he ain't got th' nerve to do it himself. He saved her life, or she thinks he did, or some romantic nonsense like that. So yu better go around an' get him away, an' keep him away, too."

"Who, me?" Inquired Red in indignation. "Me go around an' tote him off? I ain't no wagon: yu go, or send Johnny."

"Johnny would say something real pert an' get knocked into th' middle of next week for it. He won't do, so I reckon yu better go yoreself," responded Buck, smiling broadly and moving off.

"Hey, yu! Wait a minute!" cried Red in consternation. Buck paused and Red groped for an excuse: "Why don't you send Billy?" He blurted in desperation.

The foreman's smile assumed alarming proportions and he slapped his thigh in joy: "Good boy!" he laughed. "Billy's th' man-good Lord, but won't he give Cupid cold feet! Rustle around an' send th' pessimistic soul to me."

Red, grinning and happy, rapidly visited door after door, shouted, "Hey, Billy!" and proceeded to the next one. He was getting pugnacious at his lack of success when he espied Mr. Billy Williams tacking along the accidental street as if he owned it. Mr. Williams was executing fancy steps and was trying to sing many songs at once.

Red stopped and grabbed his bibulous friend as that person veered to starboard: "Yore a peach of a life-preserver, yu are!" he exclaimed.

Billy balanced himself, swayed back and forth and frowned his displeasure at this unwarranted action: "I ain't no wife-deserter!" he shouted. "Unrope me an' give me th' trail! No tenderfoot can ride me!" Then he recognized his friend and grinned joyously: "Shore I will, but only one. Jus' one more, jus' one more. Yu see, m'friend, it was all Jimmy's fault. He —"

Red secured a chancery hold and dragged his wailing and remonstrating friend to Buck, who frowned with displeasure.

"This yere," said Red in belligerent disgust, "is th' dod-blasted hero what's a-goin' to save Hopalong from a mournful future. What are we a-goin' to do?"

Buck slipped the Colt's from Billy's holster and yanked the erring one to his feet: "Fill him full of sweet oil, source him in th' trough, walk him around for awhile an' see what it does," he ordered.

Two hours later Billy walked up to his foreman and weakly asked what was wanted. He looked as though he had just been released from a six-months' stay in a hospital.

"Yu go over to th' hotel an' find Hopalong," said the foreman sternly. "Stay with him all th' time, for there is a plot on foot to wing him on th' sly. If yu ain't mighty spry he'll be dead by night."

Having delivered the above instructions and prevarications, Buck throttled the laugh which threatened to injure him and scowled at Red, who again fled into the saloon for fear of spoiling it all with revealed mirth.

The convalescent stared in open-mouthed astonishment:

"What's he doin' in th' hotel, an' who's goin' to plug him?" He asked.

"Yu leave that to me," replied Buck, "All yu has to do is to get on th' job with yore gun," handing the weapon to him, "an' freeze to him like a flea on a cow. Mebby there'll be a woman in th' game, but that ain't none of yore funeral-yu do what I said."

"Blast th' women!" exploded Billy, moving off. When he had entered the hotel Buck went in to Red.

"For Pete's sake!" moaned that person in senseless reiteration. "Th' Lord help Billy! Holy Mackinaw!" he shouted. "Gimme a drink an' let me tell th' boys."

The members of the outfit were told of the plot and they gave their uproarious sanction, all needing bracers to sustain them.

Billy found the clerk swapping lies with the bartender and, procuring the desired information, climbed the stairs and hunted for room No. 6. Discovering it, he dispensed with formality, pushed open the door and entered.

He found his friend engaged in conversation with a pretty young woman, and on a couch at the far side of the room lay an elderly white-whiskered gentleman who was reading a magazine. Billy felt like a criminal for a few seconds and then there came to him the thought that his was a mission of great import and he braced himself to face any ordeal. "Anyway," he thought, "th' prettier they are th' more dust they can raise."

"What are yu doing here?" Cried Hopalong in amazement.

"That's all right," averred the protector, confidentially.

"What's all right?"

"Why, everything," replied Billy, feeling uncomfortable.

The elderly man hastily sat up and dropped his magazine when he saw the armed intruder, his eyes as wide open as his mouth. He felt for his spectacles, but did not need them, for he could see nothing but the Colt's which Billy jabbed at him.

"None of that!" snapped Billy. "'ands up!" he ordered, and the hands went up so quick that when they stopped the jerk shook the room. Peering over the gentleman's leg, Billy saw the spectacles and backed to the wall as he apologized: "It's shore on me, Stranger —I reckoned yu was contemplatin' some gun-play."

Hopalong, blazing with wrath, arose and shoved Billy toward the hail, when Mr. Johnny Nelson, oozing fight and importance, intruded his person into the zone of action.

"Lord!" ejaculated the newcomer, staring at the vision of female loveliness which so suddenly greeted him. "Mamma," he added under his breath. Then he tore off his sombrero: "Come out of this, Billy, yu chump!" he exploded, backing toward the door, being followed by the protector.

Hopalong slammed the door and turned to his hostess, apologizing for the disturbance.

"Who are they?" Palpitated Miss Deane.

"What the deuce are they doing up here!" blazed her father. Hopalong disclaimed any knowledge of them and just then Billy opened the door and looked in.

"There he is again!" cried Miss Deane, and her father gasped. Hopalong ran out into the hall and narrowly missed kicking Billy into Kingdom Come as that person slid down the stairs, surprised and indignant.

Mr. Billy Williams, who sat at the top of the stairs, was feeling hungry and thirsty when he saw his friend, Mr. Pete Wilson, the slow witted, approaching.

"Hey, Pete," he called, "come up here an' watch this door while I rustles some grub. Keep yore eyes open," he cautioned.

As Pete began to feel restless the door opened and a dignified gentleman with white whiskers came out into the hall and then retreated with great haste and no dignity. Pete got the drop on the door and waited. Hopalong yanked it open and kissed the muzzle of the weapon before he could stop, and Pete grinned.

"Coming to th' fight?" He loudly asked. "It's going to be a shore 'nough sumptious scrap-just th' kind yu allus like. Come on, th' boys are waitin' for yu."

"Keep quiet!" hissed Hopalong.

"What for?" Asked Pete in surprise. "Didn't yu say yu shore wanted to see that scrap?"

"Shut yore face an' get scarce, or yu'll go home in cans!"

As Hopalong seated himself once more Red strolled up to the door and knocked. Hopalong ripped it open and Red, looking as fierce and worried as he could, asked Hopalong if he was all right. Upon being assured by smoking adjectives that he was, the caller looked relieved and turned thoughtfully away.

"Hey, yu! Come here!" called Hopalong.

Red waved his hand and said that he had to meet a man and clattered down the stairs. Hopalong thought that he, also, had to meet a man and, excusing himself, hastened after his friend and overtook him in the Street, where he forced a confession. Returning to his hostess he told her of the whole outrage, and she was angry at first, but seeing the humorous side of it, she became convulsed with laughter. Her father re-read his paragraph for the thirteenth time and then, slamming the magazine on the floor, asked how many times he was expected to read ten lines before he knew what was in them, and went down to the bar.

Miss Deane regarded her companion with laughing eyes and then became suddenly sober as he came toward her.

"Go to your foreman and tell him that you will shoot to-morrow, for I will see that you do, and I will bring luck to the Bar-20. Be sure to call for me at one o'clock: I will be ready."

He hesitated, bowed, and slowly departed, making his way to Tom Lee's, where his entrance hushed the hilarity which had reigned. Striding to where Buck stood, he placed his hands on his hips and searched the foreman's eyes.

Buck smiled: "Yu ain't mad, are yu?" He asked.

Hopalong relaxed: "No, but blame near it."

Red and the others grabbed him from the rear, and when he had been "buffaloed" into good humor he threw them from him, laughed and waved his hand toward the bar:

"Come up, yu sons-of-guns. Yore a cussed nuisance sometimes, but yore a bully gang all th' same."

Chapter XXV

Mr. Ewalt Draws Cards

Tex Ewalt, cow-puncher, prospector, sometimes a rustler, but always a dude, rode from El Paso in deep disgust at his steady losses at faro and monte. The pecuniary side of these caused him no worry, for he was flush. This pleasing opulence was due to his business ability, for he had recently sold a claim for several thousand dollars. The first operation was simple, being known in Western phraseology as "jumping"; and the second, somewhat more complicated, was known as "salting."

The first of the money spent went for a complete new outfit, and he had parted with just three hundred and seventy dollars to feed his vanity. He desired something contrasty and he procured it. His sombrero, of gray felt a quarter of an inch thick, flaunted a band of black leather, on which was conspicuously displayed a solid silver buckle. His neck was protected by a crimson kerchief of the finest, heaviest silk. His shirt, in pattern the same as those commonly worn in the cow country, was of buckskin, soft as a baby's cheek and impervious to water, and the Angora goatskin chaps, with the long silken hair worn outside, were as white as snow. Around his waist ran loosely a broad, black leather belt supporting a heavy black holster, in which lay its walnut-handled burden, a .44 caliber six-shooter; and thirty center-fire cartridges peeked from their loops, fifteen on a side. His boots, the soles thin and narrow and the heels high, were black and of the finest leather. Huge spurs, having two-inch rowels, were held in place by buckskin straps, on which, also, were silver buckles. Protecting his hands were heavy buckskin gloves, also waterproof, having wide, black gauntlets.

Each dainty hock of his dainty eight-hundred-pound buckskin pony was black, and a black star graced its forehead. Well groomed, with flowing mane and tail, and with the brand on its flank being almost imperceptible, the animal was far different in appearance from most of the cow-ponies. Vicious and high-spirited, it cavorted just enough to show its lines to the best advantage.

The saddle, a famous Cheyenne and forty pounds in weight, was black, richly embossed, and decorated with bits of beaten silver which flashed back the sunlight. At the pommel hung a thirty-foot coil of braided horsehair rope, and at the rear was a Sharp's .50-caliber, breech-loading rifle, its owner having small use for any other make. The color of the bridle was the same as the saddle and it supported a heavy U bit which was capable of a leverage sufficient to break the animal's jaw.

Tex was proud of his outfit, but his face wore a frown-not there only on acount of his losses, but also by reason of his mission, for under all his finery beat a heart as black as any in the cow country. For months he had smothered hot hatred and he was now on his way to ease himself of it.

He and Slim Travennes had once exchanged shots with Hopalong in Santa Fe, and the month which he had spent in bed was not pleasing, and from that encounter had sprung the hatred. That he had been in the wrong made no difference with him. Some months later he had learned of the death of Slim, and it was due to the same man. That Slim had again been in the wrong also made no difference, for he realized the fact and nothing else.

Lately he had been told of the death of Slippery Trendley and Deacon Rankin, and he accepted their passing as a personal affront. That they had been caught red-handed in cattle stealing of huge proportions and received only what was customary under the conditions formed no excuse in his mind for their passing. He was now on his way to attend the carnival at Muddy Wells, knowing that his enemy would be sure to be there.

While passing through Las Cruces he met Porous Johnson and Silent Somes, who were thirsty and who proclaimed that fact, whereupon he relieved them of their torment and, looking forward to more treatment of a similar nature, they gladly accompanied him without asking why or where.

As they left the town in their rear Tex turned in his saddle and surveyed them with a cynical smile.

"Have yu heard anything of Trendley?" He asked.

They shook their heads.

"Him an' th' Deacon was killed over in th' Panhandle," he said.

"What!" chorused the pair.

"Jack Dorman, Shorty Danvers, Charley Teale, Stiffhat Bailey, Billy Jackson, Terry Nolan an' Sailor Carson was lynched."

"What!" they shouted.

"Fish O'Brien, Pinochle Schmidt, Tom Wilkins, Apache Gordon, Charley of th' Bar Y, Penobscot Hughes an' about twenty others died fightin'."

Porous looked his astonishment: "Cavalry?"

"An' I'm going after th' dogs who did it," he continued, ignoring the question. "Are yu with me? —Yu used to pal with some of them, didn't yu?"

"We did, an' we're shore with yu!" cried Porous.

"Yore right," endorsed Silent. "But who done it?"

"That gang what's punchin' for th' Bar-20-Hopalong Cassidy is th' one I'm pining for. Yu fellers can take care of Peters an' Connors."

The two stiffened and exchanged glances of uncertainty and apprehension. The outfit of the Bar-20 was too well known to cause exuberant joy to spring from the idea of war with it, and well in the center of all the tales concerning it were the persons Tex had named. To deliberately set forth with the avowed intention of planting these was not at all calculated to induce sweet dreams.

Tex sneered his contempt.

"Yore shore uneasy: yu ain't a-scared, are yu?" He drawled. Porous relaxed and made a show of subduing his horse: "I reckon I ain't scared plumb to death. Yu can deal me a hand," he asserted.

"I'll draw cards too," hastily announced Silent, buttoning his vest. "Tell us about that jamboree over in th' Panhandle."

Tex repeated the story as he had heard it from a bibulous member of the Barred Horseshoe, and then added a little of torture as a sauce to whet their appetites for revenge.

"How did Trendley cash in?" Asked Porous.

"Nobody knows except that bum from th' Tin-Cup. I'll get him later. I'd a got Cassidy up in Santa Fe, too, if it wasn't for th' sun in my eyes. Me an' Slim loosened up on him in th' Plaza, but we couldn't see nothing with him a-standin' against th' sun."

"Where's Slim now?" Asked Porous. "I ain't seen him for some time."

"Slim's with Trendley," replied Tex. "Cassidy handed him over to St. Pete at Cactus Springs. Him an' Connors sicked their outfit on him an' his vigilantes, bein helped some by th' O-Bar-O. They wiped th' town plumb off th' earth, an' now I'm going to do some wipin' of my own account. I'll prune that gang of some of its blossoms afore long. It's cost me seventeen friends so far, an' I'm going to stop th' leak, or make another."

They entered Muddy Wells at sunrise on the day of the carnival and, eating a hearty breakfast, sallied forth to do their share toward making the festivities a success.

The first step considered necessary for the acquirement of case and polish was begun at the nearest bar, and Tex, being the host, was so liberal that his friends had reached a most auspicious state when they followed him to Tom Lee's.

Tex was too wise to lose his head through drink and had taken only enough to make him careless of consequences. Porous was determined to sing "Annie Laurie," although he hung on the last word of the first line until out of breath and then began anew. Silent, not wishing to be outdone, bawled at the top of his lungs a medley of music-hall words to the air of a hymn.

Tex, walking as awkwardly as any cow-puncher, approached Tom Lee's, his two friends trailing erratically, arm in arm, in his rear. Swinging his arm he struck the door a resounding blow and entered, hand on gun, as it crashed back. Porous and Silent stood in the doorway and quarreled as to what each should drink and, compromising, lurched in and seated themselves on a table and resumed their vocal perpetrations.

Tex swaggered over to the bar and tossed a quarter upon it: "Corn juice," he laconically exclaimed. Tossing off the liquor and glancing at his howling friends, he shrugged his shoulders and strode out by the rear door, slamming it after him. Porous and Silent, recounting friends who had "cashed in" fell to weeping and they were thus occupied when Hopalong and Buck entered, closely followed by the rest of the outfit.

Buck walked to the bar and was followed by Hopalong, who declined his foreman's offer to treat. Tom Lee set a bottle at Buck's elbow and placed his hands against the bar.

"Friend of yourn just hit the back trail," he remarked to Hopalong. "He was primed some for trouble, too," he added.

"Yaas?" Drawled Hopalong with little interest.

The proprietor restacked the few glasses and wiped off the bar. "Them's his pardners," he said, indicating the pair on the table.

Hopalong turned his head and gravely scrutinized them. Porous was bemoaning the death of Slim Travennes and Hopalong frowned.

"Don't reckon he's no relation of mine," he grunted.

"Well, he ain't yore sister," replied Tom Lee, grinning.

"What's his brand?" Asked the puncher.

"I reckon he's a maverick, 'though yu put yore brand on him up to Santa Fe a couple of years back. Since he's throwed back on yore range I reckon he's yourn if yu wants him."

"I reckon Tex is some sore," remarked Hopalong, rolling a cigarette.

"I reckon he is," replied the proprietor, tossing Buck's quarter in the cash box. "But, say, you should oughter see his rig."

"Yaas?"

"He's shore a cow-punch dude-my, but he's some sumptious an' highfalutin'. An' bad? Why, he reckons th' Lord never brewed a more high-toned brand of cussedness than his'n. He shore reckons he's the baddest man that ever simmered."

"How'd he look as th' leadin' man in a necktie festival?" Blazed Johnny from across the room, feeling called upon to help the conversation.

"He'd be a howlin' success, son," replied Skinny Thompson, "judgin' by his friends what we elevated over in th' Panhandle."

Lanky Smith leaned forward with his elbow on the table, resting his chin in the palm of his hand: "Is Ewalt still a-layin' for yu, Hopalong?" He asked.

Hopalong turned wearily and tossed his half-consumed cigarette into the box of sand which did duty as a cuspidore: "I reckon so; an' he shore can hatch whenever he gets good an ready, too."

"He's probably a-broodin' over past grievances," offered Johnny, as he suddenly pushed Lanky's elbow from the table, nearly causing a catastrophe.

"Yu'll be broodin' over present grievances if yu don't look out, yu everlastin' nuisance yu," growled Lanky, planting his elbow in its former position with an emphasis which conveyed a warning.

"These bantams ruffle my feathers," remarked Red. "They go around braggin' about th' egg they're goin' to lay an' do enough cacklin' to furnish music for a dozen. Then when th' affair comes off yu'll generally find they's been settin' on a door-knob."

"Did yu ever see a hen leave th' walks of peace an' bugs an' rustle hell-bent across th' trail plumb in front of a cayuse?" Asked Buck. "They'll leave off rustlin' grub an' become candidates for th' graveyard just for cussedness. Well, a whole lot of men are th' same way. How many times have I seen them swagger into a gin shop an' try to run things sudden an' hard, an' that with half a dozen better men in th' same room? There's shore a-plenty of trouble a-comin' to every man without rustlin' around for more.

"'Member that time yu an' Frenchy tried to run th' little town of Frozen Nose, up in Montana?" Asked Johnny, winking at the rest.

"An' we did run it, for a while," responded Buck. "But that only goes to show that most young men are chumps-we were just about yore age then."

Red laughed at the youngster's discomfiture: "That little squib of yourn shore touched her off—I reckon we irrigates on yu this time, don't we?"

"Th' more th' Kid talks, th' more money he needs," remarked Lanky, placing his glass on the bar. "He had to blow me an' Skinny twice last night."

"I got two more after yu left," added Skinny "He shore oughter practice keeping still."

At one o'clock sharp Hopalong walked up to the clerk of the hotel and grinned. The clerk looked up:

"Hullo, Cassidy?" He exclaimed, genially. "What was all that fuss about this mornin' when I was away? I haven't seen you for a long time, have I? How are you?"

"That fuss was a fool joke of Buck's, an' I wish they had been throwed out," Hopalong replied. "What I want to know is if Miss Deane is in her room. Yu see, I have a date with her."

The clerk grinned:

"So she's roped you, too, has she?"

"What do yu mean?" Asked Hopalong in surprise. "Well, well," laughed the clerk. "You punchers are easy. Any third-rate actress that looks good to eat can rope you fellows, all right. Now look here, Laura, you keep shy of her corral, or you'll be broke so quick you won't believe you ever had a cent: that's straight. This is the third year that she's been here and I know what I'm talking about. How did you come to meet her?"

Hopalong explained the meeting and his friend laughed again:

"Why, she knows this country like a book. She can't get lost anywhere around here. But she's blame clever at catching punchers."

"Well, I reckon I'd better take her, go broke or not," replied Hopalong. "Is she in her room?"

"She is, but she is not alone," responded the clerk. "There is a dude puncher up there with her and she left word here that she was indisposed, which means that you are outlawed."

"Who is he?" Asked Hopalong, having his suspicions. "That friend of yours: Ewalt. He sported a wad this morning when she passed him, and she let him make her acquaintance. He's another easy mark. He'll be busted wide open to-night."

"I reckon I'll see Tex," suggested Hopalong, starting for the stairs.

"Come back, you chump!" cried the clerk. "I don't want any shooting here. What do you care about it? Let her have him, for it's an easy way out of it for you. Let him think he's cut you out, for he'll spend all the more freely. Get your crowd and enlighten them-it'll be better than a circus. This may sound like a steer, but it's straight."

Hopalong thought for a minute and then leaned on the cigar case:

"I reckon I'll take about a dozen of yore very best cigars, Charley. Got any real high-toned brands?"

"Cortez panatella-two for a simoleon," Chancy replied. "But, seein' that it's you, I'll throw off a dollar on a dozen. They're a fool notion of the old man, for we can't sell one in a month."

Hopalong dug up a handful and threw one on the counter, lighting another: "Yu light a Cortez panatella with me," he said, pocketing the remainder. "That's five simoleons she didn't get. So long."

He journeyed to Tom Lee's and found his outfit making merry. Passing around his cigars he leaned against the bar and delighted in the first really good smoke he had since he came home from Kansas City.

Johnny Nelson blew a cloud of smoke at the ceiling and paused with a pleased expression on his face:

"This is a lalapoloosa of a cigar," he cried. "Where'd yu get it, an' how many's left?"

"I got it from Charley, an' there's more than yu can buy at fifty a shot."

"Well, I'll just take a few for luck," Johnny responded, running out into the street. Returning in five minutes with both hands full of cigars he passed them around and grinned: "They're birds, all right!"

Hopalong smiled, turned to Buck and related his conversation with Chancy. "What do yu think of that?" He asked as he finished.

"I think Charley oughter be yore guardian," replied the foreman.

"He was," replied Hopalong.

"If we sees Tex we'll all grin hard," laughed Red, making for the door. "Come on to th' contests-Lanky's gone already."

Muddy Wells streamed to the carnival grounds and relieved itself of its enthusiasm and money at the booths on the way. Cow-punchers rubbed elbows with Indians and Mexicans, and the few tourists that were present were delighted with the picturesque scene. The town was full of fakirs and before one of them stood a group of cow-punchers, apparently drinking in the words of a barker.

"Right this way, gents, and see the woman who don't eat. Lived for two years without food, gents. Right this way, gents. Only a quarter of a dollar. Get your tickets, gents, and see —"

Red pushed forward:

"What did yu say, pard?" He asked. "I'm a little off in my near ear. What's that about eatin' a woman for two years?"

"The greatest wonder of the age, gents. The wom —"

"Any discount for th' gang?" Asked Buck, gawking.

"Why don't yu quit smokin' an' buy th' lady a meal?" Asked Johnny from the center of the group.

"Th' cane yu ring th' cane yu get!" came from the other side of the street and Hopalong purchased rings for the outfit. Twenty-four rings got one cane, and it was divided between them as they wended their way toward the grounds.

"That makes six wheels she didn't get," murmured Hopalong. As they passed the snake charmer's booth they saw Tex and his companion ahead of them in the crowd, and they grinned broadly. "I like th' front row in th' balcony," remarked Johnny, who had been to Kansas City. "Don't cry in th' second act-it ain't real," laughed Red. "We'll hang John Brown on a sour appletree-in th' Panhandle," sang Skinny as they passed them.

Arriving at the grounds they hunted up the registration committee and entered in the contests. As Hopalong signed for the revolver competition he was rudely pushed aside and Tex wrote his name under that of his enemy. Hopalong was about to show quick resentment for the insult, but thought of what Charley had said, and he grinned sympathetically. The seats were filling rapidly, and the outfit went along the ground looking for friends. A bugle sounded and a hush swept over the crowd as the announcement was made for the first event.

"Broncho-busting-Red Devil, never ridden: Frenchy McAllister, Tin-Cup, Montana; Meteor, killed his man: Skinny Thompson, Bar-20, Texas; Vixen, never ridden: Lefty Allen, O-Bar-O, Texas."

All eyes were focused on the plain where the horse was being led out for the first trial. After the usual preliminaries had been gone through Frenchy walked over to it, vaulted in the saddle and the bandage was torn from the animal's eyes. For ten minutes the onlookers were held spellbound by the fight before them, and then the horse kicked and galloped away and Frenchy was picked up and carried from the field.

"Too bad!" cried Buck, running from the outfit.

"Did yu see it?" asked Johnny excitedly, "Th' cinch busted." Another horse was led out and Skinny Thompson vaulted to the saddle, and after a fight of half an hour rode the animal from the enclosure to the clamorous shouts of his friends. Lefty Allen also rode his mount from the same gate, but took ten minutes more in which to do it.

The announcer conferred with the timekeepers and then stepped forward: "First, Skinny Thompson, Bar-20, thirty minutes and ten seconds; second, Lefty Allen, O-Bar-O, forty minutes and seven seconds."

Skinny returned to his friends shamefacedly and did not look as if he had just won a championship. They made way for him, and Johnny, who could not restrain his enthusiasm pounded him on the back and cried: "Yu old son-of-a-gun!"

The announcer again came forward and gave out the competitors for the next contest, steer-roping and tying. Lanky Smith arose and, coiling his rope carefully, disappeared into the crowd. The fun was not so great in this, but when he returned to his outfit with the phenomenal time of six minutes and eight seconds for his string of ten steers, with twenty-two seconds for one of them, they gave him vociferous greeting. Three of his steers had gotten up after he had leaped from his saddle to tie them, but his horse had taken care of that. His nearest rival was one minute over him and Lanky retained the championship.

Red Connors shot with such accuracy in the rifle contest as to run his points twenty per cent higher than Waffles, of the O-Bar-O, and won the new rifle.

The main interest centered in the revolver contest, for it was known that the present champion was to defend his title against an enemy and fears were expressed in the crowd that there would be an "accident." Buck Peters and Red stood just behind the firing line with their hands on hips, and Tex, seeing the precautions, smiled grimly as he advanced to the line.

Six bottles, with their necks an inch above a board, stood twenty paces from him, and he broke them all in as many shots, taking twelve seconds in which to do it. Hopalong followed him and tied the score. Three tin balls rolling erratically in a blanket supported by two men were sent flying into the air in four shots, Tex taking six seconds. His competitor sent them from the blanket in three shots and in the same time. In slow shooting from sights Tex passed his rival in points and stood to win. There was but one more event to be contested and in it Hopalong found his joy.

Shooting from the hip when the draw is timed is not the sport of even good shots, and when Tex made sixty points out of a possible hundred, he felt that he had shot well. When Hopalong went to the line his friends knew that they would now see shooting such as would be almost unbelievable, that the best draw-and-shoot marksman in their State was the man who limped slightly as he advanced and who chewed reflectively on his fifty-cent cigar. He wore two guns and he stepped with confidence before the marshal of the town, who was also judge of the contest.

The iron ball which lay on the ground was small enough for the use of a rifle and could hardly be seen from the rear seats of the amphitheater. There was a word spoken by the timekeeper, and a gloved hand flashed down and up, and the ball danced and spun and leaped and rolled as shot after shot followed it with a precision and speed which brought the audience to a heavy silence. Taking the gun which Buck tossed to him and throwing it into the empty holster, he awaited the signal, and then smoke poured from his hips and the ball jumped continuously. Both guns emptied in the two-hand shooting, he wheeled and jerked loose the guns which the marshal wore, spinning around without a pause, the target hardly ceasing in its rolling. Under his arms he shot, backward and between his legs; leaping from side to side, ducking and dodging, following the ball wherever it went. Reloading the weapons quickly, he stepped forward and followed the ball until once more his guns were empty. Then he turned and walked back to the side of the marshal, smiling a little. His friends, and there were many in the crowd, torn from their affected nonchalance by shooting the like of which they had not attributed even to him, roared and shouted and danced in a frenzy of delight.

Red also threw his guns to Hopalong, who caught them in the air and turning, faced Tex, who stood white of face and completely lost in the forgetfulness of admiration and amazement. The guns jerked again and a button flew from the buckskin shirt of his enemy; another tore a flower from his breast and another drove it into the ground at his feet as others stirred his hair and cut the buckle off his pretty sombrero. Tex, dazed, but wise enough to stand quiet, felt his belt tear loose and drop to his feet, felt a spur rip from its strap and saw his cigarette leap from his lips. Throwing the guns to Red, Hopalong laughed and abruptly turned and was lost in the crowd.

For several seconds there was silence, but when the dazed minds realized what their eyes had seen, there arose a roar which shook the houses in the town. Roar after roar thundered forth and was sent crashing back again by the distant walls, sweeping down on the discomfited dude and causing him to slink into the crowd to find a place less conspicuous. He was white yet and keen fear gripped his heart as he realized that he had come to the carnival with the expressed purpose of killing his enemy in fair combat. The whole town knew it, for he had taken pains to spread the news.

The woman he had been with knew it from words which she had overheard while on her way to the grounds with him. His friends knew it and would laugh him into forgetfulness as the fool who boasted. Now he understood why he had lost so many friends: they had attempted what he had sworn to attempt. Look where he would he could see only a smoke-wrapped demon who moved and shot with a speed incredible. There was reason why Slim had died. There was reason why Porous and Silent had paled when they learned of their mission.

He hated his conspicuous clothes and his pretty broncho, and the woman who had gotten him to squander his money, and who was doubtless convulsed with laughter at his expense. He worked himself into a passion which knew no fear and he ran for the streets of the town, there to make good his boast or to die. When he found his enemy he felt himself grasped with a grip of steel and Buck Peters swung him around and grinned maliciously in his face:

"You plaything!" hoarsely whispered the foreman. "Why don't yu get away while yu can? Why do yu want to throw yoreself against certain death? I don't want my pleasure marred by a murder, an' that is what it will be if yu makes a gun-play at Hopalong. He'll shoot yu as he did yore buttons. Take yore pretty clothes an' yore pretty cayuse an' go where this is not known, an' if ever again yu feels like killing Hopalong, get drunk an' forget it."

The Coming of Cassidy and Others

Suddenly a rope .   .   .   yanked him from the saddle

[Page 342]

Preface

It was on one of my annual visits to the ranch that Red, whose welcome always seemed a little warmer than that of the others, finally took me back to the beginning. My friendship with

112

the outfit did not begin until some years after the fight at Buckskin, and, while I was familiar with that affair and with the history of the outfit from that time on, I had never seemed to make much headway back of that encounter. And I must confess that if I had depended upon the rest of the outfit for enlightenment I should have learned very little of its earlier exploits. A more secretive and bashful crowd, when it came to their own achievements, would be hard to find. But Red, the big, smiling, under-foreman, at last completely thawed and during the last few weeks of my stay, told me story after story about the earlier days of the ranch and the parts played by each member of the outfit. Names that I had heard mentioned casually now meant something to me; the characters stepped out of the obscurity of the past to act their parts again. To my mind's eye came Jimmy Price, even more mischievous than Johnny Nelson; "Butch" Lynch and Charley James, who erred in judgment; the coming and going of Sammy Porter, and why "You-Bet" Somes never arrived; and others who did their best, or worst, and went their way. The tales will follow, as closely as possible, in chronological order. Between some of them the interval is short; between others, long; the less interesting stories that should fill those gaps may well be omitted.

It was in the '70s, when the buffalo were fast disappearing from the state, and the hunters were beginning to turn to other ways of earning a living, that Buck Peters stopped his wagon on the banks of Snake Creek and built himself a sod dugout in the heart of a country forbidding and full of perils. It was said that he was only the agent for an eastern syndicate that, carried away by the prospects of the cattle industry, bought a "ranch," which later was found to be entirely strange to cattle. As a matter of fact there were no cows within three hundred miles of it, and there never had been. Somehow the syndicate got in touch with Buck and sent him out to look things over and make a report to them. This he did, and in his report he stated that the "ranch" was split in two parts by about forty square miles of public land, which he recommended that he be allowed to buy according to his judgment. When everything was settled the syndicate found that they owned the west, and best, bank of an unfailing river and both banks of an unfailing creek for a distance of about thirty miles. The strip was not very wide then, but it did not need to be, for it cut off the back-lying range from water and rendered it useless to anyone but his employers. Westward there was no water to amount to anything for one hundred miles. When this had been digested thoroughly by the syndicate it caused Buck's next pay check to be twice the size of the first.

He managed to live through the winter, and the following spring a herd of about two thousand or more poor cattle was delivered to him, and he noticed at once that fully half of them were unbranded; but mavericks were cows, and in those days it was not questionable to brand them. Persuading two members of the drive outfit to work for him he settled down to face the work and perils of ranching in a wild country. One of these two men, George Travis, did not work long; the other was the man who told me these tales. Red went back with the drive outfit, but in Buck's wagon, to return in four weeks with it heaped full of necessities, and to find that troubles already had begun. Buck's trust was not misplaced. It was during Red's absence that Bill Cassidy, later to be known by a more descriptive name, appeared upon the scene and played his cards.

C. E. M.

I

The Coming of Cassidy

The trail boss shook his fist after the departing puncher and swore softly. He hated to lose a man at this time and he had been a little reckless in threatening to "fire" him; but in a gun-fighting outfit there was no room for a hothead. "Cimarron" was boss of the outfit that was driving a large herd of cattle to California, a feat that had been accomplished before, but that no man cared to attempt the second time. Had his soul been enriched by the gift of prophecy he would have turned back. As it was he returned to the work ahead of him. "Aw, let him go," he growled. "He 's wuss off 'n I am, an' he 'll find it out quick. I never did see nobody what got crazy mad so quick as him."

"Bill" Cassidy, not yet of age, but a man in stature and strength, rode north because it promised him civilization quicker than any other way except the back trail, and he was tired of the coast range. He had forgotten the trail-boss during the last three days of his solitary journeying and the fact that he was in the center of an uninhabited country nearly as large as a good-sized state gave him no concern; he was equipped for two weeks, and fortified by youth's confidence.

All day long he rode, around mesas and through draws, detouring to avoid canyons and bearing steadily northward with a certainty that was a heritage. Gradually the great bulk of mesas swung off to the west, and to the east the range grew steadily more level as it swept toward the peaceful river lying in the distant valley like a carelessly flung rope of silver. The forest vegetation, so luxuriant along the rivers and draws a day or two before, was now rarely seen, while chaparrals and stunted mesquite became more common.

He was more than twenty-five hundred feet above the ocean, on a great plateau broken by mesas that stretched away for miles in a vast sea of grass. There was just enough tang in the dry April air to make riding a pleasure and he did not mind the dryness of the season. Twice that day he detoured to ride around prairie-dog towns and the sight of buffalo skeletons lying in groups was not rare. Alert and contemptuous gray wolves gave him a passing glance, but the coyotes, slinking a little farther off, watched him with more interest. Occasionally he had a shot at antelope and once was successful.

Warned by the gathering dusk he was casting about for the most favorable spot for his blanket and fire when a horseman swung into sight out of a draw and reined in quickly. Bill's hand fell carelessly to his side while he regarded the stranger, who spoke first, and with a restrained welcoming gladness in his voice. "Howd'y, Stranger! You plumb surprised me."

Bill's examination told him that the other was stocky, compactly built, with a pleasing face and a "good eye." His age was about thirty and the surface indications were very favorable. "Some surprised myself," he replied. "Ridin' my way?"

"Far's th' house," smiled the other. "Better join us. Couple of buffalo hunters dropped in awhile back."

"They 'll go a long way before they 'll find buffalo," Bill responded, suspiciously. Glancing around he readily picked out the rectangular blot in the valley, though it was no easy feat. "Huntin' or ranchin'?" he inquired in tones devoid of curiosity.

"Ranchin'," smiled the other. "Hefty proposition, up here, I reckon. Th' wolves 'll walk in under yore nose. But I ain't seen no Injuns."

"You will," was the calm reply. "You 'll see a couple, first; an' then th' whole cussed tribe. *They* ain't got no buffalo no more, neither."

Buck glanced at him sharply and thought of the hunters, but he nodded. "Yes. But if that couple don't go back?" he asked, referring to the Indians.

"Then you 'll save a little time."

"Well, let 'em come. I 'm here to stay, one way or th' other. But, anyhow, I ain't got no border ruffians like they have over in th' Panhandle. They 're worse 'n Injuns."

"Yes," agreed Bill. "Th' war ain't ended yet for some of them fellers. Ex-guerrillas, lots of 'em."

When they reached the house the buffalo hunters were arguing about their next day's ride and the elder, looking up, appealed to Bill. "Howd'y, Stranger. Ain't come 'cross no buffaler signs, hev ye?"

Bill smiled. "Bones an' old chips. But th' gray wolves was headin' southwest."

"What 'd I tell you?" triumphantly exclaimed the younger hunter.

"Well, they ain't much dif'rence, is they?" growled his companion.

Bill missed nothing the hunters said or did and during the silent meal had a good chance to study their faces. When the pipes were going and the supper wreck cleaned away, Buck leaned against the wall and looked across the room at the latest arrival. "Don't want a job, do you?" he asked.

Bill shook his head slowly, wondering why the hunters had frowned at a job being offered on another man's ranch. "I 'm headed north. But I 'll give you a hand for a week if you need me," he offered.

Buck smiled. "Much obliged, friend; but it 'll leave me worse off than before. My other puncher 'll be back in a few weeks with th' supplies, but I need four men all year 'round. I got a thousand head to brand yet."

The elder hunter looked up. "Drive 'em back to cow-country an' sell 'em, or locate there," he suggested.

Buck's glance was as sharp as his reply, for he could n't believe that the hunter had so soon forgotten what he had been told regarding the ownership of the cattle. "I don't own 'em. This range is bought an' paid for. I won't lay down."

"I done forgot they ain't yourn," hastily replied the hunter, smiling to himself. Stolen cattle cannot go back.

"If they was I 'd stay," crisply retorted Buck. "I ain't quittin' nothin' I starts."

"How many 'll you have nex' spring?" grinned the younger hunter. He was surprised by the sharpness of the response. "More 'n I 've got now, in spite of h —!"

Bill nodded approval. He felt a sudden, warm liking for this rugged man who would not quit in the face of such handicaps. He liked game men, better if they were square, and he believed this foreman was as square as he was game. "By th' Lord!" he ejaculated. "For a plugged peso I 'd stay with you!"

Buck smiled warmly. "Would good money do? But don't you stay if you oughtn't, son."

When the light was out Bill lay awake for a long time, his mind busy with his evening's observations, and they pleased him so little that he did not close his eyes until assured by the breathing of the hunters that they were asleep. His Colt, which should have been hanging in its holster on the wall where he had left it, lay unsheathed close to his thigh and he awakened frequently during the night so keyed was he for the slightest sound. Up first in the morning, he replaced the gun in its scabbard before the others opened their eyes, and it was not until the hunters had ridden out of sight into the southwest that he entirely relaxed his vigilance. Saying good-by to the two cowmen was not without regrets, but he shook hands heartily with them and swung decisively northward.

He had been riding perhaps two hours, thinking about the little ranch and the hunters, when he stopped suddenly on the very brink of a sheer drop of two hundred feet. In his abstraction he had ridden up the sloping southern face of the mesa without noticing it. "Bet there ain't another like this for a hundred miles," he laughed, and then ceased abruptly and started with unbelieving eyes at the mouth of a draw not far away. A trotting line of gray wolves was emerging from it and swinging toward the south-west ten abreast. He had never heard of such a thing before and watched them in amazement. "Well, I'm —!" he exclaimed, and his Colt flashed rapidly at the pack. Two or three dropped, but the trotting line only swerved a little without pause or a change of pace and soon was lost in another draw. "Why, they 're single hunters," he muttered. "Huh! I won't never tell this. I can't hardly believe it myself. How 'bout you, Ring-Bone?" he asked the horse.

Turning, he rode around a rugged pinnacle of rock and stopped again, gazing steadily along the back trail. Far away in a valley two black dots were crawling over a patch of sand and he knew them to be horsemen. His face slowly reddened with anger at the espionage, for he had not thought the cowmen could doubt his good will and honesty. Then suddenly he swore and spurred forward to cover those miles as speedily as possible. "Come on, ol' Hammer-Head!" he cried. "We're goin' back!"

The hunters had finally decided they would ride into the southwest and had ridden off in that direction. But they had detoured and swung north to see him pass and be sure he was not in their way. Now, satisfied upon that point, they were going back to that herd of cattle, easily turned from skinning buffalo to cattle, and on a large scale. To do this they would have to kill two men and then, waiting for the absent puncher to return with the wagon, kill him and load down the vehicle with skins. "Like h—l they will!" he gritted. "Three or none, you piruts. Come on, White-Eye! Don't sleep all th' time; an' don't light often'r once every ten yards, you saddle-galled, barrel-bellied runt!"

Into hollows, out again; shooting down steep-banked draws and avoiding cacti and chaparral with cat-like agility, the much-described little pony butted the wind in front and left a low-lying cloud of dust swirling behind as it whirred at top speed with choppy, tied-in stride in a winding circle for the humble sod hut on Snake Creek. The rider growled at the evident speed of the two men ahead, for he had not gained upon them despite his efforts. "If I 'm too late to stop it, I 'll clean th' slate, anyhow," he snapped. "Even if I has to ambush! Will you run?" he demanded, and the wild-eyed little bundle of whalebone and steel found a little more speed in its flashing legs.

The rider now began to accept what cover he could find and when he neared the hut left the shelter of the last, low hill for that afforded by a draw leading to within a hundred yards of the dugout's rear wall. Dismounting, he ran lightly forward on foot, alert and with every sense strained for a warning.

Reaching the wall he peered around the corner and stifled an exclamation. Buck's puncher, a knife in his back, lay head down the sloping path. Placing his ear to the wall he listened intently for some moments and then suddenly caught sight of a shadow slowly creeping past his toes. Quickly as he sprang aside he barely missed the flashing knife and the bulk of the man behind it, whose hand, outflung to save his balance, accidentally knocked the Colt from Bill's grasp and sent it spinning twenty feet away.

Without a word they leaped together, fighting silently, both trying to gain the gun in the hunter's holster and trying to keep the other from it. Bill, forcing the fighting in hopes that his youth would stand a hot pace better than the other's years, pushed his enemy back against the low roof of the dugout; but as the hunter tripped over it and fell backward, he pulled Bill with him. Fighting desperately they rolled across the roof and dropped to the sloping earth at the doorway, so tightly locked in each other's arms that the jar did not separate them. The hunter, falling underneath, got the worst of the fall but kept on fighting. Crashing into the door head first, they sent it swinging back against the wall and followed it, bumping down the two steps still locked together.

Bill possessed strength remarkable for his years and build and he was hard as iron; but he had met a man who had the sinewy strength of the plainsman, whose greater age was offset by greater weight and the youth was constantly so close to defeat that a single false move would have been fatal. But luck favored him, for as they surged around the room they crashed into the heavy table and fell with it on top of them. The hunter got its full weight and the gash in his forehead filled his eyes with blood. By a desperate effort he pinned Bill's arm under his knee and with his left hand secured a throat grip, but the under man wriggled furiously and bridged so suddenly as to throw the hunter off him and Bill's freed hand, crashing full into the other's stomach, flashed back to release the weakened throat grip and jam the tensed fingers between his teeth, holding them there with all the power of his jaws. The dazed and gasping hunter, bending forward instinctively, felt his own throat seized and was dragged underneath his furious opponent.

In his Berserker rage Bill had forgotten about the gun, his fury sweeping everything from him but the primal desire to kill with his hands, to rend and crush like an animal. He was brought to his senses very sharply by the jarring, crashing roar of the six-shooter, the powder blowing away part of his shirt and burning his side. Twisting sideways he grasped the weapon with one hand, the wrist with the other and bent the gun slowly back, forcing its muzzle farther and farther from him. The hunter, at last managing to free his left hand from the other's teeth, found it useless when he tried to release the younger man's grip of the gun; and the Colt, roaring again, dropped from its owner's hand as he relaxed.

The victor leaned against the wall, his breath coming in great, sobbing gulps, his knees sagging and his head near bursting. He reeled across the wrecked room, gulped down a drink of whisky from the bottle on the shelf and, stumbling, groped his way to the outer air where he flung himself down on the ground, dazed and dizzy. When he opened his eyes the air seemed to be filled with flashes of fire and huge, black fantastic blots that changed form with great swiftness and the hut danced and shifted like a thing of life. Hot bands seemed to encircle his throat and the throbbing in his temples was like blows of a hammer. While he writhed and fought for breath a faint gunshot reached his ears and found him apathetic. But the second, following closely upon the first, seemed clearer and brought him to himself long enough to make him arise and stumble to his horse, and claw his way into the saddle. The animal, maddened by the steady thrust of the spurs, pitched viciously and bolted; but the rider had learned his art in the sternest school in the world, the "busting" corrals of the great Southwest, and he not only stuck to the saddle, but guided the fighting animal through a barranca almost choked with obstructions.

Stretched full length in a crevice near the top of a mesa lay the other hunter, his rifle trained on a small bowlder several hundred yards down and across the draw. His first shot had been an inexcusable blunder for a marksman like himself and now he had a desperate man and a very capable shot opposing him. If Buck could hold out until nightfall he could slip away in the darkness and do some stalking on his own account.

For half an hour they had lain thus, neither daring to take sight. Buck could not leave the shelter of the bowlder because the high ground behind him offered no cover; but the hunter, tiring of the fruitless wait, wriggled back into the crevice, arose and slipped away, intending to crawl to the edge of the mesa further down and get in a shot from a new angle before his enemy learned of the shift; and this shot would not be a blunder. He had just lowered himself down a steep wall when the noise of rolling pebbles caused him to look around, expecting to see his friend. Bill was just turning the corner of the wall and their eyes met at the same instant.

"'Nds up!" snapped the youth, his Colt glinting as it swung up. The hunter, gripping the rifle firmly, looked into the angry eyes of the other, and slowly obeyed. Bill, watching the rifle intently, forthwith learned a lesson he never forgot: never to watch a gun, but the eyes of the man who has it. The left hand of the hunter seemed to melt into smoke, and Bill, firing at the same instant, blundered into a hit when his surprise and carelessness should have cost him dearly. His bullet, missing its intended mark by inches, struck the still moving Colt of the other, knocking it into the air and numbing the hand that held it. A searing pain in his shoulder told him of the closeness of the call and set his lips into a thin, white line. The hunter, needing no words to interpret the look in the youth's eyes, swiftly raised his hands, holding the rifle high above his head, but neglected to take his finger from the trigger.

Bill was not overlooking anything now and he noticed the crooked finger. "Stick th' muzzle *up*, an' pull that trigger," he commanded, sharply. "Now!" he grated. The report came crashing back from half a dozen points as he nodded. "Drop it, an' turn 'round." As the other obeyed he stepped cautiously forward, jammed his Colt into the hunter's back and took possession of a skinning knife. A few moments later the hunter, trussed securely by a forty-foot lariat, lay cursing at the foot of the rock wall.

Bill, collecting the weapons, went off to cache them and then peered over the mesa's edge to look into the draw. A leaden splotch appeared on the rock almost under his nose and launched a crescendo scream into the sky to whine into silence. He ducked and leaped back, grinning foolishly as he realized Buck's error. Turning to approach the edge from another point he felt his sombrero jerk at his head as another bullet, screaming plaintively, followed the first. He dropped like a shot, and commented caustically upon his paucity of brains as he gravely examined the hole in his head gear. "Huh!" he grunted. "I had a fool's luck three times in twenty minutes, —d —d if I 'm goin' to risk th' next turn. *Three* of 'em," he repeated. "I 'm a' Injun from now on. An' that foreman shore can shoot!"

He wriggled to the edge and called out, careful not to let any of his anatomy show above the sky-line. "Hey, Buck! I ain't no buffalo hunter! This is Cassidy, who you wanted to punch for you. Savvy?" He listened, and grinned at the eloquent silence. "You talk too rapid," he laughed. Repeating his statements he listened again, with the same success. "Now I wonder is he stalkin' *me*? Hey, *Buck*!" he shouted.

"Stick yore hands up an' foller 'em with yore face," said Buck's voice from below. Bill raised his arms and slowly stood up. "Now what 'n blazes do *you* want?" demanded the foreman, belligerently.

"Nothin'. Just got them hunters, one of 'em alive. I reckoned mebby you 'd sorta like to know it." He paused, cogitating. "Reckon we better turn him loose when we gets back to th' hut," he suggested. "I'll keep his guns," he added, grinning.

The foreman stuck his head out in sight. "Well, I'm d —d!" he exclaimed, and sank weakly back against the bowlder. "Can you give me a hand?" he muttered.

The words did not carry to the youth on the skyline, but he saw, understood, and, slipping and bumping down the steep wall with more speed than sense, dashed across the draw and up the other side. He nodded sagely as he examined the wound and bound it carefully with the sleeve of his own shirt. "'T ain't much-loss of blood, mostly. Yo 're better off than Travis."

"Travis dead?" whispered Buck. "In th' back! Pore feller, pore feller; didn't have no show. Tell me about it." At the end of the story he nodded. "Yo 're all right, Cassidy; yo 're a white man. He 'd 'a' stood a good chance of gettin' me, 'cept for you." A frown clouded his face and he looked weakly about him as if for an answer to the question that bothered him. "Now what am I goin' to do up here with all these cows?" he muttered.

Bill rolled the wounded man a cigarette and lit it for him, after which he fell to tossing pebbles at a rock further down the hill.

"I reckon it *will* be sorta tough," he replied, slowly. "But I sorta reckoned me an' you, an' that other feller, can make a big ranch out of yore little one. Anyhow, I 'll bet we can have a mighty big time tryin'. A mighty fine time. What you think?"

Buck smiled weakly and shoved out his hand with a visible effort. "We can! Shake, Bill!" he said, contentedly.

II
The Weasel

The winter that followed the coming of Bill Cassidy to the Bar-20 ranch was none too mild to suit the little outfit in the cabin on Snake Creek, but it was not severe enough to cause complaint and they weathered it without trouble to speak of. Down on the big ranges lying closer to the Gulf the winter was so mild as to seem but a brief interruption of summer. It was on this warm, southern range that Skinny Thompson, one bright day of early spring, loped along the trail to Scoria, where he hoped to find his friend, Lanky Smith, and where he determined to put an end to certain rumors that had filtered down to him on the range and filled his days with anger.

He was within sight of the little cow-town when he met Frank Lewis, but recently returned from a cattle drive. Exchanging gossip of a harmless nature, Skinny mildly scored his missing friend and complained about his flea-like ability to get scarce. Lewis, laughing, told him that Lanky had left town two days before bound north. Skinny gravely explained that he always had to look after his missing friend, who was childish, irresponsible and helpless when alone. Lewis laughed heartily as he pictured the absent puncher, and he laughed harder as he pictured the two together. Both lean as bean poles, Skinny stood six feet four, while Lanky was fortunate if he topped five feet by many inches. Also they were inseparable, which made Lewis ask a question. "But how does it come you ain't with him?"

"Well, we was punchin' down south an' has a li'l run-in. When I rid in that night I found he had flitted. What I want to know is what business has he got, siftin' out like that an' makin' me chase after him?"

"I dunno," replied Lewis, amused. "You 're sort of gardjean to him, hey?"

"Well, he gets sort of homesick if I ain't with him, anyhow," replied Skinny, grinning broadly. "An' who 's goin' to look after him when I ain't around?"

"That puts me up a tree," replied Lewis. "I shore can't guess. But you two should ought to 'a' been stuck together, like them other twins was. But if he 'd do a thing like that I 'd think you would n't waste no time on him."

"Well, he *is* too ornery an' downright cussed for any human bein' to worry about very much, or 'sociate with steady an' reg'lar. Why, lookit him gettin' sore on me, an' for nothin'! But I 'm so used to bein' abused I get sort of lost when he ain't around."

"Well," smiled Lewis, "he's went up north to punch for Buck Peters on his li'l ranch on Snake Creek. If you want to go after him, this is th' way I told him to go," and he gave instructions hopelessly inadequate to anyone not a plainsman. Skinny nodded, irritated by what he regarded as the other's painful and unnecessary details and wheeled to ride on. He had started for town when Lewis stopped him with a word.

"Hey," he called. Skinny drew rein and looked around.

"Better ride in cautious like," Lewis remarked, casually. "Somebody was in town when I left-he shore was thirsty. He ain't drinkin' a drop, which has riled him considerable. So-long."

"Huh!" grunted Skinny. "Much obliged. That's one of th' reasons I 'm goin' to town," and he started forward again, tight-lipped and grim.

He rode slowly into Scoria, alert, watching windows, doors and corners, and dismounted before Quiggs' saloon, which was the really "high-toned" thirst parlor in the town. He noticed that the proprietor had put black shades to the windows and door and then, glancing quickly around, entered. He made straight for the partition in the rear of the building, but the proprietor's voice checked him. "You needn't bother, Skinny-there ain't nobody in there; an' I locked th' back door an hour ago." He glanced around the room and added, with studied carelessness: "You don't want to get any reckless today." He mopped the bar slowly and coughed apologetically. "Don't get careless."

"I won't —it's me that's doin' th' hunting today," Skinny replied, meaningly. "Him a-hunting for me yesterday, when he shore knowed I was n't in town, when he knowed he could n't find me! I was getting good an' tired of him, an' so when Walt rode over to see me last night an' told me what th' coyote was doing yesterday, an' what he was yelling around, I just natchurly had to straddle leather an' come in. I can't let him put that onto me. Nobody can call me a card cheat an' a coward an' a few other choice things like he did without seeing me, an' seeing me quick. An' I shore hope he 's sober. Are both of 'em in town, Larry?"

"No; only Dick. But he's making noise enough for two. He shore raised th' devil yesterday."

"Well, I 'm goin' North trailin' Lanky, but before I leave I 'm shore goin' to sweeten things around here. If I go away without getting him he 'll say he scared me out, so I 'll have to do it when I come back, anyhow. You see, it might just as well be today. But th' next time I sit in a game with fellers that can't drop fifty dollars without saying they was cheated I 'll be a blamed sight bigger fool than I am right now. I should n't 'a' taken cards with 'em after what has passed. Why didn't they say they was cheated, then an' there, an' not wait till three days after I left town? All that's bothering me is Sam: if I get his brother when he ain't around, an' then goes North, he 'll say I had to jump th' town to get away from him. But I 'll stop that by giving him his chance at me when I get back."

"Say, why don't you wait a day an' get 'em both before you go?" asked Quigg hopefully.

"Can't: Lanky 's got two days' start on me an' I want to catch him soon as I can."

"I can't get it through my head, nohow," Quigg remarked. "Everybody knows you play square. I reckon they're hard losers."

Skinny laughed shortly: "Why, can't you see it? Last year I beat Dick Bradley out with a woman over in Ballard. Then his fool brother tried to cut in an' beat me out. Cards? H—l!" he snorted, walking towards the door. "You an' everybody else knows—" he stopped suddenly and jerked his gun loose as a shadow fell across the doorsill. Then he laughed and slapped the newcomer on the shoulder: "Hullo, Ace, my boy! You had a narrow squeak then. You want to make more noise when you turn corners, unless somebody 's looking for you with a gun. How are you, anyhow? An' how's yore dad? I 've been going over to see him regular, right along, but I 've been so busy I kept putting it off."

"Dad's better, Skinny; an' I'm feeling too good to be true. What 'll you have?"

"Reckon it's my treat; you wet last th' other time. Ain't that right, Quigg? Shore, I knowed it was."

"All right, here's luck," Ace smiled. "Quigg, that's better stock; an' would you look at th' style-real curtains!"

Quigg grinned. "Got to have 'em. I 'm on th' sunny side of th' street."

"I hear yo 're goin' North," Ace remarked.

"Yes, I am; but how 'd you know about it?"

"Why, it ain't no secret, is it?" asked Ace in surprise. "If it is, you must 'a' told a woman. I heard of it from th' crowd-everybody seems to know about it. Yo 're going up alone, too, ain't you?"

"Well, no, it ain't no secret; an' I am going alone," slowly replied Skinny. "Here, have another."

"All right-this is on me. Here's more luck."

"Where is th' crowd?"

"Keeping under cover for a while to give you plenty of elbow room," Ace replied. "He's sober as a judge, Skinny, an' mad as a rattler. Swears he 'll kill you on sight. An' his brother ain't with him; if he does come in too soon I 'll see he don't make it two to one. Good luck, an' so-long," he said quickly, shaking hands and walking towards the door. He put one hand out first and waved it, slowly stepping to the street and then walking rapidly out of sight.

Skinny looked after him and smiled. "Larry, there 's a blamed fine youngster," he remarked, reflectively. "Well, he ought to be-he had th' best mother God ever put breath into." He thought for a moment and then went slowly towards the door. "I 've heard so much about Bradley's gun-play that I 'm some curious. Reckon I 'll see if it's all true—" and he had leaped through the doorway, gun in hand. There was no shot, no sign of his enemy. A group of men lounged in the door of the "hash house" farther down the street, all friends of his, and he nodded to them. One of them turned quickly and looked down the intersecting street, saying something that made his companions turn and look with him. The man who had been standing quietly by the corner saloon had disappeared. Skinny smiling knowingly, moved closer to Quigg's shack so as to be better able to see around the indicated corner, and half drew the Colt which he had just replaced in the holster. As he drew even with the corner of the building he heard Quigg's warning shout and dropped instantly, a bullet singing over him and into a window of a near-by store. He rolled around the corner, scrambled to his feet and dashed around the rear of the saloon and the corral behind it, crossed the street in four bounds and began to work up behind the buildings on his enemy's side of the street, cold with anger.

"Pot shooting, hey!" he gritted, savagely.

"Says I 'm a-scared to face him, an' then tries *that*. *There*, d—n you!" His Colt exploded and a piece of wood sprang from the corner board of Wright's store. "Missed!" he swore. "Anyhow, I 've notified you, you coyote."

He sprang forward, turned the corner of the store and followed it to the street. When he came to the street end of the wall he leaped past it, his Colt preceding him. Finding no one to dispute with him he moved cautiously towards the other corner and stopped. Giving a quick glance around, he smiled suddenly, for the glass in Quigg's half-open door, with the black curtain behind it, made a fair mirror. He could see the reflection of Wright's corral and Ace leaning against it, ready to handle the brother if he should appear as a belligerent; and he could see along the other side of the store, where Dick Bradley, crouched, was half-way to the street and coming nearer at each slow step.

Skinny, remembering the shot which he had so narrowly escaped, resolved that he would n't take chances with a man who would pot-shoot. He wheeled, slipped back along his side of the building, turned the rear corner and then, spurting, sprang out beyond the other wall, crying: "Here!"

Bradley, startled, fired under his arm as he leaped aside. Turning while in the air, his half-raised Colt described a swift, short arc and roared as he alighted. As the bullet sang past his enemy's ear he staggered and fell, —and Skinny's smoking gun chocked into its holster.

"There, you coyote!" muttered the victor. "Yore brother is next if he wants to take it up."

* * * * *

As night fell Skinny rode into a small grove and prepared to camp there. Picketing his horse, he removed the saddle and dropped it where he would sleep, for a saddle makes a fair pillow. He threw his blanket after it and then started a quick, hot fire for his coffee-making. While gathering fuel for it he came across a large log and determined to use it for his night fire, and for that purpose carried it back to camp with him. It was not long before he had reduced the provisions in his saddle-bags and leaned back against a tree to enjoy a smoke. Suddenly he knocked the ashes from his pipe and grew thoughtful, finally slipping it into his pocket and getting up.

"That coyote's brother will know I went North an' all about it," he muttered. "He knows I 've got to camp tonight an' he can foller a trail as good as th' next man. An' he knows I shot his brother. I reckon, mebby, he 'll be some surprised."

An hour later a blanket-covered figure lay with its carefully covered feet to the fire, and its head, sheltered from the night air by a sombrero, lay on the saddle. A rifle barrel projected above the saddle, the dim flickering light of the green-wood fire and a stray beam or two from the moon glinted from its rustless surface. The fire was badly constructed, giving almost no light, while the leaves overhead shut out most of the moonlight.

Thirty yards away, in another clearing, a horse moved about at the end of a lariat and contentedly cropped the rich grass, enjoying a good night's rest. An hour passed, another, and a third and fourth, and then the horse's ears flicked forward as it turned its head to see what approached.

A crouched figure moved stealthily forward to the edge of the clearing, paused to read the brand on the animal's flank and then moved off towards the fitful light of the smoking fire. Closer and closer it drew until it made out the indistinct blanketed figure on the ground. A glint from the rifle barrel caused it to shrink back deeper into the shadows and raise the weapon it carried. For half a minute it stood thus and then, holding back the trigger of the rifle so there would be no warning clicks, drew the hammer to a full cock and let the trigger fall into place, slowly moving forward all the while. A passing breeze fanned the fire for an instant and threw the grotesque shadow of a stump across the quiet figure in the clearing.

The skulker raised his rifle and waited until he had figured out the exact mark and then a burst of fire and smoke leaped into the brush. He bent low to look under the smoke cloud and saw that the figure had not moved. Another flash split the night and then, assured beyond a doubt, he moved forward quickly.

"First shot!" he exclaimed with satisfaction. "I reckons you won't do no boastin' 'bout killin' Dick, d —n you!"

As he was about to drop to his knees to search the body he started and sprang back, glancing fearfully around as he drew his Colt.

"Han's up!" came the command from the edge of the clearing as a man stepped into sight. "I reckon —" Skinny leaped aside as the other's gun roared out and fired from his hip; and Sam Bradley plunged across the blanket-covered log and leaves.

"There," Skinny soliloquized, moving forward. "I knowed they was coyotes, *both* of 'em. Knowed it all th' time."

Two days north of Skinny on the bank of Little Wind River a fire was burning itself out, while four men lay on the sand or squatted on their heels and watched it contentedly. "Yes, I got plumb sick of that country," Lanky Smith was saying, "an' when Buck sent for me to go up an' help him out, I pulls up, an' here I am."

"I never heard of th' Bar-20," replied a little, wizened man, whose eyes were so bright they seemed to be on fire. "Did n't know there was any ranches in that country."

"Buck 's got th' only one," responded Lanky, packing his pipe. "He's located on Snake Creek, an' he 's got four thousand head. Reckon there ain't nobody within two hundred mile of him. Lewis said he 's got a fine range an' all th' water he can use; but three men can't handle all them cows in *that* country, so I 'm goin' up."

The little man's eyes seldom left Lanky's face, and he seemed to be studying the stranger very closely. When Lanky had ridden upon their noon-day camp the little man had not lost a movement that the stranger made and the other two, disappearing quietly, returned a little later and nodded reassuringly to their leader.

The wizened leader glanced at one of his companions, but spoke to Lanky. "George, here, said as how they finally got Butch Lynch. You did n't hear nothin' about it, did you?"

"They was a rumor down on Mesquite range that Butch was got. I heard his gang was wiped out. Well, it had to come sometime-he was carryin' things with a purty high hand for a long time. But I 've done heard that before; more 'n once, too. I reckon Butch is a li'l too slick to get hisself killed."

"Ever see him?" asked George carelessly.

"Never; an' don't want to. If them fellers can't clean their own range an' pertect their own cows, I ain't got no call to edge in."

"He 's only a couple of inches taller 'n Jim," observed the third man, glancing at his leader, "an' about th' same build. But he 's h —l on th' shoot. I saw him twice, but I was mindin' my own business."

Lanky nodded at the leader. "That 'd make him about as tall as me. Size don't make no dif'rence no more-King Colt makes 'em look all alike."

Jim tossed away his cigarette and arose, stretching and grunting. "I shore ate too much," he complained. "Well, there's one thing about yore friend's ranch: he ain't got no rustlers to fight, so he ain't as bad off as he might be. I reckon he done named that crick hisself, did n't he? I never heard tell of it."

"Yes; so Lewis says. He says *he 'd* called it Split Mesa Crick, 'cause it empties into Mesa River plumb acrost from a big mesa what's split in two as clean as a knife could 'a' done it."

There was a sharp report

"The Bar-20 expectin' you?" casually asked Jim as he picked up his saddle.

"Shore; they done sent for me. Me an' Buck is old friends. He was up in Montana ranchin' with a pardner, but Slippery Trendley kills his pardner's wife an' drove th' feller loco. Buck an' him hunted Slippery for two years an' finally drifted back south again. I dunno where Frenchy is. If it wasn't for me I reckon Buck 'd still be on th' warpath. You bet he 's expectin' me!" He turned and threw his saddle on the evil-tempered horse he rode and, cinching deftly, slung himself up by the stirrup. As he struck the saddle there was a sharp report and he pitched off and sprawled grotesquely on the sand. The little man peered through the smoke and slid his gun back into the holster. He turned to his companions, who looked on idly and with but little interest. "Yo 're d —d right Butch Lynch is too slick to get killed. I ain't takin' no chances with nobody that rides over my trail these days. An', boys, I got a great scheme! It comes to me like a flash when he 's talkin'. Come on, pull out; an' don't open yore traps till I says so. I want to figger this thing out to th' last card. George, shoot his cayuse; an' not another sound."

"But that's a good cayuse; worth easy —"

"Shoot it!" shouted Jim, his eyes snapping. It was unnecessary to add the alternative, for George and his companion had great respect for the lightning-like, deadly-accurate gun hands. He started to draw, but was too late. The crashing report seemed to come from the leader's holster, so quick had been the draw, and the horse sank slowly down, but unobserved. Two pairs of eyes asked a question of the little man and he sneered in reply as he lowered the gun. "It might 'a' been you. Hereafter do what I say. Now, go on ahead, an' keep quiet."

After riding along in silence for a little while the leader looked at his companions and called one of them to him. "George, this job is too big for the three of us; we can handle the ranch end, but not the drive. You know where Longhorn an' his bunch are holdin' out on th' Tortilla? All right; I 've got a proposition for 'em, an' you are goin' up with it. It won't take you so long if you wake up an' don't loaf like you have been. Now you listen close, an' don't forget a word": and the little man shared the plan he had worked out, much to his companion's delight. Having made the messenger repeat it, the little man waved him off: "Get a-goin'; you bust some records or I 'll bust you, savvy? Charley 'll wait for you at that Split Mesa that fool puncher was a-talkin' about. An' don't you ride nowheres near it goin' up-keep to th' east of it. So-long!"

He watched the departing horseman swing in and pass Charley and saw the playful blow and counter. He smiled tolerantly as their words came back to him, George's growing fainter and fainter and Charley's louder and louder until they rang in his ears. The smile changed subtly and cynicism touched his face and lingered for a moment. "Fine, big bodies-nothing else," he muttered. "Big children, with children's heads. A little courage, if steadied; but what a paucity of brains! Good G —d, what a paucity of brains; what a lack of original thought!"

Of some localities it is said their inhabitants do not die, but dry up and blow away; this, so far as appearances went, seemed true of the horseman who loped along the north bank of Snake Creek, only he had not arrived at the "blow away" period. No one would have guessed his age as forty, for his leathery, wrinkled skin, thin, sun-bleached hair and wizened body justified a guess of sixty. A shrewd observer looking him over would find about the man a subtle air of potential destruction, which might have been caused by the way he wore his guns. A second look and the observer would turn away oppressed by a disquieting feeling that evaded analysis by lurking annoyingly just beyond the horizon of thought. But a man strong in intuition would not have turned away; he would have backed off, alert and tense. Nearing a corral which loomed up ahead, he pulled rein and went on at a walk, his brilliant eyes searching the surroundings with a thoroughness that missed nothing.

Buck Peters was complaining as he loafed for a precious half hour in front of the corral, but Red Connors and Bill Cassidy, his "outfit," discussed the low prices cattle were selling for, the over-stocked southern ranges and the crash that would come to the more heavily mortgaged ranches when the market broke. This was a golden opportunity to stock the little ranch, and Buck was taking advantage of it. But their foreman persisted in telling his troubles and finally, out of politeness, they listened. The burden of the foreman's plaint was the non-appearance of one Lanky Smith, an old friend. When the second herd had been delivered several weeks before, Buck, failing to persuade one of the drive outfit to remain, had asked the trail boss to send up Lanky, and the trail boss had promised.

Red stretched and yawned. "Mebby he's lost th' way."

The foreman snorted. "He can foller a plain trail, can't he? An' if he can ride past Split Mesa, he's a bigger fool than I ever heard of."

"Well, mebby he got drunk an —"

"He don't get that drunk." Astonishment killed whatever else he might have said, for a stranger had ridden around the corral and sat smiling at the surprise depicted on the faces of the three.

Buck and Red, too surprised to speak, smiled foolishly; Bill, also wordless, went upon his toes and tensed himself for that speed which had given to him hands never beaten on the draw. The stranger glanced at him, but saw nothing more than the level gaze that searched his squinting eyes for the soul back of them. The squint increased and he made a mental note concerning Bill Cassidy, which Bill Cassidy already had done regarding him.

"I'm called Tom Jayne," drawled the stranger. "I 'm lookin' for Peters."

"Yes?" inquired Buck restlessly. "I 'm him."

"Lewis sent me up to punch for you."

"You plumb surprised us," replied Buck. "We don't see nobody up here."

"Reckon not," agreed Jayne smiling. "I ain't been pestered a hull lot by th' inhabitants on my way up. I reckon there 's more *buffalo* than men in this country."

Buck nodded. "An' blamed few buffalo, too. But Lewis did n't say nothin' about Lanky Smith, did he?"

"Yes; Smith, he goes up in th' Panhandle for to be a foreman. Lewis missed him. Th' Panhandle must be purty nigh as crowded as this country, I reckon," he smiled.

"Well," replied Buck, "anybody Lewis sends up is good enough for me. I 'm payin' forty a month. Some day I 'll pay more, if I 'm able to an' it 's earned."

Jayne nodded. "I 'm aimin' to be here when th' pay is raised; an' I 'll earn it."

"Then shake han's with Red an' Bill, an' come with me," said Buck. He led the way to the dugout, Bill and Red looking after him and the little newcomer. Red shook his head. "I dunno," he soliloquized, his eyes on the recruit's guns. They were worn low on the thighs, and the lower ends of the holsters were securely tied to the trousers. They were low enough to have the butts even with the swinging hands, so that no time would have to be wasted in reaching for them; and the sheaths were tied down, so they would not cling to the guns and come up with them on the draw. Bill wore his guns the same way for the same reasons. Red glanced at his friend. "He 's a queer li'l cuss, Bill," he suggested. Receiving no reply, he grinned and tried again. "I said as how he 's a queer li'l cuss." Bill stirred. "Huh?" he muttered. Red snorted. "Why, I says he's a drunk Injun mendin' socks. What in blazes you reckon I 'd say!"

"Oh, somethin' like that; but; you should 'a' said he's a —a weasel. A cold-blooded, ferocious li'l rat that 'd kill for th' joy of it," and Bill moved leisurely to rope his horse.

Red looked after him, cogitating deeply. "Cussed if I hadn't, too! An' so he's a two-gun man, like Bill. Wears 'em plumb low an' tied. Yessir, he's a shore 'nuff weasel, all right." He turned and watched Bill riding away and he grinned as two pictures came to his mind. In the first he saw a youth enveloped in swirling clouds of acrid smoke as two Colts flashed and roared with a speed incredible; in the second there was no smoke, only the flashing of hands and the cold glitter of steel, so quick as to baffle the eye. And even now Bill practiced the draw, which pleased the foreman; cartridges were hard to get and cost money. Red roped his horse and threw on the saddle. As he swung off toward his section of the range he shook his head and scowled.

The Weasel had the eastern section, the wildest part of the ranch. It was cut and seared by arroyos, barrancas and draws; covered with mesquite and chaparral and broken by hills and mesas. The cattle on it were lost in the chaotic roughness and heavy vegetation and only showed themselves when they straggled down to the river or the creek to drink. A thousand head were supposed to be under his charge, but ten times that number would have been but a little more noticeable. He quickly learned ways of riding from one end of the section to the other without showing himself to anyone who might be a hundred yards from any point of the ride; he learned the best grazing portions and the safest trails from them to the ford opposite Split Mesa.

He was very careful not to show any interest in Split Hill Canyon and hardly even looked at it for the first week; then George returned from his journey and reported favorably. He also, with Longhorn's assistance, had picked out and learned a good drive route, and it was decided then and there to start things moving in earnest.

There were two thousand unbranded cattle on the ranch, the entire second drive herd; most of these were on the south section under Bill Cassidy, and the remainder were along the river. The Weasel learned that most of Bill's cows preferred the river to the creek and crossed his section to get there. That few returned was due, perhaps, to their preference for the eastern pasture. In a week the Weasel found the really good grazing portions of his section feeding more cows than they could keep on feeding; but suddenly the numbers fell to the pastures' capacity, without adding a head to Bill's herd.

Then came a day when Red had been riding so near the Weasel's section that he decided to go on down and meet him as he rode in for dinner. When Red finally caught sight of him the Weasel was riding slowly toward the bunkhouse, buried in thought. When his two men had returned from their scouting trip and reported the best way to drive, his and their work had begun in earnest. One small herd had been driven north and turned over to friends not far away, who took charge of the herd for the rest of the drive while the Weasel's companions returned to Split Hill.

Day after day he had noticed the diminishing number of cows on his sections, which was ideally created by nature to hide such a deficit, but from now on it would require all his cleverness and luck to hide the losses and he would be so busy shifting cattle that the rustling would have to ease up. One thing bothered him: Bill Cassidy was getting very suspicious, and he was not altogether satisfied that it was due to rivalry in gun-play. He was so deeply engrossed in this phase of the situation that he did not hear Red approaching over the soft sand and before Red could make his presence known something occurred that made him keep silent.

The Weasel, jarred by his horse, which shied and reared with a vigor and suddenness its rider believed entirely unwarranted under the circumstances, grabbed the reins in his left hand and jerked viciously, while his right, a blur of speed, drew and fired the heavy Colt with such deadly accuracy that the offending rattler's head dropped under its writhing, glistening coils, severed clean.

Red backed swiftly behind a chaparral and cogitated, shaking his head slowly. "Funny how bashful these gun-artists are!" he muttered. "Now has he been layin' for big bets, or was he —?" the words ceased, but the thoughts ran on and brought a scowl to Red's face as he debated the question.

* * * * *

The following day, a little before noon, two men stopped with sighs of relief at the corral and looked around. The little man riding the horse smiled as he glanced at his tall companion. "You won't have to hoof it no more, Skinny," he said gladly. "It's been a' awful experience for both of us, but you had th' worst end."

"Why, you stubborn li'l fool!" retorted Skinny. "I can walk back an' do it all over again!" He helped his companion down, stripped off the saddle and turned the animal loose with a resounding slap. "Huh!" he grunted as it kicked up its heels. "You oughta feel frisky, after loafin' for two weeks an' walkin' for another. Come on, Lanky," he said, turning. "There ain't nobody home, so we 'll get a fire goin' an' rustle chuck for all han's."

They entered the dugout and looked around, Lanky sitting down to rest. His companion glanced at the mussed bunks and started a fire to get dinner for six. "Mebby they don't ride in at noon," suggested the convalescent. "Then we 'll eat it all," grinned the cook. "It's comin' to us by this time."

The Weasel, riding toward the rear wall of the dugout, increased the pace when he saw the smoke pouring out of the chimney, but as he neared the hut he drew suddenly and listened, his expression of incredulity followed by one of amazement.

A hearty laugh and some shouted words sent him spinning around and back to the chaparral. As soon as he dared he swung north to the creek and risked its quicksands to ride down its middle. Reaching the river he still kept to the water until he had crossed the ford and scrambled up the further bank to become lost in the windings of the canyon.

Very soon after the Weasel's departure Buck dismounted at the corral and stopped to listen. "Strangers," he muttered. "Glad they got th' fire goin', anyhow." Walking to the hut he entered and a yell met him at the instant recognition.

"Hullo, Buck!"

"Lanky!" he cried, leaping forward.

"Easy!" cautioned the convalescent, evading the hand. "I 've been all shot up an' I ain't right yet."

"That so! How 'd it happen?"

"Shake han's with Skinny Thompson, my fool nurse," laughed Lanky.

"I 'm a fool, all right, helpin' *him*," grinned Skinny, gripping the hand. "But when I picks him up down in th' Li'l Wind River country I was a' angel. Looked after him for two weeks down there, an' put in another gettin' up here. Served him right, too, for runnin' away from me."

"Little Wind River country!" exclaimed Buck. "Why, I thought you was a foreman in th' Panhandle."

"Foreman nothin'," replied Lanky. "I was shot up by a li'l runt of a rustler an' left to die two hundred mile from nowhere. I was n't expectin' no gun-play."

"He's ridin' up here," explained Skinny. "Meets three fellers an' gets friendly. They learns his business, an' drops him sudden when he's mountin'. Butch Lynch did th' shootin'. Butch got his name butcherin th' law. He could n't make a livin' at it. Then he got chased out of New Mexico for bein' mixed up in a free-love sect, an' pulls for Chicago. He reckoned he owned th' West, so he drifts down here again an' turns rustler. I dunno why he plugs Lanky, less 'n he thinks Lanky knows him an' might try to hand him over. I 'm honin' for to meet Butch."

Buck looked from one to the other in amazement, suspicion raging in his mind. "Why, I heard you went to th' Panhandle!" he ejaculated.

Skinny grinned: "A fine foreman he 'd make, less 'n for a hawg ranch!"

"Who told you that?" demanded Lanky, with sudden interest.

"Th' feller Lewis sent up in yore place."

"What?" shouted both in one voice, and Lanky gave a terse description of Butch Lynch. "That him?"

"That's him," answered Buck. "But he was alone. He 'll be in soon, 'long with Bill an' Red-which way did you come?" he demanded eagerly. "Why, that was through his section-bet he saw you an' pulled out!"

Skinny reached for his rifle: "I'm goin' to see," he remarked.

"I 'm with you," replied Buck.

"Me, too," asserted Lanky, but he was pushed back.

"You stay here," ordered Buck. "He might ride in. An' you 've got to send Bill an' Red after us."

Lanky growled, but obeyed, and trained his rifle on the door. But the only man he saw was Red, whose exit was prompt when he had learned the facts.

Down on the south section Bill, unaware of the trend of events, looked over the little pasture that nestled between the hills and wondered where the small herd was. Up to within the last few days he always had found it here, loath to leave the heavy grass and the trickling spring, and watched over by "Old Mosshead," a very pugnacious steer. He scowled as he looked east and shook his head. "Bet they 're crowdin' on th' Weasel's section, too. Reckon I 'll go over and look into it. He 'll be passin' remarks about th' way I ride sign." But he reached the river without being rewarded by the sight of many of the missing cows and he became pugnaciously inquisitive. He had searched in vain for awhile when he paused and glanced up the river, catching sight of a horseman who was pushing across at the ford. "Now, what's th' Weasel doin' over there?" he growled. "An' what's his hurry? I never did put no trust in him an' I 'm going to see what's up."

Not far behind him a tall, lean man peered over the grass-fringed bank of a draw and watched him cross the river and disappear over the further bank. "Huh!" muttered Skinny, riding forward toward the river. "That *might* be one of Peters' punchers; but I 'll trail him to make shore."

Down the river Red watched Bill cross the stream and then saw a stranger follow. "What th' h —l!" he growled, pushing on. "That's one of 'em trailin' Bill!" and he, in turn, forded the river, hot on the trail of the stranger.

Bill finally dismounted near the mesa, proceeded on foot to the top of the nearest rise, and looked down into the canyon at a point where it widened into a circular basin half a mile across. Dust was arising in thin clouds as the missing cows, rounded up by three men, constantly increased the rustlers' herd. To the northwest lay the mesa, where the canyon narrowed to wind its tortuous way through; to the southeast lay the narrow gateway, where the towering, perpendicular cliffs began to melt into the sloping sides of hills and changed the canyon into a swiftly widening valley. The sight sent the puncher running toward the pass, for the herd had begun to move toward that outlet, urged by the Weasel and his nervous companions.

Back in the hills Skinny was disgusted and called himself names. To lose a man in less than a minute after trailing him for an hour was more than his sensitive soul could stand without protest. Bill had disappeared as completely as if he had taken wings and flown away. The disgusted trailer, dropping to all-fours because of his great height, went ahead, hoping to blunder upon the man he had lost.

Back of him was Red, whose grin was not so much caused by Skinny's dilemma, which he had sensed instantly, as it was by the inartistic spectacle Skinny's mode of locomotion presented to the man behind. There was humor a-plenty in Red's make-up and the germ of mischief in his soul was always alert and willing; his finger itched to pull the trigger, and the grin spread as he pondered over the probable antics of the man ahead if he should be suddenly grazed by a bullet from the rear. "Bet he 'd go right up on his head an' kick," Red chuckled-and it took all his will power to keep from experimenting. Then, suddenly, Skinny disappeared, and Red's fretful nature clawed at his tropical vocabulary with great success. It was only too true-Skinny had become absolutely lost, and the angry Bar-20 puncher crawled furiously this way and that without success, until Skinny gave him a hot clew that stung his face with grit and pebbles. He backed, sneezing, around a rock and wrestled with his dignity. Skinny, holed up not far from the canyon's rim, was throwing a mental fit and calling himself outrageous names. "An' he's been trailin' *me*! H —l of a fine fool I am; I 'm awful smart today, I am! I done gave up my teethin' ring too soon, I did." He paused and scratched his head reflectively. "Huh! *This* is some populous region, an' th' inhabitants have pe-culiar ways. Now I wonder who's trailin' him? I 'm due to get cross-eyed if I try to stalk 'em both."

A bullet, fired from an unexpected direction, removed the skin from the tip of Skinny's nose and sent a shock jarring clean through him. "Is that him, th' other feller, or somebody else?" he fretfully pondered, raising his hand to the crimson spot in the center of his face. He did not rub it-he rubbed the air immediately in front of it, and was careful to make no mistake in distance. The second bullet struck a rock just outside the gully and caromed over his head with a scream of baffled rage. He shrunk, lengthwise and sidewise, wishing he were not so long; but he kept on wriggling, backward. "Not enough English," he muttered. "Thank th' Lord he can't massé!"

The firing put a different aspect on things down in the basin. The Weasel crowded the herd into the gap too suddenly and caused a bad jam, while his companions, slipping away among the bowlders and thickets, worked swiftly but cautiously up the cliff by taking advantage of the crevices and seams that scored the wall. Climbing like goats, they slipped over the top and began a game of hide and seek over the bowlder-strewn, chaparral-covered plateau to cover the Weasel, who worked, without cover of any kind, in the basin.

Red was deep in some fine calculations of angles when his sombrero slid off his head and displayed a new hole, which ogled at him with Cyclopean ferocity. He ducked, and shattered all existing records for the crawl, stopping finally when he had covered twenty yards and collected many thorns and bruises. He had worked close to the edge of the cliff and as he turned to circle back of his enemy he chanced to glance over the rim, swore angrily and fired. The Weasel, saving himself from being pinned under his stricken horse, leaped for the shelter of the cover near the foot of the basin's wall. Red was about to fire again when he swayed and slipped down behind a bowlder. The rustler, twenty yards away, began to maneuver for another shot when Skinny's rifle cracked viciously and the cattle thief, staggering to the edge of the cliff, stumbled, fought for his balance, and plunged down into the basin. His companion, crawling swiftly toward Skinny's smoke, showed himself long enough for Red to swing his rifle and shoot offhand. At that moment Skinny caught sight of him and believed he understood the situation. "You Conners or Cassidy?" he demanded over the sights. Red's answer made him leap forward and in a few moments the wounded man, bandaged and supported by his new friend, hobbled to the rim of the basin in time to see the last act of the tragedy.

The gateway, now free of cattle, lay open and the Weasel dashed for it in an attempt to gain the horses picketed on the other side. He had seen George plunge off the cliff and knew that the game was up. As he leaped from his cover Skinny's head showed over the rim of the cliff and his bullet sang shrilly over the rustler's head. The second shot was closer, but before Skinny could try again Red's warning cry made him lower the rifle and stare at the gateway.

The Weasel saw it at the same time, slowed to a rapid walk, but kept on for the pass, his eyes riveted malevolently on the youth who had suddenly arisen from behind a bowlder and started to meet him.

"It's easy to get him now," growled Skinny, starting to raise the rifle, a picture of Lanky's narrow escape coming to his mind.

"Bill's right in line," whispered Red, leaning forward tensely and robbing his other senses to strengthen sight. "They 're th' best in th' Southwest," he breathed.

Below them Bill and the Weasel calmly advanced, neither hurried nor touching a gun. Sixty yards separated them-fifty-forty-thirty —"G —d A'mighty!" whispered Skinny, his nails cutting into his calloused palms. Red only quivered. Twenty-five —twenty. Then the Weasel slowed down, crouching a little, and his swinging hands kept closer to his thighs. Bill, though moving slowly, stood erect and did not change his pace. Perspiration beaded the faces of the watchers on the cliff and they almost stopped breathing. This was worse than they had expected-forty yards would have been close enough to start shooting. "It's a pure case of speed now," whispered Red, suddenly understanding. The promised lesson was due-the lesson the Weasel had promised to give Bill on the draw. Accuracy deliberately was being eliminated by that cold-blooded advance. Fifteen yards-ten-eight-six-five-and a flurry of smoke. There had been no movement to the eyes of the watchers-just smoke, and the flat reports, that came to them like two beats of a snare drum's roll. Then they saw Bill step back as the Weasel pitched forward. He raised his eyes to meet them and nodded. "Come on, get th' cayuses. We gotta round up th' herd afore it scatters," he shouted.

Red leaned against Skinny and laughed senselessly. "Ain't he a d —d fool?"

Skinny stirred and nodded. "He shore is; but come on. I don't want no argument with *him*."

III
Jimmy Price

On a range far to the north, Jimmy Price, a youth as time measures age, followed the barranca's edge and whistled cheerfully. He had never heard of the Bar-20, and would have showed no interest if he had heard of it, so long as it lay so far away. He was abroad in search of adventure and work, and while his finances were almost at ebb tide he had youth, health, courage and that temperament that laughs at hard luck and believes in miracles. The tide was so low it must turn soon and work would be forthcoming when he needed it. Sitting in the saddle with characteristic erectness he loped down a hill and glanced at the faint trail that led into the hills to the west. Cogitating a moment he followed it and soon saw a cow, and soon after others.

"I 'll round up th' ranch house, get a job for awhile an' then drift on south again," he thought, and the whistle rang out with renewed cheerfulness.

He noticed that the trail kept to the low ground, skirting even little hills and showing marked preference for arroyos and draws with but little regard, apparently, for direction or miles. He had just begun to cross a small pasture between two hills when a sharp voice asked a question: "Where you goin'?"

He wheeled and saw a bewhiskered horseman sitting quietly behind a thicket. The stranger held a rifle at the ready and was examining him critically. "Where you goin'?" repeated the stranger, ominously. "An' what's yore business?"

Jimmy bridled at the other's impudent curiosity and the tones in which it was voiced, and as he looked the stranger over a contemptuous smile flickered about his thin lips. "Why, I 'm goin' west, an' I 'm lookin' for th' sunset," he answered with an exasperating drawl. "Ain't seen it, have you?"

The other's expression remained unchanged, as if he had not heard the flippant and pugnacious answer. "Where you goin' an' what for?" he demanded again.

Jimmy turned further around in the saddle and his eyes narrowed. "I 'm goin' to mind my own business, because it's healthy," he retorted. "You th' President, or only a king?" he demanded, sarcastically.

"I 'm boss of Tortilla range," came the even reply. "You answer my question."

"Then you can gimme a job an' save me a lot of fool ridin'," smiled Jimmy. "It 'll be some experience workin' for a sour dough as ornery as you are. Fifty per', an' all th' rest of it. Where do I eat an' sleep?"

The stranger gazed steadily at the cool, impudent youngster, who returned the look with an ironical smile. "Who sent you out here?" he demanded with blunt directness.

"Nobody," smiled Jimmy. "Nobody sends me nowhere, never, 'less 'n I want to go. Purty near time to eat, ain't it?"

"Come over here," commanded the Boss of Tortilla range.

"It's closer from you to me than from me to you."

"Yo 're some sassy, now ain't you? I 've got a notion to drop you an' save somebody else th' job."

"He 'll be lucky if you do, 'cause when that gent drifts along I 'm natchurally goin' to get there first. It's been tried already."

Anger glinted in the Boss's eyes, but slowly faded as a grim smile fought its way into view. "I 've a mind to give you a job just for th' great pleasure of bustin' yore spirit."

"If yo 're bettin' on that card you wants to have a copper handy," bantered Jimmy. "It's awful fatal when it's played to win."

"What's yore name, you cub?"

"Elijah—ain't I done prophesied? When do I start punchin' yore eight cows, Boss?"

"Right now! I like yore infernal gall; an' there's a pleasant time comin' when I starts again' that spirit."

"Then my name's Jimmy, which is enough for you to know. Which cow do I punch first?" he grinned.

"You ride ahead along th' trail. I 'll show you where you eat," smiled the Boss, riding toward him.

Jimmy's face took on an expression of innocence that was ludicrous.

"I allus let age go first," he slowly responded. "I might get lost if I lead. I 'm plumb polite, I am."

The Boss looked searchingly at him and the smile faded. "What you mean by that?"

"Just what I said. I 'm plumb polite, an' hereby provin' it. I allus insist on bein' polite. Otherwise, gimme my month's pay an' I 'll resign. But I 'm shore some puncher," he laughed.

"I observed yore politeness. I 'm surprised you even know th' term. But are you shore you won't get lost if you foller me?" asked the Boss with great sarcasm.

"Oh, that's a chance I gotta take," Jimmy replied as his new employer drew up alongside. "Anyhow, yo 're better lookin' from behind."

"Jimmy, my lad," observed the Boss, sorrowfully shaking his head, "I shore sympathize with th' shortness of yore sweet, young life. Somebody 's natchurally goin' to spread you all over some dismal landscape one of these days."

"An' he 'll be a whole lot lucky if I ain't around when he tries it," grinned Jimmy. "I got a' awful temper when I 'm riled, an' I reckons that would rile me up quite a lot."

The Boss laughed softly and pushed on ahead, Jimmy flushing a little from shame of his suspicions. But a hundred yards behind him, riding noiselessly on the sand and grass, was a man who had emerged from another thicket when he saw the Boss go ahead; and he did not for one instant remove his eyes from the new member of the outfit. Jimmy, due to an uncanny instinct, soon realized it, though he did not look around. "Huh! Reckon I 'm th' meat in this sandwich. Say, Boss, who's th' Injun ridin' behind me?" he asked.

"That's Longhorn. Look out or he 'll gore you," replied the Boss.

"'That 'd be a bloody shame,' as th' Englishman said. Are all his habits as pleasant an' sociable?"

"They 're mostly worse; he's a two-gun man."

"Now ain't that lovely! Wonder what he'd do if I scratch my laig sudden?"

"Let me know ahead of time, so I can get out of th' way. If you do that it 'll save me fifty dollars an' a lot of worry."

"Huh! I won't save it for you. But I wish I could get out my smokin' what's in my hip pocket, without Longhorn gamblin' on th' move."

The next day Jimmy rode the west section harassed by many emotions. He was weaponless, much to his chagrin and rage. He rode a horse that was such a ludicrous excuse that it made escape out of the question, and they even locked it in the corral at night. He was always under the eyes of a man who believed him ignorant of the surveillance. He already knew that three different brands of cattle "belonged" to the "ranch," and his meager experience was sufficient to acquaint him with a blotted brand when the work had been carelessly done. The Boss was the foreman and his outfit, so far as Jimmy knew, consisted of Brazo Charley and Longhorn, both of whom worked nights. The smiling explanation of the Boss, when Jimmy's guns had been locked up, he knew to be only part truth. "Yo 're so plumb fighty we dass n't let you have 'em," the Boss had said. "If we got to bust yore high-strung, unlovely spirit without killin' you, you can't have no guns. An' th' corral gate is shore padlocked, so keep th' cayuse I gave you."

Jimmy, enraged, sprang forward to grab at his gun, but Longhorn, dexterously tripping him, leaned against the wall and grinned evilly as the angry youth scrambled to his feet. "Easy, Kid," remarked the gun-man, a Colt swinging carelessly in his hand. "You 'll get as you give," he grunted. "Mind yore own affairs an' work, an' we 'll treat you right. Otherwise —" the shrugging shoulders made further explanations unnecessary.

Jimmy looked from one to the other and silently wheeled, gained the decrepit horse and rode out to his allotted range, where he saturated the air with impotent profanity. Chancing to look back he saw a steer wheel and face the south; and at other times during the day he saw that repeated by other cattle-nor was this the only signs of trailing. Having nothing to do but ride and observe the cattle, which showed no desire to stray beyond the range allotted to them, he observed very thoroughly; and when he rode back to the bunkhouse that night he had deciphered the original brand on his cows and also the foundation for that worn by Brazo Charley's herd on the section next to him. "I dunno where mine come from, but Charley's uster belong to th' C I, over near Sagebrush basin. That's a good hundred miles from here, too. Just wait till I get a gun! Trip me an' steal my guns, huh? If I had a good cayuse I 'd have that C I bunch over here right quick! I reckon they 'd like to see this herd."

When he reached the bunkhouse all traces of his anger had disappeared and he ate hungrily during the silent meal.

When Longhorn and Brazo pushed away from the table Jimmy followed suit and talked pleasantly of things common to cowmen, until the two picked up their saddles and rifles and departed in the direction of the corral, the Boss staying with Jimmy and effectually blocking the door. But he could not block Jimmy's hearing so easily and when the faint sound of hoofbeats rolled past the bunkhouse Jimmy knew that there were more than two men doing the riding. He concluded the number to be five, and perhaps six; but his face gave no indication of his mind's occupation.

"Play crib?" abruptly demanded the Boss, taking a well-worn deck of cards from a shelf. Jimmy nodded and the game was soon going on. "Seventeen," grunted the Boss, pegging slowly. "Pair of fools, they are," he growled. "Both plumb stuck on one gal an' they go courtin' together. She reminds *me* of a slab of bacon, she 's that homely."

Jimmy laughed at the obvious lie. "Well, a gal's a gal out here," he replied. "Twenty for a pair," he remarked. He wondered, as he pegged, if it was necessary to take along an escort when one went courting on the Tortilla. The idea of Brazo and Longhorn tolerating any rival or any company when courting struck him as ludicrous. "An' which is goin' to win out, do you reckon?"

"Longhorn-he 's bad; an' a better gun-man. Twenty-three for six. Got th' other tray?" anxiously grinned the Boss.

"Nothin' but an eight-that's two for th' go. My crib?"

The Boss nodded. "Ugly as blazes," he mused. "*I* would n't court her, not even in th' dark-huh! Fifteen two an' a pair. That's bad goin', very bad goin'," he sighed as he pegged.

"But you can't tell nothin' 'bout wimmen from their looks," remarked Jimmy, with the grave assurance of a man whose experience in that line covered years instead of weeks. "Now I knowed a right purty gal once. She was plumb sweet an' tender an' clingin', she was. An' she had high ideas, she did. She went an' told me she would n't have nothin' to do with no man what wasn't honest, an' all that. But when a feller I knowed rid in to her place one night she shore hid him under her bed for three days an' nights. He had got real popular with a certain posse because he was careless with a straight iron. Folks fairly yearned for to get a good look at him. They rid up to her place and she lied so sweet an' perfect they shore apologized for even botherin' her. Who 'd 'a' thought to look under *her* bed, anyhow? Some day he 'll go back an' natchurally run off with that li'l gal." He scanned his hand and reached for the pegs. "Got eight here," he grunted.

The Boss regarded him closely. "She stood off a posse with her eyes an' mouth, eh?"

"Didn't have to stand 'em off. They was plumb ashamed th' minute they saw her blushes. An' they was plumb sorry for her bein' even a li'l interested in a no-account brand-blotter like-him." He turned the crib over and spread it out with a sort of disgust. "Come purty near bein' somethin' in that crib," he growled.

"An' did you know that feller?" the Boss asked carelessly.

Jimmy started a little. "Why, yes; he was once a pal of mine. But he got so he could blot a brand plumb clever. Us cow-punchers shore like to gamble. We are plumb childish th' way we bust into trouble. I never seen one yet that was worth anythin' that would n't take 'most any kind of a fool chance just for th' devilment of it."

The Boss ruffled his cards reflectively. "Yes; we are a careless breed. Sort of flighty an' reckless. Do you think that gal's still in love with you? Wimmin' is fickle," he laughed.

"*She* ain't," retorted Jimmy with spirit. "She 'll wait all right-for him."

The Boss smiled cynically. "You can't hide it, Jimmy. Yo 're th' man what got so popular with th' sheriff. Ain't you?"

Jimmy half arose, but the Boss waved him to be seated again. "Why, you ain't got nothin' to fear out here," he assured him. "We sorta like fellers that 'll take a chance. I reckon we all have took th' short end one time or another. An' I got th' idea mebby yo 're worth more 'n fifty a month. Take any chances for a hundred?"

Jimmy relaxed and grinned cheerfully. "I reckon I 'd do a whole lot for a hundred real dollars every month."

"Yo 're on, fur 's I 'm concerned. I 'll have to speak to th' boys about it, first. Well, I 'm goin' to turn in. You ride Brazo's an' yore own range for th' next couple of days. Good night."

Jimmy arose and sauntered carelessly to the door, watched the Boss enter his own house, and then sat down on the wash bench and gazed contentedly across the moonlit range. "Gosh," he laughed as he went over his story of the beautiful girl with the high ideals. "I 'm gettin' to be a sumptuous liar, I am. It comes so easy I gotta look out or I'll get th' habit. I'd do mor'n lie, too, to get my gun back, all right."

He stretched ecstatically and then sat up straight. The Boss was coming toward him and something in his hand glittered in the soft moonlight as it swung back and forth. "Forget somethin'?" called Jimmy.

"You better stop watchin' th' moonlight," laughed the Boss as he drew near. "That's a bad sign —'specially while that gal's waitin' for you. Here's yore gun an' belt —I reckoned mebby you might need it."

Jimmy chuckled as he took the weapon. "I ain't so shore 'bout needin' it, but I was plumb lost without it. Kept feelin' for it all th' time an' it was gettin' on my nerves." He weighed it critically and spun the cylinder, carelessly feeling for the lead in the chambers as the cylinder stopped. Every one was loaded and a thrill of fierce joy surged over him. But he was suspicious-the offer was too quick and transparent. Slipping on the belt he let the gun slide into the blackened holster and grinned up at the Boss. "Much obliged. It feels right, now." He drew the Colt again and emptied the cartridges into his hand. "Them 's th' only pills as will cure troubles a doctor can't touch," he observed, holding one up close to his face and shaking it at the smiling Boss in the way of emphasis. His quick ear caught the sound he strained to hear, the soft swish inside the shell. "Them 's Law in this country," he soliloquized as he slid the tested shell in one particular chamber and filled all the others. "Yessir," he remarked as the cylinder slowly revolved until he had counted the right number of clicks and knew that the tested shell was in the right place. "Yessir, them's The Law." The soft moonlight suddenly kissed the leveled barrel and showed the determination that marked the youthful face behind it. "An' it shore works both ways, Boss," he said harshly. "Put up yore paws!"

As the Boss leaped forward the hammer fell and caused a faint, cap-like report. Then the stars streamed across Jimmy's vision and became blotted out by an inky-black curtain that suddenly enveloped him. The Boss picked up the gun and, tossing it on the bench, waited for the prostrate youth to regain his senses.

Jimmy stirred and looked around, his eyes losing their look of vacancy and slowly filling with murderous hatred as he saw the man above him and remembered what had occurred. "Sand *sounds* like powder, my youthful friend," the Boss was saying, "but it don't *work* like powder. I purty near swallowed yore gal story; but I sorta reckoned mebby I better make shore about you. Yo 're clever, Jimmy; so clever that I dass n't take no chances with you. I 'll just tie you up till th' boys come back-we both know what they 'll say. I 'd 'a' done it then only I like you; an' I wish you had been in earnest about joinin' us. Now get up."

Jimmy arose slowly and cautiously and then moved like a flash, only to look down the barrel of a Colt. His clenched hands fell to his side and he bowed his head; but the Boss was too wary to be caught by any pretenses of a broken spirit. "Turn 'round an' hol' up yore han's," he ordered. "I 'll blow you apart if you even squirms."

Jimmy obeyed, seething with impotent fury, but the steady pressure of the Colt on his back told him how useless it was to resist. Life was good, even a few hours of it, for in those few hours perhaps a chance would come to him. The rope that had hung on the wall passed over his wrists and in a few moments he was helpless. "Now sit down," came the order and the prisoner obeyed sullenly. The Boss went in the bunkhouse and soon returned, picked up the captive and, carrying him to the bunk prepared for him, dumped him in it, tied a few more knots and, closing the door, securely propped it shut and strode toward his own quarters, swearing savagely under his breath.

An hour later, while a string of horsemen rode along the crooked, low-lying trail across the Tortilla, plain in the moonlight, a figure at the bunkhouse turned the corner, slipped to the door and carefully removed the props.

Waiting a moment it opened the door slowly and slipped into the black interior, and chuckled at the sarcastic challenge from the bunk. "Sneakin' back again, hey?" blazed Jimmy, trying in vain to bridge on his head and heels and turn over to face the intruder. "Turn me loose an' gimme a gun —I oughta have a chance!"

"All right," said a quiet, strange voice. "That's what I'm here for; but don't talk so loud."

"Who 're you?"

"My name 's Cassidy. I 'm from th' Bar-20, what owns them cows you been abusin'. Huh! he shore tied some knots! Wasn't takin' no more chances with you, all right!"

"G'wan! He never did take none."

"So I 've observed. Get th' blood circulatin' an' I 'll give you some war-medicine for that useless gun of yourn what ain't sand."

"Good for you! I'll sidle up agin' that shack an' fill him so full of lead he won't know what hit him!"

"Well, every man does things in his own way; but I 've been thinkin' he oughta have a chance. He shore gave you some. Take it all in all, he 's been purty white to you, Kid. Longhorn 'd 'a' shot you quick tonight."

"Yes; an' I 'm goin' to get him, too!"

"Now you ain't got no gratitude," sighed Cassidy. "You want to hog it all. I was figgerin' to clean out this place by myself, but now you cut in an' want to freeze me out. But, Kid, mebby Longhorn won't come back no more. My outfit's a-layin' for his li'l party. I sent 'em down word to expect a call on our north section; an' I reckon they got a purty good idea of th' way up here, in case they don't receive Longhorn an' his friends as per schedule."

"How long you been up here?" asked Jimmy in surprise, pausing in his operation of starting his blood to circulating.

"Long enough to know a lot about this layout. For instance, I know yo 're honest. That's why I cut you loose tonight. You see, my friends might drop in here any minute an' if you was in bad company they might make a mistake. They acts some hasty, at times. I 'm also offerin' you a good job if you wants it. We need another man."

"I 'm yourn, all right. An' I reckon I will give th' Boss a chance. He'll be more surprised, that way."

Cassidy nodded in the dark. "Yes, I reckon so; he 'll have time to wonder a li'l. Now you tell me how yo 're goin' at this game."

But he didn't get a chance then, for his companion, listening intently, whistled softly and received an answer. In another moment the room was full of figures and the soft buzz of animated conversation held his interest. "All right," said a deep voice. "We 'll keep on an' get that herd started back at daylight. If Longhorn shows up you can handle him; if you can't, there 's yore friend Jimmy," and the soft laugh warmed Jimmy's heart. "Why, Buck," replied Jimmy's friend, "he 's spoke for that job already." The foreman turned and paused as he stood in the door. "Don't forget; you ain't to wait for us. Take Jimmy, if you wants, an' head for Oleson's. I ain't shore that herd of hissn is good enough for us. We 'll handle this li'l drive-herd easy. So long."

Red Connors stuck his head through a small window: "Hey, if Longhorn shows up, give him my compliments. I shore bungled that shot."

" 'Tain't th' first," chuckled Cassidy. But Buck cut short the arguments and led the way to Jimmy's pasture.

At daylight the Boss rolled out of his bunk, started a fire and put on a kettle of water to get hot. Buckling on his gun he opened the door and started toward the bunkhouse, where everything appeared to be as he had left it the night before.

"It's a cussed shame," he growled. "But I can't risk him bringin' a posse out here. *What* th' devil!" he shouted as he ducked. A bullet sang over his head, high above him, and he glanced at the bunkhouse with renewed interest.

Having notified the Boss of his intentions and of the change in the situation, Jimmy walked around the corner of the house and sent one dangerously close to strengthen the idea that sand was no longer sand. But the Boss had surmised this instantly and was greatly shocked by such miraculous happenings on his range. He nodded cheerfully at the nearing youth and as cheerfully raised his gun. "An' he gave me a chance, too! He could 'a' got me easy if he didn't warn me! Well, here goes, Kid," he muttered, firing.

Jimmy promptly replied and scored a hit. It was not much of a hit, but it carried reflection in its sting. The Boss's heart hardened as he flinched instinctively and he sent forth his shots with cool deliberation. Jimmy swayed and stopped, which sent the Boss forward on the jump. But the youth was only further proving his cleverness against a man whom he could not beat at so long a range. As the Boss stopped again to get the work over with, a flash of smoke spurted from Jimmy's hand and the rustler spun half way around, stumbled and fell. Jimmy paused in indecision, a little suspicious of the fall, but a noise behind him made him wheel around to look.

A horseman, having topped the little hill just behind the bunkhouse, was racing down the slope as fast as his worn-out horse could carry him, and in his upraised hand a Colt glittered as it swung down to become lost in a spurt of smoke. Longhorn, returning to warn his chief, felt savage elation at this opportunity to unload quite a cargo of accumulated grouches of various kinds and sizes, which collection he had picked up from the Bar-20 northward in a running fight of twenty miles. Only a lucky cross trail, that had led him off at a tangent and somehow escaped the eyes of his pursuers, had saved him from the fate of his companions.

Jimmy swung his gun on the newcomer, but it only clicked, and the vexed youth darted and dodged and ducked with a speed and agility very creditable as he jammed cartridges into the empty chambers. Jimmy's interest in the new conditions made him forget that he had a gun and he stared in rapt and delighted anticipation at the cloud of dust that swirled suddenly from behind the corral and raced toward the disgruntled Mr. Longhorn, shouting Red's message as it came.

Mr. Cassidy sat jauntily erect and guided his fresh, gingery mount by the pressure of cunning knees. The brim of his big sombrero, pinned back against the crown by the pressure of the wind, revealed the determination and optimism that struggled to show itself around his firmly set lips; his neckerchief flapped and cracked behind his head and the hairs of his snow-white goatskin chaps rippled like a thing of life and caused Jimmy, even in his fascinated interest, to covet them.

But Longhorn's soul held no reverence for goatskin and he cursed harder when Red's compliments struck his ear about the time one of Cassidy's struck his shoulder. He was firing hastily against a man who shot as though the devil had been his teacher. The man from the Bar-20 used two guns and they roared like the roll of a drum and flashed through the heavy, low-lying cloud of swirling smoke like the darting tongue of an angry snake.

Longhorn, enveloped in the acrid smoke of his own gun, which wrapped him like a gaseous shroud, knew that his end had come. He was being shot to pieces by a two-gun man, the like of whose skill he had never before seen or heard of. As the last note of the short, five second, cracking tattoo died away Mr. Cassidy slipped his empty guns in their holsters and turned his pony's head toward the fascinated spectator, whose mouth offered easy entry to smoke and dust. As Cassidy glanced carelessly back at the late rustler Jimmy shut his mouth, gulped, opened it to speak, shut it again and cleared his dry throat. Looking from Cassidy to Longhorn and back again, he opened his mouth once more. "You-you-what'd'ju pay for them chaps?" he blurted, idiotically.

IV

Jimmy Visits Sharpsville

Bill Cassidy rode slowly into Sharpsville and dismounted in front of Carter's Emporium, nodding carelessly to the loungers hugging the shade of the store. "Howd'y," he said. "Seen anything of Jimmy Price —a kid, but about my height, with brown hair and a devilish disposition?"

Carter stretched and yawned, a signal for a salvo of yawns. "Nope, thank God. You need n't describe nothin' about that Price cub to none of us. *We* know him. He spent three days here about a year ago, an' th' town 's been sorta restin' up ever since. You don't mean for to tell us he 's comin' here again!" he exclaimed, sitting up with a jerk.

Bill laughed at the expression. "As long as you yearn for him so powerful hard, why I gotta tell you he 's on his way, anyhow. I had to go east for a day's ride an' he headed this way. He 's to meet me here."

Carter turned and looked at the others blankly. Old Dad Johnson nervously stroked his chin. "Well, then he 'll git here, all right," he prophesied pessimistically. "He usually gets where he starts for; an' I 'm plumb glad I 'm goin' on to-morrow."

"Ha, ha!" laughed George Bruce. "So 'm I goin' on, by Scott!"

Grunts and envious looks came from the group and Carter squirmed uneasily. "That's just like you fellers, runnin' away an' leavin' me to face it. An' it was you fellers what played most of th' tricks on him last time he was here. Huh! now I gotta pay for 'em," he growled.

Bill glanced over the gloomy circle and laughed heartily. Two faces out of seven were bright, Dad's particularly so. "Well, he seems to be quite a favorite around here," he grinned.

Carter snorted. "Huh! Seems to be nothin'."

"He ain't exactly a favorite," muttered Dawson. "He 's a —a —an event; that's what he is!"

Carter nodded. "Yep; that's what he is, 'though you just can't help likin' th' cub, he 's that cheerful in his devilment."

Charley Logan stretched and yawned. "Didn't hear nothin' about no Injuns, did you? A feller rid through here yesterday an' said they was out again."

Bill nodded. "Yes; I did. An' there 's a lot of rumors goin' around. They 've been over in th' Crazy Butte country an' I heard they raided through th' Little Mountain Valley last week. Anyhow, th' Seventh is out after 'em, in four sections."

"Th' Seventh is *a* regiment," asserted George Bruce. "Leastawise it was when I was in it. It is th' best in th' Service."

Dad snorted. "Listen to him! It was when he was in it! Lordy, Lordy, Lordy!" he chuckled.

"There hain't no cavalry slick enough to ketch Apaches," declared Hank, dogmatically. "Troops has too many fixin's an' sech. You gotta travel light an' live without eatin' an' drinkin' to ketch them Injuns; an' then you never hardly sometimes see 'em, at that."

"Lemme tell you, Mosshead, th' Seventh can lick all th' Injuns ever spawned!" asserted Bruce with heat. "It wiped out Black Kettle's camp, in th' dead of winter, too!"

"That was Custer as did that," snorted Carter.

"Well, he was leadin' th' Seventh, same as he is now!"

Charley Logan shook his head. "We are talking about ketchin' 'em, not fightin' 'em. An' no cavalry in th' hull country can ketch 'Paches in *this* country-it's too rough. 'Paches are only scared of punchers."

"Shore," asserted Carter. "Apaches laugh at troops, less 'n it's a pitched battle, when they don't. Cavalry chases 'em so fur an' no farther; punchers chase 'em inter h —l, out of it an' back again."

"They shore is 'lusive," cogitated Lefty Dawson, carefully deluging a fly ten feet away and shifting his cud for another shot. "An' I, for one, admits I ain't hankerin' for to chase 'em close."

"Wish we could get that cub Jimmy to chase some," exclaimed Carter. "Afore he gits here," he explained, thoughtfully.

"Oh, he 's all right, Carter," spoke up Lefty. "We was all of us young and playful onct."

"But we all war n't he-devils workin' day an' night tryin' to make our betters miserable!"

"Oh, he 's a good kid," remarked Dad. "I sorta hates to miss him. Anyhow, we got th' best of him, last time."

Bill finished rolling a cigarette, lit it and slowly addressed them. "Well, all I got to say is that he suits me right plumb down to th' ground. Now, just lemme tell you somethin' about Jimmy," and he gave them the story of Jimmy's part in the happenings on Tortilla Range, to the great delight of his audience.

"By Scott, it's just like him!" chuckled George Bruce.

"That's shore Jimmy, all right," laughed Lefty.

"What did *I* tell you?" beamed Dad. "He 's a heller, he is. He 's all right!"

"Then why don't you stay an' see him?" demanded Carter.

"I gotta go on, or I would. Yessir, I would!"

"Reckon them Injuns won't git so fur north as here," suggested Carter hopefully, and harking back to the subject which lay heaviest on his mind. "They 've only been here twict in ten years."

"Which was twice too often," asserted Lefty.

"Th' last time they was here," remarked Dad, reminiscently, "they didn't stop long; though where they went to I dunno. We gave 'em more 'n they could handle. That was th' time I just bought that new Sharps rifle, an' what I done with that gun was turrible." He paused to gather the facts in the right order before he told the story, and when he looked around again he flushed and swore. The audience had silently faded away to escape the moth-eaten story they knew by heart. The fact that Dad usually improved it and his part in it, each time he told it, did not lure them. "Cussed ingrates!" he swore, turning to Bill. "They 're plumb jealous!"

"They act like it, anyhow," agreed Bill soberly. "I 'd like to hear it, but I 'm too thirsty. Come in an' have one with me?" The story was indefinitely postponed.

An accordion wheezed down the street and a mouth-organ tried desperately to join in from the saloon next door, but, owing to a great difference in memory, did not harmonize. A roar of laughter from Dawson's, and the loud clink of glasses told where Dad's would-have-been audience then was. Carter walked around his counter and seated himself in his favorite place against the door jamb. Bill, having eluded Dad, sat on a keg of edibles and smoked in silence and content, occasionally slapping at the flies which buzzed persistently around his head. Knocking the ashes from the cigarette he leaned back lazily and looked at Carter. "Wonder where he is?" he muttered.

"Huh?" grunted the proprietor, glancing around. "Oh, you worryin' about that yearlin'? Well, you needn't! Nothin' never sidetracks Jimmy."

A fusillade of shots made Bill stand up, and Carter leaped to his feet and dashed toward the counter. But he paused and looked around foolishly. "That's his yell," he explained. "Didn't I tell you? He's arrove, same as usual."

The drumming of hoofs came rapidly nearer and heads popped out of windows and doors, each head flanked by a rifle barrel. Above a swirling cloud of dust glinted a spurting Colt and thrust through the smudge was a hand waving a strange collection of articles.

"Hullo, Kid!" shouted Dawson. "What you got? See any Injuns?"

"It's a G-string an' a medicine-bag, by all that's holy!" cried Dad from the harness shop. "Where 'd you git 'em, Jimmy?"

Jimmy drew rein and slid to a stand, pricking his nettlesome "Calico" until it pranced to suit him. Waving the Apache breech-cloth, the medicine-bag and a stocking-shaped moccasin in one hand, he proudly held up an old, dirty, battered Winchester repeater in the other and whooped a war-cry.

"Blame my hide!" shouted Dad, running out into the street. "It is a G-string! He 's gone an' got one of 'em! He 's gone an' got a 'Pache! Good boy, Kid! An' how 'd you do it?"

Carter plodded through the dust with Bill close behind. "*Where'd* you do it?" demanded the proprietor eagerly. To Carter location meant more than method. He was plainly nervous. When he reached the crowd he, in turn, examined the trophies. They were genuine, and on the G-string was a splotch of crimson, muddy with dust.

"What's in the war-bag, Kid?" demanded Lefty, preparing to see for himself. Jimmy snatched it from his hands. "You never mind what's in it, Freckle-face!" he snapped. "That's my bag, *now.* Want to spoil my luck?"

"How'd you do it?" demanded Dad breathlessly.

"*Where* 'd you do it?" snapped Carter. He glanced hurriedly around the horizon and repeated the question with vehemence. "Where 'd you get him?"

"In th' groin, first. Then through th' —"

"I don't mean where, I mean *where* —near here?" interrupted Carter.

"Oh, fifteen mile east," answered Jimmy. "He was crawlin' down on a bunch of cattle. He saw me just as I saw him. But he missed an' I did n't," he gloated proudly. "I met a Pawnee scout just afterward an' he near got shot before he signaled. He says hell's a-poppin'. Th' 'Paches are raidin' all over th' country, down —"

"I knowed it!" shouted Carter. "Yessir, I knowed it! I felt it all along! Where you finds one you finds a bunch!"

"We'll give 'em blazes, like th' last time!" cried Dad, hurrying away to the harness shop where he had left his rifle.

"I 've been needin' some excitement for a long time," laughed Dawson. "I shore hope they come."

Carter paused long enough to retort over his shoulder: "An' I hopes you drop dead! You never did have no sense! Not nohow!"

Bill smiled at the sudden awakening and watched the scrambling for weapons. "Why, there 's enough men here to wipe out a tribe. I reckon we 'll stay an' see th' fun. Anyhow, it 'll be a whole lot safer here than fightin' by ourselves out in th' open somewhere. What you say?"

"You could n't drag me away from this town right now with a cayuse," Jimmy replied, gravely hanging the medicine-bag around his neck and then stuffing the gory G-string in the folds of the slicker he carried strapped behind the cantle of the saddle. "We 'll see it out right here. But I do wish that 'Pache owned a better gun than this thing. It's most fallin' apart an' ain't worth nothin'."

Bill took it and examined the rifling and the breech-block. He laughed as he handed it back. "You oughta be glad it was n't a better gun, Kid. I don't reckon he could put two in the same place at two hundred paces with this thing. I ain't even anxious to shoot it off on a bet."

Jimmy gasped suddenly and grinned until the safety of his ears was threatened. "Would you look at Carter?" he chuckled, pointing. Bill turned and saw the proprietor of Carter's Emporium carrying water into his store, and with a speed that would lead one to infer that he was doing it on a wager. Emerging again he saw the punchers looking at him and, dropping the buckets, he wiped his face on his sleeve and shook his head. "I 'm fillin' everything," he called. "I reckon we better stand 'em off from my store-th' walls are thicker."

Bill smiled at the excuse and looked down the street at the adobe buildings. "What about th' 'dobes, Carter?" he asked. The walls of some of them were more than two feet thick.

Carter scowled, scratched his head and made a gesture of impatience. "They ain't big enough to hold us all," he replied, with triumph. "This here store is th' best place. An', besides, it's all stocked with water an' grub, an' everything."

Jimmy nodded. "Yo 're right, Carter; it's th' best place." To Bill he said in an aside, "He 's plumb anxious to protect that shack, now ain't he?"

Lefty Dawson came sauntering up. "Wonder if Carter 'll let us hold out in his store?"

"He 'll pay you to," laughed Bill.

"It's loop-holed. Been so since th' last raid," explained Lefty. "An' it's chock full of grub," he grinned.

They heard Dad's voice around the corner. "Just like last time," he was saying. "We oughta put four men in Dick's 'dobe across th' street. Then we'd have a strategy position. You see-oh, hullo," he said as he rounded the corner ahead of George Bruce. "Who 's goin' on picket duty?" he demanded.

Under the blazing sun a yellow dog wandered aimlessly down the deserted street, his main interest in life centered on his skin, which he frequently sat down to chew. During the brief respites he lounged in the doors of deserted buildings, frequently exploring the quiet interiors for food. Emerging from the "hotel" he looked across the street at the Emporium and barked tentatively at the man sitting on its flat roof. Wriggling apologetically, he slowly gained the middle of the street and then sat down to investigate a sharp attack. A can sailed out of the open door and a flurry of yellow streaked around the corner of the "hotel" and vanished.

In the Emporium grave men played poker for nails, Bill Cassidy having corralled all the available cash long before this, and conversed in low tones. The walls, reinforced breast high by boxes, barrels and bags, were divided into regular intervals by the open loopholes, each opening further indicated by a leaning rifle or two and generous piles of cartridges. Two tubs and half a dozen buckets filled with water stood in the center of the room, carefully covered over with boards and wrapping paper. Clouds of tobacco smoke lay in filmy stratums in the heated air and drifted up the resin-streaked sides of the building. The shimmering, gray sand stretched away in a glare of sunlight and seemed to writhe under the heated air, while droning flies flitted lazily through the windows and held caucuses on the sugar barrel. A slight, grating sound overhead caused several of the more irritable or energetic men to glance up lazily, grateful they were not in Hank's place. It was hot enough under the roof, and they stretched ecstatically as they thought of Hank. Three days' vigil and anxiety had become trying even to the most stolid.

John Carter fretfully damned solitaire and pushed the cards away to pick up pencil and paper and figure thoughtfully. This seemed to furnish him with even less amusement, for he scowled and turned to watch the poker game. "Huh," he sniffed, "playin' poker for nails! An' you don't even own th' nails," he grinned facetiously, and glanced around to see if his point was taken. He suddenly stiffened when he noticed the man who sat on his counter and labored patiently and zealously with a pocket knife. "Hey, you!" he exclaimed excitedly, his wrath quickly aroused. "Ain't you never had no bringin' up? If yo 're so plumb sot on whittlin', you tackle that sugar barrel!"

Jimmy looked the barrel over critically and then regarded the peeved proprietor, shaking his head sorrowfully. "This here is a better medjum for the ex-position of my art," he replied gravely. "An' as for bringin' up, lemme observe to these gents here assembled that you ain't never had no artistic trainin'. Yore skimpy soul is dwarfed an' narrowed by false weights and dented measures. You can look a sunset in th' face an' not see it for countin' yore profits." Carter glanced instinctively at the figures as Jimmy continued. "An' you can't see no beauty in a daisy's grace-which last is from a book. I 'm here carvin' th' very image of my cayuse an' givin' you a work of art, free an' gratis. I 'm timid an' sensitive, I am; an' I 'll feel hurt if—"

"Stop that noise," snorted a man in the corner, turning over to try again. "Sensitive an' timid? Yes; as a mule! Shut up an' lemme get a little sleep."

"A-men," sighed a poker-player. "An' let him sleep-he 's a cussed nuisance when he 's awake."

"Two mules," amended the dealer. "Which is worse than one," he added thoughtfully.

"We oughta put four men in that 'dobe —" began Dad persistently.

"An' will you shut up about that 'dobe an' yore four men?" snapped Lefty. "Can't you say nothin' less 'n it's about that mud hut?"

Jimmy smiled maddeningly at the irritated crowd. "As I was sayin' before you all interrupted me, I 'll feel hurt —"

"You *will*; an' quick!" snapped Carter. "You quit gougin' that counter!"

Bill craned his neck to examine the carving, and forthwith held out a derisively pointing forefinger.

"Cayuse?" he inquired sarcastically. "Looks more like th' map of th' United States, with some almost necessary parts missin'. Your geography musta been different from mine."

The artist smiled brightly. "Here 's a man with imagination, th' emancipator of thought. It's crude an' untrained, but it's there. Imagination is a hopeful sign, for it is only given to human bein's. From this we surmise an' must conclude that Bill is human."

"Will somebody be liar enough to say th' same of you?" politely inquired the dealer.

"Will you fools shut up?" demanded the man who would sleep. He had been on guard half the night.

"But you oughta label it, Jimmy," said Bill. "You 've got California bulgin' too high up, an' Florida sticks out th' wrong way. Th' Great Lakes is *all* wrong-looks like a kidney slippin' off of Canada. An' where's Texas?"

"Huh! It 'd have to be a cow to show Texas," grinned Dad Johnson, who, it appeared, also had an imagination and wanted people to know it.

"You cuttin' in on this teet-a-teet?" demanded Jimmy, dodging the compliments of the sleepy individual.

"As a map it is no good," decided Bill decisively.

"It is no map," retorted Jimmy. "I know where California bulges an' how Florida sticks out. What you call California is th' south end of th' cayuse, above which I 'm goin' to put th' tail —"

"Not if I'm man enough, you ain't!" interposed Carter, with no regard for politeness.

" —where I 'm goin' to put th' tail," repeated Jimmy. "Florida is one front laig raised off th' ground —"

"Trick cayuse, by Scott!" grunted George Bruce. "No wonder it looks like a map."

"Th' Great Lakes is th' saddle, an' Maine is where th' mane goes —*Ouch*!"

"Mangy pun," grinned Bill.

"Kentucky ought to be under th' saddle," laughed Dad, smacking his lips. "Pass th' bottle, John."

"You take too much an' we'll all be Ill-o'-noise," said Charley Logan alertly.

"Them Injuns can't come too soon to suit *me*," growled Fred Thomas. "Who started this, anyhow?"

The sleepy man arose on one elbow, his eyes glinting. "After th' fight, you ask *me* th' same thing! Th' answer will be ME!" he snapped. "I 'm goin' to clean house in about two minutes, an' fire you all out in th' street!"

Jimmy smiled down at him. "Well, you needn't be so sweepin' an' extensive in yore cleanin' operations," he retorted. "All you gotta do is go outside an' roll in th' dust like a chicken."

The crowd roared its appreciation and the sleepy individual turned over again, growling sweeping opinions.

"But if them Injuns are comin' I shore wish they 'd hurry up an' do it," asserted Dad. "I ought to 'a' been home three days ago."

"Wish to G —d you was!" came from the floor.

Bill tossed away his half-smoked cigarette, Carter promptly plunging into the sugar barrel after it. "They ain't comin'," Bill asserted. "Every time some drunk Injun gets in a fight or beats his squaw th' rumor starts. An' by th' time it gets to us it says that all th' Apaches are out follerin' old Geronimo on th' war trail. He can be more places at once than anybody *I* ever heard of. I 'm ridin' on tomorrow morning, 'Paches or no 'Paches."

"Good!" exclaimed Jimmy, glancing at Carter. "I 'll have this here carving all done by then."

There was a sudden scrambling and thumping overhead and hot exclamations zephyred down to them. Carter dashed to the door, while the others reached for rifles and began to take up positions.

"See 'em, Hank?" cried Carter anxiously.

"See what?" came a growl from above.

"Injuns, of course, you d —d fool!"

"Naw," snorted Hank. "There ain't no Injuns out at all, not after Jimmy got that one."

"Then what's th' matter?"

"My dawg's lickin' yore dawg. *Sic* him, Pete! Hi, there! Don't you run!"

"My dawg still gettin' licked?" grinned Carter.

"I 'll swap you," offered Hank promptly. "Mine can lick yourn, anyhow."

"In a race, mebby."

"H —l!" growled Hank, cautiously separating himself from a patch of hot resin that had exuded generously from a pine knot. "I 'm purty nigh cooked an' I 'm comin' down, Injuns or no Injuns. If they was comin' this way they'd 'a' been here long afore this."

"But that Pawnee told Price they was out," objected Carter. "Cassidy heard th' same thing, too. An' didn't Jimmy get one!" he finished triumphantly.

"Th' Pawnee was drunk!" retorted Hank, collecting splinters as he slipped a little down the roof. "Great Mavericks! This here is awful!" He grabbed a protruding nail and checked himself. "Price might 'a' shot a 'Pache, or he might not. I don't take him serious no more. An' that feller Cassidy can't help what scared folks tells him. Sufferin' *toads*, what a roof!"

Carter turned and looked back in the store. "Jimmy, you shore they are out? An' *will* you quit cuttin' that counter!"

Jimmy slid off the counter and closed the knife. "That's what th' Pawnee said. When I told you fellers about it, you was so plumb anxious to fight, an' eager to interrupt an' ask fool questions that I shore hated to spoil it all. What that scout says was that th' 'Paches was out raidin' down Colby way, an' was headin' south when last re —"

"*Colby*!" yelled Lefty Dawson, as the others stared foolishly. "*Colby*! Why, that's three hundred miles south of here! An' you let us make fools of ourselves for *three* days! I 'll bust you open!" and he arose to carry out his threat. "Where 'd you git them trophies?" shouted Dad angrily. "Them was genuine!" Jimmy slipped through the door as Dawson leaped and he fled at top speed to the corral, mounted in one bound and dashed off a short distance. "Why, I got them trophies in a poker game from that same Pawnee scout, you Mosshead! He could n't play th' game no better 'n you fellers. An' th' blood is snake's blood, fresh put on. You *will* drive me out of town, hey?" he jeered, and, wheeling, forthwith rode for his life. Back in the store Bill knocked aside the rifle barrel that Carter shoved through a loop hole. "A joke 's a joke, Carter," he said sternly. "You don't aim to hit him, but you might," and Carter, surprised at the strength of the twist, grinned, muttered something and went to the door without his rifle, which Bill suddenly recognized. It was the weapon that had made up Jimmy's "trophies"!

"Blame his hide!" spluttered Lefty, not knowing whether to shoot or laugh. A queer noise behind him made him turn, a movement imitated by the rest. They saw Bill rolling over and over on the floor in an agony of mirth. One by one the enraged garrison caught the infection and one by one lay down on the floor and wept. Lefty, propping himself against the sugar barrel, swayed to and fro, senselessly gasping. "They *allus* are raidin' down Colby way! Blame my hide, *oh*, blame my hide! Ha-ha-ha! Ha-ha-ha! They *allus* are raidin' down *Colby* way!"

"Three days, an' Hank *on* th' roof!" gurgled George Bruce. "*Three* days, by Scott!"

"Hank on th' roof," sobbed Carter, "settin' on splinters an hot rosim! Whee-hee-hee! Three-hee-hee days hatchin' pine knots an' rosim!"

"Gimme a drink! Gimme a drink!" whispered Dad, doubled up in a corner. "Gimme a ho-ho-ho!" he roared in a fresh paroxysm of mirth. "Lefty an' George settin' up nights watchin' th' shadders! Ho-ho-ho!"

"An' Carter boardin' us *free*!" yelled Baldy; Martin. "Oh, my G —d! He'll never get over it!"

"Yessir!" squeaked Dad. "*Free*; an' scared we 'd let 'em burn his store. 'Better stand 'em off in my place,' he says. 'It's full of grub,' he says. He-he-he!"

"An' did you see Hank squattin' on th' roof like a horned toad waitin' for his dinner?" shouted Dickinson. "I'm goin' to die! I'm goin' to die!" he sobbed.

"No sich luck!" snorted Hank belligerently. "I 'll skin him alive! Yessir; *alive*!"

Carter paused in his calculations of his loss in food and tobacco. "Better let him alone, Hank," he warned earnestly. "Anyhow, we pestered him nigh to death las' time, an' he 's shore come back at us. Better let him alone!"

Up the street Jimmy stood beside his horse and thumped and scratched the yellow dog until its rolling eyes bespoke a bliss unutterable and its tail could not wag because of sheer ecstasy.

"Purp," he said gravely, "never play jokes on a pore unfortunate an' git careless. Don't never forget it. Last time I was here they abused me shameful. Now that th' storm has busted an' this is gettin' calm-like, you an' me 'll go back an' get a good look at th' asylum," he suggested, vaulting into the saddle and starting toward the store. No invitation was needed because the dog had adopted him on the spot. And the next morning, when Jimmy and Bill, loaded with poker-gained wealth, rode out of town and headed south, the dog trotted along in the shadow made by Jimmy's horse and glanced up from time to time in hopeful expectancy and great affection.

A distant, flat pistol shot made them turn around in the saddle and look back. A group of the leading citizens of Sharpsville stood in front of the Emporium and waved hats in one last, and glad farewell. Now that Jimmy had left town, they altered their sudden plans and decided to continue to populate the town of Sharpsville.

V
The Luck of Fools

"Did you ever see a dog like Asylum?" demanded Jimmy, looking fondly at the mongrel as they rode slowly the second day after leaving Sharpsville.

Bill shook his head emphatically. "Never, nowheres."

Jimmy turned reproachfully. "Lookit how he 's follered us."

"Follered *you*," hastily corrected Bill. "He ought to. You feed an' scratch him, an' he 'll go anywhere for that. But he 's big," he conceded.

"Mostly wolf-hound," guessed Jimmy, proudly.

"He looks like a wolf-God help it-at th' end of a hard winter."

"Well, he ain't yourn!"

"An' won't be, not if I can help it."

"He ain't no good, is he?" sneered Jimmy.

"I wouldn't say that, Kid," grunted Bill. "You know there 's good *Injuns*; but he looks purty healthy right now. Why did n't you call him Hank? They look-Good G —d!" he exclaimed as he glanced through an opening in the hills. The ring of ashes that had been a corral still smoldered, and smoke arose fitfully from the caved-in roof of the adobe bunkhouse, whose beams, weakened by fire, had fallen under their heavy load.

"Injuns!" whispered Jimmy. "Not gone long, neither. Mebby they ain't all-ain't all —" he faltered, thinking of what might lie under the roof. Bill, nodding, rode hurriedly to the ruins, wheeled sharply and returned, shaking his head slowly. There was no need to explain Apache methods to his companion, and he spoke of the Indians instead. "They split. About a dozen in th' big party an' about eight in th' other. It looks sorta serious, Kid."

Jimmy nodded. "I reckon so. An' they 're usually where nobody wants 'em, anyhow. Would n't Sharpsville be disgusted if they went north? But let's get out of here, 'less you got some plan to bag a couple."

"I like you more all th' time," Bill smiled. "But I ain't got no plan, except to move."

"Now, if they ain't funny," muttered Jimmy. "If they only knowed what they was runnin' into!"

Bill turned in surprise. "I reckon I 'm easy, but I 'll bite: what are they runnin' into?"

"I don't mean th' Injuns; I mean that wagon," replied Jimmy, nodding to a canvas-covered "schooner" on the opposite hill. "Come here, 'Sylum!" he thundered. Bill wheeled, and smothered a curse when he saw the woman. "Fools!" he snarled. "Don't let *her* know," and he was galloping toward the newcomers.

"They shore is innercent," soliloquized Jimmy, following. "Just like a baby chasin' a rattler for to play with it."

Bill drew rein at the wagon and removed his sombrero. "Howd'y," he said. "Where you headin' for?" he asked pleasantly.

Tom French shifted the reins. "Sharpsville. And where in-thunder-is it?"

His brother stuck his head out through the opening in the canvas. "Yes; where?"

"You see, we are lost," explained the woman, glancing from Bill to Jimmy, whose spectacular sliding stop was purely for her benefit, though she knew it not. "We left Logan four days ago and have been wandering about ever since."

"Well, you ain't a-goin' to wander no more, ma'am," smiled Bill. "We 're goin' to Logan an' we 'll take you as far as th' Logan-Sharpsville trail," he said, wondering where it was. "You must 'a' crossed it without knowin' it."

"Then, thank goodness, everything is all right. We are very fortunate in having met you gentlemen and we will be very grateful to you," she smiled.

"You bet!" exclaimed Tom. "But where is Sharpsville?" he persisted.

"Sixty miles north," replied Jimmy, making a great effort to stop with the reins what he was causing with his shielded spur. His horse could cavort beautifully under persuasion. "Logan, ma'am," he said, indifferent to the antics of his horse, "is about thirty miles east. You must 'a' sashayed some to get only this far in four days," he grinned.

"And we would be 'sashaying' yet, if I had n't found this trail," grunted Tom. There was a sudden disturbance behind his shoulder and the canvas was opened wider. "*You* found it!" snorted George. "You mean, *I* found it. Leave it to Mollie if I did n't! And I told you that you were going wrong. Didn't I?" he demanded.

"Hush, George," chided his sister.

"But *did n't* I? Did n't I say we should have followed that moth-eaten road running-er-north?"

"Did you?" shouted Tom, turning savagely. "You told me so many fool things I couldn't pick out those having a flicker of intelligence hovering around their outer edges. *You* drove two days out of the four, did n't you?"

"Tom!" pleaded Mollie, earnestly.

"Oh, let him rave, Sis," rejoined George, and he turned to the punchers. "Friends, I beg thee to take charge of this itinerant asylum and its charming nurse, for the good of our being and the salvation of our souls. Amen."

Tom found a weak grin. "Yes, so be it. We place ourselves and guide under your orders, though I reserve the right to beat him to a pleasing pulp when he gets sober enough to feel it. At present he reclines ungracefully within."

"You mean you got a drunk guide, in there?" demanded Bill angrily.

"He feels the yearning right away," observed George. "We 'll have to take turns thrashing Bacchus, I fear."

"How long's he been that way?" demanded Bill.

"I have n't known him long enough to answer that," responded Tom. "I doubt if he were ever really sober. He is a peripatetic distillery and I believe he lived on blotters even as a child. The first day —"

" —hour," inserted George.

" —he became anxious about the condition of the rear axle and examined it so frequently that by night he had slipped back into the Stone Age-he was ossified and petrified. He could neither see, eat nor talk. Strange creatures peopled his imagination. He shot at one before we could get his gun away from him, and it was our best skillet. How the devil he could hit it is more than I know. At this moment he may be fleeing from green tigers."

"Beg pardon," murmured George. "At this moment I have my foot on his large, unwashed face."

"Why, George! You'll hurt him!" gasped Mollie.

"No such luck. He 's beyond feeling."

"But you will! It isn't right to —"

"Don't bother your head about him, Sis," interrupted Tom, savagely.

"Sure," grinned George. "Save your sympathy until he gets sober. He'll need some then."

"Now, George, there is no use of having an argument," she retorted, turning to face him. And as she turned Bill took quick advantage. One finger slipped around his scalp and ended in a jerky, lifting motion that was horribly suggestive. His other hand and arm swept back and around, the gesture taking in the hills; and at the same time he nodded emphatically toward the rear of the wagon, where Jimmy was slowly going. Across the faces of the brothers there flashed in quick succession mystification, apprehensive doubt, fear and again doubt. But a sudden backward jerk of Bill's head made them glance at the ruined 'dobe and the doubt melted into fear, and remained. George was the first to reply and he spoke to his sister. "As long as you fear for his facial beauty, Sis, I 'll look for a better place for my foot," and he disappeared behind the drooping canvas. Jimmy's words were powerful, if terse, and George returned to the seat a very thoughtful man. He took instant advantage of his sister's conversation with Bill and whispered hurriedly into his brother's ear. A faint furrow showed momentarily on Tom's forehead, but swiftly disappeared, and he calmly filled his pipe as he replied. "Oh, he 'll sober up," he said. "We poured the last of it out. And I have a great deal of confidence in these two gentlemen."

Bill smiled as he answered Mollie's question. "Yes, we did have a bad fire," he said. "It plumb burned us out, ma'am."

"But *how* did it happen?" she insisted.

"Yes, yes; how did it happen —I mean it happened like this, ma'am," he floundered. "You see, I —that is, *we-we* had some trouble, ma'am."

"So I surmised," she pleasantly replied. "I presume it was a fire, was it not?"

Bill squirmed at the sarcasm and hesitated, but he was saved by Jimmy, who turned the corner of the wagon and swung into the breach with promptness and assurance. "We fired a Greaser yesterday," he explained. "An' last night th' Greaser slipped back an' fired us. He got away, this time, ma'am; but we 're shore comin' back for him, all right."

"But is n't he far away by this time?" she asked in surprise.

"Greasers, ma'am, is funny animals. I could tell you lots of funny things about 'em, if I had time. This particular coyote is nervy an' graspin'. I reckon he was a heap disappointed when he found we got out alive, an' I reckon he 's in these hills waitin' for us to go to Logan for supplies. When we do he 'll round up th' cows an' run 'em off. Savvy? I means, understand?" he hurriedly explained.

"But why don't you hunt him now?"

Jimmy shook his head hopelessly. "You just don't understand Greasers, ma'am," he asserted, and looked around. "Does she?" he demanded.

There was a chorus of negatives, and he continued. "You see, he's plannin' to steal our cows."

"That's what he 's doin'," cheerfully assented Bill.

"I believe you said that before," smiled Mollie.

"Ha, ha!" laughed Bill. "He shore did!"

"Yes, I did!" snapped Jimmy, glaring at him.

"Then, for goodness' sake, are you going away and let him do it?" demanded Mollie.

Jimmy grinned easily, and drawled effectively. "We 're aimin' to stop him, ma'am. You see," he half whispered, whereat Bill leaned forward eagerly to learn the facts. "He won't show hisself an' we can't track him in th' hills without gettin' picked off at long range. It would be us that 'd have to do th' movin', an' that ain't healthy in rough country. So we starts to Logan, but circles back an' gets him when he 's plumb wrapped up in them cows he 's honin' for."

"That's it," asserted Bill, promptly and proudly. Jimmy was the smoothest liar he had ever listened to. "An' th' plan is all Jimmy's, too," he enthused, truthfully.

"Doubtless it is quite brilliant," she responded, "but I certainly wish *I* were that 'Greaser'!"

"Sis!" exploded George, "I'm surprised!"

"Very well; you may remain so, if you wish. But will someone tell me this: How can these gentlemen take us to Logan if they are going only part way and then returning after that dense, but lucky, 'Greaser'?"

"I should 'a' told you, ma'am," replied Jimmy, "that th' Logan-Sharpsville trail is about half way. We 'll put you on it an' turn back."

The strain was telling on Bill and he raised his arm. "Sorry to cut off this interestin' conversation, but I reckon we better move. Jimmy, tie that wolf-hound to th' axle-it won't make him drunk-an' then go ahead an' pick a new trail to Logan. Keep north of th' other, an' stay down from sky-lines. I 'll foller back a ways. Get a-goin'," and he was obeyed.

Jimmy rode a quarter of a mile in advance, unjustly escaping the remarks that Mollie was directing at him, her brothers, Bill, the dog and the situation in general. A backward glance as he left the wagon apprised him that the dangers of scouting were to be taken thankfully. He rode carelessly up the side of a hill and glanced over the top, ducked quickly and backed down with undignified haste. He fervently endorsed Bill's wisdom in taking a different route to Logan, for the Apaches certainly would strike the other trail and follow hard; and to have run into them would have been disastrous. He approached the wagon leisurely, swept off his sombrero and grinned. "Reckon you could hit any game?" he inquired. The brothers nodded glumly. "Well, get yore guns handy." There was really no need for the order. "There 's lots of it, an' fresh meat 'll come in good. Don't shoot till I says so," he warned, earnestly.

"O.K., Hawkeye," replied Tom coolly.

"We 'll wait for the whites of their eyes, *à la Bunker Hill*," replied George, uneasily, "before we wipe out the game of this large section of God's accusing and forgotten wilderness. Any *big* game loose?"

Jimmy nodded emphatically. "You bet! I just saw a bunch of copperhead snakes that 'd give you chills." The tones were very suggestive and George stroked his rifle nervously and felt little drops of cold water trickle from his armpits. Mollie instinctively drew her skirts tighter around her and placed her feet on the edge of the wagon box under the seat. "They can't climb into the wagon, can they?" she asked apprehensively.

"Oh, no, ma'am," reassured Jimmy. "Anyhow, th' dog will keep them away." He turned to the brothers. "I ain't shore about th' way, so I 'm goin' to see Bill. Wait till I come back," and he was gone. Tom gripped the reins more firmly and waited. Nothing short of an earthquake would move that wagon until he had been told to drive on. George searched the surrounding country with anxious eyes while his sister gazed fascinatedly at the ground close to the wagon. She suddenly had remembered that the dog was tied.

Bill drummed past, waving his arm, and swept out of sight around a bend, the wagon lurching and rocking after him. Out of the little valley and across a rocky plateau, down into an arroyo and up its steep, further bank went the wagon at an angle that forced a scream from Mollie. The dog, having broken loose, ran with it, eyeing it suspiciously from time to time. Jeff Purdy, the oblivious guide, slid swiftly from the front of the wagon box and stopped suddenly with a thump against the tailboard. George, playing rear guard, managed to hold on and then with a sigh of relief sat upon the guide and jammed his feet against the corners of the box.

"So he-went back for-his friend to-find the way!" gasped Mollie in jerks. "What a pity-he did-it. I could-do better myself. I 'm being jolted-into a thousand-pieces!" Her hair, loosening more with each jolt, uncoiled and streamed behind her in a glorious flame of gold. Suddenly the wagon stopped so quickly that she gasped in dismay and almost left the seat. Then she screamed and jumped for the dashboard. But it was only Mr. Purdy sliding back again.

Before them was the perpendicular wall of a mesa and another lay several hundred yards away. Bill, careful of where he walked, led the horses past a bowlder until the seat was even with it. "Step on nothing but rock," he quietly ordered, and had lifted Mollie in his arms before she knew it. Despite her protests he swiftly carried her to the wall and then slowly up its scored face to a ledge that lay half way to the top. Back of the ledge was a horizontal fissure that was almost screened from the sight of anyone below. Gaining the cave, he lowered her gently to the floor and stood up. "Do not move," he ordered.

Her face was crimson, streaked with white lanes of anger and her eyes snapped. "What does this mean?" she demanded.

He looked at her a moment, considering. "Ma'am, I was n't goin' to tell you till I had to. But it don't make no difference now. It's Injuns, close after us. Don't show yoreself."

"It's Injuns, close after us"

She regarded him calmly. "I beg your pardon-if I had only known-is there great danger?" He nodded. "If you show yoreself. There's allus danger with Injuns, ma'am." She pushed the hair back from her face. "My brothers? Are they coming up?"

Her courage set him afire with rage for the Apaches, but he replied calmly. "Yes. Mebby th' Injuns won't know yo 're here, Ma'am. Me an' Jimmy 'll try to lead 'em past. Just lay low an' don't make no noise."

Her eyes glowed suddenly as she realized what he would try to do. "But yourself, and Jimmy? Would n't it be better to stay up here?"

"Yo 're a thoroughbred, ma'am," he replied in a low voice. "Me an' Jimmy has staked our lives more 'n onct out of pure devilment, with nothin' to gain. I reckon we got a reason this time, th' best we ever had. I 'm most proud, ma'am, to play my cards as I get them." He bent swiftly and touched her head, and was gone.

Meeting the brothers as they toiled up with supplies, he gave them a few terse orders and went on. Taking a handful of sand from behind a bowlder and scattering it with judicious care, he climbed to the wagon seat and waited, glancing back at the faint line that marked the arroyo's rim. In a few minutes a figure popped over it and whirled toward him in a high-flung, swirling cloud of dust. Overtaking the lurching wagon, Jimmy shouted a query and kept on, his pony picking its way with the agility and certainty of a mountain cat. The wagon, lurching this way and that, first on the wheels of one side and then on those of the other, bouncing and jumping at such speed that it was a miracle it was not smashed to splinters, careened after the hard-riding horseman. A rifle bounced over the tailboard, followed swiftly by a box of cartridges and an ebony-backed mirror, which settled on its back and glared into the sky like an angry Cyclops.

Mr. Purdy, bruised from head to foot and rapidly getting sober, emitted language in jerks and grabbed at the tailboard as the wagon box dropped two feet, leaving him in the air. But it met him half way and jolted him almost to the canvas top. He slid against the side and then jammed against the tailboard again and reached for it in desperation. Another drop in the trail made him miss it, and as the wagon arose again like a steel spring Mr. Purdy, wondering what caused all the earthquakes, arose on his hands and knees in the dust and spat angrily after the careening vehicle. He scrambled unsteadily to his feet and shook eager fists after the four-wheeled jumping-jack, and gave the Recording Angel great anguish of mind and writer's cramp. Pausing as he caught sight of the objects on the ground, he stared at them thoughtfully. He had seen many things during the past few days and was not to be fooled again. He looked at the sky, and back to the rifle. Then he examined the mesa wall, and quickly looked back at the weapon. It was still there and had not moved. He closed his eyes and opened them suddenly and grunted. "Huh, bet a ten spot it's real." He approached it cautiously, ready to pounce on it if it moved, but it did not and he picked it up. Seeing the cartridges, he secured them and then gasped with fear at the glaring mirror. After a moment's thought he grabbed at it and put it in his pocket just before a sudden, swirling cloud of dust drove him, choking and gasping, to seek the shelter of the bowlders close to the wall. When he raised his head again and looked out he caught sight of a sudden movement in the open, and promptly ducked, and swore. Apaches! Twelve of them!

He had seen strange things during the last few days, and just because the rifle and other objects had turned out to be real was no reason that he should absolutely trust his eyes in this particular instance. There was a limit, which in this case was Apaches in full war dress; so he arose swaggeringly and fired at the last, and saw the third from the last slide limply from his horse. As the rest paused and half of them wheeled and started back he rubbed his eyes in amazement, damned himself for a fool and sprinted for the mesa wall, up which he climbed with the frantic speed of fear. He was favored by the proverbial luck of fools and squirmed over a wide ledge without being hit. There was but one way to get him and he knew he could pick them off as fast as they showed above the rim. He rolled over and a look of mystification crept across his face. Digging into his pockets to see what the bumps were, he produced the mirror and a flask. The former he placed carelessly against the wall and the latter he raised hastily to his lips. The mirror glared out over the plain, its rays constantly interrupted by Mr. Purdy's cautious movements as he settled himself more comfortably for defense.

A bullet screamed up the face of the wall and he flattened, intently watching the rim. Chancing to glance over the plain, he noticed that the wagon was still moving, but slowly, while far to the south two horsemen galloped back toward the mesa on a wide circle, six Apaches tearing to intercept them before they could gain cover. "I was shore wise to leave th' schooner," he grinned. "I allus know when to jump," he said, and then swung the rifle toward the rim as a faint sound reached his ears. Its smoke blotted out the piercing black eyes that looked for an instant over the edge and found eternity, and Mr. Purdy grinned when the sound of impact floated up from below. "They won't try that no more," he grunted, and forthwith dozed in a drunken stupor. A sober man might have been tempted to try a shot over the rim, and would have been dead before he could have pulled the trigger. Mr. Purdy was again favored by luck.

Leaving two braves to watch him, the other two searched for a better way up the wall.

The race over the plain was interesting but not deadly or very dangerous for Bill and Jimmy. Armed with Winchesters and wornout Spencer carbines and not able to get close to the two punchers, the Apaches did no harm, and suffered because of Mr. Cassidy's use of a new, long-range Sharps. "You allus want to keep Injuns on long range, Kid," Bill remarked as another fell from its horse. The shot was a lucky one, but just as effective. "They ain't worth a d—n figurin' windage an' th' drift of a fast-movin' target, 'specially when it's goin' over ground like this. It's a white man's weapon, Jimmy. Them repeaters ain't no good for over five hundred; they don't use enough powder. An' I reckon them Spencers was wore out long ago. They ain't even shootin' close." He whirled past the projecting spur of the mesa and leaped from his horse, Jimmy following quickly. Three hundred yards down the canyon two Apaches showed themselves for a moment as they squirmed around a projection high up on the wall and not more than ten feet below the ledge. The expressions which they carried into eternity were those of great surprise. The two who kept Mr. Purdy treed on his ledge saw their friends fall, and squirmed swiftly toward their horses. It could only be cowpunchers entering the canyon at the other end and they preferred the company of their friends until they could determine numbers. When half way to the animals they changed their minds and crept toward the scene of action. Mr. Purdy, feeling for his flask, knocked it over the ledge and looked over after it in angry dismay. Then he shouted and pointed down. Bill and Jimmy stared for a moment, nodded emphatically, and separated hastily. Mr. Purdy ducked and hugged the ledge with renewed affection. Glancing around, he was almost blinded by the mirror and threw it angrily into the canyon, and then rubbed his eyes again. Far away on the plain was a moving blot which he believed to be horsemen. He fired his rifle into the air on a chance and turned again to the events taking place close at hand. "Other way, Hombre!" he warned, and Jimmy, obeying, came upon the Apache from the rear, and saved Bill's life. At hide and seek among rocks the Apache has no equal, but here they did not have a chance with Mr. Purdy calling the moves in a language they did not well understand. A bird's-eye view is a distinct asset and Mr. Purdy was playing his novel game with delighted interest and a plainsman's instinct. Consumed with rage, the remaining Indian whirled around and sent the guide reeling against the wall and then down in a limp heap. But Bill paid the debt and continued to worm among the rocks.

There was a sudden report to the westward and Jimmy staggered and dived behind a bowlder. The other four, having discovered the trick that had been played upon them on the other side of the mesa, were anxious to pay for it. Bill hurriedly crawled to Jimmy's side as the youth brushed the blood out of his eyes and picked up his rifle. "It's th' others, Kid," said Bill. "An' they 're gettin' close. Don't move an inch, for this is their game." A roar above him made him glance upward and swear angrily. "Now they 've gone an' done it! After all we 've done to hide 'em!" Another shot from the ledge and a hot, answering fire broke out from below. "My G—d!" said a voice, weakly. Bill shook his head. "That was Tom," he muttered. "Come on, Kid," he growled. "We got to drive 'em out, d—n it!" They were too interested in picking their way in the direction of the Apaches to glance at Mr. Purdy's elevated perch or they would have seen him on his knees at the very edge making frantic motions with his one good arm. He was facing the east and the plain. Beaming with joy, he waved his arm toward Bill and Jimmy, shouted instructions in a weak voice, that barely carried to the canyon floor, and collapsed, his duty done.

Bill was surprised fifteen minutes later to hear strange voices calling to him from the rear and he turned like a flash, his Colt swinging first. "Well, I 'm d —d!" he ejaculated. Four punchers were crawling toward him. "Glad to see you," he said, foolishly.

"I reckon so," came the smiling reply. "That lookin' glass of yourn shore bothered us. We could n't read it, but we did n't have to. Where are they?"

"Plumb ahead, som'ers. Four of 'em," Bill replied. "There 's two tender feet up on that ledge, with their sister. We was gettin' plumb worried for 'em."

"Not them as hired Whiskey Jeff for to guide 'em?" asked Dickinson, the leader.

"Th' same. But how 'n h —l did Logan ever come to let 'em start?" demanded Bill, angrily.

"We did n't pay no attention to th' rumors that has been flyin' around for th' last two months. Nobody had seen no signs of 'em," answered the Logan man. "We did n't reckon there was no danger till last night, when we learned they had n't showed up in Sharpsville, nor been seen anywhere near th' trail. Then we remembers Jeff's habits, an', while we debates it, we gets word that th' Injuns was seen north of Cook's ranch yesterday. We moves sudden. Here comes th' boys back —I reckon th' job 's done. They 're a fine crowd, a'right. You should 'a seen 'em cut loose an' raise th' dust when we saw that lookin' glass a-winkin'. We could n't read it none, but we didn't have to. We just cut loose."

"Lookin' glass!" exclaimed Bill, staring. "That's twice you 've mentioned it. What glass? We didn't have no lookin' glass, nohow."

"Well, Whiskey Jeff had one, a'right. An' he shore keeps her a-talkin', too. Ain't it a cussed funny thing that a feller that's got a hardboiled face like his'n would go an' tote a lookin' glass around with him? We never done reckoned he was that vain."

Bill shook his head and gave it up. He glanced above him at the ledge and started for it as Jimmy pushed up to him through the little crowd. "Hello, Kid," Bill smiled. "Come on up an' help me get her down," he invited. Jimmy shook his head and refused. "Ah, what's th' use? She 'll only gimme h —l for handin' her that blamed Greaser lie," he snapped. "An' you can do it alone-didn't you tote her up th' cussed wall?" It had been a long-range view, but Jimmy had seen it, just the same, and resented it.

Bill turned and looked at him. "Well, I 'm cussed!" he muttered, and forthwith climbed the wall. A few minutes later he stuck his head over the rim of the ledge and looked down upon a good-natured crowd that lounged in the shadow of the wall and told each other all about it. Jimmy was the important center of interest and he was flushed with pride. It would take a great deal to make him cut short his hour of triumph and take him away from the admiring circle that hedged him in and listened intently to his words. "Yessir, by G —d," he was saying, "just then I looks over th' top of a li'l hill an' what I sees makes me duck a-plenty. There was a dozen of 'em, stringin' south. I knowed they 'd shore hit that —"

"Hey, Kid," said a humorous voice from above. Jimmy glanced up, vexed at the interruption. "Well, what?" he growled. Bill grinned down at him in a manner that bid fair to destroy the dignity that Jimmy had striven so hard to build up. "She says all right for you. She 's done let you down easy for that whoppin' big Greaser lie you went an' spun her. She wants to know ain't you comin' up so she can talk to you? How about it?"

"Go on, Kid," urged a low and friendly voice at his elbow.

"Betcha!" grinned another. "Wish it was me! I done seen her in Logan."

Jimmy loosed a throbbing phrase, but obeyed, whereat Bill withdrew his grinning face from the sight of the grinning faces below. "He 's comin' ma'am; but he's shore plumb bashful." He looked down the canyon and laughed. "There they go to get Purdy off 'n his perch. I 'm natchurally goin' to lick anybody as tries to thrash that man," he muttered, glancing at George as he passed Jimmy on the ledge. George grinned and shook his head. "I 'm going to give him the spree of his sinful, long life," he promised, thoughtfully.

Far to the west, silhouetted for a moment against the crimson sunset, appeared a row of mounted figures. It looked long and searchingly at the mesa and slowly disappeared from view. Bill saw it and pointed it out to Lefty Dickinson. "There 's th' other eight," he said, smiling cheerfully. "If it was n't for Whiskey Jeff's lookin' glass that eight 'd mean a whole lot to us. We 've had the luck of fools!"

VI
Hopalong's Hop

Having sent Jimmy to the Bar-20 with a message for Buck Peters and seen the tenderfeet start for Sharpsville on the right trail and under escort, Bill Cassidy set out for the Crazy M ranch, by the way of Clay Gulch. He was to report on the condition of some cattle that Buck had been offered cheap and he was anxious to get back to the ranch. It was in the early evening when he reached Clay Gulch and rode slowly down the dusty, shack-lined street in search of a hotel. The town and the street were hardly different from other towns and streets that he had seen all over the cow-country, but nevertheless he felt uneasy. The air seemed to be charged with danger, and it caused him to sit even more erect in the saddle and assume his habit of indifferent alertness. The first man he saw confirmed the feeling by staring at him insolently and sneering in a veiled way at the low-hung, tied-down holsters that graced Bill's thighs. The guns proclaimed the gun-man as surely as it would have been proclaimed by a sign; and it appeared that gun-men were not at that time held in high esteem by the citizens of Clay Gulch. Bill was growing fretful and peevish when the man, with a knowing shake of his head, turned away and entered the harness shop. "Trouble's brewin' somewheres around," muttered Bill, as he went on. He had singled out the first of two hotels when another citizen, turning the corner, stopped in his tracks and looked Bill over with a deliberate scrutiny that left but little to the imagination. He frowned and started away, but Bill spurred forward, determined to make him speak.

"*Might* I inquire if this is Clay Gulch?" he asked, in tones that made the other wince.

"You might," was the reply. "It is," added the citizen, "an' th' Crazy M lays fifteen mile west." Having complied with the requirements of common politeness the citizen of Clay Gulch turned and walked into the nearest saloon. Bill squinted after him and shook his head in indecision.

"He wasn't guessin', neither. He shore knowed where I wants to go. I reckon Oleson must 'a' said he was expectin' me." He would have been somewhat surprised had he known that Mr. Oleson, foreman of the Crazy M, had said nothing to anyone about the expected visitor, and that no one, not even on the ranch, knew of it. Mr. Oleson was blessed with taciturnity to a remarkable degree; and he had given up expecting to see anyone from Mr. Peters.

As Bill dismounted in front of the "Victoria" he noticed that two men further down the street had evidently changed their conversation and were examining him with frank interest and discussing him earnestly. As a matter of fact they had not changed the subject of their conversation, but had simply fitted him in the place of a certain unknown. Before he had arrived they discussed in the abstract; now they could talk in the concrete. One of them laughed and called softly over his shoulder, whereupon a third man appeared in the door, wiping his lips with the back of a hairy, grimy hand, and focused evil eyes upon the innocent stranger. He grunted contemptuously and, turning on his heel, went back to his liquid pleasures. Bill covertly felt of his clothes and stole a glance at his horse, but could see nothing wrong. He hesitated: should he saunter over for information or wait until the matter was brought to his attention? A sound inside the hotel made him choose the latter course, for his stomach threatened to become estranged and it simply howled for food. Pushing open the door he dropped his saddle in a corner and leaned against the bar.

"Have one with me to get acquainted?" he invited. "Then I 'll eat, for I 'm hungry. An' I 'll use one of yore beds to-night, too."

The man behind the bar nodded cheerfully and poured out his drink. As he raised the liquor he noticed Bill's guns and carelessly let the glass return to the bar.

"Sorry, sir," he said coldly. "I 'm hall out of grub, the fire 's hout, *hand* the beds are taken. But mebby 'Awley, down the strite, can tyke care of you."

Bill was looking at him with an expression that said much and he slowly extended his arm and pointed to the untasted liquor.

"Allus finish what you start, English," he said slowly and clearly. "When a man goes to take a drink with me, and suddenly changes his mind, why I gets riled. I don't know what ails this town, an' I don't care; I don't give a cuss about yore grub an' your beds; but if you don't drink that liquor you poured out *to* drink, why I 'll natchurally shove it down yore British throat so cussed hard it 'll strain yore neck. Get to it!"

The proprietor glanced apprehensively from the glass to Bill, then on to the business-like guns and back to the glass, and the liquor disappeared at a gulp. "W'y," he explained, aggrieved. "There hain't no call for to get riled hup like that, strainger. I bloody well forgot it."

"Then don't you go an' 'bloody well' forget this: Th' next time I drops in here for grub an' a bed, you have 'em both, an' be plumb polite about it. Do you get me?" he demanded icily.

The proprietor stared at the angry puncher as he gathered up his saddle and rifle and started for the door. He turned to put away the bottle and the sound came near being unfortunate for him. Bill leaped sideways, turning while in the air and landed on his feet like a cat, his left hand gripping a heavy Colt that covered the short ribs of the frightened proprietor before that worthy could hardly realize the move.

"Oh, all right," growled Bill, appearing to be disappointed. "I reckoned mebby you was gamblin' on a shore thing. I feels impelled to offer you my sincere apology; you ain't th' kind as would even gamble *on* a shore thing. You 'll see me again," he promised. The sound of his steps on the porch ended in a thud as he leaped to the ground and then he passed the window leading his horse and scowling darkly. The proprietor mopped his head and reached twice for the glass before he found it. "Gawd, what a bloody 'eathen," he grunted. "*'E* won't be as easy as the lawst was, blime 'im."

Mr. Hawley looked up and frowned, but there was something in the suspicious eyes that searched his face that made him cautious. Bill dropped his load on the floor and spoke sharply. "I want supper an' a bed. You ain't full up, an' you ain't out of grub. So I 'm goin' to get 'em both right here. Yes?"

"You shore called th' turn, stranger," replied Mr. Hawley in his Sunday voice. "That's what I 'm in business for. An' business is shore dull these days."

He wondered at the sudden smile that illuminated Bill's face and half guessed it; but he said nothing and went to work. When Bill pushed back from the table he was more at peace with the world and he treated, closely watching his companion. Mr. Hawley drank with a show of pleasure and forthwith brought out cigars. He seated himself beside his guest and sighed with relief.

"I 'm plumb tired out," he offered. "An' I ain't done much. You look tired, too. Come a long way?"

"Logan," replied Bill. "Do *you* know where I 'm goin'? An' why?" he asked.

Mr. Hawley looked surprised and almost answered the first part of the question correctly before he thought. "Well," he grinned, "if I could tell where strangers was goin', an' why, I would n't never ask 'em where they come from. An' I 'd shore hunt up a li'l game of faro, you bet!"

Bill smiled. "Well, that might be a good idea. But, say, what ails this town, anyhow?"

"What ails it? Hum! Why, lack of money for one thing; scenery, for another; wimmin, for another. Oh, h—l, I ain't got time to tell you what ails it. Why?"

"Is there anything th' matter with me?"

"I don't know you well enough for to answer that kerrect."

"Well, would you turn around an' stare at me, an' seem pained an' hurt? Do I look funny? Has anybody put a sign on my back?"

"You looks all right to me. What's th' matter?"

"Nothin', yet," reflected Bill slowly. "But there will be, mebby. You was mentionin' faro. Here 's a turn you can call: somebody in this wart of a two-by-nothin' town is goin' to run plumb into a big surprise. There 'll mebby be a loud noise an' some smoke where it starts from; an' a li'l round hole where it stops. When th' curious delegation now holdin' forth on th' street slips in here after I 'm in bed, an' makes inquiries about me, you can tell 'em that. An' if Mr. —Mr. Victoria drops in casual, tell him I 'm cleanin' my guns. Now then, show me where I 'm goin' to sleep."

Mr. Hawley very carefully led the way into the hall and turned into a room opposite the bar. "Here she is, stranger," he said, stepping back. But Bill was out in the hall listening. He looked into the room and felt oppressed.

"No she ain't," he answered, backing his intuition. "She is upstairs, where there is a li'l breeze. By th' Lord," he muttered under his breath. "This is some puzzle." He mounted the stairs shaking his head thoughtfully. "It shore is, it shore is."

The next morning when Bill whirled up to the Crazy M bunkhouse and dismounted before the door a puncher was emerging. He started to say something, noticed Bill's guns and went on without a word. Bill turned around and looked after him in amazement. "Well, what th' devil!" he growled. Before he could do anything, had he wished to, Mr. Oleson stepped quickly from the house, nodded and hurried toward the ranch house, motioning for Bill to follow. Entering the house, the foreman of the Crazy M waited impatiently for Bill to get inside, and then hurriedly closed the door.

"They 've got onto it some way," he said, his taciturnity gone; "but that don't make no difference if you 've got th' sand. I 'll pay you one hundred an' fifty a month, furnish yore cayuses an' feed you. I 'm losin' more 'n two hundred cows every month an' can't get a trace of th' thieves. Harris, Marshal of Clay Gulch, is stumped, too. *He* can't move without proof; *you* can. Th' first man to get is George Thomas, then his brother Art. By that time you 'll know how things lay. George Thomas is keepin' out of Harris' way. He killed a man last week over in Tuxedo an' Harris wants to take him over there. He 'll not help you, so don't ask him to." Before Bill could reply or recover from his astonishment Oleson continued and described several men. "Look out for ambushes. It 'll be th' hardest game you ever went up ag'in, an' if you ain't got th' sand to go through with it, say so."

Bill shook his head. "I got th' sand to go through with anythin' I starts, but I don't start here. I reckon you got th' wrong man. I come up here to look over a herd for Buck Peters; an' here you go shovin' wages like that at me. When I tells Buck what I 've been offered he 'll fall dead." He laughed. "Now I knows th' answer to a lot of things.

"Here, here!" he exclaimed as Oleson began to rave. "Don't you go an' get all het up like that. I reckon I can keep my face shut. An' lemme observe in yore hat-like ear that if th' rest of this gang is like th' samples I seen in town, a good gun-man would shore be robbin' you to take all that money for th' job. Fifty a month, for two months, would be a-plenty."

Oleson's dismay was fading, and he accepted the situation with a grim smile. "You don't know them fellers," he replied. "They 're a bad lot, an' won't stop at nothin'."

"All right. Let's take a look at them cows. I want to get home soon as I can."

Oleson shook his head. "I gave you up, an' when I got a better offer I let 'em go. I 'm sorry you had th' ride for nothin', but I could n't get word to you."

Bill led the way in silence back to the bunk house and mounted his horse. "All right," he nodded. "I shore was late. Well, I 'll be goin'."

"That gun-man is late, too," said Oleson. "Mebby he ain't comin'. You want th' job at *my* figgers?"

"Nope. I got a better job, though it don't pay so much money. It's steady, an' a hull lot cleaner. So-long," and Bill loped away, closely watched by Shorty Allen from the corral. And after an interval, Shorty mounted and swung out of the other gate of the corral and rode along the bottom of an arroyo until he felt it was safe to follow Bill's trail. When Shorty turned back he was almost to town, and he would not have been pleased had he known that Bill knew of the trailing for the last ten miles. Bill had doubled back and was within a hundred yards of Shorty when that person turned ranchward.

"Huh! I must be popular," grunted Bill. "I reckon I will stay in Clay Gulch till t'morrow mornin'; an' at the Victoria," he grinned. Then he laughed heartily. "Victoria! I got a better name for it than that, all right."

When he pulled up before the Victoria and looked in the proprietor scowled at him, which made Bill frown as he went on to Hawley's. Putting his horse in the corral he carried his saddle and rifle into the barroom and looked around. There was no one in sight, and he smiled. Putting the saddle and rifle back in one corner under the bar and covering them with gunny sacks he strolled to the Victoria and entered through the rear door. The proprietor reached for his gun but reconsidered in time and picked up a glass, which he polished with exaggerated care. There was something about the stranger that obtruded upon his peace of mind and confidence. He would let some one else try the stranger out.

Bill walked slowly forward, by force of will ironing out the humor in his face and assuming his sternest expression. "I want supper an' a bed, an' don't forget to be plumb polite," he rumbled, sitting down by the side of a small table in such a manner that it did not in the least interfere with the movement of his right hand. The observing proprietor observed and gave strict attention to the preparation of the meal. The gun-man, glancing around, slowly arose and walked carelessly to a chair that had blank wall behind it, and from where he could watch windows and doors.

When the meal was placed before him he glanced up. "Go over there an' sit down," he ordered, motioning to a chair that stood close to the rifle that leaned against the wall. "Loaded?" he demanded. The proprietor could only nod. "Then sling it acrost yore knees an' keep still. Well, start movin'."

The proprietor walked as though he were in a trance but when he seated himself and reached for the weapon a sudden flash of understanding illumined him and caused cold sweat to bead upon his wrinkled brow. He put the weapon down again, but the noise made Bill look up.

"Acrost yore knees," growled the puncher, and the proprietor hastily obeyed, but when it touched his legs he let loose of it as though it were hot. He felt a great awe steal through his fear, for here was a gun-man such as he had read about. This man gave him all the best of it just to tempt him to make a break. The rifle had been in his hands, and while it was there the gun-man was calmly eating with both hands on the table and had not even looked up until the noise of the gun made him!

"My Gawd, 'e must be a wizard with 'em. I 'opes I don't forget!" With the thought came a great itching of his kneecap; then his foot itched so as to make him squirm and wear horrible expressions. Bill, chancing to glance up carelessly, caught sight of the expressions and growled, whereupon they became angelic. Fearing that he could no longer hold in the laughter that tortured him, Bill arose.

"Shoulder, *arms!*" he ordered, crisply. The gun went up with trained precision. "Been a sojer," thought Bill. "Carry, *arms!* About, *face!* To a bedroom, *march!*" He followed, holding his sides, and stopped before the room. "This th' best?" he demanded. "Well, it ain't good enough for me. About, *face!* Forward, *march!* Column, *left!* Ground, *arms!* Fall out." Tossing a coin on the floor as payment for the supper Bill turned sharply and went out without even a backward glance.

The proprietor wiped the perspiration from his face and walked unsteadily to the bar, where he poured out a generous drink and gulped it down. Peering out of the door to see if the coast was clear, he scurried across the street and told his troubles to the harness-maker.

Bill leaned weakly against Hawley's and laughed until the tears rolled down his cheeks. Pushing weakly from the building he returned to the Victoria to play another joke on its proprietor.

Finding it vacant he slipped upstairs and hunted for a room to suit him. The bed was the softest he had seen for a long time and it lured him into removing his boots and chaps and guns, after he had propped a chair against the door as a warning signal, and stretching out flat on his back, he prepared to enjoy solid comfort. It was not yet dark, and as he was not sleepy he lay there thinking over the events of the past twenty-four hours, often laughing so hard as to shake the bed. What a reputation he would have in the morning! The softness of the bed got in its work and he fell asleep, for how long he did not know; but when he awakened it was dark and he heard voices coming up from below. They came from the room he had refused to take. One expression banished all thoughts of sleep from his mind and he listened intently. "'Red-headed Irish gunman.' Why, they means me! 'Make him hop into h —l.' I don't reckon I 'd do that for anybody, even my friends."

"I tried to give 'im this room, but 'e would n't tyke it" protested the proprietor, hurriedly. "'E says the bloody room was n't good enough for 'im, *hand* 'e marches me out hand makes off. Likely 'e 's in *'Awley's*."

"No, he ain't," growled a strange voice. "You 've gone an' bungled th' whole thing."

"But I s'y I did n't, you know. I tries to give 'im this werry room, George, but 'e would n't 'ave it. D'y think I wants 'im running haround this blooming town? 'E 's worse nor the other, *hand* Gawd knows 'e was bad enough. 'E 's a cold-*blooded* beggar, 'e is!"

"You missed yore chance," grunted the other. "Wish *I* had that gun you had."

"I was wishing to Gawd you did," retorted the proprietor. "It never looked so bloody big before, d —n 'is *'ide!*"

"Well, his cayuse is in Hawley's corral," said the first speaker. "If I ever finds Hawley kept him under cover I 'll blow his head off. Come on; we 'll get Harris first. He ought to be gettin' close to town if he got th' word I sent over to Tuxedo. He won't let us call him. He's a man of his word."

"He 'll be here, all right. Fred an' Tom is watchin' his shack, an' we better take th' other end of town-there 's no tellin' how he 'll come in now," suggested Art Thomas. "But I wish I knowed where that cussed gun-man is."

As they went out Bill, his chaps on and his boots in his hand, crept down the stairs, and stopped as he neared the hall door. The proprietor was coming back. The others were outside, going to their stations and did not hear the choking gasp that the proprietor made as a pair of strong hands reached out and throttled him. When he came to he was lying face down on a bed, gagged and bound by a rope that cut into his flesh with every movement. Bill, waiting a moment, slipped into the darkness and was swallowed up. He was looking for Mr. Harris, and looking eagerly.

The moon arose and bathed the dusty street and its crude shacks in silver, cunningly and charitably hiding its ugliness; and passed on as the skirmishing rays of the sun burst into the sky in close and eternal pursuit. As the dawn spread swiftly and long, thin shadows sprang across the sandy street, there arose from the dissipated darkness close to the wall of a building an armed man, weary and slow from a tiresome vigil. Another emerged from behind a pile of boards that faced the marshal's abode, while down the street another crept over the edge of a dried-out water course and swore softly as he stood up slowly to flex away the stiffness of cramped limbs. Of vain speculation he was empty; he had exhausted all the whys and hows long before and now only muttered discontentedly as he reviewed the hours of fruitless waiting. And he was uneasy; it was not like Harris to take a dare and swallow his own threats without a struggle. He looked around apprehensively, shrugged his shoulders and stalked behind the shacks across from the two hotels.

Another figure crept from the protection of Hawley's corral like a slinking coyote, gun in hand and nervously alert. He was just in time to escape the challenge that would have been hurled at him by Hawley, himself, had that gentleman seen the skulker as he grouchily opened one shutter and scowled sleepily at the kindling eastern sky. Mr. Hawley was one of those who go to bed with regret and get up with remorse, and his temper was always easily disturbed before breakfast. The skulker, safe from the remorseful gentleman's eyes, and gun, kept close to the building as he walked and was again fortunate, for he had passed when Mr. Hawley strode heavily into his kitchen to curse the cold, rusty stove, a rite he faithfully performed each morning. Across the street George and Art Thomas walked to meet each other behind the row of shacks and stopped near the harness shop to hold a consultation. The subject was so interesting that for a few moments they were oblivious to all else.

A man softly stepped to the door of the Victoria and watched the two across the street with an expression on his face that showed his smiling contempt for them and their kind. He was a small man, so far as physical measurements go, but he was lithe, sinewy and compact. On his opened vest, hanging slovenly and blinking in the growing light as if to prepare itself for the blinding glare of midday, glinted a five-pointed star of nickel, a lowly badge that every rural community knows and holds in an awe far above the metal or design. Swinging low on his hip gleamed the ivory butt of a silver-plated Colt, the one weakness that his vanity seized upon. But under the silver and its engraving, above and before the cracked and stained ivory handles, lay the power of a great force; and under the casing of the marshal's small body lay a virile manhood, strong in courage and determination. Toby Harris watched, smilingly; he loved the dramatic and found keen enjoyment in the situation. Out of the corner of his eye he saw a carelessly dressed cowpuncher slouching indolently along close to the buildings on the other side of the street with the misleading sluggishness of a panther. The red hair, kissed by the slanting rays of the sun where it showed beneath the soiled sombrero, seemed to be a flaming warning; the half-closed eyes, squinting under the brim of the big hat, missed nothing as they darted from point to point.

The marshal stepped silently to the porch and then on to the ground, his back to the rear of the hotel, waiting to be discovered. He had been in sight perhaps a minute. The cowpuncher made a sudden, eye-baffling movement and smoke whirled about his hips. Fred, turning the corner behind the marshal, dropped his gun with a scream of rage and pain and crashed against the window in sudden sickness, his gunhand hanging by a tendon from his wrist. The marshal stepped quickly forward at the shot and for an instant gazed deeply into the eyes of the startled rustlers. Then his Colt leaped out and crashed a fraction of a second before the brothers fired. George Thomas reeled, caught sight of the puncher and fired by instinct. Bill, leaving Harris to watch the other side of the street, was watching the rear corner of the Victoria and was unprepared for the shot. He crumpled and dropped and then the marshal, enraged, ended the rustler's earthly career in a stream of flame and smoke. Tom, turning into the street further down, wheeled and dashed for his horse, and Art, having leaped behind the harness shop, turned and fled for his life. He had nearly reached his horse and was going at top speed with great leaps when the prostrate man in the street, raising on his elbow, emptied his gun after him, the five shots sounding almost as one. Art Thomas arose convulsively, steadied himself and managed to gain the saddle. Harris looked hastily down the street and saw a cloud of dust racing northward, and grunted. "Let them go —*they* won't never come back no more." Running to the cowpuncher he raised him after a hurried examination of the wounded thigh. "Hop along, Cassidy," he smiled in encouragement. "You 'll be a better man with one good laig than th' whole gang was all put together."

The puncher smiled faintly as Hawley, running to them, helped him toward his hotel. "Th' bone is plumb smashed. I reckon I 'll hop along through life. It 'll be hop along, for me, all right. That's *my* name, all right. Huh! Hopalong Cassidy! But I didn't hop into h —l, did I, Harris?" he grinned bravely.

And thus was born a nickname that found honor and fame in the cow-country —a name that stood for loyalty, courage and most amazing gun-play. I have Red's word for this, and the endorsement of those who knew him at the time. And from this on, up to the time he died, and after, we will forsake "Bill" and speak of him as Hopalong Cassidy, a cowpuncher who lived and worked in the days when the West was wild and rough and lawless; and who, like others, through the medium of the only court at hand, Judge Colt, enforced justice as he believed it should be enforced.

"Dealing the Odd"

Faro-bank is an expensive game when luck turns a cold shoulder on any player, and "going broke" is as easy as ruffling a deck. When a man finds he has two dollars left out of more than two months' pay and that it has taken him less than thirty minutes to get down to that mark, he cannot be censored much if he rails at that Will-o'-the-wisp, the Goddess of Luck. Put him a good ten days' ride from home, acquaintances and money and perhaps he will be justified in adding heat in plenty to his denunciation. He had played to win when he should have coppered, coppered when he should have played to win, he had backed both ends against the middle and played the high card as well-but only when his bets were small did the turn show him what he wanted to see. Perhaps the case-keeper had hoodooed him, for he never did have any luck at cards when a tow-headed man had a finger in the game.

Fuming impotently at his helplessness, a man limped across the main street in Colby, constrained and a little awkward in his new store clothes and new, squeaking boots that were clumsy with stiffness. The only things on him that he could regard as old and tried friends were the battered sombrero and the heavy, walnut-handled Colt's .45 which rubbed comfortably with each movement of his thigh. The weapon, to be sure, had a ready cash value-but he could not afford to part with it. The horse belonged to his ranch, and the saddle must not be sold; to part with it would be to lose his mark of caste and become a walking man, which all good punchers despised.

"Ten days from home, knowin' nobody, two measly dollars in my pocket, an' luck dead agin me," he growled with pugnacious pessimism. "Oh, I 'm a wise old bird, I am! A h —l of a wise bird. Real smart an' cute an' shiny, a cache of wisdom, a real, bonyfied Smart Aleck with a head full of spavined brains. I copper th' deuce an' th' deuce wins; I play th' King to win for ten dollars when I ought to copper it. I lay two-bits and it comes right-ten dollars an' I see my guess go *loco*. Reckon I better slip these here twin bucks down in my kill-me-soon boots afore some blind papoose takes 'em away from me. Wiser 'n Solomon, I am; I 've got old Caesar climbin' a cactus for pleasure an' joy. S-u-c-k-e-r is my middle name-an' I 'm busted."

He almost stumbled over a little tray of a three-legged table on the corner of the street and his face went hard as he saw the layout. Three halves of English walnut shells lay on the faded and soiled green cloth and a blackened, shriveled pea was still rolling from the shaking he had given the table. He stopped and regarded it gravely, jingling his two dollars disconsolately. "Don't this town do nothin' else besides gamble?" he muttered, looking around.

"Howd'y, stranger!" cheerfully cried a man who hastened up. "Want to see me fool you?"

The puncher's anger was aroused to a thin, licking flame; but it passed swiftly and a cold, calculating look came into his eyes. He glanced around swiftly, trying to locate the cappers, but they were not to be seen, which worried him a little. He always liked to have possible danger where he could keep an eye on it. Perhaps they were eating or drinking-the thought stirred him again to anger: two dollars would not feed him very long, nor quench his thirst.

"Pick it out, stranger," invited the proprietor, idly shifting the shells. "It's easy if yo 're right smart-but lots of folks just can't do it; they can't seem to get th' hang of it, somehow. That's why it's a bettin' proposition. Here it is, right before yore eyes! One little pea, three little shells, right here plumb in front of yore eyes! Th' little pea hides under one of th' little shells, right in plain sight: But can you tell which one? That's th' whole game, right there. See how it's done?" and the three little shells moved swiftly but clumsily and the little pea disappeared. "Now, then; where would *you* say it was?" demanded the hopeful operator, genially.

The puncher gripped his two dollars firmly, shifted his weight as much as possible on his sound leg, and scowled: he knew where it was. "Do I look like a kid? Do you reckon you have to coax like a fool to get me all primed up to show how re-markably smart an' quick I am? You don't; I know how smart I am. Say, you ain't, not by any kinda miracle, a blind papoose, are you?" he demanded.

"What you mean?" asked the other, smiling as he waited for the joke. It did not come, so he continued. "Don't take no harm in my fool wind-jammin', stranger. It's in th' game. It's a habit; I 've said it so much I just can't help it no more —I up an' says it at a funeral once; that is, part of it-th' first part. That's dead right! But I reckon I 'm wastin' my time-unless you happen to feel coltish an' hain't got nothin' to do for an age. I 've been playin' in hard luck th' last week or so-you see, I ain't as good as I uster be. I ain't quite so quick, an' a little bit off my quickness is a whole lot off my chances. But th' game's square-an' that's a good deal more'n you can say about most of 'em."

The puncher hesitated, a grin flickering about his thin lips and a calm joy warming him comfortably. He knew the operator. He knew that face, the peculiar, crescent-shaped scar over one brow, and the big, blue eyes that years of life had not entirely robbed of their baby-like innocence. The past, sorted thoroughly and quickly by his memory, shoved out that face before a crowd of others. Five years is not a long time to remember something unpleasant; he had reasons to remember that countenance. Knowing the face he also knew that the man had been, at one time, far from "square." The associations and means of livelihood during the past five years, judging from the man's present occupation, had not been the kind to correct any evil tendency. He laid a forefinger on the edge of the tray. "Start th' machinery —I 'll risk a couple of dollars, anyhow. That ain't much to lose. I bet two dollars I can call it right," he said, watching closely.

He won, as he knew he would; and the result told him that the gambler had not reformed. The dexterous fingers shifting the shells were slower than others he had seen operate and when he had won again he stopped, as if to leave. "When I hit town a short time ago I didn't know I 'd be so lucky. I went an' drawed two months' pay when I left th' ranch: I shore don't need it. Shuffle 'em again-it's yore money, anyhow," he laughed. "You should 'a' quit th' game before you got so slow."

"Goin' back to work purty soon?" queried the shell-man, wondering how much this "sucker" had left unspent.

"Not me! I 've only just had a couple of drinks since I hit town-an' *I* 'm due to celebrate."

The other's face gave no hint of his thoughts, which were that the fool before him had about a hundred dollars on his person. "Well, luck's with you today-you 've called it right twice. I 'll bet you a cool hundred that you can't call it th' third time. It's th' quickness of my hands agin yore eyes-an' you can't beat me three straight. Make it a hundred? I hate to play all day."

"I 'll lay you my winnings an' have some more of yore money," replied the puncher, feverishly. "Ain't scared, are you?"

"Don't know what it means to be scared," laughed the other. "But I ain't got no small change, nothin' but tens. Play a hundred an' let's have some real excitement."

"Nope; eight or nothin'."

He won again. "Now, sixteen even. Come on; I 've got you beat."

"But what's th' use of stringin' 'long like that?" demanded the shell-man.

"Gimme a chance to get my hand in, won't you?" retorted the puncher.

"Well, all right," replied the gambler, and he lost the sixteen.

"Now thirty," suggested the puncher. "Next time all I 've got, every red cent. Once more to practice-then every red," he repeated, shifting his feet nervously. "I 'll clean you out an' have a real, genuine blow-out on yore money. Come on, I 'm in a hurry."

"I 'll fool you *this* time, by th' Lord!" swore the gambler, angrily. "You've got more luck than sense. An' I 'll fool you next time, too. Yo 're quicker 'n most men I 've run up agin, but I can beat you, shore as shootin'. Th' game's square, th' play fair-my hand agin yore eye. Ready? Then watch me!"

He swore luridly and shoved the money across the board to the winner, bewailing his slowness and getting angrier every moment. "Yo 're th' cussedest man I ever bet agin! But I'll get you *this* time. You can't guess right all th' time, an' I know it."

"There she is; sixty-two bucks, three score an' two simoleons; all I 've got, every cent. Let's see you take it away from me!"

The gambler frowned and choked back a curse. He had risked sixty dollars to win two, and the fact that he had to let this fool play again with the fire hurt his pride. He had no fear for his money-he knew he could win at every throw-but to play that long for two dollars! And suppose the sucker had quit with the sixty!

"Do you get a dollar a month?" he demanded, sarcastically. "Well, I reckon you earn it, at that. Thought you had money, thought you drew down two months' pay an' hain't had nothin' more'n two drinks? Did you go an' lose it on th' way?"

"Oh, I drew it a month ago," replied the sucker, surprised. "I 've only had two drinks in this town, which I hit 'bout an hour ago. But I shore lost a wad playin' faro-bank agin a towhead. Come on-lemme take sixty more of yore money, anyhow."

"Sixty-*two*!" snapped the proprietor, determined to have those two miserable dollars and break the sucker for revenge. "Every cent, you remember."

"*All* right; I don't care! I ain't no tin-horn," grumbled the other. "Think I care 'bout two dollars?" But he appeared to be very nervous, nevertheless.

"Well, put it on th' table."

"After you put yourn down."

"There it is. Now watch me close!" A gleam of joy flashed up in the angry man's eyes as he played with the shells. "Watch me close! Mebby it is, an' mebby it ain't —th' game's square, th' play 's fair. It's my hand agin yore eye. Watch me close!"

"Oh, go ahead! I'm watchin', all right. Think I 'd go to sleep now!"

The shifting hands stopped, the shells lay quiet, and the gambler gazed blankly down the unsympathetic barrel of a Colt.

"Now, Thomas, old thimble-rigger," crisply remarked the supposed sucker as he cautiously slid the money off the table, to be picked up later when conditions would be more favorable. "Th' little pea ain't under *no* shell. *Stop*! Step back one pace an' elevate them paws. Don't make no more funny motions with that hand, savvy? But you can drop th' pea if it hurts them two fingers. Now we 'll see if I win; I allus like to be shore," and he cautiously turned over the shells, revealing nothing but the dirty green cloth. "I win; it ain't there-just like I thought."

"Who are you, an' how 'd you know my name?" demanded the gambler, mentally cursing his two missing cappers. They were drinking once too often and things were going to happen in their vicinity, and very soon.

"Why, you took twenty-five dollars from me up in Alameda onct, when I could n't afford to lose it," grinned the puncher. "I was something of a kid then. I remember you, all right. My foreman told me about yore bang-up fight agin th' Johnson brothers, who gave you that scar. I thought then that you were a great man-now I know you ain't. I would n't 'a' played at all if I had n't knowed how crooked you was. Take yore layout an' yore crookedness, find th' pea an' yore cappers, an' clear out. An' if anybody asks you if you 've seen Hopalong Cassidy you tell 'em I 'm up here in Colby makin' some easy money beatin' crooked games. So-long, an' *don't* look back!"

Hopalong watched him go and then went to the nearest place where he could get something to eat. In due time, having disposed of a square meal, Hopalong called for a drink and a cigar, and sat quietly smoking for nearly half an hour, so lost in thought that his cigar went out repeatedly. As he reviewed his disastrous play at faro many small details came to him and now he found them interesting. The dealer was not a master at his trade and Hopalong had seen many better; in fact the man was not even second class, and this fact hurt his pride. He had played a careful game, and the great majority of his small bets had won-it was only when he risked twenty or thirty dollars that he lost. The only big bet that he had been at all lucky on was one where doubles showed on the turn and he had been split, losing half of his stake. But when he had played his last fifty dollars on the Jack, open, the final blow fell and he had left the table in disgust.

Why weren't there cue-cards, so the players could keep their own tally of the cards instead of having to depend on the cue-box kept by the case-keeper? This made him suspicious; a crooked dealer and case-keeper can trim a big bet at will, unless the players keep their own cases or are exceptionally wise; and even then a really good dealer will get away with his play nine times out of ten. While he seldom played a system, he had backed one that morning; but he was cured of that weakness now. If the game were square he figured he could get at least an even break; if crooked, nothing but a gun could beat it, and he had a very good gun. When he thought of the gun, he reviewed the arrangement of the room and estimated the weight of the rough, deal table on which rested the faro layout. He smiled and turned to the bartender. "Hey, barkeeper! Got any paper an' a pencil?"

After some rummaging the taciturn dispenser of liquid forget-it produced the articles in question and Hopalong, drawing some hurried lines, paid his bill, treated, kept the pencil and headed for the faro game across the street.

When he entered the room the table was deserted and he nodded to the dealer as he seated himself at the right of the case-keeper, who now took his place, and opposite the dealer and the lookout. He was not surprised to find no other players in the room, for the hour was wrong; later in the afternoon there would be many and at night the place would be crowded. This suited him perfectly and he settled himself to begin playing.

When the deck was shuffled and placed in the deal box Hopalong put his ruled paper in front of him on the table, tallied once against the King for the soda card and started to play quarters and half dollars. He caught the fugitive look that passed between the men as they saw his cue-card but he gave no sign of having observed it. After that he never looked up from the cards while his bets were small. Two deals did not alter his money much and he knew that so far the game was straight. If it were not to remain straight the crookedness would not come more than once in a deal if the frame-up was "single-odd" and then not until the bet was large enough to practically break him. His high-card play ran in his favor and kept him gradually drawing ahead. He lost twice in calling the last turn and guessed it right once, at four to one, which made him win in that department of the game.

When the fifth deal began he was quite a little ahead and his play became bolder, some of the bets going as high as ten dollars. He broke even and then played heavier on the following deal. His first high bet, twenty dollars, was on the eight, open, only one eight having shown. Double eights showed on the next turn and he was split, losing half the stake.

It was about this time that the look-out discovered that Mr. Cassidy was getting a little excited and several times had nearly forgotten to keep his cases. This information was cautiously passed to the dealer and case-keeper and from then on they evinced a little more interest in the game. Finally the player, after studying his cue-card, placed fifty dollars on the Queen, open, and coppered the deuce, a case-card, and then put ten more on the high card. This came in the middle of the game and he was prepared for trouble as the turn was made, but fortune was kind to him and he raked in sixty dollars. He was mildly surprised that he had won, but explained it to himself by thinking that the stakes were not yet high enough. From then on he was keenly alert, for the crookedness would come soon if it ever did, but he strung small sums on the next dozen turns and waited for a new deal before plunging.

As the dealer shuffled the cards the door opened and closed noisily and a surprised and doubting voice exclaimed: "Ain't you Hopalong Cassidy? Cassidy, of th' Bar-20?"

Hopalong glanced up swiftly and back to the cards again: "Yes; what of it?"

"Oh, nothin'. I saw you onct an' I wondered if I was right."

"Ain't got time now; see you later, mebby. You might stick around outside so I can borrow some money if I go broke." The man who knew Mr. Cassidy silently faded, but did not stick around, thereby proving that the player knew human nature and also how to get rid of a pest.

When the dealer heard the name he glanced keenly at the owner of it, exchanged significant looks with the case-keeper and faltered for an instant as he shoved the cards together. He was not sure that he had shuffled them right, and an anxious look came into his eyes as he realized that the deal must go on. It was far from reassuring to set out to cheat a man so well known for expert short-gun work as the Bar-20 puncher and he wished he could be relieved. There was no other dealer around at that time of the day and he had to go through with it. He did not dare to shuffle again and chance losing the card beyond hope, and for the reason that the player was watching him like a hawk.

A ten lay face up on the deck and Hopalong, tallying against it on his sheet, began to play small sums. Luck was variable and remained so until the first twenty dollar bet, when he reached out excitedly and raked in his winnings, his coat sleeve at the same time brushing the cue-card off the table. But he had forgotten all about the tally sheet in his eagerness to win and played several more cards before he noticed it was missing and sought for it. Smothering a curse he glanced at the case-keeper's tally and went on with the play. He did not see the look of relief that showed momentarily on the faces of the dealer and his associates, but he guessed it.

He had no use for cue-cards when he felt like doing without them; he liked to see them in use by the players because it showed the game to be more or less straight, and it also saved him from over-heating his memory. When he had brushed his tally sheet off the table he knew what he was doing, and he knew every card that had been drawn out of the box. So far he had seen no signs of cheating and he wished to give the dealer a chance. There should now remain in the deal box three cards, a deuce, five and a four, with a Queen in sight as the last winner. He knew this to be true because he had given all his attention to memorizing the cards as they showed in the deal box, and had made his bets small so he would not have to bother about them. As he had lost three times on a four he now believed it was due to win.

Taking all his money he placed it on the four: "Two hundred and seventy on th' four to win," he remarked, crisply.

The dealer sniffed almost inaudibly and the case-keeper prepared to cover him on the cue-rack under cover of the excitement of the turn. If the four lay under the Queen, Cassidy lost; if not he either won or was in hock. The dealer was unusually grave as he grasped the deal box to make the turn and as the Queen slid off a five-spot showed.

The dealer's hand trembled as he slid the five off, showing a four, and a winner for Hopalong. He went white-he had bungled the shuffle in his indecision and now he did n't know what might develop. And in his agitation he exposed the hock card before he realized what he was doing, and showed another five. He had made the mistake of showing the "odd."

Hopalong, ready for trouble, was more prepared than the others and he was well under way before they started. His left hand swung hard against the case-keeper's jaw, his Colt roared at the drawing bartender, crumpling the trouble-hunter into a heap on the floor dazed from shock of a ball that "creased" his head. He had done this as he sprang to his feet and his left hand, dropping swiftly to the heavy table, threw it over onto the lookout and the dealer at the instant their hands found their guns. Caught off their balance they went down under it and before they could move sufficiently to do any damage, Hopalong vaulted the table and kicked their guns out of their hands. When they realized just what had happened a still-smoking Colt covered them. Many of Hopalong's most successful and spectacular plays had been less carefully thought out beforehand than this one and he laughed sneeringly as he looked at the men who had been so greedy as to try to clean him out the second time.

"Get up!" he snarled.

They crawled out of their trap and sullenly obeyed his hand, backing against the wall. The case-keeper was still unconscious and Hopalong, disarming him, dragged him to the wall with the others.

"I wondered where that deuce had crawled to," Mr. Cassidy remarked, grimly, "an' I was goin' to see, only it's plain now. I knowed you was clumsy, but my G —d! Any man as can't deal 'single-odd' ought to quit th' business, or play straight. So you had five fives agin me, eh? Instead of keepin' th' five under th' Queen, you bungled th' deuce in its place. When you went to pull off th' Queen an' five like they was one card, you had th' deuce under her. You see, I keep cases in my old red head an' I did n't have to believe what th' cue-rack was all fixed to show me. An' I was waitin', all ready for th' play that 'd make me lose.

"As long as this deal was framed up, we 'll say it was this mornin'. You cough up th' hundred an' ten I lost then, an' another hundred an' ten that I 'd won if it was n't crooked. An' don't forget that two-seventy I just pulled down, neither. Make it in double eagles an' don't be slow 'bout it. Money or lead-with *you* callin' th' turn." It was not a very large amount and it took only a moment to count it out. The eleven double eagles representing the mornin's play seemed to slide from the dealer's hand with reluctance-but a man lives only once, and they slid without stopping.

The winner, taking the money, picked up the last money he had bet and, distributing it over his person to equalize the weight, gathered up the guns from the floor. Backing toward the door he noticed that the bartender moved and a keen glance at that unfortunate assured him that he would live.

When he reached the door he stopped a moment to ask a question, the tenseness of his expression relaxing into a broad, apologetic grin. "Would you mind tellin' me where I can find some more frame-ups? I shore can use th' money."

The mumbled replies mentioned a locality not to be found on any map of the surface of the globe, and grinning still more broadly, Mr. Cassidy side-stepped and disappeared to find his horse and go on his way rejoicing.

VIII
The Norther

Johnny knew I had a notebook crammed with the stories his friends had told me; but Johnny, being a wise youth, also knew that there was always room for one more. Perhaps that explains his sarcasm, for, as he calmly turned his back on his fuming friend, he winked at me and sauntered off, whistling cheerfully.

Red spread his feet apart, jammed his fists against his thighs and stared after the youngster. His expression was a study and his open mouth struggled for a retort, but in vain. After a moment he shook his head and slowly turned to me. "Hear th' fool? He 's from *Idyho*, he is. It never gets cold nowhere else on earth. Ain't it terrible to be so ignorant?" He glanced at the bunkhouse, into which Johnny had gone for dry clothing. "So I ain't never seen no cold weather?" he mused thoughtfully. Snapping his fingers irritably, he wheeled toward the corral. "I 'm goin' down to look at th' dam-there 's been lots of water leanin' ag'in it th' last week. Throw th' leather on Saint, if you wants, an' come along. I 'll tell you about some cold weather that had th' *Idyho* brand faded. *Cold* weather! Huh!"

As he swung past the bunkhouse we saw Johnny and Billy Jordan leaning in the doorway ragging each other, as cubs will. Johnny grinned at Red and executed a one-hand phrase of the sign language that is universally known, which Red returned with a chuckle. "Wish he 'd been here th' time God took a hand in a big game on this ranch," he said. "I 'm minus two toes on each foot in consequence thereof. They can't scare me none by preachin' a red-hot hell. No, sir; not any."

He was silent a moment. "Mebby it ain't so bad when a feller is used to it; but we ain't. An' it frequent hits us goin' over th' fence, with both feet off th' ground. Anyhow, that Norther was n't no storm-it was th' attendant agitation caused by th' North Pole visitin' th' Gulf.

"Cowan had just put Buckskin on th' map by buildin' th' first shack. John Bartlett an' Shorty Jones, d —n him, was startin' th' Double Arrow with two hundred head. When th' aforementioned agitation was over they had less 'n one hundred. We lost a lot of cows, too; but our range is sheltered good, an' that rock wall down past Meeker's bunkhouse stopped our drifts, though lots of th' cows died there.

"We 'd had a mild winter for two weeks, an' a lot of rain. We was chirpin' like li'l fool birds about winter bein' over. Ever notice how many times winter is over before it is? But Buck did n't think so; an' he shore can smell weather. We was also discussin' a certain campin' party Jimmy had discovered across th' river. Jimmy was at th' bunkhouse that shift an' he was a great hand for snoopin' around kickin' up trouble. He reports there's twelve in th' party an' they 're camped back of Split Hill. Now, Split Hill is no place for a camp, even in th' summer; an' what got us was th' idea of campin' at all in th' winter. It riled Buck till he forgot to cross off three days on th' calendar, which we later discovered by help of th' almanac an' th' moon. Buck sends Hoppy over to scout around Split Hill. You know Hoppy. He scouted for two days without bein' seen, an' without discoverin' any lawful an' sane reason why twelve hard-lookin' fellers should be campin' back of Split Hill in th' winter time. He also found they had come from th' south, an' he swore there was n't no cow tracks leadin' toward them from our range. But there was lots of hoss tracks back and forth. An' when he reports that th' campers had left an' gone on north we all feel better. Then he adds they turned east below th' Double Arrow an' went back south again. That's different. It's plain to some of us they was lookin' us over for future use; learnin' our ways an' th' lay of th' land. There was seven of us at th' time, but we could 'a' licked 'em in a fair fight.

"In them days we only had two line houses. Number One was near Big Coulee, with Cowan's at th' far end of its fifteen miles of north line; th' west line was a twenty-five-mile ride south to Lookout Peak. Number Two was where th' Jumpin' Bear empties into th' river, now part of Meeker's range. From it th' riders went west twenty-five miles to th' Peak an' north from it twenty-five miles along th' east line. There was a hundred thousan' acres in Conroy Valley an' thirty thousan' in th' Meeker triangle, which made up Section Two. At that time mebby ten thousan' cows was on this section-two-thirds of all of 'em. When we built Number Three on th' Peak this section was cut down to a reasonable size. Th' third headquarters then was th' bunkhouse, with only th' east line to ride. One part, th' shortest, ran north to Cowan's; th' other run about seventeen miles south to Li'l Timber, where th' line went on as part of Number Two's. We paired off an' had two weeks in each of 'em in them days.

"When we shifted at th' end of that week Jimmy Price an' Ace Fisher got Number One; Skinny an' Lanky was in Number Two; an' me an' Buck an' Hoppy took life easy in th' bunkhouse, with th' cook to feed us. Buck, he scouted all over th' ranch between th' lines an' worked harder than any of us, spendin' his nights in th' nearest house.

"One mornin', about a week after th' campers left, Buck looked out of th' bunkhouse door an' cautions me an' Hoppy to ride prepared for cold weather. I can see he 's worried, an' to please him we straps a blanket an' a buffalo robe behind our saddles, cussin' th' size of 'em under our breath. I 've got th' short ride that day, an' Buck says he 'll wait for me to come back, after which we 'll scout around Medicine Bend. He 's still worried about them campers. In th' Valley th' cows are thicker 'n th' other parts of th' range, an' it would n't take no time to get a big herd together. He 's got a few things to mend, so he says he 'll do th' work before I get back.

"Down on Section Two things is happenin' fast, like they mostly do out here. Twelve rustlers can do a lot if they have things planned, an' 'most any fair plan will work once. They only wanted one day-after that it would be a runnin' fight, with eight or nine of 'em layin' back to hold us off while th' others drove th' cows hard. Why, Slippery Trendley an' Tamale Jose was th' only ones that ever slid across our lines with that many men.

"Three rustlers slipped up to Number Two at night an' waited. When Skinny opened th' door in th' mornin' he was drove back with a hole in his shoulder. Then there was h —l a-poppin' in that li'l mud shack. But it did n't do no good, for neither of 'em could get out alive until after dark. They learned that with sorrow, an' pain. An' they shore was het up about it. Ace Fisher, ridin' along th' west line from Number One, was dropped from ambush. Two more rustlers lay back of Medicine Bend lookin' for any of us that might ride down from the bunkhouse. An' they sent two more over to Li'l Timber to lay under that ledge of rock that sticks out of th' south side of th' bluff like a porch roof. Either me or Hoppy would be ridin' that way. They stacked th' deck clever; but Providence cut it square.

"Th' first miss-cue comes when a pert gray wolf lopes past ahead of Hoppy when he 's quite some distance above Li'l Timber. This gray wolf was a whopper, an' Hoppy was all set to get him. He wanted that sassy devil more 'n he wanted money just then, so he starts after it. Mr. Gray Wolf leads him a long chase over th' middle of th' range an' then suddenly disappears. Hoppy hunts around quite a spell, an' then heads back for th' line. While he's huntin' for th' wolf it gets cold, an' it keeps on gettin' colder fast.

"Me, I leaves later 'n usual that mornin'. An' I don't get to Cowan's until late. I 'm there when I notices how cussed cold it's got all of a sudden. Cowan looks at his thermometer, which Jimmy later busts, an' says she has gone down thirty degrees since daylight. He gives me a bottle of liquor Buck wanted, an' I ride west along th' north line, hopin' to meet Jimmy or Ace for a short talk.

"All at once I notice somebody 's pullin' a slate-covered blanket over th' north sky, an' I drag *my* blanket out an' wrap it around me. I 'm gettin' blamed cold, an' also a li'l worried. Shall I go back to Cowan's or head straight for th' bunkhouse? Cowan's the nearest by three miles, but what's three miles out here? It's got a lot colder than it was when I was at Cowan's, an' while I 'm debatin' about it th' wind dies out. I look up an' see that th' slate-covered blanket has traveled fast. It's 'most over my head, an' th' light is gettin' poor. When I look down again I notice my cayuses's ears movin' back an' forth, an' he starts pawin' an' actin' restless. That settles it. I 'm backin' instinct just then, an' I head for home. I ain't cussin' that blanket none now, an' I 'm glad I got th' robe handy; an' that quart of liquor ain't bulky no more.

"All at once th' bottom falls out of that lead sky, an' flakes as big as quarters sift down so fast they hurts my eyes, an' so thick I can't see twenty feet. In ten minutes everythin' is white, an' in ten more I 'm in a strange country. My hands an' feet ache with cold, an' I 'm drawin' th' blanket closer, when there 's a puff of wind so cold it cuts into my back like a knife. It passes quick, but it don't fool me. I know what's behind it. I reach for th' robe an' has it 'most unfastened when there 's a roar an' I 'm 'most unseated by th' wind before I can get set. I did n't know then that it's goin' to blow that hard for three days, an' it's just as well. It's full of ice-li'l slivers that are sharp as needles an' cut an' sting till they make th' skin raw. I let loose of th' robe an' tie my bandanna around my face, so my nose an' mouth is covered. My throat burns already almost to my lungs. Good Lord, but it *is* cold! My hands are stiff when I go back for th' robe, an' it's all I can do to keep it from blowin' away from me. It takes me a long time to get it over th' blanket, an' my hands are 'most froze when it's fastened. That was a good robe, but it did n't make much difference that day. Th' cold cuts through it an' into my back as if it was n't there. My feet are gettin' worse all th' time, an' it ain't long before I ain't got none, for th' achin' stops at th' ankles. Purty soon only my knees ache, an' I know it won't be long till they won't ache no more.

"I 'm squirmin' in my clothes tryin' to rub myself warm when I remember that flask of liquor. Th' cork was out far enough for my teeth to get at it, an' I drink a quarter of it quick. It's an awful load-any other time it would 'a' knocked me cold, for Cowan sold a lot worse stuff then than he does now. But it don't phase me, except for takin' most of th' linin' out of my mouth an' throat. It warms me a li'l, an' it makes my knees ache a li'l harder. But it don't last long-th' cold eats through me just as hard as ever a li'l later, an' then I begin to see things an' get sleepy. Cows an' cayuses float around in th' air, an' I 'm countin' money, piles of it. I get warm an' drowsy an' find myself noddin'. That scares me a li'l, an' I fight hard ag'in it. If I go to sleep it's all over. It keeps gettin' worse, an' I finds my eyes shuttin' more an' more frequent, an' more an' more frequent thinkin' I don't care, anyhow. An' so I drifts along pullin' at th' bottle till it's empty. That should 'a' killed me, then an' there-but it don't even make me real drunk. Mebby I spilled some of it, my hands bein' nothin' but sticks. I can't see more 'n five feet now, an' my eyes water, which freezes on 'em. I 've given up all hope of hearin' any shootin'. So I close th' peekhole in th' blanket an' robe, drawin' 'em tight to keep out some of th' cold. I am sittin' up stiff in th' saddle, like a soldier, just from force of habit, and after a li'l while I don't know nothin' more. Pete says I was a corpse, froze stiff as a ramrod, an' he calls me ghost for a long time in fun. But Pete was n't none too clear in his head about that time.

"Down at Li'l Timber, Hoppy managed to get under th' shelter of that projectin' ledge of rock on th' south side of th' bluff. Th' snow an' ice is whirlin' under it because of a sort of back draft, but th' wind don't hit so hard. He 's fightin' that cayuse every foot, tryin' to get to th' cave at th' west end, an' disputin' th' right of way with th' cows that are packed under it.

There 's firewood under that ledge an' there 's food on th' hoof, an' snow water for drink; so if he can make th' cave he 's safe. He 's more worried about his supply of smokin' tobacco than anythin' else, so far as he 's concerned.

"All at once he runs onto four men huddled half-froze in a bunch right ahead of him. He knows in a flash who they are, an' he draws fumblingly, an' holds th' gun in his two hands, they are so cold. One clean hit an' five clean misses in twenty feet! They're gropin' for their guns when a sudden gust of wind whirls down from th' top of th' hill, pilin' snow an' ice on 'em till they can't see nor breathe. An' a couple of old trees come down to make things nicer. Hoppy is blinded, an' when he gets so he can see again there's one rustler's arm stickin' up out of th' snow, but no signs of th' other three. They blundered out into th' open tryin' to get away from th' stuff comin' down on 'em, an' that means they won't be back no more.

"Hoppy manages to get to th' cave, tie his cayuse to a fallen tree, an' gather enough firewood for a good blaze, which he puts in front of th' cave. It takes him a long time to use up his matches one by one, an' then he pulls th' lead out of a cartridge with his teeth, shakes th' powder loose in it an' along th' barrel. Usin' his cigarette papers for tinder he gets th' fire started an' goin' good an' is feelin' some cheerful when he remembers th' three rustlers driftin' south. They was bound to hit a big arroyo that would lead 'em almost ag'in' Number Two's door. With th' wind drivin' 'em straight for it, Hoppy thinks it might mean trouble for Lanky or Skinny. He did n't think about 'em only havin' wool-lined slickers on, or he 'd 'a' knowed they couldn't live till they got halfway. They left their blankets in camp so they could work fast.

"People have called us clannish, an' said we was a lovin' bunch' because we stick together so tight. We 've faced so much together that us of th' old bunch has got th' same blood in our veins. We ain't eight men-we 're one man in eight different kinds of bodies. G —d help anybody that tries to make us less! It's one thing to stand up an' swap shots with a gunman; but it's another to turn yore back on a cave an' a fire like that an' go out into what is purty nigh shore death on a long chance of helpin' a couple of friends that was able to take care of themselves. That's one of th' things that explains why we made Shorty Jones an' his eleven men pay with their lives for takin' Jimmy's life. Twelve for one! That fight at Buckskin ain't generally understood, even by our friends. An' Hoppy crowns his courage twice in that one storm. Ain't he an old son-of-a-gun?

"He leaves that fire an' forces his cayuse to take him out in th' storm again, finds that th' arroyo is level full of snow, but has both banks swept bare. He passes them three rustlers in th' next ten minutes-they won't do no more cow-liftin'. Then he tries to turn back, but that's foolish. So he drifts on, gettin' a li'l loco by now. He 's purty near asleep when he thinks he hears a shot. He fights his cayuse again, but can't stop it, so he falls off an' lets it drift, an' crawls an' fights his way back to where that shot was fired from. G —d only knows how he does it, but he falls over a cow an' sees Lanky huggin' its belly for th' li'l warmth in th' carcass. An' he ought to 'a' found him, after leavin' his cayuse an' turnin' back on foot in that h —l storm! Th' drifts was beginnin' to make then-when th' storm was over I saw drifts thirty feet high in th' open; an' in th' valley there was some that run 'most to th' top of th' bluffs, an' they're near sixty feet high.

"Well, Lanky is as crazy as him, an' won't let go of that cow, an' they have a fight, which is good for both of 'em. Finally Lanky gets some sense in his head an' realizes what Hoppy is tryin' to do for him, an' they go staggerin' down wind, first one fallin' an' then th' other. But they keep fightin' like th' game boys they are, neither givin' a cuss for himself, but shore obstinate that he 's goin' to get th' other out of it. That's *our* spirit; an' we 're proud of it, by G —d! Hoppy wraps th' robe around Lanky, an' so they stagger on, neither one knowin' very much by that time. Th' Lord must 'a' pitied that pair, an' admired th' stuff He 'd put in 'em, for they bump into th' line house kerslam, an' drop, all done an' exhausted.

"Meanwhile Skinny's hoppin' around inside, prayin' an' cussin' by streaks, every five minutes openin' th' door an' firm' off his Colt. He has tied th' two ropes together, an' frequent he ties one end to th' door, th' other to hisself, an' goes out pokin' around in th' snow, hopin' to stumble over his pardner. He 's plumb forgot his bad shoulder long ago. Purty soon he opens th' door again to shoot off th' gun, an' in streaks somethin' between his laigs. He slams th' door as he jumps aside, an' then looks scared at Lanky's sombrero! Mebby he's slow hoppin' outside an' diggin' them out of th' drift that's near covered 'em! Now, don't think bad of Skinny. He dass n't leave th' house to search any distance, even if he could 'a' seen anythin'. His best play is to stick there an' shoot off his gun-Lanky might drift past if he was not there to signal. Skinny thought more of Lanky any time than he did of hisself, th' emaciated match!

"It don't take long to kick in a lot of snow with that wind blowin' an' he rubs them two till he 's got tears in his eyes. Then he fills 'em with hot stew an' whisky, rolls 'em up together an' heaves 'em in th' same bunk. It ain't warm enough in that house, even with th' fire goin', to make 'em lose no arms or laigs.

"It seems that Lanky, watchin' his chance as soon as th' snow fell heavy enough to cover his movements, slipped out of th' house an' started to circle out around them festive rustlers that held him an' his friend prisoners. He made Skinny stay behind to hold th' house an' keep a gun poppin'. Lanky has worked up behind where th' rustlers was layin' when th' Norther strikes full force. It near blows him over, an', not havin' on nothin' but an old army overcoat that was wore out, th' cold gets him quick. He can't see, an' he can't hear Skinny's shots no more! He does th' best he can an' tries to fight back along his trail, but in no time there ain't no tracks to follow. Then he loses his head an' starts wanderin' until a cow blunders down on him. He shoots th' cow an' hugs its belly to keep warm an' then he don't really remember nothin' 'till he wakes up in th' bunk alongside of Hoppy, both gettin' over an awful drunk. Skinny kept feedin' liquor to 'em till it was gone, an' he had a plenty when he began.

"Jimmy Price was at Number One when th' blow started, an' Buck was in th' bunkhouse, an' it was three weeks before they could get out an' around, on account of th' snow fallin' so steady an' hard they could n't see nothin'.

"Well, getting back to me explains how Pete Wilson came to th' Bar-20. He is migratin' south, just havin' had th' pleasure of learnin' that his wife sloped with a better-lookin' man. He was scared she might get tired of th' other feller an' sift back, so he sells out his li'l store, loads a waggin with blankets, grub, an' firewood, an' starts south, winter or no winter. He moves fast for a new range, where he can make a new beginnin' an' start life fresh, with five years of burnin' matrimonial experience as his valuablest asset. Pete says he reckoned mebby he would n't have so many harness sores if he run single th' rest of his life; heretofore he 'd been so busy applyin' salve that he did n't have time to find out just what was th' trouble with th' double harness. Lots of men feel that way, but they ain't got Pete's unlovely outspoken habit of thought. We used to reckon mebby he was n't as smart as th' rest of us, him bein' slow an' blunderin' in his retorts. We 've played that with coppers lots of times since, though. While he ain't what you 'd call quick at retortin', his retorts usually is heard by th' whole county. It ain't every collar-galled husband that's got th' gumption or smartness to jump th' minute th' hat is lifted. Pete had.

"He's drivin' across our range, an' when th' wind dies out sudden an' th' snow sifts down, he 's just smart enough to get out his beddin' an' wrap it around him till he looks like a bale of cotton. An' even at that he 's near froze an' lookin' for a place to make a stand when he feels a bump. It's me, fallin' off my cayuse, against his front wheel. He emerges from his beddin', lifts me into th' waggin, puts most of his blankets around me, an' stops. Knowin' he can't save th' cayuses, he shoots 'em. That means grub for us, anyhow, if we run short of th' good stuff. Nobody but Pete could 'a' got th' canvas off that waggin in such a gale, but he did it. He busts th' arches an' slats off th' top of th' waggin an' uses 'em for firewood. Th' canvas he drapes over th' box, lettin' it hang down on both sides to th' ground. An' in about five minutes th' whole thing was covered over with snow. Pete 's the strongest man we ever saw, an' we 've seen some good ones. Wrastlin' that canvas with stiff hands was a whole lot more than what he done to Big Sandy up there on Thunder Mesa.

"Pete says I was dead when he grabbed me, an' smellin' disgraceful of liquor. But th' first thing I know is lookin' up in th' gloom at a ceilin' that's right close to my head, an' at a sorta rafter. That rafter gives me a shock. It don't even touch th' ceilin', but runs along 'most a foot below it. I close my eyes an' do a lot of thinkin'. I remember freezin' to death, but that's all. An' just then I hears a faint voice say: 'He shore was dead.' I don't know Pete then, or that he talked to hisself sometimes. An' I reckon I was a li'l off in my head, at that. I begin to wonder if he means me, an' purty soon I 'm shore of it. An' don't I sympathize with myself? I 'm dead an' gone somewhere; but no preacher I ever heard ever described no place like this. Then I smell smoke an' burnin' meat-which gives me a clew to th' range I 'm on. Mebby I 'm shelved in th' ice box, waitin' my turn, or somethin'. I knew I 'd led a sinful life. But there wasn't no use of rubbin' it in-it's awful to be dead an' know it.

"Th' next time I opens my eyes I can't see nothin'; but I can feel somethin' layin' alongside of me. It's breathin' slow an' regular, an it bothers me till I get th' idea all of a sudden. It's another dead one, cut out of th' herd an' shoved in my corral to wait for subsequent events. I felt sorry for him, an' lay there tryin' to figger it out, an' I 'm still figgerin' when it starts to get light. Th' other feller grunts an' sits up, bumpin' his head solid against that fool rafter. No dead man that was shoved in a herd consigned to heaven ever used such language, which makes me all the shorer of where I am. But if hell's hot we 've still got a long way to go.

"He sits there rubbin' his head an' cussin' steadily, an' I 'm so moved by it that I compliments him. He jumps an' bumps his head again, an' looks at me close. 'D —d if you ain't a husky corpse,' he says. That settles it. I ain't crazy, like I was hopin', but I 'in dead. 'You an' me is on th' ragged edge of h —l,' he adds.

"'But who tipped *you* off?' I asks. 'They just shoved me in here an' did n't tell me nothin' at all.'

"'Crazy as th' devil,' he grunts, lookin' at me harder.

"'Yo 're a liar,' I replies. 'I may be dead, but d —d if I 'm crazy!'

"'An' I don't blame you, either,' he mused, sorrowful. 'Now you keep quiet till I gets somethin' to eat,' an' he crawls into a li'l round hole at th' other end of th' room.

"Purty soon I smell smoke again, an' after a long time he comes back with some hot coffee an' burned meat. I grab for th' grub, an' while I 'm eatin' I demands to know where I am.

"He laughs, real cheerful, an' tells me. I 'm under his waggin, surrounded by canvas an' any G —d's quantity of snow. Th' drift over us is fifteen foot high, th' wind has died down, an' it's still snowin' so hard he can't see twenty feet. It is also away down below freezin'.

"We stayed under that drift 'most three weeks, livin' on raw meat after our firewood gave out. We didn't suffer none from th' cold, though, under all that snow an' with all th' blankets we had. When it stopped snowin' we discovered a drift shamefully high about a mile northeast of us, an' from th' smoke comin' out of it I knew it was th' bunkhouse.

"Well, to cut it short, it was. An' mebby Buck wasn't glad to see me! He was worried 'most sick an' as soon as we could, we got cayuses and started out to look for th' others, scared stiff at what we expected to find."

He paused and was silent a moment. "But only Ace was missin'," he added. "We found him an' th' rustlers later, when th' snow went off."

He paused again and shook his head. "It shore was a miracle that we did n't go with 'em, all of us, except Buck. Pete was so plumb disgusted with travelin' in th' winter, an' had lost his cayuses, that when Buck offers him Ace's bunk he stays. An' he ain't never left us since. Huh! Cold? That cub don't know nothin'—mebby he will when he grows up, but I dunno, at that. *Idyho!*"

IX
The Drive

The Norther was a thing of the past, but it left its mark on Buck Peters, whose grimness of face told what the winter had been to him. His daily rides over the range, the reports of his men since that deadly storm had done a great deal to lift the sagging weight that rested on his shoulders; but he would not be sure until the round-up supplied facts and figures.

That the losses had not been greater he gave full credit to the valley with its arroyos, rock walls, draws, heavily grassed range and groves of timber; for the valley, checking the great southward drift by its steep ridges of rock, sheltered the herds in timber and arroyos and fed them on the rich profusion of its grasses, which, by some trick of the rushing winds, had been whirled clean of snow.

But over the cow-country, north, east, south and west, where vast ranges were unprotected against the whistling blasts from the north, the losses had been stupendous, appalling, stunning. Outfits had been driven on and on before the furious winds, sleepy and apathetic, drifting steadily southward in the white, stinging shroud to a drowsy death. Whole herds, blindly moving before the wind, left their weaker units in constantly growing numbers to mark the trail, and at last lay down to a sleep eternal. And astonishing and incredible were the distances traveled by some of those herds.

Following the Norther came another menace and one which easily might surpass the worst efforts of the blizzard. Warm winds blew steadily, a hot sun glared down on the snow-covered plain and then came torrents of rain which continued for days, turning the range into a huge expanse of water and mud and swelling the water-courses with turgid floods that swirled and roared above their banks. Should this be quickly followed by cold, even the splendid valley would avail nothing. Ice, forming over the grasses, would prove as deadly as a pestilence; the cattle, already weakened by the hardships of the Norther, and not having the instinct to break through the glassy sheet and feed on the grass underneath, would search in vain for food, and starve to death. The week that followed the cessation of the rains started gray hairs on the foreman's head; but a warm, constant sun and warm winds dried off the water before the return of freezing weather. The herds were saved.

Relieved, Buck reviewed the situation. The previous summer had seen such great northern drives to the railroad shipping points in Kansas that prices fell until the cattlemen refused to sell. Rather than drive home again, the great herds were wintered on the Kansas ranges, ready to be hurled on the market when Spring came with better prices. Many ranches, mortgaged heavily to buy cattle, had been on the verge of bankruptcy, hoping feverishly for better prices the following year. Buck had taken advantage of the situation to stock his ranch at a cost far less than he had dared to dream. Then came the Norther and in the three weeks of devastating cold and high winds the Kansas ranges were swept clean of cattle, and even the ranges in the South were badly crippled. Knowing this, Buck also knew that the following Spring would show record high prices. If he had the cattle he could clean up a fortune for his ranch; and if his herd was the first big one to reach the railroad at Sandy Creek it would practically mean a bonus on every cow.

Under the long siege of uncertainty his impatience smashed through and possessed him as a fever and he ordered the calf round-up three weeks earlier than it ever had been held on the ranch. There was no need of urging his men to the task-they, like himself, sprang to the call like springs freed from a restraining weight, and the work went on in a fever of haste. And he took his place on the firing line and worked even harder than his outfit of fanatics.

One day shortly after the work began a stranger rode up to him and nodded cheerfully. "Li'l early, ain't you?" Buck grunted in reply and sent Skinny off at top speed to close a threatened gap in the lengthy driving line. "Goin' to git 'em on th' trail early this year?" persisted the stranger. Buck, swayed by some swift intuition, changed his reply. "Oh, I dunno; I 'm mainly anxious to see just what that storm did. An' I hate th' calf burnin' so much I allus like to get it over quick." He shouted angrily at the cook and waved his arms frantically to banish the chuck wagon. "He can make more trouble with that waggin than anybody I ever saw," he snorted. "Get out of there, you fool!" he yelled, dashing off to see his words obeyed. The cook, grinning cheerfully at his foreman's language and heat, forthwith chose a spot that was not destined to be the center of the cut-out herd. And when Buck again thought of the stranger he saw a black dot moving toward the eastern skyline.

The crowded days rolled on, measured full from dawn to dark, each one of them a panting, straining, trying ordeal. Worn out, the horses were turned back into the temporary corral or to graze under the eyes of the horse wranglers, and fresh ones took up their work; and woe unto the wranglers if the supply fell below the demand. For the tired men there was no relief, only a shifting in the kind of work they did, and they drove themselves with grave determination, their iron wills overruling their aching bodies. First came the big herds in the valley; then, sweeping north, they combed the range to the northern line in one grand, mad fury of effort that lasted day after day until the tally man joyously threw away his chewed pencil and gladly surrendered the last sheet to the foreman. The first half of the game was over. Gone as if it were a nightmare was the confusion of noise and dust and cows that hid a remarkable certainty of method. But as if to prove it not a dream, four thousand cows were held in three herds on the great range, in charge of the extra men.

Buck, leading the regular outfit from the north line and toward the bunkhouse, added the figures of the last tally sheet to the totals he had in a little book, and smiled with content. Behind him, cheerful as fools, their bodies racking with weariness, their faces drawn and gaunt, knowing that their labors were not half over, rode the outfit, exchanging chaff and banter in an effort to fool themselves into the delusion that they were fresh and "chipper." Nearing the bunkhouse they cheered lustily as they caught sight of the hectic cook laboring profanely with two balking pintos that had backed his wagon half over the edge of a barranca and then refused to pull it back again. Cookie's reply, though not a cheer, was loud and pregnant with feeling. To think that he had driven those two animals for the last two weeks from one end of the ranch to the other without a mishap, and then have them balance him and his wagon on the crumbling edge of a twenty-foot drop when not a half mile from the bunkhouse, thus threatening the loss of the wagon and all it contained and the mangling of his sacred person! And to make it worse, here came a crowd of whooping idiots to feast upon his discomfiture.

The outfit, slowing so as not to frighten the devilish pintos and start them backing again, drew near; and suddenly the air became filled with darting ropes, one of which settled affectionately around Cookie's apoplectic neck. In no time the strangling, furious dough-king was beyond the menace of the crumbling bank, flat on his back in the wagon, where he had managed to throw himself to escape the whistling hoofs that quickly turned the dashboard into matchwood. When he managed to get the rope from his neck he arose, unsteady with rage, and choked as he tried to speak before the grinning and advising outfit. Before he could get command over his tongue the happy bunch wheeled and sped on its way, shrieking with mirth unholy. They had saved him from probable death, for Cookie was too obstinate to have jumped from the wagon; but they not only forfeited all right to thanks and gratitude, but deserved horrible deaths for the conversation they had so audibly carried on while they worked out the cook's problem. And their departing words and gestures made homicide justifiable and a duty. It was in this frame of mind that Cookie watched them go.

Buck, emerging from the bunkhouse in time to see the rescue, leaned against the door and laughed as he had not laughed for one heart-breaking winter. Drying his eyes on the back of his hand, he looked at the bouncing, happy crowd tearing southward with an energy of arms and legs and lungs that seemed a miracle after the strain of the round-up. Just then a strange voice made him wheel like a flash, and he saw Billy Williams sitting solemnly on his horse near the corner of the house.

"Hullo, Williams," Buck grunted, with no welcoming warmth in his voice. "What th' devil brings *you* up here?"

"I want a job," replied Billy. The two, while never enemies nor interested in any mutual disagreements, had never been friends. They never denied a nodding acquaintance, nor boasted of it. "That Norther shore raised h —l. There 's ten men for every job, where I came from."

The foreman, with that quick decision that was his in his earlier days, replied crisply. "It's your'n. Fifty a month, to start."

"Keno. Lemme chuck my war-bag through that door an' I'm ready," smiled Billy. He believed he would like this man when he knew him better. "I thought th' Diamond Bar, over east a hundred mile, had weathered th' storm lucky. You got 'em beat. They 're movin' heaven an' earth to get a herd on the trail, but they did n't have no job for *me*," he laughed, flushing slightly. "Sam Crawford owns it," he explained naïvely.

Buck laughed outright. "I reckon you did n't have much show with Sam, after that li'l trick you worked on him in Fenton. So Sam is in this country? How are they fixed?"

"They aims to shove three thousan' east right soon. It's fancy prices for th' first herd that gets to Sandy Creek," he offered. "I heard they 're havin' lots of wet weather along th' Comanchee; mebby Sam 'll have trouble a-plenty gettin' his herd acrost. Cows is plumb aggervatin' when it comes to crossin' rivers," he grinned.

Buck nodded. "See that V openin' on th' sky line?" he asked, pointing westward. "Ride for it till you see th' herd. Help 'em with it. We 'll pick it up t'morrow." He turned on his heel and entered the house, grave with a new worry. He had not known that there was a ranch where Billy had said the Diamond Bar was located; and a hundred miles handicap meant much in a race to Sandy Creek. Crawford was sure to drive as fast as he dared. He was glad that Billy had mentioned it, and the wet weather along the Comanchee-Billy already had earned his first month's pay.

All that day and the next the consolidation of the three herds and the preparation for the drive went on. Sweeping up from the valley the two thousand three- and four-year-olds met and joined the thousand that waited between Little Timber and Three Rocks; and by nightfall the three herds were one by the addition of the thousand head from Big Coulee. Four thousand head of the best cattle on the ranch spent the night within gunshot of the bunkhouse and corrals on Snake Creek.

Buck, returning from the big herd, smiled as he passed the chuck-wagon and heard Cookie's snores, and went on, growing serious all too quickly. At the bunkhouse he held a short consultation with his regular outfit and then returned to the herd again while his drive crew turned eagerly to their bunks. Breakfast was eaten by candle light and when the eastern sky faded into a silver gray Skinny Thompson vaulted into the saddle and loped eastward without a backward glance. The sounds of his going scarcely had died out before Hopalong, relieved of the responsibilities of trail boss, shouldered others as weighty and rode into the north-east with Lanky at his side. Behind him, under charge of Red, the herd started on its long and weary journey to Sandy Creek, every man of the outfit so imbued with the spirit of the race that even with its hundred miles' advantage the Diamond Bar could not afford to waste an hour if it hoped to win.

Out of the side of a verdant hill, whispering and purling, flowed a small stream and shyly sought the crystal depths of a rock-bound pool before gaining courage enough to flow gently over the smooth granite lip and scurry down the gentle slope of the arroyo. To one side of it towered a splinter of rock, slender and gray, washed clean by the recent rains. To the south of it lay a baffling streak a little lighter than the surrounding grass lands. It was, perhaps, a quarter of a mile wide and ended only at the horizon. This faint band was the Dunton trail, not used enough to show the strong characteristics of the depressed bands found in other parts of the cow-country. If followed it would lead one to Dunton's Ford on the Comanchee, forty miles above West Bend, where the Diamond Bar aimed to cross the river.

The shadow of the pinnacle drew closer to its base and had crossed the pool when Skinny Thompson rode slowly up the near bank of the ravine, his eyes fixed smilingly on the splinter of rock. He let his mount nuzzle and play with the pool for a moment before stripping off the saddle and turning the animal loose to graze. Taking his rifle in the hope of seeing game, he went up to the top of the hill, glanced westward and then turned and gazed steadily into the northeast, sweeping slowly over an arc of thirty degrees. He stood so for several minutes and then grunted with satisfaction and returned to the pool. He had caught sight of a black dot far away on the edge of the skyline that split into two parts and showed a sidewise drift. Evidently his friends would be on time. Of the herd he had seen no sign, which was what he had expected.

When at last he heard hoofbeats he arose lazily and stretched, chiding himself for falling asleep, and met his friends as they turned into sight around the bend of the hill. "Reckoned you might 'a' got lost," he grinned sleepily.

"G'wan!" snorted Lanky.

"What'd you find?" eagerly demanded Hopalong.

"Three thousan' head on th' West Bend trail five days ahead of us," replied Skinny. "Ol' Sam is drivin' hard." He paused a moment. "Acts like he knows we 're after him. Anyhow, I saw that feller that visited us on th' third day of th' round-up. So I reckon Sam knows."

Lanky grinned. "He won't drive so hard later. I 'd like to see him when he sees th' Comanchee! Bet it's a lake south of Dunton's 'cordin' to what we found. But it ain't goin' to bother us a whole lot."

Hopalong nodded, dismounted and drew a crude map in the sand of the trail. Skinny watched it, grave and thoughtful until, all at once, he understood. His sudden burst of laughter startled his companions and they exchanged foolish grins. It appeared that from Dunton's Ford north, in a distance of forty miles, the Comanchee was practically born. So many feeders, none of them formidable, poured into it that in that distance it attained the dignity of a river. Hopalong's plan was to drive off at a tangent running a little north from the regular trail and thus cross numerous small streams in preference to going on straight and facing the swollen Comanchee at Dunton's Ford. As the regular trail turned northward when not far from Sandy Creek they were not losing time. Laughing gaily they mounted and started west for the herd which toiled toward them many miles away. Thanks to the forethought that had prompted their scouting expedition the new trail was picked out in advance and there would be no indecision on the drive.

Eighty miles to the south lay the fresh trail of the Diamond Bar herd, and five days' drive eastward on it, facing the water-covered lowlands at West Bend, Sam Crawford held his herd, certain that the river would fall rapidly in the next two days. It was the regular ford, and the best on the river. The water did fall, just enough to lure him to stay; but, having given orders at dark on the second night for an attempt at crossing at daylight the next morning, he was amazed when dawn showed him the river was back to its first level.

Sam was American born, but affected things English and delighted in spelling "labor" and like words with a "u." He hated hair chaps and maintained that the gun-play of the West was mythical and existed only in the minds of effete Easterners. Knowing that, it was startling to hear him tell of Plummer, Hickock, Roberts, Thompson and a host of other gunmen who had splotched the West with blood. Not only did every man of that section pack a gun, but Crawford, himself, packed one, thus proving himself either a malicious liar or an imbecile. He acted as though the West belonged to him and that he was the arbiter of its destiny and its chosen historian-which made him troublesome on the great, free ranges. Only that his pretensions and his crabbed, irascible, childish temper made him ludicrous he might have been taken seriously, to his sorrow. Failing miserably at law, he fled from such a precarious livelihood, beset with a haunting fear that he had lost his grip, to an inherited ranch. This fear that pursued him turned him into a carping critic of those who excelled him in most things, except in fits of lying about the West as it existed at that time.

When he found that the river was over the lowlands again he became furious and, carried away by rage, shouted down the wiser counsel of his clear-headed night boss and ordered the herd into the water. Here and there desperate, wild-eyed steers wheeled and dashed back through the cordon of riders, their numbers constantly growing as the panic spread. The cattle in the front ranks, forced into the swirling stream by the pressure from the rear, swam with the current and clambered out below, adding to the confusion. Steers fought throughout the press and suddenly, out of the right wing of the herd, a dozen crazed animals dashed out in a bunch for the safety of the higher ground; and after them came the herd, an irresistible avalanche of maddened beef. It was not before dark that they were rounded up into a nervous, panicky herd once more. The next morning they were started north along the river, to try again at Dunton's Ford, which they reached in three days, and where another attempt at crossing the river proved in vain.

Meanwhile the Bar-20 herd pushed on steadily with no confusion. It crossed the West Run one noon and the upper waters of the Little Comanchee just before dark on the same day. Next came East Run, Pawnee Creek and Ten Mile Creek, none of them larger than the stream the cattle were accustomed to back on the ranch. Another day's drive brought them to the west branch of the Comanchee itself, the largest of all the rivers they would meet. Here they were handled cautiously and "nudged" across with such care that a day was spent in the work. The following afternoon the east branch held them up until the next day and then, with a clear trail, they were sent along on the last part of the long journey.

When Sam Crawford, forced to keep on driving north along the Little Comanchee, saw that wide, fresh trail, he barely escaped apoplexy and added the finishing touches to the sullenness of his outfit. Seeing the herd across, he gave orders for top speed and drove as he never had driven before; and when the last river had been left behind he put the night boss in charge of the cattle and rode on ahead to locate his rivals of the drive. Three days later, when he returned to his herd, he was in a towering fury and talked constantly of his rights and an appeal to law, and so nagged his men that mutiny stalked in his shadow.

When the Bar-20 herd was passing to the south of the little village of Depau, Hopalong turned back along the trail to find the Diamond Bar herd. So hard had Sam pushed on that he was only two days' drive behind Red and his outfit when Hopalong rode smilingly into the Diamond Bar camp. He was talking pleasantly of shop to some of the Diamond Bar punchers when Sam dashed up and began upbraiding him and threatening dire punishment. Hopalong, maintaining a grave countenance, took the lacing meekly and humbly as he winked at the grinning punchers. Finally, after exasperating Sam to a point but one degree removed from explosion, he bowed cynically, said "so-long" to the friendly outfit and loped away toward his friends. Sam, choking with rage, berated his punchers for not having thrown out the insulting visitor and commanded more speed, which was impossible. Reporting to Red the proximity of their rivals, Hopalong fell in line and helped drive the herd a little faster. The cattle were in such condition from the easy traveling of the last week that they could easily stand the pace if Crawford's herd could. So the race went on, Red keeping the same distance ahead day after day.

Then came the night when Sandy Creek lay but two days' drive away. A storm had threatened since morning and the first lightning of the drive was seen. The cattle were mildly restless when Hopalong rode in at midnight and he was cheerfully optimistic. He was also very much awake, and after trying in vain to get to sleep he finally arose and rode back along the trail toward the stragglers, which Jimmy and Lanky were holding a mile away. Red had pushed on to the last minute of daylight and Lanky had decided to hold the stragglers instead of driving them up to the main herd so they would start even with it the following morning. It was made up of the cattle that had found the drive too much for them and was smaller than the outfit had dared to hope for.

Hopalong had just begun to look around for the herd when it passed him with sudden uproar. Shouting to a horseman who rode furiously past, he swung around and raced after him, desperately anxious to get in front of the stampede to try to check it before it struck the main herd and made the disaster complete. For the next hour he was in a riot of maddened cattle and shaved death many times by the breadth of a hand. He could hear Jimmy and Lanky shouting in the black void, now close and now far away. Then the turmoil gradually ceased and the remnant of the herd paused, undecided whether to stop or go on. He flung himself at it and by driving cleverly managed to start a number of cows to milling, which soon had the rest following suit. The stampede was over. A cursing blot emerged from the darkness and hailed. It was Lanky, coldly ferocious. He had not heard Jimmy for a long time and feared that the boy might be lying out on the black plain, trampled into a shapeless mass of flesh. One stumble in front of the charging herd would have been sufficient.

Daylight disclosed the missing Jimmy hobbling toward the breakfast fire at the cook wagon. He was bruised and bleeding and covered with dirt, his clothes ripped and covered with mud; and every bone and muscle in his body was alive with pain.

The Diamond Bar's second squad had ridden in to breakfast when a horseman was seen approaching at a leisurely lope. Sam, cursing hotly, instinctively fumbled at the gun he wore at his thigh in defiance to his belief concerning the wearing of guns. He blinked anxiously as the puncher stopped at the wagon and smiled a heavy-eyed salutation. The night boss emerged from the shelter of the wagon and grinned a sheepish welcome. "Well, Cassidy, you fellers got th' trail somehow. We was some surprised when we hit yore trail. How you makin' it?"

"All right, up to last night," replied Hopalong, shaking hands with the night boss. "Got a match, Barnes?" he asked, holding up an unlighted cigarette. They talked of things connected with the drive and Hopalong cautiously swung the conversation around to mishaps, mentioning several catastrophes of past years. After telling of a certain stampede he had once seen, he turned to Barnes and asked a blunt question. "What would you do to anybody as stampeded yore stragglers within a mile of th' main herd on a stormy night?" The answer was throaty and rumbling. "Why, shoot him, I reckon." The others intruded their ideas and Crawford squirmed, his hand seeking his gun under the pretense of tightening his belt.

Hopalong arose and went to his horse, where a large bundle of canvas was strapped behind the saddle. He loosened it and unrolled it on the ground. "Ever see this afore, boys?" he asked, stepping back. Barnes leaped to his feet with an ejaculation of surprise and stared at the canvas. "Where'd you git it?" he demanded. "That's our old wagon cover!"

Hopalong, ignoring Crawford, looked around the little group and smiled grimly. "Well, last night our stragglers was stampeded. Lanky told me he saw somethin' gray blow past him in th' darkness, an' then th' herd started. We managed to turn it from th' trail an' so it did n't set off our main herd. Jimmy was near killed-well, you know what it is to ride afore stampeded cows. I found this cover blowed agin' a li'l clump of trees, an' when I sees yore mark, I reckoned I ought to bring it back." He dug into his pocket and brought out a heavy clasp knife. "I just happened to see this not far from where th' herd started from, so I reckoned I 'd return it, too." He held it out to Barnes, who took it with an oath and wheeled like a flash to face his employer.

Crawford was backing toward the wagon, his hand resting on the butt of his gun, and a whiteness of face told of the fear that gripped him. "I 'll take my time, right now," growled Barnes. "D —d if I works another day for a low-lived coyote that 'd do a thing like that!" The punchers behind him joined in and demanded their wages. Hopalong, still smiling, waved his hand and spoke. "Don't leave him with all these cows on his hands, out here on th' range. If you quits him, wait till you get to Sandy Creek. He ain't no man, he ain't; he 's a nasty lil brat of a kid that couldn't never grow up into a man. So, that bein' true, he ain't goin' to get handled like a man. I 'm goin' to lick him, 'stead of shootin' him like he was a man. You know," he smiled, glancing around the little circle, "us cowpunchers don't never carry guns. We don't swear, nor wear chaps, even if all of us has got 'em on right now. We say 'please' an' 'thank you' an' never get mad. Not never wearin' a gun I can't shoot him; but, by G —d, I can lick him th' worst he's ever been licked, an' I 'm goin' to do it right now." He wheeled to start after the still-backing cowman, and leaped sideways as a cloud of smoke swirled around his hips. Crawford screamed with fear and pain as his Colt tore loose from his fingers and dropped near the wheel of the wagon. Terror gripped him and made him incapable of flight. Who was this man, *what* was he, when he could draw and fire with such speed and remarkable accuracy? Crawford's gun had been half raised before the other had seen it. And before his legs could perform one of their most cherished functions the limping cowpuncher was on him, doing his best to make good his promise. The other half of the Diamond Bar drive crew, attracted by the commotion at the chuck wagon, rode in with ready guns, saw their friends making no attempt at interference, asked a few terse questions and, putting up their guns, forthwith joined the circle of interested and pleased spectators to root for the limping redhead.

Crawford's Colt tore loose from his fingers and dropped near
the wagon wheel

Red, back at the Bar-20 wagon, inquired of Cookie the whereabouts of Hopalong. Cookie, still smarting under Jimmy's galling fire of language, grunted ignorance and a wish. Red looked at him, scowling. "You can talk to th' Kid like that, mebby; but you get a civil tongue in yore head when any of us grown-ups ask questions." He turned on his heel, looked searchingly around the plain and mounting, returned to the herd, perplexed and vexed. As he left the camp, Jimmy hobbled around the wagon and stared after him. "Kid!" he snorted. "Grown-ups!" he sneered. "Huh!" He turned and regarded Cookie evilly. "Yo 're gonna get a good lickin' when I get so I can move better," he promised. Cookie lifted the red flannel dish-rag out of the pan and regarded it thoughtfully. "You better wait," he agreed pleasantly. "You can't run now. I 'm honin' for to drape this mop all over yore wall-eyed face; but I can wait." He sighed and went back to work. "Wish Red would shove you in with th' rest of th' cripples back yonder, an' get you off'n my frazzled nerves."

Jimmy shook his head sorrowfully and limped around the wagon again, where he resumed his sun bath. He dozed off and was surprised to be called for dinner. As he arose, grunting and growling, he chanced to look westward, and his shout apprised his friends of the return of the missing red-head.

Hopalong dismounted at the wagon and grinned cheerfully, despite the suspicious marks on his face. Giving an account of events as they occurred at the Diamond Bar chuck wagon, he wound up with: "Needn't push on so hard, Red. Crawford's herd is due to stay right where it is an' graze peaceful for a week. I heard Barnes give th' order before I left. How's things been out here while I was away?"

Red glared at him, ready to tell his opinion of reckless fools that went up against a gun-packing crowd alone when his friends had never been known to refuse to back up one of their outfit. The words hung on his lips as he waited for a chance to launch them. But when that chance came he had been disarmed by the cheerfulness of his happy friend. "Hoppy," he said, trying to be severe, "yo 're nothing' but a crazy, d —d fool. But what did they say when you started for huffy Sam like that?"

X
The Hold-Up

The herd delivered at Sandy Creek had traveled only half way, for the remaining part of the journey would be on the railroad. The work of loading the cars was fast, furious fun to anyone who could find humor enough in his make-up to regard it so. Then came a long, wearying ride for the five men picked from the drive outfit to attend to the cattle on the way to the cattle pens of the city. Their work at last done, they "saw the sights" and were now returning to Sandy Creek.

The baggage smoking-car reeked with strong tobacco, the clouds of smoke shifting with the air currents, and dimly through the haze could be seen several men. Three of these were playing cards near the baggage-room door, while two more lounged in a seat half way down the aisle and on the other side of the car. Across from the card-players, reading a magazine, was a fat man, and near the water cooler was a dyspeptic-looking individual who was grumbling about the country through which he was passing.

The first five, as their wearing apparel proclaimed, were not of the kind usually found on trains, not the drummer, the tourist, or the farmer. Their heads were covered with heavy sombreros, their coats were of thick, black woolens, and their shirts were also of wool. Around the throat of each was a large handkerchief, knotted at the back; their trousers were protected by "chaps," of which three were of goatskin. The boots were tight-fitting, narrow, and with high heels, and to them were strapped heavy spurs. Around the waist, hanging loosely from one hip, each wore a wide belt containing fifty cartridges in the loops, and supporting a huge Colt's revolver, which rested against the thigh.

They were happy and were trying to sing but, owing to different tastes, there was noticeable a lack of harmony. "Oh Susanna" never did go well with "Annie Laurie," and as for "Dixie," it was hopelessly at odds with the other two. But they were happy, exuberantly so, for they had enjoyed their relaxation in the city and now were returning to the station where their horses were waiting to carry them over the two hundred miles which lay between their ranch and the nearest railroad-station.

For a change the city had been pleasant, but after they had spent several days there it lost its charm and would not have been acceptable to them even as a place in which to die. They had spent their money, smoked "top-notcher" cigars, seen the "shows" and feasted each as his fancy dictated, and as behooved cowpunchers with money in their pockets. Now they were glad that every hour reduced the time of their stay in the smoky, jolting, rocking train, for they did not like trains, and this train was particularly bad. So they passed the hours as best they might and waited impatiently for the stop at Sandy Creek, where they had left their horses. Their trip to the "fence country" was now a memory, and they chafed to be again in the saddle on the open, wind-swept range, where miles were insignificant and the silence soothing.

The fat man, despairing of reading, watched the card-players and smiled in good humor as he listened to their conversation, while the dyspeptic, nervously twisting his newspaper, wished that he were at his destination. The baggage-room door opened and the conductor looked down on the card-players and grinned. Skinny moved over in the seat to make room for the genial conductor.

"Sit down, Simms, an' take a hand," he invited. Laughter arose continually and the fat man joined in it, leaning forward more closely to watch the play.

Lanky tossed his cards face down on the board and grinned at the onlooker.

"Billy shore bluffs more on a varigated flush than any man I ever saw."

"Call him once in a while and he 'll get cured of it," laughed the fat man, bracing himself as the train swung around a sharp turn.

"He 's too smart," growled Billy Williams. "He tried that an' found I did n't have no varigated flushes. Come on, Lanky, if yo 're playing cards, put up."

Farther down the car, their feet resting easily on the seat in front of them, Hopalong and Red puffed slowly at their large, black cigars and spoke infrequently, both idly watching the plain flit by in wearying sameness, and both tired and lazy from doing nothing but ride.

"Blast th' cars, anyhow," grunted Hopalong, but he received no reply, for his companion was too disgusted to say anything.

A startling, sudden increase in the roar of the train and a gust of hot, sulphurous smoke caused Hopalong to look up at the brakeman, who came down the swaying aisle as the door slammed shut.

"Phew!" he exclaimed, genially. "Why in thunder don't you fellows smoke up?"

Hopalong blew a heavy ring, stretched energetically and grinned: "Much farther to Sandy Creek?"

"Oh, you don't get off for three hours yet," laughed the brakeman.

"That's shore a long time to ride this bronc train," moodily complained Red as the singing began again. "She shore pitches a-plenty," he added.

The train-hand smiled and seated himself on the arm of the front seat:

"Oh, it might be worse."

"Not this side of hades," replied Red with decision, watching his friend, who was slapping the cushions to see the dust fly out: "Hey, let up on that, will you! There's dust a-plenty without no help from you!"

The brakeman glanced at the card-players and then at Hopalong.

"Do your friends always sing like that?" he inquired.

"Mostly, but sometimes it's worse."

"On the level?"

"Shore enough; they're singing 'Dixie,' now. It's their best song."

"That ain't 'Dixie!'"

"Yes it is: that is, most of it."

"Well, then, what's the rest of it?"

"Oh, them's variations of their own," remarked Red, yawning and stretching. "Just wait till they start something sentimental; you 'll shore weep."

"I hope they stick to the variations. Say, you must be a pretty nifty gang on the shoot, ain't you?"

"Oh, some," answered Hopalong.

"I wish you fellers had been aboard with us one day about a month ago. We was the wrong end of a hold-up, and we got cleaned out proper, too."

"An' how many of 'em did you get?" asked Hopalong quickly, sitting bolt upright.

The fat man suddenly lost his interest in the card-game and turned an eager ear to the brakeman, while the dyspeptic stopped punching holes in his time-card and listened. The card-players glanced up and then returned to their game, but they, too, were listening.

The brakeman was surprised: "How many did we get! Gosh! we didn't get none! They was six to our five."

"How many cards did you draw, you Piute?" asked Lanky.

"None of yore business; I ain't dealing, an' I would n't tell you if I was," retorted Billy.

"Well, I can ask, can't I?"

"Yes-you can, an' did."

"You didn't get none?" cried Hopalong, doubting his ears.

"I should say not!"

"An' they owned th' whole train?"

"They did."

Red laughed. "Th' cleaning-up must have been sumptuous an' elevating."

"Every time I holds threes he allus has better," growled Lanky to Simms.

"On th' level, we couldn't do a thing," the brakeman ran on. "There 's a water tank a little farther on, and they must 'a' climbed aboard there when we stopped to connect. When we got into the gulch the train slowed down and stopped and I started to get up to go out and see what was the matter; but I saw that when I looked down a gun-barrel. The man at the throttle end of it told me to put up my hands, but they were up as high then as I could get 'em without climbin' on the top of the seat.

"Can't you listen and play at th' same time?" Lanky asked Billy.

"I wasn't countin' on takin' the gun away from him," the brakeman continued, "for I was too busy watchin' for the slug to come out of the hole. Pretty soon somebody on the outside whistled and then another feller come in the car; he was the one that did the cleanin' up. All this time there had been a lot of shootin' outside, but now it got worse. Then I heard another whistle and the engine puffed up the track, and about five minutes later there was a big explosion, and then our two robbers backed out of the car among the rocks shootin' back regardless. They busted a lot of windows."

"An' you did n't git none," grumbled Hopalong, regretfully.

"When we got to the express-car, what had been pulled around the turn," continued the brakeman, not heeding the interruption, "we found a wreck. And we found the engineer and fireman standin' over the express-messenger, too scared to know he would n't come back no more. The car had been blowed up with dynamite, and his fighting soul went with it. He never knowed he was licked."

"An' nobody tried to help him!" Hopalong exclaimed, wrathfully now.

"Nobody wanted to die with him," replied the brakeman.

"Well," cried the fat man, suddenly reaching for his valise, "I 'd like to see anybody try to hold me up!" Saying which he brought forth a small revolver.

"You 'd be praying out of your bald spot about that time," muttered the brakeman.

Hopalong and Red turned, perceived the weapon, and then exchanged winks.

"That's a fine shootin'-iron, stranger," gravely remarked Hopalong.

"You bet it is!" purred the owner, proudly. "I paid six dollars for that gun."

Lanky smothered a laugh and his friend grinned broadly: "I reckon that'd kill a man-if you stuck it in his ear."

"Pshaw!" snorted the dyspeptic, scornfully. "You wouldn't have time to get it out of that grip. Think a train-robber is going to let you unpack? Why don't you carry it in your hip-pocket, where you can get at it quickly?"

There were smiles at the stranger's belief in the hip-pocket fallacy but no one commented upon it.

"Was n't there no passengers aboard when you was stuck up?" Lanky asked the conductor.

"Yes, but you can't count passengers in on a deal like that."

Hopalong looked around aggressively: "We 're passengers, ain't we?"

"You certainly are."

"Well, if any misguided maverick gets it into his fool head to stick *us* up, you see what happens. Don't you know th' fellers outside have all th' worst o' th' deal?"

"They have not!" cried the brakeman.

"They 've got all the best of it," asserted the conductor emphatically. "I 've been inside, and I know."

"Best nothing!" cried Hopalong. "They are on th' ground, watching a danger-line over a hundred yards long, full of windows and doors. Then they brace th' door of a car full of people. While they climb up the steps they can't see inside, an' then they go an' stick their heads in plain sight. It's an even break who sees th' other first, with th' men inside training their guns on th' glass in th' door!"

"Darned if you ain't right!" enthusiastically cried the fat man.

Hopalong laughed: "It all depends on th' men inside. If they ain't used to handling guns, 'course they won't try to fight. We 've been in so many gun-festivals that we would n't stop to think. If any coin-collector went an' stuck his ugly face against th' glass in that door he 'd turn a back-flip off 'n th' platform before he knowed he was hit. Is there any chance for a stick-up to-day, d'y think?"

"Can't tell," replied the brakeman. "But this is about the time we have the section-camps' pay on board," he said, going into the baggage end of the car.

Simms leaned over close to Skinny. "It's on this train now, and I 'm worried to death about it. I wish we were at Sandy Creek."

"Don't you go to worryin' none, then," the puncher replied. "It 'll get to Sandy Creek all right."

Hopalong looked out of the window again and saw that there was a gradual change in the nature of the scenery, for the plain was becoming more broken each succeeding mile. Small woods occasionally hurtled past and banks of cuts flashed by like mottled yellow curtains, shutting off the view. Scrub timber stretched away on both sides, a billowy sea of green, and miniature valleys lay under the increasing number of trestles twisting and winding toward a high horizon.

Hopalong yawned again: "Well, it's none o' our funeral. If they let us alone I don't reckon we 'll take a hand, not even to bust up this monotony."

Red laughed derisively: "Oh, no! Why, you could n't sit still nohow with a fight going on, an' you know it. An' if it's a stick-up! Wow!"

"Who gave you any say in this?" demanded his friend. "Anyhow, you ain't no angel o' peace, not nohow!"

"Mebby they 'll plug yore new sombrero," laughed Red.

Hopalong felt of the article in question: "If any two-laigged wolf plugs my war-bonnet he 'll be some sorry, an' so 'll his folks," he asserted, rising and going down the aisle for a drink.

Red turned to the brakeman, who had just returned: "Say," he whispered, "get off at th' next stop, shoot off a gun, an' yell, just for fun. Go ahead, it 'll be better 'n a circus."

"Nix on the circus, says I," hastily replied the other. "I ain't looking for no excitement, an' I ain't paid to amuse th' passengers. I hope we don't even run over a track-torpedo this side of Sandy Creek."

Hopalong returned, and as he came even with them the train slowed.

"What are we stopping for?" he asked, his hand going to his holster.

"To take on water; the tank 's right ahead."

"What have you got?" asked Billy, ruffling his cards.

"None of yore business," replied Lanky. "You call when you gets any curious."

"Oh, th' devil!" yawned Hopalong, leaning back lazily. "I shore wish I was on my cayuse pounding leather on th' home trail."

"Me, too," grumbled Red, staring out of the window. "Well, we 're moving again. It won't be long now before we gets out of this."

The card-game continued, the low-spoken terms being interspersed with casual comment; Hopalong exchanged infrequent remarks with Red, while the brakeman and conductor stared out of the same window. There was noticeable an air of anxiety, and the fat man tried to read his magazine with his thoughts far from the printed page. He read and re-read a single paragraph several times without gaining the slightest knowledge of what it meant, while the dyspeptic passenger fidgeted more and more in his seat, like one sitting on hot coals, anxious and alert.

"We 're there now," suddenly remarked the conductor, as the bank of a cut blanked out the view. "It was right here where it happened; the turn's farther on."

"How many cards did you draw, Skinny?" asked Lanky.

"Three; drawin' to a straight flush," laughed the dealer.

"Here 's the turn! We 're through all right," exclaimed the brakeman.

Suddenly there was a rumbling bump, a screeching of air-brakes and the grinding and rattle of couplings and pins as the train slowed down and stopped with a suddenness that snapped the passengers forward and back. The conductor and brakeman leaped to their feet, where the latter stood quietly during a moment of indecision.

A shot was heard and the conductor's hand, raised quickly to the whistle-rope sent blast after blast shrieking over the land. A babel of shouting burst from the other coaches and, as the whistle shrieked without pause, a shot was heard close at hand and the conductor reeled suddenly and sank into a seat, limp and silent.

At the first jerk of the train the card-players threw the board from across their knees, scattering the cards over the floor, and crouching, gained the center of the aisle, intently peering through the windows, their Colts ready for instant use. Hopalong and Red were also in the aisle, and when the conductor had reeled Hopalong's Colt exploded and the man outside threw up his arms and pitched forward.

"Good boy, Hopalong!" cried Skinny, who was fighting mad.

Hopalong wheeled and crouched, watching the door, and it was not long before a masked face appeared on the farther side of the glass. Hopalong fired and a splotch of red stained the white mask as the robber fell against the door and slid to the platform.

"Hear that shooting?" cried the brakeman. "They 're at the messenger. They 'll blow him up!"

"Come on, fellers!" cried Hopalong, leaping toward the door, closely followed by his friends.

They stepped over the obstruction on the platform and jumped to the ground on the side of the car farthest from the robbers.

"Shoot under the cars for legs," whispered Skinny. "That 'll bring 'em down where we can get 'em."

"Which is a good idea," replied Red, dropping quickly and looking under the car.

"Somebody's going to be surprised, all right," exulted Hopalong.

The firing on the other side of the train was heavy, being for the purpose of terrifying the passengers and to forestall concerted resistance. The robbers could not distinguish between the many reports and did not know they were being opposed, or that two of their number were dead.

A whinny reached Hopalong's ears and he located it in a small grove ahead of him: "Well, we know where th' cayuses are in case they make a break."

A white and scared face peered out of the cab-window and Hopalong stopped his finger just in time, for the inquisitive man wore the cap of fireman.

"You idiot!" muttered the gunman, angrily. "Get back!" he ordered.

A pair of legs ran swiftly along the other side of the car and Red and Skinny fired instantly. The legs bent, their owner falling forward behind the rear truck, where he was screened from sight.

"They had it their own way before!" gritted Skinny. "Now we 'll see if they can stand th' iron!"

By this time Hopalong and Red were crawling under the express-car and were so preoccupied that they did not notice the faint blue streak of smoke immediately over their heads. Then Red glanced up to see what it was that sizzed, saw the glowing end of a three-inch fuse, and blanched. It was death not to dare and his hand shot up and back, and the dynamite cartridge sailed far behind him to the edge of the embankment, where it hung on a bush.

"Good!" panted Hopalong. "We 'll pay 'em for that!"

"They 're worse 'n rustlers!"

They could hear the messenger running about over their heads, dragging and up-ending heavy objects against the doors of the car, and Hopalong laughed grimly:

"Luck's with this messenger, all right."

"It ought to be-he 's a fighter."

"Where are they? Have they tumbled to our game?"

"They're waiting for the explosion, you chump."

"Stay where you are then. Wait till they come out to see what's th' matter with it."

Red snorted: "Wait nothing!"

"All right, then; I 'm with you. Get out of my way."

"I 've been in situations some peculiar, but this beats 'em all," Red chuckled, crawling forward.

The robber by the car truck revived enough to realize that something was radically wrong, and shouted a warning as he raised himself on his elbow to fire at Skinny but the alert puncher shot first.

As Hopalong and Red emerged from beneath the car and rose to their feet there was a terrific explosion and they were knocked to the ground, while a sudden, heavy shower of stones and earth rained down over everything. The two punchers were not hurt and they arose to their feet in time to see the engineer and fireman roll out of the cab and crawl along the track on their hands and knees, dazed and weakened by the concussion.

Suddenly, from one of the day-coaches, a masked man looked out, saw the two punchers, and cried:

"It's all up! Save yourselves!"

As Hopalong and Red looked around, still dazed, he fired at them, the bullet singing past Hopalong's ear. Red smothered a curse and reeled as his friend grasped him. A wound over his right eye was bleeding profusely and Hopalong's face cleared of its look of anxiety when he realized that it was not serious.

"They creased you! Blamed near got you for keeps!" he cried, wiping away the blood with his sleeve.

Red, slightly stunned, opened his eyes and looked about confusedly. "Who done that? Where is he?"

"Don't know, but I'll shore find out," Hopalong replied. "Can you stand alone?"

Red pushed himself free and leaned against the car for support: "Course I can! Git that cuss!"

When Skinny heard the robber shout the warning he wheeled and ran back, intently watching the windows and doors of the car for trouble.

"We 'll finish yore tally right here!" he muttered.

When he reached the smoker he turned and went towards the rear, where he found Lanky and Billy lying under the platform. Billy was looking back and guarding their rear, while his companion watched the clump of trees where the second herd of horses was known to be. Just as they were joined by their foreman, they saw two men run across the track, fifty yards distant, and into the grove, both going so rapidly as to give no chance for a shot at them.

"There they are!" shouted Skinny, opening fire on the grove.

At that instant Hopalong turned the rear platform and saw the brakeman leap out of the door with a Winchester in his hands. The puncher sprang up the steps, wrenched the rifle from its owner, and, tossing it to Skinny, cried: "Here, this is better!"

"Too late," grunted the puncher, looking up, but Hopalong had become lost to sight among the rocks along the right of way. "If I only had this a minute ago!" he grumbled.

The men in the grove, now in the saddle, turned and opened fire on the group by the train, driving them back to shelter. Skinny, taking advantage of the cover afforded, ran towards the grove, ordering his friends to spread out and surround it; but it was too late, for at that minute galloping was heard and it grew rapidly fainter.

Red appeared at the end of the train: "Where's th' rest of the coyotes?"

"Two of 'em got away," Lanky replied.

"Ya-ho!" shouted Hopalong from the grove. "Don't none of you fools shoot! I'm coming out. They plumb got away!"

"They near got *you*, Red," Skinny cried.

"Nears don't count," Red laughed.

"Did you ever notice Hopalong when he 's fighting mad?" asked Lanky, grinning at the man who was leaving the woods. "He allus wears his sombrero hanging on one ear. Look at it now!"

"Who touched off that cannon some time back?" asked Billy.

"I did. It was an anti-gravity cartridge what I found sizzling on a rod under th' floor of th' express car," replied Red.

"Why did n't you pinch out th' fuse 'stead of blowing everything up, you half-breed?" Lanky asked.

"I reckon I was some hasty," grinned Red.

"It blowed me under th' car an' my lid through a windy," cried Billy. "An' Skinny, he went up in th' air like a shore-'nough grasshopper."

Hopalong joined them, grinning broadly: "Hey, reckon ridin' in th' cars ain't so bad after all, is it?"

"Holy smoke!" cried Skinny. "What's that a-popping?"

Hopalong, Colt in hand, leaped to the side of the train and looked along it, the others close behind him, and saw the fat man with his head and arm out of the window, blazing away into the air, which increased the panic in the coaches. Hopalong grinned and fired into the ground, and the fat man nearly dislocated parts of his anatomy by his hasty disappearance.

"Reckon he plumb forgot all about his fine, six-dollar gun till just now," Skinny laughed.

"Oh, he 's making good," Red replied. "He said he 'd take a hand if anything busted loose. It's a good thing he did n't come to life while me an' Hoppy was under his windy looking for laigs."

"Reckon some of us better go in th' cars an' quiet th' stampede," Skinny remarked, mounting the steps, followed by Hopalong. "They're shore *loco*."

The uproar in the coach ceased abruptly when the two punchers stepped through the door, the inmates shrinking into their seats, frightened into silence. Skinny and his companion did not make a reassuring sight, for they were grimy with burned powder and dust, and Hopalong's sleeve was stained with Red's blood.

"Oh, my jewels, my pretty jewels," sobbed a woman, staring at Skinny and wringing her hands.

"Ma'am, we shore don't want yore jewelry," replied Skinny, earnestly. "Ca'm yoreself; we don't want nothin'."

"*I* don't want that!" growled Hopalong, pushing a wallet from him. "How many times do you want us to tell you we don't want nothin'? We ain't robbers; we licked th' robbers."

Suddenly he stooped and, grasping a pair of legs which protruded into the aisle obstructing the passage, straightened up and backed towards Red, who had just entered the car, dragging into sight a portly gentleman, who kicked and struggled and squealed, as he grabbed at the stanchions of seats to stay his progress. Red stepped aside between two seats and let his friend pass, and then leaned over and grasped the portly gentleman's coat-collar. He tugged energetically and lifted the frightened man clear of the aisle and deposited him across the back of a seat, face down, where he hung balanced, yelling and kicking.

"Shut yore face, you cave-hunter!" cried Red in disgust. "Stop that infernal noise! You fat fellers make all yore noise after th' fighting is all over!"

The man on the seat, suddenly realizing what a sight he made, rolled off his perch and sat up, now more angry than frightened. He glared at Red's grinning face and sputtered:

"It's an outrage! It's an outrage! I'll have you hung for this day's work, young man!"

"That's right," grinned Hopalong. "He shore deserves it. I told him more 'n once that he 'd get strung up some day."

"Yes, and you, too!"

"Please don't," begged Hopalong. "I don't want t' die!"

Tense as the past quarter of an hour had been a titter ran along the car and, fuming impotently, the portly gentleman fled into the smoker.

"I 'll bet he had a six-dollar gun, too," laughed Red.

"I 'll bet he 's calling hisself names right about now," Hopalong replied. Then he turned to reply to a woman: "Yes, ma'am, we did. But they was n't real badmen."

At this a young woman, who was about as pretty as any young woman could be, arose and ran to Hopalong and, impulsively throwing her arms around his neck, cried: "You brave man! You hero! You dear!"

"Skinny! Red! Help!" cried the frightened and embarrassed puncher, struggling to get free.

She kissed him on the cheek, which flamed even more red as he made frantic efforts to keep his head back.

"Ma'am!" he cried, desperately. "Leggo, ma'am! Leggo!"

"Oh! Ho! Ho!" roared Red, weak from his mirth and, not looking to see what he was doing, he dropped into a seat beside another woman. He was on his feet instantly; fearing that he would have to go through the ordeal his friend was going through, he fled down the aisle, closely followed by Hopalong, who by this time had managed to break away. Skinny backed off suspiciously and kept close watch on Hopalong's admirer.

Just then the brakeman entered the car, grinning, and Skinny asked about the condition of the conductor.

"Oh, he 's all right now," the brakeman replied. "They shot him through the arm, but he 's repaired and out bossin' the job of clearin' the rocks off the track. He 's a little shaky yet, but he 'll come around all right."

"That's good. I 'm shore glad to hear it."

"Won't you wear this pin as a small token of my gratitude?" asked a voice at Skinny's shoulder.

He wheeled and raised his sombrero, a flush stealing over his face:

"Thank you, ma'am, but I don't want no pay. We was plumb glad to do it."

"But this is not pay! It's just a trifling token of my appreciation of your courage, just something to remind you of it. I shall feel hurt if you refuse."

Her quick fingers had pinned it to his shirt while she spoke and he thanked her as well as his embarrassment would permit. Then there was a rush toward him and, having visions of a shirt looking like a jeweler's window, he turned and fled from the car, crying: "Pin 'em on th' brakeman!"

He found the outfit working at a pile of rocks on the track, under the supervision of the conductor, and Hopalong looked up apprehensively at Skinny's approach.

"Lord!" he ejaculated, grinning sheepishly, "I was some scairt you was a woman."

Red dropped the rock he was carrying and laughed derisively.

"Oh, yo're a brave man, you are! scared to death by a purty female girl! If I 'd 'a' been you I would n't 'a' run, not a step!"

Hopalong looked at him witheringly: "Oh, no! You wouldn't 'a' run! You'd dropped dead in your tracks, you would!"

"You was both of you a whole lot scared," Skinny laughed. Then, turning to the conductor: "How do you feel, Simms?"

"Oh, I 'm all right: but it took the starch out of me for awhile."

"Well, I don't wonder, not a bit."

"You fellows certainly don't waste any time getting busy," Simms laughed.

"That's the secret of gun-fightin'," replied Skinny.

"Well, you 're a fine crowd all right. Any time you want to go any place when you 're broke, climb aboard my train and I 'll see't you get there."

"Much obliged."

Simms turned to the express-car: "Hey, Jackson! You can open up now if you want to."

But the express-messenger was suspicious, fearing that the conductor was talking with a gun at his head: "You go to h —l!" he called back.

"Honest!" laughed Simms. "Some cowboy friends o' mine licked the gang. Didn't you hear that dynamite go off? If they hadn't fished it out from under your feet you 'd be communing with the angels 'bout now."

For a moment there was no response, and then Jackson could be heard dragging things away from the door. When he was told of the cartridge and Red had been pointed out to him as the man who had saved his life, he leaped to the ground and ran to where that puncher was engaged in carrying the ever-silenced robbers to the baggage-car. He shook hands with Red, who laughed deprecatingly, and then turned and assisted him.

Hopalong came up and grinned: "Say, there 's some cayuses in that grove up th' track; shall I go up an' get 'em?"

"Shore! I 'll go an' get 'em with you," replied Skinny.

In the grove they found seven horses picketed, two of them being pack-animals, and they led them forth and reached the train as the others came up.

"Well, here 's five saddled cayuses, an' two others," Skinny grinned.

"Then we can ride th' rest of th' way in th' saddle instead of in that blamed train," Red eagerly suggested.

"That's just what we can do," replied Skinny. "Leather beats car-seats any time. How far are we from Sandy Creek, Simms?"

"About twenty miles."

"An' we can ride along th' track, too," suggested Hopalong.

"We shore can," laughed Skinny, shaking hands with the train-crew: "We 're some glad we rode with you this trip: we 've had a fine time."

"And we're glad you did," Simms replied, "for that ain't no joke, either."

Hopalong and the others had mounted and were busy waving their sombreros and bowing to the heads and handkerchiefs which were decorating the car-windows.

"All aboard!" shouted the conductor, and cheers and good wishes rang out and were replied to by bows and waving of sombreros. Then Hopalong jerked his gun loose and emptied it into the air, his companions doing likewise. Suddenly five reports rang out from the smoker and they cheered the fat man as he waved at them. They sat quietly and watched the train until the last handkerchief became lost to sight around a curve, but the screeching whistle could be heard for a long time.

"Gee!" laughed Hopalong as they rode on after the train, "won't th' fellers home on th' ranch be a whole lot sore when they hears about the good time what they missed!"

XI

Sammy Finds a Friend

The long train ride and the excitement were over and the outfit, homeward bound, loped along the trail, noisily discussing their exciting and humorous experiences and laughingly commented upon Hopalong's decision to follow them later. They could not understand why he should be interested in a town like Sandy Creek after a week spent in the city.

Back in the little cow-town their friend was standing in the office of the hotel, gazing abstractedly out of the window. His eyes caught and focused on a woman who was walking slowly along the other side of the square and finally paused before McCall's "Palace," a combination saloon, dance and gambling hall. He smiled cynically as his memory ran back over those other women he had seen in cow-towns and wondered how it was that the men of the ranges could rise to a chivalry that was famed. At that distance she was strikingly pretty. Her complexion was an alluring blend of color that the gold of her hair crowned like a burst of sunshine. He noticed that her eyebrows were too prominent, too black and heavy to be Nature's contribution. And there was about her a certain forwardness, a dash that bespoke no bashful Miss; and her clothes, though well-fitting, somehow did not please his untrained eye. A sudden impulse seized him and he strode to the door and crossed the dusty square, avoiding the piles of rusted cans, broken bottles and other rubbish that littered it.

She had become interested in a dingy window but turned to greet him with a resplendent smile as he stepped to the wooden walk. He noted with displeasure that the white teeth displayed two shining panels of gold that drew his eyes irresistibly; and then and there he hated gold teeth.

"Hello," she laughed. "I 'm glad to see somebody that's alive in this town. Ain't it awful?"

He instinctively removed his sombrero and was conscious that his habitual bashfulness in the presence of members of her sex was somehow lacking. "Why, I don't see nothin' extra dead about it," he replied. "Most of these towns are this way in daylight. Th' moths ain't out yet. You should 'a' been here last night!"

"Yes? But you 're out; an' you look like you might be able to fly," she replied.

"Yes; I suppose so," he laughed.

"I see you wear *two* of 'em," she said, glancing at his guns. "Ain't one of them things enough?"

"One usually is, mostly," he assented. "But I 'm pig-headed, so I wears two."

"Ain't it awrful hard to use two of 'em at once?" she asked, her tone flattering. "Then you 're one of them two-gun men I 've heard about, ain't you?"

"An' seen?" he smiled.

"Yes, I 've seen a couple. Where you goin' so early?"

"Just lookin' th' town over," he answered, glancing over her shoulder at a cub of a cowpuncher who had opened the door of the "Retreat," but stopped in his tracks when he saw the couple in front of McCall's. There was a look of surprised interest on the cub's face, and it swiftly changed to one of envious interest. Hopalong's glance did not linger, but swept carelessly along the row of shacks and back to his companion's face without betraying his discovery.

"Well; you can look it over in about ten seconds, from th' outside," she rejoined. "An' it's so dusty out here. My throat is awful dry already."

He had n't noticed any dust in the air, but he nodded. "Yes; thirsty?"

"Well, it ain't polite or ladylike to say yes," she demurred, "but I really am."

He held open the door of the "Palace" and preceded her to the dance hall, where she rippled the keys of the old piano as she swept past it. The order given and served, he sipped at his glass and carried on his share of a light conversation until, suddenly, he arose and made his apologies. "I got to attend to something" he regretted as he picked up his sombrero and turned. "See you later."

"Why!" she exclaimed. "I was just beginnin' to get acquainted!"

"A moth without money ain't no good," he smiled. "I 'm goin' out to find th' money. When I 'm in good company I like to spend. See you later?" He bowed as she nodded, and departed.

Emerging from McCall's he glanced at the "Retreat" and sauntered toward it. When he entered he found the cub resting his elbows on the pine bar, arguing with the bartender about the cigars sold in the establishment. The cub glanced up and appealed to the newcomer. "Ain't they?" he demanded.

Hopalong nodded. "I reckon so. But what is it about?"

"These cigars," explained the cub, ruefully. "I was just sayin' there ain't a good one in town."

"You lose," replied Hopalong. "Are you shore you knows a good cigar when you smokes it?"

"I know it so well that I ain't found one since I left Kansas City. You said I lose. Do you know one well enough to be a judge?"

Hopalong reached to his vest pocket, extracted a cigar and handed it to the cub, who took it hesitatingly. "Why, I'm much obliged. I —I did n't mean that-you know."

Hopalong nodded and rearranged the cigar's twin-brothers in his pocket. He would be relieved when they were smoked, for they made him nervous with their frailty. The cub lighted the cigar and an unaffected grin of delight wreathed his features as the smoke issued from his nostrils. "Who sells 'em?" he demanded, excitedly.

"Corson an' Lukins, up th' hill from th' depot," answered Hopalong. "Like it?"

"Like it! Why, stranger, I used to spend most of my week's pocket money for these." He paused and stared at the smiling puncher. "Did you say Corson an' Lukins?" he demanded incredulously. "Well, I 'll be hanged! When was you there?"

"Last week. Here, bartender; liquor for all hands."

The cub touched the glass to his lips and waved his hand at a table. Seated across from the stranger with the heaven-sent cigars he ordered the second round, and when he went to pay for it he drew out a big roll of bills and peeled off the one on the outside.

Hopalong frowned. "Sonny," he said in a low voice, "it ain't none of my affair, but you oughta put that wad away an' forget you have it when out in public. You shouldn't tempt yore feller men like that."

The cub laughed: "Oh, I had my eye teeth cut long ago. Play a little game?"

Hopalong was amused. "Didn't I just tell you not to tempt yore feller men?"

The cub grinned. "I reckon it 'll fade quick, anyhow; but it took me six months' hard work to get it together. It 'll last about six days, I suppose."

"Six hours, if you plays every man that comes along," corrected Hopalong.

"Well, mebby," admitted the cub. "Say: that was one fine girl you was talkin' to, all right," he grinned.

Hopalong studied him a moment. "Not meanin' no offense, what's yore name?"

"Sammy Porter; why?"

"Well, Sammy," remarked Hopalong as he arose. "I reckon we 'll meet again before I leave. You was remarkin' she was a fine girl. I admit it; she was. So long," and he started for the door.

Sammy flushed. "Why, I —I didn't mean nothin'!" he exclaimed. "I just happened to think about her-that's all! You know, I saw you talkin' to her. Of course, you saw her first," he explained.

Hopalong turned and smiled kindly. "You didn't say nothin' to offend me. I was just startin' when you spoke. But as long as you mentioned it I 'll say that my interest in th' lady was only brief. Her interest in me was th' same. Beyond lettin' you know that I 'll add that I don't generally discuss wimmin. I 'll see you later," and, nodding cheerily, he went out and closed the door behind him.

Hopalong leaned lazily against the hotel, out of reach of the spring wind, which was still sharp, and basked in the warmth of the timid sun. He regarded the little cow-town cynically but smilingly and found no particular fault with it. Existing because the railroad construction work of the season before had chanced to stop on the eastern bank of the deceptive creek, and because of the nearness of three drive trails, one of them important, the town had sprung up, mushroom-like, almost in a night. Facing on the square were two general stores, the railroad station and buildings, two restaurants, a dozen saloons where gambling either was the main attraction or an ambitious side-line, McCall's place and a barber shop with a dingy, bullet-peppered red-and-white pole set close to the door. Between the barber shop and McCall's was a narrow space, and the windows of the two buildings, while not opposite, opened on the little strip of ground separating them.

Rubbing a hand across his chin he regarded the barber shop thoughtfully and finally pushed away from the sun-warmed wall of the hotel and started lazily toward the red-and-white pole. As he did so the tin-panny notes of a piano redoubled and a woman's voice shrilly arose to a high note, flatted, broke and swiftly dropped an octave. He squirmed and looked speculatively along the westward trail, wondering how far away his outfit was and why he had not gone with them. Another soaring note that did not flat and a crashing chord from the piano were followed by a burst of uproarious, reckless laughter. Hopalong frowned, snapped his fingers in sudden decision and stepped briskly toward the barber shop as the piano began anew.

Entering quietly and closing the door softly, he glanced appraisingly through the windows and made known his wants in a low voice. "I want a shave, haircut, shampoo, an' anythin' else you can think of. I 'm tired an' don't want to talk. Take yore own time an' do a good job; an' if I 'm asleep when yo're through, don't wake me till somebody else wants th' chair. Savvy? All right-start in."

In McCall's a stolid bartender listened to the snatches of conversation that filtered under the door to the dance hall alongside and on his face there at times flickered the suggestion of a cynical smile. A heavy, dark complexioned man entered from the street and glanced at the closed door of the dance hall. The bartender nodded and held up a staying hand, after which he shoved a drink across the bar. The heavy-set man carefully wiped a few drops of spilled liquor from his white, tapering hands and seated himself with a sigh of relief, and became busy with his thoughts until the time should come when he would be needed.

On the other side of that door a little comedy was being enacted. The musician, a woman, toyed with the keys of the warped and scratched piano, the dim light from the shaded windows mercifully hiding the paint and the hardness of her face and helping the jewelry, with which her hands were covered, keep its tawdry secret.

"I don't see what makes you so touchy," grumbled Sammy in a pout. "I ain't goin' to hurt you if I touch yore arm." He was flushed and there was a suspicious unsteadiness in his voice.

She laughed. "Why, I thought you wanted to talk?"

"I did," he admitted, sullenly; "but there's a limit to most wants. Oh, well: go ahead an' play. That last piece was all right; but give us a gallop or a mazurka-anything lively. Better yet, a caprice: it's in keepin' with yore temperament. If you was to try to interpert mine you 'd have to dig it out of Verdi an' toll a funeral bell."

"Say; who told you so much about music?" she demanded.

"Th' man that makes harmonicas," he grinned. He arose and took a step toward her, but she retreated swiftly, smiling. "Now behave yourself, for a little while, at least. What's th' matter with you, anyhow? What makes you so silly?"

"You, of course. I don't see no purty wimmin out on th' range, an' you went to my head th' minute I laid eyes on you. *I* ain't in no hurry to leave this town, now nohow."

"I 'm afraid you 're going to be awful when you grow up. But you 're a nice boy to say such pretty things. Here," she said, filling his glass and handing it to him, "let's drink another toast-you know such nice ones."

"Yes; an' if I don't run out of 'em purty soon I 'll have to hunt a solid, immovable corner somewheres; an' there ain't nothin' solid or immovable about *this* room at present," he growled. "What you allus drinkin' to somethin' for? Well, here's a toast —I don't know any more fancy ones. Here's to —*you!*"

"That's nicer than-oh, pshaw!" she exclaimed, pouting. "An' you would n't drink a full glass to *that* one. You must think I 'm nice, when you renig like that! Don't tell me any more pretty things-an' stop right where you are! Think you can hang onto me after that? Well, that's better; why didn't you do it th' first time? You can be a nice boy when you want to."

He flushed angrily. "Will you stop callin' me a boy?" he demanded unsteadily. "I ain't no kid! I do a man's work, earn a man's pay, an' I spend it like a man."

"An' drink a boy's drink," she teased. "You 'll grow up some day." She reached forward and filled his glass again, for an instant letting her cheek touch his. Swiftly evading him she laughed and patted him on the head. "Here, *man*," she taunted, "drink this if you dare!"

He frowned at her but gulped down the liquor. "There, like a fool!" he grumbled, bitterly. "You tryin' to get me drunk?" he demanded suddenly in a heavy voice.

She threw back her head and regarded him coldly. "It will do me no good. Why should I? I merely wanted to see if you would take a dare, if you were a man. You are either not sober now, or you are insultingly impolite. I don't care to waste any more words or time with you," and she turned haughtily toward the door.

He had leaned against the piano, but now he lurched forward and cried out. "I 'm sorry if I hurt yore feelin's that way —I shore didn't mean to. Ain't we goin' to make up?" he asked, anxiously.

"Do you mean that?" she demanded, pausing and looking around.

"You know I do, Annie. Le's make up-come on; le's make up."

"Well; I'll try you, an' see."

"Play some more. You play beautiful," he assured her with heavy gravity.

"I'm tired of-but, say: Can you play poker?" she asked, eagerly.

"Why, shore; who can't?"

"Well, I can't, for one. I want to learn, so I can win my money back from Jim. He taught me, but all I had time to learn was how to lose."

Sammy regarded her in puzzled surprise and gradually the idea became plain. "Did he teach you, an' win money from you? Did he keep it?" he finally blurted, his face flushed a deeper red from anger.

She nodded. "Why, yes; why?"

He looked around for his sombrero, muttering savagely.

"Where you goin'?" she asked in surprise.

"To get it back. He ain't goin' to keep it, th' coyote!"

"Why, he won't give it back to you if he would n't to me. Anyhow, he won it."

"*Won* it!" he snapped. "He stole it, that's how much he won it. He 'll give it back or get shot."

"Now look here," she said, quickly. "You ain't goin' gunnin' for no friend of mine. If you want to get that money for me, an' I certainly can use it about now, you got to try some other way. Say! Why don't you win it from him?" she exulted. "That's th' way-get it back th' way it went."

He weighed her words and a grin slowly crept across his face. "Why, I reckon you called it, that time, Annie. That's th' way I 'll try first, anyhow, Li'l Girl. Where is this good friend of yourn that steals yore money? Where is this feller?"

As if in answer to his inquiry the heavy-set man strolled in, humming cheerily. And as he did so the sleepy occupant of the barber's chair slowly awoke, rubbed his eyes, stretched luxuriously and, paying his bill, loafed out and lazily sauntered down the street, swearing softly.

"Why, here he is now," laughed the woman. "You must 'a' heard us talkin' about you, Jim. I'm goin' to get my money back-this is Mr. Porter, Jim, who 's goin' to do it."

The gambler smiled and held out his hand. "Howd'y, Mr. Porter," he said.

Sammy glared at him: "Put yore paw down," he said, thickly. "I ain't shakin' han's with no dogs or tin-horns."

The gambler recoiled and flushed, fighting hard to repress his anger. "What you mean?" he growled, furiously.

"What I said. If you want revenge sit down there an' play, if you 've got th' nerve to play with a man. I never let no coyote steal a woman's money, an' I 'm goin' to get Annie her twenty. Savvy?"

The gambler's reply was a snarl. "Play!" he sneered. "I'll play, all right. It'll take more 'n a sassy kid to get that money back, too. I 'm goin' to take yore last red cent. You can't talk to me like that an' get it over. An' don't let me hear you call her 'Annie' no more, neither. Yo 're too cussed familiar!"

Her hand on Sammy's arm stopped the draw and he let the gun drop back into the holster. "*No!*" she whispered. "Make a fool of him, Sammy! Beat him at his own game."

Sammy nodded and scowled blackly. "I call th' names as suits me," he retorted. "When I see you on th' street I 'm goin' to call you some that I 'm savin' up now because a lady 's present. They 're hefty, too."

At first he won, but always small amounts. Becoming reckless, he plunged heavily on a fair hand and lost. He plunged again on a better hand and lost. Then he steadied as much as his befuddled brain would permit and played a careful game, winning a small pot. Another small winning destroyed his caution and he plunged again, losing heavily. Steadying himself once more he began a new deal with excess caution and was bluffed out of the pot, the gambler sneeringly showing his cards as he threw them down. Sammy glanced around to say something to the woman, but found she had gone. "Aw, never mind her!" growled his opponent. "She 'll be back-she can't stay away from a kid like you."

The woman was passing through the barroom and, winking at the bartender, opened the door and stepped to the street. She smiled as she caught sight of the limping stranger coming toward her. He might have found money, but she was certain he had found something else and in generous quantities. He removed his sombrero with an exaggerated sweep of his hand and hastened to meet her, walking with the conscious erectness of a man whose feet are the last part of him to succumb. "Hullo, Sugar," he grinned. "I found some, a'right. Now we 'll have some music. Come long."

"There ain't no hurry," she answered. "We 'll take a little walk first."

"No, we won't. We 'll have some music an' somethin' to drink. If you won't make th' music, I will; or shoot up th' machine. Come 'long, Sugar," he leered, pushing open the door with a resounding slam. He nodded to the bartender and apologized. "No harm meant, Friend. It sorta slipped; jus' slipped, tha's all. Th' young lady an' me is goin' to have some music. What? All right for you, Sugar! Then I'll make it myself," and he paraded stiffly toward the inner door.

The bartender leaned suddenly forward. "Keep out of there! You 'll bust that pianner!"

The puncher stopped with a jerk, swung ponderously on his heel and leveled a forefinger at the dispenser of drinks. "I won't," he said. "An' if I do, I 'll pay for it. Come on, Sugar-le's play th' old thing, jus' for spite." Grasping her arm he gently but firmly escorted her into the dance hall and seated her at the piano. As he straightened up he noticed the card players and, bowing low to her, turned and addressed them.

"Gents," he announced, bowing again, "we are goin' to have a li'l music an' we hopes you won't objec'. Not that we gives a d —n, but we jus' hopes you won't." He laughed loudly at his joke and leaned against the piano. "Let 'er go," he cried, beating time. "Allaman lef an' ladies change! Swing yore partner's gal —I mean, swing some other gal: but what's th' difference? All join han's an' hop to th' middle-nope! It's all han's roun' an' swing 'em again. But it don't make no difference, does it, Lulu?" He whooped loudly and marched across the room, executed a few fancy steps and marched back again. As he passed the card table Sammy threw down his hand and arose with a curse. The marcher stopped, fiddled a bit with his feet until obtaining his balance, and then regarded the youth quizzically. "S'matter, Sonny?" he inquired.

Sammy scowled, slowly recognized the owner of the imported cigars and shook his head. "Big han's, but not big enough; an' I lost my pile." Staggering to the piano he plumped down on a chair near it and watched the rippling fingers of the player in drunken interest.

The hilarious cowpuncher, leaning backward perilously, recovered his poise for a moment and then lurched forward into the chair the youth had just left. "Come on, pardner," he grinned across at the gambler. "Le's gamble. I been honin' for a game, an' here she is." He picked up the cards, shuffled them clumsily and pushed them out for the cut. The gambler hesitated, considered and then turned over a jack. He lost the deal and shoved out a quarter without interest.

The puncher leaned over, looked at it closely and grinned. "Two bits? That ain't poker; that's —that's dominoes!" he blurted, angrily, with the quick change of mood of a man in his cups.

"I ain't anxious to play," replied the gambler. "I 'll kill a li'l time at a two-bit game, though. Otherwise I 'll quit."

"A'right," replied the dealer. "I did n't expec' nothin' else from a tin-horn, no-how. I want two cards after you get yourn." The gambler called on the second raise and smiled to himself when he saw that his opponent had drawn to a pair and an ace. He won on his own deal and on the one following.

The puncher increased the ante on the fourth deal and looked up inquiringly, a grin on his face. "Le's move out th' infant class," he suggested.

The gambler regarded him sharply. "Well, th' other *was* sorta tender," he admitted, nodding.

The puncher pulled out a handful of gold coins and clumsily tried to stalk them, which he succeeded in doing after three attempts. He was so busy that he did not notice the look in the other's eyes. Picking up his hand he winked at it and discarded one. "Goin' to raise th' ante a few," he chuckled. "I got a feelin' I 'm goin' t' be lucky." When the card was dealt to him he let it lay and bet heavily. The gambler saw it and raised in turn, and the puncher, frowning in indecision, nodded his head wisely and met it, calling as he did so. His four fives were just two spots shy to win and he grumbled loudly at his luck. "Huh," he finished, "she 's a jack pot, eh?" He slid a double eagle out to the center of the table and laughed recklessly. The deals went around rapidly, each one calling for a ten-dollar sweetener and when the seventh hand was dealt the puncher picked his cards and laughed. "She 's open," he cried, "for fifty," and shoved out the money with one hand while he dug up a reserve pile from his pocket with the other.

The gambler saw the opener and raised it fifty, smiling at his opponent's expression. The puncher grunted his surprise, studied his hand, glanced at the pot and shrugging his shoulders, saw the raise. He drew two cards and chuckled as he slid them into his hand; but before the dealer could make his own draw the puncher's chuckle died out and he stared over the gambler's shoulder. With an oath he jerked out his gun and fired. The gambler leaped to his feet and whirled around to look behind. Then he angrily faced the frowning puncher. "What you think yo 're doin'?" he demanded, his hand resting inside his coat, the thumb hooked over the edge of the vest.

The puncher waved his hand apologetically. "I never have no luck when I sees a cat," he explained. "A black cat is worse; but a yaller one's bad enough. I 'll bet that yaller devil won't come back in a hurry-judgin' by th' way it started. I won't miss him, if he does."

The gambler, still frowning, glanced at the deck suspiciously and saw that it lay as he had dropped it. The bartender, grinning at them from the door, cracked a joke and went back to the bar. Sammy, after a wild look around, settled back in his chair and soothed the pianist a little before going back to sleep.

Drawing two cards the gambler shoved them in his hand without a change in his expression- but he was greatly puzzled. It was seldom that he bungled and he was not certain that he had. The discard contained the right number of cards and his opponent's face gave no hint to the thoughts behind it. He hesitated before he saw the bet-ten dollars was not much, for the size of the pot justified more. He slowly saw it, willing to lose the ten in order to see his opponent's cards. There was something he wished to know, and he wanted to know it as soon as he could. "I call that," he said. The puncher's expression of tenseness relaxed into one of great relief and he hurriedly dropped his cards. Three kings, an eight, and a deuce was his offering. The gambler laid down a pair of queens, a ten, an eight and a four, waved his hand and smiled. "It's just as well I did n't draw another queen," he observed, calmly. "I might 'a' raised once for luck."

The puncher raked in the pot and turned around in his chair. "I cleaned up that time," he exulted to the woman. She had stopped playing and was stroking Sammy's forehead. Smiling at the exuberant winner she nodded. "You should have let the cat stay—I think it really brought you luck." He shook his head emphatically. "*No*, ma'am! It was chasin' it away as did that. That's what did it, a'right."

The gambler glanced quickly at the two top cards on the deck and was picking up those scattered on the table when his opponent turned around again. How that queen and ten had got two cards too deep puzzled him greatly-he was willing to wager even money that he would not look away again until the game was finished, not if all the cats in the world were being slaughtered. One hundred and ninety dollars was too much money to pay for being caught off his guard, as he was tempted to believe he had been. He did not know how much liquor the other had consumed, but he seemed to be sobering rapidly.

The next few deals did not amount to much. Then a jackpot came around and was pushed hard. The puncher was dealing and as he picked up the deck after the cut he grinned and winked. "Th' skirmishin' now bein' over, th' battle begins. If that cat stays away long enough mebby I 'll make a killin'."

"All right; but don't make no more gun-plays," warned the gambler, coldly. "I allus get excited when I smells gun-powder an' I do reckless things sometimes," he added, significantly.

"Then I shore hopes you keep ca'm," laughed the puncher, loud enough to be heard over the noise of the piano, which was now going again.

The pot was sweetened three times and then the gambler dealt his opponent openers. The puncher looked anxiously through the door, grinning coltishly. He slowly pushed out twenty dollars. "There's th' key," he grunted. "A'right; see that an' raise you back. Good for you! I'm stayin' an' boostin' same as ever. Fine! See it again, an' add this. I 'm playin' with yore money, so I c'n afford to be reckless. All right; I'm satisfied, too. Gimme one li'l card. I shore am glad I don't need th' king of hearts-that was shore on th' bottom when th' deal *begun*."

The gambler, having drawn, cursed and reached swiftly toward his vest pocket; but he stopped suddenly and contemplated the Colt that peeked over the edge of the table. It looked squarely at his short ribs and was backed by a sober, angry man who gazed steadily into his eyes. "Drop that hand," said the puncher in a whisper just loud enough to be heard by the other over the noise of the piano. "I never did like them shoulder holsters—I carry my irons where everybody can see 'em." Leaning forward swiftly he reached out his left hand and cautiously turned over the other's cards. The fourth one was the king of hearts. "Don't move," he whispered, not wishing to have the bartender take a hand from behind. "An' don't talk," he warned as he leaned farther forward and shoved his Colt against the other's vest and with his left hand extracted a short-barreled gun from the sheath under the gambler's armpit. Sinking back in his chair he listened a moment and, raking in the pot, stowed it away with the other winnings in his pockets.

The gambler stirred, but stopped as the Colt leaped like a flash of light to the edge of the table. "Tin-horn," said the puncher, softly, "you ain't slick enough. I did n't stop you when you wanted that queen an' ten because I wanted you to go on with th' crookedness. Yaller cats is more unlucky to you than they are to me. But when I saw that last play I lost my temper; an' I stopped you. Now if you 'll cheat with me, you 'll cheat with a drunk boy. So, havin' cheated him, you really stole his money away from him. That bein' so, you will dig up six month's wages at about fifty per month. I 'd shoot you just as quick as I 'd shoot a snake; so don't get no fool notions in yore head. Dig it right up."

The gambler studied the man across from him, but after a moment he silently placed some money on the table. "It was only two forty," he observed, holding to three double eagles. The puncher nodded: "I 'll take yore word for that. Now, in th' beginnin' I only wanted to get th' boy his money; but when you started cheatin' against me I changed my mind. I played fair. Now here's your short-five," he said as he slid the gun across the table. "Mebby you might want to use it sometime," he smiled. "Now you vamoose; an' if I see you in town after th' next train leaves, I 'll *make* you use that shoulder holster. An' tell yore friends that Hopalong Cassidy says, that for a country where men can tote their hardware in plain sight, a shoulder layout ain't no good: you gotta reach too high. Adios."

He watched the silent, philosophical man-of-cards walk slowly toward the door, upright, dignified and calm. Then he turned and approached the piano. "Sister," he said, politely, "yore gamblin' friend is leavin' town on th' next train. He has pressin' business back east a couple of stations an' wonders if you 'll join him at th' depot in time for th' next train."

She had stopped playing and was staring at him in amazement. "Why didn't he come an' tell me himself, 'stead of sneakin' away an' sendin' you over?" she at last demanded, angrily.

"Well, he wanted to, but he saw a man an' slipped out with his gun in his hand. Mebby there'll be trouble; but I dunno. I'm just tellin' you. Gee," he laughed, looking at the snoring youth in the chair, "he got *that* quick. Why, I saw him less 'n two hours ago an' he was sober as a judge. Reckon I 'll take him over to th' hotel an' put him to bed." He went over to the helpless Sammy, shook him and made him get on his feet. "Come along, Kid," he said, slipping his arm under the sagging shoulder. "We'll get along. Good-by, Sugar," and, supporting the feebly protesting cub, he slowly made his way to the rear door and was gone, a grin wreathing his face as he heard the chink of gold coins in his several pockets.

XII
Sammy Knows the Game

A clean-cut, good-looking cowpuncher limped slightly as he passed the postoffice and found a seat on a box in front of the store next door. He sighed with relief and gazed cheerfully at the littered square as though it was something worth looking at. The night had not been a pleasant one because Sammy Porter had insisted upon either singing or snoring; and when breakfast was announced the youth almost had recovered his senses and was full of remorse and a raging thirst. Being flatly denied the hair of the dog that bit him he grew eloquently profane and very abusive. Hence Mr. Cassidy's fondness for the box.

Sounds obtruded. They were husky and had dimensions and they came from the hotel bar. After increasing in volume and carrying power they were followed to the street by a disheveled youth who kicked open the door and blinked in the sunlight. Espying the contented individual on the box he shook an earnest fist at that person and tried next door. In a moment he followed a new burst of noise to the street and shook the other fist. Trying the saloon on the other side of the hotel without success he shook both fists and once again tried the hotel bar, where he proceeded along lines tactful, flattering and diplomatic. Only yesterday he had owned a gun, horse and other personal belongings; he had possessed plenty of money, a clear head and his sins sat lightly on his youthful soul. He still had the sins, but they had grown in weight. Tact availed him nothing, flattery was futile and diplomacy was in vain. To all his arguments the bartender sadly shook his head, not because Sammy had no money, which was the reason he gave, but because of vivid remembrance of the grimness with which a certain red-haired, straight-lipped, two-gun cowpuncher had made known his request. "Let him suffer," had said the gunman. "It 'll be a good lesson for him. Understand; not a drop!" And the bartender had understood. To the drink-dispenser's refusal Sammy replied with a masterpiece of eloquence and during its delivery the bartender stood with his hand on a mallet, but too spellbound to throw it. Wheeling at the close of a vivid, soaring climax, Sammy yanked open the door again and stood transfixed with amazement and hostile envy. His new and officious friend surely knew the right system with women. To the burning indignities of the morning this added the last straw and Sammy bitterly resolved not to forget his wrongs.

Had Mr. Cassidy been a kitten he would have purred with delight as he watched his youthful friend's vain search for the hair of the dog, and his grin was threatening to engulf his ears when the Cub slammed into the hotel. Hearing the beating of hoofs he glanced around and saw a trim, pretty young lady astride a trim, high-spirited pony; and both were thoroughbreds if he was any judge. They bore down upon him at a smart lope and stopped at the edge of the walk. The rider leaped from the saddle and ran toward him with her hand outstretched and her face aglow with a delighted surprise. Her eyes fairly danced with welcome and relief and her cheeks, reddened by the thrust of the wind for more than twenty miles, flamed a deeper red, through which streaks of creamy white played fascinatingly. "Dick Ellsworth!" she cried. "When did you get here?"

Mr. Cassidy stumbled to his feet, one hand instinctively going out to the one held out to him, the other fiercely gripping his sombrero. His face flamed under its tan and he mumbled an incoherent reply.

"Don't you remember *me?*" she chided, a roguish, half-serious expression flashing over her countenance. "Not little Annie, whom you taught to ride? I used to think I needed you then, Dick; but oh, how I need you now. It's Providence, nothing else, that sent you. Father's gone steadily worse and now all he cares for is a bottle. Joe, the new foreman, has full charge of everything and he's not only robbing us right and left, but he 's—he 's bothering *me!* When I complain to father of his attentions all I get is a foolish grin. If you only knew how I have prayed for you to come back, Dick! Two bitter years of it. But now everything is all right. Tell me about yourself while I get the mail and then we 'll ride home together. I suppose Joe will be waiting for me somewhere on the trail; he usually does. Did you ever hate anyone so much you wanted to kill him?" she demanded fiercely, beside herself for the moment.

Hopalong nodded. "Well, yes; I have," he answered. "But you must n't. What's his name? We 'll have to look into this."

"Joe Worth; but let's forget him for awhile," she smiled. "I 'll get the mail while you go after your horse."

He nodded and watched her enter the post-office and then turned and walked thoughtfully away. She was mounted when he returned and they swung out of the town at a lope.

"Where have you been, and what have you been doing?" she asked as they pushed along the firm, hard trail.

"Punchin' for th' Bar-20, southwest of here. I wouldn't 'a' been here today only I let th' outfit ride on without me. We just got back from Kansas City a couple of days back. But let's get at this here Joe Worth prop'sition. I 'm plumb curious. How long's he been pesterin' you?"

"Nearly two years—I can't stand it much longer."

"An' th' outfit don't cut in?"

"They 're his friends, and they understand that father wants it so. You 'll not know father, Dick: I never thought a man could change so. Mother's death broke him as though he were a reed."

"Hum!" he grunted. "You ain't carin' how this coyote is stopped, just so he is?"

"No!" she flashed.

"An' he 'll be waitin' for you?"

"He usually is."

He grinned. "Le 's hope he is this time." He was silent a moment and looked at her curiously. "I don't know how you 'll take it, but I got a surprise for you—a big one. I 'm shore sorry to admit it, but I ain't th' man you think. I ain't Dick What 's-his-name, though it shore ain't *my* fault. I reckon I must look a heap like him; an' I hope I can *act* like him in this here matter. I want to see it through like *he* would. I can do as good a job, too. But it ain't no-wise fair nor right to pretend I 'm him. I ain't."

She was staring at him in a way he did not like. "Not Dick Ellsworth!" she gasped. "You are *not* Dick?"

"I 'm shore sorry-but I 'd like to play his cards. I 'm honin' for to see this here Joe Worth," he nodded, cheerfully.

"And you let me believe you were?" she demanded coldly. "You deliberately led me to talk as I did?"

"Well, now; I didn't just know what to do. You shore was in trouble, which was bad. I reckoned mebby I could get you out of it an' then go along 'bout my business. You ain't goin' to stop me a-doin' it, are you?" he asked anxiously.

Her reply was a slow, contemptuous look that missed nothing and that left nothing to be said. Her horse did not like to stand, anyway, and sprang eagerly forward in answer to the sudden pressure of her knees. She rode the high-strung bay with superb art, angry, defiant, and erect as a statue. Hopalong, shaking his head slowly, gazed after her and when she had become a speck on the plain he growled a question to his horse and turned sullenly toward the town. Riding straight to the hotel he held a short, low-voiced conversation with the clerk and then sought his friend, the Cub. This youthful grouch was glaring across the bar at the red-faced, angry man behind it, and the atmosphere was not one of peace. The Cub turned to see who the newcomer was and thereupon transferred his glare to the smiling puncher.

"Hullo, Kid," breezed Hopalong.

"You go to h —l!" growled Sammy, remembering to speak respectfully to his elders. He backed off cautiously until he could keep both of his enemies under his eyes.

Hopalong's grin broadened. He dug into his pockets and produced a large sum of money. "Here, Kid," said he, stepping forward and thrusting it into Sammy's paralyzed hands. "Take it an' buy all th' liquor you wants. You can get yore gun off 'n th' clerk, an' he 'll tell you where to find yore cayuse an' other belongings. I gotta leave town."

Sammy stared at the money in his hand. "What's this?" he demanded, his face flushing angrily.

"Money," replied Hopalong. "It's that shiny stuff you buys things with. Spondulix, cash, mazuma. You spend it, you know."

Sammy sputtered. He might have frothed had his mouth not been so dry. "Is it?" he demanded with great sarcasm. "I thought mebby it was cows, or buttons. What you handin' it to me for? I ain't no d —d beggar!"

Hopalong chuckled. "That money's yourn. I pried it loose from th' tin-horn that stole it from you. I also, besides, pried off a few chunks more; but them 's mine. I allus pays myself good wages; an' th' aforesaid chunks is plenty an' generous. Amen."

Sammy regarded his smiling friend with a frank suspicion that was brutal. The pleasing bulge of the pockets reassured him and he slowly pocketed his rescued wealth. He growled something doubtless meant for thanks and turned to the bar. "A large chunk of th' Mojave Desert slid down my throat las' night an' I 'm so dry I rustles in th' breeze. Let's wet down a li'l." Having extracted some of the rustle he eyed his companion suspiciously. "Thought you was a stranger hereabouts?"

"You 've called it."

"Huh! Then I 'm goin' to stick close to you an get acquainted with th' female population of th' towns we hit. An' I had allus reckoned lightnin' was quick!" he soliloquized, regretfully. "How 'd you do it?" he demanded.

Hopalong was gazing over his friend's head at a lurid chromo portraying the Battle of Bull Run and he pursed his lips thoughtfully. "That shore was some slaughter," he commented. "Well, Kid," he said, holding out his hand, "I 'm leavin'. If you ever gets down my way an' wants a good job, drop in an' see us. Th' clerk 'll tell you how to get there. An' th' next time you gambles, stay sober."

"Hey! Wait a minute!" exclaimed Sammy. "Goin' home now?"

"Can't say as I am, direct."

"Comin' back here before you do?"

"Can't say that, neither. Life is plumb oncertain an' gunplay 's even worse. Mebby I will if I 'm alive."

"Who you gunnin' for? Can't I take a hand?"

"Reckon not, Sammy. Why, I 'm cuttin' in where I ain't wanted, even if I am needed. But it's my duty. It's a h —l of a community as waits for a total stranger to do its work for it. If yo 're around an' I come back, why I 'll see you again. Meanwhile, look out for tin-horns."

Sammy followed him outside and grasped his arm. "I can hold up my end in an argument," he asserted fiercely. "You went an' did me a good turn-lemme do *you* one. If it's anythin' to do with that li'l girl you met to-day I won't cut in-only on th' trouble end. I'm particular strong on th' trouble part. Look here: Ain't a friend got no rights?"

Hopalong warmed to the eager youngster-he was so much like Jimmy; and Jimmy, be it known, could bedevil Hopalong as much as any man alive and not even get an unkind word for it. "I 'm scared to let you come, Kid; she 'd fumigate th' ranch when you left. Th' last twenty-four hours has outlawed you, all right. You keep to th' brush trails in th' draws-don't cavort none on skylines till you lose that biled owl look." He laughed at the other's expression and placed his hands on the youth's shoulders. "That ain't it, Kid; I never apologizes, serious, for th' looks of my friends. They 're my friends, drunk or sober, in h —l or out of it. I just can't see how you can cut in proper. Better wait for me here —I 'll turn up, all right. Meanwhile, as I says before, look out for tin-horns."

Sammy watched him ride away, and then slammed his sombrero on the ground and jumped on it, after which he felt relieved. Procuring his gun from the clerk he paused to cross-examine, but after a fruitless half hour he sauntered out, hiding his vexation, to wrestle with the problem in the open. Passing the window of a general store he idly glanced at the meager display behind the dusty glass and a sudden grin transfigured his countenance. He would find out about the girl first and that would help him solve the puzzle. Thinking thus he wandered in carelessly and he wandered out again gravely clutching a small package. Slipping behind the next building he tore off the paper and carefully crumpled and soiled with dust the purchase. Then he went down to the depot and followed the railroad tracks toward the other side of the square. Reaching the place where the south trail crossed the tracks he left them and walked slowly toward a small depression that was surrounded by hoofprints. He stooped quickly and straightened up with a woman's handkerchief dangling from his fingers. He grinned foolishly, examined it, sniffed at it and scratched his head while he cogitated. A decisive wave of his hand apprised the two spectators that he had arrived at a conclusion, which he bore out by heading straight for the postoffice, which was a part of the grocery store. The postmaster and grocer, in person one, watched his approach with frank curiosity.

Sammy nodded and went in the store, followed by the proprietor. "Howd'y," he remarked, producing the handkerchief. "Just picked this up over on th' trail. Know who dropped it?"

"Annie Allison, I reckon," replied the other. "She came in that way from th' Bar-U. Want to leave it?"

Sammy considered. "Why, I might as well take it to her —I'm goin' down there purty soon. Don't know any other ranch that might use a broncho-buster, do you?"

The proprietor shook his head. "No; most folks 'round here bust their own. Perfessional?"

Sammy nodded. "Yes. Here, gimme two-bits' worth of them pep'mint lozengers. Yes, it shore is fine; but it 'll rain before long. Well, by-by."

The bartender of the "Retreat" sniffed suspiciously and eyed the open door thoughtfully, holding aloft the bar-mop while he considered. Then he put the mop on the bar and went to the door, where he peered out. "Huh!" he grunted. "Hogin' that?" he sarcastically inquired. Sammy held out the bag and led the way to the bar. "Where's th' Bar-U? Yes? Do their own broncho-bustin'? Who, me? Ain't nothin' on laigs can throw me, includin' humans an' bartenders. What? Well, what you want to get all skinned up for, for nothin'? Five dollars? If you must lose it I might as well have it. One fall? All right; come out here an' get it."

The bartender chuckled and vaulted the counter as advance notice of his agility and physical condition, and immediately there ensued a soft shuffling. Suddenly the building shook and dusted itself and Sammy arose and stepped back, smiling at his victim. "Thanks," he remarked.

"Good money was spent on part of my education-boxin' bein' th' other half. Now, for five more, where can't I hit you?"

"Behind th' bar," grinned the other; "I got deadly weapons there. Look here!" he exclaimed hurriedly as a great idea struck him. "Everybody 'round here will back their wrastlin' reckless; le 's team up an' make some easy money. I 'll make th' bets an' you win 'em. Split even. What say?"

"Later on, mebby. What'd you say that Bar-U foreman's name was?"

The bartender's reply was supplemented by a pious suggestion. "An' if you wrastles *him*, bust his cussed neck!"

"Why this friendship?" queried Sammy, laughing.

"Oh, just for general principles."

Sammy bought cigars, left some lozenges and went out to search for his horse, which he duly found. Inwardly he was elated and he flexed his muscles and made curious motions with his arms, which caused the pie-bald to show the whites of its eyes wickedly and flatten its ragged ears. Its actions were justified, for a left hand darted out and slapped the wrinkling muzzle, deftly escaping the clicking teeth. Then the warlike pie-bald reflected judiciously as it chewed the lozenge. The eyes showed less white and the ears, moving forward and back, compromised by one staying forward. The candy was old and stale and the sting of the mint was negligible, but the sugar was much in evidence. When the hand darted out again the answering nip was playful and the ears were set rigidly forward. Sammy laughed, slipped several more lozenges into the ready mouth, vaulted lightly to the saddle and rode slowly toward the square. The pie-bald kicked mildly and reached around to nip at the stirrup, and then went on about its business as any well-broken cow pony should. Reaching the square Sammy drew rein suddenly and watched a horseman who was riding away from the "Retreat." Waiting a few minutes Sammy spurred forward to the saloon and called the bartender out to him. "Who was that feller that just left?" he asked, curiously.

"Joe Worth, th' man yo 're goin' to strike for that job. Why don't you catch him now an' mebby save yoreself a day's ride?"

"Good idea," endorsed Sammy. "See you later," and the youth wheeled and loped toward the trail, but drew rein when hidden from the "Retreat" by some buildings. He watched the distant horseman until he became a mere dot and then Sammy pushed on after him. There was a satisfied look on his face and he chuckled as he cogitated. "I shore got th' drift of this; I know th' game! Wonder how Cassidy got onto it?" He laughed contentedly. "Well, five hundred ain't too little to split two ways; an' mebby it is a two-man job. Mr. Joe Worth, who was once Mr. George Atkins, I would n't give a peso for yore chances after I get th' lay of th' ground an' find out yore habits. Yo 're goin' back to Willow Springs as shore as 'dogies' hang 'round water holes. An' you 'll shore dance their tune when you gets there."

Mr. Cassidy, arriving at the Bar-U, asked for the foreman and was told that the boss was in town, but would be back sometime in the afternoon. The newcomer replied that he would return later and, carefully keeping out of sight of the ranch house as well as he could, he wheeled and rode back the way he had come, being very desirous to have a good look at the foreman before they met. Arriving at an arroyo several miles north of the ranch he turned into it and, leaving his horse picketed on good grass along the bottom, he climbed to a position where he could see the trail without being seen. Having settled himself comfortably he improved the wait by trying to think out the best way to accomplish the work he had set himself to do. Shooting was too common and hardly justifiable unless Mr. Worth forced the issue with weapons of war.

The time passed slowly and he was relieved when a horseman appeared far to the north and jogged toward him, riding with the careless grace of one at home in the saddle. Being thoroughly familiar with the trail and the surrounding country the rider looked straight ahead as if attention to the distance yet untraveled might make it less. He passed within twenty feet of the watcher and went on his way undisturbed. Hopalong waited until he was out of sight around a hill and then, vaulting into the saddle, rode after him, still puzzled as to how he would proceed about the business in hand. He dismounted at the bunkhouse and nodded to those who lingered near the wash bench awaiting their turn.

"Just in time to feed," remarked one of the punchers. "Watch yore turn at th' basins-every man for hisself 's th' rule."

"All right," Hopalong laughed. "But is there any chance to get a job here?" he asked, anxiously.

"You 'll have to quiz th' Ol' Man-here he comes now," and the puncher waved at the approaching foreman. "Hey, Joe! Got a job for this hombre?" he called.

The foreman keenly scrutinized the newcomer, as he always examined strangers. The two guns swinging low on the hips caught his eyes instantly but he showed no particular interest in them, notwithstanding the fact that they proclaimed a gunman. "Why I reckon I got a job for you," he said. "I been waitin' to keep somebody over on Cherokee Range. But it's time to eat: we'll talk later."

After the meal the outfit passed the time in various ways until bed-time, the foreman talking to the new member of his family. During the night the foreman awakened several times and looked toward the newcomer's bunk but found nothing suspicious. After breakfast he called Hopalong and one of the others to him. "Ned," he said, "take Cassidy over to his range and come right back. Hey, Charley! You an' Jim take them poles down to th' ford an' fence in that quicksand just south of it. Ben says he 's been doin' nothin' but pullin' cows outen it. All right, Tim; comin' right away."

Ned and the new puncher lost no time but headed east at once with a packhorse carrying a week's provisions for one man. The country grew rougher rapidly and when they finally reached the divide a beautiful sight lay below them, stretching as far as eye could see to the east. In the middle distance gleamed the Cherokee, flowing toward the south through its valley of rocks, canyons, cliffs, draws and timber.

"There 's th' hut," said Ned, pointing to a small gray blot against the dead black of a towering cliff. "Th' spring's just south of it. Bucket Hill, up north there, is th' north boundary; Twin Spires, south yonder is th' other end; an' th' Cherokee will stop you on th' east side. You ride in every Sat'day if you wants. Don't get lonesome," he grinned and, wheeling abruptly, went back the way they had come.

Hopalong shook his head in disgust. To be sidetracked like this was maddening. It had taken three hours of hard traveling over rough country to get where he was and it would take as long to return; and all for nothing! He regarded the pack animal with a grin, shrugged his shoulders and led the way toward the hut, the pack horse following obediently. It was another hour before he finally reached the little cabin, for the way was strange and rough. During this time he had talked aloud, for he had the tricks of his kind and when alone he talked to himself. When he reached the hut he relieved the pack horse of its load, carrying the stuff inside. Closing the door and blocking it with a rock he found the spring, drank his fill and then let the horses do likewise. Then he mounted and started back over the rough trail, thinking out loud and confiding to his horse and he entered a narrow defile close to the top of the divide, promising dire things to the foreman. Suddenly a rope settled over him, pinned his arms to his sides and yanked him from the saddle before he had time to think. He landed on his head and was dazed as he sat up and looked around. The foreman's rifle confronted him, and behind the foreman's feet were his two Colts.

"You talks too much," sneered the man with the drop. "I suspicioned you th' minute I laid eyes on you. It 'll take a better man than you to get that five hundred reward. I reckon th' Sheriff was too scared to come hisself."

Hopalong shook his head as if to clear it. What was the man talking about? Who was the sheriff? He gave it up, but would not betray his ignorance. Yes; he had talked too much. He felt of his head and was mildly surprised to see his hand covered with blood when he glanced at it. "Five hundred 's a lot of money," he muttered.

"Blood money!" snapped the foreman. "You had a gall tryin' to get me. Why, I been lookin' for somebody to try it for two years. An' I was ready every minute of all that time."

Slowly it came to Hopalong and with it the realization of how foolish it would be to deny the part ascribed to himself. The rope was loose and his arms were practically free; the foreman had dropped the lariat and was depending upon his gun. The captive felt of his head again and, putting his hands behind him for assistance in getting up, arose slowly to his feet. In one of the hands was a small rock that it had rested upon during the effort of rising. At the movement the foreman watched him closely and ordered him not to take a step if he wanted to live a little longer.

"I reckon I 'll have to shoot you," he announced. "I dass n't let you loose to foller me all over th' country. Anyhow, I 'd have to do it sooner or later. I wish you was Phelps, d —n him; but he's a wise sheriff. Better stand up agin' that wall. I gotta do it; an' you deserve it, you Judas!"

"Meanin' yo're Christ?" sneered Hopalong. "Did you kill th' other feller like that? If I 'd 'a' knowed that I 'd 'a' slapped yore dawg's face at th' bunkhouse an' made you take an even break. Shore you got nerve enough to shoot straight if I looks at you while yo 're aimin'?" He laughed cynically. "I don't want to close my eyes."

The foreman's face went white and he half lowered the rifle as he took a step forward. Hopalong leaped sideways and his arm straightened out, the other staggering under the blow of the missile. Leaping forward Hopalong ran into a cloud of smoke and staggered as he jumped to close quarters. His hand smashed full in the foreman's face and his knee sank in the foreman's groin. They went down, the foreman weak from the kick and Hopalong sick and weak from the bullet that had grazed the bone of his bad thigh. And lying on the ground they fought in a daze, each incapable of inflicting serious injury for awhile. But the foreman grew stronger as his enemy grew weaker from loss of blood and, wriggling from under his furious antagonist, he reached for his Colt. Hopalong threw himself forward and gripped the gun wrist between his teeth and closed his jaws until they ached. But the foreman, pounding ceaselessly on the other's face with his free hand, made the jaws relax and drew the weapon. Then he saw all the stars in the heavens as Hopalong's head crashed full against his jaw and before he could recover the gun was pinned under his enemy's knee. Hopalong's head crashed again against the foreman's jaw and his right hand gripped the corded throat while the left, its thumb inside the foreman's cheek and its fingers behind an ear, tugged and strained at the distorted face. Growling like wild beasts they strained and panted, and then, suddenly, Hopalong's grip relaxed and he made one last, desperate effort to bring his strength back into one furious attack; but in vain. The battered foreman, quick to sense the situation, wrestled his adversary to one side long enough to grab the Colt from under the shifting knee. As he clutched it a shot rang out and the weapon dropped from his nerveless hand before he could pull the trigger. An exulting, savage yell roared in his ears and in the next instant he seemed to leave the ground and soar through space. He dropped ten feet away and lay dazed and helpless as a knee crashed against his chest. Sammy Porter, his face working curiously with relief and rage, rolled him against the wall of the defile and struck him over the head with a rifle butt, first disarming him.

Hopalong opened his eyes and looked around, dazed and sick. The foreman, bound hand and foot by a forty-five foot lariat, lay close to the base of the wall and stared sullenly at the sky. Sammy was coming up the trail with a dripping sombrero held carefully in his hands and was growling and talking it all over. Hopalong looked down at his thigh and saw a heavy, blood-splotched bandage fastened clumsily in place. Glancing at Sammy again he idly noted that part of the youth's blue-flannel shirt was missing. Curiously, it matched the bandage. He closed his eyes and tried to think what it was all about.

Sammy ambled up to him, threw some water in the bruised face and then grinned cheerfully at the language he evoked. Producing a flask and holding it up to the light, Sammy slid his thumb to a certain level and then shoved the bottle against his friend's teeth. "Huh!" he chuckled, yanking the bottle away. "You'll be all right in a couple of days. But you shore are one h —l of a sight-it's a toss-up between you an' Atkins."

* * * * *

It was night. Hopalong stirred and arose on one elbow and noticed that he was lying on a blanket that covered a generous depth of leaves and pine boughs. The sap-filled firewood crackled and popped and hissed and whistled under the licking attack of the greedy flames, which flared up and died down in endless alternation, and which grotesquely revealed to Hopalong's throbbing eyes a bound figure lying on another blanket. That, he decided, was the foreman. Letting his gaze wander around the lighted circle he made out a figure squatting on the other side of the fire, and concluded it was Sammy Porter. "What you doin', Kid?" he asked.

Sammy arose and walked over to him. "Oh, just watchin' a fool puncher an' five hundred dollars," he grinned. "How you feelin' now, you ol' sage hen?"

"Good," replied the invalid, and, comparatively, it was the truth. "Fine an' strong," he added, which was not the truth.

"That's the way to talk," cheered the Cub. "You shore had one fine séance. You earned that five hundred, all right."

Hopalong reflected and then looked across at the prisoner. "He can fight like the devil," he muttered. "Why, I kicked him hard enough to kill anybody else." He turned again and looked Sammy in the eyes, smiling as best he could. "There ain't no five hundred for me, Kid. I did n't come for that, did n't know nothin' about it. An' it's blood money, besides. We 'll turn him loose if he 'll get out of the country, hey? We 'll give him a chance; either that or you take th' reward."

Sammy stared, grunted and stared again. "What you ravin' about?" he demanded. "An' you didn't come after him for that money?" he asked, sarcastically.

Hopalong nodded and smiled again. "That's right, Kid," he answered, thoughtfully. "I come down to make him get out of th' country. You let him go after we get out of this. I reckon I got yore share of the reward right here in my pocket; purty near that much, anyhow. You take it an' let him vamoose. What you say?"

Sammy rose, angry and disgusted. His anger spoke first. "You go to h —l with yore money! I don't want it!" Then, slowly and wonderingly spoke his disgust. "He 's yourn; do what you want. But I here remarks, frank an' candid, open an' so all may hear, that yo 're a large, puzzlin' d —d fool. Now lay back on that blanket an' go to sleep afore I changes my mind!"

Sammy drifted past the prisoner and looked down at him. "Hear that?" he demanded. There was no answer and he grunted. "Huh! You heard it, all right; an' it plumb stunned you." Passing on he grabbed the last blanket in sight, it was on the foreman's horse, and rolled up in it, feet to the fire. His gun he placed under the saddle he had leaned against, which now made his pillow. As he squirmed into the most comfortable position he could find under the circumstances he raised his head and glanced across at his friend. "Huh!" he growled softly. "That's th' worst of them sentimental fellers. That gal shore wrapped him 'round her li'l finger all right. Oh, well," he sighed. "'Tain't none of my doin's, thank the Lord; I got sense!" And with the satisfaction of this thought still warm upon him he closed his eyes and went to sleep, confident that the slightest sound would awaken him; and fully justified in his confidence.

XIII

His Code

Mr. "Youbet" Somes, erstwhile foreman of the Two-X-Two ranch, in Arizona, and now out of a job, rode gloomily toward Kit, a town between him and his destination.

Needless to say, he was a cowman through and through. More than that, he was so saturated with cowmen's traditions as to resent pugnaciously anything which flouted them.

He was of the old school, and would not submit quietly to two things, among others, which an old-school cowman hated-wire fences and sheep. To this he owed his present ride, for he

197

hated wire fences cordially. They meant the passing of the free, open range, of straight trails across country; they meant a great change, an intolerable condition.

"Yessir, bronch! Things are gettin' damnabler every year, with th' railroads, tourists, nesters, barb' wire, an' sheep. Last year, it was a windmill, that screeched till our hair riz up. It would n't work when we wanted it to, an' we could n't stop it when it once got started.

"It gave us no sleep, no peace; an' it killed Bob Cousins-swung round with th' wind an' knocked him off 'n th' platform, sixty feet, to th' ground. Bob allus did like to monkey with th' buzz saw. I shore told him not to go up there, because th' cussed thing was loaded; but, bein' mule-headed, he knowed more 'n me.

"But this year! Lord-but that was an awful pile of wire, bronch! Three strands high, an' over a hundred an' fifty miles round that pasture. That was a' insult, bronch; an' I never swaller 'em. That's what put me an' you out here, in th' middle of nowhere, tryin' to find a way out. G'wan, now! You ain't goin' to rest till I gets off you. G'wan, I told you!"

Mr. Somes was riding east, bound for the Bar-20, where he had friends. For a year or two, he had heard persistent rumors to the effect that Buck Peters had more cows than he knew what to do with; and he argued rightly that the Bar-20 foreman could find a place for an old friend, whose ability was unquestioned. Of one thing he was certain-there were no wire fences, down there.

It was dusk when he dismounted in front of Logan's, in Kit, and went inside. The bartender glanced up, reaching for a bottle on the shelf beside him.

Youbet nodded. "You got it first pop. Have one with me. I 'm countin' on staying over in town tonight. Got a place for me?"

"Shore have-upstairs in th' attic. Want grub, too?"

"Well, I sorter hope to have somethin' to eat afore I pull out. Here's how!" And when Mr. Somes placed his empty glass on the bar, he smiled good-naturedly. "That's good stuff. Much goin' on in town?"

"Reckon you can get a game most anywhere."

"Where do I get that grub? Here?"

"No-down th' street. Ridin' far?"

"Yes —a little. Goin' down to th' Bar-20 for a job punchin'. I hear Peters has got more cows than he can handle. Know anybody down there you wants to send any word to?"

"I 'll be hanged if I know," laughed the bartender. "I know a lot of fellers, but they shift so I can't keep track of 'em, nohow."

A man in a far corner pushed back his chair, and approached the bar, scowling as he glanced at Youbet. "Gimme another," he ordered.

"Why, hullo, stranger!" exclaimed Youbet. "I did n't see you before. Have one with me."

The other looked him squarely in the eyes. "Ex-cuse me, stranger —I 'm a sheepman, an' I don't drink with cowmen."

"Well, ex-cuse *me*!" retorted Youbet, like a flash. "If I 'd 'a' knowed you was a sheepman, I wouldn't 'a' asked you!"

The sheepman drank his liquor and, returning to his corner, placed his elbows on the table, and his chin in his hands, apparently paying no further attention to the others.

"If I can't get a job with Peters, I can try th' C-80 or Double Arrow," continued Youbet, as he toyed with his glass. "If I can't get on with one of them, I reckons Waffles, of th' O-Bar-O, will find a place for me, though I don't like that country a whole lot."

The bartender hesitated for a moment. "Do you know Waffles?" he asked.

"Shore-know 'em all. Why? Do you know him, too?"

"No; but I 've heard of him."

"That so? He 's a good feller, he is. I 've punched with both him an' Peters."

"I heard he wasn't," replied the bartender, slowly but carelessly.

"Then you heard wrong, all right," rejoined Youbet. "He's one of us old fellers-hates sheep, barb' wire, an' nesters as bad as I do; an' sonny," he continued, warming as he went on. "Th' cow country ain't what it used to be-not no way. I can remember when there war n't no wire, no nesters, an' no sheep. An', between you and me, I don't know which is th' worst. Every time I runs up agin' one of 'em, I says it's th' worst; but I guess it's just about a even break."

"I heard about yore friend Waffles through sheep," replied the bartender. "He chased a sheep outfit out of a hill range near his ranch, an' killed a couple of 'em, a-doin' it."

"Served 'em right-served 'em right," responded Youbet, turning and walking toward the door. "They ain't got no business on a cattle range-not nohow."

The man in the corner started to follow, half raising his hand, as though to emphasize something he was about to say; but changed his mind, and sullenly resumed his brooding attitude.

"Reckon I 'll put my cayuse in yore corral, an' look th' town over," Youbet remarked, over his shoulder. "Remember, yo 're savin' a bed for me."

As he stepped to the street, the man in the corner lazily arose and looked out of the window, swearing softly while he watched the man who hated sheep.

"Well, there 's another friend of yore business," laughed the bartender, leaning back to enjoy the other's discomfiture. *"He* don't like 'em, neither."

"He 's a fool of a mossback, so far behind th' times he don't know who 's President," retorted the other, still staring down the street.

"Well, he don't know that this has got to be a purty fair sheep town-that's shore."

"He 'll find out, if he makes many more talks like that-an' that ain't no dream, neither!" snapped the sheepman. He wheeled, and frowned at the man behind the bar. "You see what he gets, if he opens his cow mouth in here tonight. Th' boys hate this kind real fervent; an' when they finds out that he 's a side pardner of that coyote Waffles, they won't need much excuse. You wait-that's all!"

"Oh, what's th' use of gettin' all riled up about it?" demanded the bartender easily. "He did n't know *you* was a sheepman, when he made his first break. An' lemme tell you somethin' you want to remember-them old-time cowmen can use a short gun somethin' slick. They 've got 'em trained. Bet *he* can work th' double roll without shootin' hisself full of lead." The speaker grinned exasperatingly.

"Yes!" exploded the sheepman, who had tried to roll two guns at once, and had spent ten days in bed as a result of it.

The bartender laughed softly as he recalled the incident. "Have you tried it since?" he inquired.

"Go to th' devil!" grinned the other, heading for the door. "But he 'll get in trouble, if he spouts about hatin' sheep, when th' boys come in. You better get him drunk an' lock him in th' attic, before then."

"G'wan! I ain't playin' guardian to nobody," rejoined the bartender. "But remember what I said-them old fellers can use 'em slick an' rapid."

The sheepman went out as Youbet returned; and the latter seated himself, crossing his legs and drawing out his pipe.

The bartender perfunctorily drew a cloth across the bar, and smiled. "So you don't like wire, sheep, or nesters," he remarked.

Mr. Somes looked up, in surprise, forgetting that he held a lighted match between thumb and finger. "Like 'em! Huh, I reckon not. I 'm lookin' for a job because of wire. H —l!" he exclaimed, dropping the match, and rubbing his finger. "That's twice I did that fool thing in a week," he remarked, in apology and self-condemnation, and struck another match.

"I was foreman of my ranch for nigh onto ten years. It was a good ranch, an' I was satisfied till last year, when they made me put up a windmill that did n't mill, but screeched awful. I stood for that because I could get away from it in th' daytime.

"But this year! One day, not very long ago, I got a letter from th' owners, an' it says for me to build a wire fence around our range. It went on to say that there was two carloads of barb' wire at Mesquite. We was to tote that wire home, an' start in. If two carloads wasn't enough, they 'd send us more. We had one busted-down grub waggin, an' Mesquite shore was fifty miles away-which meant a whoppin' long job totin'.

"When I saw th' boys, that night, I told 'em that I 'd got orders to raise their pay five dollars a month-which made 'em cheer. Then I told 'em that was so providin' they helped me build a barb' wire fence around th' range-which did n't make 'em cheer.

"Th' boundary lines of th' range we was usin' was close onto a hundred an' fifty miles long, an' three strands of wire along a trail like that is some job. We was to put th' posts twelve feet apart, an' they was to be five feet outen th' ground an' four feet in it-which makes 'em nine feet over all.

"There was n't no posts at Mesquite. Them posts was supposed to be growin' freelike on th' range, just waitin' for us to cut 'em, skin 'em, tote an' drop 'em every twelve feet along a line a hundred an' fifty miles long. An' then there was to be a hole dug for every post, an' tampin', staplin', an' stringin' that hell-wire. An' don't forget that lone, busted-down grub waggin that was to do that totin'!

"There was some excitement on th' Two-X-Two that night, an' a lot of figgerin'; us bein' some curious about how many posts was needed, an' how many holes we was to dig to fit th' aforesaid posts. We made it sixty-six thousand. Think of it! An' only eight of us to tackle a job like that, an' ride range at th' same time!"

"Oh, ho!" roared the bartender, hugging himself, and trying to carry a drink to the narrator at the same time. "Go on! That's good!"

"Is, is it?" snorted Youbet. "Huh! You wouldn't 'a' thought so, if you was one of us eight. Well, I set right down an' writ a long letter-took six cents' worth of stamps-an' gave our views regardin' wire fences in general an' this one of ourn in particular. I hated fences, an' do yet; an' so 'd my boys hate 'em, an' they do yet.

"In due time, I got a answer, which come for two cents. It says: 'Build that fence.'

"I sent Charley over to Mesquite to look over them cars of wire. He saw 'em, both of 'em. An' th' agent saw him.

"Th' agent was a' important man, an' he grabs Charley quick. 'Hey, you Two-X-Two puncher- you get that wire home quick. It went past here three times before they switched it, an' I 've been gettin' blazes from th' company ever since. We needs th' cars.'

"'Don't belong to me,' says Charley. 'I shore don't want it. I 'm eatin' beans an' bacon instead.'

"'You send for that wire!' yells th' agent, wild-like.

"Charley winks. 'Can't you keep it passin' this station till it snows hard? Have a drink.'

"Well, th' agent wouldn't drink, an' he wouldn't send that pore wire out into a cold world no more; an' so Charley comes home an' reports, him lookin' wanlike. When he told us, he looked sort of funny, an' blurts out that his mother went an' died up in Laramie, an' he must shore 'nuff rustle up there an' bury her. He went.

"Then Fred Ball begun to have pains in his stomach, an' said it was appendix somethin', what he had been readin' about in th' papers. He had to go to Denver, an' get a good doctor, or he 'd shore die. He went.

"Carson had to go to Santa Fé to keep some of his numerous city lots from bein' sold off by th' sheriff. He went.

"Th' rest, bein' handicapped by th' good start th' others had made in corrallin' all th' excuses, said they 'd go for th' wire. They went.

"I waited four days, an' then I went after 'em. When I got to th' station, I sees th' agent out sizin' up our wire; an' when I hails, he jumps my way quick, an' grabs my laig tight.

"'You take that wire home!' he yells.

"'Shore,' says I soothingly. 'You looks mad,' I adds.

"'Mad! Mad!' he shouts, hoppin' round, but hangin' onto my laig like grim death. 'Mad! I 'm goin' *loco* —crazy! I can't sleep! There 's twenty letters an' messages on my table, tellin' me to get that wire off'n th' cars an' send th' empties back on th' next freight! You've got to take it —*got to!*'"

The bartender shocked his nervous system by drinking plain water by mistake, but he listened eagerly. "Yes? What then?"

"Well, then I asks him where I can find my men, an' team, an' waggin'. He tells me. Th' team an' waggin is in a corral down th' street, but he don't know where th' men are. They held a gun to his head, an' said they 'd kill him if he didn't flag th' next train for 'em. Th' next train was a through express, carryin' mail. He was n't dead.

"He showed me ten more letters an' messages, regardin' th' flaggin' of a contract-mail train for four fares; an' some of them letters must 'a' been written by a old-time cowman, they was that eloquent an' God-fearin'. Then I went.

"Why, Charley was twenty years old; an' we figgered that, when th' last staple was drove in th' last post, he 'd 'a' been dead ten years! Where did I come in, the —?"

"Oh, Lord!" sighed the bartender, holding his sides, and trying to straighten his face so that he could talk out of the middle of it. "That's th' best ever! Have another drink!"

"I ain't tellin' my troubles for liquor," snorted Youbet. "You have one with me. Here comes some customers down th' street, I reckon."

"Say!" exclaimed the bartender hurriedly. "You keep mum about sheep. This is a red-hot sheep town, an' it hates Waffles an' all his friends. Hullo, boys!" he called to four men, who filed into the room. "Where 's th' rest of you?"

"Comin' in later. Same thing, Jimmy," replied Clayton, chief herder. "An' give us th' cards."

"Have you seen Price?" asked Towne.

"Yes; he was in here a few minutes ago. What 'd you say, Schultz?" the bartender asked, turning to the man who pulled at his sleeve.

"I said dot you vas nod right aboud vat you said de odder day. Chust now I ask Clayton, und he said you vas nod."

"All right, Dutchy-all right!" laughed the bartender. "Then it's on me this time, ain't it?"

Youbet walked to the bar. "Say, where do I get that grub? It's about time for me to mosey off an' feed."

"Next building-and you'll take mutton if yo 're wise," replied the bartender, in a low voice. "Th' hash is awful, an' the beef is tough," he added, a little louder.

"Mutton be damned!" snorted Youbet, stamping out. "I eat what I punch!" And his growls became lost in the street.

Schultz glanced up. "Yah! Und he shoot vat I eat, tarn him, ven he gan!"

"Oh, put yore ante in, an' don't talk so much!" rejoined Towne. "He ain't going to shoot *you*."

"It 'll cost you two bits to come in," remarked Clayton.

"An' two more," added Towne, raising the ante.

"Goot! I blay mit you. But binochle iss der game!"

"I 'll tell you a good story about a barb' wire fence tomorrow, fellers," promised the bartender, grinning.

The poker game had been going for some time before further remarks were made about the cowman who had left, and then it was Clayton who spoke.

"Say, Jimmy!" he remarked, as Schultz dealt. "Who is yore leather-pants friend who don't like mutton?"

The bartender lifted a bottle, and replaced it with great care. "Oh, just a ranch foreman, out of a job. He's a funny old feller."

"So? An' what's so funny about him? Get in there, Towne, if you wants to do any playin' with us."

"Why, he was ordered to build a hundred an' fifty miles of wire fence around his range, an' he jumped ruther than do it."

"Yas-an' most of it government land, I reckon," interposed Towne.

"Pshaw! It's an old game with them," laughed Clayton. "Th' law don't get to them; an' if they 've got a good outfit, nobody has got any chance agin 'em."

"Py Gott, dot's right!" grunted Schultz.

"Shore, it is," responded Towne, forgetting the game. "Take that Apache Hills run-in. Waffles did n't have no more right to that range than anybody else, but that did n't make no difference. He threw a couple of outfits in there, penned us in th' cabin, killed MacKay, an' shot th' rest of us up plenty. Then he threatened to slaughter our herd if we did n't pull out. By God, I 'd like to get a cowman like him up here, where th' tables are turned around on th' friends proposition."

"Hullo, boys!" remarked the bartender to the pair who came in.

"Just in time. Get chairs, an' take hands," invited Clayton, moving over.

"Who's th' cowman yo're talkin' about?" asked Baxter, as he leaned lazily against the bar.

"Oh, all of 'em," rejoined Towne surlily. "There 's one in town, now, who don't like sheep."

"That so?" queried Baxter slowly. "I reckon he better keep his mouth shut, then."

"Oh, he 's all right! He 's a jolly old geezer," assured the bartender. "He just talks to hear hisself-one of them old-timers what can't get right to th' way things has changed on th' range. It was them boys that did great work when th' range was wild."

"Yes, an' it's them bull-headed old fools what are raisin' all th' hell with th' sheep," retorted Towne, frowning darkly as he remembered some of the indignities he had borne at the hands of cowmen.

"I wish his name was Waffles." Clayton smiled significantly.

"Rainin' again," remarked a man in the doorway, stamping in. "Reckon it ain't never goin' to stop."

"Where you been so long, Price?" asked Clayton, as a salutation.

"Oh, just shiftin' about. That cow wrastler raised th' devil in th' hotel," Price replied. "Old fool! They brought him mutton, an' he wanted to clean out th' place. Said he 'd as soon eat barb' wire. They 're feedin' him hash an' canned stuff, now."

"He 'll get hurt, if he don't look out," remarked Clayton. "Who is he, anyhow, Price?"

"Don't know his name; but he 's from Arizona, on his way to th' Pecos country. Says he 's a friend of Buck Peters an' Waffles. To use one of his own expressions, he 's a old mosshead."

"Friend of Waffles, hey?" exclaimed Towne.

"Yumpin' Yimminy!" cried Oleson, in the same breath.

"Well, if he knows when he's well off, he 'll stay away from here, an' keep his mouth closed," said Clayton.

"Aw, let him alone! He's one agin' th' whole town-an' a good old feller, at that," hastily assured the bartender. "It ain't his fault that Waffles buffaloed you fellers out of th' Hills, is it? He's goin' on early tomorrow; so let him be."

"You 'll get yoreself in trouble, Jimmy, m' boy, if you inserts yoreself in this," warned Towne. "It was us agin' a whole section, an' we got ours. Let him take his, if he talks too much."

"Shore," replied Price. "I heard him shoot off his mouth, an hour ago, an' he's got altogether too much to say. You mind th' bar an' yore own business, Jimmy. We ain't kids."

"Go you two bits better," said Clayton, shoving out a coin. "Gimme some cards, Towne. It 'll cost you a dollar to see our raises."

Baxter walked over to watch the play. "I 'm comin' in next game. Who 's winnin', now?"

"Reckon I am; but we ain't much more 'n got started," Clayton replied. "Did you call, Towne? Why, I 've got three little tens. You got anythin' better?"

"Never saw such luck!" exclaimed Towne disgustedly. "Dutchy, yo 're a Jonah."

"Damn th' mutton, says I. It was even in that hash!" growled a voice, just outside the door.

A moment later, Youbet Somes entered, swinging his sombrero energetically to shake off the water.

"Damn th' rain, too, an' this wart of a town. A man can't get nothin' fit to eat for love or money, on a sheep range. Gimme a drink, sonny! Mebby it 'll cut th' taste of that rank tallow out 'n my mouth. Th' reason there is sheep on this earth of our'n is that th' devil chased 'em out 'n his place-an' no blame to him."

He drank half his liquor, and, placing the glass on the bar beside him, turned to watch the game. "Ah, strangers-that's th' only game, after all. I 've dabbled in 'em all from faro to roulette, but that's th' boss of 'em all."

"See you an' call," remarked Clayton, ignoring the newcomer. "What you got, you Dutch pagan?"

"*Zwei Kaisers* und a bair of chackasses, mit a deuce."

"Kings up!" exclaimed Clayton. "Why, say-you bet th' worst of anybody I ever knew! You 'll balk on bettin' two bits on threes, and plunge on a bluff. I reckoned you did n't have nothin'. Why ain't you more consistent?" he asked, winking at Towne.

"Gonsisdency iss no chewel in dis game-it means go broke," placidly grunted Schultz, raking in his winnings.

His friend Schneider smiled.

"Coyotes are gettin' too numerous, this year," Baxter remarked, shuffling.

Youbet pushed his sombrero back on his head. "They don't get numerous on a cow range," he said significantly.

"Huh!" snorted Baxter. "They've got too much respect to stay on one longer than they 've got to."

"They'd ruther be with their woolly-coated cousins," rejoined the cowman quietly. It was beneath his dignity as a cowman to pay much attention to what sheepmen said, yet he could not remain silent under such a remark.

He regarded sheep herders, those human beings who walked at their work, as men who had reached the lowest rung in the ladder of human endeavors. His belief was not original with him, but was that of many of his school. He was a horseman, a mounted man, and one of the aristocracy of the range; they were, to him, the rabble, and almost beneath his contempt.

Besides, it was commonly believed by cowmen that sheep destroyed the grass as far as cattle grazing was concerned-and this was the chief reason for the animosity against sheep and their herders, which burned so strongly in the hearts of cattle owners and their outfits.

Youbet drained his glass, and continued: "The coyote leaves th' cattle range for th' same good reason yore sheep leave it-because they are chased out, or killed. Naturally, blood kin will hang together in banishment."

"You know a whole lot, don't you?" snorted Clayton, with sarcasm. "Yo 're shore wise, you are!"

"He is so vise as a —a gow," remarked Schultz, grinning.

"You 'll know more, when you get as old as me," replied the ex-foreman, carefully placing the empty glass on the bar.

"I don't want to get as old as you, if I have to lose all my common sense," retorted Clayton angrily.

"An' be a damned nuisance generally," observed Towne.

"I 've seen a lot of things in my life," Youbet began, trying to ignore the tones of the others. They were young men, and he knew that youth grew unduly heated in argument. "I saw th' comin' of th' Texas drive herds, till th' range was crowded where th' year before there was nothin'. I saw th' comin' of th' sheep-an' barb' wire, I 'm sorry to say. Th' sheep came like locusts, leavin' a dyin' range behind 'em. Thin, half-starved cattle showed which way they went. You can't tell me nothin' I don't know about sheep."

"An' *I* 've seen sheep dyin' in piles on th' open range," cried Clayton, his own wrongs lashing him into a rage. "*I* 've seen 'em dynamited, an' drowned and driven hell-to-split over canyons! I 've had my men taunted, an' chased, an' killed —*killed*, by God! —just because they tried to make a' honest livin'! Who did it all? Who killed my men an' my sheep? *Who did it?*" he shouted, taking a short step forward, while an endorsing growl ran along the line of sheepmen at his side.

"Cowpunchers-they did it! They killed 'em-an' why? Because we tried to use th' grass that we had as much right to as they had —*that 's* why!"

"Th' cows was here first," replied Youbet, keenly alert, but not one whit abashed by the odds, long as they were. "It was theirs because they was there first."

"It was not theirs, no more'n th' sun was!" cried Towne, unable to allow his chief to do all the talking.

"You said you knowed Waffles," continued Clayton loudly. "Well, he 's another of you old-time cowmen! He killed MacKay-murdered him-because we was usin' a hill range a day's ride from his own grass! He had twenty men like hisself to back him up. If we 'd been as many as them, they would n't 'a' tried it-an' you know it!"

"I don't know anything of th' kind, but I do know —" began Youbet; but Schultz interrupted him with a remark intended to contain humor.

"Ven you say you doand know anyt'ing, you know somedings; ven you know dot you doand know noddings, den you know somedings. Und das iss so-yah."

"Who th' devil told you to stick yore Dutch mouth —" retorted Youbet; but Clayton cut him short.

"So *yo 're* a old-timer, hey?" cried the sheepman. "Well, by God, yore old-time friend Waffles is a coward, a murderer, an' —"

"Yo're a liar!" rang out the vibrant voice of the cowman

"Yo 're a liar!" rang out the vibrant voice of the cowman, his gun out and leveled in a flash. The seven had moved forward as one man, actuated by the same impulse; and their hands were moving toward their guns when the crashes of Youbet's weapon reverberated in the small room, the acrid smoke swirling around him as though to shield him from the result of his folly —a result which he had weighed and then ignored.

Clayton dropped, with his mouth still open. Towne's gun chocked back in the scabbard as its owner stumbled blindly over a chair and went down, never to rise. Schultz fired once, and fell back across the table.

The three shots had followed one another with incredible quickness; and the seven, not believing that one man would dare attack so many, had not expected his play. Before the stunned sheepmen could begin firing, three were dead.

Price, badly wounded, fired as he plunged to the wall for support; and the other three were now wrapped in their own smoke.

Wounded in several places, with his gun empty, Youbet hurled the weapon at Price, and missed by so narrow a margin that the sheepman's aim was spoiled. Youbet now sprang to the bar, and tried to vault over it, to get to the gun which he knew always lay on the shelf behind it. As his feet touched the upper edge of the counter, he grunted and, collapsing like a jackknife, loosed his hold, and fell to the floor.

"Mein Gott!" groaned Schneider, as he tried to raise himself. He looked around in a dazed manner, hardly understanding just what had happened. "He vas mat; crazy mat!"

Oleson arose unsteadily to his feet, and groped his way along, the wall to where Price lay.

The fallen man looked up, in response to the touch on his shoulder; and he swore feebly: "Damn that fool-that idiot!"

"Shut up, an' git out!" shouted the bartender, standing rigidly upright, with a heavy Colt in his upraised hand. There were tears in his eyes, and his voice broke from excitement. "He wouldn't swaller yore insults! He knowed he was a better man! Get out of here, every damned one of you, or I 'll begin where he stopped. G 'wan —*get out!*"

The four looked at him, befuddled and sorely hurt; but they understood the attitude, if they did not quite grasp the words-and they knew that he meant what he looked. Staggering and hobbling, they finally found the door, and plunged out to the street, to meet the crowd of men who were running toward the building.

Jimmy, choking with anger and with respect for the man who had preferred death to insults, slammed shut the door and, dropping the bar into place, turned and gazed at the quiet figure huddled at the base of the counter.

"Old man," he muttered, "now I understands why th' sheep don't stay long on a cattle range."

XIV
Sammy Hunts a Job

Sammy Porter, detailed by Hopalong, the trail-boss, rode into Truxton three days before the herd was due, to notify the agent that cars were wanted. Three thousand three-year-olds were on their way to the packing houses and must be sent through speedily. Sammy saw the agent and, leaving him much less sweeter in temper than when he had found him, rode down the dismal street kicking up a prodigious amount of dust. One other duty demanded attention and its fulfillment was promised by the sign over the faded pine front of the first building.

"Restaurant," he read aloud. "That's mine. Beans, bacon an' biscuits for 'most a month! But now I 'm goin' to forget that Blinky Thompkins ever bossed a trail wagon an' tried to cook."

Dismounting, he glanced in the window and pulled at the downy fuzz trying to make a showing on his upper lip. "Purty, all right. Brown hair an' I reckon brown eyes. Nice li'l girl. Well, they don't make no dents on me no more," he congratulated himself, and entered. His twenty years fairly sagged with animosity toward the fair sex, the intermittent smoke from the ruins of his last love affair still painfully in evidence at times. But careless as he tried to be he could not banish the swaggering mannerisms of Youth in the presence of Maid, or change his habit of speech under such conditions.

"Well, well," he smiled. "Here I 'are' again. Li'l Sammy in search of his grub. An' if it's as nice as you he 'll shore have to flag his outfit an' keep this town all to hisself. Got any chicken?"

The maid's nose went up and Sammy noticed that it tilted a trifle, and he cocked his head on one side to see it better. And the eyes were brown, very big and very deep-they possessed a melting quality he had never observed before. The maid shrugged her shoulders and swung around, the tip-tilt nose going a bit higher.

Sammy leaned back against the door and nodded approval of the slender figure in spic-and-span white. "Li'l Sammy is a fer-o-cious cow-punch from a chickenless land," he observed, sorrowfully. "There ain't *no* kinds of chickens. Nothin' but men an' cattle an' misguided cooks; an' beans, bacon an' biscuits. Li'l Miss, have you a chicken for me?"

"No!" The head went around again, Sammy bending to one side to see it as long as he could. The pink, shell-like ear that flirted with him through the loosely-gathered, rebellious hair caught his attention and he leveled an accusing finger at it. "Naughty li'l ear, peekin' at Sammy that-a-way! Oh, you stingy girl!" he chided as the back of her head confronted him. "Well, Sammy don't like girls, no matter how pink their ears are, or turned up their noses, or wonderful their eyes. He just wants chicken, an' all th' fixin's. He 'll be very humble an' grateful to Li'l Miss if she 'll tell him what he can have. An' he 'll behave just like a Sunday-school boy.

"Aw, you don't want to get mad at only me," he continued after she refused to answer. "Got any chicken? Got any-eggs? Lucky Sammy! An' some nice ham? Two lucky Sammies. An' some mashed potatoes? Fried? Good. An' will Li'l Miss please make a brand new cup of strong coffee? Then he 'll go over an' sit in that nice chair an' watch an' listen. But you ought n't get mad at him. Are you really-an'-truly mad?"

She swept down the room, into the kitchen partitioned off at the farther end and slammed the door. Sammy grinned, tugged at his upper lip and fancy-stepped to the table. He smoothed his tumbled hair, retied his neck-kerchief and dusted himself off with his red bandanna hand-kerchief. "Nice li'l town," he soliloquized. "*Fine* li'l town. Dunno as I ought to go back to th' herd-Hoppy did n't tell me to. Reckon I 'll stick in town an' argue with th' agent. If I argue with th' agent I 'll be busy; an' I can't leave while I 'm busy." He leaned back and chuckled. "Lucky me! If Hoppy had gone an' picked Johnny to argue with th' agent for three whole days where would *I* be? But I gotta keep Johnny outa here, th' son-of-a-gun. He ain't like me-he *likes* girls; an' he ain't bashful."

He picked up a paper lying on a chair near him and looked it over until the kitchen door squeaked. She carried a tray covered with a snow-white napkin which looked like a topographical map with its mountains and valleys and plains. His chuckle was infectious to the extent of a smile and her eyes danced as she placed his dinner before him.

"Betcha it's fine," he grinned, shoveling sugar into the inky coffee. "Blinky oughta have a good look at *this* layout."

"Don't be too sure," she retorted. "Mrs. Olmstead is sick and I 'm taking charge of things for her. I 'm not a good cook."

"Nothin 's th' matter with this," he assured her between bites. "Lots better 'n most purty girls can do. If Hopalong goes up against this he 'll offer you a hundred a month an' throw Blinky in to wash th' dishes. But he 'd have to 'point me guard, or you would n't have no time to do no cookin'."

"You 'd make a fine guard," she retorted.

"Don't believe it, huh? Jus' wait till you know me better."

"How do you know I 'm going to?"

"I 'm a good guesser. Jus' put a li'l pepper right there on that yalla spot. Say, any chance to get a job in this town?"

"Why, I don't know."

"Goin' to stay long?"

"I can't say. I won't go till Mrs. Olmstead is well."

"Not meanin' no harm to Mrs. Olmstead, of course-but you don't *have* to go, do you?"

"I do as I please."

"So I was thinkin'. Now, 'bout that job: any chance? Any ranches near here?"

"Several. But they want *men*. Are you a real cowboy?"

Sammy folded his hands and shook his head sorrowfully. "Huh! Want *men*! Now if I only had whiskers like Blinky. Why, 'course I 'm a cowboy. Regular one-but I can outgrow it easy. I 'm a sorta maverick an' I 'm willin' to wear a nice brand. My name's Sammy Porter," he suggested.

"That's nice. Mine is n't nice."

"Easy to change it. Really like mine?"

"Coffee strong enough?"

"Sumptious. How long's Mrs. Olmstead going to be sick?"

Her face clouded. "I don't know. I hope it will not be for long. She 's had *so* much trouble the past year. Oh, wait! I forgot the toast!" and she sped lightly away to rescue the burning bread.

The front door opened and slammed shut, the newcomer dropping into the nearest chair. He pounded on the table. "Hello, there! I want somethin' to eat, quick!"

Sammy turned and saw a portly, flashily dressed drummer whose importance was written large all over him. "Hey!" barked the drummer, "gimme something to eat. I can't wait all day!"

A vicious clang in the kitchen told that his presence was known and resented.

As Sammy turned from the stranger he caught sight of a pretty flushed face disappearing behind the door jamb, the brown eyes snapping and the red lips straight and compressed. His glance, again traveling to the drummer, began with the dusty patent leathers and went slowly upward, resting boldly on the heavy face. Sammy's expression told nothing and the newcomer, glaring at him for an instant, looked over the menu card and then stared at the partition, fidgeting in his chair, thumping meanwhile on the table with his fingers.

At a sound from the kitchen Sammy turned back to his table and smiled reassuringly as the toast was placed before him. "I burned it and had to make new," she said, the pink spots in her cheeks a little deeper in color.

"Why, th' other was good enough for me," he replied. "Know Mrs. Olmstead a long time?" he asked.

"Ever since I was a little girl. She lived near us in Clev —"

"Cleveland," he finished. "State of Ohio," he added, laughingly. "I 'll get it all before I go."

"Indeed you won't!"

"Miss," interrupted the drummer, "if you ain't too busy, would you mind gettin' me a steak an' some coffee?" The tones were weighted with sarcasm and Sammy writhed in his chair. The girl flushed, turned abruptly and went slowly into the kitchen, from where considerable noise now emanated. In a short time she emerged with the drummer's order, placed it in front of him and started back again. But he stopped her. "I said I wanted it rare an' it's well done. An' also that I wanted fried potatoes. Take it back."

The girl's eyes blazed: "You gave no instructions," she retorted.

"Don't tell me that! I know what I said!" snapped the drummer. "I won't eat it an' I won't pay for it. If you was n't so *busy* you 'd heard what I said."

Sammy was arising before he saw the tears of vexation in her eyes, but they settled it for him. He placed his hand lightly on her shoulder. "You get me some pie an' take a li'l walk. Me an' this here gent is goin' to hold a palaver. Ain't we, stranger?"

The drummer glared at him. "We ain't!" he retorted.

Sammy grinned ingratiatingly. "Oh, my; but we are." He slung a leg over a chair back and leaned forward, resting his elbow on his knee. "Yes, indeed we are-least-a-wise, *I* am." His tones became very soft and confiding. "An' I 'm shore goin' to watch you eat that steak."

"What's that you 're going to do?" the drummer demanded, half rising.

"Sit down," begged Sammy, his gun swinging at his knee. He picked up a toothpick with his left hand and chewed it reflectively. "These here Colts make a' awful muss, sometimes," he remarked. "'Specially at close range. Why," he confided, "I once knowed a man what was shot 'most in two. He was a moss-head an' would n't do what he was told. Better sorta lead off at that steak, *hombre*," he suggested, chewing evenly on the toothpick. Noticing that the girl still lingered, hypnotized by fear and curiosity, he spoke to her over his shoulder. "Won't you please get me that pie, or somethin'? Run out an' borrow a pan, or somethin'," he pleaded. "I don't like to be handicapped when I 'm feedin' cattle."

The drummer's red face paled a little and one hand stole cautiously under his coat-and froze there. Sammy hardly had moved, but the Colt was now horizontal and glowered at the gaudy waistcoat. He was between it and the girl and she did not see the movement. His smile was placid and fixed and he spoke so that she should get no inkling of what was going on. "Never drink on an empty stomach," he advised. "After you eat that meal, then you can fuss with yore flask all you wants." He glanced out of the corner of his eye at the girl and nodded. "Still there! Oh, I most forgot, stranger. You take off yore hat an' 'pologize, so she can go. Jus' say yo 're a dawg an never did have no manners. *Say* it!" he ordered, softly. The drummer gulped and muttered something, but the Colt, still hidden from the girl by its owner's body, moved forward a little and Sammy's throaty growl put an end to the muttering. "Say it plain," he ordered, the color fading from his face and leaving pink spots against the white. "That's better-now, Li'l Miss, you get me that pie-please!" he begged.

When they were alone Sammy let the gun swing at his knee again. "I don't know how they treats wimmin where you came from, stranger; but out here we 're plumb polite. 'Course you did n't know that, an' that's why you did n't get all mussed up. Yo 're jus' plain ignorant an' can't help yore bringin' up. Now, you eat that steak, *pronto!*"

"It's too cold, now," grumbled the drummer, fidgeting in the chair.

The puncher's left hand moved to the table again and when it returned to his side there was a generous layer of red pepper on the meat. "Easy to fix things when you know how," he grinned. "If it gets any colder I 'll fix it some more." His tones became sharper and the words lost their drawled softness. "You goin' to start ag'in that by yoreself, or am I goin' to help you?" he demanded, lifting his leg off the chair and standing erect. All the humor had left his face and there was a grimness about the tight lips and a menace in the squinting eyes that sent a chill rippling down the drummer's spine. He tasted a forkful of the meat and gulped hastily, tears welling into his eyes. The puncher moved a little nearer and watched the frantic gulps with critical attention. "'Course, you can eat any way you wants-yo're payin' for it; but boltin' like a coyote ain't good for th' stummick. Howsomever, it's yore grub," he admitted.

A cup of cold coffee and a pitcher of water followed the meat in the same gulping haste. Tears streamed down the drummer's red face as he arose and turned toward the door. "Hol' on, stranger!" snapped Sammy. "That costs six bits," he prompted. The coins rang out on the nearest table, the door slammed and the agonized stranger ran madly down the street, cursing at every jump. Sammy sauntered to the door and craned his neck. "Somebody 's jus' naturally goin' to bust him wide open one of these days. He ain't got no sense," he muttered, turning back to get his pie.

A cloud of dust rolled up from the south, causing Briggs a little uneasiness, and he scowled through the door at the long empty siding and the pens sprawled along it.

Steps clacked across the platform and a grinning cowpuncher stopped at the open window. "They're here," he announced. "How 'bout th' cars?"

Briggs looked around wearily. For three days his life had been made miserable by this pest, who carried a laugh in his eyes, a sting on his tongue and a chip on his shoulder. "They 'll be here soon," he replied, with little interest. "But there 's th' pens."

"Yes, there's th' pens," smiled Sammy. "They'll hold 'bout one-tenth of that herd. Ain't I been pesterin' you to get them cars?"

The agent sighed expressively and listened to the instrument on his table. When it ceased he grabbed the key and asked a question. Then he smiled for the first time that day. "They 're passing Franklin. Be here in two hours. Now get out of here or I 'll lick you."

"There 's a nice place in one of them pens," smiled Sammy.

"I see you 're eating at Olmstead's," parried the agent.

"Yea."

"Nice girl. Come up last summer when Mrs. Olmstead petered out. I ate there last winter."

Sammy grinned at him. "Why 'd you stop?"

Briggs grew red and glanced at the nearing cloud of dust. "Better help your outfit, had n't you?"

Sammy was thoughtful. "Say, that's a plumb favorite eatin' place, ain't it?"

Briggs laughed. "Wait till Saturday when th' boys come in. There 's a dozen shinin' up to that girl. Tom Clarke is real persistent."

Sammy forsook the building as a prop. "Who 's he? Puncher?"

"Yes; an' bad," replied the agent. "But I reckon she don't know it."

Sammy looked at the dust cloud and turned to ask one more question. "What does this persistent gent look like, an' where's he hang out?" He nodded at the verbose reply and strode to his horse to ride toward the approaching herd. He espied Red first, and hailed. "Cars here in two hours. Where 's Hoppy?"

"Back in th' dust. But what happened to *you*?" demanded Red, with virile interest. Sammy ignored the challenge and loped along the edge of the cloud until he found the trail boss. "Them cars 'll be here in two hours," he reported.

"Take you three days to find it out?" snapped Hopalong.

"Took me three days to get 'em. I just about unraveled that agent. He swears every time he hears a noise, thinkin' it's me."

"Broke?" demanded Hopalong.

Sammy flushed. "I ain't gambled a cent since I hit town. An' say, them pens won't hold a tenth of 'em," he replied, looking over the dark blur that heaved under the dust cloud like a fog-covered, choppy sea.

"I 'm goin' to hold 'em on grass," replied the trail boss. "They ain't got enough cars on this toy road to move all them cows in less 'n a week. I ain't goin' to let 'em lose no weight in pens. Wait a minute! You 're on night herd for stayin' away."

When Sammy rode into camp the following morning he scorned Blinky's food, much to the open-mouthed amazement of that worthy and Johnny Nelson. Blinky thought of doctors and death; but Johnny, noticing his bunkmate's restlessness and the careful grooming of his person, had grave suspicions. "Good grub in this town?" he asked, saddling to go on his shift.

Sammy wiped a fleck of dust off his boot and looked up casually. "Shore. Best is at the Dutchman's at th' far end of th' street."

Johnny mounted, nodded and departed for the herd, where Red was pleasantly cursing his tardiness. Red would eat Blinky's grub and gladly. Johnny was cogitating. "There 's a girl in this town, an' he 's got three days' head start. No wonder them cars just got here!" Red's sarcastic voice intruded. "Think I eat grass, or my stummick 's made of rubber?" he snapped. "Think I feed onct a month like a snake?"

"No, Reddie," smiled Johnny, watching the eyebrows lift at the name. "More like a hawg."

Friday morning, a day ahead of the agent's promise, the cars backed onto the siding and by noon the last cow of the herd was taking its first-and last-ride. Sammy slipped away from the outfit at the pens and approached the restaurant from the rear. He would sit behind the partition this time and escape his friends.

The soft sand deadened his steps and when he looked in at the door, a cheery greeting on the tip of his tongue, he stopped and stared unnoticed by the sobbing girl bent over the table. One hand, outflung in dejected abandon, hung over the side and Sammy's eyes, glancing at it, narrowed as he looked. His involuntary, throaty exclamation sent the bowed head up with a jerk, but the look of hate and fear quickly died out of her eyes as she recognized him.

"An' all th' world tumbled down in a heap," he smiled. "But it 'll be all right again, same as it allus was," he assured her. "Will Li'l Miss tell Sammy all about it so he can put it together again?"

She looked at him through tear-dimmed eyes, the sobs slowly drying to a spasmodic catching in the rounded throat. She shook her head and the tears welled up again in answer to his sympathy. He walked softly to the table and placed a hand on her bowed head. "Li'l Miss will tell Sammy all about it when she dries her eyes an' gets comfy. Sammy will make things all right again an' laugh with her. Don't you mind him a mite-jus' cry hard, an' when all th' tears are used up, then you tell Sammy what it's all about." She shook her head and would not look up. He bent down carefully and examined the bruised wrist-and his eyes glinted with rage; but he did not speak. The minutes passed in silence, the girl ashamed to show her reddened and tear-stained face; the boy stubbornly determined to stay and learn the facts. He heard his friends tramp past, wondering where he was, but he did not move.

Finally she brushed back her hair and looked up at him and the misery in her eyes made him catch his breath. "Won't you go?" she pleaded.

He shook his head.

"Please!"

"Not till I finds out whose fingers made them marks," he replied. The look of fear flashed up again, but he checked it with a smile he far from felt. "Nobody 's goin' to make you cry, an' get away with it," he told her. "Who was it?"

"I won't tell you. I can't tell you! I don't know!"

"Li'l Miss, look me in th' eyes an' say it again. I thought so. You mustn't say things that ain't true. Who did that?"

"What do you want to know for?"

"Oh, jus' because."

"What will you do?"

"Oh, I 'll sorta talk to him. All I want to know is his name."

"I won't tell you; you 'll fight with him."

He turned his sombrero over and looked gravely into its crown. "Well," he admitted, "he *might* not like me talkin' 'bout it. Of course, you can't never tell."

"But he did n't mean to hurt me. He 's only rough and boisterous; and he wasn't himself," she pleaded, looking down.

"Uh-huh," grunted Sammy, cogitating. "So 'm I. *I 'm* awful rough an' boisterous, *I* am; only I don't hurt wimmin. What's his name?"

"I'll not tell you!"

"Well, all right; but if he ever comes in here again an' gets rough an' boisterous he 'll lose a hull lot of future. I 'll naturally blow most of his head off, which is frequent fatal. What's that? Oh, he's a bad man, is he? Uh-huh; so 'm I. Well, I 'm goin' to run along now an' see th' boss. If you won't tell, you won't. I 'll be back soon," and he sauntered to the street and headed for Pete's saloon, where the agent had said Mr. Clarke was wont to pass his fretful hours.

As he turned the corner he bumped into Hopalong and Johnny, who grabbed at him, and missed. He backed off and rested on his toes, gingery and alert. "Keep yore dusty han's off'n me," he said, quietly. "I 'm goin' down to palaver with a gent what I don't like."

Hopalong's shrewd glance looked him over. "What did this gent do?" he asked, and he would not be evaded.

"Oh, he insulted a nice li'l girl, an' I 'm in a hurry."

"G'way!" exclaimed Johnny. "That straight?"

"Too d —n straight," snapped Sammy. "He went an' bruised her wrists an' made her cry."

"Lead th' way, Kid," rejoined Johnny, readjusting his belt. "Mebby he 's got some friends," he suggested, hopefully.

"Yes," smiled Hopalong, "mebby he has. An' anyhow, Sammy; you *know* yo're plumb careless with that gun. You might miss him. Lead th' way."

As they started toward Pete's Johnny nudged his bunkmate in the ribs: "Say; she ain't got no sisters, has she?" he whispered.

One hour later Sammy, his face slightly scratched, lounged into the kitchen and tossed his sombrero on a chair, grinning cheerfully at the flushed, saucy face that looked out from under a mass of rebellious, brown hair. "Well, I saw th' boss, an' I come back to make everythin' well again," he asserted, laughing softly. "That rough an' boisterous Mr. Clarke has sloped. He won't come back no more."

"Why, *Sammy*!" she cried, aghast. "What *have* you done?"

"Well, for one thing, I 've got you callin' me Sammy," he chuckled, trying to sneak a hand over hers. "I told th' boss I 'm goin' to get a job up here, so I 'll know Mr. Clarke won't come back. But you know, he only thought he was bad. I shore had to take his ol' gun away from him so he would n't go an' shoot hisself, an' when las' seen he was feelin' for his cayuse, intendin' to leave these parts. That's what I *done*," he nodded, brightly. "Now comes what I 'm goin' to do. Oh, Li'l Miss," he whispered, eagerly. "I 'm jus' all mixed up an' millin'. My own feet plumb get in my way. So I jus' gotta stick aroun' an' change yore name, what you don't like. Uh-huh; that's jus' what I gotta do," he smiled.

She tossed her head and the tip-tilt nose went up indignantly. "Indeed you 'll do nothing of the kind, Sammy Porter!" she retorted. "I'll choose my own name when the time comes, and it will not be Porter!"

He arose slowly and looked around. Picking up the pencil that lay on the shelf he lounged over to the partition and printed his name three times in large letters. "All right, Li'l Miss," he agreed. "I 'll jus' leave a list where you can see it while you 're selectin'. I 'm now goin' out to get that job we spoke about. You have th' name all picked out when I get back," he suggested, waving his hand at the wall. "An' did anybody ever tell you it was plumb risky to stick yore li'l nose up thataway?"

"Sammy Porter!" she stormed, stamping in vexation near the crying point. "You get right out of here! I 'll *never* speak to you again!"

"You won't get a chance to talk much if you don't sorta bring that snubby nose down a li'l lower. I 'm plumb weak at times." He laughed joyously and edged to the door. "Don't forget that list. I 'm goin' after that job. So-long, Li'l Miss."

"Sammy!"

"Oh, all right; I'll go after it later on," he laughed, returning.

XV
When Johnny Sloped

Johnny Nelson hastened to the corner of the bunkhouse and then changed his pace until he seemed to ooze from there to the cook shack door, where he lazily leaned against the door jamb and ostentatiously picked his teeth with the negative end of a match. The cook looked up calmly, and calmly went on with his work; but if there was anything rasping enough to cause his calloused soul to quiver it was the aforesaid calisthenics executed by Johnny and the match; for Cookie's blunt nature hated hints. If Johnny had demanded, even profanely and with large personal animus, why meals were not ahead of time, it would be a simple matter to heave something and enlarge upon his short cut speech. But the subtleties left the cook floundering in a mire of rage-which he was very careful to conceal from Johnny. The youthful nuisance had been evincing undue interest in early suppers for nearly a month; and judging from the lightness of his repasts he was entirely unjustified in showing any interest at all in the evening meal. So Cookie strangled the biscuit in his hand, but smiled blandly at his tormentor.

"Well, all through?" he pleasantly inquired, glancing carelessly at Johnny's clothes.

"I 'm hopin' to begin," retorted Johnny, and the toothpick moved rapidly up and down.

Cookie condensed another biscuit and gulped. "That's shore some stone," he said, enviously, eying the two-caret diamond in Johnny's new, blue tie. Johnny never had worn a tie before he became owner of the diamond, but with the stone came the keen realization of how lost it was in a neck-kerchief, how often covered by the wind-blown folds; so he had hastened to Buckskin and spent a dollar that belonged to Red for the tie, thus exhausting both the supply of ties and Red's dollars. The honor of wearing the only tie and diamond in that section of the cow-country brought responsibilities, for he had spoken hastily to several humorous friends and stood a good chance of being soundly thrashed therefor.

He threw away the match and scratched his back ecstatically on the door jamb while he strained his eyes trying to look under his chin. Fixed chins and short ties are trials one must learn to accept philosophically-and Johnny might have been spared the effort were it not for the fact that the tie had been made for a boy, and was awesomely shortened by encircling a sixteen-inch neck. Evidently it had been made for a boy violently inclined toward a sea-faring life, as suggested by the anchors embroidered in white down its middle.

"Lemme see it," urged Cookie, sighing because its owner had resolutely refused to play poker when he had no cash. This had become a blighting sorrow in the life of a naturally exuberant and very fair cook.

"An' for how long?" demanded Johnny, a cold and calculating light glinting in his eyes.

"Oh, till supper 's ready," replied Cookie with great carelessness.

"Nix; but you can wear it twenty minutes if you 'll get my grub quick," he replied. "Got to meet Lucas at half-past five." He cautiously dropped the match he had thoughtlessly produced.

The cook tried to look his belief and accepted the offer. Johnny's remarkably clean face, plastered hair and general gala attire suggested that Lucas was a woman-which Lucas profanely would have denied. Also, Johnny had been seen washing Ginger, and when a puncher washes a cayuse it's a sign of insanity. Besides, Ginger belonged to Red, who also had owned that lone dollar. Red's clothes did not fit Johnny.

"Goin' to surprise Lucas?" inquired the cook.

"What you mean?"

Cookie glanced meaningly at the attire: "Er-you ain't in th' habit of puttin' on war paint for to see Lucas, are you?"

Johnny's mental faculties produced: "Oh, we 're goin' to a dance."

"Where 'bouts?" exploded the cook.

"*Way* up north!" One's mind needs to be active as a flea to lie properly to a man like the cook. He had made a ghastly mistake.

"By golly! I 'll give th' boys cold grub an' go with you," and the cook began to save time.

Johnny gulped and shook his head: "Got a invite?"

Cookie caught the pan on his foot before it struck the floor and gasped: "Invite? Ain't it free-fer-all?"

"No; this is a high-toned thing-a-bob. Costs a dollar a head, too."

"High-toned?" snorted the cook, derisively. "Don't they know you? An' I thought Red was broke. Show me that permit!"

"Lucas 's got it-that's why I 've got to catch him."

"Oh! An' is *he* goin' all feathered up, too?"

"Shore, he 's got to."

"Huh! He wouldn't dress like that to see a *fight*. Has she got any sisters?" Cookie finished, hopefully.

"Now what you talkin' about?"

"Why, Lucas," answered the cook, placidly. "Lemme tell you something. When you want to lose me have a invite to a water-drinkin' contest. An' before you go, be shore to rub Hoppy's

boots some more; that's such a pasty shine it 'll look like sand-paper before you get to th' —
dance. You want to make it hard an' slippery. An' I 've read som'ers that only wimmin ought
to smell like a drug-store. You better let her do th' fumigatin'."

Johnny surrendered and dolefully whiffed the crushed violets he had paid two bits a pint for
at El Paso-it was not necessary to whiff them, but he did so.

"You ought to hone yore razor, too," continued the cook, critically.

"I told Buck it was dull, I ain't goin' to sharpen it for him. But, say, are you shore about
th' perfumery?"

"Why, of course."

"But how 'll I git it off?"

"Bury th' clothes," suggested Cookie, grinning.

"I like yore gall! Which clothes are best, Pete's or Billy's?"

"Pete's would fit you like th' wide, wide world. You don't want blankets on when you go
courtin'. Try Billy's. An' I got a pair of socks, though one 's green-but th' boots 'll hide it."

"I did n't put none on my socks, you chump!"

"How'd *I* know? But, say! Has she got any sisters?"

"No!" yelled Johnny, halfway through the gallery in search of Billy's clothes. When he
emerged Cookie looked him over. "Ain't it funny, Kid, how a pipe 'll stink up clothes?" he
smiled. Johnny's retort was made over several yards of ground and when he had mounted Cookie
yelled and waved him to return. When Johnny had obeyed and impatiently demanded the
reason, Cookie pleasantly remarked: "Now, be shore an' give her my love, Kid."

Johnny's reply covered half a mile of trail.

Johnny rode alertly through Perry's Bend, for Sheriff Nolan was no friend of his; and Nolan
was not only a discarded suitor of Miss Joyce, but a warm personal friend of George Greener,
the one rival Johnny feared. Greener was a widower as wealthy as he was unscrupulous, and a
power on that range: when he said "jump," Nolan soared.

The sheriff was standing before the Palace saloon when Johnny rode past, and he could not
keep quiet. His comment was so judiciously chosen as to bring white spots on Johnny's flushed
cheeks. The Bar-20 puncher was not famed for his self-control, and, wheeling in the saddle,
he pointed a quivering forefinger at Mr. Nolan's badge of office, so conspicuously displayed:
"Better men than you have hid behind a badge and banked on a man's regard for th' law savin'
'em from their just deserts. Politics is a h —l of a thing when it opens th' door to anything
that might roll in on th' wind. You come down across th' line tomorrow an' see me, without
th' nickel-plated ornament you disgraces," he invited. "Any dog can tell a lie in his kennel, but
it takes guts to bark outside th' yard."

Mr. Nolan flushed, went white, hesitated, and walked away. To fight in defense of the law
was his duty; but no sane man warred on the Bar-20 unless he must. Mr. Nolan was a man
whose ideas of necessity followed strange curves, and not to his credit. One might censure Mr.
Cassidy or Mr. Connors, or pick a fight with some of the others of that outfit and not get
killed; but he must not harm their protégé. Mr. Nolan not only walked away but he sought
the darkest shadows and held conversation with himself. If it were only possible to get the
pugnacious and very much spoiled Mr. Nelson to fracture, smash, pulverize some law! This,
indeed, would be sweet.

Meanwhile Johnny, having watched the sheriff slip away, loosed a few more words into the
air and went on his way, whistling cheerfully. Reaching the Joyce cottage he was admitted by
Miss Joyce herself and at sight of her blushing face his exuberant confidence melted and left
him timid. This he was wont to rout by big words and a dashing air he did not feel.

"Oh! Come right in," she invited. "But you are late," she laughed, chidingly.

He critically regarded the dimples, while he replied that he had drawn rein to slay the sheriff
but, knowing that it would cost him more valuable time, he had consented with himself to
postpone the event.

"But you must not do that!" she cried. "Why, that's terrible! You shouldn't even think of such things."

"Well, of course-if yo 're agin' it I wont."

"But what did he do?"

"Oh, I don't reckon I can tell that. But do you really want him to live?"

"Why, certainly! What a foolish question."

"But why do you? Do you —*like* him?"

"I like everybody."

"Yes; an' everybody likes you, too," he growled, the smile fading. "That's th' trouble. Do you like him very much?"

"I wish you wouldn't ask such foolish questions."

"Yes; I know. But do you?"

"I prefer not to answer."

"Huh! That's an answer in itself. You do."

"I don't think you 're very nice tonight," she retorted, a little pout spoiling the bow in her lips. "You 're awfully jealous, and I don't like it."

"Gee! Don't like it! I should think you 'd want me to be jealous. I only wish you was jealous of *me*. Norah, I 've just got to say it now, an' find out —"

"Yes; tell me," she interrupted eagerly. "What *did* he do?"

"Who?"

"Mr. Nolan, of course."

"Nolan?" he demanded in surprise.

"Yes, yes; tell me."

"I ain't talkin' about him. I was goin' to tell you something that I 've —"

"That you 've done and now regret? Have you ever-ever killed a man?" she breathed. "Have you?"

"No; *yes*! Lots of 'em," he confessed, remembering that once she had expressed admiration for brave and daring men. "Most half as many as Hopalong; an' I ain't near as old as him, neither."

"You mean Mr. Cassidy? Why don't you bring him with you some evening? I 'd like to meet him."

"Not *me*. I went an' brought a friend along once, an' had to lick him th' next day to keep him away from here. He 'd 'a' camped right out there in front if I had n't. No, ma'am; not any."

"Why, the idea! But Mr. Greener's very much like your friend, Mr. Cassidy. He 's very brave, and a wonderful shot. He told me so himself."

"What! He told you so hisself! Well, well. Beggin' yore pardon, he ain't nowise like Hoppy, not even in th' topics of his conversation. Why, he 's a child; an' blinks when he shoots off a gun. Here-can he show a gun like mine?" and forthwith he held out his Colt, butt foremost, and indicated the notches he had cut that afternoon. A fleeting doubt went through his mind at what his outfit would say when it saw those notches. The Bar-20 cut no notches. It wanted to forget.

She looked at them curiously and suddenly drew back. "Oh! Are they —*are* they?" she whispered.

He nodded: "They are. There is plenty of room for Nolan's, an' mebby his owner, too," he suggested. "Can't you see, Norah?" he asked in a swift change of tone. "Can't you see? Don't you know how much I —"

"Yes. It must be terrible to have such remorse," she quickly interposed. "And I sympathize with you deeply, too."

"Remorse nothin'! Them fellers was lookin' for it, an' they got just what they deserved. If I had n't 'a' done it somebody else would."

"And *you* a murderer! I never thought that of *you*. I can hardly believe it of you. And you calmly confess it to me as though it were nothing!"

"Why, I —I —"

"Don't talk to me! To think you have human blood on your hands. To think —"

"Norah! Norah, listen; won't you?"

" —that you are that sort of a man! How dare you call here as you have? How dare you?"

"But I tell you they were tryin' to get *me*! I just *had* to. Why, I didn't do it for nothin'. I 've got a right to defend myself, ain't I?"

"You *had* to? Is that true?" she demanded.

"Why, shore! Think I go 'round killin' men, like Greener does, just for th' fun of it?"

"He doesn't do anything of the kind," she retorted. "You know he does n't! Did n't you just say he blinks when he shoots off a gun?"

"Yes; I did. But I didn't want you to think he was a murderer like Nolan," he explained. Even Cookie, he thought, would find it hard to get around that neat little effort.

"I 'm so relieved," she laughed, delighted at her success in twisting him. "I am so glad he does n't blink when he shoots. I 'd hate a man who was afraid to shoot."

Johnny's chest arose a little. "Well, how 'bout me?"

"But you've killed men; you've shot down your fellow men; and have ghastly marks on your revolver to brag about."

"Well-say-but how can I shoot without shootin' or kill without killin'?" he demanded. "An' I don't brag about 'em, neither; it makes me feel too sad to do any braggin'. An' Greener's killed 'em, too; an' he brags about it."

"Yes; but he doesn't blink!" she exclaimed triumphantly.

"Neither do *I*."

"Yes; but you shoot to kill."

"Lord pity us-don't *he*?"

"Y-e-s, but that's different," she replied, smiling brightly.

Johnny looked around the room, his eyes finally resting on his hat.

"Yes, I see it's different. Greener can kill, an' blink! I can't. If he kills a man he's a hero; I 'm a murderer. I kinda reckon he 's got th' trail. But I love you, an' you 've got to pick my trail-does it lead up or down?"

"Johnny Nelson! What are you saying?" she demanded, arising.

"Something turrible, mebby. I don't know; an' I don't care. It's true-so there you are. Norah, can't you see I do?" he pleaded, holding out his hands. "Won't you marry me?"

She looked down, her cheeks the color of fire, and Johnny continued hurriedly: "I 've loved you a whole month! When I 'm ridin' around I sorta' see you, an' hear you. Why, I talk to you lots when I 'm alone. I 've saved up some money, an' I had to work hard to save it, too. I 've got some cows runnin' with our'n —in a little while I 'll have a ranch of my own. Buck 'll let me use th' east part of th' ranch, an' there 's a hill over there that 'd look fine with a house on it. I can't wait no longer, Norah, I 've got to know. Will you let me put this on yore finger?" He swiftly bent the pin into a ring and held it out eagerly: "Can I?"

She pushed him away and yielded to a sudden pricking of her conscience, speaking swiftly, as if forcing herself to do a disagreeable duty, and hating herself at the moment. "Johnny, I 've been a —a flirt! When I saw you were beginning to care too much for me I should have stopped it; but I did n't. I amused myself-but I want you to believe one thing, to give me a little credit for just one thing; I never thought what it might mean to you. It was carelessness with me. But I was flirting, just the same-and it hurts to admit it. I 'm not good enough for you, Johnny Nelson; it's hard to say, but it's true. Can you, *will* you forgive me?"

He choked and stepped forward holding out his hands imploringly, but she eluded him. When he saw the shame in her face, the tears in her eyes, he stopped and laughed gently: "But we can begin right, now, can't we? I don't care, not if you 'll let me see you same as ever. You might get to care for me. And, anyhow, it ain't yore fault. I reckon it's me that's to blame."

At that moment he was nearer to victory than he had ever been; but he did not realize it and opportunity died when he failed to press his advantage.

"I *am* to blame," she said, so low he could hardly catch the words. When she continued it was with a rush: "I am not free —I haven't been for a week. I 'm not free any more-and I 've been leading you on!"

His face hardened, for now the meaning of Greener's sneering laugh came to him, and a seething rage swept over him against the man who had won. He knew Greener, knew him well-the meanness of the man's nature, his cold cruelty; the many things to the man's discredit loomed up large against the frailty of the woman before him.

Norah stepped forward and laid a pleading hand on his arm, for she knew the mettle of the men who worked under Buck Peters: "What are you thinking? Tell me!"

"Why, I 'm thinking what Nolan said. An', Norah, listen. You say you want me to forgive you? Well, I do, if there's anything to forgive. But I want you to primise me that if Greener don't treat you right you 'll tell me."

"What do you mean?"

"Only what I said. Do you promise?"

"Perhaps you would better speak to him about it!" she retorted.

"I will-an' plain. But don't worry 'bout me. It was my fault for bein' a tenderfoot. I never played this game before, an' don't know th' cards. Good-by."

He rode away slowly, and made the rounds, and by the time he reached Lacey's he was so unsteady that he was refused a drink and told to go home. But he headed for the Palace instead, and when he stepped high over the doorsill Nolan was seated in a chair tipped back against one of the side walls, and behind the bar on the other side of the room Jed Terry drummed on the counter and expressed his views on local matters. The sheriff was listening in a bored way until he saw Johnny enter and head his way, feet high and chest out; and at that moment Nolan's interest in local affairs flashed up brightly.

Johnny lost no time: "Nolan," he said, rocking on his heels, "tell Greener I 'll kill him if he marries that girl. He killed his first wife by abuse an' he don't kill no more. Savvy?"

The sheriff warily arose, for here was the opportunity he had sought. The threat to kill had a witness.

"An' if you opens yore toad's mouth about her like you did tonight, I 'll kill you, too." The tones were dispassionate, the words deliberate.

"Hear that, Jed?" cried the sheriff, excitedly. "Nelson, yo 're under ar —"

"Shut up!" snapped Johnny loudly, this time with feeling. "When yo 're betters are talkin' you keep yore face closed. Now, it ain't hardly healthy to slander wimmin in this country, 'specially *good* wimmin. You lied like a dog to me tonight, an' I let you off; don't try it again."

"I told th' truth!" snapped Nolan, heatedly. "I said she was a flirt, an' by th' great horned spoon she is a flirt, an' you —"

The sheriff prided himself upon his quickness, but the leaping gun was kicked out of his hand before he knew what was coming; a chair glanced off Jed's face and wrapped the front window about itself in its passing, leaving the bar-tender in the throbbing darkness of inter-planetary space; and as the sheriff opened his eyes and recovered from the hard swings his face had stopped, a galloping horse drummed southward toward the Bar-20; and the silence of the night was shattered by lusty war-whoops and a spurting .45.

When the sheriff and his posse called at the Bar-20 before breakfast the following morning they found a grouchy outfit and learned some facts.

"Where 's Johnny?" repeated Hopalong, with a rising inflection. "Only wish I knowed!"

A murmur of wistful desire arose and Lanky Smith restlessly explained it: "He rampages in 'bout midnight an' wakes us up with his racket. When we asks what he 's doin' with *our* possessions he suggests we go to h —l. He takes *his* rifle, Pete's rifle, Buck's brand new canteen, 'bout eighty pounds of catridges an' other useful duffle, *all* th' tobacco, an' blows away quick."

"On my cayuse," murmured Red.

"Wearin' my *good* clothes," added Billy, sorrowfully.

"An' *my* boots," sighed Hopalong.

"I ain't got no field glasses no more," grumbled Lanky.

"But he only got one laig of my new pants," chuckled Skinny. "I was too strong for him."

"He yanked my blanket off'n me, which makes me steal Red's," grinned Pete.

"Which you didn't keep very long!" retorted Red, with derision.

"Which makes us all peevish," plaintively muttered Buck.

"Now ain't it a h —l of a note?" laughed Cookie, loudly, forthwith getting scarce. He had nothing good enough to be taken.

"An' whichever was it run ag'in' yore face, Sheriff?" sympathetically inquired Hopalong. "Mighty good thing it stopped," he added thoughtfully.

"Never mind my face!" snorted the peace officer hotly as his deputies smoothed out their grins. "I want to know where Nelson is, an' d —d quick! We 'll search the house first."

"Hold on," responded Buck. "North of Salt Spring Creek yo 're a sheriff; down here yo 're nothin'. Don't search no house. He ain't here."

"How do I know he ain't?" snapped Nolan.

"My word 's good; or there 'll be another election stolen up in yore county," rejoined Buck ominously. "An' I would n't hunt him too hard, neither. We 'll punish him."

Nolan wheeled and rode toward the hills without another word, his posse pressing close behind. When they entered Apache Pass one of them accidentally exploded his rifle, calling forth an angry tirade from the sheriff. Johnny heard it, and cared little for the warning from his friend Lucas; he waited and then rode down the rocky slope of the pass on the trail of the posse, squinting wickedly at the distant group as he caught glimpses of them now and again, and with no anxiety regarding backward glances. "Lot's wife 'll have nothing on them if they look back," he muttered, fingering his rifle lovingly. At nightfall he watched them depart and grinned at the chase he would lead them when they returned.

But he did not see them again, although his friends reported that they were turning the range upside down to find him. One of his outfit rode out to him with supplies and information every few days and it was Pete who told him that six posses were in the hills. "An' you can't leave, 'cause one of th' cordon would get you shore. I had a h —l of a time getting in today." Red reported that the sheriff had sworn to take him dead or alive. Then came the blow. The sheriff was at the point of death from lockjaw caused by complete paralysis of the curea-frend nerve just above the phlagmatic diaphragm, which Johnny had fractured. It was Hopalong who imparted this sad news, and withered Johnny's hope of returning to a comfortable bunkhouse and square meals. So the fugitive clung to the hills, shunned sky-lines and wondered if the sheriff would recover before snow flew. He was hungry most of the time now because the outfit was getting stingy with the food supplies-and he dared not shoot any game.

Four weeks passed, weeks of hunger and nervous strain, and he was getting desperate. He had learned that Greener and his fiancée were going down to Linnville soon, since Perry's Bend had no parson; and his cup of bitterness, overflowing, drove him to risk an attempt to leave that part of the country. He had seen none of Pete's "cordon" although he had looked for them, and he believed he could get away. So he rode cautiously down Apache Pass one noon, thoughtfully planning his flight. The sand, washed down the rock walls by the last rain, deadened all sounds of his progress, and as he turned a sharp bend in the cut he almost bumped into Greener and Norah Joyce. They were laughing at how they had eluded the crowd of friends who were eager to accompany them-but the laughter froze when Johnny's gun swung up.

"'Nds up, Greener!" he snapped, viciously, remembering his promise to Sheriff Nolan. "Miss Joyce, if you make any trouble it 'll cost him his life."

"Turned highwayman, eh?" sneered Greener, keenly alert for the necessary fraction of a second's carelessness on the part of the other. He was gunman enough to need no more.

"Miss Joyce, will you please ride along? I want to talk to him alone," said Johnny, his eyes fastened intently on those of his enemy.

"Yes, Norah; that's best. I 'll join you in a few minutes," urged Greener, smiling at her.

Johnny had a sudden thought and his warning was grave and cold. "Don't get very far away an' don't make no sounds, or signals; if you do it 'll be th' quickest way to *need* 'em. He 'll pay for any mistakes like that."

"You coward!" she cried, angrily, and then delivered an impromptu lecture that sent the blood surging into the fugitive's wan cheeks. But she obeyed, slowly, at Greener's signal, and when she was out of sight Johnny spoke.

"Greener, yo 're not going to marry her. You know what you are, you know how yore first wife died–an' I don't intend that Norah shall be abused as the other was. I 'm a fugitive, hard pressed; I 'm weak from want of food, and from hardships; all I have left is a slim chance of gettin' away. I 've reached the point where I can't harm myself by shooting you, an' I 'm goin' to do it rather than let any trouble come to her. But you'll get an even break, because I ain't never going to shoot a man when he 's helpless. Got anything to say?"

"Yes; yo 're th' biggest fool I ever saw," replied Greener. "Yo're locoed through an' through; an' I 'm goin' to take great pleasure in putting you away. But I want to thank you for one thing you did. You were drunk at the time an' may not remember it. When you hit Nolan for talking like he did I liked you for it, an' I 'm goin' to tell you so. Now we 'll get at th' matter before us so I can move along."

Neither had paid any attention to Norah in the earnestness and keen-eyed scrutiny of each other and the first sign they had of her actions was when she threw her arms around Greener's neck and shielded him. He was too much of a man to fire from cover and Johnny realized it while the other tried to get her to leave the scene.

"I won't leave you to be murdered —I *know* what it means, I *know* it," she cried. "My place is here, and you can't deny your wife's first request! What will I do without you! Oh, dear, let me stay! I *will* stay! What woman ever had such a wedding day before! Dear, dear, what can I do? Tell me what to do!"

Johnny sniffled and wished the posse had taken him. This was a side he had never thought of. His wife! Greener's wife! Then he was too late, and to go on would be a greater evil than the one he wished to eliminate. When she turned on him like a tigress and tore him to pieces word by word, tears rolling down her pallid cheeks and untold misery in her eyes, he shook his head and held up his hand.

"Greener, you win; I can't stop what's happened," he said, slowly. "But I 'll tell you this, an' I mean every word: If you don't treat her like she deserves, I 'll come back some of these days and kill you *shore*. Nolan got his because he talked ill of her; an' you 'll get yours if I die the next minute, if you ain't square with her."

"I don't need no instructions on how to treat my wife," retorted the other. "An' I 'm beginnin' to see th' cause of yore insanity, and it pardons you as nothing else will. Put up yore gun an' get back to th' ranch, where you belong–an' *keep away from me*. Savvy?"

"Not much danger of me gettin' in yore way," growled Johnny, "when I 'm hunted like a dog for doing what any man would 'a' done. When th' sheriff gets well, if he ever does, mebby I 'll come back an' take my medicine. How was he, anyhow, when you left?"

"Dead tired, an' some under th' influence of liquor," replied Greener, a smile breaking over his frown. He knew the whole story well, as did the whole range, and he had laughed over it with the Bar-20 outfit.

"What's that? Ain't he near dead?" cried Johnny, amazed.

"Well, purty nigh dead of fatigue dancin' at our weddin' last night; but I reckon he 'll be driftin' home purty soon, an' all recovered." Greener suddenly gave way and roared with laughter. There was a large amount of humor in his make-up and it took possession of him, shaking him from head to foot. He had always liked Johnny, not because he ever wanted to but because no one could know the Bar-20 protégé and keep from it. This climax was too much for him, and his wife, gradually recovering herself, caught the infection and joined in.

Johnny's eyes were staring and his mouth wide open, but Greener's next words closed the eyes to a squint and snapped shut the open mouth.

"That there paralysis of th' cure-a-friend nerve did n't last; an' when I heard why you licked him I said a few words that made him a wiser man. He didn't hunt you after th' first day. Now you go up an' shake han's with him. He knows he got what was coming to him and so does everybody else know it. Go home an' quit playin' th' fool for th' whole blamed range to laugh at."

Johnny stirred and came back to the scene before him. His face was livid with rage and he could not speak at first. Finally, however, he mastered himself and looked up: "I 'm cured, all right, but *they* ain't! Wait till my turn comes! What a fool I was to believe 'em; but they usually tell th' truth. 'Cura-a-friend nerve'! They 'll pay me dollar for cent before I 'm finished!" He caught the sparkle of his diamond pin, the pin he had won, when drunk, at El Paso, and a sickly grin flickered over the black frown. "I 'm a little late, I reckon; but I 'd like to give th' bride a present to show there ain't no hard feelin's on my part, an' to bring her luck. This here pin ain't no fit ornament for a fool like me, so if it's all right, I 'll be plumb tickled to see her have it. How 'bout it, Greener?"

The happy pair exchanged glances and Mrs. Greener, hesitating and blushing, accepted the gift: "You can bend it into a ring easy," Johnny hastily remarked, to cut off her thanks.

Greener extended his hand: "I reckon we can be friends, at that, Nelson. You squared up with me when you licked Nolan. Come up an' see us when you can."

Johnny thanked him and shook hands and then watched them ride slowly down the canyon, hand in hand, happy as little children. He sat silently, lost in thought, his anger rising by leaps and bounds against the men who had kept him on the anxious seat for a month. Straightening up suddenly, he tore off the navy blue necktie and, hurling it from him, fell into another reverie, staring at the canyon wall, but seeing in his mind's eye the outfit planning his punishment; and his eyes grew redder and redder with fury. But it was a long way home and his temper cooled as he rode; that is why no one knew of his return until they saw him asleep in his bunk when they awakened at daylight the following morning. And no one ever asked about the diamond, or made any explanations-for some things are better unmentioned. But they paid for it all before Johnny considered the matter closed.

Hopalong Cassidy

Chapter I
Antonio's Scheme

The raw and mighty West, the greatest stage in all the history of the world for so many deeds of daring which verged on the insane, was seared and cross-barred with grave-lined trails and dotted with presumptuous, mushroom towns of brief stay, whose inhabitants flung their primal passions in the face of humanity and laughed in condescending contempt at what humanity had to say about it. In many localities the real bad-man, the man of the gun, whose claims to the appellation he was ready to prove against the rancorous doubting of all comers, made history in a terse and business-like way, and also made the first law for the locality-that of the gun.

There were good bad-men and bad bad-men, the killer by necessity and the wanton murderer; and the shifting of these to their proper strata evolved the foundation for the law of to-day. The good bad-men, those in whose souls lived the germs of law and order and justice, gradually became arrayed against the other class, and stood up manfully for their principles, let the odds be what they might; and bitter, indeed, was the struggle, and great the price.

From the gold camps of the Rockies to the shrieking towns of the coast, where wantonness stalked unchecked; from the vast stretches of the cattle ranges to the ever-advancing terminals of the persistent railroads, to the cow towns, boiling and seething in the loosed passions of men who brooked no restraint in their revels, no one section of country ever boasted of such numbers of genuine bad-men of both classes as the great, semi-arid Southwest. Here was one of the worst collections of raw humanity ever broadcast in one locality; here the crack of the gun would have sickened except that moralists were few and the individual so calloused and so busy in protecting his own life and wiping out his own scores that he gave no heed to the sum total of the killings; it was a word and a shot, a shot and a laugh or a curse.

In this red setting was stuck a town which we will call Eagle, the riffle which caught all the dregs of passing humanity, where men danced as souls were freed. Unmapped, known only to those who had visited it, it reared its flimsy buildings in the face of God and rioted day and night with no thought of reckoning; mad, insane with hellishness unlimited.

Late in the afternoon of a glorious day towards this town rode Antonio, "broncho-buster" for the H2, a Mexican of little courage, much avarice, and great capacity for hatred. Crafty, filled with cunning of the coyote kind, shifty-eyed, gloomy, taciturn, and scowling, he was well fitted for the part he had elected to play in the range dispute between his ranch and the Bar-20. He was absolutely without mercy or conscience; indeed, one might aptly say that his conscience, if he had ever known one, had been pulled out by the roots and its place filled with viciousness. Cold-blooded in his ferocity, easily angered and quick to commit murder if the risk were small, he embraced within his husk of soul the putrescence of all that was evil.

In Eagle he had friends who were only a shade less evil than himself; but they had what he lacked and because of it were entitled to a forced respect of small weight-they had courage, that spontaneous, initiative, heedless courage which toned the atmosphere of the whole West to a magnificent crimson. Were it not for the reason that they had drifted to his social level they would have spurned his acquaintance and shot him for a buzzard; but, while they secretly held him in great contempt for his cowardice, they admired his criminal cunning, and profited by it. He was too wise to show himself in the true light to his foreman and the outfit, knowing full well that death would be the response, and so lived a lie until he met his friends of the town, when he threw off his cloak and became himself, and where he plotted against the man who treated him fairly.

Riding into the town, he stopped before a saloon and slouched in to the bar, where the proprietor was placing a new stock of liquors on the shelves.

"Where's Benito, an' th' rest?" he asked.

"Back there," replied the other, nodding toward a rear room.

"Who's in there?"

"Benito, Hall, Archer an' Frisco."

"Where's Shaw?"

"Him an' Clausen an' Cavalry went out 'bout ten minutes ago."

"I want to see 'em when they come in," Antonio remarked, shambling towards the door, where he listened, and then went in.

In the small room four men were grouped around a table, drinking and talking, and at his entry they looked up and nodded. He nodded in reply and seated himself apart from them, where he soon became wrapped in thought.

Benito arose and went to the door. *"Mescal, pronto,"* he said to the man outside.

"D——d *pronto*, too," growled Antonio. "A man would die of alkali in this place before he's waited on."

The proprietor brought a bottle and filled the glasses, giving Antonio his drink first, and silently withdrew.

The broncho-buster tossed off the fiery stuff and then turned his shifty eyes on the group. "Where's Shaw?"

"Don't know-back soon," replied Benito.

"Why didn't he wait, when he knowed I was comin' in?"

Hall leaned back from the table and replied, keenly watching the inquisitor, "Because he don't give a d—n."

"You——!" shouted the Mexican, half arising, but the others interfered and he sank back again, content to let it pass. But not so Hall, whose Colt was half drawn.

"I'll kill you some day, you whelp," he gritted, but before anything could come of it Shaw and his companions entered the room and the trouble was quelled.

Soon the group was deep in discussion over the merits of a scheme which Antonio unfolded to them, and the more it was weighed the better it appeared. Finally Shaw leaned back and filled his pipe. "You've got th' brains of th' devil, 'Tony."

"Eet ees not'ing," replied Antonio.

"Oh, drop that lingo an' talk straight-you ain't on th' H2 now," growled Hall.

"Benito, you know this country like a book," Shaw continued. "Where's a good place for us to work from, or ain't there no choice?"

"Thunder Mesa."

"Well, what of it?"

"On de edge of de desert, high, beeg. De walls are stone, an' so ver' smooth. Nobody can get up."

"How can we get up then?"

"There's a trail at one end," replied Antonio, crossing his legs and preparing to roll a cigarette. "It's too steep for cayuses, an' too narrow; but we can crawl up. An' once up, all h—l can't follow as long as our cartridges hold out."

"Water?" inquired Frisco.

"At th' bottom of th' trail, an' th' spring is on top," Antonio replied. "Not much, but enough."

"Can you work yore end all right?" asked Shaw.

"Si," laughed the other. "I am 'that fool, Antonio,' on th' ranch. But they're th' fools. We can steal them blind an' if they find it out-well," here he shrugged his shoulders, "th' Bar-20 can take th' blame. I'll fix that, all right. This trouble about th' line is just what I've been waitin' for, an' I'll help it along. If we can get 'em fightin' we'll run off with th' bone *we* want. That'll be easy."

"But can you get 'em fightin'?" asked Cavalry, so called because he had spent several years in that branch of the Government service, and deserted because of the discipline.

Antonio laughed and ordered more *mescal* and for some time took no part in the discussion which went on about him. He was dreaming of success and plenty and a ranch of his own which he would start in Old Mexico, in a place far removed from the border, and where no questions would be asked. He would be a rich man, according to the standards of that locality, and what he said would be law among the peons. He liked to daydream, for everything came out just as he wished; there was no discordant note. He was so certain of success, so conceited as not to ask himself if any of the Bar-20 or H2 outfits were not his equal or superior in intelligence. It was only a matter of time, he told himself, for he could easily get the two ranches embroiled in a range war, and once embroiled, his plan would succeed and he would be safe.

"What do you want for your share, 'Tony?" suddenly asked Shaw.

"Half."

"What! *Half?*"

"*Si.*"

"You're loco!" cried the other. "Do you reckon we're going to buck up agin th' biggest an' hardest fightin' outfit in this country an' take all sorts of chances for a measly half, to be divided up among seven of us!" He brought his fist down on the table with a resounding thump. "You an' yore game can go to h —l first!" he shouted.

"I like a hog, all right," sneered Clausen, angrily.

"I thought it out an' I got to look after th' worst an' most important part of it, an' take three chances to you fellers' one," replied Antonio, frowning. "I said half, an' it goes."

"Run all th' ends, an' keep it all," exclaimed Hall. "An', by God, we've got a hand in it, now. If you try to hog it we'll drop a word where it'll do th' most good, an' don't you forget it, neither."

"Anton ees right," asserted Benito, excitedly. "Eet ees one reesk for Anton."

"Keep yore yaller mouth shut," growled Cavalry. "Who gave you any say in this?"

"Half," said Antonio, shrugging his shoulders.

"Look here, you," cried Shaw, who was, in reality, the leader of the crowd, inasmuch as he controlled all the others with the exception of Benito and Antonio, and these at times by the judicious use of flattery. "We'll admit that you've got a right to th' biggest share, but not to no half. You have a chance to get away, because you can watch 'em, but how about us, out there on th' edge of h —l? If they come for us we won't know nothing about it till we're surrounded. Now we want to play square with you, an' we'll give you twice as much as any one of th' rest of us. That'll make nine shares an' give you two of 'em. What more do you want, when you've got to have us to run th' game at all?"

Antonio laughed ironically. "Yes. I'm where I can watch, an' get killed first. You can hold th' mesa for a month. I ain't as easy as I look. It's my game, not yourn; an' if you don't like what I ask, stay out."

"We will!" cried Hall, arising, followed by the others. His hand rested on the butt of his revolver and trouble seemed imminent. Benito wavered and then slid nearer to Antonio. "You can run yore game all by yore lonesome, as *long* as you *can!*" Hall shouted. "I know a feller what knows Cassidy, an' I'll spoil yore little play right now. You'll look nice at th' end of a rope, won't you? It's this: share like Shaw said or get out of here, an' look out for trouble a-plenty to-morrow morning. I've put up with yore gall an' swallered yore insultin' actions just as long as I'm going to, an' I've got a powerful notion to fix you right here and now!"

"No fightin', you fools!" cried the proprietor, grabbing his Colt and running to the door of the room. "It's up to you fellers to stick together!"

"I'll be d — —d if I'll stand —" began Frisco.

"They want too much," interrupted Antonio, angrily, keeping close watch over Hall.

"We want a fair share, an' that's all!" retorted Shaw. "Sit down, all of you. We can wrastle this out without no gun-play."

"You-all been yappin' like a set of fools," said the proprietor. "I've heard every word you-all said. If you got a mite of sense you'll be some tender how you shout about it. It's shore risky enough without tellin' everybody this side of sun-up."

"I mean just what I said," asserted Hall. "It's Shaw's offer, or nothin'. We ain't playing fool for no Greaser. *Yes,* that's th' word-Greaser!" he repeated in answer to Antonio's exclamation. "If you don't like it, lump it!"

"Here! Here!" cried Shaw, pushing Hall into a seat. "If you two have got anything to settle, wait till some other time."

"That's more like it," growled the proprietor, shuffling back to the bar.

"Good Lord, 'Tony," cried Shaw in a low voice. "That's fair enough; we've got a right to something, ain't we? Don't let a good thing fall through just because you want th' whole earth. Better have a little than none."

"Well, gimme a third, then."

"I'll give you a slug in th' eye, you hog!" promised Hall, starting to rise again, but Shaw held him back. "Sit down, you fool!" he ordered, angrily. Then he turned to the Mexican. "Third don't go; take my offer or leave it."

"Gimme a fourth; that's fair enough."

Shaw thought for a moment and then looked up. "Well, that's more like it. What do you say, fellers?"

"No!" cried Hall. "Two-ninths, or nothin'!"

"A fourth is two-eighths, only a little more," Shaw replied.

"Well, all right," muttered Hall, sullenly.

"That ees ver' good," laughed Benito, glad that things were clearing. All his sympathies were with his countryman, but he hesitated to take his part in the face of such odds.

The others gave their consent to the division and Shaw smiled. "Well, that's more like it. Now we'll go into this thing an' sift it out. Keep mum about it-there's twenty men in town that would want to join us if they knowed."

"I'm goin' to be boss; what I say goes," spoke up Antonio. "It's my game an' I'm takin' th' most risky end."

"You ain't got sand enough to be boss of anything," sneered Hall. "Yore sand is chalk."

"You'll say too much someday," retorted Antonio, glaring.

"Oh, not to *you*, I reckon," rejoined Hall, easily.

"Shut up, both of you!" snapped Shaw. "You can be boss, 'Tony," he said, winking at Hall. "You've got more brains for a thing like this than any of us. I don't see how you can figger it out like you do."

Antonio laughed in a self-satisfied way, for it was pleasant to hear such an admission from the lips of a Gringo, and he was ready to discuss things in a better spirit. But he remembered one thing, and swore to take payment if the plan leaked out; the proprietor had confessed hearing every word, which was not at all to his liking. If Quinn should tell, well, Quinn would die; he would see to that, he and Benito.

Chapter II
Mary Meeker Rides North

Mary Meeker, daughter of the H2 owner and foreman, found pleasure in riding on little tours of investigation. She had given the southern portions her attention first and found, after the newness had worn off, that she did not care for the level, sandy stretches of half-desert land which lay so flat for miles. The prospect was always the same, always uninteresting and wearying and hot. Now she determined upon a step which she had wished to take for a long time, and her father's request that she should not take it grew less and less of a deterrent factor. He had given so much thought and worry to that mysterious valley, dropped so many remarks about it, that she at last gave rein to her curiosity and made ready to see for herself. It was green and hilly, like the rugged Montana she had quitted to come down to the desert, and it should be a small Montana to her. There were hills of respectable size, for these she saw daily from the ranch house door, and she loved hills; anything would be better than the limitless sand.

She had known little of restraint; her corner of the world had been filled entirely by men and she had absorbed much of their better traits. Self-reliant as a cowgirl should be, expert with either Colt or Winchester, and at home in the saddle, she feared nothing the desert might hold, except thirst. She was not only expert with weapons, but she did not fear to use them against men, as she had proved on one occasion in wild Montana. So she would ride to the hills which called her so insistently and examine the valley.

One bright morning just before the roundup began she went to the corral and looked at her horse, a cross between Kentucky stock and cow-pony and having in a great degree the speed of the first and the hardiness of the last, and sighed to think that she could not ride it for days to come. Teuton was crippled and she must choose some other animal. She had overheard Doc Riley tell Ed Joyce that the piebald in the smaller corral was well broken, and this was the horse she would take. The truth of the matter was that the piebald was crafty and permitted the saddle to be fixed and himself ridden for varying periods of time before showing what he thought of such things. Doc, unprepared for the piebald's sudden change in demeanor, had taken a tumble, which made him anxious to have his wounded conceit soothed by seeing Ed Joyce receive the same treatment.

Mary found no trouble in mounting and riding the animal and she was glad that she had overheard Doc, for now she had two horses which were thoroughly reliable, although, of course, Teuton was the only really good horse on the range. She rode out of the corral and headed for the White Horse Hills, scarcely twelve miles away. What if her father had warned her not to ride near the lawless punchers who rode the northern range? They were only men and she was sure that to a woman they would prove to be gentlemen.

The southern boundary of the Bar-20 ran along the top of the hills and from them east to the river, and it was being patrolled by three Bar-20 punchers, Hopalong, Johnny, and Red, all on the lookout for straying cattle of both ranches. Neither Hopalong nor Red had ever seen Mary Meeker, but Johnny had upon the occasion of his scout over the H2 range, and he had felt eminently qualified to describe her. He had finished his eulogistic monologue by asserting that as soon as his more unfortunate friends saw her they would lose sleep and sigh often, which prophecy was received in various ways and called forth widely differing comment. Red had snorted outright and Pete swore to learn that a woman was on the range; for Pete had been married, and his wife preferred another man. Hopalong, remembering a former experience of his own, smiled in knowing cynicism when told that he again would fall under the feminine spell.

Red was near the river and Johnny half-way to the hills when Hopalong began the ascent of Long Hill, wondering why it was that Meeker had made no attempt to cross the boundary in force and bring on a crisis; and from Meeker his mind turned to the daughter.

"So there's a woman down here now," he muttered, riding down into an arroyo and up the other bank. "This country is gettin' as bad as Kansas, d——d if it ain't. First thing we know it'll be nursin' bottles an' school houses, an' h—l loose all th' time instead of once in a while."

He heard hoofbeats and glanced up quickly, alert and ready for trouble, for who would be riding where he was but some H2 puncher?

"What th'——!" he exclaimed under his breath, for riding towards him at an angle was Mary Meeker; and Johnny was wrong in his description of her, but, he thought, the Kid had done as well as his limited vocabulary would allow. She *was* pretty, pretty as-she was more than pretty!

She had seen him at the same time and flashed a quick glance which embraced everything; and she was surprised, for he was not only passably good-looking, barring the red hair, but very different from the men her father had told her made up the outfit of the Bar-20. He removed his sombrero instantly and drew up to let her pass, a queer expression on his face. Yes, he thought, Johnny had wronged her, for no other woman could have such jet-black hair crowning such a face.

"By God!" he whispered, and went no farther, for that was the summing up of his whole opinion of her.

"He *is* a gentleman," she thought triumphantly, for he had proved that she was right in her surmise regarding the men of the northern ranch. She spurred to pass him and then her piebald took part in the proceedings. The prick of the spur awakened in him a sudden desire to assert his rights, and he promptly pitched to make up for his hitherto gentle behavior. So taken up with what the last minute had brought forth she was unprepared for the vicious bucking and when she opened her eyes her head was propped against Hopalong's knee and her face dripping with the contents of his canteen.

"D —n yore ugly skin!" he was saying to the piebald, which stood quietly a short distance away, evidently enjoying the result of his activity. "Just you wait! I'll show you what's due to come yore way purty soon!" He turned again to the woman and saw that her eyes were closed as before. "By God, yore-yore beautiful!" he exclaimed triumphantly, for he had found the word at last.

She moved slightly and color came into her cheeks with a sudden rush and he watched her anxiously. Soon she moved again and then, opening her eyes, struggled to gain her feet. He helped her up and held her until she drew away from him.

"What was it?" she asked.

"That ugly cayuse went an' pitched when you wasn't lookin' for it," he told her. "Are you hurt much?"

"No, just dizzy. I don't want to make you no trouble," she replied.

"You ain't makin' me any trouble, not a bit," he assured her earnestly. "But I'd like to make some trouble for that ornery cayuse of yourn. Let me tone him down some."

"No; it was my fault. I should 'a been looking —I never rode him before."

"Well, you've got to take my cayuse to get home on," he said. "He's bad, but he's a regular angel when stacked up agin that bronc. I'll ride the festive piebald, an' we can trade when you get home." Under his breath he said, "Oh, just wait till I get on you, you wall-eyed pinto! I'll give you what you need, all right!"

"Thank you, but I can ride him now that I know just what he is," she said, her eyes flashing with determination. "I've never let a bronc get th' best of me in th' long run, an' I ain't goin' to begin now. I came up here to look at th' hills an' th' valley, an' I'm not going back home till I've done it."

"That's th' way to talk!" he cried in admiration. "I'll get him for you," he finished, swinging into his saddle. He loosened the lariat at the saddle horn while he rode towards the animal, which showed sudden renewed interest in the proceedings, but it tarried too long. Just as it wheeled and leaped forward the rope settled and the next thing it knew was that the sky had somehow slid under its stomach, for it had been thrown over backward and flat on its back. When it had struggled to its feet it found Hopalong astride it, spurring vigorously on the side farthest from Mary, and for five minutes the air was greatly disturbed. At the end of that time he dismounted and led a penitent pony to its mistress, who vaulted lightly into the saddle and waited for her companion to mount. When he had joined her they rode up the hill together side by side.

Johnny, shortly after he had passed Hopalong on the line, wished to smoke and felt for his tobacco pouch, which he found to be empty. He rode on for a short distance, angry with himself for his neglect, and then remembered that Hopalong had a plentiful supply. He could overtake the man on the hill much quicker than he could Red, who had said that he was going to ride south along the river to see if Jumping Bear Creek was dry. If it were, Meeker could be expected to become active in his aggression. Johnny wheeled and cantered back along the boundary trail, alertly watching for trespassing cattle.

It was not long before he came within sight of the thicket which stood a little east of the base of Long Hill, and he nearly fell from the saddle in astonishment, for his friend was on the ground, holding a woman's head on his knee! Johnny didn't care to intrude, and cautiously withdrew to the shelter of the small chaparral, where he waited impatiently. Wishing to stretch his legs, he dismounted and picketed his horse and walked around the thicket until satisfied that he was out of sight of his friend.

Suddenly he fancied that he heard something suspicious and he crept back around the thicket, keeping close to its base. When he turned the corner he saw the head of a man on the other side of the chaparral which lay a little southwest of his position. It was Antonio, and he was intently watching the two on the slope of the hill, and entirely unaware that he was being watched in turn.

Johnny carefully drew his Colt and covered the Mexican, for he hated "Greasers" instinctively, but on Antonio he lavished a hatred far above the stock kind. He had seen the shifty-eyed broncho-buster on more than one occasion and never without struggling with himself to keep from shooting. Now his finger pressed gently against the trigger of the weapon and he wished for a passable excuse to send the other into eternity; but Antonio gave him no cause, only watching eagerly and intently, his face set in such an expression of malignancy as to cause Johnny's finger to tremble.

Johnny arose slightly until he could see Hopalong and his companion and he smothered an exclamation. "Gosh A'mighty!" he whispered, again watching the Mexican. "That's Meeker's gal or I'm a liar! Th' son-of-a-gun, keeping quiet about it all this time. An' no wonder th' Greaser's on th' trail!"

It was not long before Johnny looked again for Hopalong and saw him riding up the hill with his companion. Then he crept forward, watching the Mexican closely, his Colt ready for instant use. Antonio slowly drew down until he was lost to sight of the Bar-20 puncher, who ran swiftly forward and gained the side of the other thicket, where he again crept forward, and around the chaparral. When he next caught sight of the broncho-buster the latter was walking towards his horse and his back was turned to Johnny.

"Hey, you!" called the Bar-20 puncher, arising and starting after the other.

Antonio wheeled, leaped to one side and half drew his revolver, but he was covered and he let the weapon slide back into the holster.

"What was you doing?"

Antonio's reply was a scowl and his inquisitor continued without waiting for words from the other.

"Never mind that, for I saw what you was doing," Johnny said. "An' I shore knew what you wanted to do, because I came near doing it to you. Now it ain't a whole lot healthy for you to go snooping around this line like you was, for I'll plug you on suspicion next time. Get on that cayuse of yourn an' hit th' trail south-go on, make tracks!"

The Mexican mounted and slowly wheeled. "You hab drop, now," he said significantly. "Nex' time, *quien sabe?*"

Johnny dropped his Colt into the holster and removed his hand from the butt. "You're a liar!" he shouted, savagely. "I ain't got th' drop. It's an even break, an' what are you going to do about it?"

Antonio shrugged his shoulders and rode on without replying, quite content to let things stand as they were. He had learned something which he might be able to use to advantage later on and he had strained the situation just a little more.

"Huh! Next time!" snorted Johnny in contempt as he turned to go back to his horse. "It'll allus be 'nex' time' with that Greaser, 'less he gets a good pot shot at me, which he won't. He ain't got sand enough to put up a square fight. Now for Red; he'll shore be riding this way purty soon, an' that'll never do. Hoppy won't want anybody foolin' around th' hills for a while, lucky devil."

More than an hour had passed before he met Red and he forthwith told him that he had caught the Mexican scouting on foot along the line.

"I ain't none surprised, Kid," Red replied, frowning. "You've seen how th' H2 cows are being driven north agin us an' that means we'll be tolerable busy purty soon. Th' Jumping Bear is dry as tinder, an' it won't be long before Meeker'll be driving to get in th' valley."

"Well, I'm some glad of that," Johnny replied, frankly. "It's been peaceful too blamed long down here. Come on, we'll ride east an' see if we can find any cows to turn. Hey! Look there!" he cried, spurring forward.

Chapter III
The Roundup

The Texan sky seemed a huge mirror upon which were reflected the white fleecy clouds sailing northward; the warm spring air was full of that magnetism which calls forth from their earthy beds the gramma grass and the flowers; the scant vegetation had taken on new dress and traces of green now showed against the more sombre-colored stems; while in the distance, rippling in glistening patches where, disturbed by the wind, the river sparkled like a tinsel ribbon flung carelessly on the grays and greens of the plain. Birds winged their joyous way and filled the air with song; and far overhead a battalion of tardy geese flew, arrow-like, towards the cool lakes of the north, their faint honking pathetic and continuous. Skulking in the coulees or speeding across the skyline of some distant rise occasionally could be seen a coyote or gray wolf. The cattle, less gregarious than they had been in the colder months, made tentative sorties from the lessening herd, and began to stray off in search of the tender green grass which pushed up recklessly from the closely cropped, withered tufts. Rattlesnakes slid out and uncoiled their sinuous lengths in the warm sunlight, and copperheads raised their burnished armor from their winter retreats. All nature had felt the magic touch of the warm winds, and life in its multitudinous forms was discernible on all sides. The gaunt tragedy of a hard winter for that southern range had added its chilling share to the horrors of the past and now the cattle took heart and lost their weakness in the sunlight, hungry but contented.

The winter had indeed been hard, one to be remembered for years to come, and many cattle had died because of it; many skeletons, stripped clean by coyotes and wolves, dotted the arroyos and coulees. The cold weather had broken suddenly, and several days of rain, followed by sleet, had drenched the cattle thoroughly. Then from out of the north came one of those unusual rages of nature, locally known as a "Norther," freezing pitilessly; and the cattle, weakened by cold and starvation, had dumbly succumbed to this last blow. Their backs were covered with an icy shroud, and the deadly cold gripped their vitals with a power not to be resisted. A glittering sheet formed over the grasses as far as eye could see, and the cattle, unlike the horses, not knowing enough to stamp through it, nosed in vain at the sustenance beneath, until weakness compelled them to lie down in the driving snow, and once down, they never arose. The storm had raged for the greater part of a week, and then suddenly one morning the sun shown down on a velvety plain, blinding in its whiteness; and when spring had sent the snow mantle roaring through the arroyos and water courses in a turmoil of yellow water and driftwood, and when the range riders rode forth to read the losses on the plain, the remaining cattle were staggering weakly in search of food. Skeletons in the coulees told the story of the hopeless fight, how the unfortunate cattle had drifted before the wind to what shelter they could find and how, huddled together for warmth, they had died one by one. The valley along Conroy Creek had provided a rough shelter with its scattered groves and these had stopped the cattle drift, so much dreaded by cowmen.

It had grieved Buck Peters and his men to the heart to see so many cattle swept away in one storm, but they had done all that courage and brains could do to save them. So now, when the plain was green again and the warm air made riding a joy, they were to hold the calf roundup. When Buck left his blanket after the first night spent in the roundup camp and rode off to the horse herd, he smiled from suppressed elation, and was glad that he was alive.

Peaceful as the scene appeared there was trouble brewing, and it was in expectation of this that Buck had begun the roundup earlier than usual. The unreasoning stubbornness of one man, and the cunning machinations of a natural rogue, threatened to bring about, from what should have been only a misunderstanding, as pretty a range war as the Southwest had seen. Those immediately involved were only a few when compared to the number which might eventually be brought into the strife, but if this had been pointed out to Jim Meeker he would have replied that he "didn't give a d —n."

Jim Meeker was a Montana man who thought to carry out on the H2 range, of which he was foreman, the same system of things which had served where he had come from. This meant trouble right away, for the Bar-20, already short in range, would not stand idly by and see him encroach upon their land for grass and water, more especially when he broke a solemn compact as to range rights which had been made by the former owners of the H2 with the Bar-20. It meant not only the forcible use of Bar-20 range, but also a great hardship upon the herds for which Buck Peters was responsible.

Meeker's obstinacy was covertly prodded by Antonio for his own personal gains, but this the Bar-20 foreman did not know; if he had known it there would have been much trouble averted, and one more Mexican sent to the spirit world.

Buck Peters was probably the only man of all of them who realized just what such a war would mean, to what an extent rustling would flourish while the cowmen fought. His best efforts had been used to avert trouble, so far successfully; but that he would continue to do so was doubtful. He had an outfit which, while meaning to obey him in all things and to turn from any overt act of war, was not of the kind to stand much forcing or personal abuse; their nervous systems were constructed on the hair-trigger plan, and their very loyalty might set the range ablaze with war. However, on this most perfect of mornings Meeker's persistent aggression did not bother him, he was free from worry for the time.

Just north of Big Coulee, in which was a goodly sized water hole, a group of blanket-swathed figures lay about a fire near the chuck wagon, while the sleepy cook prepared breakfast for his own outfit, and for the eight men which the foreman of the C80 and the Double Arrow had insisted upon Buck taking. The sun had not yet risen, but the morning glow showed gray over the plain, and it would not be long before the increasing daylight broke suddenly. The cook fires crackled and blazed steadily, the iron pots hissing under their dancing and noisy lids, while the coffee pots bubbled and sent up an aromatic steam, and the odor of freshly baked biscuits swept forth as the cook uncovered a pan. A pile of tin plates was stacked on the tail-board of the wagon while a large sheet-iron pail contained tin cups. The figures, feet to the fire, looked like huge, grotesque cocoons, for the men had rolled themselves in their blankets, their heads resting on their saddles, and in many cases folded sombreros next to the leather made softer pillows.

Back of the chuck wagon the eastern sky grew rapidly brighter, and suddenly daylight in all its power dissipated the grayish light of the moment before. As the rim of the golden sun arose above the low sand hills to the east the foreman rode into camp. Some distance behind him Harry Jones and two other C80 men drove up the horse herd and enclosed it in a flimsy corral quickly extemporized from lariats; flimsy it was, but it sufficed for cow-ponies that had learned the lesson of the rope.

"All ready, Buck," called Harry before his words were literally true.

With assumed ferocity but real vociferation Buck uttered a shout and watched the effect. The cocoons became animated, stirred and rapidly unrolled, with the exception of one, and the sleepers leaped to their feet and folded the blankets. The exception stirred, subsided, stirred again and then was quiet. Buck and Red stepped forward while the others looked on grinning to see the fun, grasped the free end of the blanket and suddenly straightened up, their hands going high above their heads. Johnny Nelson, squawking, rolled over and over and, with a yell of surprise, sat bolt upright and felt for his gun.

"Huh!" he snorted. "Reckon yo're smart, don't you!"

"Purty near a shore 'nuf pin-wheel, Kid," laughed Red.

"Don't you care, Johnny; you can finish it to-night," consoled Frenchy McAllister, now one of Buck's outfit.

"Breakfast, Kid, breakfast!" sang out Hopalong as he finished drying his face.

The breakfast was speedily out of the way, and pipes were started for a short smoke as the punchers walked over to the horse herd to make their selections. By exercising patience, profanity, and perseverance they roped their horses and began to saddle up. Ed Porter, of the C80, and Skinny Thompson, Bar-20, cast their ropes with a sweeping, preliminary whirl over their heads, but the others used only a quick flit and twist of the wrist. A few mildly exciting struggles for the mastery took place between riders and mounts, for some cow-ponies are not always ready to accept their proper place in the scheme of things.

"Slab-sided jumpin' jack!" yelled Rich Finn, a Double Arrow puncher, as he fought his horse. "Allus raisin' th' devil afore I'm all awake!"

"Lemme hold her head, Rich," jeered Billy Williams.

"Her laigs, Billy, not her head," corrected Lanky Smith, the Bar-20 rope expert, whose own horse had just become sensible.

"Don't hurt him, bronc; we need him," cautioned Red.

"Come on, fellers; gettin' late," called Buck.

Away they went, tearing across the plain, Buck in the lead. After some time had passed the foreman raised his arm and Pete Wilson stopped and filled his pipe anew, the west-end man of the cordon. Again Buck's arm went up and Skinny Thompson dropped out, and so on until the last man had been placed and the line completed. At a signal from Buck the whole line rode forward, gradually converging on a central point and driving the scattered cattle before it.

Hopalong, on the east end of the line, sharing with Billy the posts of honor, was now kept busy dashing here and there, wheeling, stopping, and manœuvring as certain strong-minded cattle, preferring the freedom of the range they had just quitted, tried to break through the cordon. All but branded steers and cows without calves had their labors in vain, although the escape of these often set examples for ambitious cows with calves. Here was where reckless and expert riding saved the day, for the cow-ponies, trained in the art of punching cows, entered into the game with zest and executed quick turns which more than once threatened a catastrophe to themselves and riders. Range cattle can run away from their domesticated kin, covering the ground with an awkward gait that is deceiving; but the ponies can run faster and turn as quickly.

Hopalong, determined to turn back one stubborn mother cow, pushed her too hard, and she wheeled to attack him. Again the nimble pony had reason to move quickly and Hopalong swore as he felt the horns touch his leg.

"On th' prod, hey! Well, stay on it!" he shouted, well knowing that she would. "Pig-headed old fool—*all right*, Johnny; I'm comin'!" and he raced away to turn a handful of cows which were proving too much for his friend. "*Ki-yi-yeow-eow-eow-eow-eow!*" he yelled, imitating the coyote howl.

The cook had moved his wagon as soon as breakfast was over and journeyed southeast with the cavvieyh; and as the cordon neared its objective the punchers could see his camp about half a mile from the level pasture where the herd would be held for the cutting-out and branding. Cookie regarded himself as the most important unit of the roundup and acted accordingly, and he was not far wrong.

"Hey, Hoppy!" called Johnny through the dust of the herd, "there's cookie. I was 'most scared he'd get lost."

"Can't you think of anythin' else but grub?" asked Billy Jordan from the rear.

"Can you tell me anything better to think of?"

There were from three to four thousand cattle in the herd when it neared the stopping point, and dust arose in low-hanging clouds above it. Its pattern of differing shades of brown, with yellow and black and white relieving it, constantly shifted like a kaleidoscope as the cattle changed positions; and the rattle of horns on horns and the muffled bellowing could be heard for many rods.

Gradually the cordon surrounded the herd and, when the destination was reached, the punchers rode before the front ranks of cattle and stopped them. There was a sudden tremor, a compactness in the herd, and the cattle in the rear crowded forward against those before; another tremor, and the herd was quiet. Cow-punchers took their places around it, and kept the cattle from breaking out and back to the range, while every second man, told off by the foreman, raced at top speed towards the camp, there to eat a hasty dinner and get a fresh horse from his *remuda*, as his string of from five to seven horses was called. Then he galloped back to the herd and relieved his nearest neighbor. When all had reassembled at the herd the work of cutting-out began.

Lanky Smith, Panhandle Lukins, and two more Bar-20 men rode some distance east of the herd, there to take care of the cow-and-calf cut as it grew by the cutting-out. Hopalong, Red, Johnny, and three others were assigned to the task of getting the mother cows and their calves out of the main herd and into the new one, while the other punchers held the herd and took care of the stray herd when they should be needed. Each of the cutters-out rode after some calf, and the victim, led by its mother, worked its way after her into the very heart of the mass; and in getting the pair out again care must be taken not to unduly excite the other cattle. Wiry, happy, and conceited cow-ponies unerringly and patiently followed mother and calf into the press, nipping the pursued when too slow and gradually forcing them to the outer edge of the herd; and when the mother tried to lead its offspring back into the herd to repeat the performance, she was in almost every case cleverly blocked and driven out on the plain where the other punchers took charge of her and added her to the cow-and-calf cut.

Johnny jammed his sombrero on his head with reckless strength and swore luridly as he wheeled to go back into the herd.

"What's th' matter, Kid?" laughingly asked Skinny as he turned his charges over to another man.

"None of yore d———d business!" blazed Johnny. Under his breath he made a resolve. "If I get you two out here again I'll keep you here if I have to shoot you!"

"Are they slippery, Johnny?" jibed Red, whose guess was correct. Johnny refused to heed such asinine remarks and stood on his dignity.

As the cow-and-calf herd grew in size and the main herd dwindled, more punchers were shifted to hold it; and it was not long before the main herd was comprised entirely of cattle without calves, when it was driven off to freedom after being examined for other brands. As soon as the second herd became of any size it was not necessary to drive the cows and calves to it when they were driven out of the first herd, as they made straight for it. The main herd, driven away, broke up as it would, while the guarded cows stood idly beside their resting offspring awaiting further indignities.

The drive had covered so much ground and taken so much time that approaching darkness warned Buck not to attempt the branding until the morrow, and he divided his force into three shifts. Two of these hastened to the camp, gulped down their supper, and rolling into their blankets, were soon sound asleep. The horse herd was driven off to where the grazing was better, and night soon fell over the plain.

The cook's fires gleamed through the darkness and piles of biscuits were heaped on the tailboard of the wagon, while pots of beef and coffee simmered over the fires, handy for the guards as they rode in during the night to awaken brother punchers, who would take their places while they slept. Soon the cocoons were quiet in the grotesque shadows caused by the fires and a deep silence reigned over the camp. Occasionally some puncher would awaken long enough to look at the sky to see if the weather had changed, and satisfied, return to sleep.

Over the plain sleepy cowboys rode slowly around the herd, glad to be relieved by some other member of the outfit, who always sang as he approached the cattle to reassure them and save a possible stampede. For cattle, if suddenly disturbed at night by anything, even the waving of a slicker in the hands of some careless rider, or a wind-blown paper, will rise in a body-all up at once, frightened and nervous. The sky was clear and the stars bright and when the moon rose it flooded the plain with a silvery light and made fairy patterns in the shadows.

Snatches of song floated down the gentle wind as the riders slowly circled the herd, for the human voice, no matter how discordant, was quieting. A low and plaintive "Don't let this par-ting grieve y-o-u" passed from hearing around the resting cows, soon to be followed by "When-n in thy dream-ing, nights like t-h-e-s-e shall come a-gain —" as another watcher made the circuit. The serene cows, trusting in the prowess and vigilance of these low-voiced centaurs to protect them from danger, dozed and chewed their cuds in peace and quiet, while the natural noises of the night relieved the silence in unobtruding harmony.

Far out on the plain a solitary rider watched the herd from cover and swore because it was guarded so closely. He glanced aloft to see if there was any hope of a storm and finding that there was not, muttered savagely and rode away. It was Antonio, wishing that he could start a stampede and so undo the work of the day and inflict heavy losses on the Bar-20. He did not dare to start a grass fire for at the first flicker of a light he would be charged by one or more of the night riders and if caught, death would be his reward.

While the third shift rode and sang the eastern sky became a dome of light reflected from below and the sunrise, majestic in all its fiery splendor, heralded the birth of another perfect day.

Through the early morning hours the branding continued, and the bleating of the cattle told of the hot stamping irons indelibly burning the sign of the Bar-20 on the tender hides of calves. Mother cows fought and plunged and called in reply to the terrified bawling of their offspring, and sympathetically licked the burns when the frightened calves had been allowed to join them. Cowboys were deftly roping calves by their hind legs and dragging them to the fires of the branding men. Two men would hold a calf, one doubling the foreleg back on itself at the knee and the other, planting one booted foot against the calf's under hind leg close to its body, pulled back on the other leg while his companion, who held the foreleg, rested on the animal's head. The third man, drawing the hot iron from the fire, raised and held it suspended for a second over the calf's flank, and then there was an odor and a puff of smoke; and the calf was branded with a mark which neither water nor age would wipe out.

Pete Wilson came riding up dragging a calf at the end of his rope, and turned the captive over to Billy Williams and his two helpers, none of them paying any attention to the cow which followed a short distance behind him. Lanky seized the unfortunate calf and leaned over to secure the belly hold, when someone shouted a warning and he dropped the struggling animal and leaped back and to one side as the mother charged past. Wheeling to return the attack, the cow suddenly flopped over and struck the earth with a thud as Buck's rope went home. He dragged her away and then releasing her, chased her back into the herd.

"*Hi!* Get that little devil!" shouted Billy to Hopalong, pointing to the fleeing calf.

"Why didn't you watch for her, you half-breed!" demanded the indignant Lanky of Pete. "Do you think this is a ten-pin alley!"

Hopalong came riding up with the calf, which swiftly became recorded property.

"Bar-20; tally one," sang out the monotonous voice of the tally-man. "Why didn't you grab her when she went by, Lanky?" he asked, putting a new point on his pencil.

"Hope th' next one heads yore way!" retorted Lanky, grinning.

"Won't. I ain't abusin' th' kids."

"Bar-20; tally one," droned a voice at the next fire.

All was noise, laughter, dust, and a seeming confusion, but every man knew his work thoroughly and was doing it in a methodical way, and the confusion was confined to the victims and their mothers.

When the herd had been branded and allowed to return to the plain, the outfit moved on into a new territory and the work was repeated until the whole range, with the exception of the valley, had been covered. When the valley was worked it required more time in comparison with the amount of ground covered than had been heretofore spent on any part of the range; for the cattle were far more numerous, and it was no unusual thing to have a herd of great size before the roundup place had been reached. This heavy increase in the numbers of the cattle to be herded made a corresponding increase in the time and labor required for the cutting-out and branding. Five days were required in working the eastern and central parts of the valley and it took three more days to clean up around the White Horse Hills, where the ground was rougher and the riding harder. And at every cutting-out there was a large stray-herd made up of H2 and Three Triangle cattle. The H2 had been formerly the Three Triangle. Buck had been earnest in his instructions to his men regarding the strays, for now was the opportunity to rid his range of Meeker's cattle in a way natural and without especial significance; once over the line it would be a comparatively easy matter to keep them there.

For taking care of this extra herd and also because Buck courted scrutiny during the branding, the foreman accepted the services of three H2 men. This addition to his forces made the work move somewhat more rapidly and when, at the end of each day's cutting-out, the stray herd was complete, it was driven south across the boundary line by Meeker's men. When the last stray-herd started south Buck rode over to the H2 punchers and told them to tell their foreman to let him know when he could assist in the southern roundup and thus return the favor.

As the Bar-20 outfit and the C80 and Double Arrow men rode north towards the ranch house they were met by Lucas, foreman of the C80, who joined them near Medicine Bend.

"Well, got it all over, hey?" he cried as he rode up.

"Yep; bigger job than I thought, too. It gets bigger every year an' that blizzard didn't make much difference in th' work, neither," Buck replied. "I'll help you out when you get ready to drive."

"No you won't; you can help me an' Bartlett more by keeping all yore men watchin' that line," quickly responded Lucas. "We'll work together, me an' Bartlett, an' we'll have all th' men we want. You just show that man Meeker that range grabbin' ain't healthy down here-that's all we want. Did he send you any help in th' valley?"

"Yes, three men," Buck replied. "But we'll break even on that when he works along th' boundary."

"Have any trouble with 'em?"

"Not a bit."

"I sent Wood Wright down to Eagle th' other day, an' he says th' town is shore there'll be a big range war," remarked Lucas. "He said there's lots of excitement down there an' they act like they wish th' trouble would hurry up an' happen. We've got to watch that town, all right."

"If there's a war th' rustlers'll flock here from all over," interposed Rich Finn.

"Huh!" snorted Hopalong. "They'll flock out again if we get a chance to look for 'em. An' that town'll shore get into trouble if it don't live plumb easy. You know what happened th' last time rustlin' got to be th' style, don't you?"

"Well," replied Lucas, "I've fixed it with Cowan to get news to me an' Bartlett if anything sudden comes up. If you need us just let him know an' we'll be with you in two shakes."

"That's good, but I don't reckon I'll need any help, leastwise not for a long time," Buck responded. "But I tell you what you might do, when you can; make up a vigilance committee from yore outfits an' ride range for rustlers. We can take care of all that comes on us, but we won't have no time to bother about th' rest of th' range. An' if you do that it'll shut 'em out of our north range."

"We'll do it," Lucas promised. "Bartlett is going to watch th' trails north to see if he can catch anybody runnin' cattle to th' railroad construction camps. Every suspicious lookin' stranger is going to be held up an' asked questions; an' if we find any runnin' irons, you know what that means."

"I reckon we can handle th' situation, all right, no matter how hard it gets," laughed the Bar-20 foreman.

"Well, I'll be leavin' you now," Lucas remarked as they reached the Bar-20 bunk house. "We begin to round up next week, an' there's lots to be done before then. Say, can I use yore chuck wagon? Mine is shore done for."

"Why, of course," replied Buck heartily. "Take it now, if you want, or any time you send for it."

"Much obliged; come on, fellers," Lucas cried to his men. "We're goin' home."

Chapter IV
In West Arroyo

Hopalong was heading for Lookout Peak, the highest of the White Horse Hills, by way of West Arroyo, which he entered half an hour after he had forded the creek, and was half way to the line when, rounding a sharp turn, he saw Mary Meeker ahead of him. She was off her horse picking flowers when she heard him and she stood erect, smiling.

"Why, I didn't think I'd see you," she said. "I've been picking flowers-see them? Ain't they pretty?" she asked, holding them out for his inspection.

"They shore are," he replied, not looking at the flowers at all, but into her big, brown eyes. "An' they're some lucky, too," he asserted, grinning.

She lowered her head, burying her face in the blossoms and then picked a few petals and let them fall one by one from her fingers. "You didn't look at them at all," she chided.

"Oh, yes, I did," he laughed. "But I see flowers all th' time, and not much of you."

"That's nice-they are so pretty. I just love them."

"Yes. I reckon they are," doubtfully.

She looked up at him, her eyes laughing and her white teeth glistening between their red frames. "Why don't you scold me?" she asked.

"Scold you! What for?"

"Why, for being on yore ranch, for being across th' line an' in th' valley."

"Good Lord! Why, there ain't no lines for you! You can go anywhere."

"In th' valley?" she asked, again hiding her face in the flowers.

"Why, of course. What ever made you think you can't?"

"I'm one of th' H2," she responded. "Paw says I run it. But I'm awful glad you won't care."

"Well, as far as riding where you please is concerned, you run this ranch, too."

"There's a pretty flower," she said, looking at the top of the bank. "That purple one; see it?" she asked, pointing.

"Yes. I'll get it for you," he replied, leaping from the saddle and half way up the bank before she knew it. He slid down again and handed the blossom to her. "There."

"Thank you."

"See any more you wants?"

"No; this is enough. Thank you for getting it for me."

"Oh, shucks; that was nothing," he laughed awkwardly. "That was shore easy."

"I'm going to give it to you for not scolding me about being over th' line," she said, holding it out to him.

"No; not for that," he said slowly. "Can't you think of some other reason?"

"Don't you want it?"

"Want it!" he exclaimed, eagerly. "Shore I want it. But not for what you said."

"Will you wear it because we're friends?"

"Now yo're talking!"

She looked up and laughed, her cheeks dimpling, and then pinned it to his shirt, while he held his breath lest the inflation of his lungs bother her. It was nice to have a flower pinned on one's shirt by a pretty girl.

"There," she laughed, stepping back to look at it.

"Gosh!" he complained, ruefully. "You've pinned it up so high I can't see it. Why not put it lower down?"

She changed it while he grinned at how his scheming had born fruit. He was a hog, he knew that, but he did not care.

"Oh, I reckon *I'm* all right!" he exulted. "Shore you don't see no more you want?"

"Yes; an' I must go now," she replied, going towards her horse. "I'll be late with th' dinner if I don't hurry."

"What! Do you cook for that hungry outfit?"

"No, not for them-just for Paw an' me."

"When are you comin' up again for more flowers?"

"I don't know. You see, I'm going to make cookies some day this week, but I don't know just when. Do you like cookies, an' cake?"

"You bet I do! Why?"

"I'll bring some with me th' next time. Paw says they're th' best he ever ate."

"Bet I'll say so, too," he replied, stepping forward to help her into the saddle, but she sprang into it before he reached her side, and he vaulted on his own horse and joined her.

She suddenly turned and looked him straight in the eyes. "Tell me, honest, has yore ranch any right to keep our cows south of that line?"

"Yes, we have. Our boundaries are fixed. We gave th' Three Triangle about eighty square miles of range so our valley would be free from all cows but our own. That's all th' land between th' line an' th' Jumping Bear, an' it was a big price, too. They never drove a cow over on us."

She looked disappointed and toyed with her quirt.

"Why don't you want to let Paw use th' valley?"

"It ain't big enough for our own cows, an' we can't share it. As it is, we'll have to drive ten thousand on leased range next year to give our grass a rest."

"Well, —" she stopped and he waited to hear what she would say, and then asked her when she would be up again.

"I don't know! I don't know!" she cried.

"Why, what's the matter?"

"Nothing. I'm foolish-that's all," she replied, smiling, and trying to forget the picture which arose in her mind, a picture of desperate fighting along the line; of her father-and him.

"You scared me then," he said.

"Did I? Why, it wasn't anything."

"Are you shore?"

"Please don't ask me any questions," she requested.

"Will you be up here again soon?"

"If th' baking turns out all right."

"Hang the baking! come anyway."

"I'll try; but I'm afraid," she faltered.

"Of what?" he demanded, sitting up very straight.

"Why, that I can't," she replied, hurriedly. "You see, it's far coming up here."

"That's easy. I'll meet you west of th' hills."

"No, no! I'll come up here."

"Look here," he said, slowly and kindly. "If yo're afraid of bein' seen with me, don't you try it. I want to see you a whole lot, but I don't want you to have no trouble with yore father about it. I can wait till everything is all right if you want me to."

She turned and faced him, her cheeks red. "No, it ain't that, exactly. Don't ask me any more. Don't talk about it. I'll come, all right, just as soon as I can."

They were on the line now and she held out her hand.

"Good-bye."

"Good-bye for now. Try to come up an' see me as soon as you can. If yo're worryin' because that Greaser don't like me, stop it. I've been in too many tight places to get piped out where there's elbow room."

"I asked you not to say nothing more about it," she chided. "I'll come when I can. Good-bye."

"Good-bye," he replied, his sombrero under his arm. He watched her until she became lost to sight and then, suspicious, wheeled, and saw Johnny sitting quietly on his horse several hundred yards away. He called his friend to him by one wide sweep of his arm and Johnny spurred forward.

"Follow me, Johnny," he cried, dashing towards the arroyo. "Take th' other side an' look for that Greaser. I'll take this side. Edge off; yo're too close. Three hundred yards is about right."

They raced away at top speed, reckless and grim, Johnny not knowing just what it was all about; but the word Greaser needed no sauce to whet his appetite since the day he had caught Antonio watching his friend on the hill, and he scanned the plain eagerly. When they reached the other end of the arroyo Hopalong called to him: "Sweep east an' back to th' line on a circle. If you catch him, shoot off yore Colt an' hold him for *me*. I'm going west."

When they saw each other again it was on the line, and neither had seen any traces of Antonio, to Johnny's vexation and Hopalong's great satisfaction.

"What's up, Hoppy?" shouted Johnny.

"I reckoned that Greaser might 'a followed her so he could tell tales to Meeker," Hopalong called.

Johnny swept up recklessly, jauntily, a swagger almost in the very actions of his horse, which seemed to have caught the spirit of its rider.

"Caught you that time," he laughed-and Johnny, when in a teasing mood, could weave into his laughter an affectionate note which found swift pardon for any words he might utter. "You an' her shore make a good —" and then he saw the flower on his friend's shirt and for the moment was rendered speechless by surprise. But in him the faculty of speech was well developed and he recovered quickly. "Sufferin' coyotes! Would you look at that! What's comin' to us down here, anyway? Are you loco? Do you mean to let th' rest of th' outfit see *that*?"

"Calamity is comin' to th' misguided mavericks that get gay about it!" retorted Hopalong. "I wear what I feels like, an' don't you forget it, neither."

"'In thy d-a-r-k eyes splendor, where th' l-o-v-e light longs to dwel-l,'" Johnny hummed, grinning. Then his hand went out. "Good luck, Hoppy! Th' best of luck!" he cried. "She's a dandy, all right, but she ain't too good for you."

"Much obliged," Hopalong replied, shaking hands. "But suppose you tell me what all th' good luck is for. To hear you talk anybody'd think all a feller had to do was to ride with a woman to be married to her."

"Well, then take off that wart of a flower an' come on," Johnny responded.

"What? Not to save yore spotted soul! An' that ain't no wart of a flower, neither."

Johnny burst out laughing, a laugh from the soul of him, welling up in infectious spontaneity, triumphant and hearty. "Oh, oh! You bit that time! Anybody'd think about right in yore case, as far as *wantin'* to be married is concerned. Why, yo're hittin' th' lovely trail to matri-mony as hard as you can."

In spite of himself Hopalong had to laugh at the jibing of his friend, the Kid. He thumped him heartily across the shoulders to show how he felt about it and Johnny's breath was interfered with at a critical moment.

"Oh, just wait till th' crowd sees that blossom! Just wait," Johnny coughed.

"You keep mum about what you saw, d'y' hear?"

"Shore; but it'll be on my mind all th' time, an' I talk in my sleep when anything's on my mind."

"Then that's why I never heard you talk in yore sleep."

"Aw, g'wan! But they'll see th' flower, won't they?"

"Shore they will; but as long as they don't know how it got there they can't say much."

"They can't, hey!" Johnny exclaimed. "That's a new one on me. It's usually what they don't know about that they talks of most. What they don't know they can guess in this case, all right. Most of 'em are good on readin' signs, an' that's plain as th' devil."

"But don't you tell 'em!" Hopalong warned.

"No. I won't tell 'em, honest," Johnny replied. He could convey the information in a negative way and he grinned hopefully at the fun there would be.

"I mean it, Kid," Hopalong responded, reading the grin. "I don't care about myself; they can joke all they wants with me. But it ain't nowise right to drag her into it, savvy? She don't want to be talked about like that."

"Yo're right; they won't find out nothin' from me," and Johnny saw his fun slip from him. "I'm goin' east; comin' along?"

"No; th' other way. So long."

"Hey!" cried Johnny anxiously, drawing rein, "Frenchy said Buck was going to put some of us up in Number Five so Frenchy an' his four could ride th' line. Did Buck say anything to you about it?"

Line house Number Five was too far from the zone of excitement, if fighting should break out along the line, to please Johnny.

"He was stringin' you, Kid," Hopalong laughed. "He won't take any of th' old outfit away from here."

"Oh, I knowed that; but I thought I'd ask, that's all," and Johnny cantered away, whistling happily.

Hopalong looked after him and smiled, for Johnny had laughed and fought and teased himself into the heart of every man of the outfit: "He's shore a good Kid; an' how he likes a fight!"

Chapter V
Hopalong Asserts Himself

Paralleling West Arroyo and two miles east of it was another arroyo, through which Hopalong was riding the day following his meeting with Mary. Coming to a place where he could look over the bank he saw a herd of H2 and Three Triangle cows grazing not far away, and Antonio was in charge of them. Hopalong did not know how long they had been in the valley, nor how they had crossed the line, but their presence was enough. It angered him, for here was open and, it appeared, authorized defiance. Not content to let his herds run as they wished, Meeker was actually sending them into the valley under guard, presumably to find out what would be done about it. The H2 foreman would find that out very soon.

The Mexican looked around and wheeled sharply to face the danger, his listlessness gone in a flash. He was not there because of any orders from Meeker, but for reasons of his own. So when the Bar-20 puncher raised his arm and swept it towards the line he sat in sullen indifference, alert and crafty.

"You've got gall!" cried Hopalong. "Who told you to herd up here!"

Antonio frowned but did not reply.

"Yo're three miles too far north," continued Hopalong, riding slowly forward until their stirrups almost touched.

Antonio shrugged his shoulders.

"I ain't warbling for my health!" cried Hopalong. "You start them cows south right away."

"I can't."

Hopalong stared. "You can't! Got a sore thumb, mebby! Well, I reckon you can, an' will."

"I can't. Boss won't let me."

"Oh, he won't! Well, I feel sorry for yore boss but yo're going to push 'em just th' same."

Antonio again shrugged his shoulders and lifted his hands in a gesture of helplessness.

"How long you been here, an' how'd you get in?"

"'N'our. By de *rio*."

"Oh, yore foreman's goin' to raise h —l, ain't he!" Hopalong snorted. "He's going to pasture on us whether we like it or not, is he? He's a land thief, that's what he is!"

"De boss ees all right!" asserted Antonio, heatedly.

"If he is he's lop-sided, but he'll be *left* if he banks on this play going through without a smash-up. You chase them cows home an' keep 'em there. If I find you flittin' around th' ends of th' line or herdin' on this side of it I'll give you something to nurse-an' you'll be lucky if you can nurse it. Come on, get a-going!"

Antonio waved his arm excitedly and was about to expostulate, but Hopalong cut him short by hitting him across the face with his quirt: "D —n you!" he cried, angrily. "Shut yore mouth! Get them cows going! You coffee-colored half-breed of a Greaser, I've a mind to stop you right now. Come on, get a move on!"

The Mexican's face grew livid and he tried to back away, swearing in Spanish. Stung to action by the blow, he jerked at his gun, but found Hopalong's Colt pushing against his neck.

"Drop that gun!" the Bar-20 puncher ordered, his eyes flashing. "Don't you know better'n that? We've put up with yore crowd as long as we're going to, an' th' next thing will be a slaughter if that foreman of yourn don't get some sense, an' get it sudden. Don't talk back! Just start them cows!"

The Mexican could do nothing but obey. His triumph at the success of his effort was torn with rabid hatred for the man who had struck him; but he could not fight with the Colt at his neck, and so sullenly obeyed. As they neared the line Hopalong ceased his personal remarks and, smiling grimly, turned to another topic.

"I let you off easy; but no more. Th' next herd we find in our valley will go sudden an' hard. If anybody is guardin' it they'll never know what hit 'em." He paused for a moment and then continued, cold contempt in his voice: "I reckon you had to obey orders, but you won't do it again if you know what's good for you. If yore boss, as you calls him, don't like what I've done, you tell him I said to drive th' next herd hisself. If he ain't man enough to bring 'em in hisself, tell him that Cassidy says to quit orderin' his men to take risks he's a-scared of."

"He ees brafe; he ain't 'fraid," Antonio rejoined. "He weel keel you ef I tell heem what you say."

"Tell him jus' th' same. I'll be riding th' line mostly, an' if he wants to hunt me up an' confab about it he can find me any time."

Antonio shrugged his shoulders and rode south, filled with elation at his success in stirring up hostility between the two ranches, but his heart seethed with murder for the blow. He would carry a message to Meeker that would call for harsh measures, and the war would be on.

As the Mexican departed Lanky Smith rode into sight and cantered forward to meet his friend.

"What's up?" he asked.

"I don't know, yet," replied Hopalong. "Greasers are such liars I don't know what to think," and he related the matter to his companion.

"Lord, but you sent a stiff message to Meeker!" Lanky exclaimed. "You keep yore eyes plumb open from now on. Meeker'll be wild, an' th' Greaser won't forget that blow."

"Was anybody on th' east end this morning?"

"Shore; me an' Pete," Lanky replied, frowning. "He couldn't get a cow acrost without us seein' him-he lied."

"Well, it makes no difference how he got across; he was there, an' that's all I care about."

"There's one of his outfit now," Lanky said.

Hopalong looked around and saw an H2 puncher riding slowly past them, about two hundred yards to the south.

"Who is he?" Lanky asked.

"Doc Riley. Meeker got him an' Curley out of a bad scrape up north an' took them both to punch for him. I hear he is some bad with th' Colt. Sort of reckons he's a whole war-party in breech-cloths an' war-paint just 'cause he's got his man."

"He's gettin' close to th' line," Lanky remarked.

"Yes, because we've been turnin' their cows."

"Reckon he won't stop us none to speak of."

Doc had stopped and was watching them and while he looked a cow blundered out of the brush and started to cross the line. Hopalong spurred forward to stop it, followed by Lanky, and Doc rode to intercept them.

"G'wan back, you bone-yard!" Hopalong shouted, firing his Colt in front of the animal, which now turned and ran back.

Doc slid to a stand, his Colt out. "What do you think you're doing with that cow?"

"None of yore business!" Hopalong retorted.

Doc backed away so he could watch Lanky, his hand leaping up, and Hopalong fired. Doc dropped the weapon and grabbed at his right arm, cursing wildly.

"You half-breed!" cried Hopalong, riding closer. "Next time you gets any curious about what I'm doing, you better write. You're a fine specimen to pull a gun on me, you are!"

"You'll stop turnin' our cows, or you'll get a pass to h —l!" retorted Doc. "We won't stand for it no more, an' when th' boys hears about this you'll have all you can take care of."

"I ain't got nothing to do but ride th' line an' answer questions like I did yourn," Hopalong rejoined. "I will have lots of time to take care of any little trouble that blows up from yore way. But *Meeker's* th' man I want to see. Tell him to take a herd across this line, will you?"

"You'll see him!" snapped Doc. "An' you'll need to see him first, too."

"I don't pot-shoot —I'll leave that for you fellers. All I want is an even break."

"You'll get it," replied Doc, wheeling and riding off.

"Things are movin' so fast you better send for Buck," Lanky suggested. "Hell'll be poppin' down here purty soon."

"I'll tell him what's going on, but there ain't no use of bringing him down here till we has to," Hopalong replied. "We can handle 'em. But I reckon Johnny had better go up an' tell him."

"Johnny ought to be riding this way purty quick; he's coming from th' hills."

"We'll meet him an' get him off."

They met Johnny and when he had learned of his mission he protested against being sent away from the line when things were getting crowded. "I don't want to miss th' fun!" he exclaimed. "Send Red, or Lanky."

"Red's too handy with th' Winchester; we might need him," Hopalong replied, smiling.

"Then you go, Lanky," Johnny suggested. "I'm better'n you with th' Colt."

"You're better'n nothing!" retorted Lanky. "You do what you're told, an' quick. Nothing will happen while you're gone, anyhow."

"Then why don't you want to go?"

"I don't want th' ride," Lanky replied. "It's too fur."

"Huh!" snorted Johnny. "Too bad about you an' th' ride! Poor old man, scared of sixty miles. I'll toss up with you."

"One of you has got to ride to Red an' tell him. He mustn't get caught unexpected," Hopalong remarked.

"What do you call?" asked Johnny, flipping a coin and catching it when it came down.

"All right, that's fair enough. Heads," Lanky replied.

"Whoop! It's tails!" cried Johnny, wheeling. "I'm going for Red," and he was gone before Lanky had time to object.

"Blasted Kid!" Lanky snorted. "How'd I know it was tails?"

"That's yore lookout," laughed Hopalong. "You ought to know him by this time. It's yore own fault."

"I'll tan his hide some of these fine days," Lanky promised. "He's too fresh," and he galloped off to cover the thirty miles between him and the bunk house in the least possible time so as to return as soon as he could.

Chapter VI
Meeker is Told

When Antonio had covered half of the distance between the line and the H2 bunk house he was hailed from a chaparral and saw Benito ride into view. He told his satellite what had occurred in the valley, gave him a message for Shaw, who was now on the mesa, and cantered on to tell Meeker his version of the morning's happenings.

The H2 foreman was standing by the corral when his broncho-buster rode up, and he stared. "Where'd you get that welt on th' face?" he demanded.

Antonio told him, with many exclamations and angry gestures, that he had ridden through the valley to see if there were any H2 cows grazing on it, that he had found a small herd and was about to return to his own range when he was held up and struck by Hopalong, who accused him of having driven the cattle across the line. When he had denied this he had been called a liar and threatened with death if he was ever again caught on that side of the line.

"By G-d!" cried the foreman. "That's purty high-handed! I'll give 'em something to beller about when I finds out just what I want to do!"

"He say, 'Tell that boss of yourn to no send you, send heemself nex' time.' He say he weel keel you on sight. I say he can't. He laugh, *so!*" laughing in a blood-curdling manner. "He say he keel nex' man an' cows that cross line. He ees *uno* devil!"

"He will, hey!" Meeker exclaimed, thoroughly angered. "We'll give him all th' chance he wants when we get things fixed. 'Tony, what did you do about getting those two men you spoke of? You went down to Eagle, didn't you?"

"*Si, si,*" assured the Mexican. "They come, *pronto*. They can keel heem. They come to-day; *quien sabe?*"

"I'll do my own killin' —but here comes Doc," Meeker replied. "Looks mad, too. Mebby they was going to kill him an' he objected. Hullo, Doc; what's th' matter?"

"That Cassidy d —n near blowed my arm off," Doc replied. "Caught him turnin' back one of our cows an' told him not to. When I backed off so I could keep one eye on his friend he up an' plugs me through my gun arm."

"I see; they owns th' earth!" Meeker roared. "Shootin' up my men 'cause they stick up for me! Come in th' house an' get that wing fixed. We can talk in there," he said, glancing at Antonio. "They cut 'Tony across th' face with a quirt 'cause he was ridin' in their valley!"

"Let's get th' gang together an' wipe 'em off th' earth," Doc suggested, following Meeker towards the house.

Mary looked up when they entered: "What's th' matter, Dad? Why, are you hurt, Doc?"

"Don't ask questions, girl," Meeker ordered. "Get us some hot water an' some clean cloth. Sit down, Doc; we'll fix it in no time."

"We better clean 'em up to-morrow," Doc remarked.

"No; there ain't no use of losin' men fighting if there's any other way. You know there's a good strong line house on th' top of Lookout Peak, don't you?"

"Shore; reg'lar fort. They calls it Number Three."

Mary had returned and was tearing a bandage, listening intently to what was being said.

"What's th' matter with getting in that some day soon an' holdin' it for good?" asked the foreman. "It overlooks a lot of range, an' once we're in it it'll cost 'em a lot of lives to get it back-if they can get it back."

"You're right!" cried Doc, eagerly. "Let me an' Curley get in there to-night an' hold her for you. We can do it."

"You can't do that. Somebody sleeps in it nights. Nope, we've got to work some scheme to get it in th' daylight. They are bound to have it guarded, an' we've got to coax him out somehow. I don't know how, but I will before many hours pass. Hullo, who's this?" he asked, seeing two strangers approach the house.

"Couple of Greasers," grunted Doc.

"Hey, you," cried Meeker through the open door. "You go down to th' corral an' wait for me."

"*Si, señor.*"

"What's th' matter, Dad?" asked Mary. "How did Doc get shot?"

Meeker looked up angrily, but his face softened.

"There's a whole lot th' matter, Mary. That Bar-20 shore is gettin' hot-headed. Cassidy hit 'Tony acrost th' face with a quirt an' shot Doc. 'Tony was riding through that valley, an' Doc told Cassidy not to drive back a cow of ourn."

She flushed. "There must 'a been more'n that, Dad. He wouldn't 'a shot for that. I know it."

"You know it!" cried Meeker, astonished. "How do you know it?"

"He ain't that kind. I know he ain't."

"I asked how you knew it!"

She looked down and then faced him. "Because I know him, because he ain't that kind. What did you say to him, Doc?"

Meeker's face was a study and Doc flushed, for she was looking him squarely in the eyes.

"What did you say to him?" she repeated. "Did you make a gun-play?"

"Well, by G-d!" shouted Meeker, leaping to his feet. "You know him, hey! 'He ain't that kind!' How long have you known him, an' where'd you meet him?"

"This is no time to talk of that," she replied, her spirit aroused. "Ask Doc what he did an' said to get shot. Look at him; he lied when he told you about it."

"I told him to quit driving our cows back," Doc cried. "Of course I had my hand on my gun when I said it. I'd been a fool if I hadn't, wouldn't I?"

"That ain't all," she remarked. "Did you try to use it?"

Meeker was staring first at one and then at the other, not knowing just what to say. Doc looked at him and his mind was made up.

"What'd you do, Doc?" he asked.

"I said: 'What are you doing with that cow?' an' he said it wasn't none of my business. I got mad then an' jerked my gun loose, but he got me first. I wasn't going to shoot. I was only getting ready for him if he tried to."

"How did he know you wasn't going to shoot?" Meeker demanded. "Reckon I can't blame him for that. He must be quick on th' draw."

"Quickest I ever saw. He had his gun out to shoot in front of a cow. At th' time I thought he was going to kill it. That's what made me get in so quick. He slid it back in th' holster an' faced me. I told you what happened then."

"Well, we've got to show them fellers they can't fool with us an' get away with it," Meeker replied. "An' I've got to have th' use of that crick somehow. I'll think of some way to square things."

"Wait, I'll go with you," Doc remarked, following the other towards the door.

"You go in th' bunk house an' wait for me. I want to see what them Greasers want."

"Wonder how much 'Tony didn't tell," mused the foreman, as he went towards the corral. "Reckon Cassidy cut him 'cause he was a Greaser. Come purty nigh doing it myself, once. Well, I don't care, but I've got to notice plays like that or they'll think I'm scared of 'em. I'll go up an' have it out, an' when I get ready I'll show them swaggerin' bucks what's what."

When he returned he saw Antonio leaning against his shack, for the Mexican was not tolerated by the rest of the outfit and so lived alone. He looked at his foreman and leered knowingly, and then went inside the building, where he laughed silently. "That's a joke, all right! Meeker hiring two of my brothers to watch his cows an' do his spying! We'll skin this range before we're through."

Meeker frowned when he caught his broncho-buster's look and he growled: "You never did look good, an' that welt shore makes you look more like th' devil than ever." He glanced at the house and the frown deepened. "So you know Cassidy! That's a *nice* thing to tell me! I'll just go up an' see that coyote, right now," and he went for his horse, muttering and scowling.

Antonio knew of a herd of cows and calves which had not been included in the H2 roundup, and which were fattening on an outlying range. There was also a large herd of Bar-20 cattle growing larger every day on the western range far outside the boundaries. Benito was scouting, Shaw and the others were nearly ready for work on the mesa, and now Meeker had hired Antonio's brothers to help him to be robbed. Added to this was the constantly growing hostility along the line, and this would blaze before he and Benito had finished their work. Everything considered he was very much pleased and even his personal vengeance was provided for. Doc had more cause for animosity against Hopalong than he had, and if the Bar-20 puncher should be killed some day when Doc rode the northern range Doc would be blamed for it. But Meeker had not acted as he should have done when two of his men had been hurt on the same day, and that must be remedied. The faster things moved towards fighting the less chance there would be of the plot becoming known.

Antonio was the broncho-buster of the H2 because he was a positive genius at the work, and he was a good, all-around cowman when he overcame his inherent laziness; but he was cruel to a degree with both horses and cattle. Because of his fitness Meeker had overlooked his undesirable qualities, which he had in plenty. He was entirely too fond of liquor and gambling, was uncertain in his hours, and used his time as he saw fit when not engaged in breaking horses. A natural liar, exceedingly unclean in his habits, vindictive and with a temper dry as tinder, he was shunned by the other members of the outfit. This filled his heart with hatred for them and for Meeker, who did not interfere. He swore many times that he would square up everything some day, and the day was getting closer.

In appearance he was about medium height, but his sloping shoulders and lax carriage gave his arms the appearance of being abnormally long. His face was sharp and narrow, while his thin, wiry body seemed almost devoid of flesh. Like most cowboys he was a poor walker and his toes turned in like those of an Indian. Such was Antonio, who longed to gamble with Fortune in a dangerous game for stakes which to him were large, and who had already suggested to Meeker that the line house on Lookout Peak was the key to the situation. It was the germ, which grew slowly in the foreman's brain and became more feasible and insistent day by day, and it accounted for his fits of abstraction; it would not do to fail if the attempt were made.

Chapter VII
Hopalong Meets Meeker

When Meeker was within a mile of the line he met Curley, told him what had occurred and that he was going to find Hopalong. Curley smiled and replied that he had seen that person less than ten minutes ago and that he was riding towards the peak, and alone.

"We'll go after him," Meeker replied. "You come because I want to face him in force so he won't start no gun-play an' make me kill him. That'd set hell to pop."

Hopalong espied Johnny far to the east and he smiled as he remembered the celerity with which that individual had departed after glancing at the coin.

"There ain't no flies on th' Kid, all right," he laughed, riding slowly so Johnny could join him. He saw Curley riding south and looked over the rough plain for other H2 punchers. Some time later as he passed a chaparral he glanced back to see what had become of his friend, but found that he had disappeared. When he wheeled to watch for him he saw Meeker and Curley coming towards him and he shook his holster to be sure his Colt was not jammed in it too tightly.

"Well, here's where th' orchestry tunes up, all right," he muttered grimly. "Licked th' Greaser, plugged Doc, an' sent word to Meeker to come up if he wasn't scared. He's come, an' now I'll have to lick two more. If they push me I'll shoot to kill!"

The H2 foreman rode ahead of his companion and stopped when fifty yards from the alert line-rider. Pushing his sombrero back on his head, he lost no time in skirmishing. "Did you chase my broncho-buster out of yore valley, cut his face with yore quirt, an' shoot Doc? Did you send word to me that you'd kill me if I showed myself?"

"Was you ever an auctioneer," calmly asked Hopalong, "or a book agent?"

"What's that got to do with it?" Meeker demanded. "You heard what I said."

"I don't know nothing about yore broncho-buster, taking one thing at a time, which is proper."

"What! You didn't drive him out, or cut him?"

"No; why?" asked Hopalong, chuckling.

"He says you did-an' somebody quirted him."

"He's loco-he wasn't in th' valley," Hopalong replied. "Think he could get in that valley? Him, or any other man we didn't want in?"

"You're devilish funny!" retorted Meeker, riding slowly forward, followed by his companion, who began to edge away from his foreman. "Since you are so exact, did you chase him off yore range an' push him over th' line at th' point of yore gun?"

"You've got me. Better not come too close-my cayuse don't like gettin' crowded."

"That's all right," Meeker retorted, not heeding the warning. "Do you mean to tell me you don't know? Yore name's Cassidy, ain't it?" he asked, angrily, his determination to avoid fighting rapidly becoming lost.

"That's my own, shore 'nuf name," Hopalong answered, and then: "Do you mean that cross-eyed, bone-yard of a yellow-faced Greaser I caught stealing our range?"

"Yes!" snapped Meeker, stopping again.

"Why didn't you say so, then, 'stead of calling him yore broncho-buster?" Hopalong demanded. "How do I know who yore broncho-buster is? I don't know what every land pirate does in this country."

"Then you shot Doc-do you know who I mean this time?" sarcastically asked the H2 foreman.

"Oh, shore. He didn't get his gun out quick enough when he went after it, did he? Any more I can tell you before I begins to say things, too?"

Meeker, angered greatly by Hopalong's contemptuous inflection and the reckless assertiveness of his every word and look, began to ride to describe a circle around the Bar-20 puncher, Curley going the other way.

"You said you'd kill me when you saw me, didn't you, you —"

Hopalong was backing away so as to keep both men in front of him, alert, eager, and waiting for the signal to begin his two-handed shooting. "I ain't a whole lot deaf —I can hear you from where you are. You better stop, for I've ridden out of tighter holes than this, an' you'll shore get a pass to h —l if you crowd me too much!"

> Adown th' road, an' gun in hand,
> Comes Whiskey Bill, mad Whiskey Bill —

This fragment of song floated out of a chaparral about twenty yards behind Hopalong, who grinned pleasantly when he heard it. Now he knew where Johnny was, and now he had the whip hand without touching his guns; while the youngster was not in sight he was all the more dangerous, since he presented no target. Johnny knew this and was greatly pleased thereby, and he was more than pleased by the way Hopalong had been talking.

The effect of the singing was instant and marked on Meeker and his companion, for they not only stopped suddenly and swore, but began to back away, glancing around in an endeavor to locate the joker in the deck. This they failed to do because Johnny was far too wise to advertise his exact whereabouts. Meeker looked at Curley and Curley looked at Meeker, both uneasy and angry.

"As I was sayin' before th' concert began," Hopalong remarked, laughing shortly, "it's a pass to h —l if you crowd me too much. Now, Meeker, you'll listen to me an' I'll tell you what I didn't have time to say before: I told that shifty-eyed mud-image of a Greaser that th' next herd of yourn to cross th' line should be brought in by you, 'less you was scared to run th' risks yore men had to take. He said you'd kill me for that message, an' I told him you knew where you could find me. Now about Doc: When a man pulls a gun on me he wants to be quicker than *he* was or he'll shore get hurt. I could 'a killed him just as easy as to plug his gun arm, an' just as easy as I could 'a plugged both of you if you pulled on me. You came up here looking for my scalp an' if you still wants it I'll go away from th' song bird in the chaparral an' give you th' chance. I'd ruther let things stay as they are, though if you wants, I'll take both you an' Curley, half-mile run together, with Colts."

"No, I didn't come up here after your scalp, but I got mad after I found you. How long is this going to last? I won't stand for it much longer, nohow."

"You'll have to see Buck. I'm obeyin' orders, which are to hold th' line against you, which I'll do."

"H'm!" replied Meeker, and then: "Do you know my girl?"

Hopalong thought quickly. "Why, I've seen her ridin' around some. But why?"

"She says she knows you," persisted Meeker, frowning.

The frown gave Hopalong his cue, but he hardly knew what to say, not knowing what she had said about it.

"Hey, you!" he suddenly cried to Curley. "Keep yore hand from that gun!"

"I didn't —"

"You're lying! Any more of that an' I'll gimlet you!"

"What in h —l are you doing, Curley?" demanded Meeker, the girl question out of his mind instantly. He had been looking closely at Hopalong and didn't know that Curley was innocent of any attempt to use his Colt.

"I tell —"

"Get out of here! I've wasted too much time already. Go home, where that gun won't worry you. You, too, Meeker! Bring an imitation bad-man up here an' sayin' you didn't want my scalp! Flit!"

"I'll go when I'm d — —d good and ready!" retorted Meeker, angry again. "You're too blasted bossy, you are!" he added, riding towards the man who had shot Doc.

A-looking for some place to land — —

floated out of the chaparral and he stiffened in the saddle and stopped.

"Come on, Curley! We can't lick pot-shooters. An' let that gun alone!"

"D —n it! I tell you I wasn't going for my gun!" Curley yelled.

"Get out of here!" blazed Hopalong, riding forward.

They rode away slowly, consulting in low voices. Then the foreman turned and looked back. "You better be careful how you shoot my punchers! They ain't all like Doc, an' they ain't all Greasers, neither."

"Then you're lucky," Hopalong retorted. "You keep yore cows on yore side an' we won't hurt none of yore outfit."

When they had gone Hopalong wheeled to look for Johnny and saw him crawling out of a chaparral, dragging a rifle after him. He capered about, waving the rifle and laughing with joy and Hopalong had to laugh with him. When they were rid of the surplus of the merriment Johnny patted the rifle. "Reckon they was shore up against a marked deck that time! Did you see 'em stiffen when I warbled? Acted like they had roped a puma an' didn't know what to do with it. Gee, it was funny!"

"You're all right, Kid," laughed Hopalong. "It was yore best play-you couldn't 'a done better."

"Shore," replied Johnny. "I had my sights glued to Curley's shirt pocket, an' he'd been plumb disgusted if he'd tried to do what you said he did. I couldn't 'a missed him with a club at that range. I nearly died when you pushed Meeker's girl question up that blind canyon. It was a peach of a throw, all right. Bet he ain't remembered yet that he didn't get no answer to it. We're going to have some blamed fine times down here before everything is settled, ain't we?"

"I reckon so, Kid. I'm going to leave you now an' look around by West Arroyo. You hang around th' line."

"All right-so long."

"Can you catch yore cayuse?"

"Shore I can; he's hobbled," came the reply from behind a spur of the chaparral. *"Stand still, you hen!* All right, Hoppy."

Johnny cantered away and, feeling happy, began, singing:

> Adown th' road, an' gun in hand,
> Comes Whiskey Bill, mad Whiskey Bill;
> A-looking for some place to land
> Comes Whiskey Bill.
> An' everybody'd like to be
> Ten miles away behind a tree
> When on his joyous, achin' spree
> Starts Whiskey Bill.

> Th' times have changed since you made love,
> Oh, Whiskey Bill, oh, Whiskey Bill;
> Th' happy sun grinned up above
> At Whiskey Bill.
> An' down th' middle of th' street
> Th' sheriff comes on toe-in feet,
> A-wishing for one fretful peek
> At Whiskey Bill.

> Th' cows go grazin' o'er th' lea —
> Pore Whiskey Bill, pore Whiskey Bill;
> An' aching thoughts pour in on me
> Of Whiskey Bill.
> Th' sheriff up an' found his stride,
> Bill's soul went shootin' down th' slide —
> How are things on th' Great Divide,
> Oh, Whiskey Bill?

Chapter VIII
On the Edge of the Desert

Thunder Mesa was surrounded by almost impenetrable chaparrals, impenetrable to horse and rider except along certain alleys, but not too dense for a man on foot. These stretched away on all sides as far as the eye could see and made the desolate prospect all the more forbidding. It rose a sheer hundred feet into the air, its sides smooth rock and affording no footing except a narrow, precarious ledge which slanted up the face of the southern end, too broken and narrow to permit of a horse ascending, but passable to a man.

The top of the mesa was about eight acres in extent and was rocky and uneven, cut by several half-filled fissures which did not show on the walls. Uninviting as the top might be considered it had one feature which was uncommon, for the cataclysm of nature which had caused this mass of rock to tower above the plain had given to it a spring which bubbled out of a crack in the rock and into a basin cut by itself; from there it flowed down the wall and into a shallow depression in the rock below, where it made a small water hole before flowing through the chaparrals, where it sank into the sand and became lost half a mile from its source.

At the point where the slanting ledge met the top of the mesa was a hut built of stones and adobe, its rear wall being part of a projecting wall of rock. Narrow, deep loopholes had been made in the other walls and a rough door, massive and tight fitting, closed the small doorway. The roof, laid across cedar poles which ran from wall to wall, was thick and flat and had a generous layer of adobe to repel the rays of the scorching sun. Placed as it was the hut overlooked the trail leading to it from the plain, and should it be defended by determined men, assault by that path would be foolhardy.

On the plain around the mesa extended a belt of sparse grass, some hundreds of feet wide at the narrowest point and nearly a mile at the widest, over which numerous rocks and bowlders and clumps of chaparral lay scattered. On this pasture were about three score cattle, most of them being yearlings, but all bearing the brand HQQ and a diagonal ear cut. These were being watched by a careless cowboy, although it was belittling their scanty intelligence to suppose that they would leave the water and grass, poor as the latter was, to stray off onto the surrounding desert.

At the base of the east wall of the mesa was a rough corral of cedar poles set on end, held together by rawhide strips, which, put on green, tightened with the strength of steel cables when dried by the sun. In its shadow another man watched the cattle while he worked in a desultory way at repairing a saddle. Within the corral a man was bending over a cow while two others held it down. Its feet were tied and it was panting, wild-eyed and frightened. The man above it stepped to a glowing fire a few paces away and took from it a hot iron, with which he carefully traced over the small brand already borne by the animal. With a final flourish he stepped back, regarding the work with approval, and thrust the iron into the sand. Taking a knife from his pocket he trimmed the V notch in its ear to the same slanting cut seen on the cattle outside on the pasture. He tossed the bit of cartilage from him, stepping back and nodding to his companions, who loosened the ropes and leaped back, allowing the animal to escape.

Shaw, who had altered the H2 brand, turned to one of the others and laughed heartily. "Good job, eh Manuel? Th' H2 won't know their cow now!"

Manuel grinned. *"Si, si*; eet ees!" he cried. He was cook for the gang, a bosom friend of Benito and Antonio, slight, cadaverous, and as shifty-eyed as his friends. In his claw-like fingers he held a husk cigarette, without which he was seldom seen. He spoke very little but watched always, his eyes usually turned eastward. He seemed to be almost as much afraid of the east as Cavalry was of the west, where the desert lay. He ridiculed Cavalry's terror of the desert and explained why the east was to be feared the more, for the eastern danger rode horses and could come to them [Transcriber's note: Text seems to be missing here in the original.] "Hope 'Tony fixes up that line war purty soon, eh, Cavalry?" remarked Shaw, suddenly turning to the third man in the group.

Cavalry was staring moodily towards the desert and did not hear him.

"Cavalry! Get that desert off yore mind! Do you want to go loco? Who's going to take th' next drive an' bring back th' flour, you or Clausen?"

"It's Clausen's turn next."

Manuel slouched away and began to climb the slanting path up the mesa. Shaw watched him reflectively and laughed. "There he goes again. Beats th' devil how scared he is, spending most of his time on th' lookout. Why, he's blamed near as scared of them punchers as you are of that skillet out yonder."

"We ain't got no kick, have we?" retorted Cavalry. "Ain't he looking out for us at th' same time?"

"I don't know about that," Shaw replied, frowning. "I ain't got no love for Manuel. If he saw 'em coming an' could get away he'd sneak off without saying a word. It'd give him a chance to get away while we held 'em."

"We'll see him go, then; there's only one way down."

"Oh, th' devil with him!" Shaw exclaimed. "What do you think of th' chances of startin' that range war?"

"From what th' Greaser says it looks good."

"Yes. But he'll get caught some day, or night, an' pay for it with his life."

Cavalry shrugged his shoulders. "I reckon so; but he's only a Greaser," he said, coldly. "I'd ruther they'd get him out there than to follow him here. If he goes, I hope it's sudden, so he won't have time to squeal."

"He's a malignant devil, an' he hates that H2 outfit like blazes," replied Shaw. "An' now he's got a pizen grudge agin' th' Bar-20. He might let his hate get th' upper hand an' start in to square things; if he does that he'll over-reach, an' get killed."

"I reckon so; but he's clever as th' devil hisself."

"Well, if he gets too big-headed out here Hall will take care of him, all right," Shaw laughed.

"I don't like th' Greasers he's saddled us with," Cavalry remarked. "There's Manuel an' Benito. One of 'em is here all th' time an' close to you, too, if you remember. Then he's going to put two or three on th' range; why?"

"Suspects we'll steal some of his share, I reckon. An' if he gets in trouble with us they'll be on his side. Oh, he's no fool."

"If he 'tends to business an' forgets his grudges it'll be a good thing for us. That Bar-20 has got an awful number of cows. An' there's th' H2, an' th' other two up north."

"We've tackled th' hardest job first-th' Bar-20," replied Shaw, laughing. "I used to know some fellers what said that outfit couldn't be licked. They died trying to prove themselves liars."

"Wonder how much money 'Tony totes around on him?" asked Cavalry.

"Not much; he's too wise. He's cached it somewhere. Was you reckonin' on takin' it away from him at th' end?"

"No, no. I just wondered what he did with it."

The man at the gate looked up. "Here comes 'Tony."

Shaw and his companion rode forward to meet him.

"What's up?" cried Shaw.

"I have started th' war," Antonio replied, a cruel smile playing over his sharp face. "They'll be fightin' purty soon."

"That's good," responded Shaw. "Tell us about it."

Antonio, with many gestures and much conceit, told of the trick he had played on Hopalong, and he took care to lose no credit in the telling. He passed lightly over the trouble between Doc and the Bar-20 puncher, but intimated that he had caused it. He finished by saying: "You send to th' same place to-morrow an' Benito'll have some cows for you. They'll soon give us our chance, an' it'll be easy then."

"Mebby it will be easy," replied Shaw, "but that rests with you. You've got to play yore cards plumb cautious. You've done fine so far, but if you ain't careful you'll go to h —l in a hurry an' take us with you. You can't fool 'em all th' time, for someday they'll get suspicious an' swap ideas. An' when they do that it means fight for us."

Antonio smiled and thought how easy it might be, if the outfits grew suspicious and he learned of it in time, to discover tracks and other things and tell Meeker he was sure there was organized rustling and that all tracks pointed to Thunder Mesa. He could ride across the border before any of his partners had time to confess and implicate him. But he assured Shaw that he would be careful, adding: "No, I won't make no mistakes. I hate 'em all too much to grow careless."

"That's just where you'll miss fire," the other rejoined. "You'll pamper yore grouch till you forget everything else. You better be satisfied to get square by taking their cows."

"Don't worry about that."

"All right. Here's yore money for th' last herd," he said, digging down into his pocket and handing the Mexican some gold coins. "You know how to get more."

Antonio took the money, considered a moment and then pocketed it, laughing. "Good! But I mus' go back now. I won't be out here again very soon; it's too risky. Send me my share by Benito," he called over his shoulder as he started off.

The two rustlers watched him and Cavalry shook his head slowly. "I'm plumb scairt he'll bungle it. If he does we'll get caught like rats in a trap."

"If we're up there we can hold off a thousand," Shaw replied, looking up the wall.

"Here comes Hall," announced the man at the gate.

The newcomer swept up and leaped from his hot and tired horse. "I found them other ranches are keeping their men ridin' over th' range an' along th' trails —I near got caught once," he reported. "We'll have to be careful how we drives to th' construction camps."

"They'll get tired watchin' after a while," replied the leader. "'Tony was just here."

"I don't care if he's in h —l," retorted Hall. "He'll peach on us to save his mangy skin, one of these days."

"We've got to chance it."

"Where's Frisco?"

"Down to Eagle for grub to tide us over for a few days."

"Huh!" exclaimed Hall. "Everything considered we're goin' to fight like th' devil out here someday. Down to Eagle!"

"We can fight!" retorted Shaw. "An' if we has to run for it, there's th' desert."

"I'd ruther die right here fighting than on that desert," remarked Cavalry, shuddering. "When I go I want to go quick, an' not be tortured for 'most a week." He had an insistent and strong horror of that gray void of sand and alkali so near at hand and so far across. He was nervous and superstitious, and it seemed always to be calling him. Many nights he had awakened in a cold sweat because he had dreamed it had him, and often it was all he could do to resist going out to it.

Shaw laughed gratingly. "You don't like it, do you?"

Hall smiled and walked towards the slanting trail.

"Why, it ain't bad," he called over his shoulder.

"It's an earthly hell!" Cavalry exclaimed. He glanced up the mesa wall. "We can hold that till we starve, or run out of cartridges-then what?"

"You're a calamity howler!" snapped Shaw. "That desert has wore a saddle sore on yore nerves somethin' awful. Don't think about it so much! It can't come to you, an' you ain't going to it," he laughed, trying to wipe out the suggestion of fear that had been awakened in him by the thought of the desert as a place of refuge. He had found a wanderer, denuded of clothes, sweating blood and hopelessly mad one day when he and Cavalry had ridden towards the desert; and the sight of the unfortunate's dying agonies had remained with him ever since. "We ain't going to die out here-they won't look for us where they don't think there's any grass or water."

Fragments of Manuel's song floated down to them as they strode towards the trail, and reassured that all would be well, their momentary depression was banished by the courage of their hearts.

The desert lay beyond, quiet; ominous by its very silence and inertia; a ghastly, malevolent aspect in its every hollow; patient, illimitable, scorching; fascinating in its horrible calm, sinister, forbidding, hellish. It had waited through centuries-and was still waiting, like the gigantic web of the Spider of Thirst.

Chapter IX

Hopalong Cassidy had the most striking personality of all the men in his outfit; humorous, courageous to the point of foolishness, eager for fight or frolic, nonchalant when one would expect him to be quite otherwise, curious, loyal to a fault, and the best man with a Colt in the Southwest, he was a paradox, and a puzzle even to his most intimate friends. With him life was a humorous recurrence of sensations, a huge pleasant joke instinctively tolerated, but not worth the price cowards pay to keep it. He had come onto the range when a boy and since that time he had laughingly carried his life in his open hand, and although there had been many attempts to snatch it he still carried it there, and just as recklessly.

Quick in decisions and quick to suspect evil designs against him and his ranch, he was different from his foreman, whose temperament was more optimistic. When Buck had made him foreman of the line riders he had no fear that Meeker or his men would take many tricks, for his faith in Hopalong's wits and ability was absolute. He had such faith that he attended to what he had to do about the ranch house and did not appear on the line until he had decided to call on Meeker and put the question before him once and for all. If the H2 foreman did not admit the agreement and promise to abide by it then he would be told to look for trouble.

While Buck rode towards Lookout Peak, Hopalong dismounted at the line house perched on its top and found Red Connors seated on the rough bench by the door. Red, human firebrand both in hair and temper, was Hopalong's loyal chum-in the eyes of the other neither could do wrong. Red was cleaning his rifle, the pride of his heart, a wicked-shooting Winchester which used the Government cartridge containing seventy grains of powder and five hundred grains of lead. With his rifle he was as expert as his friend was with the Colt, and up to six hundred yards, its limit with accuracy, he could do about what he wished with it.

"Hullo, you," said Red, pleasantly. "You looks peevish."

"An' you look foolish. What you doing?"

"Minding my business."

"Hard work?" sweetly asked Hopalong, carelessly seating himself on the small wooden box which lay close to his friend.

"Hey, you!" cried Red, leaping up and hauling him away. "You bust them sights an' you'll be sorry! Ain't you got no sense?"

"Sights? What are you going to do with 'em?"

"Wear 'em 'round my neck for a charm! What'd you reckon I'd do with 'em!"

"Didn't know. I didn't think you'd put 'em on that thing," Hopalong replied, looking with contempt at his friend's rifle. "Honest, you ain't a-goin' to put 'em on that lead ranch, are you? You're like th' Indians-want a lot of shots to waste without re-loadin'."

"I ain't wasting no shots, an' I'm going to put sights on that lead ranch, too. These old ones are too coarse," Red replied, carefully placing the box out of danger. "Now you can sit down."

"Thanks; please can I smoke?"

Red grunted, pushed down the lever of the rifle, and began to re-assemble the parts, his friend watching the operation. When Red tried to slip the barrel into its socket Hopalong laughed and told him to first draw out the magazine, if he wanted to have any success.

The line foreman took a cartridge from the pile on the bench and compared it with one which he took from his belt, a huge, 45-caliber Sharps special, shooting five hundred and fifty grains of lead with one hundred and twenty grains of powder out of a shell over three inches long; a cartridge which shot with terrific force and for a great distance, the weight of the large ball assuring accuracy at long ranges. Beside this four-inch cartridge the Government ammunition appeared dwarfed.

"When are you going to wean yoreself from popping these musket caps, Red?" he asked, tossing the smaller cartridge away and putting his own back in his belt.

"Well, you've got gall!" snorted Red, going out for his cartridge. Returning with it he went back to work on his gun, his friend laughing at his clumsy fingers.

"Yore fingers are all thumbs, an' sore at that."

"Never mind my fingers. Have you seen Johnny around?"

"Yes; he was watching one of them new H2 Greasers. He'll go off th' handle one of these days, for he hates Greasers worse'n I do, an' that coffee face'll drive him to gun-play. He reminds me a whole lot of a bull-pup chained with a corral-ful of cats when there's Greasers around."

Red laughed and nodded. "Where's Lanky?"

"Johnny said he was at Number Four fixin' that saddle again. He ain't done nothin' for th' last month but fix it. Purty soon there won't be none of it left to fix."

"There certainly won't!"

"His saddle an' yore gun make a good pair."

"Let up about the gun. You can't say nothin' more about it without repeatin' yoreself."

"It's a sawed-off carbine. I'd ruther have a Spencer any day."

"You remind me a whole lot of a feller I once knowed," Red retorted.

"That so?" asked Hopalong, suspiciously. "Was he so nice?"

"No; he was a fool," Red responded, going into the house.

"Then that's where you got it, for they say it's catching."

Red stuck his head out of the door. "On second thought you remind me of another feller."

"You must 'a knowed some good people."

"An' he was a liar."

"Hullo, Hop Wah!" came from the edge of the hilltop and Hopalong wheeled to see Skinny Thompson approaching.

"What you doing?" Skinny asked, using his stock question for beginning a conversation.

"Painting white spots on pink elephants!"

"Where's Red?"

"In th' shack, rubbin' 'em off again."

"Johnny chased that Greaser off'n th' ranch," Skinny offered, grinning.

"Good for him!" cried Hopalong.

"Johnny's all right-here comes Buck," Red said, coming out of the house. "Johnny's with him, too. Hullo, Kid!"

"Hullo, Brick-top!" retorted Johnny, who did not like his nickname. No one treated him as anything but a boy and he resented it at times.

"Did he chase you far?" Hopalong queried.

"I'd like to see anybody chase me!"

Buck smiled. "How are things down here?"

Hopalong related what had occurred and the foreman nodded. "I'm going down to see Meeker-he's th' only man who can tell me what we're to look for. I don't want to keep so many men down here. Frenchy has got all he can handle, an' I want somebody up in Two. So long."

"Let me an' Red go with you, Buck," cried Hopalong.

"Me, too!" exclaimed Johnny, excitedly.

"You stay home, an' don't worry about me," replied the foreman, riding off.

"I don't like to see him go alone," Hopalong muttered. "He may get a raw deal down there. But if he does we'll wipe 'em off'n th' earth."

"Mamma! Look there!" softly cried Johnny, staring towards the other side of the plateau, where Mary Meeker rode past. Red and Skinny were astonished and Johnny and Hopalong pretended to be; but all removed their sombreros while she remained in sight. Johnny was watching Hopalong's face, but when Red glanced around he was staring over the hill.

"Gosh, ain't she a ripper!" he exclaimed softly.

"She is," admitted Skinny. "She shore is."

Hopalong rubbed his nose reflectively and turned to Red. "Did you ever notice how pretty a freckle is?"

Red stared, for he had only toleration for the fair sex, and his friend continued:

"Take a purty girl an' stick a freckle on her nose an' it sort of takes yore breath."

Red grinned. "I ain't never took a purty girl an' stuck a freckle on her nose, so I can't say."

Hopalong flushed at the laughter and Skinny cried, joyously: "She's got two of us already! Meeker's got us licked if he'll let her show herself once in a while. Oh, these young fellers! Nothing can rope 'em so quick as a female, an' th' purtier she is th' quicker she can do it."

A warning light came into Hopalong's eyes. "Nobody in this outfit'll go back on Buck for all th' purty women in th' world!"

"Good boy!" thought Johnny.

"We've got to watch th' Kid, just th' same," laughed Skinny.

"I'll knock yore head off!" cried Johnny. "You're sore 'cause you know you ain't got no chance with women while me an' Hoppy are around!"

Red looked critically at Hopalong and snickered. "If we've got to look like him to catch th' women, thank God we don't want 'em!"

"Is that so!" retorted Hopalong.

"Say," drawled Skinny. "Wouldn't th' Kid look nice hobbled with matrimony? That is, after he grows up."

"You go to th' devil!"

"Gee, Kid, you look bloodthirsty," laughed Red. "You can fool them Greasers easy if you looks like that."

"You go to," Johnny retorted, swinging into the saddle. "I'm going along th' line to see what's loose."

"I'll lick you when I see you again!" shouted Red, grinning.

Johnny turned and twirled his fingers at his red-haired friend. "Yah, you ain't man enough!"

"Johnny's gettin' more hungry for a fight every day," Hopalong remarked. "He's itching for one."

"So was you a few years back, an' you ain't changed none," replied Red. "You used to ride around looking for fights."

"To hear you talk, anybody'd think you was a Angel of Peace," Hopalong retorted.

"One's as bad as th' other, so shut up," Skinny remarked, going into the house for a drink.

Chapter X
Buck Visits Meeker

As Buck rode south he went over the boundary trouble in all its phases, and the more he thought about it the firmer his resolution grew to hold the line at any cost. He had gone to great expense and labor to improve the water supply in the valley and he saw no reason why the H2 could not do the same; and to him an agreement was an agreement, and ran with the land. What Meeker thought about it was not the question-the point at issue was whether or not the H2 could take the line and use the valley, and if they could they were welcome to it.

But while there was any possibility for a peaceable settlement it would be foolish to start fighting, for one range war had spread to alarming proportions and had been costly to life and property. Then there was the certainty that once war had begun, rustling would develop. But, be the consequences what they might, he would fight to the last to hold that which was rightfully his. He was not going to Meeker to beg a compromise, or to beg him to let the valley alone; he was riding to tell the H2 foreman what he could expect if he forced matters.

When he rode past the H2 corrals he was curiously regarded by a group of punchers who lounged near them, and he went straight up to them without heeding their frowns.

"Is Meeker here?"

"No, he ain't here," replied Curley, who was regarded by his companions as being something of a humorist.

"Where is he?"

"Since you asks, I reckon he's in th' bunk house," Curley replied. "Where he ought to be," he added, pointedly, while his companions grinned.

"That's wise," responded Buck. "He ought to stay there more often. I hope his cows will take after him. Much obliged for th' information," he finished, riding on.

"His cows an' his punchers'll do as they wants," asserted Curley, frowning.

"Excuse me. I reckoned *he* was boss around here," Buck apologized, a grim smile playing about his lips. "But you better change that 'will' to 'won't' when you mean th' valley."

"I mean *will!*" Curley retorted, leaping to his feet. "An' what's more, I ain't through with that game laig puncher of yourn, neither."

Buck laughed and rode forward again. "You have my sympathy, then," he called over his shoulder.

Buck stopped before the bunk house and called out, and in response to his hail Jim Meeker came and stood in the door.

The H2 foreman believed he was right, and he was too obstinate to admit that there was any side but his which should be considered. He wanted water and better grass, and both were close at hand. Where he had been raised there had been no boundaries, for it had been free grass and water, and he would not and could not see that it was any different on his new range. He had made no agreement, and if one had been made it did not concern him; it concerned only those who had made it. He did not buy the ranch from the old owners, but from a syndicate, and there had been nothing said about lines or restrictions. When he made any agreements he lived up to them, but he did not propose to observe those made by others.

"How'dy, Meeker," said Buck, nodding.

"How'dy, Peters; come in?"

"I reckon it ain't worth while. I won't stay long," Buck replied. "I came down to tell you that some of yore cows are crossing our line. They're gettin' worse every day."

"That so?" asked Meeker, carelessly.

"Yes."

"Um; well, what's th' reason they shouldn't? An' what is that 'line,' that we shouldn't go over it?"

"Dawson, th' old foreman of th' Three Triangle, told you all about that," Buck replied, his whole mind given to the task of reading what sort of a man he had to deal with. "It's our boundary; an' yourn."

"Yes? But I don't recognize no boundary. What have they got to do with me?"

"It has this much, whether you recognize it or not: It marks th' north limit of yore grazin'. *We* don't cross it."

"Huh! You don't have to, while you've got that crick."

"We won't have th' crick, nor th' grass, either, if you drive yore cows on us. That valley is our best grazing, an' it ain't in th' agreement that you can eat it all off."

"What agreement?"

"I didn't come down here to tell you what you know," Buck replied, slowly. "I came to tell you to keep yore Greasers an' yore cows on yore own side, that's whatever."

"How do you know my cows are over there?"

"How do I know th' sun is shining?"

"What do you want me to do?" Meeker asked, leaning against the house and grinning.

"Hold yore herds where they belong. Of course some are shore to stray over, but strays don't count —I ain't talkin' about them."

"Well, I've punched a lot of cows in my day," replied Meeker, "an' over a lot of range, but I never seen no boundary lines afore. An' nobody ever told me to keep on one range, if they knowed me. I've run up against a wire fence or two in th' last few years, but they didn't last long when I hit 'em."

"If you want to know what a boundary line looks like I can show you. There's a plain trail along it where my men have rode for years."

"So you say; but I've got to have water."

"You've got it; twenty miles of river. An' if you'll put down a well or two th' Jumping Bear won't go dry."

"I don't know nothing about wells," Meeker replied. "Natural water's good enough for me without fooling with wet holes in th' ground."

"No; but, by G-d, yo're willin' enough to use them what I put down! Do you think I spent good time an' money just to supply *you* with water? Why don't you get yore own, 'stead of hoggin' mine!"

"There's water enough, an' it ain't yourn, neither."

"It's mine till somebody takes it away from me, an' you can gamble on that."

"Oh, I reckon you'll share it."

"I reckon I won't!" Buck retorted. "Look here; my men have held that range for many years against all kinds of propositions an' didn't get pushed into th' discard once; an' they'll go right on holding it. Hell has busted loose down here purty often during that time, but we've allus roped an' branded it; an' we hain't forgot how!"

"Well, I don't want no trouble, but I've got to use that water, an' my men are some hard to handle."

"You'll find mine worse to handle before you gets through," Buck rejoined. "They're restless now, an' once they start, all h —l can't stop 'em." Meeker started to reply, but Buck gave him no chance. "Do you know why I haven't driven you back by force? It wasn't because I figgered on what *you'd* do. It was on account of th' rustling that'll blossom on this range just as soon as we get too busy to watch things. That's why, but if yo're willing to take a chance with cow thieves, I am."

"I'm willing. I've got to have water on my northwest corner," Meeker replied. "An' I'm going to have it! If my cows get on yore private reservation, it's up to you to drive 'em off; but I wouldn't be none hasty doing it if I was you. You see, my men are plumb touchy."

"That's final, is it?"

"I ain't never swallered nothing I ever said."

"All right. I can draw on forty men to fill up gaps, an' I'll do it before I let any range jumper cheat me out of what's mine. When you buck that line, come ready for trouble."

"Yore line'll burn you before you get through pampering it," retorted Meeker, angrily.

"So? We'll pamper anybody that tries to keep us from pampering our line. If there are any burns they'll not be salved in *our* bunk house. So long."

Meeker laughed, stretched, and slipped his thumbs in the arm-holes of his vest, watching the Bar-20 foreman ride away. Then he frowned and snapped his fingers angrily. "We'll keep you busy on yore 'line' when I get ready to play th' cards I'm looking for!" he exclaimed. "Th' gall of him! Telling me I can't pasture where I wants! By G-d, I'll be told I'm using his sunlight an' breathing his air!"

He stepped forward. "Curley! Chick! Dan!"

A moment later the three men stood before him.

"What is it, Jim?" asked Curley.

"You fellers drive north to-morrow. Pick up th' stragglers an' herd 'em close to that infernal line. Don't drive 'em over till I tell you, but don't let none stray south again; savvy? If they want to stray north it's none of our business."

"Good!"

"Fine!"

"That's th' way to talk!"

"Don't start nothing, but if trouble comes yore way take care of yoreselves," Meeker remarked. "I'm telling you to herd up on our north range, that's all."

"Shore; we'll do it!" laughed Curley.

"Is that house on th' peak guarded?" Meeker asked.

"Somebody's there most of th' time," replied Dan Morgan.

"Yes; it's their bunk house now," explained Chick.

"All right; don't forget to-morrow."

Chapter XI
Three is a Crowd

When Buck reached the line on his return Hopalong was the first man he met and his orders were to the point: "Hold this line till h —l freezes, drive all H2 cows across it, an' don't start a fight; but be shore to finish any that zephyrs up. Keep yore eyes open."

Hopalong grinned and replied that he would hold the line that long and then skate on the ice, that any cow found trying to cross would get indignant, and that he and trouble were old friends. Buck laughed and rode on.

"Red Eagle, old cayuse!" cried the line rider, slapping the animal resoundingly. "We're shore ready!" And Red Eagle, to show how ready he was to resent such stinging familiarities, pitched viciously and bit at his rider's leg.

"Hit her up, old devil!" yelled Hopalong, grabbing his sombrero and applying the spurs. Red Eagle settled back to earth and then shot forward at top speed along the line trail, bucking as often as he could.

It was not long before Hopalong saw a small herd of H2 cows on Bar-20 land and he rode off to head them. When he got in front of the herd he wheeled and dashed straight at it, yelling and firing his Colt, the horse squealing and pitching at every jump.

"Ki-yi, yeow-eow-eow-eow!" he yelled, and the herd, terror-stricken, wheeled and dashed towards their ranch. He followed to the line and saw them meet and terrorize another herd, and he gleefully cried that it would be a "shore 'nuf stampede."

"Look at 'em go, old Skyrocket," he laughed. The horse began to pitch again but he soon convinced it that play time had passed.

"You old, ugly wart of a cayuse!" he cried, fighting it viciously as it reared and plunged and bit. "Don't you know I can lick four like you an' not touch leather! There, that's better. If you bite me again I'll kick yore corrugations in! But we made 'em hit th' high trail, didn't we, old hinge-back?"

He looked up and stiffened, feeling so foolish that he hardly knew enough to tear off his sombrero, for before him, sitting quietly in her saddle and looking clean through him, was Mary Meeker, a contemptuous firmness about her lips.

"Good-afternoon, Miss Meeker," he said, wondering how much she had seen and heard.

"I'll not spoil yore fun," she icily replied, riding away.

He stared after her until she had ridden around a chaparral and out of his sight, and he slammed his sombrero on the ground and swore.

"D —n th' luck!"

Then he spurred to overtake her and when he saw her again she was talking to Antonio, who was all smiles.

"Coffee-colored galoot!" Hopalong muttered, savagely. "I'll spill him all over hisself some day, th' squint-eyed mud-image! Th' devil with him, if he don't like my company he can amble."

He swept up to them, his hair stirred by the breeze and his right hand resting on the butt of his Colt. Antonio was talking when he arrived, but he had no regard for "Greasers" and interrupted without loss of time.

"Miss Meeker," he began, backing his horse so he could watch the Mexican. "I shore hope you ain't mad. Are you?"

She looked at him coldly, and her companion muttered something in Spanish; and found Hopalong's eyes looking into his soul, which hushed the Spanish.

"You talk United States if you've got anything to say, which you ain't," Hopalong commanded and then turned to the woman. "I'm shore sorry you heard me. I didn't think you was anywhere around."

"Which accounts for you terrorizing our cows an' calves," she retorted. "An' for trying to start a stampede."

Antonio stiffened at this, but did nothing because Hopalong was watching him.

"You ought to be ashamed of yoreself!" she cried, her eyes flashing and deep color surging into her cheeks. "You had no right to treat them calves that way, or to start a stampede!"

"I didn't try to start no stampede, honest," he replied, fascinated by the color playing across her face.

"You did!" she insisted, vehemently. "You may think it's funny to scare calves, but it ain't!"

"I was in a hurry," he replied, apologetically. "I shore didn't think nothing about th' calves. They was over on us an' I had to drive 'em back before I went on."

"You have no right to drive 'em back," she retorted. "They have every right to graze where th' grass is good an' where they can get water. They can't live without water."

"They shore can't," he replied in swift accord, as if the needs of cattle had never before crossed his mind. "But they can get it at th' river."

"You have no right to drive 'em away from it!"

"I ain't going to argue none with you, Miss," he responded. "My orders are to drive 'em back, which I'll do."

"Do you mean to tell me that you'll keep them from water?" she demanded, her eyes flashing again.

"It ain't my fault that yore men don't hold 'em closer to th' river," he replied. "There's water a-plenty there. Yore father's keeping 'em on a dry range."

"Don't say anything about my father," she angrily retorted. "He knows his business better'n you can tell it to him."

"I'm sorry if I've gone an' said anything to make you mad," he earnestly replied. "I just wanted to show you that I'm only obeying orders. I don't want to argue with you."

"I didn't come here to argue," she quickly retorted. "I don't want you to drive our calves so hard, that's all."

"I'll be plumb tender with 'em," he assured her, grinning. "An' I didn't try to scare that other herd, honest."

"I saw you trying to scare them just before you saw me."

"Oh!" he exclaimed, chuckling as he recalled his fight with Red Eagle. "That was all th' fault of this ornery cayuse. He got th' idea into his fool head that he could throw me, so me an' him had it out right there."

She had been watching his face while he spoke and she remembered that he had fought with his horse, and believed that he was telling the truth. Then, suddenly, the humorous side struck her and brought a smile to her face. "I'm sorry I didn't understand," she replied in a low voice.

"Then you ain't mad no more?" he asked eagerly.

"No; not a bit."

"I'm glad of that," he laughed, leaning forward. "You had me plumb scared to death."

"I didn't know I could scare a puncher so easy, 'specially you," she replied, flushing. "But where's yore sombrero?"

"Back where I throwed it," he grinned.

"Where you threw it?"

"Shore. I got sore when you rode away, an' didn't care much what happened," he replied, coolly. Then he transfixed the Mexican with his keen eyes. "If yo're so anxious to get that gun out, say so or do it," he said, slowly. "That's th' second time."

Mary watched them breathlessly, but Hopalong didn't intend to have any fighting in her presence.

"You let it alone before I take it away from you," he said. "An' I reckon you better pull out-you ain't needed around here. Go on, flit!"

Antonio glanced at Mary for orders and she nodded her head. "I don't need you; go."

Hopalong watched him depart and turned to his companion. "What's eating him, anyhow?"

"I don't know. I never saw him act that way before."

"H'm. I reckon I know; but he don't want to act that way again," he said, decisively. "Greasers are shore funny animals."

"All men are funny," she replied. "Th' idea of being scared by me when you ain't afraid of a man like him."

"That's a different kind of a scare, an' I never felt like that before. It made me want to kill somebody. I don't want you to get mad at me. I like you too much. You won't, will you?"

She smiled. "No."

"Never? No matter what happens?"

"Do you care?"

"Do I care! You know I do. Look at me, Mary!"

"No; don't come any nearer. I must go-good-bye."

"Don't go; let's ride around for a while."

"But 'Tony may tell Dad; an' if he does Dad'll come up here an' make trouble. No, I must go."

"Tell 'Tony I want to see him," he replied. "If he says anything I'll make him pay for it; an' he won't do it again."

"You mustn't do that! It would make things all th' worse."

"Will you come up again to-morrow?"

She laughed. "That'll be too soon, won't it?"

"Not by a blamed sight."

"Well, I don't know. Good-bye."

"Good-bye," he said, holding out his hand.

She gave him her hand and then tried to push him away. "No, no! No, I say! I won't come any more if you do that!"

Despite her struggles he drew her to him and kissed her again and again.

"I hate you! I hate you!" she cried, her face the color of fire. "What made you do it! You've spoiled everything, an' I'll never see you again! I hate you!" and she wheeled and galloped away.

He spurred in pursuit and when he had overtaken her he grasped her horse by the bridle and stopped her. "Mary! Don't be mad —I love you!"

"Will you let me go?" she demanded, her face crimson.

"Not till you say yo're not mad."

"Please let me go," she replied, looking in his eyes, "I'm not mad at you; but you mustn't do that again. Won't you let me go before some one sees us?"

He released her and she impulsively put her hand on his arm. "Look out-an' watch 'Tony," and she was gone.

"Yo're th' best girl ever rode a cayuse," he muttered, joyously. " 'Look out-an' watch 'Tony,' " he cried. "What do I care about that Greaser? I can clean out th' whole gang now. Just let 'em start something."

When he neared the place where his sombrero lay he saw Johnny in the act of picking it up, and Johnny might take a notion to make a race out of it before giving it up. "Hey, you!" Hopalong cried, dashing forward, "gimme that cover!"

"Come an' get it; I don't want it," Johnny retorted. "What made you lose it?"

"Fighting."

"Fighting! Fighting who?"

"Just fighting, Kid."

"Ah, come on an' tell me," begged Johnny. Then, like a shot: "Was it that Greaser?"

"Nope."

"Who was it?"

"None of yore business," laughed Hopalong, delighted to be able to tease him.

"All right!" Johnny cried. "You wait; th' boys will be glad to learn about you an' her!"

Hopalong's hand shot out and gripped his friend's shoulder. "Don't you say a word about it, do you hear?"

"Shore. I was only fooling," replied Johnny. "Think I tell them kind of things! Yo're a big fool, you are."

"I was too quick, Kid. I know yo're a thoroughbred. An' now I'll tell you who I was fighting. Its was Red Eagle. He got a fit of pitching, an' I had to take it out of him."

"I might 'a knowed it," responded Johnny, eying the tracks in the sand. "But I reckoned you might 'a had a run-in with that Greaser. I was saving him for myself."

"Why do you hate him so much more'n th' other Greasers?"

"Never mind that now. I'll tell you after I get him."

"Have you seen Buck since he came back?"

"No; why?"

Hopalong told him what the foreman had said and his friend grinned. "The good old days are coming back again, Hoppy!" he exulted. "Now I can kick th' shirt off'n that Greaser, can't I, if he gets gay?"

"If he don't kick yourn off first."

"I'd like to see him try it; or you, either! Mebbe you'd like to try it now?"

"Shoo, fly! Shoo, fly," laughed Hopalong.

"Where are you going now?" asked Johnny.

"Where I please."

"Shore. I knowed that. That's where you want to go," grinned Johnny. "But where do you want to go?"

"Where I can't go now."

"Ah, shut up! Come on. I'll go with you."

"Well, I'm going east to tell th' fellers what Buck said."

"Go ahead. I'm with you," Johnny said, wheeling.

"I didn't ask you to come."

"I didn't ask you to go," retorted Johnny. "Here," he said, holding out a cigar and putting another in his mouth. "Have a smoke; they're all right."

"Where the devil did you get 'em?"

"Up in Number Five."

"In Number Five!"

"Shore. Frenchy, th' son-o'-a-gun, had three of 'em hid over th' windy," Johnny explained. "I hooked 'em."

"So I reckoned; did you take 'em all?"

"Was you going up?"

"No; but did you?"

"Well, I looked good, but I didn't see none to leave."

"You wait till he finds it out," Hopalong warned.

"He won't do nothing," assured Johnny, easily. "Anyhow, yo're as guilty as me. He ain't got no right to cache cigars when we can't get to town for any. Besides, he's afraid of me."

"Scared of you! Oh, Lord, that's good!"

"Quit fooling an' get started," Johnny said, kicking his friend's horse.

"You behave, or I'll get that Greaser to lick you good," threatened Hopalong as he quieted Red Eagle.

"Huh! He don't like fights."

"How do you know?"

"Because my grub is his poison; get a-going."

They cantered eastward, driving back Meeker's cows whenever they were found too close to the line or over it, and it was not long before they made out Lanky riding towards them. He had not yet seen them and Johnny eagerly proposed that they prepare an ambush and scare him.

"He don't scare, you fool," replied Hopalong. "A joke is a joke, but there ain't no use getting shot at when you can't shoot back. No use getting killed for a lark."

"He might shoot, mightn't he," Johnny laughed. "I didn't think about that."

Lanky looked around, waved his hand and soon joined them. "I see yo're taking care of th' Kid, Hopalong. Hullo, Kid."

"Go to blazes!" snorted Johnny.

"Has he been a good boy, Hoppy?"

"No more'n usual. He's looking for Antonio."

"*Again?*" asked Lanky, grinning. "Ain't you found him yet?"

"Ah, go on. I'll find him when I want him," Johnny retorted.

When Lanky had heard Buck's orders he frowned.

"We'll hold it all right. Wait for Billy, he'll be along purty soon. I left him chasing some cows."

"Got yore saddle so it'll stay together for more'n ten minutes at a time?" asked Johnny.

"I bought Billy's old one," Lanky replied. "Got anything to say about it?"

Billy Williams, pessimist by nature and choice, rode up and joined them and, laughing and joking, they rode towards the Peak, to see if Buck had any further orders. But they had not gone far before Hopalong stopped and thought. "You go on. I'll stay out here an' watch things."

"I'm with you, Hoppy," Johnny offered. "You fellers go on; me an' Hopalong'll take care of th' line out here."

"All right," replied Lanky. "So long."

A few minutes later Johnny turned in his saddle. "Hey, Billy!" he shouted.

"What?"

"Has Lanky paid you for that saddle, yet?"

"Shore; why?"

"Oh, nothing. But yo're lucky."

Billy turned and said something to Lanky and they cantered on their way.

"Hey, Hoppy; don't you tell Frenchy about them cigars," Johnny suddenly remarked some time later.

Chapter XII
Hobble Burns and Sleepers

The western part of the Bar-20 ranch was poor range and but few cattle were to be found on it until Big Coulee had been reached. This portion of the ranch fed quite a large number of cattle, many of which were outlaws, but because of the heavy work demanded on the more fertile southern and eastern sections it was the custom with Buck to pay little attention to the Big Coulee herds; if a man rode up there once in a while he was satisfied. This time it was Skinny who was to look over the condition of affairs around Number Two, which was not far from Big Coulee.

Detouring here and there he took his own time and followed the general direction of the western line, and about four hours after he had quitted the Peak he passed line house Number Two and shortly afterward stopped on the rim of the coulee, a brush-grown depression of a score of acres in extent, in which was a pond covering half an acre and fed by springs on the bottom, its outlet being a deep gorge cut in the soft stone. Half a mile from the pond the small stream disappeared in the sand and was lost.

He rode through the coulee without seeing a single cow and an exploration lasting over an hour resulted no better. Beyond a bear track or two among the berry bushes he saw no signs of animal life. This did not disturb him because he took it for granted that the herds had wandered back to where the grass was better. Stopping at the line house to eat, he mounted and rode towards the hills to report to Hopalong.

Suddenly it struck him that he had seen no cow tracks in the mud around the water hole and he began to hunt for cattle. Using Pete's glasses constantly to sweep the plain for the missing herds, it was not until he had reached a point half-way to the Peak that his search was rewarded by seeing a calf far to the east of him. Watching it until it stood out boldly to his sight he followed an impulse and rode towards it to examine it at close range.

Upon getting near it he saw that it bore the V notch of the H2 cut in its ear, and that it was not branded. He thought it strange that an H2 "sleeper" should be so far from home, without a mother to lead it astray, and he roped it to look more closely at the notch. His opinion was that it had been done very recently, for the cartilage had not yet dried on the edges. Releasing the animal he mounted and started for the line, muttering to himself.

As he swung into the line trail he saw a lame cow limping around a thicket and he spurred forward, roped and threw it, this time giving no thought to the ears, for its brand was that of the Bar-20. He looked at the hocks and found them swollen and inflamed, and his experience told him that it had been done by hobbles. This, to him, explained why the calf was alone, and it gave him the choice of two explanations for the hobbling and the newly cut ear notch on the calf. Either the H2 was sleepering Bar-20 calves for their irons later on, or rustlers were at work. It seemed incredible that any H2 puncher should come that distance to make a few sleepers-but the herd had not been to the water hole! He was greatly wrought up and it was none the more pleasant to be unable to say where the blame lay. There was only one thing to do and that was to scout around and try to find a clue to the perpetrators-and, perhaps, catch the thieves at work. This proved to be unfruitful until he came to North Hill, where he found a cow dead from gunshot. He put spurs to his horse and rode straight for the Peak, which he reached as night fell and as Hopalong, Red, Pete, and Lanky were eating supper and debating the line conditions.

Skinny joined them and listened to the conversation, wordless, nodding or shaking his head at the points made. When he had finished eating he leaned back against his saddle and fumbled for tobacco and pipe, gazing reflectively into the fire, at which he spat. Hopalong turned in time to see the act and, knowing Skinny's peculiarities, asked abruptly: "What's on yore mind, Skinny?"

"Little piece of h —l," was the slow reply, and it gained the attention of the others at once. "I saw a H2 sleeper, up just above th' Bend and half way between it an' th' line."

"That so!" exclaimed Hopalong.

"Long way from home-starting in young to ramble," Red laughed. "Lazy trick, that sleeper-ing."

"This here calf had a brand new V —hadn't healed yet," Skinny remarked, lighting his pipe. "An' it didn't —*puff* —have no —*puff* —mother," he added, significantly.

"Huh, weaned, you chump-but that fresh V is shore funny."

"Go on, Skinny," ordered Hopalong, eagerly.

"I found its mother an hour later-hobble-burned an' limping; an' it wasn't no H2 cow, nei-ther; it was one of ourn."

"Rustling!" cried Hopalong.

"Th' H2 is doing it," contradicted Red, quickly.

"They wouldn't take a chance like that," replied Hopalong.

"There ain't no rule for taking chances," Red rejoined. "Some men'll gamble with h —l itself-you, for instance, in gun-play."

"What else?" demanded Hopalong of Skinny.

"That Big Coulee herd ain't up there, an' hain't been near th' water hole for so long th' mud's smooth around the edges of th' pond; kin savvy?"

"It's rustlers, by G-d!" cried Hopalong, looking triumphantly at Red.

"An' I found a dead cow-shot-on th' upper end of North Hill," Skinny added.

"H2!" Red shouted. "They're doing it!"

"Yes, likely; it was an H2 cow," Skinny placidly explained.

"Why in h —l can't you tell things in a herd, 'stead of stringin' 'em out like a stiff reata trailing to soften!" Red cried. "Yo're the damndest talker that ever opened a mouth!"

Skinny took the pipe from his mouth and looked at Red.

"I allus get it all out, don't I? What are you kicking about?"

"Yes, you do; like a five thousand herd filtering through a two-foot gate!"

"Mebby th' herd drifted to th' valley," Pete offered.

"Mebby nothing!" Red retorted. "Why, we can't drive 'em down here without 'em acting loco about it."

"Cows are shore fool animals," Pete suggested in defence.

"There's more than cows that are fool animals," Red snapped, while Skinny laughed to see Pete get his share.

Sixteen miles to the southeast of the Peak, Meeker sat on a soap box and listened, with the rest of his outfit, to what Curley was saying, —"an' when I got down a good ways south I found two young calves bellering for their maws. They was sleepers; an' an hour later I found them same maws bellering for them calves-they was limping a-plenty an' their hocks looked burned-hobble burns."

Meeker mused for a moment and then arose. "You ride that range regular, an' be cautious. Watch towards Eagle. If you catch any sons-of-skunks gamboling reckless, an' they can't explain why they are flitting over our range, shoot off yore gun accidental-there won't be no inquest."

Chapter XIII
Hopalong Grows Suspicious

The eastern sky grew brighter and the dim morning light showed a group of men at breakfast on the Peak. They already had been given their orders and as soon as each man finished eating he strode off to where his horse was picketed with the others, mounted, and rode away. Pete had ridden in late the night before and was still sleeping in the house, Hopalong not wishing to awaken him until it was absolutely necessary.

Red Connors, riding back to the house from the horse herd, drew rein for a final word. "I'm going out to watch that unholy drift of Meeker's cows, just this side of th' half-way point. They was purty thick last night when I rode in. I told Johnny to keep on that part of th' line, for I reckon things will get too crowded for one man to handle. Th' two of us can take care of 'em, all right. You knows where you can find us if you need us."

"I don't like that drift, but I'll stay here an' give Pete an hour more sleep," Hopalong replied. "Buck didn't know just when he'd be down again, but I'm looking for him before noon, just th' same."

"Well, me an' Johnny'll stop th' drift. So long," and Red cantered away, whistling softly.

Hopalong kicked out the fire and walked restlessly around the plateau, puzzled by the massing of the H2 cows along the line. The play was obvious enough on its face, for it meant that Meeker, tired of inaction, had decided to force the issue by driving into the valley. But Hopalong, suspicious to a degree, was not satisfied with that solution.

On more than one occasion he had searched past the obvious and found deeper motives, and to this ferment of thought he owed his life many times. He, himself, essentially a schemer and trusting no one but the members of his outfit, accused others of scheming and bent his mind to outwit them. Buck often irritated him greatly, for the foreman, optimistic and believing all men honest until they proved to be otherwise, held that Meeker thought himself to be in the right and so was justified in his attempt to use the valley. Hopalong believed that Meeker was not square, that he knew he had no right to the valley and was trying to steal range; he maintained that the wiser way was to believe all men crooked and put the burden on them of proving otherwise; then he was prepared for anything.

A better cow-man than Buck Peters never lived; he knew the cattle industry thoroughly, was honest, fair, and fearless, maintained an even temper and tried to avoid fighting until the last ditch had been reached. But it was an indisputable fact that Hopalong Cassidy had proved himself to be the best man on the ranch when danger threatened. He grasped situations quickly and clearly and his companions looked to him for suggestions when the sky was clouded by impending conflict. Buck realized that his line-foreman was eminently better qualified to handle the skirmish line than himself, that Hopalong could carry out things which would fall flat if any one else attempted them. Back of Buck's confidence was the pleasing knowledge that no man had ever yet got in the first shot against Hopalong on an "even break," and that when his puncher's gun exploded it was all over; this is why Hopalong could, single-handed, win out in any reasonable situation.

While Hopalong turned the matter over in his mind he thought he saw a figure move among the chaparrals far to the south and he whipped out his glasses, peering long and steadily at the place. Then he put them away and laughed softly. "You can't fool me, by G-d! I'll let you make yore play-an' if Pete don't kill a few of you I'm a liar. Here are th' shells-pick out th' pea."

Returning to the house he shook Pete. "Hey, get up!"

Pete bounded up, wide awake in an instant. "Yes?"

"Put on yore clothes an' come outside a minute," he ordered, going out.

Pete finished buttoning his vest when he joined his friend, who was pointing south. "Pete, they're playing for this house, an' I can't stay-Red an' Johnny may need me any minute. Down there a Greaser is watching this house. Meeker is massing his cows along th' line for two reasons; he's trying to draw us away from here so he can get in, an' he's going to push over th' line if he falls down here. You stay in that shack. Don't leave it for a second, understand? Stop anybody that comes up here if you have to kill him. But don't leave this house for nothing, savvy?"

"Go ahead. I savvy."

Hopalong vaulted to his saddle and started away. "I'll get somebody to help you as soon as I can," he called.

"Don't need anybody!" Pete shouted, going inside and barring the door.

Hopalong was elated by the way he had forestalled Meeker, and also because it was Pete who guarded the house. He knew his companions only as a man can know friends with whom he has lived for nearly a score of years. Red was too good a fighter to be cooped up while trouble threatened in the open; Johnny, rash and hot-tempered, could be tempted to leave the house to indulge in personal combat if taunted enough, and he, too, was too good a man in a *mêlée* to remain on the Peak. The man for the house was Pete, for he was accurate enough for that short range, he was unemotional and did not do much thinking for himself when it ran counter to his instructions; he had been told to stay in the house and hold it, and that, Hopalong felt certain, he would do.

"Pete'll hold 'em with one leg in th' air if they happen to be taking a step when he sees 'em," he laughed.

But Pete was to be confronted with a situation so unexpected and of such a nature that for once in his life he was going to forget orders-and small blame to him.

Chapter XIV
The Compromise

It was night and on the H2 sickly, yellow lights gleamed from the ranch houses. From the bunk house came occasional bursts of song, the swinging choruses thundering out on the night air, deep-toned and strong. In the foreman's quarters the clatter of dishes was soon stilled and shortly afterward the light in the kitchen could be seen no more. A girl stood in the kitchen door for a moment and then, singing, went inside and the door closed. The strumming of a guitar and much laughter came from Antonio's shack, for now he had Juan and Sanchez to help him pass the time.

Meeker emerged from a corral, glanced above him for signs of the morrow's weather, and then stood and gazed at the Mexican's shack. Turning abruptly on his heel he strode to the bunk house and smiled grimly as the chorus roared out, for he had determined upon measures which might easily change the merriment to mourning before another day passed. He had made up his mind to remain inactive no longer, but to put things to the test-his outfit and himself against the Bar-20.

He entered the building and slamming the door shut behind him, waited until the chorus was finished. When the last note died away he issued his orders for the next day, orders which pleased his men, who had chafed even more than he under the galling inaction, since they did not thoroughly understand the reasons for it.

"I had them cows herded up north for th' last three days so they'd be ready for us when we wanted 'em," he said, and then leaped at the door and jerked it open, peering about outside. The guitar was still strumming in the Mexican's shack and he recognized the voices of three in the singing. Turning, he beckoned Doc Riley to him and the two stepped outside, closing the door behind them. Great noise broke out within the house as his orders were repeated and commented on. Meeker and Doc moved to the corner of the building and consulted earnestly for several minutes, the foreman gesticulating slowly.

"But Juan said they had a man to guard it," Doc replied.

"Yes; he told me," Meeker responded. "I'm going to fix that before I go to bed-we've got to coax him out on some excuse. Once we get him out of th' house we can cover him, an' th' rest'll be easy. I won't be able to be with you —I'll have to stay outside where I can move around an' look out for th' line trouble, an' where they can see me. But you an' Jack can hold it once you get in. By G-d, you *must* get in, an' you *must* hold it!"

"We'll do it if it's possible."

"That's th' way to talk. Th' boys seem pleased about it," Meeker laughed, listening to the joy loose in the house.

"Pleased! They're tickled plumb to death," Doc cried. "They've got so sore about having to keep their guns quiet that when they cut loose-well, something's due to happen."

"I don't want that if there's any other way," Meeker replied earnestly. "If this thing can be done without wholesale slaughter we've got to do it that way. Remember, Doc, this whole country is backing Peters. He's got thirteen men now, an' he can call on thirty more in two days. Easy is th' way, easy."

"I'll spend th' next hour pounding that into their hot heads," Doc replied. "They're itching for a chance to square up for everything. They're some sore, been so for a couple of days, about that line house being guarded-they get sore plumb easy now, you know."

"Well, good-night, Doc."

"Good-night, Jim."

Meeker went towards his own house and as he neared the kitchen door a deep-throated wolf-hound bayed from the kennels, inciting a clamorous chorus from the others. Meeker shouted and the noise changed to low, deep, rumbling growls which soon became hushed. Chains rattled over wood and the fierce animals returned to their grass beds to snarl at each other. The frightened crickets took up their song again and poured it on the silence of the night.

The foreman opened the door and strode through the kitchen and into the living room, his eyes squinting momentarily because of the light. His daughter was sitting in a rocking chair, sewing industriously, and she looked up, welcoming him. He replied to her and, dexterously tossing his sombrero on a peg in the wall where it caught and hung swinging, walked heavily to the southern window and stood before it, hands clasped behind his back, staring moodily

into the star-stabbed darkness. Down the wind came the faint, wailing howl of a wolf, quavering and distant, and the hounds again shattered the peaceful quiet. But he heard neither,
so absorbed was he by his thoughts. Mary looked at him for a moment and then took up her
work again and resumed sewing, for he had done this before when things had gone wrong,
and frequently of late.

He turned suddenly and in response to the movement she looked up, again laying her sewing
aside. "What it is?" she asked.

"Trouble, Mary. I want to talk to you."

"I'm always ready to listen, Daddy," she replied. "I wish you wouldn't worry so. That's all
you've done since we left Montana."

"I know; but I can't help it," he responded, smiling faintly. "But I don't care much as long as
I've got you to talk it over with. Yo're like yore mother that way, Mary; she allus made things
easy, somehow. An' she knew more'n most women do about things."

"Yo're my own Daddy," she replied affectionately. "Now tell me all about it."

"Well," he began, sitting on the table, "I'm being cheated out of my rights. I find lines where
none exist. I'm hemmed in from water, th' best grazing is held from me, my cows are driven
helter-skelter, my pride hurt, an' my men mocked. When I say I must have water I'm told
to go to th' river for it, twenty miles from my main range, an' lined with quicksands; an' yet
there is water close to me, water enough for double th' number of cows of both ranches! It is
good, clean water, unfailing an' over a firm bottom, flowing through thirty miles of th' best
grass valley in this whole sun-cursed section. Two hundred miles in any direction won't show
another as good. An' yet, I dassn't set my foot in it —I can't drive a cow across that line!"

He paused and then continued: "I'm good an' sick of it all. I ain't going to swaller it no
longer, not a day. Peace is all right, but not at th' price I'm paying! I'd ruther die fighting for
what's mine than put up with what I have since I came down here."

"What are you going to do?" she asked quietly.

"I'm going to have a force on that line by to-morrow night!" he cried, gradually working
himself into a temper. "*I'm* going to hold them hills, an' th' springs at th' bottom of 'em. *I'm*
going to use that valley an' I'll fight until th' last man goes under!"

"Don't say that, Daddy," she quickly objected. "There ain't no line worth yore life. What
good will it do you when yo're dead? You can get along without it if it comes to that. An'
what'll happen to me if you get killed?"

"No, girl," he replied. "You've held me back too long. I should 'a struck in th' beginning,
before they got so set. It would 'a been easier then. I don't like range wars any more'n anybody,
but it's come, an' I've got to hold up my end-an' my head!"

"But th' agreement?" she queried, fearful for his safety. She loved her father with all her
heart, for he had been more than a father to her; he had always confided in her and weighed
her judgment; they had been companions since her mother died, which was almost beyond her
memory; and now he would risk his life in a range war, a vindictive, unmerciful conflict which
usually died out when the last opponent died-and perhaps he was in the wrong. She knew
the fighting ability of that shaggy, tight-lipped breed of men that mocked Death with derisive,
profane words, who jibed whether in *mêlée* or duel with as light hearts as if engaged in nothing
more dangerous than dancing. And she had heard, even in Montana, of the fighting qualities
of the outfit that rode range for the Bar-20. If they must be fought, then let it be for the right
principles and not otherwise. And there was Hopalong! —she knew in her heart that she loved
him, and feared it and fought it, but it was true; and he was the active leader of his outfit, the
man who was almost the foreman, and who would be in the thickest of the fighting. She didn't
purpose to have him killed if he was in the right, or in the wrong, either.

"Agreement!" he cried, hotly. "Agreement! I hear that every time I say anything to that
crowd, an' now you give it to me! Agreement be d ———d! Nason never said nothing about any
agreement when he told me he had found a ranch for me. He wouldn't 'a dealt me a hand like

that, one that'd give me th' worst of it in a show-down! He found out all about everything before he turned over my check to 'em."

"But they say there is one, an' from th' way they act it looks that way."

"I don't believe anything of th' sort! It's just a trick to hog that grass an' water!"

"Hopalong Cassidy told me there was one-he told me all about it. He was a witness."

"Hopalong h —l!" he cried, remembering the day that Doc had been shot, and certain hints which Antonio had let fall.

"Father!" she exclaimed, her eyes flashing.

"Oh, don't mind me," he replied. "I don't know what I'm saying half th' time. I'm all mixed up, now-a-days."

"I believe he was telling the truth-he wouldn't lie to me," she remarked, decisively.

He looked at her sharply. "Well, am I to be tied down by something I don't know about? Am I to swaller everything I hear? *I* don't know about no agreement, except what th' Bar-20 tells me. An' if there was one it was made by th' Three Triangle, wasn't it? —an' not by Nason or me? Am I th' Three Triangle? Am I to walk th' line on something I didn't make? *I* didn't make it! —oh, I'm tired arguing about it."

"Well, even if there wasn't no agreement you can't blame them for trying to keep their land, can you?" she asked, idly fingering her sewing. "The land is theirs, ain't it?"

"Did you ever hear of free grass an' free water?"

"I never heard of nothing else till I came down here," she admitted. "But it may be different here."

"Well, it ain't different!" he retorted. "An' if it is it won't stay so. What goes in Montanny will go down here. Anyhow, I don't want their land-all I want is th' use of it, same as they have. But they're hogs, an' want it all."

"They say it ain't big enough for their herds."

"Thirty-five miles long, and five miles wide, in th' valley alone, an' it ain't big enough! Don't talk to me like that! You know better."

"I'm only trying to show it to you in every light," she responded. "Mebby yo're right, an' mebby you ain't; that's what we've got to find out. I don't want to think of you fightin', 'specially if yo're wrong. Suppose yo're killed, —an' you might be. Ain't there some other way to get what you want, if yo're determined to go ahead?"

"Yes, I might be killed, but I won't go alone!" he cried savagely. "Fifty years, man an' boy, I've lived on th' range, taking every kick of fortune, riding hard an' fightin' hard when I had to. I ain't no yearling at any game about cows, girl."

"But can't you think of some other way?" she repeated.

"I've got to get that line house on th' hill," he went on, not heeding her question. "Juan told me three days ago, that they've put a guard in it now-but I'll have it by noon to-morrow, for I've been thinking hard since then. An' once in it, they can't take it from me! With that in my hands I can laugh at 'em, for I can drive my cows over th' line close by it, down th' other side of th' hill, an' into th' valley near th' springs. They'll be under my guns in th' line house, an' let anybody try to drive 'em out again! Two men can hold that house-it was built for defence against Indians. Th' top of th' hill is level as a floor an' only two hundred yards to th' edge. Nobody can cross that space under fire an' live."

"If they can't cross it an' live, how can *you* cross it, when th' house is guarded? An' when th' first shot is fired you'll have th' whole outfit down on you from behind like wild fire. Then what'll you do? You can't fight between two fires."

"By G-d, yo're right! Yo're th' brains of this ranch," he cried, his eyes squinting to hide his elation. He paced back and forth, thinking deeply. Five minutes passed, then ten, and he suddenly turned and faced her, to unfold the plan he had worked out the day before. He had been leading up to it and now he knew how to propose it. "I've got it. I've got it! Not a shot, not a single shot!"

"Tell me," she said smiling.

He slowly unfolded it, telling her of the herds waiting to be driven across the line to draw the Bar-20 men from the Peak, and of the part she was to play. She listened quietly, a troubled frown on her face, and when he had finished and asked her what she thought of it she looked at him earnestly and slowly replied:

"Do you think that's fair? Do you want *me* to do that?"

"What's unfair about it? They're yore enemies as much as they are mine, ain't they? Ain't everything fair in love an' war, as th' books say?"

"In war, perhaps; but not in love," she replied in a low voice, thinking of the man who wore her flower.

"Now look here!" he cried, leaning forward. "Don't you go an' get soft on any of that crowd! Do you hear?"

"We won't mix love an' war, Daddy," she said, decisively. "You take care of yore end, that's war; an' let me run my part. I'll do what I want to when it comes to falling in love; an' I'll help you to-morrow. I don't want to do it, but I will; you've got to have th' line house, an' without getting between two fires. I'll do it, Daddy."

"Good girl! Yo're just like yore mother-all grit!" he cried, going towards the door. "An' I reckon I won't have to take no hand in *yore* courting," he said, grabbing his sombrero. "Yo're shore able to run yore own."

"But *promise* me you won't interfere," she said, calmly, hiding her triumph.

"It's a go. I'll keep away from th' sparking game," he promised. "I'm going out to see th' boys for a minute," and the door slammed, inciting the clamor of the kennels again, which he again hushed. "D —n 'em!" he muttered, exultantly. "They tried to hog th' range, an' then they want my girl! But they *won't* hog th' range no more, an' I'll put a stop to th' courting when she plays her cards to-morrow, an' without having any hand in it. Lord, I win, every trick!" he laughed.

Chapter XV
Antonio Meets Friends

Before daylight the next morning Antonio left the ranch and rode south, bearing slightly to the west, so as not to leave his trail in Curley's path. He was to meet some of Shaw's men who would come for more cattle. When a dozen miles southwest of the ranch house he espied them at work on the edge of an arroyo. They had a fire going and were re-branding a calf. Far out on the plain was a dead cow, the calf's mother, shot because they had become angered by its belligerency when it had gone "on th' prod." They had driven cow and calf hard and when they tried to separate the two the mother had charged viciously, narrowly missing one of them, to die by a shot from the man most concerned. Meanwhile the calf had run back over its trail and they had roped it as it was about to plunge over the bank of the arroyo.

"You fools!" yelled Antonio, galloping towards them. "Don't you know better'n to blot on this range! How many times have I told you that Curley rides south!"

"He never gets this far west-we've watched him," retorted Clausen, angrily.

"Is that any reason why he can't!" demanded the Mexican. "How do we know what he'll do?"

"Yes!" rejoined Clausen. "An' I reckon he can find that steep-bank hollow with th' rope gate, can't he? Suppose he finds th' herds you holds in it for us-what then?"

"It's a whole lot farther west than here!" retorted Antonio, hotly. "They never go to Little Muddy, an' if they do, that's a chance we've got to take. But you can wait till you get to th' mesa before you change brands, can't you!"

"Aw, close yore pie-sump!" cried Frisco. "Who th' devil is doing this, anyhow? You make more noise than Cheyenne on th' Fourth of July!"

"What right have you fellers got to take chances an' hobble *me* with trouble?"

"Who's been doing all th' sleepering, hey?" sarcastically demanded Dick Archer. "Let Meeker's gang see the God-forsaken bunch of sleepers running on their range an' you'll be hobbled with trouble, all right."

Through laziness, carelessness, or haste calves might not be branded when found with branded cows. Feeling was strong against the use of the "running iron," a straight iron rod about eighteen inches long which was heated and used as a pencil on the calf's hide, and a man caught with one in his possession could expect to be dealt with harshly; it was a very easy task to light a fire and "run" a brand, and the running iron was easily concealed under the saddle flap. But it was not often that a puncher would carry a stamping iron, for it was cumbersome. With a running iron a brand could be changed, or the wrong mark put on unbranded cattle; but the stamping iron would give only one pattern.

When a puncher came across an unbranded calf with its branded mother, and the number which escaped the roundup was often large, he branded it, if he had an iron; if he did not have the iron he might cut the calf's ears to conform to the notch in its mother's ears. When the calf was again seen it might have attained its full growth. In that case there was no branded mother to show to whom it belonged; but its cut ears would tell.

These unbranded, ear-cut calves were known as "sleepers" and, in localities where cattle stealing was being or had been carried on to any extent, such sleepering was regarded with strong suspicion, and more than one man had paid a dear price for doing the work.

The ear mark of the H2 was a V, while the Bar-20 depended entirely on the brand, and part of its punchers' saddle equipment was a stamping iron.

Cowmen held sleepering in strong disfavor because it was an easy matter for a maverick hunter or a rustler to drive off these sleepers and, after altering the ear cut, to brand them with his own or some strange brand; and it was easy to make sleepers.

In the case of rustling the separation of branded calves and mothers was imperative, for should any one see a cow of one brand with a calf of another, it was very probable that a committee of discretionary powers would look into the matter. Hobbling and laming mothers and then driving away the calves were not the only ways of separating them and of weaning the calves, for a shot was often as good a way as any; but as dead cows, if found, were certain to tell the true story, this was not generally employed.

"Yes," laughed Frisco. "What about th' sleepers?"

They were discreetly silent about the cow they had killed, for they were ashamed of having left such a sign; but they would not stand Antonio's scorn and anger, and that of the other members of the band, and so said nothing about it.

"Where's th' mother of this calf?" demanded the Mexican, not heeding the remarks about sleepers.

"Hanged if I know," replied Clausen, easily; "an' hanged if I care-we can leave *one* cow, I reckon."

"Got many for us this time?" asked Archer as they rode west, driving before them the newly branded calf.

"Not many," replied Antonio. "It's risky, with Curley loose. We won't be able to do much till th' fighting starts."

When they reached their destination they came to a deep, steep-walled depression, exit from which was had at only one end where a narrow trail wound up to the plain. Across this trail at its narrowest point was stretched a lariat.

The depression itself was some ten acres in extent and was well covered with grass, while near the southwest corner was a muddy pool providing water for the herd which was now held captive.

Clausen rode down and removed the rope, riding into the basin to hasten the egress of the herd. When the last cow had scrambled out and joined its fellows, Archer and Frisco drove them west, leaving Clausen to say a few final words with Antonio before joining them.

"How's th' range war coming on?"

"Fine!" laughed Antonio. "Meeker's going to attack th' line house on th' Peak, though what good it'll do him is more than I can figure out. I put it in his head because it'll start th' fight. I had to grin when I heard Meeker and Doc planning it last night-they're easy."

"Gee!" laughed Clausen. "It's a stiff play. Who's going to win? Meeker?"

"Meeker's going to get th' licking of his life. I know that Bar-20 gang, every one. I've lived down here for some time, an' I know what they've done. Don't never get in a six-shooter argument with that feller Cassidy; an' if his friend Connors tells you to stop under eight hundred yards, you do it, an' trust to yore tongue, or Colt. He's th' devil hisself with a Winchester."

"Much obliged-but I ain't so bad that way myself. Well, I'm going to ooze west. Got any word for Shaw?"

"I'll send word by Benito —I'll know more about it to-morrow."

"All right," and Clausen was being jerked over the scenery by his impatient mount.

Antonio wheeled and rode at a gallop, anxious to be found on northern range, and eager to learn the result of his foreman's attack.

"Salem," once a harpooner on a whaling vessel, now cook for the H2, drove home from Eagle in the chuck wagon, which contained food supplies for his ranch. He was in that state hovering between tears and song, which accounts for the winding trail his wagon wheels left, and also for him being late. He had tarried in Eagle longer than he should have, for he was reluctant to quit the society of his several newly made friends, who so pleasantly allowed him to "buy" for them. When he realized how the time had flown and that his outfit would be clamoring for the noonday meal, such clamoring being spicy and personal in its expression, he left the river trail before he should and essayed a shorter way home, chanting a sea song.

> A pirate bold, on th' Spanish Main —
> Set sail, yo-ho, an' away we go —

"Starboard yore helm, you lubbers!" he shouted when the horses headed towards Mexico. Then he saw a large bulk lying on the sand a short distance ahead and he sat bolt upright.

"There she blows! No, blast me, it's a dead cow!"

He drove closer to it and, stopping the team, staggered over to see what had killed it.

"D —n me, if it ain't shot in th' port eye!" he ejaculated. "If I find the lubber what's sinkin' our cows, I'll send him to Davy Jones' locker!"

He returned to the wagon and steered nor' by nor' east, once more certain of his bearings, for he knew the locality now, and sometime later he saw Curley riding towards him.

"Ahoy!" he yelled. "Ahoy, you wind-jammer!"

"What's eating you? Why are you so late?" demanded Curley, approaching. "You needn't say —I know."

"Foller my wake an' you'll see a dead cow," cried Salem. "Deader'n dead, too! Shot in th' starboard-no, was it starboard? Now, d — —d if I know-reckon it was in th' port eye, though I didn't see no port light; aye, 'twas in th' port —"

"What in h —l do I care what eye it was!" shouted Curley. "Where is it?"

"Eight knots astern. Shot in th' port eye, an', as I said, deader'n dead. Flew our flag, too."

Curley, believing that the cook had seen what he claimed, wheeled abruptly and galloped away to report it to Meeker.

"Hey! Ain't you going to *see* it?" yelled Salem, and as he received no reply, turned to his team. "Come on, weigh anchor! Think I want to lay out here all night? 'A-sailing out of Salem town, —'" he began, and then stopped short and thought. "I *knowed* it! —it *was* th' port eye! Same side th' flag was on!" he exclaimed, triumphantly.

On the boundary line alert and eager punchers rode at a canter to and fro, watching the herds to the south of them, and quick to turn back all that strayed across the line. Just east of the middle point of the boundary Red and Johnny met and compared notes, and both reported the same state of affairs, which was that the cattle came constantly nearer.

Johnny removed his field glasses from his eyes.

"There's punchers with that herd, Red. Three of 'em."

"I reckoned so."

"Wonder what they think they're going to do?"

"We'll know purty soon."

"They're coming this way."

"If you had th' brains of a calf you'd know they wouldn't go south."

"Think they're going to rush us?" Johnny asked, eagerly.

"No; course not!" retorted Red. "They're going to make 'em stand on their heads!"

Johnny began to hum —

> Joyous Joe got a juniper jag,
> A-jogging out of Jaytown;
> Joyous Joe got a juniper jag —

"We'll show that prickly pear from Montanny some fine points."

"Now, look here, Kid; don't you let 'em get a cow across th' line. Shoot every one, but keep yore eyes on th' gang."

"'Joyous Joe got a juniper jag, —' Come on, you half-breeds!"

"Wonder where Hopalong is?" Red asked.

"Up on th' Peak, I reckon. *Hey*, Billy!" he yelled. "Here comes Billy, Red."

"I guessed as much when you yelled; if you don't yell away from my ear next time I'll kick yore pants over yore hat. D——d idiot, you!"

"Hullo, Billy," cried Johnny, ignoring Red's remarks. "Just in time for th' pie. Where's Hopalong?"

"In th' hills."

"You get along an' tell him what's doing out here," ordered Red. "Go lively!"

"Reckon I'd better stay an' give you a hand; you'll need it before long," Billy replied.

"You know what Hopalong said, don't you?" blazed Red. "What do you think me an' th' Kid are made of, anyhow? You go on, an' quick!"

"Send Johnny," Billy suggested, hopefully.

"Why, you coyote!" cried Johnny, excitedly. "Th' idea! You go on!"

"Yo're a pair of hogs," grumbled Billy, riding off. "I'll get square, someday. Hope they lick you!"

"Run along, little boy," jeered Johnny. "Oh, gee! Here they come!" he cried as Billy rode behind the chaparral. "Look at 'em!"

"*Let* 'em come!" cried Billy, returning. "We'll lick 'em!"

"Get out of here!" shouted Red, drawing his Winchester from its sheath. "For G-d's sake, do what yo're told! Want to let Meeker win out?"

"Nope; so long," and Billy galloped away.

"That ain't a herd!" cried Johnny, elated. "That's only a handful. It's a scrawny looking bunch, men an' all. Come on, you coyotes!" he yelled, waving his rifle.

"You chump; this ain't the real play-it's a blind, a wedge," Red replied. "They're pushing a big one through somewhere else."

"I'm shore glad Billy went, an' not me," Johnny remarked.

"There's Morgan," Red remarked. "I know his riding."

"Bet you won't know it when th' show's over. An' there's Chick, too. He needs a licking. You won't know his riding, neither."

The herd came rapidly forward and the men who were guarding it waved their sombreros and urged it on. Red, knowing that he would be crowded if he waited until the cows were upon him, threw his rifle to his shoulder and began to shoot rapidly, and cow after cow dropped, and the rush was stopped. Before the H2 men could get free from the panic-stricken herd Red and Johnny were within a hundred yards of them and when they looked up it was to see Red covering them, while Johnny, pleased by the reduced range, was dropping more cows.

"Stop!" Red shouted, angrily.

"Huh!" exclaimed Johnny, looking up. "Oh, I thought you was talking to me," he muttered, and then dropped another cow.

"What in h —l do you think yo're doing?" yelled Morgan.

"Just practising," retorted Johnny. He quickly swung his rifle on Chick. "Hands up! No more of that!"

"You've got gall, shooting our cows!" replied Chick.

"Get 'em up, boy!" snapped Johnny, and Chick slowly raised his arms, speaking rapidly.

"What do you take us for!" shouted Ed Joyce, frantic at his helplessness.

"Coyotes," replied Red. "An' since coyotes don't ride, you get off'n them cayuses, *pronto*."

"Like h —l!" retorted Ed.

Johnny's rifle cracked and Ed tumbled off his dead horse, and when he arose the air was blue.

"Nex' gent say 'I,'" called Johnny.

"I'll be d — —d if I'll stand for that!" yelled Morgan, reaching for his gun. The next thing he knew was that the air was full of comets, and that his horse was dead.

Chick sullenly dismounted and stood watching Red, who was now in vastly better spirits, since the H2 rifles were on the horses and too far away from their owners to be of any use. The range was too great for good revolver shooting even if they could get them into action.

"Watch 'em," said Red, firing. Chick's horse, stung to frenzy by the wound, kicked up its heels and bolted, leaving the three punchers stranded ten miles from home.

"Turn around an' hit th' back trail," ordered Red. "No back talk!"

"I'll bust you wide open, someday, you red-headed wart!" threatened Dan, shaking his fist at the grinning line man. "That's a h —l of a thing to do, that is!"

"Shut up an' go home. Ain't you got enough?" shouted Red.

"Just wait, you half-breed!" yelled Ed Joyce.

"That's two with th' waiting habit," laughed Johnny.

"What do —" began Chick, stepping forward.

"Shut up! Who told you to open yore face!" cried Red, savagely. "Get home! G'wan!"

"Walk, you coyotes, walk!" exulted Johnny.

He and his companion watched the three angry punchers stride off towards the H2 and then Red told Johnny to ride west while he, himself, would go east to help his friends if they should need him. They had just begun to separate when Johnny uttered a shout of joy. Antonio had joined the trio of walkers and they were pulling him from his horse. He waved his arms excitedly, but Chick had him covered. Dan and Ed were already on the animal and they quickly pulled Chick up behind them, narrowly watching the Mexican all the while. The horse fought for some time and then started south, the riders shouting while Antonio, still waving his arms, plodded homeward on foot.

Great joy filled Johnny's heart as he gloated over the Mexican's predicament. "Hoof it, you greasy snake! Kick up th' dust, you lazy lizard!"

"They can't get in th' game again for some time, till they get cayuses," remarked Red. "That makes four less to deal with, counting th' Greaser as a whole man."

"Three an' a third," corrected his companion. "He acts like he had all eternity to get nowhere-look at him! Let's go down an' rope him. He's on th' prod now-we can have a lot of fun."

"If I go down there it'll be to plug him good," Red replied. "You hang around out here for a while. I'm goin' west-Pete's in that house alone-so long, Kid."

Johnny grinned a farewell to Antonio and followed instructions while his friend rode towards the Peak to assist Pete, the lonely, who as it happened, would be very glad to see him.

Chapter XVII
Pete is Tricked

Pete Wilson grumbled, for he was tiring of his monotonous vigil, and almost hoped the H2 would take the house because of the excitement incident to its re-capture. At first his assignment had pleased, but as hour after hour passed with growing weariness, he chafed more and more and his temper grew constantly shorter.

With the exception of smoking he had exhausted every means of passing the time; he knew to a certainty how many bushes and large stones were on the plateau, the ranges between him and distant objects, and other things, and now he had to fall back on his pipe.

"Wish some son-of-a-thief would zephyr up an' start something," he muttered. "If I stays in this fly-corral much longer I'll go loco. A couple of years back we wouldn't have waited ten minutes in a case like this-we'd 'a chased that crowd off th' range quick. What's getting into us has got me picking out th' festive pea, all right."

He stopped at the east window and scrutinized the line as far as he could see the dim, dusty, winding trail, hoping that some of the outfit would come into sight. Then he slid the Sharps out of the window and held it on an imaginary enemy, whom he pretended was going to try to take the house. While he thought of caustic remarks, with which to greet such a person, he saw the head of a horse push up into view over the edge of the hill.

Sudden hope surged through him and shocked him to action. He cocked the rifle, the metallic clicks sweet to his ears. Then he saw the rider, and it was-Mary Meeker.

Astonishment and quick suspicion filled his mind and he held the weapon ready to use on her escort, should she have one. Her horse reared and plunged and, deciding that she was alone, and ashamed to be covering a woman, he slid the gun back into the room, leaning it against the wall close at his hand, not losing sight of the rider for a moment.

"Now, what th' devil is she doing up here, anyhow?" he puzzled, and then a grin flickered across his face as the possible solution came to him. "Mebby she wants Hopalong," he muttered, and added quickly, "Purty as blazes, too!" And she did make a pretty picture even to his scoffing and woman-hating mind.

She was having trouble with her mount, due to the spurring it was getting on the side farther from the watcher. It reared and plunged, bucking sideways, up-and-down and fence-cornered, zig-zagging over the ground forward and back, and then began to pitch "stiff-legged." Pete's eyes glowed with the appreciation of a master rider and he was filled with admiration, which soon became enthusiastic, over her saddle-ease and cool mastery. She seemed to be a part of the horse.

"She'd 'a been gone long ago if she was fool enough to sit one of them side saddle contraptions," he mused. "A-straddle is th' only —*Good!* All right! Yo're a stayer!" he exclaimed as she stepped from one stirrup and stood up in the other when the animal reared up on its hind legs.

He glanced out of the other windows of the house and fell to watching her again, his face darkening as he saw that she appeared to be tiring, while her mount grew steadily worse. Then she "touched leather," and again and again. Her foot slipped from the stirrup, but found it again, while she frantically clung to the saddle horn.

"Four-legged devil!" Pete exclaimed. "Wish *I* was on you, you ornery dog! Hey! Don't you bite like that! Keep yore teeth away from that leg or I'll blow yore d — —d head off!" he cried wrathfully as the animal bit viciously several times at the stirrup leather. "I'll whale th' stuffin' outen you, you wall-eyed clay-bank! Yo're too bronc for *her* to ride, all right."

Then, during another and more vicious fit of stiff-legged pitching the rider held to the saddle horn with both hands, while her foot, again out of the stirrup, sought for it in vain. She was rapidly losing her grip on the saddle and suddenly she was thrown off, a cry reaching Pete's ears. The victorious animal kicked several times and shook its head vigorously in celebration of its freedom and then buck-jumped across the plateau and out of sight down the hill, Pete strongly tempted to stop its exuberance with a bullet.

Pete glanced at the figure huddled in the dust and then, swearing savagely and fearing the worst, threw down the bar and jerked open the door and ran as rapidly as his awkward legs would take him to see what he could do for her, his hand still grasping his rifle. As he knelt beside her he remembered that he had been told not to leave the house under any circumstances and he glanced over his shoulder, and just in time to see a chap-covered leg disappear through the doorway. His heart sank as the crash of the bar falling into place told him that he had been unworthy of the trust his best friend had reposed in him. It was plain enough, now, that he had been fooled, to understand it all and to know that as he left the house one or more H2 punchers had sprinted for it from the other side of the plateau.

Red fury filled him in an instant and tearing the revolver from the girl's belt he threw it away and then, grasping her with both hands, he raised her up as though she weighed nothing and threw her over his shoulder, sprinting for the protection of the hillside, which he reached in a few bounds. Throwing her down as he would throw a bag of flour he snarled at her as she arose and brushed her clothes. Years ago in Pete's life a woman had outraged his love and trust and sent him through a very hell of sorrow; and since then he had had no love for the sex-only a bitter, scathing cynicism, which now found its outlet in words.

"Yo're a nice one, you are!" he yelled. "You've done yore part! Yo're all alike, every d — —d one of you-Judas wasn't no man, not by a d — —d sight! You know a man won't stand by an' see you hurt without trying to help you-an' you play it against him!"

She was about to retort, but smiled instead and went on with her dusting.

"Tickled, hey! Well, you watch an' see what *we* do to coyotes! You'll see what happens to line-thieves down here!"

She looked up quickly and suspected that instead of averting a fight she had precipitated one. Both Hopalong and her father were in as much danger now as if she had taken no part in the trouble.

Pete emptied his revolver into the air as rapidly as he could work the hammer and hurriedly reloaded it, all the time watching his prisoner and the top of the hill. Three quick reports, muffled by distance, replied from Long Hill and he turned to her.

"Now why don't you laugh?" he gritted savagely. He caught sight of her horse grazing calmly further down the hill and his Sharps leaped to his shoulder and crashed. The animal stiffened, erect for a moment, and then sank slowly back on its quivering haunches and dropped.

"*You* won't pitch no more, d —n you!" he growled, reloading.

Her eyes snapped with anger and she caught at her holster. "You coward! You coward!" she cried, stamping her foot. "To kill that horse, an' steal my gun-afraid of a woman!" she taunted. "Coward!"

"I'll pull a snake's fangs rather than get bit by one, when I can't shoot 'em!" he retorted, stung by her words. "You'll see how big a coward I am purty soon-an' you'll stay right here an' see it, too!"

"*I* won't run away," she replied, sitting down and tucking her feet under her skirts. "*I'm* not afraid of a coward!"

Another shot rang out just over the top of Stepping Stone Hill and he replied to it. Far to the west a faint report was heard and Pete knew that Skinny was roweling the lathered sides of his straining horse. Yet another sounded flatly from the direction of the dam, the hills multiplying it into a distant fusillade.

"Hear 'em!" he demanded, fierce joy ringing in his voice. "Hear 'em! You've kicked th' dynamite, all right-you'll smell th' smoke of yore little squib clean down to yore ranch house!"

"That's grand-yo're doing it fine," she laughed, strangling the fear which crept slowly through her. "Go on-it's grand!"

"It'll be a whole lot grander when th' boys get here an' find out what's happened," he promised. "There'll be some funerals start out from what's left of yore ranch house purty soon."

"Ki-i-i-e-e-p! Ki-ip ki-ip!" came the hair-raising yell from the top of Stepping Stone Hill, and Pete withheld the rest of his remarks to reply to it in kind. Suddenly Red Connors, his quirt rising and falling, bounded over the top of the hill and shot down the other side at full speed. Close behind him came Billy Williams, who rode as recklessly until his horse stepped into a hole and went down, throwing him forward like a shot out of a catapult. He rolled down the hill some distance before he could check his impetus and then, scrambling to his feet, drew his Colt and put his broken-legged mount out of its misery before hobbling on again.

Red slid to a stand and leaped to the ground, his eyes on the woman, but his first thought was for the house. "What's th' matter? Why ain't you in that shack? Didn't Hopalong tell you to hold it?" he demanded. Turning to Mary Meeker he frowned. "What are you doing up here? Don't you know this ain't no place for you to-day?"

Pete grasped his shoulder and swung him around so sharply that he nearly lost his balance, crying: "Don't talk to her, she's a d ———d snake!"

Red's hand moved towards his holster and then stopped, for it was a friend who spoke. "What do you mean, d —n you? Who's a snake? What's wrong here, anyhow?"

Billy limped up and stood amazed at the strange scene, for besides the presence of the woman, his friends were quarrelling and he had never seen that before. Seeing Mary look at him he flushed and sneaked off his sombrero, ashamed because he had forgotten it.

Pete swiftly related all that had occurred, and ended with another curse flung at his prisoner, who looked him over with a keen, critical glance and then smiled contemptuously.

"That's a fine note!" Red cried, his sombrero also coming off. He looked at Mary and saw no fear in her face, no sign of any weakness, but rather a grimness in the firmness of her lips and a battling light in her eyes, which gained her immunity from his tongue, for he admired grit. "Here, you, stop that cussing! You can't cuss no woman while I'm around!" he cried hotly. "Hopalong'll break you wide open if he hears you. Cussing won't do no good; what we want is thinking, an' fighting!" Catching sight of Billy, who looked self-conscious and a little uncomfortable, he cried: "An' what's th' matter with you?"

Billy jerked his thumb over his shoulder in the direction of the dead horse and Red, following the motion, knew. "By th' Lord, you got off easy! Pete, you watch yore prisoner; keep her out of danger, an' there'll be lots of it purty soon. We'll get th' house for you."

"Send up to Cowan's saloon; he had some dynamite, an' if we can get any we can blow them sneaks off th' face of th' earth," Pete exclaimed, his anger and shame urging him against his better nature. "Go ahead. I'll take th' chances using th' stuff—I lost th' house."

The pathetic note of self-condemnation in his last words stopped Red's reprimand and he said, instead: "We'll talk about that later. But don't you lose no sleep-they can't hold it, dynamite or no dynamite. We'll have it before sundown."

Dynamite! Mary caught her breath and sudden fear gripped her heart. Dynamite! And two men were in the house, Doc Riley and Jack Curtis, men who would not be there if she had not made it possible for them-she was responsible.

"Here comes Skinny!" cried Billy, waving his arm.

"An' here's Hopalong!" joyously cried Pete, elated, for he pinned his faith in his line-fore-man's ability to get out of any kind of a hole, no matter how deep and wide. "Now things 'll happen! We're going to get busy *now*, all right!"

The two arrived at the same instant and both asked the same question. Then Hopalong saw Mary and he was at her side in a trice.

"Hullo! What are *you* doing up here?" he cried in astonishment.

"I'm a prisoner-of *that*!" she replied, pointing at Pete.

Hopalong wheeled. "What! What have you been doing to her? Why ain't you in th' house, where you belongs?"

Pete told him, briefly, and he turned to the prisoner, a smile of admiration struggling to get through his frown. She looked at him bravely, for now was the crisis, which she had feared, and welcomed.

"By th' Lord!" he cried, softly. "Yo're a thoroughbred, a fighter from start to finish. But you shouldn't come up here to-day; there's no telling, sometimes, where bullets go after they start." Turning, he said, "Pete, you chump, stay on this side of th' hill an' watch th' house. Billy, lay so you can watch th' door. Red, come with me. An' if anybody gets a shot at them range stealers, shoot to kill. Understand? Shoot to kill-it's time."

"Dynamite?" queried Pete, hopefully. "I'll use it. Cowan —"

Hopalong stared. "Dynamite! Dynamite! We ain't fighting 'em that way, even if they are coyotes. You go an' do what I told you."

"Yes, but —"

"Shut up!" snapped Hopalong. "I know how you feel *now*, but you'll think different to-morrow."

"Let's swap th' girl for th' house," suggested Skinny, grinning. "It's a shore cinch," he added, winking at Billy, who laughed.

Hopalong wheeled to retort, caught Skinny's eye closing, and laughed instead. "I reckon that would work all right, Skinny. It'd be a good joke on 'em to take th' house back with th' same card they got it by. But this ain't no time for joking. Pete, you better stay here an' watch th' window on this side; Billy, take th' window on th' south side. Skinny can go around west an' Red'll take th' door. They won't be so joyous after they get what's coming their way. This ain't no picnic; shoot to kill. We've been peaceful too blamed long!"

"That's th' way to talk!" cried Pete. "If we'd acted that way from th' very first day they crossed our line we wouldn't be fighting to capture our own line house! You know how to handle 'em all right!"

"Pete, how much water is in there?" Hopalong asked.

"'Bout a hatful-nobody brought me any this morning, th' lazy cusses."

"All right; they won't hold it for long, then. Take yore places as I said, fellers, an' get busy," he replied, and then turned to Mary. "Where's yore father? Is *he* in that house?"

"I don't know-an' I wouldn't tell if I did!"

"Say, yo're a regular hummer! Th' more you talk th' better I like you," he laughed, admiringly. "You've shore stampeded me worse than ever —I'm so loco I can't wait much longer-when are you going to marry me? Of course you know that you've got to someday."

"Indeed I have *not*!" she retorted, her face crimson. "If you wait for me to marry you you will die of old age! An' I'm shore somebody's listening."

"Then *I'll* marry *you* —of course, that's what I meant."

"Indeed you *won't*!"

"Then th' minister will. After this line fighting is over I won't wait. I'll just rope you an' drive you down to Perry's Bend to th' hobbling man, if you won't go any other way. We'll come back a team. Oh, I mean just what I say," and she knew that he did, and she was glad at heart that he thought none the less of her for the trick she had played on Pete. He seemed to take everything as a matter of course, and as a matter of course was going to re-take the house.

"You just *dare* try it! Just *dare*!" she cried, hotly.

"Now you have gone an' done it, for I never take a dare, *never*," he laughed. "It's us for th' sky pilot, an' then th' same range for life. Yo're shore purty, an' that fighting spunk doubles it. You can begin to practise calling yourself Mrs. Hopalong Cassidy, of th' Bar-20."

Pete fired, swore, and turned his head. "How th' devil can I hit a house with all that fool talk!" and the two, suddenly realizing that Pete had been ordered to remain close by, looked foolish, and both laughed.

"It gets on my nerves," Pete growled, and then: "Here comes Johnny like a greased coyote."

They looked and saw Johnny tearing down Stepping Stone Hill as if he were afraid that the fighting would be over before he could take a hand in it. When he came within hailing distance he stood up in his stirrups, shouting, "What's up?" and then, seeing Pete, understood. Leaping from the saddle he jerked his rifle out of the sheath and ran to him, jeering. "Oh, you Pete! Oh you d — —d fool!"

"Hey, Johnny! How's things east?" Hopalong demanded.

Johnny stopped and hastily recounted how he and Red had driven back the herd, adding: "Her dad is out there now looking at his dead cows —I saw him when I came back from East Arroyo. An' I saw them three punchers ride over that ridge down south; and they shore made good time. Say, how did they get Pete out?" he asked eagerly.

"I'll tell you that later-Pete, you go an' tell Red to come here, an' take his place. We can't swap Mary for th' house, but we can swap her dad! Mary, you better go home-this won't be no place for you in a little while. Where's yore cayuse?" he asked, looking around.

"It's down there-he shot it," she replied, nodding at Pete.

"Shot it? Lord, but he must 'a been mad! Well, you can get square-Pete, where's yore cayuse?"

"How th' devil do *I* know!" Pete blazed, indignantly. "*I* wasn't keeping track of no cayuse after they got th' house!"

"It's down there on th' hill-see it?" volunteered Johnny. "Shall I get it?" he asked, grinning at the disgruntled Pete.

"Yes; an' strip th' fixings off her cayuse while yo're about it-lively."

Johnny vaulted into his saddle and loped down the hill, shortly returning with Mary's saddle and bridle in front of him and Pete's horse at the end of his rope. Hopalong quickly removed Pete's saddle and put the other in its place, Pete eloquent in his silence, and Johnny manifestly pleased by the proceedings.

"Now you can ride," Hopalong smiled, helping her into the saddle. "Pete don't care at all-he ain't saying a word," whereat Pete said a word, several of them in fact, under his breath and vowed that he would kill the men in the house to get square.

"I'll send it back as soon as I can," she promised, and then, when Hopalong leaned closer and whispered something to her, she flushed and spurred the animal, leaving him standing in a cloud of dust, a smile on his face.

Johnny, grinning until his face threatened to be ruptured, wheeled on Pete. "Yo're a lucky fool, even if you did go an' lose th' house for us-wish she'd ride *my* cayuse!"

Pete replied in keeping with his feelings now that there was no woman present, and walked away to change places with Red, who soon came up. Then the three mounted and cantered east to find the H2 foreman, Johnny mauling "Whiskey Bill" in his exuberance. Suddenly he turned in his saddle and slapped his thigh: "I'll bet four cents to a tooth brush that she's telling her dad to get scarce. She heard what you said, Hoppy!"

"Right! Come on!" exclaimed Hopalong, spurring into a gallop, his companions racing behind, spurring and quirting to catch him.

"Say, Red, she's a straight flush," Johnny shouted to his companion. "Can't be beat-if she turns Hoppy down I'm next in th' line-up!"

"You don't want no wife-you wants a nurse!" Red retorted.

Chapter XVIII
The Line House Re-captured

After Chick, Dan Morgan, and Ed Joyce had commandeered Antonio's horse and left him on foot they rode as rapidly as they could to the corrals of their ranch, where they saddled fresh mounts and galloped back to try conclusions with the men who had humbled them. They also wished to find their foreman, who they knew was somewhere along the line. Chick rode to the west, Dan to the east, and Ed Joyce straight ahead; intending to search for Meeker and then ride together again.

Meanwhile Antonio, tired of walking, returned to the line and lay in ambush to waylay the first Bar-20 puncher to ride past him, hoping to get a horse and also to leave a dead man for the Bar-20 to find and lay the blame on the H2. He knew that his rustler allies had scouts in the chaparrals and were ready to run off a big herd as soon as conditions were propitious, and he was anxious to give them the word to begin.

It chanced, however, that Ed Joyce was the first man to approach the Mexican, and he paid dearly for being a party to taking Antonio's horse. The dead man would not inflame the Bar-20, but the H2, and the results would be the same in the end. Mounting Ed's horse Antonio galloped north into the valley through West Arroyo so as to leave tracks in the direction of the Bar-20, intending to describe a semi-circle and return to his ranch by way of the river trail, leaving the horse where the trail crossed the Jumping Bear. By going the remainder of the way on foot he would not be seen on the horse of the murdered puncher, which might naturally enough stray in that direction, and so be free from suspicion.

Lanky Smith, wondering why none of his friends had passed him on the line, followed the trail west to see if things were as they should be. He was almost in sight of a point opposite West Arroyo, his view being obstructed by chaparrals, when he heard a faint shot, and spurred forward, his rifle in the hollow of his arm ready for action. It could mean only one thing-one of his friends was shooting H2 cows, and complications might easily follow. When he had turned out of an arroyo which made part of the line for a short distance he saw a body huddled on the sand several hundred feet ahead of him. At that instant Meeker, with Chick and Dan close at his heels, came into view on the other side, saw the body and, drawing their own conclusions, opened a hot fire on the Bar-20 puncher, riding to encircle him. Surprised for an instant, and then filled with rage because they had killed one of his friends, as he thought, he returned their fire and raced at Chick, who was now some distance from his companions. Dan and Meeker wheeled instantly and rode to the aid of their friend, and Lanky's horse dropped from under him. Luckily for him he felt a warning tremor go through the animal and jerked his feet free from the stirrups as it sank down, quickly crawling behind it for protection.

Immediately thereafter Chick lost his hat, then the use of his right arm, followed by being deprived of the services of a very good cow-pony, for Lanky now had a rest for his rifle and while his marksmanship was not equal to that of his friend Red, it was good enough for his present needs. Dan Morgan started to shout to his foreman and then swore luridly instead, for Lanky was pleased to drill him at five hundred yards, the bullet tearing a disconcerting hole in Dan's thigh.

Meeker had been most zealously engaged all this time in making his rifle go off at regular intervals, his bullets kicking up the dust, humming viciously about Lanky's head, and thudding into the carcass of the dead horse. Then Lanky swore and shook the blood from his cheek, telling Meeker what he thought about the matter. Settling down again he determined to husk Meeker's body from its immortal soul, when he found his magazine empty. Reaching to his belt for the wherewithal for the husking he discovered the lamentable fact that he had only three cartridges left for the Winchester, and the Colt was more ornamental than useful at that range. To make matters worse both Chick and Dan were now sitting up wasting cartridges in his direction, while Meeker seemed to have an unending supply. Just then the H2 foreman found his mark again and rendered his enemy's arm useless. At that point the clouds of misfortune parted and Hopalong, Red and Johnny at his heels, whirled into sight from the west, firing with burning zeal.

Meeker's horse went down, pinning its rider under it; Dan Morgan threw up his arms as he sat in the saddle, for his rifle was shattered; Chick, popping up his good arm first, arose from behind his fleshy breastwork and announced that he could not fight, although he certainly wanted to; but Meeker said nothing.

Riding first to Lanky, his friends joked him into a better humor while they attended to his wounds. Then they divided to extend the wound-dressing courtesy. First they tried to kill a man, then to save him; but, of course, they desired mostly to render him incapable of injuring them and as long as this was accomplished it was not necessary to deprive him of life.

Hopalong, being in command, went over to look at the H2 foreman and found him unconscious. Dragging him from under the body of his horse Hopalong felt along the pinned leg and found it was not broken. Pouring a generous amount of whiskey down the unconscious man's throat he managed to revive him and then immediately disarmed him. Meeker complained of pains in his groin, not by words but by actions. His left leg seemed paralyzed and would not obey him. Hopalong called Red, who took the injured man up in front of him, where Hopalong bound his hands to the pommel of the saddle.

Meeker preserved a stolid silence until Lanky joined them and then his rage poured out in a torrent of abuse and accusations for the killing of Ed Joyce. Lanky retorted by asking who Ed Joyce was, and wanted to know whose body he had found just before Meeker had come onto the scene. When he found that they were the same he explained that he had not seen it before Meeker had, which the H2 foreman would not believe. Red captured Dan Morgan's horse and led it up. After Chick and Dan had been helped to mount the Bar-20 men's horses, placed before the saddles and bound there, all started towards Lookout Peak, Lanky riding Dan's horse.

When they had arrived at their destination Meeker suddenly realized what he was to be used for and stormed impotently against it. He heard the intermittent firing around the plateau and knew that Doc and Jack still held the house, and believed they could continue to hold it, since the thick adobe walls were impenetrable to rifle fire.

"Well, Meeker, it's you for th' house," Hopalong remarked after he had sent Red to stop the fire of the others. "You got off d — —d lucky to-day; th' next time you raise the dickens along our line we'll pay yore ranch houses a visit in a body an' give you something to think about. We handled you to-day with six of us up north, an' what th' whole crowd can do you can guess. Now walk up there an' tell them range-jumpers to vamoose th' house!"

"They'll shoot me before they sees who I am," Meeker retorted, sullenly. "If yo're so anxious to get 'em out, do it yoreself—I don't want 'em."

By this time the others were coming up and heard Meeker's words, and Hopalong, turning to Skinny and Billy, curtly ordered them to mount. "Take this royal American fool up to th' bunk house to Buck. Tell Buck what's took place down here, an' also that we're going to shoot h —l out of th' fellers in th' house before he sees us. After that those of us who can ride are going down to th' H2 an' clean up that part of th' game, buildings an' all. Go on, lively! Red, Johnny, Pete; cover th' windows an' fill that shack plumb full of lead. It's clouding up now an' when it gets good an' dark we'll bust in th' door an' end it. Skinny, you come back again, quick, with all th' grub an' cartridges you can carry. Meeker started this, but *I'm* going to finish it an' do it right. There won't be no more line fights down here for a long time to come."

"I reckon I'll have to order 'em out," Meeker growled. "What'll you do to 'em if I do?"

"Send 'em home so quick they won't have any time to say 'good-bye,'" Hopalong rejoined. "We've seen too much of you fellers now. An' after I send 'em home you see that they stays away from that line-we'll shoot on sight if they gets within gunshot of it! You've shore had a gall, pushing us, you an' yore hatful of men an' cows! If it wasn't for th' rustling we'd 'a pushed you into th' discard th' day I found yore Greaser herding on us."

Meeker, holding his side because of the pain there from the fall, limped slowly up the hill, waving his sombrero over his head as he advanced.

"What do you want now? —*Meeker!*" cried a voice from the building. "What's wrong?"

"Everything; come on out-we lose," the foreman cried, shame in his voice.

"Don't you tell us that if you wants us to stay here," came the swift reply. "We're game as long as we last, an' we'll last a long time, too."

"I know it, Doc —" his voice broke —"they've killed Ed an' captured Chick, Dan, an' me. I'd say fight it out, an' I'd fight to th' end, only they'll attack th' ranch house if we do. We're licked, *this time!*"

"First sensible words you've said since you've been on this range," growled Lanky. "You was licked before you began, if you only knowed it. An' you'll get licked *every* time, too!"

"Well, we'll come out an' give up if they'll let us all go, including you," cried Doc. "I ain't going to get picked off in th' open while I've got this shack to fight in, not by a blamed sight!"

"It's all right, Doc," Meeker replied. "How's Jack?" he asked, anxiously, not having heard Doc's companion speak.

"Wait an' see," was the reply, and the door opened and the two defenders stepped into sight, bandaged with strips torn from their woollen shirts, the remains of which they did not bother to carry away.

"Who played that gun through th' west window?" asked Doc, angrily.

"Me!" cried Skinny, belligerently. "Why?"

"Muzzle th' talk-you can hold yore pow-wow some other time," interposed Hopalong. "You fellers get off this range, an' do it quick. An' stay off, savvy?"

Meeker, his face flushed by rage and hatred for the men who had so humiliated him, climbed up on Dan's horse and Dan was helped up behind. Then Chick was helped to mount in front of his foreman and they rode down the hill, followed by Doc and Jack. The intention was to let Dan ride to the ranch after they had all got off the Bar-20 range, and send up the cook with spare horses. Just then Doc remembered that he and Jack had left their mounts below when they walked up the hill to take the house, and they went after them.

At this instant Curley was seen galloping up and he soon reported what Salem had seen. Meeker flew into a rage at this and swore that he would never give in to either foe. While Curley was learning of the fighting, Doc and his companion returned on foot, reporting that their horses had strayed, whereupon Meeker got off the horse he rode and told Doc and Chick to ride it home, Curley being despatched for mounts, while the others sat down on the ground and waited.

When Curley returned with the horses he was very much excited, crying that during his absence Salem had seen six men run off a herd of several hundred head towards Eagle and had tried to overtake them in the chuck wagon.

"God A'mighty!" cried Meeker, furiously. "Ain't I got enough, *now*! Rustling, an' on a scale like that! Peters was right after all about th' rustling, d —n him. A whole herd! Why didn't they take th' rest, an' th' houses, an' th' whole ranch? An' Salem, th' fool, chasing 'em in th' chuck wagon! Wonder they didn't take him, too."

"I reckon he wished he had his harpoon with him," Chick snorted, the ridiculousness of Salem's action bringing a faint grin to his face, angry and wounded as he was. "He's the lo-coedest thing that wears pants in this section, or any other!"

"It was a shore fizzle all around," Meeker grumbled. "But I ain't through with that line yet-no, by th' Lord, I ain't got started yet! But this rustling has got to be cleaned up first of all-th' line can wait; an' if we don't pay no attention to th' valley for a while they'll think we've given it up an' get off their guard."

"Shore!" cried Dan, whose fury had been aroused almost to madness by the sting of the bitter defeat, and who itched to kill, whether puncher or rustler it little mattered; he only wanted a vent for his rage.

"We'll parade over that south range like buzzards sighting carrion," Meeker continued, leading the way homeward. "I ain't a-going to get robbed all th' time!"

"Wonder if Smith did shoot Ed?" queried Dan, thoughtfully. "There was quite a spell between th' shot I heard an' us seeing him, an' he acted like he had just seen Ed. But it's tough, all right. Ed was a blamed good feller."

"Who did shoot him, then?" snapped Meeker, savagely. "There's no telling what happened out there before we got there. Here, Curley, you ain't full of holes like us-you ride up there an' get him while we go home. He's laying near that S arroyo right close to th' line-th' one we scouted through that time."

"Shore, I'll get him," replied Curley, wheeling. "See you later."

Chapter XIX
Antonio Leaves the H2

On the H2 Jim Meeker rolled and muttered in his sleep, which had been more or less fitful because of his aching groin and strained leg. Gazing confusedly about him he sat bolt upright, swearing softly at the pain and then, realizing that he was where he should be, grumbled at the kaleidoscopic dreams that had beset him during his few hours of sleep, and glanced out of the window. Hastily dressing he strode to the kitchen door, calling his daughter as he passed her room, and looked out. The bunk house and the corrals were beginning to loom up in the early light and the noise in the cook shack told him that Salem was preparing breakfast for the men. He did not like the looks of the low, huge, black cloud east of him and as he figured that it would not pass over the ranch houses unless the wind shifted sharply he suddenly stared at a corral and then hastened back to his room for the Colt which lay on the floor beside his bunk. He had seen a man flit past the further corral, speed across the open, and disappear behind the corral nearest to the bunk house. This ordinarily would have provoked no further thought, for his men were crazy-headed enough to do anything, but while rustling flourished, and so audaciously, and while a line war was on, it would stand prompt investigation.

Peering again from the door, Colt in hand, Meeker slipped out silently and ran to the corral wall as rapidly as his injuries would allow. When he reached it he leaned close to it and waited, his gun levelled at the corner not ten feet from him. Half a minute later and without a sound a man suddenly turned it, crouching and alertly watching the bunk house and cook shack at his left, and then stopped with a jerk and reached to his thigh as he became aware that he was being watched at such close range. Straightening up and smothering an exclamation he faced the foreman and laughed, but to Meeker's suspicious ears it sounded very much forced and strained.

"No *sabe* Anton?" asked the prowler, smiling innocently and raising his hand from the gun.

Meeker stood silent and motionless, the Colt as steady as a rock, and a heavy frown covered his face as he searched the evil eyes of his broncho-buster, whose smile remained fixed.

"No *sabe Anton?*" somewhat hastily repeated the other, a faint trace of anxiety in his voice, but the smile did not waver, and his eyes did not shift. He began to realize that it was about time for him to leave the H2, for he knew that few things grow so rapidly as suspicion. And he knew that the outfit would do very little weighing in his case.

Meeker slowly lowered his weapon and swore; he did not like the prowling any better than he did the smile and the laugh and the treacherous eyes.

"I no savvy why yo're flitting around th' scenery when you should ought to be in bed," he replied, his words ominously low and distinct. "You've shore had a narrow squeak, for I came nigh on to letting drive from th' door on a gamble. An' I'll own that I'm some curious as to why yo're prowling around so early before breakfast. It ain't a whole lot like you to be out so early before grub time. What dragged you from th' bunk so d——d early, anyhow?"

Antonio rolled a cigarette to gain time, being elaborately exacting, and thought quickly for an excuse. Tossing the match in the air and letting the smoke curl slowly from his nostrils he grinned pleasantly. "I no sleep-have bad dreams. I wake up, *uno, dos* times an' teenk someteeng ees wrong. Then I ride to see. Eet ees soon light after that an' I am hungry, so I come back. Eet ees no more, at all."

"Oh, it ain't!" retorted the foreman, still frowning, for he strongly doubted the truth of what he had heard, so strongly that he almost passed the lie. "It's some peculiar how this ranch has been shedding dreams last night, all right. However, since I had some few myself I won't say I had all there was loose. But you listen to me, an' listen good, too. When I want any scouting done before daylight I'll take care of it myself, savvy? An' if yo're any wise you'll cure yoreself of th' habit of being out nights percolating around when you ought to be asleep. You ain't acted none too wide awake lately an' yore string of cayuses has shore been used hard, so I want it stopped, an' stopped *sudden*; hear me? I ain't paying you to work nights an' loaf days an' use up good cayuses riding hell-bent for nothing. You ain't never around no more when I want you, so you get weaned of flitting around in th' night air like a whip-poor-will; you might go an' catch malaria!"

"I no been out bafo'—Juan, he tell you that ees so, *si*."

"Is that so? I sort of reckon he'd tell me anything you want him to if he thought I'd believe it. Henceforth an' hereafter you mind what *I've* just told *you*. You might run up against some rustler what you don't know very well, an' get shot on suspicion," Meeker hazarded, but he found no change in the other's face, although he had hit Antonio hard, and he limped off to the ranch house to get his breakfast, swearing every time he put his sore leg forward, and at the ranch responsible for its condition.

Antonio leaned against the corral wall and smoked, gazing off into space as the foreman left him, for he had much to think about. He smiled cynically and shrugged his shoulders as he shambled to his shack, making up his mind to leave the H2 and join Shaw on the mesa as soon as he could do so, and the sooner the better. Meeker's remark about meeting strange rustlers, thieves he did not know, was very disquieting, and it was possible that things might happen suddenly to the broncho-buster of the H2. Soon emerging from his hut he walked leisurely to the fartherest corral and returned with his saddle and bridle. After holding a whispered consultation with Juan and Sanchez, who both showed great alarm at what he told them, and who called his attention to the fact that he had lost one of the big brass buttons from the sleeve of his coat, the three walked to the cook shack for their breakfast, where, every morning, they fought with Salem.

"Here comes them Lascars again to fill their holds with white man's grub," the cook growled as he espied them. "If I was th' old man I'd maroon them, or make 'em walk th' plank. Here, *you*! Get away from that bench!" he shouted, running out of the shack. "That's *my* grub! If you ain't good enough to eat longside of th' crew, d——d if you can eat with th' cook! Some day I'll slit you open, tail to gills, see if I don't! Here's yore grub-take it out on th' deck an' fight for it," and Salem, mounting guard over the bench, waved a huge butcher knife at them and ordered them off. "Bilgy smelling lubbers! I'll run afoul of 'em some morning an' make shark's food out of th' whole lot!"

Meanwhile Meeker, finding his breakfast not yet ready, went to Antonio's shack and glanced in it. The bunk his broncho-buster used was made up, which struck him as peculiar, since it was well known that Antonio never made up his bunk until after supper. As he turned to leave he espied the saddle and saw that the stirrups were streaked with clay. "Now what was he doing over at th' river last night?" he soliloquized. Shrugging his shoulders he wheeled and went to the bunk house, where he stumbled over a box, whacking his shins soundly. His heartfelt and extemporaneous remarks regarding stiff legs and malicious boxes awakened Curley, who sat up and vigorously rubbed his eyes with his rough knuckles. Grunts and profanity came from the other bunks, Dan swearing with exceptional loquacity and fervor at his wounded thigh.

"Somebody'll shore have to lift me out like a baby," he grumbled. "I'll get square for this, all right!"

"Aw, what you cussing about?" demanded Chick, whose arm throbbed with renewed energy when he sat up. "How'd you like to have an arm like mine so you can't use it for grub, hey?"

"You an' yore arm can—"

"What's matter, Jim?" interrupted Curley, dropping his feet to the floor and groping for his trousers. "You got my pants?" he asked Dan, whereupon Dan told him many things, ending with: "In th' name of heaven what do I want with pants on this leg! I can't get my own on, let alone yourn. Mebby Chick has put 'em on his scratched wing!" he added, with great sarcasm, whereupon Curley found them under his bunk and muttered a profane request to be told why they had crawled so far back.

"Yo're a hard luck bunch if yo're as sore as me," growled Meeker, kicking the offending box out of doors. "I cuss every time I hobble."

"Oh, I ain't sore, not a bit —I'm feeling fine," exulted Curley, putting one foot into a twisted trouser leg while he hopped recklessly about to keep his balance, Dan watching him enviously. He grabbed Chick's shoulder to steady himself and then arose from the floor to find Chick calling him every name in the language and offering to whip him with one hand if he grabbed the wounded arm again.

"Aw, what's th' matter with you!" he demanded, getting the foot through without further trouble. "I didn't stop to think, you chump!"

"Why didn't you?" snapped Chick, aggressively.

"Curley, yo're a plain, d — —d nuisance-get outside where you'll have plenty of room to get that other leg in," remarked Dan.

"Not satisfied with keeping us all awake by his cussed snoring an' talking, he goes an' *hops* right on my bad arm!" Chick remarked. "He snores something awful, Jim; like a wagon rumbling over a wooden bridge; an' he whistles every lap."

"You keep away from *me*, you cow!" warned Doc, weighing a Colt in his hand by the muzzle. "I'll shore bend this right around yore face if you don't!"

"Aw, go to th' devil! Yo're a bunch of sore-heads, just a bunch of—" Curley snapped, his words becoming inaudible as he went out to the wash bench, where Meeker followed him, glad to get away from the grunting, swearing crowd inside.

"Curley," the foreman began, leaning against the house to ease his thigh and groin, "that Greaser of our'n is either going *loco*, or he is up to some devilment, an' I a whole lot favors th' devilment. I thought of telling him to clean out, get off th' range an' stay off, but I reckon I'll let him hang around a while longer to see just what his game is. Of course if he is crooked, it's rustling. I'd like an awful lot to ketch him rustling; it'd wipe out a lot of guessing, an' him at th' same time."

"They're all of 'em crooked," Curley replied, refilling the basin. "Every blasted one, an' he's worse than all th' others-he's a coyote!"

"Yes, I reckon you ain't far from right," replied Meeker. "Well, anyway, I put in a bad night an' rolled out earlier'n usual. I looked out an' saw somebody sneaking around th' corral, an', gettin' my gun, I went after him hot foot. It was Antonio, an' when I asks for whys an' wherefores, he gives me a fool yarn about having a dream. He woke up an' was plumb scared to death somebody was running off with th' ranch, an', being so all-fired worried about th' safety of th' ranch he's too lazy to work for, he just couldn't sleep, but had to get up an' *saddle his cayuse* an' *ride* around th' corrals to see if it was here. Now, what do you think of that?"

"Huh!" snorted Curley. "He don't care a continental cuss about this ranch or anybody on it, an' never did."

"Which same I endorses; it shore was a sudden change," Meeker replied, glancing at the Mexican's shack. "I looked in his hut an' saw his bunk hadn't been used since night afore last, so he must 'a had his dreams then. There was yaller clay on his stirrups-he must 'a been scared somebody was going to run off with th' river, too. Now he shore was rampaging all over creation last night-he didn't have no dreams nor no sleep in that bunk last night, nohow. Now, th' question is, where was he, an' what th' devil was he doing? I'd give twenty-five dollars if I knowed for shore."

"That's easy!" snorted Curley, trying to get water out of his ear. "Where'd I 'a been last night if I wasn't broke? Why, down in Eagle having a good time-there's lots of good times in that town if you've got th' price of more than a look-in. Or, mebby, he was off seeing his girl, his *dulce*, as he calls her. That's a good way to pass th' evening, too." Then, seeing the frown on Meeker's face he swiftly contradicted himself, realizing that it was no time for jesting. "Why, it looks to me like he might be a little interested in some of th' promiscuous cattle lifting that's going on 'round here. I'll pump him easy so he won't know what I'm driving at."

"Yes, you might do that if yo're shore you won't scare him away, but I want you to pass th' horse corral, anyhow, an' see what horse he rode. See how hard he pushed it riding around th' corrals, an' if there's any yellow clay on its legs. Don't let him see you doing it or he'll get gun-shy an' jump th' country. I'm going up to breakfast—Mary's calling me."

Curley looked up. "Shore I'll do it. Holy cats! It's raining some on th' hills, all right. Look yonder!"

"Yes. I saw it this morning early. It passed to th' northeast of us. I'll be back soon," and the foreman limped away. "Hey, Curley," he called over his shoulder for Antonio's benefit, "take a look at them sore yearlings in th' corral," referring to several calves they had quarantined.

"All right, Jim. They was some better last night. I don't think it's anything that's catching."

"O-o-h!" yawned Jack in the doorway. "Seems like I just turned in—gosh, but I'm sleepy."

"Nothing like cold water for that feeling," laughed Curley. "We stayed up too late last night talking it over. Hullo, Chick; still going to lick me one-handed?"

"You get away from that water, so I can wash one-handed," replied Chick. "But you shouldn't ought to 'a done that. No, Jack—go ahead; but I'm next. Hey, Dan!" he cried, laughing, "shall I bring some water in to you?"

"I won't stay here an' listen to such language as Dan's ripping off," Curley grinned, starting away. "I'm going up to look at them sick yearlings in Number Two corral."

True to his word Curley looked the animals over thoroughly and then dodged into the horse corral, where he quickly examined the horses as he passed them, alert for trouble, for a man on foot takes chances when he goes among cow-ponies in a corral. Not one of the animals forming Antonio's *remuda* appeared to have been ridden and it was not until he espied Pete, Doc's favorite horse, that he found any signs. Pete's hair was roughened and still wet from perspiration, there was a streak of yellow clay along its belly on one side but none on its hoofs, and dried lather still clung to its jaws. Pete made no effort to get away, for he was one of the best trained and most intelligent animals on the ranch, a veteran of many roundups and drives, and he knew from experience that he would not be called on to do double duty; he had done his trick while the others rested.

"An' you know I ain't a-going to ride you, hey?" Curley muttered. "You've had yore turn, an' you know you won't be called on to-day, you wise old devil. Pete, some people say cayuses ain't got no sense, that they can't reason—they never knowed you, did they? Well, boy, you'll have yore turn grazing with th' rest purty soon."

He returned to the bunk house and spent a few minutes inside and then sauntered easily towards the ranch house, where the foreman met him.

"So there wasn't no clay on his hoofs, hey?" Meeker exclaimed. "Some on his belly, an' none on his hoofs. Hum! I reckon Pete was left by hisself while th' Greaser wrastled with th' mud. Must 'a thought he was prospecting. Well, he's a liar, an' a sneak; watch him close, an' tell th' rest to do th' same. Mebby we'll get th' chance soon of stretching his yellow neck some bright morning. I'll be down purty soon to tell you fellers where to ride."

Curley returned to the wash bench and cleansed his hands, and because the cold water felt so good, he dipped his face into it again, blowing like a porpoise. As he squilgeed his face to lessen the duty of the overworked towel, he heard a step and looked up quickly. Antonio was leaning against the house and scowling at him, for he had looked through a crack in the corral wall and had seen Pete being examined.

"Eet ees *bueno* thees mornin'," the Mexican offered.

"What's good?" Curley retorted, staring because of Antonio's unusual loquacity.

"*Madre de Dios*, de weatha."

"Oh, salubrious," replied Curley, evading a hole in the towel. "Plumb sumptuous an' high-falutin', so to speak. You had a nice night for Eagle, all right. Who-all was down there?"

"Antone not en Eagle-he no leev de rancho," the Mexican replied, surprised. He hesitated as if to continue and Curley noticed it.

"What's on yore mind, 'Tony? What's eating you? *Pronto*, I'm hungry. Next!"

"No nex'—I no *sabe*."

"You talkee likum Chinee!" retorted Curley. "Why don't you learn how to talk English? It's easy enough. An' what do you want, anyhow, getting so friendly all of a sudden?"

Antonio hesitated again. "What you do een de corral thees mornin'?"

"Oh, I was looking at them yearlings-they was purty bad, but they're gettin' along all right. What do you think about 'em?"

"No; een de *beeg* corral."

"Oh, you do!" snapped Curley. "Well, I remembered you was riding around this morning before sun-up so I reckoned I'd look in an' see if you rid my cayuse, which you didn't, an' which is good for you. I ain't a whole lot intending to go moping about on no tired-out bronc, an' don't you forget it, neither. An' seeing as how it ain't none of your d———d business what I do or where I go, that's about all for you."

"You no spik true—*Pah*! eet ees a lie!" cried the Mexican excitedly, advancing a step, and running into the wash water and a fist, both of which met him in the face. Curley, reaching for his holster and finding that he had forgotten to buckle it on, snatched the Remington from Antonio's sheath while the fallen man was half dazed. Pointing it at the Mexican's stomach, he ordered him up and then told him things.

"I reckon you got off easy, Greaser-th' next time you calls me a liar shoot first, or there'll be one less unwashed, shifty-eyed coyote of a Greaser to ride range nights."

Antonio, drenched and seething with fury, his discolored face working with passion and his small, cruel eyes snapping, sprang to the wall and glared at the man who had knocked him down. But for the gun in Curley's hand there would have been the flash of a knife, but the Remington was master of the situation. Knife throwing is a useful art at times, but it has its limitations. Cursing in Spanish, he backed away and slunk into his shack as Doc Riley stuck his head out of the bunk house doorway, hoping to be entertained.

"Worth while hanging 'round, Curley? Any chance of seeing a scrap?" Doc asked, eying the gun in his friend's hand.

"You could 'a seen th' beginning of a scrap a couple of minutes earlier," Curley replied. "I didn't give him a chance to throw. Why, he was out all night on Pete, yore cayuse-rode him hard, too. He said—"

"My Pete! Out all night on Pete!" yelled Doc, taking a quick step towards Antonio's hut, the door of which slammed shut, whereupon Doc shouted out his opinions of "Greasers" in general and of Antonio in particular. "Is that right?" he asked, turning to Curley. "Was he out on Pete?"

"He shore was-used him up, too."

"I'll break every bone in his yaller carcass!" Doc shouted, shaking his fist at the hut. "Every time I see him I want to get my gun going, an' it's getting worse all th' time. Unwashed pup! I'll fill him full of lead pills surer than anything some of these days, you see if I don't!"

"If you don't I will," replied Curley. "I just don't know why I didn't then because—"

"Four bells-grub pile!" rang out the stentorian voice of Salem, who could shout louder than any man on the ranch, and the conversation came to an abrupt end, to be renewed at the table.

When Antonio heard the cook's shout he opened the door a trifle and then, seeing that the coast was clear, picked up the bundle which contained his belongings, shouldered his saddle, slipped his rifle under his arm, and ran to the corral. Juan and Sanchez had been there before him and he found that they not only had taken four of the best horses, but that they had also picketed two good ones for him, and had driven off the remainder to graze, which would delay pursuit should it be instituted. Saddling the better of the two, he left the other and cantered northwest until hidden from the sight of any one at the ranch, and then galloped for safety.

Meeker, returning to the bunk house, found his men in far better humor than they were in when he left them, although the death and burial of Ed Joyce and the other misfortunes of the day before had quieted them a little. As he entered the room he heard Salem in the cook shack, droning a mournful dirge-like air as he slammed things about.

"Hey, cook!" shouted the foreman, standing in the door of the gallery. "Cook!"

"Aye, aye, sir!"

"You are shore you didn't recognize none of them thieves that ran off our herd yesterday?"

"Nary a one, sir. They was running with all sails set two points off my port bow, which left me astarn of 'em. I was in that water-logged, four-wheeled hulk of a chuck wagon an' I couldn't overhaul 'em, sir, 'though I gave chase. I tried a shot with th' chaser, but I was rolling so hard I couldn't hull 'em. But I'll try again when I'm sober, sir."

"All right, Salem," laughed Meeker. "Curley, you take yore regular range. Doc, suppose you take th' west, next to Curley? Chick an' Dan will have to stay here till they get well enough to ride, an' I'll need somebody on th' ranch after yesterday, anyhow. Jack, how do you feel? Good! Ride between here an' Eagle. I'm going to go down to that town an' see what I can find out."

"But I can ride, Jim," offered Chick, eagerly. "This arm won't bother me much. Let me stick close to Doc, or one of th' boys. Maybe they might need me, Jim."

"You stay right here, like I said. We'll have to wait till we're all right before we can get down to work in earnest. An' every one of you look out for trouble—shoot first an' talk after." He turned again to the gallery. "Salem, kill a cow an' sun cure th' meat; we might want it in a hurry sometime soon. That'll be one cow they don't get, anyway."

"Who's going to ride north, Jim?" asked Doc.

"Nobody; th' Bar-20 has been so d — —d anxious to turn our cows an' do our herding for us, an' run th' earth, we'll just let 'em for a while. Not much danger of any rustlers buzzing reckless around *that* neighborhood; they'll earn all they steal if they get away with it."

> I saw her face grow cold in death,
> I saw her —

came Salem's voice in a new wail. Meeker grabbed a quirt and, leaping to the gallery, threw it. The song stopped short and other words, less tuneful, finished the cook's efforts.

"You never mind what you saw!" shouted the foreman. "If you can't sing anything but grave-yard howls, you shut up yore singer!"

Chapter XX
What the Dam Told

About the time Meeker caught Antonio prowling around the corral, Hopalong stepped out of the line house on the Peak and saw the approaching storm, which gladdened him, notwithstanding the fact that he and Red would ride through it to the bunk house. The range was fast drying up, the grass was burning under the fierce heat of the sun, and the reservoir, evaporating as rapidly as it was supplied, sent but little water down the creek through the valley. This storm, if it broke over the valley, promised to be almost a flood, and would not only replenish the water supply, but would fortify the range for quite a while against the merciless sun.

After he had sent Meeker and his men on their homeward journey he ordered all but Red to report to Buck at the bunk house, believing that the line fighting was at an end for a while, at least. But to circumvent any contingency to the contrary, he and Red remained to guard the house and discuss the situation. The rest of the line riders were glad to get away for a day, as there was washing and mending to be done, clothes to be changed, and their supply of cartridges and tobacco to be replenished.

After throwing his saddle on his horse he went back to the house to get his "slicker," a yellow water-proof coat, and saw Red gathering up their few belongings.

"Going to rain like th' devil, Red," he said. "We'll get soaked before we reach th' dam, but it'll give th' grass a chance, all right. It's due us, an' we're going to get it."

Red glanced out of the window and saw the onrushing, low black mass of clouds. "Gee! I reckon yes! Going to be some fireworks, too."

Hopalong, slipping into the hideous slicker, followed Red outside and watched him saddle up. "It'll seem good to be in th' house again with all th' boys, an' eat cook's grub once more. I reckon Frenchy an' some of his squad will drift in-Johnny said he was going to ride out that way on his way back an' tell 'em all th' news."

"Yes. Mind yore business, Ginger!" Red added as his horse turned its head and nipped at his arm, half in earnest and half in playful expostulation. Ginger could not accustom himself to the broad, hind cinch which gripped his soft stomach, and he was wont to object to it in his own way. "Yes, it's going to be a shore enough cloud-burst!" Red exclaimed, glancing apprehensively at the storm. "Mebby we better take th' hill trail-we won't have no cinch fording at th' Bend if *that* lets loose before we get there. We should 'a gone home with th' crowd last night, 'stead of staying up here. I knowed they wouldn't try it again-it's all yore fault."

"Oh, yo're a regular old woman!" retorted Hopalong. "A wetting will do us good-an' as for th' ford, I feel like having a swim."

The close, humid air stirred and moaned, and fitful gusts bent the sparse grass and rustled across the plateau, picking up dust and sending it eddying along the ground. A sudden current of air whined around the corners of the line house, slamming the door violently and awakening the embers of the fire into a mass of glowing coals, which crackled and gave off flying sparks. Several larger embers burst into flame and tumbled end over end across the ground, and Hopalong, running them down, stamped them out, returning and kicking dust over the fire, actuated by the plainsman's instinct. Red watched him and grinned.

"Of course that cloud-burst won't put the fire out," he remarked, sarcastically, although he would have done the same thing if his friend had not.

"Never go away an' leave a fire lit," Hopalong replied, sententiously, closing the banging door and fastening it shut. A streak of lightning quivered between earth and clouds and the thunder rolled in many reverberations along the cliffs of the valley's edge, to die out on the flat void to the west. Down the wind came the haunting wail of a coyote, sounding so close at hand that Red instinctively reached for his rifle and looked around.

"Take *mine!*" jeered Hopalong, mounting, having in mind the greater range of his weapon. "You'll shore need it if you want to get that feller. Gee, but it's dark!"

It was dark and the air was so charged with electricity that blue points of flame quivered on the ears of their horses.

"We're going to get h —l!" shouted Red above the roar of the storm. "Every time I spits I make a streak in th' air-an' ain't it hot!"

One minute it was dark; another, the lightning showed things in a ghastly light, crackling and booming like a huge fireworks exhibition. The two men could feel the hearts of their horses pounding against their sides, and the animals, nervous as cats, kept their ears moving back and forth, the blue sparks ghostly in the darkness.

"Come on, get out of this," shouted Hopalong. "D —n it, there goes my hat!" and he shot after it.

For reply Red spurred forward and they rode down the steep hill at a canter, which soon changed to a gallop, then to a dead run. Suddenly there came a roar that shook them and the storm broke in earnest, the rain pouring down in slanting sheets, drenching them to the skin in a minute, for their slickers were no protection against that deluge. Hopalong stripped his off, to see it torn from his grasp and disappear in the darkness like a frightened thing.

"Go, then!" he snapped. "I was roasting in you, anyhow! I won't have no clothes left by th' time I hits th' Bend-which is all th' better for swimming."

Red slackened pace, rode at his friend's side, their stirrups almost touching, for it was safer to canter than to gallop when they could not see ahead of them. The darkness gradually lessened and when they got close to the dam they could see as well as they could on any dull day, except for a distance-the sheets of water forbade that.

"What's that?" Hopalong suddenly demanded, drawing rein and listening. A dull roar came from the dam and he instinctively felt that something was radically wrong.

"Water, of course," Red replied, impatiently. "This is a *storm*," he explained.

Hopalong rode out along the dam, followed by Red, peering ahead. Suddenly he stopped and swore.

"She's *busted*! Look there!"

A turbulent flood poured through a cut ten feet wide and roared down the other side of the embankment, roiled and yellow.

"Good G-d! She's a goner shore!" cried Red excitedly.

"It shore is —*No*, Red! It's over th' stone work-see where that ripple runs? We can save it if we hustle," Hopalong replied, wheeling. "Come on! Dead cows'll choke it-get a move on!"

When Buck had decided to build the dam he had sent for an engineer to come out and look the valley over and to lay out the lines to be followed. The west end, which would be built against the bluff, would be strong; but Buck was advised to build a core of rubble masonry for a hundred feet east of the centre, where the embankment must run almost straight to avoid a quicksand bottom. This had been done at a great increase over the original estimate of the cost of the dam, but now it more than paid for itself, for Antonio had dug his trench over the rubble core-had he gone down a foot deeper he would have struck it and discovered his mistake.

Hopalong and Red raced along the dam and separated when they struck the plain, soon returning with a cow apiece dragging from their lariats, which they released and pushed into the torrent. The bodies floated with the stream and both men feared their efforts were in vain. Then Hopalong uttered a shout of joy, for the carcasses, stranding against the top of the masonry core, stopped, the water surging over them. Racing away again they dragged up more cows until the bodies choked the gap, when they brought up armfuls of brush and threw them before the bodies. Then Red espied a shovel, swore furiously at what it told him, and fell to throwing dirt into the breach before the brush. He had to take it from different places so as not to weaken the dam, and an hour elapsed before they stopped work and regarded the results of their efforts with satisfaction.

"Well, she's there yet, and she'll stay, all right. Good thing we didn't take th' hill trail," Hopalong remarked.

"Somebody cut it, all right," Red avowed, looking at the shovel in his hands. "*H2*! Hoppy, see here! This is *their* work!"

"Shore enough H2 on th' handle, but Meeker an' his crowd never did that," Hopalong replied. "I ain't got no love for any of 'em, but they're too square for this sort of a thing. Besides, they want to use this water too much to cheat themselves out of every chance to get it."

"You may be right-but it's d — —d funny that we find their shovel on th' job," Red rejoined, scowling at the brand burned into the wooden handle.

"What's that yo're treading on?" Hopalong asked, pointing to a bright object on the ground.

Red stooped and then shouted, holding up the object so his friend could see it. "It's a brass button as big as a half-dollar —bet it belonged to th' snake that used this shovel!"

"Yo're safe. I won't bet you-an' Antonio was th' only one I've seen wearing buttons like that in these parts," Hopalong replied. "I'm going to kill him on sight!" and he meant what he said.

"Same here, th' ornery coyote!" Red gritted.

"That Greaser has had me guessing, but I'm beginning to see a great big light," Hopalong remarked, taking the button and looking it over. "Yep, it's hissen, all right."

"Well, we've filled her," Red remarked after a final inspection.

"She'll hold until to-morrow, anyhow, or till we can bring th' chuck wagon full of tools an' rocks down here," Hopalong replied. "We'll make her solid for keeps when we begin. You better take th' evidence with you, Red, an' let Buck look 'em over. It's a good thing Buck spent that extra money putting in that stone core! Besides losing th' reservoir we'd have had plenty of dead cows by this time if it wasn't for that."

"An' that Greaser went an' picked out the weakest spot in th' whole thing, or th' spot what would be th' weakest if that wall wasn't there," Red remarked. "He ain't no fool, but a stacked deck can beat a good head time after time."

When they reached the ford they found a driftwood-dotted flood roaring around the bend, three times as wide as it was ordinarily, for the hills made a watershed that gave quick results in such a rain.

"Now Red Eagle, old cayuse, here's where you swim," Hopalong laughed, riding up stream so he would not be carried past the bottom of the hill trail on the farther side. Plunging in, the two horses swam gallantly across, landing within a few feet of the point aimed at, and scrambled up the slippery path, down which poured a stream of water.

When they reached the half-way point between the ford and the ranch houses the storm slackened, evolving into an ordinary rain, which Hopalong remarked would last all day. Red nodded and then pointed to a miserable, rain-soaked calf, which moved away at their approach.

"Do you see that!" he exclaimed. "Our brand, an' Meeker's ear notch!"

"That explains th' shovel being left on th' dam," quickly replied Hopalong. "It would be plumb crazy for th' H2 to make a combination like that ear notch an' our brand, an' you can gamble they don't know nothing about it. Th' gent that left Meeker's shovel *for us to find* did that, too. You know if any of th' H2 cut th' dam they wouldn't forget to take th' shovel with 'em, Red. It's Antonio, that's who it is. He's trying to make a bigger fight along th' line an' stir things up generally so he can rustle promiscuous. Well, we'll give all our time to th' rustling end from now on, if I have got any voice in th' matter. An' I hope to th' Lord I can get within gun range of that coyote of a Greaser. Why, by th' A'mighty, I'll go down an' plug him on his own ground just as soon as I can get away, which will be to-morrow! That's just what I'll do! I'll stop his plays or know th' reason why."

"An' I'm with you-you'll take a big chance going down there alone," Red replied. "*After* Meeker hears what we've got to say he'll be blamed glad we came."

An hour later they stopped at the ranch house, a squat, square building, flat of roof, its adobe walls three feet thick and impenetrable to heat. Stripping saddles and bridles from their streaming mounts, they drove the animals into a large corral and ran to the bunk house, where laughter greeted their appearance.

"Swimming?" queried Johnny, putting aside his harmonica.

"Hey, you! Get out of here an' lean up against th' corral till you shed some of that water!" cried Lanky, the wounded, watching the streams from their clothes run over the floor. "We'll be afloat in a minute if you don't get out-we ain't no fishes."

"You shut up," retorted Red. "We'll put you out there to catch what water we missed if you gets funny," he threatened, stripping as rapidly as he could. He hung the saturated garments on pegs in the gallery wall and had Pete rub him down briskly, while Billy did the same for his soaked companion.

Around them were their best friends, all laughing and contented, chaffing and exchanging personal banter with each other, engaged in various occupations, from sewing buttons on shirts to playing cards and mending riding gear. Snatches of songs burst forth at odd intervals, while laughter was continually heard. This was the atmosphere they loved, this repaid them for their hard work, this and the unswerving loyalty, the true, deep affection, and good-natured banter that pricked but left no sting. Here was one of the lures of the range, the perfect fellowship that long acquaintance and the sharing of hard work and ubiquitous danger breeds among the members of a good, square outfit. Not one of them ever counted personal safety before duty to his ranch and his companions, taking his hard life laughingly and without complaint, generous to a fault, truthful and loyal and considerate. There was manhood for you, there was contempt for restricting conventions, for danger; there was a unity of thought and purpose that set the rough-spoken, ready-fighting men of the saddle and rope in a niche by themselves, a niche where fair play, unselfishness, and a rough but sterling honor abides always. Their occupation gave more than it exacted and they loved it and the open, wind-swept range where they were the dominating living forces.

Buck came in with Frenchy McAllister and Pie Willis and grinned at his crowd of happy "boys," who gave warm welcome. The foreman was not their "boss," their taskmaster, but he was their best friend, and he shared with them the dangers and joys which were their lot, sympathetic in his rough way, kind and trusting.

Hopalong struggling to get his head through a dry shirt, succeeded, and swiftly related to his foreman the occurrences of the morning, pointing to the shovel and button as the total exhibit of his proofs against the Mexican. The laughter died out, the banter was hushed, and the atmosphere became that of tense hostility and anger. When he had ceased speaking angry exclamations and threats filled the room, coming from men who always "made good." When Red had told of the H2-Bar-20 calf, an air of finality, of conviction, settled on them; and it behooved Antonio to hunt a new range, for his death would be sudden and merciless if he met any of the Bar-20 outfit, no matter when or where. They never forgot.

After brief argument they came to the decision that he was connected with the rustling going on around them, and this clinched his fate. Several, from the evidence and from things which they had observed and now understood, were of the opinion that he was the ringleader of the cattle thieves, the head and the moving spirit.

"Boys," Buck remarked, "we won't bother about th' line very much for a while. It's been a peaceable sort of a fracas, anyhow, an' I don't expect much further trouble. If H2 cows straggle across an' yo're right handy to 'em an' ain't got nothing pressing to do, drive 'em back; but don't look for 'em particularly. There won't be no more drives against us for a long time. We've got to hunt rustlers from now on, an' hunt hard, or they'll get too numerous to handle very easy. Let th' cows take care of themselves along th' river, Frenchy, an' put your men up near Big Coulee, staying nights in Number Two. Pete an' Billy will go with you. That'll protect th' west, an' there won't be no rustling going on from th' river, nohow. Don't waste no time herding-put it all in hunting. Hopalong, you, Johnny, Red, an' Skinny take th' hills country an' make yore headquarters in Number Three an' Four. Lanky will stay up here until he can handle hisself good again. I'll ride promiscuous, but if any of you learn anything you want me to know, leave it with Lanky or th' cook if you can't find me. Just as soon as we have anything to go on, we'll start on th' war path hot foot an' clean things up right an' proper."

"What'll we do if we catches anybody rustling?" asked Johnny, assuming an air of ignorance and curiosity, and ducking quickly as Red swung at him.

"Give 'em ten dollars reward an' let 'em go," Buck grinned.

"Give me ten if I brings th' Greaser to you?"

"I'll fine you twenty if you waste that much time over him," Buck replied.

"Whoop!" Johnny exulted. "Th' good old times are coming back again! Remember Bye-an'-Bye an' Cactus Springs, Buckskin an' Slippery Trendley? Remember th' good old scraps? Now we'll have something else to do besides chasing cows an' wiping th' rust off our guns!"

Lanky, who took keen delight in teasing the youngster, frowned severely. "Yo're just a fool kid, just a happy idiot!" he snorted, and Johnny looked at him, surprised but grinning. "Yes, you are! I never seen such a bloody-minded animal in all my born days as you! After all th' fighting you've gone an' got mixed up in, you still yap for more! You makes me plumb disgusted, you do!"

"He *is* awful gory," remarked Hopalong soberly. "Just a animated massacre in pants."

"Regular Comanche," amended Red, frowning. "What do you think about him, Frenchy?"

"I'd ruther not say it," Frenchy replied. "You ask Pie-he ain't scared of nothing, massacre *or* Comanche."

Johnny looked around the room and blurted out, "You all think th' same as me, every one of you, even if you are a lot of pussy-cats, an' you know it, too!"

"Crazy as a locoed cow," Red whispered across the room to Buck, who nodded sorrowfully and went into the cook shack.

"You wait till I sees Antonio an' you'll find out how crazy I am!" promised Johnny.

"I shore hopes he spanks you an' sends you home a-bawling," Lanky snorted. "You needs a good licking, you young cub!"

"Yah, yah!" jibed Johnny. "Needing an' getting are two different tunes, grand-pop!"

"You wasn't down here, was you, Frenchy, when Johnny managed to rope a sleepy gray wolf that was two years old, an' tried to make a pet out of him?" asked Hopalong, grinning at his recollection of the affair.

"No!" exclaimed Frenchy in surprise. "Did he do it?"

"Oh, yes, he did it; with a gun, after th' pet had torn his pants off an' chewed him up real well. He's looking for another, because he says that was too mean a beast to have any luck with."

Buck stepped into the room again. "Who wants to go with me to th' dam in th' wagon?" he asked. "I want to look at that cut an' fix it for keeps if it needs fixing. All right! All right! Anybody'd think I asked you to go to a dance," he laughed. "Pete, you an' Billy an' Pie will be enough."

"Can't we ride alongside?" asked Pie. "Do we have to sit in that thing?"

"You can walk, if you want to. I don't care how you go," Buck replied, stepping into the rain with the three men close behind him. Soon the rattling of the wagon was heard growing fainter on the plain.

The banter and the laughter ran on all the rest of the morning. After dinner Hopalong built a fire in the huge stove and put a ladleful of lead on the coals, while Frenchy and Skinny re-sized and re-capped shells from the boxes on the wall. Hopalong watched the fire and smoked the bullet moulds, while Lanky managed to measure powder and fill the shells after Frenchy and Skinny had finished with them. Hopalong filled the moulds rapidly while Johnny took out the bullets and cooled them by dropping them into cold rain water, being cautioned by Hopalong not to splash any water into the row of moulds. As soon as he found them cool enough, Johnny wiped them dry and passed them on to Red, who crimped them into the charged shells. Soon the piles of cartridges grew to a goodly size, and when the last one had been finished the crowd fell to playing cards until supper was ready. Hopalong, who had kept on running bullets, sorted them, and then dropped them into the boxes made for each size. Finally he stopped and went to the door to look for signs of the morrow's weather.

"Clearing up in th' west an' south-here comes Buck an' th' others," he called over his shoulder. "How was it, Buck?" he shouted, and out of the gathering dusk came the happy reply:

"Bully!"

Chapter XXI
Hopalong Rides South

The morning broke clear and showed a clean, freshened plain to the men who rode to the line house on the Peak, there to take up their quarters and from there to ride as scouts. Hopalong sent Red to ride along the line for the purpose of seeing how things were in that vicinity and, leaving the others to go where they wished, struck south down the side of the hill, intending to hunt Antonio on his own ground. Tied to his saddle was the shovel and in his pocket he carried the brass button, his evidence for Meeker. As he rode at an easy lope he kept a constant lookout for signs of rustling. Suddenly he leaned forward and tightened his knee grip, the horse responding by breaking into a gallop, while its rider took up his lariat, shaking it into a long loop, his twisting right wrist imparting enough motion to it to keep it clear of the vegetation and rocks.

A distant cow wheeled sharply and watched him for a moment and then, snorting, its head down and its tail up, galloped away at a speed not to be found among domesticated cattle. It was bent upon only one thing-to escape that dreaded, whirling loop of rawhide, so pliant and yet so strong. Hopalong, not as expert as Lanky, who carried a rope nearly sixty feet long and who could place it where he wished, used one longer than the more common lariats.

The cow did its best, but the pony steadily gained, nimbly executing quick turns and jumping gullies, up one side of a hill and down the other, threading its way with precision through the chaparrals and deftly avoiding the holes in its path. Closer and closer together came the pursued and pursuers, and then the long rope shot out and sailed through the air, straight for the animal's hind legs. As it settled, a quick upward jerk of the arm did the rest and there was a snubbing of rope around the saddle horn, a sudden stopping and dropping back on haunches on the part of the pony, and the cow went down heavily. The rider did not wait for the horse to get set, but left the saddle as soon as the rope had been securely snubbed, and ran to the side of his victim.

The cow was absolutely helpless, for the rope was taut, the intelligent pony leaning back and being too well trained to allow the least amount of slack to bow the rawhide closer to the earth. Therefore Hopalong gave no thought to his horse, for while cinches, pommel, and rope held, the small, wiry, wild-eyed bundle of galvanic cussedness would hold the cow despite all its efforts to get up.

"Never saw *that* brand before, an' I've rid all over this country for a good many years, too," he soliloquized. "There sure ain't no HQQ herd down this way, nor no place close enough for a stray. Somebody is shore starting a herd on his own hook; from th' cows on this range, too.

"By th' great horned spoon! I can see Bar-20 in them marks!" he cried, bending closer. "All he had to do was to make a H out of th' Bar, close up th' 2, an' put a tail on th' O! Hum-whoop! There is H2 in it, too! Close th' 2 an' add a Q, an' there you are! I don't mind a hog once in a while, but working both ranches to a common mark is shore too much for me. Stealing from both ranches an' markin 'em all HQQ!"

He moved up to look at the ears and swore when he saw them. "D —n it! That's all I want to know! Mebby a sheriff wouldn't get busy on th' evidence, but I ain't no sheriff—I'm just a plain cow-punch with good common sense. Meeker's cut is a V in one ear-here I finds a slant like Skinny saw, an' in both ears. If that don't cut under Meeker's notch I'm a liar! All framed up to make a new herd out of our cows. Just let me catch some coyote with a running iron under his saddle flap an' see what happens!"

He quickly slacked the rope and slipped off the noose, running as fast as he could go to his pony, for some cows get "on the prod" very easily, and few cows are afraid of a man on foot; and when a long-horned Texas cow has "its dander up," it is not safe for an unmounted man to take a chance with its horns, unless he is willing to shoot it down. This Hopalong would not do, for he did not want to let the rustlers know that the new brand had been discovered. Vaulting into his saddle he eluded the charge of the indignant cow and loped south, coiling up his rope as he went.

Half an hour after leaving the HQQ cow he saw a horseman ahead of him, threading his way through a chaparral. As Hopalong overtook him the other emerged and stopped, uncertain whether to reach for his gun or not. It was Juan, who had not gone to Mesa overnight, scouting to learn if any new developments had taken place along the boundary. Juan looked at the shovel and then at the puncher, his face expressionless.

Hopalong glanced at the other's cuff, found it was all right, and then forced himself to smile. "Looking for rustlers?" he bantered.

"*Si.*"

"What! There ain't no rustlers loose on this range, is there?" asked Hopalong, surprised.

"*Quien sabe?*"

"Oh, them sleepers were made by yore own, lazy outfit, an' you might as well own up to it," Hopalong grinned, deprecatingly. "You can fool Meeker, all right, he's easy; but you can't throw dust in my eyes like that. On th' level, now, ain't I right? Didn't you fellers make them sleepers?"

Juan shrugged his shoulders. "*Quien sabe?*"

"That *'Quien sabe'* is th' handiest an' most used pair of words in yore cussed language," replied Hopalong grinning. "Ask one of you fellers something you don't want to tell an' it's *'Quien sabe?'* ain't it?"

"*Si,*" laughed the Mexican.

"I thought so," Hopalong retorted. "You can't tell me that any gang that would cut a dam like they did ourn wouldn't sleeper, an' don't you forget it, neither!"

Juan's face cleared for a moment as he gloated over how Antonio's scheme had worked out, and he laughed. "No can fool you, hey?" Then he pressed his knee tighter against his saddle skirt and a worried look came into his eyes.

Hopalong took no apparent notice of the action, but he saw it, and it sent one word burning through his brain. They were riding at a walk now and Hopalong, not knowing that Juan had left the H2, suggested that they ride to the ranch together. He was watching the Mexican closely, for it would not be unusual for a man in Juan's position to try to get out of it by shooting. The Mexican refused to ride south and Hopalong, who was determined to stay with his companion until he found out what he wanted to know, proposed a race to a barranca that cut into the plain several hundred yards ahead. He would let Juan beat him, and all the way, so he could watch the saddle flap, and if this failed he would waste no more time in strategy, but would find out about it quickly. Juan also declined to race, and very hurriedly, for the less his saddle was jolted the better it would be for him. He knew Hopalong's reputation as a revolver fighter and would take no chances.

"That ain't a bad cayuse you got there. I was wondering if it could beat mine, what's purty good itself. Is it very bronc?" he asked, kicking the animal in the ribs whereupon it reared and pranced. Juan's left hand went to the assistance of his knee, his right grasped the cantle of his saddle, where it was nearer the butt of his Colt, and a look of fear came into his eyes.

Hopalong watched his chance and as the restive animal swung towards him he spurred it viciously, at the same time crying: "Take yore hand from off that flap, you d ———d cow-lifter!"

The command was unnecessary, for a thin, straight rod of iron slipped down and stuck in the sand, having worked loose from its lashings. Mexican-like, Juan had put off until to-morrow to heat it and bend a loop in one end for more secure fastening.

At the instant it fell Juan leaned back and dropped over on the far side of his horse, his right leg coming up level with his enemy, and reached for his gun, intending to shoot through the end of the holster and save time. But he went farther than he had intended, not stopping until he struck the earth, his bullet missing Hopalong by only a few inches.

The Bar-20 puncher slipped his Colt back into the sheath and, leaning down, deftly picked up the iron and fastened it to his saddle. Roping the Mexican's horse he continued on his way to the H2, leaving Juan where he had fallen.

When he arrived at the ranch he turned the horse into the corral and started to ride to the bunk house; but Salem, enjoying a respite from cooking and washing dishes, saw him and started for him on an awkward run, crying:

"Where'd you git that hoss? Where'd you clear from, an' who are you?"

"Th' cayuse belongs to Meeker—Juan was riding it. Is anybody around?"

"I'm around, ain't I, you fog-eyed lubber! Where's th' Lascar? Who are you?"

"Well, Duke, I'm from th' Bar-20, an' my name is Hop—"

"Weigh anchor an' 'bout ship! You can't make this port, you wind-jamming pirate!"

"I want to see yore foreman. This is his shovel, an' I—"

"Then where'd you get it, hey? How'd you get his—"

"Hang it!" interrupted Hopalong, losing his patience. "I tell you I want to see Meeker! I want to see him about some—"

"An' where's th' coolie that rid that hoss?" demanded the cook, belligerently.

"You won't see that thief no more. That's one of th' things I want to—"

"Hooray!" cried Salem. "Was he drowned, or shanghaied?"

"Was he what? What are you talking about, anyhow? Where did you ever learn how to talk Chinese?"

"What! Chinese! You whale-bellied, barnacle-brained bilge pirate, I've got a good notion —"

"Say, is there anybody around here that ain't loco? Are they all as crazy as you?" Hopalong asked.

Salem grabbed up one of the bars of the corral gate and, roaring strange oaths, ran at the stranger, but Hopalong spurred his horse and kept clear of the pole while Salem grew short winded and more profane. Then the puncher thought of Mary and cantered towards the ranch house intending to ask her where he could find her father, thus combining business with pleasure. Salem shook the pole at him and then espied the saddled horse in the corral. He disliked horses as much as they disliked him, so much, in fact, that he said the only reason he did not get out of the country and go back to the sea was because he had to ride a horse to do it. But any way was acceptable under the present exigencies, so he clambered into the saddle after more or less effort and found it not quite roomy enough for one of his growing corpulency. Shouting "Let fall!" he cantered after the invader of his ranch, waving the pole valiantly. He did not see that the ears of his mount were flattened or that its eyes were growing murderous in their expression, and he did not know that the lower end of the pole was pounding lustily against the horse's legs every time he waved the weapon. All he thought about was getting his pleasant duty over with as soon as possible, and he gripped the pole more firmly.

Hopalong looked around curiously to see what the cook was doing to make all that noise, and when he saw he held his sides. "Well, if th' locoed son-of-a-gun ain't after me! Lord! Hey, stranger," he shouted, "if you want him to run fast, take hold of his tail an' pull it three times!"

He was not averse to having a little fun at the tenderfoot's expense and he deferred his visit to the house to circle around the angry cook and shout advice. Instead of laying the reins against his mount's neck to turn it, Salem jerked on them, which the indignant animal instantly resented. It had felt all along that it was being made a fool of and imposed upon, but now it would have a sweet revenge. Leaping forward suddenly it stopped stiff-legged and arched its back several times with all the force it was capable of; but it could have stopped immediately after the first pitch, for Salem, still holding to the pole, executed a more or less graceful parabola and landed in a sitting posture amid much dust.

"*Whoof!* What'd we strike?" he demanded dazedly. Then, catching sight of the cause of his flight, which was at that moment cropping an overlooked tuft of grass as if it were accustomed to upsetting pole-waving cooks, Salem scrambled to his feet and ran at it, getting in one good whack before the indignant and groping pony could move.

"There, blast you!" he yelled. "I'll show you what you get for a trick like that!" Turning, and seeing Hopalong laughing until the tears ran down his face, he roared, "What are you laughing at, d —n you?"

A rope sailed out and tightened around Salem's feet and he once more sat down, unable to arise this time, because of Hopalong's horse, which backed slowly, step by step, dragging the captive, who was now absolutely helpless.

"Now I want to talk to you for a few minutes, an' I'm going to," Hopalong remarked. "Will you listen quietly or will you risk losing th' seat of yore pants? You've *got* to listen, anyhow."

"Wha-what ——go ahead, only stop th' headway of yore craft! Lay to! I'm on th' rocks!"

Laughing, Hopalong rode closer to him. "Where's Antonio?"

"In h —l, I hope, leastwise that's where he ought to be."

"Well, I just sent his friend Juan there-had to; he toted a running iron an' —"

"Did you? Did you?" cried Salem in accents of joy. "Why didn't you say so before! Come in an' splice th' main brace, shipmate! That cross between a nigger an' a Chinee is in Davy Jones' locker, is he? Hey, wait till I get these lashings cast off-yo're a good hand after all. Come in an' have some grog-best stuff this side of Kentucky, where it was made."

"I ain't got time," replied Hopalong, smiling. "Where's that Greaser broncho-buster?"

"Going to send *him* down too? D —n my tops'ls, wish I knowed! He deserted, took shore leave, an' ain't reported since. Yo're clipper-rigged, a regular AB, you are! Spin us th' yarn, matey."

Hopalong told him about the dam and the shooting of Juan and gave him the shovel and button for Meeker, Salem's mouth wide open at the recital. When he had finished the cook grabbed his stirrup and urged him towards the grog, but Hopalong laughingly declined and, looking towards the ranch house, saw Jim Meeker riding like mad in their direction.

"What do you want?" blazed the foreman, drawing rein, his face dark with anger.

"I want to plug Antonio, an' his friend Sanchez," Hopalong replied calmly. "I just caught Juan with a running iron under his saddle flap an' I drilled him for good. Here's th' iron."

"Good for you!" cried Meeker, taking the rod. "They've jumped, all of 'em. I'm looking for 'em myself, an' we're all looking for coyotes toting these irons. I'm glad you got one of 'em!"

"Antonio scuttled their dike-here's th' shovel he did it with," interrupted Salem eagerly. "An' here's th' button off th' Greaser's jacket. He left it by th' shovel. My mate, here, is cruising to fall in with 'em, an' when he does there'll be —"

"Why, that's *my* shovel!" cried Meeker. "An' that's his button, all right."

Hopalong told him all about the attempt to cut the dam and when he had ceased Meeker swore angrily. "Them Greasers are on th' rustle, shore! They're trying to keep th' fighting going on along th' line so we'll be too busy to bother 'em in their stealing. I've been losing cows right an' left-why, they run off a herd of beef right here by th' houses. Salem saw 'em. They killed cows down south an' covered my range with sleepers an' lame mothers. How did you come to guess he had an iron?"

Hopalong told of the HQQ cow he had found and, dismounting, traced the brand in the sand, Meeker bending over eagerly.

"You see this Bar-20?" he asked, pointing it out, and his interested companion interrupted him with a curse.

"Yes, I do; an' do *you* see this H2?" he demanded. "They've merged our brands into one-stealing from both of us!"

"Yes. I figgered that out when I saw th' mark; that's one of th' things I came down to tell you about," Hopalong replied, mounting again. "An' Red an' me found a Bar-20 calf with a V ear notch, too. That proves what th' dam was cut for, don't it?"

"Why didn't I drop that coyote when I caught him skulking th' other morning!" growled Meeker, regretfully. "He had just come back from yore dam then-had yaller mud on his cayuse an' his stirrups. Out all night on a played-out bronc, an' me too thick to guess he was up to some devilment an' shoot him for it! Oh, h —l! I thought purty hard of you, Cassidy, but I reckon we all make mistakes. Any man what would stop to think out th' real play when he found that shovel is square."

"Oh, that's all right. I allus did hate Greasers, an' mebby that was why I suspected him, that an' th' button."

Meeker turned to the cook. "Where's Chick an' Dan?" he asked, impatiently. "I ain't seen 'em around."

"Why, Chick rid off down south an' Dan cleared about an hour ago."

"What! With that leg of hissen!"

"Aye, aye, sir; he couldn't leave it behind, you know, sir."

"All right, Cassidy; much obliged. I'll put a stop to th' rustling on *my* range, or know th' reason why. D —n th' day I ever left Montanny!" Meeker swore, riding towards the ranch house.

"Say, I hope you find them Lascars," remarked Salem. "Yo're th' boy that'll give 'em what they needs. Wish you had caught 'em all four instead of only one."

Hopalong smiled. "Then they might 'a got me instead."

"No, no, siree!" exclaimed the cook. "You can lick 'em all, an' I'll gamble on it, too! But you better come in an' have a swig o' grog before you weighs anchor, matey. As I was saying, it's th' best grog west of Kentucky. Come on in!"

Chapter XXII
Lucas Visits the Peak

When Hopalong returned to the line house on the Peak he saw Johnny and Skinny talking with Lucas, the C80 foreman, and he hailed them.

"Hullo, Lucas!" he cried. "What are you doing down here?"

"Glad to see you, Hopalong," Lucas replied, shaking hands. "Came down to see Buck, but Lanky, up in th' bunk house, said he was off somewhere scouting. From what Lanky said I reckon you fellers had a little joke down here last week."

"Yes," responded Hopalong, dismounting. "It was a sort of a joke, except that somebody killed one of Meeker's men. I'll be blamed if I know who done it. Lanky says he didn't an' he don't have to deny a thing like that neither. Looks to me like he caught some brand-blotter dead to rights, like I did a little while ago, an' like he got th' worst of th' argument. Lanky would 'a told me if he did it, an' don't you forget it, neither."

"What's that about catching somebody dead to rights?" eagerly asked Johnny.

"Who was it?" asked Skinny.

"Juan. He toted a running iron an' I caught him just after I looked over a cow with a new brand —"

"Did you get him good?" quickly asked Johnny. "Did he put up a fight?"

"Yes; an' what was th' brand?" Skinny interposed.

"Here, here!" laughed Hopalong. "I reckon I'll save time if I tell you th' whole story," and he gave a short account of his ride, interrupted often by the inquisitive and insistent Johnny.

"An' who is Salem?" Johnny asked.

"Meeker's cook."

"What did Meeker say about it when you told him?"

"Gimme a chance to talk an' I'll tell you!" and Johnny remained silent for a moment. Finally the story was told and Johnny, who had been swearing vengeance on all "Greasers," asked one more question, grinning broadly:

"An' what did Mary say?"

"You say Meeker lost a whole herd?" asked Lucas. "Let me tell you there's more people mixed up in this rustling than we think. But I'll tell you one thing; that herd didn't go north, unless they drove ten miles east or west of our range."

"Well, I reckon it's under one man, all right," Hopalong replied. "If it was a lot of separate fellers running it by themselves there'd 'a been a lot of blunders an' some few of 'em would 'a been shot before Juan went. It's a gang, all right. But why th' devil did they turn loose that H2 rebranded cow, that HQQ that I found? They might 'a knowed it would cause some hot thinking when it was found. That cow is just about going to lick 'em."

"Stray," sententiously remarked Skinny.

"Shore, that's what it was," Lucas endorsed.

"An' do you know what that means?" asked Hopalong, looking from face to face. "It means that they can't be holding their herds very far away. It's three to one that I'm right."

"Mebby they're down in Eagle," suggested Johnny hopefully, for Eagle would be a good, exciting proposition in a fight.

"No, it ain't there," Hopalong replied. "There's too many people down there. They would all know about it an' want a share in th' profits; but it ain't a whole lot foolish to say that Eagle men are in it."

"Look here!" cried Skinny. "Mebby that HQQ is their road brand-that cow might 'a strayed from their drive. They've got to have some brand on cows they sell, an' they can't leave ours on an' get back alive."

"You are right, but not necessarily so about th' road brand," Hopalong rejoined. "But that don't tell us where they are, does it?"

"We've got to hunt HQQ cows on th' drive," Johnny interposed as Skinny was about to speak. "I'll go down to Eagle an' see if I can't get on to a drive. Then I'll trail th' gang all th' way an' back to where they hangs out. That'll tell us where to go, all right."

"You keep out of Eagle-you'd be shot before you reached Quinn's saloon," Hopalong said. "No; it ain't Eagle, not at all. See here, Lucas; have you watched them construction camps along that railroad? There ain't a better market nowhere than them layouts; they don't ask no questions if th' beef is cheap."

"Yes, I've watched th' trails leading to 'em."

"Why, they wouldn't cross yore range!" Hopalong cried. "They'd drive around you an' hit th' camp from above; they ain't fools. Hey! I've got it! They can't go around th' Double Arrow unless they are willing to cross th' Staked Plain, an' you can bet they ain't. That leaves th' west, an' there's a desert out there they wouldn't want to tackle. They drive between th' desert an' yore range."

"If they drive to th' camps, yo're right without a doubt," Skinny remarked. "But mebby they are driving south-mebby they're starting a ranch along th' Grande, or across it."

"Well, we'll take th' camps first," Hopalong replied. "Lucas, can you spare a man to look them camps over? Somebody that can live in 'em a month, if he has to?"

"Shore. Wood Wright is just th' man."

"No, he ain't th' man," contradicted Hopalong quickly. "Anybody that wears chaps, or walks like he does would arouse suspicion in no time, an' get piped out some night. This man has got to have business up there, like looking for a job. Say! Can you get along without yore cook for a while? If you can't we will!"

"You bet yore life I can!" exulted Lucas. "That's good. He can get a job right where th' meat is used, an' where th' hides will be kicking around. He goes to-morrow!"

"That's th' way; th' sooner th' better," Hopalong responded. "But we won't wait for him. We'll scout around lively down here an' if we don't find anything he may. But for th' Lord's sake, don't let him ride a cayuse into that camp that has brands of this section. Cowan will be glad to lend you his cayuse; he got it up north too far to make 'em suspicious."

"Yes; I reckon that'll be about the thing."

"Here comes Red," Johnny remarked. "Hey, Red, Hoppy got Juan this morning. Caught him toting a straight iron!"

"Johnny, you get away lively an' tell Frenchy to scout west," Hopalong ordered. "You can stay up in Number Two with them to-night, but come down here again in th' morning. Red, to-morrow at daylight we go west an' comb that country."

"That's th' way," remarked Lucas, mounting. "Get right at it. Have you got any word for Buck? I'll go past th' house an' leave it if you have."

"Yes; tell him what we've talked over. An' you might send yore outfit further west, too," Hopalong responded. "I'll bet a month's pay we end this cow-lifting before two more weeks roll by. We've got to!"

"Oh, yes; I near forgot it-Bartlett thinks we-all ought to get together after th' rustling is stopped an' shoot that town of Eagle plumb off th' earth," Lucas said. "It's only a hell hole, anyhow, an' it won't do no harm to wipe it out." He looked around the group. "What do you fellers think about it?" he asked.

"Well, we might, then; we've got too many irons in th' fire now, though," Hopalong replied. "Hey, Johnny! Get a-going! We'll talk about Eagle later."

"I'm forgetting lots of things," laughed Lucas. "We had a little fight up our way th' other day. Caught a feller skinning one of Bartlett's cows, what had strayed over on us. Got him dead to rights, too. He put up a fight while he lasted. Said his name was Hawkins."

"Hawkins!" exclaimed Hopalong. "I've heard that name somewhere."

"Why, that's th' name on th' notice of reward posted in Cowan's," Red supplied. "He's wanted for desertion from th' army, an' for other things. They want him bad up at Roswell, an' they'll pay for him, dead or alive."

"Well, they won't get him; he ain't keeping good enough," Lucas replied. "An' we don't want that kind of money. So long," and he was off.

"So you got Juan," Red remarked. "You ought to have took him alive-we could get it all out of him an' find out where his friends are hanging out."

"He went after his gun, an' he had an iron," Hopalong replied. "I didn't know he had left Meeker, an' I didn't stop to think. You see, he was a brand-blotter."

"What's Meeker going to do about th' line?" Red asked.

"Nothing for a while; he's too worried an' busy looking after his sleepers. He ain't so bad, after all."

"Say," remarked Skinny, thoughtfully. "Mebby that gang is over east, like Trendley was. There's lots of water thereabouts, an' good grass, too, in th' Panhandle. Look how close it is to Fort Worth an' th' railroad."

"Too many people over there," Hopalong replied. "An' *they* know all about th' time we killed Trendley an' wiped out his gang. They won't go where they are shore we'll look."

"If I can get sight of one of them Greasers I'll find out where they are," Red growled. "I'll put green rawhide around his face if I have to, an' when he savvys what th' sun is going to do to that hide an' him, he'll talk, all right, an' be glad of th' chance."

"To hear you, anybody would think you'd do a thing like that," Hopalong laughed. "I reckon he'd drop at eight hundred, clean an' at th' first shot. But, say, green rawhide wouldn't do a thing to a man's face, would it! When it shrunk he'd know it, all right."

"Crush it to a pulp," Skinny remarked. "But who is going to cook th' supper? I'm starved."

Hopalong awakened suddenly and listened and found Red also awake. Hoofbeats were coming towards the house and Hopalong peered out into the darkness to see who it was, his Colt ready.

"Who's that?" he challenged, sharply, the clicks of his gun ringing clear in the night air.

"Why, me," replied a well-known voice. "Who'd you think it was?"

"Why didn't you stay up in Number Two, like I told you? What's wrong?"

"Nothing," Johnny replied, stripping off his saddle and bridle.

"An' you came all th' way down here in th' dark, just to wake us up?" Hopalong asked, incredulously. "Twenty miles just for that!"

"No. I ain't got here yet —I'm only half way," Johnny retorted. "Can't you see I'm here? An' I didn't care about you waking up. I wanted to get here, an' here I am."

"In th' name of heaven, are you drunk, or crazy?" asked Red. "Of all th' d —n fools I ever —"

"Oh, shut up, all of you!" growled Skinny, turning over in his bunk. "Lot of locoed cusses that don't know enough to keep still! Let th' Kid alone, why don't you!" he muttered, and was sound asleep again.

"No, I ain't drunk or crazy! Think I was going to stay up there when you two fellers are going off scouting to-morrow? Not by a jugful! I ain't letting nothing get past me, all right," Johnny rejoined.

"Well, you ain't a-going, anyhow," muttered Hopalong, crawling into his bunk again. "You've got to stay with Skinny —" he did not speak very loud, because he knew it would cause an argument, and he wished to sleep instead of talk.

"What'd you say?" demanded Johnny.

"For G-d's sake!" marvelled Red. "Can't nobody go an' scratch 'emselves unless th' Kid is on th' ground? Come in here an' get to sleep, you coyote!"

> Adown th' road, his gun in hand,
> Comes Whiskey Bill, mad Whiskey —

Johnny hummed. "Hey! What you doing?" he yelled, leaping back.

"You heave any more guns on my face an' you'll find out!" roared Skinny, sitting up and throwing Johnny's Colt and belt to the floor. "Fool infant!"

"Tumble in an' shut up!" cried Red. "We want some sleep, you sage hen!"

"Yo're a lot of tumble-bugs!" retorted Johnny, indignantly. "How did I know Skinny had his face where I threw my gun! He's so cussed thin I can't hardly see him in daylight, th' chalk mark! Why didn't he say so? Think I can see in th' dark?"

"I don't talk in my sleep!" retorted Skinny, "or go flea-hopping around in th' dark like a —"

"*Shut up!*" shouted Hopalong, and silence at last ensued.

Chapter XXIII
Hopalong and Red Go Scouting

As Hopalong and Red rode down the slope of the Peak the rays of the sun flashed over the hills, giving promise of a very hot day. They were prepared to stay several days, if need be, on the semi-arid plain to the west of them, for it would be combed thoroughly before they returned. On they loped, looking keenly over the plain and occasionally using their field glasses to more closely scrutinize distant objects, searching the barrancas and coulees and threading through mesquite and cactus growths. Hopalong momentarily expected to find signs of what they were looking for, while Red, according to his habit, was consistently contradictory in his words and disproportionately pessimistic.

Moving forward at a swinging lope they began to circle to the west and as they advanced Hopalong became eager and hopeful, while his companion grumbled more and more. In his heart he believed as Hopalong did, but there had to be something to talk about to pass the time more pleasantly; so when they met in some barranca to ride together for a short distance they exchanged pleasantries.

"Yo're showing even more than yore usual amount of pig-headed ignorance to-day," Hopalong grumbled. "Yore blasted, ingrowing disposition has been shedding cussedness at every step. I'll own up to being some curious as to when it's going to peter out."

"As if that's any of yore business," retorted Red. "But I'll just tell you, since you asks; it's going to stop when I get good an' ready, savvy?"

"Yo're awful cheerful at times," sarcastically snorted his companion.

Red's eyes had been roving over the plain and now he raised his glasses and looked steadily ahead.

"What's that out there? Dead cow?" he asked, calmly.

Hopalong put his glasses on it instantly. "Cow?" he asked, witheringly. "No; it's an overgrown lizard! Come on," he cried, spurring forward, Red close behind him.

Riding around it they saw that it bore the brand of the H2, and Hopalong, dismounting, glanced it over quickly and swore.

"Shot in th' head-what did I tell you!"

"You didn't have to get off yore cayuse to see that," retorted Red. "But get on again, an' come along. There's more out here. I'll take th' south end of this-don't get out of hearing."

"Wait! Wonder why they shot it, instead of driving it off after they got it this far?" Hopalong mused.

"Got on th' prod, I reckon, leaving its calf an' being run so hard. I've seen many a one I'd like to have shot. Looks to me like they hang out around that water hole-they drove it that way."

"You can bet yore head they didn't drive it straight to their hang-out —they ain't doing nothing like that," Hopalong replied. "They struck south after they thought they had throwed off any pursuit. They drove it almost north, so far; savvy?"

"Well, they've got to have water if they're holding cows out on this stove," Red rejoined. "An' I just told you where th' water is."

"G'wan! Ten cows would drain that hole in two days!" Hopalong responded. "They've also got to have grass, though mebby you never knew that. An' what about that herd Meeker lost? They wouldn't circle so far to a one-by-nothing water hole like that one is."

"Well, then, where'll they find grass an' water out here?" demanded Red, impatiently. "Th' desert's west, though mebby you never knew that!"

"Red, we've been a pair of fools!" Hopalong cried, slapping his thigh by way of emphasis. "Here we are skating around up here when Thunder Mesa lays south, with plenty of water an' a fair pasture on all sides of it! That's where we'll go."

"Hoppy, once in a great while you do show some intelligence, an' you've shown some now; but we better go up to that water hole first," Red replied. "We can swing south then. We're so close to it now that there ain't nothing to be gained by not taking a look at it. Mebby we'll find a trail, or something."

"Right you are; come on. There ain't no use of us riding separate no more."

Half an hour later Hopalong pointed to one side, to a few half-burned greasewood and mesquite sticks which radiated like the spokes of a wheel.

"Yes, I saw 'em," Red remarked. "They couldn't wait till they got home before they changed th' brand, blamed fools."

"Yes, an' that explains th' HQQ cow I discovered," Hopalong quickly replied. "They got too blamed hasty to blot it an' it got away from 'em."

"Well, it shore beats th' devil how Meeker had to go an' stir up this nest of rattlers," Red grumbled, angrily.

"If these fellers hang out at Thunder Mesa an' drive to th' railroad camps we ought to strike their trail purty close to th' water hole," Hopalong remarked. "It's right in their path."

Red nodded his head. "Yes, we ought to."

An hour later they rode around a chaparral and came within sight of the water hole, which lay a few hundred yards away. As they did so a man rode up out of the depression and started north, unconscious of his danger.

The two men spurred to overtake him, both drawing their rifles and getting ready for action. He turned in his saddle, saw them, and heading westward, quirted and spurred his horse into a dead run, both of his pursuers shouting for him to stop as they followed at top speed. He glanced around again and, seeing that they were slowly but surely gaining, whipped up his rifle and fired at them several times, both replying. He kept bearing more and more to the west and Red rode away at an angle to intercept him. Ten minutes later the fleeing man turned and rode north again, but Red had gained fifty yards over Hopalong and suddenly stopping his horse to permit better shooting, he took quick aim and fired. The pursued man found that his horse was useful only as a breastwork as Red's report died away, and hastily picked himself up and crawled behind it.

"Look out, Red!" warned Hopalong as he flung himself off his horse and led it down into a deep coulee for protection. "That's Dick Archer, an' he can shoot like th' very devil!"

Red, already in a gully, laughed. "An' so can I."

"Hey, I'm going around on th' other side-look out for him," Hopalong called, starting away. "We can't waste no more time up here than we has to."

"All right; go ahead," Red replied, pushing his sombrero over the edge of the gully where the rustler could see it; and he laughed softly when he saw the new hole in it. "He shore can shoot, all right," he muttered. Working down the gully until he came to a clump of greasewood he crawled up the bank and looked out at the man behind the dead horse, who was intently watching the place where he had seen Red's sombrero. "I knowed Eagle was holding cards in this game," Red remarked, smiling grimly. "Wonder how many are in it, anyhow?"

Hearing the crack of a gun he squinted along the sights of his Winchester and waited patiently for a chance to shoot. Then he heard another shot and saw the rustler raise himself to change his position, and Red fired. "I knowed, too, that Hoppy would drive him into range for me, even if he didn't hit him. Wonder what Mr. Dick Archer thinks about *my* shooting about now? Ah!" he cried as the smoke from his second shot drifted away. "Got you again!" he grunted. Then he dropped below the edge of the gully and grinned as he listened to the bullets whining overhead, for the rustler, wounded twice inside of a minute by one man, was greatly incensed thereby and petulantly bombarded the greasewood clump. He knew that he was done for, but that was no reason why he shouldn't do as much damage as he could while he was able.

"Bet he's mad," grinned Red. "An' there goes that Sharps —I could tell Hoppy's gun in a fusillade."

Crawling back up the gully to his first position Red peered out between some gramma grass tufts and again slid his rifle to his shoulder, laughing softly at the regular reports of the Sharps.

A puff of smoke enveloped his head and drifted behind him as he worked the lever of his rifle and, arising, he walked out towards the prostrate man and waved for his friend to join him. As he drew near the rustler struggled up on one elbow, and Red, running forward with his gun raised half-way to his shoulder, cried: "Don't make no gun-play, or I'll blow you apart! Where's th' rest of yore gang?"

"Go to h —l!" coughed the other, trying to get his Colt out, for his rifle was empty. He stiffened and fell flat.

Ten minutes later Hopalong and Red were riding southwest along a plain and well beaten trail, both silent and thoughtful. And at the end of an hour they saw the ragged top of Thunder Mesa towering against the horizon. They went forward cautiously now and took advantage of the unevenness of the plain, riding through barrancas and keeping close to chaparrals.

"Well, Red, I reckon we better stop," Hopalong remarked at last, his glasses glued to his eyes. "No use letting them see us."

"Is that smoke up there?" asked Red.

"Yes; an' there's somebody moving around near th' edge."

"I see him now."

"I reckon we know all that's necessary," Hopalong remarked. "That trail is enough, anyhow. Now we've got to get back to th' ranch without letting them fellers see us."

"We can lead th' cayuses till we can get in that barranca back there," Red replied. "We won't stick up so prominent if we do that. After we make it we'll find it easy to keep from being seen if we've any caution."

Hopalong threw himself out of the saddle. "Dismount!" he cried. "That feller up there is coming towards this end. He's their lookout, I bet."

They remained hidden and quiet for an hour while the lookout gazed around the plain, both impatient and angry at the time he gave to his examination. When he turned and disappeared they waited for a few minutes to see if he was coming back, and satisfied that the way was clear, led their horses to the barranca and rode through it until far enough away to be safe from observation.

Darkness caught them before they had covered half of the distance between the mesa and the ranch, and there being no moon to light the way, they picketed their mounts, had supper, and rolling up in their blankets, spent the night on the open plain.

Chapter XXIV

Red's Discomfiture

On their return they separated and Red, coming to an arroyo, rode along its edge for a mile and then turned north. Ten minutes after he had changed his course he espied an indistinct black speck moving among a clump of cottonwoods over half a mile ahead of him, and as he swung his glasses on it a cloud of smoke spurted out. His horse reared, plunged, and then sank to earth where it kicked spasmodically and lay quiet. As the horse died Red, who had dismounted at the first tremor, threw himself down behind it and shoved his rifle across the body, swearing at the range, for at that distance his Winchester was useless. A small handful of sand flew into the air close beside him with a vicious spat, and the bullet hummed away into the brush as a small pebble struck him sharply on the cheek. A few seconds later he heard the faint, flat report.

"It's a clean thousand, an' more," he growled. "Wish I had Hopalong's gun. I'd make that feller jump!"

He looked around to see how close he was to cover and when he glanced again at the cottonwoods they seemed to be free of an enemy. Then a shot came from a point to the north of the trees and thudded into the carcass of the horse. Red suddenly gave way to his accumulated anger which now seethed at a white heat and, scrambling to his feet, ran to the brush behind him. When he gained it he plunged forward to top speed, leaping from cover to cover as he zig-zagged towards the man who had killed Ginger, and who had tried his best to kill him.

He ran on and on, his rifle balanced in his right hand and ready for instant use, his breath coming sharply now. Red was in no way at home out of the saddle. His high-heeled, tight-fitting boots cramped his toes and the sand made running doubly hard. He was not far from the cottonwoods; they lay before him and to his right.

Turning quickly he went north, so as to go around the plot of ground on which he hoped to find his accurate, long-range assailant, and as he came to a break in the hitherto close-growing brush he stopped short and dropped to one knee behind a hillock of sand, the rifle going to his shoulder as part of the movement.

Several hundred yards east of him he saw two men, who were hastily mounting, and running from them was a frightened calf. One of the pair waved an arm towards the place where Ginger lay and as he did so a puff of smoke lazily arose from behind the hillock of sand to the west and he jumped up in his saddle, his left arm falling to his side. Another puff of smoke arose and his companion fought his wounded and frightened horse, and then suddenly grasped his side and groaned. The puffs were rising rapidly behind the hillock and bullets sang sharply about them; the horse of the first man hit leaped forward with a bullet-stung rump. Spurring madly the two rustlers dashed into the brush, lying close along the necks of their mounts, and soon were lost to the sight of the angry marksman.

Red leaped up, mechanically refilling the magazine of his rifle, and watched them out of sight, helpless either to stop or pursue them. He shook his rifle, almost blind with rage, crying: "I hope you get to Thunder Mesa before *we* do, an' stay there; or run into Frenchy an' his men on yore way back! If I could get to Number Two ahead of you you'd never cross that boundary."

As he returned to his horse his rage cooled and left him, a quiet, deep animosity taking its place, and he even smiled with savage elation when he thought how he had shot at eight hundred yards-they had not escaped entirely free from punishment and his accuracy had impressed them so much that they had not lingered to have it out with him, even as they were two to one, mounted, and armed with long-range rifles. And he could well allow them to escape, for he would find them again at the mesa, if they managed to cross the line unseen by his friends, and he could pay the debt there.

He swore when he came to the body of his horse and anger again took possession of him. Ginger had been the peer of any animal on the range and, contrary to custom, he had felt no little affection for it. At cutting out it had been unequalled and made the work a pleasure to its rider; at stopping when the rope went home and turning short when on the dead run it had not been excelled by any horse on the ranch. He had taught it several tricks, such as coming to him in response to a whistle, lying down quickly at a slap on the shoulder, and bucking with whole-hearted zeal and viciousness when mounted by a stranger. Now he slapped the carcass and removed the saddle and bridle which had so often displeased it.

"Ginger, old boy," he said, slinging the forty-pound saddle to his shoulder and turning to begin his long tramp towards the dam, "I shore hate to hoof it, but I'd do it with a lot better temper if I knowed you was munching grass with th' rest of the cavvieyh. You've been a good old friend, an' I hates to leave you; but if I get any kind of a chance at th' thief that plugged you I'll square up for you good an' plenty."

To the most zealous for exercise, carrying a forty-pound double-cinched saddle for over five miles across a hot, sandy plain and under a blazing, scorching sun, with the cinches all the time working loose and falling to drag behind and catch in the vegetation, was no pleasant task; and add to that a bridle, full magazine rifle, field glasses, canteen, and a three-pound Colt revolver swinging from a belt heavily weighted with cartridges, and it becomes decidedly irksome, to say the least. Red's temper can be excused when it is remembered that for years his walking had been restricted to getting to his horse, that his footwear was unsuited for walking, that he had been shot at and had lost his best horse. Each mile added greatly to his weariness and temper and by the time he caught sight of Hopalong, who rode recklessly over the range blazing at a panic-stricken coyote, he was near the point of spontaneous combustion.

He heaved the saddle from him, kicked savagely at it as it dropped, for which he was instantly sorry, and straightened his back slowly for fear that any sudden exertion would break it. His rifle exploded, twice, thrice; and Hopalong sat bolt upright and turned, his rifle going instinctively to his shoulder before he saw his friend's waving sombrero.

The coyote-chaser slid the smoking Sharps into its sheath and galloped to meet his friend who, filling the air with sulphurous remarks, now seated himself on the roundly cursed saddle.

Hopalong swept up and stopped, grinning expectantly and, to Red, exasperatingly. "Where's yore cayuse?" he asked. "Why are you toting yore possessions on th' hoof? Are you emigrating?"

Red's reply was a look wonderfully expressive of all the evils in human nature, it was fairly crowded with murder and torture, and Hopalong held his head on one side while he weighed it.

"Phew!" he exclaimed in wondering awe. "Yo're shore mad! You'd freeze old Geronimo's blood if he saw that look!"

"An' I'll freeze yourn; I'll let it soak into th' sand if you don't change yore front!" blazed Red. "What's the matter? Where's Ginger?"

A rapid-fire string of expletives replied and then Hopalong began to hear sensible words, which more and more interspersed the profanity, and it was not long before he learned of Red's ride along the arroyo's rim.

"When I turned north," Red continued, wrathfully, "I saw something in them dozen cottonwoods around that come-an'-go spring; an' then what do you think happened?" he cried. Not waiting for any reply he continued hastily: "Why, some murdering squaw's dog went an' squibbed at me at long range! With me on my own ranch, too! An' he killed Ginger first shot. He missed me three straight an' *I* couldn't do nothing at a thousand an' over with this gun."

"Th' d —n pirate!" exclaimed Hopalong, hotly.

"I was a whole lot mad by that time, so I jumped back into th' brush an' ran for th' grove, hoping to get square when I got in range. After I'd run about a thousand miles I came to th' edge of th' clearing west of th' trees an' d — —d if I didn't see two fellers climbing on their cayuses, an' some hasty, too. Reckon they didn't know how many friends I might have behind me. Well, I was some shaky from running like I did, an' they was a good eight hundred away, but I let drive just th' same an' got one in th' arm, th' other somewhere else, an' hit both of their cayuses. I wish I'd 'a filled 'em so full of holes they couldn't hang together, th' thieves!"

"I'd shore like to go after them, Red," Hopalong remarked. "We could ride west an' get 'em when they pass that water hole if you had a cayuse."

"Oh, we'll get 'em, all right-at th' mesa," Red rejoined. "I'm so tired I wouldn't go now if I could. Walking all th' way down here with that saddle! You get off that cayuse an' let me ride him," he suggested, mopping his face with his sleeve.

"What! Me? *Me* get off an' walk! I reckon not!" replied Hopalong, and then his face softened. "You pore, unfortunate cow-punch," he said, sympathetically. "You toss up yore belongings an' climb up here behind me. I'll take you to th' dam, where Johnny has picketed his cayuse. Th' Kid's going in for a swim; said he didn't know how soon he'd get a chance to take a bath. We can rustle his cayuse for a joke-come on."

"Oh, wait a minute, can't you?" Red replied, wearily. "I can't lift my legs high enough to get up there-they're like lead. That trail was hell strung out."

"You should 'a cached yore saddle an' everything but th' gun an' come down light," Hopalong remarked. "Or you could a' gone to th' line an' waited for somebody to come along. Why didn't you do that?"

"I ain't leaving that saddle nowhere," Red responded. "Besides I was too blamed mad to stop an' think."

"Well, don't wait very long-Johnny may skin out if you do," Hopalong replied, and then, suddenly: "Just where was it you shot at them snakes?" Red told him and Hopalong wheeled as if to ride after them.

"Here, you!" cried Red, the horseless. "Where th' devil are you going so sudden?"

"Up to get them cow-lifters that you couldn't, of course," his companion replied. "I'm shore going to show you how easy it is when you know how."

"Like h —l you are!" Red cried, springing up, his lariat in his hand. "Yo're going to stay right here with me, that's what yo're going to do! I've got something for you to do, you compact bundle of gall! You try to get away without me and I'll make you look like an interrupted spasm, you wart-headed Algernon!"

"Do you want 'em to get plumb away?" cried the man in the saddle, concealing his mirth.

"I want you to stick right here an' tote me to a cayuse!" Red retorted, swinging the rope. "*I'm* going to be around when anybody goes after them Siwashes, an' don't you forget it. There ain't no hurry-we'll get 'em quick enough when we starts west. An' if you try any get-away play an' leave me out here on my two feet with all these contraptions, I'll pick you off'n that piebald like hell greased with calamity!"

Hopalong laughed heartily. "Why, I was only a-fooling, Red. Do you reckon I'd go away an' leave you standing out here like a busted-down pack mule?"

"I hoped you was only fooling, but I wasn't taking no chances with a cuss like you," Red replied, grinning. "Not with this load of woe, you bet."

"Say, it's too bad you didn't have my gun up there," Hopalong said, regretfully. "You could 'a got 'em both then, an' had two cayuses to ride home on."

"Well, *I* could 'a got 'em with it," Red replied, grinning, his good nature returning under the chaffing. "But you can't hit th' mesa with it over six hundred. They'd 'a got away from you without getting hit."

Hopalong laughed derisively and then sobered and became anxious. "Yo're right, Red, yo're right," he asserted with tender solicitude. "Now you get right up here behind me an' I'll take you to th' dam where th' Kid is. Pore feller," he sighed. "Well, I ain't a-wondering after all you've been through. It was enough to make a *strong*-minded man loco." He smiled reassuringly. "Now climb right up behind me, Reddie. Gimme yore little saddle an' yore no-account gun-Ouch!"

"I'll give you th' butt of it again if you don't act like you've made th' best of them gravy brains!" Red snorted. "Here, you lop-eared cow-wrastler —catch this!" throwing the saddle so sudden and hard that Hopalong almost lost his balance from the impact. "Now you gimme a little room in front of th' tail —I ain't no blasted fly."

Hopalong gave his friend a hand and Red landed across the horse's back, to the instant and strong dislike of that animal, which showed its displeasure by bucking mildly.

"Glory be!" cried Hopalong, laughing. "Riding double on a bucking hinge ain't no play, is it? Suppose he felt like pitching real strong-where would you be with that tail holt?"

"You bump my nose again with th' back of yore head an' you'll see how much play it is!" Red retorted. "Come on-pull out. We ain't glued fast. Th' world moves, all right, but if yo're counting on it sliding under you till th' dam comes around you're way off; it ain't moving that way. Hey! Stop that spurring!"

"I'll hook 'em in you again if you don't shut up!" Hopalong promised, jabbing them into the horse, which gave one farewell kick, to Red's disgust, and cantered south with ears flattened.

"Whoop! I'm riding again!" Red exulted.

"I'm glad it wasn't Red Eagle they went an' killed," Hopalong remarked.

"Red Eagle!" snorted Red, indignantly. "What good is this cayuse, anyhow? Ginger was worth three like this."

"Well, if you don't like this cayuse you can get off an' hoof it, you know," Hopalong retorted. "But I'll tell you what you know a'ready; there ain't no cayuse in this part of th' country that can lose him in long-distance running. He ain't no fancy, parlor animal like Ginger was; he don't know how to smoke a cig or wash dishes, or do any of th' fool things yore cayuse did, but he is right on th' job when it comes to going hard an' long. An' it's them two things that tell how much a cayuse is worth, down here in this country. If I could 'a jumped on him up there when they made their get-away from you, me an' th' Sharps would 'a fixed 'em. They wouldn't be laughing now at how easy you was."

"They ain't laughing, not a bit of it-an' they won't even be able to swear after I get out to th' mesa," Red asserted. "Have you seen Buck, or anybody 'cept th' Kid?"

"Yes. I told Buck an' Frenchy about it, an' Skinny, too," Hopalong replied. "Buck an' Frenchy went north along th' west line to get th' boys from Number Two. Buck says we'll go after 'em just as soon as we can get ready, which most of us are now. Pore Lanky; he's got to stay home an' pet his wounds-Buck said he couldn't go."

"Did Buck say who was going an' who was going to stay home?"

"Yes; you, Johnny, Billy, Pete, Skinny, Frenchy, me, Buck, an' Pie Willis are going-th' rest will have to watch th' ranch. That makes nine of us. Wonder how many are up that mesa?"

"There'll be plenty, don't you worry," Red replied. "When we go after anybody we generally has to mix up with a whole company. I wouldn't be a whole lot surprised if they give us an awful fight before they peter out. They'll be up in th' air a hundred feet. We'll have plenty to do, all right."

"Well, two won't be there, anyhow-Archer an' Juan. I bet we'll find most of th' people of Eagle up there waiting for us."

"Lord, I hope they are!" cried Red. "Then we can clean up everything at once, town an' all."

"There's th' Kid-see th' splash?" Hopalong laughed. "He shore is stuck on swimming. He don't care if there's cotton-mouths in there with him. One of them snakes will get him some day, an' if one does, then we'll plant him, quick."

"Oh, I dunno. I ain't seen none at th' dam," Red replied. "They don't like th' sand there as much as they do th' mud up at th' other end, an' along th' sides. Gee! There's his cayuse!"

Johnny dove out of sight, turned over and came up again, happy as a lark, and saw his friends riding towards him, and he trod water and grinned. "Hullo, fellers. Coming in? —it's fine! Hey, Red. We're all going out to Thunder Mesa as soon as we can! But what are you riding double for? Where's yore cayuse?" Something in Red's expression made him suspicious of his friends' intentions and, fearing that he might have to do some walking, he made a few quick strokes and climbed out, dressing as rapidly as his wet skin would permit.

Red briefly related his experience and Johnny swore as he struggled through his shirt. "What are you going to do?" he asked, poking his head out into sight.

"I'm going to ride yore cayuse to th' line house-you ain't as tired as me," replied Red.

"Not while I'm alive, you ain't!" cried Johnny, running to his horse. Then he grinned and went back to his clothes. "You take him an' rope th' cayuse I saw down in that barranca-there's two of 'em there, both belonging to Meeker. But you be shore to come back!"

"Shore, Kid," Red replied, vaulting into the saddle and riding away.

Johnny fastened his belt around him and looked up. "Say, Hoppy," he laughed, "Buck said Cowan sent my new gun down to th' bunk house yesterday. He's going to bring it with him when he comes down to-morrow. But I only got fifty cartridges for it-will you lend me some of yourn if I run short?"

"Where did Cowan get it?"

"Why, don't you remember he said he'd get me one like yourn th' next time he went north? He got back yesterday-bought it off some feller up on th' XS. Cost me twenty-five dollars without th' cartridges. But I've got fifty empties I can load when I get time, so I'll be all right later on. Will you lend me some?"

"Fifty is enough, you chump," laughed Hopalong. "You won't get that many good chances out there."

"I know; but I want to practise a little. It'll shoot flatter than my Winchester," Johnny grinned, hardly able to keep from riding to the bunk house to get his new gun.

Red rode up leading a horse. "That's a good rope, Kid, 'though th' hondo is purty heavy," he said, saddling the captured animal. "Is Buck going to bring down any food an' cartridges when he comes?" he asked.

"Yes; three cayuses will pack 'em. We can send back for more if we stay out there long enough to need more. Buck says that freak spring up on top flows about half a mile through th' chaparral before it peters out. What do you know about it, Red?" Hopalong asked.

"Seems to me that he's right. I think it flows through a twisting arroyo. But there'll be water enough for us, all right."

"I got a .45-120 Sharps just like Hopalong's, Red," Johnny grinned. "He said he'd lend me fifty cartridges for it, didn't you, Hoppy?"

"Well, I'll be blamed!" exclaimed Hopalong. "First thing *I* knowed about it, if I did. I tell you you won't need 'em."

"Where'd you get it?" asked Red.

"Cowan got it. I told you all about it three weeks ago."

"Well, you better give it back an' use yore Winchester," replied Red. "It ain't no good, an' you'll shoot some of us with it, too. What do *you* want with a gun that'll shoot eighteen hundred? You can't hit anything now above three hundred."

"Yo're another —I can, an' you know it, too. Three hundred!" he snorted. "Huh! Here comes Skinny!"

Skinny rode up and joined them, all going to the Peak. Finally he turned and winked at Johnny.

"Hey, Kid. Hopalong ought to go right down to th' H2 while he's got time. He hadn't ought to go off fighting without saying good-bye to his girl, had he?"

"She'd keep him home-wouldn't let him take no chances of getting shot," Red asserted. "Anyhow, if he went down there he'd forget to come back."

"Ow-wow!" cried Johnny. "You hit him! You hit him! Look at his face!"

"He shore can't do no courting while he's away," Skinny remarked. "He wouldn't let Red go with him when he went to give Meeker th' shovel, an' I didn't know why till just now."

"You go to blazes, all of you!" exclaimed Hopalong, red and uncomfortable. "I ain't doing no courting, you chump! An' Red knows why I went down there alone."

"Yes; you gave me a fool reason, an' went alone," Red retorted. "An' if that ain't courting, for th' Lord's sake what is it? Or is she doing all of it, you being bashful?"

"Yes, Hoppy; tell us what it is," asked Skinny.

"Oh, don't mind them, Hoppy; they're jealous," Johnny interposed. "Don't you make no excuses, not one. Admit that yo're courting an' tell 'em that yo're going to keep right on a-doing it an' get all th' honey you can."

Red and Skinny grinned and Hopalong, swearing at Johnny, made a quick grab for him, but missed, for Johnny knew the strength of that grip. "I ain't courting! I'm only trying to-trying to be-sociable; that's all!"

"Sociable!" yelled Red. "Oh, Lord!"

"It must be nice to be sociable," replied Johnny. "Since you ain't courting, an' are only trying to be sociable, then you won't care if we go down an' try it. Me for th' H2!"

"You bet; an' I'm going down, too," asserted Red, who was very much afraid of women, and who wouldn't have called on Mary Meeker for a hundred dollars.

Hopalong knew his friend's weakness and he quickly replied: "Red, I dare you to do that. I dare you to go down there an' talk to her for five minutes. When I say talk, I don't mean stammer. I dare you!"

"Do you dare *me?*" asked Johnny, quickly, glancing at the sun to see how much time he had.

"Oh, I ain't got time," replied Red, grinning.

"You ain't got th' nerve, you mean," jeered Skinny.

"I dare you, Red," Hopalong repeated, grimly.

"I asked you if you dared *me?*" hastily repeated Johnny.

"*You!* Not on yore life, Kid. But you stay away from there!" Hopalong warned.

"Gee-wish you'd lend me them cartridges," sighed Johnny. "Mebbe Meeker has got some he ain't so stingy with," he added, thoughtfully.

"I'll lend you th' cartridges, Kid," Hopalong offered. "But you stay away from th' H2. D'y hear?"

Chapter XXV
Antonio's Revenge

While Red had been trudging southward under his saddle and other possessions a scene was being enacted on a remote part of the H2 range which showed how completely a cowboy leased his very life to the man who paid him his monthly wage, one which serves to illustrate in a way how a ranchman was almost a feudal lord. There are songs of men who gave up their lives to save their fellows, one life for many, and they are well sung; but what of him who risks his life to save one small, insignificantly small portion of his employer's possessions, risks it without hesitation or fear, as a part of his daily work? What of the man who, not content with taking his share of danger in blizzard, fire, and stampede, on drive, roundup, and range-riding, leaps fearlessly at the risk of his life to save a paltry head or two of cattle to his ranch's tally sheet? Such men were the rule, and such a one was Curley, who, with all his faults, was a man as a man should be.

Following out his orders he rode his part of the range with alertness, and decided to explore the more remote southwestern angle of the ranch. Doc had left him an hour before to search the range nearer Eagle and would not be back again until time to return to the ranch house for the night. This was against Meeker's orders, for they had been told to keep together for their own protection, but they had agreed that there was little risk and that it would be better to separate and cover more ground.

The day was bright and, with the exception of the heat, all he could desire. His spirits bubbled over in snatches of song as he cantered hither and yon, but all the time moving in the general direction of the little-ridden territory. On all sides stretched the same monotonous view, sage brush, mesquite, cactus, scattered tufts of grass, and the brown plain, endless, flat, wearying.

The surroundings did not depress him, but only gradually slowed the exultant surge of his blood and, as he hummed at random, an old favorite came to him out of the past, and he sung it joyously:

My taste is that of an aristocrat,
My purse that of a pauper:
I scorn the gold her parents hold —
But shore I love their daughter.
Hey de diddle de, hey de dee,
But shore I love their daughter.

When silvery nights my courting light
An' souls of flowers wander,
Then who's to blame if I loved th' game
An' did not pause to ponder?
Hey de diddle de, hey de dee,
An' did not pause to ponder.

Her eyes are blue, an' oh, so true —
Th' words were said ere thought, Lad.
Her father swore we'd meet no more —
But I am not distraught, Lad.
Hey de diddle de, hey de de —
But I am not distraught, Lad.

He ceased abruptly, rigidly erect, staring straight ahead as the significance of the well trodden trail impressed itself on his mind. He was close to the edge of a steep-walled basin; and leading to it was a narrow, steep gully, down which the beaten trail went. Riding closer he saw that two poles were set close to the wall of the gully, and from one of them dangled a short, frayed hempen rope. There was a water hole in the basin, surrounded by a muddy flat, and everywhere were the tracks of cattle.

As he hesitated to decide whether or not it would be worth while to ride through the depression he chanced to look south, and the question decided itself. Spurring savagely, he leaned forward in the saddle, the wind playing a stern song in his ears, a call to battle for his ranch, his pride, and his hatred for foul work. He felt the peculiar, compelling delight, the surging, irresistible intoxication of his kind for fighting, the ecstasy of the blood lust, handed down from his Saxon forefathers.

A mile ahead of him was a small herd of cattle, being driven west by two men. Did he stop to return to the ranch for assistance? Did he count the odds? Not he, for he saw the perpetrators of the insults he and his companions had chafed under-the way was clear, the quarry plain, and he asked naught else.

They saw him coming-one of them raised a pair of glasses to his eyes and looked closely at him and from him all around the plain. All the time they were driving the cattle harder, shouting and whipping about them with their rawhide quirts; and constantly nearer came the cowboy, now standing up in his stirrups and lashing his straining mount without mercy. Soon he thought he recognized one of the herders, and he flung the name on the whistling wind in one contemptuous shout: "Antonio! D —n his soul!" and fell to beating the horse all the harder.

It was Antonio, and a puff of smoke arose from the Mexican's shoulder and streaked behind, soon followed by another. Curley knew the rifle, a .40-90 Sharps, and did not waste a shot, for he must be on equal terms before he could hope to cope with it. Another puff, then another and another, but still he was not hit. Now he drew his own rifle from its holster and hazarded a shot, but to no avail. Then the second herder, who had not as yet fired, snatching the rifle from Antonio's hands and, checking his horse, leaped off and rested the weapon across the saddle. Taking deliberate aim, he fired, and Curley pitched out of the saddle as his horse stumbled and fell. The rider scrambled to his feet, dazed and hurt, and ran to his horse, but one look told the story and he ended the animal's misery with a shot from his Colt.

The herder and the cattle were rapidly growing smaller in the distance but the Mexican rode slowly around the man on foot, following the circumference of a large circle and shooting with calm deliberation. The bullets hummed and whined viciously past the H2 puncher, kicking up the dust in little spurts, and cold ferocity filled his heart as he realized the rustler's purpose. He raised his own rifle and fired-and leaded the barrel. When he had fallen the barrel had become choked with sand and dust and he was at the mercy of his gloating enemy, who would now wipe out the insult put upon him at the bunk house. Slowly Antonio rode and carefully he fired and then, seeing that there was something wrong with Curley's rifle, which the puncher threw aside, he drew closer, determined to shoot him to pieces.

Curley was stung with rage now. He knew that it was only a question of waiting until the right bullet came, and scorning to hug the sand for the "Greaser" he held in such contempt, and vaguely realizing that such an act would not change the result, he put all his faith in a dash. He ran swiftly towards his astonished enemy, who expected him to seek what cover the dead horse would give him, Colt in hand, cursing at every jump and hoping to be spared long enough to get within range with his six-shooter, if only for one shot. Antonio did not like this close work and cantered away, glancing back from time to time. When Curley finally was forced to stop because of exhaustion the rider also stopped and slipped off his horse to have a rest for the rifle. Curley emptied the Colt in a futile, enraged effort to make a lucky hit while his enemy calmly aimed from across the saddle. Hastily reloading the Colt as he ran, the puncher dashed forward again, zig-zagging to avoid being hit. There was a puff of gray smoke, but Curley did not hear the report. He threw one arm half up as if to ward off the shot and pitched forward, face down in the dust, free from all pain and strife.

Antonio fired again and then cautiously drew nearer to his victim, the rifle at the ready. Turning shortly he made a quick grab at his horse, fearing that it might leave him on foot to be caught by some wandering H2 puncher. Springing into the saddle he rode forward warily to get a closer look at the man he had murdered, proud of his work, but fearful that Curley was playing dead.

When assured that he had nothing to fear from the prostrate form, he rode close. "Knock me down, will you!" he gritted, urging the horse to trample on the body, which the animal refused to do. "Call me an unwashed Greaser coyote, hey! Come out looking for us, did you? Well, you found us, all right, but a h—l of a lot of good it did you, you American dog! You ain't saying a word, are you, you carrion? You ain't got no smart come-back now, an' you ain't throwing no wash water on me, are you?"

He started and looked around nervously, fearful that he might be caught and left lying on the sand as he had left Curley. One or two of the H2 outfit carried single-shot rifles which shot as far if not farther than his own, and the owners of them knew how to shoot. Wheeling abruptly he galloped after the herd, looking back constantly and thinking only of putting as great a distance as possible between himself and the scene of the killing.

A lizard crawled out of a hillock and stared steadily at the quiet figure and then, making a tentative sortie, disappeared under the sand; but the man who had sung so buoyantly did not mind it, he lay wrapped in the Sleep Eternal. He had died as he had lived, fearlessly and without a whimper.

Late in the afternoon Doc Riley, sweeping on a circling course, rode through chaparrals, alert even after his fruitless search, looking around on all sides, and wondered if Curley and he would meet before they reached the ranch proper. Suddenly something caught his eye and he stood up in the stirrups to see it better, a ready curse leaping from his lips. He could not make out who it was, but he had fears and he spurred forward as hard as he could go. Then he saw the horse and knew.

Riding close to the figure so as to be absolutely sure, he knew beyond a hope of mistake and looked around the plain, his expression malevolent and murderous.

"Curley! Curley!" he cried, leaping off his horse and placing a heavy, kindly hand on the broad, sloping shoulder of the man who had been his best friend for years. "So they got you, lad! They got you! In God's name, why did I leave you?" he cried in bitter self-condemnation. "It's my fault, it's my fault, lad!" He straightened up suddenly and glared around through tear-dimmed eyes. *"But by th' living God I'll pay them for this,* I'll pay them for this! D —n their murdering souls!"

He caught sight of an empty cartridge shell and snatched it up eagerly. ".40-90, by G-d! That's Antonio's! Curley, my lad, I'll get him for you-an' when I *do!* I'll send his soul to th' blackest pit in h —l, an' send it *slow!*"

He noticed and followed the tracks in the sand, reading them easily. He found the Winchester and quickly learned its story, which told him the whole thing. Returning to the body of his friend he sat by it quietly, looking down at it for several minutes, his sombrero in his hand.

"Well, wishing won't do no good," he muttered, dismounting. "I'll take you home, lad, an' see you put down too deep for coyotes to bother you. An' I'll square yore scores or join you trying."

He lifted the body across the withers of his horse and picked up the Colt. Mounting, he rode at a walk towards the bunk house, afire with rage and sorrow.

For the third time Meeker strode to the door of the bunk house and looked out into the darkness, uneasy and anxious. Chick sauntered over to him and leaned against the frame of the door. "They'll show up purty soon, Jim," he remarked.

"Yes. I reckon so-Salem!" the foreman called. "Put their grub where it'll keep warm."

"Aye, aye, sir. I was just thinking I ought to. They're late, ain't they, sir?" he asked. "An' it's dark, too," he added, gratis.

"Why, is it, Salem?" queried Dan, winking at Jack Curtis, but Salem disappeared into the gallery.

"Listen! —I hear 'em!" exclaimed Chick.

"You hear one of 'em," corrected Meeker, turning to the table to finish drinking his coffee. "Hey, Salem! Never mind warming that grub-rustle it in here. One of 'em's here, an' he'll be starved, too."

Suddenly Chick started back with an exclamation as Doc Riley loomed up in the light of the door, carrying a body over his shoulder. Stepping into the room while his friends leaped to their feet in amazement and incredulity, he lowered his burden to a bench and faced them, bloody and furious.

"What's th' matter?" exclaimed Meeker, the first to find his voice, leaping forward and dropping the cup to the floor. "Who did that?"

Doc placed his sombrero over the upturned face and ripped out a savage reply. "Antonio! Yore broncho-buster! Th' snake that's raising all th' devil on this range! Here-see for yoreself!" tossing the cartridge shell to his foreman, who caught it clumsily, looked at it, and then handed it to Dan. Exclamations and short, fierce questions burst from the others, who crowded up to see the shell.

"Tell me about it, Doc," requested Meeker, pacing from wall to wall.

"He was shot down like a dog!" Doc cried, his rage sweeping over him anew in all its savagery. "I saw th' whole thing in th' sand, plain as day. Th' Greaser got his cayuse first an' then rode rings around him, keeping out of range of Curley's Colt, for Curley had leaded his rifle. It was Colt against Sharps at five hundred, that was what it was! He didn't have a show, not a measly show for his life! Shot down like *a dog!*"

"Where'd it happen?" asked Chick, breathlessly, while the low-voiced threats and imprecations swelled to an angry, humming chorus.

"Away down in th' southwest corner," replied Doc, and he continued almost inaudibly, speaking to himself and forgetful of the others. "Me an' him went to school together an' I used to lick every kid that bullied him till he got big enough to do it hisself. We run away together an' shared th' same hard luck. We went through that Sioux campaign together, side by side, an' to think that after he pulled out of *that* alive he had to be murdered by a yaller coward of a Greaser! If he'd been killed by a human being an' in a fair fight it would be all right; but by that coyote-it don't seem possible, not noway. I licked th' feller that hurt him on his first day at school—I'm going to kill th' last!

"Meeker," he said, coming to himself and facing the angry foreman, "I'm quitting to-night. I won't punch no more till I get that Greaser. I take up that trail at daylight an' push it to a finish even if it takes me into Mexico-it's got to be him or me, now."

"You don't have to quit *me* to do that, an' you *know* it!" Meeker cried. "I don't care if yo're gone for six months-yore pay goes on just th' same. He went down fighting for me, an' I'll be everlastingly condemned if I don't have a hand in squaring up for it. Yo're going on special duty for th' H2, Doc, an' yore orders are to get Antonio. Why, by th' Lord, I'll take up th' trail with you, Doc, an' with th' rest of th' boys behind me. This ranch can go galley-west an' crooked till we get that snake. Dan an' Salem stays with my girl an' to watch th' ranch-th' rest of us are with you-we're as anxious as you to push him Yonder, Doc."

"If I can get him alive, get my two hands on his skinny neck," Doc muttered, his fingers twitching, "I'll kill him slow, so he'll feel it longer, so he'll be shore to know why he's going. I want to *feel* his murdering soul dribble hell-wards, an' let him come back a couple of times so I can laugh in his yaller face when he begs! I want to get him —*so!*" and Chick shuddered as the knotted, steel-like fingers opened and shut, for Doc was half devil now. While Chick stared, the transformed man walked over to the bench and picked up the body in his brawny arms and strode into the blackness-Curley was going to lie in the open, with the stars and the sky and the sighing wind.

"God!" breathed Chick, looking around, "I never saw a man like *that* before!"

"I hope he gets what he wants!" exclaimed Dan, fiercely.

"You fellers get yore traps ready for a chase," Meeker ordered as he strode to the door of the gallery. "Fifty rounds for six-shooters an' fifty for rifle, an' plenty of grub. It's a whole lot likely that th' Greaser headed for his gang, an' we've got to be ready to handle everything that comes up. Hey, Salem!" he shouted.

"Aye, aye, sir!" replied Salem, who had just come in from one of the corrals and knew nothing of what had occurred.

"Did you cure that beef I told you to?" demanded the foreman.

"Yes, sir; but it ain't had time to cure-th' weather's not been right. Howsomever, I smoked some. That'll be ship-shape."

"Well, have it on our cayuses at daylight. Did you cut this beef in strips, or in twenty-pound chunks, like you did th' last?"

"Strips, *little* strips —I ain't trying to sun-cure no more big hunks, not me, sir."

Meeker turned and went towards the outer door.

"Don't waste no time, boys," he said. "Get all th' sleep you can to-night —you'll need it if I reckon right. Good-night," and he stepped out into the darkness. "D —n them dogs!" he muttered, disappearing in the direction of the kennels, from which came quavering, long-drawn howls.

Chapter XXVI

Frisco Visits Eagle

Eagle did not thoroughly awaken until the sun began to set, for it was not until dark that its inhabitants, largely transient, cared to venture forth. Then it was that the town seethed, boldly, openly, restrained by nothing save the might of the individual.

Prosperity had blessed the town, for there had been an abrupt and pleasing change in local conditions since the disagreement between the two ranches north of the town had assumed warlike aspect. Men who heretofore had no standing with the proprietors of the town's places of amusement and who had seldom been able to pay for as much liquor as they were capable of drinking, now swaggered importantly where they pleased, and found welcome where formerly it had been denied them; for their hands were thrust deep into pockets from which came the cheerful and open-sesame clinking of gold. Even Big Sandy, who had earned his food by sweeping out the saloons and doing odd jobs about them, and who was popularly believed to be too lazy to earn a better living by real work, now drank his fill and failed to recognize a broom when he saw it. While the inhabitants could not "get in" on the big plums which they were certain were being shaken down on the range, they could and did take care of the windfalls, and thrived well. They would stay in town until their money was gone and then disappear for a week, and return to spend recklessly. It is not out of place to state, in passing, that numerous small herds bearing strange brands frequently passed around the town at a speed greater than that common to drives, and left clouds of dust on the southeastern horizon.

The town debated the probable whereabouts of ten men who had suddenly disappeared in a body, along with Antonio of the H2. It was obvious what they were doing and the conjectures were limited as to their whereabouts and success. For a while after they had left one or two had ridden in occasionally to buy flour and other necessities, and at that time they had caused no particular thought. But now even these visits had ceased. It was common belief that Quinn knew all about them, but Quinn for good reasons was not urged to talk about the matter. Big Sandy acted as though he knew, which increased his importance for a time, and discredited him thereafter.

While the citizens had been able to rustle as they pleased they had given but little thought to the ten men, being too busy to trail. But now that the H2 punchers rode range with rifles across their arms rustling had become very risky and had fallen off. Then it was that the idlers renewed their conjectures about Shaw and his men and thrashed that matter over and over again. The majority being, as we have said, transients, knew nothing about Thunder Mesa, and those who did know of it were silent, for Shaw and some of his companions knew only one way to close a man's mouth, and were very capable.

So it happened that about noon of the day Curley lost his life six men met in the shadow cast by the front of the "Rawhide" a hundred yards from Quinn's, and exercised squatter sovereignty on the bench just outside the door, while inside the saloon Big Sandy and Nevada played cards close to the bar and talked in low tones. When they were aware of the presence of those on the bench they played silently and listened. The six men outside made up one of the groups of the town's society, having ridden in together and stuck together ever since they had arrived, which was wise.

Big Sandy and Nevada made a team more feared than any other combination. The former, while fair with weapons, was endowed with prodigious strength; by some it was hailed as being greater than that of Pete Wilson, the squat giant of the Bar-20, whose strength was proverbial, as it had good right to be. Nevada was the opposite type, slender, short, wiry, and soft-spoken, but the quickest man in town on the draw and of uncertain temper.

Chet Bates, on the bench, replied to a companion and gave vent to his soft, Southern laugh. "Yuh still wondering 'bout thet man Shaw, an' th' othas?"

"Nothing else to do, is there?" retorted Dal Gilbert. "We can't run no more cattle, can we?"

"I reckon we can't."

"They're running a big game an' I want to get in it," remarked John Elder. "Frisco was allus friendly. We've got to go trailing for 'em."

"Yes; an' get shot," interposed George Lewis. "They're ten to our six. An' that ain't all of our troubles, neither. We'll find ourselves in a big fight some day, an' right here. Them ranches will wake up, patch up their troubles, an' come down here. You remember what Quinn said about th' time Peters led a lot of mad punchers agin Trendley an' his crowd, don't you? In a day he can raise men enough to wipe this town off th' map."

"Yuh forget, suh, that they are fighting foh principles, an' men who fight foh principles don't call truces," said Chet Bates.

"You've said that till it's old," laughed Sam Austin.

"*I* say we've got to keep our eyes open," warned Lewis.

"Th' devil with that!" broke in Con Irwin. "What *I* want to know is how we're going to get some of th' easy money Shaw's getting."

"We'll have to wait for one of his men to come to town an' trail him back," replied Gilbert.

"What do you say that we try to run one more good herd an' then scout for them, or their trails?" asked Irwin.

"Heah comes somebody," remarked Chet, listening.

The sound of galloping grew rapidly louder and soon they saw Frisco turn into the street and ride towards them. As they saw him a quiet voice was heard behind them and looking up, they saw Nevada smiling at them. "Get him drunk an' keep him away from Quinn's," he counselled.

They exchanged looks and then Elder stepped out into the street and held up his hand. "Hullo, Frisco!" he cried.

"Where yuh been keeping yuhself foh so long?" asked Chet, affably. "Holed up som'ers?"

"Hullo, fellers," grinned Frisco, drawing rein.

"Everybody have a drink on me," laughed Chet. "Ah'm pow'ful thirsty."

Frisco was escorted inside to the bar, where Chet did the honors, and where such a spirit of hospitality and joviality surrounded him that he forgot how many drinks he had taken. He dug up a handful of gold and silver and spread it out on the bar and waved at the bartender. "Bes' you got-ver' bes'," he grinned. "Me an' my fren's want th' ver' bes'; don't we, fellers? I got money-helluva lot of money-an' thersh more where it came from, ain't that so, boys?"

When the noise had subsided he turned around and levelled an unsteady finger at the bartender. "I never go-back onsh fren', never. An' we're all frensh-ain't we, fellers? Tha's right. I got s'more frensh-good fellesh, an' lots of money cached in sand."

"Ah'll bet yuh have!" cried Chet.

"You allus could find pay-dirt," marvelled Nevada, glancing warningly around him. "Yo're a fine prospector, all right."

Frisco stared for a moment and then laughed loudly and leaned against the bar for support. "Proshpector! Proshpector! W'y, we earned tha's money-run a helluva lot of risks. Mebby tha's Bar-20 outfit'll jump us an' make us fight 'em. No; they can't jump us-they can't get up at us!"

"On a mesa, shore!" whispered Elder to Lewis.

"Wha's you shay?"

"Said they couldn't lick you."

"Who couldn't —lick us?"

"Th' Bar-20," explained Elder.

Frisco rubbed his head and drew himself up, suspicion percolating through his muddled brain. "Never shaid nozzing 'bout no Bar-Twensh!" he asserted, angrily. "Nozzing 'tall. I'm going out of here-don't like you! Gotta get some flour an' ozzer stuff. Never shaid nozzing 'bout —" he muttered, staggering out.

Nevada turned to Elder. "You go with him an' quiet his suspicions. Keep him away from Quinn, for that coyote'll hold him till he gets sober if you don't. This is the chance we've been wanting. Don't try to pump him-his trail will be all we need."

"Wonder what mesa they're on?" asked Lewis.

"Don't know, an' don't care," Nevada replied. "We'll find out quick enough. There's eight of us an' we can put up a stiff argument if they won't take us in. You know they ain't going to welcome us, don't you?"

"Hey, go out th' back way," growled Big Sandy, interposing his huge bulk between Bates and the door. "An' don't let Frisco see you near a cayuse, neither," he added.

Nevada walked quickly over to his friend and said a few hurried words in a low voice and Big Sandy nodded. "Shore, Nevada; he might try that, but I'll watch him. If he tries to sneak I'll let you know hasty. We're in this to stay," and he followed the others to the door.

Nevada turned and faced the bartender. "Mike, you keep quiet about what you saw an' heard to-day; understand? If you don't, me an' you won't fit in this town at th' same time."

Mike grinned. "I forgot how to talk after one exciting day up in Cheyenne, an' I ain't been drunk since, neither."

"Yo're a wise man," replied the other, stepping out by the back door and hastening up the street where he could keep watch over Quinn's saloon. It was an hour before he caught sight of Frisco, and he was riding west, singing at the top of his lungs. Then Quinn slipped into his corral and threw a saddle on a horse.

"Drop it!" said a quiet voice behind him and he turned to see Nevada watching him.

"What do you mean?" demanded Quinn, ominously.

"Let loose of that cayuse an' go back inside," was the reply.

"You get th' h —l out of here an' mind yore own —" Quinn leaped aside and jerked at his Colt; but was too late, and he fell, badly wounded. Nevada sprang forward and disarmed him and then, mounting, galloped off to join his friends.

Chapter XXVII
Shaw has Visitors

When Frisco reached the edge of the clearing around the mesa he saw Antonio and Shaw toiling cautiously up the steep, precarious trail leading to the top, and he hailed vociferously. Both looked around, Antonio scowling and his companion swearing at their friend's condition. Frisco's pack horse, which he had sense enough to bring back, was loaded down with bags and packages which had been put on recklessly, inasmuch as a slab of bacon hung from the animal's neck and swayed to and fro with each step; and the animal he rode had a bartender's apron hanging down before its shoulders.

"Had a rip-snorting time-rip-snorting time," he announced pleasantly, in a roar. "Salubrious-rip-snorting-helluva time!"

"Nobody'd guess it!" retorted Shaw. "Look at them bundles! An' him an expert pack-horse man, too. An' that cayuse with a shirt! For anybody that can throw as neat a diamond hitch as him, that pack horse is a howling disgrace!"

"Hang th' pack horse!" growled Antonio. "I bet th' whole town knows our business now! He ought to be shot. Where you going?"

"Down to help him up," Shaw replied. "He'll bust his fool neck if he wrestles with that trail alone. You go on up an' send a couple of th' boys down to bring up th' grub," he ordered, starting down the path.

"Let him bust his fool neck!" cried the Mexican. "He should 'a done that before he left."

"What's th' ruction?" asked Clausen, looking down over the edge at the Mexican.

"Oh, Frisco's come back howling drunk. Go down an' help him tote th' grub up. Shaw said for somebody else to help you."

"Hey, Cavalry," cried Clausen. "Come on an' gimme a hand," and the two disappeared down the trail.

The leader returned, heralded by singing and swearing, and pushed Frisco over the mesa top to sprawl full-length on the ground. Shaw looked down at him with an expression of anger and anxiety and then turned abruptly on his heel as a quavering snore floated up from the other.

"Here, Manuel!" he called, sharply. "Take my glasses an' go out to yore lookout rock. Look towards Eagle an' call me if you see anybody."

The Mexican shuffled away as Cavalry and Clausen, loaded down, appeared over the edge of the mesa wall and dropped their loads at Shaw's feet.

"What did you tell him to get?" asked Clausen, marvelling.

"What do you think I told him to get?" snapped Shaw.

"I don't know, seeing what he brought back," was the reply.

Shaw examined the pile. "G-d's name, what's all this stuff?" he roared. "Bacon! An' all th' meat we want is down below. Canned milk! Two bottles XXX Cough Syrup, four bottles of whiskey, bottle vaniller extract, plug tobacco, an' three harmonicas! Is *that* flour!" he yelled, glaring at a small bag. "Twenty pounds! Five pounds of salt!"

"I reckon he bought all th' cartridges in town," Cavalry announced, staggering into sight with a box on his shoulder. "Lord, but it's heavy!"

"Twenty pounds of flour to last nine men a month!" Shaw shouted, kicking at the bag. "An' look at this coffee-two pounds! I'll teach him a lesson when he gets sober."

"Well, he made up th' weight in th' cartridges," Cavalry grinned. He grasped Shaw's arm. "What's got into Manuel?"

The leader looked and sprinted to the lookout rock, where Manuel was gesticulating, and took the glasses. Half a minute later he returned them to the Mexican and rejoined his companions near the pile of supplies.

"What is it?" asked Cavalry.

"Some of our Eagle friends. Mebby they want cards in this game, but we'll waste little time with 'em. Post th' fellers along th' edge, Clausen, an' you watch th' trail up. Keep 'em covered while I talks with 'em. Don't be slow to burn powder if they gets to pushing things."

"They trailed Frisco," growled Cavalry.

"Shore; oh, he was a great success!" snapped Shaw, going to the edge of the mesa to await the eight newcomers, his men finding convenient places along the top of the wall, their rifles ready for action.

They did not have long to wait for soon Nevada and Chet Bates rode into the clearing and made for the trail.

"That's far enough, Nevada!" shouted Shaw, holding up his hand.

"Why, hullo, Shaw!" cried the man below. "Yo're up a good tree, all right," he laughed.

"Yes."

"Can we ride up, or do we have to take shank's mare?"

"Neither."

"Well, we want some water after that ride," replied Nevada.

"Plenty of it below. Nobody asked you to take that ride. What do you want, anyhow?"

"Why, when Frisco said you was out here we thought we'd drop in on you an' pay you a little visit."

"You have paid us a little visit. Call again next summer."

"Running many cows?" asked Nevada.

"Nope; educating coyotes. Didn't see none, did you?"

Nevada exchanged a few words with his companion and then looked up again. "I reckon you need us, Shaw. Eight more men means twice as many cows; an' we can all fight a little if th' ranches get busy out here."

"We're crowded now. Better water up an' hit th' back trail. It's hard riding in th' dark."

"We didn't come out here for a drink," replied Nevada. "We came out to help you rustle, which same we'll do. I tell you that you need us, man!"

"When I need you I'll send for you. *Adios.*"

"You ain't going to let us come up?"

"Not a little bit. Pull yore stakes an' hit th' back trail. *Adios!*"

"Well, we'll hang around to-night an' talk it over again to-morrow. Mebby you'll change yore mind. So long," and the two wheeled and disappeared into the chaparrals, Nevada chuckling. "I didn't spring that little joker, Chet, because it's a good card to play last. When we tell him that we won't let nobody come down off'n th' mesa it'll be after we can't do nothing else. No use making him mad."

Up on the mesa Shaw wheeled, scowling. "I knowed that fool would fire off something big! Why can't he get drunk out here, where it's all right?"

"That Nevada is a shore bad proposition," Clausen remarked.

"So'm I!" snapped Shaw. "He can't come up, an' pursooant to that idee I reckon you an' Hall better arrange to watch th' trail to-night."

He walked away and paced slowly along the edge of the wall, studying every yard of it. He had done this thing before and had decided that no man sat a saddle who could scale the sheer hundred feet of rock which dropped so straight below him. But somehow he felt oppressed, and the sinking sun threw into bold relief the furrows of his weather-beaten, leathery face and showed the trouble marks which sat above his eyes. At one part of the wall he stopped and peered over, marshalling imaginative forces in attack after attack against it. But at the end he smiled and moved on-that was the weakest point in his defence, but he would consider himself fortunate if he should find no weaker defence in future conflicts. As he returned to the hut he glanced at the lookout rock and saw Manuel in his characteristic pose, unmoving, silent, watchful.

"I'm getting as bad as Cavalry and his desert," he grumbled. "Still, they can't lick us while we stay up here."

Chapter XXVIII
Nevada Joins Shaw

Late in the forenoon of the day after Nevada had argued with Shaw, Manuel shifted his position on the lookout rock and turned to face the hut. "Señor! Señor Shaw! He ees here."

Shaw strode to the edge of the mesa and looked down, seeing Nevada sitting quietly on a horse and looking up at him. Manuel, his duty performed, turned and looked eastward, shrinking back as Shaw stepped close to him. Lying prone along the edge half a dozen men idly fingered rifles as they covered the man below, Antonio's face in particular showing intense aversion to any more recruits.

"Morning, Shaw," shouted Nevada. "Going to let us come up?"

The leader was about to reply when he felt a tug at his ankle and saw Manuel's lips moving. "What is it, Greaser?"

"Look, Señor, look!" whispered the frightened Mexican, pointing eastward. "Eet ees de Bar-20! They be here *poco tiempo!*"

"Shut up!" retorted Shaw in a whisper, glancing east, and what he saw changed his reply to the man below. "Well, Nevada, we are purty crowded up here as it is, but I'll ask th' boys about it. They ain't quite decided. Be back in a minute," and he stepped back out of sight of those below and waved his companions to him. Briefly stating the facts he asked that Nevada and his force be allowed up to help repulse the Bar-20, and the men who only a short time before had sworn that they would take in no partners nodded assent and talked over the new conditions while their leader again went to the edge.

"We can get along without you fellers," he called down, "but we don't reckon you'll cut any hole in our profits as long as you do yore share of work. If yo're willin' to share an' share alike, in work, grub, profits, an' fighting, why I reckon you can come up. But I'm leader here an' what I says goes; are you agreeable?"

"That's fair," Nevada replied. "Th' harder th' work th' bigger th' pay-come on, boys," he cried, turning and waving his arm. "We're in!"

While the newcomers put their horses in the corral and toiled carefully up the steep trail Manuel stared steadily into the east and again saw the force that had filled him with fear. Hall, who was now watching with him, abruptly arose and returned to the hut, reporting: "Seven men out there-it's th' Bar-20, all right, I reckon"; and almost immediately afterward Manuel found a moving speck far to the east which Shaw's powerful glasses soon showed to be three pack horses driven by two men.

Nevada looked curiously about him as he gained his goal and then sought a place in the hut for his bunk. This, however, was full, and he cast around outside to find the best place for his blankets. Finding it, he stepped to the spring and had just quenched his thirst when he saw Shaw standing on a ledge of rock above him, looking down. "What is it, Shaw?" he asked.

"Well, you fellers shore enough raised h —l, now didn't you!" demanded the leader, a rising anger in his voice. "Yo're a fine collection of fools, you are —"

"What do —"

" —Leading that Bar-20 gang out here by th' nice, plain trail you left," Shaw continued, sarcastically, not heeding the other's explosive interjection. "That's a nice thing to saddle us with! D —n it, don't you know you've queered th' game for good?"

"Yo're drunk!" retorted Nevada, heatedly. "We came up from th' south! How th' devil could that crowd hit *our* trail?"

"They must 'a hit southwest on a circle," lied Shaw. "Manuel just now saw 'em pass a clearing an' heading this way-nine of 'em!"

"Th' devil!" exclaimed Nevada. "How many are up here now?" he asked quickly.

"Sixteen."

"All right! Let 'em come!" cried the other. "Sixteen to nine-it's easy!" he laughed. "Look here; we can clean up them fellers an' then raid their ranch, for there's only four left at home. We can run off a whopping big herd, sell 'em, an' divvy even. Then we separates, savvy? Why, it couldn't be better!"

Shaw showed his astonishment and his companion continued. "Th' H2 is shy men, an' th' C80 and th' Double Arrow is too far away to bother us. As soon as we lick this aggregation of trouble hunters, what's left will ride hell-bent for that valley. Then th' biggest herd ever rustled in these parts, a trip to a new range, an' plenty of money to spend there."

"That sounds good-but this pleasing cleaning-up is due to be full of knots," Shaw rejoined. "Them nine men come from th' craggiest outfit of high-toned gun-artists in these parts, an' you can bet that they are th' pick of th' crowd! Cassidy, Connors, Peters-an' they've got forty friends purty nigh as bad, an' eager to join in. I ain't no ways a quitter, but this looks to me like Custer's Last Stand, us being th' Custers."

"Ah, yo're loco!" retorted Nevada. "Look here! Send a dozen picked men down quick an' let 'em lose 'emselves in th' chaparral, far back. When th' terrible man-killers of th' great Bar-20 get plugging this way, our trouble-gang slips up from behind an' it's all over! Go on, before it's too late! Or one of us will ride like th' devil to Eagle for help-but it's got to be quick! You say I got you in this, which I know well I didn't, but now I'll get you out an' put you in th' way of a barrel of money."

The crack of a rifle sounded from the plain and the next instant Clausen dashed up, crying, "Manuel tried to cut an' run, but somebody down below dropped him off'n th' trail. They're all around us!"

"Good for th' somebody!" cried Shaw. "I'll kill th' next man that tries to leave us-that goes, so pass it along." Then he turned to Nevada, a sneer on his face. "That means anybody riding for help, too!" and he backed away.

Hall turned the corner, looking Nevada squarely in the eyes. "Say, Shaw, wonder what's got into Archer? He's been gone a long time for that trip."

"Reckon he's got tired an' quit," replied Shaw.

"You know he ain't that kind!" Hall cried, angrily.

"All right, all right. If he comes back an' finds out what's up he'll probably hustle to Eagle for some of th' boys," Shaw responded. Neither would ever see Dick Archer again-his bones were whitening near a small water hole miles to the north, as Hopalong and Red could testify.

"As long as one of us is outside we've got a chance," Nevada remarked. "How're we fixed for grub, Hall?"

"Got enough jerked beef to last us a month," and Hall departed.

A shot hummed over Nevada's head and, ducking quickly, he followed Hall. Close behind him went Shaw, muttering. "Well, it had to come sometime-an' we're better fixed than I ever reckoned we'd be. Now we'll see who gets wiped out!"

Chapter XXIX
Surrounded

Above, a pale, hot sky with only a wisp of cloud; below, a semi-arid "pasture," scant in grass, seamed by tortuous gullies and studded with small, compact thickets and bulky bowlders. A wall of chaparral, appearing solid when viewed from a distance, fenced the pasture, and rising boldly from the southwest end of the clearing a towering mass of rock flung its rugged ramparts skyward. Nature had been in a sullen mood when this scene had been perpetrated and there was no need of men trying to heighten the gloomy aspect by killing each other. Yet they were trying and had been for a week, and they could have found no surroundings more in keeping with their occupation.

Minute clouds of smoke spurted from the top of the wall and from the many points of vantage on the pasture to hang wavering for an instant before lazily dissipating in the hot, close air. In such a sombre setting men had elected to joke and curse and kill, perhaps to die; men hot with passion and blood-lust plied rifles with deliberate intent to kill. On one side there was fierce deep joy, an exultation in forcing the issue, much as if they had tugged vainly at a leash and suddenly found themselves free. They had been baited, tricked, robbed, and fired upon and now, their tormentors penned before them, there would be no cessation in their efforts to wipe out the indignities under which they had chafed for so long a time.

On the other side, high up on a natural fortress which was considered impregnable, lay those who had brought this angry pack about them. There was no joy there, no glad eagerness to force the battle, no jokes nor laughter, but only a grim desperation, a tenacious holding to that which the others would try to take. On one side aggression; on the other, defence. Fighters all, they now were inspired by the merciless end always in their minds; they were trapped like rats and would fight while mind could lay a plan or move a muscle. Of the type which had out-roughed, out-fought for so long even the sturdy, rough men who had laid the foundation for an inland empire amid dangers superlative, they knew nothing of yielding; and to yield was to die. It was survivor against survivor in an even game.

"Ah, God!" moaned a man on the mesa's lofty rim, staggering back aimlessly before he fell, never to rise again. His companions regarded him curiously, stolidly, without sympathy, as is often the case where death is constantly expected. Dal Gilbert turned back to his rifle and the problems before him. "So you've gone, too. An' I reckon we'll follow" —such was Chet Bates' obituary.

In a thicket two hundred yards south of the mesa Red Connors worked the lever of his rifle, a frown on his face. "I got him, all right. Do you know who he is?"

"No; but I've seen him in Eagle," replied Hopalong, lowering the glasses. "What's worrying me is water-my throat's drying awful."

"You shouldn't 'a forgot it," chided Red. "Now we've got to go without it all day."

Hopalong ducked and swore as he felt of his bleeding face. "Purty close, that!"

"Mind what yo're doing!" replied Red. "Get off my hand."

"This scrap is shore slow," Hopalong growled. "Here we've been doing this for a whole week, all of us shot up, an' only got two of them fellers."

"Well, yo're right; but there ain't a man up there that ain't got a few bullet holes in him," Red replied. "But it is slow, that's shore."

"I've got to get a drink, an' that's all about it," Hopalong asserted. "I can crawl in that gully most of th' way, an' then trust a side-hopping dash. Anyhow, I'm tired of this place. Johnny's got th' place for *me*."

"You better stay here till it's dark, you fool."

"Aw, stay nothing-so long," and Hopalong, rifle in hand, crawled towards the gully. Red watched the mesa intently, hoping to be able to stop some of the firing his rash friend was sure to call forth.

Twenty minutes passed and then two puffs of smoke sailed against the sky, Red replying. Then half a dozen puffs burst into sight. A faint shout came to Red's ears and he smiled, for his friend was safe.

As Hopalong gained the chaparral he felt himself heartily kicked and, wheeling pugnaciously, looked into Buck Peters' scowling face. "Yo're a healthy fool!" growled the foreman. "Ain't you got no sense at all? Hereafter you flit over that pasture after dark, d'y hear!"

"He's th' biggest fool I ever saw, an' th' coolest," said a voice in the chaparral at the left.

"Why, hullo, Meeker," Hopalong laughed, turning from Buck. "How do you like our little party now?"

"I'm getting tired of it, an' it's some costly for me," grumbled the H2 foreman. "Bet them skunks in Eagle have cleaned out every head I owned." Then he added as an afterthought: "But I don't care a whole lot if I can see this gang wiped out —*Antonio* is th' coyote *I'm* itching to stop."

"He'll be stopped," replied Hopalong. "Hey, Buck, Red's shore thirsty."

"He can stay thirsty, then. An' don't you try to take no water to him. You stay off that pasture during daylight."

"But it was all my fault —" Hopalong began, and then he was off like a shot across the open, leaping gullies and dodging around bowlders.

"Here you!" roared Buck, and stopped to stare, Meeker at his side. A man was staggering in circles near a thicket which lay a hundred yards from them. He dropped and began to crawl aimlessly about, a good target for the eager rifles on the mesa. Bullets whined and shrilled and kicked up the dust on the plain, but still the rushing Bar-20 puncher was unhit. From the mesa came the faint crackling of rifle fire and clouds of smoke hovered over the cover sheltering Red Connors. Here and there over the pasture and along the chaparral's rim rifles cracked in hot endeavor to drive the rustlers from their positions long enough to save the reckless puncher. Buck and Meeker both were firing now, rapidly but carefully, muttering words of hope and anxiety as they worked the levers of their spurting guns. Then they saw Hopalong gain the prostrate man's side, drag him back to cover, and wave his arm. The fire from the mesa was growing weaker and as it stopped Hopalong, with the wounded man on his back, ran to the shelter of a gully and called for water.

"He's th' best man in this whole country!" cried Meeker, grabbing up a canteen and starting to go through the chaparral to give them water. "To do that for one of *my* men!"

"I've knowed that for nigh onto fifteen years," replied Buck.

Near the Eagle trail Billy Williams and Doc Riley lay side by side, friendly now.

"I tell you we've been shooting high," Doc grumbled. "It's no cinch picking range against that skyline."

"Hey! Look at Hopalong!" cried Billy, excitedly. "Blamed idiot-why, he's going out to that feller. Lord! Get busy!"

"That's Curtis out there!" ejaculated Doc, angrily. "They've got him, d —n 'em!"

"My gun's jammed!" cursed Billy, in his excitement and anger standing up to tear at the cartridge. "I allus go an' —" he pitched sideways to the sand, where he lay quiet.

Doc dropped his rifle and leaped to drag his companion back to the shelter of the cover. As he did so his left arm was hit, but he accomplished his purpose and as he reached for his canteen the Bar-20 pessimist saved him the trouble by opening his eyes and staring around. "Oh, my head! It's shore burning up, Doc!" he groaned. "What th' devil happened that time, anyhow?"

"Here; swaller this," Doc replied, handing him the canteen.

"Who got me?" asked Billy, laying the vessel aside.

"How do I know? Whoever he was he creased you nice. His friends got me in th' arm, too. You can help me fix it soon."

"Shore I will! We can lick them thieves, Doc," Billy expounded without much interest. "Yessir," he added.

"You make me tired," Doc retorted. "You talking about being careful when you stand up in plain sight of them fellers like you just did."

"Yes, I know. I was mad, an' sort of forgot about 'em being able to shoot at me-but what happened out there, anyhow?"

Doc craned his neck. "There's Cassidy now, in that gully-Meeker's just joined him. Good men, both of 'em."

"You bet," replied Billy, satisfied. "Yessir, we can lick 'em-we've got to."

On the west side of the mesa, back in the chaparral and out of sight of the rustlers, Pie Willis lay face down in the sand, quiet. Near him lay Frenchy McAllister, firing at intervals, aflame with anger and a desire to kill. Opposite him on the mesa, a scant three hundred yards away, two rustlers gloated and fired, eager to kill the other puncher, who shot so well.

"That other feller knows his business, Elder," remarked Nevada as a slug ricochetted past his head. "Wonder who he is."

"Wonder *where* he is," growled Elder, firing at a new place. "He's been shifting a lot. Anyhow, we got one. There's so much smoke down there I can't seem to place him. Mebby —" he fell back, limp, his rifle clattering down a hundred feet of rock.

Nevada looked at him closely and then drew back to a more secure position. "We're even, stranger, but we ain't quits, by a good deal!" He swore. *Zing-ing-ing!* "Oh, you know I moved, do you!" he gritted. "Well, how's *that!*" *Spat!* a new, bright leaden splotch showed on the rock above his head and hot lead stung his neck and face as the bullet spattered. "I'll get you yet, you coyote!" he muttered, changing his position again. "Ah, *h —l!*" he sobbed and dropped his rifle to grasp his right elbow, shattered by a Winchester .45. Pain shot through every fibre of his body and weakened him so he could not crawl for shelter or assistance. He swayed, lost his balance and swayed further, and as his side showed beyond the edge of his rocky rampart he quivered and sank back, helpless, pain-racked, and bleeding to death from two desperate wounds.

"We was-tricked-up here!" he moaned. "That must-be Red-Connors out there. Ah!" *Spat! Chug! Spat!* But Nevada did not hear them now.

Down in the chaparral, Frenchy, getting no response to his shots, picked up his glasses and examined the mesa. A moment later he put them back in the case, picked up his rifle and crawled towards his companion.

"Pie!" he called, touching the body. "Pie, old feller! I got 'em both for you, Pie-got 'em —" screened by the surrounding chaparral he stood up and shook a clenched fist at the sombre, smoke-wreathed pile of rock and shouted: "An' they won't be all! Do you hear, you thieves? *They won't be all!*"

Lying in a crack on the apex of a pinnacle of rock a hundred yards northwest of the mesa Johnny Nelson cursed the sun and squirmed around on the hot stone, vainly trying to find a spot comparatively cool, while two panic-stricken lizards huddled miserably as far back in the crack as they could force themselves. Long bright splotches marked the stone all around the youthful puncher and shrill whinings came to him out of the air, to hurtle away in the distance ten times as loud and high-pitched. For an hour he had not dared to raise his head to aim, and his sombrero, which he had used as a dummy, was shot full of holes. Johnny, at first elated because of his aerial position, now cursed it fervently and was filled with disgust. When he had begun firing at sunrise he had only one man to face. But the news went around among the rustlers that a fool had volunteered to be a target and now three good shots vied with each other to get the work over with quickly, and return to their former positions.

"I reckon I can squirm over th' edge an' drop down that split," Johnny soliloquized, eying a ragged, sharp edge in the rock close at hand. "Don't know where it goes to, or how far down, but it's cool, that's shore."

He wriggled over to it, flattened as much as possible, and looked over the edge, seeing a four-inch ledge ten feet below him. From the ledge it was ten feet more to the bottom, but the ledge was what interested him.

"Shore I can-just land on that shelf, hug th' wall an' they can't touch me," he grinned, slipping over and hanging for an instant until he stopped swinging. The rock bulged out between him and the ledge, but he did not give that any thought. Letting go he dropped down the face of the rock, shot out along the bulge and over his cherished ledge, and landed with a grunt on a mass of sand and debris twenty feet below. As he pitched forward to his hands he heard the metallic warning of a rattlesnake and all his fears of being shot were knocked out of his head by the sound. When he landed from his jump he was on the wrong side of the crevice and among hot lead. Ducking and dodging he worked back to the right side and then blew off the offending rattler's head with his Colt. Other rattlers now became prominent and Johnny, realizing that he was an unwelcome guest in a rattlesnake den, made good use of his eyes and Colt as he edged towards the mouth of the crevice. Behind him were rattlers; before him, rustlers who could and would shoot. To say that he was disgusted is to put it mildly.

"Cussed joint!" he grunted. "This is a measly place for me. If I stay I get bit to death; if I leave I get shot. Wonder if I can get to that ledge-ugh!" he cried as the tip of a rattler's tail hung down from it for an instant. "Come on! Bring 'em all out! Trot out th' tarantulas, copper heads, an' Gilas! Th' more th' merrier! Blasted snake hang-out!"

He glanced about him rapidly, apprehensively, and shivered. "No more of this for Little Johnny! I'll chance th' sharp-shooters," he yelled, and dashed out and around the pile so quickly as to be unhit. But he was not hit for another reason, also. Skinny Thompson and Pete Wilson, having grown restless, were encircling the mesa by keeping inside the chaparral and came opposite the pinnacle about the time Johnny discovered his reptilian neighbors. Hearing the noise they both stopped and threw their rifles to their shoulders. Here was a fine opportunity to lessen the numbers of the enemy, for the rustlers, careless for the moment, were peering over their breastwork to see what all the noise was about, not dreaming that two pairs of eyes three hundred yards away were calculating the range. Two puffs of smoke burst from the chaparral and the rustlers ducked out of sight, one of them hard hit. At that moment Johnny made his dash and caused smiles to flit across the faces of his friends.

"We might 'a knowed it was him!" laughed Skinny. "Nobody else would be loco enough to pick out that thing."

"Yes; but now what's he doing?" asked Pete, seeing Johnny poking around among the rocks, Colt in hand.

"Hunting rustlers, I reckon," Skinny replied. "Thinks they are tunnelling an' coming up under him, I suppose. Hey! Johnny!"

Johnny turned, peering at the chaparral.

"What are you doing?" yelled Skinny.

"Hunting snakes."

Skinny laughed and turned to watch the mesa, from which lead was coming.

"Can you cover me if I make a break?" shouted Johnny, hopefully.

"No; stay where you are!" shouted Pete, and then ducked.

"Stop yelling and move about some or you'll get us both hit," ordered Skinny. "Them fellers can *shoot*!"

"Come on; let's go ahead. Johnny can stay out there till dark an' hunt snakes," Pete was getting sarcastic. "Wonder if he reckons we came here to get shot at just to hunt snakes!"

"No; we'll help him in," Skinny replied. "You'll find th' rattlers made it too hot for him up there. Start shooting."

Johnny hearing the rapid firing of his friends, ran backwards, keeping the pinnacle between him and his enemies as long as he could. Then, once out of its shelter, he leaped erratically over the plain and gained a clump of chaparral. He now had only about a hundred yards to go, and Johnny could sprint when need was. He sprinted. Joining his friends the three disappeared in the chaparral and two disgusted rustlers helped a badly wounded companion to the rough hospital in the hut at the top of the mesa trail.

Johnny and his friends had not gone far before Johnny, eager to find a rustler to shoot at, left them to go to the edge of the chaparral and while he was away his friends stumbled on the body of Pie Willis. Johnny, moving cautiously along the edge of the chaparral, soon met Buck and Hopalong, who were examining every square foot of the mesa wall for a way up.

"Hullo, Johnny!" cried Hopalong. "What you doing here? Thought you was plumb stuck on that freak rock up north."

"I was-an' *stuck*, for shore," grinned Johnny. "That rock is a nest of snakes, besides being a fine place to get plugged by them fellers. An' hot!"

"How'd you get away?"

"Pete an' Skinny drove 'em back an' I made my get-away. They're in th' chaparral some-where close," Johnny replied. "But why are you telescoping at th' joker? Think you see money out there?"

"Looking for a place to climb it," Hopalong responded. "We're disgusted with this long-range squibbing. You didn't see no breaks in th' wall up where you was, did you?"

"Lemme see," and Johnny cogitated for a moment. Then his face cleared. "Shore I did; there's lots of cracks in it, running up an' down, an' a couple of ledges. I ain't so shore about th' ledges, though-you see I was too busy to look for ledges during th' first part of th' seance, and I dassn't look during th' last of it. There was three of 'em a-popping at me!"

"Hey, Johnny!" came a hail; "Johnny!"

"That's Pete an' Skinny-Hullo!" Johnny shouted.

"Come here-Pie Willis is done for!"

"What?"

"Pie-Willis-is-done-for!"

The three turned and hastened towards the voice, shouting questions. They found Skinny and Pete standing over the body and sombreros came off as the foreman knelt to examine it. Pie had been greatly liked by the members of the outfit he had lately joined, having been known to them for years.

"Clean temple shot," Buck remarked, covering the face and arising. "There's some fine shots up on that rock. Well, here's another reason why we've got to get up there an' wipe 'em out quick. Pie was a white man, square as a die and a good puncher —I wouldn't have asked for a better pardner. You fellers take him to camp-we're going to find a way to square things if there is one. No, Pete, you an' Johnny carry him in-Skinny is going with us."

Buck, Hopalong, and Skinny returned to the edge of the pasture and the foreman again swept the wall through his glasses. "Hey! What's that? A body?"

Hopalong looked. "Yes, two of 'em! I reckon Pie died game, all right."

"Well, come on-we've got to move along," and Buck led the way north, Skinny bringing up the rear. Next to Lanky Smith, at present nursing wounds at the ranch, Skinny was the best man with a rope in the Bar-20 outfit and the lariat he used so deftly was one hundred and fifty feet in length, much longer than any used by those around the mesa. Buck had asked him to go with them because he wished to have his opinion as to the possibility of getting a rope up the mesa wall.

When they came opposite the rock which had sheltered Johnny they sortied to see if that part of the mesa was guarded, but there was no sign of life upon it. Then, separating, they dashed to the midway cover, the thicket, which they reached without incident. From there they continued to the pinnacle and now could see every rock and seam of the wall with their naked eyes. But they used the glasses and after a few minutes' examination of the ledges Hopalong turned to his companions. "Just as Johnny said. Skinny, do you reckon if you was under them to-night that you could get yore rope fast to th' bottom one?"

"Shore; that's easy. But it won't be no cinch roping th' other," Skinny replied. "She sticks out over th' first by two feet. It'll be hard to jerk a rope from that narrow foothold."

"Somebody can hang onto you so you can lean out," Buck replied. "Pete can hold you easy."

"But what'll he hold on to?"

Hopalong pointed. "See that spur up there, close to th' first ledge? He can hitch a rope around that an' hang to th' rope. I tell you it's *got* to be done. We can't lose no more men in this everlasting pot-shooting game. We've got to get close an' clean up!"

"Well, I ain't saying nothing different, am I?" snapped Skinny. "I'm saying it'll be hard, an' it will. Now suppose one of them fellers goes on sentry duty along this end; what then?"

"We'll solve that when we come to it," Hopalong replied. "I reckon if Red lays on this rock in th' moonlight that he can drop any sentry that stands up against th' sky at a hundred yards. We've got to try it, anyhow."

"*Down!*" whispered Buck, warningly. "Don't let 'em know we're here. Drop that gun, Hoppy!"

They dropped down behind the loose bowlders while the rustler passed along the edge, his face turned towards the pinnacle. Then, deciding that Johnny had not returned, he swept the chaparral with a pair of glasses. Satisfied at length that all was well he turned and disappeared over a rocky ledge ten feet from the edge of the wall.

"I could 'a dropped him easy," grumbled Hopalong, regretfully, and Skinny backed him up.

"Shore you could; but I don't want them to think we are looking at this end," Buck replied. "We'll have th' boys raise th' devil down south till dark an' keep that gang away from this end."

"I reckon they read yore mind-hear th' shooting?" Skinny queried.

"That must be Red out there —I can see half of him from here," Hopalong remarked, lowering his glasses. "Look at th' smoke he's making! Wonder what's up? Hear th' others, too!"

"Come on-we'll get out of this," Buck responded. "We'll go to camp an' plan for to-night, an' talk it over with th' rest. I want to hear what Meeker's going to do about it an' how we can place his men."

"By thunder! If we *can* get up there, half a dozen of us with Colts, an' sneak up on 'em, we'll have this fight tied up in a bag so quick they won't know what's up," Skinny remarked. "You can bet yore life that if there's any way to get a rope up that wall I'll do it!"

Chapter XXX
Up the Wall

Pipes were glowing in the shadows away from the fire, where men lay in various attitudes of ease. A few were examining wounds while others cleaned rifles and saw that their revolvers were in good condition. Around the fire but well back from it four men sat cross-legged, two others stretched out on their elbows and stomachs near them.

"You say everything is all right on th' ranch?" asked Buck of a man who, covered with alkali, had just come from the Bar-20. "No trouble, hey?"

"Nope; no trouble at all," replied Cross, tossing his sombrero aside. "Lucas an' Bartlett each sent us four men to help out when they learned you had come out here. We shipped four of 'em right on to th' H2, which is too short-handed to do any damage to rustlers."

"Much obliged for that," spoke up Meeker, relief in his voice. "I'm blamed glad to hear things are quiet back home-but I don't know how long they'll stay that way with Eagle so close."

"Well, Eagle ain't a whole lot anxious to dip in no more," laughed Cross, looking at the H2 foreman. "Leastawise, that's what Lucas said. He sent a delegation down there which made a good impression. There was ten men in it an' they let it be known that if they came back again there would be ten more with 'em. In that case Eagle wouldn't be no more than a charred memory. Since Quinn died, being shot hard by Nevada, who I reckons is out here, th' town ain't got nobody to tell it how to do things right, which is shore pleasant."

"You bring blamed good news —I'm glad Lucas went down there," Buck replied. "I can't tell as good news about us out here, yet. We've had a hard time for a week. They got Pie to-day, an' most of us are shot up plentiful. Yo're just in time for th' festival, Cross-we're going to try to rush 'em to-night an' get it over. We reckon Skinny an' Pete can get us a way up that wall before dawn."

"Me for th' rush," laughed Cross. "I'm fresh as a daisy, which most of you fellers ain't. How many of 'em have you got so far? Are there many still up there?"

"We've got four of 'em that I knows of, an' how many of 'em died from their wounds I can't say," replied Hopalong. "But a whole lot of 'em have been plugged, an' plugged hard."

"But how many are up there still able to fight?"

"I should say about nine," Hopalong remarked, thoughtfully.

"Ten," corrected Red. "I've been watching th' positions an' I know."

"About nine or ten-they shift so nobody can really tell," Buck replied. "I reckon we've seen 'em all in Eagle, too."

"Frenchy got Nevada an' another to-day, on th' west side," Johnny interposed.

"I'm glad Nevada is gone-he's a terror in a mix-up," Cross rejoined. "Best two-handed gun man in Eagle, he was."

"Huh!" snorted Johnny. "Stack him up against Hoppy an' see how long he'd last!"

"I said in Eagle!" retorted Cross.

Buck suddenly stood up and stretched. "You fellers all turn in now an' snatch some sleep. I'm going out to see how things are with Billy. I'll call you in time. Doc, you an' Curtis are too shot up to do any climbing-you turn in too. When I come back I'll wake you an' send you out to help Billy watch th' trail. Where's Red?"

"Over here-what do you want?" came from the shadows.

"Nothing, only get to sleep. I reckoned you might be off somewheres scouting. Skinny, where's yore rope? Got that manilla one? Good! Put three more hemp lariats out here where I can find 'em when I come back. Now don't none of you waste no time; turn in right now!" He started to walk away and then hesitated, turning around. "Doc, you an' Curtis better come with me now so you won't lose no time hunting Billy in th' dark when yore eyes are sleepy-it's hard enough to find him now in th' dark, when I'm wide awake. You can get yore sleep out there-he'll wake you when yo're needed."

The two punchers arose and joined him, Doc with his left arm bandaged and his companion with three bandages on him. When they joined Buck Doc protested. "Let me go with you an' th' rest of th' boys, Peters, when you go up that wall. I came out here to get th' Greaser that murdered Curley, an' I hate to miss him now. If I can't climb th' boys will be glad to pull me up, an' it won't take no time to speak of. My gun arm is sound as a dollar —I want that Greaser!"

Buck glanced at Meeker, who refused to give any sign of his thoughts on the matter. "Well, all right, Doc. But if we should have to fight as soon as we get up an' don't have no time to pull you after us, you'll miss everything. But you can do what you want."

"I'll just gamble on that. I ain't hurt much, an' if I can't climb I'll manage to get in th' scrap someway, even if I has to hunt up Billy," replied Doc, contentedly, returning to the fire.

Buck and his companion moved away into the darkness while those around the fire lay down to get a few hours' rest, which they needed badly. George Cross, who was not sleepy, remained awake in a shadow and kept guard, although none was needed.

Buck and Curtis found Billy by whistling and the wounded H2 puncher found a place to lie down and was soon asleep, while the foreman and his friend sat up, watching the faint glow on the mesa, the camp-fire of the besieged. Once they heard the clatter of a rifle from the head of the trail and later they saw a dim figure pass quickly across the lighted space. They were content to watch on such a night, for the air had cooled rapidly after the sun went down and the sky was one twinkling mass of stars.

Twice during the wait Buck disappeared into the black chaparral close at hand and struck a match under his coat to see the time, and on the last occasion he returned to Billy, remarking: "Got half an hour yet before I leave you. Are you sleepy?"

"No, not very; my head hurts too much to sleep," Billy replied, re-crossing his legs and settling himself in a more comfortable position. "When you leave I'll get up on my hoofs so I won't feel like dosing off. I won't wake Curtis unless I have to-he's about played out."

"You wake him when you think I've been gone half an hour," Buck ordered. "It'll take him some time to get his eyes open-we mustn't let any get away. They've got friends in Eagle, you know."

"Wish I could smoke," Billy remarked, wistfully.

"Why, you can," replied Buck, quickly. "Go back there in th' chaparral an' get away with a pipeful. I'll watch things till you come back, an' if I need you quick I can call. You've got near half an hour-make th' best of it."

"Here's th' gun-much obliged, Buck," and Billy disappeared, leaving the foreman to plan and watch. Buck glanced at the sleeping man occasionally when he heard him toss or mutter and wished he could let him sleep on undisturbed.

Suddenly a flash lighted up the top of the trail for an instant and the sharp report of a rifle rang out loudly on the still, night air. Buck, grabbing the Winchester, sprang to his feet as an excited chorus came from the rustlers' stronghold. Then he heard laughter and a few curses and quiet again ensued.

"What was that, Buck?" came a low, anxious hail from behind.

The foreman laughed softly and replied: "Nothing, Billy, except that th' guard up there reckoned he saw something to shoot at. It's funny how staring at th' dark will get a feller seeing things that ain't. Why, had yore smoke so soon?" he asked in surprise as Billy sat down beside him.

"Shore," replied Billy. "Two of 'em. I reckon yore time is about up. Gimme th' gun now."

"Well, good luck, Billy. Better move up closer to th' trail if you can find any cover. You don't want to miss none. So long," and Billy was alone with his sleeping companion.

When the foreman returned to the camp he was challenged, and stopped, surprised. "It's Peters," he called.

"Oh, all right. Time to go yet?" asked Cross, emerging from the darkness.

"Purty near; but I thought I told you to go to sleep?"

"I know, but I ain't sleepy, not a bit. So I reckoned I'd keep watch over th' rest of th' gang."

"Well, since yo're wide awake, you help me knot these ropes an' let th' others have a few minutes more," Buck responded, picking up Skinny's fifty-foot lariat and placing it to one side. He picked up the three shorter ropes and threw one to his companion. "Put a knot every foot an' a half-make 'em tight an' big."

In a few minutes the work was finished and Buck awakened the sleeping men, who groped their way to the little stream close by and washed the sleep out of their tired eyes, grabbing a bit of food on their return to the fire.

"Now, fellers," said the foreman, "leave yore rifles here-it's Colts this trip, except in Red's case. Got plenty of cartridges? Everybody had a drink an' some grub? All right; single file after me an' don't make no noise."

When the moon came up an hour later Red Connors, lying full length on the apex of the pinnacle which Johnny had tried and found wanting, watched an indistinct blurr of men in the shadow of the mesa wall. He saw one of them step out into the moonlight, lean back and then straighten up suddenly, his arm going above his head. The silence was so intense that Red could faintly hear the falling rope as it struck the ground. Another cast, and yet another, both unsuccessful, and then the fourth, which held. The puncher stepped back into the shadow again and another figure appeared, to go jerking himself up the face of the wall. While he watched the scaling operations Red was not missing anything on the top of the mesa, where the moon bathed everything in a silvery light.

Then he saw another figure follow the first and kick energetically as it clambered over onto the ledge. Soon a rope fell to the plain and the last man up, who was Skinny, leaned far out and cast at the second ledge, Pete holding him. After some time he was successful and again he and his companion went up the wall. Pete climbed rapidly, his heavy body but small weight for the huge, muscular arms which rose and fell so rapidly. On the second ledge the same casting was gone through with, but it was not until the eighth attempt that the rope stayed up. Then Red, rising on his elbows, put his head closer to the stock of his rifle and peered into the shadows back of the lighted space on the rocky pile. He saw Pete pull his companion back to safety and then, leaping forward, grasp the rope and climb to the top. Already one of the others was part way up the second rope while another was squirming over the lower ledge, and below him a third kicked and hauled, half way up the first lariat.

"String of monkeys," chuckled Red. "But they can't none of 'em touch Pete in that sort of a game. Wonder what Pete's doing?" he queried as he saw the man on the top of the mesa bend, fumble around for a moment, and then toss his arm out over the edge. "Oh, it's a knotted rope-he's throwing it down for th' others. Well, Pete, old feller, you was th' first man to get —*Lord!*"

He saw Pete wheel, leap forward into a shadow, and then a heaving, twisting, bending bulk emerged into the moonlight. It swayed back and forth, separated into two figures and then became one again.

"They're fighting, rough an' tumble!" Red exclaimed. "Lord have mercy on th' man who's closing with that Pete of ourn!"

He could hear the scuffling and he knew that the others had heard it, too, for Skinny was desperately anxious to wriggle over the edge, while down the line of ropes the others acted like men crazed. Still the pair on the mesa top swayed back and forth, this way and that, bending, twisting, and Red imagined he could hear their labored breathing. Then Skinny managed to pull himself to the top of the wall and sprang forward, to sink down from a kick in the stomach.

"God A'mighty!" cried Red excitedly. "Who is it that can give Pete a fight like that? Well, I'm glad he's so busy he can't use his gun!"

Skinny was crawling around on his hands and knees as Buck's head arose over the edge. The foreman, well along in years, and heavy, was too tired to draw himself over the rim without a moment's rest. He had no fear for Pete, but he was worried lest some rustler might sound an alarm. Skinny now sat up and felt for his Colt, but the foreman's voice stopped him. "No shooting, yet! Want to tell 'em what's up? You let them fellers alone for a minute, an' give me a hand here."

Pete, his steel-like fingers darting in for hold after hold, managed to jerk his opponent's gun from its sheath and throw it aside, where Skinny quickly picked it up. He was astonished by the skill and strength of his adversary, who blocked every move, every attempt to get a dangerous hold. Pete, for a man reputed as being slow, which he was in some things, was darting his arms in and out with remarkable quickness, but without avail. Then, realizing that his cleaner living was standing him in good stead, and hearing the labored breathing of the rustler, he leaped in and clinched. By this time Hopalong and three more of the attacking force had gained the mesa top and were sent forward by the foreman, who was now intent upon the struggle at hand.

"It's Big Sandy!" Hopalong whispered to Skinny, pausing to watch for a moment before he disappeared into the shadows.

He was right, and Big Sandy, breathless and tired, was fighting a splendid fight for his life against a younger, fresher, and stronger man. The rustler tried several times for a throat hold but in vain, and in a fury of rage threw his weight against his opponent to bear him to the ground, incautiously bringing his feet close together as he felt the other yield. In that instant Pete dropped to a crouch, his vice-like hands tightened about Big Sandy's ankles, and with a sudden, great surge of his powerful back and shoulders he straightened up and Sandy plunged forward to a crashing fall on the very edge of the mesa, scrambled to his feet, staggered, lost his balance, and fell backwards a hundred feet to the rocks below.

The victor would have followed him but for Buck, who grasped him in time. Pete, steady on his feet again, threw Buck from him by one sweep of his arms and wheeled to renew the fight, surprise flashing across his face at not seeing his opponent.

"He's down below, Pete," Buck cried as Johnny, white-faced, crawled over the edge.

"What was that?" exclaimed the Kid. "Who fell?"

"Big Sandy," replied the foreman. "He —" the report of a shot cut him short. "Come on!" he cried. "They're at it!" and he dashed away, closely followed by Johnny and Pete as Jim Meeker came into view. The H2 foreman slid over the mesa rim, leaped to his feet and sprinted forward, Colt in hand, to be quickly lost in the shadows, and after him came Red Connors, the last.

Down below Doc, hearing a thud not far from him, hurried around a spur of rock in the wall, sick at heart when he saw the body. Bending over quickly he recognized the mass as once having been Big Sandy, and he forthwith returned to the rope to be pulled up. When he at last realized that his friends had forgotten him there was loud, lurid cursing and he stamped around like a wild man, waving a Colt in his right hand. Finally he dropped heavily on a rock, too enraged to think, and called the attacking force, collectively and individually, every name that sprang to his lips. As he grew calmer he arose from the rock, intending to join Billy and Curtis at the other end of the pasture, and as he took a step in that direction he heard a sharp click and a pebble bounced past him. He stepped backwards quickly and looked up, seeing a figure sliding rapidly down the highest rope. He was immediately filled with satisfaction and easily forgave his companions for the anxiety they had caused him, and as he was about to call out he heard a Spanish oath. Slipping quickly and noiselessly into the deeper shadow at the base of the wall he flattened himself behind the spur of rock close to the rope, where he waited tensely, a grim smile transforming his face.

Chapter XXXI
Fortune Snickers at Doc

Antonio was restless and could not sleep. He turned from side to side on the ground near the fire before the hut and was one of the first to run to the top of the trail when the guard there discharged his rifle at nothing. Returning to his blanket the Mexican tried to compose himself to rest, but was unsuccessful. Finally he arose, picked up his rifle, and slouched off into the shadows to wander about from point to point.

Cavalry, coming in from his post to get a drink, caught sight of the Mexican before he was swallowed up by the darkness and, suspicious as ever of Antonio, forgot the drink and followed.

After wandering about all unconscious of espionage Antonio finally drifted to the western edge and seated himself comfortably against a bowlder, Cavalry not fifty feet away in a shadow. Time passed slowly and as the Mexican was about to return to the fire he chanced to glance across the mesa along a moon-lighted path and stiffened at what he saw. A figure ran across the lighted space, silently, cautiously, Colt in hand, and then another, then two together, and the Mexican knew that the enemy had found a way up the wall and were hurrying forward to fight at close quarters, to effect a surprise on the unsuspecting men about the fire and in the hut. There remained, perhaps, time enough for him to escape and he arose and ran north, crouching as he zig-zagged from cover to cover, cautious and alert.

Cavalry, because of his position, had not seen the flitting punchers and, his suspicions now fully aroused, he slipped after the Mexican to find out just what he was going to do. When the firing burst out behind him he paused and stood up, amazed. As he struggled to understand what it meant he saw three men run past a bowlder at his left and then he knew, and still hesitated. He was not a man who thought quickly and his first natural impulse, due to his army training, was to try to join his friends, but gradually the true situation came to him. How many men there were in the attacking force he did not know, but he had seen three after the fighting had begun; and it was evident that the cowmen would not rush into the lion's jaws unless they were strong enough to batter down all resistance. Four of his friends were dead, another had evidently deserted, and the remainder were all more or less severely wounded-there could be no hope of driving the ranchmen back, and small chance of him being able to work through their line to join his friends. There remained only one thing to be done, to save himself while he might.

As he moved forward slowly and cautiously to find a way down the wall he remembered the Mexican's peculiar actions and wondered if he had a hand in helping the cowmen up.

Meanwhile Antonio, reaching the edge of the open space where Pete and Big Sandy had fought, saw Red Connors appear over the rim and dash away to join in the fighting. Waiting long enough to assure himself that there were none following Red he ran to the edge and knelt by the rope. Leaving his rifle behind and seeing that the flap of his holster was fastened securely, he lowered himself over, sliding rapidly down to the first ledge. Here he spent a minute, a minute that seemed an eternity, hunting for the second rope in the shadows, found it and went on.

Sliding and bumping down the rough wall he at last reached the plain and, with a sigh of relief, turned to run. At that instant a figure leaped upon him from behind and a hand gripped his throat and jerked him over backwards. Antonio instinctively reached for his Colt with one hand while he tore at the gripping fingers with the other, but he found himself pinned down between two rocks in such a manner that his whole weight and that of his enemy was on the holster and made his effort useless. Then, terrified and choking for breath, he dug wildly at the vice-like fingers which not for a moment relaxed, but in vain, for he was growing weaker with each passing second.

Doc leaned forward, peering into the face before him, his fingers gripping with all their power, gripping with a force which made the muscles of the brawny forearm stand out like cords, his face malevolent and his heart full of savage joy. Here was the end of his hunt, here was the man who had murdered Curley in cold blood, cowardly, deliberately. The face, already dark, was turning black and the eyes were growing wide open and bulging out. He felt the surge of the Mexican's pulse, steadily growing weaker. But he said no word as he watched and gloated, he was too intent to speak, too centred upon the man under him, too busy keeping his fingers tight-gripped. He would make good his threat, he would keep his word and kill the murderer of his best friend with his naked hand, as he had sworn.

Up above the two, Cavalry, working along the edge, had come across Antonio's rifle and then as he glanced about, saw the rope. Here was where the cowmen had come up and here was where he could go down. From the way the shooting continued he knew that the fight was desperate and he believed himself to be cut off from his friends. He hated to desert in the face of the enemy, to leave his companions of a dangerous business to fight for their lives without him, but there was only one thing to do since he could not help them-he must save himself.

Dropping his rifle beside the other he lowered himself over the edge and slid rapidly down. When half-way down the last rope his burning hands slipped and he fell head over heels, and landed on Doc, knocking him over and partially stunning him. Cavalry's only idea now was to escape from the men who, as he thought, were guarding the rope and, hastily picking himself up, he dashed towards the chaparral to the west as fast as he could run, every moment expecting to feel the hot sting of a bullet. At last, when the chaparral closed about him he plunged through it recklessly and ran until sheer exhaustion made him drop insensible to the sand. He had run far, much farther than he could have gone were it not for the stimulus of the fear which gripped him; and had he noticed where he was going he would have known that he was running up a slope, a slope which eventually reached a level higher than the top of the mesa. And when he dropped if he had been capable of observation he would have found himself in a chaparral which arose above his head, and seen the narrow lane through it which led to a great expanse of sand, tawney and blotched with ash-colored alkali, an expanse which stretched away to the desolate horizon.

Shortly after Cavalry's descent Antonio stirred, opened his eyes, stared vaguely about him and, feeling his bruised and aching throat, staggered to his feet and stumbled to the east, hardly conscious of what he was doing. As he proceeded his breath came easier and he began to remember having seen Doc lying quiet against a rock. He hesitated a moment as he wondered if Doc was dead and if so, who had killed him. Then he swore because he had not given him a shot to make sure that he would not rejoin his friends. Hesitating a moment he suddenly decided that he would be better off if he put a good distance between himself and the mesa, and ran on again, eager to gain the shelter of the chaparral.

When Doc opened his eyes and groped around he slowly remembered what had occurred and his first conscious act was to look to see if his expected victim were dead or alive. It did not take him long to realize that he was alone and his hand leaped for his Colt as he peered around. Limping out on the plain he caught sight of the running Mexican, rapidly growing indistinct, and hazarded two shots after him. Antonio leaped into a new speed as though struck with a whip and cursed himself for not having killed the H2 puncher when he had the chance. A moment more and he was lost in the thickets. Doc tried to follow, but his leg, hurt by Cavalry's meteoric descent, was not equal to any great demand for speed and so, turning, he made his way towards the camp to get a horse and return to take up the Mexican's trail.

He lost an hour in this, a feverishly impatient hour, punctuated with curses as he limped along and with an unsparing quirt once he was astride. What devilish Humpty Dumpty had cheated him this time? "All the king's horses and all the king's men couldn't put Humpty Dumpty together again"—they couldn't if he once caught up with the Mexican. He laughed grimly and swore again as the cranky beast beneath him shied a pain into his sore leg. "Go on, you!" he yelled, as he swept up to where the ropes still dangled against the wall. "Th' Mexican first," he muttered. The world was not big enough to hide the murderer of Curley, to save him from his just deserts. The two trails lay plain before him in the brilliant moonlight and his pony sprang forward toward the spot where Antonio had disappeared in the chaparral.

Chapter XXXII
Nature Takes a Hand

When Hopalong caught up with his four companions he was astonished by the conditions on the mesa. Instead of a bowlder-strewn, rocky plain as he had believed it to be he found himself on a table-land cut and barred by fissures which ran in all directions. At one time these had been open almost to the level of the surrounding pasture but the winds had swept sand and debris into the gashes until now none were much more than ten feet deep. Narrow alleyways which led in every direction, twisting and turning, now blocked and now open for many feet in depth, their walls sand-beaten to a smoothness baffling the grip of one who would scale them, were not the same in a fight as a comparatively flat plain broken only by miscellaneous bowlders and hummocks. There could be no concerted dash for the reason that one group of the attacking force might be delayed until after another had begun to fight. And it was possible, even probable, that the turns in the alleyways might be guarded; and once separated in the heat of battle it would be easy enough to shoot each other. Instead of a dashing fight soon to be over, it looked as though it would be a deadly game of hide and seek to wear out the players and which might last for an indefinite length of time. It was disconcerting to find that what had been regarded as the hardest part of the whole affair, the gaining of the mesa top, was the easiest.

"Here, fellows!" Hopalong growled. "We'll stick together till we get right close, an' then if we have time an' these infernal gorges don't stop us, we may be able to spread out. We've got to move easy, too. If we go galloping reckless we'll run into some guard an' there won't be no surprise party on Thunder Mesa. We can count on having light, though not as much as we might have, for th' moon won't go back on us till th' sun fades it."

"It's light enough," growled Skinny. "Come on-we've got to go ahead an' every minute counts. *I* didn't think we'd lose so much time roping them knobs an' getting up."

They moved forward cautiously in single file, alert and straining eyes and ears, and had covered half of the distance when a shot was heard ahead and they listened, expecting an uproar. Waiting a minute and hearing nothing further, they moved on again, angry and disgruntled. Then another shot rang out and they heard Billy and Curtis reply.

"Shooting before daylight, before they get their morning's grub," grumbled George Cross.

"Yes; sort of eye-opener, I reckon," softly laughed Chick Travers, who was nervous and impatient. "Get a move on an' let's start something," he added.

As they separated to take advantage of a spoke-like radiation of several intersecting fissures another shot rang out ahead and there was an angry *spat*! close to Hopalong's head. Another shot and then a rattling volley sent the punchers hunting cover on the run, but they were moving forward all the time. It was a case of getting close or be killed at a range too great for Colts, and their rifles were in the camp. Had the light been better the invaders might have paid dearly right there for the attack.

Confusion was rife among the defenders and the noise of the shouts and firing made one jumble of sound. Bullets whistled along the fissures in the dim light and hummed and whizzed as they ricochetted from wall to wall. As yet the attacking force had made no reply, being too busily occupied in getting close to lose time in wasting lead at that range, and being only five against an unknown number protected by a stone hut and who knew every bowlder, crevice, and other points of vantage.

Hopalong slid over a bowlder which choked his particular and personal fissure and saw Jim Meeker sliding down the wall in front of it. And as Meeker picked himself up Skinny Thompson slid down the other wall.

"Well, I'm hanged!" grunted Hopalong in astonishment.

"Same here," retorted Skinny. "What you doing 'way over here?"

"Thought you was going to lead th' other end of th' line!" rejoined Hopalong.

"This is it-yo're off yore range."

"Well, I reckon not!" Hopalong responded, indignantly.

"An' say, Meeker, how'd you get over here so quick?" Skinny asked, turning to the other. "You was down below when I saw you last."

"*Me?* Why, I just follered my nose, that's all," Meeker replied, surprised.

"You've got a blamed crooked nose, then," Skinny snorted, and turned to Hopalong. "Why don't you untangle yoreself an' go where you belong, you carrot-headed blunderer!"

"Hang it! I tell you I —" Hopalong began, and then ducked quickly. "Lord, but somebody's got us mapped out good!"

"Well, some of our fellers have started up-hear 'em over there?" exclaimed Skinny as firing broke out on the east. "Them's Colts, all right. Mebby it's plumb lucky for us it *ain't* so blamed light, after all; we'll have time to pick our places before they can see us real good."

"Pick our places!" snorted Hopalong. "Get tangled up, you mean!" he added.

"Hullo! What you doing, fellers?" asked a pained and surprised voice above them. "Why ain't you in it?"

"For th' love of heaven-it's Frenchy!" cried Hopalong. "Skinny, I reckon them Colts you heard belonged to th' rustlers. *We're* all here but a couple."

"Didn't I leave you over east about five minutes ago, Frenchy?" demanded Skinny, his mouth almost refusing to shut.

"Shore. I'm east-what's eating at you?" asked Frenchy.

"Come on-get out of this!" ordered Hopalong, scrambling ahead. "You foller me an' you'll be all right."

"We'll be back to th' ropes if we foller you," growled Skinny. "Of all th' locoed layouts I ever run up against this here mesa top takes th' prize," he finished in disgust.

Bullets whined and droned above them and frequently hummed down the fissure to search them out, the high, falsetto whine changing quickly to an angry *spang*! as they struck the wall a slanting blow. They seemed to spring away again with renewed strength as they sang the loud, whirring hum of the ricochette, not the almost musical, sad note of the uninterrupted bullet, but venomous, assertive, insistent. The shots could be distinguished now, for on one side were the sharp cracks of rifles; on the other a different note, the roar of Colts.

"This ain't no fit society for six-shooters," Meeker remarked in a low voice as they slid over a ridge, and dropped ten feet before they knew it.

"For th' Lord's sake!" ejaculated Hopalong as he arose to his feet. "Step over a rock an' you need wings! Foller a nice trail an' you can't get out of th' cussed thing! Go west an' you land east, say 'so-long' to a friend an' you meet him a minute later!"

"We ought to have rifles in this game," Meeker remarked, rubbing his knee-cap ruefully.

"Yes; an' ladders, ropes, an' balloons," snorted Skinny.

"Send somebody back for th' guns," suggested Frenchy.

"Who?" demanded Hopalong. "Will *you* go?"

"Me? Why, I don't want no rifle!"

"Huh! Neither do I," remarked Skinny. "Here, Frenchy, give me a boost up this wall, —take my foot!"

"Well, don't wiggle so, you piece of string!"

"That's right! Walk backwards! I ain't no folding step-ladder! How do you think I'm going to grab that edge if you takes me ten feet away from it?"

Spang! Spang! Zing-ing-ing!

"Here, you! Lemme down! Want me to get plugged!" yelled Skinny, executing ungraceful and rapid contortions. "Lower me, you fool!"

"Let go that ridge, then!" retorted Frenchy.

During the comedy Hopalong had been crawling up a rough part of the wall and he fired before he lost his balance. As he landed on Meeker a yell rang out and the sound of a rifle clattering on rock came to them. "I got him, Skinny-go ahead now," he grunted, picking himself up.

It was not long until they were out of the fissure and crawling down a bowlder-strewn slope. As they came to the bottom they saw a rustler trying to drag himself to cover and Meeker fired instantly, stopping the other short.

"Why, I thought *I* stopped him!" exclaimed Hopalong.

"Reckon you won't rustle no more cows, you thief," growled Meeker, rising to his knees.

Hopalong pulled him down again as a bullet whizzed through the space just occupied by his head. "Don't you get so curious," he warned. "Come on—I see Red. He's got his rifle, lucky cuss."

"Good for him! Wish I had mine," replied Meeker, grinning at Red, who wriggled an elbow as a salutation. In his position Red could hardly be expected to do much more, since two men were waiting for a shot at him.

"Well, you can get that gun down there an' have a rifle," Hopalong suggested, pointing to the Winchester lying close to its former owner. "You can do it, all right."

"Good idea-shoot 'em with their own lead," and the H2 foreman departed on his hands and knees for the weapon.

"I hit one-he's trying to put his shoulder together," cried Red, grinning. "What makes you so late —I was th' last one up, an' I've been here a couple of hours."

"Yo're a sinful liar!" retorted Hopalong. "We stopped to pick blackberries back at that farm house," he finished with withering sarcasm.

"You fellers had time to get married an' raise a family," Red replied. He ducked and looked around. "Ah, you coyote-hit him, but not very hard, I reckon."

It was daylight when Pete, on the other end of the line, turned and scourged Johnny. "Ain't you got no sense in yore fool head? How can I see to shoot when you kick around like that an' fill my eyes with dirt! Come down from up there or I'll lick you!"

"Ah, shut up!" retorted Johnny with a curse. "You'd kick around if somebody nicked *yore* ear!"

"Well, it serves you right for being so unholy curious!" Pete replied. "You come down before he nicks yore eye!"

"Not before I get square —*Wow!*" and Johnny came down rapidly.

"Where'd he get you that time?"

"None of yore business!" growled Johnny.

"I told you to come —"

"Shut up!" roared Johnny, glaring at him. "Wish I had that new Sharps of mine!"

"Go an' get it, Kid. Yo're nimble," Pete responded. "An' bring up some of th' others, too, while yo're about it."

"But how long will this fight last, do you reckon?" the other asked, with an air of weighing something.

"All day with rifles —a week without 'em."

"Shore yo're right?"

"Yes; go ahead. There'll be some of th' scrap left for you when you get back."

"All right, —but don't you get that feller. I want him for what he did to me," and Johnny hastened away. He returned in fifteen minutes with two rifles and gave one of them to his companion.

"They're .45-70's —an' full, too," he remarked. "But I ain't got no more cartridges for 'em."

"How'd you get 'em so quick?"

"Found 'em by th' rope where we come up-didn't have to stop; just picked 'em up an' came right back," Johnny laughed. "But I wonder how they got there?"

"Bet four dollars an' a tooth-pick they means that two thieves got away down them ropes. Where's Doc?"

"Don't know-but I don't think anybody pulled him up here."

"Then he might 'a stopped them two what owned th' rifles-he would be mad enough to stay there a month if Red forgot him."

"Yes; waiting to lick Red when he came down," and Johnny crawled up again to his former position. "Now, you cow-stealing coyote, watch out!" As he settled down he caught sight of his foreman. "Hullo, Buck! What you doing?"

"Stringing beads for my night shirt," retorted Buck. "You get down from up there, you fool!"

"Can't. I got to pay for —" he ducked, and then fired twice. "Just missed th' other ear, Pete. But I made him jump a foot-plugged him where he sits down. He was moving away. An' blamed if he ain't a Greaser!"

"Yes; an' you took two shots to do it, when cartridges are so scarce," Pete grumbled.

At first several of the rustlers had defended the hut but the concentrated fire of the attacking force had poured through its north window from so many angles that evacuation became necessary. This was accomplished through the south window, which opened behind the natural breastwork, and at a great cost, for Con Irwin and Sam Austin were killed in the move.

The high, steep ridge which formed the rear wall of the hut and overlooked the roof of the building ran at right angles to the low breastwork and extended from the north end of the hut to the edge of the mesa, a distance of perhaps fifty feet. On the side farthest from the breastwork it sloped to the stream made by the spring and its surface was covered with bowlders. The rustlers, if they attempted to scale its steep face, would be picked off at short range, but they realized that once the enemy gained its top their position would be untenable except around the turn in the breastwork at the other side of the mesa. In order to keep the punchers from gaining this position they covered the wide cut which separated the ridge from the enemy's line, and so long as they could command this they were safe.

After wandering from point to point Hopalong finally came to the edge of the cut and found Red Connors ensconced in a narrow, shallow depression on a comparatively high hummock. While they talked his eyes rested on the ridge across the cut and took in the possibilities that holding it would give.

"Say, Red, if we could get up on that hill behind th' shack we'd have this fight over in no time-see how it overlooks everything?"

"Yes," slowly replied Red. "But we can't cross this barranca-they sweep it from end to end. I tried to get over there, an' I know."

"But we can try again," Hopalong replied. "You cover me."

"Now don't be a fool, Hoppy!" his friend retorted. "We can't afford to lose you for no gang of rustlers. It's shore death to try it."

"Well, you can bet I ain't going to be fool enough to run twenty yards in th' open," Hopalong replied, starting away. "But I'm going to look for a way across, just th' same. Keep me covered."

"All right, I'll do my best-but don't you try no dash!"

But the rustlers had not given up the idea of holding the ridge themselves, and there was another and just as important reason why they must have it; their only water was in the hut and the spring. To enter the building was certain death, but if they could command the ridge it would be possible to get water, for the spring and rivulet lay on the other side at its base. Hall, well knowing the folly of trying to scale the steep bank under fire, set about finding another way to gain the coveted position. He found a narrow ledge on the face of the mesa wall, at no place more than eight inches wide, and he believed that it led to the rear of the ridge. Finding that the wall above the narrow foothold was rough and offered precarious finger holds, he began to edge along it, a hundred feet above the plain. When he had almost reached the end of his trying labors he was discovered by Billy and Curtis, who lay four hundred yards away in the chaparral, and at once became the target for their rifles. Were it not for the fact that they could not shoot at their best because of their wounds Hall would never have finished his attempt, and as it was the bullets flattened against the wall so close to him that on two occasions he was struck by spattering lead and flecks of stone. Then he moved around the turn and was free from that danger, but found that he must get fifty yards north before he could gain the plateau again. To make matters worse the ledge he was on began to grow narrower and at one place disappeared altogether. When he got to the gap he had to cling to the rough wall and move forward inch by inch, twice narrowly missing a drop to the plain below. But he managed to get across it and strike the ledge again and in a few minutes more he stepped into a crevice and sat down to rest before he pushed on. When he looked around he found that the crevice led northeast and did not run to the ridge, and he swore as he realized that he must go through the enemy's line to gain the position. He would not risk going back the way he had come, for he was pretty well tired out. He thought of trying to get to the other end of the mesa so as to escape by the way the attacking force had come up, but immediately put it out of his mind as being too contemptible for further consideration. He arose and moved forward, seeking a way up the wall of the crevice-and turning a corner, bumped into Jim Meeker.

There was no time for weapons and they clinched. Meeker scorned to call for help and Hall dared make no unnecessary noise while in the enemy's line and so they fought silently. Both tried to draw their Colts, Meeker to use his either as a gun or a club, Hall as a club only, and neither succeeded. Both were getting tired when Hall slipped and fell, the H2 foreman on top of him. At that instant Buck Peters peered down at them from the edge of the fissure and then dropped lightly. He struck Hall over the head with the butt of his Colt and stepped back, grinning.

"There'll be a lot more of these duets if this fight drags out very long," Buck said. "This layout is shore loco with all its hidden trails. Have you got a rope, Jim? We'll tie this gent so he won't hurt hisself if you can find one."

"No. Much obliged, Peters," Meeker replied. "Why, yes I have, too. Here, use this," and he quickly untied his neck-kerchief and gave it to his friend. Buck took the one from around

Hall's neck and the two foremen gave a deft and practical exhibition of how to tie a man so he cannot get loose. Meeker took the Winchester from Hall's back, the Colt and the cartridge belt, and gave them to Buck, laughing.

"Seventy-three model; .44 caliber," he explained. "You'll find it better than th' six-shooter, an' you'll have plenty of cartridges for it, too."

"But don't you want it?" asked Buck, hesitating.

"Nope. I left one around th' corner here. I can get along with it till I get my own from th' camp."

"All right, Jim. I'll be glad to keep this-it'll come in handy."

"Tough luck, finding them fellers in such a strong layout," Meeker growled, glancing around at the prisoner. "Ah, got yore eyes open, hey?" he ejaculated as Hall glared at him. "How many of you fellers are up here, anyhow?"

"Five thousand!" snapped Hall. "It took two of you to get me!" he blazed. "Got my guns, too, ain't you? Hope they bust an' blow yore cussed heads off!"

"Thanks, stranger, thanks," Buck replied, turning to leave. "But Meeker had you licked good —I only hurried it to save time. Coming, Jim?"

"Shore. But do you think this thief can get loose?"

Buck paused, searching his pockets, and smiled as he brought to light a small, tight roll of rawhide thongs. "Here, this'll keep him down," and when they had finished their prisoner could move neither hands nor feet. They looked at him critically and then went away towards the firing, the rustler cursing them heartily.

"What's th' matter, Meeker?" asked Buck suddenly, noticing a drawn look on his companion's face.

"Oh, I can't help worrying about my girl. She ain't scared of nothing an' she likes to ride. She's too purty to go breezing over a range that's covered with rustling skunks. I told her to stay in th' house, but —"

"Well, why in thunder don't you go back where you can take care of her?" Buck demanded, sharply. "She's worth more than all th' cows an' rustlers on earth. You ain't needed bad out here, for we can clean this up, all right. You know as long as there are fellers like us to handle a thing like this no man with a girl depending on him has really got any right to take chances. I never thought of it before, or I'd 'a told you so. You cut loose for home to-day, an' leave us to finish this."

"Well, I'll see how things go to-morrow, then. I can pull out th' next morning if everything is all right out here." He hesitated a moment, looking Buck steadily in the eyes, a peculiar expression on his face. "Peters, yo're a white man, one of th' whitest I ever met, an' you've got a white outfit. I don't reckon we'll have no more trouble about that line of yourn, not nohow. When we settle down to peace an' punching again I'm going to let you show me how to put down some wells at th' southern base of yore hills, like you said one day. If I can get water, a half as much as you got in th' Jumping Bear, I'll be fixed all right. But I want to ask you a fair question, man to man. I ain't no real fool an' I've seen more than I'm supposed to, but I want to be shore about this, dead shore. What kind of a man is Hopalong Cassidy when it comes to women?"

Buck looked at him frankly. "If I had a daughter I wouldn't want a better man for her."

Chapter XXXIII
Doc Trails

Doc had not gone far into the chaparral before he realized that his work was going to be hard. The trail was much fainter than it would have been if the Mexican were mounted; the moonlight failed to penetrate the chaparral except in irregular patches which made the surrounding shadows all the deeper by contrast; what little he saw of the trail led through places far too small and turning too sharply to permit being followed by a man on horseback, and lastly, he expected every minute to be fired upon, and at close range. He paused and thought a while-Antonio would head for Eagle, that being the only place where he could get assistance, and there he would find friends. Doc picked his way out of the labyrinth of tortuous alleys and finally came to a comparatively wide lane leading southeast. He rode at a canter now and planned how he would strike the fugitive's trail further down, and after he had ridden a few miles he was struck by a thought that stopped him at once.

"Hang it all, he might 'a headed for them construction camps or for one of th' north ranches, to steal a cayuse," he muttered. "Th' only safe thing for me to do is to jump his trail an' stop guessing, an' even then mebby he'll get me before I get him. That's a clean gamble, an' so here goes," wheeling and retracing his course. When he again found the trail at the place he had quit it, he dismounted and crawled along on his hands and knees in order to follow the foot-prints among the shadows. Then some animal bounded up in front of him and leaped away, and as he turned to look after it he caught sight of his horse standing on its hind legs, and the next instant it was crashing through the chaparral. Drawing his Colt and cursing he ran back in time to see the horse gain an alleyway and gallop off. Angered thoroughly he sent a shot after it and then followed it, finally capturing it in a blind alley. Roundly cursing the frightened beast he led it back to where he had left the trail and, keeping one hand on the reins, continued to follow the foot-prints. Day broke when he had reached the edge of the chaparral and he mounted with a sigh of relief and rode forward along the now plainly marked trail.

As he cantered along he kept his eyes searching every possible cover ahead of and on both sides of him, watching the trail as far ahead as he could see it, for the Mexican might have doubled back to get a pursuer as he rode past. After an hour of this caution he slapped his thigh and grinned at his foolishness.

"Now ain't I a cussed fool!" he exclaimed. "A regular, old-woman of a cow-puncher! That Greaser won't do no doubling back or ambushing. He'll shore reckon on being trailed by a bunch an' not by a locoed, prize-winning idiot. Why, he's making th' best time he can, an' that's a-plenty, too. Besides he ain't got no rifle. Lift yore feet, you four-legged sage hen," he cried, spurring his horse into a lope. He mechanically felt at the long rifle holster at the saddle flap and then looked at it quickly. "An' no rifle for *me*, neither! Oh, well, that's all right, too. I don't need any better gun than he's got, th' coyote. Canteen full of water an' saddle flaps stuffed with grub. Why, old cayuse, if you can do without drinking till we get back to th' mesa we'll be plumb happy. Wonder when you was watered last?"

The trail had been swinging to the north more and more and when Doc noted this fact he grinned again.

"Nice fool I'd 'a been hunting for these tracks down towards Eagle, wouldn't I? But I wonder where he reckons he's going, anyhow?"

Sometime later he had his answer, for he found himself riding towards a water hole and then he knew the reason for the trail swinging north. He let his mount drink its fill and while he waited he noticed a torn sombrero, then a spur, and further away the skeleton of a horse. Looking further he saw the skeleton of a man, all that the coyotes had left of the body of Dick Archer, the man killed by Red on the day when he and Hopalong had discovered that Thunder Mesa was inhabited. He pushed around the water hole and then caught sight of something in the sand. Edging his mount over to it he leaned down from the saddle and picked up a Colt's revolver, fully loaded and as good as the day Archer died. That air contained no moisture. As he slipped it in a saddle bag he spurred forward at top speed, for on the other side of a hummock he saw the head and then the full figure of a man plodding away from him, and it was Antonio.

The fugitive, hearing hoofbeats, looked back and then dropped to one knee, his rifle going to his shoulder with the movement.

"Where in h —l did *he* get a rifle?" ejaculated Doc, forcing his horse to buck-jump and pitch so as to be an erratic target. "He didn't have none when *I* grabbed him! Th' devil! That cussed skeleton back there gave *me* a six-shooter, an' *him* a rifle!"

There was a dull smothered report and he saw the Mexican drop the gun and rock back and forth, apparently in agony, and he rode forward at top speed. Jerking his horse to its haunches he leaped off it just as Antonio wiped the blood from his eyes and jerked loose his Remington six-shooter. But his first shot missed and before he could fire again Doc grappled with him.

This time it was nearly an even break and Doc found that the slim figure of his enemy was made up of muscles of steel, that the lazy Greaser of the H2 ranch was, when necessary, quick as a cat and filled with the courage of desperation. It required all of Doc's attention and skill to keep himself from being shot by the other's gun and when he finally managed to wrest the weapon loose he was forced to drop it quickly and grab the same hand, which by some miracle of speed and dexterity now held a knife, a weapon far more deadly in hand-to-hand fighting. Once when believing himself to be gone the buckle of his belt stayed the slashing thrust and he again fought until the knife was above his head. Then, suddenly, two fingers flashed at his eyes and missed by so close a margin that Doc's eyebrows were torn open and his eyes blinded with blood. Instinct stronger than the effect of the disconcerting blindness made him hold his grip on the knife hand, else he would have been missing when his foreman looked for him at the mesa. He dug the fingers of his left hand, that had gripped around the Mexican's waist, into his enemy's side and squeezed the writhing man tighter to him, wiping the blood from his eyes on the shirt of the other. As he did so he felt Antonio's teeth sink into his shoulder and a sudden great burst of rage swept over him and turned a man already desperate into a berserker, a mad man.

The grip tightened and then the brawny, bandaged left arm quickly slipped up and around the Mexican's neck, pressing against the back of it with all the power of the swelling, knotted muscles. A smothered cry sobbed into his chest and he bent the knife hand back until the muscles were handicapped by their unnatural position and then, suddenly releasing both neck and hand, leaped back a step and the next instant his heavy boot thudded into the Mexican's stomach and he watched the gasping, ghastly-faced rustler sink down in a nerveless heap, fighting desperately for the breath that almost refused to return.

Doc wiped his eyes free of blood and hastily bound his neck-kerchief around the bleeding eyebrows. As he knotted the bandage he stepped forward and picked up both the revolver and knife and threw them far from him. Glancing at the rifle he saw that it had burst and knew that the greased, dirty barrel had been choked with sand. He remembered how Curley's rifle had been leaded by the same cause and fierce joy surged through him at this act of retributive justice. He waited patiently, sneering at the groaning Mexican and taunting him until the desperate man had gained his feet.

Doc stepped back a pace, tossing the burst rifle from him, and grinned malignantly. "Take yore own time, Greaser. Get all yore wind an' strength. *I* ain't no murderer —I don't ride circles around a man an' pot-shoot him. I'm going to kill you fair, with my hands, like I said. Th' stronger you are th' better I'll feel when I leave you. An' if you should leave me out here on th' sand, all right-but it's got to be fair."

When fully recovered Antonio began the struggle by leaping forward, thinking his enemy unprepared. Doc faced him like a flash and bent low, barely escaping the other's kick. They clinched and swayed to and fro, panting, straining, every ounce of strength called into play. Then Doc got the throat hold again and took a shower of blows unflinchingly. His eyebrows, bleeding again, blinded him, but he could feel if he could not see. Slowly the resistance weakened and finally Doc wrestled Antonio to his knees, bending over the Mexican and slowly tightening his grip; and the man who had murdered Curley went through all he had felt at the base of the mesa wall, at last paying with his life for his career of murder, theft, fear, and hypocrisy.

Doc arose and went to his horse. Leading the animal back to the scene of the struggle he stood a while, quietly watching the Mexican for any sign of life, although he knew there would be none.

"Well, bronc, Curley's squared," he muttered, swinging into the saddle and turning the animal's head. "Come on, get out of this!" he exclaimed, quirting hard. As he passed the water hole he bowed to the broken skeleton. "Much obliged, stranger, whoever you was. Yore last play was a good one."

Chapter XXXIV
Discoveries

When the two foremen entered the firing line again they saw Red Connors and they cautiously went towards him. As they came within twenty feet of him Buck chanced to glance across the cut and what he saw brought a sudden smile to his face.

"Meeker, Red has got that spring under his gun!" he exclaimed in a low voice. "They can't get within ten feet of it or within ten feet of th' water at any point along its course. This is too good to bungle-wait for me," and he ran out of sight around a bend in the crevice, Meeker staring across at the spring, his eyes following the rivulet until it flowed into the deep, narrow cut it had worn in the side of the mesa.

Red looked around. "Why, hullo, Meeker! Where's Buck? Thought I heard him a minute ago. If you have got any water to spare I can use some of it good. Some thief drilled my canteen when I went fooling along this barranca, an' I ain't got a drop left."

Meeker began to move closer to him, Red warning him to be careful, and adding, "Three of them fellers ain't doing nothing but watch this cut. Scared we'll get across it an' flank 'em, I reckon."

"Do you know that yo're covering their water supply?" Meeker asked, handing his canteen to his thirsty companion. "They can't get to it as long as you stay here. That's why they're after you so hard."

Red wiped his lips on his sleeve and sighed contentedly. "It's blamed hot, but it's wet. But is that right? Am I keeping 'em thirsty? Where's th' water?"

"Shore you are; it's right over there-see that little ditch?" Meeker replied, pointing.

Bing! Spat!

The H2 foreman dropped his arm and grinned. "They're watching us purty close, ain't they? Didn't miss me far, at that," showing his companion a torn sleeve and a lead splotch on the rock behind him.

"Not a whole lot. Two of them fellers can shoot like blazes. Yo're plumb lucky," Red responded. "If you'd showed more'n yore sleeve that time they'd 'a hit you." He looked across the cut and puckered his brow. "Well, if that's where their water is they don't get none. Mebby we can force 'em out if we watches that spring right smart."

"Here comes Buck now, with Skinny."

"It's too good a card to lose, Skinny," the Bar-20 foreman was saying as he approached. "You settle some place near here where you can pot anybody that tries for a drink. Mebby this little trick wins th' game for us —*quien sabe?* Hullo, Red; where's yore side pardner?"

"Oh, he went prospecting along this barranca to see if he could get across," Red replied. "He wants to get up on top of that ridge behind th' shack. Says if he can do it th' fight won't last long. See how it overlooks their layout?"

Buck looked and his eyes glistened. "An' he's right, too, like he is generally. That's th' key, an' it lies between them an' th' spring. Beats all how quick that feller can size up a hand. If he could play poker as well as he can fight he could quit working for a living."

"Yes; yo're shore right," Red replied.

Several shots rang out from the breastwork and the bullets hummed past them down the cut. A burst of derisive laughter replied fifty yards to their right and a taunt followed it. More shots were fired and answered by another laugh and taunt, inducing profanity from the marksman, and then Hopalong called to Red. "Six out of seven went plumb through my sombrero, Red, when I poked it out to find if they was looking. They was. Purty good for 'em, eh?"

"Too blamed good to suit me-lucky yore head wasn't in it," Red replied.

Hopalong, singing in stentorian voice an original version of "Mary and Her Little Lamb" in which it seemed he aspired to be the lamb, finally came into view with a perforated sombrero in his hand, which he eyed ruefully. "A good roof gone up, but I didn't reckon everybody was looking my way," he grumbled. "Somebody shore has got to pay for that lid, too," then he glanced up, saw Meeker, and looked foolish. "Howd'y, Meeker; what's new, Buck?"

"Hey, Hoppy! Did you know I was covering their drinking water?" asked Red, triumphantly.

"I knowed you was covering some of it, but you needn't take on no airs about it, for you didn't know it," Hopalong retorted. "What I want to know is why you wasn't covering *me*, like you said you would!" he cried, eying Red's sombrero, which lay at his feet. "It's all yore fault that my Stetson's bust wide open, an' that being so, we'll just swap, right now, too!" suiting the action to the words.

"Hey! Gimme that war-bonnet, you bunch of gall!" yelled Red kicking at his tormentor and missing. "Gimme that, d'y hear!"

"Give you a punch in th' eye, you sheep!" retorted Hopalong, backing away. "Think you can get away with a play like that after saying you was going to cover me? *I* ain't no papoose, you animated carrot!"

"Gimme that Stetson!" Red commanded, starting to arise. There was a sharp hum and he dropped back again, blood flowing from his cheek, that being the extent of his person he had so inadvertently exposed. "There, blank you! See what you made me do! Going to drop that hat?"

"Why don't you give 'em a good shot at you? That ain't no way to treat 'em-but honest, Red, you shouldn't get so excited over a little thing like that," Hopalong replied. "Now, I'll leave it to Meeker, here-hadn't I ought to take his roof?"

Meeker laughed. "Th' Court reserves its decision, but possession is nine points in law."

"Huh! Possession is everything. Since I can keep it, why, then, according to th' Court, th' hat belongs to me. Hear that, Red?"

"Yes, I hear it! An' if I wasn't so cussed busy I'd show you how long you'd keep it," Red rejoined. "I'll bet you a hat you don't keep it a day after we get this off'n our hands. Bow-legged Algernon, you!"

"Done-then I'll have two hats; one for work an' one to wear when I'm visiting," Hopalong laughed. "But you've got th' best of th' swap, anyhow. That new lid of yourn, holes an' all, is worth twice as much as this wool thing I'm getting for it. My old one is a *hat!*"

Red refused to lower his dignity by replying and soon fired. "Huh! Reckon that feller won't shoot no more with his right hand."

"Say, I near forgot to tell you Meeker captured one of them fellers out back; got him tied up now," Buck remarked, relating the incident, Meeker interrupting to give the Bar-20 foreman all the credit.

"Good!" exclaimed Red. "It's a rope necktie for him. An' one less to shoot at me."

"An' *you* here, Buck!" cried Hopalong in surprise. "Come on, lead th' way! How do you know he was th' only one to get behind us! Good Lord!"

"Gosh, yo're right!" Buck exclaimed, running off. "Come on, Jim. We're a pair of fools, after all!"

At the other end of the line Chick Travers and George Cross did as well as they could with their Colts, but found their efforts unavailing. Their positions were marked by the rustlers and they had several narrow escapes, both being wounded, Cross twice. Ten yards west of them Frenchy McAllister was crawling forward a foot at a time from cover to cover and so far he had not been hit. His position also had been marked and he was now trying to find a new one unobserved, where he could have a chance to shoot once without instantly being fired upon. Pete and Johnny had separated, the latter having given up his attempt to make the rustler pay for his wounded ear. He had emptied the magazine of the rifle he had found and now only used his Colt. As he worked along the firing line he saw Frenchy ten yards in front of him, covered nicely by a steep rise in the ground.

"How are you doing out there, Frenchy?" he asked in a low voice.

"Not very good; wish I had my rifle," came the soft-spoken reply.

"I had one that I found, but I used up all th' cartridges there was in th' magazine."

"What kind an' caliber?"

".45-70 Winchester. I found it by th' ropes. Pete says he reckoned some rustler must have left it behind an' got away down th' —"

"Get it for me, Kid, will you?" interrupted Frenchy, eagerly. "I plumb forgot to leave my belt of rifle cartridges back in th' camp. Got it on now, an' it's chock full, too. Hurry up, an' I'll work back to you for it."

"What luck! In a second," Johnny exulted, disappearing. Returning with the rifle he handed it to his friend and gazed longingly at the beltful of rifle cartridges. "Say, Frenchy," he began. "You know we'll all have our rifles to-night, an' you've got more cartridges for that than you can use before then. It won't be more than three hours before we send for ours. Suppose you gimme some of them for Pete-he's got th' mate to that gun, an' can't use it no more because it's empty."

"Shore, Kid," and Frenchy slipped a handful of cartridges out of his belt and gave them to Johnny. "With my compliments to Pete. What was that you was saying about rustlers an' th' ropes?"

Johnny told of Pete's deductions regarding the finding of the rifles and Frenchy agreed with them, and also that Doc had taken care of the owners of the weapons when they had reached the plain.

"Well, I'm going further away from them thieves now that I've got something to shoot with," Frenchy asserted. "They won't be looking for any of us a hundred yards or more farther back. Mebbe I can catch some of 'em unawares."

"I'll chase off an' give Pete these pills," Johnny replied. "He'll be tickled plumb to death. He was cussing bad when I left him."

George Cross, crawling along a steep, smooth rock barely under the shelter of a bowlder, endeavored to grasp the top, but under-reached and slipped, rolling down to the bottom and in plain sight of the rustlers. As his companion, Chick Travers, tried to help him two shots rang out and Cross, sitting up with his hands to his head, toppled back to arise no more. Chick leaped up and fired twice at one of the marksmen, and missed. His actions had been so sudden and unexpected that he escaped the return shot which passed over him by a foot as he dropped back to cover. Somehow the whole line seemed to feel that there had been a death among them, as evidenced by the burst of firing along it. And the whole line felt another thing; that the cartridges of the rustlers were getting low, for they seemed to be saving their shots. But it was Hopalong who found the cause of the diminishing fire. After hunting fruitlessly with the two foremen and finding that Hall was the only man to get back of the firing line he left his two companions in order to learn the condition of his friends. As he made his way along the line he chanced to look towards the hut and saw four rifles on the floor of it, and back of them, piled against the wall, was the rustlers' main supply of ammunition. Calling out, he was answered by Pete, who soon joined him.

"Pete, you lucky devil, turn that rifle through th' door of th' shack an' keep it on them cartridges," he ordered. "They ain't been shooting as fast as they was at first, an' there's th' reason for it. Oh, just wait till daylight to-morrow! They won't last long after that!"

"They won't get them cartridges, anyhow," Pete replied with conviction.

"Hey, fellers," cried a voice, and they looked around to see Chick Travers coming towards them. "Yore man Cross has passed. He rolled off his ledge an' couldn't stop. They got him when he hit th' bottom of it."

"D —n 'em!" growled Hopalong. "We'll square our accounts to-morrow morning. Pete, you watch them cartridges."

"Shore —" *Bang!* "Did you see that?" Pete asked, frantically pumping the lever of his rifle.

"Yes!" cried Chick. "Some feller tried to get in that south window! Bet he won't try again after that hint. Hear him cuss? There-Red must 'a fired then, too!"

"Good boy, Pete!—keep 'em out. We'll have somebody in there after dark," Hopalong responded. "They've got th' best covers now, but we'll turn th' table on 'em when th' sun comes up to-morrow."

"Here comes Buck an' Meeker," remarked Chick. "Them two are getting a whole lot chummy lately, all right. They're allus together."

"That's good, too. They're both of 'em all right," Hopalong replied, running to meet them. Chick saw the three engage in a consultation and look towards the hut and the ridge behind it, Buck and Meeker nodding slowly at what Hopalong was saying. Then they moved off towards the west where they could examine the building at closer range.

Chapter XXXV
Johnny Takes the Hut

As the day waned the dropping shots became less and less frequent and the increasing darkness began to work its magic. The unsightly plain with its crevices and bowlders and scrawny vegetation would soon be changed into one smooth blot, to be lighted with the lurid flashes of rifles as Red and Pete fired at irregular intervals through the south windows of the hut to keep back any rustler who tried to get the ammunition within its walls. Two were trying and had approached the window just as a bullet hummed through it. They stopped and looked at each other and moved forward again. Then a bullet from Pete's rifle, entering through the open door, hummed out the window and struck against the rocky ridge.

"Say! Them coyotes can see us through that windy," remarked Clausen. "Th' sky at our backs is too light yet."

"They can't see us standing here," objected Shaw.

"Then what are they shooting at?"

"Cuss me if I know. Looks like they was using th' winder for a target. Reckon we better wait till it gets darker."

"If we wait till it's dark we can sneak in through th' door," suggested Clausen. "If we go in crawling we ain't likely to stop no shot high enough to go through that windy."

"You can if you wants, but I ain't taking no chances like that, none whatever."

Another shot whined through the window and stopped with an angry spat against the ridge. Shaw scratched his head reflectively. "It shore beats me why they keeps that up. There ain't no sense to it," he declared in aggrieved tones. "They don't know nothing about them cartridges in there."

"That's it!" exclaimed Clausen, excitedly. "I bet a stack of blues they do know. An' they're covering somebody going in to steal 'em. Oh, h—l!" and he slammed his hat to the ground in bitter anger. "An' us a-standing here like a couple of mired cows! I'm going to risk it."

"Wait," advised Shaw. "Let's try a hat an' see if they plug at it."

"Wait be d———d! My feet are growing roots right now. I'm going in," and Clausen broke away from his friend and ran towards the hut, a crouching run, comical to look at but effective because it kept his head below the level of the window; without pausing in his stride his body lengthened into a supple curve as he plunged head foremost through the window, landing on the cabin floor with hands and feet bunched under him, his passing seen only as a fleeting, puzzling shadow, by the watchful eyes outside.

Across the cut Johnny was giving Red instructions and turned to leave. "Th' cut is full of shadows an' th' moon ain't up yet. Now, remember, one more shot through that window—I'm going to foller it right in. Get word to Pete as soon as you can, though I won't pass th' door. He's only got three cartridges left an' he'll be getting some anxious about now. So long."

"So long, an' good luck, Kid," Red replied.

Johnny wriggled across the cut on his stomach, picking out the shadows and gaining the shelter of the opposite bank, stood up, and ran to the hut. Red fired and then Johnny cautiously climbed through the window and dropped to the floor.

He had anticipated Clausen by the fraction of a second. As his feet touched the floor the noise of Clausen's arrival saluted him and the startled Johnny jerked his gun loose and sent a shot in the other's direction, leaping aside on the instant. The flash of the discharge was gone too quickly for him to distinguish anything and the scrambling sound that followed mystified him further. That there had been no return shot did not cause him to dance with joy, far otherwise; it made him drop silently to his stomach and hunt the darkest part of the hut, the west wall. He lay still for a minute, eyes and ears strained for a sound to tell him where to shoot. Then Red called to him and wanted an answer, whereupon Johnny thought of things he ached to call Red. Then he heard a low voice outside the south window, and it called: "Clausen, Clausen-what happened? Why don't you answer?"

"Oh, so my guest is Clausen, hey?" Johnny thought. "Wonder if Clausen can see in th' dark? 'Nother d — —d fool wanting an answer! I'll bet Clausen is hugging th' dark spots, too. Wonder if I scared him as much as he scared me?"

The suspense was becoming too much of a strain and, poking his Colt out in front of him, he began to move forward, his eyes staring ahead of him at the place where Clausen ought to be.

Inch by inch he advanced, holding his breath as well as he could, every moment expecting to have Clausen salute him in the face with a hot .45. Johnny was scared, and well scared, but it only proves courage to go on when scared stiff, and Johnny went on and along the wall he thought Clausen was using for a highway.

"Wonder how it feels to have yore brains blowed out," he shivered. "For God's sake, Clausen, make a noise-sneeze, cough, choke, yell, anything!" he prayed, but Clausen remained ominously silent. Johnny pushed his Colt out farther and poked it all around. Touching the wall it made a slight scraping sound and Johnny's blood froze. Still no move from Clausen, and his fright went down a notch-Clausen was evidently even more scared than he was. That was consoling. Perhaps he was so scared that he couldn't pull a trigger, which would be far more consoling.

"Johnny! Johnny! Answer, can't you!" came Red's stentorian voice, causing Johnny to jump a few inches off the floor.

"Clausen! Clausen!" came another voice.

"For God's sake, answer, Clausen! Tell 'em yo're here!" prayed Johnny. "Yo're d — —d unpolite, anyhow."

By this time he was opposite the door and he wondered if Pete had been told not to bombard it. He stopped and looked, and stared. What was that thing on the floor? Or was it anything at all? He blinked and moved closer. It looked like a head, but Johnny was taking no chances. He stared steadily into the blackest part of the hut for a moment and then looked again at the object. He could see it a little plainer now, for it was not quite as dark outside as it was in the building; but he was not sure about it.

"Can't fool me, you coyote," he thought. "Yo're hugging this wall as tight as a tick on a cow, a blamed sight tighter than I am, an' in about a minute I'm going to shoot along it about four inches from th' floor. I'd just as soon get shot as be scared to death, anyhow. Mebby we've passed each other! An' Holy Medicine! Mebby there's two of 'em!"

He regarded the object again. "That shore looks like a head, all right." He felt a pebble under his hand and drawing back a little he covered the questionable object and then tossed the pebble at it. "Huh, if it's a head, why in thunder didn't it move?"

There were footsteps outside the south window and he listened, the Colt ready to stop any one rash enough to look in, Clausen or no Clausen.

"Where's Clausen, Shaw?" said a voice, and the reply was so low Johnny could not make it out.

"Yes; that's just what I want to know," and Johnny stared in frowning intentness at the supposed head. He moved closer to the object and by dint of staring thought he saw the head and shoulders of a man face down in a black, shallow pool. Then his hand became wet and he jerked it back and wiped it on his sleeve; he could hardly believe his senses. As he grasped the significance of his discovery he grinned sheepishly and moved back to the north wall, where no rustler's bullet could find him. "Lord! An' I got him th' first crack! Got him shooting by ear!"

"Johnny! Johnny!" came Red's roar, anxious and querulous.

Johnny wheeled and shook his Colt out of the window, for the moment forgetting the peril of losing sight of the opening in the other wall. "I'll Johnny *you*, you blankety-blank fool!" he shouted. Then he heard a curse at the south window and turned quickly, his Colt covering the opening. "An' I'll Johnny you too, you cow-stealing coyotes! Stick yore thieving heads in that windy an' holler for yore Clausen! *I* can show you where he is, an' send you after him if you'll just take a look! Want them cartridges, hey? Well, come an' get 'em!"

A bullet, fired at an angle through the window, was the reply and several hummed through the open door and glanced off the steep sides of the ridge. Waiting until they stopped coming he dropped and wriggled forward along the west wall, feeling in front of him until he touched a box. Grasping it he dragged the important cartridges to him and then backed to the north window with them.

He fell to stuffing his pockets with the captured ammunition and then stopped short and grinned happily. "Might as well *hold* this shack an' wait for somebody to look in that windy. They can't get me."

He dropped the box and walked to the heavy plank door, slamming it shut. He heard the thud of bullets in it as he propped it, and laughed. "Can't shoot through them planks, they're double thick." He smelled his sticky fingers. "An' they're full of resin, besides."

He stopped suddenly and frowned as a fear entered his mind; and then smiled, reassured. "Nope; no rustling snake can climb up that ridge-not with Red an' Pete watching it."

Chapter XXXVI
The Last Night

Fifty yards behind the firing line of the besiegers a small fire burned brightly in a steep-walled basin, casting grotesque shadows on the rock walls as men passed and re-passed. Overhead a silvery moon looked down at the cheerful blaze and from the cracks and crevices of the plain came the tuneful chorus of Nature's tiny musicians, sounding startlingly out of place where men were killing and dying. A little aside from the others three men in consultation reached a mutual understanding and turned to face their waiting friends just as Pete Wilson ran into the lighted circle.

"Hey, Johnny is in th' hut with th' cartridges," he exclaimed, telling the story in a few words.
"Good for th' Kid!"
"It's easy now, thanks to him."
"Why didn't he tell us he was going to try that?" demanded Buck. "Taking a chance like that on his own hook!"
"Scared you wouldn't let him," Pete laughed. "Red an' me backed him up with our rifles th' best we could. He had a fight in there, too, judging from th' shot. He had me an' Red worried, thinking he might 'a been hit, but he was cussing Red when I left."
"Well, that helps us a lot," Buck replied. "Now I want three of you to go to camp an' bring back grub, rifles, an' cartridges. Pete, Skinny, Chick-yo're th' ones. Leave yore canteens here an' hustle! Hopalong, you an' Meeker go off somewhere an' get some sleep. I'll call you before it gets light. Frenchy, me an' you will take all th' canteens at hand an' fill 'em while we've got time. They won't be able to see us now. We'll pass Red an' get his, too. Come on."

When they returned they dropped the dripping vessels and began cleaning their Colts. That done they filled their pipes and sat cross-legged, staring into the fire. A snatch of Johnny's exultant song floated to them and Buck smiled, laying his pipe aside and rising. "Well, Frenchy, things'll happen in chunks when th' sun comes up. Something like old times, eh? There ain't no Deacon Rankin or Slippery Trendley here —" he stopped, having mentioned a name he had promised himself never to say in Frenchy's presence, and then continued in a subdued voice, bitterly scourging himself for his blunder. "They're stronger than I thought, an' they've shot us up purty well, killed Willis an' Cross, an' made fools of us for weeks on th' range; but this is th' end of it all. *We* deal to-morrow, an' we cut th' cards to-night."

Frenchy was strangely silent, staring fixedly at the fire. Buck glanced at him in strong sympathy, for he knew what his slip of the tongue had awakened in his friend's heart. Frenchy had adored his young wife and since the day he had found her foully murdered in his cabin on the Double Y he had been another man. When the moment of his vengeance had come, when he had her murderer in his power and saw his friends ride away to leave him alone with Trendley that day over in the Panhandle, to exact what payment he wished, then he had become his old self for a while, but it was not long before he again sank into his habitual carelessness, waiting patiently for death to remove his burden and make him free. His vengeance did not bring him back his wife.

Buck shook his head slowly and affectionately placed a heavy hand on his friend's shoulder. "Frenchy, won't you ever forget it? It hurts me to see you this way so much. It's over twenty years now an' day after day I've grieved to see you so unhappy. You paid him for it in yore own way. Can't you forget it now?"

"Yes; I killed him, an' slow. He never thought a man could make th' payment so hard, not even his black heart could realize it till he felt it," Frenchy replied, slowly and calmly. "He took th' heart out of me; he killed my wife and made my life a living hell. All I had worth living for went that day, an' if I could kill him over again every day for a year it wouldn't square th' score. I reckon I ain't built like other men. You never heard me whimper. I kept my poison to myself an' tried to do the best that was in me. An' you ain't never heard me say what I'm going to tell you now. I never believed in hunches, but something tells me that I'll leave all this behind me before another day passes. I felt it somehow when we left th' ranch an' it's been growing stronger every hour since. If I do pass out to-morrow, I want you to be glad of it, same as I would be if I could know. I'm going back to th' line now an' watch them fellers. So long."

The two men, bosom friends for thirty years, looked in each other's eyes as they grasped hands, and it was Buck's eyes that grew moist and dropped first. "So long, Frenchy-an' good luck, as you see it."

The foreman watched his friend until lost in the darkness and he thought he heard him singing, but of this he was not sure. He turned and stared at the fire for a minute, silent, immovable, and then breathed heavily.

"I never saw anybody carry a grief so long, never," he soliloquized. "I reckon it sort of turned his brain, coming so sudden an' in such a damnable way. I know it made me see red for a week. If I had only stayed there that day! When he got Trendley in th' Panhandle I hoped he would change, an' he did for a while, but that was all. He lived for that alone, an' since then I reckon he's felt he hadn't nothing to do with his life. He has been mixed up in a bunch of gun-arguments since then; but he didn't have no luck. Well, Frenchy, I hate to lose a friend like you, but here's better luck to-morrow, luck as you see it, friend!"

He kicked the fire together and was about to add fuel when he heard two quick shots and raised his head to listen. Then a ringing whoop came from the front and he recognized Johnny's voice. He heard Red call out and Johnny reply and he smiled grimly as he went towards the sounds. "Reckon somebody tried to get in that shack, like a fool. He must 'a been disgusted. How that Kid shore does love a fight!"

> Joyous Joe got a juniper jag,
> A-jogging out of Jaytown,

came down the wind.

"Did you get him, Kid?" cried Buck from the firing line.

"Nope; got his hat, though-but I shore got Clausen an' all of their cartridges!"

"Can you keep them shells alone?"

"*Can* I? *Wow*, ask th' other fellers! An' I'm eating jerked beef-sorry I can't give you some."

"Shut up about eating, you pig!" blazed Red, who was hungry.

"You'll eat hot lead to-morrow, all of you!" jeered a rustler's voice.

Red fired at the sound. "Take yourn now!" he shouted.

"You can't hit a cow!" came the taunt, while other strange voices joined in.

Buck found Red and ordered him to camp to get some sleep before Pete and the others returned, feeling that he and Frenchy were enough to watch. Red demurred sleepily and finally compromised by lying down at Buck's side, where he would be handy in case of trouble. Buck waited patiently, too heavily laden with responsibility to feel the need of rest, and when he judged that three hours had passed began to worry about the men he had sent to camp. Drawing back into a crevice he struck a match and looked at his watch.

"Twelve o'clock!" he muttered. "I'll wake Red an' see how Frenchy is getting on. Time them fellers were back too."

Frenchy changed his position uneasily and peered at the distant breastwork, hearing the low murmur of voices behind it. All night he had heard their curses, but a new note made him sit up and watch more closely. The moon was coming up now and he could see better. Suddenly he caught the soft flash of a silver sombrero buckle and fired instantly. Curses and a few shots replied and a new, querulous voice was added to the murmur, a voice expressing pain.

"I reckon you got him," remarked a quiet voice at his side as Buck lay down beside him. The foreman had lost some time in wandering along the whole line of defence and was later than he had expected.

"Yes; I reckon so," Frenchy replied without interest, and they lapsed into silence, the eloquent silence of men who understand each other. They heard a shot from below and knew that Billy or Curtis was about and smiled grimly at the rising murmur it caused among the rustlers. Buck glanced at the sky and frowned. "There can't be more'n five or six left by now, an' if it wasn't for th' moon I'd get th' boys together an' rush that bunch." He was silent for a moment and then added, half to himself, "but it won't be long now, an' we can wait."

Distant voices heralded the return of Pete and his companions and the foreman arose. "Frenchy, I'm going to place th' boys an' start things right away. We've been quiet too long."

"Might as well," Frenchy replied, "I'm getting sleepy-straining my eyes too much, I reckon, trying to see a little better than I can."

"Here's th' stuff, Buck," Skinny remarked as the foreman entered the circle of light. "Two days' fighting rations, fifty rounds for th' rifles an' fifty for th' Colts. Chick is coming back there with th' rifles."

"Good. Had yore grub yet?" Buck asked. "All right-didn't reckon you'd wait for it. What kept you so long? You've been gone over three hours."

"We was talking to Billy an' Curtis," Skinny remarked. "They're anxious to have it over. They've been spelling each other an' getting some sleep. We saw Doc's saddle piled on top of th' grub when we got to camp. It wasn't there when we all left th' other night. Billy says Doc came running past last night, saddled up an' rode off. He got back this afternoon wearing a bandage around his head. He didn't say where he had been, but now he is at th' bottom of th' trail waiting for a shot, so Billy says. Pete reckons he went after somebody that got down last night, one of them fellers that left their rifles up here by th' ropes."

"Mebby yo're right," replied Buck, hurriedly. "Get ready to fight. I ain't going to wait for daylight when this moonlight will answer. Pete, Skinny, Chick-you get settled out on th' east end, where me an' Frenchy will join you. We'll have this game over before long."

He strode away and returned with Hopalong and Meeker, who hastily ate and drank and, filling their belts with cartridges and taking their own rifles from the pile Chick had brought, departed toward the cut with orders for Red to come in.

Pete and his companions moved away as Frenchy, shortly followed by Red, came in and reported.

"Eat an' drink, lively. Red, you get back to yore place an' take care of th' cut," Buck ordered. "Frenchy, you come out east with th' rest. There's cartridges for you both an' there's yore own rifle, Frenchy."

"Glad yo're going to start things," chewed Red through a mouthful of food. "It's about time we show them fellers we can live up to our reputations. Any of 'em coming my way won't go far."

Frenchy filled his pipe and lighted it from a stick he took out of the fire and as it began to draw well he stepped quickly forward and held out his hand. "Good luck, Red. They can't fight long."

"Same to you, Frenchy," Red cried, grasping the hand. "Yo're right, there. You look plumb wide awake, like Buck-how'd you do it?"

Frenchy laughed and strode after his foreman, Red watching him. "He's acting funny-reckon it's th' sleep he's missed. Well, here goes," and he, too, went off to the firing line.

—An' aching thoughts pour in on me,

Of Whiskey Bill,

came Johnny's song from the hut-and the fight began again.

Chapter XXXVII
Their Last Fight

A figure suddenly appeared on the top of the flanking ridge, outlined against the sky, and flashes of flame spurted from its hands, while kneeling beside it was another, rapidly working a rifle, the roar of the guns deafening because of the silence which preceded it. Shouts, curses, and a few random, futile shots replied from the breastworks, its defenders, panic-stricken by the surprise and the deadly accuracy of the two marksmen, scurrying around the bend in their fortifications, so busy in seeking shelter that they failed to make their shots tell. Two men, riddled by bullets, lay where they had fallen and the remaining three, each of them wounded more than once, crouched under cover and turned their weapons against the new factors; but these had already slid down the face of the ridge and were crawling along the breastwork, alert and cautious.

In front of the rustlers heavy firing burst out along the cowmen's line and Red Connors, from his old position above the cut, swung part way around and turned his rifle against the remnant of the defenders at another angle, and fired at every mark, whether it was hand, foot, or head; while Johnny, tumbling out of the south window of the hut, followed in the wake of Hopalong and Meeker. The east end of the line was wrapped in smoke, where Buck and his companions labored zealously.

Along the narrow trail up the mesa's face a man toiled heavily and it was not long before Doc Riley opened fire from the rear. The three rustlers, besieged from all sides, found their positions to be most desperate and knew then that only a few minutes intervened between them and eternity. They had three choices-to surrender, to die fighting, or to leap from the mesa to instant death below.

Shaw, to his credit, chose the second and like a cornered wolf goaded to despair leaped up and forward to take a gambler's chance of gaining the hut. Before him were Hopalong, Meeker, Johnny, and Doc. Doc was hastily reloading his Colt, Johnny was temporarily out of sight as he crawled around a bowlder, and Hopalong was greatly worried by ricochettes and wild shots from the rifles of his friends which threatened to end his career. Meeker alone was watching at that moment but his attention was held by the rustler near the edge of the mesa who was trying to shrink himself to fit the small rock in front of him and to use his gun at the same time.

Shaw sprang from his cover and straight at the H2 foreman, his foot slipping slightly as he fired. The bullet grazed Meeker's waist, but the second, fired as the rustler was recovering his balance, bored through Meeker's shoulder. The H2 foreman, bending forward for a shot at the man behind the small rock, was caught unawares and his balance, already strained, was destroyed by the shock of the second bullet, and he flopped down to all fours. Shaw sprang over him just as Hopalong and Johnny caught sight of him and he swung his revolver on Hopalong at the moment when the latter's bullet crashed through his brain.

Buck Peters, trying for a better position, slipped on the rock which had been the cause of the death of George Cross and before he could gain his feet a figure leaped down in front of him and raised a Colt in his defence, but spun half way around and fell, shot through the head. A cry of rage went up at this and a rush was made against the breastworks from front and side. Frenchy McAllister's forebodings had come true.

Sanchez, finding his revolver empty and with no time to reload, held up his hands. Frisco, blinded by blood, wounded in half a dozen places, desperate, snarling, and still unbeaten, wheeled viciously, but before he could pull his trigger, Hopalong grasped him and hurled him down, Johnny going with them. Doc, a second too late, waved his sombrero. "Come on, it's all over!"

In another second the rushing punchers from the front slid and rolled and plunged over the breastwork and eyed the results of their fire.

Meeker staggered around the corner and leaned against Buck for support. "My G-d! This is awful! I didn't think we were doing so much damage."

"I did!" retorted Buck. "I know what happens when my outfit burns powder. Where's Red?" he asked anxiously.

"Here I am," replied a voice behind him.

"All right; take that Greaser to th' hut, somebody," the foreman ordered. "Johnny, you an' Pete take this feller there, too," pointing to Frisco. "He's th' one that killed Frenchy. Hopalong, take Red, an' bring in that feller me an' Meeker tied up in that crevice, if he ain't got away."

Hopalong and Red went off to bring in Hall and Buck turned to the others. "You fellers doctor yore wounds. Meeker, yo're hard hit," he remarked, more closely looking at the H2 foreman.

"Yes. I know it-loss of blood, mostly," Meeker replied. "An' if it hadn't been for Cassidy I'd been hit a d — —d sight harder. Where's Doc? He knows what to do —*Doc!*"

"Coming," replied a voice and Doc turned the corner. He had a limited knowledge of the work he was called upon to do, and practice, though infrequent, had kept it more or less fresh.

"Reckon yo're named about right, Doc," Buck remarked as he passed the busy man. "You got me beat an' I ain't no slouch."

"I'd 'a been a real Doc if I hadn't left college like a fool to punch cows, —you've got to keep still, Jim," he chided.

"Hey, Buck," remarked Hopalong, joining the crowd and grinning at the injured, "we've got that feller in th' shack. When th' feller I grabbed out here saw him he called him Hall. Th' other is Frisco an' th' Greaser ain't got no name, I reckon. How you feeling, Meeker? That was Shaw plugged you."

"Feeling better'n him," Meeker growled. "Yo're a good man to work with, Cassidy."

"Well, Cassidy, got any slugs in you?" affably asked Doc, the man Hopalong had wounded on the line a few weeks before. Doc brandished a knife and cleaning rod and appeared to be anxious to use them on somebody else.

"No; but what do you do with them things?" Hopalong rejoined, feeling of his bandage.

"Take out bullets," Doc grinned.

"Oh, I see; you cut a hole in th' back an' then push 'em right through," Hopalong laughed. "Reckon I'd ruther have 'em go right through without stopping. Who's that calling?"

"Billy an' Curtis. Tell 'em to come up," Buck replied, walking towards the place where Frenchy's body lay.

Hopalong went to the edge and replied to the shouts and it was not long before they appeared. When Doc saw them he grinned pleasantly and drew them aside, trying to coax them to let him repair them. But Billy, eying the implements, sidestepped and declined with alacrity; Curtis was the victim.

"After *him* th' undertaker," Billy growled, going towards the hut.

Chapter XXXVIII
A Disagreeable Task

Two men, Hall and Frisco, sat with their backs against the wall of the hut, weaponless, wounded, nervous, one sullen and enraged, the other growling querulously to himself about his numerous wounds. The third prisoner, the Mexican, was pacing to and fro with restless strides, vicious and defiant, his burning eyes quick, searching, calculating. It seemed as though he was filled with a tremendous amount of energy which would not let him remain quiet. When his companions spoke to him he flashed them a quick glance but did not answer; thinking, scheming, plotting, he missed not the slightest movement of those about him. Wounded as he was he did not appear to know it, so intent was he upon his thoughts.

Hall, saved from the dangers of the last night's fight, loosed his cumulative rage frequently in caustic and profane verbal abuse of his captors, his defeat, his companions, and the guard. Frisco, courageous as any under fire, was dejected because of the wait; merely a difference of temperament.

The guard, seated carelessly on a nearby rock, kept watch over the three and cogitated upon the whole affair, his Colt swinging from a hand between his knees. Twenty paces to his right was a stack of rifles and Sanchez, lengthening his panther stride with barely perceptible effort, drew nearer to them on each northward lap. He typified the class of men who never give up hope, and as he gained each yard he glanced furtively at the guard and then estimated the number of leaps necessary to reach the coveted rifles. His rippling muscles were bunching up for the desperate attempt when the guard interfered, the sharp clicks of his Colt bringing the Mexican to an abrupt stop. Sanchez shrugged his shoulders and wheeling, resumed his restless walk, being careful to keep it within safe limits.

Hall, lighting his pipe, blew a cloud of smoke into the air and looked at the guard, who was still cogitating.

"How did you fools finally figger we was out here?"

Hopalong looked up and smiled. "Oh, we just figgered you fools would be here, and would stay up here. Yore friend Antonio worked too hard."

Hall carefully packed his pipe and puffed quickly. "I knowed he'd bungle it, d — —d Greaser. It was th' Greasers that busted up th' game. Sixteen men an' four of 'em Greasers. By G-d, if we was all white men we'd 'a given you fellers a hot tune to dance to. Greasers are all cowards, any —"

"You lie!" snapped Sanchez, stepping forward.

"Stop it!" shouted Hopalong, half arising, his Colt on the two. "You keep peaceful-there's been too much fighting now. But if them other Greasers had been like this one here I reckon you wouldn't 'a lost nothing by having 'em."

"What happened to Cavalry an' Antonio?" asked Hall. "Did you get 'em when you came up?"

"They got down th' way we came up-Doc trailed th' Greaser an' got him at that water hole up north," Hopalong replied. "Don't know nothing about th' other feller. Reckon he got away, but one don't make much difference, anyhow. He'll never come back to this country."

"Say, how much longer will it take yore friends to do th' buryin' act?" asked Frisco, irritably. "I'm plumb tired of waiting-these wounds hurt like blazes, too."

"Reckon they're coming now," was the reply. "I hear-yes, here they are."

"I owe you ten dollars, Hall," Frisco remarked, trivial things now entering his mind. "Reckon you won't get it, neither."

"Oh, pay me in h —l!" Hall snapped.

"Yes," Buck was saying, "he shore was white. He knowed he was going an' he went like th' man he was-saving a friend. 'Tain't th' first time Frenchy McAllister's saved my life, neither."

Frisco glanced around and his face flashed with a look of recognition, but he held his tongue; not so with Curtis, who stared at him in surprise and stepped forward.

"Good G-d! It's Davis! What ever got you into this?"

"Easy money an' a gun fight," Davis, alias Frisco, replied.

"Tough luck, tough luck," Curtis muttered slowly.

"D —n tough, if you asks me," Frisco growled.

"What happened to th' others?" Curtis asked, referring to three men with whom he and Frisco had punched and prospected several years before.

"Little Dan went out in that same gun fight, Joe Baird was got by th' posse next day, an' George Wild an' I got into th' mountains an' was separated. I got free after a sixty-mile chase, but I don't know how George made out. We had stuck up a gold caravan an' killed two men what was with it. They was th' only fellers to pull their guns against us."

"Well, I'm d — —d!" ejaculated Curtis. "An' so that crowd went bad!"

"Say, for th' Lord's sake, get things moving," cried Hall, angrily. "If we've got to die make it quick-or else shoot that infernal Greaser-he's got on my nerves with his tramp, tramp, tramp! Wish I'd 'a gone with Shaw 'stead of waiting for my own funeral."

Buck surveyed them. "Got anything to say?"

"Not me —I've had mine," replied Frisco, toying with a bandage. Then he started to say something but changed his mind. "Oh, well, what's th' use! Go ahead."

"Don't drag it out," growled Hall. "Say, you got *my* rope there?" he demanded suddenly, eying the coils slung over Skinny's shoulder. "No, you ain't. I want my own, savvy?"

"Oh, we ain't got time to hunt for no ropes," rejoined Skinny. "One's as good as another, ain't it?"

"Yes, I reckon so-hustle it through," Hall replied, sullenly.

"Go ahead, you fellers," ordered Hopalong as some of his friends went first down the trail after the two sent to the camp for the horses. "Come on, Sanchez! Fall in there!"

When the procession reached the bottom of the trail Buck halted it to wait for the horses and his prisoners took one more look around.

"Say, Peters, where's th' cayuses we had in that corral?" asked Hall, surprised.

"Oh, we got them out th' first night-we wasn't taking no chances," replied the foreman. "They're somewhere near th' camp now."

As the horse herd was driven up Sanchez made his last play. All were intent upon tightening cinches, the more intent because of the impending and disagreeable task, when he slipped like a shadow through the group and throwing himself across a likely looking pinto (he knew the horse), headed in a circular track for the not too distant chaparral.

"*Take* him, Red!" shouted Buck, who was the first to recover.

Red's rifle leaped to his shoulder and steadied; in three more jumps the speedy pinto would have shielded Sanchez, clinging like a burr to the further side; but the rifle spoke once and the fleeing Mexican dropped and lay quiet on the sand.

Hopalong rode out to him and glancing at the still form, wheeled and returned. "Got him clean, Red."

A group of horsemen rode eastward towards the chaparral and as it was about to enclose them one of the riders bringing up the rear turned in his saddle and looked back at two dangling forms outlined against the darker background of the frowning mesa, two where he had expected to see three.

"Well, th' rustling is over," he remarked. "Say, that Greaser wasn't no coward. I reckoned Greasers was all yaller dogs."

"Have you known many of 'em?" asked Skinny, quietly.

"No," replied Chick. "Didn't ever see none till I came down here. Reckon there ain't many up in Montanny. But I heard lots about 'em. *He* was all grit! I allus reckoned they was coyotes, an' mostly scared."

"If you stay down here for long you'll meet some more that ain't cowards," Skinny replied. "I have-more'n once. A Greaser is a man, same as me an' you, an' I've known some that would look th' devil hisself in th' eye an' call him a liar."

"Gee!" exclaimed Chick, thoughtfully.

Chapter XXXIX
Thirst

The stars grow dim and a streak of color paints the eastern sky, sweeping through the upper reaches of the darkness and tingeing the earth's curtain until the dim gray light outlines spectral yuccas and twisted, grotesque cacti leaning in the hushed air like drunken sentries of some monstrous army. The dark carpet which stretched away on all sides begins to show its characteristics and soon develops into greasewood brush. As if curtains were drawn aside objects which a moment before were lost to sight in the darkness emerge out of the light like ghosts, bulky, indistinct, grotesque, and array themselves to complete the scene.

The silence seems to deepen and become strained, as if in fear of what is to come; the dark ground is now gray and tawny in places and the vegetation is plain to the eye. Then out of the east comes a flash and a red, coppery sun flares above the horizon, molten, quivering, blinding; the cool of the night swiftly departs and a caldron-like heat bursts upon the plain. The silence seems almost to shrink and become portentous with evil, the air is hushed, the plants stand without the movement of a leaf, and nowhere is seen any living creature. The whole is unreal, a panorama, with vegetation of wax and a painted, faded blue sky, the only movement being the shortening shadows and the rising sun.

Across the sand is an erratic trail of shoe prints, coming from the east. For a dozen yards it runs evenly and straight, then a few close prints straggle to and fro, zig-zagging hither and yon for a distance, finally going on straight again. But the erratic prints grow more frequent and become more pronounced as they go on, circling and weaving, crossing, re-crossing and doubling back as their maker staggered hopelessly on his way, urged only by the instinct of thirst, to find water, if it were only a mouthful. The trail is here blurred, for he fell, and the prints of his hands and knees and shoe-tips tell how he went on for some distance. He gained his feet here and threw away his Colt, and later his holster and belt.

The sun is overhead now and the sand shimmers, the heated air quivering and glistening, and the desolate void takes on an air of mystery and fear, and death. No living thing moves across the heat-cursed sand, but here is a tangled mass of sand and clay and greasewood twigs, in the heart of which mice sleep and wait for night, and over there is a hillock sheltering lizards. Stay! Under that greasewood bush a foolish gray wolf is waiting for night-but he has little to fear, for he can cover forty miles between dark and dawn, and his instinct is infallible; no wandering trail will mark his passing, but one as straight as the flight of a bullet. The shadows shrink close to the stems of the plants and the thin air dances with heat.

Behind that clump of greasewood, back beyond those crippled cacti, a man staggers on and on. His hair is matted, his fingers bleeding from digging frantically in the sand for water; his lips, cracked and bleeding and swollen, hide the shrivelled, stiff tongue which clicks against his teeth at every painful step. His eyelids are stiff and the staring, unblinking eyes are set and swollen. He clutches at his throat time and time again,—a drowning sensation is there. Ha! He drops to his knees and digs frantically again, for the sand is moist! A few days ago a water hole lay there. He throws off his shirt and finally staggers on again.

His tongue begins to swell and forces itself beyond the swollen, festering lips; the eyelids split and the protruding eyeballs weep tears of blood. His skin cracks and curls up, the clefts going constantly deeper into the flesh, and the exuding blood quickly dries and leaves a tough coating over the wounds. Wherever the exudation touches it stings and burns, and the cracks and clefts, irritated more and more each minute, deepen and widen and lengthen, smarting and nerve-racking with their pain.

There! A grove of beautiful green trees is before him, and in it a fountain splashes with musical babbling. He yells and dances and then, casting aside the rest of his clothes, staggers towards it. Water, water, at last! Water and shade! It grows indistinct, wavers-and is gone! But it must be there. It was there only a moment ago-and on and on he runs, hands tearing at his choking, drowning throat. Here is water-close at hand —a purling, cold brook, whispering and tinkling over its rocky bed-he jumps into it-it moved! It's over there, ten paces to his right. On and on he staggers, the stream just ahead. He falls more frequently and wavers now. Oh, for just a canteen of water, just a swallow, just a drop! The gold of the world would not buy it from him-just a drop of water!

He is dying from within, from the inside out. The liquids of his body exude through the clefts and evaporate. His brain burns and bands of white-hot steel crush his throbbing head and his burning lungs. No amount of water will save him now-only death, merciful death can end his sufferings.

Water at last! Real water, a noisome pool of stagnant liquid lies at the bottom of a slight depression, the dregs of a larger pool concentrated by evaporation. Around it are the prints of many kinds of feet. It is water, water!—he plunges forward into it and lies motionless, half submerged. A grayback lizard darts out of the greasewood near at hand, blinks rapidly and darts back again, glad to escape the intolerable heat.

Cavalry had escaped.

Chapter XL
Changes

With the passing of the weeks the two ranches had settled down to routine duty. On the H2 conditions were changed greatly for the better and Meeker gloated over his gushing wells and the dam which gave him a reservoir on his north range, the early completion of which he owed largely to the experience and willing assistance of Buck and the Bar-20 outfit.

It was getting along towards Fall when a letter came to the Bar-20 addressed to John McAllister. Buck looked at it long and curiously. "Wonder who's writing to Frenchy?" he mused. "Well, I've got to find out," and he opened the envelope and looked at the signature; it made him stare still more and he read the letter carefully. George McAllister, through the aid of the courts, had gained possession of the old Double Y in the name of its owners and was going to put an outfit on the ground to evict and hold off those who had jumped it. He knew nothing about ranching and wanted Frenchy McAllister, who owned half of it, to take charge of it and to give him the address of Buck Peters, the other half-owner. He advised that Peters' share be bought because the range was near a railroad and was growing more valuable every day.

Buck's decision was taken instantly. Much as he disliked to leave the old outfit here was the chance he had been waiting for without knowing it. He would never have set foot on the Double Y during Frenchy's lifetime because of loyalty to his old friend. Had he at any time desired possession of the property he and his friends could have taken it and left court actions to the other side. But Frenchy was gone, and he still owned half of a valuable piece of property and one that he could make pay well. He was getting on in years and it would be pleasant to have his cherished dream come true, to be the over-lord and half-owner of a good cattle ranch and to know that when he became too old to work with any degree of pleasure he need not worry about his remaining years. If he left the Bar-20 one of his friends would take his place and he was sure it would be Hopalong. The advancement in pay and authority would please the man whom he had looked upon as his son. And perhaps it would bring to Hopalong that which now kept his eyes turned towards the H2. Yes, it was time to go to his own and let another man come into *his* own; to move along and give a younger man a chance.

He replied to George McAllister at length, covering everything, and took the letter to the bunk house to have it mailed.

"Billy," he said, "here's a letter to go to Cowan's th' first thing to-morrow. Don't forget."

Buck started the fall work early and pushed it harder than usual for he wished to have everything done before the new foreman took charge. The beef roundup and drives were over with quickly, considering the time and labor involved, and when the chill blasts of early Winter swept across the range and whined around the ranch buildings Buck smiled with the satisfaction which comes with work well done. George McAllister, failing to buy Buck's interest, now implored him to go to the Double Y at once and take charge, which he had promised to do in time to become familiar with conditions on the winter-bound northern range before the new herds were driven to it.

As yet he had told his men nothing of his plans for fear they would persuade him to stay where he was, but he could tell Meeker, and one crisp morning he called at the H2 and led its foreman aside. When he had finished Meeker grasped his hand, told him how sorry he was to lose so good a friend and neighbor, and how glad he was at that friend's good fortune.

"I hope Cassidy *is* th' man to take yore place, Peters," he remarked, thoughtfully. "He's a good man, th' best in th' country, white, square, and nervy. I've had my eyes on him for some time an' I'll back him to bust anything he throws his rope on. He can handle that ranch easy an' well."

"Yo're right," replied Buck, slowly. "He ain't never failed to make good yet. Whoever th' boys pick out to be foreman will be foreman, for th' owners have left that question with me. But Meeker, it's like pulling teeth for me to go up to Montana without him. I can't take him 'less I take 'em all, an' I've got reasons why I can't do that. An' I ain't quite shore he'd go with me now-yore ranch holds something that ties him tight to this range. He'll be lonely up in our ranch house, an' it's plenty big enough for two," he finished, smiling interrogatively at his companion.

"Well, I reckon it'll not be lonely if he wants to change it," laughed Meeker. "Leastawise, them's th' symptoms plentiful enough down here. I was dead set agin it at first, but now I don't want nothing else but to see my girl fixed for life. An' when I pass out, all I have is hers."

Chapter XLI
Hopalong's Reward

Seven men loitered about the line house on Lookout Peak, wondering why they, the old outfit, had been told to await their foreman there. Why were the others, all good fellows, excluded? What could it mean? Foreboding grew upon them as they talked the matter over and when Buck approached they waited eagerly for him to speak.

He dismounted and looked at them with pride and affection and a trace of sorrow showed in his voice and face when he began to talk.

"Boys," he said, slowly, "we've got things ready for snow when it comes. Th' cattle are strong an' fat, there's plenty of grass curing on th' range, an' th' biggest drive ever sent north from this ranch has been taken care of. There's seven of you here, two on th' north range, an' four more good men coming next week; an' thirteen men can handle this ranch with some time to spare.

"I've been with you for a long time now. Some of you I've had for over twelve years, an' no man ever had a better outfit. You've never turned back on any game, an' you've never had no trouble among yoreselves. You've seen me sending an' getting letters purty regular for some time, an' you've been surprised at how I've pushed you to get ready for winter. I'm going to tell you all about it now, an' when I've finished I want you to vote on something," and they listened in dumb surprise and sorrow while he told them of his decision. When he had finished they crowded about him and begged him to stay with them, telling him they would not allow him to leave. But if he must go, then they, too, must go and help him whip a wild and lawless range into submission. He would need them badly in Montana, and nowhere could he get men who would work and fight so hard and cheerfully for him as his old outfit. They would not let him talk and he could not if they would, for there was something in his throat which choked and pained him. Johnny Nelson and Hopalong were tugging at his shoulders and the others stormed and pleaded and swore, tears in the eyes of all. He wavered and would have thrown away all his resolutions, when he thought of Hopalong and the girl. Pushing them back he told them he could not stay and begged them, as they loved him, to consider his future. They looked at one another strangely and then realized how selfish they were, and said so profanely.

"*Now* yo're my old outfit," he cried, striking while the iron was hot. "I've told you why I must go, an' why I can't take *all* of you with me, an' why I won't take a few an' leave th' rest. Don't think I don't want you! Why, with you at my back I'd buck that range into shape in no time, an' chase th' festive gun-fighters off th' earth. Mebby some day you can come up to me, but not now. Now I want th' new foreman of th' Bar-20 to be one of th' men who worked so hard an' loyally an' long for me an' th' ranch. I want one of you to take my place. Th' owners have left th' choice to me, an' say th' man I appoint will be their choice; an' I ain't a-going to do it —I can't do it. One last favor, boys; go in that house an' pick yore foreman. Go now, an' I'll wait for you here."

"We'll do it right here-Red Connors!" cried Hopalong.

"Hopalong!" yelled Red and Johnny in the same voice, and only a breath ahead of the others. "Hopalong! Hopalong!" was the cry, his own voice lost, buried, swept under. He tried to argue, tried to show that he was unfit, but he could make no headway, for his exploits were shouted to convince him. As fast as he tried to speak some one remembered something else he had done-they ranged over a period of ten years and from Mexico to Cheyenne; from Dodge City and Leavenworth to the Rockies.

Buck laughed and clapped his hands on Hopalong's shoulders. "I appoint you foreman, an' you can't get out of it, nohow! Lemme shake hands with th' new foreman of th' Bar-20 —I'm one of th' boys now, an' glad to get rid of th' responsibility for a while. Good luck, son!"

"No you ain't going to get rid of 'em," laughed Hopalong, but serious withal. "Yo're th' foreman of this ranch till you leave us-ain't he, boys?" he appealed.

Buck put his hands to his ears and yelled for less noise. "All right, I'll play at breaking you in —'though th' Lord knows I can't show you nothing you don't know now. My first order under these conditions is that you ride south, Hopalong, an' tell th' news to Meeker, an' to his girl. An' tell 'em separate, too. An' don't forget I want to see you hobbled before I leave next month-tell her to make it soon!"

Hopalong reddened and grinned under the rapid-fire advice and chaffing of his friends and tried to retort.

Johnny sprang forward. "Come on, fellers! Put him on his cayuse an' start him south! We've got to have *some* hand in his courting, anyhow!"

"Right!"

"Good idea!"

"Look out! *Grab* him, Red!"

"Up with him!"

"We ought to escort him on his first love trail," yelled Skinny above the uproar. "Come on! *Saddles*, boys!"

"Like h —l!" cried Hopalong, spurring forward his nettlesome mount. "You've got to grow wings to catch me an' Red Eagle! *Go, bronc!*" and he shot forward like an arrow from a bow, cheers and good wishes thundering after him.

———————————————————

Buck moved about restlessly in his sleep and then awakened suddenly and lay quiet as a hand touched his shoulder. "What is it? Who are you?" he demanded, ominously.

"I reckoned you'd like to know that yo're going to be best man in two weeks, Buck," said a happy voice. "She said a month, but I told her you was going away before then, an' you *might*, you know. I shore feel joyous!"

The huge hand of the elder man closed over his in a grip which made him wince. "Good boy, an' good luck, Hoppy! It was due you an' I knowed you'd win. Good luck, an' happiness, son!"

Bar-20 Days

Chapter I
On a Strange Range

Two tired but happy punchers rode into the coast town and dismounted in front of the best hotel. Putting up their horses as quickly as possible they made arrangements for sleeping quarters and then hastened out to attend to business. Buck had been kind to delegate this mission to them and they would feel free to enjoy what pleasures the town might afford. While at that time the city was not what it is now, nevertheless it was capable of satisfying what demands might be made upon it by two very active and zealous cow-punchers. Their first experience began as they left the hotel.

"Hey, you cow-wrastlers!" said a not unpleasant voice, and they turned suspiciously as it continued: "You've shore got to hang up them guns with the hotel clerk while you cavorts around on this range. This is *fence* country."

They regarded the speaker's smiling face and twinkling eyes and laughed. "Well, yo're the foreman if you owns that badge," grinned Hopalong, cheerfully. "We don't need no guns, no-how, in this town, we don't. Plumb forgot we was toting them. But mebby you can tell us where lawyer Jeremiah T. Jones grazes in daylight?"

"Right over yonder, second floor," replied the marshal. "An' come to think of it, mebby you better leave most of yore cash with the guns-somebody'll take it away from you if you don't. It'd be an awful temptation, an' flesh is weak."

"Huh!" laughed Johnny, moving back into the hotel to leave his gun, closely followed by Hopalong. "Anybody that can turn that little trick on me an' Hoppy will shore earn every red cent; why, we've been to Kansas City!"

As they emerged again Johnny slapped his pocket, from which sounded a musical jingling. "If them weak people try anything on us, we may come between them and *their* money!" he boasted.

"From the bottom of my heart I pity you," called the marshal, watching them depart, a broad smile illuminating his face. "In about twenty-four hours they'll put up a holler for me to go git it back for 'em," he muttered. "An' I almost believe I'll do it, too. I ain't never seen none of that breed what ever left a town without empty pockets an' aching heads-an' the smarter they think they are the easier they fall." A fleeting expression of discontent clouded the smile, for the lure of the open range is hard to resist when once a man has ridden free under its sky and watched its stars. "An' I wish I was one of 'em again," he muttered, sauntering on.

Jeremiah T. Jones, Esq., was busy when his door opened, but he leaned back in his chair and smiled pleasantly at their bow-legged entry, waving them towards two chairs. Hopalong hung his sombrero on a letter press and tipped his chair back against the wall; Johnny hung grimly to his hat, sat stiffly upright until he noticed his companion's pose, and then, deciding that everything was all right, and that Hopalong was better up in etiquette than himself, pitched his sombrero dexterously over the water pitcher and also leaned against the wall. Nobody could lose him when it came to doing the right thing.

"Well, gentlemen, you look tired and thirsty. This is considered good for all human ailments of whatsoever nature, degree, or wheresoever located, in part or entirety, *ab initio*," Mr. Jones remarked, filling glasses. There was no argument and when the glasses were empty, he continued: "Now what can I do for you? From the Bar-20? Ah, yes; I was expecting you. We'll get right at it," and they did. Half an hour later they emerged on the street, free to take in the town, or to have the town take them in, —which was usually the case.

"What was that he said for us to keep away from?" asked Johnny with keen interest.

"Sh! Not so loud," chuckled Hopalong, winking prodigiously.

Johnny pulled tentatively at his upper lip but before he could reply his companion had accosted a stranger.

"Friend, we're pilgrims in a strange land, an' we don't know the trails. Can you tell us where the docks are?"

"Certainly; glad to. You'll find them at the end of this street," and he smilingly waved them towards the section of the town which Jeremiah T. Jones had specifically and earnestly warned them to avoid.

"Wonder if you're as thirsty as me?" solicitously inquired Hopalong of his companion.

"I was just wondering the same," replied Johnny. "Say," he confided in a lower voice, "blamed if I don't feel sort of lost without that Colt. Every time I lifts my right laig she goes too high-don't feel natural, nohow."

"Same here; I'm allus feeling to see if I lost it," Hopalong responded. "There ain't no rubbing, no weight, nor nothing."

"Wish I had something to put in its place, blamed if I don't."

"Why, now yo're talking-mebby we can buy something," grinned Hopalong, happily. "Here's a hardware store-come on in."

The clerk looked up and laid aside his novel. "Good-morning, gentlemen; what can I do for you? We've just got in some fine new rifles," he suggested.

The customers exchanged looks and it was Hopalong who first found his voice. "Nope, don't want no rifles," he replied, glancing around. "To tell the truth, I don't know just what we do want, but we want something, all right-got to have it. It's a funny thing, come to think of it; I can't never pass a hardware store without going in an' buying something. I've been told my father was the same way, so I must inherit it. It's the same with my pardner, here, only he gets his weakness from his whole family, and it's different from mine. He can't pass a saloon without going in an' buying something."

"Yo're a cheerful liar, an' you know it," retorted Johnny. "You know the reason why I goes in saloons so much-you'd never leave 'em if I didn't drag you out. He inherits that weakness from his grandfather, twice removed," he confided to the astonished clerk, whose expression didn't know what to express.

"Let's see: a saw?" soliloquized Hopalong. "Nope; got lots of 'em, an' they're all genuine Colts," he mused thoughtfully. "Axe? Nails? Augurs? Corkscrews? Can we use a corkscrew, Johnny? Ah, thought I'd wake you up. Now, what was it Cookie said for us to bring him? Bacon? Got any bacon? Too bad-oh, don't apologize; it's all right. Cold chisels-that's the thing if you ain't got no bacon. Let me see a three-pound cold chisel about as big as that," — extending a huge and crooked forefinger, —"an' with a big bulge at one end. Straight in the middle, circling off into a three-cornered wavy edge on the other side. What? Look here! You can't tell us nothing about saloons that we don't know. I want a three-pound cold chisel, any kind, so it's cold."

Johnny nudged him. "How about them wedges?"

"Twenty-five cents a pound," explained the clerk, groping for his bearings.

"They might do," Hopalong muttered, forcing the article mentioned into his holster. "Why, they're quite hocus-pocus. You take the brother to mine, Johnny."

"Feels good, but I dunno," his companion muttered. "Little wide at the sharp end. Hey, got any loose shot?" he suddenly asked, whereat Hopalong beamed and the clerk gasped. It didn't seem to matter whether they bought bacon, cold chisels, wedges, or shot; yet they looked sober.

"Yes, sir; what size?"

"Three pounds of shot, I said!" Johnny rumbled in his throat. "Never mind what size."

"We never care about size when we buy shot," Hopalong smiled. "But, Johnny, wouldn't them little screws be better?" he asked, pointing eagerly.

"Mebby; reckon we better get 'em mixed-half of each," Johnny gravely replied. "Anyhow, there ain't much difference."

The clerk had been behind that counter for four years, and executing and filling orders had become a habit with him; else he would have given them six pounds of cold chisels and corkscrews, mixed. His mouth was still open when he weighed out the screws.

"Mix 'em! Mix 'em!" roared Hopalong, and the stunned clerk complied, and charged them for the whole purchase at the rate set down for screws.

Hopalong started to pour his purchase into the holster which, being open at the bottom, gayly passed the first instalment through to the floor. He stopped and looked appealingly at Johnny, and Johnny, in pain from holding back screams of laughter, looked at him indignantly. Then a guileless smile crept over Hopalong's face and he stopped the opening with a wad of wrapping paper and disposed of the shot and screws, Johnny following his laudable example. After haggling a moment over the bill they paid it and walked out, to the apparent joy of the clerk.

"Don't laugh, Kid; you'll spoil it all," warned Hopalong, as he noted signs of distress on his companion's face. "Now, then; what was it we said about thirst? Come on; I see one already."

Having entered the saloon and ordered, Hopalong beamed upon the bartender and shoved his glass back again. "One more, kind stranger; it's good stuff."

"Yes, feels like a shore-enough gun," remarked Johnny, combining two thoughts in one expression, which is brevity.

The bartender looked at him quickly and then stood quite still and listened, a puzzled expression on his face.

Tic-tickety-tick-tic-tic, came strange sounds from the other side of the bar. Hopalong was intently studying a chromo on the wall and Johnny gazed vacantly out of the window.

"What's that? What in the deuce is that?" quickly demanded the man with the apron, swiftly reaching for his bung-starter.

Tickety-tic-tic-tic-tic-tic, the noise went on, and Hopalong, slowly rolling his eyes, looked at the floor. A screw rebounded and struck his foot, while shot were rolling recklessly.

"Them's making the noise," Johnny explained after critical survey.

"Hang it! I knowed we ought to 'a' got them wedges!" Hopalong exclaimed, petulantly, closing the bottom of the sheath. "Why, I won't have no gun left soon 'less I holds it in." The complaint was plaintive.

"Must be filtering through the stopper," Johnny remarked. "But don't it sound nice, especially when it hits that brass cuspidor!"

The bartender, grasping the mallet even more firmly, arose on his toes and peered over the bar, not quite sure of what he might discover. He had read of infernal machines although he had never seen one. "What the blazes!" he exclaimed in almost a whisper; and then his face went hard. "You get out of here, quick! You've had too much already! I've seen drunks, but —G'wan! Get out!"

"But we ain't begun yet," Hopalong interposed hastily. "You see —"

"Never mind what I see! I'd hate to see what you'll be seeing before long. God help you when you finish!" rather impolitely interrupted the bartender. He waved the mallet and made for the end of the counter with no hesitancy and lots of purpose in his stride. "G'wan, now! Get out!"

"Come on, Johnny; I'd shoot him only we didn't put no powder with the shot," Hopalong remarked sadly, leading the way out of the saloon and towards the hardware store.

"You better get out!" shouted the man with the mallet, waving the weapon defiantly. "An' don't you never come back again, neither," he warned.

"Hey, it leaked," Hopalong said pleasantly as he closed the door of the hardware store behind him, whereupon the clerk jumped and reached for the sawed-off shotgun behind the counter. Sawed-off shotguns are great institutions for arguing at short range, almost as effective as dynamite in clearing away obstacles.

"Don't you come no nearer!" he cried, white of face. "You git out, or I'll let *this* leak, an' give you *all* shot, an' more than you can carry!"

"Easy! Easy there, pardner; we want them wedges," Hopalong replied, somewhat hurriedly. "The others ain't no good; I choked on the very first screw. Why, I wouldn't hurt you for the world," Hopalong assured him, gazing interestedly down the twin tunnels.

Johnny leaned over a nail keg and loosed the shot and screws into it, smiling with childlike simplicity as he listened to the tintinnabulation of the metal shower among the nails. "It *does* drop when you let go of it," he observed.

"Didn't I tell you it would? I allus said so," replied Hopalong, looking back to the clerk and the shotgun. "Didn't I, stranger?"

The clerk's reply was a guttural rumbling, ninety per cent profanity, and Hopalong, nodding wisely, picked up two wedges. "Johnny, here's yore gun. If this man will stop talking to hisself and drop that lead-sprayer long enough to take our good money, we'll wear em."

He tossed a gold coin on the table, and the clerk, still holding tightly to the shotgun, tossed the coin into the cash box and cautiously slid the change across the counter. Hopalong picked up the money and, emptying his holster into the nail keg, followed his companion to the street, in turn followed slowly by the suspicious clerk. The door slammed shut behind them, the bolt shot home, and the clerk sat down on a box and cogitated.

Hopalong hooked his arm through Johnny's and started down the street. "I wonder what that feller thinks about us, anyhow. I'm glad Buck sent Red over to El Paso instead of us. Won't he be mad when we tell him all the fun we've had?" he asked, grinning broadly.

They were to meet Red at Dent's store on the way back and ride home together.

They were strangely clad for their surroundings, the chaps glaringly out of place in the Seaman's Port, and winks were exchanged by the regular *habitues* when the two punchers entered the room and called for drinks. They were very tired and a little under the weather, for they had made the most of their time and spent almost all of their money; but any one counting on robbing them would have found them sober enough to look out for themselves. Night had found them ready to go to the hotel, but on the way they felt that they must have one more bracer, and finish their exploration of Jeremiah T. Jones' tabooed section. The town had begun to grow wearisome and they were vastly relieved when they realized that the rising sun would see them in the saddle and homeward bound, headed for God's country, which was the only place for cow-punchers after all.

"Long way from the home port, ain't you, mates?" queried a tar of Hopalong. Another seaman went to the bar to hold a short, whispered consultation with the bartender, who at first frowned and then finally nodded assent.

"Too far from home, if that's what yo're driving at," Hopalong replied. "Blast these hard trails-my feet are shore on the prod. Ever meet my side pardner? Johnny, here's a friend of mine, a salt-water puncher, an' he's welcome to the job, too."

Johnny turned his head ponderously and nodded. "Pleased to meet you, stranger. An' what'll you all have?"

"Old Holland, mate," replied the other, joining them.

"All up!" invited Hopalong, waving them forward. "Might as well do things right or not at all. Them's my sentiments, which I holds as proper. Plain rye, general, if you means me," he replied to the bartender's look of inquiry.

He drained the glass and then made a grimace. "Tastes a little off-reckon it's my mouth; nothing tastes right in this cussed town. Now, up on our —" He stopped and caught at the bar. "Holy smoke! That's shore alcohol!"

Johnny was relaxing and vainly trying to command his will power. "Something's wrong; what's the matter?" he muttered sleepily.

"Guess you meant beer; you ain't used to drinking whiskey," grinned the bartender, derisively, and watching him closely.

"I can-drink as much whiskey as —" and, muttering, Johnny slipped to the floor.

"That wasn't whiskey!" cried Hopalong, sleepily, "that liquor was *fixed*!" he shouted, sudden anger bracing him. "An' I'm going to fix *you*, too!" he added, reaching for his gun, and drawing forth a wedge. His sailor friend leaped at him, to go down like a log, and Hopalong, seething with rage, wheeled and threw the weapon at the man behind the bar, who also went down. The wedge, glancing from his skull, swept a row of bottles and glasses from the shelf and, caroming, went through the window.

In an instant Hopalong was the vortex of a mass of struggling men and, handicapped as he was, fought valiantly, his rage for the time neutralizing the effects of the drug. But at last, too sleepy to stand or think, he, too, went down.

"By the Lord, that man's a fighter!" enthusiastically remarked the leader, gently touching his swollen eye. "George must 'a' put an awful dose in that grog."

"Lucky for us he didn't have no gun-the wedge was bad enough," groaned a man on the floor, slowly sitting up. "Whoever swapped him that wedge for his gun did us a good turn, all right."

A companion tentatively readjusted his lip. "I don't envy Wilkins his job breaking in that man when he gets awake."

"Don't waste no time, mates," came the order. "Up with 'em an' aboard. We've done our share; let the mate do his, an' be hanged. Hullo, Portsmouth; coming around, eh?" he asked the man who had first felt the wedge. "I was scared you was done for that time."

"No more shanghaiing hair pants for me, no more!" thickly replied Portsmouth. "Oh, my head, it's bust open!"

"Never mind about the bartender-let him alone; we can't waste no time with him now!" commanded the leader sharply. "Get these fellers on board before we're caught with 'em. We want our money after that."

"All clear!" came a low call from the lookout at the door, and soon a shadowy mass surged across the street and along a wharf. There was a short pause as a boat emerged out of the gloom, some whispered orders, and then the squeaking of oars grew steadily fainter in the direction of a ship which lay indistinct in the darkness.

Chapter II
The Rebound

A man moaned and stirred restlessly in a bunk, muttering incoherently. A stampeded herd was thundering over him, the grinding hoofs beating him slowly to death. He saw one mad steer stop and lower its head to gore him and just as the sharp horns touched his skin, he awakened. Slowly opening his bloodshot eyes he squinted about him, sick, weak, racking with pain where heavy shoes had struck him in the melee, his head reverberating with roars which seemed almost to split it open. Slowly he regained his full senses and began to make out his surroundings. He was in a bunk which moved up and down, from side to side, and was never still. There was a small, round window near his feet-thank heaven it was open, for he was almost suffocated by the foul air and the heat. Where was he? What had happened? Was there a salty odor in the air, or was he still dreaming? Painfully raising himself on one elbow he looked around and caught sight of a man in the bunk across. It was Johnny Nelson! Then, bit by bit, the whole thing came to him and he cursed heartily as he reviewed it and reached the only possible conclusion. He was at sea! He, Hopalong Cassidy, the best fighting unit of a good fighting outfit, shanghaied and at sea! Drugged, beaten, and stolen to labor on a ship.

Johnny was muttering and moaning and Hopalong slowly climbed out of the narrow bunk, unsteadily crossed the moving floor, and shook him. "Reckon he's in a stampede, too!" he growled. "They shore raised h —l with us. Oh, what a beating we got! But we'll pass it along with trimmings."

Johnny's eyes opened and he looked around in confusion. "Wha', Hopalong!"

"Yes; it's me, the prize idiot of a blamed good pair of 'em. How'd you feel?"

"Sleepy an' sick. My eyes ache an' my head's splitting. Where's Buck an' the rest?"

Hopalong sat down on the edge of the bunk and sore luridly, eloquently, beautifully, with a fervor and polish which left nothing to be desired in that line, and caused his companion to gaze at him in astonishment.

"I had a mighty bad dream, but you must 'a' had one a whole lot worse, to listen to you," Johnny remarked. "Gee, you're going some! What's the matter with you. You sick, too?"

Thereupon Hopalong unfolded the tale of woe and when Johnny had grasped its import and knew that his dream had been a stern reality, he straightway loosed his vocabulary and earned a draw. "Well, I'm going back again," he finished, with great decision, arising to make good his assertion.

"Swim or walk?" asked Hopalong nonchalantly.

"Huh! Oh, Lord!"

"Well, I ain't going to either swim or walk," Hopalong soliloquized. "I'm just going to stay right here in this one-by-nothing cellar an' spoil the health an' good looks of any pirate that comes down that ladder to get me out." He looked around, interested in life once more, and his trained eye grasped the strategic worth of their position. "Only one at a time, an' down that ladder," he mused, thoughtfully. "Why, Johnny, we owns this range as long as we wants to. They can't get us out. But, say, if only we had our guns!" he sighed, regretfully.

"You're right as far as you go; but you don't go to the eating part. We'll starve, an' we ain't got no water. I can drink about a bucketful right now," moodily replied his companion.

"Well, yo're right; but mebby we can find food an' water."

"Don't see no signs of none. Hey!" Johnny exclaimed, smiling faintly in his misery. "Let's get busy an' burn the cussed thing up! Got any matches?"

"First you want to drown yoreself swimming, an' now you want to roast the pair of us to death," Hopalong retorted, eyeing the rear wall of the room. "Wonder what's on the other side of that partition?"

Johnny looked. "Why, water; an' lots of it, too."

"Naw; the water is on the other sides."

"Then how do I know?—sh! I hear somebody coming on the roof."

"Tumble back in yore bunk-quick!" Hopalong hurriedly whispered. "Be asleep-if he comes down here it'll be our deal."

The steps overhead stopped at the companionway and a shadow appeared across the small patch of sunlight on the floor of the forecastle. "Tumble up here, you blasted loafers!" roared a deep voice.

No reply came from the forecastle-the silence was unbroken.

"If I have to come down there I'll —" the first mate made promises in no uncertain tones and in very impolite language. He listened for a moment, and having very good ears and hearing nothing, made more promises and came down the ladder quickly and nimbly.

"*I'll* bring you to," he muttered, reaching a brawny hand for Hopalong's nose, and missing. But he made contact with his own face, which stopped a short-arm blow from the owner of the aforesaid nose, a jolt full of enthusiasm and purpose. Beautiful and dazzling flashes of fire filled the air and just then something landed behind his ear and prolonged the pyrotechnic display. When the skyrockets went up he lost interest in the proceedings and dropped to the floor like a bag of meal.

Hopalong cut another piece from the rope in his hand and watched his companion's busy fingers. "Tie him good, Johnny; he's the only ace we've drawn in this game so far, an' we mustn't lose him."

Johnny tied an extra knot for luck and leaned forward, his eyes riveted on the bump under the victim's coat. His darting hand brought into sight that which pleased him greatly. "Oh, joy! Here, Hoppy; you take it."

Hopalong turned the weapon over in his hand, spun the cylinder and gloated, the clicking sweet music to his ears. "Plumb full, too! I never reckoned I'd ever be so tickled over a snub-nosed gun like this-but I feel like singing!"

"An' I feel like dying," grunted Johnny, grabbing at his stomach. "If the blamed shack would only stand still!" he groaned, gazing at the floor with strong disgust. "I don't reckon I've ever been so blamed sick in all my —" the sentence was unfinished, for the open porthole caught his eye and he leaped forward to use it for a collar.

Hopalong gazed at him in astonishment and sudden pity took possession of him as his pallid companion left the porthole and faced him.

"You ought to have something to eat, Kid —I'm purty hungry myself-what the blazes!" he exclaimed, for Johnny's protesting wail was finished outside the port. Then a light broke upon him and he wondered how soon it would be his turn to pay tribute to Neptune.

"Mr. Wilkins!" shouted a voice from the deck, and Hopalong moved back a step. "Mr. Wilkins!" After a short silence the voice soliloquized: "Guess he changed his mind about it; I'll get 'em up for him," and feet came into view. When halfway down the ladder the second mate turned his head and looked blankly down a gun barrel while a quiet but angry voice urged him further: "Keep a-coming, keep a-coming!" The second mate complained, but complied.

"Stick 'em up higher-now, Johnny, wobble around behind the nice man an' take *his* gun-you shut yore yap! I'm bossing this trick, not you. Got it, Kid? There's the rope-that's right. Nobody'd think you sick to see you work. Well, that's a good draw; but it's only a pair of aces against a full, at that. Wonder who'll be the next. Hope it's the foreman."

Johnny, keeping up by sheer grit, pointed to the rear wall. "What about that?"

For reply his companion walked over to it, put his shoulder to it and pushed. He stepped back and hurled his weight against it, but it was firm despite its squeaking protest. Then he examined it foot by foot and found a large knot, which he drove in by a blow of the gun. Bending, he squinted through the opening for a full minute and then reported:

"Purty black in there at this end, but up at the other there's a light from a hole in the roof, an' I could see boxes an' things like that. I reckon it's the main cellar."

"If we could get out at the other end with that gun you've got we could raise blazes for a while," suggested Johnny. "Anyhow, mebby they can come at us that way when they find out what we've gone an' done."

"Yo're right," Hopalong replied, looking around. Seeing an iron bar he procured it and, pushing it through the knot hole in the partition, pulled. The board, splitting and cracking under the attack, finally broke from its fastenings with a sharp report, and Hopalong, pulling it aside, stepped out of sight of his companion. Johnny was grinning at the success of his plan when he was interrupted.

"Ahoy, down there!" yelled a stentorian voice from above. "Mr. Wilkins! What the devil are you doing so long?" and after a very short wait other feet came into sight. Just then the second mate, having managed to slip off the gag, shouted warning:

"Look out, Captain! They've got us and our guns! One of them has —" but Johnny's knee thudded into his chest and ended the sentence as a bullet sent a splinter flying from under the captain's foot.

"Hang these guns!" Johnny swore, and quickly turned to secure the gag in the mouth of the offending second mate. "You make any more yaps like that an' I'll wing you for keeps with yore own gun!" he snapped. "We're caught in yore trap an' we'll fight to a finish. You'll be the first to go under if you gets any smart."

"Ahoy, men!" roared the captain in a towering rage, dancing frantically about on the deck and shouting for the crew to join him. He filled the air with picturesque profanity and stamped and yelled in passion at such rank mutiny.

"Hand grenades! Hand grenades!" he cried. Then he remembered that his two mates were also below and would share in the mutineers' fate, and his rage increased at his galling helplessness. When he had calmed sufficiently to think clearly he realized that it was certain death for any one to attempt going down the ladder, and that his must be a waiting game. He glanced at his crew, thirteen good men, all armed with windlass bars and belaying pins, and gave them orders. Two were to watch the hatch and break the first head to appear, while the others returned to work. Hunger and thirst would do the rest. And what joy would be his when they were forced to surrender!

Hopalong groped his way slowly towards the patch of light, barking his shins, stumbling and falling over the barrels and crates and finally, losing his footing at a critical moment, tumbled down upon a box marked "Cotton." There was a splintering crash and the very faint clink of metal. Dazed and bruised, he sat up and felt of himself-and found that he had lost his gun in the fall.

"Now, where in blazes did it fly to?" he muttered angrily, peering about anxiously. His eyes suddenly opened their widest and he stared in surprise at a field gun which covered him; and then he saw parts of two more.

"Good Lord! Is this a gunboat?" he cried. "Are we up against bluejackets an' Uncle Sam?" He glanced quickly back the way he had come when he heard Johnny's shot, but he could see nothing. He figured that Johnny had sense enough to call for help if he needed it, and put that possibility out of his mind. "Naw, this ain't no gunboat-the Government don't steal men; it enlists 'em. But it's a funny pile of junk, all the same. Where in blazes is that toy gun? *Well*, I'll be hanged!" and he plunged toward the "Cotton" box he had burst in his descent, and worked at it frantically.

"Winchesters! Winchesters!" he cried, dragging out two of them. "Whoop! Now for the cartridges-there shore must be some to go with these guns!" He saw a keg marked "Nails," and managed to open it after great labor-and found it full of army Colts. Forcing down the desire to turn a handspring, he slipped one of the six-shooters in his empty holster and patted it lovingly. "Old friend, I'm shore glad to see you, all right. You've been used, but that don't make no difference." Searching further, he opened a full box of *machetes*, and soon after found cartridges of many kinds and calibres. It took him but a few minutes to make his selection and cram his pockets with them. Then he filled two Colts and two Winchesters-and executed a short jig to work off the dangerous pressure of his exuberance.

"But what an unholy lot of weapons," he soliloquized on his way back to Johnny. "An' they're all second-hand. Cannons, too-an' *machetes*!" he exclaimed, suddenly understanding. "Jumping Jerusalem! —a filibustering expedition bound for Cuba, or one of them wildcat republics down south! Oh, ho, my friends; I see where you have bit off more'n you can chew." In his haste to impart the joyous news to his companion, he barked his shins shamefully.

"'Way down south in the land o' cotton, cinnamon seed an'" —whoa, blast you!" and Hopalong stuck his head through the opening in the partition and grinned. "Heard you shoot, Kid; I reckoned you might need me-an' these!" he finished, looking fondly upon the weapons as he shoved them into the forecastle.

Johnny groaned and held his stomach, but his eyes lighted up when he saw the guns, and he eagerly took one of each kind, a faint smile wreathing his lips. "Now we'll show these water snakes what kind of men they stole," he threatened.

Up on the deck the choleric captain still stamped and swore, and his crew, with well-concealed mirth, went about their various duties as if they were accustomed to have shanghaied men act this way. They sympathized with the unfortunate pair, realizing how they themselves would feel if shanghaied to break broncos.

Hogan, A. B., stated the feelings of his companions very well in his remarks to the men who worked alongside: "In me hear-rt I'm dommed glad av it, Yensen. I hope they bate the old man at his own game. 'T is a shame in these days for honest men to be took in that unlawful way. I've heard me father tell of the press gangs on the other side, an' 't is small business."

Yensen looked up to reply, chanced to glance aft, and dropped his calking iron in his astonishment. "Yumping Yimminy! Luk at dat fallar!"

Hogan looked. "The deuce! That's a man after me own heat-rt! Kape yore pagan mouth shut! If ye take a hand agin 'em I'll swab up the deck wid yez. G'wan wor-rking like a sane man, ye ijit!"

"Ay ent ban fight wit dat fallar! Luk at the gun!"

A man had climbed out of the after hatch and was walking rapidly towards them, a rifle in his hands, while at his thigh swung a Colt. He watched the two seamen closely and caught sight of Hogan's twinkling blue eyes, and a smile quivered about his mouth. Hogan shut and opened one eye and went on working.

As soon as Hopalong caught sight of the captain, the rifle went up and he announced his presence without loss of time. "Throw up yore hands, you pole-cat! I'm running this ranch from now on!"

The captain wheeled with a jerk and his mouth opened, and then clicked shut as he started forward, his rage acting galvanically. But he stopped quickly enough when he looked down the barrel of the Winchester and glared at the cool man behind it.

"What the blank are you doing?" he yelled.

"Well, I ain't kidnapping cow-punchers to steal my boat," replied Hopalong. "An' you fellers stand still or I'll drop you cold!" he ordered to the assembled and restless crew. "Johnny!" he shouted, and his companion popped up through the hatch like a jack-in-the-box. "Good boy, Johnny. Tie this coyote foreman like you did the others," he ordered. While Johnny obeyed, Hopalong looked around the circle, and his eyes rested on Hogan's face, studying it, and found something there which warmed his heart. "Friend, do you know the back trail? Can you find that runt of a town we left?"

"Aye, aye."

"Shore, you; who'd you think I was talking to? Can you find the way back, the way we came?"

"Shure an' I can that, if I'm made to."

"You'll swing for mutiny if you do, you bilge-wallering pirate!" roared the trussed captain. "Take that gun away from him, d'ye hear!" he yelled at the crew. "I'm captain of this ship, an' I'll hang every last one of you if you don't obey orders! This is mutiny!"

"You won't do no hanging with that load of weapons below!" retorted Hopalong. "Uncle Sam is looking for filibusters-this here gun is 'cotton,'" he said, grinning. He turned to the crew. "But you fellers are due to get shot if you sees her through," he added.

"I'm captain of this ship —" began the helpless autocrat.

"You shore look like it, all right," Hopalong replied, smiling. "If yo're the captain you order her turned around and headed over the back trail, or I'll drop you overboard off yore own ship!" Then fierce anger at the thought of the indignities and injuries he and his companion had suffered swept over him and prompted a one-minute speech which left no doubt as to what he would do if his demand was not complied with. Johnny, now free to watch the crew, added a word or two of endorsement, and he acted a little as if he rather hoped it would not be complied with: he itched for an excuse.

The captain did some quick thinking; the true situation could not be disguised, and with a final oath of rage he gave in. "'Bout ship, Hogan; nor' by nor'west," he growled, and the seaman started away to execute the command, but was quickly stopped by Hopalong.

"Hogan, is that right?" he demanded. "No funny business, or we'll clean up the whole bunch, an' blamed quick, too!"

"That's the course, sor. That's the way back to town. I can navigate, an' me orders are plain. Ye're Irish, by the way av ye, and 't is back to town ye go, sor!" He turned to the crew: "Stand by, me boys." And in a short time the course was nor' by nor'west.

The return journey was uneventful and at nightfall the ship lay at anchor off the low Texas coast, and a boat loaded with men grounded on the sandy beach. Four of them arose and leaped out into the mild surf and dragged the boat as high up on the sand as it would go. Then the two cow-punchers followed and one of them gave a low-spoken order to the Irishman at his side.

"Yes, sor," replied Hogan, and hastened to help the captain out onto the sand and to cut the ropes which bound him. "Do ye want the mates, too, sor?" he asked, glancing at the trussed men in the boat.

"No; the foreman's enough," Hopalong responded, handing his weapons to Johnny and turning to face the captain, who was looking into Johnny's gun as he rubbed his arms to restore perfect circulation.

"Now, you flat-faced coyote, yo're going to get the beating of yore life, an' I'm going to give it to you!" Hopalong cried, warily advancing upon the man whom he held to be responsible for the miseries of the past twenty-four hours. "You didn't give me a square deal, but I'm man enough to give you one! When you drug an' steal any more cow-punchers —" action stopped his words.

It was a great fight. A filibustering sea captain is no more peaceful than a wild boar and about as dangerous; and while this one was not at his best, neither was Hopalong. The latter luckily had acquired some knowledge of the rudiments of the game and had the vigor of youth to oppose to the captain's experience and his infuriated but well-timed rushes. The seamen, for the honor of their calling and perhaps with a mind to the future, cheered on the captain and danced up and down in their delight and excitement. They had a lot of respect for the prowess of their master, and for the man who could stand up against him in a fair and square fist fight. To give assistance to either in a fair fight was not to be thought of, and Johnny's gun was sufficient after-excuse for non-interference.

The *sop! sop!* of the punishing blows as they got home and the steady circling of Hopalong in avoiding the dangerous attacks, went on minute after minute. Slowly the captain's strength was giving out, and he resorted to trickery as his last chance. Retreating, he half raised his arms and lowered them as if weary, ready as a cat to strike with all his weight if the other gave an opening. It ought to have worked-it had worked before-but Hopalong was there to win, and without the momentary hesitation of the suspicious fighter he followed the retreat and his hard hand flashed in over the captain's guard a fraction of a second sooner than that surprised gentleman anticipated. The ferocious frown gave way to placid peace and the captain reclined at the feet of the battered victor, who stood waiting for him to get up and fight. The captain lay without a sign of movement and as Hopalong wondered, Hogan was the first to speak.

"Fer the love av hiven, let him be! Ye needn't wait-he's done; I know by the sound av it!" he exclaimed, stepping forward. "'T was a purty blow, an' 't was a gr-rand foight ye put up, sor! A gr-rand foight, but any more av that is murder! 'T is an Irishman's game, sor, an' ye did yersilf proud. But now let him be-no man, least av all a Dootchman, iver tuk more than that an' lived!"

Hopalong looked at him and slowly replied between swollen lips, "Yo're right, Hogan; we're square now, I reckon."

"That's right, sor," Hogan replied, and turned to his companions. "Put him in the boat; an' mind ye handle him gintly-we'll be sailing under him soon. Now, sor, if it's yer pleasure, I'll be after saying good-bye to ye, sor; an' to ye, too," he said, shaking hands with both punches. "Fer a sick la-ad ye're a wonder, ye are that," he smiled at Johnny, "but ye want to kape away from the water fronts. Good-bye to ye both, an' a pleasant journey home. The town is tin miles to me right, over beyant them hills."

"Good-bye, Hogan," mumbled Hopalong gratefully. "Yo're square all the way through; an' if you ever get out of a job or in any kind of trouble that I can help you out of, come up to the Bar-20 an' you won't have to ask twice. Good luck!" And the two sore and aching punchers, wiser in the ways of the world, plodded doggedly towards the town, ten miles away.

The next morning found them in the saddle, bound for Dent's hotel and store near the San Miguel Canyon. When they arrived at their destination and Johnny found there was some hours to wait for Red, his restlessness sent him roaming about the country, not so much "seeking what he might devour" as hoping something might seek to devour him. He was so sore over his recent kidnapping that he longed to find a salve. He faithfully promised Hopalong that he would return at noon.

Chapter III
Dick Martin Starts Something

Dick Martin slowly turned, leaned his back against the bar, and languidly regarded a group of Mexicans at the other end of the room. Singly, or in combinations of two or more, each was imparting all he knew, or thought he knew about the ghost of San Miguel Canyon. Their fellow-countryman, new to the locality, seemed properly impressed. That it was the ghost of

Carlos Martinez, murdered nearly one hundred years before at the big bend in the canyon, was conceded by all; but there was a dispute as to why it showed itself only on Friday nights, and why it was never seen by any but a Mexican. Never had a Gringo seen it. The Mexican stranger was appealed to: Did this not prove that the murder had been committed by a Mexican? The stranger affected to consider the question.

Martin surveyed them with outward impassiveness and inward contempt. A realist, a cynic, and an absolute genius with a Colt .45, he was well known along the border for his dare-devil exploits and reckless courage. The brainiest men in the Secret Service, Lewis, Thomas, Sayre, and even old Jim Lane, the local chief, whose fingers at El Paso felt every vibration along the Rio Grande, were not as well known-except to those who had seen the inside of Government penitentiaries-and they were quite satisfied to be so eclipsed. But the Service knew of the ghost, as it knew everything pertaining to the border, and gave it no serious thought; if it took interest in all the ghosts and superstitions peculiar to the Mexican temperament it would have no time for serious work. Martin once, in a spirit of savage denial, had wasted the better part of several successive Friday nights in the San Miguel, but to no avail. When told that the ghost showed itself only to Mexicans he had shrugged his shoulders eloquently and laughed, also eloquently.

"A Greaser," he replied, "is one-half fear and superstition, an' the other half imagination. There ain't no ghosts, but I know the *Greasers* have seen 'em, all right. A Greaser can see anything scary if he makes up his mind to. If *I* ever see one an' he keeps on being one after I shoot, I'll either believe in ghosts, or quit drinking." His eyes twinkled as he added: "An' of the two, I think I'd *prefer* to see ghosts!"

He was flushed and restless with deviltry. His fifth glass always made him so; and to-night there was an added stimulus. He believed the strange Mexican to be Juan Alvarez, who was so clever that the Government had never been able to convict him. Alvarez was fearless to recklessness and Martin, eager to test him, addressed the group with the blunt terseness for which he was famed, and hated.

"Greasers are cowards," he asserted quietly, and with a smile which invited excitement. He took a keen delight in analyzing the expressions on the faces of those hit. It was one of his favorite pastimes when feeling coltish.

The group was shocked into silence, quickly followed by great unrest and hot, muttered words. Martin did not move a muscle, the smile was set, but between the half-closed eyelids crouched Combat, on its toes. The Mexicans knew it was there without looking for it-the tone of his voice, the caressing purr of his words, and his unnatural languor were signs well known to them. Not a criminal sneaking back from voluntary banishment in Mexico who had seen those signs ever forgot them, if he lived. Martin watched the group cat-like, keenly scrutinizing each face, reading the changing emotions in every shifting expression; he had this art down so well that he could tell when a man was debating the pull of a gun, and beat him on the draw by a fraction of a second.

"De senor ees meestak," came the reply, as quiet and caressing as the words which provoked it. The strange Mexican was standing proudly and looking into the squinting eyes with only a grayness of face and a tigerish litheness to tell what he felt.

"None go through the canyon after dark on Fridays," purred Martin.

"*I* go tro' de canyon nex' Friday night. Eef I do, then you mak apology to me?"

"I'll limit my remark to all but one Greaser."

The Mexican stepped forward. "I tak' thees gloove an' leave eet at de Beeg Ben', for you to fin' in daylight," he said, tapping one of Martin's gauntlets which lay on the bar. "You geev' me eet befo' I go?"

"Yes; at nine o'clock to-morrow night," Martin replied, hiding his elation. He was sure that he knew the man now.

The Mexican, cool and smiling, bowed and left the room, his companions hastening after him.

"Well, I'll bet twenty-five dollars he flunks!" breathed the bartender, straightening up.

Martin turned languidly and smiled at him. "I'll take that, Charley," he replied.

Johnny Nelson was always late, and on this occasion he was later than usual. He was to have joined Hopalong and Red, if Red had arrived, at Dent's at noon the day before, and now it was after nine o'clock at night as he rode through San Felippe without pausing and struck east for the canyon. The dropping trail down the canyon was serious enough in broad daylight, but at night to attempt its passage was foolhardy, unless one knew every turn and slant by heart, which Johnny did not. He was thirty-three hours late now, and he was determined to make up what he could in the next three.

When Johnny left Hopalong at Dent's he had given his word to be back on time and not to keep his companions waiting, for Red might be on time and he would chafe if he were delayed. But, alas for Johnny's good intentions, his course took him through a small Mexican hamlet in which lived a senorita of remarkable beauty and rebellious eyes; and Johnny tarried in the town most of the day, riding up and down the streets, practising the nice things he would say if he met her. She watched him from the heavily draped window, and sighed as she wondered if her dashing Americano would storm the house and carry her off like the knights of old. Finally he had to turn away with heavy and reluctant heart, promising himself that he would return when no petulant and sarcastic companions were waiting for him. Then-ah! what dreams youth knows.

Half an hour ahead of him on another trail rode Juan, smiling with satisfaction. He had come to San Felippe to get a look at the canyon on Friday nights, and Martin had given him an excuse entirely unexpected. For this he was truly grateful, even while he knew that the American had tried to pick a quarrel with him and thus rid the border of a man entirely too clever for the good of customs receipts; and failing in that, had hoped the treacherous canyon trail would gain that end in another manner. Old Jim Lane's fingers touched wires not one whit more sensitive than those which had sent Juan Alvarez to look over the San Miguel-and Lane's wires had been slow this time. When Juan had left the saloon the night before and had seen Manuel slip away from the group and ride off into the north, he had known that the ghost would show itself the following night.

But Juan was to be disappointed. He was still some distance from the canyon when a snarling bulk landed on the haunches of his horse. He jerked loose his gun and fired twice and then knew nothing. When he opened his eyes he lay quietly, trying to figure it out with a head throbbing with pain from his fall. The cougar must have been desperate for food to attack a man. He moved his foot and struck something soft and heavy. His shots had been lucky, but they had not saved him his horse and a sprained arm and leg. There would be no gauntlet found at the Big Bend at daylight.

When Johnny Nelson reached the twin boulders marking the beginning of the sloping run where the trail pitched down, he grinned happily at sight of the moon rising over the low hills and then grabbed at his holster, while every hair in his head stood up curiously. A wild, haunting, feminine scream arose to a quavering soprano and sobbed away into silence. No words can adequately describe the unearthly wail in that cry and it took a full half-minute for Johnny to become himself again and to understand what it was. Once more it arose, nearer, and Johnny peered into the shadows along a rough backbone of rock, his Colt balanced in his half-raised hand.

"You come 'round me an' you'll get hurt," he muttered, straining his eyes to peer into the blackness of the shadows. "Come on out, Soft-foot; the moon's yore finish. You an' me will have it out right here an' now —I don't want no cougar trailing me through that ink-black canyon on a two-foot ledge —" he thought he saw a shadow glide across a dim patch of moonlight, but when his smoke rifted he knew he had missed. "Damn it! You've got a mate 'round here somewhere," he complained. "Well, I'll have to chance it, anyhow. Come on, bronc! Yo're shaking like a leaf-get out of this!"

When he began to descend into the canyon he allowed his horse to pick its own way without any guidance from him, and gave all of his attention to the trail behind him. The horse could get along better by itself in the dark, and it was more than possible that one or two lithe cougars might be slinking behind him on velvet paws. The horse scraped along gingerly, feeling its way step by step, and sending stones rattling and clattering down the precipice at his left to tinkle into the stream at the bottom.

"Gee, but I wish I'd not wasted so much time," muttered the rider uneasily. "This here canyon-cougar combination is the worst *I* ever butted up against. I'll never be late again, not never; not for all the girls in the world. Easy, bronc," he cautioned, as he felt the animal slip and quiver. "Won't this trail ever start going up again?" he growled petulantly, taking his eyes off the black back trail, where no amount of scrutiny showed him anything, and turned in the saddle to peer ahead-and a yell of surprise and fear burst from him, while chills ran up and down his spine. An unearthly, piercing shriek suddenly rang out and filled the canyon with ear-splitting uproar and a glowing, sheeted half-figure of a man floated and danced twenty feet from him and over the chasm. He jerked his gun and fired, but only once, for his mount had its own ideas about some things and this particular one easily headed the list. The startled rider grabbed reins and pommel, his blood congealed with fear of the precipice less than a foot from his side, and he gave all his attention to the horse. But scared as he was he heard, or thought that he heard, a peculiar sound when he fired, and he would have sworn that he hit the mark-the striking of the bullet was not drowned in the uproar and he would never forget the sound of that impact. He rounded Big Bend as if he were coming up to the judge's stand, and when he struck the upslant of the emerging trail he had made a record. Cold sweat beaded his forehead and he was trembling from head to foot when he again rode into the moonlight on the level plain, where he tried to break another record.

Chapter IV
Johnny Arrives

Meanwhile Hopalong and Red quarrelled petulantly and damned the erring Johnny with enthusiastic abandon, while Dent smiled at them and joked; but his efforts at levity made little impression on the irate pair. Red, true to his word, had turned up at the time set, in fact, he was half an hour ahead of time, for which miracle he endeavored to take great and disproportionate credit. Dent was secretly glad about the delay, for he found his place lonesome. He thoroughly enjoyed the company of the two gentlemen from the Bar-20, whose actions seemed to be governed by whims and who appeared to lack all regard for consequences; and they squabbled so refreshingly, and spent their money cheerfully. Now, if they would only wind up the day by fighting! Such a finish would be joy indeed. And speaking of fights, Dent was certain that Mr. Cassidy had been in one recently, for his face bore marks that could only be acquired in that way.

After supper the two guests had relapsed into a silence which endured only as long as the pleasing fulness. Then the squabbling began again, growing worse until they fell silent from lack of adequate expression. Finally Red once again spoke of their absent friend.

"We oughtn't get peevish, Hoppy-he's only thirty-six hours late," suggested Red. "An' he might be a week," he added thoughtfully, as his mind ran back over a long list of Johnny's misdeeds.

"Yes, he might. An' won't he have a fine cock-an'-bull tale to explain it," growled Hopalong, reminiscently. "His excuses are the worst part of it generally."

"Eh, does he-make excuses?" asked Dent, mildly surprised.

"He does to *us*," retorted Red savagely. "He's worse than a woman; take him all in all an' you've got the toughest proposition that ever wore pants. But he's a good feller, at that."

"Well, you've got a lot of nerve, you have!" retorted Hopalong. "You don't want to say anything about the Kid-if there's anybody that can beat him in being late an' acting the fool generally, it's you. An' what's more, you know it!"

Red wheeled to reply, but was interrupted by a sudden uproar outside, fluent swearing coming towards the house. The door opened with a bang, admitting a white-faced, big-eyed man with one leg jammed through the box he had landed on in dismounting.

"Gimme a drink, quick!" he shouted wildly, dragging the box over to the bar with a cheerful disregard for chairs and other temporary obstructions. "Gimme a drink!" he reiterated.

"Give you six hops in the neck!" yelled Red, missing and almost sitting down because of the enthusiasm he had put into his effort. Johnny side-stepped and ducked, and as he straightened up to ask for whys and wherefores, Red's eyes opened wide and he paused in his further intentions to stare at the apparition.

"Sick?" queried Hopalong, who was frightened.

"Gimme that drink!" demanded Johnny feverishly, and when he had it he leaned against the bar and mopped his face with a trembling hand.

"What's the matter with you, anyhow?" asked Red, with deep anxiety.

"Yes; for God's sake, what's happened to you?" demanded Hopalong.

Johnny breathed deeply and threw back his shoulders as if to shake off a weight. "Fellers, I had a cougar soft-footing after me in that dark canyon, my cayuse ran away on a two-foot ledge up the wall, —an'—I—saw—a—ghost!"

There was a respectful silence. Johnny, waiting a reasonable length of time for replies and exclamations, flushed a bit and repeated his frank and candid statement, adding a few adjectives to it. "*A real, screeching, flying ghost!* An' I'm going *home*, an' I'm going to *stay* there. I ain't never coming back no more, not for anything. Damn this border country, *anyhow!*"

The silence continued, whereupon Johnny grew properly indignant. "You act like I told you it was going to rain! Why don't you say something? Didn't you hear what I said, you fools!" he asked pugnaciously. "Are you in the habit of having a thing like that told you? Why don't you show some interest, you dod-blasted, thick-skulled wooden-heads?"

Red looked at Hopalong, Hopalong looked at Red, and then they both looked at Dent, whose eyes were fixed in a stare on Johnny.

"Huh!" snorted Hopalong, warily arising. "Was that all?" he asked, nodding at Red, who also arose and began to move cautiously toward their erring friend. "Didn't you see no more'n one ghost? Anybody that can see one ghost, an' no more, is wrong somewhere. Now, stop, an' think; didn't you see *two*?" He was advancing carefully while he talked, and Red was now behind the man who saw one ghost.

"Why, you —" there was a sudden flurry and Johnny's words were cut short in the melee.

"Good, Red! Ouch!" shouted Hopalong. "Look out! Got any rope, Dent? Well, hurry up: there ain't no telling what he'll do if he's loose. The mescal they sells down in this country ain't liquor-it's poison," he panted. "An' he can't even stand whiskey!"

Finding the rope was easier than finding a place to put it, and the unequal battle raged across the room and into the next, where it sounded as if the house were falling down. Johnny's voice was shrill and full of vexation and his words were extremely impolite and lacked censoring. His feet appeared to be numerous and growing rapidly, judging from the amount of territory they covered and defended, and Red joyfully kicked Hopalong in the melee, which in this instance also stands for stomach; Red always took great pains to do more than his share in a scrimmage. Dent hovered on the flanks, his hands full of rope, and begged with great earnestness to be allowed to apply it to parts of Johnny's thrashing anatomy. But as the flanks continued to change with bewildering swiftness he begged in vain, and began to make suggestions and give advice pleasing to the three combatants. Dent knew just how it should be done, and was generous with the knowledge until Johnny zealously planted five knuckles on his one good eye, when the engagement became general.

The table skidded through the door on one leg and caromed off the bar at a graceful angle, collecting three chairs and one sand-box cuspidor on the way. The box on Johnny's leg had long since departed, as Hopalong's shin could testify. One chair dissolved unity and distributed itself lavishly over the room, while the bed shrunk silently and folded itself on top of Dent, who bucked it up and down with burning zeal and finally had sense enough to crawl from under it. He immediately celebrated his liberation by getting a strangle hold on two legs, one of which happened to be the personal property of Hopalong Cassidy; and the battle raged on a lower plane. Red raised one hand as he carefully traced a neck to its own proper head and then his steel fingers opened and swooped down and shut off the dialect. Hopalong pushed Dent off him and managed to catch Johnny's flaying arm on the third attempt, while Dent made tentative sorties against Johnny's spurred boots.

"Phew! Can he fight like that when he's sober?" reverently asked Dent, seeing how close his fingers could come to his gaudy eye without touching it. "I won't be able to see at all in an hour," he added, gloomily.

Hopalong, seated on Johnny's chest, soberly made reply as he tenderly flirted with a raw shin. "It's the mescal. I'm going to slip some of that stuff into Pete's cayuse some of these days," he promised, happy with a new idea. Pete Wilson had no sense of humor.

"That ghost was plumb lucky," grunted Red, "an' so was the sea-captain," he finished as an afterthought, limping off toward the bar, slowly and painfully followed by his disfigured companions. "One drink; then to bed."

After Red had departed, Hopalong and Dent smoked a while and then, knocking the ashes out of his pipe, Hopalong arose. "An' yet, Dent, there are people that believe in ghosts," he remarked, with a vast and settled contempt.

Dent gave critical scrutiny to the scratched bar for a moment. "Well, the Greasers all say there *is* a ghost in the San Miguel, though I never saw it. But some of them have seen it, an' no Greasers ride that trail no more."

"Huh!" snorted Hopalong. "Some Greasers must have filled the Kid up on ghosts while he was filling hisself up on mescal. Ghosts? R-a-t-s!"

"It shows itself only to Greasers, an' then only on Friday nights," explained Dent, thoughtfully. This was Friday night. Others had seen that ghost, but they were all Mexicans; now that a "white" man of Johnny's undisputed calibre had been so honored Dent's skepticism wavered and he had something to think about for days to come. True, Johnny was not a Greaser; but even ghosts might make mistakes once in a while.

Hopalong laughed, dismissing the subject from his mind as being beneath further comment. "Well, we won't argue —I'm too tired. An' I'm sorry you got that eye, Dent."

"Oh, that's all right," hastily assured the store-keeper, smiling faintly. "I was just spoiling for a fight, an' now I've had it. Feels sort of good. Yes, first thing in the morning-breakfast'll be ready soon as you are. Good-night."

But the proprietor couldn't sleep. Finally he arose and tiptoed into the room where Johnny lay wrapped in the sleep of the exhausted. After cautious and critical inspection, which was made hard because of his damaged eye, he tiptoed back to his bunk, shaking his head slowly. "He wasn't drunk," he muttered. "He saw that ghost all right; an' I'll bet everything I've got on it!"

At daybreak three quarrelling punchers rode homeward and after a monotonous journey arrived at the bunk house and reported. It took them two nights adequately to describe their experiences to an envious audience. The morning after the telling of the ghost story things began to happen. Red starting it by erecting a sign.

NOTISE-NO GHOSTS ALOWED

An exuberant handful of the outfit watched him drive the last nail and step back to admire his work, and the running fire of comment covered all degrees of humor, and promised much hilarity in the future at the expense of the only man on the Bar-20 who had seen a ghost.

In a week Johnny and his acute vision had become a bye-word in that part of the country and his friends had made it a practice to stop him and gravely discuss spirit manifestations of all kinds. He had thrashed Wood Wright and been thrashed by Sandy Lucas in two beautiful and memorable fights and was only waiting to recover from the last affair before having the matter out with Rich Finn. These facts were beginning to have the effect he strove for; though Cowan still sold a new concoction of gin, brandy, and whiskey which he called "Flying Ghost," and which he proudly guaranteed would show more ghosts per drink than any liquor south of the Rio Grande-and some of his patrons were eager to back up his claims with real money.

This was the condition of affairs when Hopalong Cassidy strolled into Cowan's and forgot his thirst in the story being told by a strange Mexican. It was Johnny's ghost, without a doubt, and when he had carelessly asked a few questions he was convinced that Johnny had really seen something. On the way home he cogitated upon it and two points challenged his intelligence with renewed insistence: the ghost showed itself only on Friday, and then only to "Greasers." His suspicious mind would not rest until he had reviewed the question from all sides, and his opinion was that there was something more than spiritual about the ghost of the San Miguel-and a cold, practical reason for it.

When he rode into the corral at the ranch he saw that another sign had been put on the corral wall. He had destroyed the first, speaking his mind in full at the time. He swept his gloved hand upward with a rush, tore the flimsy board from its fastenings, broke it to pieces across his saddle, and tossed the fragments from him. He was angry, for he had warned the outfit that they were carrying the joke too far, that Johnny was giving way to hysterical rage more frequently, and might easily do something that they all would regret. And he felt sorry for the Kid; he knew what Johnny's feelings were and he made up his mind to start a few fights himself if the persecution did not cease. When he stepped into the bunk house and faced his friends they listened to a three-minute speech that made them squirm, and as he finished talking the deep voice of the foreman endorsed the promises he had just heard made, for Buck had entered the gallery without being noticed. The joke had come to an end.

When Johnny rode in that evening he was surprised to find Hopalong waiting for him a short distance from the corral and he replied to his friend's gesture by riding over to him. "What's up now?" he asked.

"Come along with me. I want to talk to you for a few minutes," and Hopalong led the way toward the open, followed by Johnny, who was more or less suspicious. Finally Hopalong stopped, turned, and looked his companion squarely in the eyes. "Kid, I'm in dead earnest. This ain't no fool joke-now you tell me what that ghost looked like, how he acted, an' all about it. I mean what I say, because now I know that you saw *something*. If it wasn't a ghost it was made to look like one, anyhow. Now go ahead."

"I've told you a dozen times already," retorted Johnny, his face flushing. "I've begged you to believe me an' told you that I wasn't fooling. How do I know you ain't now? I'm not going to tell —"

"Hold on; yes, you are. Yo're going to tell it slow, an' just like you saw it," Hopalong interrupted hastily. "I know I've doubted it, but who wouldn't! Wait a minute —I've done a heap of thinking in the past few days an' I know that you saw a ghost. Now, everybody knows that there ain't no such thing as ghosts; then what was it you saw? There's a game on, Kid, an' it's a dandy; an' you an' me are going to bust it up an' get the laugh on the whole blasted crowd, from Buck to Cowan."

Johnny's suspicions left him with a rush, for his old Hoppy was one man in a thousand, and when he spoke like that, with such sharp decision, Johnny knew what it meant. Hopalong listened intently and when the short account was finished he put out his hand and smiled.

"We're the fools, Kid; not you. There's something crooked going on in that canyon, an' I know it! But keep mum about what we think."

Johnny lost his grouch so suddenly and beamed upon his friends with such a superior air that they began to worry about what was in the wind. The suspense wore on them, for with Hopalong's assistance, Johnny might spring some game on them all that would more than pay up for the fun they had enjoyed at his expense; and the longer the suspense lasted the worse it became. They never lost sight of him while he was around and Hopalong had to endure the same surveillance; and it was no uncommon thing to see small groups of the anxious men engaged in deep discussion. When they found that Buck must have been told and noticed his smile was as fixed as Hopalong's or Johnny's, they were certain that trouble of some nature was in store for them.

Several weeks later Buck Peters drew rein and waited for a stranger to join him.

"Howdy. Is yore name Peters?" asked the newcomer, sizing him up in one trained glance.

"Well, who are you, an' what do you want?"

"I want to see Peters, Buck Peters. That yore name?"

"Yes; what of it?"

"My name's Fox. Old Jim Lane gave me a message for you," and the stranger spoke earnestly to some length. "There; that's the situation. We've got to have shrewd men that they don't know an' won't suspect. Lane wants to pay a couple of yore men their wages for a month or two. He said he was shore he could count on you to help him out."

"He's right; he can. I don't forget favors. I've got a couple of men that-there's one of 'em now. Hey, Hoppy! Whoop-e, Hoppy!"

Mr. Cassidy arrived quickly, listened eagerly, named Red and Johnny to accompany him, overruled his companions by insisting that if Johnny didn't go the whole thing was off, carried his point, and galloped off to find the lucky two, his eyes gleaming with anticipation and joy. Fox laughed, thanked the foreman, and rode on his way north; and that night three cow-punchers rode south, all strangely elated. And the friends who watched them go heaved signs of relief, for the reprisals evidently were to be postponed for a while.

Chapter V
The Ghost of the San Miguel

Juan Alvarez had not been in San Felippe since Dick Martin left, which meant for over a month. Martin was down the river looking for a man who did not wish to be found; and some said that Martin cared nothing about international boundaries when he wanted any one real bad. And there was that geologist who wore blue glasses and was always puttering around in the canyon and hammering chips of rock off the steep walls; he must have slipped one noon, because his body was found on a flat boulder at the edge of the stream. Manuel had found it and wanted to be paid for his trouble in bringing it to town-but Manuel was a fool. Who, indeed, would pay good money for a dead Gringo, especially after he was dead? And there were three cow-punchers holding a herd of 6-X cattle up north, an hour or so from the town. They wanted to buy steers from Senor Rodriguez, but said that he was a robber and threatened to cut his ears off. Cannot a man name his own price? These cow-punchers liked to get drunk and gallop through San Felippe, shooting like crazy men. They got drunk one Friday night and went shouting and singing to the Big Bend in the canyon to see the flying ghost, and they called it names and fired off their pistols and sang loudly; and for a week they insulted all the Mexicans in town by calling them liars and cowards. Was it the fault of any one that the ghost would show itself only to Mexicans? Oh, these Gringos-might the good God punish them for their sins!

Thus the peons complained to the padre while they kept one eye open for the advent of the rowdy cow-punchers, who always wanted to drink, and then to fight with some one, either with fists or pistols. Why should any one fight with them, especially with such things as fists?

"Let them fight among themselves. What have you to do with heretics?" reproved the good padre, who ostracized himself from the pleasant parts of the wide world that he might make easier the life and struggles of his ignorant flock. "God is not hasty-He will punish in His own way when it best suits Him. And perhaps you will profit much if you are more regular to mass instead of wasting the cool hours of the morning in bed. Think well of what I have said, my children."

But the cow-punchers were not punished and they swore they would not leave the vicinity until they had all the steers they wanted, and at their own price. And one night their herd stampeded and was checked only in time to save it from going over the canyon's edge. And for some reason Sanchez kept out of the padre's way and did not go to confess when he should, for the padre spoke plainly and set hard obligations for penance.

The cow-punchers swore that it had been done by some Mexican and said that they would come to town some day soon and kill three Mexicans unless the guilty one was found and brought to them. Then the padre mounted his donkey and went out to them to argue and they finally told him they would wait for two weeks. But the padre was too smart for them-he sent a messenger to find Senor Dick Martin, and in one week Senor Martin came to town. There was no fight. The Gringo rowdies were cowards at heart and Martin could not shoot them down in cold blood, and he could not arrest them, because he was not a policeman or even a sheriff, but only a revenue officer, which was a most foolish law. But he watched them all the time and wanted them to fight-there was no more shooting or drunkenness in town. Nobody wanted to fight Senor Martin, for he was a great man. He even went so far as to talk with them about it and wave his arms, but they were as frightened at him as little children might be.

So the Mexicans gossiped and exulted, some of the bolder of them even swaggering out to the Gringo camp; but Martin drove them back again, saying he would not allow them to bully men who could not retaliate, which was right and fair. Then, afraid to go away and leave the mad cow-punchers so close to town, he ordered them to drive their herd farther east, nearer to Dent's store, and never to return to San Felippe unless they needed the padre; and they obeyed him after a long talk. After seeing them settled in their new camp, which was on Monday morning, Martin returned to San Felippe and told the padre where he could be found and then rode away again. San Felippe celebrated for a whole day and two Mexican babies were christened after Senor Dick Martin, which was honor all around.

Friday, when Manuel went over to spy upon the cow-punchers in their new camp, he found them so drunk that they could not stand, and before he crept away at dusk two of them were sleeping like gorged snakes and the third was firing off his revolver at random, which diversion had not a little to do with Manuel's departure.

When Manuel crept away he headed straight for a crevice near the wall of the canyon at the Big Bend and, reaching it, looked all around and then dropped into it. Not long thereafter another Mexican appeared, this one from San Felippe, and also disappeared into the crevice. As darkness fell Manuel reappeared with something under his jacket and a moment later a light gleamed at the base of a slender sapling which grew on the edge of the canyon wall and leaned out over the abyss. It was cleverly placed, for only at one spot on the Mexican side of the distant Rio Grande could it be seen-the high canyon walls farther down screened it from any one who might be riding on the north bank of the river. In a moment there came an answering twinkle and Manuel, covering the lantern with a blanket, was swallowed up in the darkness of the crevice.

Without a trace of emotion, Dick Martin, from his place of concealment, caught the answering gleam, and he watched Manuel disappear. "Cassidy was right in every point; Lewis or Sayre couldn't 'a' done this better. I hope he won't be late," he muttered, and settled himself more comfortably to wait for the cue for action, smiling as the moon poked its rim over the low hills to his right. "This means promotion for me, or I've very much mistaken," he chuckled.

Hopalong was not late and as soon as it was dark he and his companions stole into the canyon on foot. They felt their way down the east end of the trail, not far from Dent's, toward the Big Bend, which they gained without a mishap. Johnny was sent up to a place they had noticed and marked in their memories at the time they had rioted down to defy the ghost. He was to stop any one trying to escape up the San Felippe end of the canyon trail, and his confidence in his ability to do this was exuberant. Hopalong and Red slowly and laboriously worked their way down the perilous path leading to the bottom, forded the stream, and crept up the other side, where they found cover not far from a wide crack in the canyon wall. Upon the occasion of their hilarious visit to the Big Bend they had observed that a faint trail led to the crack and had cogitated deeply upon this fact.

Three hours passed before the watchers in and above the canyon were rewarded by anything further; and then a light flickered far down the canyon and close to the edge of the stream. Immediately strange noises were heard and suddenly the ghost swung out of the opening in the rock wall near Hopalong and Red and danced above their heads, while the shrieking which had so frightened Johnny and his horse filled the canyon with uproar and sent Martin wriggling nearer to the crevice which he had watched so closely. The noise soon ceased, but the ghost danced on, and the sound of men stumbling along the rocky ledge bordering the stream became more and more audible. Four were in the party and they all carried bulky loads on their backs and grunted with pleasure and relief as they entered the entrance in the wall. When the last man had disappeared and the noise of their passing had died out, Johnny's rope sailed up and out, and the ghost swayed violently and then began to sag in an unaccountable manner towards the trail as the owner of the rope hitched its free end around a spur of rock and made it fast. Then he feverishly scrambled down the steep path to join his friends.

Hopalong and Red, wriggling on their stomachs towards the crack in the wall, paused in amazement and stared across the canyon; and then the former chuckled and whispered something in his companion's ear. "That was why he lugged his rope along! He's just idiot enough to want a souveneer an' plaything at the risk of losing the game. Come on! —they'll tumble to what's up an' get away if we don't hustle."

When the two punchers cautiously and noiselessly entered the crack and felt their way along its rock walls they heard fluent swearing in Spanish by the man who worked the ghost, and who could not understand its sudden ambition to take root. It was made painfully clear to him a moment later when a pair of brawny hands reached out of the darkness behind him and encircled his throat a hand's width below his gleaming cigarette. Another pair used cords with deftness and despatch and he was left by himself to browse upon the gag when all his senses returned.

Hopalong, with Red inconsiderately stepping on his heels, felt his way along the wall of the crevice, alert and silent, his Colt nestling comfortably in his right hand, while the left was pushed out ahead feeling for trouble. As they worked farther away from the canyon distant voices could be heard and they forthwith proceeded even more cautiously. When Hopalong came to the second bend in the narrow passage he peered around it and stopped so abruptly that Red's nose almost spread itself over the back of his head. Red's indignation was all the harder to bear because it must bloom unheard.

In a huge, irregular room, whose roof could not be discerned in the dim light of the few candles, five men were resting in various attitudes of ease as they discussed the events of the night and tried to compute their profits. They were secure, for Manuel, having by this time put away the ghost and megaphone, was on duty at the mouth of the crevice, and he was as sensitive to danger as a hound.

"The risk is not much and the profits are large," remarked Pedro, in Spanish. "We must burn a candle for the repose of the soul of Carlos Martinez. It is he that made our plans safe. And a candle is not much when we —"

"Hands up!" said a quiet voice, followed by grim commands. The Mexicans jumped as if stung by a scorpion, and could just discern two of the rowdy gringo cow-punchers in the heavy shadows of the opposite wall, but the candle light glinted in rings on the muzzles of their six-shooters. Had Manuel betrayed them? But they had little time or inclination for cogitation regarding Manuel.

"Easy there!" shouted Red, and Pedro's hand stopped when half way to his chest. Pedro was a gambler by nature, but the odds were too heavy and he sullenly obeyed the command.

"Stick 'em up! Stick 'em up! Higher yet, an' hold 'em there," purred a soft voice from the other end of the room, where Dick Martin smiled pleasantly upon them and wondered if there was anything on earth harder to pound good common sense into than a "Greaser's" head. His gun was blue, but it was, nevertheless, the most prominent part of his make-up, even if the light was poor.

One of the Mexicans reached involuntarily for his gun, for he was a gun-man by training; while his companions felt for their knives, deadly weapons in a melee. Martin, crying, "Watch 'em, Cassidy!" side-stepped and lunged forward with the speed and skill of a boxer, and his hard left hand landed on the point of Juan Alvarez' jaw with a force and precision not to be withstood. But to make more certain that the Mexican would not take part in any possible demonstration of resistance, Martin's right circled up in a short half-hook and stopped against Juan's short ribs. Martin weighed one hundred and eighty pounds and packed no fat on his well-knit frame.

At this moment a two-legged cyclone burst upon the scene in the person of Johnny Nelson, whose rage had been worked up almost to the weeping point because he had lost so much time hunting for the crevice where it was not. Seeing Juan fall, and the glint of knives, he started in to clean things up, yelling, "I'm a ghost! I'm a ghost! Take 'em alive! Take 'em alive!"

Hopalong and Red felt that they were in his way, and taking care of one Mexican between them, while Martin knocked out another, they watched the exits,—for anything was possible in such a chaotic mix-up,—and gave Johnny plenty of room. The latter paused, triumphant, looked around to see if he had missed any, and then advanced upon his friends and shoved his jaw up close to Hopalong's face. "Tried to lose me, didn't you! Wouldn't wait for me! For seven cents an' a toothbrush I'd give you what's left!"

Red grabbed him by trousers and collar and heaved him into the passageway. "Go out an' play with yore souveneer or we'll step on you!"

Johnny sat up, rubbed certain portions of his anatomy, and grinned. "Oh, I've got it, all right! I'm shore going to take that ghost home an' make some of them fools *eat* it!"

Martin smiled as he finished tying the last prisoner. "That's right, Nelson; you've got it on 'em this time. Make 'em chew it."

Chapter VI
Hopalong Loses a Horse

For a month after their return from the San Miguel, Hopalong and his companions worked with renewed zest, and told and retold the other members of the outfit of their unusual experiences near the Mexican border. Word had come up to them that Martin had secured the conviction of the smugglers and was in line for immediate advancement. No one on the range had the heart to meet Johnny Nelson, for Johnny carried with him a piece of the ghost, and became pugnacious if his once-jeering friends and acquaintances refused to nibble on it. Cowan still sold his remarkable drink, but he had yielded to Johnny's persuasive methods and now called it "Nelson's Pet."

One bright day the outfit started rounding up a small herd of three-year-olds, which Buck had sold, and by the end of the week the herd was complete and ready for the drive. This took two weeks and when Hopalong led his drive outfit through Hoyt's Corners on its homeward journey he felt the pull of the town of Grant, some miles distant, and it was too strong to be resisted. Flinging a word of explanation to the nearest puncher, he turned to lope away, when Red's voice checked him. Red wanted to delay his home-coming for a day or two and attend to a purely personal matter at a ranch lying to the west. Hopalong, knowing the reason for Red's wish, grinned and told him to go, and not to propose until he had thought the matter over very carefully. Red's reply was characteristic, and after arranging a rendezvous and naming the time, the two separated and rode toward their destinations, while the rest of the outfit kept on towards their ranch.

"A man owes something to *all* his friends," Hopalong mused. In this case he owed a return game of draw poker to certain of Grant's leading citizens, and he liked to pay his obligations when opportunity offered.

It was mid-afternoon when he topped a rise and saw below him the handful of shacks making up the town. A look of pleased interest flickered across his face as he noticed a patched and dirty tent pitched close up to the nearest shack. "Show!" he exclaimed. "Now, ain't that luck! I'll shore take it in. If it's a circus, mebby it has a trick mule to ride —I'll never forget that one up in Kansas City," he grinned. But almost instantly a doubt arose and tempered the grin. "Huh! Mebby it's the branding chute of some gospel sharp." As he drew near he focussed his eyes on the canvas and found that his fears were justified.

"All Are Welcome," he spelled out slowly. "Shore they are!" he muttered. "I never nowhere saw such hard-working, all-embracing rustlers as them fellers. They'll stick their iron on any-thing from a wobbly calf or dying dogie to a staggering-with-age mosshead, an' shout 'tally one' with the same joy. Well, not for mine, *this* trip. I'm going to graze loose an' buck-jump all I wants. Anyhow, if I did let him brand me I'd only backslide in a week," and Hopalong pressed his pony to a more rapid gait as two men emerged from the tent. "There's the sky-pilot now," he muttered —"an' there's Dave!" he shouted, waving his arm. "Oh, Dave! Dave!"

Dave Wilkes looked up, and his grin of delight threatened to engulf his ears. "Hullo, Cassidy! Glad to see you! Keep right on for the store —I'll be with you in a minute." When David told his companion the visitor's name the evangelist held up his hand eloquently and spoke.

"I know all about him!" he exclaimed sorrowfully. "If I can lead him out of his wickedness I will rest content though I save no more souls this fortnight. Is it all true?"

"Huh! What true?"

"All that I have heard about him."

"Well, I dunno what you've heard," replied Dave, with grave caution, "but I reckon it might be if it didn't cover lying, stealing, cowardice, an' such coyote traits. He's shore a holy terror with a short gun, all right, but lemme tell you something mebby you *ain't* heard: There ain't a square man in this part of the country that won't feel some honored an' proud to be called a friend of Hopalong Cassidy. Them's the sentiments rampaging hereabouts. I ain't denying that he's gone an' killed off a lot of men first an' last-but the only trouble there is that he didn't get 'em soon enough. They all had lived too blamed long when they went an' stacked up agin him an' that lightning short gun of hissn. But, say, if yo're calculating to tackle him at yore game, lead him gentle-don't push none. He comes to life real sudden when he's shoved. So long; see you later, mebby."

The revivalist looked after him and mused, "I hope I was informed wrong, but this much I have to be thankful for: The wickedness of most of these men, these over-grown children, is manly, stalwart, and open; few of them are vicious or contemptible. Their one great curse is drink."

When Hopalong entered the store he was vociferously welcomed by two men, and the propri-etor joining them, the circle was complete. When the conversation threatened to repeat itself cards were brought and the next two hours passed very rapidly. They were expensive hours to the Bar-20 puncher, who finally arose with an apologetic grin and slapped his thigh significantly.

"Well, you've got it all; I'm busted wide open, except for a measly dollar, an' I shore hopes you don't want that," he laughed. "You play a whole lot better than you did the last time I was here. I've got to move along. I'm going east an' see Wallace an' from there I've got to meet Red an' ride home with him. But you come an' see us when you can-it's *me* that wants revenge this time."

"Huh; you'll be wanting it worse than ever if we do," smiled Dave.

"Say, Hoppy," advised Tom Lawrence, "better drop in an' hear the sky-pilot's palaver before you go. It'll do you a whole lot of good, an' it can't do you no harm, anyhow."

"You going?" asked Hopalong suspiciously.

"Can't —got too much work to do," quickly responded Tom, his brother Art nodding happy confirmation.

"Huh; I reckoned so!" snorted Hopalong sarcastically, as he shook hands all around. "You all know where to find us-drop in an' see us when you get down our way," he invited.

"Sorry you can't stay longer, Cassidy," remarked Dave, as his friend mounted. "But come up again soon-an' be shore to tell all the boys we was asking for 'em," he called.

Considering the speed with which Hopalong started for Wallace's, he might have been expecting a relay of "quarter" horses to keep it going, but he pulled up short at the tent. Such inconsistency is trying to the temper of the best-mannered horse, and this particular animal was not in the least good-mannered, wherefore its rider was obliged to soothe its resentment in his own peculiar way, listening meanwhile to the loud and impassioned voice of the evangelist haranguing his small audience.

"I wonder," said Hopalong, glancing through the door, "if them friends of mine reckon I'm any ascared to go in that tent? Huh, I'll just show 'em anyhow!" whereupon he dismounted, flung the reins over his horse's head, and strode through the doorway.

The nearest seat, a bench made by placing a bottom board of the evangelist's wagon across two up-ended boxes, was close enough to the exhorter and he dropped into it and glanced carelessly at his nearest neighbor. The carelessness went out of his bearing as his eyes fastened themselves in a stare on the man's neck-kerchief. Hopalong was hardened to awful sights and at his best was not an artistic soul, but the villainous riot of fiery crimson, gaudy yellow, and pugnacious and domineering green which flaunted defiance and insolence from the stranger's neck caused his breath to hang over one count and then come double strong at the next exhalation. "Gee whiz!" he whispered.

The stranger slowly turned his head and looked coldly upon the impudent disturber of his reverent reflections. "Meaning?" he questioned, with an upward slant in his voice. The neck-kerchief seemed to grow suddenly malignant and about to spring. "Meaning?" repeated the other with great insolence, while his eyes looked a challenge.

While Hopalong's eyes left the scrambled color-insult and tried to banish the horrible after-image, his mind groped for the rules of etiquette governing free fist fights in gospel tents, and while he hesitated as to whether he should dent the classic profile of the color-bearer or just twist his nose as a sign of displeasure, the voice of the evangelist arose to a roar and thundered out. Hopalong ducked instinctively.

"—Stop! Stop before it is too late, before death takes you in the wallow of your sins! Repent and gain salvation —"

Hopalong felt relieved, but his face retained its expression of childlike innocence even after he realized that he was not being personally addressed; and he glanced around. It took him ninety-seven seconds to see everything there was to be seen, and his eyes were drawn irresistibly back to the stranger's kerchief. "Awful! Awful thing for a drinking man to wear, or run up against unexpectedly!" he muttered, blinking. "Worse than snakes," he added thoughtfully.

"Look ahere, you —" began the owner of the offensive decoration, if it might be called such, but the evangelist drowned his voice in another flight of eloquence.

"—*Peace*! *Peace* is the message of the Lord to His children," roared the voice from the upturned soap box, and when the speaker turned and looked in the direction of the two men-with-a-difference he found them sitting up very straight and apparently drinking in his words with great relish; whereupon he felt that he was making gratifying progress toward the salvation of their spotted souls. He was very glad, indeed, that he had been so grievously misinformed about the personal attributes of one Hopalong Cassidy, —glad and thankful.

"Death cometh as a thief in the night," the voice went on. "Think of the friends who have gone before; who were well one minute and gone the next! And it must come to all of us, to all of us, to me and to you —"

The man with the afflicted neck started rocking the bench.

"Something is coming to somebody purty soon," murmured Hopalong. He began to sidle over towards his neighbor, his near hand doubled up into a huge knot of protuberant knuckles and white-streaked fingers; but as he was about to deliver his hint that he was greatly displeased at the antics of the bench, a sob came to his ears. Turning his head swiftly, he caught sight of the stranger's face, and sorrow was marked so strongly upon it that the sight made Hopalong gape. His hand opened slowly and he cautiously sidled back again, disgruntled, puzzled, and vexed at himself for having strayed into a game where he was so hopelessly at sea. He thought it all over carefully and then gave it up as being too deep for him to solve. But he determined one thing: He was not going to leave before the other man did, anyhow.

"An' if I catch that howling kerchief outside," he muttered, smacking his lips with satisfaction at what was in store for it. His visit to Wallace was not very important, anyway, and it could wait on more important events.

"There sits a sinner!" thundered out the exhorter, and Hopalong looked stealthily around for a sight of a villain. "God only has the right to punish. 'Vengeance is mine,' saith the Lord, and whosoever takes the law into his own hands, whosoever takes human life, defies the Creator. There sits a man who has killed his fellow-men, his brothers! Are you not a sinner, *Cassidy*?"

Cassidy jumped clear of the bench as he jerked his head around and stared over the suddenly outstretched arm and pointing finger of the speaker and into his accusing eyes.

"Answer me! Are you not a sinner?"

Hopalong stood up, confused, bewildered, and then his suspended thoughts stirred and formed. "Guilty, I reckon, an' in the first degree. But they didn't get no more'n what was coming to 'em, no more'n they earned. An' that's straight!"

"How do you know they didn't? How do you know they earned it? How do you *know*?" demanded the evangelist, who was delighted with the chance to argue with a sinner. He had great faith in "personal contact," and his was the assurance of training, of the man well rehearsed and fully prepared. And he knew that if he should be pinned into a corner by logic and asked for *his* proofs, that he could squirm out easily and take the offensive again by appealing to faith, the last word in sophistry, and a greater and more powerful weapon than intelligence. *This* was his game, and it was fixed; he could not lose if he could arouse enough interest in a man to hold him to the end of the argument. He continued to drive, to crowd. "What right have you to think so? What right have you to judge them? Have you divine insight? Are you inspired? 'Judge not lest ye be judged,' saith the Lord, and you *dare* to fly in the face of that great command!"

"You've got me picking the pea in *this* game, all right," responded Hopalong, dropping back on the bench. "But lemme tell you one thing; Command or no command, devine or not devine, I know when a man has lived too long, an' when he's going to try to get me. An' all the gospel sharps south of heaven can't stop me from handing a thief what he's earned. Go on with the show, but count me out."

While the evangelist warmed to the attack, vaguely realizing that he had made a mistake in not heeding Dave Wilkes' tip, Hopalong became conscious of a sense of relief stealing over him and he looked around wonderingly for the cause. The man with the kerchief had "folded his tents" and departed; and Hopalong, heaving a sigh of satisfaction, settled himself more comfortably and gave real attention to the discourse, although he did not reply to the warm and eloquent man on the soap box. Suddenly he sat up with a start as he remembered that he had a long and hard ride before him if he wished to see Wallace, and arising, strode towards the exit, his chest up and his chin thrust out. The only reply he made to the excited and personal remarks of the revivalist was to stop at the door and drop his last dollar into the yeast box before passing out.

For a moment he stood still and pondered, his head too full of what he had heard to notice that anything out of the ordinary had happened. Although the evangelist had adopted the wrong method he had gained more than he knew and Hopalong had something to take home with him and wrestle out for himself in spare moments; that is, he would have had but for one thing: As he slowly looked around for his horse he came to himself with a sharp jerk, and hot profanity routed the germ of religion incubating in his soul. His horse was missing! Here was a pretty mess, he thought savagely; and then his expression of anger and perplexity gave way to a flickering grin as the probable solution came to his mind.

"By the Lord, I never saw such a bunch to play jokes," he laughed. "Won't they never grow up? They was watching me when I went inside an' sneaked up and rustled my cayuse. Well, I'll get back again without much trouble, all right. They ought to know me better by this time."

"Hey, stranger!" he called to a man who was riding past, "have you seen anything of a skinny roan cayuse fifteen han's high, white stocking on the near foreleg, an' a bandage on the off fetlock, Bar-20 being the brand?"

The stranger, knowing the grinning inquisitor by sight, suspected that a joke was being played: he also knew Dave Wilkes and that gentleman's friends. He chuckled and determined to help it along a little. "Shore did, pardner; saw a man leading him real cautious. Was he yourn?"

"Oh, no; not at all. He belonged to my great-great-grandfather, who left him to my second cousin. You see, I borrowed it," he grinned, making his way leisurely towards the general store, kept by his friend Dave, the joker. "Funny how everybody likes a joke," he muttered, opening the door of the store. "Hey, Dave," he called.

Mr. Wilkes wheeled suddenly and stared. "Why, I thought you was half-way to Wallace's by now!" he exclaimed. "Did you come back to lose that lone dollar?"

"Oh, I lost that too. But yo're a real smart cuss, now ain't you?" queried Hopalong, his eyes twinkling and his face wreathed with good humor. "An' how innocent you act, too. Thought you could scare me, didn't you? Thought I'd go tearing 'round this fool town like a house afire, hey? Well, I reckon you can guess again. Now, I'm owning up that the joke's on me, so you hand over my cayuse, an' I'll make up for lost time."

Dave Wilkes' face expressed several things, but surprise was dominant. "Why, I ain't even seen yore ol' cayuse, you chump! Last time I saw it you was on him, going like the devil. Did somebody pull you off it an' take it away from you?" he demanded with great sarcasm. "Is somebody abusing you?"

Hopalong bit into a generous handful of dried apricots, chewed complacently for a moment, and replied: "'At's aw right; I want my cayuse." Swallowing hastily, he continued: "I want it, an' I've come to the right place for it, too. Hand it over, David."

"Dod blast it, I tell you I ain't got it!" retorted Dave, beginning to suspect that something was radically wrong. "I ain't seen it, an' I don't know nothing about it."

Hopalong wiped his mouth with his sleeve. "Well, then, Tom or Art does, all right."

"No, they don't, neither; I watched 'em leave an' they rode straight out of town, an' went the other way, same as they allus do." Dave was getting irritated. "Look here, you; are you joking or drunk, or both, or is that animule of yourn really missing?"

"Huh!" snorted Hopalong, trying some new prunes. "'Ese prunes er purty good," he mumbled, in grave congratulation. "I don' get prunes like 'ese very of'n."

"I reckon you don't! They ought to be good! Cost me thirty cents a half-pound," Dave retorted with asperity, anxiously shifting his feet. It didn't take much of a loss to wipe out a day's profits with him.

"An' I don't reckon you paid none too much for 'em, at that," Mr. Cassidy responded, nodding his head in comprehension. "Ain't no worms in 'em, is there?"

"Shore there is!" exploded Dave. "Plumb full of 'em!"

"You don't say! Hardly know whether to take a chance with the worms or try the apricots. Ain't no worms in them, anyhow. But when am I going to get my cayuse? I've got a long way to go, an' delay is costly-how much did you say these yaller fellers cost?" he asked significantly, trying another handful of apricots.

"On the dead level, cross my heart an' hope to die, but I ain't seen yore cayuse since you left here," earnestly replied Dave. "If you don't know where it is, then somebody went an' lifted it. It looks like it's up to you to do some hunting, 'stead of cultivating a belly-ache at *my* expense. *I* ain't trying to keep you, God knows!"

Hopalong glanced out of the window as he considered, and saw, entering the saloon, the same puncher who had confessed to seeing his horse. "Hey Dave; wait a minute!" and he dashed out of the store and made good time towards the liquid refreshment parlor. Dave promptly nailed the covers on the boxes of prunes and apricots and leaned innocently against the cracker box to await results, thinking hard all the while. It looked like a plain case of horse-stealing to him.

"Stranger," cried Hopalong, bouncing into the bar-room, "where did you see that cayuse of mine?"

"The ancient relic of yore family was aheading towards Hoyt's Corners," the stranger replied, grinning broadly. "It's a long walk. Have something before you starts?"

"Damn the walk! Who was riding him?"

"Nobody at all."

"What do you mean?"

"He wasn't being rid when I saw him."

"Hang it, man; that cayuse was stole from me!"

"Somewhat in the nature of a calamity, now ain't it?" smiled the stranger, enjoying his contributions to the success of the joke.

"You bet yore life it is!" shouted Hopalong, growing red and then pale. "You tell me who was leading him, understand?"

"Well, I couldn't see his face, honest I couldn't," replied the stranger. "Every time I tried it I was shore blinded by the most awful an' horrible neck-kerchief I've ever had the hard luck to lay my eyes on. Of all the drunks I ever met, them there colors was-Hey! Wait a minute!" he shouted at Hopalong's back.

"Dave, gimme yore cayuse an' a rifle-quick!" cried Hopalong from the middle of the street as he ran towards the store. "Hypocrite son-of-a-hoss-thief went an' run mine off. Might 'a' knowed nobody but a thief could wear such a kerchief!"

"I'm with you!" shouted Dave, leading the way on the run towards the corral in the rear of his store.

"No, you ain't with me, neither!" replied Hopalong, deftly saddling. "This ain't no plain hoss-thief case-it's a private grudge. See you later, mebby," and he was pacing a cloud of dust towards the outskirts of the town.

Dave looked after him. "Well, that feller has shore got a big start on you, but he can't keep ahead of that Doll of mine for very long. She can out-run anything in these parts. 'Sides, Cassidy's cayuse looked sort of done up, while mine's as fresh as a bird. That thief will get what's coming to him, all right."

Chapter VII
Mr. Cassidy Cogitates

While Hopalong tried to find his horse, Ben Ferris pushed forward, circling steadily to the east and away from the direction of Hoyt's corners, which was as much a menace to his health and happiness as the town of Grant, twenty miles to his rear. If he could have been certain that no danger was nearer to him than these two towns, he would have felt vastly relieved, even if his horse was not fresh. During the last hour he had not urged it as hard as he had in the beginning of his flight and it had dropped to a walk for minutes at a stretch. This was not because he felt that he had plenty of time, but for the reason that he understood horses and could not afford to exhaust his mount so early in the chase. He glanced back from time to time as if fearing what might be on his trail, and well he might fear. According to all the traditions and customs of the range, both of which he knew well, somewhere between him and Grant was a posse of hard-riding cow-punchers, all anxious and eager for a glance at him over their sights. In his mind's eye he could see them, silent, grim, tenacious, reeling off the miles on that distance-eating lope. He had stolen a horse, and that meant death if they caught him. He loosened his gaudy kerchief and gulped in fear, not of what pursued, but of what was miles before him. His own saddle, strapped behind the one he sat in, bumped against him with each reach of the horse and had already made his back sore-but he must endure it for a time. Never in all his life had minutes been so precious.

Another hour passed and the horse seemed to be doing well, much better than he had hoped-he would rest it for a few minutes at the next water while he drank his fill and changed the bumping saddle. As he rounded a turn and entered a heavily grassed valley he saw a stream close at hand and, leaping off, fixed the saddle first. As he knelt to drink he caught a movement and jumped up to catch his mount. Time after time he almost touched it, but it evaded him and kept up the game, cropping a mouthful of grass during each respite.

"All right!" he muttered as he let it eat. "I'll get my drink while you eat an' then I'll get you!"

He knelt by the stream again and drank long and deep. As he paused for breath something made him leap up and to one side, reaching for his Colt at the same instant. His fingers found only leather and he swore fiercely as he remembered-he had sold the Colt for food and kept the rifle for defence. As he faced the rear a horseman rounded the turn and the fugitive, wheeling, dashed for the stolen horse forty yards away, where his rifle lay in its saddle sheath. But an angry command and the sharp hum of a bullet fired in front of him checked his flight and he stopped short and swore.

"I reckon the jig's up," remarked Mr. Cassidy, balancing the up-raised Colt with nicety and indifference.

"Yea; I reckon so," sullenly replied the other, tears running into his eyes.

"Well, I'm damned!" snorted Hopalong with cutting contempt. "Crying like a li'l baby! Got nerve enough to steal my cayuse, an' then go an' beller like a lost calf when I catch you. Yo're a fine specimen of a hoss-thief, I don't think!"

"Yo're a liar!" retorted the other, clenching his fists and growing red.

Mr. Cassidy's mouth opened and then clicked shut as his Colt swung down. But he did not shoot; something inside of him held his trigger finger and he swore instead. The idea of a man stealing his horse, being caught red-handed and unarmed, and still possessed of sufficient courage to call his captor a name never tolerated or overlooked in that country! And the idea that he, Hopalong Cassidy, of the Bar-20, could not shoot such a thief! "Damn that sky pilot! He's shore gone an' made me loco," he muttered, savagely, and then addressed his prisoner. "Oh, you ain't crying? Wind got in yore eyes, I reckon, an' sort of made 'em leak a little-that it? Or mebby them unholy green roses an' yaller grass on that blasted fool neck-kerchief of yourn are too much for *your* eyes, too!"

"Look ahere!" snapped the man on the ground, stepping forward, one fist upraised. "I came nigh onto licking you this noon in that gospel sharp's tent for making fun of that scarf, an' I'll do it yet if you get any smart about it! You mind yore own business an' close yore fool eyes if you don't like my clothes!"

"Say! You ain't no cry-baby after all. Hanged if I even think yo're a real genuine hoss-thief!" enthused Mr. Cassidy. "You act like a twin brother; but what the devil ever made you steal that cayuse, anyhow?"

"An' that's none of yore business, neither; but I'll tell you, just the same," replied the thief. "I had to have it; that's why. I'll fight you rough-an'-tumble to see if I keep it, or if you take the cayuse an' shoot me besides: is it a go?"

Hopalong stared at him and then a grin struggled for life, got it, and spread slowly over his tanned countenance. "Yore gall is refreshing! Damned if it ain't worse than the scarf. Here, you tell me what made you take a chance like stealing a cayuse this noon —I'm getting to like you, bad as you are, hanged if I ain't!"

"Oh, what's the use?" demanded the other, tears again coming into his eyes. "You'll think I'm lying an' trying to crawl out-an' I won't do neither."

"*I* didn't say *you* was a liar," replied Hopalong. "It was the other way about. Reckon you can try me, anyhow; can't you?"

"Yes; I s'pose so," responded the other, slowly, and in a milder tone of voice. "An' when I called you that I was mad and desperate. I was hasty-you see, my wife's dying, or dead, over in Winchester. I was riding hard to get to her before it was too late when my cayuse stepped into a hole just the other side of Grant-you know what happened. I shot the animal, stripped off my saddle an' hoofed it to town, an' dropped into that gospel dealer's layout to see if he could make me feel any better-which he could not. I just couldn't stand his palaver about death an' slipped out. I was going to lay for you an' lick you for the way you acted about this scarf-had to do something or go loco. But when I got outside there was yore cayuse, all saddled an' ready to go. I just up an' threw my saddle on it, followed suit with myself an' was ten miles out of town before I realized just what I'd done. But the realizing part of it didn't make no difference to me —I'd 'a' done it just the same if I had stopped to think it over. That's flat, an' straight. I've got to get to that li'l woman as quick as I can, an' I'd steal all the cayuses in the whole damned country if they'd do me any good. That's all of it-take it or leave it. I put it up to you. That's yore cayuse, but you ain't going to get it without fighting me for it! If you shoot me down without giving me a chance, all right! I'll cut a throat for that wore-out bronc!"

Hopalong was buried in thought and came to himself just in time to cover the other and stop him not six feet away. "Just a minute, before you make me shoot you! I want to think about it."

"Damn that gun!" swore the fugitive, nervously shifting his feet and preparing to spring. "We'd 'a' been fighting by this time if it wasn't for that!"

"You stand still or I'll blow you apart," retorted Hopalong, grimly. "A man's got a right to think, ain't he? An' if I had somebody here to mind these guns so you couldn't sneak 'em on me I'd fight you so blamed quick that you'd be licked before you knew you was at it. But we ain't going to fight —*stand still*! You ain't got no show at all when yo're dead!"

"Then you gimme that cayuse-my God, man! Do you know the hell I've been through for the last two days? Got the word up at Daly's Crossing an' ain't slept since. I'll go loco if the strain lasts much longer! She asking for me, begging to see me: an' me, like a damned idiot, wasting time out here talking to another. Ride with me, behind me-it's only forty miles more-tie me to the saddle an' blow me to pieces if you find I'm lying-do anything you wants; but let me get to Winchester before dark!"

Hopalong was watching him closely and at the end of the other's outburst threw back his head. "I reckon I'm a plain fool, a jackass; but I don't care. I'll rope that cayuse for you. You come along to save time," Hopalong ordered, spurring forward. His borrowed rope sailed out, tightened, and in a moment he was working at the saddle. "Here, you; I'm going to swamp mounts with you-this one is fresher an' faster." He had his own saddle off and the other on in record time, and stepped back. "There; don't stand there like a fool-wake up an' hustle! I might change my mind-that's the way to move! Gimme that neck-kerchief for a souveneer, an' get out. Send that cayuse back to Dave Wilkes, at Grant-it's hissn. Don't thank me; just gimme that scarf an' ride like the devil."

The other, already mounted, tore the kerchief from his throat and handed it quickly to his benefactor. "If you ever want a man to take you out of hell, send to Winchester for Ben Ferris-that's me. So long!"

Mr. Cassidy sat on his saddle where he had dropped it after making the exchange and looked after the galloping horseman, and when a distant rise had shut him from sight, turned his eyes on the scarf in his hand and cogitated. Finally, with a long-drawn sigh he arose, and, placing the scarf on the ground, caught and saddled his horse. Riding gloomily back to where the riot of color fluttered on the grass he drew his Colt and sent six bullets through it with a great amount of satisfaction. Not content with the damage he had inflicted, he leaned over and swooped it up. Riding further he also swooped up a stone and tied the kerchief around it, and then stood up in his stirrups and drew back his arm with critical judgment. He sat quietly for a time after the gaudy missile had disappeared into the stream and then, wheeling, cantered away. But he did not return to the town of Grant-he lacked the nerve to face Dave Wilkes and tell his childish and improbable story. He would ride on and meet Red as they had agreed; a letter would do for Mr. Wilkes, and after he had broken the shock in that manner he could pay him a personal visit sometime soon. Dave would never believe the story and when it was told Hopalong wanted to have the value of the horse in his trousers pocket. Of course, Ben Ferris *might* have told the truth and he might return the horse according to directions. Hopalong emerged from his reverie long enough to appeal to his mount:

"Bronc, I've been thinking: am I or am I not a jackass?"

Chapter VIII
Red Brings Trouble

After a night spent on the plain and a cigarette for his breakfast, Hopalong, grouchy and hungry, rode slowly to the place appointed for his meeting with Red, but Mr. Connors was over two hours late. It was now mid-forenoon and Hopalong occupied his time for a while by riding out fancy designs on the sand; but he soon tired of this makeshift diversion and grew petulant. Red's tardiness was all the worse because the erring party to the agreement had turned in his saddle at Hoyt's Corners and loosed a flippant and entirely uncalled-for remark about his friend's ideas regarding appointments.

"Well, that red-headed Romeo is shore late this time," Hopalong muttered. "Why don't he find a girl closer to home, anyhow? Thank the Lord I ain't got no use for shell games of any kind. Here I am, without anything to eat an' no prospects of anything, sitting up on this locoed layout like a sore thumb, an' can't move without hitting myself! An' it'll be late to-day before I can get any grub, too. Oh, well," he sighed, "I ain't in love, so things might be a whole lot worse with me. An' he ain't in love, neither, only he won't listen to reason. He gets mad an' calls me a sage hen an' says I'm stuck on myself because some fool told me I had brains."

He laughed as he pictured the object of his friend's affections. "Huh; anybody that got one good, square look at her wouldn't ever accuse him of having brains. But he'll forget her in a month. That was the life of his last hobbling fit an' it was the worst he ever had."

Grinning at his friend's peculiarly human characteristics he leaned back in the saddle and felt for tobacco and papers. As he finished pouring the chopped alfalfa into the paper he glanced up and saw a mounted man top the sky-line of the distant hills and shoot down the slope at full speed.

"I knowed it: started three hours late an' now he's trying to make it up in the last mile," Hopalong muttered, dexterously spreading the tobacco along the groove and quickly rolling the cigarette. Lighting it he looked up again and saw that the horseman was wildly waving a sombrero.

"Huh! Wigwagging for forgiveness," laughed the man who waited. "Old son-of-a-gun, I'd wait a week if I had some grub, an' he knows it. Couldn't get mad at him if I tried."

Mr. Connors' antics now became frantic and he shouted something at the top of his voice. His friend spurred his mount. "Come on, bronc; wake up. His girl said 'yes' an' now he wants me to get him out of his trouble." Whereupon he jogged forward. "What's that?" he shouted, sitting up very straight. "What's that?"

Red energetically swept the sombrero behind him and pointed to the rear. "War-whoops! W-a-r w-h-o-o-p-s! Injuns, you chump!" Mr. Connors appeared to be mildly exasperated.

"Yes?" sarcastically rejoined Mr. Cassidy in his throat, and then shouted in reply: "Love an' liquor don't mix very well in you. Wake up! Come out of it!"

"That's straight —I mean it!" cried Mr. Connors, close enough now to save the remainder of his lungs. "It's a bunch of young bucks on their first war-trail, I reckon. 'T ain't Geronimo, all right; I wouldn't be here now if it was. Three of 'em chased me an' the two that are left are coming hot-foot somewhere the other side of them hills. They act sort of mad, too."

"Mebby they ain't acting at all," cheerily replied his companion. "An' then that's the way you got that graze?" pointing to a bloody furrow on Mr. Connors' cheek. "But just the same it looks like the trail left by a woman's finger nail."

"Finger nail nothing," retorted Mr. Connors, flushing a little. "But, for God's sake, are you going to sit here like a wart on a dead dog an' wait for 'em?" he demanded with a rising inflection. "Do you reckon yo're running a dance, or a party, or something like that?"

"How many?" placidly inquired Mr. Cassidy, gazing intently towards the high sky-line of the distant hills.

"Two-an' I won't tell you again, neither!" snapped the owner of the furrowed cheek. "The others are 'way behind now-but we're standing *still!*"

"Why didn't you say there was others?" reproved Hopalong. "Naturally I didn't see no use of getting all het up just because two sprouted papooses feel like crowding us a bit; it wouldn't be none of *our* funeral, would it?" and the indignant Mr. Cassidy hurriedly dismounted and hid his horse in a nearby chaparral and returned to his companion at a run.

"Red, gimme yore Winchester an' then hustle on for a ways, have an accident, fall off yore cayuse, an' act scared to death, if you know how. It's that little trick Buck told us about, an' it shore ought to work fine here. We'll see if two infant feather-dusters can lick the Bar-20. Get a-going!"

They traded rifles, Hopalong taking the repeater in place of the single-shot gun he carried, and Red departed as bidden, his face gradually breaking into an enthusiastic grin as he ruminated upon the plan. "Level-headed old cuss; he's a wonder when it comes to planning or fighting. An' lucky,—well, I reckon!"

Hopalong ran forward for a short distance and slid down the steep bank of a narrow arroyo and waited, the repeater thrust out through the dense fringe of grass and shrubs which bordered the edge. When settled to his complete satisfaction and certain that he was effectually screened from the sight of any one in front of him, he arose on his toes and looked around for his companion, and laughed. Mr. Connors was bending very dejectedly apparently over his prostrate horse, but in reality was swearing heartily at the ignorant quadruped because it strove with might and main to get its master's foot off its head so it could arise. The man in the arroyo turned again and watched the hills and it was not long before he saw two Indians burst into view over the crest and gallop towards his friend. They were not to be blamed because they did not know the pursued had joined a friend, for the second trail was yet some distance in front of them.

"Pair of budding warriors, all right; an' awful important. Somebody must 'a' told *them* they had brains," Mr. Cassidy muttered. "They're just at the age when they knows it all an' have to go 'round raising hell all the time. Wonder when they jumped the reservation."

The Indians, seeing Mr. Connors arguing with his prostrate horse, and taking it for granted that he was not stopping for pleasure or to view the scenery, let out a yell and dashed ahead at grater speed, at the same time separating so as to encircle him and attack him front and rear at the same time. They had a great amount of respect for cowboys.

This manoeuvre was entirely unexpected and clashed violently with Mr. Cassidy's plan of procedure, so two irate punchers swore heartily at their rank stupidity in not counting on it. Of course everybody that knew anything at all about such warfare knew that they would do just such a thing, which made it all the more bitter. But Red had cultivated the habit of thinking quickly and he saw at once that the remedy lay with him; he astonished the exultant savages by straddling his disgruntled horse as it scrambled to its feet and galloping away from them, bearing slightly to the south, because he wished to lure his pursuers to ride closer to his anxious and eager friend.

This action was a success, for the yelling warriors, slowing perceptibly because of their natural astonishment at the resurrection and speed of an animal regarded as dead or useless, spurred on again, drawing closer together, and along the chord of the arc made by Mr. Connors' trail. Evidently the fool white man was either crazy or had original and startling ideas about the way to rest a horse when hard pressed, which pleased them much, since he had lost so much time. The pleasures of the war-trail would be vastly greater if all white men had similar ideas.

Hopalong, the light of fighting burning strong in his eyes, watched them sweep nearer and nearer, splendid examples of their type and seeming to be a part of their mounts. Then two shots rang out in quick succession and a cloud of pungent smoke arose lazily from the edge of the arroyo as the warriors fell from their mounts not sixty yards from the hidden marksman.

Mr. Connors' rifle spat fire once to make assurance doubly sure and he hastily rejoined his friend as that person climbed out of the arroyo.

"Huh! They must have been half-breeds!" snorted Red in great disgust, watching his friend shed sand from his clothes. "I allus opined that 'Paches was too blamed slick to bite on a game like that."

"Well, they are purty 'lusive animals, 'Paches; but there are exceptions," replied Hopalong, smiling at the success of their scheme. "Them two ain't 'Paches-they're the exceptions. But let me tell you that's a good game, just the same. It is as long as they don't see the second trail in time. Didn't Buck and Skinny get two that way?"

"Yes, I reckon so. But what'll we do now? What's the next play?" asked Red, hurriedly, his eyes searching the sky-line of the hills. "The rest of the coyotes will be here purty soon, an' they'll be madder than ever now. An' you better gimme back that gun, too."

"Take yore old gun-who wants the blamed thing, anyhow?" Hopalong demanded, throwing the weapon at his friend as he ran to bring up the hidden horse. When he returned he grinned pleasantly. "Why, we'll go on like we was greased for calamity, that's what we'll do. Did you reckon we was going to play leap-frog around here an' wait for the rest of them paint-shops, like a blamed fool pair of idiots?"

"I didn't know what *you* might do, remembering how you acted when I met you," retorted Red, shifting his cartridge belt so the empty loops were behind and out of the way. "But I shore knowed what we ought to do, all right."

"Well, mebby you also know how many's headed this way; do you?"

"You've got me stumped there; but there's a round dozen, anyway," Red replied. "You see, the three that chased me were out scouting ahead of the main bunch; an' I didn't have no time to take no blasted census."

"Then we've got to hit the home trail, an' hit it hard. Wind up that four-laigged excuse of yourn, an' take my dust," Hopalong responded, leading the way. "If we can get home there'll be a lot of disgusted braves hitting the high spots on the back trail trying to find a way out. Buck an' the rest of the boys will be a whole lot pleased, too. We can muster thirty men in two hours if we gets to Buckskin, an' that's twenty more than we'll need."

"Tell you one thing, Hoppy; we can get as far as Powers' old ranch house, an' that's shore," replied Red, thoughtfully.

"Yes!" exploded his companion in scorn and pity. "That old sieve of a shack ain't good enough for *me* to die in, no matter what you think about it. Why, it's as full of holes as a stiff hat in a melee. Yo're on the wrong trail; think again."

Mr. Cassidy objected not because he believed that Powers' old ranch house was unworthy of serious consideration as a place of refuge and defence, but for the reason that he wished to reach Buckskin so his friends might all get in on the treat. Times were very dull on the ranch, and this was an occasion far too precious to let slip by. Besides, he then would have the pleasure of leading his friends against the enemy and battling on even terms. If he sought shelter he and Red would have to fight on the defensive, which was a game he hated cordially because it put him in a relatively subordinate position and thereby hurt his pride.

"Let me tell you that it's a whole lot better than thin air with a hard-working circle around us-an' you know what that means," retorted Mr. Connors. "But if you don't want to take a chance in the shack, why mebby we can make Wallace's, or the Cross-O-Cross. That is, if we don't get turned out of our way."

"We don't head for no Cross-O-Cross or Wallace's," rejoined his friend with emphasis, "an' we won't waste no time in Powers' shack, neither; we'll push right through as hard as we can go for Buckskin. Let them fellers find their own hunting-our outfit comes first. An' besides that'll mean a detour in a country fine for ambushes. We'd never get through."

"Well, have it yore own way, then!" snapped Red. "You allus was a hard-headed old mule, any-how." In his heart Red knew that Hopalong was right about Wallace's and the Cross-O-Cross.

Some time after the two punchers had quitted the scene of their trap, several Apaches loped up, read the story of the tragedy at a glance, and galloped on in pursuit. They had left the reservation a fortnight before under the able leadership of that veteran of many war-trails — Black Bear. Their leader, chafing at inaction and sick of the monotony of reservation life, had yielded to the entreaties of a score of restless young men and slipped away at their head, eager for the joys of raiding and plundering. But instead of stealing horses and murdering isolated whites as they had expected, they met with heavy repulses and were now without the mind of their leader. They had fled from one defeat to another and twice had barely eluded the cavalry which pursued them. Now two more of their dwindling force were dead and another had been found but an hour before. Rage and ferocity seethed in each savage heart and they determined to get the puncher they had chased, and that other whose trail they now saw for the first time. They would place at least one victory against the string of their defeats, and at any cost. Whips rose and fell and the war-party shot forward in a compact group, two scouts thrown ahead to feel the way.

Red and Hopalong rode on rejoicing, for there were three less Apaches loose in the South-west for the inhabitants to swear about and fear, and there was an excellent chance of more to follow. The Southwest had no toleration for the Government's policy of dealing with Indians and derived a great amount of satisfaction every time an Apache was killed. It still clung to the time-honored belief that the only good Indian was a dead one. Mr. Cassidy voiced his elation and then rubbed an empty stomach in vain regret, —when a bullet shrilled past his head, so unexpectedly as to cause him to duck instinctively and then glance apologetically at his red-haired friend; and both spurred their mounts to greater speed. Next Mr. Connors grabbed frantically at his perforated sombrero and grew petulant and loquacious.

"Both them shots was lucky, Hoppy; the feller that fired at me did it on the dead run; but that won't help us none if one of 'em connects with us. You gimme that Sharps-got to show 'em that they're taking big chances crowding us this way." He took the heavy rifle and turned in the saddle. "It's an even thousand, if it's a yard. He don't look very big, can't hardly tell him from his cayuse; an' the wind's puffy. Why don't you dirty or rust this gun? The sun glitters all along the barrel. Well, here goes."

"Missed by a mile," reproved Hopalong, who would have been stunned by such a thing as a hit under the circumstances, even if his good-shooting friend had made it.

"Yes! Missed the coyote I aimed for, but I got the cayuse of his off pardner; see it?"

"Talk about luck!"

"That's all right: it takes blamed good shooting to miss that close in this case. Look! It's slowed 'em up a bit, an' that's about all I hoped to do. Bet they think I'm a real, shore-'nuff medicine-man. Now gimme another cartridge."

"I will not; no use wasting lead at this range. We'll need all the cartridges we got before we get out of this hole. You can't do nothing without stopping-an' that takes time."

"Then I'll stop! The blazes with the time! Gimme another, d'ye hear?"

Mr. Cassidy heard, complied, and stopped beside his companion, who was very intent upon the matter at hand. It took some figuring to make a hit when the range was so great and the sun so blinding and the wind so capricious. He lowered the rifle and peered through the smoke at the confusion he had caused by dropping the nearest warrior. He was said to be the best rifle shot in the Southwest, which means a great deal, and his enemies did not deny it. But since the Sharps shot a special cartridge and was reliable up to the limit of its sight gauge, a matter of eighteen hundred yards, he did not regard the hit as anything worthy of especial mention. Not so his friend, who grinned joyously and loosed his admiration.

"Yo're a shore wonder with that gun, Red! Why don't you lose that repeater an' get a gun like mine? Lord, if I could use a rifle like you, I wouldn't have that gun of yourn for a gift. Just look at what you did with it! Please get one like it."

"I'm plumb satisfied with the repeater," replied Red. "I don't miss very often at eight hundred with it, an' that's long enough range for most anybody. An' if I do miss, I can send another that won't, an' right on the tail of the first, too."

"Ah, the devil! You make me disgusted with yore fool talk about that carbine!" snapped his companion, and the subject was dropped.

The merits of their respective rifles had always been a bone of contention between them and one well chewed, at that. Red was very well satisfied with his Winchester, and he was a good judge.

"You did stop 'em a little," asserted Mr. Cassidy some time later when he looked back. "You stopped 'em coming straight, but they're spreading out to work up around us. Now, if we had good cayuses instead of these wooden wonders, we could run away from 'em dead easy, draw their best mounted warriors to the front an' then close with 'em. Good thing their cayuses are well tired out, for as it is we've got to make a stand purty soon. Gee! They don't like you, Red; they're calling you names in the sign language. Just look at 'em cuss you!"

"How much water have you got?" inquired his friend with anxiety.

"Canteen plumb full. How're you fixed?"

"I got the same, less one drink. That gives us enough for a couple of days with some to spare, if we're careful," Mr. Connors replied. New Mexican canteens are built on generous lines and are known as life-preservers.

"Look at that glory-hunter go!" exclaimed Red, watching a brave who was riding half a mile to their right and rapidly coming abreast of them. "Wonder how he got over there without us seeing him."

"Here; stop him!" suggested Hopalong, holding out his Sharps. "We can't let him get ahead of us and lay in ambush-that's what he's playing to do."

"My gun's good, and better, for me, at this range; but you know, I can't hit a jack-rabbit going over rough country as fast as that feller is," replied his companion, standing up in his stirrups and firing.

"Huh! Never touched him! But he's edging off a-plenty. See him cuss you. What's he calling you, anyhow?"

"Aw, shut up! How the devil do *I* know? I don't talk with my arms."

"Are you superstitious, Red?"

"No! Shut up!"

"Well, I am. See that feller over there? If he gets in front of us it's a shore sign that somebody's going to get hurt. He'll have plenty of time to get cover an' pick us off as we come up."

"Don't you worry-his cayuse is deader'n ours. They must 'a' been pushing on purty hard the last few days. See it stumble? —what'd I tell you!"

"Yes; but they're gaining on us slow but shore. We've got to make a stand purty soon-how much further do you reckon that infernal shack is, anyhow?" Hopalong asked sharply.

"'T ain't fur off-see it any minute now."

"Here," remarked Hopalong, holding out his rifle, "stencil yore mark on his hide; catch him just as he strikes the top of that little rise."

"Ain't got time-that shack can't be much further."

And it wasn't, for as they galloped over a rise they saw, half a mile ahead of them, an adobe building in poor state of preservation. It was Powers' old ranch house, and as they neared it, they saw that there was no doubt about the holes.

"Told you it was a sieve," grunted Hopalong, swinging in on the tail of his companion. "Not worth a hang for anything," he added bitterly.

"It'll answer, all right," retorted Red grimly.

Chapter IX
Mr. Holden Drops In

Mr. Cassidy dismounted and viewed the building with open disgust, walking around it to see what held it up, and when he finally realized that it was self-supporting his astonishment was profound. Undoubtedly there were shacks in the United States in worse condition, but he hoped their number was small. Of course he knew that the building was small. Of course he knew that the building would make a very good place of defence, but for the sake of argument he called to his companion and urged that they be satisfied with what defence they could extemporize in the open. Mr. Connors hotly and hastily dissented as he led the horses into the building, and straightway the subject was arbitrated with much feeling and snappy eloquence. Finally Hopalong thought that Red was a chump, and said so out loud, whereat Red said unpleasant things about his good friend's pedigree, attributes, intelligence, et al., even going so far as to prognosticate his friend's place of eternal abode. The remarks were fast getting to be somewhat personal in tenor when a whine in the air swept up the scale to a vicious shriek as it passed between them, dropped rapidly to a whine again and quickly died out in the distance, a flat report coming to their ears a few seconds later. Invisible bees seemed to be winging through the air, the angry and venomous droning becoming more pronounced each passing moment, and the irregular cracking of rifles grew louder rapidly. An angry *s-p-a-t!* told of where a stone behind them had launched the ricochet which hurled skyward with a wheezing scream. A handful of 'dobe dust sprang from the corner of the building and sifted down upon them, causing Red to cough.

"That ricochet was a Sharps!" exclaimed Hopalong, and they lost no time in getting into the building, where the discussion was renewed as they prepared for the final struggle. Red grunted his cheerful approval, for now he was out of the blazing sun and where he could better appreciate the musical tones of the flying bullets; but his companion, slamming shut the door and propping it with a fallen roof-beam, grumbled and finally gave rein to his rancor by sneering at the Winchester.

"It shore gets me that after all I have said about that gun you will tote it around with you and force yoreself into a suicide's grave," quoth Mr. Cassidy, with exuberant pugnacity. "I ain't in no way objecting to the suicide part of it, but I can't see that it's at all fair to drag *me* onto the edge of everlasting eternity with you. If you ain't got no regard for yore own life you shore ought to think a little about yore friend's. Now you'll waste all yore cartridges an' then come snooping around me to borrow my gun. Why don't you lose the damned thing?"

"What I pack ain't none of yore business, which same I'll uphold," retorted Mr. Connors, at last able to make himself heard. "You get over on yore own side an' use yore Colt; I've wondered a whole lot where you ever got the sense to use a Colt —*I* wouldn't be a heap surprised to see you toting a pearl-handled .22, like the kids use. Now you 'tend to yore grave-yard aspirants, an' lemme do the same with mine."

"The Lord knows I've stood a whole lot from you because you just can't help being foolish, but I've got plumb weary and sick of it. It stops right here or you won't get no 'Paches," snorted Hopalong, peering intently through a hole in the shack. The more they squabbled the better they liked it, —controversies had become so common that they were merely a habit; and they served to take the grimness out of desperate situations.

"Aw, you can't lick one side of me," averred Red loftily. "You never did stop anybody that was anything," he jeered as he fired from his window. "Why, you couldn't even hit the bottom of the Grand Canyon if you leaned over the edge."

"You could, if you leaned too far, you red-headed wart of a half-breed," snapped Hopalong. "But how about the Joneses, Tarantula Charley, Slim Travennes, an' all the rest? How about them, hey?"

"Huh! You couldn't 'a' got any of 'em if they had been sober," and Mr. Connors shook so with mirth that the Indian at whom he had fired got away with a whole skin and cheerfully derided the marksman. "That 'Pache shore reckons it was you shooting at him, I missed him so far. Now, you shut up—I want to get some so we can go home. I don't want to stay out here all night an' the next day as well," Red grumbled, his words dying slowly in his throat as he voiced other thoughts.

Hopalong caught sight of an Apache who moved cautiously through a chaparral lying about nine hundred yards away. As long as the distant enemy lay quietly he could not be discerned, but he was not content with assured safety and took a chance. Hopalong raised his rifle to his shoulder as the Indian fired and the latter's bullet, striking the edge of the hole through which Mr. Cassidy peered, kicked up a generous handful of dust, some of which found lodgment in that individual's eyes.

"Oh! Oh! Oh! Wow!" yelled the unfortunate, dancing blindly around the room in rage and pain, and dropping his rifle to grab at his eyes. "Oh! Oh! Oh!"

His companion wheeled like a flash and grabbed him as he stumbled past. "Are you plugged bad, Hoppy? Where did they get you? Are you hit bad?" and Red's heart was in his voice.

"No, I ain't plugged bad!" mimicked Hopalong. "I ain't plugged at all!" he blazed, kicking enthusiastically at his solicitous friend. "Get me some water, you jackass! Don't stand there like a fool! I ain't going to fall down. Don't you know my eyes are full of 'dobe?"

Red, avoiding another kick, hastily complied, and as hastily left Mr. Cassidy to wash out the dirt while he returned to his post by the window. "Anybody'd think you was full of red-eye, the way you act," muttered Red peevishly.

Hopalong, rubbing his eyes of the dirt, went back to the hole in the wall and looked out. "Hey, Red! Come over here an' spill that brave's conceit. I can't keep my eyes open long enough to aim, an' it's a nice shot, too. It'd serve him right if you got him!"

Mr. Connors obeyed the summons and peered out cautiously. "I can't see him, nohow; where is the coyote?"

"Over there in that little chaparral; see him now? *There!* See him moving. Do you mean to tell me—"

"Yep; I see him, all right. You watch," was the reply. "He's just over nine hundred-where's yore Sharps?" He took the weapon, glanced at the Buffington sight, which he found to be set right, and aimed carefully.

Hopalong blinked through another hole as his friend fired and saw the Indian flop down and crawl aimlessly about on hands and knees. "What's he doing now, Red?"

"Playing marbles, you chump; an' here goes for his agate," replied the man with the Sharps, firing again. "There! Gee!" he exclaimed, as a bullet hummed in through the window he had quitted for the moment, and thudded into the wall, making the dry adobe fly. It had missed him by only a few inches and he now crept along the floor to the rear of the room and shoved his rifle out among the branches of a stunted mesquite which grew before a fissure in the wall. "You keep away from that windy for a minute, Hoppy," he warned as he waited.

A terror-stricken lizard flashed out of the fissure and along the wall where the roof had fallen in and flitted into a hole, while a fly buzzed loudly and hovered persistently around Red's head, to the rage of that individual. "Ah, ha!" he grunted, lowering the rifle and peering through the smoke. A yell reached his ears and he forthwith returned to his window, whistling softly.

Evidently Mr. Cassidy's eyes were better and his temper sweeter, for he hummed "Dixie" and then jumped to "Yankee Doodle," mixing the two airs with careless impartiality, which was a sign that he was thinking deeply. "Wonder what ever became of Powers, Red. Peculiar feller, he was."

"In jail, I reckon, if drink hasn't killed him."

"Yes; I reckon so," and Mr. Cassidy continued his medley, which prompted his friend quickly to announce his unqualified disapproval.

"You can make more of a mess of them two songs than anybody I ever heard murder 'em! *Shut up!*" —and the concert stopped, the vocalist venting his feelings at an Indian, and killing the horse instead.

"Did you get him?" queried Red.

"Nope; but I got his cayuse," Hopalong replied, shoving a fresh cartridge into the foul, greasy breech of the Sharps. "An' here's where I get him-got to square up for my eyes some way," he muttered, firing. "Missed! Now what do you think of that!" he exclaimed.

"Better take my Winchester," suggested Red, in a matter-of-fact way, but he chuckled softly and listened for the reply.

"Aw, you go to the devil!" snapped Mr. Cassidy, firing again. "Whoop! Got him that time!"

"Where?" asked his companion, with strong suspicion.

"None of yore business!"

"Aw, darn it! Who spilled the water?" yelled Red, staring blankly at the overturned canteen.

"Pshaw! Reckon I did, Red," apologized his friend ruefully. "Now of all the cussed luck!"

"Oh, well; we've got another, an' you had to wash out yore eyes. Lucky we each had one — *Holy smoke!* It's most all gone! The top is loose!"

Heartfelt profanity filled the room and the two disgusted punchers went sullenly back to their posts. It was a calamity of no small magnitude, for, while food could be dispensed with for a long time if necessary, going without water was another question. It was as necessary as cartridges.

Then Hopalong laughed at the ludicrous side of the whole affair, thereby revealing one of the characteristics which endeared him to his friends. No matter how desperate a situation might be, he could always find in it something at which to laugh. He laughed going into danger and coming out of it, with a joke or a pleasantry always trembling on the end of his tongue.

"Red, did it ever strike you how cussed thirsty a feller gets just as soon as he knows he can't have no drink? But it don't make much difference, nohow. We'll get out of this little scrape just as we've allus got out of trouble. There's some mad war-whoops outside that are worse off than we are, because they are at the wrong end of yore gun. I feel sort of sorry for 'em."

"Yo're shore a happy idiot," grinned Red. "Hey! Listen!"

Galloping was heard and Hopalong, running to the door, looked out through a crack as sudden firing broke out around the rear of the shack, and fell to pulling away the props, crying, "It's a puncher, Red; he's riding this way! Come on an' help him in!"

"He's a blamed fool to ride this way! I'm with you!" replied Red, running to his side.

Half a mile from the house, coming across the open space as fast as he could urge his horse, rode a cowboy, and not far behind him raced about a dozen Apaches, yelling and firing.

Red picked up his companion's rifle, and steadying it against the jamb of the door, fired, dropping one of the foremost of the pursuers. Quickly reloading again, he fired and missed. The third shot struck another horse, and then taking up his own gun he began to fire rapidly, as rapidly as he could work the lever and yet make his shots tell. Hopalong drew his Colt and ran back to watch the rear of the house, and it was well that he did so, for an Apache in that direction, believing that the trapped punchers were so busily engaged with the new developments as to forget for the moment, sprinted towards the back window; and he had gotten within twenty paces of the goal when Hopalong's Colt cracked a protest. Seeing that the warrior was no longer a combatant, Mr. Cassidy ran back to the door just as the stranger fell from his horse and crawled past Red. The door slammed shut, the props fell against it, and the two friends turned to the work of driving back the second band, which, however, had given up all hope of rushing the house in the face of Red's telling fire, and had sought cover instead.

The stranger dragged himself to the canteens and drank what little water remained, and then turned to watch the two men moving from place to place, firing coolly and methodically. He thought he recognized one of them from the descriptions he had heard, but he was not sure.

"My name's Holden," he whispered hoarsely, but the cracking of the rifles drowned his voice. During a lull he tried again. "My name's Holden," he repeated weakly. "I'm from the Cross-O-Cross, an' can't get back there again."

"Mine's Cassidy, an' that's Connors, of the Bar-20. Are you hurt very bad?"

"No; not very bad," lied Holden, trying to smile. "Gee, but I'm glad I fell in with you two fellers," he exclaimed. He was but little more than a boy, and to him Hopalong Cassidy and Red Connors were names with which to conjure. "But I'm plumb sorry I went an' brought you more trouble," he added regretfully.

"Oh, pshaw! We had it before you came-you needn't do no worrying about that, Holden; besides, I reckon you couldn't help it," Hopalong grinned facetiously. "But tell us how you came to mix up with that bunch," he continued.

Holden shuddered and hesitated a moment, his companions alertly shifting from crack to crack, window to window, their rifles cracking at intervals. They appeared to him to act as if they had done nothing else all their lives but fight Indians from that shack, and he braced up a little at their example of coolness.

"It's an awful story, awful!" he began. "I was riding towards Hoyt's Corners an' when I got about half way there I topped a rise an' saw a nester's house about half a mile away. It wasn't there the last time I rode that way, an' it looked so peaceful an' home-like that I stopped an' looked at it a few minutes. I was just going to start again when that war-party rode out of a barranca close to the house an' went straight for it at top speed. It seemed like a dream, 'cause I thought Apaches never got so far east. They don't, do they? I thought not-these must 'a' got turned out of their way an' had to hustle for safety. Well, it was all over purty quick. I saw 'em drag out two women an' —an' —purty soon a man. He was fighting like fury, but he didn't last long. Then they set fire to the house an' threw the man's body up on the roof. I couldn't seem to move till the flames shot up, but then I must 'a' went sort of loco, because I emptied my gun at 'em, which was plumb foolish at that distance, for me. The next thing I knowed was that half of 'em was coming my way as hard as they could ride, an' I lit out instanter; an' here I am. I can't get that sight outen my head nohow-it'll drive me loco!" he screamed, sobbing like a child from the horror of it all.

His auditors still moved around the room, growing more and more vindictive all the while and more zealously endeavoring to create a still greater deficit in one Apache war-party. They knew what he had looked upon, for they themselves had become familiar with the work of Apaches in Arizona. They could picture it vividly in all its devilish horror. Neither of them paid any apparent attention to their companion, for they could not spare the time, and, also, they believed it best to let him fight out his own battles unassisted.

Holden sobbed and muttered as the minutes dragged along, at times acting so strangely as to draw a covert side-glance from one or both of the Bar-20 punchers. Then Mr. Connors saw his boon companion suddenly lean out of a window and immediately become the target for the hard-working enemy. He swore angrily at the criminal recklessness of it. "Hey, you! Come in out of that! Ain't you got no brains at all, you blasted idiot! Don't you know that we need every gun?"

"Yes; that's right. I sort of forgot," grinned the reckless one, obeying with alacrity and looking sheepish. "But you know there's two thundering big tarantulas out there fighting like blazes. You ought to see 'em jump! It's a sort of a leap-frog fight, Red."

"Fool!" snorted Mr. Connors belligerently. "*You'd* 'a' jumped if one of them slugs had 'a' got you! Yo're the damnedest fool that ever walked on two laigs, you blasted sage-hen!" Mr. Connors was beginning to lose his temper and talk in his throat.

"Well, they didn't get me, did they? What you yelling about, anyhow?" growled Hopalong, trying to brazen it out.

"An' *you* talking about suicide to me!" snapped Mr. Connors, determined to rub it in and have the last word.

Mr. Holden stared, open-mouthed, at the man who could enjoy a miserable spider fight under such distressing circumstances, and his shaken nerves became steadier as he gave thought to the fact that he was a companion of the two men about whose exploits he had heard so much. Evidently the stories had not been exaggerated. What must they think of him for giving way as he had? He rose to his feet in time to see a horse blunder into the open on Red's side of the house, and after it blundered its owner, who immediately lost all need of earthly conveyances. Holden laughed from the joy of being with a man who could shoot like that, and he took up his rifle and turned to a crack in the wall, filled with the determination to let his companions know that he was built of the right kind of timber after all, wounded as he was.

Red's only comment, as he pumped a fresh cartridge into the barrel, was, "He must 'a' thought he saw a spider fight, too."

"Hey, Red," called Hopalong. "The big one is dead."

"What big one?"

"Why, don't you remember? That big tarantula I was watching. One was bigger than the other, but the little feller shore waded into him an' —"

"Go to the devil!" shouted Red, who had to grin, despite his anger.

"Presently, presently," replied Hopalong, laughing.

So the day passed, and when darkness came upon them all of the defenders were wounded, Holden desperately so.

"Red, one of us has got to try to make the ranch," Hopalong suddenly announced, and his friend knew he was right. Since Holden had appeared upon the scene they had known that they could not try a dash; one of them had to stay.

"We'll toss for it; heads, I go," Red suggested, flipping a coin.

"Tails!" cried Hopalong. "It's only thirty miles to Buckskin, an' if I can get away from here I'm good to make it by eleven to-night. I'll stop at Cowan's an' have him send word to Lucas an' Bartlett, so there'll be enough in case any of our boys are out on the range in some line house. We can pick 'em up on the way back, so there won't be no time lost. If I get through you can expect excitement on the outside of this sieve by daylight. You an' Holden can hold her till then, because they never attack at night. It's the only way out of this for us-we ain't got cartridges or water enough to last another day."

Red, knowing that Hopalong was taking a desperate chance in working through the cordon of Indians which surrounded them, and that the house was safe when compared to running such a gantlet, offered to go through the danger line with him. For several minutes a wordy war raged and finally Red accepted a compromise; he was to help, but not to work through the line.

"But what's the use of all this argument?" feebly demanded Holden. "Why don't you both go? I ain't a-going to live nohow, so there ain't no use of anybody staying here with me, to die with me. Put a bullet through me so them devils can't play with me like they do with others, an' then get away while you've got a chance. Two men can get through as easy as one." He sank back, exhausted by the effort.

"No more of that!" cried Red, trying to be stern. "I'm going to stay with you an' see things through. I'd be a fine sort of a coyote to sneak off an' leave you for them fiends. An', besides, I can't get away; my cayuse is hit too hard an' yourn is dead," he lied cheerfully. "An' yo're going to get well, all right. I've seen fellers hit harder than you are pull through."

Hopalong walked over to the prostrate man and shook hands with him. "I'm awful glad I met you, Holden. Yo're pure grit all the way through, an' I like to tie to that kind of a man. Don't you worry about nothing; Red can handle this proposition, an' we'll have you in Buckskin by to-morrow night; you'll be riding again in two weeks. So long."

He turned to Red and shook hands silently, led his horse out of the building and mounted, glad that the moon had not yet come up, for in the darkness he had a chance.

"Good luck, Hoppy!" cried Red, running to the door. "Good luck!"

"You bet-an' lots of it, too," groaned Holden, but he was gone. Then Red wheeled. "Holden, keep yore eyes an' ears open. I'm going out to see that he gets off. He may run into a —" and he, too, was gone.

Holden watched the doors and windows, striving to resist the weak, giddy feeling in his head, and ten minutes later he heard a shot and then several more in quick succession. Shortly afterward Red called out, and almost immediately the Bar-20 puncher crawled in through a window.

"Well?" anxiously cried the man on the floor. "Did he make it?"

"I reckon so. He got away from the first crowd, anyhow. I wasn't very far behind him, an' by the time they woke up to what was going on he was through an' riding like blazes. I heard him call 'em half-breeds a moment later an' it sounded far off. They hit me, —fired at my flash, like I drilled one of them. But it ain't much, anyhow. How are you feeling now?"

"Fine!" lied the other. "That Cassidy is shore a wonder-he's all right, an' so are you. I'll never see him again, but I shore hope he gets through!"

"Don't be foolish. Here, you finish the water in yore canteen —I picked it up outside by yore cayuse. Then go to sleep," ordered Red. "I'll do all the watching that's necessary."

"I will if you'll call me when you get sleepy."

"Why, shore I will. But don't you want the rest of the water? I ain't a bit thirsty —I had all I could hold just before you came," Red remarked as his companion pushed the canteen against him in the dark. He was choking with thirst. "Well, then; all right," and Red pretended to drink. "Now, then, you go to sleep; a good snooze will do you a world of good-it's just what you need."

Chapter X
Buck Takes a Hand

Cowan's saloon, club, and place of general assembly for the town of Buckskin and the nearby ranches, held a merry crowd, for it was pay-day on the range and laughter and liquor ran a close race. Buck Peters, his hands full of cigars, passed through the happy-go-lucky, do-as-you-please crowd and invited everybody to smoke, which nobody refused to do. Wood Wright, of the C-80, tuned his fiddle anew and swung into a rousing quick-step. Partners were chosen, the "women" wearing handkerchiefs on their arms to indicate the fact, and the room shook and quivered as the scraping of heavy boots filled the air with a cloud of dust. "Allaman left!" cried the prompter, and then the dance stopped as if by magic. The door had crashed open and a blood-stained man staggered in and towards the bar, crying, "Buck! Red's hemmed in by 'Paches!"

"Good God!" roared the foreman of the Bar-20, leaping forward, the cigars falling to the floor to be crushed and ground into powder by careless feet. He grasped his puncher and steadied him while Cowan slid an extra generous glassful of brandy across the bar for the wounded man. The room was in an uproar, men grabbing rifles and running out to get their horses, for it was plain to be seen that there was hard work to be done, and quickly. Questions, threats, curses filled the air, those who remained inside to get the story listening intently to the jerky narrative; those outside, caring less for the facts of an action past than for the action to come, shouted impatiently for a start to be made, even threatening to go on and tackle the proposition by themselves if there were not more haste. Hopalong told in a graphic, terse manner all that was necessary, while Buck and Cowan hurriedly bandaged his wounds.

"Come on! Come on!" shouted the mounted crowd outside, angry, and impatient for a start, the prancing of horses and the clinking of metal adding to the noise. "Get a move on! *Will* you hurry up!"

"Listen, Hoppy!" pleaded Buck, in a furore. "Shut up, you outside!" he yelled. "You say they know that you got away, Hoppy?" he asked. "All right —*Lanky!*" he shouted. "*Lanky!*"

"All right, Buck!" and Lanky Smith roughly pushed his way through the crowd to his foreman's side. "Here I am."

"Take Skinny and Pete with you, an' a lead horse apiece. Strike straight for Powers' old ranch house. Them Injuns'll have pickets out looking for Hoppy's friends. You three get the pickets nearest the old trail through that arroyo to the southeast, an' then wait for us. We'll come along the high bank on the left. Don't make no noise doing it, neither, if you can help it. Understand? Good! Now ride like the devil!"

Lanky grabbed Pete and Skinny on his way out and disappeared into the corral; and very soon thereafter hoof-beats thudded softly in the sandy street and pounded into the darkness of the north, soon lost to the ear. An uproar of advice and good wishes crashed after them, for the game had begun.

"It's Powers' old shack, boys!" shouted a man in the door to the restless force outside, which immediately became more restless. "Hey! Don't go yet!" he begged. "Wait for me an' the rest. Don't be a lot of idiots!"

Excited and impatient voices replied from the darkness, vexed, grouchy, and querulous. "Then get a move on —*whoa!* —it'll be light before we get there if you don't hustle!" roared one voice above the confusion. "You know what *that* means!"

"Come on! Come on! For God's sake, are you tied to the bar?"

"Yo're a lot of old grandmothers! Come on!"

Hopalong appeared in the door. "I'll show you the way, boys!" he shouted. "Cowan, put my saddle on yore cayuse —*pronto!*"

"Good for you, Hoppy!" came from the street. "We'll wait!"

"You stay here; yo're hurt too much!" cried Buck to his puncher, as he grabbed up a box of cartridges from a shelf behind the bar. "Ain't you got no sense? There's enough of us to take care of this without you!"

Hopalong wheeled and looked his foreman squarely in the eyes. "Red's out there, waiting for me —I'm going! I'd be a fine sort of a coyote to leave him in that hell hole an' not go back, wouldn't I!" he said, with quiet determination.

"Good for you, Cassidy!" cried a man who hastened out to mount.

"Well, then, come on," replied Buck. "There's blamed few like you," he muttered, following Hopalong outside.

"Here's the cayuse, Cassidy," cried Cowan, turning the animal over to him. "*Wait*, Buck!" and he leaped into the building and ran out again, shoving a bottle of brandy and a package of food into the impatient foreman's hand. "Mebby Red or Hoppy'll need it-so long, an' good luck!" and he was alone in a choking cloud of dust, peering through the darkness along the river trail after a black mass that was swallowed up almost instantly. Then, as he watched, the moon pushed its rim up over the hills and he laughed joyously as he realized what its light would mean to the crowd. "There'll be great doings when *that* gang cuts loose," he muttered with savage elation. "Wish I was with 'em. Damn Injuns, anyhow!"

Far ahead of the main fighting force rode the three special-duty men, reeling off the miles at top speed and constantly distancing their friends, for they changed mounts at need, thanks to the lead horses provided by Mr. Peters' cool-headed foresight. It was a race against dawn, and every effort was made to win-the life of Red Connors hung in the balance and a minute might turn the scale.

In Powers' old ranch house the night dragged along slowly to the grim watcher, and the man huddled in the corner stirred uneasily and babbled, ofttimes crying out in horror at the vivid dreams of his disordered mind. Pacing ceaselessly from window to window, crack to crack, when the moon came up, Mr. Connors scanned the bare, level plain with anxious eyes, searching out the few covers and looking for dark spots on the dull gray sand. They never attacked at night, but still —. Through the void came the quavering call of a coyote, and he listened for the reply, which soon came from the black chaparral across the clearing. He knew where two of them were hiding, anyhow. Holden was muttering and tried to answer the calls, and Red looked at him for the hundredth time that night. He glanced out of the window again and noticed that there was a glow in the eastern sky, and shortly afterwards dawn swiftly developed.

Pouring the last few drops of the precious water between the wounded man's parched and swollen lips, he tossed the empty canteen from him and stood erect.

"Pore devil," he muttered, shaking his head sorrowfully, as he realized that Holden's delirium was getting worse all the time. "If you was all right we could give them wolves hell to dance to. Well, you won't know nothing about it if we go under, an' that's some consolation." He examined his rifle and saw that the Colt at his thigh was fully loaded and in good working order. "An' they'll pay us for their victory, by God! They'll pay for it!" He stepped closer to the window, throwing the rifle into the hollow of his arm. "It's about time for the rush; about time for the game —"

There was movement by that small chaparral to the south! To the east something stirred into bounding life and action; a coyote called twice-and then they came, on foot and silently as fleeting shadows, leaning forward to bring into play every ounce of energy in the slim, red legs. Smoke filled the room with its acrid sting. The crashing of the Winchester, worked with wonderful speed and deadly accuracy by the best rifle shot in the Southwest, brought the prostrate man to his feet in an instinctive response to the call to action, the necessity of defence. He grasped his Colt and stumbled blindly to a window to help the man who had stayed with him.

On Red's side of the house one warrior threw up his arms and fell forward, sprawling with arms and legs extended; another pitched to one side and rolled over twice before he lay still; the legs of the third collapsed and threw him headlong, bunched up in a grotesque pile of lifeless flesh; the fourth leaped high into the air and turned a somersault before he struck the sand, badly wounded, and out of the fight. Holden, steadying himself against the wall, leaned in a window on the other side of the shack and emptied his Colt in a dazed manner-doing his very best. Then the man with the rifle staggered back with a muttered curse, his right arm useless, and dropped the weapon to draw his Colt with the other hand.

Holden shrieked once and sank down, wagging his head slowly from side to side, blood oozing from his mouth and nostrils; and his companion, goaded into a frenzy of blood-lust and insane rage at the sight, threw himself against the door and out into the open, to die under the clear sky, to go like the man he was if he must die. "Damn you! It'll cost you more yet!" he screamed, wheeling to place his back against the wall.

The triumphant yells of the exultant savages were cut short and turned to howls of dismay by a fusillade which thundered from the south where a crowd of hard-riding, hard-shooting cow-punchers tore out of the thicket like an avalanche and swept over the open sand, yelling and cursing, and then separated to go in hot pursuit of the sprinting Apaches. Some stood up in their stirrups and fired down at a slant, making a short, chopping motion with their heavy Colts; others leaned forward, far over the necks of their horses, and shot with stationary guns; while yet others, with reins dangling free, worked the levers of blue Winchesters so rapidly that the flashes seemed to merge into a continuous flame.

"Thank God! Thank God-an' Hoppy!" groaned the man at the door of the shack, staggering forward to meet the two men who had lost no time in pursuit of the enemy, but had ridden straight to him.

"I was scared stiff you was done fer!" cried Hopalong, leaping off his horse and shaking hands with his friend, whose hand-clasp was not as strong as usual. "How's Holden?" he demanded, anxiously.

"He passed. It was a close —" began Red, weakly, but his foreman interposed.

"Shut up, an' drink this!" ordered Buck, kindly but sternly. "We'll do the talking for a while; you can tell us all about it later on. Why, *bullo!*" he cried as Lanky Smith and his two happy companions rode up. "Reckon you must 'a' got them pickets."

"Shore we did! Stalked 'em on our bellies, didn't we, Skinny?" modestly replied Mr. Smith, the roping expert of the Bar-20. "Ropes an' clubbed guns did the rest. Anyhow, there was only two anywhere near the trail."

"We didn't see you," responded the foreman, tying the knot of a bandage on Mr. Connors' arm. "An' we looked sharp, too."

"Reckon we was hunting for more; we sort of forgot what you said about waiting for you," Mr. Smith replied, grinning broadly.

"An' you've got a good memory now," smiled Mr. Peters.

"We didn't find no more, though," offered Mr. Pete Wilson, with grave regret. "An' we looked good, too. But we got Red, an' that's the whole game. Red, you old son-of-a-gun, you can lick yore weight in powder!"

"It's too bad about Holden," muttered Red, sullenly.

Chapter XI
Hopalong Nurses a Grouch

After the excitement incident to the affair at Powers' shack had died down and the Bar-20 outfit worked over its range in the old, placid way, there began to be heard low mutterings, and an air of peevish discontent began to be manifested in various childish ways. And it was all caused by the fact that Hopalong Cassidy had a grouch, and a big one. It was two months old and growing worse daily, and the signs threatened contagion. His foreman, tired and sick of the snarling, fidgety, petulant atmosphere that Hopalong had created on the ranch, and driven to desperation, eagerly sought some chance to get rid of the "sore-thumb" temporarily and give him an opportunity to shed his generous mantle of the blues. And at last it came.

No one knew the cause for Hoppy's unusual state of mind, although there were many conjectures, and they covered the field rather thoroughly; but they did not strike on the cause. Even Red Connors, now well over all ill effects of the wounds acquired in the old ranch house, was forced to guess; and when Red had to do that about anything concerning Hopalong he was well warranted in believing the matter to be very serious.

Johnny Nelson made no secret of his opinion and derived from it a great amount of satisfaction, which he admitted with a grin to his foreman.

"Buck," he said, "Hoppy told me he went broke playing poker over in Grant with Dave Wilkes and them two Lawrence boys, an' that shore explains it all. He's got pack sores from carrying his unholy licking. It was due to come for him, an' Dave Wilkes is just the boy to deliver it. That's the whole trouble, an' I know it, an' I'm damned glad they trimmed him. But he ain't got no right of making *us* miserable because he lost a few measly dollars."

"Yo're wrong, son; dead, dead wrong," Buck replied. "He takes his beatings with a grin, an' money never did bother him. No poker game that ever was played could leave a welt on him like the one we all mourn, an' cuss. He's been doing something that he don't want us to know-made a fool of hisself some way, most likely, an' feels so ashamed that he's sore. I've knowed him too long an' well to believe that gambling had anything to do with it. But this little trip he's taking will fix him up all right, an' I couldn't 'a' picked a better man-or one that I'd rather get rid of just now."

"Well, lemme tell you it's blamed lucky for him that you picked him to go," rejoined Johnny, who thought more of the woeful absentee than he did of his own skin. "I was going to lick him, shore, if it went on much longer. Me an' Red an' Billy was going to beat him up good till he forgot his dead injuries an' took more interest in his friends."

Buck laughed heartily. "Well, the three of you might 'a' done it if you worked hard an' didn't get careless, but I have my doubts. Now look here-you've been hanging around the bunk house too blamed much lately. Henceforth an' hereafter you've got to earn your grub. Get out on that west line an' hustle."

"You know I've had a toothache!" snorted Johnny with a show of indignation, his face as sober as that of a judge.

"An' you'll have a stomach ache from lack of grub if you don't earn yore right to eat purty soon," retorted Buck. "You ain't had a toothache in yore whole life, an' you don't know what one is. G'wan, now, or I'll give you a backache that'll ache!"

"Huh! Devil of a way to treat a sick man!" Johnny retorted, but he departed exultantly, whistling with much noise and no music. But he was sorry for one thing: he sincerely regretted that he had not been present when Hopalong met his Waterloo. It would have been pleasing to look upon.

While the outfit blessed the proposed lease of range that took him out of their small circle for a time, Hopalong rode farther and farther into the northwest, frequently lost in abstraction which, judging by its effect upon him, must have been caused by something serious. He had not heard from Dave Wilkes about that individual's good horse which had been loaned to Ben Ferris, of Winchester. Did Dave think he had been killed or was still pursuing the man whose neck-kerchief had aroused such animosity in Hopalong's heart? Or had the horse actually been returned? The animal was a good one, a successful contender in all distances from one to five miles, and had earned its owner and backers much money-and Hopalong had parted with it as easily as he would have borrowed five dollars from Red. The story, as he had often reflected since, was as old as lying—a broken-legged horse, a wife dying forty miles away, and a horse all saddled which needed only to be mounted and ridden.

These thoughts kept him company for a day and when he dismounted before Stevenson's "Hotel" in Hoyt's Corners he summed up his feelings for the enlightenment of his horse.

"Damn it, bronc! I'd give ten dollars right now to know if I was a jackass or not," he growled. "But he was an awful slick talker if he lied. An' I've got to go up an' face Dave Wilkes to find out about it!"

Mr. Cassidy was not known by sight to the citizens of Hoyt's Corners, however well versed they might be in his numerous exploits of wisdom and folly. Therefore the habitues of Stevenson's Hotel did not recognize him in the gloomy and morose individual who dropped his saddle on the floor with a crash and stamped over to the three-legged table at dusk and surlily demanded shelter for the night.

"Gimme a bed an' something to eat," he demanded, eyeing the three men seated with their chairs tilted against the wall. "Do I get 'em?" he asked, impatiently.

"You do," replied a one-eyed man, lazily arising and approaching him. "One dollar, now."

"An' take the rocks outen that bed —I want to sleep."

"A dollar per for every rock you find," grinned Stevenson, pleasantly. "There ain't no rocks in *my* beds," he added.

"Some folks likes to be rocked to sleep," facetiously remarked one of the pair by the wall, laughing contentedly at his own pun. He bore all the ear-marks of being regarded as the wit of the locality-every hamlet has one; I have seen some myself.

"Hee, hee, hee! Yo're a droll feller, Charley," chuckled Old John Ferris, rubbing his ear with unconcealed delight. "That's a good un."

"One drink, now," growled Hopalong, mimicking the proprietor, and glaring savagely at the "droll feller" and his companion. "An' mind that it's a good one," he admonished the host.

"It's better," smiled Stevenson, whereat Old John crossed his legs and chuckled again. Stevenson winked.

"Riding long?" he asked.

"Since I started."

"Going fur?"

"Till I stop."

"Where do you belong?" Stevenson's pique was urging him against the ethics of the range, which forbade personal questions.

Hopalong looked at him with a light in his eye that told the host he had gone too far. "Under my sombrero!" he snapped.

"Hee, hee, hee!" chortled Old John, rubbing his ear again and nudging Charley. "He ain't no fool, hey?"

"Why, I don't know, John; he won't tell," replied Charley.

Hopalong wheeled and glared at him, and Charley, smiling uneasily, made an appeal: "Ain't mad, are you?"

"Not yet," and Hopalong turned to the bar again, took up his liquor and tossed it off. Considering a moment he shoved the glass back again, while Old John tongued his lips in anticipation of a treat. "It is good—fill it again."

The third was even better and by the time the fourth and fifth had joined their predecessors Hopalong began to feel a little more cheerful. But even the liquor and an exceptionally well-cooked supper could not separate him from his persistent and set grouch. And of liquor he had already taken more than his limit. He had always boasted, with truth, that he had never been drunk, although there had been two occasions when he was not far from it. That was one doubtful luxury which he could not afford for the reason that there were men who would have been glad to see him, if only for a few seconds, when liquor had dulled his brain and slowed his speed of hand. He could never tell when and where he might meet one of these.

He dropped into a chair by a card table and, baffling all attempts to engage him in conversation, reviewed his troubles in a mumbled soliloquy, the liquor gradually making him careless. But of all the jumbled words his companions' diligent ears heard they recognized and retained only the bare term "Winchester"; and their conjectures were limited only by their imaginations.

Hopalong stirred and looked up, shaking off the hand which had aroused him. "Better go to bed, stranger," the proprietor was saying. "You an' me are the last two up. It's after twelve, an' you look tired and sleepy."

"Said his wife was sick," muttered the puncher. "Oh, what you saying?"

"You'll find a bed better'n this table, stranger—it's after twelve an' I want to close up an' get some sleep. I'm tired myself."

"Oh, that all? Shore I'll go to bed—like to see anybody stop me! Ain't no rocks in it, hey?"

"Nary a rock," laughingly reassured the host, picking up Hopalong's saddle and leading the way to a small room off the "office," his guest stumbling after him and growling about the rocks that lived in Winchester. When Stevenson had dropped the saddle by the window and departed, Hopalong sat on the edge of the bed to close his eyes for just a moment before tackling the labor of removing his clothes. A crash and a jar awakened him and he found himself on the floor with his back to the bed. He was hot and his head ached, and his back was skinned a little—and how hot and stuffy and choking the room had become! He thought he had blown out the light, but it still burned, and three-quarters of the chimney was thickly covered with soot. He was stifling and could not endure it any longer. After three attempts he put out the light, stumbled against his saddle and, opening the window, leaned out to breathe the pure air. As his lungs filled he chuckled wisely and, picking up the saddle, managed to get it and himself through the window and on the ground without serious mishap. He would ride for an hour, give the room time to freshen and cool off, and come back feeling much better. Not a star could be seen as he groped his way unsteadily towards the rear of the building, where he vaguely remembered having seen the corral as he rode up.

"Huh! Said he lived in Winchester an' his name was Bill—no, Ben Ferris," he muttered, stumbling towards a noise he knew was made by a horse rubbing against the corral fence. Then his feet got tangled up in the cinch of his saddle, which he had kicked before him, and after great labor he arose, muttering savagely, and continued on his wobbly way. "Goo' Lord, it's darker'n cats in —*oof!*" he grunted, recoiling from forcible contact with the fence he sought. Growling words unholy he felt his way along it and finally his arm slipped through an opening and he bumped his head solidly against the top bar of the gate. As he righted himself his hand struck the nose of a horse and closed mechanically over it. Cow-ponies look alike in the dark and he grinned jubilantly as he complimented himself upon finding his own so unerringly.

"Anything is easy, when you know how. Can't fool me, ol' cayuse," he beamed, fumbling at the bars with his free hand and getting them down with a fool's luck. "You can't do it —I got you firs', las', an' always; an' I got you good. Yessir, I got you good. Quit that rearing, you ol' fool! Stan' still, can't you?" The pony sidled as the saddle hit its back and evoked profane abuse from the indignant puncher as he risked his balance in picking it up to try again, this time successfully. He began to fasten the girth, and then paused in wonder and thought deeply, for the pin in the buckle would slide to no hole but the first. "Huh! Getting fat, ain't you, piebald?" he demanded with withering sarcasm. "You blow yoreself up any more'n I'll bust you wide open!" heaving up with all his might on the free end of the strap, one knee pushing against the animal's side. The "fat" disappeared and Hopalong laughed. "Been learnin' new tricks, ain't you? Got smart since you been travellin', hey?" He fumbled with the bars again and got two of them back in place and then, throwing himself across the saddle as the horse started forward as hard as it could go, slipped off, but managed to save himself by hopping along the ground. As soon as he had secured the grip he wished he mounted with the ease of habit and felt for the reins. "G'wan now, an' easy-it's plumb dark an' my head's bustin'."

When he saddled his mount at the corral he was not aware that two of the three remaining horses had taken advantage of their opportunity and had walked out and made off in the darkness before he replaced the bars, and he was too drunk to care if he had known it.

The night air felt so good that it moved him to song, but it was not long before the words faltered more and more and soon ceased altogether and a subdued snore rasped from him. He awakened from time to time, but only for a moment, for he was tired and sleepy.

His mount very quickly learned that something was wrong and that it was being given its head. As long as it could go where it pleased it could do nothing better than head for home, and it quickened its pace towards Winchester. Some time after daylight it pricked up its ears and broke into a canter, which soon developed signs of irritation in its rider. Finally Hopalong opened his heavy eyes and looked around for his bearings. Not knowing where he was and too tired and miserable to give much thought to a matter of such slight importance, he glanced around for a place to finish his sleep. A tree some distance ahead of him looked inviting and towards it he rode. Habit made him picket the horse before he lay down and as he fell asleep he had vague recollections of handling a strange picket rope some time recently. The horse slowly turned and stared at the already snoring figure, glanced over the landscape, back the to queerest man it had ever met, and then fell to grazing in quiet content. A slinking coyote topped a rise a short distance away and stopped instantly, regarding the sleeping man with grave curiosity and strong suspicion. Deciding that there was nothing good to eat in that vicinity and that the man was carrying out a fell plot for the death of coyotes, it backed away out of sight and loped on to other hunting grounds.

Chapter XII
A Friend in Need

Stevenson, having started the fire for breakfast, took a pail and departed towards the spring; but he got no farther than the corral gate, where he dropped the pail and stared. There was only one horse in the enclosure where the night before there had been four. He wasted no time in surmises, but wheeled and dashed back towards the hotel, and his vigorous shouts brought Old John to the door, sleepy and peevish. Old John's mouth dropped open as he beheld his habitually indolent host marking off long distances on the sand with each falling foot.

"What's got inter you?" demanded Old John.

"Our broncs are gone! Our broncs are gone!" yelled Stevenson, shoving Old John roughly to one side as he dashed through the doorway and on into the room he had assigned to the sullen and bibulous stranger. "I knowed it! I knowed it!" he wailed, popping out again as if on springs. "He's gone, an' he's took our broncs with him, the measly, low-down dog! I knowed he wasn't no good! I could see it in his eye; an' he wasn't drunk, not by a darn sight. Go out an' see for yoreself if they ain't gone!" he snapped in reply to Old John's look. "Go on out, while I throw some cold grub on the table-won't have no time this morning to do no cooking. He's got five hours' start on us, an' it'll take some right smart riding to get him before dark; but we'll do it, an' hang him, too!"

"What's all this here rumpus?" demanded a sleepy voice from upstairs. "Who's hanged?" and Charley entered the room, very much interested. His interest increased remarkably when the calamity was made known and he lost no time in joining Old John in the corral to verify the news.

Old John waved his hands over the scene and carefully explained what he had read in the tracks, to his companion's great irritation, for Charley's keen eyes and good training had already told him all there was to learn; and his reading did not exactly agree with that of his companion.

"Charley, he's gone and took our cayuses; an' that's the very way he came —'round the corner of the hotel. He got all tangled up an' fell over there, an' here he bumped inter the palisade, an' dropped his saddle. When he opened the bars he took my roan gelding because it was the best an' fastest, an' then he let out the others to mix us up on the tracks. See how he went? Had to hop four times on one foot afore he could get inter the saddle. An' that proves he was sober, for no drunk could hop four times like that without falling down an' being drug to death. An' he left his own critter behind because he knowed it wasn't no good. It's all as plain as the nose on your face, Charley," and Old John proudly rubbed his ear. "Hee, hee, hee! You can't fool Old John, even if he is getting old. No, sir, b' gum."

Charley had just returned from inside the corral, where he had looked at the brand on the far side of the one horse left, and he waited impatiently for his companion to cease talking. He took quick advantage of the first pause Old John made and spoke crisply.

"I don't care what corner he came 'round, or what he bumped inter; an' any fool can see that. An' if he left that cayuse behind because he thought it wasn't no good, he *was* drunk. That's a Bar-20 cayuse, an' no hoss-thief ever worked for that ranch. He left it behind because he stole it; that's why. An' he didn't let them others out because he wanted to mix us up, neither. How'd he know if we couldn't tell the tracks of our own animals? He did that to make us lose time; that's what he did it for. An' he couldn't tell what bronc he took last night-it was too dark. He must 'a' struck a match an' seen where that Bar-20 cayuse was an' then took the first one nearest that wasn't it. An' now you tell me how the devil he knowed yourn was the fastest, which it ain't," he finished, sarcastically, gloating over a chance to rub it into the man he had always regarded as a windy old nuisance.

"Well, mebby what you said is —"

"Mebby nothing!" snapped Charley. "If he wanted to mix the tracks would he 'a' hopped like that so we couldn't help telling what cayuse he rode? He knowed we'd pick his trail quick, an' he knowed that every minute counted; that's why he hopped-why, yore roan was going like the wind afore he got in the saddle. If you don't believe it, look at them toe-prints!"

"H'm; reckon yo're right, Charley. My eyes ain't nigh as good as they once was. But I heard him say something 'bout Winchester," replied Old John, glad to change the subject. "Bet he's going over there, too. He won't get through that town on no critter wearing my brand. Everybody knows that roan, an' —"

"Quit guessing!" snapped Charley, beginning to lose some of the tattered remnant of his respect for old age. "He's a whole lot likely to head for a town on a stolen cayuse, now ain't he! But we don't care where he's heading; we'll foller the trail."

"Grub pile!" shouted Stevenson, and the two made haste to obey.

"Charley, gimme a chaw of yore tobacker," and Old John, biting off a generous chunk, quietly slipped it into his pocket, there to lay until after he had eaten his breakfast.

All talk was tabled while the three men gulped down a cold and uninviting meal. Ten minutes later they had finished and separated to find horses and spread the news; in fifteen more they had them and were riding along the plain trail at top speed, with three other men close at their heels. Three hundred yards from the corral they pounded out of an arroyo, and Charley, who was leading, stood up in his stirrups and looked keenly ahead. Another trail joined the one they were following and ran with and on top of it. This, he reasoned, had been made by one of the strays and would turn away soon. He kept his eyes looking well ahead and soon saw that he was right in his surmise, and without checking the speed of his horse in the slightest degree he went ahead on the trail of the smaller hoof-prints. In a moment Old John spurred forward and gained his side and began to argue hot-headedly.

"Hey! Charley!" he cried. "Why are you follering this track?" he demanded.

"Because it's his; that's why."

"Well, here, wait a minute!" and Old John was getting red from excitement. "How do you know it is? Mebby he took the other!"

"He started out on the cayuse that made these little tracks," retorted Charley, "an' I don't see no reason to think he swapped animules. Don't you know the prints of yore own cayuse?"

"Lawd, no!" answered Old John. "Why, I don't hardly ride the same cayuse the second day, straight hand-running. I tell you we ought to foller that other trail. He's just cute enough to play some trick on us."

"Well, you better do that for us," Charley replied, hoping against hope that the old man would chase off on the other and give his companions a rest.

"He ain't got sand enough to tackle a thing like that single-handed," laughed Jed White, winking to the others.

Old John wheeled. "Ain't, hey! I am going to do that same thing an' prove that you are a pack of fools. I'm too old to be fooled by a common trick like that. An' I don't need no help —I'll ketch him all by myself, an' hang him, too!" And he wheeled to follow the other trail, angry and outraged. "Young fools," he muttered. "Why, I was fighting all around these parts afore any of 'em knowed the difference between day an' night!"

"Hard-headed old fool," remarked Charley, frowning, as he led the way again.

"He's gittin' old an' childish," excused Stevenson. "They say warn't nobody in these parts could hold a candle to him in his prime."

Hopalong muttered and stirred and opened his eyes to gaze blankly into those of one of the men who were tugging at his hands, and as he stared he started his stupefied brain sluggishly to work in an endeavor to explain the unusual experience. There were five men around him and the two who hauled at his hands stepped back and kicked him. A look of pained indignation slowly spread over his countenance as he realized beyond doubt that they were really kicking him, and with sturdy vigor. He considered a moment and then decided that such treatment was most unwarranted and outrageous and, furthermore, that he must defend himself and chastise the perpetrators.

"Hey!" he snorted, "what do you reckon yo're doing, anyhow? If you want to do any kicking, why kick each other, an' I'll help you! But I'll lick the whole bunch of you if you don't quite mauling me. Ain't you got no manners? Don't you know anything? Come 'round waking a feller up an' man-handling —"

"Get up!" snapped Stevenson, angrily.

"Why, ain't I seen you before? Somewhere? Sometime?" queried Hopalong, his brow wrinkling from intense concentration of thought. "I ain't dreaming; I've seen a one-eyed coyote som'ers, lately, ain't I?" he appealed, anxiously, to the others.

"Get up!" ordered Charley, shortly.

"An' I've seen you, too. Funny, all right."

"You've seen me, all right," retorted Stevenson. "Get up, damn you! Get up!"

"Why, I can't —my han's are tied!" exclaimed Hopalong in great wonder, pausing in his exertions to cogitate deeply upon this most remarkable phenomenon. "Tied up! Now what the devil do you think —"

"Use yore feet, you thief!" rejoined Stevenson roughly, stepping forward and delivering another kick. "Use yore feet!" he reiterated.

"Thief! Me a thief! Shore I'll use my feet, you yaller dog!" yelled the prostrate man, and his boot heel sank into the stomach of the offending Mr. Stevenson with sickening force and laudable precision. He drew it back slowly, as if debating shoving it farther. "Call me a thief, hey! Come poking 'round kicking honest punchers an' calling 'em names! Anybody want the other boot?" he inquired with grave solicitation.

Stevenson sat down forcibly and rocked to and fro, doubled up and gasping for breath, and Hopalong squinted at him and grinned with happiness. "Hear him sing! Reg'lar ol' brass band. Sounds like a cow pulling its hoofs outen the mud. Called me a thief, he did, just now. An' I won't let nobody kick me an' call me names. He's a liar, just a plain, squaw's dog liar, he —"

Two men grabbed him and raised him up, holding him tightly, and they were not over careful to handle him gently, which he naturally resented. Charley stepped in front of him to go to the aid of Stevenson and caught the other boot in his groin, dropping as if he had been shot. The man on the prisoner's left emitted a yell and loosed his hold to sympathize with a bruised shinbone, and his companion promptly knocked the bound and still intoxicated man down. Bill Thomas swore and eyed the prostrate figure with resentment and regret. "Hate to hit a man who can fight like that when he's loaded an' tied. I'm glad, all the same, that he ain't sober an' loose."

"An' you ain't going to hit him no more!" snapped Jed White, reddening with anger. "I'm ready to hang him, 'cause that's what he deserves, an' what we're here for, but I'm damned if I'll stand for any more mauling. I don't blame him for fighting, an' they didn't have no right to kick him in the beginning."

"Didn't kick him in the beginning," grinned Bill. "Kicked him in the ending. Anyhow," he continued seriously, "I didn't hit him hard-didn't have to. Just let him go an' shoved him quick."

"I'm just naturally going to clean house," muttered the prisoner, sitting up and glaring around. "Untie my han's an' gimme a gun or a club or anything, an' watch yoreselves get licked. Called me a thief! What are you fellers, then? —sticking me up an' busting me for a few measly dollars. Why didn't you take my money an' lemme sleep, 'stead of waking me up an' kicking me? I wouldn't 'a' cared then."

"Come on, now; get up. We ain't through with you yet, not by a whole lot," growled Bill, helping him to his feet and steadying him. "I'm plumb glad you kicked 'em; it was coming to 'em."

"No, you ain't; you can't fool me," gravely assured Hopalong. "Yo're lying, an' you know it. What you going to do now? Ain't I got money enough? Wish I had an even break with you fellers! Wish my outfit was here!"

Stevenson, on his feet again, walked painfully up and shook his fist at the captive, from the side. "You'll find out what we want of you, you damned hoss-thief!" he cried. "We're going to tie you to that there limb so yore feet'll swing above the grass, that's what we're going to do."

Bill and Jed had their hands full for a moment and as they finally mastered the puncher, Charley came up with a rope. "Hurry up-no use dragging it out this way. I want to get back to the ranch some time before next week."

"Why I ain't no hoss-thief, you liar!" Hopalong yelled. "My name's Hopalong Cassidy of the Bar-20, an' when I tell my friends about what you've gone an' done they'll make you hard to find! You gimme any kind of a chance an' I'll do it all by myself, sick as I am, you yaller dogs!"

"Is that yore cayuse?" demanded Charley, pointing.

Hopalong squinted towards the animal indicated. "Which one?"

"There's only one there, you fool!"

"That so?" replied Hopalong, surprised. "Well, I never seen it afore. My cayuse is-is-where the devil *is* it?" he asked, looking around anxiously.

"How'd you get that one, then, if it ain't yours?"

"Never had it —'t ain't mine, nohow," replied Hopalong, with strong conviction. "Mine was a *hoss.*"

"You stole that cayuse last night outen Stevenson's corral," continued Charley, merely as a matter of form. Charley believed that a man had the right to be heard before he died-it wouldn't change the result and so could not do any harm.

"Did I? Why —" his forehead became furrowed again, but the events of the night before were vague in his memory and he only stumbled in his soliloquy. "But *I* wouldn't swap my cayuse for that spavined, saddle-galled, ring-boned bone-yard! Why, it interferes, an' it's got the heaves something awful!" he finished triumphantly, as if an appeal to common sense would clinch things. But he made no headway against them, for the rope went around his neck almost before he had finished talking and a flurry of excitement ensued. When the dust settled he was on his back again and the rope was being tossed over the limb.

The crowd had been too busily occupied to notice anything away from the scene of their strife and were greatly surprised when they heard a hail and saw a stranger sliding to a stand not twenty feet from them. "What's this?" demanded the newcomer, angrily.

Charley's gun glinted as it swung up and the stranger swore again. "What you doing?" he shouted. "Take that gun off'n me or I'll blow you apart!"

"Mind yore business an' sit still!" Charley snapped. "You ain't in no position to blow anything apart. We've got a hoss-thief an' we're shore going to hang him regardless."

"An' if there's any trouble about it we can hang two as well as we can one," suggested Stevenson, placidly. "You sit tight an' mind yore own affairs, stranger," he warned.

Hopalong turned his head slowly. "He's a liar, stranger; just a plain, squaw's dog of a liar. An' I'll be much obliged if you'll lick hell outen 'em an' let —*why, hullo, hoss-thief!*" he shouted, at once recognizing the other. It was the man he had met in the gospel tent, the man he had chased for a horse-thief and then swapped mounts with. "Stole any more cayuses?" he asked, grinning, believing that everything was all right now. "Did you take that cayuse back to Grant?" he finished.

"Han's up!" roared Stevenson, also covering the stranger. "So yo're another one of 'em, hey? We're in luck to-day. Watch him, boys, till I get his gun. If he moves, drop him quick."

"You damned fool!" cried Ferris, white with rage. "He ain't no thief, an' neither am I! My name's Ben Ferris an' I live in Winchester. Why, that man you've got is Hopalong Cassidy-Cassidy, of the Bar-20!"

"Sit still-you can talk later, mebby," replied Stevenson, warily approaching him. "Watch him, boys!"

"Hold on!" shouted Ferris, murder in his eyes. "Don't you try that on me! I'll get one of you before I go; I'll shore get one! You can listen a minute, an' I can't get away."

"All right; talk quick."

Ferris pleaded as hard as he knew how and called attention to the condition of the prisoner. "If he did take the wrong cayuse he was too blind drunk to know it! Can't you *see* he was!" he cried.

"Yep; through yet?" asked Stevenson, quietly.

"No! I ain't started yet!" Ferris yelled. "He did me a good turn once, one that I can't never repay, an' I'm going to stop this murder or go with him. If I go I'll take one of you with me, an' my friends an' outfit'll get the rest."

"Wait till Old John gets here," suggested Jed to Charley. "He ought to know this feller."

"For the Lord's sake!" snorted Charley. "He won't show up for a week. Did you hear that, fellers?" he laughed, turning to the others.

"Stranger," began Stevenson, moving slowly ahead again. "You give us yore guns an' sit quiet till we gets this feller out of the way. We'll wait till Old John Ferris comes before doing anything with you. He ought to know you."

"He knows me all right; an' he'd like to see me hung," replied the stranger. "I won't give up my guns, an' you won't lynch Hopalong Cassidy while I can pull a trigger. That's flat!" He began to talk feverishly to gain time and his eyes lighted suddenly. Seeing that Jed White was wavering, Stevenson ordered them to go on with the work they had come to perform, and he watched Ferris as a cat watches a mouse, knowing that he would be the first man hit if the stranger got a chance to shoot. But Ferris stood up very slowly in his stirrups so as not to alarm the five with any quick movement, and shouted at the top of his voice, grabbing off his sombrero and waving it frantically. A faint cheer reached his ears and made the lynchers turn quickly and look behind them. Nine men were tearing towards them at a dead gallop and had already begun to forsake their bunched-up formation in favor of an extended line. They were due to arrive in a very few minutes and caused Mr. Ferris' heart to overflow with joy.

"Me an' my outfit," he said, laughing softly and waving his hand towards the newcomers, "started out this morning to round up a bunch of cows, an' we got jackasses instead. Now lynch him, damn you!"

The nine swept up in skirmish order, guns out and ready for anything in the nature of trouble that might zephyr up. "What's the matter, Ben?" asked Tom Murphy ominously. As under-foreman of the ranch he regarded himself as spokesman. And at that instant catching sight of the rope, he swore savagely under his breath.

"Nothing, Tom; nothing now," responded Mr. Ferris. "They was going to hang my friend there, Mr. Hopalong Cassidy, of the Bar-20. He's the feller that lent me his cayuse to get home on when Molly was sick. I'm going to take him back to the ranch when he gets sober an' introduce him to some very good friends of hissn that he ain't never seen. Ain't I, Cassidy?" he demanded with a laugh.

But Mr. Cassidy made no reply. He was sound asleep, as he had been since the advent of his very good and capable friend, Mr. Ben Ferris, of Winchester.

Chapter XIII
Mr. Townsend, Marshal

Mr. Cassidy went to the ranch and lived like a lord until shame drove him away. He had no business to live on cake and pie and wonderful dishes that Mrs. Ferris and her sister literally forced on him, and let Buck's mission wait on his convenience. So he tore himself away and made up for lost time as he continued his journey on his own horse, for which Tom Murphy and three men had faced down the scowling population of Hoyt's Corners. The rest of his journey was without incident until, on his return home along another route, he rode into Rawhide and heard about the marshal, Mr. Townsend.

This individual was unanimously regarded as an affliction upon society and there had been objections to his continued existence, which had been overruled by the object himself. Then word had gone forth that a substantial reward and the undying gratitude of a considerable number of people awaited the man who would rid the community of the pest who seemed to be ubiquitous. Several had come in response to the call, one had returned in a wagon, and the others were now looked upon as martyrs, and as examples of asinine foolhardiness. Then it had been decided to elect a marshal, or perhaps two or three, to preserve the peace of the town; but this was a flat failure. In the first place, Mr. Townsend had dispersed the meeting with no date set for a new one; in the second, no man wanted the office; and as a finish to the comedy, Mr. Townsend cheerfully announced that hereafter and henceforth he was the marshal, self-appointed and self-sustained. Those who did not like it could easily move to other localities.

With this touch of office-holding came ambition, and of stern stuff. The marshal asked himself why he could not be more officers than one and found no reason. Thereupon he announced that he was marshal, town council, mayor, justice, and pound-keeper. He did not go to the trouble of incorporating himself as the Town of Rawhide, because he knew nothing of such immaterial things; but he was the town, and that sufficed.

He had been grievously troubled about finances in the past, and he firmly believed that genius such as his should be above such petty annoyances as being "broke." That was why he constituted himself the keeper of the public pound, which contented him for a short time, but later, feeling that he needed more money than the pound was giving him, he decided that the spirit of the times demanded public improvements, and therefore, as the executive head of the town, he levied taxes and improved the town by improving his wardrobe and the manner of his living. Each saloon must pay into the town treasury the sum of one hundred dollars per year, which entitled it to police protection and assured it that no new competitors would be allowed to do business in Rawhide.

Needless to say he was not furiously popular, and the crowds congregated where he was not. His tyranny was based upon his uncanny faculty of anticipating the other man's draw. The citizens were not unaccustomed to seeing swift death result to the slower man from misplaced confidence in his speed of hand-that was in the game-an even break; but to oppose an individual who *always* knew what you were going to do before you knew it yourself-this was very discouraging. Therefore, he flourished and waxed fat.

Of late, however, he had been very low in finances and could expect no taxes to be paid for three months. Even the pound had yielded him nothing for over a week, the old patrons of Rawhide's stores and saloons preferring to ride twenty miles farther in another direction than to redeem impounded horses. Perhaps his prices had been too high, he thought; so he assembled the town council, the mayor, the marshal, and the keeper of the public pound to consult upon the matter. He decided that the prices were too high and at once posted a new notice announcing the cut. It was hard to fall from a dollar to "two bits," but the treasury was low-the times were panicky.

As soon as he had changed the notice he strolled up to the Paradise to inform the bartender that impounding fines had been cut to bargain prices and to ask him to make the fact generally known through his patrons. As he came within sight of the building he jumped with pleasure, for a horse was standing dejectedly before the door. Joy of joys, trade was picking up —a stranger had come to town! Hastening back to the corral, he added a cipher to the posted figure, added a decimal point, and changed the cents sign to that of a dollar. Two dollars and fifty cents was now the price prescribed by law. Returning hastily to the Paradise, he led the animal away, impounded it, and then sat down in front of the corral gate with his Winchester across his knees. Two dollars and fifty cents! Prosperity had indeed returned!

"Where the CG ranch is I dunno, but I do know where one of their cayuses is," he mused, glancing between two of the corral posts at the sleepy animal. "If I has to auction it off to pay for its keep and the fine, the saddle will bring a good, round sum. I allus knowed that a dollar wasn't enough, nohow."

Nat Fisher, punching cows for the CG and tired of his job, leaned comfortably back in his chair in the Paradise and swapped lies with the all-wise bartender. After a while he realized that he was hopelessly outclassed at this diversion and he dug down into his pocket and brought to light some loose silver and regarded it thoughtfully. It was all the money he had and was beginning to grow interesting.

"Say, was you ever broke?" he asked suddenly, a trace of sadness in his voice.

The bartender glanced at him quickly, but remained judiciously silent, smelling the preamble of an attempt to "touch."

"Well, I have been, am now, an' allus will be, more or less," continued Fisher, in soliloquy, not waiting for an answer to his question. "Money an' me don't ride the same range, not any. Here I am fifty miles away from my ranch, with four dollars and ninety-five cents between me an' starvation an' thirst, an' me not going home for three days yet. I was going to quit the CG this month, but now I gotta go on working for it till another pay-day. I don't even own a cayuse. Now, just to show you what kind of a prickly pear I am, I'll cut the cards with you to see who owns this," he suggested, smiling brightly at his companion.

The bartender laughed, treated on the house, and shuffled out from behind the bar with a pack of greasy playing cards. "All at once, or a dollar a shot?" he asked, shuffling deftly.

"Any way it suits you," responded Fisher, nonchalantly. He knew how a sport should talk; and once he had cut the cards to see who should own his full month's pay. He hoped he would be more successful this time.

"Don't make no difference to me," rejoined the bartender.

"All right; all at once, an' have it over with. It's a kid's game, at that."

"High wins, of course?"

"High wins."

The bartender pushed the cards across the table for his companion to cut. Nat did so, and turned up a deuce. "Oh, don't bother," he said, sliding the four dollars and ninety-five cents across the table.

"Wait," grinned the bartender, who was a stickler for rules. He reached over and turned up a card, and then laughed. "Matched, by George!"

"Try again," grinned Fisher, his face clearing with hope.

The bartender shuffled, and Fisher turned a five, which proved to be just one point shy when his companion had shown his card.

"Now," remarked Fisher, watching his money disappear into the bartender's pocket, "I'll put up my gun agin ten of yore dollars if yo're game. How about it?"

"Done-that's a good weapon."

"None better. Ah, a jack!"

"I say queen-nope, *king*!" exulted the dispenser of liquids. "Say, mebby you can get a job around here when you quit the CG," he suggested.

"That's a good idea," replied Fisher. "But let's finish this while we're at it. I got a good saddle outside on my cayuse-go look it over an' tell me how much you'll put up agin it. If you win it an' can't use it, you can sell it. It's first class."

The bartender walked to the door, looked carefully around for a moment, his eyes fastening upon a trail in the sandy street. Then he laughed. "There ain't no saddle out here," he reported, well knowing where it could be found.

"What! Has that ornery piebald-well, what do you think of that!" exclaimed Fisher, looking up and down the street. "This is the first time that ever happened to me. Why, some coyote stole it! Look at the tracks!"

"No; it ain't stolen," the bartender responded. He considered a moment and then made a suggestion. "Mebby the marshal can tell you where it is-he knows everything like that. Nobody can take a cayuse out of this town while the marshal is up an' well."

"Lucky town, all right," chirped Fisher. "An' where is the marshal?"

"You'll find him down the back way a couple of hundred yards; can't miss him. He allus hangs out there when there are cayuses in town."

"Good for him! I'll chase right down an' see him; an' when I get that piebald ——!"

The bartender watched him go around the corner and shook his head sadly. "Yes; hell of a lucky town," he snorted bitterly, listening for the riot to begin.

The marshal still sat against the corral gate and stroked the Winchester in beatific contemplation. He had a fine job and he was happy. Suddenly leaning forward to look up the road, he smiled derisively and shifted the gun. A cow-puncher was coming his way rapidly, and on foot.

"Are you the marshal of this flea of a town?" politely inquired the newcomer.

"I am the same," replied the man with the rifle. "Anything I kin do for you?"

"Yes; have you seen a piebald cayuse straying around loose-like, or anybody leading one-CG being the brand?"

"I did; it was straying."

"An' which way did it go?"

"Into the town pound."

"What! Pond! What'n blazes is it doing with a pond? Couldn't it drink without getting in? Where's the pond?"

"Right here. It's eating its fool head off. I said pound, not pond. P-o-u-n-d; which means that it's pawned, in hock, for destroying the vegetation of Rawhide, an' disturbing the public peace."

"Good joke on the piebald, all right; it was never locked up before," laughed Fisher, trying to read a sign that faced away from him at a slight angle. "Get it out for me an' I'll disturb *its* peace. Sorry it put you to all that trouble," he sympathized.

"Two dollars an' four bits, an' a dollar initiation fee-it wasn't never in the pound before. That makes three an' a half. Got the money with you?"

"What!" yelled Fisher, emerging from his trance. "What!" he yelled again.

"I ain't none deaf," placidly replied the marshal. "Got the money, the three an' a half?"

"If you think yo're going to skin me outen three-fifty, one-fifty, or one measly cent, you need some medicine, an' I'll give it to you in pill form! You'd make a bum-looking angel, so get up an' hand over that cayuse, *an' do it damned quick!*"

"Three-fifty, an' two bits extry for feed. It'll cost you 'bout a dollar a day for feed. At the end of the week I'll sell that cayuse at auction to pay its bills if you don't cough up. Got the money?"

"I've got a lead slug for you if I can borrow my gun for five minutes!" retorted Fisher, seething double from anger.

"Five dollars more for contempt of court," pleasantly responded Mr. Townsend. "As Justice of the Peace of this community I must allow no disrespect, no contempt of the sovereign law of this town to go unpunished. That makes it eight-seventy-five."

"An' to think I lost my gun!" shouted Fisher, dancing with rage. "I'll get that cayuse out an' I won't pay a cent, not a damned cent! An' I'll get you at the same time!"

"Now you dust around for fifteen dollars even an' stop yore contempt of court an' threats or I'll drill you just for luck!" rejoined Mr. Townsend, angrily. "If you keep on working yore mouth like that there won't be nothing coming to you when I sell that cayuse of yourn. Turn around an' strike out or I'll put you with yore ancestors!"

Chapter XIV
The Stranger's Plan

Fisher, wild with rage, returned to the Paradise and profanely unfolded the tale of his burning wrongs to the bartender and demanded the loan of his gun, which the bartender promptly refused. The present owner of the gun liked Fisher very much for being such a sport and sympathized with him deeply, but he did not want to have such a pleasing acquaintance killed.

"Now, see here: you cool down an' I'll lend you fifteen dollars on that saddle of yourn. You go up an' get that cayuse out before the price goes up any higher-you don't know that man like I do," remarked the man behind the bar earnestly. "That feller Townsend can shoot the eyes out of a small dog at ten miles, purty nigh. Do you savvy my drift?"

"I won't pay him a cussed cent, an' when he goes to sell that piebald at auction, I'll be on hand with a gun; I'll get one somewhere, all right, even if I have to steal it. Then I'll shoot out *his* eyes at ten paces. Why, he's a two-laigged hold-up! That man would —" he stopped as a stranger entered the room. "Hey, stranger! Don't you leave that cayuse of yourn outside all alone or that coyote of a marshal will steal it, shore. He's the biggest thief I ever knowed. He'll lift yore animal quick as a wink!" Fisher warned, excitedly.

The stranger looked at him in surprise and then smiled. "Is it usual for a marshal to steal cayuses? Somewhat out of line, ain't it?" he asked Fisher, glancing at the bartender for light.

"I don't care what's the rule-that marshal just stole my cayuse; an' he'll take yourn, too, if you ain't careful," Fisher replied.

"Well," drawled the stranger, smiling still more, "I reckon I ain't going to stay out there an' watch it, an' I can't bring it in here. But I reckon it'll be all right. You see, I carry 'big medicine' agin hoss-thieves," he replied, tapping his holster and smiling as he remembered the time, not long past, when he himself had been accused of being one. "I'll take a chance if he will-what'll you all have?"

"Little whiskey," replied Fisher, uneasily, worrying because he could not stand for a return treat. "But, say; you keep yore eye on that animal, just the same," he added, and then hurriedly gave his reasons. "An' the worst part of the whole thing is that I ain't got no gun, an' can't seem to borrow none, neither," he added, wistfully eyeing the stranger's Colt. "I gambled mine away to the bartender here an' he won't lemme borrow it for five minutes!"

"Why, I never heard tell of such a thing before!" exclaimed the stranger, hardly believing his ears, and aghast at the thought that such conditions could exist. "Friend," he said, addressing the bartender, "how is it that this sort of thing can go on in this town?" When the bartender had explained at some length, his interested listener smote the bar with a heavy fist and voiced his outraged feelings. "I'll shore be plumb happy to spread that coyote marshal all over his cussed pound! Say, come with me; I'm going down there right now an' get that cayuse, an' if the marshal opens his mouth to peep I'll get him, too. I'm itching for a chance to tunnel a man like him. Come on an' see the show!"

"Not much!" retorted Fisher. "While I am some pleased to meet a white man, an' have a deep an' abiding gratitude for yore noble offer, I can't let you do it. He put it over on me, an' I'm the one that's got to shoot him up. He's mine, my pudding; an' I'm hogging him all to myself. That is one luxury I can indulge in even if I am broke; an' I'm sorry, but I can't give you cards. Seeing, however, as you are so friendly to the cause of liberty an' justice, suppose you lend me yore gun for about three minutes by the watch. From what I've been told about this town such an act will win for you the eternal love an' gratitude of a down-trodden people; yore gun will blaze the way to liberty an' light, freedom an' the right to own yore own property, an' keep it. All I ask is that I be the undeserving medium."

"A-men," sighed the bartender. "Deacon Jones will now pass down the aisle an' collect the buttons an' tin money."

"Stranger," continued Fisher, warming up, when he saw that his words had not produced the desired result, "King James the Twelfth, on the memorable an' blood-soaked field of Trafalgar, gave men their rights. On that great day he signed the Magnet Charter, and proved himself as great a liberator as the sainted Lincoln. You, on this most auspicious occasion, hold in yore strong hand the destiny of this town-the women an' children in this cursed community will rise up an' bless you forever an' pass yore name down to their ancestors as a man of deeds an' honor! Let us pause to consider this —"

"Hold that pause!" interrupted the astounded bartender hurriedly, and with shaking voice. "String it out till I get untangled! I ain't up much on history, so I won't take no chance with that; but I want to tell our eloquent guest that there ain't no women *or* children in this town. An' if there was, I sort of reckon their ancestors would be born first. What do you think about it —"

"Let us pause to consider the shameful an' burning *indignity* perpetrated upon us to-day!" continued Fisher, unheeding the bartender's words. "I, a peaceful, law-abiding *citizen* of this *glorious* Commonwealth, a free an' *equal* member of a liberty-loving nation, a nation whose standard is, *now* and forever, 'Gimme liberty or gimme det', a *nation* that stands for all the conceivable benefits that mankind may enjoy, a *nation* that scintillates pyrotechnically over the prostitution of power —"

Bang! went the bartender's fist on the counter. "Hey! Pause again! Wait a minute! Go back to 'shameful an' burning,' and gimme a chance!"

"—that stands for an even break, I, Nathaniel G. Fisher, have been deprived of one of my inalienable rights, the right of locomotion to distant an' other parts. *An"* I say, right here an' now, that I won't allow no spavined individual with thieving prehensils to —"

"Has that pound-keeper got a rifle?" calmly interrupted the stranger, without a pang of remorse.

"He has. Thus has it allus been with tyrants-well armed, fortified by habit an' tradition —"

"Then you won't get my gun, savvy? We'll find another way to get that cayuse as long as you feel that the marshal is yore hunting. Besides, this man's gall deserves some respect; it is genius, an' to pump genius full of cold lead is to act rash. Now, suppose you tell me when this auction is due to come off."

"Oh, not for a week; he wants to run up the board an' keep expenses. Tyrants, such as him —"

"Shore," interposed the bartender, "he'll make the expenses equal what he gets for the cayuse, no matter what it comes to. An' he's the whole town, an' the justice of the peace, besides. What he says goes."

"Well, I'm the Governor of the State an' I've got the Supreme Court right here in my holster, so I reckon I can reverse his official acts an' fill his legal opinions full of holes," the stranger replied, laughing heartily. "Bartender, will you help me play a little joke on His Honore, the Town, —just a little harmless joke?"

"Well, that all depends whether the joke is harmless on *me*. You see, he can shoot like the devil-he allus knows when a man is going to draw, an' gets his gun out first. I ain't got no respect for him, but I take off my hat to his gunplay, all right."

The stranger smiled. "Well, I can shoot a bit myself. But I shore wish he'd hold that auction quick —I've got to go on home without losing any more time. Fisher, suppose you go down to the pound and dare that tumble-bug to hold the auction this afternoon. Tell him that you'll shoot him full of holes if he goes pulling off any auction to-day, an' dare him to try it. I want it to come off before night, an' I reckon that'll hustle it along."

"I'll do anything to get the edge on that thief," replied Fisher, quickly, "but don't you reckon I'd better tote a gun, going down an' bearding such a thief in his own den? You know I allus like to shoot when I'm being shot at."

"Well, I don't blame you; it's only a petty weakness," grinned the stranger, hanging onto his Colt as if fearing that the other would snatch it and run. "But you'll do better without any gun-me an' the bartender don't want to have to go down there an' bring you back on a plank."

"All right, then," sighed Fisher, reluctantly, "but he'll jump the price again. He'll fine me for contempt of court an' make me pay money I ain't got for disturbing him. But I'm game-so long."

When he had gained the street, the stranger turned to the bartender. "Now, friend, you tell me if this man of gall, this Mr. Townsend, has got many friends in town-anybody that'll be likely to pot shoot from the back when things get warm. I can't watch both ends unless I know what I'm up against."

"*No!* Every man in town hates him," answered the bartender, hastily, and with emphasis.

"Ah, that's good. Now, I wonder if you could see 'most everybody that's in town now an' get 'em to promise to help me by letting me run this all by myself. All I want them to do is not to say a word. It ain't hard to keep still when you want to."

"Why, I reckon I might see 'em-there ain't many here this time of day," responded the bartender. "But what's yore game, anyhow?" he asked, suddenly growing suspicious.

"It's just a little scheme I figgered out," the stranger replied, and then he confided in the bartender, who jigged a few fancy steps to show his appreciation of the other's genius. His suspicions left him at once, and he hastened out to tell the inhabitants of the town to follow his instructions to the letter, and he knew they would obey, and be glad, hilariously glad, to do so. While he was hurrying around giving his instructions, the CG puncher returned to the hotel and reported.

"Well, it worked, all right," Fisher growled. "I told him what I'd do to him if he tried to auction that cayuse off an' he retorted that if I didn't shut up an' mind my own business, that he'd sell the horse this noon, at twelve o'clock, in the public square, wherever that is. I told him he was a coyote and dared him to do it. Told him I'd pump him full of air ducts if he didn't wait till next week. Said I had the promise of a gun an' that it'd give me great pleasure to use it on him if he tried any auctioneering at my expense this noon. Then he fined me five dollars more, swore that he'd show me what it meant to dare the marshal of Rawhide an' insult the dignity of the court an' town council, an' also that he'd shoot my liver all through my system if I didn't leave him to his reflections. Now, look here, stranger; noon is only two hours away an' I'm due to lose my outfit: what are *you* going to do to get me out of this mess?" he finished anxiously, hands on hips.

"You did real well, very fine, indeed," replied the stranger, smiling with content. "An' don't you worry about that outfit —I'm going to get it back for you an' a little bit more. So, as long as you don't lose nothing, you ain't got no kick coming, have you? An' you ain't got no interest in what I'm going to do. Just sit tight an' keep yore eyes an' ears open at noon. Meantime, if you want something to do to keep you busy, practise making speeches-you ought to be ashamed to be punching cows an' working for a living when you could use yore talents an' get a lot of graft besides. Any man who can say as much on nothing as you can ought to be in the Senate representing some railroad company or waterpower steal-you don't have to work there, just loaf an' take easy money for cheating the people what put you there. Now, don't get mad —I'm only stringing you: I wouldn't be mean enough to call you a senator. To tell the truth, I think yo're too honest to even think of such a thing. But go ahead an' practise —*I* don't mind it a bit."

"Huh! I couldn't go to Congress," laughed Fisher. "I'd have to practise by getting elected mayor of some town an' then go to the Legislature for the finishing touches."

"Mr. Townsend would beat you out," murmured the stranger, looking out of the window and wishing for noon. He sauntered over to a chair, placed it where he could see his horse, and took things easy. The bartender returned with several men at his heels, and all were grinning and joking. They took up their places against the bar and indulged in frequent fits of chuckling, not letting their eyes stray from the man in the chair and the open street through the door, where the auction was to be held. They regarded the stranger in the light of a would-be public benefactor, a martyr, who was to provide the town with a little excitement before he followed his predecessors into the grave. Perhaps he would *not* be killed, perhaps he would shoot the pound-keeper and general public nuisance-but ah, this was the stuff of which dreams were made: the marshal would never be killed, he would thrive and outlive his fellow-townsmen, and die in bed at a ripe old age.

One of the citizens, dangling his legs from the card table, again looked closely at the man with the plan, and then turned to a companion beside him. "I've seen that there feller som'ers, sometime," he whispered. "I *know* I have. But I'll be teetotally dod-blasted if I can place him."

"Well, Jim; I never saw him afore, an' I don't know who he is," replied the other, refilling his pipe with elaborate care, "but if he can kill Townsend to-day, I'll be so plumb joyous I won't know what to do with m'self."

"I'm afraid he won't, though," remarked another, lolling back against the bar. "The marshal was born to hang-nobody can beat him on the draw. But, anyhow, we're going to see some fun."

The first speaker, still straining his memory for a clue to the stranger's identity, pulled out a handful of silver and placed it on the table. "I'll bet that he makes good," he offered, but there were no takers.

The stranger now lazily arose and stepped into the doorway, leaning against the jamb and shaking his holster sharply to loosen the gun for action. He glanced quickly behind him and spoke curtly: "Remember, now —*I* am to do all the talking at this auction; you fellers just look on."

A mumble of assent replied to him, and the townsmen craned their necks to look out. A procession slowly wended its way up the street, led by the marshal, astride a piebald horse bearing the crude brand of the CG. Three men followed him and numerous dogs of several colors, sizes, and ages roamed at will, in a listless, bored way, between the horse and the men. The dust arose sluggishly and slowly dissipated in the hot, shimmering air, and a fly buzzed with wearying persistence against the dirty glass in the front window.

The marshal, peering out from under the pulled-down brim of his Stetson, looked critically at the sleepy horse standing near the open door of the Paradise and sought its brand, but in vain, for it was standing with the wrong side towards him. Then he glanced at the man in the door, a puzzled expression stealing over his face. He had known that man once, but time and events had wiped him nearly out of his memory and he could not place him. He decided that the other horse could wait until he had sold the one he was on, and, stopping before the door of the Paradise, he raised his left arm, his right arm lying close to his side, not far from the holster on his thigh.

"Gentlemen an' feller-citizens," he began: "As marshal of this booming city, I am about to offer for sale to the highest bidder this A Number 1 piebald, pursooant to the decree of the local court an' with the sanction of the town council an' the mayor. This same sale is for to pay the town for the board an' keep of this animal, an' to square the fine in such cases made an' provided. It's sound in wind an' limb, fourteen han's high, an' in all ways a beautiful piece of hoss-flesh. Now, gentlemen, how much am I bid for this cayuse? Remember, before you make me any offer, that this animal is broke to punching cows an' is a first-class cayuse."

The crowd in the Paradise had flocked out into the street and oozed along the front of the building, while the stranger now leaned carelessly against his own horse, critically looking over the one on sale. Fisher, uneasy and worried, squirmed close at hand and glanced covertly from his horse and saddle to the guns in the belts on the members of the crowd.

It was the stranger who broke the silence: "Two bits I bid-two bits," he said, very quietly, whereat the crowd indulged in a faint snicker and a few nudges.

The marshal looked at him and then ignored him. "How much, gentlemen?" he asked, facing the crowd again.

"Two bits," repeated the stranger, as the crowd remained silent.

"Two bits!" yelled the marshal, glaring at him angrily: "*Two bits!* Why, the *look* in this cayuse's eyes is worth four! Look at the spirit in them eyes, look at the intelligence! The saddle alone is worth a clean forty dollars of any man's money. I am out here to sell this animal to the highest bidder; the sale's begun, an' I want bids, not jokes. Now, who'll start it off?" he demanded, glancing around; but no one had anything to say except the terse stranger, who appeared to be getting irritated.

"You've got a starter —I've given you a bid. I bid two bits —t-w-o b-i-t-s, twenty-five cents. Now go ahead with yore auction."

The marshal thought he saw an attempt at humor, and since he was feeling quite happy, and since he knew that good humor is conducive to good bidding, he smiled, all the time, however, racking his memory for the name of the humorist. So he accepted the bid: "All right, this gentleman bids two bits. Two bits I am bid-two bits. Twenty-five cents. Who'll make it twenty-five dollars? Two bits-who says twenty-five dollars? Ah, did *you* say twenty-five dollars?" he snapped, leveling an accusing and threatening fore-finger at the man nearest him, who squirmed restlessly and glanced at the stranger. "*Did you say twenty-five dollars?*" he shouted.

The stranger came to the rescue. "He did not. He hasn't opened his mouth. But *I* said twenty-five *cents*," quietly observed the humorist.

"Who'll gimme thirty? Who'll gimme thirty dollars? Did I hear thirty dollars? Did I hear twenty-five dollars bid? Who said thirty dollars? Did *you* say twenty-five dollars?"

"How could he when he was talking politics to the man behind him?" asked the stranger. "I said two bits," he added complacently, as he watched the auctioneer closely.

"I want twenty-five dollars-an' you shut yore blasted mouth!" snapped the marshal at the persistent twenty-five-cent man. He did not see the fire smouldering in the squinting eyes so alertly watching him. "Twenty-five dollars-not a cent less takes the cayuse. Why, gentlemen, he's worth twenty in *cans*! Gimme twenty-five dollars, somebody. *I* bid twenty-five. I want thirty. I want thirty, gentlemen; you must gimme thirty. *I* bid twenty-five dollars-who's going to make it thirty?"

"Show us yore twenty-five an' she's yourn," remarked the stranger, with exasperating assurance, while Fisher grew pale with excitement. The stranger was standing clear of his horse now, and alert readiness was stamped all over him. "You accepted my bid-show yore twenty-five dollars or take my two bits."

"You close that face of yourn!" exploded the marshal, angrily. "I don't mind a little fun, but you've got altogether too damned much to say. You've queered the bidding, an' now you shut up!"

"I said two bits an' I mean just that. You show yore twenty-five or gimme that cayuse on my bid," retorted the stranger.

"By the pans of Julius Caesar!" shouted the marshal. "I'll put you to sleep so you'll never wake up if I hears any more about you an' yore two bits!"

"Show me, Rednose," snapped the other, his gun out in a flash. "I want that cayuse, an' I want it quick. You show me twenty-five dollars or I'll take it out from under you on my bid, you yaller dog! *Stop it!* Shut up! That's suicide, that is. Others have tried it an' failed, an' yo're no sleight-of-hand gun-man. This is the first time I ever paid a hoss-thief in *silver*, or bought stolen goods, but everything has to have a beginning. You get nervous with that hand of yourn an' I'll cure you of it! Git off that piebald, an' quick!"

The marshal felt stunned and groped for a way out, but the gun under his nose was as steady as a rock. He sat there stupidly, not knowing enough to obey orders.

"Come, get off that cayuse," sharply commanded the stranger. "An' I'll take yore Winchester as a fine for this high-handed business you've been carrying on. You may be the local court an' all the town officials, but I'm the Governor, an' here's my Supreme Court, as I was saying to the boys a little while ago. Yo're overruled. Get off that cayuse, an' don't waste no more time about it, neither!"

The marshal glared into the muzzle of the weapon and felt a sinking in the pit of his stomach. Never before had he failed to anticipate the pull of a gun. As the stranger said, there must always be a beginning, a first time. He was thinking quickly now; he was master of himself again, but he realized that he was in a tight place unless he obeyed the man with the drop. Not a man in town would help him; on the other hand, they were all against him, and hugely enjoying his discomfiture. With some men he could afford to take chances and jerk at his gun even when at such a disadvantage, but —

"Stranger," he said slowly, "what's yore name?"

The crowd listened eagerly.

"My *friends* call me Hopalong Cassidy; other people, other things-you gimme that cayuse an' that Winchester. Here! Hand the gun to Fisher, so there won't be no lamentable accidents: I don't want to shoot you, 'less I have to."

"They're both yourn," sighed Mr. Townsend, remembering a certain day over near Alameda, when he had seen Mr. Cassidy at gun-play. He dismounted slowly and sorrowfully. "Do I —do I get my two bits?" he asked.

"You shore do-yore gall is worth it," said Mr. Cassidy, turning the piebald over to its overjoyed owner, who was already arranging further gambling with his friend, the bartender.

Mr. Townsend pocketed the one bid, surveyed glumly the hilarious crowd flocking in to the bar to drink to their joy in his defeat, and wandered disconsolately back to the pound. He was never again seen in that locality, or by any of the citizens of Rawhide, for between dark and dawn he resumed his travels, bound for some locality far removed from limping, red-headed drawbacks.

Chapter XV

Johnny Learns Something

For several weeks after Hopalong got back to the ranch, full of interesting stories and minus the grouch, things went on in a way placid enough for the most peacefully inclined individual that ever sat a saddle. And then trouble drifted down from the north and caused a look of anxiety to spoil Buck Peters' pleasant expression, and began to show on the faces of his men. When one finds the carcasses of two cows on the same day, and both are skinned, there can be only one conclusion. The killing and skinning of two cows out of herds that are numbered by thousands need not, in themselves, bring lines of worry to any foreman's brow; but there is the sting of being cheated, the possibility of the losses going higher unless a sharp lesson be given upon the folly of fooling with a very keen and active buzz-saw,—and it was the determination of the outfit of the Bar-20 to teach that lesson, and as quickly as circumstances would permit.

It was common knowledge that there was a more or less organized band of shiftless malcontents making its headquarters in and near Perry's Bend, some distance up the river, and the deduction in this case was easy. The Bar-20 cared very little about what went on at Perry's Bend-that was a matter which concerned only the ranches near that town-as long as no vexatious happenings sifted too far south. But they had so sifted, and Perry's Bend, or rather the undesirable class hanging out there, was due to receive a shock before long.

About a week after the finding of the first skinned cows, Pete Wilson tornadoed up to the bunk house with a perforated arm. Pete was on foot, having lost his horse at the first exchange of shots, which accounts for the expression describing his arrival. Pete hated to walk, he hated still more to get shot, and most of all he hated to have to admit that his rifle-shooting was so far below par. He had seen the thief at work and, too eager to work up close to the cattle skinner before announcing his displeasure, had missed the first shot. When he dragged himself out from under his deceased horse the scenery was undisturbed save for a small cloud of dust hovering over a distant rise to the north of him. After delivering a short and bitter monologue he struck out for the ranch and arrived in a very hot and wrathful condition. It was contagious, that condition, and before long the entire outfit was in the saddle and pounding north, Pete overjoyed because his wound was so slight as not to bar him from the chase. The shock was on the way, and as events proved, was to be one long to linger in the minds of the inhabitants of Perry's Bend and the surrounding range.

The patrons of the Oasis liked their tobacco strong. The pungent smoke drifted in sluggish clouds along the low, black ceiling, following its upward slant toward the east wall and away from the high bar at the other end. This bar, rough and strong, ran from the north wall to within a scant two feet of the south wall, the opening bridged by a hinged board which served as an extension to the counter. Behind the bar was a rear door, low and double, the upper part barred securely-the lower part was used most. In front of and near the bar was a large round table, at which four men played cards silently, while two smaller tables were located along the north wall. Besides dilapidated chairs there were half a dozen low wooden boxes partly filled with sand, and attention was directed to the existence and purpose of these by a roughly lettered sign on the wall, reading: "Gents will look for a box first," which the "gents" sometimes did. The majority of the "gents" preferred to aim at various knotholes in the floor and bet on the result, chancing the outpouring of the proprietor's wrath if they missed.

On the wall behind the bar was a smaller and neater request: "Leave your guns with the bartender. —Edwards." This, although a month old, still called forth caustic and profane remarks from the regular frequenters of the saloon, for hitherto restraint in the matter of carrying weapons had been unknown. They forthwith evaded the order in a manner consistent with their characteristics-by carrying smaller guns where they could not be seen. The majority had simply sawed off a generous part of the long barrels of their Colts and Remingtons, which did not improve their accuracy.

Edwards, the new marshal of Perry's Bend, had come direct from Kansas and his reputation as a fighter had preceded him. When he took up his first day's work he was kept busy proving that he was the rightful owner of it and that it had not been exaggerated in any manner or degree. With the exception of one instance the proof had been bloodless, for he reasoned that gun-play should give way, whenever possible, to a crushing "right" or "left" to the point of the jaw or the pit of the stomach. His proficiency in the manly art was polished and thorough and bespoke earnest application. The last doubting Thomas to be convinced came to five minutes after his diaphragm had been rudely and suddenly raised several inches by a low right hook, and as he groped for his bearings and got his wind back again he asked, very feebly, where "Kansas" was; and the name stuck.

When Harlan heard the nickname for the first time he stopped pulling the cork out of a whiskey bottle long enough to remark, casually, "I allus reckoned Kansas was purty close to hell," and said no more about it. Harlan was the proprietor and bartender of the Oasis and catered to the excessive and uncritical thirsts of the ruck of range society, and he had objected vigorously to the placing of the second sign in his place of business; but at the close of an incisive if inelegant reply from the marshal, the sign went up, and stayed up. Edwards' language and delivery were as convincing as his fists.

The marshal did not like the Oasis; indeed, he went further and cordially hated it. Harlan's saloon was a thorn in his side and he was only waiting for a good excuse to wipe it off the local map. He was the Law, and behind him were the range riders, who would be only too glad to have the nest of rustlers wiped out and its gang of ne'er-do-wells scattered to the four winds. Indeed, he had been given to understand in a most polite and diplomatic way that if this were not done lawfully they would try to do it themselves, and they had great faith in their ability to handle the situation in a thorough and workmanlike manner. This would not do in a law-abiding community, as he called the town, and so he had replied that the work was his, and that it would be performed as soon as he believed himself justified to act. Harlan and his friends were fully conversant with the feeling against them and had become a little more cautious, alertly watching out for trouble.

On the evening of the day which saw Pete Wilson's discomfiture most of the habitues had assembled in the Oasis where, besides the card-players already mentioned, eight men lounged against the bar. There was some laughter, much subdued talking, and a little whispering. More whispering went on under that roof than in all the other places in town put together; for here rustling was planned, wayfaring strangers were "trimmed" in "frame-ups" at cards, and a hunted man was certain to find assistance. Harlan had once boasted that no fugitive had ever been taken from his saloon, and he was behind the bar and standing on the trap door which led to the six-by-six cellar when he made the assertion. It was true, for only those in his confidence knew of the place of refuge under the floor; it had been dug at night and the dirt carefully disposed of.

It had not been dark very long before talking ceased and card-playing was suspended while all looked up as the front door crashed open and two punchers entered, looking the crowd over with critical care.

"Stay here, Johnny," Hopalong told his youthful companion, and then walked forward, scrutinizing each scowling face in turn, while Johnny stood with his back to the door, keenly alert, his right hand resting lightly on his belt not far from the holster.

Harlan's thick neck grew crimson and his eyes hard. "Looking fer something?" he asked with bitter sarcasm, his hands under the bar. Johnny grinned hopefully and a sudden tenseness took possession of him as he watched for the first hostile move.

"Yes," Hopalong replied coolly, appraising Harlan's attitude and look in one swift glance, "but it ain't here, now. Johnny, get out," he ordered, backing after his companion, and safely outside, the two walked towards Jackson's store, Johnny complaining about the little time spent in the Oasis.

As they entered the store they saw Edwards, whose eye asked a question.

"No; he ain't in there yet," Hopalong replied.

"Did you look all over? Behind the bar?" Edwards asked, slowly. "He can't get out of town through that cordon you've got strung around it, an' he ain't nowhere else. Leastwise, I couldn't find him."

"Come on back!" excitedly exclaimed Johnny, turning towards the door. "You didn't look behind the bar! Come on-bet you ten dollars that's where he is!"

"Mebby yo're right, Kid," replied Hopalong, and the marshal's nodding head decided it.

In the saloon there was strong language, and Jack Quinn, expert skinner of other men's cows, looked inquiringly at the proprietor. "What's up now, Harlan?"

The proprietor laughed harshly but said nothing-taciturnity was his one redeeming trait. "Did you say cigars?" he asked, pushing a box across the bar to an impatient customer. Another beckoned to him and he leaned over to hear the whispered request, a frown struggling to show itself on his face. "Nix; you know my rule. No trust in here."

But the man at the far end of the line was unlike the proprietor and he prefaced his remarks with a curse. "*I* know what's up! They want Jerry Brown, that's what! An' I hopes they don't get him, the bullies!"

"What did he do? Why do they want him?" asked the man who had wanted trust.

"Skinning. He was careless or crazy, working so close to their ranch houses. Nobody that had any sense would take a chance like that," replied Boston, adept at sleight-of-hand with cards and very much in demand when a frame-up was to be rung in on some unsuspecting stranger. His one great fault in the eyes of his partners was that he hated to divvy his winnings and at times had to be coerced into sharing equally.

"Aw, them big ranches make me mad," announced the first speaker. "Ten years ago there was a lot of little ranchers, an' every one of 'em had his own herd, an' plenty of free grass an' water for it. Where are the little herds now? Where are the cows that *we* used to own?" he cried, hotly. "What happens to a maverick-hunter now-a-days? By God, if a man helps hisself to a pore, sick dogie he's hunted down! It can't go on much longer, an' that's shore."

Cries of approbation arose on all sides, for his auditors ignored the fact that their kind, by avarice and thievery, had forever killed the occupation of maverick-hunting. That belonged to the old days, before the demand for cows and their easy and cheap transportation had boosted the prices and made them valuable.

Slivers Lowe leaped up from his chair. "Yo're right, Harper! Dead right! *I* was a little cattle owner once, so was you, an' Jerry, an' most of us!" Slivers found it convenient to forget that fully half of his small herd had perished in the bitter and long winter of five years before, and that the remainder had either flowed down his parched throat or been lost across the big round table near the bar. Not a few of his cows were banked in the east under Harlan's name.

The rear door opened slightly and one of the loungers looked up and nodded. "It's all right, Jerry. But get a move on!"

"Here, *you!*" called Harlan, quickly bending over the trap door, "*Lively!*"

Jerry was half way to the proprietor when the front door swung open and Hopalong, closely followed by the marshal, leaped into the room, and immediately thereafter the back door banged open and admitted Johnny. Jerry's right hand was in his side coat pocket and Johnny, young and self-confident, and with a lot to learn, was certain that he could beat the fugitive on the draw.

"I reckon you won't blot no more brands!" he cried, triumphantly, watching both Jerry and Harlan.

The card-players had leaped to their feet and at a signal from Harlan they surged forward to the bar and formed a barrier between Johnny and his friends; and as they did so that puncher jerked at his gun, twisting to half face the crowd. At that instant fire and smoke spurted from Jerry's side coat pocket and the odor of burning cloth arose. As Johnny fell, the rustler ducked low and sprang for the door. A gun roared twice in the front of the room and Jerry staggered a little and cursed as he gained the opening, but he plunged into the darkness and threw himself into the saddle on the first horse he found in the small corral.

When the crowd massed, Hopalong leaped at it and strove to tear his way to the opening at the end of the bar, while the marshal covered Harlan and the others. Finding that he could not get through. Hopalong sprang on the shoulder of the nearest man and succeeded in winging the fugitive at the first shot, the other going wild. Then, frantic with rage and anxiety, he beat his way through the crowd, hammering mercilessly at heads with the butt of his Colt, and knelt at his friend's side.

Edwards, angered almost to the point of killing, ordered the crowd to stand against the wall, and laughed viciously when he saw two men senseless on the floor. "Hope he beat in yore heads!" he gritted, savagely. "Harlan, put yore paws up in sight or I'll drill you clean! Now climb over an' get in line-quick!"

Johnny moaned and opened his eyes. "Did-did I —get him?"

"No; but he gimleted you, all right," Hopalong replied. "You'll come 'round if you keep quiet." He arose, his face hard with the desire to kill. "I'm coming back for *you*, Harlan, after I get yore friend! An' all the rest of you pups, too!"

"Get me out of here," whispered Johnny.

"Shore enough, Kid; but keep quiet," replied Hopalong, picking him up in his arms and moving carefully towards the door. "We'll get him, Johnny; an' all the rest, too, when ——" The voice died out in the direction of Jackson's and the marshal, backing to the front door, slipped out and to one side, running backward, his eyes on the saloon.

"Yore day's about over, Harlan," he muttered. "There's going to be some few funerals around here before many hours pass."

When he reached the store he found the owner and two Double-Arrow punchers taking care of Johnny. "Where's Hopalong?" he asked.

"Gone to tell his foreman," replied Jackson. "Hey, youngster, you let them bandages alone! Hear me?"

"Hullo, Kansas," remarked John Bartlett, foreman of the Double-Arrow. "I come nigh getting yore man; somebody rode past me like a streak in the dark, so I just ups an' lets drive for luck, an' so did he. I heard him cuss an' I emptied my gun after him."

"The rest was a-passing the word along to ride in when I left the line," remarked one of the other punchers. "How you feeling now, Johnny?"

Chapter XVI
The End of the Trail

The rain slanted down in sheets and the broken plain, thoroughly saturated, held the water in pools or sent it down the steep sides of the arroyo, to feed the turbulent flood which swept along the bottom, foam-flecked and covered with swiftly moving driftwood. Around a bend in the arroyo, where the angry water flung itself against the ragged bulwark of rock and flashed away in a gleaming line of foam, a horseman appeared bending low in the saddle for better protection against the storm. He rode along the edge of the stream on the farther bank, opposite the steep bluff on the northern side, forcing his wounded and jaded horse to keep fetlock deep in the water which swirled and sucked about its legs. He was trying his hardest to hide his trail. Lower down the hard, rocky ground extended to the water's edge, and if he could delay his pursuers for an hour or so, he felt that, even with his tired horse, he would have more than an even chance.

But they had gained more than he knew. Suddenly above him on the top of the steep bluff across the torrent a man loomed up against the clouds, peered intently into the arroyo, and then waved his sombrero to an unseen companion. A puff of smoke flashed from his shoulder and streaked away, the report of the shot lost in the gale. The fugitive's horse reared and plunged into the deep water and with its rider was swept rapidly towards the bend, the way they had come.

"That makes the fourth time I've missed that coyote!" angrily exclaimed Hopalong as Red Connors joined him.

The other quickly raised his rifle and fired; and the horse, spilling its rider out of the saddle, floated away tail first. The fugitive, gripping his rifle, bobbed and whirled at the whim of the greedy water as shots struck near him. Making a desperate effort, he staggered up the bank and fell exhausted behind a boulder.

"Well, the coyote is afoot, anyhow," said Red, with great satisfaction.

"Yes; but how are we going to get to him?" asked Hopalong. "We can't get the cayuses down here, an' we can't swim *that* water without them. An' if we could, he'd pot us easy."

"There's a way out of it somewhere," Red replied, disappearing over the edge of the bluff to gamble with Fate.

"Hey! Come back here, you chump!" cried Hopalong, running forward. "He'll get you, shore!"

"That's a chance I've got to take if I get him," was the reply.

A puff of smoke sailed from behind the boulder on the other bank and Hopalong, kneeling for steadier aim, fired and then followed his friend. Red was downstream casting at a rock across the torrent but the wind toyed with the heavy, water-soaked *reata* as though it were a string. As Hopalong reached his side a piece of driftwood ducked under the water and an angry humming sound died away downstream. As the report reached their ears a jet of water spurted up into Red's face and he stepped back involuntarily.

"He's so shaky," Hopalong remarked, looking back at the wreath of smoke above the boulder. "I reckon I must have hit him harder than I thought in Harlan's. Gee! He's wild as blazes!" he yelled as a bullet hummed high above his head and struck sharply against the rock wall.

"Yes," Red replied, coiling the rope. "I was trying to rope that rock over there. If I could anchor to that, the current would push us over quick. But it's too far with this wind blowing."

"We can't do nothing here 'cept get plugged. He'll be getting steadier as he rests from his fight with the water," Hopalong remarked, and added quickly, "Say, remember that meadow back there a ways? We can make her from there, all right."

"Yo're right; that's what we've got to do. He's sending 'em nearer every shot-Gee! I could 'most feel the wind of that one. An' blamed if it ain't stopped raining. Come on."

They clambered up the slippery, muddy bank to where they had left their horses, and cantered back over their trail. Minute after minute passed before the cautious skulker among the rocks across the stream could believe in his good fortune. When he at last decided that he was alone again he left his shelter and started away, with slowly weakening stride, over cleanly washed rock where he left no trail.

It was late in the afternoon before the two irate punchers appeared upon the scene, and their comments, as they hunted slowly over the hard ground, were numerous and bitter. Deciding that it was hopeless in that vicinity, they began casting in great circles on the chance of crossing the trail further back from the river. But they had little faith in their success. As Red remarked, snorting like a horse in his disgust, "I'll bet four dollars an' a match he's swum down the river clean to hell just to have the laugh on us." Red had long since given it up as a bad job, though continuing to search, when a shout from the distant Hopalong sent him forward on a run.

"Hey, Red!" cried Hopalong, pointing ahead of them. "Look there! Ain't that a house?"

"Naw; course not! It's a—it's a ship!" Red snorted sarcastically. "What did you think it might be?"

"G'wan!" retorted his companion. "It's a mission."

"Ah, g'wan yoreself! What's a mission doing up here?" Red snapped.

"What do you think they do? What do they do anywhere?" hotly rejoined Hopalong, thinking about Johnny. "There! See the cross?"

"Shore enough!"

"An' there's tracks at last-mighty wobbly, but tracks just the same. Them rocks couldn't go on forever. Red, I'll bet he's cashed in by this time."

"Cashed nothing! Them fellers don't."

"Well, if he's in that joint we might as well go back home. We won't get him, not nohow," declared Hopalong.

"Huh! You wait an' see!" replied Red, pugnaciously.

"Reckon you never run up agin a mission real hard," Hopalong responded, his memory harking back to the time he had disagreed with a convent, and they both meant about the same to him as far as winning out was concerned.

"Think I'm a fool kid?" snapped Red, aggressively.

"Well, you ain't no *kid*."

"You let *me* do the talking; *I'll* get him."

"All right; an' I'll do the laughing," snickered Hopalong, at the door. "Sic 'em, Red!"

The other boldly stepped into a small vestibule, Hopalong close at his heels. Red hitched his holster and walked heavily into a room at his left. With the exception of a bench, a table, and a small altar, the room was devoid of furnishings, and the effect of these was lost in the dim light from the narrow windows. The peculiar, not unpleasant odor of burning incense and the dim light awakened a latent reverence and awe in Hopalong, and he sneaked off his sombrero, an inexplicable feeling of guilt stealing over him. There were three doors in the walls, deeply shrouded in the dusk of the room, and it was very hard to watch all three at once.

Red was peering into the dark corners, his hand on the butt of his Colt, and hardly knew what he was looking for. "This joint must 'a' looked plumb good to that coyote, all right. He had a hell of a lot of luck, but he won't keep it for long, damn him!" he remarked.

"Quit cussing!" tersely ordered Hopalong. "An' for God's sake, throw out that damned cigarette! Ain't you got no manners?"

Red listened intently and then grinned. "Hear that? They're playing dominoes in there—come on!"

"Aw, you chump! 'Dominee' means 'mother' in Latin, which is what they speaks."

"How do you know?"

"Hanged if I can tell —I've heard it somewhere, that's all."

"Well, I don't care what it means. This is a frame-up so that coyote can get away. I'll bet they gave him a cayuse an' started him off while we've been losing time in here. I'm going inside an' ask some questions."

Before he could put his plan into execution, Hopalong nudged him and he turned to see his friend staring at one of the doors. There had been no sound, but he would swear that a monk stood gravely regarding them, and he rubbed his eyes. He stepped back suspiciously and then started forward again.

"Look here, stranger," he remarked, with quiet emphasis, "we're after that cow-lifter, an' we mean to get him. Savvy?"

The monk did not appear to hear him, so he tried another tack. "*Habla Espanola?*" he asked, experimentally.

"You have ridden far?" replied the monk in perfect English.

"All the way from the Bend," Red replied, relieved. "We're after Jerry Brown. He tried to kill Johnny, an' near made good. An' I reckon we've treed him, judging from the tracks."

"And if you capture him?"

"He won't have no more use for no side pocket shooting."

"I see; you will kill him."

"Shore's it's wet outside."

"I'm afraid you are doomed to disappointment."

"Ya-as?" asked Red with a rising inflection.

"You will not want him now," replied the monk.

Red laughed sarcastically and Hopalong smiled.

"There ain't a-going to be no argument about it. Trot him out," ordered Red, grimly.

The monk turned to Hopalong. "Do you, too, want him?"

Hopalong nodded.

"My friends, he is safe from your punishment."

Red wheeled instantly and ran outside, returning in a few moments, smiling triumphantly. "There are tracks coming in, but there ain't none going away. He's here. If you don't lead us to him we'll shore have to rummage around an' poke him out for ourselves: which is it?"

"You are right-he is here, and he is not here."

"We're waiting," Red replied, grinning.

"When I tell you that you will not want him, do you still insist on seeing him?"

"We'll see him, an' we'll want him, too."

As the rain poured down again the sound of approaching horses was heard, and Hopalong ran to the door in time to see Buck Peters swing off his mount and step forward to enter the building. Hopalong stopped him and briefly outlined the situation, begging him to keep the men outside. The monk met his return with a grateful smile and, stepping forward, opened the chapel door, saying, "Follow me."

The unpretentious chapel was small and nearly dark, for the usual dimness was increased by the lowering clouds outside. The deep, narrow window openings, fitted with stained glass, ran almost to the rough-hewn rafters supporting the steep-pitched roof, upon which the heavy rain beat again with a sound like that of distant drums. Gusts of rain and the water from the roof beat against the south windows, while the wailing wind played its mournful cadences about the eaves, and the stanch timbers added their creaking notes to swell the dirge-like chorus.

At the farther end of the room two figures knelt and moved before the white altar, the soft light of flickering candles playing fitfully upon them and glinting from the altar ornaments, while before a rough coffin, which rested upon two pedestals, stood a third, whose rich, sonorous Latin filled the chapel with impressive sadness. "Give eternal rest to them, O Lord," —the words seeming to become a part of the room. The ineffably sad, haunting melody of the mass whispered back from the room between the assaults of the enraged wind, while from the altar came the responses in a low, Gregorian chant, and through it all the clinking of the censer chains added intermittent notes. Aloft streamed the vapor of the incense, wavering with the air currents, now lost in the deep twilight of the sanctuary, and now faintly revealed by the glow of the candles, perfuming the air with its aromatic odor.

As the last deep-toned words died away the celebrant moved slowly around the coffin, swinging the censer over it and then, sprinkling the body and making the sign of the cross above its head, solemnly withdrew.

From the shadows along the side walls other figures silently emerged and grouped around the coffin. Raising it they turned it slowly around and carried it down the dim aisle in measured tread, moving silently as ghosts.

"He is with God, Who will punish according to his sins," said a low voice, and Hopalong started, for he had forgotten the presence of the guide. "God be with you, and may you die as he died-repentant and in peace."

Buck chafed impatiently before the chapel door leading to a small, well-kept graveyard, wondering what it was that kept quiet for so long a time his two most assertive men, when he had momentarily expected to hear more or less turmoil and confusion.

C-r-e-a-k! He glanced up, gun in hand and raised as the door swung slowly open. His hand dropped suddenly and he took a short step forward; six black-robed figures shouldering a long box stepped slowly past him, and his nostrils were assailed by the pungent odor of the incense. Behind them came his fighting punchers, humble, awed, reverent, their sombreros in their hands, and their heads bowed.

"What in blazes!" exclaimed Buck, wonder and surprise struggling for the mastery as the others cantered up.

"He's cashed," Red replied, putting on his sombrero and nodding toward the procession.

Buck turned like a flash and spoke sharply: "Skinny! Lanky! Follow that glory-outfit, an' see what's in that box!"

Billy Williams grinned at Red. "Yo're shore pious, Red."

"Shut up!" snapped Red, anger glinting in his eyes, and Billy subsided.

Lanky and Skinny soon returned from accompanying the procession.

"I had to look twice to be shore it was him. His face was plumb happy, like a baby. But he's gone, all right," Lanky reported.

"Deader'n hell," remarked Skinny, looking around curiously. "This here is some shack, ain't it?" he finished.

"All right-he knowed how he'd finish when he began. Now for that dear Mr. Harlan," Buck replied, vaulting into the saddle. He turned and looked at Hopalong, and his wonder grew. "Hey, *you*! Yes, *you*! Come out of that an' put on yore lid! Straddle leather-we can't stay here all night."

Hopalong started, looked at his sombrero and silently obeyed. As they rode down the trail and around a corner he turned in his saddle and looked back; and then rode on, buried in thought.

Billy, grinning, turned and playfully punched him in the ribs. "Getting glory, Hoppy?"

Hopalong raised his head and looked him steadily in the eyes; and Billy, losing his curiosity and the grin at the same instant, looked ahead, whistling softly.

Chapter XVII
Edwards' Ultimatum

Edwards slid off the counter in Jackson's store and glowered at the pelting rain outside, perturbed and grouchy. The wounded man in the corner stirred and looked at him without interest and forthwith renewed his profane monologue, while the proprietor, finishing his task, leaned back against the shelves and swore softly. It was a lovely atmosphere.

"Seems to me they've been gone a long time," grumbled the wounded man. "Reckon he led 'em a long chase-had six hours' start, the toad." He paused and then as an afterthought said with conviction: "But they'll get him-they allus do when they make up their minds to it."

Edwards nodded moodily and Jackson replied with a monosyllable.

"Wish I could 'a' gone with 'em," Johnny growled. "I like to square my own accounts. It's allus that way. I get plugged an' my friends clean the slate. There was that time Bye-an'-Bye went an' ambushed me-ah, the devil! But I tell you one thing: when I get well I'm going down to Harlan's an' clean house proper."

"Yo're in hard luck again: that'll be done as soon as yore friends get back," Jackson replied, carefully selecting a dried apricot from a box on the counter and glancing at the marshal to see how he took the remark.

"That'll be done before then," Edwards said crisply, with the air of a man who has just settled a doubt. "They won't be back much before to-morrow if he headed for the country I think he did. I'm going down to the Oasis an' tell that gang to clear out of this town. They've been here too long now. I never had 'em dead to rights before, but I've got it on 'em this time. I'd 'a' sent 'em packing yesterday only I sort of hated to take a man's business away from him an' make him lose his belongings. But I've wrastled it all out an' they've got to go." He buttoned his coat about him and pulled his sombrero more firmly on his head, starting for the door. "I'll be back soon," he said over his shoulder as he grasped the handle.

"You better wait till you get help-there's too many down there for one man to watch an' handle," Jackson hastily remarked. "Here, I'll go with you," he offered, looking for his hat.

Edwards laughed shortly. "You stay here. I do my own work by myself when I can-that's what I'm here for, an' I can do this, all right. If I took any help they'd reckon I was scared," and the door slammed shut behind him.

"He's got sand a plenty," Jackson remarked. "He'd try to push back a stampede by main strength if he reckoned it was his duty. It's his good luck that he wasn't killed long ago — *I'd 'a' been.*"

"They're a bunch of cowards," replied Johnny. "As long as you ain't afraid of 'em, none of 'em wants to start anything. Bunch of sheep!" he snorted. "Didn't Jerry shoot me through his pocket?"

"Yes; an' yo're another lucky dog," Jackson responded, having in mind that at first Johnny had been thought to be desperately wounded. "Why, yore friends have got the worst of this game; they're worse off than you are-out all day an' night in this cussed storm."

While they talked Edwards made his way through the cold downpour to Harlan's saloon, alone and unafraid, and greatly pleased by the order he would give. At last he had proof enough to work on, to satisfy his conscience, for the inevitable had come as the culmination of continued and clever defiance of law and order.

He deliberately approached the front door of the Oasis and, opening it, stepped inside, his hands resting on his guns-he had packed two Colts for the last twenty-four hours. His appearance caused a ripple of excitement to run around the room. After what had taken place, a visit from him could mean only one thing-trouble. And it was entirely possible that he had others within call to help him out if necessary.

Harlan knew that he would be the one held responsible and he ceased wiping a glass and held the cloth suspended in one hand and the glass in the other. "Well?" he snapped, angrily, his eyes smouldering with fixed hatred.

"Mebby you think it's well, but it's going to be a blamed sight better before sundown tomorrow night," evenly replied the marshal. "I just dropped in sort of free-like to tell you to pack up an' get out of town before dark-load yore wagon an' vamoose; an' take yore friends with you, too. If you don't —" he did not finish in words, for his tightening lips made them unnecessary.

"*What!*" yelled Harlan, red with anger. He placed his hands on the bar and leaned over it as if to give emphasis to his words. "*Me* pack up an' git! *Me* leave this shack! Who's going to pay me for it, hey? *Me* leave town! You drop out again an' go back to Kansas where you come from-they're easier back there!"

"Well, so far I ain't found nothing very craggy 'round here," retorted Edwards, closely watching the muttering crowd by the bar. "Takes more than a loud voice an' a pack of sneaking coyotes to send me looking for something easier. An' let me tell you this: *You* stay away from Kansas-they hangs people like you back there. That's whatever. You pack up an' git out of this town or I'll start a burying plot with you on yore own land."

The low, angry buzz of Harlan's friends and their savage, scowling faces would have deterred a less determined man; but Edwards knew they were afraid of him, and the men on whom he could call to back him up. And he knew that there must always be a start, there must be one man to show the way; and each of the men he faced was waiting for some one else to lead.

"You all slip over the horizon before dark to-night, an' it's dark early these days," he continued. "*Don't get restless with yore hands!*" he snapped ominously at the crowd. "I means what I say-you shake the mud from this town off yore boots before dark-before that Bar-20 outfit gets back," he finished meaningly.

Questions, imprecations, and threats filled the room, and the crowd began to spread out slowly. His guns came out like a flash and he laughed with the elation that comes with impending battle. "The first man to start it'll drop," he said evenly. "Who's going to be the martyr?"

"I *won't* leave town!" shouted Harlan. "I'll stay here if I'm killed for it!"

"I admire yore loyalty to principle, but you've got damned little sense," retorted the marshal. "You ain't no practical man. *Keep yore hands where they are!*" —his vibrant voice turned the shifting crowd to stone-like rigidity and he backed slowly toward the door, the poor light gleaming dully from the polished blue steel of his Colts. Rugged, lion-like, charged to the finger tips with reckless courage and dare-devil self-confidence, his personality overflowed and dominated the room, almost hypnotic in its effect. He was but one against many, but he was the master, and they knew it; they had known it long enough to accept it without question, and the training now stood him in good stead.

For a moment he stood in the open doorway, keenly scrutinizing them for signs of danger, his unwavering guns charged with certain death and his strong face made stronger by the shadows in its hollows. "Before dark!"—and he was gone.

He left behind him deep silence, which endured for several moments.

"By the Lord, I *won't!*" cried Harlan, still staring at the door.

The spell was broken and a babel of voices filled the room, threats mingling with excuses, hot, vibrant, profane. These men were not cowards all the way through, but only when face to face with the master. They had flourished in a way by their wits alone on the same range with the outfits of the C-80 and the Double-Arrow, for individually they were "bad," and collectively they made a force of no mean strength. Edwards had landed among them like a thunderbolt and had proved his prowess, and they still held him in awesome respect. His reckless audacity and grim singleness of purpose had saved him on more than one occasion, for had he wavered once he would have been shot down without mercy. But gradually his enforcement of hampering laws became more and more intolerable, and their subordinated spirits were nearly on the point of revolt. When he faced them they resumed their former positions in relation to him-but once out of his sight they plotted to destroy him. Here was the crisis: it was now or never. They could not evade his ultimatum-it was obey or fight.

Submission was not to be thought of, for to flee would be to lose caste, and the story of such an act would follow them wherever they went, and brand them as cowards. Here they had lived, and here they would stay if possible, and to this end they discussed ways and means.

"Harlan's right!" emphatically announced Laramie Joe. "We can't pull out and have this foller us."

"We should have started it with a rush when he was in here," remarked Boston, regretfully.

Harlan stopped his pacing and faced them, shoving out a bottle of whiskey as an aid to his logic.

"That chance is past, an' I don't know but what it is a good thing," he began. "He was primed an' looking fer trouble, an' he'd shore got a few of us afore he went under. What we want is strategy-that's the game. You fellers have got as much brains as him, an' if we thrash this thing out we can find a way to call his play-an' get him! No use of any of us getting plugged 'less we have to. But whatever we do we've got to start it right quick an' have it over before that Bar-20 gang comes back. Harper, you an' Quinn go scouting-an' don't take no guns with you, neither. Act like you was hitting the long trail out, an' work back here on a circle. See how many of his friends are in town. While you are gone the rest of us will hold a pow-wow an' take the kinks out of this game. Chase along, an' don't waste no time."

"Good!" cried Slivers Lowe emphatically. "There's blamed few fellers in town now that have any use for him, for most of them are off on the ranges. Bet we won't have more than six to fight, an' there's that many of us here."

The scouts departed at once and the remaining four drew close in consultation.

"One more drink around and then no more till this trouble is over," Harlan said, passing the bottle. The drinks, in view of the coming drought and the thirsty work ahead, were long and deep, and new courage and vindictiveness crept through their veins.

"Now here's the way it looks to me," Harlan continued, placing the bottle, untasted by himself, on the floor behind him. "We've got to work a surprise an' take Edwards an' his friends off their guard. That'll be easy if we're careful, because they think we ain't looking for fight. When we get them out of the way we can take Jackson's store an' use one of the other shacks and wait for the Bar-20 to ride in. They'll canter right in, like they allus do, an' when they get close enough we'll open the game with a volley an' make every shot tell. 'T won't last long, 'cause every one of us will have his man named before they get here. Then the few straddlers in town, seeing how easy we've gone an' handled it'll join us. We've got four men to come in yet, an' by the time the C-80 an' Double-Arrow hears about it we'll be fixed to drive 'em back home. We ought to be over a dozen strong by dark."

"That sounds good, all right," remarked Slivers, thoughtfully, "but can we do it that easy?"

"Course we can! We ain't fools, an' we all can shoot as well as them," snapped Laramie Joe, the most courageous of the lot. Laramie had taken only one drink, and that a small one, for he was wise enough to realize that he needed his wits as keen as he could have them.

"We can do it easy, if Edwards goes under first," hastily replied Harlan. "An' me an' Laramie will see to that part of it. If we don't get him, you all can hit the trail an' we won't be sore about it. That is, unless you are made of the stuff that stands up an' fights 'stead of running away. I reckon I ain't none mistaken in any of you. You'll all be there when things get hot."

"You can bet the shack *I* won't do no trail-hitting," growled Boston, glancing at Slivers, who squirmed a little under the hint.

"Well, I'm glued to the crowd; you can't lose me, fellers," Slivers remarked, re-crossing his legs uneasily. "Are we going to begin it from here?"

"We ought to spread out cautions and surround Jackson's, or wherever Edwards is," Laramie Joe suggested. "That's my —"

"Yo're right! Now you've hit it plumb on the head!" interrupted Harlan, slapping Laramie heartily across the back. "What did I tell you about our brains?" he cried, enthusiastically. He had been on the point of suggesting that plan of operations when Laramie took the words out of his mouth. "I'd never thought of that, Laramie," he lied, his face beaming. "Why, we've got 'em licked to a finish right now!"

"This *is* a hummer of a game," laughed Slivers. "But how about the Bar-20 crowd?"

"I've told you that already," replied the proprietor.

"You bet it's a hummer," cried Boston, reaching for the whiskey bottle under cover of the excitement and enthusiasm.

Harlan pushed it away with his foot and raised his clenched fist. "Do you wonder I didn't think of that plan?" he demanded. "Ain't I been too mad to think at all? Hain't I seen my friends treated like dogs, an' made to swaller insults when I couldn't raise my hand to stop it? Didn't I see Jerry Brown chased out of my place like a wild beast? If we are what we've been called, then we'll sneak out of town with our tails atween our laigs; but if we're men we'll stay right here an' cram the insults down the throats of them that made 'em! If we're *men* let's prove it an' make them liars swaller our lead."

"My sentiments an' allus was!" roared Slivers, slapping Harlan's shoulder.

"We're men, all right, an' we'll show 'em it, too!"

At that instant the door opened and four guns covered it before it had swung a foot.

"Put 'em down-it's Quinn!" exclaimed the man in the doorway, flinching a bit. "All right, Jed," he called over his shoulder to the man who crowded him. After Quinn came Big Jed and Harper brought up the rear. They had no more than shaken the water from their sombreros when the back door let in Charley Rich and his two companions, Frank and Tom Nolan. While greetings were being exchanged and the existing conditions explained to the newcomers, Harper and Quinn led Harlan to one side and reported, the proprietor smiling and nodding his head wisely. And while he listened, Slivers surreptitiously corralled the whiskey bottle and when the last man finished with it there was nothing in it but air.

"Well, boys," exclaimed Harlan, "things are our way. Quinn, here, met Joe Barr, of the C-80, who said Converse an' four other fellers, all friends of Edwards, stopped at the ranch an' won't be back home till the storm stops. Harper saw Fred Neil going back to his ranch, so all we've got to figger on is the marshal, Barr, an' Jackson, an' they're all in Jackson's store. Lacey might cut in, since he'd sell more liquor if I went under, but he can't do very much if he does take a hand. Now we'll get right at it." The whole thing was gone over thoroughly and in detail, positions assigned and a signal agreed upon. Seeing that weapons were in good condition after their long storage in the cellar, and that cartridge belts were full, the ten men left the room one at a time or in pairs, Harlan and Laramie Joe being the last. And both Harlan and Laramie delayed long enough to take the precaution of placing horses where they would be handy in case of need.

Chapter XVIII
Harlan Strikes

Joe Barr laughingly replied to Johnny Nelson's growled remarks about the condition of things in general and tried to soothe him, but Johnny was unsoothable.

"An' I've been telling him right along that he's got the best of it," complained Jackson in a weary voice. "Got a measly hole through his shoulder-good Lord! if it had gone a little lower!" he finished with a show of exasperation.

"An' ain't I been telling you all along that it ain't the measly hole in my shoulder that's got me on the prod?" retorted Johnny, with more earnestness than politeness. "But why couldn't I go with my friends after Jerry an' get shot later if I had to get it at all? Look what I'm missing, roped an' throwed in this cussed ten-by-ten shack while they're having a little excitement."

"Yo're missing some blamed nasty weather, Kid," replied the marshal. "You ain't got no kick coming at all. Why, I got soaked clean through just going down to the Oasis."

"Well, I'm kicking, just the same," snapped Johnny. "An' furthermore, I don't see nobody big enough to stop me, neither-did you all get that?"

The rear door opened and Fred Neal looked in. "Hey, Barr; come out an' gimme a hand in the corral. Busted my cinch all to pieces half a mile out-an' how the devil it ever busted like that is —" the door slammed shut and softened his monologue.

"Would you listen to that!" snorted Barr in an injured tone. "Didn't I go an' tell him near a month ago that his cussed cinch wouldn't hold no better'n a piece of wet paper?" His complaint added materially to the atmosphere of sullen discontent pervading the room. "An' now I gotter go out in this rain an' —" the slam of the door surpassed anything yet attempted in that line of endeavor. Jackson grabbed a can of corn as it jarred off the shelf behind him and directed a pleasing phrase after the peevish Barr.

"Say, won't somebody please smile?" gravely asked Edwards. "I never saw such a happy, cheerful bunch before."

"I might smile if I wasn't so blamed hungry," retorted Johnny. "Doesn't anybody ever eat in this town?" he asked in great sarcasm. "Mebby a good feed won't do me no good, but I'm going to fill myself regardless. An' after that, if the grub don't shock me to death, I'm shore going to trim somebody at Ol' Sledge-for two bits a hand."

"If I could play you enough hands at that price I could sell out an' live high without working," grinned Jackson, preparing to give the reckless invalid all he could eat. "That's purty high, Kid; but I just feel real devilish, an' I'm coming in."

"An' I'll go over to my shack, get some money, an' bust the pair of you," laughed Edwards, again buttoning his coat and going towards the door. "Holy Cats! A log must 'a' got jammed in the sluice-gate up there," he muttered, scowling at the black sky. "It's coming down harder'n ever, but here goes," and he stepped quickly into the storm.

Jackson paused with a frying pan in his hands and looked through the window after the departing marshal, and saw him stagger, stumble forward, then jerk out his guns and begin firing. Hard firing now burst out in front and Jackson, cursing angrily, dropped the pan and reached for his rifle-to drop it also and sink down, struck by the bullet which drilled through the window. Johnny let out a yell of rage, grabbed his Colt, and ran to the door in time to see Edwards slowly raise up on one elbow, fire his last shot, and fall back riddled by bullets.

Jackson crawled to his rifle and then to the side window, where he propped his back against a box and prepared to do his best. "It was shore a surprise," he swore. "An' they went an' got Edwards before he could do anything."

"They did not!" retorted Johnny. "He —" the glass in the door vibrated sharply and the speaker, stepping to one side out of sight, with a new and superficial wound, opened fire on the building down the street. Two men were lying on the ground across the street-these Edwards had shot-and another was trying to drag himself to the shelter of a building. A man sprinted from an old corral close by in a brave and foolhardy attempt to save his friend, and Johnny swore because he had to fire twice at the same mark.

The rear door crashed open and shut as Barr, closely followed by Neal, ran in. They had been caught in the corral but, thanks to Harlan's whiskey, had managed to hold their own until they had a chance to make a rush for the store.

"Where's the marshal?" cried Barr, catching sight of Jackson. "Are you plugged bad?" he asked, anxiously.

"Well, I ain't plugged a whole lot *good*!" snapped Jackson. "An' Edwards is dead. They shot him down without warning. We're going to get ours, too-these walls don't stop them bullets. How many out there?"

"Must be a dozen," hastily replied Neal, who had not remained idle. Both he and Barr were working like mad men moving boxes and barrels against the walls to make a breastwork capable of stopping the bullets which came through the boards.

"I reckon —I'm bleeding inside," Jackson muttered, wearily and without hope. "Wonder how-long we-can hold out?"

"We'll hold out till we're good an' dead!" replied Johnny, hotly. "They ain't got us yet an' they'll pay for it before they do. If we can hold 'em off till Buck an' the rest come back we'll have the pleasure of seeing 'em buried."

"Oh, I'll get you next time!" assured Barr to an enemy, slipping a fresh cartridge into the Sharps and peering intently at a slight rise on the muddy plain. "You shoot like yo're drunk," he mumbled.

"But what is it all about, anyhow?" asked Neal, finding time for an immaterial question. "Who are they? —can't see nothing but blurs through this rain!"

"Yes; what's the game?" asked Barr, mildly surprised that he had not thought of it before.

"It's that Oasis gang," Johnny responded. He fired, and growled with disappointment. "Harlan's at the head of it," he added.

"Edwards-told Harlan to-get out of-town," Jackson began.

"An' to take his gang with him," Johnny interposed quickly to save Jackson from the strain. "They had till dark. Guess the rest. Oh, you *coyote*!" he shouted, staggering back. There was a report farther down the barricade and Neal called out, "I got him, Nelson; he's done. How are you?"

"Mad! Mad!" yelled Johnny, touching his twice-wounded shoulder and dancing with rage and pain. "Right in the same place! Oh, wait! *Wait!* Hey, gimme a rifle —I can't do nothing with a Colt at this range; my name ain't Hopalong," and he went slamming around the room in hot search of what he wanted.

"There ain't —no more-Johnny," feebly called Jackson, raising slightly to ease himself. "You can have-my gun purty-soon. I won't be able-to use it-much longer."

"Why don't Buck an' Hoppy hurry up!" snarled Johnny.

"Be a long time-mebby," mumbled Jackson, his trembling hands trying to steady the rifle. "They're all-around us. *Ah*, missed!" he intoned hoarsely, trying to pump the lever with un-obeying hands. "I can't last-much —" the words ceased abruptly and the clatter of the rifle on the floor told the story.

Johnny stumbled over to him and dragged him aside, covering the upturned face with his own sombrero, and picked up the rifle. Rolling a barrel of flour against the wall below the window he fixed himself as comfortably as possible and threw a shell into the chamber.

"Now, you coyotes; you pay *me* for *that*!" he gritted, resting the gun on the window sill and holding it so he could work it with one hand and shoulder.

"Wonder how them pups ever pumped up enough courage to cut loose like this?" queried Neal from behind his flour barrel.

"Whiskey," hazarded Barr. "Harlan must 'a' got 'em drunk. An' that's three times I've missed that snake. Wish it would stop raining so I could see better."

"Why don't you wish they'd all drop dead? Wish good when you wish at all: got as much chance of having it come true," responded Neal, sarcastically. He smothered a curse and looked curiously at his left arm, and from it to the new, yellow-splintered hole in the wall, which was already turning dark from the water soaking into it. "Hey, Joe; we need some more boxes!" he exclaimed, again looking at his arm.

"Yes," came Johnny's voice. "Three of 'em-five of 'em, an' about six feet long an' a foot deep. But if my outfit gets here in time we'll want more'n a dozen."

"Say! Lacey's firing now!" suddenly cried Barr. "He's shooting out of his windy. That'll stop 'em from rushing us! Good boy, Lacey!" he shouted, but Lacey did not hear him in the uproar.

"An' he's worse off than we are, being alone," commented Neal. "Hey! One of us better make a break for help-my ranch's the nearest. What d'ye say?"

"It's suicide; they'll get you before you get ten feet," Barr replied with conviction.

"No; they won't —the corral hides the back door, an' all the firing is on this side. I can sneak along the back wall an' by keeping the buildings atween me an' them, get a long ways off before they know anything about it. Then it's a dash-an' they can't catch me. But can you fellers hold out if I do?"

"Two can hold out as good as three-go ahead," Johnny replied. "Leave me some of yore Colt cartridges, though. You can't use 'em all before you get home."

"Don't stop fer that; there's a shelfful of all kinds behind the counter," Barr interposed.

"Well, so long an' good luck," and the rear door closed, and softly this time.

"Two hours is some wait under the present circumstances," Barr muttered, shifting his position behind his barricade. "He can't do it in less, nohow."

Johnny ducked and looked foolish. "Missed me by a foot," he explained. "He can't do it in two-not there an' back," he replied. "The trail is mud over the fetlocks. Give him three at the least."

"They ain't shooting as much as they was before."

"Waiting till they gets sober, I reckon," Johnny replied.

"If we don't hear no ruction in a few minutes we'll know he got away all right," Barr soliloquized. "An' he's got a fine cayuse for mud, too."

"Hey, why can't you do the same thing if he makes it?" Johnny suddenly asked. "I can hold her alone, all right."

"Yo're a cheerful liar, you are," laughed Barr. "But can *you* ride?"

"Reckon so, but I ain't a-going to."

"Why, we *both* can go-it's a cinch!" Barr cried. "Come on!"

"Lord! —an' I never even thought of that! Reckon I was too mad," Johnny replied. "But I sort of hates to leave Jackson an' Edwards," he added, sullenly.

"But they're gone! You can't do them no good by staying."

"Yes; I know. An' how about Lacey chipping in on our fight?" demanded Johnny. "I ain't a-going to leave him to take it all. You go, Barr; it wasn't yore fight, nohow. You didn't even know what you was fighting for!"

"Huh! When anybody shoots at me it's my fight, all right," replied Barr, seating himself on the floor behind the breastwork. "I forgot all about Lacey," he apologized. At that instant a tomato can went *spang!* and fell off the shelf. "An' it's too late, anyhow; they ain't a-going to let nobody else get away on that side."

"An' they're tuning up again, too," Johnny replied, preparing for trouble. "Look out for a rush, Barr."

Hopalong Cassidy stopped swearing at the weather and looked up and along the trail in front of him, seeing a hard-riding man approach. He turned his head and spoke to Buck Peters, who rode close behind him. "Somebody's shore in a hurry-why, it's Fred Neal."

It was. Mr. Neal was making his arms move and was also shouting something at the top of his voice. The noise of the rain and of the horses' hoofs splashing in the mud and water at first made his words unintelligible, but it was not long before Hopalong heard something which made him sit up even straighter. In a moment Neal was near enough to be heard distinctly and the outfit shook itself out of its weariness and physical misery and followed its leader at reckless speed. As they rode, bunched close together, Neal briefly and graphically outlined the relative positions of the combatants, and while Buck's more cautious mind was debating the best way to proceed against the enemy, Hopalong cried out the plan to be followed. There would be no strategy-Johnny, wounded and desperate, was fighting for his life. The simplest way was the best —a dash regardless of consequences to those making it, for time was a big factor to the two men in Jackson's store.

"Ride right at 'em!" Hopalong cried. "I know that bunch. They'll be too scared to shoot straight. Paralyze 'em! Three or four are gone now-an' the whole crowd wasn't worth one of the men they went out to get. The quicker it's over the better."

"Right you are," came from the rear.

"Ride up the arroyo as close as we can get, an' then over the edge an' straight at 'em," Buck ordered. "Their shooting an' the rain will cover what noise we make on the soft ground. An' boys, *no quarter!*"

"Reckon *not!*" gritted Red, savagely. "Not with Edwards an' Jackson dead, an' the Kid fighting for his life!"

"They're still at it!" cried Lanky Smith, as the faint and intermittent sound of firing was heard; the driving wind was blowing from the town, and this, also, would deaden the noise of their approach.

"Thank the Lord! That means that there's somebody left to fight 'em," exclaimed Red. "Hope it's the Kid," he muttered.

"They can't rush the store till they get Lacey, an' they can't rush him till they get the store," shouted Neal over his shoulder. "They'd be in a cross fire if they tried either-an' that's what licks 'em."

"They'll be in a cross fire purty soon," promised Pete, grimly.

Hopalong and Red reached the edge of the arroyo first and plunged over the bank into the yellow storm-water swirling along the bottom like a miniature flood. After them came Buck, Neal, and the others, the water shooting up in sheets as each successive horse plunged in. Out again on the farther side they strung out into single file along the narrow foot-hold between water and bank and raced towards the sharp bend some hundreds of yards ahead, the point in the arroyo's course nearest the town. The dripping horses scrambled up the slippery incline and then, under the goading of spurs and quirts, leaped forward as fast as they could go across the level, soggy plain.

A quarter of a mile ahead of them lay the scattered shacks of the town, and as they drew nearer to it the riders could see the flashes of guns and the smoke-fog lying close to the ground. Fire spat from Jackson's store and a cloud of smoke still lingered around a window in Lacey's saloon. Then a yell reached their ears, a yell of rage, consternation and warning. Figures scurried to seek cover and the firing from Jackson's and Lacey's grew more rapid.

A mounted man emerged from a corral and tore away, others following his example, and the outfit separated to take up the chase individually. Harlan, wounded hard, was trying to run to where he had left his horse, and after him fled Slivers Lowe. Hopalong was gaining on them when he saw Slivers raise his arm and fire deliberately into the back of the proprietor of the Oasis, leap over the falling body, vault into the saddle of Harlan's horse and gallop for safety. Hopalong's shots went wide and the last view any one had of Slivers in that part of the country was when he dropped into an arroyo to follow it for safety. Laramie Joe fled before Red Connors and Red's rage was so great that it spoiled his accuracy, and he had the sorrow of seeing the pursued grow faint in the mist and fog. Pursuit was tried until the pursuers realized that their mounts were too worn out to stand a show against the fresh animals ridden by the survivors of the Oasis crowd.

Red circled and joined Hopalong. "Blasted coyotes," he growled. "Killed Jackson an' Edwards, an' wanted the Kid! He's shore showed 'em what fighting is, all right. But I wonder what got into 'em all at once to give 'em nerve enough to start things?"

"Edwards paid his way, all right," replied Hopalong. "If I do as well when my time comes I won't do no kicking."

"Yore time ain't coming that way," responded Red, grinning. "You'll die a natural death in bed, unless you gets to cussing me."

"Shore there ain't no more, Buck?" Hopalong called.

"Yes. There was only five, I reckon, an' they was purty well shot up when we took a hand. You know, Johnny was in it all the time," replied the foreman, smiling. "This town's had the cleaning up it's needed for some time," he added.

They were at Jackson's store now, and hurriedly dismounted and ran in to see Johnny. They found him lying across some boxes, which brought him almost to the level of a window sill. He was too weak to stand, while near him in similar condition lay Barr, too weak from loss of blood to do more than look his welcome.

"How are you, Kid?" cried Buck anxiously, bending over him, while others looked to Barr's injuries.

"Tired, Buck, awful tired; an' all shot up," Johnny slowly replied. "When I saw you fellers-streak past this windy—I sort of went flat-something seemed to break inside me," he said, faintly and with an effort, and the foreman ordered him not to talk. Deft fingers, schooled by practice in rough and ready surgery, were busy over him and in half an hour he lay on Jackson's cot, covered with bandages.

"Why, hullo, Lacey!" exclaimed Hopalong, leaping forward to shake hands with the man Red and Billy had gone to help. "Purty well scratched up, but lively yet, hey?"

"I'm able to hobble over here an' shake han's with these scrappers-they're shore wonders," Lacey replied. "Fought like a whole regiment! Hullo, Johnny!" and his hand-clasp told much.

"Yore cross fire did it, Lacey; that was the whole thing," Johnny smiled. "Yo're all right!"

Red turned and looked out of the window toward the Oasis and then glanced at Buck. "Reckon we better burn Harlan's place-it's all that's left of that gang now," he suggested.

"Why, yes; I reckon so," replied the foreman. "That's as —"

"No, we won't!" Hopalong interposed quickly. "That stands till Johnny sets it off. It's the Kid's celebration-he was shot in it."

Johnny smiled.

Chapter XX
Barb Wire

After the flurry at Perry's Bend the Bar-20 settled down to the calm routine work and sent several drive herds to their destination without any unusual incidents. Buck thought that the last herd had been driven when, late in the summer, he received an order that he made haste to fill. The outfit was told to get busy and soon rounded up the necessary number of three-year-olds. Then came the road branding, the final step except inspection, and this was done not far from the ranch house, where the facilities were best for speedy work.

Entirely recovered from all ill effects of his afternoon in Jackson's store up in Perry's bend, Johnny Nelson waited with Red Connors on the platform of the branding chute and growled petulantly at the sun, the dust, but most of all at the choking, smarting odor of burned hair which filled their throats and caused them to rub the backs of grimy hands across their eyes. Chute-branding robbed them of the excitement, the leaven of fun and frolic, which they always took from open or corral branding-and the work of a day in the corral or open was condensed into an hour or two by the chute. This was one cow wide, narrow at the bottom and flared out as it went up, so the animal could not turn, and when filled was, to use Johnny's graphic phrase, "like a chain of cows in a ditch." Eight of the wondering and crowded animals, guided into the pen by men who knew their work to the smallest detail and lost no time in its performance, filed into the pen after those branded had filed out. As the first to enter reached the farther end a stout bar dropped into place, just missing the animal's nose; and as the last cow discovered that it could go no farther and made up its mind to back out, it was stopped by another bar, which fell behind it. The iron heaters tossed a hot iron each to Red and Johnny and the eight were marked in short order, making about two hundred and fifty they had branded in three hours. This number compared very favorably with that of the second chute where Lanky Smith and Frenchy McAlister waved cold irons and sarcastically asked their iron men if the sun was supposed to provide the heat; whereat the down-trodden heaters provided heat with great generosity in their caustic retorts.

"Oh, Susanna, don't you cry for me," sang Billy Williams, one of the feeders. "But why in Jericho don't you fellers get a move on you? You ain't no good on the platform-you ought to be mixing biscuits for Cookie. Frenchy and Lanky are the boys to turn 'em out," he offered, gratis.

Red's weary air bespoke a vast and settled contempt for such inanities and his iron descended against the side of the victim below him-he would not deign to reply. Not so with Johnny, who could not refrain from hot retort.

"Don't be a fool *all* the time," snapped Johnny. "Mind yore own business, you shorthorn. Big-mouthed old woman, that's what —" his tone dropped and the words sank into vague mutterings which a strangling cough cut short. "Blasted idiot," he whispered, tears coming into his eyes at the effort. Burning hair is bad for throat and temper alike.

Red deftly knocked his companion's iron up and spoke sharply. "You mind yourn better-that makes the third you've tried to brand twice. Why don't you look what yo're doing? Hot iron! Hot iron! What're you fellers doing?" he shouted down at the heaters. "This ain't no time to go to sleep. How d'ye expect us to do any work when you ain't doing any yoreselves!" Red's temper was also on the ragged edge.

"You've got one in yore other hand, you sheep!" snorted one of the iron heaters with restless pugnacity. "Go tearing into us when you —" he growled the rest and kicked viciously at the fire.

"Lovely bunch," grinned Billy who, followed by Pete Wilson, mounted the platform to relieve the branders. "Chase yoreselves-me an' Pete are shore going to show you cranky bugs how to do a hundred an hour. Ain't we, Pete? An' look here, you," he remarked to the heaters, "don't you fellers keep *us* waiting for hot irons!"

"That's right! Make a fool out of yoreself first thing!" snapped one of the pair on the ground.

"Billy, I never loved you as much as I do this minute," grinned Johnny wearily. "Wish you'd 'a' come along to show us how to do it an hour ago."

"I would, only —"

"Quit chinning an' get busy," remarked Red, climbing down. "The chute's full; an' it's all yourn."

Billy caught the iron, gave it a preliminary flourish, and started to work with a speed that would not endure for long. He branded five out of the eight and jeered at his companion for being so slow.

"Have yore fun now, Billy," Pete replied with placid good nature. "Before we're through with this job you'll be lucky if you can do two of the string, if you keep up that pace."

"He'll be missing every other one," growled his heater with overflowing malice. "That iron ain't cold, you Chinaman!"

"Too cold for me-don't miss none," chuckled Billy sweetly. "Fill the chute! Fill the chute! Don't keep us waiting!" he cried to the guiders, hopping around with feigned eagerness and impatience.

Hopalong Cassidy rode up and stopped as Red returned to take the place of one of the iron heaters. "How they coming, Red?" he inquired.

"Fast. You can sic that inspector on 'em the first thing to-morrow morning, if he gets here on time. Bet he's off som'ers getting full of redeye. Who're going with you on this drive?"

"The inspector is all right-he's here now an' is going to spend the night with us so as to be on hand the first thing to-morrow," replied Hopalong, grinning at the hard-working pair on the platform. "Why, I reckon I'll take you, Johnny, Lanky, Billy, Pete, an' Skinny, an' we'll have two hoss-wranglers an' a cook, of course. We'll drive up the right-hand trail through West Valley this time. It's longer, but there'll be more water that way at this time of the year. Besides, I don't want no more foot-sore cattle to nurse along. Even the West Valley trail will be dry enough before we strike Bennett's Creek."

"Yes; we'll have to drive 'em purty hard till we reach the creek," replied Red, thoughtfully. "Say; we're going to have three thousand of the finest three-year-old steers ever sent north out of these parts. An' we ought to do it in a month an' deliver 'em fat an' frisky. We can feed 'em good for the last week."

"I just sent some of the boys out to drive in the cayuses," Hopalong remarked, "an' when they get here you fellers match for choice an' pick yore remuda. No use taking too few. About eight apiece'll do us nice. I shore like a good cavvieyeh."

"Hullo, Hoppy!" came from the platform as Billy grinned his welcome through the dust on his face. "Want a job?"

"Hullo yoreself," growled Pete. "Stick yore iron on that fourth steer before he gets out, an' talk less with yore mouth."

"Pete's still rabid," called Billy, performing the duty Pete suggested.

"That may be the polite name for it," snorted one of the iron heaters, testing an iron, "but that ain't what I'd say. Might as well cover the subject thoroughly while yo're on it."

"Yes, verily," endorsed his companion.

"Here comes the last of 'em," smiled Pete, watching several cattle being driven towards the chute. "We'll have to brand 'em on the move, Billy; there ain't enough to fill the chute."

"All right; hot iron, you!"

Early the next morning the inspector looked them over and made his count, the herd was started north and at nightfall had covered twelve miles. For the next week everything went smoothly, but after that, water began to be scarce and the herd was pushed harder, and became harder to handle.

On the night of the twelfth day out four men sat around the fire in West Valley at a point a dozen miles south of Bennett's Creek, and ate heartily. The night was black-not a star could be seen and the south wind hardly stirred the trampled and burned grass. They were thoroughly tired out and their tempers were not in the sweetest state imaginable, for the heat during the last four days had been almost unbearable even to them and they had had their hands full with the cranky herd. They ate silently, hungrily-there would be time enough for the few words they had to say when the pipes were going for a short smoke before turning in.

"I feel like hell," growled Red, reaching for another cup of coffee, but there was no reply; he had voiced the feelings of all.

Hopalong listened intently and looked up, staring into the darkness, and soon a horseman was seen approaching the fire. Hopalong nodded welcome and waved his hand towards the food, and the stranger, dismounting, picketed his horse and joined the circle. When the pipes were lighted he sighed with satisfaction and looked around the group. "Driving north, I see."

"Yes; an' blamed glad to get off this dry range," Hopalong replied. "The herd's getting cranky an' hard to hold-but when we pass the creek everything'll be all right again. An' ain't it hot! When you hear us kick about the heat it means something."

"I'm going yore way," remarked the stranger. "I came down this trail about two weeks ago. Reckon I was the last to ride through before the fence went up. Damned outrage, says I, an' I told 'em so, too. They couldn't see it that way an' we had a little disagreement about it. They said as how they was going to patrol it."

"Fence! What fence?" exclaimed Red.

"Where's there any fence?" demanded Hopalong sharply.

"Twenty mile north of the creek," replied the stranger, carefully packing his pipe.

"What? Twenty miles north of the creek?" cried Hopalong. "What creek?"

"Bennett's. The 4X has strung three strands of barb wire from Coyote Pass to the North Arm. Thirty mile long, without a gate, so they says."

"But it don't close this trail!" cried Hopalong in blank astonishment.

"It shore does. They say they owns that range an' can fence it in all they wants. I told 'em different, but naturally they didn't listen to me. An' they'll fight about it, too."

"But they *can't* shut off this trail!" exclaimed Billy, with angry emphasis. "They don't own it no more'n we do!"

"I know all about that-you heard me tell you what they said."

"But how can we get past it?" demanded Hopalong.

"Around it, over the hills. You'll lose about three days doing it, too."

"I can't take no sand-range herd over them rocks, an' I ain't going to drive 'round no North Arm or Coyote Pass if I could," Hopalong replied with quiet emphasis. "There's poison springs on the east an' nothing but rocks on the west. We go straight through."

"I'm afraid that you'll have to fight if you do," remarked the stranger.

"Then we'll fight!" cried Johnny, leaning forward. "Blasted coyotes! What right have they got to block a drive trail that's as old as cattle-raising in these parts! That trail was here before I was born, it's allus been open, an' it's going to stay open! You watch us go through!"

"Yo're dead right, Kid; we'll cut that fence an' stick to this trail, an' fight if we has to," endorsed Red. "The Bar-20 ain't crawling out of no hole that it can walk out of. They're bluffing; that's all."

"I don't think they are; an' there's twelve men in that outfit," suggested the stranger, offhand.

"We ain't got time to count odds; we never do down our way when we know we're right. An' we're right enough in this game," retorted Hopalong, quickly. "For the last twelve days we've had good luck, barring the few on this dry range; an' now we're in for the other kind. By the Lord, I wish we was here without the cows to take care of-we'd show 'em something about blocking drive trails that ain't in their little book!"

"Blast it all! Wire fences coming down this way now," mused Johnny, sullenly. He hated them by training as much as he hated horse-thieves and sheep; and his companions had been brought up in the same school. Barb wire, the death-knell to the old-time punching, the bar to riding at will, a steel insult to fire the blood-it had come at last.

"We've shore got to cut it, Red, —" began Hopalong, but the cook had to rid himself of some of his indignation and interrupted with heat.

"Shore we have!" came explosively from the tail board of the chuck wagon. "Got to lay it agin my li'l axe an' swat it with my big ol' monkey wrench! An' won't them posts save me a lot of trouble hunting chips an' firewood!"

"We've shore got to cut it, Red," Hopalong repeated slowly. "You an' Johnny an' me'll ride ahead after we cross the creek to-morrow an' do it. I don't hanker after no fight with all these cows on my han's, but we've got to risk one."

"Shore!" cried Johnny, hotly. "I can't get over the gall of them fellers closing up the West Valley drive trail. Why, I never heard tell of such a thing afore!"

"We're short-handed; we ought to have more'n we have to guard the herd if there's a fight. If it stampedes-oh, well, that'll work out to-morrow. The creek's only about twelve miles away an' we'll start at daylight, so tumble in," Hopalong said as he arose. "Red, I'm going out to take my shift —I'll send Pete in. Stranger," he added, turning, "I'm much obliged to you for the warning. They might 'a' caught us with our hands tied."

"Oh, that's all right," hastily replied the stranger, who was in hearty accord with the plans, such as they were. "My name's Hawkins, an' I don't like range fences no more'n you do. I used to hunt buffalo all over this part of the country before they was all killed off, an' I allus rode where I pleased. I'm purty old, but I can still see an' shoot; an' I'm going to stick right along with you fellers an' see it through. Every man counts in this game."

"Well, that's blamed white of you," Hopalong replied, greatly pleased by the other's offer. "But I can't let you do it. I don't want to drag you into no trouble, an' —"

"You ain't dragging me none; I'm doing it myself. I'm about as mad as you are over it. I ain't good for much no more, an' if I shuffles off fighting barb wire I'll be doing my duty. First it was nesters, then railroads an' more nesters, then sheep, an' now it's wire-won't it never stop? By the Lord, it's got to stop, or this country will go to the devil an' won't be fit to live in. Besides, I've heard of your fellers before —I'll tie to the Bar-20 any day."

"Well, I reckon you must if you must; yo're welcome enough," laughed Hopalong, and he strode off to his picketed horse, leaving the others to discuss the fence, with the assistance of the cook, until Pete rode in.

Chapter XXI
The Fence

When Hopalong rode in at midnight to arouse the others and send them out to relieve Skinny and his two companions, the cattle were quieter than he had expected to leave them, and he could see no change of weather threatening. He was asleep when the others turned in, or he would have been further assured in that direction.

Out on the plain where the herd was being held, Red and the three other guards had been optimistic until half of their shift was over and it was only then that they began to worry. The knowledge that running water was only twelve miles away had the opposite effect than the one expected, for instead of making them cheerful, it caused them to be beset with worry and fear. Water was all right, and they could not have got along without it for another day; but it was, in this case, filled with the possibility of grave danger.

Johnny was thinking hard about it as he rode around the now restless herd, and then pulled up suddenly, peered into the darkness and went on again. "Damn that disreputable li'l rounder! Why the devil can't he behave, 'stead of stirring things up when they're ticklish?" he muttered, but he had to grin despite himself. A lumbering form had blundered past him from the direction of the camp and was swallowed up by the night as it sought the herd, annoying and arousing the thirsty and irritable cattle along its trail, throwing challenges right and left and stirring up trouble as it passed. The fact that the challenges were bluffs made no difference to the pawing steers, for they were anxious to have things out with the rounder.

This frisky disturber of bovine peace was a yearling that had slipped into the herd before it left the ranch and had kept quiet and respectable and out of sight in the middle of the mass for the first few days and nights. But keeping quiet and respectable had been an awful strain, and his mischievous deviltry grew constantly harder to hold in check. Finally he could stand the repression no longer, and when he gave way to his accumulated energy it had the snap and ginger of a tightly stretched rubber band recoiling on itself. On the fourth night out he had thrown off his mask and announced his presence in his true light by butting a sleepy steer out of its bed, which bed he straightway proceeded to appropriate for himself. This was folly, for the ground was not cold and he had no excuse for stealing a body-warmed place to lie down; it was pure cussedness, and retribution followed hard upon the act. In about half a minute he had discovered the great difference between bullying poor, miserable, defenceless dogies and trying to bully a healthy, fully developed, and pugnacious steer. After assimilating the preliminary punishment of what promised to be the most thorough and workmanlike thrashing he had ever known, the indignant and frightened bummer wheeled and fled incontinently with the aroused steer in angry pursuit. The best way out was the most puzzling to the vengeful steer, so the bummer cavorted recklessly through the herd, turning and twisting and doubling, stepping on any steer that happened to be lying down in his path, butting others, and leavening things with great success. Under other conditions he would have relished the effect of his efforts, for the herd had arisen as one animal and seemed to be debating the advisability of stampeding; but he was in no mood to relish anything and thought only of getting away. Finally escaping from his pursuer, that had paused to fight with a belligerent brother, he rambled off into the darkness to figure it all out and to maintain a sullen and chastened demeanor for the rest of the night. This was the first time a brick had been under the hat.

But the spirits of youth recover quickly-his recovered so quickly that he was banished from the herd the very next night, which banishment, not being at all to his liking, was enforced only by rigid watchfulness and hard riding; and he was roundly cursed from dark to dawn by the worried men, most of whom disliked the bumming youngster less than they pretended. He was only a cub, a wild youth having his fling, and there was something irresistibly likable and comical in his awkward antics and eternal persistence, even though he was a pest. Johnny saw more in him than his companions could find, and had quite a little sport with him: he made fine practice for roping, for he was about as elusive as a grasshopper and uncertain as a flea. Johnny was in the same general class and he could sympathize with the irrepressible nuisance in its efforts to stir up a little life and excitement in so dull a crowd; Johnny hoped to be as successful in his mischievous deviltry when he reached the town at the end of the drive.

But to-night it was dark, and the bummer gained his coveted goal with ridiculous ease, after which he started right in to work off the high pressure of the energy he had accumulated during the last two nights. He had desisted in his efforts to gain the herd early in the evening and had rambled off and rested during the first part of the night, and the herders breathed softly lest they should stir him to renewed trials. But now he had succeeded, and although only Johnny had seen him lumber past, the other three guards were aware of it immediately by the results and swore in their throats, for the cattle were now on their feet, snorting and moving about restlessly, and the rattling of horns grew slowly louder.

"Ain't he having a devil of a good time!" grinned Johnny. But it was not long before he realized the possibilities of the bummer's efforts and he lost his grin. "If we get through the night without trouble I'll see that you are picketed if it takes me all day to get you," he muttered. "Fun is fun, but it's getting a little too serious for comfort."

Sometime after the middle of the second shift the herd, already irritable, nervous, and cranky because of the thirst they were enduring, and worked up to the fever pitch by the devilish manoeuvres of the exuberant and hard-working bummer, wanted only the flimsiest kind of an excuse to stampede, and they might go without an excuse. A flash of lightning, a crash of thunder, a wind-blown paper, a flapping wagon cover, the sudden and unheralded approach of a careless rider, the cracking and flare of a match, or the scent of a wolf or coyote-or water, would send an avalanche of three thousand crazed steers crashing its irresistible way over a pitch-black plain.

Red had warned Pete and Billy, and now he rode to find Johnny and send him to camp for the others. As he got halfway around the circle he heard Johnny singing a mournful lay, and soon a black bulk loomed up in the dark ahead of him. "That you, Kid?" he asked. "That you, Johnny?" he repeated, a little louder.

The song stopped abruptly. "Shore," replied Johnny. "We're going to have trouble aplenty to-night. Glad daylight ain't so very far off. That cussed li'l rake of a bummer got by me an' into the herd. He's shore raising Ned to-night, the li'l monkey: it's getting serious, Red."

"I'll shoot that yearling at daylight, damn him!" retorted Red. "I should 'a' done it a week ago. He's picked the worst time for his cussed devilment! You ride right in an' get the boys, an' get 'em out here quick. The whole herd's on its toes waiting for the signal; an' the wink of an eye'll send 'em off. God only knows what'll happen between now and daylight! If the wind should change an' blow down from the north, they'll be off as shore as shooting. One whiff of Bennett's Creek is all that's needed, Kid; an' —"

"Oh, pshaw!" interposed Johnny. "There ain't no wind at all now. It's been quiet for an hour."

"Yes; an' that's one of the things that's worrying me. It means a change, shore."

"Not always; we'll come out of this all right," assured Johnny, but he spoke without his usual confidence. "There ain't no use —" he paused as he felt the air stir, and he was conscious of Red's heavy breathing. There was a peculiar hush in the air that he did not like, a closeness that sent his heart up in his throat, and as he was about to continue a sudden gust snapped his neck-kerchief out straight. He felt that refreshing coolness which so often precedes a storm and as he weighed it in his mind a low rumble of thunder rolled in the north and sent a chill down his back.

"Good God! Get the boys!" cried Red, wheeling. "It's *changed*! An' Pete an' Billy out there in front of—*there they go!*" he shouted as a sudden tremor shook the earth and a roaring sound filled the air. He was instantly lost to ear and eye, swallowed by the oppressive darkness as he spurred and quirted into a great, choking cloud of dust which swept down from the north, unseen in the night. The deep thunder of hoofs and the faint and occasional flash of a six-shooter told him the direction, and he hurled his mount after the uproar with no thought of the death which lurked in every hole and rock and gully on the uneven and unseen plain beneath him. His mouth and nose were lined with dust, his throat choked with it, and he opened his burning eyes only at intervals, and then only to a slit, to catch a fleeting glance of-nothing. He realized vaguely that he was riding north, because the cattle would head for water, but that was all, save that he was animated by a desperate eagerness to gain the firing line, to join Pete and Billy, the two men who rode before that crazed mass of horns and hoofs and who were pleading and swearing and yelling in vain only a few feet ahead of annihilation-if they were still alive. A stumble, a moment's indecision, and the avalanche would roll over them as if they were straws and trample them flat beneath the pounding hoofs, a modern Juggernaut. If he, or they, managed to escape with life, it would make a good tale for the bunk house some night; if they were killed it was in doing their duty-it was all in a day's work.

Johnny shouted after him and then wheeled and raced towards the camp, emptying his Colt in the air as a warning. He saw figures scurrying across the lighted place, and before he had gained it his friends raced past him and gave him hard work catching up to them. And just behind him rode the stranger, to do what he could for his new friends, and as reckless of consequences as they.

It seemed an age before they caught up to the stragglers, and when they realized how true they had ridden in the dark they believed that at last their luck was turning for the better, and pushed on with renewed hope. Hopalong shouted to those nearest him that Bennett's Creek could not be far away and hazarded the belief that the steers would slow up and stop when they found the water they craved; but his words were lost to all but himself.

Suddenly the punchers were almost trapped and their escape made miraculous, for without warning the herd swerved and turned sharply to the right, crossing the path of the riders and forcing them to the east, showing Hopalong their silhouettes against the streak of pale gray low down in the eastern sky. When free from the sudden press of cattle they slowed perceptibly, and Hopalong did likewise to avoid running them down. At that instant the uproar took on a new note and increased threefold. He could hear the shock of impact, whip-like reports, the bellowing of cattle in pain, and he arose in his stirrups to peer ahead for the reason, seeing, as he did so, the silhouettes of his friends arise and then drop from his sight. Without additional warning his horse pitched forward and crashed to the earth, sending him over its head. Slight as was the warning it served to ease his fall, for instinct freed his feet from the stirrups, and when he struck the ground it was feet first, and although he fell flat at the next instant, the shock had been broken. Even as it was, he was partly stunned, and groped as he arose on his hands and knees. Arising painfully he took a short step forward, tripped and fell again; and felt a sharp pain shoot through his hand as it went first to break the fall. Perhaps it was ten seconds before he knew what it was that had thrown him, and when he learned that he also learned the reason for the whole calamity-in his torn and bleeding hand he held a piece of barb wire.

"Barb wire!" he muttered, amazed. "Barb wire! Why, what the *—Damn that ranch!*" he shouted, sudden rage sweeping over him as the situation flashed through his mind and banished all the mental effects of the fall. "They've gone an' strung it south of the creek as well! Red! Johnny! Lanky!" he shouted at the top of his voice, hoping to be heard over the groaning of injured cattle and the general confusion. "Good Lord! *are they killed!*"

They were not, thanks to the forced slowing up, and to the pool of water and mud which formed an arm of the creek, a back-water away from the pull of the current. They had pitched into the mud and water up to their waists, some head first, some feet first, and others as they would go into a chair. Those who had been fortunate enough to strike feet first pulled out the divers, and the others gained their feet as best they might and with varying degrees of haste, but all mixed profanity and thankfulness equally well; and were equally and effectually disguised.

Hopalong, expecting the silence of death or at least the groaning of injured and dying, was taken aback by the fluent stream of profanity which greeted his ears. But all efforts in that line were eclipsed when the drive foreman tersely explained about the wire, and the providential mud bath was forgotten in the new idea. They forthwith clamored for war, and the sooner it came the better they would like it.

"Not now, boys; we've got work to do first," replied Hopalong, who, nevertheless, was troubled grievously by the same itching trigger finger. They subsided-as a steel spring subsides when held down by a weight-and went off in search of their mounts. Daylight had won the skirmish in the east and was now attacking in force, and revealed a sight which, stilling the profanity for the moment, caused it to flow again with renewed energy. The plain was a shambles near the creek, and dead and dying steers showed where the fence had stood. The rest of the herd had passed over these. The wounded cattle and three horses were put out of their misery as the first duty. The horse that Hopalong had ridden had a broken back; the other two, broken legs. When this work was out of the way the bruised and shaken men gave their attention to the scattered cattle on the other side of the creek, and when Hawkins rode up after wasting time in hunting for the trail in the dark, he saw four men with the herd, which was still scattered; four others near the creek, of whom only Johnny was mounted, and a group of six strangers riding towards them from the west and along the fence, or what was left of that portion of it.

"That's awful!" he cried, stopping his limping horse near Hopalong. "An' here come the fools that done it."

"Yes," replied Johnny, his voice breaking from rage, "but they won't go back again! I don't care if I'm killed if I can get one or two of that crowd —"

"Shut up, Kid!" snapped Hopalong as the 4X outfit drew near. "I know just how you feel about it; feel that way myself. But there ain't a-going to be no fighting while I've got these cows on my han's. That gang'll be here when we come back, all right."

"Mebby one or two of 'em won't," remarked Hawkins, as he looked again over the carnage along the fence. "I never did much pot-shooting, 'cept agin Injuns; but I dunno —" He did not finish, for the strangers were almost at his elbow.

Cranky Joe led the 4X contingent and he did the talking for it without waste of time. "Who the hell busted that fence?" he demanded, belligerently, looking around savagely. Johnny's hand twitched at the words and the way they were spoken.

"I did; did you think somebody leaned agin it?" replied Hopalong, very calmly,—so calmly that it was about one step short of an explosion.

"Well, why didn't you go around?"

"Three thousand stampeding cattle don't go 'round wire fences in the dark."

"Well, that's not our fault. Reckon you better dig down an' settle up for the damages, an' half a cent a head for water; an' then go 'round. You can't stampede through the other fence."

"That so?" asked Hopalong.

"Reckon it is."

"Yo're real shore it is?"

"Well there's only six of us here, but there's six more that we can get blamed quick if we need 'em. It's so, all right."

"Well, coming down to figures, there's eight here, with two hoss-wranglers an' a cook to come," retorted Hopalong, kicking the belligerent Johnny on the shins. "We're just about mad enough to tackle anything: ever feel that way?"

"Oh, no use getting all het up," rejoined Cranky Joe. "We ain't a-going to fight 'less we has to. Better pay up."

"Send yore bills to the ranch-if they're O. K., Buck'll pay 'em."

"Nix; I take it when I can get it."

"I ain't got no money with me that I can spare."

"Then you can leave enough cows to buy back again."

"I'm not going to pay you one damned cent, an' the only cows I'll leave are the dead ones-an' if I could take them with me I'd do it. An' I'm not going around the fence, neither."

"Oh, yes; you are. An' yo're going to pay," snapped Cranky Joe.

"Take it out of the price of two hundred dead cows an' gimme what's left," Hopalong retorted. "It'll cost you nine of them twelve men to pry it out'n me."

"You won't pay?" demanded the other, coldly.

"Not a plugged peso."

"Well, as I said before, I don't want to fight nobody 'less I has to," replied Cranky Joe. "I'll give you a chance to change yore mind. We'll be out here after it to-morrow, cash or cows. That'll give you twenty-four hours to rest yore herd an' get ready to drive. Then you pay, an' go back, 'round the fence."

"All right; to-morrow suits me," responded Hopalong, who was boiling with rage and felt constrained to hold it back. If it wasn't for the cows—!

Red and three companions swept up and stopped in a swirl of dust and asked questions until Hopalong shut them up. Their arrival and the manner of their speech riled Cranky Joe, who turned around and loosed one more remark; and he never knew how near to death he was at that moment.

"You fellers must own the earth, the way you act," he said to Red and his three companions.

"We ain't fencing it in to prove it," rejoined Hopalong, his hand on Red's arm.

Cranky Joe wheeled to rejoin his friends. "To-morrow," he said, significantly.

Hopalong and his men watched the six ride away, too enraged to speak for a moment. Then the drive foreman mastered himself and turned to Hawkins. "Where's their ranch house?" he demanded, sharply. "There must be some way out of this, an' we've got to find it; an' before to-morrow."

"West; three hours' ride along the fence. I could find 'em the darkest night what ever happened; I was out there once," Hawkins replied.

"Describe 'em as exact as you can," demanded Hopalong, and when Hawkins had done so the Bar-20 drive foreman slapped his thigh and laughed nastily. "One house with one door an' only two windows-are you shore? Good! Where's the corrals? Good again! So they'll take pay for their blasted fence, eh? Cash or cows, hey! Don't want no fight 'less it's necessary, but they're going to make us pay for the fence that killed two hundred head, an' blamed nigh got us, too. An' half a cent a head for drinking water! I've paid that more'n once-some of the poor devils squatting on the range ain't got nothing to sell but water, but I don't buy none out of Bennett's Creek! Pete, you mounted fellers round up a little-bunch the herd a little closer, an' drive straight along the trail towards that other fence. We'll all help you as soon as the wranglers bring us up something to ride. Push 'em hard, limp or no limp, till dark. They'll be too tired to go crow-hopping 'round any in the dark to-night. An' say! When you see that bummer, if he wasn't got by the fence, drop him clean. So they've got twelve men, hey! Huh!"

"What you going to do?" asked Red, beginning to cool down, and very curious.

"Yes; tell us," urged Johnny.

"Why, I'm going to cut that fence, an' cut it all to hell. Then I'm going to push the herd through it as far out of danger as I can. When they're all right Cookie an' the hoss-wranglers will have to hold 'em during the night while we do the rest."

"What's the rest?" demanded Johnny.

"Oh, I'll tell you that later; it can wait," replied Hopalong. "Meanwhile, you get out there with Pete an' help get the herd in shape. We'll be with you soon-here comes the wranglers an' the cavvieyeh. 'Bout time, too."

Chapter XXII
Mr. Boggs is Disgusted

The herd gained twelve miles by dark and would pass through the northern fence by noon of the next day, for Cook's axe and monkey wrench had been put to good use. For quite a distance there was no fence: about a mile of barb wire had been pulled loose and was tangled up into several large piles, while rings of burned grass and ashes surrounded what was left of the posts. The cook had embraced this opportunity to lay in a good supply of firewood and was the happiest man in the outfit.

At ten o'clock that night eight figures loped westward along the southern fence and three hours later dismounted near the first corral of the 4X ranch. They put their horses in a depression on the plain and then hastened to seek cover, being careful to make no noise.

At dawn the door of the bunk house opened quickly and as quickly slammed shut again, three bullets in it being the reason. An uproar ensued and guns spat from the two windows in the general direction of the unseen besiegers, who did not bother about replying; they had given notification of their presence and until it was necessary to shoot there was no earthly use of wasting ammunition. Besides, the drive outfit had cooled down rapidly when it found that its herd was in no immediate danger and was not anxious to kill any one unless there was need. The situation was conducive to humor rather than anger. But every time the door moved it collected more lead, and it finally remained shut.

The noise in the bunk house continued and finally a sombrero was waved frantically at the south window and a moment later Nat Boggs, foreman of the incarcerated 4X outfit, stuck his head out very cautiously and yelled questions which bore directly on the situation and were to the point. He appeared to be excited and unduly heated, if one might judge from his words and voice. There was no reply, which still further added to his heat and excitement. Becoming bolder and a little angrier he allowed his impetuous nature to get the upper hand and forthwith attempted the feat of getting through that same window; but a sharp *pat!* sounded on a board not a foot from him, and he reconsidered hastily. His sombrero again waved to insist on a truce, and collected two holes, causing him much mental anguish and threatening the loss of his worthy soul. He danced up and down with great agility and no grace and made remarks, thereby leading a full-voiced chorus.

"Ain't that a hell of a note?" he demanded plaintively as he paused for breath. "Stick *yore* hat out, Cranky, an' see what *you* can do," he suggested, irritably.

Cranky Joe regarded him with pity and reproach, and moved back towards the other end of the room, muttering softly to himself. "I know it ain't much of a bonnet, but he needn't rub it in," he growled, peevishly.

"Try again; mebby they didn't see you," suggested Jim Larkin, who had a reputation for never making a joke. He escaped with his life and checked himself at the side of Cranky Joe, with whom he conferred on the harshness of the world towards unfortunates.

The rest of the morning was spent in snipe-shooting at random, trusting to luck to hit some one, and trusting in vain. At noon Cranky Joe could stand the strain no longer and opened the door just a little to relive the monotony. He succeeded, being blessed with a smashed shoulder, and immediately became a general nuisance, adding greatly to the prevailing atmosphere. Boggs called him a few kinds of fools and hastened to nail the door shut; he hit his thumb and his heart became filled with venom.

"*Now* look at what they went an' done!" he yelled, running around in a circle. "Damned outrage!"

"Huh!" snorted Cranky Joe with maddening superiority. "That ain't nothing-just look at me!"

Boggs looked, very fixedly, and showed signs of apoplexy, and Cranky Joe returned to his end of the room to resume his soliloquy.

"Why don't you come out an' take them cows!" inquired an unkind voice from without. "Ain't changed yore mind, have you?"

"We'll give you a drink for half a cent a head-that's the regular price for watering cows," called another.

The faint ripple of mirth which ran around the plain was lost in opinions loudly expressed within the room; and Boggs, tears of rage in his eyes, flung himself down on a chair and invented new terms for describing human beings.

John Terry was observing. He had been fluttering around the north window, constantly getting bolder, and had not been disturbed. When he withdrew his sombrero and found that it was intact he smiled to himself and leaned his elbows on the sill, looking carefully around the plain. The discovery that there was no cover on the north side cheered him greatly and he called to Boggs, outlining a plan of action.

Boggs listened intently and then smiled for the first time since dawn. "Bully for you, Terry!" he enthused. "Wait till dark-we'll fool 'em."

A bullet chipped the 'dobe at Terry's side and he ducked as he leaped back. "From an angle-what did I tell you?" he laughed. "We'll drop out here an' sneak behind the house after dark. They'll be watching the door-an' they won't be able to see us, anyhow."

Boggs sucked his thumb tenderly and grinned. "After which —," he elated.

"After which —," gravely repeated Terry, the others echoing it with unrestrained joy.

"Then, mebby, I can get a drink," chuckled Larkin, brightening under the thought.

"The moon comes up at ten," warned a voice. "It'll be full to-night —an' there ain't many clouds in sight."

"*Ol' King Cole was a merry ol' soul,*" hummed McQuade, lightly.

"An' —a —merry-ol' —soul-was-he! —was-he!" thundered the chorus, deep-toned and strong. "*He had a wife for every toe, an' some toes counted three!*"

"Listen!" cried Meade, holding up his hand.

"*An' every wife had sixteen dogs, an' every dog a flea!*" shouted a voice from the besiegers, followed by a roar of laughter.

The hilarity continued until dark, only stopping when John Terry slipped out of the window, dropped to all-fours and stuck his head around the corner of the rear wall. He saw many stars and was silently handed to Pete Wilson.

"What was that noise?" exclaimed Boggs in a low tone. "Are you all right, Terry?" he asked, anxiously.

Three knocks on the wall replied to his question and then McQuade went out, and three more knocks were heard.

"Wonder why they make that funny noise," muttered Boggs.

"Bumped inter something, I reckon," replied Jim Larkin. "Get out of my way —I'm next."

Boggs listened intently and then pushed Duke Lane back. "Don't like that-sounds like a crack on the head. Hey, Jim! *Say* something!" he called softly. The three knocks were repeated, but Boggs was suspicious and he shook his head decisively. "To 'ell with the knocking —*say* something!"

"Still got them twelve men?" asked a strange voice, pleasantly.

"*An' every dog a flea,*" hummed another around the corner.

"Hell!" shouted Boggs. "To the door, fellers! To the door-quick!"

A whistle shrilled from behind the house and a leaden tattoo began on the door. "Other window!" whispered O'Neill. The foreman got there before him and, shoving his Colt out first to clear the way, yelled with rage and pain as a pole hit his wrist and knocked the weapon out of his hand. He was still commenting when Duke Lane pried open the door and, dropping quickly on his stomach, wriggled out, followed closely by Charley Beal and Tim. At that instant the tattoo drummed with greater vigor and such a hail of lead poured in through the opening that the door was promptly closed, leaving the three men outside to shift for themselves with the darkness their only cover.

Duke and his companions whispered together as they lay flat and agreed upon a plan of action. Going around the ends of the house was suicide and no better than waiting for the rising moon to show them to the enemy; but there was no reason why the roof could not be utilized. Tim and Charley boosted Duke up, then Tim followed, and the pair on the roof pulled Charley to their side. Flat roofs were great institutions they decided as they crawled cautiously towards the other side. This roof was of hard, sun-baked adobe, over two feet thick, and they did not care if their friends shot up on a gamble.

"Fine place, all right," thought Charley, grinning broadly. Then he turned an agonized face to Tim, his chest rising. "*Hitch! Hitch!*" he choked, fighting with all his will to master it. "*Hitch-chew! Hitch-chew! Hitch-chew!*" he sneezed, loudly. There was a scramble below and a ripple of mirth floated up to them.

"*Hitch-chew?*" jeered a voice. "What do we want to hit you for?"

"Look us over, children," invited another.

"Wait until the moon comes up," chuckled the third. "Be like knocking the nigger baby down for Red an' the others. Ladies and gents: We'll now have a little sketch entitled 'Shooting snipe by moonlight.'"

"Jack-snipe, too," laughed Pete. "Will somebody please hold the bag?"

The silence on the roof was profound and the three on the ground tried again.

"Let me call yore attention to the trained coyotes, ladies an' gents," remarked Johnny in a deep, solemn voice. "Coyotes are not birds; they do not roost on roofs as a general thing; but they are some intelligent an' can be trained to do lots of foolish tricks. These ani-mules were —"

"Step this way, people; on-ly ten cents, two nickels," interrupted Pete. "They bark like dogs, an' howl like hell."

"Shut up!" snapped Tim, angrily.

"After the moon comes up," said Hopalong, "when you fellers get tired dodging, you can chuck us yore guns an' come down. An' don't forget that this side of the house is much the safest," he warned.

"Go to hell!" snarled Duke, bitterly.

"Won't; they're laying for me down there."

Johnny crawled to the north end of the wall and, looking cautiously around the corner, funnelled his hands: "On the roof, Red! On the roof!"

"Yes, dear," was the reply, followed by gun-shots.

"Hey! Move over!" snapped Tim, working towards the edge furthest from the cheerful Red, whose bullets were not as accurate in the dark as they promised to become in a few minutes when the moon should come up.

"Want to shove me off?" snarled Charley, angrily. "For heaven's sake, Duke, do you want the whole earth?" he demanded of his second companion.

"You just bet yore shirt I do! An' I want a hole in it, too!"

"Ain't you got no sense?"

"Would I be up here if I had?"

"It's going to be hot as blazes up here when the sun gets high," cheerfully prophesied Tim: "an' dry, too," he added for a finishing touch.

"We'll be lucky if we're live enough to worry about the sun's heat —*say,* that was a *close* one!" exclaimed Duke, frantically trying to flatten a little more. "Ah, thought so-there's that blamed moon!"

"Wish I'd gone out the window instead," growled Charley, worming behind Duke, to the latter's prompt displeasure.

"You fellers better come down, one at a time," came from below. "Send yore guns down first, too. Red's a blamed good shot."

"Hope he croaks," muttered Duke. "*That's* closer yet!"

Tim's hand raised and a flash of fire singed Charley's hair. "Got to do something, anyhow," he explained, lowering the Colt and peering across the plain.

"You damned near succeeded!" shouted Charley, grabbing at his head. "Why, they're three hundred, an' you trying for 'em with a —*oh!*" he moaned, writhing.

"Locoed fool!" swore Duke, "showing 'em where we are! They're doing good enough as it is! You ought-got *you,* too!"

"*I'm* going down-that blamed fool out there ain't caring what he hits," mumbled Charley, clenching his hands from pain. He slid over the edge and Pete grabbed him.

"Next," suggested Pete, expectantly.

Tim tossed his Colt over the edge. "Here's another," he swore, following the weapon. He was grabbed and bound in a trice.

"When may we expect you, Mr. Duke?" asked Johnny, looking up.

"Presently, friend, presently. I want to —*wow!*" he finished, and lost no time in his descent, which was meteoric. "That feller'll *kill* somebody if he ain't careful!" he complained as Pete tied his hands behind his back.

"You wait till daylight an' see," cheerily replied Pete as the three were led off to join their friends in the corral.

There was no further action until the sun arose and then Hopalong hailed the house and demanded a parley, and soon he and Boggs met midway between the shack and the line.

"What d'you want?" asked Boggs, sullenly.

"Want you to stop this farce so I can go on with my drive."

"Well, I ain't holding you!" exploded the 4X foreman.

"Oh, yes; but you are. I can't let you an' yore men out to hang on our flanks an' worry us; an' I don't want to hold you in that shack till you all die of thirst, or come out to be all shot up. Besides, I can't fool around here for a week; I got business to look after."

"Don't you worry about us dying with thirst; that ain't worrying us none."

"I heard different," replied Hopalong, smiling. "Them fellers in the corral drank a quart apiece. See here, Boggs; you can't win, an' you know it. Yo're not bucking me, but the whole range, the whole country. It's a fight between conditions-the fence idea agin the open range idea, an' open trails. The fence will lose. You closed a drive trail that's 'most as old as cow-raising. Will the punchers of this part of the country stand for it? Suppose you lick us, —which you won't —can you lick all the rest of us, the JD, Wallace's, Double-Arrow, C-80, Cross-O-Cross, an' the others! That's just what it amounts to, an' you better stop right now, before somebody gets killed. You know what that means in this section. Yo're six to our eight, you ain't got a drink in that shack, an' you dasn't try to get one. You can't do a thing agin us, an' you know it."

Boggs rested his hands on his hips and considered, Hopalong waiting for him to reply. He knew that the Bar-20 man was right but he hated to admit it, he hated to say he was whipped.

"Are any of them six hurt?" he finally asked.

"Only scratches an' sore heads," responded Hopalong, smiling. "We ain't tried to kill anybody, yet. I'm putting that up to you."

Boggs made no reply and Hopalong continued: "I got six of yore twelve men prisoners, an' all yore cayuses are in my han's. I'll shoot every animal before I'll leave 'em for you to use against me, an' I'll take enough of yore cows to make up for what I lost by that fence. You've got to pay for them dead cows, anyhow. If I do let you out you'll have to road-brand me two hundred, or pay cash. My herd ain't worrying me-it's moving all the time. It's through that other fence by now. An' if I have to keep my outfit here to pen you in or shoot you off I can send to the JD for a gang to push the herd. Don't make no mistake: yo're getting off easy. Suppose one of my men had been killed at the fence-what then?"

"Well, what do you want me to do?"

"Stop this foolishness an' take down them fences for a mile each side of the trail. If Buck has to come up here the whole thing'll go down. Road-brand me two hundred of yore three-year-olds. Now as soon as you agree, an' say that the fight's over, it will be. You can't win out; an' what's the use of having yore men killed off?"

"I hate to quit," replied the other, gloomily.

"I know how that is; but yo're wrong on this question, dead wrong. You don't own this range or the trail. You ain't got no right to close that old drive trail. Honest, now; have you?"

"You say them six ain't hurt?"

"No more'n I said."

"An' if I give in will you treat my men right?"

"Shore."

"When will you leave."

"Just as soon as I get them two hundred three-year-olds."

"Well, I hate a quitter; but I can't do nothing, nohow," mused the 4X foreman. He cleared his throat and turned to look at the house. "All right; when you get them cows you get out of here, an' don't never come back!"

Hopalong flung his arm with a shout to his men and the other kicked savagely at an inoffensive stick and slouched back to his bunk house, a beaten man.

Chapter XXIII
Tex Ewalt Hunts Trouble

Not more than a few weeks after the Bar-20 drive outfit returned to the ranch a solitary horseman pushed on towards the trail they had followed, bound for Buckskin and the Bar-20 range. His name was Tex Ewalt and he cordially hated all of the Bar-20 outfit and Hopalong in particular. He had nursed a grudge for several years and now, as he rode south to rid himself of it and to pay a long-standing debt, it grew stronger until he thrilled with anticipation and the sauce of danger. This grudge had been acquired when he and Slim Travennes had enjoyed a duel with Hopalong Cassidy up in Santa Fe, and had been worsted; it had increased when he learned of Slim's death at Cactus Springs at the hands of Hopalong; and, some time later, hearing that two friends of his, "Slippery" Trendley and "Deacon" Rankin, with their gang, had "gone out" in the Panhandle with the same man and his friends responsible for it, Tex hastened to Muddy Wells to even the score and clean his slate. Even now his face burned when he remembered his experiences on that never-to-be-forgotten occasion. He had been played with, ridiculed, and shamed, until he fled from the town as a place accursed, hating everything and everybody. It galled him to think that he had allowed Buck Peters' momentary sympathy to turn him from his purpose, even though he was convinced that the foreman's action had saved his life. And now Tex was returning, not to Muddy Wells, but to the range where the Bar-20 outfit held sway.

Several years of clean living had improved Tex, morally and physically. The liquor he had once been in the habit of consuming had been reduced to a negligible quantity; he spent the money on cartridges instead, and his pistol work showed the results of careful and dogged practice, particularly in the quickness of the draw. Punching cows on a remote northern range had repaid him in health far more than his old game of living on his wits and other people's lack of them, as proved by his clear eye and the pink showing through the tan above his beard; while his somber, steady gaze, due to long-held fixity of purpose, indicated the resourcefulness of a perfectly reliable set of nerves. His low-hung holster tied securely to his trousers leg to assure smoothness in drawing, the restrained swing of his right hand, never far from the well-worn scabbard which sheathed a triggerless Colt's "Frontier"—these showed the confident and ready gun-man, the man who seldom missed. "Frontiers" left the factory with triggers attached, but the absence of that part did not always incapacitate a weapon. Some men found that the regular method was too slow, and painstakingly cultivated the art of thumbing the hammer. "Thumbing" was believed to save the split second so valuable to a man in argument with his peers. Tex was riding with the set purpose of picking a fair fight with the best six-shooter expert it had ever been his misfortune to meet, and he needed that split second. He knew that he needed it and the knowledge thrilled him with a peculiar elation; he had changed greatly in the past year and now he wanted an "even break" where once he would have called all his wits into play to avoid it. He had found himself and now he acknowledged no superior in anything.

On his way south he met and talked with men who had known him, the old Tex, in the days when he had made his living precariously. They did not recognize him behind his beard, and he was content to let the oversight pass. But from these few he learned what he wished to know, and he was glad that Hopalong Cassidy was where he had always been, and that his gun-work had improved rather than depreciated with the passing of time. He wished to prove himself master of The Master, and to be hailed as such by those who had jeered and laughed at his ignominy several years before. So he rode on day after day, smiling and content, neither under-rating nor over-rating his enemy's ability with one weapon, but trying to think of him as he really was. He knew that if there was any difference between Hopalong Cassidy and himself that it must be very slight-perhaps so slight as to result fatally to both; but if that were so then it would have to work out as it saw fit-he at least would have accomplished what many, many others had failed in.

In the little town of Buckskin, known hardly more than locally, and never thought of by outsiders except as the place where the Bar-20 spent their spare time and money, and neutral ground for the surrounding ranches, was Cowan's saloon, in the dozen years of its existence the scene of good stories, boisterous fun, and quick deaths. Put together roughly, of crude materials, sticking up in inartistic prominence on the dusty edge of a dustier street; warped, bleached by the sun, and patched with boards ripped from packing cases and with the flattened sides of tin cans; low of ceiling, the floor one huge brown discoloration of spring, creaking boards, knotted and split and worn into hollows, the unpretentious building offered its hospitality to all who might be tempted by the scrawled, sprawled lettering of its sign. The walls were smoke-blackened, pitted with numerous small and clear-cut holes, and decorated with initials carelessly cut by men who had come and gone.

Such was Cowan's, the best patronized place in many hot and dusty miles and the Mecca of the cowboys from the surrounding ranches. Often at night these riders of the range gathered in the humble building and told tales of exceeding interest; and on these occasions one might see a row of ponies standing before the building, heads down and quiet. It is strange how alike cow-ponies look in the dim light of the stars. On the south side of the saloon, weak, yellow lamp light filtered through the dirt on the window panes and fell in distorted patches on the plain, blotched in places by the shadows of the wooden substitutes for glass.

It was a moonlight night late in the fall, after the last beef round-up was over and the last drive outfit home again, that two cow-ponies stood in front of Cowan's while their owners lolled against the bar and talked over the latest sensation-the fencing in of the West Valley range, and the way Hopalong Cassidy and his trail outfit had opened up the old drive trail across it. The news was a month old, but it was the last event of any importance and was still good to laugh over.

"Boys," remarked the proprietor, "I want you to meet Mr. Elkins. He came down that trail last week, an' he didn't see no fence across it." The man at the table arose slowly. "Mr. Elkins, this is Sandy Lucas, an' Wood Wright, of the C-80. Mr. Elkins here has been a-looking over the country, sizing up what the beef prospects will be for next year; an' he knows all about wire fences. Here's how," he smiled, treating on the house.

Mr. Elkins touched the glass to his bearded lips and set it down untasted while he joked over the sharp rebuff so lately administered to wire fences in that part of the country. While he was an ex-cow-puncher he believed that he was above allowing prejudice to sway his judgment, and it was his opinion, after careful thought, that barb wire was harmful to the best interests of the range. He had ridden over a great part of the cattle country in the last few yeas, and after reviewing the existing conditions as he understood them, his verdict must go as stated, and emphatically. He launched gracefully into a slowly delivered and lengthy discourse upon the subject, which proved to be so entertaining that his companions were content to listen and nod with comprehension. They had never met any one who was so well qualified to discuss the pros and cons of the barb-wire fence question, and they learned many things which they had never heard before. This was very gratifying to Mr. Elkins, who drew largely upon hearsay, his own vivid imagination, and a healthy logic. He was very glad to talk to men who had the welfare of the range at heart, and he hoped soon to meet the man who had taken the initiative in giving barb wire its first serious setback on that rich and magnificent southern range.

"You shore ought to meet Cassidy-he's a fine man," remarked Lucas with enthusiasm. "You'll not find any better, no matter where you look. But you ain't touched yore liquor," he finished with surprise.

"You'll have to excuse me, gentlemen," replied Mr. Elkins, smiling deprecatingly. "When a man likes it as much as I do it ain't very easy to foller instructions an' let it alone. Sometimes I almost break loose an' indulge, regardless of whether it kills me or not. I reckon it'll get me yet." He struck the bar a resounding blow with his clenched hand. "But I ain't going to cave in till I has to!"

"That's purty tough," sympathized Wood Wright, reflectively. "I ain't so very much taken with it, but I know I would be if I knowed I couldn't have any."

"Yes, that's human nature, all right," laughed Lucas. "That reminds me of a little thing that happened to me once —"

"Listen!" exclaimed Cowan, holding up his hand for silence. "I reckon that's the Bar-20 now, or some of it-sounds like them when they're feeling frisky. There's allus something happening when them fellers are around."

The proprietor was right, as proved a moment later when Johnny Nelson, continuing his argument, pushed open the door and entered the room. "I didn't neither; an' you know it!" he flung over his shoulder.

"Then who did?" demanded Hopalong, chuckling. "Why, hullo, boys," he said, nodding to his friends at the bar. "Nobody else would do a fool thing like that; nobody but you, Kid," he added, turning to Johnny.

"I don't care a hang what you think; I say I didn't an' —"

"He shore did, all right; I seen him just afterward," laughed Billy Williams, pressing close upon Hopalong's heels. "Howdy, Lucas; an' there's that ol' coyote, Wood Wright. How's everybody feeling?"

"Where's the rest of you fellers?" inquired Cowan.

"Stayed home to-night," replied Hopalong.

"Got any loose money, you two?" asked Billy, grinning at Lucas and Wright.

"I reckon we have-an' our credit's good if we ain't. We're good for a dollar or two, ain't we, Cowan?" replied Lucas.

"Two dollars an' four bits," corrected Cowan. "I'll raise it to three dollars even when you pay me that 'leven cents you owe me."

"'Leven cents? What 'leven cents?"

"Postage stamps an' envelope for that love letter you writ."

"Go to blazes; that wasn't no love letter!" snorted Lucas, indignantly. "That was my quarterly report. I never did write no love letters, nohow."

"We'll trim you fellers to-night, if you've got the nerve to play us," grinned Johnny, expectantly.

"Yes; an' we've got that, too. Give us the cards, Cowan," requested Wood Wright, turning. "They won't give us no peace till we take all their money away from 'em."

"Open game," prompted Cowan, glancing meaningly at Elkins, who stood by idly looking on, and without showing much interest in the scene.

"Shore! Everybody can come in what wants to," replied Lucas, heartily, leading the others to the table. "I allus did like a six-handed game best-all the cards are out an' there's some excitement in it."

When the deal began Elkins was seated across the table from Hopalong, facing him for the first time since that day over in Muddy Wells, and studying him closely. He found no changes, for the few years had left no trace of their passing on the Bar-20 puncher. The sensation of facing the man he had come south expressly to kill did not interfere with Elkins' card-playing ability for he played a good game; and as if the Fates were with him it was Hopalong's night off as far as poker was concerned, for his customary good luck was not in evidence. That instinctive feeling which singles out two duellists in a card game was soon experienced by the others, who were careful, as became good players, to avoid being caught between them; in consequence, when the game broke up, Elkins had most of Hopalong's money. At one period of his life Elkins had lived on poker for five years, and lived well. But he gained more than money in this game, for he had made friends with the players and placed the first wire of his trap. Of those in the room Hopalong alone treated him with reserve, and this was cleverly swung so that it appeared to be caused by a temporary grouch due to the sting of defeat. As the Bar-20 man was known to be given to moods at times this was accepted as the true explanation and gave promise of hotly contested games for revenge later on. The banter which the defeated puncher had to endure stirred him and strengthened the reserve, although he was careful not to show it.

When the last man rode off, Elkins and the proprietor sought their bunks without delay, the former to lie awake a long time, thinking deeply. He was vexed at himself for failing to work out an acceptable plan of action, one that would show him to be in the right. He would gain nothing more than glory, and pay too dearly for it, if he killed Hopalong and was in turn killed by the dead man's friends-and he believed that he had become acquainted with the quality of the friendship which bound the units of the Bar-20 outfit into a smooth, firm whole. They were like brothers, like one man. Cassidy must do the forcing as far as appearances went, and be clearly in the wrong before the matter could be settled.

The next week was a busy one for Elkins, every day finding him in the saddle and riding over some one of the surrounding ranches with one or more of its punchers for company. In this way he became acquainted with the men who might be called on to act as his jury when the showdown came, and he proceeded to make friends of them in a manner that promised success. And some of his suggestions for the improvement of certain conditions on the range, while they might not work out right in the long run, compelled thought and showed his interest. His remarks on the condition and numbers of cattle were the same in substance in all cases and showed that he knew what he was talking about, for the punchers were all very optimistic about the next year's showing in cattle.

"If you fellers don't break all records for drive herds of quality next year I don't know nothing about cows; an' I shore don't know nothing else," he told the foreman of the Bar-20, as they rode homeward after an inspection of that ranch. "There'll be more dust hanging over the drive trails leading from this section next year when spring drops the barriers than ever before. You needn't fear for the market, neither-prices will stand. The north an' central ranges ain't doing what they ought to this year-it'll be up to you fellers down south, here, to make that up; an' you can do it." This was not a guess, but the result of thought and study based on the observations he had made on his ride south, and from what he had learned from others along the way. It paralleled Buck's own private opinion, especially in regard to the southern range; and the vague suspicions in the foreman's mind disappeared for good and all.

Needless to say Elkins was a welcome visitor at the ranch houses and was regarded as a good fellow. At the Bar-20 he found only two men who would not thaw to him, and he was possessed of too much tact to try any persuasive measures. One was Hopalong, whose original cold reserve seemed to be growing steadily, the Bar-20 puncher finding in Elkins a personality that charged the atmosphere with hostility and quietly rubbed him the wrong way. Whenever he was in the presence of the newcomer he felt the tugging of an irritating and insistent antagonism and he did not always fully conceal it. John Bartlett, Lucas, and one or two of the more observing had noticed it and they began to prophesy future trouble between the two. The other man who disliked Elkins was Red Connors; but what was more natural? Red, being Hopalong's closest companion, would be very apt to share his friend's antipathy. On the other hand, as if to prove Hopalong's dislike to be unwarranted, Johnny Nelson swung far to the other extreme and was frankly enthusiastic in his liking for the cattle scout. And Johnny did not pour oil on the waters when he laughingly twitted Hopalong for allowing "a licking at cards to make him sore." This was the idea that Elkins was quietly striving to have generally accepted.

The affair thus hung fire, Elkins chafing at the delay and cautiously working for an opening, which at last presented itself, to be promptly seized. By a sort of mutual, unspoken agreement, the men in Cowan's that night passed up the cards and sat swapping stories. Cowan, swearing at a smoking lamp, looked up with a grin and burned his fingers as a roar of laughter marked the point of a droll reminiscence told by Bartlett.

"That's a good story, Bartlett," Elkins remarked, slowing refilling his pipe. "Reminds me of the lame Greaser, Hippy Joe, an' the canned oysters. They was both bad, an' neither of 'em knew it till they came together. It was like this. . . ." The malicious side glance went unseen by all but Hopalong, who stiffened with the raging suspicion of being twitted on his own deformity. The humor of the tale failed to appeal to him, and when his full senses returned Lucas was in the midst of the story of the deadly game of tag played in a ten-acre lot of dense underbrush by two of his old-time friends. It was a tale of gripping interest and his auditors were leaning forward in their eagerness not to miss a word. "An' Pierce won," finished Lucas; "some shot up, but able to get about. He was all right in a couple of weeks. But he was bound to win; he could shoot all around Sam Hopkins."

"But the best shot won't allus win in that game," commented Elkins. "That's one of the minor factors."

"Yes, sir! It's *luck* that counts there," endorsed Bartlett, quickly. "Luck, nine times out of ten."

"Best shot ought to win," declared Skinny Thompson. "It ain't all luck, nohow. Where'd I be against Hoppy, there?"

"Won't neither!" cried Johnny, excitedly. "The man who sees the other first wins out. That's wood-craft, an' brains."

"Aw! What do you know about it, anyhow?" demanded Lucas. "If he can't shoot so good what chance has he got-if he misses the first try, what then?"

"What chance has he got! First chance, miss or no miss. If he can't see the other first, where the devil does his good shooting come in?"

"Huh!" snorted Wood Wright, belligerently. "Any fool can *see*, but he can't *shoot*! An' it's as much luck as wood-craft, too, an' don't you forget it!"

"The first shot don't win, Johnny; not in a game like that, with all the dodging an' ducking," remarked Red. "You can't put one where you want it when a feller's slipping around in the brush. It's the most that counts, an' the best shot gets in the most. I wouldn't want to have to stand up against Hoppy an' a short gun, not in that game; no, sir!" and Red shook his head with decision.

The argument waxed hot. With the exception of Hopalong, who sat silently watchful, every one spoke his opinion and repeated it without regard to the others. It appeared that in this game, the man with the strongest lungs would eventually win out, and each man tried to show his superiority in that line. Finally, above the uproar, Cowan's bellow was herd, and he kept it up until some notice was taken of it. "Shut up! *Shut up!* For God's sake, *quit!* Never saw such a bunch of tinder-let somebody drop a cold, burned-out match in this gang, an' hell's to pay. Here, *all* of you, play cards an' forget about cross-tag in the scrub. You'll be arguing about playing marbles in the dark purty soon!"

"All right," muttered Johnny, "but just the same, the man who —"

"Never mind about the man who! Did you hear *me?*" yelled Cowan, swiftly reaching for a bucket of water. "*This* is a game where *I* gets the most in, an' don't forget it!"

"Come on; play cards," growled Lucas, who did not relish having his decision questioned on his own story. Undoubtedly somewhere in the wide, wide world there was such a thing as common courtesy, but none of it had ever strayed onto that range.

The chairs scraped on the rough floor as the men pulled up to a table. "I don't care a hang," came Elkins' final comment as he shuffled the cards with careful attention. "I'm not any fancy Colt expert, but I'm damned if I won't take a chance in that game with any man as totes a gun. Leastawise, of *course*, I wouldn't take no such advantage of a lame man."

The effect would have been ludicrous but for its deadly significance. Cowan, stooping to go under the bar, remained in that hunched-up attitude, his every faculty concentrated in his ears; the match on its way to the cigarette between Red's lips was held until it burned his fingers, when it was dropped from mere reflex action, the hand still stiffly aloft; Lucas, half in and half out of his chair, seemed to have got just where he intended, making no effort to seat himself. Skinny Thompson, his hand on his gun, seemed paralyzed; his mouth was open to frame a reply that never was uttered and he stared through narrowed eyelids at the blunderer. The sole movement in the room was the slow rising of Hopalong and the markedly innocent shuffling of the cards by Elkins, who appeared to be entirely ignorant of the weight and effect of his words. He dropped the pack for the cut and then looked up and around as if surprised by the silence and the expressions he saw.

Hopalong stood facing him, leaning over with both hands on the table. His voice, when he spoke, rumbled up from his chest in a low growl. "You won't *have* no advantage, Elkins. Take it from me, you've had yore last fling. I'm glad you made it plain, this time, so it's something I can take hold of." He straightened slowly and walked to the door, and an audible sigh sounded through the room as it was realized that trouble was not immediately imminent. At the door he paused and turned back around, looking back over his shoulder. "At noon to-morrow I'm going to hoof it north through the brush between the river an' the river trail, starting at the old ford a mile down the river." He waited expectantly.

"Me too-only the other way," was the instant rejoinder. "Have it yore own way."

Hopalong nodded and the closing door shut him out into the night. Without a word the Bar-20 men arose and followed him, the only hesitant being Johnny, who was torn between loyalty and new-found friendship; but with a sorrowful shake of the head, he turned away and passed out, not far behind the others.

"Clannish, ain't they?" remarked Elkins, gravely.

Those remaining were regarding him sternly, questioningly, Cowan with a deep frown darkening his face. "You hadn't ought to 'a' said that, Elkins." The reproof was almost an accusation.

Elkins looked steadily at the speaker. "You hadn't ought to 'a' let me say it," he replied. "How did I know he was so touchy?" His gaze left Cowan and lingered in turn on each of the others. "Some of you ought to 'a' told me. I wouldn't 'a' said it only for what I said just before, an' I didn't want him to think I was challenging him to no duel in the brush. So I says so, an' then he goes an' takes it up that I *am* challenging him. I ain't got no call to fight with nobody. Ain't

I tried to keep out of trouble with him ever since I've been here? Ain't I kept out of the poker games on his account? Ain't I?" The grave, even tones were dispassionate, without a trace of animus and serenely sure of justice.

The faces around him cleared gradually and heads began to nod in comprehending consent.

"Yes, I reckon you have," agreed Cowan, slowly, but the frown was not entirely gone. "Yes, I reckon-mebby-you have."

Chapter XXIV
The Master

It was noon by the sun when Hopalong and Red shook hands south of the old ford and the former turned to enter the brush. Hopalong was cool and ominously calm while his companion was the opposite. Red was frankly suspicious of the whole affair and nursed the private opinion that Mr. Elkins would lay in ambush and shoot his enemy down like a dog. And Red had promised himself a dozen times that he would study the signs around the scene of action if Hopalong should not come back, and take a keen delight, if warranted, in shooting Mr. Elkins full of holes with no regard for an even break. He was thinking the matter over as his friend breasted the first line of brush and could not refrain from giving a slight warning. "Get him, Hoppy," he called, earnestly; "get him good. Let *him* do some of the moving about. I'll be here waiting for you."

Hopalong smiled in reply and sprang forward, the leaves and branches quickly shutting him from Red's sight. He had worked out his plan of action the night before when he was alone and the world was still, and as soon as he had it to his satisfaction he had dropped off to sleep as easily as a child-it took more than gun-play to disturb his nerves. He glanced about him to make sure of his bearings and then struck on a curving line for the river. The first hundred yards were covered with speed and then he began to move more slowly and with greater regard for caution, keeping close to the earth and showing a marked preference for low ground. Sky-lines were all right in times of peace, but under the present conditions they promised to become unhealthy. His eyes and ears told him nothing for a quarter of an hour, and then he suddenly stopped short and crouched as he saw the plain trail of a man crossing his own direction at a right angle. From the bottom of one of the heel prints a crushed leaf was slowly rising back towards its original position, telling him how new the trail was; and as if this were not enough for his trained mind he heard a twig snap sharply as he glanced along the line of prints. It sounded very close, and he dropped instantly to one knee and thought quickly. Why had the other left so plain a trail, why had he reached up and broken twigs that projected above his head as he passed? Why had he kicked aside a small stone, leaving a patch of moist, bleached grass to tell where it had lain? Elkins had stumbled here, but there were no toe marks to tell of it. Hopalong would not track, for he was no assassin; but he knew that he would do if he were, and careless. The answer leaped to his suspicious mind like a flash, and he did not care to waste any time in trying to determine whether or not Elkins was capable of such a trick. He acted on the presumption that the trail had been made plain for a good reason, and that not far ahead at some suitable place, —and there were any number of such within a hundred yards, —the maker of the plain trail lay in wait. Smiling savagely he worked backward and turning, struck off in a circle. He had no compunctions whatever now about shooting the other player of the game. It was not long before he came upon the same trail again and he started another circle. A bullet *zipped* past his ear and cut a twig not two inches from his head. He fired at the smoke as he dropped, and then wriggled rapidly backward, keeping as flat to the earth as he could. Elkins had taken up his position in a thicket which stood in the centre of a level patch of sand in the old bed of the river, —the bed it had used five years before and forsaken at the time of the big flood when it cut itself a new channel and made the U-bend which now surrounded this piece of land on three sides. Even now, during the rainy season, the thicket which sheltered Mr. Elkins was frequently an island in a sluggish, shallow overflow.

"Hole up, blast you!" jeered Hopalong, hugging the ground. The second bullet from Mr. Elkins' gun cut another twig, this one just over his head, and he laughed insolently. "I ain't ascared to do the moving, even if you are. Judging from the way you keep out o' sight the canned oysters are in the can again. *I* never did no ambushing, you coyote."

"You can't make remarks like that an' get away with 'em —I've knowed you too long," retorted Elkins, shifting quickly, and none too soon. "You went an' got Slim afore he was wide awake. I know *you*, all right."

Hopalong's surprise was but momentary, and his mind raced back over the years. Who was this man Elkins, that he knew Slim Travennes? "Yo're a liar, Elkins, an' so was the man who told you that!"

"Call me Ewalt," jeered the other, nastily. "Nobody'll hear it, an' you'll not live to tell it. Ewalt, Tex Ewalt; call me that."

"So you've come back after all this time to make me get you, have you? Well, I ain't a-going to shoot no buttons off you *this* time. I allus reckoned you learned something at Muddy Wells-but you'll learn it here," Hopalong rejoined, sliding into a depression, and working with great caution towards the dry river bed, where fallen trees and hillocks of sand provided good cover in plenty. Everything was clear now and despite the seriousness of the situation he could not repress a smile as he remembered vividly that day at the carnival when Tex Ewalt came to town with the determination to kill him and show him up as an imitation. His grievance against Elkins was petty when compared to that against Ewalt, and he began to force the issue. As he peered over a stranded log he caught sight of his enemy disappearing into another part of the thicket, and two of his three shots went home. Elkins groaned with pain and fear as he realized that his right knee-cap was broken and would make him slow in his movements. He was lamed for life, even if he did come out of the duel alive; lamed in the same way that Hopalong was-the affliction he had made cruel sport of had come to him. But he had plenty of courage and he returned the fire with remarkable quickness, his two shots sounding almost as one.

Hopalong wiped the blood from his cheek and wormed his way to a new place; when half way there he called out again, "How's yore health-Tex?" in mock sympathy.

Elkins lied manfully and when he looked to get in another shot his enemy was on the farther bank, moving up to get behind him. He did not know Hopalong's new position until he raised his head to glance down over the dried river bed, and was informed by a bullet that nicked his ear. As he ducked, another grazed his head, the third going wild. He hazarded a return shot, and heard Hopalong's laugh ring out again.

"Like the story Lucas told, the best shot is going to win out this time, too," the Bar-20 man remarked, grimly. "You thought a game like this would give you some chance against a better shot, didn't you? You are a fool."

"It ain't over yet, not by a damned sight!" came the retort.

"An' you thought you had a little the best of it if you stayed still an' let me do the moving, didn't you? You'll learn something before I get through with you: but it'll be too late to do you any good," Hopalong called, crouched below a hillock of sand so the other could not take advantage of the words and single him out for a shot.

"You can't learn me nothing, you assassin; I've got my eyes open, this time." He knew that he had had them open before, and that Hopalong was in no way an assassin; but if he could enrage his enemy and sting him into some reflex carelessness he might have the last laugh.

Elkins' retort was wasted, for the sudden and unusual, although a familiar sound, had caught Hopalong's ear and he was giving all his attention to it. While he weighed it, his incredulity holding back the decision his common sense was striving to give him, the noise grew louder rapidly and common sense won out in a cry of warning an instant before a five-foot wall of brown water burst upon his sight, sweeping swiftly down the old, dry river bed; and behind it towered another and greater wall. Tree trunks were dancing end over end in it as if they were straws.

"Cloud-burst!" he yelled. "Run, Tex! Run for yore life! Cloud-burst up the valley! Run, you fool; *Run!*"

Tex's sarcastic retort was cut short as he instinctively glanced north, and his agonized curse lashed Hopalong forward. "Can't run-knee cap's busted! Can't swim, can't do-ah, hell—!"

Hopalong saw him torn from his shelter and whisked down the raging torrent like an arrow from a bow. The Bar-20 puncher leaped from the bank, shot under the yellow flood and arose, gasping and choking many yards downstream, fighting madly to get the muddy water out of his throat and eyes. As he struck out with all his strength down the current, he caught sight of Tex being torn from a jutting tree limb, and he shouted encouragement and swam all the harder, if such a thing were possible. Tex's course was checked for a moment by a boiling back-current and as he again felt the pull of the rushing stream Hopalong's hand gripped his collar and the fight for safety began. Whirled against logs and stumps, drawn down by the weight of his clothes and the frantic efforts of Tex to grasp him-fighting the water and the man he was trying to save at the same time, his head under water as often as it was out of it, and Tex's vise-like fingers threatening him-he headed for the west shore against powerful cross-currents that made his efforts seem useless. He seemed to get the worst of every break. Once, when caught by a friendly current, they were swung under an overhanging branch, but as Hopalong's hand shot up to grasp it a submerged bush caught his feet and pulled him under, and Tex's steel-like arms around his throat almost suffocated him before he managed to beat the other into insensibility and break the hold.

"I'll let you go!" he threatened; but his hand grasped the other's collar all the tighter and his fighting jaw was set with greater determination than ever.

They shot out into the main stream, where the U-bend channel joined the short-cut, and it looked miles wide to the exhausted puncher. He was fighting only on his will now. He would not give up, though he scarce could lift an arm, and his lungs seemed on fire. He did not know whether Tex was dead or alive, but he would get the body ashore with him, or go down trying. He bumped into a log and instinctively grasped it. It turned, and when he came up again it was bobbing five feet ahead of him. Ages seemed to pass before he flung his numb arm over it and floated with it. He was not alone in the flood; a coyote was pushing steadily across his path towards the nearer bank, and on a gliding tree trunk crouched a frightened cougar, its ears flattened and its sharp claws dug solidly through the bark. Here and there were cattle and a snake wriggled smoothly past him, apparently as much at home in the water as out of it. The log turned again and he just managed to catch hold of it as he came up for the second time.

Things were growing black before his eyes and strange, weird ideas and images floated through his brain. When he regained some part of his senses he saw ahead of him a long, curling crest of yellow water and foam, and he knew, vaguely, that it was pouring over a bar. The next instant his feet struck bottom and he fought his way blindly and slowly, with the stubborn determination of his kind, towards the brush-covered point twenty feet away.

When he opened his eyes and looked around he became conscious of excruciating pains and he closed them again to rest. His outflung hand struck something that made him look around again, and he saw Tex Ewalt, face down at his side. He released his grasp on the other's collar and slowly the whole thing came to him, and then the necessity for action, unless he wished to lose what he had fought so hard to save.

Anything short of the iron man Tex had become would have been dead before this or have been finished by the mauling he now got from Hopalong. But Tex groaned, gurgled a curse, and finally opened his eyes upon his rescuer, who sank back with a grunt of satisfaction. Slowly his intelligence returned as he looked steadily into Hopalong's eyes, and with it came the realization of a strange truth: he did not hate this man at all. Months of right living, days and nights of honest labor shoulder to shoulder with men who respected him for his ability and accepted him as one of themselves, had made a new man of him, although the legacy of hatred from the old Tex had disguised him from himself until now; but the new Tex, battered, shot-up, nearly drowned, looked at his old enemy and saw him for the man he really was. He smiled faintly and reached out his hand.

"Cassidy, yo're the boss," he said. "Shake."

They shook.

Buck Peters, Ranchman

Chapter I
Tex Returns

Johnny Nelson reached up for the new, blue flannel shirt he had hung above his bunk, and then placed his hands on hips and soliloquized: "Me an' Red buy a new shirt apiece Saturday night an' one of 'em 's gone Sunday mornin'; purty fast work even for this outfit."

He strode to the gallery to ask the cook, erstwhile subject of the Most Heavenly One, but the words froze on his lips. Lee Hop's stoop-shouldered back was encased in a brand new, blue flannel shirt, the price mark chalked over one shoulder blade, and he sing-songed a Chinese classic while debating the advisability of adopting a pair of trousers and thus crossing another of the boundaries between the Orient and the Occident. He had no eyes in the back of his head but was rarely gifted in the "ways that are strange," and he felt danger before the boot left Johnny's hand. Before the missile landed in the dish pan Lee Hop was digging madly across the open, half way to the ranch house, and temporary safety.

Johnny fished out the boot and paused to watch the agile cook. "He 's got eyes all over hisself-an' no coyote ever lived as could beat him," was his regretful comment. He knew better than to follow-Hopalong's wife had a sympathetic heart, and a tongue to be feared. She had not yet forgotten Lee Hop's auspicious initiation as an *ex-officio* member of the outfit, and Johnny's part therein. And no one had been able to convince her that sympathy was wasted on a "Chink."

The shirtless puncher looked around helplessly, and then a grin slipped over his face. Glancing at the boot he dropped it back into the dish water, moved swiftly to Red's bunk, and in a moment a twin to his own shirt adorned his back. To make matters more certain he deposited on Red's blankets an old shirt of Lee Hop's, and then sauntered over to Skinny's bunk.

"Hoppy said he 'd lick me if I hurt th' Chink any more; but he did n't say nothin' to Red. May th' best man win," he muttered as he lifted Skinny's blankets and fondled a box of cigars. "One from forty-three leaves forty-two," he figured, and then, dropping to the floor and crawling under the bunk, he added a mark to Skinny's "secret" tally. Skinny always liked to know just how many of his own cigars he smoked.

"Now for a little nip, an' then th' open, where this cigar won't talk so loud," he laughed, heading towards Lanky's bunk. The most diligent search failed to produce, and a rapid repetition also failed. Lanky's clothes and boots yielded nothing and Johnny was getting sarcastic when his eyes fell upon an old boot lying under a pile of riding gear in a corner of the room. Keeping his thumb on the original level he drank, and then added enough water to bring the depleted liquor up to his thumb. "Gee —I 've saved sixty-five dollars this month, an' two days are gone already," he chuckled. He received sixty-five dollars, and what luxuries were not nailed down, every month.

Mounting his horse he rode away to enjoy the cigar, happy that the winter was nearly over. There was a feeling in the air that told of Spring, no matter what the calendar showed, and Johnny felt unrest stirring in his veins. When Johnny felt thus exuberant things promised to move swiftly about the bunk-house.

When far enough away from the ranch houses he stopped to light the cigar, but paused and, dropping the match, returned the "Maduro" to his pocket. He could not tell who the rider was at that distance, but it was wiser to be prudent. Riding slowly forward, watching the other horseman, he saw a sombrero wave, and spurred into a lope. Then he squinted hard and shook his head.

"Rides like Tex Ewalt-but it ain't, all right," he muttered. Closer inspection made him rub his eyes. "That arm swings like Tex, just th' same! An' I did n't take more'n a couple of swallows, neither. Why, d —n it! If that ain't him I 'm going' to see *who* it is!" and he pushed on at a gallop. When the faint hail floated down the wind to him he cut loose a yell and leaned forward, spurring and quirting. "Old son-of-a-gun 's come back!" he exulted. "Hey, Tex! Oh, Tex!" he yelled; and Tex was yelling just as foolishly.

They came together with a rush, but expert horsemanship averted a collision, and for a few minutes neither could hear clearly what the other was saying. When things calmed down Johnny jammed a cigar into his friend's hands and felt for a match.

"Why, I don't want to take yore last smoke, Kid," Tex objected.

"Oh, go ahead! I 've got a hull *box* of 'em in th' bunk-house," was the swift reply. "Could n't stay away, eh? Did n't like th' East, nohow, did you? Gosh, th' boys 'll be some tickled to see you, Tex. Goin' to stay? How you feelin'?"

"You bet I 'm a-stayin'," responded Tex. "Is that Lanky comin'?"

"Hey, Lanky!" yelled Johnny, standing up and waving the approaching horseman towards them. "*Pronto*! Tex 's come back!"

Lanky's pony's legs fanned a haze under him and he rammed up against Tex so hard that they had to grab each other. Everybody was talking at once and so they rode towards the bunk-house, picking up Billy on the way.

"Where's Hopalong?" demanded Tex. "Married! H —l he is!" A strange look flitted across his face. "Well, I 'm d —d! An' where 's Red?"

Johnny glanced ahead just in time to see Lee Hop sail around a corner of the corral, and he replied with assurance, "Red 's th' other side of th' corral."

"Huh!'" snorted Lanky, "You 've got remarkable eyes, Kid, if you can see through-well, I 'm hanged if he *ain't!*"

After Red came Pete, waving a water-soaked boot. They disappeared and when Tex and his friends had almost reached the corral, Lee Hop rounded the same corner again, too frightened even to squeal. As he started around the next corner he jumped away at an angle, Pete, still waving the boot, missing him by inches. Pete checked his flow of language as he noticed the laughing group and started for it with a yell. A moment later Red came into sight, panting heavily, and also forgot the cook. Lee Hop stopped and watched the crowd, taking advantage of the opportunity to gain the cook shack and bar the door. "Dlam shirt no good-sclatchee like helle," he muttered. White men were strange-they loved each other like brothers and fought one another's battles. "Led head! Led head!" he cried, derisively. "My hop you cloke! Hop you cloke chop-chop! No fliend my, savee?"

Skinny Thompson, changing his trousers in the bunkroom, heard Lee's remarks and laughed. Then he listened-somebody was doing a lot of talking. "They 're loco, plumb loco, or else somethin's wrong," and he hopped to the door. A bunched crowd of friends were tearing toward him, yelling and shooting and waving sombreros, and a second look made him again miss the trousers' leg and hop through the door to save himself. The blood swept into his face as he saw the ranch house and he very promptly hopped back again, muttering angrily.

The crowd dismounted at the door and tried to enter *en masse*; becoming sane it squirmed into separate units and entered as it should. Lee Hop hastily unbarred his door and again fled for his life. When he returned he walked boldly behind his foreman, and very close to him, gesticulating wildly and trying to teach Hopalong Cantonese. The foreman hated to chide his friends, but he and his wife were tired of turning the ranch house into a haven for Chinese cooks.

As he opened the door he was grabbed and pushed up against a man who clouted him on the back and tried to crush his hand. "Hullo, Cassidy! Best sight I've laid eyes on since I left!" yelled the other above the noise.

"Tex!" exclaimed Hopalong. "Well, I'm d —d! When did you get here? Going to stay? Got a job yet? How'd you like the East? Married? *I* am-best thing I ever did. You look white-sick?"

"City color-like the blasted collars and shirts," replied the other, still pumping the hand. "I 'm goin' to stay, I 'm lookin' for a job, an' I 'd ruther punch cows for my keep than get rich in th' East. It 's all fence-country —can't move without bumping into somebody or something-an' noise! An' crooked! They 'd steal th' fillin's out of yore teeth when you go to talk-an' you won't know it!"

"Like to see 'em fool *me!*" grunted Johnny, looking savage.

"Huh! Th' new beginners 'd pick you out to practise on," snorted Red. "That yore shirt or mine?" he asked, suspiciously.

"They 'd give you money for th' fun of taking it away from you," asserted Tex. "Why, one feller, a slick dresser, too, asks me for th' time. I was some proud of that ticker-cost nigh onto a hundred dollars. He thanks me an' slips into th' crowd. When I went to put th' watch back I did n't have none. I licked th' next man, old as he was, who asks me for th' time. He was plumb surprised when I punched him-reckon he figured I was easy."

"Ain't they got policemen?" demanded Red.

"Yes; but *they* don't carry watches-they 're too smart."

"Have a drink, Tex," suggested Lanky, bottle in hand. When the owner of it took a drink he looked at his friends and then at the bottle, disgust pictured on his face. "This liquor's shore goin' to die purty soon. It's gettin' weaker every day. Now I wonder what in h —l Cowan makes it out of?"

"It *is* sort of helpless," admitted Tex. "Now, Kid, I 'll borrow another of them cigars of yourn. Them Maduros are shore good stuff. I would n't ask you only you said you had a —"

"D'ju see any shows in th' East?" demanded Johnny, hurriedly: "Real, good, bang-up shows?"

Skinny faded into the bunk-room and soon returned, puzzled and suspicious. He slipped Tex a cigar and in a few moments sidled up close to the smoker.

"That as good as th' Kid's?" he asked, carelessly.

Tex regarded it gravely: "Yes; better. I like 'em black, but don't say nothin' to Johnny. He likes them blondes 'cause he 's young."

It was not long before Tex, having paid his respects to the foreman's wife, returned to the bunk-house, leaned luxuriously against the wall and told of his experiences in the East. He had an attentive audience and it swayed easily and heartily to laughter or sympathy as the words warranted. There was much to laugh at and a great deal to strain credulity. But the great story was not told, the story of the things pitiful in the manner in which they showed up how square a regenerated man could be, and how false a woman. It was the old story-ambition drove him out into a new world with nothing but a clean conscience, a strong, deft pair of hands, and a clever brain; a woman drove him back, beaten, disheartened, and perilously near the devious ways he had forsaken. He could not stay in the new surroundings without killing-and he knew the woman was to blame; so when he felt the ground slip under his hesitating feet, he threw the new life behind him and hastened West, feverish to gain the locality where he had learned to look himself in the face with regret and remorse, but without shame.

In turn he learned of the things that had occurred since he had left: of the bitter range-war; of his best friend's promotion and marriage; and of Buck Peters' new venture among hostile strangers. The latter touched him deeply-he knew, from his own bitter experiences, the disheartening struggle against odds great enough to mean a hard fight for Buck and all his old outfit. Something that in Tex's heart had been struggling for weeks, the vague uneasiness which drove him faster and faster towards the West, now possessed him with a strength not to be denied. He knew what it was-the old lust for battle, the game of hand and wits with life on the table, could not be resisted. The southern range was now peaceful, thanks to Buck and his men, thanks to Meeker's real nature; the Double Arrow and the C80 formed a barrier of lead and steel on the north and east, a barrier that no rustler cared to force. Peace meant solitude on the sun-kissed range and forced upon him opportunities for thought-and insanity, or suicide. But up in Montana it would be different; and the field, calling insistently for Tex to come, was one where his peculiar abilities would be particularly effective. Buck needed friends, but stubbornly forbade any of his old outfit to join him. Of course, they would disregard his commands and either half or all of the Bar Twenty force would join him; but their going would be delayed until well after the Spring round-up, for loyalty to their home ranch demanded this. Tex was free, eager, capable, and as courageous as any man. He had the cunning of a coyote, the cold savagery of a wolf, and the power of a tiger. In his lightning-fast hands a Colt rarely missed-and he gathered from what he heard that such hands were necessary to make the right kind of history on the northern range.

Finally Hopalong arose to go to the ranch house for the noon meal, taking Tex with him. The foreman and his wife did not eat with the outfit, because the outfit would not allow it. Mary had insisted at first that her husband should not desert his friends in that manner, and he stood neutral on the question. But the friends were not neutral-they earnestly contended that he belonged to his wife and they would not intrude. Lanky voiced their attitude in part when he said: "We 've had him a long time. We borrow him during workin' hours-we never learned no good from him, so we ain't goin' to chance spottin' our lily white souls." But there was another reason, which Johnny explained in naive bluntness: "Why, Ma'am, we eats in our shirt sleeves, an' we grabs regardless. We has to if we don't want Pete to get it all. An' somehow I don't think we 'd git very fat if we had to eat under wraps. You see, we 're free-an'-easy-an' we might starve, all but Pete. Why, Ma'am, Pete can eat any thin', anywheres, under any conditions. So we sticks to th' old table an' awful good appetites."

So Hopalong and Tex walked away together, the limp of the one keeping time with that of the other, for Tex's wounded knee had mended a great deal better than he had hoped for. Hopalong stopped a moment to pat his wolf hounds, briefly complimenting them to Tex, and then pushed open the kitchen door, shoving Tex in ahead of him.

"Just in time, boys," said Mary, "I hope you 're good an' hungry."

They both grinned and Hopalong replied first: "Well, I don't believe Pete can afford to give us much of a handicap to-day."

"Nor any other time, as far's I 'm concerned," added Tex, laughing. "We 'll do yore table full justice, Mrs. Cassidy," he assured her.

Mary, dish in hand, paused between the stove and the table. She looked at Tex with mischievous eyes: "Billy-Red tells me you love him like a brother. Is he deceiving me?"

Hopalong laughed and Tex replied, smiling: "More like a sister, Mrs. Cassidy —I can't find any faults in him, an' we don't fight."

Mary completed her journey to the stove, filled the dish and carried it to the table; resting her hands on the edge of the table, she leaned forward in seeming earnestness. "Well, you must know that we are one, and if you love Billy-Red —" finishing with an expressive gesture. "Those who love me call me Mary."

Tex's face was gravely wistful, but a wrinkle showed at the outer corner of his eyes. "Well," he drawled, "those who love me call me Tex."

"Good!" exclaimed Hopalong, grinning.

"An' I 'm thankful that my hair 's not th' color to cause any trustin' soul to call me by a more affectionate name," Tex finished. He ducked Hopalong's punch while Mary laughed a bird-like trill that brought to her husband's face an expression of idolizing happiness and made Tex smile in sympathy. As the dinner progressed Tex shared less and less in the conversation, preferring to listen and make occasional comments, and finally he spoke only when directly addressed.

When the meal was over and the two men started to go into the sitting-room, Mary said: "You 'll have to excuse me, Mr. —er-Tex," she amended, smiling saucily. "I guess you two men can take care of each other while I red up."

"We 'll certainly try hard, Mrs. —er-Mary," Tex replied, his face grave but his eyes twinkling. "We watched each other once before, you know."

As soon as they were alone Hopalong waved his companion to a chair and bluntly asked a question: "What's th' matter, Tex? You got plumb quiet at th' table."

The other, following his friend's example, filled a pipe before he replied.

"Well, I was thinkin' —could n't help it; an' I was drawin' a contrast that hurt. Hoppy, I 'm not goin' to stay here longer 'n I can help; you don't need me a little bit, an' if you took me in yore outfit it 'd be only because you want to help me. This ain't no place for me —I need excitement, clean, purposeful excitement, an' you fellows have made this part of th' country as quiet as a Quaker meetin'. I 've been thinkin' Buck needs somebody that 'll stick to him-an' there ain't nothin' I won't do for Buck. So I 'm goin' to pull my freight north, but *not* as Tex Ewalt."

"Tex, if you do that I 'll be able to sleep better o' nights," was the earnest reply. "We 'd like to have you. You know that, but it might mean life to Buck if he had you. Lord, but could n't you two raise h —l if you started! He 'll be tickled half to death to see you-there will be at least one man he won't have to suspect."

Tex considered a moment. "He won't see me-to know me. I 'm one man when I 'm known, when I 've declared myself; I can be two or three if I don't declare myself. One fighting man won't do him much good-if I could take th' outfit along we would n't waste no time in strategy. Th' rest of th' population, hostile to Buck, would move out as we rode in-an' they would n't come back. No, I 'm playing th' stranger to Buck. Somebody 's goin' to pay me for it, too. An' th' pay 'll not be in money but in results. I won't starve, not as long as people like to play cards. I quit that, you know; but if I do play, it 'll be part of my bigger game."

"I feel sorry for th' card-playin' population if you figger you ought to eat," smiled Hopalong, reminiscently.

"If I 'd 'a' knowed about Buck, I 'd 'a' gone to Montana 'stead of comin' here, an' saved some valuable time," Tex observed.

"But as far as that goes, Tex, they can't do much before Spring, anyhow," Hopalong remarked, thoughtfully. "An' it's yore own fault," he added. "We wanted to send you th' news occasionally, but you never let us know where you was. We 'd 'a' liked to hear from you, too."

"Yes, I reckon I 've got time enough; besides, I need th' exercise," agreed Tex.

"How is it you never wrote?" asked Hopalong, curiously.

Tex left his seat and walked to the door. "Take a walk with me-this ain't no place to tell a story like that."

"I 've got somethin' better 'n that —I want to go down to th' H2 an' see my father-in-law for a couple of minutes. Never met him, did you? We can ride slow an' have lots of time. Be with you in a minute," and Hopalong hastened to ask his wife if she had any word to send to her father. He joined Tex at the bunkhouse, now deserted except for Lee Hop, and in a minute they left for the H2. As they rode, Tex told his story.

"This is going to be short an' meaty. When I left here I struck Kansas City first, then Chicago, spending a few days in each of them. I 'd heard a lot about New York, an' headed for it. I had n't been there very long before I met a woman, an' you know they can turn us punchers into fool knots. Well, I courted her four days an' married her-oh, I was plumb in love with her, all right. She was one of them sweet, dreamy, clingin' kind-pretty as h —l, too. I had a good job by then, and for most a year I was too happy to put my feet on this common old earth. I never gambled, never drank, and found it not very hard to quit cussing, except on real, high-toned occasions. But I never could get along without my gun. Civilization be d —d! There 's more crooks an' killers in New York than you an' me ever saw or heard of. Once I was glad I had it-did n't have to shoot, though. Th' man got careless an' let his gun waver a little an' was lookin' at th' works in *mine* before he knowed it. He did n't want no money-what he needed was a match, an' he was doin' it to win a bet-or so he palavers. I takes his stubby .32 an' kicks him so he 'd *earn* that bet, an' lets him go. I had to laugh-him stackin' agin *me* at that game!

"Well, I got promoted, an' had to travel out of town every two weeks. I 'd be gone two days an' then turn up bright an' smilin' for my wife to admire. Once I was wired to come back quick on account of somethin' unexpected turnin' up, an' I lopes home to spend that second night in my own bed. I remember now that I wondered if th' wife would be there or at her mother's.

"She was there, but she was n't admirin' *me*. I saw red, an' th' fact that I did n't go loco proved that I ain't never goin'. But th' trigger hung on a breath an' *he* knowed it. He was pasty white an' could n't hardly stand up. Then th' shock wore off an' he was th' coolest man in town.

"What are you goin' to do about it?' he asks, slowly. 'Yore wife loves *me*, not you. She 's allus loved me-you never really reckoned she was in love with *you*, did you?"

”*I* was shocked then, only I was wearin' my poker face an' he could n't see nothin'. 'Why, I did think, once in a while, that she loved me,' I retorts. 'I certainly kept you hangin' 'round th' gutter an' *sneakin'* in, anyhow. When I get through with you they 'll find you in that same gutter.'

"'Goin' to shoot me? I *ought* to have a chance. I ain't got no gun-you see, I ain't wild an' woolly like you,' an' he actually grinned!

"'What kind of a chance did *I* have, out of town an' not suspectin' any thin'?' I asks.

"'But she *loves* me; don't you understand? She was *happy* with me. What good will it do *you* if you kill me an' break her heart? She 'll never look at you again.'

"'I reckon she won't anyhow,' I retorts. 'Leastwise not if I can help it. Look here: Don't you know you deserve to die?'

"'That's open to debate, but for brevity I 'll say yes; but I want a chance. I gave *you* a chance every time I came here-you did n't take it, that's all.'

"'I 'll get you a gun, d —d if I won't,' I replied, an' backed towards th' valise where my big old Colt was. But he stops me with a sneer.

"'I said a *chance*! You was *born* with a gun in your hand, an' it 'd be pure murder.'

"'I 'm glad somethin 's pure,' says I. Then I remembered that old valise again. Remember th' last thing I did for you an' Peters before I quit, Hoppy?"

Hopalong thought quickly. "Yes, you an' Pete put in two days settin' poisoned cows in th' brush on th' west line. Did a good job, too. Ain't been bothered none by wolves since."

Tex chuckled. "There was a bottle of yore stuff in that war-bag an' it was half full. I don't remember puttin' it there, but there she was. So I takes it an' holds it up for him to look at, readin' th' label out loud. That was th' only time my wife says a word, an' she says *his* name, sorrowful; then she goes on lookin' from him to me an' from me to him.

"He laughs at me an' sneers again. 'Think I 'm go in' to eat that?' he says.

"I don't answer. I 'm too busy workin' with one hand an' watchin' him. I knowed he did n't have no gun, but there was chairs an' bottles a-plenty. I got down a bottle of bitters an' poured some of it in a couple of glasses. Then I drops in some pain-killer an' stirs it up. It does n't mix very well, so I pushed th' remains of their supper to one side an' slips th' two glasses under th' table cloth, holdin' one edge of it in my teeth so it would n't touch th' glasses an' let him follow 'em. If they 'd been cards I 'd 'a' spread 'em monte-fashion under his nose-but they was n't.

"'Now, you skunk-take your pick an' don't wrangle no more about yore chances. An' you drink it before I drink mine, or I 'll blow yore cussed ribs loose!'

"I had given him credit for havin' a-plenty nerve, but now I sees it was n't nerve at all-just gall. He was pasty white again, almost green, an' his little soul plumb tried to climb out of his eyes. I was a whole lot surprised at how he went to pieces an' I was savagely elated at th' way he was a-starin' at that cloth. He looks at me for an instant and then back at th' little shell game on th' table' an' he says in a weak, thin voice: 'How 'd I know-you 'll drink-yourn?'

"'You ain't supposed to be knowin' anythin' about my habits while I 've got this gun-an' it's gettin' plumb heavy, too,' I retorts. 'You 've been yellin' about an even break, an' there it is. An' if it 'll hurry things any I 'll pick up my glass now an' drink it as soon as I see yore glass empty, an' yore Adam's apple bob enough. We won't have to wait very long before we get results. You 'll pick yore glass an' drain it or you 'll stop lead.' An' I did n't care, Hoppy, which one he got —I was worse'n dead then-what th' h —l did I care about livin'?

"I reached out to get my glass as soon as he had his'n an' I laid th' gun on my knee, knowin' he did n't have no weapon, an' that I could get th' drop before he could swing a bottle or chair. But I knowed wrong. He was a liar. As I touched my glass his hand streaks for his hip pocket. I gave him th' liquor in his eyes an' lunged for his gun hand just in time. Then I lets loose all th' rage that was boilin' in me an' when I gets tired of punishin' him, I throws him at th' feet of th' woman, picks up both guns, gets what personal duffle I need, an' blows th' ranch. His face was even all over, his nose was busted, his teeth stuck in his lips, an' he had a broken gun-wrist that gave somebody a whole lot of trouble before it worked right again, if it ever did. I 'm glad I did n't shoot him-there was a lot more of satisfaction doin' it with my naked hands. It was man to man an' I played with him, with all his extra twenty pounds. By G —d, I can feel it yet!"

During the short pause Hopalong looked steadily ahead with unseeing eyes, his face hard, his eyes narrowed, and a tightness about his lips that told plainly what he felt. To come home to that! He realized that his companion was speaking again and gave close attention.

"I don't know where I put in th' next week, but when I got rational I found myself in a cell in a Philadelphia jail, along with bums and crooks. I found that I 'd beat up a couple of policemen when I was drunk. When I got ready to leave th' town I didn't have a whole lot of money, so I played cards with what I had an' left th' town as soon as I had my fare-which did n't take long. That bunch never went up agin' such a well trained deck in their lives."

This time Hopalong broke the silence that ensued, his hand dropping unconsciously on his friend's arm in warm, impulsive sympathy. "By G —d, what a deal! It's awful, Tex; awful!"

"Yes, it was-an' it ain't exactly what you 'd call a joke right now. But I ain't worryin' none about th' woman-she killed my love stone cold that night. But when I think of how things *might* 'a' turned out if she 'd been square, of th' home I 'd 'a' had-but h —l, what's th' use, anyhow? Now what hurts me most is my pride an' conceit-an' th' way I turned to th' drink an' cheatin' so easy. It makes me mad clean through to think of what a infant I was, how I played th' fool for th' Lord knows how long; an' sometimes I want to kill somebody to sort of get square with myself. Up north I 'll be too busy tryin' to make fools out of other people to do much in th' line of sympathizin' with myself-an' too busy an' cautious to break back to drink an' cards. That was one of th' things drove me back here-there 's a whole lot more temptation facin' a man back East, an' 'specially a feller that's totin' a big load of trouble."

"Don't it beat all how different luck will run for different people?" marvelled Hopalong, thinking of his portion.

"That was runnin' in my mind while I was eatin'," replied Tex. "Reckon I *did* get sort of quiet. But I 'm plumb glad th' right kind of luck came yore way, all right."

They rode on for a short time, each busy with his own thoughts, and then Hopalong looked up. "We 're goin' up to see Buck just as soon as I feel th' ranch is in proper shape. I 've got to get th' round-up out of th' way first. You see, we ain't had no honeymoon trip yet."

"Yo 're lucky again; I never could see no joy in hikin' over th' country changin' trains, livin' in hotels, sleepin' in a different bed every night, each one worse'n th' one before, lookin' after baggage, an' workin' hard all th' time. I 've often wondered why it is that two people jump into all that trouble just as soon as they get into their own little heaven for th' first time." Then Tex's face grew earnest. "Now, look here, Hoppy: You ain't goin' up to see Buck till I tell you to come. I know you, all right; just as soon as you land you 'll be out gunnin' for th' bunch that's tryin' to bust Buck's game. You ain't single no more-yo're a married man, an' when a man 's got a wife like yourn he naturally ain't got no cussed business runnin' 'round puttin' hisself in th' way of gettin' killed. You let yore gun get plumb dusty an' when you want any excitement, go out an' try to make water run up hill, or somethin' simple like that. You handle th' trouble that comes to you, an' don't go off a-lookin' for it."

They spent the rest of the time in discussing the status of the married man, and when Mary afterward learned of the stand Tex took she shared more of her husband's affection for him. After a short stay at the H2 they turned homeward and went thoroughly into the matter of Tex's ride north. It was agreed that extra precaution would do no harm, and in order to have no blunder on the part of any one, they decided that it was best not to say anything about where he was going. Hopalong was greatly pleased and relieved now that he knew that his old foreman would have some one to help him fight his battles on that cold, distant range; but he did not appear to be as cheerful about it as was his companion. Tex looked forward to the trip with all the eagerness and impatience of a boy and it showed in his conversation and actions.

When they reached the ranch house at dusk they found Mary cooking a very small meal, and she waved them off. "You an' Billy-Red can't eat here to-night: yo 're goin' to eat with th' boys in th' bunk-house. I would n't spoil your fun for anything. Now you get right out —I mean just what I say!"

"But, girl—" began Hopalong.

"Now I 've made up my mind, an' that's all there is about it. I can get along without you this once —I won't do it again, you know-an' I want you boys to have a rousin' good time all by yoreselves. I want th' boys to like me, Billy-Red, to feel that I ain't changed *everythin'* by bein' here. Now you clear out-Lee knows all about it, an' I cooked some goodies this afternoon for th' feast. Johnny cleaned out th' cake tins an' scraped th' bowls I mixed th' fillin' in —I had to drive him away. Look! There he is, leanin' up against that tree watchin' for me to set somethin' out to cool. He purty near got away with a pie-oh, he 's terrible! But he 's a good boy, just th' same."

Tex turned, emitted a blood-curdling yell and started for the anxious Johnny, Hopalong close behind, while Mary stood in the door and watched the fun, laughing with delight. The outfit piled out of the bunk-house, caught sight of Johnny pounding towards them, and joined in, much to the Kid's disgust. They did not know anything about the affair, but they did not have to know-Johnny was legitimate prey for all, at any time and under any conditions. The fleeing youngster was nearly caught twice as he dodged and doubled, but once past them, he drew away with ease. When the winded and laughing pursuers finally stopped, he circled around to the nearest corral, found a seat on the gate and watched them straggle back to the bunk-house, deriding them with cheerful abandon, dissecting them with a shrewd and cutting tongue. He took them up in rotation and laid bare their faults and weaknesses until they leaned against the wall and laughed at each other until the tears came. Then he turned to ridicule.

"An' there's Skinny," he continued, slowly and gravely, while he rolled a cigarette. "Th' only way you can see him, except at noon, is to look at him in front, or at his feet. Why, I grabbed a broom in th' dark one time an' shore apologized before I realized that it was n't him at all. When he sits down he looks like a figger four, an' I 'm allus a-scared he 'll get into one pant's laig by mistake. When he eats solid stuff he looks like a rope with a knot in it-it's scary watchin' them knots go down-looks like he was skinnin' hisself. You can't tell whether he 's comin' or goin' —th' bumps is all alike. His laigs is so long he looks like a wishbone an' I 'm holdin' my breath most of th' time for fear he 'll split. When he goes huntin' all he has to do is to stand still so th' game won't see him; it wanders up to see what's holdin' up th' hat. He put Pete's pants on once when he fell in th' crick-after he fell in-an' I lifts my hat when I saw th' ridin' skirts. His laigs are beautiful-except for them knobs half way down where they hinge. An' when he swallers a mouthful of water he looks like a muscle dance. Why, I got into his bunk one night by mistake an' spent five minutes a-tryin' to smooth out a crease in th' blanket. Then he wakes up an' tells me to go over an' scratch Red for a change. Tells me to git off 'n him, 'cause I 'm flattenin' him out. That can't be did, an' he knew it, too.

"What *you* laughin' at, Red? You ain't got no laugh comin'. Every mornin' you sit on th' bunk an' count yore clothes an' groan. You put yore hat on first an' yore boots next. Then you takes off th' boots so yore socks can get on. Then th' boots go on again. Then they come off again to let yore pants go on, after which on go th' boots again. Then you take yore hat off to let th' shirt slip over yore head an' it goes right back on again. I 've seen you feel around for yore suspenders for five minutes before you remembered they was under th' shirt."

"Yo 're another! I don't wear no suspenders!"

"No, you don't. Not now, but you did. You quit 'em 'cause they cost a dollar a pair an' kept gettin' lost under th' shirt. Now when you dress up you lift my suspenders. Tex never saw you in love. I did; lots of times; about twice a month. You put th' saddle on th' corral wall, close th' horse, an' mount th' gate. You eat coffee with a knife an' sugar th' water. When I wake up first I see you huggin' th' pillow, which is my old coat wrapped around my old pants. If anybody says 'patience,' you bust yore neck a-lookin' for her. What did you do up to Wallace's that time when his niece came on to visit at his ranch? Wallace told me all about it, an' all about th' toothbrush, too. Lemme see if you remember good. Did n't you —"

"You never mind about me rememberin'," Red shouted, grabbing up a bucket of water off the wash bench and starting for his tormentor. Johnny leaped down and backed off, dodging behind the corral wall. As Red made the turn he fell sprawling, the water affectionately clinging to him. When he arose and looked around Johnny was entering the bunk-house door and the rest of the outfit clung together trying to hold themselves up, and voiced its misery in wails. At that moment Lee Hop buck-jumped around the corner on his trip from the cook shack to the corral, his favorite place of refuge when the ranch house was cut off from him, and he saw Red too late. When he was able to think he was minus a shirt and Red was carrying him under one arm and the shirt under the other.

"Now, you heathen-get that grub on th' table or I 'll picket you an' Johnny to th' same stake!" Red threatened, grimly.

"Him get clake. Him stealie pie. Alle same in klitchen. Eat chop-chop!" wailed the cook. He was promptly dropped and looked up in time to see a rush for the cook shack. But Johnnie was placing the delicacies on the table and close scrutiny failed to discover anything wrong with them, notwithstanding the suspicious manner in which his tongue groomed his teeth.

The supper was a howling success, and unlike the usual Bar-20 meals, was prolonged, and fun seasoned every dish. Even Lee Hop, incapable as he was of grasping most of the points in their rapid flight, and not wholly in sympathy with certain members of the outfit-even his countenance lost its expression of constant watchfulness; his mouth widened into a grin whose extremities were lost somewhere in the region of his back hair; his eyes gleamed like jet buttons in a dish of mush; and his moisture-laden skin shone until, altogether, his head resembled nothing so much as a pumpkin-bogie, a good-natured one, with an extra large candle lighted inside. He was tempted now and again to insert a remark in the short openings, but experience checked him in time. When the crowd filed into the living-room it was to tell tales of men living and dead; stories that covered a great range of human action, from the foolishness of "Aristotle" Smith to the cold ferocity and cruelty of Slippery Trendley and Deacon Rankin. The hours flew past with astonishing speed and when Tex looked at his watch he stared for a moment and returned it to his pocket with a quick, decisive movement.

"It's past midnight, fellows, an' I 'm riding' on in the mornin'," he remarked, arising.

The crowd looked its amazement and then vociferously announced its regret. These men held it a breach of etiquette to question, and because there were no "whys" or "wherefores," Tex felt impelled to explain. He was going on to see old friends, but he would return. The Bar-20 was his range and he would get back as soon as he could. In deference to his wishes and to let him get as much sleep as possible, the outfit quietly prepared for rest, and Hopalong, bidding them good-night, departed for the ranch house.

Breakfast over the next morning, Tex rode north, followed by an escort of friends of which any man would have been proud. Hopalong and Mary rode at his side and behind in a compact bunch came the boys. They stopped when the river trail was reached and Tex shook hands all around.

"I 'm sorry to leave you, Hopalong," he said earnestly; "but you know how it is: I 've been away quite a spell and things happen quick out here. You 'll see me again this Summer an' I 'll come to stay if you want me. Mary, I 'm mighty glad to see he 's got such a good foreman-he 's needed one a long time; an' I can see a big improvement in him already."

"Reckon you might profit by the example-must be girls a-plenty out in this country who 'd make good foremen," she replied, laughing.

Tex's face showed no trace of hurt as the chance arrow sped to the mark; he laughed, pointing at Johnny. "I reckon there are; but the Kid would n't give me no show."

"We 'll answer for him, Tex," chuckled Red. "We cured him once before an' we 'd be shore glad to do it again."

"Yep-kept him in the hills, starvin' an' freezin' for a whole month," sweetly added Skinny.

Johnny flushed and squirmed but had no time to retort, Pete and the others being too busy talking to Tex to let him be heard. Finally Tex backed off, raised his hat, and with a bow and a smile to Mary, wheeled and loped off along the trail to run Spring a race to Montana. Every time he looked back he waved in answer to his friends, and then, swiftly mounting a rise, was silhouetted for an instant against the white clouds on the horizon and as swiftly dropped from sight, a faint chorus of yells reaching him.

The outfit turned slowly to return to their ranch and when they missed their foreman, they saw him sitting silent where they had left him, his wife's hand on his arm. He could still see Tex against the sky, clear cut, startlingly strong and potent, and he nodded his head slowly. "He 's needed up there, an' he 's the best man to go." Turning, he was surprised to find his wife so near and he smiled joyously: "Wouldn't go an' leave me all alone, would you, Honey? Yo 're shore a thoroughbred an' I 'm plumb proud of you. Race you to th' bunch!"

Chapter II
H. Whitby Booth is Shown How

If any man of the Bar-20 punchers had been brought face to face with George McAllister he would have suffered the shock of his life. "Frenchy?" he would have hesitated, "What in —? Why, Frenchy?" And the shock would have been mutual, since Frenchy McAllister had been dead some months, a fact of which his brother George was sorrowfully aware. Yet so alike were they that any of Frenchy's old friends would have thought the dead come to life.

A distinguishing feature was the eye-glasses which George had long found necessary. He took them off and laid aside his book as the butler announced Mr. Booth.

H. Whitby Booth entered the room with the hesitating step of one who has a favor to ask. A tall, well-set-up man of the blonde type of so many of his countrymen, his usual movements were slow when compared with the nervous action of those in the hustling city of Chicago. Hesitation gave him the appearance of a mechanical figure, about to run down. Mr. McAllister's hearty welcome did not seem to reassure him.

"Ah-Miss McAllister-ah-is not at home," he volunteered, rather than questioned.

The other man eyed him quizzically. "No," he agreed, "she and Mrs. Blake are out somewhere; I am not just sure where. Shall I inquire?"

"No, oh no. I rather wanted to talk to you, you know-that is-ah —"

"Sit down, Whitby, and relieve your mind. Cigars on that table there, and some whiskey and fizz. Shall I ring for brandy?"

"Awfully good of you, really. No, I —I think I 'll go in as I am. The fact is I want Margaret-Miss McAllister-and I thought I 'd ask if you had any objections."

"Margaret has."

"Oh, I say!"

"Fact, she has. Might as well face the music, Whitby. The truth is just this: It's less than a week ago since Margaret was holding you up as a horrible example. Margaret comes from a line of hustlers; she has not had common sense and national pride bred out of her in a fashionable school; and she looks with extreme disfavor on an idler."

"But I say, Mr. McAllister, you don't think —"

"No, my boy, I don't think where Margaret is concerned-Margaret thinks. Don't misunderstand me. I like you, Whitby. Confidentially, I believe Margaret does, too. But I am quite sure she will never marry a man who does nothing and, as she expressed it herself, lives on an allowance from his father."

"Then I understand, sir, you have no objections?"

"None in the world-because I believe you will strike your gait before long and become something of a hustler yourself. But let me tell you, Margaret does n't deal in futures —I 'm used to it-but she insists on a fact, not a probability."

Whitby drew a breath which was largely expressive of relief. "In that case, sir, I 'll try my luck," and he arose to say good-night.

"You know where to find them?"

"Rather! I was going there when I had spoken to you."

"I see," said Mr. McAllister, somewhat grimly, remembering the other's greeting. "Sit down, Whitby. The night is young, you can't miss them, and I am so sure of the badness of your luck that I should like to give you a little encouragement to fall back on." Whitby resumed his seat and Mr. McAllister puffed thoughtfully at his cigar for a few moments before speaking.

"Not to go too far back," he began, "my grandfather was a boy when his father took him from Ireland, the birthplace of the family, to France, the birthplace of liberty, as the old man thought. Those were stirring times for that boy and the iron of life entered into him at an early age. He married and had one son, my father, who thought the liberty of this country so much better than that of France, that he came here, bringing his young wife with him; the wife died in giving birth to my younger brother, John. All that line were hustlers, Whitby. They had to be, to keep alive. Margaret knows their history better than I do and glories in it. You see?"

Whitby nodded mournfully. He was beginning to lose confidence again.

"My father would have been alive to-day but for an unfortunate accident which carried off both him and my mother within a few days. My brother and myself were found pretty well provided for. My share has not decreased. In fact I have done very well for a man who is not avaricious. But I had to fight; and more than once it was a close call, win or lose. Margaret knows all that, Whitby, and the dear girl is as proud of her father, I do believe, as of any who went before him. Her mother left us very soon and Margaret has been my companion ever since she could talk. Are you beginning to understand?"

"I am, indeed," was the reluctant acknowledgment.

"Very good. Then here is where you come in." His face clouded and he was silent so long that Whitby looked up inquiringly. The motion aroused McAllister and he continued:

"My brother was queer. I have always thought his birth had something to do with it; but however that may be, he was, in my opinion, peculiar in many of his ways. The choice of his path in life was quite on a par with his character: he invested every dollar he had in land out West, he and a partner whom I have never seen; bought and paid for land and stock at a time when Government land was used by any one without payment of any kind and when live-stock raising was almost an unknown industry, at least in that part of the country. But that was n't all. He went out to the ranch and took his delicate young wife with him, a bride, and lived in a wild region where they saw only Indians, outlaws, and those who were worse than either." His face hardened and the hand he laid on the table trembled as he turned to face to his listener. "Worse than either, Whitby," he repeated. "The Indians were bad enough at times, God knows, but there is excuse for their deviltry; there could be no excuse for those others.

"One reason John gave for going West was that the life would bring health to his wife. It did so. A few months' time saw her a robust woman. And then John returned to the ranch one day to come upon a scene that drove him crazy, I verily believe. No need to go into it, though I had the details from his partner at the time-John did not write me for years. They both started out after the murderers and wandered over a great part of this country before finding the chief fiend. Even his death brought no peace to John. He would never go back to the old place nor would his partner, out of feeling for him. After much persuasion I got them to put matters into my hands, but so many years had passed that I found the ownership in dispute and it is but lately that I have succeeded in regaining title. It was too late for John, who died before I came into possession, but his partner, a man named Peters, has gone up there from a Texan ranch to run the place. He is half owner and should be the best man for the job. But-and my experience with those Westerners places emphasis on that 'but' —I do not really know just what kind of a man he is. I am putting quite a large sum of money in this venture, relying upon Peters' knowledge and hoping for a square deal. And if he is the best man for the place, you are the best man I know to show me that. Don't interrupt.

"I know right well what Margaret will tell you to-night, and if you want to make her change her mind, you could have no better opportunity than I offer. My brother's history is an abiding grief with Margaret, and if you go out there and make good you will surely make good with her.

"That's all. If I 'm right, come and see me to-morrow at the office. I will have everything noted down for you in writing. Commit it to memory and then destroy the notes; because you would be valueless if any one interested discovered you were acting for me. And don't see Margaret after to-night before you go."

He arose and held out his hand. Whitby grasped it as he stood up and looked frankly at him. "It's awfully good of you, Mr. McAllister," he declared. "You 've left me deuced little hope, I must say, but there 's no knowing where you are if you don't ask, is there? And if I come a cropper I 'll try your way and chance it."

"You 'll find my way is right. I 've made mistakes in my life but never any where Margaret was concerned. Good-night."

* * * * *

Whitby stood at the top of the steps, slowly drawing his right-hand glove through his gloved left hand, time after time, casting a long look before he leaped. The driver of his hired *coupé* eyed him with calculating patience, observing to himself that if this were a specimen of the average Englishman, England must be a cinch for a cabman. Whitby had not yet arrived at the leaping stage when another *coupé*, a private one with a noticeably fine team, stopped in passing the house, and a voice hailed him: "Hello, Whit! What are you mooning there for?"

Whitby smiled: for all his consideration he had been pushed in at the last. He slowly descended the steps while he replied: "Evenin', Wallie. I was just going to drop in on the Sparrows."

"Good enough! Me, too. Jump in here and let your wagon follow. Do you hear, you driver? Trail in behind-unless you won't need him, Whit."

"Oh, let him come along. I —ah —I may be leaving rather early, don't you know."

"That so? Me, too. I'm darned glad I met you, Whit. I 'm in a regular blue funk-Brown is sulky as a bear. He 's been driving me about for an hour, I should say, and he does n't understand it. Fact is, Whit, I 'm going to ask a girl to marry me to-night, and I don't want to, not a little bit; but if I don't, some other fellow will, and that would be-well, worse."

"By Jove! Marry you *to-night*! Do you fancy she will?"

"No, you 'bloomin' Britisher.' *Ask* her, not marry her, to-night. For the love of Moses! Do you think it's an elopement?"

"Well, I did n't know, you know," and his tone was one of distinct disappointment. "You seem to be pretty certain she 'll have you."

"Oh! She 'll have me right enough, but I 've got to ask first and make sure. There 're too many others hanging around to suit me."

"I say, old chap, I hope you won't mind my asking but-it is n't Miss McAllister, by any chance, is it?"

Wallie turned in his seat and stared at the anxious face of Whitby for a few moments, then he broke into shouts of laughter. "You, too," he managed to say; and at last: "No, you trembling aspirant, it isn't, by any chance, Miss McAllister. Margie and I are good friends, all right, but not in that way. Oh, you sly Johnnie! Why, I 'll bet a hundred you 're up to the same game, yourself. Own up, now."

"I think a great deal of Miss McAllister, a very great deal. If I thought she 'd have me I 'd ask her the first opportunity."

"And that will be in a few minutes. She 's bound to be there-and here we are. Wish me luck, Whit."

"I do, with all my heart, Wallie," and he was very serious in his earnestness.

"Same to you, Whit, and many-no, not that, of course." They were in the rooms by this time, both pairs of eyes wandering, searching this way and that as they moved toward their pretty hostess whose recent marriage seemed to have increased, if possible, her popularity with the male sex; she stood so surrounded by a chaffing crowd of men that they found difficulty in getting near her. They did not linger, however, as each caught sight of the object of his pursuit at the same time, and their paths parted from that moment.

The maturity of Margaret McAllister's mind would never have been suspected from her appearance. The pale green satin gown, overhung with long draperies of silk-fringed tulle, the low round satin corsage being partly veiled by a diagonal drapery of the same transparent material, and ornamented-as was the skirt-with a satin scarf, tied with knots of ribbon and clusters of water-lilies —this formed a creation that adorned a perfect figure of medium height, whose symmetry made it seem smaller than it really was. The Irish temperament and quickness of intelligence were embodied in a brunette beauty inherited from her French ancestry; but over all, like the first flush of morning's light on a lovely garden, lay the delicate charm of her American mother. One of a group of girls, with several men hovering on the outer circle, she detached herself upon Whitby's approach and advanced to meet him.

"Good-evening, Mr. Booth. Are n't you late?"

"Yes, rather." Whitby drew comfort from the fact that she had chosen to notice it.

"Aunt Jessie is over this way. She is complaining of the heat already. Perhaps you would better mention it."

"Mrs. Blake? I will. I 've a favor to ask of Mrs. Blake. Let's join her."

Mrs. Blake was of that comfortable age, size, and appearance which expressed satisfaction with the world and its ways. She affected black at all times with quite touching consistency; doubly so, since gossip hinted at a married life not altogether happy. However, her widowhood did not permit derogatory remarks concerning the late Mr. Blake, who made up to her in dying all his short-comings when alive; and she had proven a discreet chaperon for Margaret from the assumption of that position. Her most conspicuous weakness was endeavoring to overcome a growing embonpoint with corsets, and the tight lacing undoubtedly had much to do with her susceptibility to heat. Whitby was a favorite with her and she greeted him warmly, closing her waving fan to tap him with it now and again in emphasis.

But Whitby's purpose would not wait; as soon as the chance offered he begged free, and arose to the occasion with a daring that surprised himself. "I am going to hide up with Miss McAllister for quite a time, Mrs. Blake. If any one comes bothering, just put him off, will you? That is, if Miss McAllister doesn't mind."

"Mind? Of course she doesn't mind. Run along, Margie, and for Heaven's sake, don't sit in a draft-though I don't believe you can find one in this house," and the fan was brought into more vigorous action at the reminding thought.

"Well, I don't know, Mr. Booth," remonstrated Margaret as they moved away. "They will begin to dance very soon and I promised Wallie Hartman the opening. You came in together, didn't you?"

"Oh, Wallie! Yes, he was pretty keen on getting here but I rather fancy he's forgotten about that dance, you know."

"What makes you say that? What mischief are you two brewing?"

"Ah-it's Wallie's secret, you know, —that is, his part of it is —I say, here 's the very spot."

They had made the turn behind the stairs, where a punch bowl stood; the space immediately behind the stairs being too low in which to stand comfortably upright, a mass of foliage was banked in a half circle, outside of which the stand and punch bowl were placed; inside, a thoughtful hostess had arranged a *tête-à-tête*, quite unnoticeable from without. Whitby's attention had been drawn to it by the couple who had emerged upon their approach, the girl radiant and the man walking on air, of which details Whitby was entirely oblivious. Margaret was more observing and she looked after Wallie with a dawning look of understanding and then at Whitby with a quick glance of apprehension. There was no time to protest, even if she would, as Whitby had led her behind the leafy screen before she fully realized the import of his action.

Like many slow starters, Whitby, when once in movement, set a rapid pace. He came to the point now with promptitude:

"Miss McAllister, I arrived late because I called on your father before coming here, to ask his permission to address you. I must say he rather dashed my hopes, you know. He does n't think I 'm such a bad sort-he does n't object in the least-but he seemed to fancy his daughter Margaret would. I—I hope he is mistaken."

She turned to him a face in which the eyes were slowly filling with tears, nor did she remove the hand upon which his rested, on the curving back of the seat. It was not her first proposal, by several, but there was a vibrating earnestness, an unexpected tenderness in this big, slow Englishman which told her she was going to hurt him seriously when she spoke. And she did not want to hurt him; with all her heart and soul she wished she did not have to hurt him.

"I 'm not worthy of you, Margaret. I don't think any man is worthy of a good woman, and I 'm just an ordinary man. But I 'll *be* worthy of you, from to-night. —and that whether you say yes or no.

"You know I love you. You must know I left London and came over here to follow you. But you don't know how much I care for you-and I can't tell you. I 'm a duffer at this sort of game-like everything else —I never did it before-and 'pon my word, I don't know how. But if I could say what I feel, then perhaps, you might know better. What is it to be, Margaret? Wait a bit! If you feel doubtful, I 'll wait as long as you want me to. But-but —I 'm afraid it's no go." He sat looking dumbly at her, hoping for some sign of encouragement, but there was no misreading the answer in her face.

It was a long minute before she spoke. She was unnerved by the hysterical desire to put her arms around him and soothe him as she might a hurt child. Something of her embarrassment was conveyed to him and with the wish to save her the pain of refusing in words he started as if to rise. She stopped him with a gesture.

"Wait. I *will* say what I want you to know. I like you-no! not in that way; not the way a woman should-the man she expects to marry. Perhaps if you had been —I am not sure-but I could *not* marry a drone. Oh! why don't you wake up! How *can* you go on from day to day with no thought but self-indulgence? You say you love me. Ask yourself: Is not that merely a form of self-indulgence? Oh, I know you would take care of me and defer to me and let me have my way in everything-you are that kind of a man-but to what end? That I might be the more pleasing to you. Is it your purpose to dawdle through life, taking only such pains as shall make things more pleasing to you?"

"Is that all, Margaret? Is it only because you fancy I'm a loafer?"

"But you are! You are! Oh! I don't know —I 'm not sure —"

"I 'm sure!" the exulting certainty in his voice startled her. "I 'm sure!" he repeated. "I may be a bit of an ass in some things but no woman would care as you care, what a man was or what he did unless she loved him. You love me, Margaret, thank God! Give me a chance. You 're only a girl, yet. Give me a year and if I go under, or you find I 'm wrong, I 'll thank you for the chance and never blame you. Will you?"

Her heart was pounding in suffocating throbs and she trembled like a leaf in the wind before the eager intensity of his gaze. A strong will held her in check, else she had given way then and there, but she faced him with a fine bravery. "Yes," she promised, "I will. Go away and make good."

"Make good! By Jove, that's what your father said. Make good —I 'll not forget it." His head bent low in an old-fashioned but becoming salute while her free hand rested unfelt for an instant upon the yellow hair, a gesture that was at once a blessing and a prayer.

Chapter III

Buck Makes Friends

The town of Twin River straggled with indifferent impartiality along the banks of the Black Jack and Little Jill branches where they ran together to form the Jones' Luck River, two or three houses lying farther north along the main stream. The trail from Wayback, the nearest railway point, hugged the east bank of Jones' Luck, shaded throughout its course by the trees which lined the river, as they did all the streams in this part of the country: cottonwoods mostly, with an occasional ash or elm. Looking to the east, the rolling ground sloped upward toward a chain of hills; to the west, beyond the river, the country lay level to the horizon. On both sides of the trail the underbrush grew thick; spring made of it a perfect paradise of blossoms.

Boomerang, pet hobo of Twin River and the only one who ever dared to come back, left Little Nell's with his characteristic hurried shuffle and approached the wooden bridge where the Wayback trail crossed the Jill, and continued south to Big Moose. Boomerang was errand boy just now, useful man about the hotel or one of the saloons when necessity drove, at other times just plain bum. He was suspected of having been a soldier. A sharp "'tention" would startle him into a second's upright stiffness which after a furtive look around would relax into his customary shambling lack of backbone. He had one other amusing peculiarity: let a gun be discharged in his vicinity and there was trouble right away, trouble the gunner was not looking for; Boomerang would fly into such a fury of fighting rage, it was a town wonder that some indignant citizen had not sent him long ago where he never could come back.

Coming to the bridge he looked casually and from habit along the trail and espied a horseman riding his way. He studied him reflectively a few seconds and then spat vigorously at something moving on one of the bridge planks, much as the practised gun-man snaps without appearing to aim. "Stranger," he affirmed; "Cow-punch," he added; "Old man," he shrewdly surmised, and shook his head; "Dunno 'im" and he glanced at the stain on the plank to see what he had bagged. Among his other pleasing human habits "Boom" used tobacco-as a masticant-there was the evidence of the fact. But he had missed and after a wistful look for something to inspire him to a more successful effort, he shuffled on.

The horseman came at a steady gait, his horse, a likely-looking bay with black spots, getting over the ground considerably faster than the cow-ponies common to the locality; approaching the bridge he was slowed to a walk while his rider took in the town with comprehensive glance. A tall man, lean and grizzled, with the far-seeing, almost vacant eye of the plainsman, there was nothing, to any one but such a student of humanity as "Boom," to indicate his calling, much less his position in it. The felt hat, soft shirt and rough, heavy suit, the trousers pushed into the tops of his boots, were such as a man in the town might wear and many did wear. He forded the stream near the bridge at a walk. Pop Snow, better known as Dirty, cleverly balancing himself within an inch of safety in front of the "I-Call" saloon, greeted him affably: "Come a long way, stranger?" asked Dirty.

"From Wayback," announced the other and paused in interested suspense. Dirty had become seized with some internal convulsion, which momentarily threatened disaster to his balance. His feet swung back and forth in spasmodic jerks, the while his sinful old carcass shook like a man with the Chagres fever. Finally a strangled wheeze burst from his throat and explained the crinkle about his eyes: he was laughing.

"Wayback ain't fur," he declared, licking his lips in anticipation of the kernel of his joke about to come. "You can a'most see it frum here through the bottom uv —"

"How d' you know it ain't?" the horseman abruptly interrupted.

Dirty was hurt. This was not according to Hoyle. Two more words and no self-respecting "gent" could refuse to look toward Wayback through a glass-and certainly not alone. The weather was already too cold to sit fishing for such fish as this; and here was one who had swallowed the bait, rejecting the hook.

"Why, stranger, I been there," explained Dirty, in aggrieved remonstrance.

"How long since you been there? Not since two-at-once, was you? Didn't it used to be at Drigg's Worry? Didn't it?"

Snow lost his balance. He nodded in open-mouthed silence.

"Course it was-at Drigg's Worry-and now it's way back," and with a grim chuckle the stranger pressed in his knees and loped on down the trail to the Sweet-Echo Hotel.

Dirty stared after him. "Who in hell's that?" he asked himself in profane astonishment. "It 's never Black Jack-too old; an' it ain't Lucky Jones-too young. He sure said 'two-at-once.' Two-at-once: I ain't heard that in more 'n twenty years." His air-dried throat compelled inward attention and he got up from his box and turned and looked at it. "Used to be at Drigg's Worry, did n't it?" he mimicked. "Did n't it? An' now it's way back." He kicked the box viciously against the tavern wall. "D —n yer! This yer blasted town 's gettin' too smart," and he proceeded to make the only change of base he ever undertook during the day, by stamping across the bridge to the "Why-Not."

The door of the I-Call opened and a man appeared. He glanced around carelessly until he noticed the box, which he viewed with an appearance of lively interest, coming outside and walking around it at a respectful distance. "Huh!" he grunted. Having satisfied himself of its condition he drawlingly announced it for the benefit of those inside. "Dirty 's busted his chair," he informed, and turned to look curiously after Pop Snow, who was at that moment slamming the door of the Why-Not behind him.

Through the open door three other men came out. They all looked at the box. One of them stopped and turned it over with his thumb. "Kicked it," he said, and they all looked across at the Why-Not, considering. A roar from behind them smote upon their ears like a mine blast: "Shut that door!" With one accord they turned and trooped back again.

The rider meanwhile was talking to his horse as he covered the short distance to the Sweet-Echo Hotel. "Wonderful climate, Allday. If twenty years don't wear you down no more 'n old Snow you 'll shore be a grand horse t' own," and he playfully banged him alongside the neck with his stirrup. Allday limited his resentment to a flattening of the ears and the rider shook his head sorrowfully. "Yo 're one good li'l hoss but yore patience 'd discourage a saint." He swung off the trail to ride around the building in search of a shelter of some kind, catching sight of Boomerang just disappearing through the door of the bar-room. "Things has been a-movin' 'round Twin River since Frenchy an' me went after Slippery an' his gang: bridges, reg'lar hotels, an' tramps. An' oblige me by squintin' at th' stable. If Cowan 'd wake up an' find that at th' back door, he 'd fall dead."

He dismounted and led his horse through the stable door, stopping in contemplation of the interior. He was plainly surprised. "One, two, three, four," he counted, "twenty stalls-twenty tie-'em-by-th'-head stalls-no, there 's a rope behind 'em. Well, I 'm d —d! He ain't meanin' to build again in fifty years; no, not never!"

Allday went willingly enough into one of the stalls-they were nothing new to him-and fell to eating with no loss of time. Buck watched him for a few moments and then, throwing saddle and bridle onto his shoulder, he walked back the way he had come and into the hotel bar. No one noticed him as he entered, all, even the bartender, being deeply intent on watching a game of cards. Buck grunted, dropped his belongings in a corner, and paused to examine the group. A grand collie dog, lying near the stove in the middle of the room, got up, came and sniffed at him, and went back and lay down again.

The game was going on at a table close to the bar, over which the bartender leaned, standing on some elevation to enable him to draw closer. Only two men were playing. The one facing Buck was a big man, in the forties, his brown hair and beard thickly sprinkled with gray; brown eyes, red-rimmed from dissipation, set wide apart from a big, bold nose, stared down at the cards squeezed in a big hand. The other man was of slight build, with black hair, and the motions of his hands, which Buck had caught as he entered, were those of a gambler: accurate, assured, easy with a smooth swiftness that baffled the eye. He was dressed like a cowpunch; he looked like a cow-punch —all but the hands; these, browned as they were, and dirty, exhibited a suppleness that had never been injured by hard work. Buck walked up to the bar and a soft oath escaped him as he caught sight of the thin, brown face, the straight nose, the out-standing ears, the keen black eyes-Buck's glance leaped around the circle of on-lookers in the effort to discover how many of the gambler's friends were with him. He was satisfied that the man was playing a lone hand. There was a tenseness in the air which Buck knew well, but from across the hall came a most incongruous sound. "Piano, by G—d!" breathed Buck in amazement. The intentness on the game of those in the room explained why he had seen no one about the place and he was at a loss to account for the indifference of the musician.

At the big man's left, standing in the corner between the bar and the wall, was a woman. Her blonde hair and blue eyes set off a face with some pretensions to beauty, and in point of size she was a fitting mate for the big man at whom she stared with lowering gaze. Close to her stood the hobo, and Buck rightly concluded he was a privileged character. Surrounding the table were several men quite evidently punchers, two or three who might be miners, and an unmistakable travelling salesman of that race whose business acumen brings them to the top though they start at the bottom. Buck had gauged them all in that one glance. Afterward he watched the gambler's hands and a puzzled expression gradually appeared on his face; he frowned and moved uneasily. Was the man playing fair or were his eyes getting old? Suddenly the frown disappeared and he breathed a sigh of relief: the motion itself had been invisible but Buck had caught the well-remembered preliminary flourish; thereafter he studied the faces of the others; the game had lost interest, even the low voices of the players fell on deaf ears. His interest quickened as the big man stood up.

"I 'm done," he declared. "That lets me out, Dave. You 've got th' pile. After to-night I 'll have to pound leather for forty a month and my keep." He turned to the woman, while an air of relief appeared among the others at his game acceptance of the loss. "Go on home, Nell. I won't be up yet a while."

"You won't be up at all," was the level-voiced reply.

"Eh?" he exclaimed, in surprised questioning.

She pushed past him and walked to the door. "You won't be up at all," she repeated, facing him. "You 've lost your pile and sent mine after it in a game you don't play any better than a four-year-old. I warned you not to play. Now you take the consequences." The door slammed after her. "Boom" silently opened the door into the hall and vanished.

The big man looked around, dazed. No one met his eye. Dave was sliding the cards noise-lessly through his fingers and the rest appeared fascinated by the motion. The big man turned to the bartender.

"Slick, gimme a bottle," he demanded. Slick complied without a word and he bore it in his hand to the table behind the door, where he sat drinking alone, staring out morosely at the gathering darkness.

Buck dropped into the vacated chair and laid his roll on the table. "The time to set in at a two-hand game of draw," he remarked with easy good nature, "is when th' other feller is feelin' all flushed up with winnin'. If you like to add my pile to that load you got a'ready, I 'm on." He beamed pleasantly on the surrounding faces and a cynical smile played for a moment on the thin lips of the man facing him. "Sure," he agreed, and pushed the cards across the table.

"Bar-keep, set 'em up," said Buck, flicking a bill behind him. Slick became busy at once and Buck, in a matter-of-fact manner, placed his gun on the table at his left hand and picked up the pack. "Yes," he went on with vacuous cheerfulness, "the best man with a full deck I ever saw told me that. We crossed trails down in Cheyenne. They was shore some terrors in that li'l town, but he was th' one original." He shook his head in reminiscent wonder, and raised his glass. "Here 's to a growin' pile, Bud," and nodding to the others, who responded with indistinct murmurs, the drink was drained in the customary gulp. "One more, bar-keep, before we start her," he demanded. "I never drink when I 'm a-playin'." Here he leaned forward and raised his voice. "Friend, you over there by th' winder, yo 're not drinkin'."

The big man slowly turned his head and looked at Buck with blood-shot eyes, then at the extra glass on his table. "Here 's better luck ner mine, friend-not wishin' you no harm, Dave," and he added the drink to the generous quantity he had already consumed. Buck waved his hand in acknowledgment, then he smiled again on his opponent.

"Same game you was playin', Bud?" he asked, genially.

"Suits me," was the laconic reply.

Buck raised the second drink. "Here's to Tex Ewalt, th' man who showed me th' error of my ways." The tail of his eye was on Dave.

The name of Tex must have shocked him like a bucket of ice water but he did not betray it by so much as the flicker of an eyelid. Ewalt and he had been friends in the Panhandle and both had escaped the fate of Trendley and his crowd more by luck than merit. Buck knew Dave's history in Texas, related by Ewalt himself, who had illustrated the tell-tale flourish with which Dave introduced a crooked play; but he did not know that Dave Owens was Black Jack, returned after years of wandering, to the place of his nativity.[1]

Buck shuffled the cards slowly and then with a careful exaggeration of the flourish, dealt the hand in a swift shower of dropping units. A sigh of appreciation escaped the observant group and this time Buck got results: at sight of the exaggerated flourish an involuntary contraction of the muscles hardened the deceptively boyish form and face of the younger man and the black eyes stared a challenging question at the smiling gray ones opposite before dropping to the cards he had unconsciously gathered up.

Luck smiled on Buck from the start. He meant that it should. Always a good player, his acquaintance with Tex, who had taught him all he knew of crooked plays, had made him an apt pupil in the school in which his slippery opponent was a master. With everything coming his way Buck was quite comfortable. Sooner or later the other would force the fighting. Time enough to sit up and take notice when the flourishing danger signal appeared.

It came at last. Dave leaned forward and spoke. "Cheyenne, how'd jack-pots strike yer? I got ter hit th' trail before six an' it's pretty nigh time to feed."

"Shore!" assented Buck, heartily.

The pot grew in a manner scandalous to watch. "Double the ante," softly suggested Dave.

"Shore," agreed Buck, with genial alacrity.

"Double her ag'in."

"Double she is," was Buck's agreeable response.

Pass after pass, and Slick stretched out over the bar and craned his neck. At last, with a graceful flourish a good hand fell to Buck, a suspiciously good hand, while Dave's thin lips were twisted into a one-sided smile. Buck looked at him reproachfully.

"Bud, you should oughter o' knowed better 'n that. I got six cards."

The smile faded from Dave's face and he stared at the cards like a man who sees ghosts. The stare rose slowly to Buck's face, but no one could possibly suspect such grieved reproach to be mere duplicity. It was too ridiculous-only Dave knew quite well that he had not dealt six cards. "Funny," he said. "Funny how a man 'll make mistakes."

"I forgive you this once, but don't do it no more," and Buck shuffled the cards, executed a particularly outrageous flourish, and dealt.

"Ha! Ha!" barked Bow-Wow Baker. "D —n if they ain't both makin' th' same sign. Must belong to th' same lodge."

Chesty Sutton dug him in the ribs with an elbow. "Shut up!" he hissed, never taking his eyes from the game.

Dave passed and Buck opened. Dave drew three cards to two high ones. Buck stood pat. Dave scanned his hand; whatever suspicion he might have had, vanished: he had never seen the man who could deal him a straight in that fashion. He backed his hand steadily until Buck's assurance and his own depleted cash made him pause, and he called. Buck solemnly laid down four aces. Four! —and Dave would have taken his oath the diamond ace had been on the bottom of the deck before the deal-and Buck had not drawn cards.

"They 're good," said Dave shortly, dropping his hand into the discard. "If you 're goin' to stay around here, Cheyenne, I 'll get revenge to-morrer." He started to rise.

"Nope, I guess not, Bud. I never play yore kind of a game with th' same man twice."

Dave froze in his position. "Meanin'?" he asked, coldly.

"I don't like th' way you deal," was the frank answer.

"D —n you!" cursed Dave. His hand flew to his gun-and stopped. Over the edge of the table a forty-five was threatening with steady mouth.

"Don't do it, Bud," warned Buck.

Dave's hand slowly moved forward. "A two-gun man, eh?" he sneered.

"Shore. Never bet on th' gun on th' table, Bud. You got a lot to learn. Hit her up or you 'll be late-an' down where I came from it's unhealthy to look through a winder without first makin' a noise."

"Yore argument is good. But I reckon it 'd be a good bet as how you 'll learn somethin' in Twin River you ain't never learned nowhere else." Dave sauntered carelessly to the front door.

"You ain't never too old to learn," agreed Buck, sententiously. The front door closed quietly after Dave and half a minute later his pony's hoofs were heard pounding along the trail that led toward Big Moose.

"Cheyenne, put her there! I like yore style!" Chesty Sutton, late puncher for the Circle X, shoved his hand under Buck's nose with unmistakable friendliness. "I like th' way *you* play, all right."

"Me, too," chimed in Bow-Wow. "Dave Owens has got th' lickin' of his life. An' between you an' I, Cheyenne, I ain't never seed Dave get licked afore-not reg'lar."

The chorus of congratulations that followed was so sincere that Buck's heart warmed toward the company. Chesty secured attention by pointing his finger at Buck and wagging it impressively. "But you hear me, Cheyenne," he warned. "Dave ain't no quitter. He 's got it agin' you an' he 's h —l on th' shoot. I ain't never heerd of his killin' nobody but he 's right handy spoilin' yore aim. Ain't he, Bow-Wow?"

"Look a-here. How often have I told you? You sez so. He is. Don't allus leave it to me." Bow-Wow's tone was indignant as he rubbed his right arm reflectively.

"Gentlemen, I 'm not sayin' a word against anybody, not one word," and Slick glanced from man to man, shaking his head to emphasize his perfect belief in the high standard of morality prevalent in Twin River. "But I begs leave to remark that *I* like Cheyenne's game-which it is th' first time in my brief but eventful career that I seen five dealt cards turn into six. You all seen it. It sure happened. Mr. Cheyenne, you have my joyous admiration. Let's celebrate. An' in th' meantime, might I inquire, without offence, if Cheyenne has a habit of complainin' of too many cards?"

They had lined up before the bar and all glasses were filled before Buck answered. Slick stood directly before him and every face, showing nothing beyond polite interest, was turned his way. But Buck well knew that on his reply depended his position in the community and the gravity of the occasion was in his voice when he spoke.

"Gentlemen, Mr. Slick has called. There's two ways of playin'. When I plays with any gentleman here, I plays one way. Dave Owens played th' other way. I played his game."

He glanced at the silent figure by the window, set down his glass, and started to cross the room. Chesty Sutton put out his hand and stopped him. "I would n't worry him none, Cheyenne. Ned Monroe 's th' best boss I ever worked for but hard luck has been pilin' up on him higher 'n th' Rockies since he lost his ranch. Better let him fight it out alone, friend."

Lost his ranch-Ned Monroe-Buck's intention was doubly strengthened. "Leave it to me," was his confident assurance, and he strode across the room and around the table in front of the window. The sombre eyes of the big man were forced to take notice of him.

"Friend, it's on th' house. Mr. Slick is a right pleasant man, an' he 's waitin'." A rapid glance at the bottle told him that Monroe, in his complete oblivion, had forgotten it. Ned eyed him with a puzzled frown while the words slowly illumined his clouded mind. At length he turned slowly, sensed the situation, and rose heavily to his feet. "Sure," was the simple reply.

At the bar significant looks were exchanged. "I 'm beginnin' to *like* Cheyenne," declared Slick, thoughtfully, rubbing the palm of his left hand against the bar; "which his persuadin' language is fascinatin' to see."

"It sure is," Chesty Sutton endorsed promptly, while the others about him nodded their heads in silent assent.

"Well, gentlemen," said Slick, "here 's to th' continued good health of Mr. Cheyenne." Down the line ran the salutation and Buck laughed as he replaced his empty glass.

"I shore hope you-all ain't tryin' to scare me none," he insinuated; "because I 'm aimin' to stop up here an' —who in h —l's poundin' that pie-anner?" he broke off, turning to glare in the direction of the melancholy sound.

"Ha! Ha!" barked in his ear, and Buck wheeled as if he had been kicked. "That's Sandy," explained Bow-Wow Baker. "He thinks he 's some player. An' he is. There ain't nothin' like it between here an' Salt Lake."

"Oh, yes; there is," contradicted Buck. "You an' him 's a good team. I bet if you was in th' same room you 'd set up on yore hind laigs an' howl." Bow-Wow drew back, abashed.

"Set 'em up, Mr. Slick," chuckled the salesman.

"Don't notice him, Cheyenne," advised Chesty in a disgusted aside. "He don't mean nothin' by it. It's just a habit. It's got so I 'm allus expectin' him to raise his foot an' scratch for fleas," and he withered the crestfallen Bow-Wow with a look of scorn.

"You was sayin' as how you was aimin' to stop here," suggested Ned Monroe, his interest awakened at thought of a rising star so often following the fall of his own.

"Yes," acknowledged Buck. "If I find —"

Crash! Ding-dong! Ding-dong! The noise of the bell was deafening. Buck set down his glass with extreme care and looked at Slick with an air of helpless wonder, but Bow-Bow was ready with the explanation. "Grub-pile!" he shouted, making for the side door, grasping hold of Chesty's hand as he went out and dragging that exasperated puncher after him by strength of muscle and purpose. "Come on, Cheyenne! No 'angel-in-th'-pot,' but a good, square meal, all right."

Chesty Sutton cast behind him at Buck a glance of miserable apology, seized the door-frame in passing, and delivered to Bow-Wow a well-placed and energetic kick. Relieved of the drag of Chesty's protesting weight and with the added impetus of the impact of Chesty's foot, Bow-Wow shot across the wide hall, struggling frantically to regain his equilibrium, and passed through the door of the dining-room like a quarter-horse with the blind staggers. The bell-ringing ended in a crash of broken crockery, succeeded by a fearful uproar of struggling and profanity.

The collie bounded to his feet, his hair bristling along his spine, and rushed at the door with a low growl. Ned caught him by the collar and held him. "Down, Bruce, down!" he commanded, and the dog subsided into menacing growls.

Chesty, at the door, snorted in derision. "D —n fool!" he informed those behind him. "He 's tryin' to climb th' table. Hey, Ned; let th' other dog loose," he suggested, hopefully.

By the time the highly entertained group had gathered about the dining-room door, the oaths and imprecations had resolved themselves into a steady railing. Bow-Wow sat sprawled in a chair, gazing in awed silence along the path of wreckage wrought by the flying bell; opposite him, waving a pair of pugnacious fists in close proximity to Bow-Wow's face, stood Sandy McQueen, proprietor of the Sweet-Echo. It appeared that he was angry and the spectators waited with absorbed expectancy on what would happen next.

"Ye gilravagin' deevil!" he shouted, "canna ye see an inch afore yer ain nase? Gin ye hae nae better manners na a gyte bull, gang oot to grass like thae ither cattle. Lord preserv's," he prayed, following the strained intensity of Bow-Wow's gaze, "look at the cheeny! A 'm ruined!" He started to gather up the broken crockery when the roar of laughter, no longer to be restrained, assailed his outraged ears. He looked sourly at his guests. "Ou, ay, ye maun lauch, but wha's to pay for the cheeny? Ou, ay! A ken weel eneuch!"

The hilarious company pushed into the dining-room and began to help him in his task, casting many jocose reproaches on the overburdened Bow-Wow. Slick returned to the bar-room to clean off the bar before eating, and Buck went after him. "Hey, what have I struck?" he asked, with much curiosity. "He sounds worse 'n a circus."

"He 's mad," explained Slick. "Nobody on God's green earth can understand him when he 's mad. Which a circus is music alongside o' him. When he 's ca'm, he talks purty good American."

"You shore relieves my mind. What is he-Roosian?"

"Claims to be Scotch. But I dunno —a Scotchman 's a sort of Englishman, ain't he?"

"That was allus my opinion," agreed Buck.

"Well —I dunno," and Slick shook his head doubtfully as he hung the towel onto a handy hook and stooped to come under the bar. "Sounds funny to me, all right. 'Tain't English; not by a h —l of a sight."

"Sounds funny to me," echoed Buck. "I 'm *shore* it ain't English. But, say, Slick; gimme a room. I 'm stoppin' here an' I 'd like to drop my things where I can find 'em."

"Right," said Slick, and he led the way into the hall and toward a bedroom at the rear. Chesty Sutton stood in the doorway of the dining-room. "Better git in on th' jump, Cheyenne," he advised, anxiously. "Bow-Wow 's that savage, he's boltin' his grub in chunks an' there ain't goin' to be a whole lot left for stragglers."

"Muzzle him," replied Buck, over his saddle-weighted shoulder, while Slick only grinned, "If I goes hungry, I eats Bow-Wow. Dog ain't so bad." Chesty chuckled and returned to the sulky Bow-Wow with the warning.

Despite Chesty's fears, there was plenty to eat and to spare. Little talking was done, as every one was hungry, with the possible exception of Ned, and even he would have passed for a hungry man. Sandy McQueen and the cook officiated and the race was so nearly a dead heat that the first to finish was hardly across the hall before the last pushed his chair back from the table.

An immediate adjournment to the bar-room was the customary withdrawal, and Buck, doing as the others, found Ned in his former seat beside a table. Buck joined him and showed such an evident desire for privacy that the others forbore to intrude.

"Ned," said Buck, leaning towards him across the table, "it ain't none of my business, an' it ain't as I 'm just curious, but was that straight, what you said about bein' broke?"

"That's straight," Ned assured him, gloomily.

"An' lookin' for a job?" asked Buck, quietly.

"You bet," was the emphatic reply.

"Chesty said as how he used to work for you. Was you foreman?"

"I was foreman an' boss of the NM ranch till them blood-suckers back East druv me off 'n it —d —n 'em."

"Boss, was you? Then I reckon you wouldn't refuse a job as foreman, would you?"

Ned's interest became practical. "Where 's yore ranch?" he asked, with some show of eagerness.

"Why, I was aimin' to stop 'round here some'rs."

"H —l! There ain't a foot o' ground within eighty mile o' where yo 're sittin' as ain't grazed a heap over, less 'n it's some nester hangin' on by his fingers an' toes-an' blamed few o' them, neither. Leastaways, none but th' NM an' Schatz's range, which they says belongs to th' old Double Y, both of 'em."

"What's keepin' them free?"

"'Bout a regiment o' deputies, I reckon." He smiled grimly. "It's costin' 'em somethin' to keep th' range free o' cattle. Mebby you could lease it. That McAllister feller ain't never goin' to get a man to run it for long. Some o' th' boys is feelin' mighty sore an' Schatz is a tough nut. It's goin' to be a mighty big job, when he starts, an' that's certain."

"I 'd like to see it. We 'll go t'morrow."

Buck's careless defiance of the situation pleased Ned. With the first evidence of good humor he had shown he hit Buck a resounding slap on the back. "That's you," was his admiring comment.

The door opened to admit the short, broad figure of a man who, after a glance around the room, made his bow-legged way to their table. His tone betrayed some anxiety as he asked: "Ned, haf you seen mein Fritz?"

"Nope," answered Ned, "I have n't, Dutch. Hey, boys!" he called, "Anybody seen Pickles?"

A chorus of denials arose and Chesty sauntered over to get details. "W'y, you durned ol' Dutch Onion, you ain't gone an' lost him again, have you?"

"Ach! Dot leetle *Kobold*! Alvays ven I looks, like a flea he iss someveres else."

"How 'd you lose him?" demanded Chesty.

Dutch stole a look askance at Ned and turned on Chesty a reproachful face. He laid a glove on the edge of the table. "Dot's Fritz. I turn 'round, like dot," suiting action to word, in a complete turn, his right hand reaching out, taking up the glove and whirling it behind his back as he faced the table again. He looked at the empty spot with vast surprise, in delicious pantomime.

The glove, meanwhile, had fallen against the nose of Bruce, who sniffed at it and then picked it up and carried it to Slick behind the bar, returning to his resting place with the air of a duty accomplished.

Dutch continued to stare at the table for several seconds. Then he glanced around and called: "Fritz! Fritz! *Komm' zu mir* —und Fritz iss gone," he finished, turning to those at the table an expression of comical bewilderment. He took a couple of steps in the direction where he supposed the glove to be. Bruce was just lying down. Dutch looked more carefully, stooping to see along the floor. A light broke in on him. He straightened up and excitedly declared: "Yoost like dot! Yoost like der glove iss Fritz: I know ver he iss bud I can't see him."

"Dutch, come here." Ned's voice was stern and Dutch approached with hanging countenance. "Where was you when you 'turn 'round like dot'?" asked Ned.

"Only a minute, Ned; yoost a minute!"

"Where?"

"In Ike's I vas; yoost a minute."

"Ain't I told you to keep out o' there?"

Dutch moved his feet, licked his lips, and cleared his throat; words seemed to fail him.

While he hesitated the door opened again, something more than six inches, and Boomerang squeezed through. He shuffled up to Dutch and touched him on the shoulder. "Hey, Dutch, I been chasin' you all over. Pickles went home wit' Little Nell, see? An' she sent me ter tell you."

"Vat! mit dot —" he broke off and turned to Ned. "I begs your pardon, but Fritz, he iss leetle-he learn quick. Right avay I go." He was at the door when Slick hailed him.

"Hey, Dutchy, this yourn?" The other caught the tossed glove, and nodded.

"Yah, first der glove, soon iss Fritz," and the door closed behind him.

"Good as a circus," laughingly declared Buck. "About pay now-how would eighty a month hit you, for a starter?"

"Fine," declared Ned.

"Then here she is, first month," and Buck handed it over. "Will that be enough to square up what you owe?" he added.

"W'y, I don't owe nothin'," declared Ned.

"Well-now —I was just a-thinkin' 'bout th' lady as seemed right vexed when you dropped yore roll to Dave." He looked casually at Slick, behind the bar, while he was saying it.

"Little Nell? I don't owe her nothin', neither. It was my pile, —all of it."

Buck heaved a sigh of relief. "I 'm right glad to hear it. Then you 'll be all ready to hit th' trail with me in th' mornin'?" he asked.

"Shore; but s'pos'n you can't get th' ranch?" suggested Ned.

"I 'll get it. An' when I get it I 'll run it, too, less'n they load me with lead too heavy to sit a horse-then you 'll run it." His smile was infectious.

"Cheyenne, I like yore style. Put 'er there," and he shoved a huge, hairy fist at Buck. "'Nother thing," he went on, "Chesty an' Bow-Wow was a-goin' over to th' Bitter Root. I 'll tell 'em to hang 'round for a spell. Them 's two good boys. So 's Dutchy-when he ain't a-runnin' after Pickles."

"All right; you talk to 'em. See you in th' mornin'," and with a general good-night, Buck went to his room.

Chesty and Bow-Wow joined Ned to have a "night cap" and say good-bye, intending to start early next morning. "No, boys, I 've had enough," said Ned. "I 've took a job with Cheyenne, an' you boys better hang 'round. Find Dutch in th' mornin' an' tell him. An' I 'm a-goin' to turn in, too. I 'm cussed sleepy." The other two sat staring across the table at one another. The news seemed too good to be true.

"Ha! Ha!" barked Bow-Wow, "I never did like them d —n Bitters, not nohow."

Chesty nodded his head. "Me, too," he agreed. "Son, there 's a big time due in these parts: I feel it in my bones."

Seized with a common impulse they sprang to their feet and began a war-dance around the stove, chanting some Indian gibberish that was a series of grunts, snarls, and yells. Their profane demands for information meeting with no response, the others one by one joined them, until a howling, bobbing ring of men circled the stove, and, growling and barking at their heels, the dog danced with them. Slick looked on with an indulgent grin and the row did not cease until Sandy stuck his head in at the hall door. "Deil tak' ye!" he shouted. "Canna ye let a body sleep?"

A minute later the room had settled down into its customary decorum and Bruce, with a wary look about, now and then, was preparing to resume his rudely interrupted doze.

Chapter IV
The Foreman of the Double Y

Buck cinched up his saddle on Allday and led him out of the stable. "Ned, this is shore one scrumptious hotel," he observed as he swung into his seat.

"It certainly is. Nothin' to beat it in Montany, I reckon," was Ned's hearty endorsement.

Buck shook his head as they passed through the gate together. "Most too good," he suggested.

"I dunno," Ned doubted, "th' branch from Wayback 's shore to come down th' Jones' Luck, an' then Sandy 'll rake in."

They had just turned into the trail when a rider passed them at speed, causing Ned's cayuse to shy and buck half way to the Jill. The evener-tempered Allday only pointed his ears and pulled on the bit. "Reckon you could catch that feller, eh? Well, you could n't," was Buck's careless insult. "If Hoppy could see that horse he 'd give all he 's got for him-bar Mary."

The horse merited his criticism. A powerful black, well over fifteen hands, he showed the sloping thigh bones and shoulder of a born galloper, while the deep chest gave promise of long-sustained effort. His rider had pulled up at the general store just beyond the hotel and Ned joining him, Buck expressed his admiration. A moment later he added to it: "By th' Lord, Ned, that 's a woman." The rider had dropped from the saddle and paused to wave her hand to Ned before she entered the store. Buck caught the glance from a pair of beautiful dark eyes that rested on him a moment before it fleeted past to his companion. The grave smile was well suited to the wonderfully regular features and when she turned and entered the store it was with the swinging step of perfect movement. Buck faced about with a jerk when he realized that he had actually turned in his saddle to gaze after her.

"Best horse in these parts an' th' finest woman," agreed Ned, "an' honest," he added, gruffly.

Buck stared at him, surprised. "Why, o' course! Anybody says different?" He unconsciously stiffened at the thought.

"Um-no, not as I knows of. Her daddy 's a nester; got a quarter-section 'tother side o' Twin River, off th' trail a piece. Rosa LaFrance-pretty name, ain't it? Th' boys calls her the French Rose."

"Yes, 'tis pretty," drawled Buck. "What I'm askin' about is this recommendation o' character to me."

It was Ned's turn to feel surprised. He pondered as he looked at Buck. "I reckon I warn't exactly speakin' to you, Cheyenne," he explained; "more to myself, like. You see, it's this way: Dave Owens, he won that horse from McReady of the Cyclone, one night in Wayback. I was n't there but I hears it's a regular clean up. McReady was in a streak o' bad luck and would a' lost ranch an' all but his friends hocussed his liquor an' Mac, he drops out of his chair like somebody hit him with an axe. Next day Rose rides into Twin River on that same horse. John, that's her daddy, he never bought him; he could n't. Then how did she come by it? That's her business, I says. That's one thing. For another, Dave Owens travels that way considerable, an' Dave ain't no company for the French Rose. I 'm too old to interfere or I durn soon would."

Buck brooded on this situation for some time and then burst into a laugh. Ned eyed him with stern disapproval. "I was thinkin' of a cow-punch I know," explained Buck, in apology. "He 'd interfere so quick, there would n't be time to notify th' mourners."

Ned smiled in sympathy. "That 'd do," he admitted, "but you can't jump in an' shoot up a fellow if a girl's sweet on him, can you? It 'd be just nacheraly foolish."

"That 's so," agreed Buck, "but if the French Rose can look at that son of a thief and like him, then Hopalong Cassidy has no call to be proud o' *his*self."

"Eh?" questioned Ned.

"Th' name slipped out. But now 's as good a time as any to tell you. Did you ever hear o' Frenchy McAllister?"

"Owner o' the Double Y?"

"Half owner-leastways, he was. Frenchy 's dead. You was cussin' his brother last night. I want to tell you about Frenchy."

Buck told the story in terse, graphic sentences, every one a vivid picture. He painted the scene of Trendley's crime to the accompaniment of a low-voiced growl of lurid profanity from Ned, who was quite unconscious of it. The relentless hunt for the criminals, extending through many months; the deadly retribution as one by one they were found; the baffling elusiveness of Slippery Trendley and the unknown manner of his fate when run to earth at last-one scene followed another until Buck left the arch devil in his story, as he had left him in fact, bound and helpless, looking up at the pitiless face of the man he had injured beyond the hope of pardon, their only witnesses the silent growths of Texas chaparral and the grieving eye of God.

It was a terrible story, even in the mere telling of it. Buck's level voice and expressionless face hid the seething rage which filled him now, as always, when his thoughts dwelt upon the awful drama. Ned's judgment was without restriction: "By the Eternal!" he swore, "that h —l-hound deserved whatever he got. D —d if you ain't made me sick." They rode in silence for several minutes and then: "Poor fellow! poor fellow!" he lamented. "Did you say he's dead?"

"Yes, Frenchy's gone under," answered Buck gravely. "You 'd 'a' liked him, Ned."

"Yes, I reckon I would," agreed Ned. He looked at the other, considering. "Where do you come in?" he asked. Buck's narrative had failed to connect the new-born "Cheyenne" as "Frenchy's pardner."

"I 'm Buck Peters," was the simple explanation.

Ned pulled his horse back onto its haunches and Buck wheeled and faced him. So they sat, staring, Ned inarticulate in his astonishment, Buck waiting. The power of coherent thought returned to Ned at last and he rode forward with outstretched hand. "Th' man as stuck to Frenchy McAllister through that deal is good enough for me to tie up to," he declared, and the grip of their hands was the cementing of an unfailing friendship. "An' I 'd like for Buck Peters to tell Frenchy's brother as I takes back what I said agin' him."

Their way led through an excellent grass country. The comparatively low ground surrounding Wayback rose gradually to Twin River and more rapidly after leaving that town. The undulating ground now formed in higher and more extensive mounds, rising in places to respectable-sized hills; usually the sides reached in long slopes the intervening depressions, but not infrequently they were abrupt and occasionally one was met which presented the broad, flat face of a bluff. The air was perceptibly colder but the bunch grass, hiding its wonderfully nourishing qualities under the hue it had acquired from the hot summer sun, was capable of fattening more cattle to the acre than any but the best lands of the Texan ranges with which Buck was familiar. Snow had not yet swept down over the country, though apt to come with a rush at any time. Even winter affected the range but little as a general rule; disastrous years were luckily few and far separated, so that the average of loss from severity of weather was small. The talk of the two naturally veered to this and kindred topics and Buck began stowing away nuggets of northern range wisdom as they fell from the lips of the more experienced Ned.

Studying the trail ahead of him, Buck broke the first silence by asking: "Ain't we near the boundary of the Double Y?"

"You 'll know, soon enough. Th' first big butte we come to, some cuss 'll be settin' there, hatchin' out trouble."

"That's him, then," and Buck pointed to the right where a solitary horseman showed dark against the sky-line.

"Yep, that's one of 'em. Reglar garjun, ain't he?"

"Beats me how you let 'em stand you off, Ned," wondered Buck.

"Well, when we made good and sure you owned the range, Buck, there were n't no use in fighting. That McAllister would 'a run in th' reglar army next, d —d if he would n't."

Buck chuckled. "He 's sure a hard man to beat. I don't mind fighting when I have to, but I 'm mighty glad it looks peaceful."

"We 'll have fightin'. When I was turned off my ranch, it just about foundered me. I sold th' stock, every head, an' you saw where th' last o' th' cash went. But don't forget Smiler Schatz. He 's a bigger man an' a better man nor I ever was, an' he 's a-layin' low an' a-waitin'. He calculates to get you —I dunno how."

"An' I dunno how," mused Buck. "Say, Ned, I thought th' stage line ran through to Big Moose: there ain't no tracks?"

" 'Cause it crosses th' ford at th' Jack an' goes to th' Fort; then it swings round to Big Moose, an' back th' same road. Wonder who 's that pointin' this way?"

Buck glanced ahead to see a moving speck disappear behind a knoll far along the trail. "Dunno; maybe another deputy," he suggested.

The distant rider came into sight again and Ned stared steadily at him. "No," he declared, "think I know that figger. Yessir! It's Smiler. I kin tell him 'most as far as I kin see him."

"That's the feller gave us the fight, ain't it?"

"Did his share-some over, mebbe. He 's a hard nut."

"Well, I 'm not bad at a pinch, myself, Ned; mebbe I can crack him." Ned smiled grimly at the jest and hoped he would be cracked good. Evidently there was no great liking between the quondam owners of the Double Y.

However, this was not apparent in their greeting. The steady approach had been uninterrupted and Buck looked with interest at the "hard nut" as they met.

In a land of dirty men-dirty far more frequently from necessity than from choice-Schatz was a by-word for slovenliness nearly approaching filth. If he washed at all it left no impression on the caked corrugations of his smiling countenance. His habit of smiling was constant, so much a part of him that it gave him his name. And it had been solemnly affirmed by one of his men that he never interfered with his face until the dirt interfered with his smile; then he chipped it off with a cold chisel and hammer. This must have been slander: no one had ever seen him when it looked chipped. A big man, with a fine head, he sat in his saddle with the careless ease of long practice. "Hello, Ned!" he called, with a gay wave of the hand. *"Wie geht's?"*

"Howdy, Karl!" replied Ned. "How's sheep?"

"Ach! don't say it, der grasshoppers. Never vill dey reach Big Moose. Also, I send East a good man to talk mit dat McAllister to lease der range yet. Before now he say a manager come from Texas, soon. Vat iss Texas like Montana? Nodding. Ven der snow come —"

"Hol' on! This is th' manager, Mr. Buck Peters, half owner o' the Double Y, an' he 's put me in as foreman."

"So-it pleases me greatly, Mr. Buck. Ned iss a good man. If you haf Ned, that iss different." He shook hands with Buck who took note of the blue eyes and frank smile of the blonde German, at a loss to discover where he hid that hardness Ned had referred to.

"Sorry I can't offer you a job," said Buck, matching the other's smile at the joke, "but from what I hear, one foreman will be a-plenty on the Double Y."

"It iss a good range-eggselent-und der iss mooch free grass ven you haf der Double Vy for der hard years; but dere iss not enough for you und for me, too, so I turn farmer. Also some of der boys, dey turn farmer. I take oud quarter-section alretty."

"Quarter-section! Turn farmer! You! Sufferin' cows! give me a drink," and Ned looked wildly around for the unattainable.

"Donnerwetter! Somet'ing I must do. To lend money iss good but not enough. Also my train vill not vait. So I say good-morning und vish you luck."

Ned wheeled his horse to gaze after the departing figure and Buck sat laughing at his expression. "Luck," echoed Ned; "bad luck, you mean, you grinnin' Dutchman. H—l of a farmer you 'll be. Now I wonder what's his little game."

"Aw, come on, Ned. 'Pears to me he 's easy," and Allday sprang away along the trail.

"Easy, eh!" growled Ned, when he caught up, "he 's this easy: him and me started even up here, 'bout th' same time. 'T was n't long before he begun crowdin' me. Neither of us had nuthin' at first but when we quit he could show five cows to my one. How 'd he do it?"

"Borrowed th' money and bought yearlin's," answered Buck.

"Yes, he did," Ned grudgingly admitted. "But I kep' a-watchin' him an' he allus branded more than th' natural increase, every round-up —an' I could never see how he done it."

"You-don't —say," was Buck's thoughtful comment, "Well, down our way when a man gets to doin' miracles on a free range we drops in on him casual an' asks questions-they don't do it twice"; and he unconsciously increased Allday's pace.

"Here, pull up," urged Ned; "this bronc 's beginnin' to blow. That's a bang-up horse you 've got there. No good with cattle, is he?"

"No," agreed Buck. "I got this horse because 'discretion is sometimes better than valler,' as Tex Ewalt said when somebody asked him why he did n't shoot Hoppy. Most times I finish what I start, but once in a while, on a big job, it's healthy to take a vacation. An' I naturally expected to leave some hasty an' travel fast."

"Ain't nothin' could catch you, in these parts, not if you got a good start, less'n it's French Rose an' Swallow."

"Well, I was n't aimin' to run far nor yet to stay long. That seems like it 'd be th' ranch."

"That's her," agreed Ned.

The ranch house, rectangular and of much greater dimensions than Buck expected to find it, presented two novel features, one of which he noticed at once. "What's th' idea of a slopin' roof, Ned?" he asked.

"That's Karl's notion. See that upside down trough runs along th' high part at th' back? There ain't a foot o' that roof you can't slosh with a bucket o' water. An' you can shoot along th' walls from them cubby holes built out at each corner. Th' house is a heap bigger 'n th' old one was; it used to set over yonder in that valley, but th' wipin' out o' Custer put th' fear o' God in Smiler an' he raised this place soon after. Five men could stand off five hundred Injuns."

"Where 's th' water?"

Ned chuckled. "Wait till you see it. There 's a well sunk at th' side an' you can pull it in without goin' out-door if you wants to. Karl is one o' them think-of-everything fellers. He put th' ranch house on a knoll an' th' bunk-house on another. Then, he figgers, if they wants to rush me they 'll be good an' winded when they gets here. My shack is a pig-pen 'long side o' this un', but I got it figgered out I need n't to stop if I don't want."

"How's that, Ned?"

"I could cut an' run any time-come night. I 'll show you when we goes over there."

Bare as was the interior, the ranch house gave promise of comfort and the bunk-house and the stable with its adjacent corral proved equally satisfactory. The fire-place of the bunk-house was built over the bare earth and there they repaired to make a fire and eat the food they had brought with them. The added warmth was a distinct comfort but the smoke brought company on the run. They had scarcely begun their meal when a faint sound led Buck to saunter to the door and look out. Down the steep side of a high butte dropped a horseman with considerably more speed and no more care than a dislodged boulder; arriving at the bottom, his horse straightened out into a run that showed he was expected to get somewhere right away. Buck gravely bit into a sandwich the while he admired the rider's horsemanship; an admiration that was directed into another channel when the object of it slipped rifle from holster, pumped a cartridge into the barrel, and threw it forward in business-like attitude. "'Spects to have use for it, right soon," mused Buck, and then, over his shoulder: "Better hide, Ned. Here comes a garjun an' he 's got his gun out."

"Th' h —l he has!" rumbled Ned. "Come an' push me up th' chimley, Buck; I 'm a-scared."

Buck strolled back to the fire and half a minute later the horse pounded up to the house, his rider sprang off and came through the door, gun first. He continued across the room with solemn countenance, set his gun against the wall, and went to the fire where he extended his hands to the blaze. "Howdy, Ned; howdy, stranger," was his easy greeting.

Ned, sitting cross-legged, smirked up at him. "Howdy, Jack. You were n't going to run me off'n th' range, was you?"

"Nope. Saw Cheyenne Charley headin' this way 'bout an hour since. Thought mebbe he 'd burn her up-Pipes o' peace!" His eyes widened as he gazed at Ned's upturned mouth. "Bottled beer, or I 'm a Injun. You lives high," and he swallowed involuntarily as the inspiring gurgle stimulated his salivary glands.

"I 'm taperin' off on beer," explained Ned. "Got three bottles, one for Buck and two for me. I 'm biggest. But you can have one o' mine. Buck, this is Jim's Jack, head garjun an' a right good sort. Buck Peters has come to take charge of his own ranch, Jack."

"Shake," said Jack. He glanced over the papers Buck handed him and passed them back. All three turned to look at the open door.

"Hang up a sign, Buck," advised Ned. "If we stops here long enough we can start a hotel. Come in, Charley."

The Indian stepped slowly in. "Cheyenne Charley, Buck," said Ned; "off the Reservation for a drunk at Twin River. You 'd think he 'd stop in Big Moose. Reckon he 's hungry, too; he —" Ned paused and his eyes sought the object of Charley's steady and significant gaze. "Oh, that be d —d!" he exclaimed, swooping onto the third bottle of beer beside him and holding it out to Buck. "He wants your beer. Charley is a good Injun —I *think* —but 'lead us not into temptation'" —and with the other hand he proceeded to put his share of temptation out of sight, an example that Jim's Jack emulated with dignified speed.

"Let him have it," said Buck, good naturedly. "I never hankered much for beer, nohow." He passed the bottle to the Indian, not in the least suspecting what "an anchor he had cast to windward." The other two exchanged a look of regretful disapproval.

Half an hour later they had separated, Buck and Ned going on to the more distant NM ranch, Jack to gather up his fellow deputies, and the Cheyenne hitting the trail for Twin River with a thirst largely augmented by the sop he had thrown to it.

Chapter V
"Comin' Thirty" has Notions

Up from the south, keeping Spring with him all the way, rode Tex. The stain of the smoke-grimed cities was washed out of him in the pure air; day by day his muscles toughened and limbered, his lightning nerves regained their old spontaneity of action, each special sense vied with the others in the perfection of service rendered, and gradually but surely his pulse slowed until, in another man, its infrequency of beat would have been abnormal. When he rode into Twin River, toward the end of a glorious day, he had become as tireless as the wiry pony beneath him, whose daily toll of miles since leaving the far-off Bar-20 was well nigh unbelievable.

Tex crossed the ford of the Black Jack behind the Sweet-Echo Hotel. Dirt had bespattered him from every angle; it was caked to mud on his boots, lay in broad patches along his thighs, displayed itself lavishly upon his blue flannel shirt, and had taken frequent and successful aim at his face; but two slits of sun-lit sky seemed peering out from beneath his lowered lids, the pine-tree sap bore less vitality than surged in his pulsing arteries, his lounging seat was the deceptive sloth of the panther, ready on the instant to spring; and over all, cool as the snow-capped peaks of the Rockies, ruled the calculating intelligence, unscrupulous in the determination to win, now that it was on the side of the right, as when formerly it fought against it.

One glance at the imposing Sweet-Echo and Tex turned his pony's head toward the trail. "No, no, Son John, you 'll not sleep there with your stockings on-though I shan't ask you to go much farther," Tex assured him. "I 've seen prettier, and ridden cleverer, but none more willing than you, Son John. Ah, this begins to look more like our style. 'I-Call' —sweet gamester, I prithee call some other day; I would feed, not play. 'Ike's' —thy name savors overly much of the Alkali, brother. Ha! 'By the prickling of my thumbs, something wicked that way bums.'" He had turned to cross the Jill and saw Pop Snow basking in the failing sunlight. "'Why-Not' —well, why not? I will."

"Come a long way, stranger?" asked Dirty, his gaze wandering over the tell-tale mud. He had come the wrong way for profit, but Dirty always asked, on principle: he hated to get out of practice.

Tex swung his right leg over his pony's neck and sat sideways, looking indolently at the pickled specimen who sat as indolently regarding him. "Plucked from a branch of the Mussel Shell," murmured Tex, "when Time was young"; and then drawled: "Tolerable, tolerable; been a-comin' thirty year, just about."

Dirty looked at him with frank disgust, spat carefully, and turning on his seat no more than was absolutely necessary, stuck his head in at the open door and yelled: "Hey, boys! Come on out an' meet Mr. Comin' Thirty. Comin' is some bashful 'bout drinkin' with strangers, so get acquaint."

Scenting a tenderfoot half a dozen of the inmates strolled outside. When they saw the sun-tanned Tex they expressed their opinion of Dirty in concise and vitriolic language, not forgetting his parents; after which they invited Tex to "sluice his gills." One of them, a delicate-featured, smooth-faced boy, added facetiously: "Don't be afraid; we won't eat you."

Tex released his left foot from the stirrup and slid to earth. "I was n't afraid o' bein' et, exactly," was his slow response; "I was just a-wonderin' if it would bite. I notice it 's slipped its collar."

"Go to h —l! Th' lot o' you!" screeched Pop, bouncing to his feet with surprising alacrity. "Wait till I buy th' nex' one o' you a drink-wait! That's all."

"Lord, Dirty, we *has* been a-waitin'. Since Fall round-up, ain't it?" appealing to the others who gave instant, vigorous, and profane endorsement.

"Pah!" exploded Pop. He faced about and executed a singular and superlatively indecent gesture with a nimbleness unexpected and disgracefully grotesque in so old a man; and then without a backward glance, he stamped off across the bridge to the I-Call. The others watched him in fascinated silence until he plumped down on his inevitable box, when the smooth-faced first speaker turned to his nearest neighbor and asked in hushed tones: "What do you think of him, Mike?"

"Fanny, me boy, if I thought I 'd ever conthract Dirty's partic'lar brand o' sinfulness, I 'd punch a hole in th' river-with me head," and he solemnly led the way in to the bar.

"Gentlemen, it's on me," declared Tex, " —for good and special reasons," he explained, when they began to expostulate. "Give me a large and generous glass," he requested of the barkeeper, "and fill it with 'Water for me, water for me, and whiskey for them which find it agree.' You see, gentlemen, liquor an' I don't team no better 'n a lamb an' a coyote. I must either love it or leave it alone an' I 'm dead set agin' spiritual marriage. Here 's how."

"If I 'd begun like that I 'd be a rich man this day," observed Mike, when his head resumed the perpendicular.

"If I 'd begun like that I would n't be here at all," responded Tex.

"Well, ye 'll have a cigar with me, anyhow. Putt a name to it, boys, an', Fred, whisper: Pass up that wee little box ye keep, in th' locker. Me friend, Comin', will take a good one, while he 's at it."

A blue-shirted miner next him interposed: " 'T is my trate. He 'll hev a cigar with me, he well. Das' thee thenk I be goin' to drenk with thee arl the time, and thee never taake a drenk 'long o' me? Set un up, Fred, my son, and doan't forget the lettle box."

Tex gazed curiously at the speaker. It was his first meeting with a Cornishman and Bill Tregloan was a character in more than speech. Wherever gold, or a rumor of gold, drew the feet of miner, there sooner or later would be Bill Tregloan. He had crossed the continent to California on foot and alone at a time when such an attempt was more than dangerous. That he escaped the natural perils of the trip was sufficiently wonderful; as for the Indians, there is no doubt they thought him mad.

Bill had his way in paying for the order and turned to lounge against the bar when his eye caught sight of that which drew from him a torrent of sputtering oaths and a harsh command. The only one who had failed to join the others at the bar was Charley, the Cheyenne Indian. He lay sprawled on the floor against the opposite wall, very drunk and asleep, and about to be subjected to one of the pleasing jokes of the railroad towns, in this instance very crudely prepared. The oil with which he was soaked, had been furnished far too plentifully, and he stood an excellent chance of being well roasted when the match, then burning, should be applied.

The man holding the match looked up at the Cornishman's shout. He did not understand the words but the meaning of the action that followed was plain; and when the miner, growling like a bear, started to rush at him, his hand dropped to his gun with the speed of a hawk. Fanny promptly stuck out his foot. Tregloan went down with Fanny on top of him but it takes more than one slight boy, whatever his strength, to hold down a wrestling Cornishman. The flurry that followed, even with the added weight of numbers, would have been funny but for the scowling face of the olive-skinned man who stood with ready gun until assured the struggle had gone against his opponent. Then he slipped gun in holster and felt for another match. "Take him away," he said, with a sneering smile, "he make me sick."

"What did they do that for?" asked Tex of Mike. Neither had moved during the excitement. The rest were pushing and pulling Tregloan out of the saloon.

"That's Guinea Mike," was the explanation. "He 'd murder his mother if she crossed him. First fair chanst I mane to break his d —d back-an' if ye tell him so he 'll kill me on sight."

"Interestin' specimen," observed Tex. Guinea Mike found another match and calmly lit it. Those not engaged in soothing Bill were looking in at the door and windows. Dutch Fred, behind the bar, was swearing good American oaths regarding the unjustified waste of his kerosene. Tex stepped away from the bar. "Blow that out," he said, dispassionately.

Guinea Mike looked up with a snarl. The two stares met and grappled. Guinea slowly raised the match to his lips and puffed it out, flipping it from him with a snap of one finger so that it fell almost at the feet of Tex. They watched each other steadily. A solitary snore from the Indian sounded like the rumble of overhead thunder. Slowly the hand of Guinea descended from before his lips and in unison with it descended the head of Fred until his eyes just cleared the top of the bar. Guinea's hand rested in the sagging waist of his trousers, a second, two —

The roar of the explosion was deafening. Guinea Mike's right shoulder went into retirement and his gun dropped from his nerveless fingers. Screaming with rage he stooped to grasp it with his left hand and pitched forward at full length, both knee-caps shattered, at the mercy of this stranger who shot as if at a mark.

The noise awakened Cheyenne Charley who opened his eyes and smiled foolishly at the distorted face which had so unexpectedly reached his level. "D —n drunk," he observed, and immediately went to sleep again.

Tex walked over and kicked the gun across the floor. Irish Mike picked it up and handed it to Fred. "I could a' killed you just as easy as I didn't, Guinea," said Tex. "I don't like you an' yore ways. It's just a notion. So don't you stop. An' don't send any o' yore friends. 'No Guineas need apply.' That goes, if I has to Garibaldi yore whole d —n country."

The spectators had filed back to the room and were engaged in audible comments on the justification and accuracy of the shooting, while they busied themselves in the rough surgery which had to serve. To the suggestion that he ought to be taken to the doctor at Wayback, Fred interposed the objection: "No, dake him to Nell's. Mike is a friend mit her."

Pop Snow, attracted by the excitement, stood peering in a window. Twin River crowded the room but Pop's resentment was still warm. A man rode up and stooped from the saddle to look over his shoulder. "Who 's that? What's up?" he asked.

"'T aint nothin'; *only* Guinea Mike. See th' feller Fanny 's hangin' onto? Well, that's him: Comin' Thirty has notions-an' I ain't never seen better shootin'.'"

Dave swung down, tied his pony to the rail and went inside to see the new bad-man of Twin River. It had been growing steadily colder during the past few hours; the wind, sweeping in from the west, held a sinister threat, the air a definite chill, and Dave felt he would be none the worse for a little fire-water. Dirty felt it also, but his senile annoyance had merely simmered down, not subsided, and he scurried back to the I-Call for cover until such time as he thought it fitting to go home.

* * * * *

It was very late when Dave turned a tired pony to pasture and entered the three-room cabin of Karl Schatz. The rough exterior gave no indication of the comfort with which the German had surrounded himself. Fur rugs covered the floor of the living-room; the chairs and table had travelled many miles before landing here; a fine sideboard showed several pieces of fair china; mounted horns of various kinds were on the walls, one group being utilized as a gun rack, and between them hung several good paintings. A stove had been removed but in its place smouldered a wood fire, the fireplace jutting out from the wall. When Dave came in Karl sat smoking; on the table beside him lay an open volume of poems. "Vell?" he asked, as Dave dropped into a chair and stretched his legs wearily before him.

"Double Y has got a new bunch o' cattle. Hummers. Bought 'em out of a drove come up last Fall on Government contract; the Government went back on th' deal an' they was wintered up here. Got th' pick o' th' lot, I hear." Dave fell into silence and stared at the fire. Karl puffed thoughtfully while he looked at the black head whose schemes seemed coming to nought.

"Cameron 's got back," continued Dave; "he 's brought his money with him; took up his note at the bank; paid full interest." Another pause, with no comment from Karl. Dave continued to display his items of information in sections. "I met One-eye Harris at Eccles'.

"Th' Cyclone ranch has got some with th' itch. It 'll mean a lot o' work-an' then some.

"LaFrance wants to bleed you for two hundred. Don't you. He 'll get too rich to have me for a son-in-law."

Karl nodded his head. "Farming iss goot," he murmured, "—mit vasser." Dave glanced at him.

"Them new steers o' th' Double Y oughta fetch forty in th' Fall. Will, too."

"Farming iss goot," repeated Karl, "—mit vasser. Also, to lend money. But Camerons, dey pay und der money lies idle. Ven do ve eat up der Double Y, Dave?"

Dave glanced at him sullenly. "Why don't you let me kill that d —n Peters? Are you afraid I 'll get hurt?"

"Alvays I fear. I haf no one bud you, *du Spitzbub*. But kill him? Ach! Soon anoder manager come. Killing iss not goot, Dave. You must plan besser, *aber* I do id. Dat make you feel sheep, *du Schwarzer Spitzbub, vas?*"

"I 'll get 'em. Guinea Mike 's shot up."

"Vell, he iss anoder von likes killing. Who vas id?"

"Stranger. Reminded me of a feller, somehow-an' then, again, he did n't. Deals a slick hand at cards."

"Ach, cards! Alvays der cards! Who know dem besser as me? Who pay for dem so much? Cards und killing, dey are no goot."

"Well, let's roost," suggested Dave, and led the way to the inner room. Karl fastened doors and windows, put out the light, and followed him.

Chapter VI
An Honest Man and a Rogue

How to do it? That was the question that hammered incessantly at Dave's brain until he actually dreamed of it. Dreaming of it was the only satisfactory solution, for in his dreams matters arranged themselves with the least possible effort on his part and with little or no danger-though, to do him justice, danger was the consideration which had the least weight. But the dreams presented lamentable gaps which Dave, in his waking moments, found it impossible to bridge. Winter had given way to Spring and Buck Peters, aided by the indefatigable Ned, was rounding the ranch into a shape that already cut a figure in the county and would do so in the Territory before long.

The Double Y owed nothing to Dave. His animosity was confined strictly to Buck; but he knew that Karl was resolved to usurp ownership of the range he had come to look upon as his own. And Dave had become imbued with the idea that his own interests demanded the realization of Karl's wishes.

Why the German had become interested in this handsome idler, so many years younger than himself, Karl could not have explained. True, he was alone in the world, he was a red fox where the other was a black one, while Dave's present sinfulness and inclinations were such as the elder man understood and sympathized with. Yet these were hardly reasons; Karl himself never would have advanced them as such. Perhaps he had it in mind to use him as a cat's-paw. Few of our likes or dislikes have their origin in a single root.

If only they could "eat up" the Double Y! Dave cursed the obsession which threatened his fortunes; he cursed the energetic Buck who was rearing obstacles in his way with every week that passed; and he cursed his own barren imagination which balked at the riddle.

No heat of the inward furnace showed in the cool gravity of his face. Sitting at a table in the crowded bar-room of the Sweet-Echo, he seemed intent on mastering the difficulties of a particularly intricate game of solitaire. From time to time some of those at the same table would become interested, only to turn away again, baffled by their lack of knowledge.

The usual class of patrons was present, augmented in number, since the spring round-up was at hand and strangers were dropping in every day. Later in the evening, most of those present would gravitate to the lower end of the town where forms of amusement which Sandy McQueen did not countenance, were common. To none of these did Dave give any attention, though he looked with interest at Tex Ewalt when he entered; the increased hum of voices and several loud greetings had taken his mind momentarily from his thoughts. Tex's reputation had lost nothing in force since the excitement of his advent.

Suddenly and for the first time Dave hesitated in his play. He looked fixedly at the Jack of Spades and removed it from the pile where it lay. He paused with it in his hand. The Jack of Spades was in doubt-so was Dave.

A querulous voice was damning Buck Peters. *"Donner und Blitzen*! Vas it my fault *der verruchter* bull break loose *und ist hinaus gegangen*? 'Yah!' says Buck, 'Yah!' loud, like dat. Mad? — *mein gracious*! Vot for is a bull, anyhow? 'Gimme my time,' I say; 'I go.' 'Gif you a goot kick,' says Buck; 'here, dake dis und get drunk und come back *morgen*.' I get drunk und go back und break his d —n neck-only for leetle Fritz."

"Leetle Fritz" sat swinging his legs, on the bar. He looked at his father with plain disapproval. "Ah, cheese it, Pap!" was his advice. "What's th' good o' gittin' drunk? Why can't you hol' y' likker like a man?"

A roar of laughter greeted this appeal, at which even Gerken smiled gleefully. He was glad that Fritz was smart, *"une seine Mutter."*

Dave pushed the Jack of Spades back into the pack. He arose and sauntered over to the bar. "That's th' way to talk, Pickles," he endorsed, tickling the boy playfully in the ribs. "Yo 're a-going to hold yore likker like a man, ain't you?"

"No sirree! Ther' ain't goin' to be any likker in mine. I promised mother."

"Bully for you!" Dave's admiration was genuine and the boy blushed at the compliment. Like many other rascals, Dave was easily admitted into the hearts of children and simple folk and women and dogs. Bruce, the collie, was nuzzling his hand at that moment and the broad, foolish face of Gottleib was beaming on him. "Hi, Slick! Pickles 'll have a lemonade. I 'll have a lemonade, too; better put a stick in mine, I 'm a-gettin' so 's I need one. An' Pap 'll have a lemonade, too-oh! with a stick, Pap, with a stick —I would n't go for to insult your stomach."

They drank their lemonades, Gottleib's face expressive of splinters, and a minute later Pickles sat alone while his father endeavored to win some of Dave's money and Dave endeavored to let him. Tex tilted his chair and with a fine disregard for alien fastidiousness, stuck his feet on the edge of the table and smiled. He almost crashed over backward at sight of a figure that entered the room from the hall. "God bless our Queen!" murmured Tex, "he 's a long way from 'ome. Must be a remittance man come over the line to call on Sandy."

H. Whitby Booth swept an appraising glance over the company and, without a pause, chose a seat next to Tex. "Surprisin' fine weather, isn't it?" he observed, taking a cigar-case from his pocket.

"My word!" agreed Tex, succinctly.

Whitby looked at him with suspicion. "Try a weed?" he invited.

"I don't mind if I do, old chap," and Tex selected one with a gravity he was far from feeling.

Whitby looked hard at him while Tex lit the cigar. It was a good one. Tex noted it with satisfaction.

"I say, are you chaffing me?" asked Whitby, smilingly.

It was a very good cigar. Tex had not enjoyed one as good in a regrettably long time. He blew the smoke lingeringly through his nostrils and laughed. "I 'm afraid I was," he admitted, "but you must n't mind that. It's what you 're here for, the boys 'll think-that is, if you don't stop long enough to get used to it."

"Oh, I don't mind in the least. And I expect to stop if the climate agrees with me."

"What's the matter-lunger? You don't look it."

"Not likely. But they tell me it's rather cold out here in winter."

"Some cold. You get used to it. You feel it more in the East, where the air 's damp."

"I 'm delighted to hear it. And the West is becoming quite civilized, I believe, compared with what it was."

"Oh, my, yes!" Tex choked on a mouthful of cigar smoke in his haste to assure Whitby of the engaging placidity of the population. "Why, no one has been killed about here since-well, not since I came to Twin River." Tex did not consider it necessary to state how short a time that had been. "Civilized! Well, I should opinionate. Tame as sheep. Nowadays, a man has to show a pretty plain case of self-defence if he expects to avoid subsequent annoyance."

"Ah, so I was informed. They seem quiet enough here."

"Yes, Sandy won't stand any disturbance. He's away to-night but Slick's got his orders. Know Sandy?"

"No. Is he the proprietor?"

"That's him: Sandy McQueen, proprietor, boss, head-bouncer, the only —"

"I say, what's the row?"

Tex's feet hit the floor with a bang. Gottleib Gerken was shaking his fist in Dave's face, Dave sitting very still, intently watchful. *"Du verdammter Schuft!"* shouted Gerken, *"Mein Meister verrathen, was!"* He sent the table flying, with a violent thrust of his foot: "I show you!"

Watchful as he was, Dave did not anticipate what was coming. As the table toppled over he sprang to his feet, the forward thrust of his head in this action moving in contrary direction to the hurtling fist of Gottleib, which stopped very suddenly against his nose. Dave staggered backward, stumbled over his chair and went crashing to the floor, where he lay for an instant dazed.

"By Jove! that was a facer," cried the appreciative Whitby. The others were ominously quiet.

The next moment Dave was on his feet, white with murderous rage. There was more than fallen dignity to revenge: Gottleib knew too much. Without the least hesitation his gun slanted and the roar of the discharge was echoed by Gottleib's plunging fall. A frenzied scream, feminine in shrillness, rang through the room. Dave's gun dropped from his hand and he sank to the floor; a whiskey bottle, flying the length of the room, had struck him on the head, and Boomerang, struggling with maniacal fury in the arms of several men, strove to follow his missile. At the other end of the bar the numbed Pickles suddenly came to life and leaped to the floor. Caught and stopped in his frantic rush across the room he kicked and struck at his captor. "Lemme go!" he shrieked, "lemme go! I 'll kill the —— ——" The men holding Boomerang ran him to the open hall door and gave him forcible exit and the stern command to "Git! an' keep a-goin'."

A sullen murmur swelling to low growls of anger formed an undertone to the boy's hysterical cries, as the men looked on at Tex's efforts to revive the stunned culprit. "Lynch him!" growled a voice. "Lynch him!" echoed over the room. "Lynch him!" shouted a dozen men, and Tex ceased his efforts and came on guard barely in time to stop a concerted rush. Straddling the recumbent figure, his blazing eyes shocked the crowd to a stand-still. With a motion quicker than a striking rattler a gun in either hand threatened the waverers. "Dutchy 's got a gun," he rebuked them; "he was a-reachin' for it when he dropped."

"That's correct," agreed a backward member. "Sure. I seen him a-goin' for it," affirmed another. They gathered about Gottleib to look for the proof.

Suddenly the door was flung open and Rose LaFrance stood in the opening. "What are you doing?" she questioned. "What is the matter with Fritz? Come here, Fritz."

The boy, released and subsiding into gasping sobs, staggered weakly toward her. She drew him close and folded him in her arms. The men, silent and abashed, in moving to allow the boy to pass, had disclosed to her the figure of the prone Gottleib and she understood. "Oh-h!" she breathed and looked slowly from one to another, her gaze resting last on Tex, the fallen table hiding from her the man he was protecting. Utter loathing was in her look and the innocent Tex was stung to defiance by it, throwing back his head and returning stare for stare.

"You wolf!" she accused, in low, passionately vibrant tones. "Kill, kill, kill! You and your kind. Is it then so great a pleasure to you? Shame to you for mad beasts! And greater shame to the cur dogs who let you do it." Her glance swept the averted faces with blasting scorn. "Come, Fritz." She led the boy out and the door was closed carefully after her by a sheepish-looking individual whose position behind it and out of sight of those scornful eyes had been envied by every man in the room.

"Well—I 'm—d—d!" said Tex, recovering his voice.

"'They that touch pitch will be defiled,'" observed Whitby, sententiously. Tex looked his resentment. He felt a touch on his leg and glanced down. Dave had recovered consciousness. "Get off me, Comin'," he requested. "Who hit me?"

"Boomerang flung a bottle at you," informed Tex. "How you feeling?"

"All serene. Head 's dizzy," he added, swaying on his feet. He walked to the nearest chair and sat down. "Must 'a' poured a pint o' whiskey into me."

"Boom passed you a quart bottle," replied Tex.

Dave glanced at the inert form of Gerken as it was carried out into the hall. "Sorry I had to do it," he said, "but I had to get him first or go under. He oughtn't to said I cheated him."

"I say, that's a bally lie, you know." Whitby's drawling voice electrified the company. Those behind him hastily changed their positions. Dave, with a curse, reached again for his gun-it lay on the floor against the wall, where it had fallen.

"Drop it, Dave," came Slick's grating command. "Think I got nothin' to do but clean up after you? Which yo 're too hot to stay indoors. Go outside and cool off."

"You tell me to git out?" exclaimed Dave, incredulously.

"That's what," was Slick's dogged reply. "The Britisher wants to speak his piece an' all interruptions is barred entirely. An' don't let Sandy see you for a month."

Dave walked over and picked up his gun. "To h—l with Sandy," he cursed. The door slammed open and he was gone.

Slick slid his weapon back onto the shelf and proceeded to admonish Whitby. "See here, Brit, don't you never call a man a liar 'less yo 're sure you can shoot first."

"But dash it all! the man is a liar, you know. The German chap said 'you d—n scoundrel! Traitor to my master, eh!' There 's nothing in that about cheating, is there?"

"Well, mebbe not," agreed Slick, "but comparisons is odorous, you don't want to forget that. Which we 'll drink to the memory of th' dead departed. What 'll it be, boys?"

Chapter VII
The French Rose

The home of Jean LaFrance, a small cabin built principally of the ever-ready cottonwood, was located in a corner of his quarter-section, farthest from the Jones' Luck River, which formed one boundary of his farm. He had designs upon more than one quarter-section, not at that time an unusual or impossible ambition, in so far as homestead laws went. His simple plan regarding residence was to move the cabin or build against it as occasion arose. The rolling country sloped steadily upward from the river to the chain of hills farther to the east. These sent down several tributary streams, all unreliable during the warm weather with the exception of one which passed close to the cabin. The conformation of the land gave a view from the cabin of one long stretch of the trail from Twin River and several short ones; opposite the house, continuing to Wayback, the trail was lost sight of.

Thus Buck was plainly visible as he loped along the trail on the morning following the Sweet-Echo tragedy, only no one happened to be observing him. As he disappeared behind the first rise, a pair of inquisitive young eyes, half closed in the effort of the mouth below to retain possession of far more than its capacity, arose above the level of the window sill and looked eagerly for an invitation to mischief. Seeing nothing that particularly called him, Pickles went out and into the barn.

Buck struck off the trail and rode along the path to the house. Spring had returned in force after its temporary retreat before the recent cold and the air bore whisperings of the mighty wedlock of nature; all about him the ecstatic song of the meadow-lark held a meaning that escaped him, vague, intangible, but thrillingly near to suggestion; the new green of the prairie melted into the faint purple of the distant hills, beneath a sky whose blue depths touched infinity. It was a perfect day and Buck, on his errand of aid to the helpless, forgave the fences and the evidence of land cultivation which threatened the life of the range. Riding close to the door he raised his quirt-and paused.

Rivalling the meadow-larks there flowed the music of a mellow contralto roice in song. His hand dropped to his side. That the language was strange made little difference: the meaning of life almost was discovered to him as he listened.

> "Earth has her flowers and Heaven her sun —
> But I have my heart.
> Winter will come, the sweet blossoms will die —
> But warm, ah! so warm
> Is my heart.

> "When the White King makes his truce with the Gold —
> How dances my heart!
> All the sweet perfumes that float in the Spring
> Rest close, ah! so close
> In my heart.

> "One day when Love like a bee, buzzing past,
> Wings close to my heart,
> Deep he shall drink where no winter can chill,
> Content, ah! content
> In my heart."

The low voice died away into silence; from afar came the soft cooing of a dove, soothingly insistent as the croon of a lullaby; the riotous call of the larks arose in gleeful chorus; within the cabin were the sounds of movement: footsteps, the pushing of a pan across the table, and then a subdued pounding which sent Buck's thoughts whirling back into the distant past to hover over one of his most sacred memories. He sat perfectly still. How many years had gone by since he had heard a good woman singing over her household tasks! How very long ago it seemed since his mother had made bread to the tune of that same 'punch, punch, slap-punch, punch'! His stern face softened into a tenderness that had not visited it since he was a boy. Mother-The French Rose-it was a pretty name.

Buck was not in the least aware of it but when a man thus links the name of a woman with that of his mother, it has a significance.

The faint nicker of a horse aroused Allday from his apathetic interest in flies; he raised his head and sent forth a resounding whinny in response; the blare of it was yet in the air when Rose stood in the open doorway.

I despair of picturing her to you, so difficult it is to portray in words the loveliness of a woman's beauty; and the charm of the French Rose was as many-hued as the changing sky at sunset; the modulations of her voice ranged from the grave, rich tones of an organ to the melting timbre of a flute, pitched to the note of the English thrush; her very presence was as steadfastly delightful as the fragrance of a hay field, newly mown. In a long life I have known but one such woman and this was she.

First, then, she harmonized. The simple gown, turned in at the throat, with sleeves rolled high on the arms for greater freedom in her work, the short skirt impeding but little her activity of movement, covered a form meant by God to be a mother of men; and the graceful column of her neck supported a head that did honor to her form. Lustre was in every strand of the black hair, against which the ears set like the petals of a flower; the contour of the face, the regularity of the features, were flawless, unless for an overfulness of the lips in repose; the natural olive complexion, further darkened by the sun-tan from her out-door life, could not conceal the warm color of the blood which glowed in her cheeks like the red stain on a luscious peach; and the mystery of her dark, serious eyes had drawn men miles to the solving-in vain.

So she stood, silently regarding Buck, who as silently regarded her. When she had first come upon him, in those few moments of unaccustomed softness when the hard mask of assertive manhood had been slipped aside, her questioning gaze had probed the depths of him, wondering and warming to what it found there. Her smile awoke Buck to a sense of his rudeness and he swept off his hat with the haste of embarrassment. "I 've come for Pickles," he blurted out, anxious to excuse his unwarranted presence.

"Is it-is it M'sieu Peters?" she questioned.

"That's me," admitted Buck. "Can I have him?" He smiled at the absurdity of his question. Of course she would be glad to get rid of such a mischievous little "cuss."

Rose considered. "Enter, M'sieu Peters. We will speak of it," she invited.

"I shore will," was the prompt acceptance. Buck's alacrity would have called forth hilarious chaffing from the Bar-20 punchers. It surprised himself. She set out a cup and a bottle on one end of the table and hastened to the other with an exclamation of dismay: *"Hélas, mon pain!"* and forthwith the "punch, punch!" was resumed, while Buck stared at the process and forgot to drink.

"Why do you take Fritz from me?" asked Rose.

Buck resumed his faculties with a grunt of disgust. "What's th' matter with me?" he asked himself. "Am I goin' loco or did Johnny Nelson bite me in my sleep? What was that: *'Take Fritz?'"*

This was seeing the matter in a different light. Buck ran his fingers through his hair and looked helpless. He poured himself a drink. "Take Fritz? Take anything she wants? Why, I'd give her my shirt. There I go again —" and he savagely, in imagination, kicked himself.

"You see —I sort o' reckoned," he faltered, "Dutch bein' one o' my boys-Pickles-Fritz-ought to be taken care of, an' —"

"So-and you think I will not take care of him?"

"Oh, no; ma'am. Never thought nothin' o' th' kind. You stick yore brand on him an' we 'll say no more about it. Yore health, ma'am."

Rose packed the dough into the pan and set it aside. Buck watched her with rueful countenance. "Now you 've gone an' made her mad," he told himself. "Guess you better stick to cows, you longhorn!"

She returned to her place and sat opposite him, her flour-stained arms lying along the table. "You shall take him, M'sieu Peters," she declared.

To Buck's remonstrance she nodded her head. *"Mais oui —*it is better," she insisted. "He grow up a man, a strong man-yes. Only a strong man have a chance in this so bad country. Yes, it is better, I call him."

"Let me," Buck interposed, and stepping to the door he cried out a yodelling call that brought Fritz scampering into the cabin with scared face: it was his father's well-known summons. Rose called him to her and put her arms about his shoulders.

"M'sieu Peters have come to take you with him, Fritz. You will go?" she asked him.

"Betcher life," said Pickles.

Buck grinned and Rose laughed a little at the callous desertion. *"Eh, bien, m'sieu —*you hear?" she said to Buck, and then, to the boy: "It please you more to go with M'sieu Peters than stay with me-yes?"

"Betcher life," repeated Pickles. "Yo 're all right, but I want to be a cow-punch an' rope an' shoot. Some day I 'll get that d —d ol' Dave Owens for killin' dad."

"*Dieu!*" Rose was on her feet, gripping Fritz so hard that he squirmed. "Dave kill-Dave —"

"Sure, he done it! Who'd yeh s'pose?" Fritz wriggled loose and stood rubbing his shoulder. Rose stood staring at him until Buck pushed him out of the room, when she sank back into her chair, covering her eyes with one shaking hand.

Outside Buck was questioning Pickles. "You rid yore daddy's bronc over, didn't you? Can you rope him? Bully for you. Get a-goin', then. We want to pull out o' here right smart." Pickles was off on the run and Buck slowly entered the cabin. He went over and stood looking out of the window. "I would n't take it so hard," he ventured. "These sort o' mistakes is bound to happen. An' it might a' been worse. It might a' been Dave went under."

Rose flung out a hand towards him. "I wish —" she began passionately and then caught back the words, horrified at her thought.

"Course you wish he had n't done it. He had n't oughter done it. Dutchy was a good man-an' a square man-an' Dave ain't neither-though I shore hates to hurt yore feelin's in sayin' so."

"*I* know him. He is bad-bad. No one know him like me." The deep voice seemed to hold a measureless scorn. Buck wondered at this.

"Well, if you know him I 'm right glad. I figgered it out you did n't."

"I know him," she repeated, and this time she spoke with a weariness that forbade further remark.

They remained thus silent until Fritz rode up on the Goat, shouting out that he was ready and long since forgetful of a scene he had not understood. Buck turned from the window. "Good-bye, ma'am, I reckon we 'll drift."

Rose came forward with extended hand. "Good-bye. You will guard him? But certainly. When you ride to town, maybe you ride a little more and tell me he is well and good. It is not too far?"

"Too far! Th' Double Y ain't none too far. I reckon you forget I come from Texas."

They waved to her just before they dropped from sight down the last dip to the trail. She was watching when they came into view again at the first gap and watched them out of sight at the end of the long stretch before the bend. Then she turned back into the room and removing the demijohn and cup from the table, she stood looking at the chair where Buck had sat. "*Voilà, un homme,*" she declared, patting gently the rough back of the chair: "a true man. They are not many-no."

Chapter VIII
Tex Joins the Enemy

Tex slung a leg over Son John and ambled away from Wayback, in the wake of Dave. His adroit and unobtrusive observance of Dave had been without results unless there were something suspicious in the long conversation held with a one-eyed puncher who rode away on a Cyclone-brand pony. Tex, however, was by no means cast down; he could not hope to pick up something every day and he already had learned the only quarter from which trouble might come to Buck. He delayed action in the hope that something tangible might turn up; and he fervently hoped that it might be before Hopalong found himself foot-loose from the Bar-20. Tex was quicker with his gun than most men but he possessed a real artist's love for a reason why action should occur in a certain way; if he were also able to show that it could have occurred in no other way, he found all the more satisfaction in the setting.

A loud splash in the nearby river brought his head around in the direction of the sound; through a break in the foliage a broad patch of water, seen dimly in the dusk of the evening, showed rapidly widening circles. "Walloper," commented Tex, immediately resolving to emulate that fish in the morning. "Though I certainly hope old Smiler won't come to the water below me for a drink: nice mouthful of mutton I'd make for his wolf fangs. What in thunder! —" his pony had plunged forward as if spurred. Tex got him in hand and whirled to face the unknown danger. The rush of the river, the steady wind through the trees, the elusive chirp or movement of some bird—only familiar sounds met his ear and there was still light enough to show only familiar objects. "Why, you white-legged, ghost-seeing plug-ugly!" remonstrated Tex. "Who do you think is riding you? Johnny Nelson? Then you must be looking for a lesson on behavior about now. Get along."

He rode slowly, not wishing to overtake Dave before he settled in Twin River. Tex had as much right as Dave to be riding from Wayback but he wished to avoid arousing the faintest hint of suspicion. There was no other place along the trail for Dave to stop, except the LaFrance cabin. Queer how opinions differed regarding the French Rose: from the extreme of all-bad to that of all-good. Judicious Tex, summing up, concluded her to be neither —"Just like any other woman: half heart, quarter intellect, and the balance angel and devil; extra grain of angel and she 's good; extra grain of devil and she 's bad." Tex, not knowing Rose personally, gave her the benefit of the doubt.

"If he stops in there I 'll miss him," said Tex. "But he 's bound to go on to Twin from there. If we come together in the trail, it's no harm done: Dave will never suspect me until he looks into my gun. Bet a hat he thinks I 'm a pretty good friend of his." He chuckled, recalling the arguments for and against Gerken on the night of the shooting. The consensus of opinion seemed to be that Dave had been within his rights but "some hasty." This was not Tex's opinion. He chuckled again as he recalled the lurid out-spokenness of Sandy McQueen's opinion which had turned the perfunctory trial into a farce and had kept Twin River on the grin for two days. "And all is gay when Sandy comes marching home," he hummed. "I 'm glad they found the gun on Dutch. Peck of trouble if he had n't been heeled. There 's me, just naturally obliged to pull out Dave. If he goes under I lose touch with the old thief who stops at home. Funny they don't get at it. There 's enough material in Twin River alone to wipe three Double Y's off the map, good as Buck is. Give him six months more and half Montana could n't do it-because the other half would be fighting *for* him, Lordy! The old-times! Folks have grown most surprising slow these days."

He had left the foot of the farm road half a mile in the rear when he heard the sound of a horse coming up behind him. The darkness hid Tex until the other was nearly abreast, when he hailed. "He did turn off to see Rose," reflected Tex, as he returned the greeting and Dave rode up.

"That you, Comin'?" said Dave. "I been wantin' to see you. Goin' anywhere particular?"

"No," drawled Tex. "I was just considerin' which of them shanties in Twin 'd have th' most loose money."

"Bah!" scornfully exclaimed Dave, drawing alongside him. "There ain't no money in Twin River. You an' me could make a good haul over in Wayback but I got somethin' better 'n that. Let's go into Ike's. Ike never hears nothin' an' all th' rest is deaf, too. I want to talk to you."

Ike's was primitive to a degree but once removed from a tent. The log walls of the low, single room were weather-proofed in several ingenious ways, ranging from mud to bits of broken boxes. The bar was a rough, home-made table, the front and both ends shut in by canvas on which was painted: "Don't shoot here." Ike was careful either of his legs or his kegs. A big stove stood in a shallow trough of dirt midway between the bar and the door, accepting salival tributes in winter which developed into miraculous patches of rust in summer. Several smaller tables, likewise home-made, a number of boxes, and a few very shaky chairs completed the furnishings. It was the reverse of inviting, even in the bitter cold of winter, but Ike never lacked for customers of a sort and probably made more money than any one in Twin River. Ike himself was a grizzled veteran of more than fifty years, sober, taciturn, not given to cards but always ready to "shake-'em-up." Dice was his one weakness at any time of the day or night. To be sure, he always won. He had them trained.

The regular *habitués* were a canny lot, tight-lipped, cautious, slow in speech and in movement, except at a crisis. The opening door was a target for every eye and not a straight glance in the crowd; each seemed trying, like the Irishman when he bent his gun-barrel, to make his eyes shoot around a corner. And they all took their liquor alike, squeezing the glass as if it were a poker hand and they were afraid to show the quality or quantity of the contents. It was usually easy to pick out an occasional caller or a stranger: he was drunk or on the way to it; Ike's regulars were never drunk.

The entry of Dave and Tex was noted in the usual manner. Dave had long been recognized as one of their kind. Tex, since his dramatic entry into Twin River, had shown no displeasing partiality for hard work. Both were welcomed therefore, silently or laconically, not to be confounded with sullenly. As they sauntered over to an unoccupied corner table, Tex noticed Fanny sitting in a game with Bill Tregloan, both of them much the worse for liquor, while their three companions showed the becoming gravity of sober winners. Fanny closed one of his wide, woman's eyes and nodded to them with a cheerful grin, but Bill was too far gone to notice anything but his persistent bad luck. "D —n this poker game," he bellowed, banging a huge fist on the table, "If 't was Nap I might win something, but here I 've been sittin' all night, scatting my money in the say."

Fanny laughed uproariously but the others eyed him in silent disapprobation. What "Nap" might be they did not know, but poker was good enough for them.

"What 'll you drink, Comin'?" asked Dave as a preliminary.

"I ain't drinkin', Dave, not never. But I 'm right ready an' anxious to hear o' that somethin' good you 've got to deal out."

"Y-e-e-a —well, it's this way," began Dave, sampling his liquor in the customary gulp. He set down his glass to ask abruptly: "Got any friends in Twin River?"

"Nary friend-nor anywhere else," replied Tex, indifferently. "Don't need 'em-can't afford 'em."

Dave looked hard at Tex. "What about that bunch Fanny travels with?" he suggested.

"You said friends," was the significant answer.

"All right-all th' better. I seen you play a mighty good game o' cards."

Tex snorted. He could not restrain it. Was it possible Dave was aiming to milk him? "I'm allus willin' to back my play," he declared, drily.

"You won't have to back it. If yo 're as good as I hopes, I 'll back it. It's this way: I want to back you agin' a man as thinks he can play. He 's considerable of a dealer-considerable-an' he won't play me because he beats me once an' thinks I 'm no good. He 's got money, a-plenty, an' I don't want a dollar. You keeps what you wins-an' I wants you to get it all." He turned and called across the room: "Ike, flip us a new deck." The pack in his hands, he faced Tex again. "Suppose we plays a few hands an' you gimme a sample o' yore style."

Tex thrust his hands in his pockets and tipped back in his rickety chair. "Lemme get this right," he demanded. "You backs me to play, pockets th' losses, gives up th' winnin's, all to best th' other feller-on'y he must n't win."

"You got it."

"On'y he must n't win."

"That's what I said."

"Must be a friend o' yourn."

"Y-e-s," drawled Dave, with a sardonic smile.

"Who is it?"

"Peters o' th' Double Y."

"Ah! I 've heard o' him."

"An' you an' me an' a lot more 'll hear too d —d much o' him if we don't run him out. He 's a heap too good for Twin River."

"How 'll you rope him?"

"I got a bait-best kind. They allus fall for a woman." Dave's sneering tones, as he broke open the pack, sorely taxed his companion's self-control. "What'll we play?" he continued. "Better make it 'stud.' Th' gamer a man is th' quicker he goes broke at stud an' Peters is game enough."

Tex dropped back into position and took his hands from his pockets. "I shine at stud," he remarked softly, taking the deck Dave offered him. The joker was sent spinning across the room to glance from the nose of Fanny who sat sprawlingly asleep, nodding to an empty table; the Cornishman, swearing strange oaths, had gone off some time previously; two of the others were renewing the oft-defeated attempt to dice Ike to the extent of a free drink; the rest of the inmates were attending strictly to business and if an occasional oblique glance was aimed at Tex and Dave it did not show the curiosity which may have directed it.

"He must n't win," murmured Tex. The cards rustled in the shuffle. Dave grunted. "An' you must n't win?" Tex inquired.

"I 'm a-goin' to do all I know how to win," warned Dave.

"Oh, that o' course," sanctioned Tex. "Shift this table. I likes to see th' door," he explained.

Dave complied, looking sharply for some other reason. The lamp on the wall divided its light fairly between them. Dave was satisfied.

"Is it for love or money?" asked Tex.

"Might as well make it interestin'," suggested Dave.

Tex thought for a moment. "No," he dissented, "'Dog eat dog' ain't no good. But we 'll keep count so you can see how bad you make out."

It was no game. Tex won as he liked with the deck in his hand and his remarks on Dave's dealing were neither complimentary nor soothing. "Duced bad form, as the Britisher would say," was his plaintive remonstrance at Dave's first attempt; "you palms th' pack like a professional." Sometime later, as he ran his finger nail questioningly along the edge of the cards, he shook his head in sorrow: "You shore thumbs 'em bold an' plenteous, Dave," was his caustic comment. And then, querulously: "D —n it, Dave! don't deal me seconds. Th' top card is plenty good enough for me."

It required very little of this to cross Dave's none too easy temper. He pushed the cards away from him, pleased and annoyed at the same time. "You 'll do," he declared, "if you can't clean up Peters there ain't a man in th' country as can." A sudden suspicion struck him. Tex had reached out with his left hand to pick up the deck. "Where 'd you get that ring, Comin'? I never seen it afore."

A swift movement of the fingers under the idly held pack and Tex extended his hand, palm up. The band of dark metal, almost unnoticeable on the brown hand, was as plain on the palm side as Dave had seen it to be on the back of the hand. "Belonged to my wife," said Tex, the cynical undertones in his voice bearing no expression in his face. "I wear it on our wedding anniversary."

"Excuse *me*," was Dave's hasty apology. He pushed back from the table. "Keep in trainin', Comin'. I 'll see Rose an' start things rollin'. Jean will take you in as an old friend when we 're ready. We must n't be too thick; Peters might hear of it. Good-night. I 'm goin' to roost."

"Night, Dave." Tex sat fingering the cards with something very like wonder on his face. "What sort of a babe-in-arms is this for deviltry? He used to have better ideas. The cold weather up here must have congealed his brains. Break Buck Peters at stud! Maybe he plans to get us shooting. I 'll bet a hat old Schatz never hatched that scheme." He took the cards over to Ike and strolled out, unseating Fanny with one sweep of his foot as he went.

Fanny arose to his feet, looking for trouble. He was sober in his legs but his ideas crossed. No one being near him, he surveyed his backless, up-ended chair with blinking ferocity. "Cussed, buckin' pinto! Think I can't ride you, huh? Watcher bet?" He righted the chair and took a flying seat, all in one movement. "Huh! Ride anythin' on four laigs," he boasted. Lulled by this confidence in his horsemanship, his head began to nod again, in sleep.

Tex ambled over to the Why-Not where his entry was greeted with boisterous invitations to a game. Four bright boys had come over from the Fort and were cleaning up the crowd. Tex was ashamed of them, and said so, refusing to go to the assistance of such helpless tenderfeet. He borrowed paper and pencil of Dutch Fred and rapidly composed a note to Buck. Much adroit manoeuvring secured the services of Cheyenne Charley, not yet too drunk to understand the repeated instructions of Tex. Thus it came about that Buck, without knowing how it got there, found on his table a communication of absorbing interest, signed: "A Friend." It read:

Buck Peters: Don't play cards with strangers, especially stud poker. Dave Owens aims to have Rose rope you into a frame-up. John is in it, too. Mighty easy to plug you in a row.

"A Friend," mused Buck. "An' Rose is to rope me into a crooked game. I 'm d —d if I believe it." He made as if to tear the paper but changed his mind. "No, I 'll just keep this. Mebby there 'll be more of 'em. Jake!" he roared.

"—lo!" came the answering roar.

"Who's been here this mornin'?"

"Where?"

"At th' ranch."

A huge, slouching figure with a remarkable growth of hair appeared in the doorway. Jake was a cook because he was too big to ride and too lazy to dig. He ran his fingers through his hair, considering. "At th' ranch?" he repeated. "There was Pickles an' Ned, o' course; and Cock Murray come over to ask —"

"I don't mean them, I mean some stranger."

"Stranger? Where?"

"Right here in this room."

"Ther' ain't been no stranger. What'd he do?"

"Do? Why-why, he stole all th' silver, that's what. It's gettin' so I 'll have to lock up all th' valuables every time I go out, yo 're that interested in yore cookin'. Course, you need th' practice, I agree. Sling on th' chuck, you blind, deaf elephant. I got to get."

Jake rapidly retreated. In the kitchen he paused and ran his fingers through his hair. He looked scared. "Stole th' silver! Lock up th' valuables! He must be loco." Whereupon he stole out of the back door and concealed two stones in his clothes, where they would be handy. At close quarters he was a very grizzly for strength but if Buck should start to shoot him up from a distance, he did not purpose to be altogether at a disadvantage. Thus fortified he prepared to serve the meal.

Chapter IX
Any Means to an End

Jean LaFrance carefully cleaned his boots and stepped into the cabin. *"Bon jour, ma belle Rose. Breakfast is ready, eh? But for why you make three to eat?"*

"Did you not see, on the trail?"

"No." He took up a bucket of water and a tin basin, going to a bench outside, to wash. In a few moments a horseman loped into view and disappeared again, hidden by an intervening rise. At sight of the rider a look of fear flashed across the face of Jean and he smothered a curse, hastily re-entering the cabin to dry his hands. "Dave!" he exclaimed.

"Yes," assented Rose, impassively.

"You know he come?"

"No," as expressionless as before.

"For why he come some early? But yes! Schatz, he send the money, eh? Eh?"

Rose shrugged her shoulders doubtfully and answered the consequent look of anxiety on Jean's face by placing her hands on his shoulders and gently shaking him. *"Wait till he comes, mon père,"* she encouraged him.

He nodded his head, unconsciously squaring his shoulders in response to the subtle appeal to his manhood. At the sound of the horseman's feet he went outside. Dave's smiling cheerfulness relieved his mind and he returned the greeting with newborn good humor, leading the horse off to the stable while Dave went indoors.

The handsome animal glowed with the health of youth; not a trace of his evil nature showed in the sparkle of his eyes, and the clear red of his cheek still stood proof against the assaults of a life of reckless debauchery. "Hello, Rose," he cried, "I could n't stay away no longer. I come up last night but you 'd turned in." Encircling her waist he drew her to him to kiss her on the cheek, laughing good-naturedly at the interposed hand. "All right, have it your own way. But I wants you to know I never aims to kiss a girl yet, as I don't kiss her, come kissin'-time."

"It is not kissing-time for me, Dave-no. Not for any man. Why you stay away so long?" she asked-and could have bitten her tongue for it the next instant.

"Missed me, did you?" commented Dave, delighted. "Well, you see I —" he hesitated.

"You do not want to tell for why you kill that unoffensive man and leave Fritz without a father." The contempt in her voice cut like a whip.

"Unafensive!" he repeated, the color ebbing from his face to leave it the dangerous white of the fated homicide. "He was that unafensive he knocked me off my feet an' started to pull a gun on me. It was an even break. That's more 'n yore dad allows when anybody tries to rush him."

She winced as if struck. "Is it not promise you speak nothing of this?"

"I ain't a-speakin' of it. Nobody knows 't was him. Leastwise nobody but me. I would n't 'a' dug it up on'y you go accusin' me o' killin' when I has to protect myself."

Jean was heard approaching and Rose made a weary gesture of submission. *"Eh, bien.* Me, I know nothing but what I hear. Do not be angry when father comes."

"Peters, I suppose. D —n him for a liar." His face cleared as Jean entered. "Well, I got bad news for you, Jean. Schatz says he can't let you have that money just now, but he 'll remember you."

"Good! Soon, I hope," and Jean rubbed his hands in pleased anticipation as he drew up to the table.

* * * * *

Dave sat silently watching Rose, after Jean had left them to go to his work. She went about her daily duties, patiently waiting. Something in Dave's manner told her he had come for more than the mere pleasure of seeing her.

"Rose, sit down," he said at last. "I want to talk to you." She seated herself obediently and faced him.

"Allons," she prompted him.

"You see, it's this way: Here 's me, errand boy for Schatz. I draws my time, same as I 'm a-punchin' for him, but what is it? Not enough to live on. I can make more with th' cards, a whole lot more, on'y you says no. An' there ain't nothin' reglar 'bout gamblin', anyhow. Schatz is honin' for his ranch. He 's bound to get it an' I 'm bound to help him. 'Cause why? I strike it rich. Schatz will put me on as foreman or mebby better. Now, how do we get th' ranch? Break that McAllister-Peters combine, that's how. An' how do we break 'em? You."

"Me?"

"You. It's pie. You get him here-Peters-an' I got a man as 'll clean him out like a cyclone lickin' up a haystack. You get him here, that's all. You know how. I ain't a-goin' to be jealous of a girl as breaks off a kiss in th' middle an' han's me back my end of it. You ain't woke up yet, Rose, an' when you do, I 'll be there."

"You will be there."

"You bet-with aces-four of 'em." He nodded with confident assurance. "You get Peters a-comin' here an' then some night Comin' Thirty drops in casual to see yore daddy. That 'll be all. Comin' knows his business."

"Who is Comin'?"

"Who is he?" Dave grinned. "Well, he's th' on'y man can deal a deck between th' Mississip' an' th' Rockies. When Peters gets through with him he won't think so much o' that feller he met in Cheyenne —H —l!" He sprang to his feet, consternation on his face. Rose gazed at him in mute wonder. "It can't be!" he muttered, "he went out long ago." He was silent in

491

troubled speculation for a while. "Rose," he continued abruptly, "you ask Peters, first time you see him-when 'll you go? To-day?"

"Go where?"

"Over to th' ranch," he explained, impatiently. "You 've got to set her rollin'. Go over to see Pickles, can't you?"

"Yes, if you say go."

"All right. Go to-day. An' ask Peters when he 's seen Tex Ewalt. Don't forget th' name: Tex Ewalt."

"Tex Ewalt. I go now. It may be difficult. Men do not come here like before —"

"Before I showed 'em th' way. You 'll get Peters, if you try right."

"And you? Is it to Big Moose you ride?"

"No, I got to go to Wayback. Will I throw th' leather onto Swaller?"

"No, Swallow come when I call."

"All right. Then I'll hit th' trail. What, you won't? Wait till you wake up." He went off laughing and in a minute more swung past the house with a rattle of harness and shout of farewell. Rose stood in the doorway, motionless, looking after him.

"If I try right. You beast!" The words came through her lips laden with unutterable loathing. She put her hands before her eyes to shut out the sight of him and turned back into the room, throwing out her arms in despair. "What can I do?" she asked passionately; and again: "What can I do?"

* * * * *

To Tex, grimly watchful in the bar-room of the Why-Not, her coming brought a shock. He remembered her as she appeared when publicly denouncing him for a crime he had not committed, a memory that ill prepared him for the all-pervading charm of her beauty. Approaching rapidly, a glorious figure, sitting the powerful black with unaffected grace, her grave loveliness smote him with a sort of wonder. Plunging through the ford in a series of magnificent leaps, the rifted spray flashed about her in the sunlight like bursting clouds of jewels. The solid ground once more under his feet, the black settled into his stride and they were away, the blue sky above the distant hills set wide for them, a gateway of the gods. "When she had passed it seemed like the ceasing of exquisite music," murmured Tex.

Dutch Fred laughed genially at his companion's interest. They two were alone in the room. "Der French Rose, a fine voman, yes," he remarked, with open and honest admiration. "You like her?"

Tex stared steadily out of the window as he answered:

> "'Had she been true
> If Heaven had made me such another world
> Of one entire and perfect chrysolite
> I 'd not have sold her for it.'"

"Sold her! Sold her for a —vot? Vot you talk, anyvay?"

"That, my friend, is what the nigger said when the shoe pinched. There 's a h —l of a lot of tight shoes in th' world, Fred."

Fred walked to the door and gazed solemnly after Tex as he rode away; then he walked back to the bar and solemnly mixed himself a fancy drink, which he compounded with the judgment of long experience. He set down the glass and admonished it with a pudgy forefinger: "How *he* know she vear tight shoes, vat?"

But the glass had already given up all it contained.

Swallow, meanwhile, was putting the trail behind him with praiseworthy speed, and brought Rose within hailing distance of the ranch house just as Jake, with his carefully concealed stones, re-entered the kitchen. As she dropped from her horse Buck appeared at the door and sprang forward to greet her, his stern face aglow with pleasure. "Why, ma'am, I 'm right glad to see you," he declared, appreciative of the firm clasp of the hand she gave him. "Honest as a man's," was his thought. "Jake! O-o, Jake!" he called.

Jake tip-toed to the door and peered cautiously forth, heaving a huge sigh of relief at the new development. "Better run him in the stable, Jake," advised Buck. "An' take some o' th' sweat off 'n him. Take yore time. We 'll wait. You see," he went on to Rose, "none of th' boys is up; but Ned ought to be here right soon. An' Pickles, Pickles 'll be that pleased he won't eat nothin'. Pickles says yo 're a brick an' he likes you 'most as well as Whit."

Her bubbling laughter set Buck to laughing in sympathy and they stood, one at either side the table, looking at each other like two happy children, moved to mirth by they knew not what.

"It is a disappointment I have not come before, M'sieu Peters," said Rose, "you make me so very welcome. But Whit-who is Whit?"

"Whit? Oh, he's th' Britisher we took on when-when we went short a hand. He 's willin' an' strong an' learns quick, though he shore has some amazin' ideas about cows."

The momentary clouding of her face as she recalled how he had "gone short a hand," he allowed to pass without comment and went gayly on. "Pickles, he likes to hear him tell stories; fairy stories, you might call them, but they ain't like no fairy stories I ever heard. An' he tells 'em like he believes 'em. I ain't right certain he don't. Pickles does. You would n't think a kid like that would take to fairy stories, would you, ma'am?"

"No-o. Always he is for the grand minute-to be a man, to ride, to throw the rope, —like that. And to shoot-he must not shoot, M'sieu Peters."

"Well, you see, ma'am, he-you —I —" he was clearly embarrassed, but Truth and Buck were Siamese twins and always moved in pairs. Hot and uncomfortable as it made him, he had to confess. "Why, he 's just naturally boun' to shoot. Yesterday I give him a rifle an' a big bunch o' cartridges. He won't hurt nothin', ma'am."

"*Mais non* —I hope not. Make him to be-to be good. A strong man can be good, M'sieu Peters?"

Buck frowned in thought. "Yes," he declared. "But there 's more ways than one o' bein' good. Our way 'd never do for some places, an' their way 'd never do for us. Th' quickest man with a short gun I ever knowed an' one as has killed considerable few, first an' last, he 's a good man, ma'am. He would n't lie, nor steal, nor do a mean act. An' he never killed a man 'less he was driven to it. I say it an' I know it. I 'd trust him with my life an' my honor. An' there 's more like him, ma'am, a-plenty." He stood tensely upright, an admirable figure, deep in earnest thought. And she stood watching him, silent, studying his face, absorbing his words with a thirsty soul: the firm conviction of a man who, intuition told her, was sound to the core. "This is a rough country," he continued, "with rough ways. There 's good men an' bad men. Th' bad men are th' devil's own an' it seems like th' good men are scattered soldiers with a soldier's work to do. If a bad man takes offence an' you know he means to get you if he can, it's plumb foolish to wait till yo 're shot before you begin shootin'. He did n't begin with you an' he shore won't stop with you, an' it's your plain duty to drop him at th' first threatenin' move. Mebby you won't have to kill him, but if you must, you must. I don't say it's right but it's necessary. That's all, ma'am."

He turned to her with a whimsical smile. Her face was alight with a heartfelt gratitude, for Buck, all unknowingly, had exonerated her father, in showing her a new aspect of his doubtful matter from the view-point of a man among men. She passed her hand across her eyes in a swift gesture, then laid it for an instant firmly upon his shoulder. "*Merci, mon ami*," she said quietly. That shoulder, whenever he thought of it, tingled for days after, in a way that to Buck was unaccountable.

A moment later Jake appeared. "Ready in two shakes," he promised, referring to the meal.

"Can't you rustle up somethin' extra, Jake?" asked Buck. "You know we got company."

Jake assumed an air of nonchalant capability. "Well, now, I reckon," he answered; in spite of himself a hint of boasting was in his voice. "What do you say to aigs?"

"Aigs?" repeated Buck, his eyes widening.

"Aigs!" reiterated Jake, complacently.

Rose looked on in much amusement while Buck's astonished stare wandered down half the length of Jake's lofty height and stopped. "Are you carryin' 'em in yore pockets?" asked Buck.

"In my pockets!" exclaimed Jake. He glanced down. What in blazes did he have in his pockets? A hasty investigation brought forth two large stones.

"What in-what are you carryin' *them* for?" asked Buck, with lively curiosity.

Jake turned to Rose with his explanation: "You see, ma'am, it's th' cyclone. I got a' almanac as says a cyclone is a-comin' an' due to-day, an' I did n't want to be blown onto th' top o' one o' these yer mountains an' mebby freeze to death." Rose's responsive peal of laughter repaid him, and, withering Buck with a look, he retired to the kitchen to cook his magically acquired eggs.

The meal was nearly finished when Pickles appeared, late as usual. Ned had been given up by Buck, who explained his absence as probably due to the development of some unexpected duty. Rose, awaiting a more favorable opportunity to introduce the real object of her visit, had deliberately prolonged the enjoyment of listening to his conversation. His friends would not have known the usually taciturn Buck. Quite equal to the production of a flow of language when language was desirable, his calling and environment seldom found it necessary. Indeed, if brevity were the sole ingredient of wit, few men had been wittier. But to-day he surpassed himself in eloquence; and it was in the midst of an unconsciously picturesque narrative that he was interrupted.

There came a scramble of hoofs, the slam of a door, a rapid padding of moccasined feet, followed by a yell from Jake and the taunting treble of a boyish voice, and Pickles sped into view, clutching the door frame as he ran, and swinging himself out of range. His back toward them and his head craned in the direction of Jake to insure the full effect of a truly hideous grimace, he jeered that worthy for his bad marksmanship: "Yah! you missed me ag'in! W'y don't you use a gun like a man?" and by way of emphasis he shook the light rifle he was carrying. As Jake directed a missile with unerring skill at anything short of a bird on the wing, it is to be presumed that, with Pickles as a mark, he did not try very hard. It is certain that he was chuckling gleefully as he went to pick up the dishcloth, a large remnant of what looked suspiciously like the passing of a blue flannel shirt.

Satisfied there was no immediate danger from the rear, Pickles wheeled about. "Buck, I near got —" he stopped short. "Rose!" he exclaimed and looked sharply from her to Buck and back again. "You ain't a-goin' to take me back?" he asked, doubtfully.

Rose shook her head as she looked at him. It was a new Pickles she saw. The roguish mischief had gone from the eyes which, when he faced them, had been alive with eager intensity; the air of precocious anxiety, tribute to a happy-go-lucky father (oftener "happy" than lucky) had vanished completely; motionless as he stood in his hopeful expectancy, he was aquiver with life. "No, Fritz," she assured him, "M'sieu Peters, he need you-more than me-yes."

Pickles was at the table in a moment. "Betcher life he does," he agreed. "You don't want a boy, anyhow. I 'd have a girl if I was you. Say, Buck," he informed between bites, "I seen Ned an' he says that d —n bull's broke out again. He 's gone after him. An' Cock Murray says: Can you lend him a hat. That wall-eyed pinto o' his made b — out o' his 'n."

"You young scallywag! You must n't swear afore a lady-not never. An' you must talk polite, besides. Don't you never forget it."

Pickles looked straight into Buck's stern eyes, without fear. "I won't," he promised, earnestly. "Gosh! I 'm hungry," and he proceeded to prove it. And Rose knew then that Pickles would grow up a "strong man" —and a good man, after the ideas of M'sieu Peters, which, she had become convinced, were very good ideas, indeed.

Pickles had long since departed with a hat for the far-distant Murray; the boys had straggled in and gone again from the bunk-house, where Jake ministered to their amazing appetites; and the afternoon sun was casting shadows of warning before Rose remembered the long ride home which was to come. A silence, longer than usual, had fallen upon them, which neither seemed to find embarrassing. Buck's inscrutable face, as he looked upon her, told nothing of his thoughts; but on hers was a soft wistfulness that surely sprang from pleasant imaginings. She pushed back her chair at last with a murmur of regret. Jake was glad to hear it. He had begun to have anxious misgivings regarding his job. Buck glanced through the window and really saw the outside world for the first time in two hours. He sprang to his feet and exclaimed in bewilderment. "First time in my life I ever did it," he declared. Rose looked an inquiry. "First time th' sun ever stole a march on me that way," he explained. "Reckon I must a' been some interested in your talk, ma'am," and his humorous smile was deliciously boyish. The sparkle in her eyes and the flush on her cheeks told that Rose discerned a compliment higher than the spoken one. She began to draw on her thick man's gloves with an air almost demure.

"It is very selfish that I have make you waste so much time, M'sieu Peters," she apologized, her eyes intent upon the gloves.

Buck stared. There was a certain grimness in his humor as he answered: "Hm! Well, I 'm a-goin' to waste some more. That is, I will if you don't run away from Allday. He 's good, but that black o' yourn has got th' laigs of him, I reckon."

She watched him as he strode away for the horses, deciding how best to approach the object of her visit. True to her nature it was less an approach than a direct appeal. As they set off together she spoke abruptly: "What time did you see Tex Ewalt last? I think —I am sure-it is better if you have not see him for a long time-so."

"Well, I ain't seen him in a long time." He was plainly surprised. "Do you know Tex?" he asked, wonderingly.

She shook her head. "No. Some one ask me-but you have not seen him. That is good. Once I tell you I am glad if you come to see me about Fritz."

"Shore I 'll come," he promised heartily.

"You must not," she warned him. "In the morning, a little while, yes; at night or to stay long-no."

A light broke in upon Buck, who recalled the mysteriously delivered letter of that morning. The wholesome admiration for a lovely woman, the natural pleasure in an experience infrequent in his man-surrounded life, began to concentrate and take definite shape in his mind at the promised vindication of his judgment. He tested her shrewdly: "You don't want to see me," was his brusque comment.

She looked reproachfully at his set profile. "*Mais, quelle folie*! I am glad to see you always," she assured him, "but it must be like that. It is better." She hesitated a moment and continued: "It is better *aussi*, if you will not play cards. I —I like it, much, if you will not play cards." Her heightened color and diffident manner showed what it cost her to make it a personal request.

"By G —d! I knew it," cried Buck. He whanged Allday over one eye with his hat, and that sedate animal executed a side jump that would have done credit to a real bad pony. There are limits to all things and Allday was feeling pretty good just then, anyway.

Rose was startled. "What is it you know?" she asked, doubtfully.

Buck's face was alight with smiling gratification. Oblivious of the fact that at last he had stung Allday into remonstrance, he answered by the card, "I knowed that gamblin' habit 'd grow on me so my friends could see it. An' I hereby swears off. I never touches a deck till you says so, ma'am. That goes as it lays."

Still doubtful as to his meaning-such exuberance of feeling could scarcely be induced by swearing off anything-she questioned him in some embarrassment. "Is it I ask too much, that you will not play?"

"Too much! There ain't nothin' you can't ask me, nothin'—" he paused. "It's time I was hittin' th' back trail 'fore I say mor'n I ought. Just one thing, ma'am: I can't never know you better than I do right now. An' I want to say I 'm right proud to know you." He drew Allday down to a walk and halted as she stopped and faced him, sweeping her a salute as eloquent in gesture as were his words in speech.

The color came and went in her cheeks as she regarded him. "I am glad," she said at last, "Oh, I am very glad," and turning, she left him at a speed that vied with her racing thoughts.

Buck watched her go, the definite shape in his mind assuming a seductiveness that fascinated while it scared him. "If I was only ten years younger," he muttered. He jerked Allday's head around. "Get away, boy," he cried, and the horse struck his gait at a bound.

Buck was riding wide of the ranch house when a suspicion pricked him and he headed for home. At the door he shouted for Jake.

Jake lounged out. "What's th' noise?" he asked, languidly.

"Say, Jake, where 'd you get them aigs?"

Jake looked pained. "I got 'em off Cheyenne Charley," he asserted.

"Cheyenne Charley? Where 'n blazes did he get 'em," wondered Buck.

"Well, now, I can't rightly say," drawled Jake, "but I'm certain shore o' one thing: he never laid 'em."

"No," agreed Buck, reflectively. "Did he give 'em to you?" he added.

Jake yawned elaborately to hide the weakness of his position. "Not exactly," he admitted. "I got him drunk."

"Oh," commented Buck. He turned to ride off when another question obtruded itself, but Jake had disappeared. Buck slid to the ground and entered quietly by another door, going to where he kept his private stock. A rapid inspection showed where Jake had obtained his supply. He had appropriated Buck's whiskey to pay for eggs which it was very evident he had meant to eat himself. Only his vanity had led to their disclosure. "Th' d —n scoundrel!" said Buck, and he hurriedly secured the demijohn in the one place in the house that locked.

Chapter X
Introducing a Parasite

In the northeast corner of the Cyclone ranch, not far from the Little Jill, and in a hollow, well screened by hills and timber, One-Eye sat on his horse, smoking a brown cigarette and keeping a satisfied watch over a dozen mangy-looking cattle as they grazed intermittently in a restless, nervous way. They were a pitiful-looking handful, weak, emaciated, their skins showing bald patches and scabs, and they continually licked themselves and rubbed against the trees. While they were restless, it was without snap or vim; they were spiritless and drooping, enduring patiently until death should end their misery.

One-Eye beamed upon them, his good optic glowing with satisfaction. He had gone to some trouble and risk to cut these miserable animals cut of the herd collected by the hasty round-up, and now that he was about to have them taken off his hands he sighed with deep content. To run infected cattle onto the Cyclone's non-infected northern range was very dangerous, for his foreman was direct and unhesitating in his methods. Discovery might easily mean a bullet above One-Eye's blue-red nose-and this accounts for that puncher's satisfaction. Some men will do a great deal for ten dollars.

"D —n if they ain't beauts," he chuckled. "When it comes to pickin' out th' real, high-toned wrecks, th' constant scratchers, why I reckon I 'm some strong. He says to me 'Get th' very wust, One-Eye,' —an' I shore has obeyed orders. That two-year-old tryin' to saw through that cottonwood is a prize-winner when it comes to scabs-his tail looks like a dead tree in a waste of sand, th' way th' hair 's gone. Wait till he gets rubbin' hisself through th' brush across th' river, where Peters' cows like to hang out. He 'll hang mites on every twig; an' this kind o' weather will boom things. I heard tell that Peters examined that new herd extra cautious afore he bought it-well, boxcars an' pens can hand out itch a-plenty, so he can't prove they got it from us." He pulled out a battered brass watch and gauged where the broken hands would be if they were all there to point. "He 's due in ten minutes an' he 's usually on time. Yep: here he comes now. I 'll get my ten afore I do any more work-wish I could get ten dollars as easy every day."

Dave cantered up, his eyes fastened intently on the cattle, and he laughed cynically as he turned and regarded the puncher. "Well," he grinned, "I reckon you got th' wust that could stand bein' drove. Come on; we 'll get 'em off our hands as quick as we can —I don't want to answer no questions right now. It 'll be like puttin' a match to dry grass, th' way this dozen will cut down Peters' cows."

"It shore will," replied One-Eye. "Got that ten handy?" he inquired, carelessly.

"Why, they ain't across th' river yet," replied Dave, frowning.

"They 'll get across when I gets my ten," smiled One-Eye.

"Here 's th' money!" snapped Dave, angrily, as he almost threw the gold piece at his companion. "Fust time I was ever told I could n't be trusted for ten dollars."

"Oh, I trust you, all right-on'y I worked plumb hard for that coin, an' I want to feel it, like. Come on-take th' south side —I 'll handle th' rest."

The herd moved slowly forward into a dry ravine and finally came to the river bank. They hadn't life enough to give trouble until they understood what they were expected to do. Then the everlasting, thick-headed obstinacy, the perverse whims which all cows have to an outrageous extent, asserted itself in a manner wholly unexpected in such tottering hulks of diseased flesh. They did everything but get wet, even showing a returning flash of spirit in the way they swung their heads and kicked up their heels. Time and time again they broke and ran along the bank, and always in Dave's direction, who, until now, had nursed the belief that he was something of a cow-puncher. When half-dead cows unhesitatingly picked him out, time after time, for an easy mark, and simply walked through his defence, it was time to exchange ideas on some things.

At first One-Eye was greatly amused. He liked Dave well enough but he hated Dave's conceit-and to be present at his companion's discomfiture was very gratifying. But gradually One-Eye grew restless unto peevishness and a vast contempt settled upon him, edging his temper with a keenness rare to him. He had been trying to get one dozen imitation cows to cross an ordinarily wide river, and neither coldness nor unusual depth had any bearing on the matter. As he wondered how long he had been engaged in watching Dave's blunders and jerked out the brass watch to see, his voice rumbled and boomed with a jarring timbre and suddenness that make Dave jump.

"What th' h —l d' you think yo're doin'?" demanded One-Eye. "'Allamanleft' an' 'Ladies chain' is all right for a dance, but it 's some foolish out here. An' somebody 's goin' to lope along this way an' see us, if you don't quit makin' a jackass out er yo'rself."

Stung to the quick, Dave wheeled to face his critic, his pent-up rage almost hysterical. He had held it in, choked it back, and forced himself to be calm, but now-his purpose was never disclosed, for at the instant he wheeled, the watchful cattle leaped through the opening he had made and headed for the hills, their heads down and tails up. Dave hesitated, glancing from One-Eye to the cattle and back again, his face white and pinched. One-Eye's anger melted under his impelling sense of the ridiculous and, slapping his thigh a resounding smack, he burst into roars of laughter, until he was bent in his saddle like a man drunk or sorely wounded.

"This yer 's a circus," he finally managed to cry. "Don't get mad, Dave: we 'll make 'em cross this time or they 'll float down like logs. Come on."

When they rounded up the bunch and started it toward the river again the cows were surprisingly docile and the two drivers exchanged wondering glances. At the river edge the dozen hesitated for a moment while they nosed the water and at One-Eye's wondering command, pushed into the stream, scrambled out on the farther bank, and walked slowly into the brush. Dave's hypnotized senses were all in his eyes and he barely heard his companion speak.

One-Eye prefaced his remarks with a fluent burst of profanity, and cogitated aloud: "Cows is worse than wimmin! They *is*! Of all th' crazy hens what ever a man drove, them dozen mangy critters has got 'em all roped an' tied! What in h —l do you *think* of 'em?"

"I ain't thinkin', One-Eye," softly replied Dave. "I 'm prayin' for strength an' fortitude. I figgers I can drop th' last six from where I 'm sittin', an' it's some temptation!"

One-Eye ironed out his grin. "I'm some tempted myself, Dave. There 's things in a cowman's life to drive him plumb loco. I 've been part loco more 'n once. Mum? You bet I 'll keep mum. You don't reckon I 'm hankerin' for to collect no cold lead, do you?"

Dave scarcely heard him. He was looking across the river, a smile on his face. Before him was the Rocking Horse, and south of it, so close as to appear a part of it from that angle, lay the Hog Back. He had planned well, he told himself, when he had decided to turn infected cattle on the Double Y at that point.

"Now, they ain't goin' fur to be found while they stops near ol' Hog Back, Dave," One-Eye was saying. "Nobody hardly ever rides that way, an' they 'll drift down where th' grass is better, soon as they finds out what they 're up agin. Wonder if it was true about that feller ridin' th' Rockin' Horse all day long?" he asked, curiously.

He would have talked all day if given half a chance, but his companion, knowing One-Eye's inability to gracefully terminate a conversation, or effect a parting, mercilessly performed the operation himself. "I 'm goin' south, One-Eye. See you in town, some night," and Schatz' *protégé* cantered away, and became hidden by the brush and hills of the rough country skirting the river.

One-Eye looked after him. "Black devil!" he scowled. "If anybody gets plugged for this, you can bet it won't be little Davy. I wonder what th' Dutch Onion knowed that Dave didn't want told? Well, when me an' him is together my gun hand ain't never far from home-but I 'm surprised he did n't pump lead into me when I laughed like I did. I plumb forgot, then. Come on, boss; home for us, an' sudden. I ain't hankerin' none to be seen 'round here, *now*."

Chapter XI
The Man Outside

Dave loped through Twin River in no amiable mood. An unreasoning irritability tormented and blinded him to everything but the trail ahead. But if Dave failed to notice his friends, one of them at least bore him no ill-feeling for the oversight; this one was so solicitous for Dave's welfare that he followed all the way to the LaFrance cabin; when Dave went indoors he still lingered, hugging the cabin wall close to a window, while he listened with much interest to the talk that went on inside.

"Where 's Jean?" asked Dave, briefly, as he entered.

Rose glanced at him. The even, metallic tones meant temper and she was painfully anxious to avoid crossing him when in this mood. Her voice was soothing as a summer breeze through tree branches when she answered. "He go to the station," she explained; "something about a harrow. He will be late."

"See Peters?"

"Yes."

"What 'd he say about Tex Ewalt?"

"He have not see him for many months. He ask me if I know him."

"Well?"

"You forget to tell me what to say. I forget to answer."

"Hm! Beats th' Dutch how a woman 'll crawl out of a hole. When 's he comin' to see you?"

"I do not know. He-he is very droll, that M'sieu Peters. Always he look at me strange like he suspect something."

"He ain't got nothin' to suspect. Did n't try to kiss you, did he?"

"He never come near me one time-no; only he look at me, straight, without any smile."

"Bah! I knowed you did n't take th' right way with him. You got t' tempt them gray-eyed galoots. They 'll follow you easy enough if you show 'em there's somethin' at the end o' th' trail. You go ag'in. Make him glad to see you. Won't be long afore he 's hangin' round, then."

"*Quel jour* —when I must go?"

"Oh, whenever you get th' chanst. Soon as you kin. You got Pickles for an excuse, ain't you?"

At this point the solicitous caretaker outside risked a look through the window. His glance travelled over the shoulder of Dave, sitting with his back to the window, and rested on the face of Rose. Wrhat he saw there was a revelation: scorn, contempt, loathing, the expression any good woman might bear toward a man with a mind considerably lower than the nobler beasts; it lasted but a moment; placidity swept over the regular features as she replied. *"Mais oui,"* she admitted, "Fritz is excuse."

"Well, you won't need any excuse if you play th' game right. You 'll be excuse enough, yourself."

Enthralled by the contradiction between the expression and speech of Rose, the watcher prolonged his stare beyond safety. Rose's level gaze lifted from the unnoting eyes of Dave and rested full on the face in the window. The watcher changed instantly to the listener with one hand on his gun, but not so quickly that he failed to see the brilliant smile that flashed across the face of Rose. The alert tenseness of his attitude relaxed as he realized the significance of that smile and his shoulders heaved in strangling a laugh at the way Dave was being fooled.

Dave's moodiness persisted. He sat glowering at the point of his boot, switching it venomously with his quirt, a thing he had not carried since his experience with the Cyclone cattle at the Hog Back. It reminded him of his proven lack of ability as a driver of cows; but it was "out of this nettle, Chagrin, that he plucked the flower, Complacence"; a cynical laugh announced recovery from the black mood. "Well, there 's some as help me better 'n you do," he declared. "If I can't get Peters here, I give him somethin' that 'll keep him busy at home."

"Bien, but how?" Rose's interest had just the proper amount of congratulatory warmth and a faint wheeze escaped the listener outside as he choked back a laugh of admiration.

"I give him the itch," replied Dave, with dramatic brevity.

"Itch?" repeated Rose, in perplexity.

"Yes-itch, mange, scab! His d —n cows 'll be scratchin' their hides off afore he knows it. Th' Cyclone had it an' I got One-Eye Harris to save me out some. Mangiest lot o' cows ever *I* saw. We put 'em across th' Jill, up by th' Rocking Horse, a while back."

"But the range-is it not bad?" asked Rose, wonderingly.

"Shore is. What do I care? Makes 'em trouble, don't it? An' it 'll spoil some o' their cows, you bet."

"M'sieu Schatz, he tell you do this?"

"Smiler! The cussed ol' bear! He 's been a-layin' up all winter like a bear in a hole an' he ain't woke up yet. Poetry! an' Philosophy! an' some shifty *I*talian named Mac-Mac somethin' or other. Smiler sets a heap by Mac. Jus' sits an' reads an' hol's out his han's an' says: 'Gimme th' Double Y, Dave.' Mus' think I carry it in m' hat."

"But you will get it, Dave-yes."

"You bet yo' boots I 'll get it. Peters 'll be so sick o' that range afore I 'm done with him he 'll be glad to quit. But if you get him comin' here, it 'll be done quicker."

"I will try," murmured Rose.

The flush that went with the words was wrongly interpreted by Dave. "That's you!" he exclaimed, admiringly, and was at her side before she realized it, bending over her in a swift movement that almost caught her by surprise. He laughed easily at his defeat, in no wise discomfited. "Ain't come kissin'-time yet, eh, Rose?"

She looked up coolly, careful not to give way an inch from the nearness of him. Nothing tempts a man so much as a retreat. *"Mais non, m'sieu.* When the day, then the hour-you go too far unless," was her calm warning.

"All right. Time enough," he rejoined carelessly. "Guess I 'll drift back to Twin. Have to see Comin' an' keep him on edge, or he 'll get tired o' waitin' for that good thing I promised him. He ain't a feller as you can ask questions or I 'd cussed quick find out who he is an' where he come from."

Rose stood in the doorway until the sound of his horse's feet assured her that he was certainly on his way to Twin River. Then she went in, closed the door behind her, darkened the front windows and going to the window at the back called out clearly: "Enter. I want to talk to you, Tex Ewalt."

Tex lounged forward a step, bringing himself into view, his face the picture of mischievous amusement. He rested his arms on the sill and smiled at her. "You are a good guesser," he admitted.

"Enter," she insisted. "Not the door, no; the window-hurry."

He slipped through with the suppleness of a naked Indian and she at once shut out the night at this and the other windows. "We must beware more eaves-droppers," she explained. She motioned to a bench and seated herself near him, looking at him intently.

"I think you kill Fritz' father that night," she began. "I am sorry."

Tex bowed, as if such unjust suspicions were his daily portion, and waited.

"You are M'sieu Peters' friend?" she questioned.

Tex carefully poked two depressions in the crown of his hat and carefully poked them out again, thinking swiftly. "Yes," he replied, meeting her eyes again.

"You are Tex Ewalt. Dave call you Comin'. M'sieu Peters not know you are here. You spy for M'sieu Peters, yes?"

"Buck told you, eh? Did you tell him I was in Twin River?"

She shook her head. "But no. I guess, when I see you at the window."

Tex looked incredulous. "How did you guess?" he asked.

Rose reviewed the incidents from which she had drawn her conclusion. Tex was impressed. "That's not guessing. That's pure reason," he declared.

"You will tell M'sieu Peters about the itch?" she inquired eagerly.

"Why don't you tell him? I can't risk going out to the ranch."

"No! No! Dave must not suspect. You tell him quick so Dave not think it is me."

"Why, Dave is in a hole. Harris will squeal the minute I put my fingers on him."

"He will suspect. He must not-Oh! you do not understand."

Tex indented his hat on the left side; that was Dave: then on the right side; that was Buck: then, with careful precision, in the middle of the crown; that was Rose. He studied the result with thoughtful attention. "Like Dave?" he inquired, casually.

"I —" she began with passionate intensity but paused. "No," she answered, more calmly.

"No," repeated Tex. He smoothed out the left-hand depression with an air of satisfaction. "That 's good," he continued, "because I shall have to put a crimp, a very serious crimp, in his anatomy one of these days. I can feel it coming. What do you think of Buck?"

"M'sieu Peters is a good man —a good man," she repeated, dreamily. Tex glanced at her and back at his hat, which he eyed malevolently. Then he sighed. "Oh, well, every man has to find it out for himself," was his irrelevant comment. "Where does Schatz stand in this?"

"Dave say he try to get back the range. But Dave he is so much a liar."

"Yes, I should say he was a pretty good liar. Well, I 'll be going."

"But no!" she exclaimed. "You must eat supper," and she began hastily to make preparations.

"You did n't offer Dave any," suggested Tex, with a ghost of a grin.

"No," she admitted, seriously. "Sometimes I must, but to-night it is not necessary. I am glad, always, to see him go."

"Well, so am I," agreed Tex. "Here, let me do that."

Tex learned much during the meal that went to confirm the suspicions he had already formed. Also his opinions in regard to women-kind in general seemed less plausible than before. But though shaken, they were not routed; and when he took up his hat in leaving, the two dimples in it looked at him mockingly. "Oh, well, what's the use?" he said. "Good-night, Miss LaFrance," and he threw the hat on his head as it was.

Chapter XII
A Hidden Enemy

Cock Murray had an engagement to meet Schatz at the point where the Double Y's north line touched the Black Jack, and after he had ridden up to the south line to see how the cows were doing, as Buck had ordered, he swung west to the Black Jack to follow it down to the meeting place. As he rode he neared the Hog Back, a vast upheaval of rock, not high enough to be called a mountain, flat on the top except for hollows and gullies, scantily covered with grass and stunted trees. The Hog Back would have been called a mesa in the South, for want of a better name, though it was no more a mesa than it was a mountain. A mile long and a third of that across at its widest point, it made an effective natural barrier between the Double Y and the river, hiding a pasture of great acreage which lay between it and the precipitous cliff which frowned down upon the rushing, swishing Black Jack eighty feet below. While the round-up would, of course, comb this poor-grass part of the range for outlaws and strays, the outfit never gave it any attention because cattle seldom were found upon it.

Cock Murray, knowing that he had an hour to spare, and fond of hard riding where his skill was called into play, suddenly decided to ascend the Hog Back. Antelope were still to be found even on the range itself, along the wildest part of the south line, and he might get a shot at one if he made the climb. It was an easy task to go up the northern end, where the trail arose in a succession of steep grades; but he had no time for that and guided his pony up the rough, rocky east wall. As he gained the top he rested the horse while he looked around. It was a favorite view of his; below him lay the range and the river; he could see, on a clear day, the dot that represented his ranch house; and to the west and south lay the wild, rolling range of the Cyclone. Gradually his gaze sought nearer objects and he thought of antelope. Moving forward cautiously he kept keen watch on all sides, intending if he caught sight of one, to dismount and stalk it on foot. He had ridden nearly to the northern end when he jerked his pony to a stand, and then, gazing earnestly ahead a short distance, went on as rapidly as the broken ground would permit.

"Dead cows! What 'n h—l killed 'em? Wolves would clean 'em to the bone. G'wan, you fool!" he growled at his mount. "Scared of dead cows, are you! If you are, I 've got the cure for it right here on my heel."

The horse went on, picking its footing, and soon Murray whistled in surprise: "Cyclone brand! Bet they 've got the itch, too. Yep! Died from it, by G—d! Now, how the blazes did they get over here! Cows, and sick ones especially, don't hanker to swim the Jack. Well, that will hold over a little-let 's see how many are up here" —and he began the search. Four were all he could find, two alive and two dead. The two that still stumbled weakly in search of food, dropped as if struck by lightning as the acrid gray smoke sifted past Murray's head. "Wonder how many more there was and where they went to? Must have been here some time, judging by the carcasses. Holy smoke! If any cows gone as bad as these are loose on our range may the Lord pity *us*! Come on, bronc; we 'll see what Schatz thinks about it. Wish I had time to build a fire over these itch farms."

He was careful to guide his horse on ground barren of vegetation and not let brush or grass touch the animal when he could avoid it. As he plunged down the steep northern trail, a dried water course, he reined up hard, looking closely at the tracks in the soft alluvial soil washed down by the last rain. "Must have been about a dozen; perhaps a few less-then some did get where we don't want them-holy cats! as if we have n't got enough with our regular calf round-up!"

When he galloped up to the north line he found Schatz waiting for him. "Schatz," he shouted, "I just found four itch cows on the Hog Back. Six or eight are loose on th' ranch. They was Cyclone, an' they never crossed th' Jack by themselves."

"*Mein Gott*! Did you drive dem back?"

"Two was dead; th' other two was so near it I just dropped 'em. They could n't stand a drive even to th' river. Shall I tell Peters?"

"Shall you tell him? *Gewiss*! Vat you t'ink —I vant itch on de Double Vy? How dey come?"

"I don't know. But they must 'a' been driven. Th' Jack is cold as ice an' she runs strong by th' Rocking Horse. That's where th' tracks led to. Cows ain't goin' to swim that for fun. Why, these was all et up with th' itch-wonder they did n't drown."

"*Dank Gott*! Sick cows ain't made vell mit ice vater und schwimmin'. Dey don't lif so long like de vater vas varm. Der shock help kill dem quick."

Murray nodded, his hand resting on his gun, and Schatz noticed it. "*Gewiss*, if dey vas too veak to drive in der river, it vas besser to shoot dem. But ven dey drop dey stay mit all dem parasites. Drivin' dem off de range is besser. *Aber*, you stopped dem de best vay you could."

Murray nodded again. "Yes, yo're right-but I was n't thinkin' of shootin' no cows," he asserted calmly. "I know all about that. But I was just a-wonderin' if I should ketch some skunk of a cow-punch drivin' itch cattle on us, an' shoot him, if he 'd drop any parasites when *he* fell."

"*Ach Gott*! Alvays you shoot, like Dave! Shoot, shoot, shoot! Vy in *Himmel* should you alvays grab dot gun? Brains are in your head, and *besser* as lead in dot Colt. Brains first, and if dey don't do it, den der gun. But alvays der gun should be last. *Verstanden?*"

Murray did not reply and his companion, exchanging a few terse sentences with him, waved him towards the ranch house while he followed the line towards the Little Jill.

Buck was washing for supper when Murray arrived and kept right on with his ablutions as the puncher told his tale. Murray quite expected to see some signs of its effect on the owner, but he met with surprise and looked it. Buck Peters almost made an ally when he turned, after Murray's last word. "Murray, that's good work. Prepare for *hard* work. Send Ned here right away," he said, quietly, no trace of emotion in his voice.

Murray went out, thinking hard. When a man could take such a blow as that one had been taken, then he was clean grit all through. To smile as Buck had done —"By G —d, he 's a man!" swore the puncher. "I can't *help* liking him; wish I did n't have to help throw him. And I wish he did n't trust me like he does-ah, h —l!" he growled, savagely. "He 's a range thief, after all!"

When Monroe entered the ranch house he found his employer looking out of the window in the direction of the Hog Back, but he turned at Ned's entry. "Got work ahead, Ned. Murray found some Cyclone cows dead and wobbly on th' Hog Back. Bad case of itch. He killed th' wobblers but says th' tracks show that about a dozen was in th' herd. That means eight of 'em are on our range among the cattle. Tell th' boys we start th' round-up at daylight. If we can, we 'll make this do for the spring round-up, too; if not, then th' calves 'll have to wait till we can go for 'em. Th' north range won't have no itch cows on it yet, so take th' south first. As fast as we can cut out th' cattle that are free from it, we 'll throw 'em over on th' north range. Begin in th' Hog Back country an' clean up. Drive everything out of it."

"It's d —d funny Cyclone cows swum th' Jack," commented Monroe, a black look on his face. "By G —d, let *me* ketch anybody at that game!"

"That's th' whole thing, Ned," and Buck smiled: "To ketch 'em. I know a man who 'd clean up th' mystery if he was here, an' was told he did n't have nothin' else to do." He smiled again quietly and turned to his supper. "But he ain't here, so what's th' use."

"Mebby I —" suggested Ned, nervously.

"No, yo 're goin' to help me most by curing th' evil on th' table; never mind th' dealer, nor th' game. We 've got as many cards as we 're goin' to get-use 'em, Ned. Help me lick th' itch first-th' hows an' whys can wait."

"Yo 're right, Peters; an' we *will* lick it! But it makes me fightin' mad, a thing like this. I 'll get everything all ready to-night an' th' round-up starts with th' comin' of th' sun to-morrow. Good-night."

Buck ate slowly, his thoughts far more occupied with the problem than with the food. This was the firing of the first cannon in the fight Monroe had predicted. Who was responsible? His suspicions, guided by Monroe's warning, were directed towards Schatz, but in his present absence of knowledge they could advance no farther than suspicions. Dave's half-closed eyes sneered at him as he recalled the ambiguous threat made that first night in the Sweet-Echo: still remained suspicion only. McReady, of the Cyclone, might have designs for the Double Y, but he doubted it. They had yet free grass a-plenty, though the time was not far distant when the private ownership of the Double Y would be an invaluable asset. Still, it might be any other cowman in that part of the country-or none of them. Well, he had met problems as great as this one on the Texan range-but he had fought them with an outfit loyal to the last man, every unit of it willing and eager to face all kinds of odds for him. He now recalled those men to his mind's eye, and he never loved them more than he did now, when he realized how really precious unswerving loyalty is. Hopalong, Red, Johnny and the others of the old Bar-20 outfit, made an honor roll that held his thoughts even to the temporary exclusion of the bitterness of his present situation. If only he had that outfit with him now! Even his neighbors and acquaintances on that southern range were to be trusted and depended upon more than his present outfit. His vision, knocking patiently at first upon the door of his abstraction, at this point kicked its way in and demanded attention. Buck became aware that for some time he had been staring unseeingly at a folded paper, tucked partly under his bunk blanket. With a smothered oath he sprang from his seat, strode to the bunk and snatched up the paper. The warning it contained was better founded than the first. It read:

"Buck Peters: Itch on the YY. Crossed the Jack at the Rocking Horse. A Friend."

"If you told me who sent it across, you 'd be more of a friend," muttered Buck-in which he was less wise than Tex, who did not see the sense in having the servant removed while the master remained.

Hoofbeats rolled up in the darkness and stopped at the door of the house and a moment later Whitby entered the room, his pink, English complexion aglow with the exercise and wind-beating of his ride.

Buck was glad to see him; he needed a little of the other's cheerful optimism and after a few minutes of random conversation, Buck told him of the latest developments. Whitby's surprise was genuine, and the practicability of his nature asserted itself. This was ground upon which he was thoroughly at home.

"I say, Buck, we can show these swine a thing or two they don't know," he began. "They don't know it in the States, I 'll lay, nor north of the line either, for that matter. My Governor is a cattle man, you might say; on the other side of the pond, of course. And I 've knocked about farm land a good bit, you know. Now a chap in the same county had a lot of sheep with this what-d'you-call it-scab, they said. He used a preparation of arsenic but a lot of the beggars died, poisoned, you know. He had tried a number of other things and he got jolly well tired of the game; so he wrote to a cousin, chemist or something, and told him about it; and this chap sent him a recipe, after a bit, that killed off the parasites like winking, without injuring a single sheep."

"That ain't goin' to help us none, Whit. You ain't got th' receipt an' you don't know how to make th' stuff."

"Ah! But I do though. I gave him a hand with the silly beggars and bally good fun it was, too. We passed them through a long trough and ducked their heads under as fast as they came along. But it was work, no end, mixing the solution. There was nothing funny about that part of it."

"See here, Whit, are you really in earnest? Do you think you can make the stuff and show us how to use it?"

"Absolutely certain, dear boy. Cattle are n't sheep, but I 'll be bound it 'll do the trick."

"How fast can you run 'em though?"

Whitby reflected. "We could do a thousand a day, perhaps more. It depends on how many you do at once, you know." And Whitby went into a detailed description to which Buck gave close attention. At the end he shook his head. "Reckon we 'll have to stick to th' old way," he adjudged, regretfully. "There ain't that quantity of lime and sulphur in all Montana."

"Ah, yes; your point is good," drawled Whitby, smiling. "But your partner lives in Chicago where there is any quantity of it. If we wired him to-morrow to get the stuff and ship it at once he would do it, don't you know."

"Take it too long to get here," replied Buck, gloomily.

"Don't you think the railroad will see that such an important consignment gets off and comes through quickly, especially if the consignor is willing to pay the damage? I 'll bet you a good cigar it will be here within a week after we wire. Let *me* send the wire and I 'll bet you a box. I 'm bally good at wires. I used to get money out of the Governor by wire when I could get it no other way."

"Let her go," said Buck. "If it's all you say we 'll show them coyotes we know a few tricks ourselves."

"Yes, I fancy we shall," replied Whitby. "But isn't this a rummy game? They act like savages, you know. It is all very refreshing to a sated mind-and their justice is so deuced direct, right or wrong. Fancy Blackstone in the discard, as you Americans say, and a Colt's revolver sovereign lord of the realm!"

"King Colt is all right, Whitby, when you *know* who to loose him at," declared Buck, turning toward the door to the kitchen. "Jake! Jake!" he called.

The sharp, incisive tones told their story and brought buoyancy to the cook, for he was on his feet, across the kitchen, and into the dining-room in apparently one movement, which astounded the soul of that culinary devotee when leisure gave time for reflection.

"Why, Jake, I believe yo 're gettin' to be almost a human, livin' creature," remarked Buck. "I never saw you move so fast before. It ain't pay day now, you know."

"Shore I know, but next *week is*," grinned Jake, not quite catching the meaning.

"Oh, I 'm glad you do," sighed Buck with relief. "Now as long as you ain't sufferin' no hallucernations, suppose you tell Ned to come in here. You need n't tell *him* —he knows it ain't, too."

"Knows what ain't?" demanded Jake, his fingers slowly ploughing through his mass of hair. "If I need n't tell him, what do you want me to tell him for?"

"Be calm, Jake, be calm," replied Buck, raising a warning finger. "There are *two* tells in this; one you must, th' other you need n't."

"Ah, go to h —l an' tell him yourself," retorted Jake, backing toward a handy chair so as not to be without a weapon.

"You tell Ned I want to see him —I 'll explain th' second tell later. Now —*Will* y'u tell?"

Jake backed into the kitchen, slammed shut the door behind him, and lost no time in getting to the bunkhouse.

"Hey, Ned," he blurted out, "th' boss says to tell you he wants to see you. Th' second tell can wait till later. William Tell?"

"What t'ell!" snorted Bow-Wow, arising.

"You another?" demanded the cook; then he fled, Ned following more leisurely.

Bow-Wow looked at Murray inquiringly: "What did he mean by William Tell?"

Murray put down his mended riding gear. "Why, don't you know?"

"Shore; what is it?" sarcastically responded Bow-Wow. "If I knew, do you think I 'd tell?"

"Well I know, all right. It's what he was brought up on, Bow-Wow."

"Huh! Did you know him when he was a kid?"

"Shore! He used to live in th' next street in th' same town, or was it in some other town?" he mused, thoughtfully. "H —l, that don't make no difference, 'cause he lived in th' next street. See?"

"No; I don't; not a d —d bit!"

"Bow-Wow, if I was as thick as you get sometimes, I 'd drink lots of water an' thin down a bit. This is th' story of William Tell, an' I 'll tell it to you if you won't tell: When he was a kid he had a awful yearnin' for apples, like you has for cheap whiskey, Bow-Wow. Nothin' else suited him an' th' bigger he got th' more apples he had to eat. All th' farmers was a-layin' for him with guns, so what did li'l Willie do? Why, he shot 'em down with a bow an' arrer. An' that's why he can throw a stone so straight to-day. *Now* do you see?"

Bow-Wow threw a shoe after Murray's departing figure and suggested a place to go to. Then he scowled and muttered: "If I was shore of what I suspects I 'd give you a sample of *my* shootin', *six* samples so you 'd appreciate the real thing." He grinned at the memory of Jake's message.

"You 'll say somethin' with sense in it some day if you gropes long enough, Jake. Yo 're gettin' warmer all th' time."

When Monroe reached the ranch house Buck met him with some sharp orders: "Send Bow-Wow to Twin River and Wayback first thing to-morrow. Tell him to leave word we want two dozen more punchers for our round-up —fifty dollars a month an' a full month's work guaranteed. Jake 's goin' to dig some big holes in th' ground in th' next few days-he ain't fit for nothin' else, not even cookin'.'"

A crash in the kitchen interrupted him. "Jake!" he called. There was a scramble and the cook appeared, much excited. "What's th' fuss about?"

"Fell off my chair," replied Jake. "An' it hurts, too."

"Yo 're gettin' too soft, Jake. A little exercise 'll toughen you so a chair would n't dare to tackle you. I 'm goin' to let you dig some holes first thing to-morrow."

Jake had visions of extensive excavations, dug by him, into which thousands of dead cows were being piled for burial. "Would n't it be better to burn 'em, or push 'em into th' river an' shoot 'em there?"

"I never saw holes you could handle that way, Jake," gravely replied Buck.

"Why, no," supplemented the foreman. "Most holes would ruther be slit up th' middle an' salted. That's th' way we allus used to get rid of 'em."

"I don't mean holes —I mean *cows*!" explained Jake.

"Oh, then it 's all right," responded Buck. "I ain't goin' to ask *you* to dig no cows, Jake. But yo 're goin' to dig some nice ditches to-morrow; long, deep ones, an' good an' wide."

"I ain't never dug a ditch in my life," hastily objected Jake.

"Why, did n't you tell me how you dug that railroad cut down there in Iowa, an' got a hundred dollars extra 'cause you saved th' company so much money?" inquired Buck.

"Oh, but that was a steam shovel!"

"All right; you 'll steam afore yo 're at it very long."

Jake backed out again, slipped out of his kitchen, and stood reflective under the stars. He would quit and flee to Twin River if it was n't such a long walk. "D —n it!" he growled, and forthwith threw two stones into the darkness by way of getting rid of some of his anger.

"Sa-a-y!" floated a voice out of the night. "You jerk any more rocks in *this* direction an' I 'll beat you up so you 'll wipe your feet on yoreself, thinkin' yo 're a doormat! What 'n h —l you mean, anyhow?"

"Mebby they 's *apples*!" jeered Bow-Wow from the bunk-house. "Hello, William Tell!"

The cook softly closed the door and propped a chair against it. "Gee whiskers! I ain't goin' to stay *here* much longer! *Every*body 's gettin' crazy!"

"'If a body meets a body, comin' through th' rye,'" quavered a voice from the corral and a voice in the darkness profaned the song: "Ever meet yoreself goin' t'other way, after surroundin' th' rye?"

"Never had that pleasure after you 'd been at th' booze."

Chesty Sutton entered the bunk-house and stared at Bow-Wow. "What's eatin' you?" he demanded, curiously.

"I dunno; I 've been itchin' ever since Murray told us. Wonder if I 've got it?"

Chesty considered: "Well, now I remember that chickens, cats, and dogs don't get cattle itch. You ain't got it, Bow-Wow. It 's yore imagination that's got it. But if you 're bound to scratch, do it somewhere else-you make me nervous, keepin' on one spot so long. Wait till I asks th' boys about it."

"Stop!" snapped Bow-Wow, his hand on a bottle of harness oil: "You never mind about askin' anybody! I 'll take yore word for it-remember, I 'll bust yore gizzard if you gets that pack o' coyotes barkin' at my heels!"

"Holy Smoke! We 'll have our hands full a while," growled Chesty, dropping onto a box. "Let any o' this crowd ketch anybody throwin' mangy cows over on us! An' right after it comes th' Spring combin'—this is shore a weary world."

"Jake 's got to dig some ditches," remarked the foreman, entering the house, and immediately the misery of future hours was forgotten in the merriment and satisfaction found in this news. Jake would have a lot of advisers.

In the ranch house Whitby was laughing gently and finally he voiced a wish: "I say, Peters, what a wealth of character there is out here. I wish Johnnie Beauchamp were here-what a rattling good play he could make. You know, Johnnie's last play was almost a success-and I 'm very much interested in him. I backed him to the tune of two thousand pounds."

Invited to spend the night in the ranch house, Whitby accepted with alacrity. In carrying out McAllister's wishes he could not be too near headquarters, he concluded; but added to this, he entertained a sincere admiration for Buck Peters which increased as the days went by.

Some few minutes after the lights were out, Buck was brought back from the shadowy realm of sleep by Whitby's voice coming from the other room. "I say, Peters, did you keep those calculations?"

"Yes," answered Buck. "Why?"

"There 's the lumber, you know. It might be a good idea to have McAllister send it on."

"Shore would. You tell him."

"I will," promised Whitby. A few seconds later he broke out again: "Do you know, Buck, the railroad companies of America are cheerful beggars. They take your luggage and then play ducks and drakes with it, in a very idiotic way. Why, mine was lost for two weeks and I was in a very devil of a fix. So it would not be a bad idea, you know, if I tell your partner to send a man with the consignment. He can sit on the barrels and see that they are n't placed on a siding to prove the theory that loss of movement results in inertia. Am I right?"

Buck laughed from his heart. "If there 's anything you don't think of make a note of it an' let me see it," he commended.

"What a rummy remark. I say, how-ha! ha!" and Whitby's bunk creaked to his mirth. "That's rather a neat one, you know! I did n't know you were Irish, Peters, blessed if I did! I must tell that to your man Friday-it will keep the bally ass combing his frowsy locks for a week."

Buck had one foot on the Slumberland boundary when he heard the voice again, seeming to have travelled a long distance: "And I believe I should be rewarded for my brilliancy. I 'll ask your partner to send some brandy and a box of *good* cigars with the rest of it as my fee. I 'll have to learn to smoke all over again," he complained drowsily. A raucous snore bounced off the partition and Whitby opened his eyes for a moment: "My word, if Friday could only cook as well as he snores!"

Chapter XIII
Punctuation as a Fine Art

Twin River was in full blast when Dave rode in, looking for Tex. He dropped off the pony and went into the Why-Not, but his man was not there; after a few unavoidable drinks-Dave could not have avoided one if it had invited from the middle of the Staked Plain-he looked in at Ike's and the I-Call. He sampled the liquor in both places but evidently Comin' Thirty was not in that part of the town and he jogged on up to the Sweet-Echo. He had not been in here since warned off by Slick, but fear of consequences had nothing to do with absenting himself; fear did not enter into his composition. Dave's fundamental fault lay in his hatred of being beaten. It had lead him to cheat at play; to outwit by foul means; to take the sure course to any desired end, deliberately regardless of what any one might think. The danger of such actions did not deter him in the least; he was always ready, usually overwhelmingly ready, to back them up in any manner his opponents demanded of him. The defeat, sure to be met when he opposed a superior intelligence, he confidently relied upon overcoming by sheer force of personality, mistaking violence for strength, deceit for ingenuity. The bad judgment of his failures ever wore the mantle of bad luck; and the thought and time he wasted in schemes for revenge might have been used more profitably in making success of his failure.

Since his employment by Schatz his mind had been fully occupied by the furtherance, as he considered it, of his employer's plan. Buck Peters, the Englishman, even Slick, at times pricked his memory, but he had resolutely put them aside until a more convenient season. Now, with whiskey spurring his Satanic temperament, he considered it obligatory to go into the Sweet-Echo. He wanted to find Comin' and no fancy bar-keep' nor roaring Scotchman should keep him from going wherever he wanted to go. He stepped from his stirrup onto the porch and went into the bar-room as if he owned it.

The expected trouble did not develop. Slick gave him a short nod and set up glass and bottle with praise-worthy promptitude. If Dave was without fear, so was Slick, who would have taken him on in any way whatever; preferably, as became his Irish ancestry, with his hands, but failing that, with anything from a pop-gun to a cannon. Dave, with his usual habit of ignoring the other man, imagined Slick to be overawed; this leavened his savagery with good nature. What was Slick Milligan, anyhow? Just a bar-keep'—Dave turned his back to the bar and surveyed the inmates of the room. Comin' was not there. Where in thunder was he?

Maybe bucking the tiger at Little Nell's. Dave had two or three drinks with men he knew and rode back to cross the ford. He was again out in his reckoning. He watched the cards flick from the box. Nell, herself, was dealing and Dave's fingers itched to get down, but he refrained. With the vague hints dropped by Schatz and his consequent hope of speedily winning Rose, he knew he must drop gambling-until he had won to the fulfilment of his desires, at least.

As he watched he suddenly realized he was hungry and strolled into the eating house, run by Nell as a paying adjunct to her other businesses. The whiskey, as it often does in healthy stomachs, was calling loudly for food and Dave answered the call with unstinted generosity. Being genuinely wishful to see Tex he did not linger but, as soon as finished, started to make the round again.

He got no farther than the Why-Not. His entry was met by a roar of laughter and shouts of encouragement: "Bully f' you, gran'pa!"—"Did he ever come back?"—"That's th' caper, Dirty!"—"*Let* him alone, *he* ain't chokin'."

Seated on a box on the top of a table (Dirty would be buried in a box; they would never have the heart to separate his attenuated figure from the object so long associated with it in life), old Pop Snow bent up and down, shrinking, shrinking, until his bony leanness threatened to vanish before their gaze; a wheezing gasp started him swelling again and his "he! he! he!" whistled above the uproar like a hiss in a machine shop.

He was astonishingly drunk-for Dirty. His pervious clay had developed innumerable channels for alcohol in the years of training he had given it; and he was seldom so joyously hilarious as this. For one reason it was seldom that any one would pay for it, and Dirty's means only went far enough to keep him everlastingly thirsty. The explanation appeared to Dave in the shape of a group of miners, whose voices, in their appreciation, were the loudest.

"He-he-he! He-he-he-he!" Pop Snow's shrill pipe continued, while the others demanded more. "Sawbones had n't been gone a week afore he was wanted. He-he-he! eh, dear! eh, dear! Lucky Jones come along-an' stopped. Ther' wearn't nothin' *to* do but stop. He comes to me an' he says: 'Wheer 's ther' a doctor?' 'Well,' I says, 'jedgin' from what I hears, if you jest foller th' river north fur about fifteen mile to Drigg's Worry,' I says, 'you 'll find a saw-bones as used to be yer-but when he left he swears as how he ain't never comin' back to th' P'int,' I says.

He-he-he! Send-I-may-live if he don't, though. Yep, an' Jones purty nigh goes into th' wet, too. 'Th' P'int?' roars th' Doc, 'No, siree, by G —d, no, sir! Twenty-eight mile th' last time to tend a stinkin' ole sow, on account o' a misbegotten son o' Beelzebub an th' North Pole they call Snow down there. This time I 'spose 't'ud be a skunk.' 'It's my wife,' says Jones, 'an' if yuh don't come right sudden I 'm a-goin' to blow off th' top o' yore devilish ole head,' says Jones; 'an' if she dies,' he sez, 'I blows her off, anyhow.' He-he-he! Saw-bones, he riz up an' come a-kitin'. I ain't much on Welshmen; they biles over too easy. But Saw-bones done a good job an' got away wi' his life. We hears all about it nex' day when Jones comes to me an' tells me it is two at once, boy an' a girl. Fust we knowed he 'd brung his wife. Not as she stays long. Winter 's one too many fur her an' she cashes in. Then Lucky Jones, he tries to cross th' river below th' P'int, 'stid o' th' ford, an' th' ice ain't strong enough, an' Jones, he was some drunk, I reckon. We calls th' river after him an' th' forks after th' kids. Lord, they was bad uns, both on 'em. Black Jack, he hez hisself hung for suthin' or other, an' Little Jill, she turns out just a plain —"

Every one jumped, it was so unexpected. The lead sung so close to Dirty's nose that the backward jerk almost took him off the table and he recovered his seat with a sideways wriggle and squirm that did credit to the elasticity of his aged muscles. Having managed to retain his seat, he continued to retain it. None of the others showed the least desire to move, though every last man of them yearned for absence-sudden, noiseless absence-of a kind so instantaneous as to preclude the possibility of notice: anything less were foolhardy in the face of those blazing eyes and that loosely held gun, its business end oscillating like the head of a snake and far more deadly.

"Don't be afeared, Dirty," purred Dave, in the kindliest tones. "I was jest a-puttin' in th' period. Yore eddication is shameful, Dirty, an' I grieves for you, account of it. You has a generous mixture o' commas an' semi-commas an' things like that, but yore periods is shore some scarce. You was a-sayin' as how Little Jill was a sweet, good gal, as never done wrong in her life, was n't you?"

Dirty swallowed hard and nodded. Speech was beyond him just then and perhaps he had spoken too much, already. He repeated his former contortion with equal skill and success, and every head in the crowd rose perceptibly and returned to its former level as the gun spoke again and another hole appeared in the wall, close to the first.

"A period comes after that, Dirty," said Dave. "Don't you never forgit th' kind o' gal she was-an' then comes th' period. You 'll mebby hold yore liquor better." He shoved the gun back in the holster, eyed the crowd insolently for a moment, and turning his back on it, walked calmly from the room.

Pop Snow climbed down from the table in haste and pushed his way through the detaining arms and the medley of questions that assailed him on his way to the door, which opened and closed like a stage trap as he stepped out and sprang to one side; his anger was that of a sober and far younger man and he peered about with keen eyes. His caution was uncalled for: Dave was splashing through the ford and Dirty watched him set out in a swift lope along the Big Moose trail. Dave had no stomach for further company that night.

Dirty rubbed a pair of trembling lips as he gazed. "Black Jack!" he muttered, "Black Jack! He *warn't* hung, then. No, an' he won't never be 'less it's fur killin' pore ole Pop Snow. Pore ole Pop Snow," he repeated, whimpering as he hurried across the bridge toward shelter; "Jest like Dutch Onion. Dead an' gone, pore ole Dutch. Pore ole Pop." He stopped in the middle of the trail and with a flash of his former spirit, shook his fist after the distant Dave: "Shell I?" he jeered: "shell I, then? I been yer afore you, Jack, an' I 'll be a-livin' when you rot."

Hoofbeats coming out of the darkness where Dave had disappeared, startled him and he scuttled away like a rabbit.

Chapter XIV

Fighting the Itch

Monroe and the three men left to him after Bow-Wow had departed for Twin River and Wayback, in the company of Whitby, were too small a force to attempt the round-up, so they put in the day riding over those sections of the range farthest removed from the Hog Back, examining every cow they found. At nightfall they had the pleasure of reporting to Buck that the entire portion of the range along the Little Jill, extending from the river to the middle of the ranch, was free from infection; as a matter of fact the conclusion reached in council was that only that portion of range bounded by the Black Jack, the south line, and Blackfoot Creek needed to be cleaned up. This meant that two-thirds of the ranch was free from the itch, and the infected third contained less than a fourth of the Double Y cows.

Plans for the round-up were considered and soon arrived at. All the men with the exception of three, were to be actively engaged in the round-up. They were to start from the south line and drive northwest towards the Hog Back. The Black Jack made a natural barrier on the west and would hold the herd safely on that side. The three other punchers were to ride even with the drive line, but on the other side of Blackfoot Creek, and keep ambitious cows from crossing onto the non-infected portions of the range. This arrangement would constantly force the cattle onto the wedge-shaped range at the juncture of the two waters. Here the herd could be dipped and driven across the shallow Blackfoot onto a clean territory, where they would be held for further observation. Then if the rest of the range showed signs of infection the round-up and dipping could be carried on again at other points. If a strict line could be maintained along the Blackfoot the Hog Back range would be fenced off effectually from the non-infected cattle on the other parts of the ranch. The question of building an actual fence to separate the Hog Back range from the rest was gone into thoroughly and the decision was unanimous that twelve miles of fence was too big a proposition to be attempted at that moment; if necessary it could be put up later when it was found that patrolling the creek was inadvisable. But perhaps a side light can be thrown on this quiet decision when it is remembered how fervently a cowman hated fences. These men were all of the old school and preferred to keep barb-wire as a theory and not a fact.

That evening Bow-Wow returned with a crowd of cow-punchers of varying degrees of fitness, all eager to take cards in any game at fifty dollars a month. The majority of them were not up to the standards Buck cherished; if they had been, they would not have been waiting for a job. But it was certain they knew how to punch cows, enough for the demands of the moment-and Jake waxed eloquent and sarcastic when he hazarded a guess as to when they had eaten their last square meal. Perhaps, after all, digging huge ditches would not be so bad, for cooking three meals a day for twenty-odd hungry men was more of a task than he cared to tackle. But Bow-Wow had exercised some intelligence of his own, as after events showed. Two of his squad were ex-cooks. The "ex" is used advisedly, for if ever cooks were "ex" it was these two; this was the decision voiced simultaneously by twenty hungry men at the first meal prepared by the two. Sam Hawkins suggested that they had quit cooking to save their lives, and regretted that they had so made their choice.

The drive went ahead without more than the usual bluster and confusion, and the end of the first day found the round-up well under way. Outlying free range had been thoroughly combed, in which assistance had been given by neighboring ranches; Buck, in carrying out his policy of supplying his own help, had not failed to notify other owners and foremen that they could rely on the Double Y for its contingent of men when the general round-up should take place. The drivers were divided into two squads for day work and three for night riding around the herd; the two-squad arrangement was made for meal times, one squad eating while the other worked. There was no time lost at meals because each of the ex-cooks, in a chuck wagon alloted to him, preceded the drive and was never very far from the field of operations. Thus were system and order gained the first day, which meant time saved in the end.

Buck intended to spend his nights in the ranch house as usual, and when he gained it the first night he found two things of interest. The first announced itself by sending him to his hands and knees within three feet of his front door; the second was a telegram from McAllister saying that a special had the right of way, and from the wording Buck could see it pounding into the Northwest, over crossings and past switch towers, its careening red tail lights bearing a warning to would-be range-jumpers if they did but know it. The message further stated that the consignment was under the personal attention of a puncher who, having grown sick of the stock yards, was cheerfully availing himself of the opportunity of getting back to the open range at no expense. Buck sighed with relief as he realized that the ingredients of the dip were already on the way, and could not be sidetracked or lost without the subduing of a very irritable cow-puncher. As he put the message away he remembered the first thing that had impressed itself on him, and went out to take a look at it.

The light in his hand revealed the sodless strip fifty feet long and four feet wide. Its depth was to the under side of the grass, a matter of two or three inches. There was a stake at each corner of the bare rectangle and these supported a one-strand fence made of lariats.

Buck scratched his head and then growled a profane request to feel the head of the man who was responsible. He strode into the house and stopped in the kitchen door; and Jake very wearily turned around on his chair and looked at him with intent curiosity.

"What 'n h —l is that scalped grass for?" demanded Buck, evenly.

"That's th' beginnin' of ditch number one," replied Jake. "How 'd you like them lines, eh? Straight as a die. Took me all mornin' to lay 'em out like that."

"Did it? I congratulate you, Jake-likewise I sympathize with you. I reckon you 'll get it down a foot in a couple o' weeks, eh?"

"Oh, quicker'n that," modestly rejoined Jake.

"Did n't I tell you to dig them ditches close to where th' Blackfoot empties into th' Jack?" demanded Buck. "Are you figgerin' on extendin' it from here to there? I don't want a trench no fifteen miles long. To-morrow mornin' you ride with me an' I 'll show you where to dig. An' don't you bother stakin' it off exact, neither. I want them ditches all finished in *three* days. Did you reckon I was goin' to drive two thousand head of itch cows fifteen miles so I could dip 'em bang up agin my own front door!"

Pickles bounced in, his rifle under his arm. "Hullo, Buck!" he cried. "Shot a coyote to-day!"

"Good, Pickles," smiled Buck. "Want a job shootin' a *man* to-morrow?"

"Betcher life! Is it Dave?"

"No, it's Jake, here," replied Buck. "You take yore rifle an' come with me an' Jake to-morrow. If he don't dig fast enough to suit you, you shoot him in th' laig."

"Betcher life! Which leg?" asked Pickles, agog with anticipation.

"I 'm leavin' that to you, Pickles. You 're gettin' big enough to figger things out for yoreself."

"Will he limp like Hopalong?"

"Worse, mebby."

Jake, grinning, feared Pickles might be carried away with his zeal, and he put in a laughing objection; but he sobered instantly at Buck's sharp reply.

"I mean it. He 'll shoot if he 's a friend o' mine. I ain't goin' to lose a lot of cows 'cause I 've got a man too lazy to dig. You 've got yore orders, Pickles: obey 'em like a real Bar-20 puncher."

"Betcher life I will. Just like Hopalong Cassidy!"

Jake groaned at the intense earnestness in Pickles' declaration; to emulate the great Hopalong Cassidy was enduring honor in Pickles' eyes, and from past performances and several duels with the boy, Jake reached the conclusion that he was slated to do some very rapid digging on the morrow.

"Lemme use *yore* rifle, Buck!" asked Pickles, his eyes shining with the joy of living. He knew he could do a great deal better with Buck's repeater, and the thought of exploding .45-70 cartridges was a delight beyond his wildest dreams.

Jake's heart stopped for the reply and he sighed with relief as Pickles' face fell; but the boy's spirits rose like a balloon. "All right, Buck; I can get him with my gun, though I ought to have a repeater."

* * * * *

The round-up went forward swiftly and the day that McAllister's special puffed into Wayback and snorted onto the siding, found the Hog Back country swept clean of cattle, the herd being held close to Jake's two big ditches. Buck had known the magnitude of the task he set for Jake and when the cook showed he was anxious to do his share of the work, Buck had told off men enough to help him get through in time. The digging was hard and unaccustomed work and the men were changed frequently, all but Jake; he seemed to consider it a matter of pride to stick to the job and made a point of throwing the last shovelful of dirt as well as the first; as a consequence his altitude was below normal for a week afterwards, and it was a month before he forgot to grunt with every breath.

The hauling of the lumber exercised the ingenuity and strained the resources of Jean LaFrance, the only man in the locality who possessed anything on wheels capable of carrying it. Inasmuch as he could ill spare the time, although sorely needing the money, it exhausted Jean's stock of oaths to the point where his own language failed him; even English, which he understood, seemed singularly tame and unworthy the occasion; so that he fell back on his carefully reserved specimens of German expletives, which he did not in the least understand, and these with constant repetitions carried him through. Two men, driving the two borrowed chuck wagons, succeeded in transporting the rest of the shipment, and Whitby, to his great satisfaction, found that McAllister had not forgotten his fee.

The junction of the Blackfoot with the Jack presented a busy scene. The close-packed blue-clay, which had made hard work for the diggers, now proved a help, the timbers fitting snug without backing. Meanwhile the more important part, the preparing of the solution, went on under the direction of Whitby; his calm handling and frequent active coöperation without becoming warm or soiled was a wonder to see. Under the huge caldrons, which had been the first of the consignment to arrive, wood had been piled ready for the match; on bases made of logs stood rows of whiskey barrels; shallow troughs were filled and re-filled with water until the swelling wood took up and became water-tight. Far into the night they worked, and now the crackling fires were giving the night shift trouble with the snorting cattle. Weird shadows darted out over the ground, lengthened and vanished as the men moved about the fires, worked over the lime-slaking troughs or poured off the compound paste into the steaming caldrons. When the barrels were filled with the first lot of the mixture, Whitby relented and the men stumbled off to rest.

With the dawn they were at work again; and now the dipping troughs came into use as the saturated solution was drawn off from the barrels, leaving the sediment at the bottom, and dumped into the troughs, where water was added to reduce it to the required strength. Night was approaching again before the water arose to nearly the required level; the men were thoroughly tired and Whitby, reluctantly and as a result of a direct order from Buck, called a halt. Buck knew the temper of his men better than Whitby: at anything directly connected with range duties, provided they were familiar with it, they would work until they dropped; but this was something whose usefulness remained to be proven. Buck was too wise to push them in such a case, but he grinned cheerfully as he turned away from the reluctance on Whitby's face. The Britisher was surely a glutton for work.

The prudence of Buck's reasoning was shown by the eagerness with which the men responded to the call next morning. In less than an hour Whitby announced all ready and the men entered upon a scene which they individually and collectively swore repaid them for their trouble. At Whitby's shout, two of the men riding herd cut out the first bunch of cattle and drove them toward the dipping trough; the flimsily constructed horse corral swarmed with laughing, joking punchers who roped their mounts with more or less success in the first attempt, while outside the wranglers darted forward and back, wheeling on a pie dish, checking the more ambitious of the ponies that resented a confinement limited to a single line of lariats; saddles dropped onto recalcitrant backs and were cinched with a speed nothing short of marvellous to a layman, and the whooping punchers were jerked away to the herd.

The first lot of cows, some twenty in number, flirting their tails and snorting in angry impotence, entered the wide opening between a wedge-shaped pair of fences and galloped toward the narrow vent which led to the trough. And now was seen Buck's wisdom in continuing the fence along the edge of the troughs a few feet, both at entrance and exit: the first brute, a magnificent three-year-old, appeared to realize the crush that would come and spurted for the opening; the significance of the situation did not appeal to him until he was close to the edge; he slid to the very brink and gathered himself for a leap, but the fence was too high; the next instant the cattle behind, urged on by Cock Murray, whooping like an Indian, bumped into the hesitating brute and he fell forward into the trough with a bellow of rage and started on his swim to the other end.

When Cock Murray, with Slow Jack close behind, had followed the bunch between the fences, they were assailed by a chorus of shouts to which they paid no heed whatever. Slow Jack, being in the rear, caught a glimpse out of the tail of his eye of Whitby running and waving his arms; he looked around for the cause of so much excitement and was in time to see the second bunch, instead of being driven over to the other trough as they should have been, come thundering into the wedge and drive down upon him. Slow Jack shot up to the fence, threw one leg along the neck of his pony and skimmed through the opening he made for, with nothing to spare and a scratched saddle; after which he spent several profane seconds in telling the chaffing drivers what he thought of them. His annoyance was forgotten when they suddenly doubled up, shrieking with laughter, and pointed toward the shoot.

Slow Jack looked and then looked at them. The second bunch had gone galloping madly on to the narrow opening, against which they were wedged and dropping one by one as a third bunch pressed in after them. They were coming too rapidly and Ned Monroe, riding past from the other trough, was sending the next bunch in the proper direction and going on to the herd to put some sense of order into the heads of the rollicking punchers. Slow Jack quite failed to see anything funny in all this and said so with force and directness; he added, moreover, a prophecy regarding idiots, the fulfilment of which was due to take place in the near, in fact immediate, future, which threatened complete derangement of the internal economy of said idiots. The idiots were entirely oblivious. Jack was puzzled. He glanced ahead and noticed a lot more idiots. Disgusted with his vain attempt to get an explanation, he rode forward to see for himself.

Cock Murray, having quirted the last of the first bunch into the trough, became aware of the shouting, gesticulating men who had left their duties to run toward the fence to attract his attention. In the cross-fire of warnings he failed to understand any of them, but the rumbling rush behind brought him suddenly to a realization of his position. One glance and he saw it was too late to retreat. There was just one thing to do. "Holy mackerel!" gasped Cock. He put the quirt to his pony in a frenzy of blows and landed in the dipping mixture with a jump that carried his pony's feet to the bottom of the trough. Sputtering and swearing Cock went through to the end; it was useless, as he knew, to try to climb out over those smooth abrupt walls, and he was too obstinate to leave his saddle. Which was madder, Cock or the pony, it would be hard to say. It was when he went climbing up the cleated incline at the farther end that Slow Jack got his first inkling of the cause of mirth. He gave one astonished stare, made two or three odd noises in his throat, and then, gravely and in silence, dropped from his saddle to the ground. It was not until he lay at full length, the long reins of the bridle drooping from the bit and his pony gazing at him inquiringly, that he exploded-but then he laughed steadily for half an hour.

The cattle, which had not awaited these developments, were dropping into the trough with praise-worthy regularity and making their way to the other end; when about half way there and swimming resignedly, a kind-hearted puncher, wearing a delighted grin in addition to his regular equipment, and armed with a strong pole, forked at the business end, leaned forward swiftly, jammed the fork over the unsuspecting cow's head, and pushed zealously. The result was gratifying to the few on-lookers, and disconcerting to the cow so rudely ducked; just before the unfortunate bovine touched the sloping runway to dry earth, another grinning puncher repeated the dose. The cows, reluctant to enter the bath, showed no reluctance to leave it and the scene of their humiliation, and they lumbered away with a speed surprising to those whose ideas of cows are based upon observation of domesticated "bossies" in pasture in the East. But they were not allowed to run free, being driven slowly across a roughly constructed bridge to the farther side of the Blackfoot, onto the non-infected range, and held there.

"This yere trough is shore makin' some plenty of Baptists," grinned Chesty Sutton.

"Yep; but with Mormon inclinations," amended Bow-Wow.

"Bow to th' gents," reprimanded Chesty, ducking a cow. "You look like a drowned rat," he criticised.

"Bow agin," requested Bow-Wow, and the cow obeyed, with a show of fight when its head came up.

"Some high-falutin' picklin' factory," chuckled Chesty. "Messrs. Bow-Wow Baker an' Chesty Sutton, world's greatest mite picklers. Blue-noses, red-noses an' other kinds o' cow inhabitants a specialty. Give you a whole dollar, Bow-Wow, if you fall in."

"Is that just a plain hope, or a insinooation?" demanded the cheerful Bow-Wow. "I sleep next to you, so don't get too blamed personal. But we might put Jake in-though mebby his ain't th' right kind. Hey, Jake; come here."

"If you wants to see me, you come here," retorted the cook. "I 've seen all of them ditches *I* wants to. An' I ain't takin' no chances with a couple o' fools, neither."

"Hey, Chesty!" called Bow-Wow, delighted. "Here comes that LX steer we had such a h —l of a time with in th' railroad pens. Soak him good! Ah, ha, my long-horned friend; you was some touchy an' peevish down there in Wayback. Take *that* —don't worry, Chesty 's been savin' some for you, too. *Hard*, Chesty! That's th' boy-bet he 's mad as a rattler."

"Look at that moth-eaten scab of a yearlin'," laughed Chesty, pointing. "Th' firm could declare dividends on th' mites we 'll pickle on her. *Souse* she goes! Once more for luck-look at her steam up! H —l, *this* ain't work-it's fun. Under you go, Alice dear. Next!"

"Here comes Kinkaid o' th' Cyclone," announced Cock Murray, riding up to take a hasty look at the operations before he returned to the herd for another bunch of cows.

Chesty handed his pole to Murray, grabbed up a lariat, and started for the newcomer, shouting: "Here comes some itch! Dip him, fellers! Quick!"

Kinkaid manoeuvred swiftly, grinning broadly. "If that stuff is warmer 'n th' water in th' Jack, why, I might be coaxed into it. Howd'y, boys; thought I 'd come over an' pick up some points."

"How you makin' out on th' Cyclone?" asked Buck.

"Bad —*very* bad. We tried isolatin' th' mangy ones, but they 're dyin' like flies in frost time. Lost forty million so far an' I reckon th' other two 'll die to-morrow. We thought our north range was free, but they 're on that, too. We drove clean cows up in th' Rockin' Horse territory an' now they 're showin' signs o' havin' th' itch. Beats all how it travels."

Cock Murray listened intently, but held his peace. He thought he might explain how it had travelled toward the Rocking Horse.

"That's where we noticed it first," said Buck. "We found some o' yore cows on th' Hog Back, an' their trail left th' river just below th' Rockin' Horse."

Kinkaid looked surprised and asked questions. He sat very quietly for a few moments and then looked at Buck with a peculiar expression on his face. "Sick cows don't swim th' Jack, cold as it is now. I wonder who in h —l —?" he muttered, softly.

"We 're wonderin', too, Kinkaid," replied Buck, slowly. "It's lead or rope for anybody we ketch at it." Kinkaid nodded his emphatic endorsement of this.

Whitby was keeping a close watch on the tally of cattle as they emerged, comparing it with the amount of fresh mixture constantly being added to that already in the troughs, and he found reason to be thankful that he had ordered more than he expected to use. Any left over would make all the less needed at the fall shipment when, as he knew, the dipping would have to be repeated; not until then could they be assured that the disease was stamped out.

The first day's work finished less than half the herd, but they continued, the following day, until the last cow scrambled out. After which, as a matter of precaution, Buck gave the boys the fun of driving every pony through the mixture. What had been entertaining before now became side-splitting, for tired as they were, the savage natures of the furious victims drew energy from unexpected sources and made a scene well worth watching, and a little risky for those men waiting with ropes at the end of the dripping board. The cows were angry, but had neither the intelligence nor the fighting ability of the maddened animals who had only a short time before seemed to enjoy the discomfiture of the animals they were accustomed to drive and bully; and it was only agility and good luck that the flying hoofs landed on nothing more substantial than air.

While this did not take long it was too late when finished, and the men too weary, to break camp; but the next morning saw the chuck wagon piled high with barrels and caldrons on the way to the ranch house. Some of the extra men, having in mind the wording of the guarantee of a full month's pay, cherished the hope that there was no further use for their services and that they would be paid off and told to leave. They were disappointed, for instead of loafing or leaving, half of them were set to planting posts for the fence which it was found necessary to erect along the creek, while the others rode over the range on the look-out for cows with signs of itch. A small herd of about a hundred, found scattered along and near the creek, were dipped as a precautionary measure, and after a week had elapsed without finding further signs of the disease, Buck ordered the second squad to begin the Spring or calf round-up; the fence division patrolled the creek to effect a quarantine until the wire arrived. They had a two-strand fence extending along Blackfoot Creek from its source to the river, when the round-up was half over, and were immediately put to work with the others. When the last calf was branded, the extra force was let go and Buck waited for some new deviltry. It came, and turned his hair grayer and deepened the lines of care on his face. Calves had totalled up well and proved to him that there was lots of money to be taken out of the Double Y under fair conditions, but the next blow cut into his resources with crushing effect and made him waver for a moment.

Chapter XV
The Slaughter of the Innocents

The round-up was still under way when Cock Murray was taken off and sent to Twin River in a chuck wagon to get provisions for the ranch. He had loaded his wagon and left town behind him when he saw Dave riding hard to overtake him. He drew rein and nodded when the horseman pulled up beside him.

"Howd'y, Dave."

"Howd'y, Murray," replied Dave. "Spring round-up over yet?"

"Nope; 'bout half."

"Itch all cured good?"

"Can't find no more signs of it. That dippin' play was a winner an' it's a good thing to remember."

"I 've got a little job for you an' Slow Jack," Dave remarked, after a moment's thought.

"Yeh? Hope it's better'n some o' yore schemes."

"What do you mean? I never had no schemes."

"All right—my mistake," drawled Murray. "What's th' new one?"

"New nothin'. I just want you an' Slow Jack to drive a couple o' thousand head up in th' Hog Back country some 'rs an' hold 'em hid till I can take care o' 'em."

"If yo 're goin' to start up in business for yoreself, I 'd keep away from th' Hog Back," replied Murray gravely. "Better try down on th' southeast corner. There ain't no itch hangin' 'round there."

"Business nothin'!" snapped Dave, not liking his companion's levity. "I 've got somethin' in my head that 'll make a fortune for you an' Slow Jack. I don't want no profits-just th' joy o' takin' a good punch at Peters 'll do for me. But you two ought to split 'bout twenty thousand dollars a-tween you."

"Music to my ears!" chuckled Murray. "Slow Jack's goin' to work on a salary basis on *this* job-th' profits 'll be mine. Whereabouts is this gold mine located, did you say?"

Dave did not heed him but continued hurriedly: "There 's a good pasture atween th' Hog Back an' th' river, an' th' only way to it or out of it is up that ravine. You an' Slow Jack can drive cows to it whenever you gets a chanct, an' a couple o' ropes acrost th' ravine 'll hold 'em in. When you get a couple o' thousand there we 'll drive 'em north o' th' Cyclone's line to Rankin, put 'em on th' cars there an' get 'em south into Wyoming. There 's good money in it, Murray."

The driver was staring at his companion, blank amazement on his face. "Gosh! That sounds easy! 'Bout as easy as me an' you capturin' th' Fort an' makin' th' Government pay us a big war indemnity. Slow Jack 's goin' to get th' wages an' profits, too. I 'm too generous to cut in an' spoil his chance to make a fortune. I suppose we 're goin' to tie th' herd to balloons an' get 'em to Rankin that way?"

"You collect th' herd an' I 'll attend to all th' rest o' it," declared Dave. "I 've got this thing all worked out an' it's goin' through."

"Can't be did, Dave," emphatically replied the driver, dazed by the signs of insanity manifested by his companion.

"You say that because it ain't never been done," retorted Dave, angrily. "It *can* be done, an' I 'm goin' to do it. Put that in yore pipe."

"All right-you ought to know," responded Murray, tactfully. "Who are th' miracle-men that are goin' to get th' herd off that table-land an' to Rankin without bein' seen or leavin' a trail?"

"Big Saxe, th' hunchback, is one," Dave explained. "Th' trail we 'll leave ain't botherin' us any. They won't be missed till it's too late to look for tracks-an' by that time th' cows 'll be sold."

Murray thought of one objection that would kill the plan without mercy: the railroad was not in the habit of accepting unaccredited cows for shipment; curiosity would be shown as to the brand, where it came from, who owned it, and other pertinent facts. But Dave was so hopeful, so earnest, that Murray decided to talk the matter over with Schatz before dispelling Dave's dream.

"Well, that's true, Dave," he soberly replied. "When you think it over ca'm like, it ain't so plumb foolish. Me an' Slow Jack 'll see what we can do-let you know as soon as we can. I got to poke along. But say, Dave; it's shore death to anybody tryin' to fool with *Cyclone* cows along th' river-tell th' boys so they won't try to throw over any more scabby cattle on us. Kinkaid is some peevish 'bout his north range gettin' th' itch. Got any more plans you want to tell about? All right-don't get mad at *me*, Dave; I 'm only foolin'. So long."

Murray had crossed the north line of his ranch before he emerged from his trance. Then he shook himself, laughed and looked around, urging the team to livelier efforts. He nursed his secret until after dark and then slipped away from the ranch and struck out toward Twin River. When he had gone a mile in this direction he wheeled sharply and urged his pony toward the trail along the Little Jill. Arriving at the Schatz domicile he reconnoitred a little and then slipped up to the kitchen door and drummed lightly on it. Schatz opened it and dragged the visitor inside.

"You must nod come to see me more as iss necessary," began the German. "It iss such carelessness as puts peoples in chails. Vat iss it dis time?"

Murray, grinning, unfolded Dave's plans to the astonished German, who could only grunt his surprise and disgust. Suddenly Schatz brightened and a faint twinkle came into his eye. "Dot iss a goot plan, Murray. A very goot plan. *Aber* it goes too far. Dose railroad peoples vould spoil it quick. You get der herd like Dave says, more if you can; und hold it till *I* say somet'ing. Neffer mind vat Dave say-he iss *ein verruchter Mensch*. But ven *I* say somet'ing, den you do it. *Verstanden?*"

"All right, Schatz," agreed Murray, smiling. "I 'll back yore play to th' limit, every time. But what 'll I say to Dave when he gets anxious?"

"He von't ged anxious. I vill speak der vord before he haf time to ged anxious. I vill tell vat to do mit dot herd, und it von't be vat Dave vants."

"Then I 'll tell Slow Jack that th' collection takes place. Anything else?"

"*Nein* —careful you go. Alvays you must be careful. *Goot nacht!*" and the door closed quickly.

"Ach! Dot Dave!" ejaculated Schatz, his hands upraised.

* * * * *

Slow Jack must have been told of Schatz's wishes, because during the week following Murray's visit to the German's house, cattle had been disappearing from the southwestern part of the range; this was not strange enough to cause worry even if it had been observed, because cows go where they please; and it was not observed by any one but Cock Murray and Slow Jack. The fence, extending to within a short distance of the south line, was regarded as barrier enough to keep the cattle off the infected range, and Buck gave no particular thought to it. Slow Jack rode along the fence every few days to see that there were no breaks in it and as Cock Murray had the south line under his care, it was an easy matter to round up small herds and drive them over the Hog Back, down the ravine on the river side, and hold them on the plateau pasture by the means Dave had suggested. The grass was heavy and the water plentiful along the line patrolled by Murray and there were always large numbers of cows grazing there-so many, in fact, that those driven off could not be missed under ordinary circumstances. Thus the hidden herd grew rapidly and it was not long before a large herd grazed close to the edge of the precipitous cliffs frowning down on the cold, hard-looking Black Jack.

Murray, fussing around the horse corral, had put in a hard day's riding and had no desire to stray far from the bunk-house that chilly, windy night. He had been engaged in driving cattle onto the range he had been thinning, so as to cover the missing cows, and over five hundred extra head grazed near the springs that made the swampy headquarters of the creek.

Slow Jack was getting nervous because Schatz had not been heard from and he was grouchy and touchy even to his partner in the business on hand. He and Murray would be likely to have unpleasant questions asked of them if the herd should be discovered. They were in charge of that part of the range and it would not be easy to excuse the presence of so many cows on the infected section. The fence was intact and if it were not, then it would be squarely up to them; Buck would be profanely curious how it was that a respectable herd had managed to get past Murray and go around the end of the fence. And it would be hard to explain how the cattle willingly left the best grass on the ranch and wandered up the Hog Back, all finding the ravine and herding on the cliff-top pasture. And if the rope or the tracks of the two punchers' horses should be seen, gun-play would follow with deadly certainly.

"D —n that Dutchman!" growled Slow Jack to Murray, as they met and strolled away a short distance; "Seems like we ain't got enough cows up there to suit th' hog. He wants that pasture covered with 'em, I reckon. Word or no word, them cows has got to get back on th' range. An' th' itch is among 'em, too, Murray."

Murray smoked in silence for a while and then looked up, a frown on his face. "Smiler has got to be quick. Dave, th' fool, was out to see me again to-day. I asked him when he was goin' to rustle that bunch an' he says he 's got it all fixed-mebby th' first black night. Is it black to-night?" he asked, ironically.

"Black as h —l!" growled Slow Jack. "If Dave beats th' ol' man to it, an' gets away with that herd, I 'll be plumb tickled to death. An' if he gets away with it good an' clean, without bein' caught, it 'll go down in th' history o' cattle-stealin' as th' greatest miracle since th' Dead Sea was walked on. Holy Gripes! Would n't it be a sensation?"

"Th' laurels will remain with th' Dead Sea," grunted Murray. "Dave 's shore goin' to be fertilizer for th' daisies some o' these days if he don't get sane." After a moment he growled: "An' if he don't stop comin' to see me like he has, Smiler 'll have to dig up another ass to be father to."

"He was lookin' for me, yesterday," grinned Slow Jack, "but I seen him first. He ain't goin' to *sic* no lead *my* way if I can help it."

"Jack, did you ever figger out why Smiler lets Dave mess around like he does?" suddenly asked Murray. "Th' Dutchman is one clever individual, but every clever crook makes one mistake that ropes him. I hereby prophesy that Dave is Smiler's mistake an' will make th' Dutchman lose. Want to bet on it?"

"What you allus lookin' for shore things for?" jeered Jack. "You ain't got no sportin' blood in you! In course I know it-an' that's just th' reason I've got my stuff ready to move quick an' my trail all mapped out. I might want to leave before breakfast some day. Tell you one thing—*you* can drive cows over th' Hog Back but I 'm *all through*! D—n if I drive another one!"

"I 'm th' good little boy, too, from now on," replied Murray. "An' I 'm goin' to be awful busy farther east on that line. Savvy? I ain't goin' to be able to even guess how they got over th' Hog Back, an' I 'll take th' blame for bein' careless. I 'd ruther lose my job than house any lead under my skin. Aw! I 'm goin' in an' get some sleep."

"Me, too; I 'll come right soon," and Slow Jack drifted off into the darkness as his companion started for the bunk-house.

When Slow Jack entered the bunk-house half an hour after Murray, he paused in the door and looked at the western sky, where lightning zigzagged occasionally. The barely audible roll of thunder told him how far off the storm was and he noticed that the wind was blowing less steadily, coming in gusts from varying points. Even while he stood, the sound of the thunder increased in volume and the long, thin lightning reached out nearer to him, a livid whip that lashed the heavens into roaring anger.

"Huh! Reckon Spring is shore nuff here now," he muttered. "Fust real lightnin' I seen this year." Five minutes later he was asleep.

* * * * *

The Hog Back loomed up like a condensation of the surrounding night, its huge bulk magnified and made soft in its rugged outlines. A restless wind scurried like a panic-stricken animal, sighing through the brush and whispering through the rocks. At intervals the silence was so intense that the scraping of a twig, yards away, could be plainly heard; and at other times the bellow of a steer would have been lost in a few rods.

Something moved across the plain, slowly and carefully as if feeling its way, and toiled up the precarious trail, rolling pebbles clattering down; in the noise of their fall was lost the soft thudding that marked the course of the moving smudge. The lightning in the western sky flashed nearer and gave brief illumination of the scene. Four men rode single file up the dark trail, silent, intent, wary, the leader picking his way as though he knew it well; in reply to a low-voiced question from his nearest companion, he stretched out an abnormally long arm in a sharp gesture. He did not like to have his ability doubted.

Reaching the top, the procession strung along and finally dipped into a ravine, following the steeply slanting water-course until stopped by a lariat stretched across the way. Tossing aside the rope, the leader led the force onto the walled-in pasture where each man went swiftly to work without instructions. The fire at the leader's feet, fanned by the high wind, leaped from him through the sun-cured bunches of grass in a rapidly widening circle, the heavy smoke rolling down upon the restless cattle in pungent clouds, sparks streaming through them. Every cow on the pasture was on its feet, pawing and snorting with fear at this most dreaded of all enemies. While they stood, seemingly hypnotized for a moment by the low flames, the darkness to the east of them was streaked with spurts of fire and the cracks of revolvers on their flank sent them thundering toward the river. The confusion of the stampede was indescribable as the front ranks, sensing the edge of the cliff, tried in vain to check itself and hold back against the press of the avalanche of terror-stricken animals behind. The change was magical-one moment a frenzied mass of struggling cows lighted grotesquely by the burning grass, and then only the edge of the cliff and the swishing grayness of the river below. The wind was blowing the flames toward the edge of the cliff and they would die from lack of material upon which to feed, though the four cared little about that. Their horses stumbled with them along the ravine, leaving behind a blackened plain across which sparks were driven by each gust of wind, to glow brilliantly and die. Below, once more wrapped in impenetrable darkness, swished the Black Jack, cold, cruel, deep, and fugitive, its scurrying, frightened cross currents whispering mysteriously as they discussed the tragedy. Suddenly the rain deluged everything as if wrathful at the pitiable slaughter and eager to wash out the stain of it.

* * * * *

In the middle of the forenoon of the following day Slow Jack loomed up in the fog of the driving rain and the vapors arising from the earth and slid from his saddle in front of the ranch house, his hideous yellow slicker shining as though polished. Buck opened the door and instinctively stepped back to avoid the wet gust that assailed him. "There 's a lot o' cows floating in the backwater o' th' Jack where th' creek empties in —I roped one an' drug it ashore. Just plain drowned, I reckon. There was signs of itch, too," Slow Jack reported.

Buck hastened into his storm clothes, got Monroe from the corral, and started through the storm to see for himself. When he reached the river he saw a score of Double Y cows drifting in circles in the backwater, and at intervals one would swing into the outer current and be caught in the pull of the rushing river to go sailing toward Twin. The stream was rising rapidly now, its gray waters turning brown and roiled. Sending Monroe to follow the stream to town, he and Slow Jack rode close to the water toward the hazy Hog Back. When he met Monroe at the ranch house that afternoon he learned that most of the inhabitants of Twin River were swarming upon the point behind Ike's saloon, busily engaged in roping and skinning the cattle as fast as they drifted by; the count varied from one hundred to five hundred, and he knew that the fight was on again.

There had been no clues found upon which to base action against the perpetrators. True, the pasture behind the Hog Back had been burned since he last saw it, but Slow Jack's tardy memory recalled that one morning, several days before, he had detected the smell of grass smoke in the air. He was going to investigate it but hesitated to go through the quarantined range for fear of bringing back the itch. During the day the smell had disappeared and he had seen no signs of smoke at any time. He had meant to speak of it when he returned to the bunk-house but had forgotten, as usual.

When left alone Buck stared out of the window, not noticing that the storm had ceased, burning with rage at his absolute helplessness. The loss of the cows was not great enough to cripple him seriously but this blow, following hard upon the other, showed him what little chance he had of making the Double Y a success without a large outfit of tried and trusted men. Even while he looked at the plain with unseeing eyes his cattle might be stolen or driven to death in the swollen waters of either river-and he was powerless to stop it.

To his mind again leaped the recollection of Ned's warning regarding Schatz: he was a "hard nut," Ned had said. Buck was beginning to think he would have to crack him on suspicion. He looked in the direction of the German's cabin and a curse rumbled in his throat.

Whitby opened the door and reported that everything was all right on his part of the range and asked for orders for the next day. After a few minutes' conversation he moved on to the bunk-house, troubled and ill at ease at the appearance of his employer. In a way Whitby had certain small privileges that were denied to the other members of the outfit. He was a gentleman, as Buck had instantly realized, and he could make time pass very rapidly under most conditions. He paused now and finally decided to thrust his company upon Buck for the evening; in his opinion Buck would be all the better for company. He had almost reached the ranch house door when behind him there was a sound of furious galloping and Bow-Wow flung himself from his horse and burst into the room excited and fuming, Whitby close upon his heels.

"They 've shot a lot of cows on th' southeast corner, close to th' Jill. I 'd 'a' been in sooner only I went huntin' for 'em. Lost their tracks when they swum th' river. Three of 'em did it, an' they dropped nigh onto fifty head." Winded as he was, Bow-Wow yet found breath for a string of curses that appeared to afford him little relief.

A look came into Buck's face that told of a man with his back to the wall. The piling on of the last straw was dangerously near at hand. His fingers closed convulsively around the butt of his Colt and he swayed in his tracks. No one ever knew how close to death Whitby and Bow-Wow were at that moment, by what a narrow margin the range was spared ruthless murder at the hands of a man gone fighting mad. The Texan was cut to the heart by this last news, and only a swift reaction in the form of the habitual self-restraint of thirty years saved him from running amuck. The grayness of his face gave way to its usual color, only the whipcord veins and the deep lines telling of the savage battle raging in the soul of the man. He waved the two men away and paced to and fro across the room, fighting the greatest battle of his eventful life. One man against unknown enemies who shot in the dark; his outfit was an unknown quantity and practically worse than none at all, since he had to trust it to a certain extent. He thought that Ned Monroe was loyal, but his judgment might have become poor because of the strain he had undergone; and was not Monroe one who had lost when the ranch was turned over to its rightful owners? Bow-Wow was more likely to be honest than otherwise, but he had no proof in the puncher's favor. Chesty Sutton had no cause to be a traitor, but the workings of the human mind cause queer actions at times. Cock Murray and Slow Jack could be regarded as enemies, but there was not enough proof to convict them: they had been in charge of the western part of the ranch when the herd had been stampeded into the Black Jack-yet Buck realized that two men could hardly handle so large a tract of land; and again, the stampede had occurred at night while they were asleep in the bunkhouse. If he got rid of every man he could find reason to doubt, he would have no outfit to handle the routine work of the ranch. There remained Jake and Whitby. The cook could be dismissed as of no account one way or the other, since he was a fool at best and never left the ranch house for more than a few minutes at a time. The Englishman seemed to be loyal but there was no positive assurance of it; while he had undoubtedly killed the itch, it was so dangerous a plague that every man's hand should be turned against it.

When he tried to reason the matter out he came to the conclusion he had reached so often before: the only man in Montana whom he trusted absolutely was Buck Peters. If he had some of his old outfit, or even Hopalong, Red, or Lanky, one man in whom he could place absolute trust, he felt he could win out in the end-and he would have them. He ceased his pacing to and fro and squared his shoulders: He would give his outfit one last tryout and if still in doubt of its loyalty, he would send a message to Hopalong and have him pick out a dozen men from the Bar-20 and near-by ranches and send them up to the Double Y. Lucas, Bartlett, and Meeker could spare him a few men each, men friendly to him. It would be admitting preliminary defeat to do this but the results would justify the means.

When he thought he had mastered himself and was becoming calm and self-possessed, Chesty Sutton and the foreman entered with troubled looks on their faces. Monroe spoke: "Chesty reports he found a dozen cows lyin' in a heap at th' bottom of Crow Canyon, and Murray says th' fence has been cut an' stripped o' wire for a mile on th' north end."

Buck lost himself in the fury of rage that swept over him at this news. The fence had been intact that noon when he rode out to look over the floating cows in the Jack; this blow in daylight told him that the battle was being forced from several points at once; and again he realized how absolutely helpless he was-there was no hope now. When Ned and Chesty returned to the bunk-house, drawing meagre satisfaction from the clearing weather, they left behind them a man broken in spirit, weak from fruitless anger, who shook his upraised arms at Providence and cursed every man in Montana. A desperate idea entered his head: he would force the fighting.

He slipped out of the corral, roped his horse and led it around back of the ranch house, where he tethered it and returned to the house to wait for night. Night would see him at Schatz's cabin, there to choke out the truth and strike his first blow.

Jake came in, muttering something about lights and supper, to retreat silently at the curt dismissal. The long shadows stole into the room, enveloping the brooding figure, and deepened into dark. The time was come and Buck arose and went out to his horse. With his hand on the picket he paused and listened. Across the Jill a broad moon was beginning to cast its light and from the same direction, a long way off, came the sound of singing. The singer was coming toward him and Buck stepped into the house again to await his arrival. He might be the bearer of some message.

While he paced restlessly the singing died down and in a few minutes the squeaking of a vehicle caught his ear. He wondered who cared to drive over that trail when there were so many good saddle horses to be had for the asking and he started toward the door to see. Suddenly he stopped as if shot and gripped his hat with all his strength as another song came to his ears. He doubted his senses and feared he was going crazy, hoping against hope that he heard aright. Who in Montana could know that song!

> ″'Th' cows go grazin' o'er th' lea —
> Pore Whiskey Bill, pore Whiskey Bill.
> An' achin' thoughts pour in on me
> Of Whiskey Bill.

> Th' sheriff up an' found his stride,
> Bill's soul went shootin' down th' slide —
> How are things o'er th' Great Divide,
> Oh, Whiskey Bill?'

″Hello th' house! Hey, Buck! Buck! *O*, Buck! Whoa, blame you-think I'm a fool tenderfoot? Hey, Buck! BUCK!″

Buck leaped to the door in one great bound and ran toward the creeping buckboard, yelling like an Indian. The bunk-house door flew open and the men tumbled through it, guns in hand, and sprinted toward the point of trouble. Bow-Wow led and close upon his heels ran Whitby, with Murray a close third. When the leader got near enough he saw two men wrestling near a buckboard and he manoeuvred so as to insert himself into the fracas at the first opportunity. Then he snorted and backed off in profound astonishment, colliding with the eager English-man, to the pain of both. The wrestlers were not wrestling but hugging; and a woman in the buckboard was laughing with delight. Bow-Wow shook his head as if to clear it and began to slip back toward the bunk-house. This was against all his teachings and he would have no part in it. The idea of two cowmen hugging each other!

Whitby strolled after and overtook the muttering puncher. "I fancy that's one of those Texans he 's been talking about; or, rather, two of them. Perhaps we shall see some frontier law up here now-and God knows it is time."

Slow Jack veered off and swore in his throat. ″*Texas* law, huh? We 'll send him back where he come from, in a box!″ he growled.

He stopped when he heard Buck's laughing words, and sneered: ″Hopalong Cassidy an' his wife, eh? She 'll be his widder if he cuts in *this* game. But I wonder if any more o' them terrible Texas killers is comin' up? Huh! Let 'em come-that's all.″

Chapter XVI

The Master Mind

For a while, at least, Buck seemed to cast his troubles to the four winds and was a picture of delight; his happiness, bubbling up in every word, kept his face wreathed in one vast smile. At last he had a man whom he could trust. Jake was summoned and prepared the best meal he could and the three sat down to a very good supper, Buck surprised to find how hungry he had become. His visit to Schatz was forgotten as he listened to Hopalong and Mary chatter about old times and people he wished he could see again.

After a little, Hopalong noticed how tired his wife was and sent her to get a good night's rest. The long railroad journey and the ride in the buckboard had been a great strain on her.

When left alone, Buck demanded to know all about the Bar-20 and its outfit and laughed until the tears came as he listened to some of the tales. "What deviltry has Johnny been up to since I left?" asked Buck.

"Well, it's only been six months," replied Hopalong, "so you see he ain't really had much time; but he 's made good use o' what he did have. He fell in love again, had th' prospectin' fever, wanted to go down to th' Mexican line an' help Martin. I had th' very devil of a time stoppin' him. Him an' Lucas had their third fight an' Lucas got licked this time; then they went off to Cowan's an' blew th' crowd, near havin' another scrap 'cause each wanted to pay. He dosed Pete's cayuse with whiskey an' ginger, chased Lee Hop clean to Buckskin, so we ain't got no cook. Red licked him for that, so Johnny tied all th' boys together one night, tied chairs an' things to 'em an' then stepped outside an' began shootin' at th' stars. It was some lively, that mess in th' dark, judgin' from th' hair-raisin' noises; it scared th' Kid all th' way to Perry's Bend-leastways, we has no news for a week, when we hears he 'd pulled stakes there, leavin' th' town fightin' an' th' sheriff locked up in his own jail. Th' Bend has sent numerous invitations for him to call again. From there he drifts over to th' C80, wins all their money an' then rides home loaded down with presents to square hisself with th' boys. He wanted to fight when I made Red foreman while I was away-it's Red's first good chance to get square."

"That's th' Kid, all right," laughed Buck. "Lord, how I wish he was up here!"

"Red, he's th' same grouch as ever but he's all right if Johnny 'd let him get set. As soon as Red calms down th' Kid calls his attention to somethin' excitin' an' th' trouble begins again. They all wanted to come up here an' give you a hand till you got things runnin' right. I told 'em I could get a better crowd in two days, so they stayed home to spite me. From what I 've heard I wish I 'd told 'em they could come-things 'd run smoother for you with them wild men buckjumpin' 'round lookin' for trouble. Like to turn Red an' Johnny loose up here with a good grudge to work off. Th' railroad would report that Montana was jumpin' east fast."

"What was that your wife called you?" asked Buck, curiously.

"Billy-Red," laughed Hopalong. "That 's her own name for me."

"Billy-h —l!" snorted Buck. "Billy-goat would suit you better."

"Say, Buck, Pete saw som'ers there was lots o' money in raisin' chickens, so he borrows all our money, gets about a hundred head from th' East, an' starts in. For a week there was lots of excitement 'round our place-coyotes got so they 'd get under our feet an' th' nights was plumb full o' hungry animals with a taste for chicken. We put up a bomb-proof coop but they tunnelled it th' first night an' got all that was left o' th' herd 'cept about a dozen what was roostin' high. Pete, he was broken-hearted an' give up. He makes Mary a present o' what was left of his stock, an' what do you think she give him for 'em? Two day's work diggin'. He dug a ditch, four-sided, for th' foundations of a new coop. Then he has to sink posts in it in th' ground an' fill th' ditch with stones. Johnny got th' stones in th' chuck wagon from th' creek, so as to square hisself with Mary, an' she give him a whole apricot pie for it. He 's been a nuisance ever since. Well, th' posts rose four feet above th' ground an' when that hen-corral was roofed over, you could see, any moonlight night, plenty o' coyotes trottin' 'round it, prayin' for somethin' to happen. We got some fine shootin' for a while. But I got other things to talk about, Buck-Texas can wait."

"Kind of a dry job, Hoppy," replied Buck, going to a cupboard and returning with a bottle.

"Better stuff than Cowan ever sold," smiled the visitor, and then plunged into what he considered real news.

"When we got off th' train at Wayback, I went huntin' for a wagon an' purty soon we was on our way to Twin River. I knowed we 'd have to spend th' night there: Mary could n't stand forty miles in a buckboard after that train ride. We had n't got very far from town when I hears a hail an' looks around to see Tex Ewalt comin' up. He spotted me when I left th' train but he did n't want to show he knows me there."

"What!" exclaimed Buck, in great surprise. "Tex Ewalt! Why, I thought he went East for good."

"He thought so, too, at th' time," and Hoppy gave a brief history of their friend's movements. "When he got back to th' ranch he was restless an' decided to come up here an' help you. He 's been very busy up here in a quiet way. He tells me he knows th' man that put th' itch on yore range. Tex says he could 'a' stopped it if he knew enough to add two an' two. But he says there 's another man behind him, slicker 'n a coyote. Tex 's been hopin' every day to rope an' tie him but he ain't got him yet."

"Who is it?" asked Buck, with grim simplicity.

"Tex won't tell me. He says you can't do no good shootin' on suspicion. He's tried watchin' him but he might as well be goin' to church when he does leave home, his travels is that innocent."

"Why didn't Tex come here? I been wantin' one man I could trust, an' me an' Tex could 'a' wiped out th' gang."

"He says different-an' he was afraid o' bein' seen. You see, that would kill his usefulness. Just as soon as he could get to th' bottom o' th' game an' lay his fingers on th' real boss, *then* he 'd 'a' come out for you in th' open, put th' boss in th' scrap-pile for burial, an' burned powder till you had things where you wanted 'em. We about concluded you ain't makin' good use o' th' punchers you got, Buck, though I shore hates to say it."

"How can I make use o' men I don't trust? You don't know th' worst, Hopalong—"

"About th' couple o' thousand head went swimmin'? I ain't heard much else in Twin River. How 'd it happen?"

Buck ran over the day's occurrences graphically and without missing a single point. Hopalong's thoughtful comment was characteristic of the man upon whom Buck had unconsciously leaned in crises not a few.

"The two men on yore south pasture is liars," he declared. "Yore foreman is some doubtful: 'pears like to me if he 's honest an' attendin' to business, no point o' yore range ought to go shy o' him for long. Th' Britisher 's white: it's no part o' his business to help you, th' way Tex tells me; if he ain't square he just does his work an' don't offer no suggestions. Th' other two is all right if they ain't just fools what 'll do as th' foreman says 'cause he 's th' foreman, right or wrong. That's how I reckons you stand. Now we got to prove it."

"Fire away," said Buck, earnestly. "I agrees to every word. Provin' it's th' horse I ain't been able to rope."

"Th' outlyin' free range don't count. You ain't missed no cows in th' round-up, has you?"

"No, they tallied high."

"Goes to show there 's a head to th' deviltry. You don't get no losses on'y right on yore home range. Now, we divide th' range in sections, a man to each section, an' work 'em that way a few days. There won't be no night ridin' at first. Then we set 'em night ridin' when they ain't expectin' it an' shift th' men every night. We soon know who to trust, don't we?"

"Yo 're right-plumb right-an' it's so simple I ought to be fed hay, for a cow. I got a map som'ers-or I 'll make one. We 'll lay out them sections right now."

"That's th' talk! There ain't no time like right now for doin' most things, Buck."

They were not long in laying out and perfecting their plans and had said good-night when Buck suddenly remembered the picketed pony. He turned it into the corral and went to bed.

Smiler Schatz, sleeping the sleep of the very wicked and the very innocent, did not dream how near he had come to an incident more exciting than any he had ever passed through.

Chapter XVII
Hopalong's Night Ride

Hopalong, passing the bunk-house on his way to the stable, paused to listen. Through the open window Pickles' voice had reached him quite clearly: "I don't guess I 'll ever get him, Whit, but if I do, it 'll be for keeps, you betcher."

Hopalong was interested. The death of Gottlieb Gerken was an old story and so many things of pressing moment having occurred about the time of Hopalong's arrival, he had not been told of this. The finality of decision in Pickles' murderous intention was so evident that Hopalong wondered how the boy came to conceive so deadly a hatred. He stepped to the window and stood looking at the two figures within. They neither saw nor heard him.

Both were deep in thought. Whitby's inherent regard for due process of law had received numerous shocks since he left Chicago. Like many another square man finding his niche in a raw country, he was beginning to see that right must be enforced by might, until such time as wrong became subdued by the steady march of the older civilization. And this face-about in opinion is not accomplished in a day, even when on the spot and a personal sufferer. It was this new feeling that led him to listen with respect to Pickles' confidences, boy though he was. Boys imbibed men's ideas early in this country; too early, thought Whitby, recalling his own play-time at this lad's age. He stole a look at the glum face beside him and began to draw circles with the point of the switch he held in his hand-he was never without one. "It's a pity," he said, "a pity."

"What's a pity?" asked Pickles, a note of indignation in his voice at the implied suggestion.

Whitby ignored the tone. "It's a pity you never heard of the Witch's Spell," he explained, reminiscently.

"What's that?"

"But then, of course," reasoned Whitby, "if you can't find a Witch's Ring, you can't work the Spell; and I rather fancy there is n't a Witch's Ring in all the world outside of Yorkshire."

"What's it like?" demanded Pickles, with the practical insistence of Young America.

"Why, the Old Witch makes it, you know. She runs around in a ring and blows on the grass and it never grows any more. Inside the Ring and outside, the grass is just the same, but the Ring is always bare."

Pickles was silent. He was picturing to himself the process of the Ring in the making. So was Hopalong. It seemed very matter-of-fact as Whitby told it; still, there was something —

"What's she do that for?" asked Pickles-the very question Hopalong was asking himself.

"It's the bad fairies, you know, and Wizards, and that sort of thing; she 's afraid of them. But they can't pass the Ring, no matter how deep they dig, so the Witch is quite safe, you know. They 're a bad lot, those others, no end. But the Old Witch is quite a decent sort. She lives inside the Ring, under the ground, and that's where you go to get your wish."

Pickles pondered. His eyes began to glow. "Any wish?" he questioned, in subdued excitement.

"All sorts," declared Whitby. "There was Jimmie Pickering: he always got his wish; he told me so, himself; and Arthur Cooper: he wished to be a minister and he got his wish; and George Hick: he wished to see the world and he 's always travelling up and down the earth; and Allen Ramsey, who wished to be an athlete, strong, you know: he got his wish; then there was Maggie Sheffield, who wished to marry a soldier: she married a soldier; and Vi Glades, who wished to be a singer: she can sing tears into your heart, lad, so sweet you 're glad to have them there; so she got her wish. And ever so many more: they all got their wishes. She was a rare good one, that Witch."

"Did you get yore wish, Whit?"

"I could only count to seven," explained Whitby.

Pickles' lips moved silently. "How many do you have to count?" he asked, dubiously.

"Nine," said Whitby, with a regretful sigh. "You run around the Ring nine times, holding your breath and saying your wish to yourself over and over again. Then you run into the middle and lie down. You must n't breathe until you lie down. When you put your ear to the ground you can hear the Old Witch churning out your wish. 'Ka-Chug! Ka-Chug! Ka-Chug!' goes the churn, away down in the earth. Then you know you will get your wish."

Pickles straightened up and looked fixedly at Whitby. His voice was very solemn: "Whit, I take my oath there's a Witch's Ring right here on the range!"

"Nonsense!"

"Hope I may die! I 'll show you, to-morrow. An' I 'm a-goin' to wish —"

"I say! You must n't tell your wish, you know. That breaks the Spell. If ever you tell your wish, it does n't come true."

"Jiggers! —I won't tell. Nine times 'round the Ring an' hol' yore breath an' say yore wish fast an' then to th' middle —"

Hopalong lost the rest as he continued on his way to the stable. Pickles' Ring puzzled him only for a moment, for as he turned away from the window, he was chuckling. "Means some place where th' Injuns used to war-dance, I reckon," was his conclusion. "But that Britisher seems like he believed it himself."

Two minutes later and he was in the saddle and riding south, edging over toward Big Moose trail. He melted into the surrounding darkness like a shadow, silence having been the evident aim of his unusual preparations earlier in the evening. Not a leather creaked; an impatient toss of his pony's head betrayed no clink of metal on teeth; the velvety padding of the hoofs made as little noise as the passing of one of the larger cats, in a hurry. Hopalong meant to quarter the section of range allotted him like a restless ghost and, if the others did as well, he had a strong conviction that night-deviltry would lose its attractions in this particular part of the country.

It was not long before he began to test his memory. To a man of his experience this guard duty would have presented but little difficulty in any case, but Hopalong had been careful to make a very complete mental map of this section when riding it by daylight. He went on now like a man in his own house.

He turned abruptly to the left, heading for the Jill and taking the low ground between two huge buttes. Just short of the Big Moose trail he halted, listening intently for five minutes, and then, turning west again, began to quarter the ground like a hound, gradually working south. With the plainsman's certainty of direction his course followed a series of obliques, fairly regular, though he chose the low ground, winding about the buttes, to the top of which he lent a keen scrutiny. He stopped for minutes at a time to listen and then went on again.

It was during one of these pauses that he espied a dark shape at rest not far from him. He eyed it with suspicion. It should be a cow but there was something not quite normal in its attitude. He rode forward cautiously, being in no way desirous of disturbing the brute. Circling it at a walk a similar object loomed up, some little distance from the other. "Calf!" he decided. A few steps nearer and he changed his mind. "No, another cow. I don't know as I ever see cattle look like that. 'Pears like they was shore enough tuckered out-an' I bet they ain't drifted a mile in twenty-four hours." They were very still. There was no reason why they should not be and yet-the wind being right, he hazarded a few steps nearer.

And then there came to his ears a sound that stiffened him in his saddle. His pony turned its head and gazed inquiringly into the darkness. "Injuns!" breathed Hopalong, doubt struggling with conviction. He slipped to earth and ran noiselessly to the nearest recumbent figure. A single touch told him: it was a dead cow; warm, but unquestionably dead.

With his horse under him once more, Hoppy crept forward. Careful before, his progress now had all the stealth of a stalking tiger. There it came again: the unmistakable twang of a bow-string. The pony veered to the left in response to the pressure of Hoppy's knee, when there sounded a movement to the right and he straightened his course to ride between the two. His spirits began to rise with the old-time zest at the imminence of a fight to the death. Mary, back yonder in the ranch house, with her new proud hope, Buck and his anxieties, Tex in his indefatigable hunt for evidence, the far-distant Bar-20 with its duties and its band of loyal friends, all were forgotten in the complete absorption of the coming duel. Indians! Rebellious and treacherous punchers were foemen to beware of, but these red wolves, savage from the curb of the reservation and hungry with a blood lust long denied —a grin of pure delight spread over his features as he foresaw the instant transformation from cattle-killing thieves to strategic assassins at the first crack of his Colt.

The odds could not be great and he expected to reduce them at the opening of hostilities. Warily he glanced about him as he moved slowly forward, casting, at the last, a searching look off to the right. He saw that which brought him up standing, his breath caught in his distended lungs; it escaped in a long sigh of pleased wonder: "Great Land of Freedom! Please look at that," he pleaded to his unresponsive country.

Broadside on, head up and facing him with ears pricked forward, alert yet waiting, stood a horse that filled Hopalong's soul with the sin of covetousness. So near that the obscurity failed to hide a line, the powerful quarters and grand forehand betrayed to Hopalong's discerning eyes a latent force a little superior to the best he had ever looked on. "An' a' Injun's!" sighed Hoppy, in measureless disgust. "But not if I sees th' Injun," he added hopefully. Wishing that he might, his thought back-somersaulted to Pickles and Whitby and the Witch's Spell. A whimsical smile wrinkled the corners of his mouth and at this very moment the thing happened.

A nerve-racking screech, the like of which no Indian ever made, lifted the hair on Hoppy's head, and his pony immediately entered upon a series of amazing calisthenics, an enthusiastic rendering no doubt enhanced by the inch or two of arrow-head in his rump. Hopalong caught one glimpse of a squat, mis-shapen figure that went past him with a rush and let go at it, more from habit than with the expectation of hitting. When he had subdued his horse to the exercise of some little equine sense, the rapidly decreasing sound of the fleeing marauder told him that only one had been at work and with grim hopelessness he set after him. "Might as well try to catch a comet," he growled, sinking his spurs into the pony's side and momentarily distracting its attention from the biting anguish of the lengthier spur behind.

The pony was running less silently than when he left the ranch. Portions of unaccustomed equipment, loosened in his mad flurry, were dropping from him at every jump. This, and the straining of Hopalong's hearing after the chase, allowed to pass unnoticed the coming up of a third horseman, riding at an angle to intercept the pursuit. The first intimation of his presence Hopalong received was the whine of a bullet, too close for comfort, and Hopalong was off and behind his pony to welcome the crack of the rifle when it reached him. "Shootin' at random, d —n his fool hide!" snorted Hoppy; "an' shootin' good too," he conceded, as a second bullet sped eagerly after the first. Hoppy released a bellow of angry protest: "Hey! What 'n h —l do you reckon yo 're doin'?"

There was an interval of silence and then a voice from the darkness: "Show a laig, there: who is it?"

"Show you a boot, you locoed bummer! It's Cassidy." He mounted resignedly and waited for the other to ride up. "Could n't 'a' caught him, nohow," he reflected. "Never see such a horse in my life, never. Hope to th' Lord it don't rain. Be just like it."

The unknown rode up full of apologies. Hopalong cut him short. "What d' they call you?" he asked, curtly.

"Slow Jack," was the answer.

Hoppy grunted. "Well, you camp down right here," he ordered, "an' don't let nobody blot that sign. I 'm a-goin' to be here at daylight an' foller that screech-owl th' limit. Good-night."

He headed for the ranch house, satisfied that his section of range would remain undisturbed during the next few hours, at the least.

* * * * *

"Sweet birds-o'-paradise! Would you—would you oblige me by squintin' at that!"

Straight north, from the few dead carcasses where the trail started it led to the creek bank, east of the ranch house; and like hounds with nose to scent, Hopalong, Buck, and Ned had followed it from the point where Slow Jack had been found doing sentry-go and sent, in profane relief, to breakfast and sleep. Hoppy was in the lead and as he came to the creek he raised his eyes to look across at the other bank for signs of the quarry's exit from the water. It was the sign on the north bank, coupled with that on the somewhat higher bank where they stood, that had made him exclaim.

Ned Monroe's face cleared of the frowning perplexity that had darkened it at first sight of the hoof prints they tracked. "Must be a stranger," he affirmed. "Dunno th' country or he 'd never jump when he could ride through."

"Jump!" exclaimed Buck, startled. "Why, of course," he conceded. "Hoppy, that's shore one scrumptious jump"; and the dawning admiration grew to wonder as he mentally measured the distance.

Hoppy nodded his head. "*I* never see th' horse could do it right now; an' that bird flew over there last night. He was right on it afore he knew an' he did n't stop to remember how deep it was; he just dug in a spur an' lifted him at sight of th' breakin' bubbles: they 'd show purty nigh white last night-an' th' horse, he does n't know how much he has to jump, so he jumps a good one —a d —n good one, though Ned, here, don't think it so much. Mebby you know a horse as could do it right easy, eh, Ned?"

With Hopalong's sharp eyes on his face, Ned shook his head in denial, gazing stolidly at the sign. "Too good for any in these parts; would n't be no disgrace for a thoroughbred."

Buck glanced quickly at Ned and then, pulling his hat low over his eyes, struck up the brim with two snappy blows of the back of his hand.

"Well, Buck, I reckon I 'll leave you an' Ned to foller this. I got a feelin' I 'm wanted at th' ranch. So long." Hopalong rode off in obedience to one of the signals that had helped to simplify affairs among the Bar-20 punchers.

Buck had signified his desire for Hoppy's absence. He pushed Allday to the creek and set off at a lope. "Easy as follerin' a wagon, Ned," he remarked.

"Yep," agreed Ned.

"Stopped here," observed Buck. "Listenin', I reckon. Goin' slower, now."

"Some," replied Ned.

"Right smart jump acrost that creek," said Buck, questioningly.

"Uh-huh!" consented Ned, with non-committal brevity.

They rode a couple of miles before Buck hazarded another remark. "Seems like I oughta know that hoof," he complained. "Keeps a-lookin' more 'n more like I knowed it. Durn thing purty nigh talks."

Ned threw him a startled glance and then gazed steadily ahead. "Be at th' Jill in a minute," he announced.

"Yeah. Thought he was driftin' that-away. Lay you ten to two he don't *jump* th' Jill, Ned."

"Here 's Charley," was the irrelevant response. The Indian was a welcome diversion. Buck slowed to a walk, raised his eyes and waved Charley an amiable salute. The Cheyenne promptly left the trail and rode to join them.

"Hey, Charley, whose horse is that?" asked Buck, pointing to the hoof prints.

The Indian barely glanced at them. "French Rose," he declared. "Cross trail, swim river before sun. Heap good horse."

"Where goin', Charley-ranch?" asked Buck, evenly. He did not question the Cheyenne's conclusions. *He knew.* Buck was satisfied of that.

Charley grinned sheepishly and shifted uneasily under Buck's stare. "That's all right," assured Buck, "tell Jake to give you-no, wait for me. I 'll be there as soon as you are." He turned away and Charley accepted his dismissal in high good humor, riding off with cheering visions of a cupful of the "old man's" whiskey, which was very different from that dispensed over the bar in Twin River.

"Well, Ned," said Buck.

"Well, Buck," returned Ned.

"You knew it was Rose's horse."

"I was a-feared."

"You knew it, you durn ol' grizzly."

"Look a-here, Buck. You ain't goin' to tell me as how Rose —"

"Not by a jugful! That's a flower without a stain, Ned, an' I backs her with my whole pile."

"Here, too," coincided Ned, in hearty accord.

"We lost th' trail, Ned."

"You bet!"

"In th' Jill."

"Took a boat," suggested Ned, solemnly.

Buck concealed his amusement. "Or a balloon," he offered.

"Mebby," assented Ned. "Could n't pick her up agin, nohow."

"Not if we 'd had a dog," declared Buck.

"Or a' Injun," supplemented Ned. They gazed at one another for a second and, of one mind, spun their horses around and off for the ranch like thoroughbreds at the drop of the flag.

"I just thought o' Charley," explained Buck.

"Here, too," grunted Ned.

"Might talk," said Buck.

"You bet."

Charley heard them coming. When he saw them, the explanation to his untutored mind was a race. Determined to be in at the finish, he laid the quirt to his pony with enthusiastic zeal, casting a rapid glance over his shoulder, now and then, to see if he were holding his own. It was a sight to see the tireless little pony wake up under punishment. He had covered twenty miles that day and over forty the day before, but he shot forward on his wiry legs like a startled jack-rabbit and in one-two-three order they thundered up to the ranch house with a noise that brought Mary to the door.

"Well, Buck Peters!" she exclaimed, "ain't you *never* goin' to grow up? Yo're worse'n that loco husband o' mine, right now."

Buck grinned at the abashed Ned and winked knowingly at Mary. He and Mary were very good friends, Buck long ago having gauged her sterling worth and become aware of her mischievous propensity for teasing. As he led Charley indoors he asked for Hopalong and learned that he had set off for Twin River soon after his arrival at the ranch house.

* * * * *

Hopalong had taken his cue from Buck without question but not without curiosity. On his way to the house he decided, not without a longing thought in the direction of Red Connors, foreman *pro tem* of the Bar-20, that Tex Ewalt would be all the better for a knowledge of recent events. Therefore he paused only long enough to inform Mary of his intention before starting in search of him. At Twin River he pulled up at the Why-Not and went in for a drink. Tex was standing at the bar and ten minutes after Hopalong left, Tex had overtaken him on the Wayback trail. They struck off through the undergrowth until secure from observation, and Tex was soon acquainted with the latest attempt at stock reduction.

He listened silently until Hopalong mentioned the kind of man who had done the killing. "Big Saxe," he exclaimed. "So, that's his game. Well, we got 'em now, Hopalong. I can lay my hands on that cow-killer right soon, an' he 'll squeal, you bet. An' I got a long way to go. *Adios.*"

"Blamed grasshopper!" grumbled Hopalong. "Never even guessed where that horse come from. If Big Saxe is on him yet, you shore got a long journey, Tex."

Chapter XVIII
Karl to the Rescue

Dave, harboring a fermenting acerbity beside which the Spartan boy's wolf was a tickling parasite, lay hidden behind a stunted pine, his glasses trained on the Schatz cabin. Sourly he reviewed his several plans, each coming to nought as surely as if Peters had been made aware of it in its inception. The last grand coup, from which he had expected to derive immediate benefit, had arrived prematurely and mysteriously at its unexpected denouement; and that fool Saxe, upon whom he had relied to create a diversion, must needs keep himself hidden, to turn up when his efforts would be worse than useless. And then to come to Dave to be paid for making a fool of himself! He cursed aloud at the recollection. "It was a good scheme, too," he asserted savagely. No use telling him all those cows had stampeded and hurled themselves to destruction —"When the money for 'em was as good as mine." It had never been his real intention to allow Murray and Jack to divide the profits and by a curious mental strabismus he readily saw how he had been robbed. But losing the money was not the only nor the greatest blow. The injury to his sorely tried vanity hurt the most. He had been beaten, not so much by the enemy as by one of his friends.

Clouded by that same vanity his reason had acquitted all those who might have betrayed him, excepting Schatz. Rose, a woman who loved him-he had dismissed the thought with scorn; Comin', Cock Murray; they had all to lose and nothing to gain by treachery: and all the others were bound to him by ties, the weakest of which was stronger than any Buck could have formed in the time. Schatz alone might prove a gainer. He did not know in what way, but purposed to discover. That was why he was watching now. He knew Schatz was at home: he had seen the smoke of his breakfast fire. "Allus *is* home," he grated. He anticipated the calling of Schatz' agents at the cabin and when Schatz came out and finally rode off on the Twin River trail, Dave was disconcerted. He followed with much care, making good use of his glasses. The sight of Schatz turning off the trail and riding toward the Double Y ranch house filled him with a cold fury. —He determined to intercept him on his return and have it out on the spot.

But Dave, intent upon the unconscious back of Karl, had been careless of the surrounding country; and only his luck in choosing to wait in a place remote from cover, saved him just then from a rude awakening. Dodging about in the vain effort to approach to a point of vantage, was Pickles; he had finished certain mystic incantations involving the running at speed in circles, and was returning to await the fulfilment of his wish. Filled with awe as he was at this swift response, it did not prevent him from acting upon it.

His arrival at the nearest possible point showed him that Dave was still out of range. For the first time a doubt of Buck's omniscience assailed him: it was no part of wisdom to arm a man with a rifle of that sort. With cautious speed he retraced his steps, mounted the Goat, and scurried for the ranch by a roundabout route. There was nothing haphazard about this; his ideas were clearly defined: did n't Red Connors always borrow Hopalong's Sharps for long range? That showed. Pickles had implicit faith in the rifle. All that worried him was that Dave might not wait long enough.

Karl rode leisurely up to the ranch house and called. Mary came to the door and behind her Buck, whose brow was wrinkled in the effort of composing a letter to McAllister. It was not an easy letter to write and Buck had enlisted Whitby's services. He asked Karl to climb down and come inside. Mary had disappeared with a promptitude due to instinctive dislike. Karl was not a man to invite the admiration of any woman at the best of times and now his appearance gave abundant proof of its being long past "chipping-time."

Karl entered with the unexpected lightness of step so often a compensating grace in fat men, shook hands with Whitby, accepted the proffered chair, and plunged into the reason of his visit with but little preamble. Whitby sat making idle marks with his pen; soon he began to write swiftly.

"Big lot of cows you loose, ain'd it?" he asked.

"A few," replied Buck.

"Vat you t'ink: stampede?"

"Looks like it."

"*Look* like it? *Donnerwetter*! Look like a drive."

"You seen it?"

Karl nodded. "Look like a drive," he repeated.

"Would n't surprise me none," admitted Buck. "We had Injuns shootin' 'em on th' range last night."

"*Himmel*! Vat fools!"

"Looks like they 're tryin' to drive me off 'n th' range."

"*Yah, aber* not me. Ten years und no trouble come."

"Huh! Well, what would *you* do?"

"Fight," advised Karl. "I vill fight if you let me in. I haf a plan."

"In where?" asked Buck, in some wonder.

"In der ranch —a partner. Look! Cows you must haf, money you must haf, brains you must haf: I bring dem. I bring shust so much money as you und your partner togedder. Der money in der bank *geht*. You buy der cows, goot stock, besser as before. Goot cows, goot prices, ain'd it? You pay for everyt'ing mit der money in der bank. I stay here und stop dot foolishness mit precipices und parasites und shooting. Vat you dink?"

"Let me get you. You want to buy in on the Double Y, equal partners. I put in so much, McAllister puts in so much, and you put in as much as both of us. Th' money goes in th' bank an' I have th' spendin' of it. You do yore share o' th' work an' yo 're dead certain you can stop th' deviltry on th' range. Is that it?"

"*Yah!*" assented Karl, emphatically.

Buck was astounded at the audacity of the proposal. His gaze wandered to Whitby, whose pen was moving over the paper with a speed that impressed Buck, busy as his mind was. Outside, a horseman clattered up to the house and Mary, from the kitchen door, motioned Hopalong to come in that way. The door had no sooner closed behind him than Pickles sped from the security of the stable, slipped Hoppy's rifle from the saddle holster, and half a minute later the Goat went tearing away, bearing the triumphant boy and the coveted rifle to another scene of operations. For tenacity of purpose and facility of execution, Pickles was already superior to most men.

Buck recovered his wits and faced the expectant Schatz. "I just been a-writin' to McAllister," he informed him. "You 'll have to give me time to see what he says. Let's liquor."

* * * * *

Buck stood in the door watching Karl ride away; the expressionless face gave no hint of his feelings unless it were found in a certain cold hardness of the gray eyes in their steady stare, fixed upon the broad back of the receding German. Leaving this mark, his glance fell on the horse, waiting patiently for its late rider, and he turned back into the room and called: "Hoppy!" Hopalong came in from the kitchen and Buck met his entry with the question: "What do you think that Dutch hog come for?"

Hopalong glanced meaningly at Whitby, who still appeared to be writing against time. "That's all right," asserted Buck, "I 'm a-copperin' my bets from now on. Schatz wants to buy in as a partner an' reckons he can stop th' Double Y from losin' any more stock, long 's he 's in on th' deal."

"What 'd *you* say?" asked Hopalong.

"Nothin'. I wanted a chance to get my breath."

"Well, I would n't flirt with that proposition, not any."

"Why, curse his fool hide, what do I want with him or his money? If he can stop th' deviltry mebby he 's at th' bottom of it; an' if he is, it won't be long afore we know it. Next time he comes I 'll tell him to go plumb to h —l."

"I would n't, Buck."

"What's that?" asked Buck, staring hard at Whitby.

"I would n't," repeated Whitby. "I fancy it's time you learned what I know. This German chap, now. You can't fight him yet, Buck; you can't, really."

"Oh, can't I!" exclaimed Buck. "What do you know about it?"

"I know all about it, I should say all that can be found out. Do you mind if we have in Mrs. Cassidy? Clever woman, Mrs. Cassidy."

He left the room while Buck and Hopalong eyed each other helplessly. "D —d if he ain't tellin' me what kind of a wife I 've got," complained Hopalong. Mary came in, followed by Whitby.

"Now if you two boys 'll only listen to Whitby, you 'll learn somethin'," promised Mary.

"It began in Chicago," said Whitby. "Beastly hole, Chicago. I was n't at all sorry to leave it, except-but that's neither here nor there. McAllister is a friend of mine and he rather thought Buck under-rated the difficulties here; so he asked me to run out and look it over. I soon found it was jolly well too big for me so I wrote to the Governor-my father, at home you know-and he said he 'd foot the bills. So I put it in the hands of a detective agency; very thorough people, 'pon my word. They tell me this German chap is at the bottom of the mischief but they can't prove it. He is always behind somebody else. If Ned Monroe had not been honest and given up, McAllister would never have won his case in that court: Schatz owns the judge, so they tell me. Amazin' country, is n't it? And then he is far too clever to wage a losing fight: you would have won at the last, despite his efforts. Now he 's come with his offer of partnership. Clever idea, really. He 'll jolly well use you if he can't beat you; and no doubt he expects to trick you, Buck, in some way, perhaps lending you money-then, you out of it, he has McAllister at a disadvantage.

"My idea is this: take Schatz in as a partner and he 'll grow less careful. We shall be able to trip him up. Remarkable man, really. Not one of those he employs can be made to talk; they 're entirely loyal. But sooner or later he will make a mistake: rogues all do, even the cleverest of them; and if they continue to escape, it is merely because no one happened to be watching and catch them at it. I 'll lend you the money, Buck —"

"But what in-what do I need money for, Whit? Ain't th' range an' th' cattle enough?"

"Of course they are. But the German wants to see some cash capital and it will do no harm to give him plenty of rope, will it now?"

"But, Whit," objected Hopalong, "if yo 're shore it's th' Dutchman, we can drive him out of th' country so quick he 'll burn his feet. Men 's been shot for less 'n he 's done."

"You can't do it, Cassidy. The agency has n't been able to get a bit of proof. And McAllister is set against anything rash. I thought at one time he had put on another man. There 's a chap who makes his headquarters at Twin River who 's busy, no end. The agency rather suspected he was one of Schatz's men. Sharp chap, that. And he can't be working on his own hook, can he?"

He glanced at Buck as if expecting a reply.

"That's Tex Ewalt, Whit," informed Mary. "He 's on our side."

"Ah! do you know, I thought as much. My word, I 'm thirsty; wish I had a brandy and soda here." He paused to take a drink of water, shaking his head when Buck motioned to the whiskey. "I 'm afraid I shall never get used to that rye of yours," he declared, mournfully.

Buck turned to Hopalong. "What do you make of it?" he asked.

"If it depended on you alone, Buck, it would be easier to answer. But McAllister is in th' game an' it shore ain't Frenchy: we both know what he 'd 'a' done. What does McAllister think o' this partnership deal?" he asked Whitby.

"He has n't heard of it, but I 'm sure he would agree with me."

"All right!" exclaimed Buck. "We'll let Mac make th' runnin'. If it looks like he 's goin' to lose th' race it will be all th' easier to drop th' winner if we got him in gun range. But I shore hates to pay big interest, like I must, a-puttin' up money that way."

"Let me lend it you, Buck," advised Whitby. "The Governor will cable it fast enough when I ask for it. You won't have to pay me a penny interest. And when things settle down a bit you can turn it over to McAllister. I shall stop in this country. I like it, by Jove! And I 'm jolly well sure McAllister will sell out to me, particularly if—I say, Buck, have I made good out here in the West?"

Buck laughed as he grasped Whitby's hand. "Made good!" he repeated. "Yo 're th' best Britisher I ever knew an' I 've met some good ones in my time." With Hopalong's slap on his shoulder and Mary smiling at him from her chair by the window, Whitby felt that it was likely to prove a very pleasant country "when things settled down a bit."

"Let's get at that letter to Mac," suggested Buck. "Th' sooner I hear from him th' easier I 'll be in mind."

"I 've written it," answered Whitby. "If you like I 'll get it to Wayback to-night and stop over until morning."

"Go ahead," agreed Buck.

When he had left, Hopalong turned to his wife with the query: "How did he find out yo 're a clever woman, Mary?"

"Because he 's a clever man, only he hides it," replied Mary. "He was a-gassin' 'bout you an' Buck an' I naturally found out a thing or two myself. That's how he came to tell you. He regular confided in me an' I advised him to tell you-all."

"It was a safe bet you 'd find out more 'n you 'd let go," complimented Hopalong.

"Oh, you Billy-Red!"

* * * * *

When Pickles, mounted on the Goat, had left the ranch by a roundabout way he headed for the bottom of one of the range's many depressions and followed it until close to the Jill, where he turned south and began edging nearer and nearer to the place he had seen Dave. Pickles had listened to many tales of hunting and as his associates had been grown men, experienced in stalking, the boy had absorbed a great deal of healthy knowledge which he made use of in his playing, in the great outdoors. With a grave thoughtfulness beyond his years he now proceeded to put his knowledge to a sterner use and worked cautiously toward his objective without loss of time. When he rode up the bank of a draw, alert and wary, and saw the solitary horseman still keeping his patient vigil, he swiftly dismounted, picketed the Goat and, taking the heavy rifle, crept forward, crouching as he went.

He had come to the edge of the cover and saw Dave still very far away; and after vainly trying to find some way to get closer to the man he was after, he carefully opened the breech of the heavy Sharps to be again assured it was loaded. A bigger cartridge than he had ever used confronted him: four inches of brass and lead, throwing a 600-grain bullet by the terrific force of one hundred and twenty grains of powder. The forty-five Sharps Special raised Hopalong another notch in Pickles' estimation-truly it was a man's weapon.

"Gosh!" he gloated, and then glanced thoughtfully across the open plain towards the horseman. "Twelve hundred, all right," he muttered, regretfully, for one hundred would have suited him better. But a swift smile chased away the scowl. The rifle belonging to Hopalong never missed-he had Buck's word for that-and besides, he had made his wish. One last look around for a cover nearer to Dave, and the big sight was raised and set. The gun went to his shoulder and the heavy report crashed out of a huge cloud of gray smoke as the Sharps spoke.

The rifle belonging to Hopalong never missed — and besides, he had made his wish

Dave's sullen temper was rudely jogged into fierce and righteous anger. Something hit his face. Something else screamed past him, struck a rock and whirred into the sky with a sharp, venomous burr. The pony, resenting Dave's painful appropriation of part of his ear, went up into the air and came down on stiff legs, its back arching once as it landed. The instant the hoofs were firmly on the ground it stretched out and ran as it never had before, Dave helpless to check it. The heavy, sharp report of the huge rifle in Pickles' hand had no sooner reached him than he had all he could do to hold his seat. But the sound of that bullet passing him, lingered in his mind long after he had regained control of his terrified mount.

Pickles, swallowing hard and holding one shoulder with a timidly investigating hand, blinked his dazed eyes as he looked about, inquiringly. He remembered pulling the trigger-and then the Goat had reached out thirty feet and kicked him in the neck-and if it wasn't the Goat, who threw the rock? Dave! He sat up and then struggled to his feet, looking eagerly out to see the remains of Dave scattered carelessly over the landscape. Dave was fast getting smaller, a cloud of dust drifting to the south along his trail.

"D —n it!" cried the boy, tears of vexation in his eyes. "He got away! I missed! I missed!" he shouted. "Buck lied to me! Th' old gun ain't no good!" and in the ecstasy of his rage he danced up and down on the discredited weapon. "Whitby's witches ain't no good! Nothin's no good; an' I missed him!"

Meanwhile his injuries were not becoming easier: his head displayed a large, angry lump, and ached fit to burst; his shoulder was n't broken, he decided, as he exercised it tentatively, but not far from it; and a piece of skin was missing from his bleeding cheek.

"I ought to 'a' got him," he muttered sullenly, picking up the rifle and moving slowly back to where his horse was picketed. "Well, anyhow, he was awful scared —I *knowed* he was a coward! I knowed it! If this old gun was as good as its kick I *would* 'a' got him, too." Pickles had gauged the distance perfectly and his hand had not even quivered when he pulled the trigger-but he had yet to learn of windage and how to figure it. Dave owed his life to the wind that swept the dust of his pony's feet southward.

When Pickles had turned the horse into the pasture he reloaded the rifle before slipping it back into its long leather scabbard. It must be found as he had found it and, besides, he was plainsman enough to realize how serious it might be for Hopalong if he believed the weapon was loaded and found it empty in a crisis.

"Never missed, hey?" he growled savagely as he moved away. "Huh! *Next* time, I 'll use *Buck's* gun!"

Chapter XIX
The Weak Link

The little buckskin pony stood with wide-planted feet and hanging head; his splendid bellows of lungs and powerful abdominal muscles sent the wind in and out of the distended nostrils in the effort to overcome the effect of that last mad burst of speed demanded of him; in his eyes alone, battling against the haze, shone his unconquerable spirit. Bearing saddle and bridle Dave strode away from him to the cabin.

Straight in from Wayback, without a stop, the game little buckskin had carried Dave. Jealousy consumed him. Rumors of Smiler's defection were floating about the town and, though no one but those intimately concerned, knew the actual agreement made, the presence of the principals and their several places of call had been noted and fully commented upon. From such premises the town's deductions came near the truth.

The facts as known were enough for Dave. Whatever Schatz might be planning, Dave was satisfied that he had no part in it. That Schatz intended to treat him fairly was beyond the angle of his narrow mind. He was very calm over it, his face smooth of wrinkles, his movements slow and assured. He had passed through all the stages from irritation to rage-and beyond: Calm is always beyond.

"Mein gracious, Dave, you vas in a hurry?" asked Schatz, as Dave entered.

He hung saddle and bridle on a peg in the kitchen and strode through into the other room before replying. "No," he drawled, dropping into a chair and stretching his legs full length.

"No? Schust try to kill a horse, *vas*?"

"Yes. Played a trick on me this mornin' an' I 'm showin' him who 's boss."

"*Dummer Esel*! Und vor a trick you kill him! Den no more tricks, *vas*?"

"Oh, to h —l with th' cayuse! What's all this I hear o' you an' Peters in a lovin' match?"

"*Ach*! *'Nun kommt die Wahrheit'*! If you not come to-day, I send for you. Vy you stay avay like dot?"

"I 'm busy tryin' to make Peters good an' sick o' th' range, tryin' to drive him back to Texas, where he come from. What are you doin': payin' his passage or backin' him to win?"

"Paying his passage, Dave; vere, I am not sure. Look: here iss Herr Peters," stabbing a finger into the palm of his extended right hand, "und here iss McAllister," duplicating with his left; "und ven I do so," closing both hands tightly, "nobody iss left but Schatz."

"Easy as that, eh?" said Dave, sceptically.

"Schust so easy like dot. Look! I make me a pardner by der Double Y."

"Fine," drawled Dave, with hidden sarcasm.

"Vine as gold. Peters, he get all der money vat he can. McAllister, he send der same as Peters. Me, I got dot money, already. Der money vas in der bank. Der range iss my property schust so much as Peters und McAllister."

"Fine," repeated Dave.

"Peters, he dink he spend der money. Soon he go to buy cows. Now iss de point: to-morrow I go by der bank, I dake oud all der money. Four men iss guard. I say I go over by der Bitter Root vere der Deuce Arrow herd for sale iss; und I take all der money. Because dot bank in Vayback too small. I leave der bank und stop by der Miner's Pick saloon. Ve drink. A man vot vears a mask comes in. He cover us mit a gun. He take der money, ride away to Coon River by der Red Bluff. Dere iss man und boat. Der man mit der boat take horse und ride to first relay und pretty soon he iss in Rankin. A relay every ten miles. Der man mit der money go down river in der boat five mile und dere iss man mit two horses; he ride to Vayback und den here mit der money. Vat you tink?"

"Fine," said Dave, for the third time. "An' who 's goin' to do all that ground an' lofty tumblin' with th' money?"

"Dave Owens," replied Schatz, with an air of conferring a great favor.

"Me!" exclaimed Dave. He laughed cynically. "Why, Karl, if I had somebody to do all th' hard work, I can make plans like that, myself. Talk sense."

"Hard vork! It iss easy, like a squirrel up a tree. Everybody iss by der station ven der train comes. You take all der guns und ve not make noise, *aber* some thief know you got all der money und catch you first und rob you. Ve got no horses ven ve go by train, und must run, get horses to run after you. So you get avay. You come here mit der money und who know it?"

"Who's makin' th' blind trail?"

"Denver Gus."

"I don't envy Gus none."

"Vy? I pay him goot. He vas go to Texas, anyvay, pretty quick."

"How you goin' to get out of it?"

"I don't get out of it. Peters, he gets sick und I say: 'Vell, some money I got yet, I buy you out'; *aber* he tink it iss a trick und get mad. Four men I got, gun-men, all. Dey shoot him so soon he get mad."

"An' then McAllister jumps on you with both feet for takin' that money out o' th' bank in th' first place."

"*Ach*! Vat you dink? Am I a fool? Ain'd I a pardner already?'

"What's that got to do with it?"

"I have schust so much right to take der money as Peters. I don't steal der money-it iss steal avay from me. Can I help it?"

"Is that th' law?"

"Der law iss my part. For der law, brains you must haf. Brains I got. To ride, you know. Vat you dink?"

"I go you," declared Dave. "But you shore take a big chance with th' money. I *might* get plugged an' have to drop it."

"*Mein lieber Gott!*" moaned Schatz, in despair. "Brains! Brains!" he roared. "*Ach*! Vat use? Alvays it iss der same. Von day Canada iss der United States; so England iss *gebunden*; South America iss Deutchland; soon all der continent iss Deutchland. Vat fools! No *Verstand-blos* for money. Und to make money iss der little part. Vat fools!"

"Wake up! Who 's th' fool if I drop that bundle an' somebody on a good horse gets away with it? Because you can bet yore whole pile I ain't aimin' to stop an' stand off th' beginnin' of a Judge Lynch party, not any."

"Dave, if a veek you sit und a veek you tink, und schust about von ting, you know somethings about it, *vas*?"

"Shore would."

"Und mit *your* head you must tink. Many days mit *my* head I tink und tink, everythings, possible und not possible. Den ven der plans iss made, *you* mit *your* head mistakes find. Der money vat you steal, it iss no matter, *aber* don't lose it-besser you burn it, as lose it."

"*Burn* it?"

"Yah! Paper it iss, schust paper."

"Paper!" Dave stared in doubt. "Paper," he repeated, struggling to grasp the idea. He gave it up and quite humbly asked for light. "What th' blazes am I a-goin' to run away with paper for?"

"Maybe somebody smarter as I tink. Two men, already, much questions ask. Maybe Peters take all der money before me. So I go by der bank und get der money first. Dey can't help it. It iss my bank anyvay und der check iss dere."

"You 've *got* th' money!"

"Yah, here in der house I got it. Everythings iss *vollkommen*. All der mistakes vat come I know, possible und not possible. Noding can slip, noding can break."

"Yo 're a wonder!" congratulated Dave, "th' one an' only original, sure-fire, bull's-eye wonder." He leaned forward suddenly, head bent in listening. "Somebody outside," he warned, softly. Gun in hand, he sprang to the door and passed out. The gloom of the coming night lay in wait in the valleys but it was light enough to detect any skulker. Dave made a systematic search, satisfying himself that no one was within a mile of the cabin, before returning. "It's all right," he assured, as he entered the room again. A deafening roar followed his words. Schatz gave a convulsive start and slid slowly from his chair to the floor; on his face was an overwhelming surprise.

"Huh-Huh! Huh! —" the grunting laugh spoke immeasureable contempt. "Brains!"

* * * * *

The half-open drawer of the sideboard revealed in the lamplight a number of packages, the wrappings of several being torn open. Dave sat thoughtfully contemplating them. He had removed them from their hiding place and put them in the drawer before lighting the lamp, both acts due to precaution: spying upon Karl had discovered to Dave the hiding place; he was distinctly opposed to finding himself in the same predicament regarding his suddenly acquired wealth. The still figure, resting under two feet of earth, close to the river bank, gave him no concern whatever. His mind was busy with the best way to pack the money; small bills were difficult to trace but bulky to carry. He shoved the drawer to with his foot and re-lit his pipe. His plans were already made. He had reasoned them out swiftly while hunting the supposed skulker. The disappearance of Karl would be associated with the disappearance of the money. The bank would maintain that the money had been drawn on the day the check was dated, which necessarily must be to-morrow. The four men who were to act as guards would conclude some difficulty had arisen and await further orders; it would be the same with all the others involved. The way was clear for him. There remained only Rose. He knocked the ashes from his pipe and went to bed.

Chapter XX
Misplaced Confidence

Pickles was hungry. He cocked his eye anxiously at the sun and sighed. He gazed in discouragement over the widespread furrowed earth where his best efforts left so small a trace and dropping the hoe, sighed again. With all his soul he wished he had not fled from the Double Y. Sudden resolution armed him. He shoved his hands in his pockets and marched manfully in the direction of the house. He refused to go hungry for anybody.

Topping a rise, his head barely showed against the sky-line when he dropped as if shot. The horseman making for the house might be Jean; his glance had been too hasty for recognition. Flat against the earth, Pickles pushed himself backward until he felt it safe to turn and gallop clumsily down grade on hands and feet. Far enough, he sat and thought. He could gain the barn unseen and if he ran, would have time to dash into the house, grab some chuck, and get away again before the horseman got there. He sprang to his feet and ran like a long-horn steer, gazed upon by the stock in pasture with interest: they were not accustomed to this style of locomotion in trousers.

Pickles made excellent time on the level but when he turned to breast the slope it was harder going; and Pickles was tired; he had been at work since sun-up with a short rest at breakfast. He gained the barn winded but went through and crossed to the house without pausing. Back of the house he stopped to listen. He had cut it too fine. The horse was coming up to the door. "Darn it!" said Pickles, with bitter emphasis.

The snap of the catch on the front door and Rose's voice told him she had gone outside. Maybe the rider was n't coming in; they could n't see the end window if they did and if he were quick-he squirmed over the ledge, dropped noiselessly to the floor, sped through the doorway-and almost dislocated his spine with the ferret-like turn he made in trying to get back into the room the same instant he left it: he had barely escaped the other's entry; if Rose came to the bedroom she would be certain to exclaim at sight of him. Pickles breathed a short —a very short-prayer. He put his hands to the window ledge-and stiffened.

"No, I can't stay. Rose, I 'm pullin' my freight. How soon can you come along?"

It was Dave-he was going away-and he wanted Rose to go, too. Pickles knelt silently by the bunk and muffled his rapid breathing in the blankets, while he listened.

"Where?" asked Rose.

"Anywhere you say. I 'm a-goin' to clean up a gold mine in a few hours an' yo 're goin' to help me spend it. We 'll get married first stop."

"A gold mine?"

"More money than you ever saw."

"And you want-me-to go with you?"

"Not with me. I got to get th' money first. I 'll get th' train to Helena to-night. You get on at Jackson. You can make it easy on Swaller."

"I must know more. Perhaps you tell true. Perhaps you run away. Tell me."

"Got a good opinion o' yore future husband, ain't you? Quit foolin', Rose. Have I got to show you the cards afore you take a hand?"

"Yes," was the decisive answer.

"All right. It's this way: Schatz deals to Peters from a cold deck. He gets all th' money out o' the bank, Peters', McAllister's, an' his. Then he lets me lift it, him not knowin' who I am, o' course. I do th' mysterious disappearance act an' Schatz makes foolish noises too late. A posse takes after me an' runs into a blind trail. I circle back to town. Right there is where I fool Schatz. He thinks I 'm driftin' along the Big Moose trail to hand th' money over to him graceful. 'Stead o' that I 'm snortin' along the track to Helena with you. Schatz dassent make no holler an' we leave him an' Peters to fight it out. Do you get me?"

"They will kill you."

"Oh, not a whole lot, I reckon. I 'm gettin' so used to bein' killed thataway, I sorter like it. Talk sense. Where's th' ole man?"

"I will leave a letter for him."

"Hip hooray! Mighty nigh kissin'-time, Rose. *Would* be, on'y I can't leave this blasted cayuse: 'fraid to trust him. Which way you goin'? Don't show in Wayback. Hit th' river farther west."

Pickles had heard enough. His exit through the window was rapid and silent. His retreat from the house, made along two sides of a triangle, was prompted by his knowledge of the positions of Rose and Dave and he manoeuvred so they should not be able to see him. Nevertheless the security of the barn was very welcome, although he gained it only to recall that the Goat was at pasture. Then Swallow must be in the corral. He looked from the rear door. Yes, there he was, close to the fence, gazing across the grass at the field stock and no doubt wishing he were with them. Whimpering with suppressed delight the boy ran silently to his rope, hanging in long loops over two pegs in the wall; he coiled it ready to hand, crept out the door, and was at Swallow with the rush of a bob-cat. The great stallion made one mighty bound, lashed out one foot and stood with flattened ears; he knew the meaning of a rope in that position as well as any cow-pony in Montana and the indignity vexed while it subdued him. Pickles never bridled and saddled so rapidly in his short life. Keeping the barn between him and the house, he rode a mile or more out of his course before he dared to turn; then he took his bearings, set a straight line for the Double Y ranch, and gave Swallow his head. The good horse, scarcely feeling the boy's light weight, went forward with a rush, but responded to the light hand on the bridle and settled down, travelling mile after mile with the tireless stride and ease of movement that had won him his name.

Greatly as he wished for the journey's end, Pickles rode with judgment. The first doubt assailed him as he neared the Jill: would Swallow take the water? He was not kept long in doubt. Swallow knew better than to refuse. A master rider had put him through this stream, close to that very spot, in the dark of a not long distant night. The sight of the water sent the horse's ears pricking forward; he entered readily and swam for the opposite bank the moment the ground left his feet. Pickles shouted his delight; it would have broken his heart to have been compelled to go back to the ford. Swallow scrambled out onto the bank with little trouble and stretched out once more in his sweeping gallop; he knew now where he was bound and pulled impatiently against the restraining touch. The pace was a source of wonder to Pickles; seven miles and a swim at the end of it and here he was asking for a loose rein, demanding it, and going faster than ever. "Darned if I believe he *can* get tired," said Pickles; "go on then," and he gave him his head and smiled a tired smile to note how the powerful limbs quickened their action and the horse gathered pace until Pickles was travelling faster than ever before in his life. Only the smoothness of the motion gave him confidence in his own ability to hold out. "I could never 'a' made it on th' Goat," he reflected. "Go on, boy! Eat 'em up!" One slender black ear slanted toward him and away again. Swallow was eating 'em up the best he knew how.

* * * * *

Having made her decision, Rose listened carefully to Dave's advice. The more he talked the better she understood the situation; and Dave had scarcely mounted to ride away before she began her own preparations. They appeared to be very simple, merely the apparelling for a ride and keeping watch after Dave to see that he kept on his way.

Dave's disappearance sent her hurrying to the stable. She was surprised to find her bridle missing. On the next peg was Pickles' bridle, the only one ready for instant use. She hesitated a moment at sight of the heavy bit, but took it down and hastened to the edge of the pasture, sending a clear call for Swallow as she ran. There came no answering hoof-beats and she waited to reach the fence before calling again. A glance to right and left and she put her hands to her mouth and sent forth a ringing summons that carried to the far corner of the enclosure. The wait of a few seconds told her that Swallow was not in the pasture. Vexed and wondering she glanced from one to another of the animals near her: two draft horses, a brood mare, its long-legged colt close by, all watching her with that spell-bound intensity of gaze frequently accorded the sudden appearance of a human among domestic animals running free. Swallow would never be turned in the same field as these; then where was he? Jean was riding the only saddle pony-no, there was the Goat. Suspicion awoke in Rose: was it possible Pickles had dared to ride away on Swallow!

The Goat had ideas of his own; he had positively no use for a bridle just then, but Rose had ideas of a distinctly superior order of intelligence and but little time was lost before the Goat was plunging away to where Pickles should be, carrying Rose astride and bareback. Her suspicions were confirmed in part: Pickles was not where he should be. She swung the Goat through a half circle on his hind feet and started back for the barn with a rush. Ten minutes later, the Goat, properly saddled, turned short out of the farm road with a cat-like scramble onto the Twin River trail. He had not carried so much weight since his old master rode him and he did not like it, but knew better than to shirk; he had tried that, and the spurs, two of them, clanking loosely on Rose's small boots, had ripped his sides with quite an old-time fervor. Rose had found time to adjust them after saddling; the last hole barely held them but they served. How she longed for the free-striding gallop of Swallow! The tied-in gait of the Goat was irksome to her but she kept him to his work and Twin River drew rapidly nearer. With Dave's instructions in mind she knew there was plenty of time but it would be foolish to lessen the margin of safety by loitering.

A quarter of a mile from the ford she passed the stage from Wayback. The driver was just whipping up to enter Twin River in style and the stage occupants had opportunity to appraise Rose as she forged ahead. "My heavens, what a beauty!" exclaimed a young lady on the seat beside the driver, herself no mean specimen of God's handiwork. "Who is she?"

The driver shifted his whip and swept off his hat with a flourish. He gazed admiringly after the rider. "That, ma'am, is the French Rose; an' this is certainly my lucky day. I ain't seen two such pretty women before in one day, not in a dog's age. I ain't never seen 'em," he amended with enthusiastic conviction.

The coach cut through the ford to the hiss of the swirling water and turned into the straight in time for them to see a man run out from the Sweet-Echo to meet Rose, standing with his hand on the bridle while Rose leaned forward in what looked suspiciously like a warm greeting.

Another exclamation escaped the young lady on the stage: "Whitby!" and the blush called forth by the driver's frank admiration paled as she watched the two whom they rapidly approached.

"Know him, ma'am?" asked the driver politely; but his companion was oblivious to all but the scene before her.

Rose's imperious gesture and call had brought Whitby running. They had achieved a warm regard for each other during Rose's numerous visits to the Double Y, made at Dave's instigation; visits that had not ceased until the arrival ef Hopalong and Mary, when Dave had declared it was no use to try longer. Whitby grasped the significance of Rose's hurried words in very brief time. "By Jove!" he exclaimed, thinking rapidly. "By Jove! he will do it, too. They can't refuse to honor his check, you know. Buck is the only one can stop it. Lucky Pickles was gone and you came here instead of going to the Wayback bank. Buck has n't long left me. I can catch him." He ran around to the shed at the rear and was going fast when he turned into the trail, astride his pony. His reassuring wave of the hand to Rose stopped in mid-air as he caught sight of Margaret McAllister, standing on the footboard of the coach and looking at him with an expression he did not in the least understand. He made as if to pull up, thought better of it, and sweeping off his hat, dug the spurs into his pony and shot out over the Big Moose trail at a speed that promised to get him somewhere very soon.

* * * * *

Dave had not left the LaFrance cabin far behind when he pulled up with an oath and after a short period of consideration, turned back, riding at fair speed. He found cause to congratulate himself in starting early: it gave him time to go back to Rose and furnish her money in case of need. He saw her sooner than he expected. Turning a slight bend in the trail, he had full view of the Goat, not two hundred yards away, and saw him bound forward like a racer as the spurs ripped into him; Dave gripped a shout in his throat at sight of this act: why was Rose in such a hurry? Suspicion ebbed and flowed in his mind. If she were in such a hurry, why was n't she on Swallow? But the spurring had been for speed, not for punishment. Maybe she was saving Swallow for the longer journey. But if content to tell her father by letter of her going, who in Twin River needed a personal call? She could not be going farther than Twin River-to the Double Y, for example: there was not time for that. And why should she want to go there, either? Dave shook his head impatiently. Either she was square or she was n't. If she was n't, there would be a group of hard-riding boys pounding along the trail in time to cut off Schatz at the bank. He decided to ride to within a short distance of town, lay off the trail, and wait. If no one showed up, he would stick to the original plan. If Rose played crooked, he would take a train East. If too hard pressed, he could use the relays south in place of Denver Gus. Denver might put up an argument but he had one answer to all arguments that had always silenced opposition the moment he produced it. "Get on, bronc," he commanded, heading for Wayback.

* * * * *

Buck had got farther south than Whitby suspected; so far, that Whitby was beginning to hope he had not struck off from the trail, when he sighted him. Buck was riding head on shoulder, as if he had heard the coming of his pursuer, and he pulled up at the other's wild gesture. "What's eatin' him?" said Buck, smiling for the thousandth time at Whitby's manner of riding; it was a constant wonder to Buck that a man could sit a horse like that and stick to the worst of them as Whitby did. "He shore ain't meanin' to swim the Black Jack to get to the Fort." The smile faded as he suddenly realized the appeal in the Englishman's frantic waving; he rode forward rapidly and they were soon near enough together for Whitby to be sure his words would be heard and understood.

"Twin River, Buck! Twin River! And ride like h —l!"

Buck's quirt bit into his pony's flank. Never before had he known the Englishman profane; it must be serious. Whitby turned and raced ahead of him, rapidly over-taken by Buck who rode a fresher and speedier mount. As they ran side by side, Whitby rapidly repeated Rose's news.

"I can make it, Whit," declared Buck. "They won't try to work th' game till closin' time at th' bank. Train bound west is due at Wayback about then. Wish I had Allday under me. So long."

Whitby slowed to a lope and Buck drew away rapidly. His duty accomplished, the Englishman's thoughts turned to the puzzling expression on Margaret McAllister's face, as he had last seen it. He tried in vain to analyze it and unconsciously pressed his tired horse into a faster pace in his anxiety for an explanation.

Buck did not spare his pony. He *must* be at the bank before the money was paid over. The stringing up of Schatz by Judge Lynch would not bring the money back; and Buck had grave doubts of his ability to accomplish this retribution. Schatz appeared to grow stronger the more he knew of him. Nobody but a man very sure of himself and his power would dare such deviltry. Well, it would come to a personal straightening of accounts. Buck's grim face was never sterner. But first he must get to the bank. Resolutely putting aside all other considerations he gave his whole mind to his horse. Presently he shook his head: "Never make it," he muttered; "have to relay at Twin." Even as he said it he saw ahead of him another rider approaching at an easy lope; an expression of gratified pleasure appeared on Buck's face as he saw the other dismount and begin to lengthen the stirrup leathers. It was Rose. "By G —d! What a woman!" exclaimed Buck. "She thinks as quick as Cassidy an' never overlooks a bet."

He urged his pony to its best speed. With a fresh mount in sight, his object was practically assured. As he drew near, Rose called out: "Horse wait for you at Two Fork Creek."

He pulled short beside her in two jumps. "Rose, I love you," he declared, his eyes sparkling with pleasure; "you 'd oughta been a man!" He sprang to the ground while speaking and was astride the Goat at a bound, turning in his saddle to call back to her: "But I 'm most mighty glad yo 're not." A wave of his hand and he faced about, settling in his seat for the run to Two Fork, five miles beyond Twin River.

The crimson flood that burned in her face at his first remark, to recede at his second, returned in full tide as she stood with lips apart and eyes wide, watching him ride away. A trembling seized her, so that she clung to the saddle for support. The moving figure became blurred as the tears gathered in her eyes; she brushed them away impatiently with the back of her hand. "He is not mean it that way," she murmured; "it is only that he is glad I think about the horse."

She mounted and rode soberly toward Twin River. The pony, awaiting the customary notice to attend to business and finding it long in coming, began to entertain a sneaking affection for skirts, which until then he had regarded with suspicious hostility.

Chapter XXI
Pickles Tries to Talk

Mary sat at the window sewing — a continuous performance with her these days. The sound of a horse approaching caused her to glance up just as a faint call for "Buck" reached her. One look and the sewing fell to the floor as she sprang to her feet, crying out for Jake as she ran. With Swallow nuzzling at her dress, she supported Pickles until Jake came to aid; he lifted the boy from the saddle and carried him into the house.

Mary hastily got out the whiskey and Pickles gulped down a mouthful before he realized what it was. He choked, and pushed away the cup. "Don't want it," he declared, weakly; "ain't never goin' to drink."

"Good boy," encouraged Mary, patting his head. "You stick to that."

"Where 's Buck?" asked Pickles.

"He ain't come back yet," answered Mary.

"Where is he?" insisted Pickles.

"I don't know," was the patient reply.

"I gotta find Buck," the boy declared, starting to rise.

Mary pushed him back. "How can you find him when you don't know where he is?"

"Ain't he som'er's on th' range?"

"No; him an' Whit rode off Twin River way this mornin' an' they ain't neither of 'em back yet."

"Well, I gotta find him, an' I gotta find him now," declared Pickles. "Lemme go."

"What's eatin' you?" demanded Jake. "*You* ain't fitten to ride *no* place an' I 'm mortally certain you can't walk."

"Shut yore trap, Woolly-face. What's a sheep like you know, anyhow? Nothin'! Can't even dig holes less 'n yo 're prodded with lead. Lemme go."

The whiskey was having an effect on Pickles or he never would have shown malice like this. Besides, it was not true and Pickles knew it. To all questions he had but one answer and Mary was in despair when Hopalong strode into the room. Hoppy wanted to know things —"Where'd you get that horse?" he asked, sharply.

"Huh?" queried Pickles.

"Where 'd you get that horse-that horse you was ridin'?"

"That's Rose's horse-where 's Buck?"

"Rose who?"

"Huh? French Rose. Say, where's Buck?"

"French Rose, hey? Say, Mary, that's th' horse got away from me with that cow-killin' screech-owl th' other night."

"That horse? Rose LaFrance's horse? Oh, Billy!"

It seemed that Mary was deeper in Buck's confidence than his old friend Hopalong, in this matter, at all events.

"Say you, blast you! Where's Buck? Lemme go! What's eatin' you? Ah, h —l!" Pickles relaxed under the grasp of Jake's hands and limply essayed to retrieve his reputation. "I asks yore pardon, ma'am. I promises Buck I won't never swear afore a lady an' here I goes an' does it, first time I 'm mad."

Hoppy eyed the penitent keenly. "Say, Bud; what's wrong?" he asked, quietly. "Buck ain't got no better friend than me and I 'll find him for you; but there ain't no good huntin', less 'n I got somethin' to say when I get there."

"Will you? Bully for you! Tell Buck th' Dutchman 's goin' to get all th' money-then Dave 's goin' to get it-it's in th' bank-on'y Schatz don't know who it is-nobody catches Dave runnin' into a blin' trail thataway-then Dave takes th' money to th' Dutchman-but right here 's where he fools him-he don't take it-he keeps it-an' he marries Rose on th' train to Helena-Rose rides Swaller to Jackson to get th' train-on'y she has got to get another horse 'cause I rode Swaller here. D 'you get me?" Pickles stared expectantly at Hopalong, who turned to Jake.

"Put that horse in th' barn. Saddle Allday. Rope a cayuse an' set that smoke a-rollin' —take a blanket an' ball th' smoke three times at th' end o' every minute-go through th' Gut an' up th' north side. *Pronto!*"

Jake went out of the door on the jump. He moved fast for Buck on occasion-rare, it is true-but there was a volcanic danger in Hopalong's eye that put springs in Jake's boot-heels.

"That's th' way to talk," sighed Pickles, happily. Hopalong went to the rack and took down his rifle. "Reckon yo 're goin' to want that?" asked Pickles.

"Reckon I might," admitted Hopalong, gravely. "You see, after I find Buck I 'm a-goin' to look for Dave an' th' Dutchman."

"Jiggers! I shore hopes you find 'em. I 'd sooner you get Dave than any man I know, 'ceptin' me."

"Well, I sorter count on gettin' Dave. So long, Pickles."

"So long," echoed the boy.

Mary followed her husband outside. "Don't get hurt, Billy-Red," she warned him.

"That sort o' vermin never hurt me yet, Mary. When th' boys get here send 'em after me to Wayback. Tell Ned, rifles. Let me have all th' money you got; if I miss Buck I might want it."

Mary watched him until he rode by on Allday, waving to him from the corner of the house. Then she went indoors to Pickles.

"That's a bully man, that Hopalong, ain't he?" was his enthusiastic greeting.

"He shore is; an' you 're a bully boy, Pickles," replied Mary. She took up her sewing again. The boy watched her curiously and was about to ask a question, when Sleep floated past and Pickles forgot to ask it.

Chapter XXII
"A Ministering Angel"

Mrs. Blake surveyed her surroundings with the surface calm which comes from seeing and disbelieving. These were depths to which she never had expected to descend. She allowed herself half a moment of speculation on the possibility of there existing, somewhere in the world, a real lack of accommodations as appalling as her imagination could now conceive. "I have often thought Mr. Blake somewhat careless in his choice of a hotel during our wanderings, but the worst of them never even suggested-Margie, did you ever in your life imagine such a room could exist?"

"It is only for an hour or so," returned Margaret, listlessly.

"Oh, I don't complain, my dear. You are an equal sufferer. And I am distinctly relieved at the thought of removing some of this terrible dust before we-before-we —"

Her voice trailed off into silence as she caught sight of a motto over the door; it was one of those affairs worked in colored worsted over perforated cloth; the colors had been chosen with less regard to harmony than is usually exhibited by an artist; perhaps it was contrast that was sought; as a study in contrasts it was a blasting success. Mrs. Blake glared at it with the fascinated interest of a spectator within the danger zone of a bursting bomb. "'God bless our home,'" she read, in awed undertone. "Perhaps He will, but it is more than it deserves." She mounted laboriously onto a chair and turned the motto to the wall, hastily facing it about again with a suppressed scream: if the front were chaos the back was a cataclysm. In a spasm of indignation she jerked it loose from its fastening and dropped it out of sight behind the evil-looking washstand. In this position her glance fell on the crude specimen of basin provided. She picked it up doubtfully and struck it against the side of the washstand. "Tin!" she exclaimed. "A dishpan!" and went off into peals of laughter, banging the pan and calling "Dinner!" in an unnaturally deep voice, when she could speak from laughing.

Margaret turned a sullen face from the window. She had seen the French Rose in animated conversation with a tall, good-looking man in flannel shirt and overalls, who had ridden away up the road, evidently in obedience to her orders; while Rose, herself, rode in the direction taken by Whitby. The soft, broad-brimmed hat, the waist but little different from the flannel shirt of the man, the ill-fitting skirt, the mannish gloves and clumsy boots-the superb health of the splendid figure proclaimed itself through all these disadvantages. The woman was a perfect counterfoil for Whitby, and Margaret hid the ache in her heart under a sullenness of demeanor that a less astute companion might have attributed to the annoyances and inconveniences of the journey.

"For heaven's sake, Aunt, don't make such a noise," she insisted; "my head aches as if it would split."

"Your head aches! I 'm sorry, my dear. Still, there are worse things than head-aches, now are n't there?"

Margaret stared. "No doubt," she admitted, tartly; "but it is the worst I have to submit, at present. When a greater evil befalls me I will tell you."

"Why, that's honest," said Mrs. Blake, cheerfully; "and as long as we are to be honest, you are sure it is not your conscience that is at fault?"

"My conscience?" asked Margaret. "What has my conscience to do with a head-ache?"

"First class in Physical Geography, rise. Jessie, what is the origin of the islands of head-aches that vex the pacific waters of the soul? They are due to volcanic action of bad conscience."

"Oh, Aunt! how can you be so absurd?"

"I would rather be absurd than unjust, Margaret."

"I don't understand you."

"You understood me very well. Because you see Whitby talking to a pretty woman, is that a reason to condemn him?"

"Talking! He kissed her before my very eyes, in the public street."

"You cannot say that, Margaret. I saw the meeting as plainly as you did."

"How could you? You were inside! Why has he never mentioned her in his letters?"

"Has he ever mentioned anything but business? He would scarcely mention her to George, and you know he has not written to you."

"No, he had something better to do. This is an unprofitable discussion. I am utterly indifferent to Mr. Booth's actions, past, present, and to come, as well as the reasons for them. If you intend to use that basin for something other than a dinner-call, do so. I 'm not hungry, but we might as well get it over with. We have a long drive before us."

"With all my heart, my dear; unless the water is on a par with the other-er-conveniences."

* * * * *

"Seems like Buck Peters might be in a hurry," observed Slick Milligan, sufficiently interested to come from behind the bar and walk out onto the porch. "Which it's th' first time I see him use a quirt."

"None o' thea punchers think aucht o' a horse," was Sandy's opinion, based on a wide experience.

If Margaret had chanced to overhear Slick's remark it would have explained much. Mrs. Blake was resting, preparatory to sallying forth on the last stretch of their journey, and Margaret was about to make inquiries regarding a conveyance, when the rapid drumming of a horse's feet drew her to the window as Buck went past. Margaret had never met Buck but she was far too good a horsewoman to fail to recognize the pony. She had noted every detail when she had first seen Rose and you may be sure no point, good or bad, of the Goat as a saddle pony, had escaped her critical judgment. Her first thought, as the Goat went past, was one of surprise that he should make so little of the weight of his rider, a full-grown man and no light-weight, either; lean and hard as Buck was, Margaret's estimate of the number of pounds the pony carried was very near the mark; and then, in a flash, she knew him: the very animal that the French Rose had ridden. Margaret knew it to be out of the question that he had travelled to the Double Y ranch and back; they must have exchanged horses on the road. But, why?

The consideration of this enigma and the many possibilities it offered as collateral questions, occupied her fully, to the very grateful content of Mrs. Blake, who was genuinely tired and ashamed to say so. It was a consideration so perplexing that Margaret was prepared to allow Whitby to explain, when he was so unfortunate as to appear in company with Rose. He had overtaken her, a half-mile down the trail, but Margaret could not, of course, know this. They remained in earnest conversation for two or three minutes, when Rose went on and Whitby went around to the shed to put up his pony. Margaret ran down stairs and went out onto the porch. She felt better able to face him in the open.

It was thus that Whitby, coming in at the back door, was directed out through the front one. Rapidly as Margaret moved, she was too great an attraction to escape instant notice. Whitby advanced with outstretched hand. "Ripping idea, taking us by surprise, Miss McAllister. Awful journey, you know, really."

"We wished to avoid giving trouble. You are looking very well, Mr. Booth."

"Fit as a fiddle, thank you. But —I say-you 'll excuse me, —but are n't you feeling a little-ah-seedy, now? I mean —"

"I quite understand what you mean. Am I looking a little-ah-seedy, Mr. Booth?"

"No, certainly not! Very stupid of me, I'm sure. I —ah-rather fancied-but of course I 'm wrong. This confounded dust gets in a chap's eyes so —"

"Do you mean that my eyes look dusty, Mr. Booth?"

"Oh, I say! Now you 're chaffing me. As if—"

"Not in the least. Chaffing is an art in which I fail to excel. But if you mean that I look a little pale and dragged with the journey, you must remember that I do not pretend to have the vitality of a cow-girl."

"Ah! Just so. And Mrs. Blake-she is with you, I presume."

"The presumption is justified. Aunt's vitality was even less equal to the journey than my own. She is resting and begs to be excused until she can say 'How do' at the ranch."

"Why-ah-how did Mrs. Blake know I called in?"

Margaret bit her lip. "I happened to be looking from the window as you rode up," she explained, carelessly.

"Ah! Just so. Miss McAllister, you don't know me very well, not really; perhaps no better than I know you. I 'm no good at this sort of thing, this fencing with words, you know; I discovered that long ago; and I long ago adopted the only other method: to smash right through the guard. My presumption does n't presume so far as to imagine you are jealous; I am not seeking causes; all I know is, you made me a promise when I came West, a conditional promise, I grant you: I was to make good. Well, I have n't done half bad, really. I fancy Mr. McAllister would admit as much. Buck Peters admits more; and one has to be something of a man, you know, to merit that from Peters. He 's the finest man I ever knew, myself, bar none. It is very good of you to hear me so patiently. I 'm coming to the kernel of the difficulty just now:

"Rose LaFrance, the cow-girl you mentioned, is the right sort. She brought word this morning that will save Peters a goodish bit of money; incidentally Mr. McAllister, also. Buck had to be in Wayback at the earliest possible moment and I was fortunate enough to overtake him. Miss LaFrance not only was thoughtful enough to ride to meet Buck and give him a fresh mount and to send a man ahead with whom Buck will change again, but she insists that we follow him, which is a jolly good idea; these fellows are very careless with their fire-arms and he might require help. If the blackguard he is after succeeds in withdrawing the entire deposit from the bank and it is given to him in cash, before Peters gets there, he will certainly require help. I leave you to reflect on these facts, Miss McAllister. Give my kindest regards to Mrs. Blake."

He stalked back the way he had come, in the characteristic wooden manner which precluded any appeal, if Margaret had felt like making one; but her mind was too fully occupied with what she had heard to understand that he was actually leaving. He was splashing through the ford before she realized the significance of this part of his defence. Thoughtful, and without resentment, she went to rejoin Mrs. Blake.

Whitby pushed his horse sufficiently to overtake Rose who, he knew, was riding slowly. Just outside the town he met Cock Murray, astride the Goat; the Goat was a very tired pony and showed it.

"My dear man! Why are n't you following Peters?" asked Whitby, in surprised remonstrance.

"My dear Brit! I sorta allowed it was n't healthy," answered Cock. "I tells you th' same as I tells th' French Rose: 'When Buck says "Scoot for th' ranch an' tell Cassidy to hit Wayback *pronto* an' he 'll get news o' me at th' bank,"' it 'pears like, to my soft-boiled head, that's what I oughta do."

"I beg your pardon. Of course. Rather odd Peters didn't tell me."

"He meant to. I 'm sorry he did n't. So long."

"So long," echoed Whitby, mechanically. He pulled up to shout after Cock: "You won't get far on that horse; he 's done, you know."

"I ain't goin' far on that 'oss," Cock shouted back; "an' they 're never done till they 're down, you know."

"Impudent beggar, but a good man. They grow 'em good out here. I fancy the bad-plucked ones don't last." And Whitby hastened on to overtake Rose.

He had left Two Fork Creek four miles behind him before sighting her; in her impatience she had gone faster than she knew. Whitby had almost caught up, when he saw Rose bend forward, wave to him, and then dash away, as if she were inviting him to a race.

"Buck!" exclaimed Whitby, with intuitive conviction. "It's Buck as sure as little apples Kesicks." Fifty yards' advance showed him that he was right. The figure lying huddled in the road was certainly Buck, and beside him was his dead pony. Rose flung herself from the saddle and ran to him; and Whitby, wearing the terribly savage expression of the man slow to anger, was not far behind. Together they laid the unconscious figure at full length.

Rose flung herself from the saddle and ran to him

"It is there," said Rose, dully, pointing to the right thigh.

"Ah," breathed Whitby, in a sigh of relief. He cut the cloth but forbore to tear it away, the coagulated blood having stopped the bleeding. "Drilled through!" he exclaimed. "Why, the swine must have been near enough to do better than that. How ever did he miss? We 'll bandage this as it is, Miss LaFrance, and do it properly at-now, should you say take him to the doctor at Wayback?"

"No. He is a drunken beast. I will nurse him."

"Very well. A good nurse is better than a drunken doctor. Just cut this sleeve from my shirt, will you?"

Rose took the knife and cut, instead, a three-inch strip from the bottom of her skirt, Whitby meanwhile producing a flask, from which he carefully fed Buck small quantities of whiskey. Rose tendered him the bandage. "Well rolled, Miss LaFrance! Have you been taught this sort of thing?" Rose silently nodded her head. "My word! Buck is in luck. You apply the bandage then, while I give him this. You'll make a better job of it than I should."

Buck slowly opened his eyes to see Whitby's face bending over his. "Got away, Whit," he whispered, weakly; "ambushed me, by G—d," and relapsed into unconsciousness.

"Much blood! He have lose much blood," murmured Rose.

"Yes," assented Whitby. "How shall we carry him? He can never ride."

"Travois," said Rose. "I show you."

Buck again regained consciousness and his voice was distinctly stronger. "Get after him, Whit. He must n't get away."

"Oh, nonsense, Buck. They know the cat's out of the bag by this time and they will never be such asses as to try it on now. As for Dave, he can't get away. The agency will be jolly glad to do something for the money they have had by turning over Dave if I ask it of them. And McAllister will think you are worth a good bit more than the money, I lay. I know I do."

Buck was attempting feeble remonstrance when Rose returned from her survey of the timber available and swiftly placed her hands over his lips. "Do not talk," she commanded. "It is bad to talk, now."

"What price the nurse-eh, Buck? Oh, you lucky beggar!"

"Rose," murmured Buck. "Why, that's right kind."

Admonishing him with raised forefinger, Rose gave instructions to Whitby and he hastened away to gather material for the travois.

* * * * *

When Margaret returned to Mrs. Blake she was carrying a pair of driving gloves and a jaunty sailor hat which Mrs. Blake knew had been packed in one of the trunks. "Are we going to start, Margie?" she asked, with languid interest.

"*I* am going to start but I am going the other way. We shall not be able to leave for the ranch before morning, probably."

Mrs. Blake sat up with a suddenness that surprised even herself. "The morning!" she echoed. "If you think that I shall stay in this horror of a room until morning, Margaret, you are mistaken. I will go, if I walk."

"It's a long walk," commented Margaret, carelessly.

"And may I ask why you are going the other way and when you purpose to return?"

"I am going to Wayback to telegraph. Some thief has planned to get all of papa's money from the bank there, and of course he will try to escape on the train. We shall catch him by telegraphing to the officers at the next town."

"If you do he is a fool. And who are 'we'? How did you learn all this?"

"Whitby told me."

"When?"

"Just now."

"Was Whitby here?"

"Yes."

"And never asked for me?"

"I told him you begged to be excused."

"You told him I—now see here, Margaret. There is such a thing as going too far, and this is an example of it. 'Beg to be excused'! What will he think of me? Where is he now?"

"He has gone on to Wayback. But he never will have the sense to telegraph. That is why I am going."

"Did you quarrel?"

"Well-we were n't exactly friendly."

"Oh! —oh! —oh!" The three exclamations were long-drawn, with pauses between them and in three different keys.

"Aunty!" cried Margaret, furiously, stamping her foot. "How dare you insinuate —I said I was going to *telegraph*!"

"All right, my dear. Have it your own way. I 'll immolate myself on the altar of friendship: in this case, a particularly uncomfortable bed. Please remember, Margaret, as you speed away on your errand of avarice, I said a *particularly* uncomfortable bed."

Margaret went out and slammed the door. Mrs. Blake chuckled until she laughed, and laughed until she gasped for breath and was obliged to loosen her corsets. "I am as bad as Margie," she sighed; "I don't know when I am well off. Now I shall have to stay marooned in this pesky room until Margie returns. I never can fasten these outrageous things without help."

In her fetching gown of figured brown cloth, bordered with beaver fur, with slanting drapery of plain green, above which a cutaway jacket exposed a full vest, and topped by a high beaver toque-with flush due to the recent passage-at-arms still in her cheeks and the fire of indignation in her eyes-Margaret presented a *chic* daintiness that met with the entire approval of the burly Sandy, who hastened from the bar-room at the sound of her descent.

"I want a hitch of some kind," requested Margaret; "something with speed and bottom, and the sooner the better."

"A hitch?" queried Sandy. He had ominous visions of the dainty figure being whirled to destruction behind a pair of unruly bronchos.

"A horse, a team, a rig, something to drive, and at once," explained Margaret, impatiently.

"Oh, ay! I ken ye meanin' richt enough. I ken it fine; but I hae doots o' yer abeelity."

"Very well, then I will buy it, only let me have it immediately."

"It's no' th' horses, ye ken. What would I tell yer mither, gin ye 're kilt?"

"Bosh!" said Margaret, scornfully. "I can drive anything you can harness."

"Oh, ay! Nae doot, nae doot. But it willna be ane o' Sandy's, I telt ye that."

Here a voice was heard from out front, roaring for Slick and demanding a cayuse, in a hurry.

"Losh! yon 's anither. They must theenk I keepit a leevery," and Sandy hastened out to the porch to see who was desirous of further depleting his stock. When he saw the condition of the Goat his decision was quick and to the point: "Ma certes! Ye 'll no run th' legs of ony o' my cattle, Cock Murray, gin ye crack yer throat crawin'. Tut, tut! Look at yon!" He shook his head sorrowfully as he gazed at the dejected appearance of the Goat.

"Won't, hey!" shouted Cock, slapping back the saddle, "then I 'll borrer Dutch Fred's, an' Buck Peters 'll burn yore d —d ol' shack 'bout yore ears when he knows it." A man, watching interestedly from the bar-room, left by the hall exit, running.

"Buck Peters! Weel, in that case-Slick, ye can lend him yer ain."

"I was just a-goin' to," declared Slick, hurrying off; "which yore d —very generous when it don't cost you nothin'."

Cock loosened the cinch. "Generous as-Miss McAllister!" he exclaimed, aghast.

"Why, of all the people! How delightful! What on earth are *you* doing out here?" Margaret ran down to him, extending both hands in warm greeting.

Cock took them as if in a dream. "Miss McAllister-Chicago-Oh, what a fool I 've been!"

The man who had left the bar-room tore around the corner of the hotel on a wicked-looking pinto which lashed out viciously at the Goat when brought to a stop, a compliment the Goat promptly returned, though with less vigor. "Here y' are, Cock. He 'll think he 's headin' for th' Cyclone an' he 'll burn th' earth." The Cyclone puncher pushed the straps into Murray's hand and led away the Goat to a well-earned rest.

"I have to go, Miss McAllister. See you at the ranch. I 'm punching for the Double Y. They call me Cock Murray. It-it's a name I took."

"I 'll remember. Cock Murray: it fits you like a glove," and Murray mounted to her ripple of laughter. "We shall be out there to-morrow. Aunt is with me," she called to him, while the pinto worked off a little of its superfluous deviltry, before getting down to its work. She watched him admiringly, Cock sitting firm and waiting, until presently the pony straightened out and proceeded to prove his owner's boast. "Tip-top, Ralph," praised Margaret; "but you always could ride." She turned and faced the dour Sandy. "See here! Do you *ever* intend to get out that rig?"

"Weel-gin ye 're a relative o' Buck Peters, I jalouse ye 'll gang yer ain gait, onyway," and he went grumbling through the hall to do her bidding.

A roaring volley of curses, instantly checked and rolling forth a second time with all the sulphur retained to add rancor to the percolator, drew Margaret curiously to overlook the cause. Seeing, she thought she understood Sandy's reluctance to let his team to her: a pair of perfectly matched bays, snipped with white in a manner that gave to their antics an air of rollicking mischief, they were lacking the angularity of outline Margaret already had come to expect in Western ponies, and their wild plunging seemed more the result of overflowing vitality than inherent vice. Drawn by the uproar, Slick appeared beside her.

"No team for a lady to drive," he declared, shaking his head.

"Ridiculous!" asserted Margaret. "Go help them." A devitalized imprecation from Sandy hastened his steps. Margaret was in doubt which amused her most: the trickiness of the ponies or Sandy's heroic endeavor to swear without swearing. She understood him far better than either of the others, who worked silently and with well directed efforts.

With Slick's invaluable assistance their object was soon accomplished, the team being hitched to a new buckboard that was the pride of Sandy's heart. "'T is a puir thing," he protested, eying it sourly. "I hae naething better."

"Why, it is perfect," declared Margaret, "but I shall want a whip."

"Ye 'll want nae whup," denied Sandy, shaking his head ominously.

The Cyclone puncher at the head of the nigh horse called to her: "Take 'em out o' th' corral, miss? They 'll go like antelopes when they start."

Margaret laughed in gay excitement. "No, no! please don't," she entreated, drawing on her gloves. "I could drive that pair through the eye of a needle."

Sandy glanced from her to the team and back again.

"Havers! I 'll gie ye ma ain whup," he promised. He was back in half a minute with a lash whip whose holly stock never grew in America.

"What a beauty!" exclaimed Margaret. She ran down the steps, gathered up the lines, and sprang into the buckboard, bracing herself for the inevitable jerk. "Ready," she warned. "Let go."

It was lucky for Mrs. Blake that she had loosened her corset strings and was confined to her room; had she seen the start-and she knew Margaret's skill as well as any one-she certainly would have burst them in her fright. With the three men it was otherwise; they vented their admiration in a ringing cheer. The ponies, gathering speed in the short stretch to the ford, were coaxed over so near the I-Call that Dirty Snow tumbled precipitately from his box and fled around the corner of the saloon; missing the box by a foot, the wheels began a wide arc toward the water through which the rig whirled in an avalanche of spray, to shave the front of the Why-Not as closely as it had the I-Call. To the delighted astonishment of Twin River-by this time the entire inhabitants, excepting only Mrs. Blake, were more or less interested in the proceedings-the team was no sooner going in the straight than Margaret cracked the lash to right and left and the startled ponies bellied to the ground in their efforts to escape an unknown danger. Sandy guffawed in pride of ownership; Slick gazed with his soul in his eyes; the puncher danced up and down in his joy, thumping first one and then the other.

"Did you see it?" he demanded, "Did you see it?" The others admitted eyesight equal to the occasion. "Say," asseverated the puncher, "if I owned all Montany, from here to th' line, I gives it to get that gal. That's th' kind of a hair-pin I am. You hear me!"

* * * * *

Margaret's sudden exclamation hastened the speed of the ponies but she drew them firmly in and approached the group on the trail at an easy lope. Whitby ran up from the river bank as she pulled the team to a stand.

"Who is it, Miss LaFrance? How did it happen?" asked Margaret, guessing the answer to her own questions.

"It is M'sieu Peters, ma'am'selle. He is wounded," replied Rose.

"Just in time, Miss McAllister," said Whitby, coming up at that moment. "We 'll commandeer that wagon as an ambulance."

"Miss McAllister!" exclaimed Buck, wonderingly. Then, energetically: "Whit, you get after that pole-cat. I can get to th' ranch, now. Get a-goin'."

"Buck, I 'm like Jake: 'sot in my ways.' There is no necessity to follow that pole-cat, as you so aptly call him. And you are not going to the ranch, you know. Miss LaFrance has kindly volunteered expert service in nursing and I intend that you shall get it. Miss McAllister, Miss LaFrance, whose services you already know; and Mr. Peters, your father's partner."

"You must not think of going on to the ranch, Mr. Peters," persuaded Margaret. "I only hope it is not too far to Miss LaFrance's home. If we could lift you —I 'm afraid these horses won't stand."

"Lift! I reckon I got one good laig, Miss McAllister —" he fell back with a grunt.

"Dash it all, Buck! Do you want to break open that wound? 'Pon my word, I don't envy you your patient, Miss LaFrance. You lie still, you restless beggar. I 've packed more than one man with a game leg and gone it alone. Do you think you can manage those dancing jackasses?" He looked doubtingly from them to Margaret.

Margaret dimpled. "Ask Sandy," she advised, demurely.

"Ou, ay!" quoth Whitby and Margaret broke into bubbling laughter that reflected from Rose's face in the faint shadow of a smile.

"Too bad of me to be laughing this way, Mr. Peters," apologized Margaret, correctly interpreting the expression of Rose, whose glance had turned to Buck; "but I have so much cause to be merry when I least expected it that I forgot for the moment you are wounded."

She resolutely avoided looking at Whitby who, thus unobserved, displayed a grin more fittingly adapted to the countenance of the famous Cat of Cheshire. Rose glanced swiftly from Whitby to Margaret and the two women were already aware of that which the men would never guess in each other.

"Shucks! I been shot up worse 'n this, Miss McAllister," assured Buck; "if that pig-headed Britisher would on'y take orders like he oughta. He 's obstinater nor a cow with a suckin' calf."

"Right-o!" assented Whitby, who had finished his preparations for the lift. "Now, Miss LaFrance."

He had managed to pass the blanket under Buck's middle, looping it over his own neck; while this arrangement eased but little weight from Rose, it had the advantage of keeping Buck comparatively straight. Whitby, backing up into the buckboard, his hands tightly grasping Buck beneath the arms, was ably assisted by Rose, who moved and steadied her load without apparent effort. Margaret was genuinely surprised. "How strong you are!" she exclaimed, admiringly.

"Gentle as rain," commended Buck. "If you got that flask handy, Whit, I 'd like to feel it."

Chapter XXIII
Hopalong's Move

Hopalong, nursing Allday with due regard to the miles yet to be travelled, was disagreeably surprised to recognize Cock Murray in the horseman approaching. The explanation offered did not improve his temper. He turned on Murray a hard stare that was less a probe than an exponent of destruction to a liar. There was that about Hopalong which spelled danger; no strong man is without it; and few men, honest or not, fail of the impression when in the presence of it. Cock Murray was no coward. He was distinctly not afraid to meet death at a moment's notice or with no notice at all, if it came that way; yet he was grateful to be able to face that stare with an honest purpose in his heart.

"Murray, down Texas way h —l-raisin' on a range means sudden death. It's a-goin' to stop on th' Double Y. Which side are you on?"

"If it depends on my say-so, th' Double Y is as peaceful as a' Eastern dairy from this out."

"Let 'er go at that. How 's that cayuse?"

"Good, an' fresh as paint. I on'y breathed him, comin' from Twin."

"Swap. This bay has come along right smart for twenty miles. I ain't goin' to lose you much, either. Th' boys is after us but they won't catch you."

Hopalong was well past the Sweet-Echo before the pinto was recognized. Slick let out a yell of surprise. The Cyclone puncher sauntered to the window, where Slick was pointing, glanced up the trail and laughed. "That's a friend o' Buck's," he explained, "an' he 's certainly aimin' to get there, wherever it is, as quick as he can."

"Ain't that yore pinto?" queried Slick.

"Less 'n I 'm blind," agreed the cow-punch.

"Seems to me there's a lot o' swappin' goin' on som'ers along th' Big Moose," hazarded Slick. "Which they can't *all* be backin' winners," he added, thoughtfully.

They were still seeking light in useless discussion when the long-striding Allday went past. Slick shouted to Murray for news but Cock waved his hand without speaking. Twin River was beginning to show a languid interest. Day-and-night *habitués* of the I-Call lounged out into the open and gazed after Cock inquiringly, irritated Pop Snow into a frantic change of base by their apparently earnest belief in his knowledge of these events and their demands for information, and lounged back again; Dutch Fred soothed the peevish old man by talking "like he had some sense"; having sense proved an asset once more as Dirty, no one being near, suddenly discovered a thirst. Ike, wise old wolf, though unable to solve the riddle, smelled a killing. "Stay around," he advised several of his own trustworthy satellites. Little Nell alone, who looked on and read as the others ran, came near to supplying the missing print: "The French Rose has shook Dave," she decided. "Dave has pulled his freight and the Double Y is on the prod after him. Smiler ought to show for place but the minute he looks like a winner the Texan 'll pump him full of lead. The Double Y will win out. Maybe Ned —" Little Nell's wild heart had regretted bluff, kindly Ned, these many days.

The passing of the Double Y punchers, strung out half a mile, confirmed Nell's guess. The Cyclone puncher, hurriedly throwing the leather on the Goat, loped along beside Slow Jack, the last in the string, obtaining from him such meagre information as only whetted his curiosity. He returned to the Sweet-Echo and Slick, disdaining to reply to the I-Call loungers. Ike was too wise to risk a rebuff; he already knew enough from what he had seen. "Pickin's, boys," was his laconic comment; and soon a company of five Autolycus-minded gentlemen took the Big Moose trail, openly. The break-up of this chance foray was largely due to the simple matter of direction.

Hopalong, knowing nothing of the wagging tongues at Twin River, drove the pinto for every ounce there was in him. A vague uneasiness, risen with the delivery of Buck's message by Cock Murray, rode with Hopalong; he could not shake it off. Ten minutes beyond Two Fork he saw the buckboard and the curse in his throat had its origin in a conviction as accurate as Whitby's had been. He turned and rode beside them. "Well, they got you, Buck," was his quiet comment.

"Shore did," admitted Buck. "Ambushed at four hundred-first shot-bad medicine. I lit a-runnin' an' caves in just as th' next ball drops th' bronc. I lays most mighty still. He thinks I kicked th' bucket but he 's afraid to find out. I was hopin' he 'd come to see. He gets away quiet an' I lay an' bleed a-waitin' for him. Rose an' Whit here wakes me out of a sweet dream." He smiled up at Rose whose anxiety was evident.

"Too much talk," she warned him.

"Dave?" asked Hopalong, looking at Whitby, who nodded.

"How far?"

"Two miles; possibly less," answered Whitby.

"I 'll get him," said Hopalong, with quiet certitude. "So long, Buck."

"So long, Hoppy. Go with him, Whit. Can't afford another ambush."

"Very well, Buck. You will find a medicine-chest in my kit, Miss McAllister."

Whitby turned and rode hard after Hopalong who, nevertheless, arrived at the dead pony considerably in advance, and after a searching look around, rode straight to the ambush. The signs of its recent occupancy were plain to be seen. Hopalong got down and squatted under cover as Dave must have done, from which position his shrewd mind deduced the cause of the poor shot: a swinging limb, which had deflected the bullet at the critical moment. The signs showed Dave had led his horse from the spot, finally mounting and riding off in a direction well to the east of Wayback. Minute after minute Hopalong tracked at a slow canter; suddenly his pony sprang forward with a rush: even to the Englishman's inexperienced eyes there was evidence of Dave having gone faster; very much faster, Whitby thought, as he rode his best to hold the pace, wondering meanwhile, how it was possible to track at such speed. It was n't possible: Dave had set a straight line for Wayback and gone off like a jack rabbit. Hopalong was simply backing his guess.

Exhaustive inquiries in Wayback seemed to show that Hoppy had guessed wrong. No one had seen Dave. No one had seen Schatz, either; the bank president had gone to Helena and his single clerk, single in a double sense, was an unknown number of miles distant on a journey in courtship. The station agent declared Dave had neither purchased a ticket nor taken any train from the Wayback station. Whitby became downcast but Hopalong, with each fruitless inquiry, gathered cheerfulness almost to loquacity. It was his way. "Cheer up, Whit," he encouraged: "I'd 'a' been punchin' cows an' dodgin' Injuns in th' Happy Hunting Grounds before I could rope a yearlin' if I 'd allus give up when I was beat."

Whitby looked at him gloomily. "I 'm fair stumped," he admitted. "D' you think, now, it would be wisdom to go back and follow his spoor?"

"Spoor is good. He came to Wayback, Whit, sure as yo 're a bloomin' Britisher. Keep a-lookin' at me, now: There 's a bum over by th' barber's has been watchin' us earnest ever since we hit town; he 's stuck to us like a shadow; see if you know him. Easy, now. Don't scare him off."

Whitby won his way into Hopalong's heart by the simplicity of his manoeuvre. Taking from his lips the cigar he was smoking, he waved it in the general direction of the station. "You said a bum near the barber-shop," he repeated. His pony suddenly leaped into the air and manifested an inexplicable and exuberant interest in life. When quieted, Whitby was facing the barber's and carefully examining the bum. Hopalong chuckled through serious lips. Whitby had allowed the hot end of his cigar to come in contact with the pony's hide. "No, can't say I do; but he evidently knows me. Dashed if he does n't want me to follow him," and Whitby looked his astonishment.

Hopalong's eyes sparkled. "Get a-goin', Whit. Here's where ye call th' turn. What'd I tell you?" He wheeled and rode back to the station. Whitby followed the shambling figure down the street and around the corner of a saloon, where he discovered him sunning himself on a heap of rubbish, in the rear.

"Well, my man; what is it?" asked Whitby.

The crisp, incisive tones brought him up standing; he saluted and came forward eagerly. "Youse lookin' f'r Dave?" he responded.

"What of it?"

"I seen him jump d' train down by d' pens. She wuz goin' hell-bent-f'r-election, too. Wen Dave jumps, I drops. Dave an' me don't pal."

"Why not?"

"Didn't he git me run out o' Twin? Youse was dere. Don'tcher 'member Pickles an' Dutch Onion-Pickles' old man-an' dat Come Seven guy w'at stopped d' row? Don'tcher?"

"Yes; I do. Are you the man who shied the bottle?"

"Ke-rect. I 'd done f'r him, too, but dey put d' ki-bosh on me."

"And are you sure it was Dave? Did the train stop?"

"Stop nothin'! 'T was a string o' empties. Dave jumped it, all right. An' I 'd hoof it all d' way to Sante Fe to see him swing."

"Deuced good sentiment, by Jove. Here, you need-well, a number of things, don't you know."

Boomerang gazed after the departing Englishman and blinked rapidly at the bill in his hand. Did he or did he not see a zero following that two? With a fervent prayer for sanity he carefully tucked it out of sight.

Whitby returned to Hopalong as much elated as previously he had been cast down. "We have the bally blackguard," was his glad assurance.

"Where?" asked Hopalong; "in yore pocket, or yore hat, or only in yore mind." Whitby explained and Hopalong promptly appealed to the station agent.

It was a weary wait. Whitby, a patient man himself, found occasion to admire the motionless relaxation of Hopalong, who appeared to be storing energy until such time as he would require it. To Whitby, who was well acquainted with the jungle of India, it was the inertia of the tiger, waiting for the dusk.

The station door opened again but this time with a snappier purpose that seemed promising. Whitby turned his head. The railroader nodded as one well satisfied with himself. "Got your man," he announced, with a grin of congratulation. "He dropped off at X——. Don't seem a whole lot scared. Took a room at th' hotel. Goin' to turn him over to the sheriff?"

"No," answered Hopalong, "an' I don't want nothin' to get out here, *sabe*? If it does, yo 're th' huckleberry. When 's th' next train East?"

"It's past due, but it 'll be along in twenty minutes."

"I 'll take a ticket," and Hopalong rose to his feet and followed him into the station. He returned shortly, to apologize for leaving Whitby behind. "I know you 'd like to go, Whit, but you ought to find out about that money. Better stay here an' see them bank people in th' mornin'."

Whitby acknowledged the wisdom of this and agreed to call on Buck at Jean's on his way back to the ranch. "You tell Buck Dave is at X——," said Hoppy. "An' that's where he stays," he added, grimly. "Here she comes."

Long before this, the usual crowd of idlers had gathered; and now the rest of Wayback began to ooze into the road and toward the station. As the train drew in it attracted even a half-shaved man from the barber's, hastily wiping the soap from his face as he ran; after him came the barber, closing the razor and sticking it in his pocket. The first man off the cars was a fox-faced little hunchback, whose deformity in no way detracted from his agile strength; after him, with studied carelessness, came Tex. Hopalong grunted, turned his head as the clatter of hoofs sounded through the turmoil, and signalled Chesty Sutton, first man of the rapidly arriving Double Y punchers.

"Don't you stray none, screech-owl, or I 'll drop you," he warned the captive, who shot one impish glance at the speaker and froze in his tracks. "Chesty, tell Ned to take this coyote to th' ranch, an' don't let him get away, not if you has to shoot him."

"Hold hard, stranger. He looks mighty like Big Saxe to me, an' if he is, I wants him. I got a warrant for him in my clo'es." The deputy sheriff started forward.

"Wait!" commanded Hopalong. The deputy waited. "Tex, hold that train. You an' me are goin' th' same way. Mr. Sheriff, I got a warrant ahead o' yourn an' I wants him. You 'll find him at th' Double Y ranch when I gets through with him."

Slow Jack, the last of the Double Y punchers, loped up to the station, swung from his saddle and joined the interested group surrounding the disputants.

"If that's Big Saxe I wants him now an' I 'm goin' to take him."

"Don't you, son." Kind as Hopalong's tone sounded, the deputy halted again. "Bow-Wow, hit th' trail an' have eyes in th' back of yore head. Straddle, boys." The crowd scattered as the mounted punchers moved their ponies about, to open a clear space. Hopalong met the eye of the hunchback, whose clear, shrewd glance recognized the master of the moment. "Screechy! that pinto 's a-waitin' for you an' if any son-of-a-gun gets there first, *you* won't need no bracelets. Git!"

Struggling between indecision and duty, the deputy saw the group of punchers, the pinto in advance, turn into the Twin River trail. "Looky here!" he began fiercely to Hopalong, "'pears to me —"

"Bah! Tell it to Schatz"; and Hopalong sprang up the steps, followed by Tex, to the outspoken regret of Wayback's citizens there assembled.

Chapter XXIV
The Rebellion of Cock Murray

The buckboard, wheeling off the trail, was lost to view almost as soon as Murray saw it. Rose and Margaret he had recognized at a glance but whose figure had been the second in the wagon? Suddenly misgiving assailed him. Forgetting Hopalong and his orders, he turned and followed them. Every step of his horse increased his anxiety and urged him forward; and twin-born with it smouldered a growing anger that held him back: he hesitated to have his fears confirmed in the presence of two women, one of whom-well, that was done with but it had left a scar that was beginning to throb again with the old pain. He rode slowly but gaining steadily on the trio ahead. When they reached the cabin, Rose called; receiving no answer she was about to go for help when she saw Murray and pointed to him. Margaret motioned and he hurried to obey the summons.

He recognized Buck while still some distance away and the smoulder burst into a blaze. This was the game then? Schatz had emphatically stated it was to be one of freeze-out; when they found it would n't work then the good old way was good enough. The jauntiness of carriage which had earned him his nickname (he was responsible for the surname only) was gone when he joined the others; the gay insolence of his speech was gone also, and some of his good looks. The successful concealment of his feelings had lost him much but it had gained him more: Margaret thrilled to a sense of power she had not expected in him. Rose's gesture of finger to lips was superfluous: Murray never felt less like talking.

"How'd you get here, Cock?" asked Buck, dully. The strain of the drive was telling even upon his iron frame.

"Orders," answered Cock, briefly; and Buck was not sufficiently interested to inquire further.

The team was effectually secured and they got Buck from the wagon and into the cabin with but little difficulty; Murray, though he did not look it, was a far stronger man than Whitby; and Buck was laid gently in the bunk, his head brushing the spot where Pickles had muffled his breathing a few hours before.

The removal of the bandage brought a gasp to the lips of Margaret, who pressed her hand to her heart and stared with horrified eyes. She touched Rose on the shoulder: "Can you-can you dress the wound without me?" she asked, breathlessly.

"But certainly," answered Rose, mildly surprised.

"Then I will go-back-and send on the medicine chest. I am sure you will need it."

"That is good," commended Rose, looking curiously after Margaret, who swayed as she went out of the room.

Murray hurried after her. "It is nothing, Miss McAllister, except for the pain and possible fever. Buck will tell you so himself. Drink this."

The cold water made her feel better. "I never realized before-what fighting means," she murmured. "It may be nothing but it looks-terrible."

"Nothing dangerous, I assure you, and perfect health will bring him through. Shall you go on out to the ranch?"

"Why, I must send the medicines."

"Then wait for me to join you at Twin River. I shall not be long."

He controlled the restive team until she was ready and watched her start. When he returned to Rose she had bared and was bathing the wound from which but little blood came, now. When a fresh bandage had been put in place she turned to him with expressive gesture: "Remove all," she commanded, indicating Buck's clothing. She left the room and Murray heard her moving about in the attic while he busied himself in obedience to her orders.

"Who was it, Buck?" he asked, sombrely.

"Did n't see him. Dave, I reckon."

"Was it Dave you was after?"

"That's him. Did n't you know?"

"No." Murray slit viciously through the waist band of the trousers and raised Buck with one powerful arm while he eased away the severed cloth. He said nothing more until Rose came with a garment such as Buck had not worn for more years than he liked to remember. When it was donned and Buck made comfortable, Murray spoke with decision. In his earnestness he unconsciously reverted from the slip-shod manner of speech to which he had habituated himself.

"I have a confession to make," he began; "and I want to make it now. I don't think it will harm you to hear it."

"Let 'er go," said Buck, with awakened interest.

"I am a hypocrite. I am indirectly responsible for the loss of your cattle. I have been taking your money and working for another man. I am not at all proud of it. In fact, as things have turned out, I 'm d —d sick of it. All that I can say for myself is that I honestly thought the other man was in the right; now I know better. If it will be any satisfaction to you I would give my life this minute rather than have it known by-by certain people who are bound to know of it if you talk. So it has not been easy to tell you. I have only one thing more to add: I can't be treacherous to the other man although he has been treacherous to me; but if you are not afraid to trust me, I guarantee to make the Double Y sound on the inside, at least-that is, if they don't kill me."

"By th' Lord!" breathed Buck. "I 'm right glad I got that pill. Trust you? You bet!" He reached out his hand to Murray and the grip he felt confirmed his belief that the canker was surely healed on the Double Y.

Softly as Buck spoke, the sound of his voice brought Rose to the door. She looked sternly at Murray: "You must go," she declared; "So much talk bring fever."

"All right, ma'am," assented Murray, carefully keeping from her his tell-tale face, "sure you won't need help?"

"No, my father come soon." She advanced to the bunk and improved comfort and appearance with a few deft touches.

"Good-day, then, ma'am. So long, Buck. I 'm ridin' to th' ranch with Miss McAllister."

"So long, Cock. Get at it, son. Th' Double Y needs you, you bet," and the smile on the stern face was so winning that Murray left hastily, with long strides.

Chapter XXV
Mary Receives Company

Mary's heart skipped a beat and then pulsed ninety to the minute as her first suspicion became a certainty: a wagon was coming through the dark to the ranch. With a prayer for her husband on her lips she went slowly to the door. She recognized Murray's voice and Jake's in conversation and stood with her hand on the door until Jake's rough command was followed by the sound of the wagon going to the stable. No one wounded! Her relief was so great that she walked unsteadily in crossing back to her chair. Mary was nervous and easily upset, these days.

Surprise acted as a tonic when the two ladies entered, followed by Murray. A glance at Margaret's face stirred memories in Mary. She stammered: "Why-why —I know-who —"

Murray supplied the name: "It is Miss McAllister, Mrs. Cassidy."

"Why, of co'se," said Mary; "I 'd know Miss McAllister anywhere; she favors Frenchy like she was his own daughter."

"Did you know Uncle John?" asked Margaret, breathlessly.

"Yes, indeedy. I took to him first sight," and Mary smiled at the girl's eagerness.

"Aunt Jessie! Isn't that just glorious? Mrs. Cassidy, this is my aunt, Mrs. Blake-and I want you to tell me everything you can remember about Uncle John."

"Now you have done it," declared Mrs. Blake. "You will get no peace from Margaret while she thinks there is a wag of your tongue left about her Uncle John."

"Margaret-that's a right sweet name. But I 'm afraid Billy would insist —" she flushed a dull red as Mrs. Blake sharply addressed Murray: "Ralph, see that some one gets those trunks in, will you? That is, if they did not drop off into the bosom of this blessed wilderness, somewhere *en route*."

"They did n't. But it's all Montana to an incubator Jake took them to the stable," and Murray promptly vanished.

"Certainly he would insist," agreed Mrs. Blake, resuming the thread of Mary's unconscious soliloquy. "And quite right, too. It would have to be-what did you say your name is, my dear?"

"Mary " —the shy smile made her seem very unlike the self-reliant H2 girl.

Mrs. Blake took her in her arms and mothered her. "Mary is every bit as sweet as Margaret," she declared. "And now you must came over here and sit down. That is six for me and a half dozen for myself. *How* I shall rejoice to land in a seat that neither shakes nor bumps!"

"I shore begs you-all 's pardon; but I ain't got over my surprise yet."

"Shall we put you to very much trouble, Mrs. Cassidy?" asked Margaret. "Perhaps if you get that lazy Murray to help —"

"Why, Murray ain't lazy. There ain't none of the boys lazy, 'cept maybe Jake. An' it's shore a pleasure to have you here."

"May heaven forgive my vegatative emotion in the cessation of motion," and Mrs. Blake carefully refrained from moving her foot forward one enticing inch: it was good enough as it was.

"You ain't use' to travelling, Mrs. Blake," suggested Mary.

"On the contrary, my dear," that lady assured her. "Mr. Blake hauled me over the entire country from the Mississippi to the Atlantic; but he never subjected me to the churning discomfort of a devil-drawn buckboard driven by a heartless madcap in petticoats." Mrs. Blake shifted the faintest imaginable distance to the left and back again immediately: the first position was the more comfortable, as she might have known.

The two younger women exchanged a smile, Margaret's a merry one, Mary's more sober as she thought how easily the buckboard might have carried a load indifferent for all time, to jolts. "Did you see anything o' th' boys?" she asked.

"I saw them all, I believe," answered Margaret. "They went through Twin River just before we started."

"Cock Murray came back with you. Did you see my husband? He started out to find Mr. Peters."

"Mr. Cassidy and Mr. Booth went after that Dave brute."

"Where was Buck?"

"He was wounded, Mrs. Cassidy. Not badly, they say. Dave shot him from ambush. We found him lying in the road."

"Oh! I ought to go to him," and Mary started from her seat.

"Certainly not," declared Mrs. Blake. "It is quite evident that you do not appreciate the comforts of inertia. Besides, from what Margaret tells me, he is well taken care of."

"Oh! and I forgot the medicine chest," exclaimed Margaret. "Yes, he has an attentive nurse, Mrs. Cassidy. We took him to the LaFrance place. And I must get that medicine chest from Whitby's kit and send it over. Where are Whitby's things, Mrs. Cassidy?"

"They 're in th' bunk-house. Murray will get them for you. So Buck is there? Did you see the French Rose, Miss McAllister?"

"Yes, haven't you? She is lovely; so serious and calm and strong. In some way she makes you feel that she is sure to do the right thing at the right time. Oh, I like her, immensely."

"Liking goes by contrasts," sleepily reminded Mrs. Blake. Mary smiled no less at Margaret's grimace than at Mrs. Blake's pointed sarcasm.

"She has n't been to the ranch since we-all came," said Mary. "Buck says she rid over quite often afore that. I 'm glad Rose is 'tendin' him; from what I hear of her he could n't be in better hands."

"Mr. Peters seemed glad, too," said Margaret, suggestively; "and Miss LaFrance did not seem at all sorry."

Before Mary could respond to Margaret's unspoken question, the door opened with a bang and Pickles rushed in. "Been a-helpin' them sheep with th' trunks," he informed them. "Where's Hopalong? Did he find Buck? That cacklin' Murray has forgot how to crow; he on'y grunts."

"Hopalong has gone after Dave. He shot Buck," answered Mary.

"Not dead!" Pickles was aghast.

"No, only wounded."

"I just *got* to kill that Dave. Rose has got to lemme off on that promise. I bet she will now he 's gone an' shot up Buck."

Mrs. Blake stirred in her chair and opened one eye. "Out of the mouths of babes and sucklings —"

"Sucker yoreself!" retorted Pickles. "Reckon you think I don't know nothin'. You wait." He slammed the door behind him and stamped off, greatly incensed. His advice to Jake, who told him to open the other door while he carried in a trunk, was impossible to follow, involving a journey from which no one, not even Jake, would ever be likely to return.

When Margaret, insisting that Mary direct operations from her chair, was satisfied with domestic arrangements, she asked Murray's advice about sending the medicine chest to Rose. Obeying Whitby's wishes seemed the most important thing in life at present. Cock demurred to her plan of sending him before morning; and he was opposed to leaving the ranch at all before Buck himself took charge again. Margaret was vexed at his stupidity. They had gone together to the bunk-house and argued the matter with the object of dispute on the floor between them. Glancing at them from his own especial bunk was Pickles, trying in vain to make sense from a jumble of sounds unlike any he had ever heard. Pickles' vocabulary was very limited. His snort of disgust as he gave it up and turned his back on the disputants, gave Cock an idea. "Pickles," he said, "Buck's sick and he needs this box. Buck told me to stay at the ranch. Will you take it if I saddle Swallow?"

"Shore will," and Pickles shoved one entirely nude leg from the bunk; before he could follow it with the other, he was much surprised and more embarrassed to find himself swooped upon, seized and swiftly kissed by Margaret, whose brown-clad form fled through the door like the flirt of a wood-thrush, vanishing into the dim recesses of the forest.

* * * * *

Ned Monroe and the boys, Big Saxe with them, came straggling up to the bunk-house in the early hours of the morning, Ned having acquired a change of mounts at Twin River. They secured their prisoner by the simple expedient of tying him in a lump-and a cow-punch makes knots that are exceedingly hard to struggle out of. Big Saxe did n't try.

Cock Murray was first out and he awoke Ned. In the open, safe from being overheard, they held conference, Monroe nodding his head understandingly as Cock made his points. After breakfast, Monroe delivered a speech, short and to the point, and when they separated to their duties, Cock and Slow Jack rode away together. Big Saxe, very effectually hobbled at the ankles, was put in charge of Chesty Sutton who tersely informed him that the first false move he made he would find himself humpbacked all the way to his feet.

Cock bent his powers of persuasion to the converting of Slow Jack. It proved an easy task. Secretly admiring Cock and his ways, Slow Jack also perceived the trend of events to be putting Schatz out of the running. The unbending will of Hopalong was over them all and Slow Jack was not averse to throwing his services to the winning side.

It was the middle of the afternoon when Whitby appeared. The women listened to his news with varying degrees of interest. Buck was doing well and had declared it would not be long before he was at the ranch; in the meantime, as he was obliged to be quiet, he seemed well contented where he was. Pickles had arrived safe and had constituted himself body-guard and messenger-at-need for Rose. As for Hopalong he could tell them no more than they had already learned from Monroe. Mary was not worried. She had supreme confidence in Hopalong's ability to take care of himself and would have smiled if any one had suggested danger.

The end of Whitby's budget was punctuated with a huge sigh from Jake, whose ear had never been far from the kitchen door. He now entered diffidently and addressed himself to the Englishman: "I wrastled some chuck for you, Whit; reckoned you might want some." His lumbering exit was closely followed by Whitby's, whose strangled appetite slipped the noose at Jake's invitation.

In the lively conversation of the three women, Margaret's voice groped about in Whitby's consciousness like a hand searching in the dark for a hidden spring; her sudden ringing laugh awoke him to his purpose and hastily finishing his meal he made his way to the barn. After an hour's delay, spent in selecting a pony for Margaret and taking the edge off the temper of the quietest —a favor that Margaret would have repudiated with scorn-he appeared at the house again with the offer to show her over the range if she cared to go.

It was the very thing Margaret most wanted to do and they set out with but little time lost. When she become accustomed to the saddle she suggested a race but Whitby had no intention of running any such risk. He easily held her interest in another way.

"I say, Miss McAllister, there 's one thing I did n't mention just now," he began.

"Not bad news?" questioned Margaret.

"Can't say it's good. That beastly German had the cheek to get away with the money after all. He checked against the blessed lot yesterday forenoon. I was at the bank this morning. It's right enough. They produced the check. Seems a bit odd, you know, they should be carrying that amount and pass it over in cash. I said as much; but the president-rummy chap, by the way-he explained it; something about big shipments of cattle. However, it's gone."

"Dear me! it seems very careless of somebody. Papa ought to know. What shall you do?"

"Oh, I notified the agency at once; they 've taken it in hand. But it won't do any good, you know. That bounder Schatz has it all planned out and if he loses it, why, there you are, you know."

"Yes, so it seems; but, to all intents and purposes, he steals it. Do you intend to let him triumph in such brazen robbery?"

"I rather fancy I shall have very little to say in the matter. That Cassidy chap who is trying to catch Dave, went off without knowing the money was gone. My word! I should n't care to be Schatz when Cassidy hears of it. Deuced odd no one saw him in Wayback but the banking people. However, the German will have to go. I wrote the Governor and Mr. McAllister this morning. Between them they can come to an agreement with Peters and we can buy the German out-or perhaps I should say his heirs. It's a good sporting chance that it will be his heirs. Cassidy has a proper amount of suspicion in his character and no one will ambush him, I 'll lay."

"Good gracious! But you can't afford to lose all that money, can you?"

"It is a bit of a facer. But what of it? The range can stand it. In twenty years it will bring ten times the money for farm land, or I 'm much mistaken. I 'm sure the Governor will chance it and Buck will be glad to have me an active partner. He said as much."

"Mr. Booth, did n't you advance the money to Peters in the last partnership agreement?"

"Oh, I say! Did they tell you that? Then you should know it was my advice that brought on his loss. But Buck is n't obliged to put up any money with us; his experience and services are quite equal to the money I shall put up. I fancy Mr. McAllister will agree with me in that. All Buck wants is fair play, don't you know."

Margaret pulled her pony so that she had the advantage of a few feet nearer the house when she spoke. "Whitby," she said, very clearly, "you are a dear."

Both ponies swung their noses towards home in the same moment. The burning blush on Margaret's face streamed from it on the air-currents and settled on Whitby's determined countenance, to leave him and float away to the rose clouds in the western sky. Whitby had the faster mount but Margaret rode a far lighter weight and the chase might have been a long one had she been very anxious to keep away. As it was a short half mile found them on even terms. Whitby's arm went about the girl's waist as the ponies ran stride for stride and she felt herself leaving the saddle. With reckless abandonment to the law of might she yielded and lay in his arms; their pace slowed to a walk, Whitby looking solemnly into the brilliant eyes that mockingly regarded him.

"The good old rule, the simpler plan, that he shall take who hath the power," quoted Margaret.

"And he shall keep who can," capped Whitby. "I can, Margaret, and I will," he declared, a deep note of earnestness in his voice.

Margaret reached up and covered the steady eyes whose searching threatened the unconscious secrets of her heart. But her voice reached him, fainter, fraught with the vibration of sureness: "Whitby, you are a dear."

Chapter XXVI
Hunters and Hunted

A string of empty cars backed onto the siding at X — —, bumping and grinding and squealing as the engine puffed softly; a running rattle and crash told of the shivering line coming to rest and the sibilant sighs of the engine seemed to voice its protest at being side-tracked for the passing of an engine of a higher caste. While it panted and wheezed, its crew taking advantage of the opportunity to look to and oil journals and rods, a man made his way through the brush several hundred yards down the track, swearing mildly as he brushed cinders and dust from his clothes. His only possessions besides his clothes were a revolver swinging in its buttoned holster, and a tightly rolled and securely tied gunny sack, to which he clung in grim determination.

"H —l of a ride," he growled as he headed in a circuitous course for the town a short distance away. "But it breaks th' trail. They 'll figger I went north to cross th' line, or up to Helena. Lucky they told me Denver Gus's relay was relieved. Brains, says Smiler-huh, devil a lot of good his brains done him. He is out of it, an' so is Peters, d —n 'em. Brains!"

He entered the town, looking for a place to put up. The Come-Again looked good and he entered it, securing a room on the second floor, which was under the roof. He was explicit to the proprietor: "It's got to be a back room, an' I want it for a couple of days, an' I don't want no noise, —I'm out here for my cussed nerves an' as soon as I can get a good job we 'll see about terms. Oh, I expect to pay in advance-will two days' pay keep you from layin' awake nights?"

"Reckon somebody made a mistake," replied the proprietor. "Yore nerves is purty strong."

"Have a drink and forget it," Dave smiled. When he had paid for the drinks he asked a question: "Who's got th' best horse in town? I'm a-goin' to buy it if it's good enough."

The proprietor looked him over and nodded toward a table in the farther corner: "That's him."

Dave sauntered over to the lone drinker: "Just been told you got th' best horse in town. That right?"

The other looked up slowly: "I might," he replied.

"I want to buy him. I don't give a d —n about th' price if he's good. Interested? Thought you'd be."

The other also looked the cocky stranger over: "Yes —I 'm interested —a little. I ain't h — l-bent for to sell that horse. He 's th' best ever came to these parts-that's why he 's good-he *came* here."

Dave was impatient: "Is he where I can see him?"

"Shore," drawled the horseman, arising languidly. "Come along an' you can see him if yore eyes is good."

The owner of the "best horse in town" studied Dave as they walked along and his mental comment was not flattering to the *protégé* of the late Herr Schatz. "Fake cow-puncher," was his summing up. "He don't know a *hoss* from a hoss-but he thinks he does."

When they came to the corral the owner pointed to a big gray in the corner: "That's him, stranger. He 's part cow-horse an' part Kaintuk, an' too good to be out here in this part of the country. *That's* th' hoss Bad Hawkins rid from Juniper Creek to Halfway in ten hours-one hundred an' forty miles, says th' map, an' Hawkins weighed a hundred an' seventy afore they got him. He weighed so much he broke off th' limb of th' best tree they could find. Why, *he 's* th' cuss what held up th' Montana Express down at Juniper Creek bridge-reckon you *are* a stranger to these parts."

"He don't look like no miracle to *me*," asserted Dave, closely scrutinizing the horse.

"No? Mebby you ain't up on miracles. If you want a purty hoss why did n't you say so? Dolly 's slick as silk an' fat as butter-you can have her if you wants her. Cost you about twenty-five dollars less. But you won't save nothin' on her if you wants a hoss for hard ridin', one that gets there quick, an' gets back quick."

"I ain't said nothin' 'bout savin' no money," retorted Dave. "An' it seems to me yo 're purty d —n high in yore prices, anyhow."

"Well, I sees you wants a hoss right bad; an' when a man wants a hoss bad he wants a *good* hoss-an' good hosses come high. Dolly 's gentle as a kitten," shrewdly explained the owner. "Big Gray, there, he 's some hard to ride, onless you can sit a saddle good as th' next."

"How much for Big Gray?" snapped Dave.

"One hundred dollars."

"I ain't buyin' a herd," remonstrated Dave.

"I ain't sellin' a herd," smiled the owner. "I told you good hosses come high. Mebby Dolly 'd suit you better. She 's my daughter's hoss."

"Here 's th' hundred," replied Dave, nettled. "Got a bridle or halter or piece of rope? An' I want to buy a saddle-one that's been broke in."

"There's a halter on him-good enough? All right; I got a saddle that's in purty fair shape-don't need it, so you can have it for twenty."

When Dave rode from the corral he was headed for the general store and bought a rifle, a rope, and sundry other necessaries, including food. Returning to the hotel he put his horse in the corral, had a drink, and went to his room carrying the saddle, the gunny sack, and his other purchases with him. The gunny sack had not been from under his arm an instant while he had been in town. The erstwhile owner of Big Gray drifted back to his table shortly after Dave's return and settled himself for another drink.

"Did you sell him one?" asked the proprietor, digging down for change.

"Yep," was the reply.

"Fifty, sixty, seventy-five —there 's yore change. I wonder who he is an' where he's goin'?" remarked the proprietor, in lieu of something better.

"Dunno; but he ain't no cow-punch, an' likewise he ain't no tenderfoot. Looks like a tin-horn to me. His fingers was purty slick gettin' th' bills off his roll. They was so slick I counted 'em to be sure he was n't robbin' hisself. But there was n't no folded bill there. Here, have a drink with me-business is pickin' up."

* * * * *

When the east-bound accommodation pulled into X — — at dusk two men jumped off and started toward the nearest hotel. The proprietor of the Come-Again assigned them a room and spoke of supper, to which they intimated their ability to do justice to "anythin' you got." As they turned away carelessly toward the "washroom" one of them halted: "We're expectin' a friend," and he gave a concise description of the third man.

"Why, he 's upstairs now-first door to th' left at th' top of th' flight-got in this afternoon. But he said he did n't want to be bothered none," hastily warned the proprietor.

"That's right-you can let that go for th' three of us," replied Hopalong, smiling.

"Said his nerves was all stampeded," commented the host, dubiously.

Hopalong winked, grinning: "Did n't act none that-a-way, did he?"

"Oh, I *told* him somebody was stringin' him," laughed the proprietor.

"Reckon we 'll go up an' hustle him down to his feed," Tex remarked, leading the way, with Hopalong stepping on his heels.

The proprietor studied the three names on his register, and spoke to the horseman, who now was playing solitaire in a negligent way. "Wonder what's up, Dick?"

"Dunno," replied Dick, holding aloft a queen of hearts and studying the layout. "Reckon you better let this deal go by. Keep yore chips out, Joe; don't like th' looks of th' pair of 'em. That red-head looks like a bad customer, if his corn 's stepped on. Mebby their nervous friend has did somethin' they don't like."

The knocking upstairs now reverberated through the house and a peevish voice threatened destruction to the door unless it opened speedily.

"That's th' red-head," remarked Dick. "What did I tell you?"

The proprietor hastened from behind the bar and went up the steep, narrow stairs with undignified haste. "Don't bust that door!" he cried. "Don't you bust it!"

"Aw, close yore face!" growled a voice, and Dick nodded his head wisely. "Both of 'em bad customers," he mumbled.

There was a crash and the sound of splintering wood, followed by disgusted exclamations. Dick arose and sauntered up to see the show: the host was nervously clutching a bill large enough to pay for several broken doors. The red-head was looking out of the open window while the other man rapidly searched the room.

"He dropped his belongings first," audibly commented the man at the window. "Then *he* dropped." He turned quickly to the proprietor: "Did he have a horse?"

"Yes; bought one first thing after he registered."

"We want one apiece," crisply demanded Hopalong, "with speed, bottom, an' sand. Got 'em? No? Then where can we get 'em to-night?"

"What'd he do?" blundered the host, rubbing the bill with tender fingers and looking for information instead of giving it.

"He dropped out th' winder," sharply replied Tex. "We never stand for that."

"Never, not under no circumstances," endorsed his friend. "It allus riles us. How 'bout them horses?"

"I reckon I can fix you up," offered Dick. "I sold him th' hoss he 's got. He wanted th' best in town, which he didn't get for bein' too blamed flip. But he paid for it, just th' same. I got a roan an' a bay that 'll run Big Gray off 'n his feed an' his feet. If yo 're comin' back this way I 'll buy 'em back again at a reduction —I 'd like to keep them two. I don't reckon I 'll get no chance to buy back th' other."

The horseman fell in behind the descending procession and lined up with it against the bar on Hopalong's treat. Then they left the proprietor to swear at the cook while they departed for the corral.

Dick chuckled. "Th' gray I sold yore missin' friend carried Bad Hawkins from Juniper Creek to Halfway in fourteen hours-ten miles an hour. Th' roan an' th' bay did it in ten hours even-which puts a period after th' last words of Hawkins. Bad Hawkins weighed less 'n you," he said to Tex, "an' th' gray shore sprains a laig a-doin' it. It don't show-that is, not when he was sold it did n't. That feller was too d —d flip-one of them Smart Alecks that stirs my bile somethin' awful."

Tex wearied of his voice: "Yore discernment is very creditable," he replied, with becoming gravity.

The horseman glanced at him out of the corner of his eye: "Yes —I reckon so," he hazarded.

When they reached the corral the two strangers looked in critically. Nearly a score of horses were impounded, among them several bays and roans. Hopalong pointed to one of the roans. "That looks like th' horse," he remarked, quietly, at the instant his friend singled out the bay.

"Them 's th' hosses-they 'll run th' liver out of Big Gray even if his laig does hold out," smiled their owner, glad that his first customer had not been as wise as either of these two men. The horses were cut out and accepted on the spot.

"How much?" demanded Hopalong, brusquely.

"Eighty apiece."

"That's a lot of money. But we got to have 'em. How 'bout saddles? We can do without 'em if we has to, but we ain't hankerin' very strong to do it."

"I got a couple of good ones," responded the horseman. Then he yielded to a sudden burst of generosity. "Tell you what I 'll do —I 'll sell you them saddles for forty apiece an' when I gets 'em back, you gets yore money back. An' if you don't kill th' hosses, we 'll have a little dicker over them, too. I would n't sell 'em only for a good price an' you won't have nothin' to complain about if I buys 'em back again."

"Yo 're a white man," responded Hopalong. "Now we all oughta have a drink to bind th' deal. An' I reckon supper 'll go good, too. We 'll be right glad to have you join us." The invitation was accepted with becoming alacrity.

After the meal, and a game of cards, during which both punchers had learned much about the surrounding country, they went on a tour of investigation. They had discovered that the only way south likely to be taken by a man not perfectly familiar with the several little-known mountain trails, was through Lone Tree Pass. A walk about the town, before turning in, disclosed to them the kind and amount of Dave's purchases: these showed that he expected to be in the saddle more than a few hours. Returning to the hotel they went at once to their room. Sitting on the edge of the bed Hopalong asked a question: "You 've got me on t' lay of th' land in this part of the country, Tex. Why do you figger he 'll head south?"

Tex blew out the light and settled himself snugly in his bed before replying. "Because anybody else would figger he 'd strike north for th' Canadian line, or up to Helena an' West, where a man can get lost easy. I 've sort of palled with Dave, an' I know th' skunk like a ABC book. His trail will show us th' way, but it won't tell us about th' country ahead of us. I allus like to know what I 'm goin' up against when I can."

"Shore; good-night," muttered Hopalong, and in a moment more soft snores vibrated out through the open window, to be mildly criticised by the cook in the cook shack below.

Down in the bar-room the proprietor, having said good-night to his last customer, pushed the column of figures away with a sigh of satisfaction and rested his chin on his hand while he reviewed the events of the day. "Why," he muttered, pugnaciously, coming out of his reveries and pouring himself a liberal drink on the strength of the day's profits; "why, now I know what that coyote wanted his room at the back of the house for-good thing I got th' money ahead of time! Well, he 's got a h —l of a lot of trouble chasin' him, anyhow, th' beat."

* * * * *

With three days' rations fastened to their saddles Hopalong and Tex whirled away from the Come-Again as the first streak of gray appeared in the eastern sky and after a short distance at full speed to take the devilishness out of their mounts, they slowed to a lope. Heading straight for the Pass, they picked up Dave's trail less than two miles from town and then settled into a steady gait that ate up the miles without punishing their horses. They had not made any mistake in their mounts for they were powerful and tough, spirited enough to possess temper and courage without any undue nervous waste, and the way they covered ground, with apparently no effort, brought a grim smile to Hopalong's face.

"I don't reckon I 'll do no swappin' back, Tex," he chuckled. "I 've allus wanted a cayuse like this 'n, an' I reckon he 'll stay bought, even at th' price."

"They look good-but I 'll tell you more about 'em by night," Tex replied. He glanced ahead with calm assurance: "I don't figger he's so very far, Hoppy?"

"Why no, Tex; he could n't ride hard last night, not over strange country-it was darker'n blazes. We did n't leave very long after him when you figger it in miles, an' he ain't reckonin' *shore* on bein' chased. He drops out th' winder an' sneaks that way 'cause he ain't takin' no chances.

"We 've got th' best cayuses, we 've had more sleep than him, we know this game better, we 're tougher, an' we can get more out of a cayuse than he can. I reckon we ought to get sight of him afore sundown, an' I would n't be surprised if we saw him shortly after noon. We 'll shore get him 'bout noon, if he 's had any sleep."

"I 'd ruther get him this side of Lone Tree Pass —I ain't hankerin' for no close chase through th' mountains after a cuss like Dave," Tex replied. "What do you say 'bout lettin' out another link?"

Hopalong watched his horse for a minute, glanced critically at his companion's, and tightened the grip of his knees. "That feller said a hundred an' forty in ten hours-how far is that pass? Well, might as well find out what this cayuse can do-come on, let 'em go!"

Pounding along at a gait which sent the wind whistling past their ears they dipped into hollows, shot over rises, and rounded turns side by side, stirrups touching and eyes roving as they searched the trail ahead. The turns they made were not as many as those in the trail they followed, for often they cut straight across from one turn to another. The ability to do this brought a shrewd smile to Hopalong's thin lips.

"Let his cayuse pick its way, Tex-told you he could n't go fast last night. Bet a dollar we come to where he slept afore long-an' say! luck 's with us, shore. Notice how he was bearin' —a little off th' course all th' time-that gray of his must a' come from som'ers up north. He had to correct that when he could see where th' Pass lay-come on, we 'll try another cut-off, an' a big one."

"Yo 're right-we 'll gain a hour, easy," Tex replied as they shot off at a tangent for the distant mountain range on a line for the Pass. The sun was two hours higher when Tex laughed aloud, stretching his hand across his friend's horse and pointing some distance ahead of him. "There's th' track again, Hoppy," he cried, "you was right-see it?"

Hopalong waited until they swept up along the fresh trail before he replied and the reply was characteristic of him. "Pushin' th' gray hard, Tex. Them toe prints are purty deep-an' d —d if th' gray ain't havin' trouble with his bad laig! See that off fore hoofmark? See how it ain't as deep as its mate? Th' gray's favorin' that laig, an' only for one reason: it hurts him more when he don't. Move away a little, Tex; don't do no good to be bunched so close where there 's so much cover. He ain't a long way off, judgin' from them tracks. We don't know that he ain't doubled back to pick us off as we near him."

Tex tightened his knee-grip and rowelled his spurs lightly along the side of his mount, darting ahead with Hopalong speeding up to catch him. It was a test to see how the horses were holding up and when the animals took up the new speed and held it with plenty of reserve strength, the two men let them go.

As they shot down a rough, sloping trail to a shallow creek, flowing noisily along the bottom of a wild arroyo, Hopalong looked ahead eagerly and called to Tex to slow down to a walk. Tex, surprised, obeyed and took the reins of the bay as Hopalong went ahead to cross the stream on foot. But Tex's surprise was only momentary; he quickly understood the reason for the play and he warmed to his sagacious friend while he admired his skill.

Hopalong waded the stream and looked carefully around on both side of the tracks where they left the water. Motioning Tex to come ahead, he grinned as the other obeyed. "Did n't want to splash no fresh water around here till I saw if th' water Dave splashed was all soaked up. It is; but th' spots is moist. An' another thing: see th' prints o' that hoof where he takes up an' sets down-where is he lame?"

"Shoulder," replied Tex with instant decision.

"Shore is. An' he 's been a-gettin' lamer every step. Bet he ain't an hour ahead, Tex."

"Won't take you-an' he 'll be above us all th' way till we cross th' top of th' range, so we better keep under cover as much as we can," Tex replied. "We 've trailed worse men than Dave, a whole lot worse, an' far better shots; but he ain't really due to miss twice in two days. Th' Pass ain't so far ahead now-there it is, with th' blasted pine stickin' up like a flag-pole. Half an hour more an' we 'll be in it."

Ahead of them, toiling up the Pass on a tired and limping horse rode Dave, not so fresh as he might have been with the four hours' sleep he had secured in the open at dawn. The night ride over strange, rough country had been hard and his rage at the shabby trick played upon him by the horse dealer had not helped him any. To win up to the point where success was almost his; and then to have a half-breed horse coper-one who had absolutely no connection with the game-threaten to defeat him! To fool all the players, to gain, as he thought, a big handicap and then to be delayed by a man who sought only to gain a little money and be well rid of a poor horse! Dave's temper was like that of a rattler hedged in by thorns and the rougher part of the mountain trail had been saturated with profanity. There was not much chance of meeting any one on that trail and by the time he reached a place where he could get another horse, the need for one would have gone. Let him see a horseman and he knew who would ride the horse. He struck the limping gray savagely as it flinched over a particularly rough part of the trail and he was growling and swearing as he rounded a turn in the Pass and came to a place where, by climbing a boulder just above him, he could get a good view of the way he had come. Dismounting, he made the climb and looked back over the trail. Miles of country were below him, the trail winding across it, hidden at times and then running on in plain view until some hill concealed it again. The sun was half down in the western sky and he swore again as he realized how much farther he should have been-how near the end of his ride.

"A hundred an' forty miles in ten hours!" he snarled, squirming back to descend to his horse. "No wonder Bad Hawkins got caught! Served th' d —n fool right; an' it 'd serve me right for being such a — —" the words ceased and the speaker flattened himself to the rock as he peered intently at a hill far down the trail, waiting to be sure his eyes had not deceived him.

The slanting sun had made a fairyland of the rugged scenery, bathing the rocks until they seemed to glow, finding cunningly hidden quartz and crystals and turning them into points of flame. The fresh, clean green coat that Spring had thrown over the crags as if to hide them, softened the harsher tones and would have thrilled even Dave, who was sated with scenery, if it had not been for his temper and the desperate straits in which he found himself. He lay like one dead but for the straining eyes. An eagle, drifting carelessly across the blue, missed him in its sharp scrutiny, so well did his clothes blend with the tones of the rock.

"H —l!" he muttered, for far below him something moved out into the trail again where it emerged from behind the hill, and two mounted men came into sight, riding rapidly to take advantage of the short run of level country.

Dave could not make them out-they were only two men at that distance, but he wasted no time nor gave heed to any optimism. He wriggled backwards, dropped to the trail, and looked around for a place to hide his horse. Not seeing one at hand he mounted again and forced the limping animal forward until he saw a narrow ravine cut into the mountain side by the freshets of countless years. Leading the gray into this and around a turn in the wall, he picketed the animal and then hastened back, scurrying to and fro in search of a hiding place that would give him a view of the trail for the greatest distance. His mind worked as rapidly as his feet. The coming horsemen might be innocent of all knowledge of him or of his need. If so, he preferred to ride behind them. If they were in pursuit-and he could not believe it to be a mere coincidence that any but an enemy would be following him so close through Lone Tree Pass-they had not started from the town he had just quitted-unless they had traced him by telegraph! Dave cursed softly and settled himself a little more at ease in his ambush.

Hopalong and Tex, enjoying that friendship that sets no embarrassment on silence, rode forward side by side when the trail permitted it, grim, relentless, dogged. They represented that class of men who can pursue one thing to the exclusion of all tempting side leads, needing nothing but what they themselves can supply; who approach all duties with cool, level-headed precision and gain their goal without a thought of reward and with small regard for danger. Danger they had both met in all the forms it took on the range and trail, dance-hall and saloon; both had mastered it by the speed and certainty of their hands and guns, and neither found anything exciting or fearful in this game of follow and take; on the other hand it was tiresome to have to follow, and one man, at that. If some bold, daring stroke of strategy or a reckless dash could have been hoped for, it would have made the game interesting. So they jogged on toward the opening of the pass, taciturn and sombre, but with the cold patience of Indians.

The trail narrowed again and Tex took the lead. "Closer now," he remarked, more to himself than to his companion, whose reply was a grunt, presumed to be affirmative. When they entered the pass itself it was Hopalong who led, and to see him as he sat slouching in his saddle, apparently half asleep, one would have wondered that a man whose wariness was the basis of so many famed exploits could ride thus carelessly, allowing his horse to pick the way. But in the shadow of his straight-brimmed hat, two hard, keen eyes squinted through the narrow lids, among the wrinkles, and missed nothing that could be seen; under the faded red shirt sleeve was an arm ready for the lightning draw that had never yet been beaten, and the hand-worn butt of the heavy Colt rubbed softly against the belt-strap of its holster.

Hopalong rolled a cigarette and took advantage of the movement to speak: "Goin' back to Texas, Tex?"

"Why," replied Tex, pausing to reflect. "Why, I said as how I would to all yore boys, but I reckon mebby Buck needs me worse'n you do. What think?"

"Stay up here an' run for sheriff," was the crisp reply. "This country 's sick with crooks."

"Reckon so."

"Good place for undertakers, while th' boom is on," continued Hopalong, smiling grimly at the truth in his jest. He knew Tex Ewalt.

"Th' boom 'll be busted flat afore you go home," Tex responded. "It's fallin' now. Dave was its high-water mark."

They were riding side by side now and Hopalong growled a suggestion: "Go slow, Tex; mebby he 's holin' up on us, like he did on Buck. He ain't more 'n a million miles ahead of us now."

"Uh-huh; an' if he is he ought to get us easy in this place. Got to take a chance, anyhow. Gimme a match —*Look out!*"

As he spoke he hurled his horse against Hopalong's and his left arm dropped to his side with a bullet through it, while his right hand flashed to his hip, where a pungent cloud of smoke burst out to envelop his horse's head. Off his balance from the unexpected shock, Hopalong's shot went wide, but the next five, directed at Dave's head-long rush as he came crashing down through the underbrush, gave promise of better aim.

As he spoke he hurled his horse against Hopalong's, while his right
hand flashed to his hip

"I owed him that, anyhow," muttered Tex, his ears ringing from the fusillade so close to him. "An' I owed you th' play, Hoppy, ever since that day in th' brush—"

"You don't owe me nothin' now, Tex; that's as close as any in ten years," returned Hopalong. "Well, he showed hisself a d—d ambushin' snake just as we thought he would. He could a' got us both if his nerves had n't got th' chills an' fever. We was some careless!"

"We was a pair of blasted kids," Tex remarked. "Now what 'll we do with him? We can't take him back, an' buryin' in solid rock ain't been in my schoolin'."

"We can cover him with rocks, I reckon, but we ain't got time-besides, how'd he leave Buck?" demanded Hopalong sharply. "Why, he got you, Tex! Here, you close-mouthed fool, lemme fix that hole."

Tex stood quietly thoughtful until Hopalong had finished his task. "We 'll just chuck him off th' trail, Hoppy; then we won't have to answer no question or shoot sense into no thick skulls. How 'bout it?"

"Uh-huh, go ahead," grunted Hopalong and the two walked over, picked up the unresisting bulk and placed it in a fissure in the rock wall.

"By th' Lord!" swore Tex: "Five shots out of five when you got yore balance —*that's* shootin'! *You* better run for sheriff."

"I had n't ought to 'a' done it when I knowed th' second got him-but he kept a-comin' an' I was a-thinkin' of Buck. Come on, let's get goin'." He mounted and waited impatiently for Tex, who was still standing beside his horse as if unwilling to leave the scene. "His pot-shootin' is over, so let's start back."

"Uh-huh," muttered Tex, still lost in thought. Hopalong waited, having acquired increased respect for his friend's brain capacity in the last few days.

"Hoppy, why did Dave ambush Buck an' have to run, just when he was goin' to skin Schatz for a pot of money?"

"Give it up," answered Hopalong.

"Well, why did n't Schatz turn up when everything was set for the play?"

"Got to pass again, Tex," was Hopalong's indulgent reply.

"Dave had plenty of chances to kill Buck-better chances than that one-an' no need to run, if he was careful. Th' Twin River trail is travelled some-it was shore risky-no time to waste in Wayback waitin' for Schatz after that, huh?"

"Mebby th' kid did n't get it right," suggested Hopalong.

Tex nodded his head convincingly. "Yes, he did. Told a straight story. Hoppy, Dave knew Schatz was n't comin'. Hoppy, I got —I got a feelin' —Hoppy, what 'll you bet Dave ain't got th' money right now?"

"By G —d!" exclaimed Hopalong, staring at his friend, his mind racing along the scent like a hound to the kill. "By G —d!" he repeated, softly, as he dropped from the saddle and became hidden in the crevice. "No money, Tex; only a few —"

"Where's his horse?" demanded Tex, eagerly.

"*Yo 're* goin' to run for sheriff," came the retort, and Hopalong followed the track of Dave's horse and turned into the ravine, out of sight of Tex, who waited impatiently.

Tex was surprised at the result of the quest when a crazy man came buck-jumping into sight, yelling like an Indian and frantically waving a tightly grasped saddle pad of sacking. He would have come out with more dignity if the money had been his, but belonging as it did to his old foreman, the big-hearted man who had been for so long a time on the verge of despair and defeat, allowed himself the luxury of free expression to the bubbling joy within him.

"Come on, Tex!" he cried. "Th' h —l with goin' back-we 'll take a chance of meetin' th' Dutchman as Dave Owens' personal executors an' ambassadors. If Schatz has got a wad like this, he 's th' man I want to see. Come on! We 'll bust all Montana records for hold-ups —come on, you wise old devil!"

"Now who 's goin' to be sheriff?" grinned Tex, and then allowed himself the relief of working off his joy in a short jig, which informed him that Dave had made a hit; not a bull's eye, but a hit just the same.

"Here, you drunk Apache," Hopalong cried, "let's count up an' see what we got."

Had any one drifted along a minute later he would have been torn between duty and discretion: duty to provide a sane guardian in himself for that part of the Government treasury strayed to the wilds of these western mountains, and discretion in facing the two capable-looking highwaymen who sat crossed-legged on the trail with guns on the ground close to their hands.

"Um-m-m," murmured Tex, who knew of the size of the joint account. "Schatz is lucky if he 's got carfare-th' capital of th' Peters-McAllister-Schatz combine is spread reckless under our gloatin' eyes; all except th' few miserable bills that Dave spent. Come on, you greedy hog-we 'll let Schatz have his two-bits an' be glad to get rid of him. I 'd hate to shoot any man as fat as him-no tellin' what 'd happen. Stick yore roll where it won't jar loose, load that right-hand gun, an' see that nobody holds you up."

"I 've allus been plumb a-scared o' hold-ups," grinned Hopalong, facetiously. "We all was. Lead costs money, an' there ain't no use wastin' it." The grin disappeared and a hard look focussed in his clear eyes as he thought of what a lovely time any hold-up squad would have when Buck's money was at stake.

They mounted and rode away down the pass. As they came to the first bend, Tex glanced back and saw Big Gray peacefully cropping the scanty vegetation along the trail by the ravine. He was without bridle or saddle and Tex glanced covertly at the happy man at his side who could put five bullets in a falling enemy without a pang, and immediately after release a limping horse so that it could live and grow strong, to roam free among the mountains.

Hopalong rolled both guns at once to end the celebration, the bullets striking a rock down the trail as fast as one could count and at intervals as regular as the hammer-stroke of a striking clock. To a man who looked upon a gun only as a weapon to be pointed and discharged at an object, this would have been sufficiently wonderful, but to a real gun-man, one acquainted with the delicacy of manipulation and absolute precision required to effect this result, it was far more wonderful. There are many good gun-men who never have acquired this art, and the danger of practising it is enough to deter most men from attempting it. To hold a six-shooter by a finger slipped through the trigger guard and make it spin around like a pinwheel, firing it every time the muzzle swung out and away from the body, is risky; and when two guns are going at once, it is trebly risky, while accuracy is almost impossible. Hopalong was accurate, so was Johnny, but the latter could work only one gun. Tex, being something of a master of gun-play, was capable of appreciating the feat at its true worth and his eyes glowed at the exhibition. To him came the memory of a day far back in the years when this dexterity had worked to his dishonor, yet it brought with it no malice and it was with the deep affection that a man has for a man friend-and usually for only one-that he playfully advised his companion to "load 'em up again." "Hoppy, there 's only one hand I ever see that I 'm more afraid of than that 'n o' yourn," he remarked.

Hopalong looked at him in mild surprise: "Whose is that?" he asked.

"Yore other one," and Tex grinned at his jest.

Chapter XXVII
Points of the Compass

The long-slanting shadows found Hopalong and Tex far from Lone Tree Pass, riding straight for the Double Y ranch. Their chase after Dave had taken them well to the west of south and they had concluded to keep the horses and equipment and strike for the ranch. As Hopalong sagely remarked: "Eighty dollars is eighty dollars, Tex, but these here two bronchs 'pear to me purty good stock; besides, what's eighty dollars 'longside the money-bag I 'm a-sittin' on?" and he eyed, complacently, the bloated gunny-sack that hid its wealth under so innocent an exterior.

They went ahead with that unerring instinct of the plainsman whose sense of direction seems positively uncanny to a tenderfoot, especially if the tenderfoot has ever been lost. There was no sign of a trail nor did they expect to see one, until they struck the Big Moose, north of the Reservation. This in itself was a source of gratification to them; they were quite content to meet with no one and all they asked was to be let severely alone until such time as the money was turned over to Buck and they should cease to be responsible for it.

The stumbling of the tired horses led them reluctantly to make camp. Hopalong was loath to be away from Mary longer than was necessary; only the grim determination to get Buck's money to him with as little risk as possible had decided him to ride to the ranch instead of taking the train from X ———, which would have been hours quicker. They had discussed this matter, even to the thinking of a possible train hold-up, and Hopalong expressed his very decided preference for the open. "I was in a train hold-up once," he told Tex, "an' seven of th' boys was n't none too many to break it up. Skinny got plugged-not bad-but it might be us this time, an' it might be a whole lot worse."

He entertained Tex with the story while they made their simple preparations for their supper. Tex listened with the ear of a good listener, giving voice to his amusement, or endorsement of an action, or profanely consigning the whole troupe of train robbers to that region where go the "many who are called but not chosen." But all the while, though interested in the tale which concerned so many of his old friends, his analytical mind was pondering over the reason of Dave's action: How had he got the money from Schatz? Why had no one seen Schatz in Wayback? Where had the transfer of the money been made from Schatz to Dave? What had happened to change the plans of the fake hold-up, when Dave was to relieve Schatz of the money? His busy mind approached the riddle from many angles, as in the dark of night, a man with a lantern might cover a big stretch of country, searching everywhere for the track which would lead him to the finding of a hidden treasure. Farther and farther afield went Tex, examining, comparing, and rejecting every possibility that presented itself to his inward vision. Disappointed at the failure of his efforts to discover the solution, he cast from his mind all his useless speculation and adopted the slower but surer method which he should have tried at first: He put himself in the place of Dave-little by little he cast off his own personality and changed to that of the other, picturing to himself the effect upon Dave's cupidity when told of the part he was to play in the stealing of the money. So sensitive was his intelligence, so receptive to the shadowy suggestions that beckoned to him, perhaps from that lonely, unmarked grave beside the upper waters of the Little Jill, that presently his eyes began to gleam, his lips parted, and he stretched out his hand to Hopalong in unconscious emphasis. "Th' gunny sack, Hoppy! Where did he get th' gunny sack?"

The ghost of Schatz smiled. Tex was a man after his own heart.

Tex's abstraction had not escaped Hopalong. The end of his tale reached, he had put away the balance of the food, seen to the secure picketing of the two horses, put out the fire by the simple expedient of kicking over it sufficient sand, and had arranged the saddles in such a way that they completely hid the sack and could not be disturbed without arousing both him and Tex. From time to time he glanced at his silent companion, smiling to himself at the sight of such complete absorption. He could see himself over again in Tex, who was almost as old a man, recalling how he had been wont to ponder on the probable movements of an enemy and the pleasure he took, after a victory, in reviewing what had gone before and checking the mistakes and the successes in his reasoning. He wondered idly why it had lost its attraction for him and he concluded, with a whimsical grin, that marriage gave a man other things to think about.

But however lost Hopalong might be to inward speculation, no outward manifestation of the unusual or unlooked-for failed to appeal to his always active and alert senses. The pipe he had been smoking contentedly was held between his fingers, out and almost cold, his head was bent to one side and he was listening intently. He put his head to the ground and then arose to his feet, his ear turned to the stray breeze that was bringing to him faint and disagreeable sounds. When Tex's hand went out to him and Tex's voice broke in upon those barely audible sounds, he grasped the hand and gripped it hard to enjoin silence. Tex listened with all his ears but the ground noises had ceased and he was not high enough to have the advantage of the wind that was vexing Hopalong's hearing. Hopalong silently dragged him to his feet; they stood thus for a few seconds and then the look they turned upon each other was pregnant with significance.

"Makin' quite a noise," said Hopalong. "An' we ain't near th' trail yet. What do you make of it?"

"Dunno," answered Tex. "Had n't ought to be a man within twenty miles of us, Hoppy, 'less it's a Injun-an' them's no Injuns. Sounds to me like singin'."

"Same here," agreed Hopalong. "Can't be a drive herd, can it?"

"Not as I knows of. No herd ever come this way since th' railroad put through, an' then they stuck to th' trail."

"We got to find out, Tex," declared Hopalong, decisively. "Can't roost with a noisy bunch of coyotes like them runnin' 'round an' howlin' for gore."

"I 'll go, Hoppy," said Tex, "an' if I ain't back in an hour, you take both cayuses an' hike out for th' ranch."

"An' leave you afoot?" asked Hopalong. "Not by a d —n sight."

"You must, Hoppy. I got a reputation that 'll serve me with either honest men or thieves. I can't come to no harm. 'Tother way, you might get hurt. Two of us can't get away on them bronchs, they did too much to-day already. You 'll have to go at a walk, if you do go. 'Course I don't stop with that bunch 'less I has to. It's that bag I 'm thinkin' about, Hoppy. If I has to stop, you want to put as much ground as you can between them an' you. I 'm d —d glad they did n't see our fire."

"All right, Tex. I gives you an hour. 'Tain't more 'n a mile. Get a-goin'."

Tex started away and Hopalong began to get ready for a possible flight. Even if Tex did return they might decide that another location for their camp would be healthier. As he fastened the saddles to the two animals they each turned and looked at him with a disgust as expressive as if spoken.

Tex made for the spot from which the sounds had come, walking easily but silently, his form a mere shadow in the star-lit night and invisible on the lower levels, to which he carefully kept, at a distance of two hundred yards. At the end of ten minutes he was able to distinguish words and knew that Hoppy's and his surmise had been correct: they had heard the singing of night riders around a herd. It was the un-called-for presence of a herd in this vicinity which, more than all else, had led Tex to insist upon the reconnoitre being left to him. "Honest men or thieves," he had said. He was very doubtful of finding honest men. Only the condition of the horses had checked him from advising a departure on suspicion.

He was skulking along now, bent double; in his hand, the blade lying along his arm, was a knife such as few men in the West carried at that day and in the use of which Tex was unusually expert. It was entirely characteristic of him that he should possess such a weapon: silence in action is desired by the worst class of man, and Tex had been of that class before the enforced association of better men and the heroically magnanimous action of an opponent had changed him to the man he was. He slunk forward with the stealthy prowl of a wolf, glancing to right and left as he went, hoping to sight the camp of the cattlemen and get near enough without being seen, to learn what he had come to find out. He dropped flat to earth as a sudden snort startled him: he had come upon the herd without knowing it. A disquieted animal sprang to its feet and did not lie down again until the soothing voice of the herder was raised. The song floated down the wind and Tex listened as well as the cow:

> "'Now then, young men, don't be melancholy;
> Just see, like me, if you can't be jolly;
> If anything goes wrong with me
> I never sulk nor pout;
> In fact I am and always was
> The merriest girl that's out.'"

If the cow were soothed it was quite otherwise with Tex: his hair almost bristled as the rider went past, near enough for the heavy knife to have sped through the air and sunk haft-deep between his shoulders. "Chatter Spence!" sprang to Tex's lips. "Who's he driving for?" a question that he was still asking himself when another herder neared him, whose choice of lullaby was probably influenced by that of his companion, for he was calling out in most lugubrious voice:

'Buffalo gals, are you comin' out to-night,
Comin' out to-night, comin' out to-night?
Buffalo gals, are you comin' out to-night
To dance by th' light of th' moon?'

"It's all wrong," the singer broke off to say in a sing-song voice, that, as far as the cattle were concerned, had all the effect of a melody. "It's all wrong," he repeated. "There ain't no moon. 'To dance by th' light of th' stars,'" he corrected, and then: "Gentlemen, I rises to a question of order. I don't want to dance. I 'm too blasted sore to dance —I 'm too sore to be a-sittin' on this cross-eyed, rat-tailed, flea-bitten son-of-a-dog, too; an' if I ain't relieved pretty soon, Shanghai is a-goin' to hear—" his voice trailed away and the words were no longer distinguishable.

Tex cautiously sat up. "That's Argue Bennett. And Shanghai is with them. Why, d—n it! There must be a whole brood of Ike's chickens roosting around here. I 'm going to find them, even if I miss Hoppy in doing it."

He started to arise and back away before the first singer should approach again, only to drop back into his former prone position at the sound of a third singer, coming from his right. Bennett and Spence heard him too and were more than ready to resign the herd by the time he and his companion arrived. Bennett did not hesitate to announce his bitter condemnation of the way things were being done.

"That you, Ship?" he called.

"That's me," came the answer.

"Shore it's you," agreed Bennett, in sarcastic acknowledgment. "I 'd a' bet every cow I own it's you. An' I goes on record as bettin' every cow *you* own that Cracker is a-ridin' 'longside you. Do I win?"

"You win with yore own stock but I objects to you winnin' with mine. It *might* a' been Shanghai."

"Yes, it *might*; but if it was I 'd a' dropped dead from surprise. What I want to know is: what call has Shanghai got to hold down all th' soft snaps? Is he any better'n we are? Echo answers no-Echo bein' Chatter Spence, who has n't got pride enough to disagree with a hen."

"Aw, what's eatin' you! This ain't no regular drive. An' did you ever know Shanghai to get left on a deal? How'd we ever got through th' Cyclone if it hadn't been for Shanghai? You make me tired. Did you ever know a herd to get over th' ground so fast? Been you, we 'd be some're near Big Moose right now. You leave Shanghai alone an' we 'll have th' herd in our pockets afore Peters knows they 're gone. Nice little bunch, too. Go an' get yore chuck an' you 'll feel better. 'Jennie, my own true loved one, Wait till th' clouds roll by'" —he rode on to circle the herd.

"Did you ever hear such a pill? He thinks nobody knows nothin' but Shanghai. What do you say, Cracker?"

"Well, I kind o' sides with Ship. We ain't done as much as Shanghai, if it comes to that, 'ceptin' night herd."

"H—l! I 'm wastin' my breath talkin' to you. Come on, Chatter, we-why, th' greedy hog 's gone a'ready." Bennett made haste to get back to camp. He knew the supplies to be none too plentiful. So did Chatter Spence.

Tex stole away as silently as he had come, leaving the cattle-thieves happy in their ignorance of his discovery. He pushed himself hard on his return, fearful of having overstayed the time. Hopalong was waiting for him, however, and listened to his news with quiet interest.

"Buck's cows, Hoppy," was Tex's greeting, as he arrived on the run. "We got to get 'em but it's one sweet little job. Old Ship o' State is a holy terror in a row; Chatter Spence ain't bad, an' Argue Bennett an' Cracker impressed me as bein' good men to have around. But th' one we got to watch out for is Shanghai. He never falls down an' it would n't surprise me none to know he was watchin' them four same as I was. There's two of 'em ridin' herd an' three in camp. How do we go at it?"

"Got to get th' two night-ridin'. Tie 'em up an' th' other three is easy. Hol' on a minute till I get th' bank."

Ship o' State was beginning the twenty-seventh stanza in the melodious history of an incorrigible reprobate who deserved death in every one of them, when he was utterly confounded to hear a voice, almost at his ear, command him to "throw up his hands an' climb down of 'n that cayuse, *pronto*." Contrary to what all his friends would have expected him to do, he obeyed the command instantly and to the letter. He was relieved of his gun and was being very effectually secured when the strangely quavering voice of Cracker was heard and came near. Ship eyed his captor in wonder. If Cracker were to be captured in the same manner, then this was the coolest man in the country. Nearer and nearer came the voice until Ship actually found himself worrying over the narrowness of the margin of safety. It was not until Cracker went by that he understood. The grotesque shape could only be accounted for in one way: Cracker's captor was straddling the same pony.

It was just when Ship had reached this conclusion that a very unpleasant bunch of rags was thrust into his mouth and he was lifted and thrown face down across the back of his horse. Hopalong got into the saddle and they rode away from the herd. They had not gone far before another horseman joined them and Ship could hear the singing Cracker as he circled the herd. "There's three of 'em anyway," was his thought, wherein he was wrong. Cracker, with his hands trussed high behind his back and his feet hobbled, was stumbling slowly along with the threat in his memory that if he stopped singing until he was told, his head stood a good chance of being separated from the rest of his carcass, when he would never be able to sing again; and the further information that, if the herd should stampede, he was in a fair way to be crushed to a pulp. The latter he knew to be true and he was equally convinced that the other would be quite likely to take place.

Fifty yards from the herd, Ship was quietly dumped to the ground. Far enough away from him the horses were picketed and two forms crept carefully upon the three men in camp.

Dark as it was, there was no difficulty in finding two of the three. Spence and Bennett, the latter agreeably surprised to find that Shanghai had depleted the general treasury to the extent of one cow, had both eaten a large and satisfying meal; their hunger appeased, weariness had asserted itself in double force and nothing less than a determined kick would have awakened either of them. But Hopalong and Tex prowled around looking for Shanghai without success.

Shanghai was living up to his reputation. Having made his plans and given orders to insure their carrying out, he then stayed around and saw it done. Argue Bennett might grumble to the others but he knew the futility, as also the danger, of grumbling to Shanghai. When his two subordinates had eaten their fill and gone to sleep, Shanghai still sat hunched before the dying embers of the fire, smoking a meditative pipe. When the smoke ceased to float lazily from his nostrils he knocked the warm ashes onto the palm of his hand, got to his feet and slipped quietly away from the camp.

Any one who knew Shanghai well would have reasoned that he was probably going to look over the herd because he started away in the opposite direction. Going straight to his objective point was entirely too elemental for Shanghai. He fetched a wide circle before drawing near the herd, his approach being unheralded and made with the suspicious caution which marked all his movements. He listened inattentively to the husky voice of Cracker who was mourning the demise of somebody named Brown, and moved a little nearer. Presently he became vaguely uneasy at the silence of old Ship-o'-State. It was not the lack of song on Ship's part that troubled Shanghai-the cattle were resting easy enough-but where was he? When Cracker came around again Shanghai was near enough to see him and he craned his neck in wonder at the sight: Cracker on his two feet, staggering along like a man about three whiskeys from oblivion, and Ship off post. Here was something very wrong and Shanghai cursed softly to think how far away his horse was. What in blazes made him come afoot, anyway? He started back to camp to repair the oversight and to have Chatter and Argue behind him before making an investigation of Cracker's astonishing preference for night-herding on foot.

His descent upon the camp would have been creditable to an Apache. First making sure of his horse and leaving him in shape for instant departure, he circled the two sleeping forms, viewing them from all sides. There was something wrong. Shanghai did not know what it was but the figures of his two companions seemed actually to exhale menace and the longer he hesitated the stronger the feeling became. Shanghai stole quietly back to his horse, mounted and rode off with the settled conviction that sun-up was the proper time for investigating these unusual circumstances and that the proper spot was several miles distant from below the sky-line of some convenient knoll.

At the unmistakable sound of retreating hoofbeats the figures in camp came to life. They sat up and listened and then Tex looked at Hoppy with frank disapprobation. "Hoppy, my way was best," he declared. Hopalong nodded, in silent agreement, and Tex continued: "I been a-hearin' considerable talk about this here Shanghai an' I 'm bound to say I believe all I hears. D —n if he ain't got second sight."

Hopalong nodded again. "Let's round up th' rest of th' roosters, anyhow. We got four, an' four's a plenty to take care of."

"Shore is," admitted Tex. "Let's bring 'em in an' hog-tie 'em. Them cows would n't move for anythin' 'less 'n a Norther after th' way they 've come across country."

A half hour later Ike's four pets were lying side by side in camp, trussed to the point of immovability and all apparently, in spite of their discomfort, taking advantage of the opportunity to secure the sleep they so much needed after their unsuccessful exertions.

"Hoppy," said Tex, "I think that with that Shanghai party still runnin' at large, it 'd be some wise to split up that wealth. Better take a chance of losin' half of it than all of it. What you think?"

"Same here," agreed Hopalong. He opened the sack and dumped out the packages, dividing them roughly into two parts with a sweep of his hand, and proceeded to rip up the sack, preparatory to making two parcels of the money.

"'With milk an' honey blest,'" faltered a voice and they turned to find Argue Bennett's eyes almost starting from his head at the sight he beheld.

"Playin' 'possum, eh? It'd do you no harm to stretch hemp right now," and Tex's meditative air was fringed with ferocity.

"No offence, Comin', no offence. You woke me movin'. Is that what Dave got away with?"

"Yes-an' there won't no more Daves get away with it, you can bet all th' cows you own on that."

"An' me a-riskin' my neck rustlin' that bunch when all that beautiful wealth was a-leavin' th' country easy an' graceful an' just a-shoutin' to be brought back. Excuse me, Comin'. I ain't got no call to talk. I reckon I never did talk. Th' best I ever done since I was born is bray."

Thus it came about that Shanghai suffered the acute misery of seeing his four-footed fortune headed back the way it had come. Not that he lost heart all at once. After some hours of following he had decided that a bold stroke might put him again in possession and was perfecting the details of the stratagem his ready mind conceived, when a sudden check was given by a rapidly approaching cloud of dust from the northwest. The check became check-mate when the useful field-glasses disclosed to his pained vision the hilarious meeting that took place. A certain jaunty carriage, a characteristic swagger that did not forsake him even in the saddle, made Shanghai look hard at the leader of the new-comers and suspect Cock Murray. And his suspicion was well founded. Cock Murray had already redeemed his promise to Buck and it may be pardoned him if in the joy of his heart, his swagger became so pronounced as to disclose his personality across some miles of country.

Shanghai closed his glasses and moved slowly to his horse. "Well, it had to be," he conceded, philosophically. "An' I reckon it's about time I pulled my freight."

Chapter XXVIII

The Heart of a Rose

And the evening and the morning were the second day. At a time when, through the diffused and fading light of the sun-vacant sky, the silver-pale stars blinked one by one in their awakening; when the protesting twitter of disturbed birds seeking their rest sounded sweetly clear above the steady rumble of the marshland frogs; when the velvet-footed killers stretched and yawned and gazed with dilated pupils at the near approach of night; when the men who persuaded luck to their advantage, in various ways, began to gather about the tables in cow-town and mining-camp, and there was a lighting of lamps by the foresighted and a trimming of wicks by the procrastinators-the French Rose faced her father, Jean, and did battle for love and happiness, though she knew it not.

The easy-going Jean had known nothing of the manner in which their guest was wounded, nor by whom; and Rose had not thought it wise to tell him, even if it occurred to her in the stress of that first day. But Jean had heard many rumors in Twin River, many disquieting facts and equally disturbing inferences. He had hurried home beset with fears for the outcome, alarmed at the reckless step Rose had taken and vainly asking himself why. Immediately upon his entry he had set Pickles at a task which would occupy him away from the cabin. Standing moodily at the window he watched him go. Then he turned to his daughter for an explanation.

"Is Dave here yesterday?" he asked.

"Yes," replied Rose, non-committally.

Jean turned over in his mind this new fact and fitted it into the pattern. "For why you go so fast to Twin?" he questioned.

"No one is here but me. Fritz, he go to the Two Y's ranch."

"You tell him?"

"No. He hear Dave talk an' go to tell M'sieu Peters Dave have stole all his money."

"*Diable*! Steal?"

"Yes."

Jean knitted his brows in the effort to understand the reason for this; quite naturally he came back in a circle to his first inquiry and repeated it: "For why you go to Twin?"

"I go for men to catch Dave when he steal the money." This, while not strictly true, was the nearest to truth that Jean could understand.

The trend of his thoughts was shown by his next question. "Dave-he know?" he asked, and his anxiety was apparent.

"Yes," was the brief answer.

"*Mon Dieu!*" exclaimed Jean. He turned from her and stared with unseeing eyes over the land he had struggled hard to make his own. And now he must lose it. Rapidly calculating how long his slender resources would support him until Rose could dispose of his stock and follow, despair came upon him as he realized that the vengeance of Dave was not to be escaped. "For why," he asked, hoarsely, "for why you do this?"

"For why?" repeated Rose and the thrill in her voice caused him to turn and look at her in surprise. "Figure to yourself, then: That devil he come here and he sneer at you, and he insult me-yes. Many times he insult me that I have to hold myself, so! that I do not kill him. I endure. He send me ——-*Dieu!* that I should say it-he make dirt of me to walk on, to arrive at a man who is high, good, ah, a man! *mon père*, a man like you, one time when you have no fear. He send me. I say nothing. Many times he try, like a dog, to spring at his throat, but always, it is nothing but snap at his heels. Like a dog which he is. Then he come to me and say he is triumph. He get much money. And he tell me go with him. Me! me! he command like he is master and me slave. He steal money from M'sieu Peters and him and me, we go away together, like that, like man and his squaw. And I say nothing. Ah, *mon père*! it is too much-too much. If it be some other man-not M'sieu Peters-then I go. I save you, *mon père*, though it kill me. But-it is too much."

She bowed her head, filled with self-reproach, with a knowledge that her father could never see this thing as she did. Jean stared at her, motionless; but his dumb amaze slowly lifted. He came to her and rested his hand lightly on her bowed head. *"Ma Rose-ma belle Rose* —when you have for a good man so big love as that, I would die, with gladness, to know so big happiness is come to you." And he went swiftly from the cabin.

At the closing of the door she sprang to it and threw it wide again. "You will not go-now-to-night?" she called.

The answer, low, determined, in the tones of the father of that other time, reassured her: "No. We stay. Maybe-who knows? —God is good."

She went back and with steady hand lit the lamp and placed it on the table. The noble face was aglow with hopeful pride: he would face it at last, this thing that had embittered both their lives.

"Rose!"

She started and turned in dismay toward the inner room. He was awake-how long? —and calling her.

"Rose!" the call came again, gentle but insistent. "Rose, I —I want you."

She stood a moment longer, both hands pressed against her heart, her breath coming in great gasps and in her eyes the frightened look of a child. Then she caught up the lamp and with swift step went in and stood beside the bunk. "Is it then you rest ill, my friend?" she asked softly, and then bent to re-arrange the pillow. Buck's hand closed over hers.

"Rose," he whispered, "Rose —I heard."

She slipped to her knees, hiding her face in the pillow, her figure shaking with great tremors and sobs breaking from her so that she could scarcely speak. "Oh, I am ashamed," she said brokenly, "I am ashamed."

"Ashamed! And I— —" he stopped, drawing in a deep breath at the wonder of it; then raising himself to rest on bent arm, he laid his cheek against her hair. "I 'm th' one as ought to be ashamed, Rose: a man o' my age, an' feelin' th' way I do-an' you a girl. But I 've got to have you, Rose. I just got to have you. An' if you don't say 'yes' I swear to God I 'll give up an' pull out o' this country. I don't want to stop another day if you say 'no.'"

She drew away from him and raised her head to look at him doubtfully, appealingly, believingly. A wonderful smile broke through her tears and stilled the trembling of her lips. "You mean it, Buck. Oh! You do! You do!" Her arms were about him and she lowered him gently back again. "Rest you, and get well quickly, wounded man," she murmured. "My man-my man until I die-and after."

The Bar-20 Three

Chapter I
"Put a 'T' in it"

Idaho Norton, laughing heartily, backed out of the barroom of Quayle's hotel and trod firmly on the foot of Ward Corwin, sheriff of the county, who was about to pass the door. Idaho wheeled, a casual apology trembling on his lips, to hear a biting, sarcastic flow of words, full of profanity, and out of all proportion to the careless injury. The sheriff's coppery face was a deeper color than usual and bore an expression not pleasant to see. The puncher stepped back a pace, alert, lithe, balanced, the apology forgotten, and gazed insolently into the peace officer's wrathful eyes.

"–an' why don't you look where yo're steppin'? Don't you know how to act when you come to town?" snarled the sheriff, finishing his remarks.

Idaho looked him over coolly. "I know how to act in any company, even yourn. Just now I ain't actin' I'm waitin'."

The sheriff's eyes glinted. "I got a good mind--"

"You ain't got nothin' of th' sort," cut in the puncher, contemptuously. "You ain't got nothin' good, except, mebby, yore reg'lar plea of self-defense. I'm sayin' out loud that that ain't no good, here an' now; an' I'm waitin' to take it away from you an' use it myself. You been trustin' too cussed much to that nickel badge."

Bill Trask, deputy, who had a reputation not to be over looked, now took a hand from the rear, eager to add to his list of victims from any of that outfit. The puncher was between him and the sheriff, and hardly could watch them both. Trask gently shook his belt and said three unprintable words which usually started a fight, and then glared over his shoulder at a sudden interruption, tense and angry.

"Shut up, you!" said the voice, and he saw a two-gun stranger slouching away from the hotel wall. The deputy took him in with one quick glance and then his eyes re turned to those of the stranger and rested there while a slight prickling sensation ran up his spine. He had looked into many angry eyes, and in many kinds of circumstances, but never before had his back given him a warning quite so plainly. He grew restless and wanted to look away, but dared not; and while he hung in the balance of hesitation the stranger spoke again. "Two to one ain't fair, 'specially with the lone man in th' middle; but I'll make th' odds even, for I'm honin' to claim self-defense, myself. It's right popular. I saw it all an' I'm sayin' you are three chumps to get all het up over a little thing like that. Mebby his toes are tender but what of it? He ain't no baby, leastawise he don't look like one. An' I'm tellin' you, an' yore badge-totin' friend, that I know how to act, too." A twinkle came into the hard, blue eyes. "But what's th' use of actin' like four strange dogs?"

Somewhere in the little crowd a man laughed, others joined in and pushed between the belligerents; and in a minute the peace officers had turned the corner, Idaho was slowly walking toward the two-gun stranger and the crowd was going about its business.

"Have a drink?" asked the puncher, grinning as he pushed back his hat.

"Didn't I just say that I knowed how to act?" chuckled the stranger, turning on his heel and following his companion through the door. "You must 'a' met them two before."

"Too cussed often. What'll you have? Make mine a cigar, too, Ed. No more liquor for me today Corwin –don't forget."

The bartender closed the box and slid it onto the back-bar again. "No, he don't," he said. "An' Trask is worse," he added, looking significantly at the stranger, whose cigar was now going to his satisfaction and who was smilingly regarding Idaho, and who seemed to be pleased by the frank return scrutiny.

"You ain't a stranger here no longer," said Idaho, blowing out a cloud of smoke. "You got two good enemies, an' a one-hoss friend. Stayin' long?"

"About half an hour. I got a little bunch of cows on th' drive west of here, an' they ought to be at Twitchell an' Carpenter's corrals about now. Havin' rid in to fix up bed an' board for my little outfit, I'm now on my way to finish deliverin' th' herd. See you later if yo're in town tonight."

"I don't aim to go back to th' ranch till tomorrow," replied Idaho, and he hesitated. "I'm sorry you horned in on that ruckus--there's mebby trouble bloomin' out of that for you. Don't you get careless till yo're a day's ride away from this town. Here, before you go, meet Ed Doane. He's one of th' few white men in this runt of a town."

The bartender shook hands across the bar. "Pleased to meet up with you, Mr.–Mr.?"

"Nelson," prompted the stranger. "How do you do, Mr. Doane?"

"Half an' half," answered the dispenser of liquids, and then waved a large hand at the smiling youth. "Shake han's with Idaho Norton, who was never closer to Idaho than Parsons Corners, thirty miles northwest of here. Idaho's a good boy, but shore impulsive. He's spent most of his life practicin' th' draw, et cetery; an' most of his money has went for ca'tridges. Some folks say it ain't been wasted. Will you gents smoke a cigar with me?"

After a little more careless conversation Johnny nodded his adieus, mounted and rode south. Not long thereafter he came within sight of the Question-Mark, Twitchell and Carpenter's local ranch.

Its valley sloped eastward, following the stream winding down its middle between tall cottonwoods, and the horizon was limited by the tops of the flanking hills, which dipped and climbed and zigzagged into the gray of the east, where great sand hills reared their glistening tops and the hopeful little creek sank out of sight into the dried, salty bed of a one-time lake. Near the trail were two buildings, a small stockaded corral and a wire-fenced pasture of twenty acres; and the Question-Mark brand, known wherever cattlemen congregated, even beyond the Canadian line, had been splashed with red paint on the wall of the larger building. The glaring, silent interrogation-mark challenged every passing eye and had started many curious, grim, and cynical trains of thought in the minds of tired and thirsty wayfarers along the trail. To the north of the twenty-acre pasture a herd of SV cattle grazed, spread out widely, too tired, too content with their feeding to need much attention.

Johnny saw the great, red question-mark and instantly drew rein, staring at it. "Why?" he muttered, and then grew silent for a moment. Shaking his head savagely he urged the horse on again, and again glanced at the crimson interrogation. "Damn you!" he growled. "There ain't no man livin' can answer."

He passed the herd at a distance and rode up to the larger building, where a figure suddenly appeared in the doorway, looked out from under a shielding hand and quickly stepped forward to meet him.

"Hello, Nelson!" came the cheery greeting.

"Hello, Ridley!" replied Johnny. "Glad to see you again. Thought I'd bring 'em down to you, an' save you goin' up th' trail after 'em. Why don't you paint out that glarin' question-mark on th' side of th' house?"

Ridley slapped his hands together and let out a roar of laughter. "Has it got you, too?" he demanded in unfeigned delight.

"Not as much as it would before I got married," replied Johnny. "I'm beginnin' to see a reason for livin'."

"Good!" exclaimed Ridley. "If I ever meet yore wife I'll tell her somethin' that'll make her dreams sweet." The expression of his face changed swiftly. "Do you know "he considered, and changed the form of his words. "You'd be surprised if you knew th' number of people hit by that painted question-mark. I've had 'em ride in here an' start all kinds of conservations with me; th' gospel sharps are th' worst. One man blew his brains out in Quayle's hotel because of what that sign started workin' in his mind. Go look at it: it's full of bullet holes!"

"I don't have to," replied Johnny, and quickly answered his companion's unspoken challenge. "An 1 I can sleep under it, an' smile, cuss you!" He glanced at the distant cattle. "Have you looked 'em over?"

Ridley nodded. "They're in good shape. Ready to count 'em now?"

"Be glad to, an' get 'em off my han's."

"Bring 'em up in front of th' pasture, an' I'll wait for you there," said Ridley.

Johnny wheeled and then checked his horse. "What kind of fellers are Corwin an' Trask?" he asked.

Ridley looked up at him, a curious expression on his face. "Why?"

"Oh, nothin'; I was just wonderin'."

"As long as you ain't aimin' to stop around these parts for long, th' less you know about 'em th' better. I'll be waitin' at th' pasture."

Johnny rode off and started the herd again, and when it stopped it was compacted into a long V, with the point facing the pasture gate, and it poured its units from this point in a steady stream between the two horsemen at the open gate, who faced each other across the hurrying pro cession and built up another herd on the other side, one which spread out and grazed without restraint, unless it be that of a wire fence. And with the shrinking of the first and the expanding of the second the SV ownership changed into that of the Question-Mark.

The shrewd, keen-eyed buyer for Twitchell and Carpenter looked up as the gate closed after the last steer and smiled across the gap at the SV foreman as he announced his count.

Johnny nodded. "My figgers, to a T," he said. "That 2-Star steer don't belong to us. Joined up with us some where along th' trail. You know 'em?"

"Belongs to Dawson, up on th' north fork of th' Bear. I'll drop him a check in a couple of days. This feller must 'a' wandered some to get in with yourn. Well, yourn is a good bunch of four-year-olds. You'll have to wait till I get to town, for I ain't got a blank check left, an' I shore ain't got no one thousand one hundred and forty-three dollars layin' around down here. Want cash or a check?"

"If I took a check I'd have to send somebody up to Sherman with it," replied Johnny. "I might take it at that, if I was goin' right back. Better make it cash, Ridley."

Ridley grinned. "I've swept up this part of th' country purty good."

Johnny shook his head. "I'm lookin' for weaners an' not in this part of th' country. I'll see you in town,"

"Before supper," said Ridley. "You puttin' up at Quayle's?"

"You called it," answered Johnny, wheeling. He rode off, picked up his small outfit and led the way to Mesquite, where he hoped to spend but one night. The little SV group cantered over the thin trail in the wake of their bobbing chuck wagon, several miles ahead of them, and reached the town well ahead of it, much to the cook's vexation. As they neared Quayle's hotel Johnny pulled up.

"This is our stable," he said. "Go easy, boys. We leave at daylight. See you at supper."

They answered him laughingly and swept on to Kane's place, which they seemed to sense, each for his favorite, drink and game.

The afternoon shadows were long when Ridley, just from the bank, left his rangy bay in front of the hotel and entered the office, nodding to several men he knew. He went on through and stopped at the bar.

"Howd'y, Ed," he grunted. "That SV foreman around? Nelson's his name."

Ed Doane mopped up the bar mechanically and bobbed his head toward the door. "Here he comes now. Make a deal?"

Ridley nodded as he turned. "Hello, Nelson! Read this over. If it's all right, sign it, an' we'll let Ed disfigure it as a witness. I allus like a witness."

Johnny signed it with the pen the bartender provided and then the bartender labored with it and blew on it to dry the ink.

"Disfigure it, hey?" chuckled Ed, pointing to his signature, which was beautifully written but very much over done. "That bill of sale's worth somethin' now."

Johnny admired it frankly and openly. "I allus did like shadin', an' them flourishes are plumb fetchin'. Me, now; I write like a cow."

"I'm worse," admitted Ridley, chuckling and giving Johnny a roll of bills. "Count 'em, Nelson. Folks usually turn my writin' upside down for th' first try. Speakin' of witnesses, there's another little thing I like. I allus seal documents, Ed. Take 'em out of that bottle you hide under th' bar. Three of 'em. Somehow, Ed, I allus like to see you stoop like that. Well, Nelson; does it count up right? Then, business bein' over, here's to th' end of th' drought."

It went the rounds, Ed accumulating three cigars as his favorite beverage, and as the glasses clicked down on the bar Ridley felt for the makings. "Sorry th' bank's closed, Nelson. It might be safer there over night."

"Mebby but it's safe enough, anyhow," smiled Johnny, shrugging his shoulders. "Anyhow th' bank wouldn't be open early enough in th' mornin' for us. Which reminds me that I better go out an' look around. My four-man outfit's got to leave at daylight."

"I'll go with you as far as th' street," said Ridley. As they neared the door Johnny hung back to let his companion pass through first and as he did so he heard a soft call from the bartender, and half turned.

"Come here a minute," said Doane, leaning over the bar. "It ain't none of my business, Nelson, but I'm sayin' *I* wouldn't go into Kane's with th' wad of money you got on you; an' if I did I shore wouldn't show it nor get in no game. You don't have to remember that I said anythin' about this."

"I never gamble with money that don't belong to me," replied Johnny, "nor not even while I've got it on me; an' already I've forgot you said anythin'. That place must be a sort of 'sink of iniquity,' as that sanctified parson called Abilene."

"Huh!" grunted Doane. "You can put a 'T' in that 'sink' an' there's only one place where a 'T' will fit. Th' money would be enough, but in yore case there's more. Idaho said it."

"He's only a kid," deprecated Johnny.

"'Out of th' mouths of babes'" replied Doane. "I'm tellin' you that's all."

Ridley stuck his head in at the door. "So-long, fellers," he said.

"Hey, Ridley!" called the bartender hurriedly. "Would you go into Kane's if you had Nelson's roll on you?"

"Not knowin' what I might do under th' infloonce of likker, I can't say," answered Ridley; "but if I did I wouldn't drink in there. So-long, an' I mean it, this time," and he did.

Johnny left soon afterward and wandered along the street toward the building on the northern outskirts of the town where Pecos Kane ran a gambling-house and hotel. Johnny ignored the hotel half and lolled against the door as he sized up the interior of the gambling-hall, and instantly became the center of well-disguised interest. While he paused inside the threshold a lean, tall man arose from a chair against the wall and sauntered carelessly out of sight through a narrow doorway leading to a passage in the rear. Kit Thorpe was not a man to loaf on his job when a two-gun stranger entered the place, especially when the stranger appeared to be looking for someone. Otherwise there was no change in the room, the bartender polishing his glasses without pause, the card players silently intent on their games and the man at the deserted roulette table who held a cloth against the ornate spinning wheel kept on polishing it. They seemed to draw reassurance from Thorpe's disappearance.

One slow look was enough to satisfy Johnny's curiosity. The room was about sixty feet long by half as wide and on his left-hand side lay the bar, built solidly from the floor by close-fitting planks running vertically, which appeared to be of hardwood and quite thick, and the top was of the same material. Several sand-box cuspidors lay before it. The backbar was a shelf backed by a narrow mirror running well past the middle half, and no higher than necessary to give the bartender a view of the room when he turned around, which he did but seldom. Round card-tables, heavy and crude, were scattered about the room and a row of chairs ran the full length along the other side wall. Several loungers sat at the tables, one of them an eastern tough, judging from his clothes, his peaked cap pulled well down over his eyes. At the farther end was a solid partition painted like a checkerboard and the few black squares which cunningly hid several peep holes were not to be singled out by casual observation. Those who knew said that they were closed on their inner side by black steel plates which hung on oiled pivots and were locked shut by a pin. At a table in front of the checkerboard were four men, one flung forward on it, his head resting on his crossed arms; another had slumped down on the edge of his chair, his chin on his chest, while the other two carried on a grunted, pessimistic conversation across their empty glasses.

Johnny's face flickered with a faint smile and he walked toward them, nodding carelessly at the man behind the bar.

Arch Wiggins looked up, a sickly grin on his flushed face. "Hullo," he grunted, foolishly.

"Not havin' nothin' else to do I reckoned I'd look you up," said Johnny. "Fed yet?"

Arch shrugged his shoulders and Sam Gardner sighed expressively, and then prodded the slumped individual into semblance of intelligence and erectness. This done he kicked the shins of the prostrate cook until that unfortunate raised an owlish, agonized, and protesting countenance to stare at his foreman.

"Nelson wants to know if yo're hungry," prompted Sam, grinning.

"Take it away!" mumbled the indignant cook. "I won't eat! Who's goin' to make me?" he demanded with a show of pugnacity. "I won't!"

Joe Reilly, painfully erect in his chair, blinked and focussed his eyes on the speaker. "Then don't!" he said. "Shut yore face others kin eat!" He turned his whole body, stiff as a ramrod, and looked at each of the others in turn. "Don't pay no 'tendon to him. I kin eat th' damned harness," he asserted, thereby proving that his stomach preserved family traditions.

Johnny laughed at them. "Yo're ah I of an outfit," he said without conviction. "What do you say about goin' up to th' hotel an' gettin' somethin' to eat? It's past grubtime, but let's see if they'll have th' nerve to try to tell us to get out. Broke?" he inquired, and as they silently arose to their feet, which seemed to take a great deal of concentration, he chuckled. Then his face hardened. "Where's yore guns?" he demanded.

Arch waved elaborately at the disinterested bartender. "That gent loaned us ten apiece on 'em," he said. "'Bligin' feller. Thank you, friend."

"Yo're a'right," said the cook, nodding at the dispenser of fluids.

"An' yo're a fine, locoed bunch, partin' with yore guns in a strange town," snapped Johnny. "You head for th' hotel, pronto! G'wan!"

The cook turned and waved a hand at the solemn bartender. "Goo'-bye!" he called. "I won't eat! Goo'bye."

Seeing them started in the right direction, Johnny went in and up to the bar. "Them infants don't need guns," he asserted, digging into a pocket, "but as long as they ain't shot themselves, yet, I'm takin' a chance. How much?"

The bartender, typical of his kind, looked wise when it was not necessary, finished polishing the glass in his hand and then slowly faced his inquisitor, bored and aloof. He had the condescending air of one who held himself to be mentally and physically superior to any man in town, and his air of preoccupation was so heavy that it was ludicrous. "Ten apiece," he answered nonchalantly, as behove the referee of drunken disputes, the adviser of sodden men, the student of humanity's dregs, whose philosophy of life was rotten to the core because it was based purely on the vicious and the weak, and whose knowledge, adjudged abysmal and cyclopedic by an admiring riffraff of stupefied mentality, was as shallow, warped, and perverted as the human derelicts upon which his observations were based. As Johnny's hand came up with the roll of bills the man of liquor kept his face passive by an act of will, but there crept into the ratlike eyes a strange gleam, which swiftly faded. "Put it way," he said heartily, a jovial, free-handed good fellow on the instant. "We got it back, an' more. It was worth th' money to have these where they wouldn't be too handy. We allus stake a good loser it's th' policy of th' house. Take these instead of th' stake." He slid the heavy weapons across the bar. "What'll you have?"

"Same as you," replied Johnny, and he slowly put the cigar into a pocket. "Purty quiet in here," he observed, laying two twenty-dollar bills on the bar.

"Yeah," said the bartender, pushing the money back again; "but it's a cheerful ol' beehive at night. Better put that in yore pocket an' drop in after dark, when things are movin'. I know a blonde that'll tickle you 'most to death. Come in an' meet her."

"Tell you what," said Johnny, grinning to conceal his feelings. "You keep them bills. If I keep 'em I'll have to let them fools have their guns back for nothin'. I'm aimin' to take ten apiece out of their pay. If you don't want it, give it to th' blonde, with Mr. Nelson's compliments. It won't be so hard for me to get acquainted with her, then."

The bartender chuckled and put the bills in the drawer. "Yo're no child, I'm admittin'. Reckon you been usin' yore head quite some since you was weaned."

One of the card players at the nearest table said some' thing to his two companions and one of them leaned back stretched and arose. "I'm tired. Get somebody to take my place."

The sagacious observer of the roll of bills started to object to the game being broken up, glanced at Johnny and smiled. "All right; mebby this gent will sit in an' kill a little time. How 'bout it, stranger?"

Johnny smiled at him. "My four-man outfit ain't leavin' me no time to kill," he answered. "I got to trail along behind 'em an' pick up th' strays."

The gambler grinned sympathetically. "Turn 'em loose tonight. What's th' use of herdin' with yearlin's, any how? If you get tired of their company an' feel like tryin' yore luck, come in an' join us."

"If I find that I got any heavy time on my han's I'll spend a couple of hours with you," replied Johnny. As he turned toward the door he glanced at the bartender. "Don't forget th' name when you give her th' forty," he laughed.

The bartender chuckled. "I got th' best mem'ry of any man in this section. See you later, mebby."

Johnny nodded and departed, his hands full of guns, and as he vanished through the front door Kit Thorpe reappeared from behind the partition, grinned cynically at the bartender and received a wise, very wise look in return.

Reaching the hotel Johnny entered it by the nearest door, that of the barroom, walked swiftly through with the redeemed guns dangling from his swinging hands and without pausing in his stride, flung a brief remark over his shoulder to the man behind the bar, who was the only person, besides himself, in the room: "You was shore right. It should ought to have a 'T' in it," and passed through the other door, across the office and into the dining-room, where his four men were having an argument with a sullen waiter and a wrathy cook.

Ed Doane straightened up, his ears preserving the words, his eyes retaining the picture of an angry, hurrying two-gun man from whose hands swung four more guns. He cogitated, and then the possible significance of the numerous weapons sprang into his mind. Ed did not go around the bar. He vaulted it and leaped to the door, out of which he hopefully gazed at the tranquil place of business of Pecos Kane. Slowly the look of hope faded and he returned to his place behind the bar, scratching his frowsy head in frank energy, his imagination busy with many things.

Chapter II
Well-known Strangers

The desert and a paling eastern sky. The penetrating cold of the dark hours was soon to die and give place to a punishing heat well above the hundred mark. Spectral agaves, flinging their tent-shaped crowns heavenward, seemed to spring bodily from the radiating circlet of spiny swords at their bases, their slender stems still lost in the weakening darkness. Pale spots near the ground showed where flower-massed yuccas thrust up, lancelike, from their slender, prickly leaves. Giant cacti, ghostly, bulky, indistinct, grotesque in their erect, parallel columns reached upward to a height seven times that of a tall man. They are the only growing things unmoved by winds. The sage, lost in the ground-hugging darkness, formed a dark carpet, mottled by lighter patches of sand. There were quick rustlings over the earth as swift lizards scurried hither and yon and a faint whirring told of some "side-winder" vibrating its rattles in emphatic warning against some encroachment. Tragedies were occurring in the sage, and the sudden squeak of a desert rat was its swan song.

In the east a silvery glow trembled above the horizon and to the magic of its touch silhouettes sprang suddenly from vague, blurred masses. The agave, known to most as the century plant, showed the delicate slenderness of its arrowy stem and marked its conical head with feathery detail. The flower-covered spikes of the Spanish bayonets became studies in ivory, with the black shadows on their thorny spikes deep as charcoal. The giant cacti, boldly thrown against the silver curtain, sprang from their joining bases like huge, thick telegraph poles of ebony, their thorns not yet clearly revealed. The squat sage, now resolved into tufted masses, might have been the purplish leaden hollows of a great sea. The swift rustlings became swift movements and the "side-winder" uncoiled his graceful length to round a nearby sage bush. The quaking of a small lump of sand grew violent and a long, round snoot pushed up inquiringly, the cold, beady eyes peering forth as the veined lids parted, and a Gila monster sluggishly emerged, eager for the promised warmth. To the northeast a rugged spur of mountains flashed suddenly white along its saw-toothed edge, where persistent snows crowned each thrusting peak. A moment more, and dazzling heliographic signals flashed from the snowy caps, the first of all earthly things to catch the rays of the rising sun, as yet below the far horizon. On all sides as far as eye could pierce through the morning twilight not a leaf stirred, not a stem moved, but everywhere was rigidity, unreal, uncanny, even terrifying to an imaginative mind. But wait! Was there movement in the fogging dark of the north? Rhythmic, swaying movement, rising and falling, vague and mystical? And the ghostly silence of this griddle-void was broken by strange, alien sounds, magnified by contrast with the terror-inspiring silence. A soft creaking, as of gently protesting saddle leather, interspersed with the frequent and not unmusical tinkle of metal, sounded timidly, almost hesitatingly out of the dark along the ground.

Silver turned into pink, pink into gold, and gold into crimson in almost a breath, and long crimson ribbons be came lavender high in the upper air, surely too beautiful to be a portent of evil and death. Yet the desert hush tightened, constricted, tensed as if waiting in rigid suspense for a lethal stroke. Almost without further warning a flaming, molten arc pushed up over the far horizon and grew with amazing bulk and swiftness, dispelling the chill of the night, destroying the beauty of the silhouettes, revealing the purple sage as a mangy, leaden coverlet, riddled and thin, squatting tightly against the tawny sand, across which had sprung with instant speed long, vague shadows from the base of every object which raised above the plain. The still air shuddered into a slow dance, waving and quivering, faster and faster like some mad dance of death, the rising heat waves distorting with their evil magic giant cacti until their fluted, thorny columns weaved like strange, slowly undulating snakes standing erect on curving tails. And in the distance but a few leagues off blazed the white mockery of the crystal snow, serene and secure on its lofty heights, a taunt far-flung to madden the heat-crazed brain of some swollen, clawing thing in distorted human form slowly dying on the baking sands.

The movement was there, for the sudden flare of light magically whisked it out of the void like a rabbit out of a conjurer's hat. Two men, browned, leather-skinned, erect, silent, and every line of them bespeaking reliance with a certainty not to be denied, were slowly riding south ward. Their horses, typical of their cow-herding type, were loaded down with large canteens, and suggested itinerant water peddlers. Two gallons each they held, and there were four to the horse. One could imagine these men counted on taking daily baths but they were only double-riveting a security against the hell-fires of thirst, which each of them had known intimately and too well. The first rider, as erect in his saddle as if he had just swung into it, had a face scored with a sorrow which only an iron will held back; his squinting eyes were cold and hard, and his hair, where it showed beneath the soiled, gray sombrero, was a sandy color, all of what was left of the flaming crimson of its youth. He rode doggedly with out a glance to right or left, silent, sullen, inscrutable. When the glorious happiness of a man's life has gone out there is but little left, often even to a man of strength. Behind him rode his companion, five paces to the rear and exactly in his trail, but his wandering glances flashed far afield, searching, appraising, never still. Younger in years than his friend, and so very much younger in spirit, there was an air of nonchalant recklessness about him, occasionally swiftly mellowed by pity as his eyes rested on the man ahead. Now, glancing at the sun-cowed east, his desert cunning prompted him and he pushed forward, silently took the lead and rode to a thicket of mesquite, whose sensitive leaves, hung on delicate stems, gave the most cooling shade of any desert plant. Dismounting, he picketed his horse and then added a side-line hobble as double security against being left on foot on the scorching sands. Not satisfied with that, he unfastened the three full canteens, swiftly examined them for leaks and placed them under the bush. Six gallons of water, but if need should arise he would fight to the death for it. Out of the corner of his eye he watched his companion, who mechanically was doing the same thing. Red Connors yawned, drank sparingly and then, hesitating, grinned foolishly and fastened one end of his lariat to his wrist.

"That dessicated hunk of meanness don't leave this hombre afoot, not nohow," said Red, looking at his friend; but Hopalong only stared into the bush and made no reply.

Nothing abashed at his companion's silence, Red stretched out at full length under the scant shade, his Colt at his hand in case some Gila monster should be curious as to what flavor these men would reveal to an inquisitive bite. Red's ideas of Gilas were romantic and had no scientific warrant whatever. And it was possible that a "side-winder" might blunder his way.

"It's better than a lava desert, anyhow," he remarked as he settled down, having in mind the softness of the loose sand. "One whole day of hell-to-leather fryin', an' one more shiverin' night, an' this stretch of misery will be behind, but it shore saves a lot of ridin', it does. I'll bet I'm honin' for a swim in th' Rio Placer an' I ain't carin' how much mud there is, neither. Ah, th' devil!" he growled in great disgust, slowly arising. "I done forgot to sprinkle them cayuses' insides. One apiece, they get, which is only insultin' 'em."

Hopalong tried to smile, arose and filled his hat, which his thirsty horse frantically emptied. When the canteen was also empty he went back to the sandy couch, to lay awake in the scorching heat, fighting back memories which tortured him near to madness, his mental torments making him apathetic to physical ones. And so dragged the weary, trying day until the cooling night let them go on again.

Three days later they rode into Gunsight, made care less inquiries and soon thereafter drew rein before the open door of the SV, unconscious of the excited conjectures rioting in the curious town.

Margaret Nelson went to the door, her brother trying to push past her, and looked wonderingly up at the two smiling strangers.

Red bowed and removed his hat with a flourish. "Mrs. Johnny?" he asked, and at the nodded assent smiled broadly. "My name's Red Connors, an' my friend is Hopalong Cassidy. He is th' very best friend yore fool husband ever had. We came down to make Johnny's life miserable for a little while, an' to give you a hand with his trainin', if you need it."

Margaret's breath came with a rush and she held out both hands with impulsive friendliness. "Oh!" she cried. "Come in. You must be tired and hungry let Charley turn your horses into the corral."

Charley wriggled past the barrier and jumped for Hopalong, his shrill whoop of delighted welcome bringing a smile to the stern face of the mounted man. A swoop of the rider's arm, a writhing twist of the boy's body, coming a little too late to avoid the grip of that iron hand, and Charley shot up and landed in front of the pommel, where he exchanged grins at close range with his captor.

"I knowed you first look," asserted the boy as the grip was released. "My, but I've heard a lot about you! Yo're goin' to stay here, ain't you? I know where there's some black bear, up on th' hills want to go huntin' with me?"

Hopalong's tense, wistful look broke into a smile, the first sincere, honest smile his face had known for a month. Gulping, he nodded, and turned to face his friend's wife. "Looks like I'm adopted," he said. "If you don't mind, Mrs. Johnny, Charley an' me will take care of th' cayuses while Red helps you fix up th' table." He reached out, grasped the bridle of Red's horse as its rider dismounted, and rode to the corral, Charley's excited chatter bringing an anxious smile to his sister, but a heartfelt, prayerful smile to Red Connors. He had great hopes.

Red paused just inside the door. "Mrs. Johnny," he said quietly, quickly, "I got to talk fast before Hoppy comes back. He lost his wife an' boy a month ago fever in four days. He's all broke up. Went loco a little, an' even came near shootin' me because I wouldn't let him go off by hisself. I've had one gosh-awful time with him, but finally managed to get him headed this way by talkin' about Johnny a-plenty. That got him, for th' kid allus was a sort of son to him. I'm figgerin' he'll be a lot better off down here on this south range for awhile. Even crossin' that blasted desert seemed to help he loosened up his talk considerable since then. An' from th' way he grabbed that kid, I'm say in' I'm right. Where is Johnny?"

"Oh!" Margaret's breathed exclamation did not need the sudden moisture in her eyes to interpret it, and in that instant Red Connors became her firm, unswerving friend. "We'll do our best and I think he should stay here, always. And Johnny will be delighted to have him with us, and you, too Red."

"Here he comes," warned her companion. "Where is Johnny? When will he get here?"

"Why, he took a herd down to Mesquite," she replied, smiling at Hopalong, who limped slowly into the room with Charley slung under his arm like a sack of flour. "He should be back any day now. And won't he be wild with delight when he finds you two boys here! You have no idea how he talks about you, even in his sleep--oh, if I were inclined to jealousy you might not be so welcome!"

"Ma'am," grinned Red, tickled as a boy with a new gun, "you don't never want to go an' get jealous of a couple of old horned toads like us--well, like Hoppy, anyhow. We'll sort of ride herd on him, too, every time he goes to town. Talk about revenge! Oh, you wait! So he went off an' left you all alone? Didn't he write about some trouble that was loose down here?"

"It was but it's cleaned up. He didn't leave me in any danger--every man down here is our friend," Margaret replied, quick to sense the carefully hidden thought which had prompted his words, and to defend her husband.

"Well, two more won't hurt, nohow," grunted Red. "You say he ought to get here any day?"

"I'm spending more time at the south windows every day," she smiled. "I don't know what will happen to the housework if it lasts much longer!"

"South windows?" queried Hopalong, standing Charley on his head before letting loose of him. "Th' trail is west, ain't it?" he demanded, which caused Red to chuckle inwardly at how his friend was becoming observant again.

"The idea!" retorted Margaret. "Do you think my boy will care anything about any trail that leads round about? He'll leave the trail at the Triangle and come straight for this house! What are hills and brush and a miserable little creek to him, when he's coming home? I thought you knew my boy."

"We did, an' we do," laughed Red. "I'm bettin' yore way--I hope he's got a good horse--it'll be a dead one if it ain't."

"He's saving Pepper for the homestretch if you know what that means!"

"Hey, Red," said Charley, slyly. "Yore gun works, don't it?"

"Shore thing. Why?"

"Well, mine don't," sighed the boy. "Wonder if yourn is too heavy, an' strong, for a boy like me to shoot? Bet it ain't."

Margaret's low reproof was lost in Red's burst of laughter, and again a smile crept to Hopalong's face, a smile full of heartache. This eager boy made his memories painfully alive.

"You an' me an' Hoppy will shore go out an' see," promised Red. "Mrs. Johnny will trust you with us, I bet. Hello! Here's somebody comin'," he announced, looking out of the door.

"That's my dad!" cried Charley, bolting from the house so as to be the first one to give his father the good news.

Arnold rode up laughing, dismounted and entered the house with an agility rare to him. And he was vastly relieved. "Well! Well! Well!" he shouted, shaking hands like a pump handle. "I saw you ride over the hill an' got here as fast as Lazy would bring me. Red an' Hopalong! Our household gods with us in the flesh! And that scalawag off seeing the sights of strange towns when his old friends come to visit him. I'm glad to see you boys! The place is yours. Red and Hopalong! I'm not a drinkin' man, but there are times when follow me while Peggy gets supper!"

"Can I go with you, Dad?" demanded Charley.

"You help Peggy set the table."

"Huh! *I* don't care! Me an' Hoppy an' Red are goin' after bear, an' I'm goin' to use Red's gun."

"Seems to me, Charley," reproved Arnold, "that you are pretty familiar, for a boy; and especially on such short acquaintance. You might begin practicing the use of the word 'Mister.'"

"Or say 'Uncle Red' and 'Uncle Hopalong,'" suggested Margaret.

"'Red' is my name, an' I'm shore 'Red' to him," defended that person.

"Which goes for me," spoke up his companion. "I'm Hopalong, or Hoppy to anybody in this family though 'Uncle' suits me fine."

"Then we'll have a fair exchange," retorted Margaret, smiling. "The family circle calls me 'Margaret' or 'Peggy.'"

"If you want to rile her, call her Maggie," said Charley. "She goes right on th' prod!"

"I'm plumb peaceful," laughed Red, turning to follow his host. "You help Mrs. Margaret, an' when I come back you an' me'll figger on goin' after bear as soon as we can."

Chapter III
A Question of Identity

Johnny sauntered into Quayle's barroom and leaned against the bar, talking to Ed Doane. An hour or two before he had finished his dinner, warned his outfit again about the early start on the morrow, advanced them some money, and watched them leave the hotel for one more look at the town, and now he was killing time.

"What do you think about Kane's?" asked Ed carelessly, and then looked up as a customer entered. When the man went out he repeated the question.

Johnny cogitated and shrugged his shoulders. "Same as you. Reg'lar cow-town gamblin'-hall, with th' same fixin's, wimmin', crooked games, an' wise bums hangin' 'round. Am I right?"

A group entered, and when they had been served they went into the hotel office, the bartender's eyes on them as long as they were in sight. He turned and frowned. "Purty near. You left a couple of things out. I'm not sayin' what they are, but I am sayin' this: Don't you ever pull no gun in there if you should have any trouble. Wait till you get yore man outside. Funny thing about that sort of a spell, I reckon but no stranger ever got a gun out an' workin' in Kane's place. They died too quick, or was put out of workin' order."

Johnny raised his eyebrows: "Mebby no good manever tried to get one out, an' workin'."

"You lose," retorted Ed emphatically. "Some of 'em was shore to be good. It's a cold deck with a sharp shooter. There I go again!" he snorted. "I'm certainly shootin' off my mouth today. I must be loco!"

"Then don't let that worry you. I ain't shootin' mine off," Johnny reassured him. "I'm tryin' to figger ':

A voice from the street interrupted him. "Hey, stranger! Yore outfit's in trouble down in Red Frank's!"

Johnny swung from the bar. "Where's his place?" he asked.

"One street back," nodded the bartender, indicating the rear of the room. "Turn to yore right third door. It's a Greaser dive look sharp!"

Johnny grunted and turned to obey the call. Walking out of the door, he went to the corner, turned it, and soon turned the second corner. As he rounded it he saw stars, reached for his guns by instinct, and dropped senseless. Two shadowy figures pounced upon him, rolled him over, and deftly searched him.

Back in the hotel Idaho stuck his head into the barroom. "Seen Nelson?" he asked.

"Just went to Red Frank's this minute his gang's in trouble there!" quickly replied Ed.

"I'll go 'round an' be handy, anyhow," said Idaho, loosening his gun as he went through, the door. Rounding the first corner, he saw a figure flit into the darkness across the street and disappear, and as he turned the second corner he tripped and fell over a prostrate man. One glance and his match went out. Jumping around the corner, he saw a second man run across an open space between two clumps of brush, and his quick hand chopped down, a finger of flame spitting into the night. A curse of pain answered it and he leaped forward, hot and vengeful; but his search was in vain, and he soon gave it up and hastened back to his prostrate friend, whom he found sitting up against the wall with an open jackknife in his hand.

"What happened?" demanded Idaho, stopping and bending down. "Where'd he get you?"

"Somethin' fell on my head an' my guns are gone," mumbled Johnny. "I bet I've been robbed!" His slow, fumbling search revealed the bitter truth, and he grunted. "Clean! Clean!"

"I shoved a hunk of lead under th' skin of somebody runnin' heard him yelp," Idaho said. "Lost him in th' dark. Here, grab hold of me. I'll take you to my room in th' hotel. Able to toddle?"

"Able to kill th' skunk with my bare han's," growled the unfortunate, staggering to his feet. "I'm goin' to Kane's!" he asserted, and Idaho's arguments were exhausted before he was able to have his own way.

"You come along with me I want to look at yore head. An', besides, you ought to have a gun before you go huntin'. Come, on. We'll go in through th' kitchen that's th' nearest way. It's empty now, but th' door's never locked."

"You gimme a gun, an' I'll know where to go!" blazed Johnny, trembling with weakness. "I showed my roll in there, like a fool. Eleven hundred h--l of a foreman *I* am!"

"You can't just walk into a place an' start shootin'!" retorted Idaho, angrily. "Will you listen to sense? Come on, now. After you get sensible you can do what you want, an' I'll go along an' help you do it. That's fair, ain't it? How do you know that feller belongs to Kane's crowd? May be a Greaser, an' a mile away by now. Come on be sensible!"

"Th' SV can't afford to lose that money oh, well," sighed Johnny, "yo're right. Go ahead. I'll wash off th' blood, anyhow. I must be a holy show."

They got to Idaho's room without arousing any unusual interest and Idaho examined the throbbing bump with clumsy fingers, receiving frank statements for his awkwardness.

"Shucks," he grinned, straightening up. "It's as big as an egg, but besides th' skin bein' broke an' a lot of blood, there ain't nothin' th' matter. I'll wash it off an' if you keep yore hat on, nobody '11 know it. I reckon that hat just about saved that thick skull of yourn."

"What did you see when you found me?" asked Johnny when his friend had finished the job.

Idaho told him and added: "Hoped I could tell him by th' yelp, but I can't, unless, mebby, I go around an' make everybody in this part of th' country yelp for me. But I don't reckon that's hardly reasonable."

"Yo're right," grinned Johnny. "Well," he said, after a moment's thought, "I don't go back home without eleven hundred dollars an' my guns; but I got to send th' boys back. They can't help me none, bein' known as my friends. Besides, we're all broke, an' they're needed on th' ranch. If I knowed that Kane had a hand in this, I'd cussed soon get that money back!"

"Yo're shore plumb set on that Kane dear."

"I showed that wad of bills in just two places: Ed's bar, an' Kane's joint."

"Ed's bar is out of it if nobody else was in there at th' time."

"Only Ridley, Ed, an' myself."

"Somebody could've looked in th' window," suggested Idaho.

"Nobody did, because I was lookin' around."

"If you go in Kane's an' make a gunplay, you'll never know how it happened or who done it; an' if you go in, without a gunplay, an' let 'em know what you think, some Greaser 'll hide a knife in you. Then you'll never get it 'back."

"Just th' same, that's th' place to start from," persisted Johnny doggedly. "An' from th' inside, too."

Idaho frowned. "That may be so, but startin' it from there means to end it there an' then. You can't buck Kane in his own place. It's been tried more'n once. I ain't shore you can buck him in this town, or part of th' country. Bigger people than you are suspected of payin' him money to let 'em alone. You'd be surprised if I named names. Look here: I better speak a little piece about this part of th' country. This county is unorganized an' ain't got no courts, nor nothin' else except a peace officer which we calls sheriff. It's big, but it ain't got many votes, an' what it has is one-third Greaser. Most Greasers don't amount to much in a stand-up fight, but their votes count. They are all for Kane. We've only had one election for sheriff, an' although Corwin is purty well known, he won easy. Kane did it, an' when anybody says 'Corwin,' they might as well say 'Kane.' He is boss of this section. His gamblin'-joint is his head quarters, an' it's guarded forty ways from th' jack. His gang is made up of all kinds, from th' near decent down to th' night killer. When Kane wants a man killed, that man don't live long. Corwin takes his orders before an' after a play like this one. Yo're expected to report it to him. Comin' down to cases, th' pack has got to be fed, an' they have got to make a killin' once in a while. Even if Kane ain't in on it direct, he'll get most of that money across his bar or tables. To wind up a long speech, you better go home with yore men, for that ain't enough money to get killed over."

"Mebby not if it was mine!" snapped Johnny. "An' I ain't shore about that, neither. An' there's more'n money in this, an' more than th' way I was handled. Somebody in this wart of a town has got Johnny Nelson's two guns an' nobody steals them an' keeps 'em! I got friends, lots of 'em, in Montanny, that would lend me th' money quick; but there ain't nobody can give me them six-guns but th' thief that's got 'em. I'm rooted solid.'"

"All right," said Idaho. "Yo're talkin' foolish, but cussed if I don't like to hear it. So me an' you are goin' to hog-tie that gang. If I get Corwin in th' ruckus, I'll be satisfied."

"Yo're th' one that's talkin' foolish," retorted Johnny, fighting back his grin. "An I'm cussed if *I* don't like to hear it. But there's this correction: Me an' you ain't goin' to bulldog that gang at all. *I* am. Yo're goin' to sprawl on yore saddle an' light out for wherever you belong, an' stay there. Yo're a marked man an' wouldn't last th' swish of a longhorn's tail. Yore brand is registered they got you in their brand books; but they ain't got mine. I'm not wearin' no brand. I ain't even earnotched, 'though I must 'a' been a 'sleeper' when I let 'em put this walnut on my head. I'm a plain, ornery maverick. Think I'm comin' out in th' open? I don't want no brass band playin' when I go to war. I'm a Injun."

"Yo're a little striped animal in this town one of them kind that's unpleasant up-wind from a feller," snorted Idaho. "How can you play Injun when they know yo're hangin' 'round here lookin' for yore money? Answer me that, maverick!"

"I'm comin' to that. Can you get me an old hat? One that's plumb wore out?"

"Reckon so," grunted Idaho, in surprise. "Th' clerk might be able to dig one up."

"No, not th' clerk; but Ed Doane," corrected Johnny. "Now you think hard before you answer this one: Could you see my face plain when you found me? Could they have seen it plain enough to be shore it was me?"

Idaho stared at him and a cheerful expression drifted across his face. "I'm gettin' th' drift of this Injun business," he muttered. "Mebby mebby cuss it, it will work! I couldn't see nothin' but a bump on th' ground along that wall till I lit a match. I'll get you a hat an' I'll plant it, too."

Johnny nodded. "Plant anythin' else you want that don't look like anythin' I own. Be shore that hat ain't like mine."

Idaho raised his hand as a sudden tramping sounded on the stairs. "That yore outfit?" he asked as a loud, querulous voice was heard.

Johnny went to the door and called, whereupon Arch waved his companions toward their quarters and answered the summons, following his foreman into the room. Johnny was about to close the door when Idaho arose and pushed past him.

"We been talkin' too loud," whispered the departing puncher. "You never can tell. I'm goin' out to sit on th' top step where there's more air," and he went on again, the door closing after him.

Johnny turned and smiled at Arch's expression. "You boys leave at daylight on th' jump. I got to stay here. You can say I'm waitin' for th' chance to pick up some money buyin' a herd of yearlin's cheap, or anythin' you can think of. Any thin' that'll stick. You'll have plenty of time to smooth it out before you get back home. I want you boys to scratch up every cent you've got an' turn it over to me. Any left of that I gave you after supper?"

"Shore quite some," grinned Arch. "We had better luck, down th' street. You must be aimin' to get a-plenty yearlin's, with that roll you got. What are we goin' to do, busted?"

"I want a couple of Colts, too," continued Johnny. "You won't need any money. Th' waggin is well stocked an' when you get back you can draw on Arnold."

"We was goin' to stop at Highbank for a good time," protested Arch.

"Have it in yore old man's hotel an' owe it to him," suggested Johnny.

"Have a good time in my old man's place!" exclaimed Arch. "Oh, h l!" He burst out laughing. "That'll tickle th' boys, that will!" The puncher looked searchingly at his foreman. "Hey, what's all th' trouble?"

Johnny thought it would be wiser to post his companion and crisply told what had happened.

Arch cleared his throat, hitched up his belt, and looked foolish but determined. "It's been comin' rapid, but I got it all. Yo're talkin' to th' wrong man. You want to fix up that story for th' ranch with some soft-belly that's ridin' that way. Better send a letter. We're all stayin' here. Fine bunch of-"

"You can help me more by goin' back like nothin's happened," interrupted Johnny. "Th' ranch won't be worry in' me then, an' if you stayed here it might give th' game away. Besides, one man can live longer on th' money we got than four can, only have a quarter of th' chance to drink too much, an' only talk a fourth as much. That's th' natural play, an' every thin' has got to be natural."

"That's th' worst of havin' a smooth face," grumbled Arch, ruefully rubbing his chin. "If I only had whiskers, I could shave 'em off an' be a total stranger; but I don't reckon I could grow a good enough bunch to get back here in time."

Johnny laughed, his heart warming to the puncher. "Take you a year or two; an' there's more'n whiskers needed to hide from a good man. There's little motions, gait, voice oh, lots of things. You can help me more if you go north. See Dave Green, tell him on th' quiet, an' ask him to send me down a couple hundred dollars. He can buy a check from th' Doc, payable to George Norton. There's a bank in this town. He's to send it to George Norton, general delivery."

"Dave will spread it far an' wide," objected Arch. "He tells all he knows."

"If he did," smiled Johnny, "it shore would be an eddication for th' man that heard it. He talks a lot an' says nothin'. If he told all he knew, hell would 'a' popped long ago on them ranges. I'm only wishin' he could get a job in Kane's!"

"Gosh!" exclaimed Arch. "Mebby he can. He's a bang-up bartender."

Johnny shook his head and laughed.

"Well, I reckon you know best," said Arch. "If you say so, we'll go home but it hurts bad as a toothache. An' as long as we're goin', we can start tonight this minute."

"You'll start at daylight, like honest folks," chuckled Johnny. "Think I want Kane to sit down an' figger why a lazy outfit got ambitious all at once? An' th' two boys that lend me their guns want to be ridin' close to th' waggin, on its left side, until they get out of town. I don't want anybody noticin' they ain't got their guns. Mebby their coats'll hide 'em, anyhow. But before you do anythin' else, get me a copy of that weekly newspaper down stairs. There's some layin' around th' office. Shore you got it all?"

Arch nodded, and his foreman opened the door. Idaho glanced around and then went down the stairs and through the office, stopping at the bar, where he held a low-voiced conversation with the man behind it. Ed looked a little surprised at the unusual request, but Idaho's earnestness and anxiety told him enough and he asked no questions. A few minutes later, after Idaho had disappeared into the kitchen, Ed told the clerk to watch the bar, and went up to his room, and dropped several articles out of the window before he left it again.

When Idaho had finished scouting and planting the sombrero, a broken spur, and a piece torn from a red kerchief, he went into the barroom and grinned at his friend Nelson, who leaned carelessly back against the wall; and then his eyes opened wide as he saw the size of the roll of bills from which Johnny was peeling the outer layer. For two hours they sat and played California Jack in plain sight of the street as though nothing unusual had occurred, Johnny's sombrero pushed back on his head, the walnut handle of one of his guns in plain sight, his boots not only guiltless of spurs, but showing that they never had borne them, and his faded, soiled, blue neckerchief was as it had been all day. His mood was cheerful and his laughter rang out from time to time as his friend's witticisms gave excuse. To test his roll, he pulled it out again under his friend's eyes and thumbed off a bill, changed his mind, rolled it back again, and carelessly shoved the handful into his pocket.

Idaho leaned forward. "Who th' devil did you slug?" he softly asked.

"Tell you later deal 'em up," grunted Johnny, a sigh of satisfaction slipping from him. It had been one of Tex Ewait's maxims never to be broke, even if carefully trimmed newspapers had to serve as padding, and in this instance, at least, Johnny believed his old friend to be right. The world finds bluff very useful, and opulence seldom receives a cold shoulder.

At daylight three horsemen and a wagon went slowly up the little street, two men sticking close to each other and the vehicle, and soon became lost to sight. Two or three nighthawks paused and watched the outfit, and one of them went swiftly into Kane's side door. Idaho drew back from the corner of the hotel where he had been watching, nodded wisely to himself, and went into the stable to look after his horse.

The little outfit of the SV stopped when a dozen miles had been put behind and prepared and ate a hurried break fast. As he gulped the last swallow of coffee, Arch arose and went to his horse.

"Thirty miles a day with a waggin takes too long," he said. "One of you boys ride in th' waggin an' gimme a lead hoss. Nelson's a good man, an' it's our job to help him all we can. I can do it that way between sleeps, if I can keep my eyes open to th' end of it. By gettin' a fresh cayuse from my old man at Highbank, I'll set a record for these parts."

Gardner nodded. "Take my cayuse, Arch. I'm crucify in' myself on th' cross of friendship. Cook, give him some grub."

Ten minutes later Arch left them in a cloud of dust, glad to get away from the wagon and keen to make a ride that would go down in local history.

After breakfast Johnny sauntered into the barroom, nodded carelessly to the few men there, and seated him self in his favorite chair.

"Thought mebby you might be among th' dear departed this mornin'," remarked Ed carelessly. "Heard a shot soon after you left last night, but they're so common 'round here that I didn't get none excited. Have any trouble in Red Frank's?"

"You better pinch yoreself ," retorted Johnny. "You saw me an' Idaho settin' right in this room, playin' cards long after that shot. I was upstairs when I heard it. Didn't go to Red Frank's. Changed my mind when I got around at th' side of th' hotel, an' went through th' kitchen, upstairs lookin' for Idaho. What business I got playin' nurse to four growed-up men? A lot they'd thank me for cuttin' in on their play."

"Did they have any trouble?"

"No; they wasn't in Red Frank's at all anyhow, that's what they said. Somebody playin' a joke, or seein' things, I reckon. Seen Idaho this mornin'?"

"No, I ain't," answered Ed sleepily. "Reckon he's still abed. Say, was that yore outfit under my winder before dawn? I come cussed near shootin' th' loud-mouthed fool that couldn't talk without shoutin'."

Johnny laughed. "I reckon it was. They was sore about havin' to go home. Know of any good yearlin's I can buy cheap?"

Ed yawned, rubbed his eyes, and slowly shook his head. "Too close to Ridley. Folks down here mostly let 'em grow up an' sell 'em to him. Prices would be too high, anyhow, I reckon. Better hunt for 'em nearer home."

"That's what I been doin'," growled Johnny. "Well, mebby yo're right about local prices an' conditions; but I'm goin' to poke around an' ask questions, anyhow. To tell you th' truth, a town looks good to me for a change, 'though I'm admittin' this ain't much of a town, at that. Sorta dead nothin' happens, at all."

"That's th' fault of th' visitor, then," retorted Ed, another yawn nearly disrupting his face. "Ho-hum! Some day I'm goin' out an' find me a cave, crawl in it, close it up behind me, an' sleep for a whole week. An' from th' looks of you, it wouldn't do you no harm to do th' same thing." He nodded heavily to the other customers as they went out.

"I'll have plenty of time for sleep when I get home," grinned Johnny. "I got to get some easy money out of this town before I think of sleepin'. Kane's don't get lively till dark, does it?"

Ed snorted. "Was you sayin' easy money?" he demanded with heavy sarcasm.

"I was."

"Oh, well; if you must, I reckon you must," grunted the bartender, shrugging his shoulders.

"A new man, playin' careful, allus wins in a place like Kane's, if he's got a wad of money as big as mine," chuckled Johnny, voicing another maxim of his friend Tex, and patting the bulging roll in his pocket.

Ed looked at the pocket, and frowned. "Huh! Lord help that wad!" he mourned.

"It's got all th' help it needs," countered Johnny. "I'm its guardian. I might change it for bigger bills, for it's purty prominent now. However, that can wait till it grows some more." He burst out laughing. "Big as it is, there's room for more."

"Better keep some real little ones on th' outside," suggested Ed wisely. "You show it too cussed much."

"Do you know there's allus a right an' a wrong way of doin' everythin'?" asked his companion. "A man that's got a lot of money will play safe an' stick a few little ones on th' outside; but a man that's got only little bills will try to get a big one for th' cover. One is tryin' to hide his money; th' other to run a bluff. Wise gamblers know that. I got little bills on th' outside of mine. You watch 'em welcome me."

Despite his boasts, he did not spend much time in Kane's, but slept late and hung around the hotel for a day or two, and then, one morning, he got a nibble on his bait. He was loafing on the hotel steps when he caught sight of the sheriff coming up the street. Corwin had been out of town and had returned only the night before. Seeing the lone man on the steps, the peace officer lengthened his rolling stride and headed straight for the hotel, his eyes fixed on the hat, guns, kerchief, and boots.

"Mornin'," he said, nodding and stopping.

"Mornin'," replied Johnny cheerily. "Bright an' cool, but a little mite too windy for this hour of th' day," he observed, watching a vicious little whirlwind of dust racing up the middle of the street. It suddenly swerved in its course, struck the sheriff, and broke, covering them with bits of paper and hurling dust and sand in their faces and mouths. Other furious little gusts sent the light debris of the street high in the air to be tossed about wildly before settling back to earth again.

"Yo're shore shoutin'," growled Corwin, spitting violently and rubbing his lips. "Don't like th' looks of it. Ain't got no love for a sand storm." He let his blinking eyes rest for a moment on his companion's boots, noted an entire absence of any signs of spur straps, glanced at the guns and at the opulent bump in one of the trouser pockets, noted the blue neckerchief, and gazed into the light blue eyes, which were twinkling at his expression of disgust. "D n th' sand," he grunted, spitting again. "How do you like this town of ourn, outside of th' dust, now that you've seen more of it?"

Johnny smiled broadly. "Leavin' out a few things besides th' dust such as bein' too quiet, dead, an' lackin' 'most everythin' a town should have I'd say it is a purty fair town for its kind. But, bad as it is, it ain't near as bad as that bed I've been sleepin' in. It reminds me of some of th' country I've rid over. It's full of mesas, ridges, canyons, an' valleys, an' all of 'em run th' wrong way. Cuss such a bed. I gave it up after awhile, th' first night, an' played Idaho cards till I was so sleepy I could 'a' slept on a cactus. After that, though, it ain't been so bad. It's all in gettin' used to it, I reckon."

The sheriff laughed politely. "Well, I reckon there ain't no bed like a feller's own. Speakin' of th' town bein' dead, that is yore fault; you shouldn't stay so close to th' hotel. Wander around a little an' you'll find it plumb lively. There's Red Frank's an' Kane's they are high-strung enough for 'most anybody." The momentary gleam in his eyes was not lost on his companion.

"Red Frank's," cogitated Johnny. Then he laughed. "I come near goin' in there, at that. Anyhow, I shore started."

"Why didn't you go on?" inquired the sheriff, speaking' as if from polite, idle curiosity. "You might 'a' seen some excitement in there."

"Somebody tried to play a joke on me," grinned Johnny, \" but I fooled 'em. My boys are shore growed up."

"How'd yore boys make out?"

"They said they wasn't in there at all. Reckon some body got excited or drunk if they wasn't try in' to make a fool out of me. But, come to think of it, I did hear a shot."

"They're not as rare as they're goin' to be," growled the sheriff. "But it's hard to stop th' shootin'. Takes time."

Johnny nodded. "Reckon so. You got a bad crowd of Greasers here, too, which makes it harder though they're generally strong on knifeplay. Mexicans, monte, an' mescal are a bad combination."

"Better tell yore boys to look sharp in Red Frank's. It's a bad place, 'specially if a man's got likker in him. An' they'll steal him blind."

"Don't have to tell 'em, for I sent 'em home," replied Johnny, and then he grinned. "An' there ain't no man livin' can rob 'em, neither, for I wouldn't let 'em draw any of their pay. Bein' broke, they didn't kick up as much of a fuss as they might have. I know how to handle my outfit. Say!" he exclaimed. "Yo're th' very man I been lookin' for, an' I didn't know it till just this minute. Do you know where I can pick up a herd of a couple or three hundred yearlin's at a fair figger?"

Corwin shook his head. "You might get a few here an' there, but they ain't worth botherin' about. Anyhow, prices are too high. Better look around on yore way back, up on some of them God- forsaken ranges north of here. But how'll you handle a herd with yore outfit gone?"

His companion grinned and winked knowingly. "I'll handle it by buy in' subject to delivery. Let somebody else have th' fun of drivin' a lot of crazy-headed yearlin's all that distance. Growed-up steers are bad enough, an' I've had all I want of them for awhile. Well," he chuckled, "not havin' no yearlin's to buy, I reckon I've got time to wander around nights. Six months in a ranchhouse is shore confinin'. I need a change. What do you say to a little drink?"

Corwin wiped more sand from his lips. "It's a little early in th' day for me, but I'm with you. This blasted wind looks like it's gettin' worse," he growled, scowling as he glanced about.

"It's only addin' to th' liveliness of yore little town," chuckled Johnny, leading the way.

"We ain't had a sand storm in three years," boasted the sheriff, hard on his companion's heels. "I see you know th' way," he commented.

Johnny set down his empty glass and brought up the roll of bills, peeled the outer from its companions, and tossed it on the bar. "You got to take somethin' with us, Ed," he reproved.

Ed shrugged his shoulders, slid the change across the counter, and became thoughtfully busy with the arrangement of the various articles on the backbar.

Corwin treated, talked a few moments, and then he parted, his busy brain asking many questions and becoming steadily more puzzled.

Ed mopped the bar without knowing he was doing it. and looked at his new friend. "Where'd you pick that up?" he asked.

"Meanin'?" queried Johnny, glancing at the windows, where sand was beating at the glass and pushing in through every crack in the woodwork.

"Corwin."

"Oh, he rambled up an' got talkin'. Reckon I'll go out, sand or no sand, an' see if I can get track of any yearlin's, just to prove that you don't know any thin' about th' cow business."

"Nobody but a fool would go out into that unless they shore had to," retorted Ed. "It's goin' to get worse, shore as shootin'. I know 'em. Lord help anybody that has to go very far through it!"

Johnny opened the door, stuck his head out and ducked back in again. Tying his neckerchief over his mouth and nose, he went to the rear door, closed his eyes, and plunged out into the storm, heading for the stable to look to the comfort of his horse. Pepper rubbed her nozzle against him, accepted the sugar with dignity, and followed his every move with her great, black eyes. He hung a sack over the window and, finding nails on a shelf, secured it against the assaults of the wind.

"There, Pepper Girl reckon you'll be right snug; but don't you go an' butt it out to see what's goin' on outside. I'm glad this ain't no common shed. Four walls are a heap better than three today."

"That you, Nelson?" came a voice from the door. Idaho slid in, closed the door behind him with a bang, and dropped his gun into the holster. "This is shore a reg'lar storm; an' that's shore a reg'lar hoss!" he exclaimed, spitting and blowing. He stepped toward the object of his admiration.

"Look out!" warned Johnny. "She's likely to brain a stranger. Trained her that way. She'll mebby kill any body that comes in here; but not hardly while I'm around, I reckon. Teeth an' hoofs she's a bad one if she don't know you. That's why I try to get her a stable of her own. What was you doin' with th' six-gun?"

"Keepin' th' sand out of it," lied Idaho. "Thiefproof, huh?" he chuckled. "I'm sayin' it's a good thing. Ever been tried?"

"Twice," answered Johnny. "She killed th' first one." He lowered his voice. "I'm figgerin' Corwin knows about that little fracas of th' other night. Did you tell anybody?"

"Not a word. What about yore outfit?"

"Tight as fresh-water clams, an', besides, they didn't have no chance to. They even left without their break fast. But I'm dead shore he knows. How did he find it out?"

"Looks like you might be right, after all," admitted Idaho. "I kept a lookout that mornin', like I told you, an' th' news of yore outfit leavin' was shore carried, which means that somebody in Kane's gang was plumb interested. How much do you think Corwin knows about it?"

"Don't know; but not as much now as he did before he saw me this mornin'," answered Johnny. "When he sized me up, his eyes gave him away just a little flash. But now he may be wonderin' who th' devil it was that got clubbed that night. An' he showed more signs when he saw my money. Say: How much does Ed know?"

"Not a thing," answered Idaho: "He's one of my best friends, an' none of my best friends ask me questions when I tell 'em not to. An' now I'm glad I told him not to, because, of course, you don't know any thin' about him. No, sir," he emphatically declared; "anythin' that Corwin knows come from th' other side. What you goin' to do?"

"I don't know," admitted Johnny. "I got to wrastle that out; but I do know that I ain't goin' out of th' hotel today. It looks like Californy Jack for us till this blows over. Yore cayuse fixed all right?"

"Shore; good as I can. Come on, if yo're ready."

"Hadn't you better carry yore gun in yore hand, so th' sand won't get in it?" asked Johnny gravely.

Idaho looked at him and laughed. "Come on I'm startin'," he said, and he dashed out of the building, Johnny close at his heels.

Chapter IV
A Journey Continued

Pounding into Highbank from the south, Arch turned the two fagged-out horses into his father's little corral, roped the better of the two he found there, saddled it, and rode around to the front of the hotel, where he called loudly.

Pete Wiggins went to the door and scowled at his son. "What you doin' with that hoss?" he demanded in no friendly tone.

"Breakin' records," impudently answered his young hopeful. "Left Big Creek, north of Mesquite, at sixtwenty this mornin', an' I'm due in Gunsight before dark. Left you two cayuses for this one but don't ride 'em too hard. So-long!" and he was off in a cloud of dust.

Pete Wiggins stepped forward galvanically and called, shaking his first. "Come back here! Don't you kill that hoss!"

His beloved son's reply was anything but filial, but as long as his wrathful father did not hear it, perhaps it may better be left out of the record.

The shadows were long when Arch drew up in front of the "Palace "in Gunsight, and dismounted almost in the door. He looked at his watch and proudly shouted the miles and the time of the ride before looking to see who was there to hear it. As he raised his head and saw Dave Green, Arnold, and two strangers staring at him, he called himself a fool, walked stiffly to a chair, and lowered himself gently into it.

"That's shore some ridin'," remarked Dave, surprised. "What's wrong? What's th' reason for killin' cayuses?"

"Wanted to paste somethin' up for others to shoot at," grinned Arch, making the best of the situation.

"How'd you come to leave ahead of Nelson?" demanded Arnold, his easy-going boss. "Where is he? An' where's th' rest of th' boys?" The SV owner was fast falling into the vernacular, which made him fit better into the country.

"Oh, he's tryin' to make a fortune buyin' up a herd of fine yearlin's," answered the recordmaker with con fident assurance. "It ain't nothin' to him that th' owner don't want to sell 'em. I near busted laughin' at 'em wranglin'. They was near fightin' when I left. You should 'a' heard 'em! Anybody'd think that man didn't own his own cattle. But I'm bettin' on Nelson, just th' same, for when I left they had got to wranglin' about th' price, an' that's allus a hopeful sign. He shore will tire that man out. I used a lead hoss as far as Highbank, changin' frequent', an' got a fresh off th' old man. Nelson told us all to go home, where we're needed but he'll be surprised when he knows how quick *I* got there. Sam an' th' others are with th' waggin, comin' slower."

"I should hope so!" snorted Arnold. "An' you ain't home yet. What's th' real reason for all this speed, an' for headin' here instead of goin' to th' ranch? A man that's born truthful makes a poor liar; but I'll say this for you, Arch--with a little practice you'll be near as good as Dave, here. Come on; tell it!"

Arch looked wonderingly at his employer, grinned at Dave, and then considered the two strangers. "I've done told it already," he affirmed, stiffly.

"Shake hands with Red Connors an' Hopalong Cassidy," said Arnold. "You've heard of them, haven't you?"

"Holy cats! I have!" exclaimed Arch, gripping the hands of the two in turn. "I certainly have. Have you two ever been in Mesquite?" he demanded, eagerly. "Good! Now, wait a minute; I want to think," and he went into silent consultation with himself.

"Mebby he's aimin' to improve on me," said Dave. "Judgin' from th' studyin', I figger he's trying to bust in yore class, Arnold."

Arch grinned from one to the other. "Seein' as how we're all friends of Nelson, an' his wife ought to be kept calm, I reckon I ought to spit it out straight. Here, you listen," and he told the truth as fully and completely as he knew it.

Arnold shook his head at the end of the recital. The loss of the herd money was a hard blow, but he was too much of a man to make it his chief concern. "Arch," he said slowly, "yo're so fond of breakin' records that yo're goin' to sleep in town, get another horse at daylight, an' break yore own record gettin' back to Mesquite. Tell that son-in-law of mine to come home right away, before Peggy is left a widow. It's no fault of his that he lost it it's to his credit, goin' to the aid of his men. I wouldn't 'a' had it to lose if it wasn't for what he's done for th' SV. He earned it for me; an' if he's lost it, all right"

"Most generally th' East sends us purty poor specimens," observed Dave. "Once in awhile we get a thoroughbred. Gunsight's proud of th' one it got."

"Arnold," said Arch eagerly, "I'll get to Mesquite tomorrow if it's moved to th' other side of h--l!"

Hopalong took the cigar from his mouth. "Wait a minute," he said. He slowly knocked the ashes from it and looked around. "While I'm appreciatin' what you just said, Arnold, I don't agree with it." He thought for a moment and then continued. "You don't know that son-in-law of yourn like I do. Somebody knocked him on th' head, stole his money an' his guns. Don't forget th' guns. Bein' an easterner, that mebby don't mean anythin' to you; but bein' an old Bar-20 man, it means a heap to me. He won't leave till he's squared up, all around. I know it. Seein' how it is, we got to accept it; an' figger out some way to make his wife take it easy, an' not do no worryin'. Here!" he exclaimed, leaning for ward. "Arnold, you sit down an' write him a letter. Write it now. Tell him to stay down there until he gets a good herd of yearlin's. Then Arch has got to start back in th' mornin' an' join th' waggin, an' come home like he ought to. He stays here tonight, an' nobody has seen him, at all."

"An' Dave don't need to bother with any check," said Red. "Hoppy an' me has plenty of money. We'll start for Mesquite at daylight, Arch, here, ridin' with us till we meet th' waggin. Of course, Hoppy don't mean that yo're really goin' to write a letter, Arnold," he explained.

"That's just what I do mean," said Hopalong. "He's goin' to write th' letter, but he ain't goin' to send it. He'll give it to Arch, an' then it can be torn up. What's th' use of lyin' when it's so easy to tell th' truth? 'Though I'm admittin' I wasn't thinkin' of that so much as I was that a man can allus tell th' truth better'n he can lie. When he tells about th' letter, he's goin' to be talkin' about a real letter, what won't get to changin' around in a day or two, or when he gets rattled. Mrs. Johnny is mebby goin' to ask a lot of questions."

"I'll give odds that she does," chuckled Dave, looking under the backbar. "Here's pen an' ink," he said, pushing the articles across the counter. "There's paper an' envelopes around here some here it is. Go ahead, now:

' Dear Johnny: I take my ' "

"Shut up!" barked Arnold, glaring at him. "I guess I know how to write a letter! Besides, I don't take my pen in hand. It's your pen, you grinnin' chump! As long as we're ridin' on th' tail of Truth, let's stick to it, all th' way. Shut up, now, an' gimme a chance!" He glared around at the grinning faces, jabbed the pen in the ink, and went to work. When he had finished, he read it aloud, and handed it to Arch, who tore it up and threw the pieces on the floor.

Hopalong reached down, picked up the pieces, and gravely, silently put them on the bar. Dave raked them into his hand, dropped them into a tin dish, and put a match to them. Arnold looked around the little group and snorted.

"Huh! You an' Dave must 'a' gone to th' same school!"

Dave nodded. "We have, I reckon. Experience is a good school, too."

"Th' lessons stick," said Hopalong, looking at Dave with a new interest.

Arch chuckled. "Cuss it! I'll shore hate to stop at that waggin. I'm sayin' Mesquite is goin' to be terrible upset some day soon. Why ain't I got whiskers? I'd like to see his face when he sets eyes on you fellers. Bet he'll jump up an' down an' yell!"

"Mebby," said Hopalong, "for if there's any yellin', he'll shore have to start it. He sent you fellers away because you was known to be friends of his, didn't he?"

Dave slapped the bar and laughed outright. "If I wasn't so fat, I'd go with you! I'm beginnin' to see why he thought so much of you fellers. Here it's time for a drink."

"What are we goin' to tell Margaret?" asked Arnold. "She may get suspicious if you leave so suddenly."

"You just keep repeatin' that letter to yoreself," laughed Red, "an' leave th' rest to better liars. Yo're as bad a liar as Arch, here. Me an' Hoppy may 'a' been born truthful, but we was plumb spoiled in our bringin' up. Reckon we better be leavin' now. Arch, where'll we meet you about two hours after daylight tomorrow?"

Arch groaned. "Shucks! About daylight it'll take Fanning that long to get me out of bed oh, well," he sighed, resignedly. "I'll be at th' ford, waitin' for you to come along. Come easy, in case I'm asleep."

"South of here, on this trail?" asked Red. "Thought so. All right. So-long," and he followed his slightly limping friend out to the horses.

Dave hurried to the door. "Hey!" he shouted. "Hadn't I better send him that check, anyhow? He may need it before you get there."

A roar of laughter from behind answered him, and he wheeled to face Arch. "When does th' mail leave?" asked the puncher.

"Day after tomorrow," answered Dave, and swung around as a voice from the street rubbed it in.

"You must 'a' played hookey from that school, Dave," jeered Arnold.

"He's fat clean to th' bald spot," shouted Arch. "Come on in, Dave. We ain't got time to hold back for no mail to get there first." He stuck his head out of the window. "So-long, fellers! See you at th' ford."

Dave watched the three until they were well along the trail and then he turned slowly. "I never did really doubt th' stories Nelson told about that old outfit, but if I had any doubts I ain't got them no more. Did you see th' looks in their eyes when you was tellin' about Nelson?"

"I did!" snapped Arch. "Why in hell ain't I got whiskers?"

Reaching the SV, Arnold and his companions put up the horses and walked slowly toward the house, seeing a flurry of white through the kitchen door.

"Think it'll reach him in time?" asked Red, waiting outside the door for Arnold to enter first.

"Ought to. Slim said he would mail it at Highbank as soon as he got there," answered Arnold.

"I shore hope so," said Red. "I'd hate to have that ride for nothin' an' it would just be our luck to pass him somewhere on th' way, an' get there after he left."

"He'd likely foller th' reg'lar trail up, anyhow," said Hopalong. "It ain't likely we'll miss him."

Margaret put down the dish and looked at them accusingly. "What are you boys talking about?" she demanded.

"Only wonderin' if yore father's letter will get to Johnny in time to catch him before he leaves," said Hopalong. "Dave says it will as long as that Slim feller is takin' it to Highbank with him. Slim live down there?" he asked his host.

"No; goin' down for th' Double X, I suppose," replied Arnold. "Supper ready, Peggy?"

"Not until I learn more about this," retorted Margaret, determinedly. "What letter are you talking about?"

"Oh, I told Johnny to look around and see if he could pick up a good herd of yearlings cheap," answered her father, going into the next room.

Margaret compressed her lips, but said nothing about it, whereupon Red silently swore a stronger oath of allegiance. "The table is waiting for you. I've had to keep the supper warm," she said.

Red nodded under standingly. "Men- folks are shore a trial an' tribulation," he said, passing through the door.

"Hadn't ought to take him very long, I suppose?" queried Arnold, passing the meat one way and the potatoes the other.

Red laughed. "You don't know him very well, yet," he replied. "Give him a chance to dicker over a herd an' he's happy for a week or more. He shore does like to dicker."

"I never saw anything in his nature which would indicate anything like that," said Margaret, tartly. "He always has impressed me with being quite direct Perhaps I did not understand you correctly?"

"Peggy! Peggy!" reproved her father. "It means bread and butter for us."

"I can eat my bread without butter," she retorted. "As a matter of fact I've seen very little butter out in this country."

Red screwed his face up a little and wriggled his foot. "I don't reckon you've ever seen him buyin' a herd, ma'am?"

"You are quite right, Mr. Connors. I never have."

Red did not take the trouble to inform her that he never had seen her husband buy a herd. "I reckon it's his love for gamblin'," he said, carelessly, and instantly regretted it.

"Gambling?" snapped Margaret, her eyes sparking. "Did you say gambling?"

Hopalong flashed one eloquent look at his friend, whose hair now was not the only red thing about him, and re moved the last of the peel from the potato. "Red is referrin', I reckon, to th' love of gamblin' that was born in yore husband, Margaret. It allus has been one of his, an' our, fears that it would get th' best of him. But," he said, proudly and firmly, "it never did. Johnny is gettin' past th' age, now, when a deck of cards acts strong on him. An' it's all due to Red. He used to whale him good every time he caught th' Kid playin'."

Red's sanctimonious expression made Hopalong itch to smear the hot potato over it, and the heel of his boot on Red's shin put a look of sorrow on that person's face which was not in the least simulated.

"We all had a hand in that, Margaret," generously re marked the man with the shuddering shin. "Tex Ewalt watched him closest. But, as I was sayin', out at th' corral, I don't believe he's got men enough to handle no herd of yearlin's. Them youngsters are plumb skittish, an' hard to keep on th' trail. Me an' Hoppy are aimin' to go down an' help him an' see him all th' sooner, to tell you th' truth."

"That will please him," smiled Margaret. She looked at her father, whose appetite seemed to be ravenous, judging by the attention he was giving to the meal. "What did you write, Dad?"

Arnold washed down a refractory mouthful of potato, which suffered from insufficient salivation, and looked up. He repeated the letter carelessly and reached for another swallow of coffee, silently thanking Hopalong for insisting that the letter actually be written.

The meal over they sat and chatted until after dark, Margaret doing up a bundle of things which she thought her husband might need. When morning came she had breakfast on the table at daylight for her departing friends, and she also had a fat letter for her husband, which she entrusted to Red, the sterling molder of her husband's manly character.

When they had ridden well beyond sight of the house Hopalong thoughtfully dropped the bundle to the ground, turned in the saddle and looked with scorn at his friend. "You shore are a hard-boiled jackass! For two bits I'd've choked you last night. How'd you like to have some body shoot off his mouth to yore wife about your gamblin'?"

"I've reformed, an' she knows it!"

"Yes, you've reformed! You've reformed a lot, you have!"

"You ain't got no business pickin' on th' man that taught th' Kid most all he knows about poker!" tartly retorted Red.

"Cussed little you ever taught him," rejoined Hopalong. "It was me an' Tex that eddicated his brain, an' fingers. He only used you to practice on."

And so they rode, both secretly pleased by this auspicious beginning of a new day, for the day that started without a squabble usually ended wrong, somehow. Picking up Arch, who yawningly met them at the ford, they pushed southward at a hard pace, relying on the relay which their guide promised to get at Highbank. Reaching this town Arch led them to his father's little corral, and exulted over the four fresh horses which he found there. Saddles were changed with celerity and they rolled on southward again.

Peter Wiggins in the hotel office held the jack of hearts over the ten of the same suit and cocked an ear to listen. Slowly making the play he drew another card from the deck in his hand, and listened again. Reluctant to bestir himself, but a little suspicious, he debated the matter while he played several cards mechanically. Then he arose and walked through the building, emerging from the kitchen door. Three swiftly moving riders, his son in the middle, were taking the long, gentle slope just south of town. Pete's laziness disappeared and he made good time to the corral. One look was enough and he shook a vengeful fist at his heir and pride.

"Twice!" he roared, kicking an inoffensive tomato can over the corral wall. "Twice! Mebby you'll try it again! All right; I'm willin'. I never heard of anybody around here thraskin' a twenty-three-year-old son, but as long as yo're bustin' records an' makin' th' Wigginses famous, I ought to do my share. Yo're bustin' ridin' records I'm aimin' to bust th' hidin' records, if you don't smash th' sprintin' records, you grinnin' monkey!"

Pete went into the hotel, soon returning with the cards and a box; and for the rest of the morning played solitaire with the steadily rising sun beating on his back, and swarms of flies exploring his perspiring person.

The three riders were going on, hour after hour, their speed entirely controlled by what they knew of horse flesh, and when they espied the wagon Arch suggested another change of mounts, which was instantly overruled by Hopalong.

"Some of them Mesquite hombres will be rememberin' them cayuses," he said. "We're doin' good enough as we are."

When they reached the wagon and drew rein to breathe their mounts, Joe Reilly grinned a welcome. "Thought you was goin' to Gunsight! "he jeered.

Arch laughed triumphantly. "I've done been there, but got afraid you fellers might get lost. Meet Hopalong assidy an' Red Conners, friends of th' foreman."

"Why'n h--l didn't you bring my hoss with you, you locoed cow?" blazed Sam Gardner from the wagon seat. "You never got to Gunsight. You must 'a' hit a cushion an' bounced back."

"Forgot all about yore piebald," retorted Arch. "But if you must have a cayuse you can ask my old man for one when you get to Highbank. I'd do it for you, only me an' him ain't on th' best of terms right now." He turned to his two new friends. "All you got to do now is foller th' wagon tracks to town."

"So-long," said the two, and whirled away.

They spent the night not many miles north of Big Creek and were riding again at dawn. As they drew nearer to their objective the frisking wind sent clouds of dust whirling around them to their discomfort.

"That must be th' town," grunted Red through his kerchief as his eyes, squinting between nearly closed lids, caught sight of Mesquite through a momentary opening in the dust-filled air to the southeast.

"Hope so," growled his companion. "Cussed glad of it. This is goin' to be a whizzer. Look at th' tops of them sand hills yonder streamin' into th' air like smoke from a roarin' prairie fire.

Here's where we separate. I'm takin' to th' first shack I find. Don't forget our names, an' that we're strangers, for awhile, anyhow."

Red nodded. "Bill Long an' Red Thompson," he muttered as they parted.

Not long thereafter Hopalong dismounted in the rear of Kane's and put his horse in the nearer of the two stables, doing what he could for the animal's comfort, and then stepped to the door. He paused, glanced back at the "P. W." brand on the horse and smiled. "Red's is a Horseshoe cayuse. That's what I call luck!" and plunged into the sand blasts. Bumping into the wall of Kane's big building he followed it, turned the corner, and groped his way through the front door.

At the sudden gust the bartender looked around and growled. "Close that door! Pronto!"

The newcomer slammed it shut and leaned against the wall, rubbing at his eyelids and face, and shed sand at every movement.

The bartender slid a glass of water across the bar. "Here; wash it out. You'll only make 'em worse, rubbin'," he said as the other began rubbing his lips and spit ting energetically.

Bill Long obeyed, nodded his thanks and glanced furtively at the door, and became less alert. "Much obliged. I didn't get all there was flyin', but I got a-plenty."

The dispenser of drinks smiled. "Lucky gettin' in out of it when you did."

"Yes," replied Bill, nervously. "Yes; plumb lucky. This will raise th' devil with th' scenery."

"Won't be a trail left," suggested the bartender, watching closely.

Bill glanced up quickly, sighed with satisfaction and then glanced hurriedly around the room. "Whose place is this?" he whispered out of the corner of his mouth.

"Pecos Kane's," grunted the bartender, greatly pleased about something. His pleasure was increased by the quick look of relief which flashed across the other's face, and he chuckled. "Yo're all right in here."

"Yes," said Bill, and motioned toward a bottle. Gulping the drink he paid for it and then leaned over the counter. "Say, friend," he whispered anxiously, "if any body conies around askin' for Bill Long, you ain't seen him, savvy?"

"Never even heard of th' gent," smiled the other.

"Here's where you should ought to lose yo're name," he suggested.

Bill winked at him and slouched away to become mixed up in the crowd. The checkerboard rear wall obtruded itself upon his vision and he went back and found a seat not far from it and from Kit Thorpe, bodyguard of the invisible proprietor, who sat against the door leading through the partition. Thorpe coldly acknowledged the stranger's nod and continued to keep keen watch over the crowd and the distant front door.

The day was very dull, the sun's rays baffled by the swirling sand, and the hanging kerosene lamps were lit, and as an occasional thundering gust struck the building and created air disturbances inside of it the lamps moved slightly to and fro and added a little more soot to the coating on their chimneys. Bill's natural glance at the unusual design of the rear wall caught something not usual about it and caused an unusual activity to arise in his mind. He knew that his eyes were sore and inflamed, but that did not entirely account for the persistent illusion which they saw when his roving glance, occasionally returning to the wall, swept quickly over it. There were several places where the black was a little blacker, and these spots moved on their edges, contracting and lengthening as the lamps swung gently. Pulling the brim of his hat over his eyes, he faced away from the wall and closed his burning eyelids, but his racing thoughts were keen to solve any riddle which would help to pass the monotonous time. Another veiled glance as he shifted to a more comfortable position gave him the explanation he sought. Those few black squares had been cut out, and the moving strips of black which had puzzled him were the shadows of the edges, moving across a black board which, set back the thickness of the partition, closed them.

"Peekholes," he thought, and then wondered anew. Why the lower row, then, so low that a man would have to kneel to look through the openings?" Peekholes," persisted hide-bound Experience, grabbing at the obvious. "Perhaps," doubted Suspicion; "but then, why that lower row?" Suddenly his gunman's mind exulted. "Peekholes above, an' loopholes below." A good gunman would not try to look through such small openings, nearly closed by the barrel of a rifle. But why a rifle, for a good gun man? "He'd need all of a hole to look through, an' a good gunman likes a hip shot. That's it: Eyes to th' upper, six-gun at th' lower, for a range too short to allow a miss."

He stirred, blinked at the gambling crowd and closed his eyes again. The sudden, gusty opening of the front door sent jets of soot spouting from the lamp chimneys and bits of rubbish skittering across the floor; and it also sent his hand to a gun-butt. He grunted as Red Thompson entered, folded his arms anew and dozed again, as a cynical smile flickered to Thorpe's face and quickly died. Bill shifted slightly. "Any place as careful in thinkin' out things as this place is will stand a lot of lookin' over," he thought. "Th' Lord help anybody that pulls a gun in this room. An' I'll bet a man like Kane has got more'n loop holes. I'm shore goin' to like his place."

Kit Thorpe had not missed the stranger's alert interest and motion at the opening of the door, but for awhile he did not move. Finally, however, he yawned, stretched, moved restlessly on his chair and then noisily arose and disappeared behind the partition, closing the checkered door after him. It was not his intention to sit so close to anyone who gave signs which indicated that he might be engaged in a shooting match at any moment. It would be better to keep watch from the side, well out of the line of fire.

Bill Long did not make the mistake of looking at the holes again, but dozed fitfully, starting at each gust which was strong enough to suggest the opening of the door. "I got to find th' way, an' that's all there is to it," he muttered. "How am I goin' to be welcome around here?"

Chapter V
What the Storm Hid

The squeaking of the door wakened Johnny and his gun swung toward the sound as a familiar face emerged from the dusk of the hall and smiled a little.

"Reckon it ain't no shootin' matter," said the sheriff, slowly entering. He walked over to a chair and sat down. "Just a little call in th' line of duty," he explained.

"Sorry there wasn't a bell hangin' on th' door, or a club, or something' ' replied Johnny ironically. "Then you could 'a' waited till I asked you to come in."

"That wouldn't 'a' been in th' line of duty," chuckled Corwin, his eyes darting from one piece of wearing apparel to another. "I'm lookin' around for th' fellers that robbed th' bank last night. Yore clothes don't hardly look dusty enough, though. Where was you last night, up to about one o'clock?"

"Down in th' barroom, playin' cards. Why?"

"That's what Ed says, too. That accounts for you durin' an' after th' robbery. I've got to look around, any how, for them coyotes."

"You'd show more sense if you was lookin' around for hoss tracks instead of wastin' time in here," retorted Johnny, keeping his head turned so the peace officer could not see what was left of the bump.

"There ain't none," growled Corwin, arising. "She's still blowin' sand a-plenty a couple of shacks are buried to their chimneys. I'm tellin' you this is th' worst sand storm that ever hit this town, but it looks like it's easin' up now. There won't be a trail left, an' th' scenery has shifted enough by this time to look like some place else. Idaho turn in when you did?"

"He did. Here he is now," replied Johnny, for the first time really conscious of the sand blasts which rasped against the windows.

Idaho peered around the door, nodded at Corwin and looked curious, and suspicious. "If I ain't wanted, throw me out," he said, holding up his trousers with one hand, the other held behind his back. "Hearin' voices, I thought mebby somebody was openin' a private flask an', bein' thirsty, I come over to help. My throat is shore dusty. 'An' would you listen to that wind? It shore rocked this old hotel last night. Th' floor of my room is near ankle deep in places."

"Th' bank was robbed last night," blurted Corwin, watching keenly from under his hat brim. "Whoever done it is still in town, unless he was ad d fool!"

Idaho grunted his surprise. "That so? Gee, they shore couldn't 'a' picked a better time," he declared. "Gosh, there's sand in my hair, even!"

Johnny rubbed his scalp, looked mildly surprised and slammed his sombrero on his head. "It ain't polite," he grinned, "but I got enough of it now." He sat up, crossed his legs under the sand-covered blankets and faced his visitors. "Tell us about it, Sheriff," he suggested.

"Wait till I get a belt," said Idaho, backing out of the door. When he returned he carried the rest of his clothes and started getting into them as the sheriff began his recital.

"John Reddy, th' bank watchman, says he was a little careless last night, which nobody can hardly blame him for. He sat in his chair agin' the rear wall, th' whole place under his eyes, an' listened to th' storm. To kill time he got to makin' bets with hisself about how soon th' second crack in th' floor would be covered over, an' then th' third, an' so on. 'Long about a little after twelve he says he hears a moan at th' back door. He pulls his gun an' listens close, down at th' crack just above th' sand drift. Then he hears it again, an' a scratchin' an clawin'. There's only one thing he's thinkin' about then how he'd feel if he was th' poor devil out there, lost an' near dead. I allus said a watchman should ought to have no feelin's, an' a cussed strong imagination. John ain't fillin' th' bill either way. He cleared away th' drift on his side of th' door an' opens it an' beyond rememberin' somethin' sandy jumpin' for him, that's all he knows till he come to later on an' found hisself tied up, with a welt on th' head that felt big as a doorknob."

If the sheriff expected to detect any interchange of glances between his auditors at his reference to the watch man's bump on the head he was disappointed. Johnny was looking at him with a frank interest seconded by that of Idaho, and neither did anything else during the short pause.

"John got his senses back enough to know what had happened, an' one glance around told him that he was right," continued Corwin. "Finally he managed to get his legs loose enough to hobble, an' he butted out into th' flyin' sand with his eyes shut an' his nose buried agin' his shoulder so he could breathe; an' somehow he managed to hit a buildin' in his blind driftin'. It was McNeil's, an' by throwin' his weight agin' th' door an' buttin' it with his shoulders an' elbows, he woke up Sam, who let him in, untied his arms an' th' rest of him, fixed him up as well as he could in a hurry an' then left him there. Sam got Pete Jennings, next door, sent Pete an' a scatter-gun to watch over what was left in th' bank, an' then started out to find me. He had to give it up till it got light, so he waited in th' bank with Pete. Th' bank fellers are there now, checkin' up. Th' big, burglar-proof safe was blowed open neat as a whistle but they plumb ruined th' little one. They overlooked th' biggest of all, down in th' cellar. Well," he sighed, arising, "I got to go on with my callin' an' it's one fine day to be wanderin' all over town."

"If I was sheriff I wouldn't have to do much wanderin'," said Idaho. "But, anyhow, it can't last," he grinned.

Johnny nodded endorsement. "Th' harder, th' shorter. It's gettin' less all th' time," he said, pivoting and sitting on the edge of the bed. "But, just th' same," he yawned, stretching ecstatically, "I'm shore-e-e g-l-a-d *I* can stay indoors till she peters out. Yo're plumb right, Corwin; them fellers never left town last night. An' if I was you I'd be cussed suspicious of anybody that seemed anxious to leave any time today."

"They never did leave town last night," said Idaho, a strange glint showing in his eyes.

"An' nobody can leave today, neither." said Corwin.

"If they try it they will be stopped," he added, pointedly. "I've got a deputy coverin' every way out, sand or no sand. So-long," and he tramped down the bare stairs, grumbling at every step.

Johnny removed his hat to put on his shirt, and then replaced it. "You speakin' about sand in yore hair gave me what I needed," he grinned.

"That's why I said it," laughed his companion. "I saw that yore neck was stiff an' felt sorry for you. Now what th' devil do you think about that bank?"

"Kane," grunted Johnny, pouring sand from a boot.

"That name must 'a' been cut on th' butt of th' gun that hit you," chuckled Idaho. "It's been drove in solid. Get a rustle on; I'm hungry, an' my teeth are full of sand. I'm anxious to hear what Ed knows."

An unpleasant and gritty breakfast out of the way, they went in to visit with the bartender and to while away a few hours at California Jack.

"Hello," grunted Ed. "Sheriff come pokin' his face in yore room?" he asked.

"He did," answered Johnny; "an' he'll never know how close he come to pokin' it into h< 1."

"My boot just missed him," regretted Ed. "He sung out right prompt when he felt th' wind of it. D d fourflush."

"I'm among friends an' sympathizers," chuckled Idaho. "He says as how he's goin' wanderin' around in th' sand blasts doin' his duty. Duty nothin'! I'm bettin' he's settin' in Kane's, right now, takin' it easy."

"Then he can't get much closer to 'em," snorted Ed "He can near touch th' men that did it." He paused as Johnny laughed in Idaho's face and, shrugging his shoulders, turned and rearranged the glasses on the backbar: "All right; laugh an' be damned!" he snorted; "but would you look at that shelf an' them glasses? Cuss any country that moves around like that. I bet I got some of them Dry Arroyo sand hills in them glasses!"

"There was plenty in th' hash this mornin'," said Idaho; "but it didn't taste like that Dry Arroyo sand. It wasn't salty enough. Gimme a taste of that."

"Just because you'll make a han'some corpse ain't no reason why you should be in any hurry," retorted Ed. "Here! "he snorted, tossing a pack of cards on the bar. "Go over an' begin th' wranglin' agin 'though th' Lord knows I ain't got no thin' agin' Nelson." He glanced out of the window. "Purty near bio wed out. It'll be ca'm in another half-hour; an' then you get to blazes out of here, an' stay out till dark!"

"I wish I had yore happy disposition," said Idaho. "I'd shore blow my brains out."

"There wouldn't be anythin' to clean up, anyhow!" retorted Ed. "Lord help us, here comes Silent Lewis!"

"Hello, fellers!" cried the newcomer. "Gee but it's been some storm. Sand's all over everythin'. Hear about th' bank robbery?"

"Bank robbery?" queried Ed, innocently. "What bank robbery? Sand bank?" he asked, sarcastically.

"Sand bank! Sand bank nothin'!" blurted Silent. "Ain't you heard it yet? Why, I live ten miles out of town, an' I know all about it."

"I believe every word you say," said Ed. "Tell us about it."

"Gee, where have you-all been?" demanded Silent "Why, John Reddy, settin' on his chair, watchin' th' safe, hears a moanin', so he opened th' door "

"Of th' safe?" asked Idaho, curiously.

"No, no; of th' bank. Th' bank door, th' rear one. He hears a moan "

"Which moan; first, or second?" queried Ed, anxiously.

"Th' first th' second didn't come till hey, I thought you didn't hear about it?" he accused.

"I didn't; but you mentions two moans, separate an' distinct," defended Ed.

"You shore did," said Idaho, firmly.

Johnny nodded emphatically. "Yessir; you shore did. Two moans, one at each end."

"But I didn't get to th' second moan at all!"

"Now, what's th' use of tellin' us that?" flared the bartender. "Don't you think we got ears?"

"If you can't tell it right, shut up," said Idaho.

"I can tell it right if you'll shut up!" retorted Silent. "As I said, he hears a moan, so he leaves th' safe an' goes to th' door. Then he hears a second moan, scratching an' "

"Hey I "growled Ed indignantly. "What you talkin' about? Who in h--l ever heard of a second moan scratchin' "

"It was th' first that scratched," corrected Idaho. "He said it plain. You must be listenin' with yore feet."

"If you'd gimme a chance to tell it "began Silent, bridling.

"Never mind my hearin' you," snapped Ed at Idaho.

"I know what I heard. An' lemme tell you, Silent, you can't cram nothin' like that down my throat. Before you go any further, just explain to me how a moan can scratch! I'm allus willin' to learn, but I want things explained careful an' full."

"He ain't quick-witted, like you an' me," said Johnny. "We understand how a scratch moans, but he's too dumb. Go on an' tell th' ignoramus."

"If yo're so cussed quick-witted, will you please tell me what'n blazes you are talkin' about?" demanded Silent, truculently. "What do you mean by a scratch moans?"

"That's what I want to know," growled Idaho. "You can't scratch moans. Cuss it, I reckon I ought to know, for I've tried to do it, more'n once, too."

"Yo're dumber than Nelson," jeered Ed. "It's all plain to me."

"What is?" snapped Idaho.

"Moanin' scratches, that's what!"

"Of a safe?" asked Johnny. "Then why didn't you say so? How'd *I* know that you meant that. Go on, Silent."

",You was at th' second moan," prompted Ed.

"He scratched that," said Idaho. "He got as far as leavin' th' safe, 'though what he was doin' in there with it, I'd like to know. Reddy let you in?"

"Look here, Idaho," scowled Silent. "I wasn't in there at all. You'll get me inter trouble, sayin' things like that. I was ten miles away when it happened."

"Then why didn't you say so, at th' beginnin'?" asked Ed.

"Ah!" triumphantly exclaimed Johnny. "Then you tell us how you could hear th' scratchin' an' moanin'; tell us that!"

"That's all right, Nelson," said Idaho, soothingly. "He can hear more things when he's ten miles away than any man you ever knowed. Go ahead, Silent."

"You go to h--l!" roared Silent, glaring. "You think yo're smart, don't you, all of you? I was goin' to tell you about th' robbery, but now you can cussed well find it out for yoreselves! An' don't let me hear about any of you sayin' I was in that bank last night, neither! D d fools!" and he stamped out, slamming the door behind him. "Blow an' be damned!" he growled at the storm. "I'd ruther eat sand than waste time with them ijuts. ' Scratch moans! ' Scratch."

Silent's departure left a more cheerful atmosphere in the barroom. The three men he had forsaken were grinning at each other, the petty annoyances of the storm for gotten, and the next hour passed quickly. At its expiration the wind had died down and the storm-bound town was free again. Ed finished cleaning the bar and the glassware about the time that his two friends had swept the last of the sand into the street and cleared away a drift which blocked the rear door. They were taking a congratulatory drink when Ridley, coming to town for the mail himself because he would not ask any of his men to face the discomforts of that ride, stamped in, and his face was like a thunder cloud.

"Gimme a drink!" he demanded, and when he had had it he swung around and glared at Idaho. "Lukins have any money in that bank? Yes? You better be off to let him know about it. H--l of a note: Thirty thousand stole! An' Jud Hill holdin' a gun on me when I rode into town, askin' fool questions! An' let me tell you somethin' judgin' from th' tools they forgot to take with 'em, it wasn't no amatachures that did that job. Diamond drills an' cow-country crooks don't know each other. An' that Jud Hill, a-stoppin' me!"

"Mebby he won't let you leave town," suggested Idaho. "Corwin's given orders like that."

Ridley crashed his fist on the bar, and then to better express his feelings he leaned over and stuck out his jaw. "Y-a-a-s? Then I'm invitin' you-all to Hill's funeral, an' Corwin's, too, if he cuts in! Thirty thousand! Great land of cows!"

"Corwin's out now, huntin' for 'em," said Ed.

"Is he?" sneered Ridley. "Then he wants to find 'em! Th' firm of Twitchell an' Carpenter owns near half of that bank every dollar th' Question-Mark has was in it. There's a change comin' to this part of th' country! "and he stamped out, mounted his horse and whirled down the trail. When he reached the sentry he rode so close to him that their legs rubbed and Hill's horse began to give ground.

"Do I go on?" snapped Ridley.

Jud Hill nodded pleasantly. "Shore. Seein' as how you come in this mornin' I reckon you do."

Ridley urged his horse forward without replying, reached the ranchhouse, wrote a letter which was a masterpiece of its kind and gave it to one of his men to post in Larkinville, twenty miles to the south. That done, all he could do was impatiently to await the reply.

After Ridley had left, Johnny went out to look after Pepper, found her all right, cleaned the sand out of the feed box and then went down to look at the bank. Four men with rifles were posted around it and waved him away. He could see several other men busy in the building, but beyond that there was nothing to claim his attention. Joining the small crowd of idlers across the street he listened to their conjectures, which were entirely vague and colorless, and then wandered back to look for Idaho in Quayle's. His friend was not to be seen and after exchanging a few words with the jovial proprietor he went in to talk with the bartender.

"No wind now, but my throat's dry. Gimme a drink, half water," and holding it untasted for the moment he jerked his head backward in the direction of the bank. "Nothin' to see, except some fellers inside lookin' for 'most anything an' four men with Winchesters on th' outside."

While he was speaking a man had entered and seated himself in the rear of the room. Johnny glanced carelessly at him, and the glass cracked sharply in his convulsive grip, the liquor squirting through his fingers and gathering a deeper color as it passed. A thin trickle of blood ran down his hand and wrist.

Ed had started at the sound and his head was bent forward, his unbelieving eyes staring at the dripping hand.

Johnny opened it slowly, shook the fragments from it and let it fall to his side, mechanically shaking off blood and liquor. "Cuss it, Ed," he gently reproved, looking calmly into the bartender's questioning face, "you should ought to pick out th' bad ones an' throw 'em away yes, an' bust 'em first."

Ed picked up the bottom of the glass and critically examined it, noting a discolored strip along one of the sharp edges, where dirt had accumulated from numberless washings. The largest fragment showed the greasy line to the rounded brim. "I usually do," he growled. "Thought I had this one, too. Must've got back somehow. Hurt bad?"

"Nothin' fatal, I reckon," answered Johnny, drawing the injured member up his trousers leg. "But I'm sayin' you owe me another drink; an' leave th' water out, this time. Water in whisky never does bring good luck, nohow."

Ed smiled, pushing out bottle and glass. "We might say that one was on th' house all that didn't get on you." He instinctively reached for and used the bar cloth as he looked over at the stranger. "I can promise you one that ain't cracked," he smiled.

"I'll take mine straight," said Bill Long. "I don't want no more hard luck."

"Wonder where Idaho is?" asked Johnny. "Well, if he comes in, tell him I'm exercisin' my cayuse. Reckon I'll go down an' chin with Ridley this afternoon. Th' south trail is less sandy than th' north one."

"An' give Corwin a chance to say things about you?" asked Ed, significantly. "He'll be lookin' for a peg to hang things on."

"Then mebby he won't never look for any more."

"That may be true; but what's th' use?"

"Reckon yo're right," reluctantly admitted Johnny. "Guess I'll go up to Kane's an' see what's happenin'. If Idaho comes in, or any more of my numerous friends," he grinned, "send 'em up there if they're askin' for me. I'll mebby be glad to see 'em," and he sauntered out.

Ed smiled pleasantly at the other customer. "Bad thing, a glass breakin' like that," he remarked.

Bill Long looked at him without interest. "Serves him right," he grunted, "for holdin' it so tight. Nobody was aimin' to take it away from him, was they?"

Johnny entered Kane's too busy thinking to give much notice to the room and the suppressed excitement occasioned by the robbery, and sat down at a table. As he leaned back in the chair he caught sight of a red-headed puncher talking to one of Kane's card-sharps and he got another shock. "Holy maverick!" he muttered, and looked carelessly around to see if any more of his Montana friends had dropped into town. Then he smiled as the card-sharp looking up, beckoned to him. As he passed down the room he noticed the quiet easterner hunched up in a corner, his cap well down over his eyes, and Johnny wondered if the man ever wore it any other way. He was out of place in his cow-town surroundings perhaps that was why he had not been seen outside of Kane's building. Ridley's remark about the tools came to him and he hesitated, considered, and then went on again. He had no reason to do Corwin's work for him. Dropping into a vacant chair at the gambler's table he grunted the customary greeting.

"Howd'y," replied the card-sharp, nodding pleasantly.

"No use bein' lonesome. Meet Red Thompson," he said, waving.

"Glad to meet you," said Johnny, truthfully, but hiding as well as he could the pleasure it gave him. "I once knowed a Thompson short, fat feller. Worked up on a mountain range in Colorado. Know him?"

Red shook his head. "Th' world's full of Thompsons," he explained. "You punchin'?"

"Got a job on th' SV, couple of days' ride north of here. Just come down with a little beef herd for Twitchell an' Carpenter. Ain't seen no good bunch of yearlin's that can be got cheap, have you?"

Red shook his head: "No, I ain't."

The gambler laughed and poked a lean thumb at the SV puncher. "Modest feller, he is," he said. "He's foreman, up there."

Red's mild interest grew a little. "That so? I passed yore ranch comin' down. Need another man?"

The SV foreman shook his head. "I could do with one less. Them bank fellers picked a good time for it, didn't they?"

"They shore did," agreed the gambler. "Couldn't've picked a better. Kane loses a lot by that, I reckon. Well, what do you gents say to a little game? Small enough not to cause no calamities; large enough to be interesting Nothin' else to do that I can see."

Red nodded and, the limit soon agreed upon, the game began. As the second hand was being dealt Bill Long wandered in, talked for a few moments with the bar tender and then went over to a chair. Tipping it back against the wall he pulled down his hat brim, let his chin sink on his chest and prepared to enjoy a nap. Naturally a man wishing to doze would choose the darkest corner, and if he was not successful who could tell that the narrow slit between his lids let his keen eyes watch everything worth seeing? His attention was centered mostly on the tenderfoot stranger with the low-pulled cap and the cut out squares in the great checkerboard partition at the rear of the room.

The poker game was largely a skirmish, a preliminary feeling out for a game which was among the strong probabilities of the future. Johnny and the gambler were about even with each other at the breaking up of the play, but Red Thompson had lost four really worth-while jack pots to the pleasant SV foreman. As they roughly pushed back their chairs Bill Long stirred, opened his eyes, blinked around, frowned slightly at being disturbed and settled back again. "Red couldn't 'a' got that money to him in no better way," he thought, contentedly.

The three players separated, Johnny going to the hotel, Red seeking a chair by the wall and the gambler loafing at the bar.

"An' how'd you find 'em?" softly asked the wise bar tender. "Coin' after that foreman's roll?"

The gambler grunted and shifted his weight to the other leg. "Thompson ain't very much; but I dunno about th' other feller. Sometimes I think one thing; sometimes, another. Either he's cussed innocent, or too slick for me to figger. Reckon mebby Fisher ought to go agin' him, an' find out, for shore."

"How'd you make out, last night, with Long?"

"There's a man th' boss ought to grab," replied the gambler. "He didn't win much from me but it's his first, an' last, chance with me. I don't play him no more. I'd like to see him an' Fisher go at it, with no limit. Fisher would have th' best of it on th' money end, havin' th' house behind him in case he had to weather a run of hard luck; but mebby he'd need it."

As the gambler walked away the easterner arose, slouched to the bar and held a short whispered conversation with the man behind it.

The bartender frowned. "You can't get away before night. Sandy Woods will take care of you before mornin', I reckon. Go upstairs an' quit fussin'. Yo're safe as h--l!"

The bartender's prophecy came true after dark, when Sandy Woods and the anxious stranger quietly left town together; but the stranger had good reason to be anxious, for at dawn he was careless for a moment and found him self looking into his escort's gun. He had more courage than good sense and refused to be robbed, and he died for it. Sandy dragged the body into a clump of bushes away from the trail and then rode on to kill the necessary time, leading the other's horse. He was five thousand dollars richer, and had proved wrong the old adage about honor among thieves.

Chapter VI
The Writing on the Wall

When the senior member of the firm of Twitchell and Carpenter read Ridley's letter things began to happen. It was the last straw, for besides being half-owners in the bank the firm had for several years been annoyed by depredations committed by Mesquite citizens on its herds. The depredations had ceased upon payment of "campaign funds "to the Mesquite political ring, but the blackmail levy had galled the senior member, who was not as prone as Carpenter was to buy peace. Orders flew from the firm's office and the little printing-plant at Sandy Bend broke all its hazy precedents, with the result that a hard-riding courier, relaying twice, carried the work of the job-print toward Mesquite. Reaching Ridley's domain he turned the package over to the local superintendent, who joyously mounted and carried it to town.

Tim Quayle welcomed his old friend, listened intently to what Ridley had to say and handed over an assortment of tacks and nails, and a chipped hammer. "'Tis time, Tom," he said, simply.

Ridley went out and selected a spot on the hotel wall, and the sound of the hammer and the sight of his unusual occupation caused a small crowd of curious idlers to gather around him. When the poster was unrolled there were sibilant whispers, soft curses, frank prophesies, and some commendations, which was entirely a matter of the personal viewpoint. Half an hour later, the last poster placed, Ridley took a short cut, entered the hotel through the kitchen and went into the barroom. What he had published for the enlightenment, edification, or disapprobation of his fellow-citizens was pointed and business-like, and read as follows:

$2,500.00 REWARD!

For Information Leading to the Capture and Conviction of the Men Who Robbed the Mesquite Bank.

TWITCHELL & CARPENTER

Sandy Bend TOM RIDLEY, Local Supt.

Quayle turned and smiled at the T & C man. "Ye've slapped their faces, Tom. Mind yore eye!"

"They've prodded th' old mosshead once too often," growled Ridley, looking around at Johnny, Idaho, and the others. "I reckon this stops th' blackmail to th' gang. When I wrote my letter I expected somethin' would hap pen, an' th' letter I got in return near curled my hair. Twitchell's fightin' mad."

"Th' reward's too big," criticized Idaho.

"I'm fearin' it ain't big enough," said Ed Doane, shaking his head.

Ridley laughed contentedly. "It's more than enough. There's men in this town, an' that gang, who would knife anybody for half of that. When they can get twenty-five hundred by simply openin' their mouths, without bein' known, they'll do it. Loyalty is fine to listen about, but there's few men in th' gang we're after that have any twenty-five hundred dollars' worth. This is th' beginnin' of th' end. Mark my words."

"A lot depends on how many were in on it," suggested Johnny, "an' how many of th' others know about it."

"He's throwin' money away," doggedly persisted Idaho. "A thousand would buy any of 'em, that an' secrecy."

"He ain't throwin' it away," retorted Ridley, "considerin' his letter. He's after results, amazin' results, an' he shore knows how to get 'em. It'll be sort of more pleasant if th' gang is sold out. He figgers a reward like that will save time an' be self-actin', for my orders are to stay in th' ranchhouse an' wait. That's what I'm goin' to do, too; an' I'll be settin' there with all guns loaded. No tellin' what'll happen now an', not bein' able to say how soon it will happen, I'm leavin' you boys. So-long."

He walked out to his horse and mounted. As he settled into the saddle there was a flat report, his hat flew from his head and he toppled from the horse, dead before he struck the ground.

Quayle swiftly reached over the desk and took a Winchester from its pegs, Irish tears in his eyes; and waited hopefully, Irish rage in his heart, watching the dirty windows and the open door. "It's to a finish, byes," he grated in a brogue thickened by his emotions, the veins of his forehead and neck swelling into serpentine ridges.

"They read th' writin' on th' wall, an' they read ut plain. D'ye mind what some of thim divils would be after doin' for all that money? They'd cut their own mither's throat an' Kane knows ut! An' I'm thinkin' they'll be careful now Kane has served his notice."

The idlers in the street stood as if frozen, gaping, not one of them daring to approach the body, nor even to stop the horse as it kicked up its heels and trotted down the street. Ed Doane was the third man through the door and he brought in the dead man's hat as Johnny and Idaho placed the warm body on the floor of the office. They hardly had stepped back when hurried footsteps neared the door and the sheriff, with two of his deputies, entered the office, paused instinctively at sight of the rifle in Quayle's hands, and then slowly, carefully bent over to examine the body. The sheriff reached forth a hand to turn it over, but stopped instantly and froze in his stooped position, his arm outstretched.

"Kape ut off him!" roared Quayle, his eyes blazing. "What more d'ye want to see?"

"From behind?" asked Corwin, slowly straightening up, but his eyes fixed on the proprietor.

"An' where'd ye be thinkin' 'twas from?" snarled Quayle, the veins standing out anew. "No dirty pup of that pack would dare try ut from th' front, an' ye know ut! An' need ye look twice to see where th' slug av a buffalo-gun came out? Don't touch him, anny av ye! Kape yore paws off Tom Ridley! An' I'm buryin' him, mesilf."

"But, as sheriff "began Corwin.

"Aye, but!" snapped Quayle. "We'll be after callin' things be their right names. Ye are no sheriff. Ye was choosed by th' majority av votes cast by th' citizens av an unorganized county, like byes choose a captain av their gangs. There's no laws to back ye up, an' ye took no oath. As long as th' majority will it, yore th' keeper av th' peace an' no longer. Sheriff?" he sneered. "An' 'tis a fine sheriff ye'll be makin', runnin' in circles like a locoed cow since th' robbery, questionin' every innocent man in town, an' hopin' 'twould blow over, an' die a natural death. But it's got th' breath av life in it now! What do ye think old Twitchell will be say in' to this" he thundered, his rigid arm pointing to the body on the floor. "Clear out, th' pack av ye! Ye've seen all ye need to!"

Corwin glanced at the body again, from it around the ring of set and angry faces, shrugged his shoulders and motioned to his deputies to leave. "We'll hold th' inquest here," he said, turning away.

"Ye'll hold no inquest!" roared Quayle. "Show me yore coroner! Inquest, is ut? I've held yore inquest already. There's plenty av us here an' we say, so help us God, Tom Ridley was murdered, an' by persons unknown. There's yer inquest, an' yer findin's. W r hat do ye say, byes?" he demanded. A low growl replied to him and he sneered again. "There! There's yer inquest! As long as yer playin' sheriff, go out an' do yer duty; but look out ye don't put yer han's on a friend! Clear out, an' run yer bluff!"

Corwin's eyes glinted as he looked at the fearless speaker, but with Idaho straining at a moral leash, Johnny's intent eagerness and the sight of the rifle in the proprietor's hands, he let discretion mold his course and slouched out to the street, where another quiet crowd opened silently to let him through.

Johnny passed close to Idaho. "Go to your ranch for a few days, or they'll couple you to me!" he whispered.

Bill Long, feeding his borrowed Highbank horse in the northernmost of the two stables at the rear of Kane's, heard the jarring crash of a heavy rifle so loud and near that he dropped instantly to hands and knees and crawled to a crack in the south wall. As he peered out he got a good, clear view of a pock-marked Mexican with a crescent-shaped scar over one eye and who, Sharp's in hand, wriggled out of the north window of the adjoining stable, dropped sprawling within five feet of the watcher's eyes, scrambled to his feet and fled close along the rear of Bill's stable. The watcher sprang erect, sped silently back to his horse and stirred the grain in the feed box with one hand, while the other rested on a six-gun in case the Mexican should be of an inquisitive and belligerent frame of mind. His view of the street had been shut off by the corner of the southern stable and he had not seen the result of the shot. Wishing to show no undue curiosity he did not go down the street, but returned to the gambling-hall. He had not been seated more than a few minutes when one of Kane's retainers ran in from the street with the news of Ridley's death. There was a flurry of excitement, which quickly died down, but under the rippling surface Bill sensed the deeper, more powerful currents.

"This man Kane, whoever an' wherever he is," he thought, "has shore trained this bunch of scourin's. I'm gettin' plumb curious for a look at him. Huh!" he muttered, as the window-wriggling, pock-marked Mexican emerged from behind the partition, bent swiftly over Kit Thorpe and betook his tense and nervous self to the roulette table. "I've got yore ugly face carved deep in my mem'ry, you Greaser snake!" he growled under his breath. "If it wasn't for loosin' bigger game I'd turn you over to Ridley's friends before night. You can wait."

Not long after the appearance of the Mexican, the sheriff came in by the front door, pushed through the crowd near the bar and walked swiftly toward the rear of the room. Speaking shortly to Kit Thorpe in a low voice he passed through the door of the checkerboard partition.

"I'm learnin'," muttered Bill. "I don't know who Kane is, but I'm dead shore I know where he is. An' I'm gettin' a better line on this killin'. I'll shore have to get a look behind that door, somehow."

Suddenly the doorkeeper arose and stuck his head around behind the partition and then, straightening up, closed the door, went up to the bar, spoke to several men there and led them to the rear. Opening the door again he let them through and resumed his vigil; and none of them reappeared before Bill went into the north building to eat his supper.

Chapter VII
The Third Man

Kane's gambling-hall was in full blast, reeking with the composite odor of liquor, kerosene lamps, rank tobacco, and human bodies, the tables well filled, the faro and roulette layouts crowded by eager devotees. The tenseness of the afternoon was forgotten and curses and laughter arose in all parts of the big room. The two-man Mexican orchestra strumming its guitars and the extra bartenders were earning their pay. Punchers, gamblers, storekeepers, two traveling men, a squad of cavalrymen on leave from the nearest post, Mexicans, and bums of several races made up the noisy crowd as Johnny Nelson pushed into the room and nodded to the head bartender.

"Well, well," smiled the busy barman without stopping his work. "Here's our SV foreman, out at night. Thought mebby you'd heard of some yearlin's an' hit th' trail after 'em."

"I don't reckon there was ever a yearlin' in this section," grinned Johnny.

"That so? There's several down at th' other end of th' bar," chuckled the man of liquor. "That blonde you left th' forty dollars for has shore been strainin' her eyes lookin' for you. Says she knows she's goin' to like you. Go back an' sooth her. Gin is her favorite."

"I ain't lookin' for her yet," replied Johnny. "That's somethin' you never want to do. It's th' wrong system. Don't pay no attention to 'em if you want 'em to pay attention to you. Let her wait a little longer. Where's that Thompson feller? I like th' way he plays draw, seein' as how I won some of his money. Seen him tonight?"

"Shore; he's around somewhere. Saw him a little while ago."

Johnny noticed a quiet, interested crowd in a far corner and joined it, working through until he saw two men playing poker in the middle. One was Bill Long and the other was Kane's best card-sharp, Mr. Fisher, and they were playing so intently as to be nearly oblivious of the crowd. On the other side of the ring, sitting on a table, was Red Thompson, his mouth partly open and his eyes riveted on the game.

The play was getting stiff and Fisher's eyes had a look in them that Johnny did not like. The gambler reached for the cards and began shuffling them with a speed and dexterity which bespoke weary hours of earnest practice. As he pushed them out for the cut his opponent leaned back, relaxed and smiled pleasantly.

"I allus like to play th' other fellow's game," Bill ob served. "If he plays fast *I* like to play fast; if he plays 'em close, *I* like to play 'em close; if he plays reckless, *I* like to play reckless; if he plays 'em with flourishes, *I* like to play 'em with flourishes. I'm not what you might call original. I'm a imitator." He slowly reached out his hand, held it poised over the deck, changed his mind and withdrew it. "Reckon I'll not cut this time. They're good as they are. I like yore dealin'."

Fisher yanked the deck to him and dealt swiftly. "I'm not very bright," he remarked as he glanced at his hand, "so I'm gropin' about yore meanin'. Or didn't it have none?"

"Nothin', only to show that I'm so polite I allus let th' other feller set th' pace," smiled Bill. "As he plays, I play." He picked up the cards, squared them into exact alignment and slid them from the table and close against his vest, where a deft touch spread them for a quick glance at the pips. "They look good; but, I wonder?" he muttered. "Reckon that's best, after all. Gimme two cards when you get time."

Fisher gave him two and took the same number.

"I find I'm gettin' tired," growled Bill, "an' it shore is hot an' stiflin' in here. As it stands I'm a little ahead not more'n fifty dollars. That bein' so, I quit after this hand and two more. There ain't much action, anyhow."

"If yo're lookin' for action mebby you feel like takin' off th' hobbles," suggested Fisher, carelessly.

"Hobbles, saddles an' anythin' else you can think of," nodded Bill. "Do we start now?"

Fisher nodded, saw the modest bet and doubled it.

Bill tossed his four queens and the ace of hearts face down in the discard and smiled. "Didn't get what I was lookin' for," he grinned into the set face across from him. "Got to have 'em before I can play 'em."

Fisher hid his surprise and carelessly 'tossed his four kings and the six of diamonds, also face down, into the discard, fumbled the deck as he went to pass it over and spilled it on top of the cards on the table. Cursing at his clumsiness, he scrambled the cards together and pushed them toward his opponent. "My fingers must be gettin' all thumbs," he growled as he raked in the money. What had happened? Had he bungled the deal, or wasn't four queens big enough for the talkative fool across from him?

Bill smilingly agreed. "They do get that way at times," he remarked, shuffling with a swift flourish which made Johnny hide a smile. He pushed the pack out, Fisher cut it, and the flying cards dropped swiftly into two neat piles almost flush on their edges, which seemed to merit a murmur of appreciation from the crowd. Johnny shifted his weight to the other leg and prepared to enjoy the game.

Fisher glanced at his hand and became instant prey to a turmoil of thoughts. Four queens, with an eight of clubs! He looked across at the calm, reflective dealer who was rubbing the disgraceful stubble on his chin while he drew two cards partly from his hand and considered them seriously. He seemed to be perplexed.

"I been playin' this game for more years than I feel like tellin'," Bill grumbled, whimsically; "but I ain't never been able really to decide one little thing." Becoming conscious that he might be delaying the game he looked up suddenly. "Have patience, friend. Oh, then it's all right! You ain't discarded yet," he finished cheerfully. Throwing away the two cards he waited.

"Gimme one," grunted Fisher, discarding, "an' I'm sayin' fifty dollars," he continued, shoving the money out without glancing at the card on the table. "How many you takin'?" he asked.

"Two," answered Bill, looking at him keenly. He glanced down at the single back showing on the table before him and grinned. "Th' other's under it," he explained needlessly. "Well, I'm still an imitator," he chuckled. "Here's yore fifty, and fifty more. I'm sorry I ain't playin' in my own town, so I could borrow when it all gets up."

Whatever Fisher's thoughts were he hid them well, and he was not to be the first one to weaken and look at the draw. He had a reputation to maintain, and he saw the raise and returned it Bill pushed out a hundred dollars and Fisher came back, but his tenseness was growing.

Bill considered, looked down at his unknown draw, shook his head and picked up one card. "I'm feelin' the strain," he growled, seeing the raise and repeating it. He glanced up at the crowd, which had grown considerably, and smiled grimly.

Fisher evened up and raised again, watching his worried opponent, who scowled, sucked his lips, shook his head and then, with swift decision, picked up the other card. "I can't afford to quit now," he muttered. "Here goes for another boost!"

His opponent having wilted first and saved the gambler's face, Fisher picked up his own draw and when he saw it he stiffened, his thoughts racing again. It was no coincidence, he decided. In all of his experience he had known but two men who could do that, and here was a third! But still there was a hope that there was no third, that it was a coincidence. And there was quite a sum of money on the table. The doubt must be removed and the truth known, and another fifty, sent after its brothers was not too big a price to pay for such knowledge. He pushed the money out onto the table. "I calls," he grunted.

Bill dropped his little block of cards and spread them with a sweep of one hand, while the other was ready to make the baffling draw which had made him famous in other parts of the country. Fisher glanced at the four kings and nodded, all doubts laid to rest the third man sat across from him.

He slowly pushed back as the crowd, not knowing just what to expect, scattered. "I'm tired. Shall we call it off for tonight?" he asked.

Without relaxing Bill nodded. "Suits me. I'm tired, too; an' near suffocated. See you to-morrow?"

Fisher grunted something as he arose and, turning abruptly, pushed through the thinning crowd to get a bracer at the bar, while the winner slowly hauled in the money. Gulping down the fiery liquor the gambler wheeled to go into the dark and deserted dining-room where he could sit in quiet and go over the problem again, and looked up to see the other gambler in his way.

"What did you find out?" asked the other in a low voice.

"I found th' devil has come up out of h--l!" growled Fisher. "Come along an' I'll tell you about it. He's th' third man! Old Parson Davies was th' first, but he's dead; Tex Ewalt was th' second, an' I ain't seen him in years cuss it! I wondered why this man's play seemed familiar! He's got some of Tex's tricks of handlin' th' cards."

"Shore he ain't Tex?"

"As shore as I am that you ain't," retorted Fisher; "but I'm willin' to bet he knows Tex. Come on let's get out of this hullabaloo. He's got a nerve, pickin' my cards, an' dealin' 'em alternate off th' top an' bottom, with me watchin' him!"

"We got to figger how to get it back," thoughtfully muttered the other, following closely. "Everythin's goin' wrong. They went after Nelson an' got somebody else; they stirred up th' T & C by robbin' th' bank, an' then had to go an' make it worse by gettin' Ridley! I'm admittin' I'm walkin' soft, an' ready to jump th' country right quick."

Fisher sank into a chair in the dining-room. "An' if Long hangs around here much longer Kane'll ditch me like a wore-out boot. A couple more losses like tonight an' he'll plumb forget my winnin's for th' past two years. An' me gettin' all cocked to strike him for a bigger per centage!"

Out in the reeking gambling-hall Bill put his empty glass on the bar and slid a gold piece at the smiling head man behind the counter. "Spend th' change on th' ladies in th' corner," he said. "It allus gives me luck; an' I had such luck tonight that I ain't aimin' to take no chances losin' it. Reckon I'll horn in on th' faro layout," and he did, where he managed to lose a part of his poker winnings before he turned in for the night.

Up late the next morning he hastened into the diningroom to beat the closing of the doors and saw the head bartender eating a lonely breakfast. The dispenser of liquors beckoned and pushed back a chair at his table.

Bill accepted the invitation and gave his order. "Well," he remarked, "yo're lookin' purty bright this mornin'.'"

"I'm gettin' so I don't need much sleep, I reckon," replied the bartender. "Did yore folks use a poker deck to cut yore teeth on?"

Bill laughed heartily. "My luck turned, an' Fisher happened to be th' one that got in th' way."

"He says you play a lot like a feller he used to know."

"That so? Who was he?"

"Tex Ewalt."

"Well, I ought to, for me an' Tex played a lot together, some years back. Wonder what ever happened to Tex? He ain't been down this way lately, has he?"

"No. I never saw him. Fisher knew him. He says Tex was th' greatest poker player that ever lived."

"I reckon he's right/' replied Bill. "I'm plumb grateful to Tex. It ain't his fault that I don't play a better game. But I got an idea playin' like his has got to be born in a man." He ate silently for a moment. "Now that I'm spotted I reckon my poker playin' is over in here. Oh, well, I ain't complainin'. I can eat an' sleep here, an' find enough around town to keep me goin' for a little while, anyhow. Then I'll drift."

"Unless, mebby, you play for th' house," suggested the bartender. "What kind of a game does that SV foreman play?"

"I never like to size a man up till I play with him," answered Bill. "I was sort of savin' him for myself, for he's got a fat roll. Now I reckon I'll have to let somebody else do th' brandin'." He sighed and went on with his breakfast.

"Get him into a little game an' see how good he is," suggested the other, arising. "Goin' to leave you now." He turned away and then stopped suddenly, facing around again. "Huh! I near forgot. Th' boss wants to see you."

"Who? Kane? What about?"

"He'll tell you that, I reckon."

"All right. Tell him I'm in here."

The other grinned. "I said th' boss wants to see you"

"Shore; I heard you."

"People he wants to see go to him."

"Oh, all right; why didn't you say so first off? Where is he?"

"Thorpe will show you th' way. Whatever th' boss says, don't you go on th' prod. If yore feelin's get hurt, don't relieve 'em till you get out of his sight."

"I've played poker too long to act sudden," grinned Bill, easily.

His breakfast over, he sauntered into the gambling room and stopped in front of Kit Thorpe, whose welcoming grin was quite a change from his attitude of the day before. "I've been told Kane wants to see me. Here I am."

Thorpe opened the door, followed his companion through it and paused to close and bolt it, after which he kept close to the other's heels and gave terse, grunted directions. "Straight ahead to th' left to th' right straight ahead. Don't make no false moves after you open that door. Go ahead push it open."

Bill obeyed and found himself in an oblong room which ran up to the opaque glass of a skylight fifteen feet above the floor, and five feet below the second skylight on the roof, in both of which the small panes were set in heavy metal bars. The room was cool and well ventilated.

Before him, seated at the far side of a flat-topped, walnut desk of ancient vintage sat a tall, lean, white-haired man of indeterminate age, who leaned slightly forward and whose hands were not in sight.

"Sit down," said Kane, in a voice of singular sweetness and penetrating timbre. For several minutes he looked at his visitor as a buyer might look at a horse, silent, thoughtful, his deeply-lined face devoid of any change in its austere expression.

"Why did you come here?" he suddenly snapped.

"To get out of th' storm," answered Bill.

"Why else?"

Bill looked around, up at the graven Thorpe and back again at his inquisitor, and shrugged his shoulders. "Mebby you can tell me," he answered before he remembered to be less independent.

"I think I can. Anyone who plays poker as well as you do has a very good reason for visiting strange towns. What is your name?"

"Bill Long."

"I know that. I asked, what is your name?"

Bill looked around again and then sat up stiffly. "That ain't interestin' us."

"Where are you from?"

Bill shrugged his shoulders and remained silent.

"You are not very talkative today. How did you get that Highbank horse?"

Bill acted a little surprised and anxious. "L I don't know," he answered foolishly.

"Very well. When you make up your mind to answer my questions I have a proposition to offer you which you may find to be mutually advantageous. In the mean while, do not play poker in this house. That's all."

Thorpe coughed and opened the door, and swiftly placed a hand on the shoulder of the visitor. "Time to go," he said.

Bill hesitated and then slowly turned and led the way, saying nothing until he was back in the gambling-hall and Thorpe again kept his faithful vigil over the checkered door.

"Cuss it," snorted Bill, remembering that in the part he was playing he had determined to be loquacious. "If I told him all he wanted to know I'd be puttin' a rope around my neck an' givin' him th' loose end! So he's got a proposition to make, has he? Th' devil with him an' his propositions. I don't have to play poker in his place there's plenty of it bein' played outside this buildin', I reckon. For two-bits I'd 'a' busted his neck then an' there!"

"You'd 'a' been spattered all over th' room if you'd made a play," replied Thorpe, a little contempt in his voice for such boasting words from a man who had acted far from them when in the presence of Kane. He had this stranger's measure. "An' you mind what he said about play in' in here, or I'll make you climb up th' wall, you'll be that eager to get out. You think over what he said, an' drift along. I'm busy."

Bill, his frown hiding inner smiles, slowly turned and walked defiantly away, his swagger increasing with the distance covered; and when he reached the street he was exhaling dignity, and chuckled with satisfaction he had seen behind the partition and met Kane. He passed the bank, once more normal, except for the armed guards, and bumped into Fisher, who frowned at him and kept on going.

"Hey!" called Bill. "I want to ask you somethin'."

Fisher stopped and turned. "Well?" he growled, truculently.

Bill went up close to him. "Just saw Kane. He says he has got somethin' to offer me. What is it?"

"My job, I reckon!" snapped the gambler.

"Yore job?" exclaimed his companion. "I don't want yore job. If I'd 'a' knowed that was it I'd 'a' told him so, flat. I'm playin' for myself. An' say: He orders me not to play no more poker in his place. Wouldn't that gall you?"

"Then I wouldn't do it," said the gambler, taking his arm. "Come in an' have a drink. What else did he say?"

Bill told him and wound up with a curse. "An' that Thorpe said he'd make me climb up th' wall! Wonder who he thinks he is Bill Hickok?"

Fisher laughed. "Oh, he don't mean nothin'. He's a lookin'-glass. When Kane laughs, he laughs; when Kane has a sore toe, he's plumb crippled. But, just th' same I'm tellin' you Thorpe's a bad man with a gun. Don't rile him too much. Say, was you ever paired up with Ewalt?"

Bill put down his glass with deliberate slowness. "Look here!" he growled. "I'm plumb tired of answerin' personal questions. Not meanin' to hurt yore feelin's none, I'm sayin' it's my own cussed business what my name is, where I come from, who my aunt was, an' how old I was when I was born. I never saw such an' oldwoman's town!"

Fisher laughed and slapped his shoulder. "Keep all four feet on th' ground, Long; but it is funny, now ain't it?"

Bill grinned sheepishly. "Mebby but for a little while I couldn't see it that way. Have one with me, after which I'm goin' up an' skin that SV man before you can get a crack at him. He's fair lopsided with money. If I can't play poker in Kane's, I shore can send a lot of folks to his place with nothin' left but their pants an' socks!"

"Don't overdo it," warned Fisher. "Come on I'm headin' back an' I'll leave you at Quayle's."

"How'd you ever come to let that yearlin'-mad fore man keep away from yore game?" asked Bill as they started up the street. "Strikes me you shore overlooked somethin'."

"Does look like it, from a distance," admitted Fisher, grinning. "Reckon we was goin' too easy with him; but we didn't know you was goin' to turn up an' horn in. We never like to stampede a good prospect by bein' hasty. We felt him out a little an' I was figgerin' on amusin' him right soon. There's somethin' cussed queer about him. We're all guessin', an' guessin' different"

"Yes?" inquired Bill carelessly. "I didn't notice nothin' queer about him. He acts a little too shore of hisself, which is how I like 'em. You ain't got a chance to get him now, for I'm goin' to set on his fool head an' burn a nice, big BL on his flank. So any little thing that you know shore will come in handy. I'd do th' same for you. I'm through spoilin' yore game in Kane's, an' I didn't take yore job. What's so queer about him?"

Fisher glanced at his companion and shook his head. "It ain't nothin' about cards. He figgered in a mistake that was made, an' don't know how lucky he was. Th' boss don't often slip up an' there's a white man an' some Greasers in this town that are cussed lucky too. They blundered, but they got what they went after. An' nobody's heard a word about th' gent that was unlucky, which makes me suspicious. I got a headache tryin' to figger it." He shook his head again and then exclaimed in sudden anger: "An' I've quit tryin'! Kane was all set to throw me into th' discard as soon as you come along. He can think what he wants to, for all I care. But let me tell you this: If you win a big roll in this town, an' th' one you got now is plenty big enough, be careful how you wander around after dark. I reckon I owe you that much, anyhow."

Bill stopped in front of the hotel. "I don't know what yo're talkin' about, but that don't make no difference. Th' last part was plain. Come in an' have somethin'."

Fisher looked at him and smiled. "Friend, I'd just as soon be seen goin' in there now as I would be seen rustlin' a herd; an' it might even be worse for me. Let it go till you come up to our place. Adios."

Chapter VIII
Notes Compared

Entering the barroom of the hotel Bill bought a cigar, talked aimlessly for a few minutes with Ed Doane and then wandered into the office, where Johnny was seated in a chair tipped back against the wall and talking to the proprietor. Bill nodded, took a seat and let himself into the conversation by easy stages, until Quayle was talking to him as much as he was to Johnny, and the burden of his words was Ridley's death.

Bill spat in disgust. "That ain't th' way to get a man!" he exclaimed. "Looks like some Greaser had a grudge agin' him somebody he's mebby fired off his payroll, or suspected of cattle-liftin'."

"You're a stranger here," replied the proprietor. "I can tell it."

"I am, an' glad of it," replied Bill, smiling; "but I'm learnin' th' ways of yore town rapid. I already know Fisher's poker game, Thorpe's nature, an' Pecos Kane's looks an' disposition. I cleaned Fisher at poker, Thorpe has threatened to make me climb up a wall, an' Kane told me, cold an' personal, to quit playin' poker in his place. I also learned that a white man an' some Greasers made a big mistake, but got what they went after; that Fisher riggers different from Kane an' th' others; an' that Kane won't slip up th' next time, after dark, 'specially if he don't use th' same fellers. All that I heard; but what it's about I don't know, or care."

Johnny was laughing at the humor of the newcomer, and waved from Bill to Quayle. "Tim, this is Bill Long, that we heard about, for I saw him clean out Fisher. Long, this is Quayle, an' my name's Nelson. Cuss it, man! I'd say you was gettin' acquainted fast. What was that you was sayin' about th' white man an' th' Greasers, an' some mistake? It was sort of riled up."

"It riled up," chuckled Bill, crossing his legs. "I gave it out just like I got it. As I says to Fisher last night, I'm a imitator. Any news about th' robbery?"

Quayle snorted. "Fine chance! An' d'ye think they'd be after tellin' on thimselves? That's th' only way for any news to be heard."

"I may be a stranger," replied Bill; "but I'm no stranger to human nature, which is about th' same in one place as it is in another. If that reward don't pan out some news, then I'm loco."

Quayle listened to a call from the kitchen. "It's th' only chance, then," he flung over his shoulder as he left them. "It's that damned Mick. I'll be back soon."

Johnny, with a glance at the barroom door, leaned slightly forward and whispered one word, his eyes moist: "Hoppy!"

Bill Long squirmed and grinned. "You flat-headed sage-hen!" he breathed. "*I want to see you in secret.*"

Johnny nodded. "I reckon th' reward might start somethin' out in th' open, but I wouldn't want to be th' man that tried for it." His voice dropped to a whisper.

"We'll take a ride this afternoon from Kane's, plain an' open." In his natural voice he continued. "But, Twitchell an' Carpenter are shore powerful. An' they've got th' men an' th' money."

"Do you reckon anybody had a personal grudge?" asked Bill. "I'll fix it."

"I'm near as much a stranger here as you are," answered Johnny, "though I sold Ridley some cattle. I met him before, on th' range around Gunsight. Nice feller, he was. What time?"

"He must 'a' been a good man, to work for th' T & C," replied Bill. "After dinner."

"He was."

"Oh, well; it ain't my funeral. Feel like a little game?"

"I used to think I could play poker," chuckled Johnny; "but I woke up last night. Seein' as how I still got them yearlin's to buy, I don't feel like playin'."

Quayle's voice boomed out suddenly from the kitchen. "If yer fingers was feet ye'd be as good! Hould it, now if ut slips this time I'll be after bustin' yer head. I've showed ye a dozen times how to put it back, an' still ye yell fer me. There, now hould it! Hand me th' wire annybody'd think blast th' blasted man that made ut! Some Dootchman, I'll wager."

"Shure an' we ought to get a new wan it's warped crooked, an' cracked "

"We should, should we?" roared the proprietor. "An' who are 'we'? Only tin years old, an' it's a new wan we'd be gettin', is ut? What we ought to be gettin' is a new cook, an' wan that's not cracked. Now, th' nixt time ye poke ut, poke gintly ye ain't makin' post holes with that poker. An' now look at me "A door slammed and a washbasin sounded like tin.

Ed Doane's laugh sounded from the barroom and he appeared in the doorway, where he grinned. "I hear it frequent, but it's allus funny. Sometimes they near come to blows."

"Stove?" queried Bill.

"Shore th' grate's buckled out of shape, an' it's a little short. Murphy gets mad at th' fire an' prods it good an' then th' show starts all over again. It's funnier than th' devil when th' old man gets a blister from it, for he talks so that nobody but Murphy can understand one word in ten. Easy! Here he comes."

"Buy a new wan, is ut?" muttered the proprietor, his red face bearing a diagonal streak of soot. "Shure for him to spile, like he spiled this wan. Ah, byes, I'm tellin' ye th' hotel business ain't what it used to be."

"Yore face looks funny," said Ed.

Quayle turned on him. "Oh, it does, does ut? Well, if my face don't suit ye now would ye look at that?" he demanded as he caught sight of his reflection in the dingy mirror over the desk. "But it ain't so bad, at that; th' black's above th' red!"

"Hey, Tim!" came from the kitchen. "Thought ye said ye fixed ut? Ut's down agin!"

"I--I--I!" sputtered Quayle wildly. He spread the soot over his face with a despairing sweep of his sleeve, leaped into the air and started on a lumbering run for the kitchen. "You--I--damn it!" he yelled, and the kitchen resounded to his bellowing demands for the cook.

Ed Doane wiped his eyes, looked around and shouted, his out-thrust hand pointing to a window, where a red face peered into the room.

"Shure," said the cook, apologetically, "he's the divvil himself. If I stay here wan more day me name ain't Murphy. Will wan av yez, that ain't go no interest in th' dommed stove, tell that Mick to buy a new grate? An' would ye listen to him, now?"

When he was able to Bill arose. "Well, I reckon I'll go up an' look in at Kane's. If I run this way, don't stop me."

Sauntering up the street he came to the south side of the gambling-hall and went along it, and when a certain number of paces beyond the fifth high window, the sill of which was above his head, he stumbled and fell. Swearing under his breath he picked up a Colt which had slipped from its holster and, arising to hands and knees, looked around and then stood up.

He could see under the entire building except at the point where he had fallen, and there he saw that under Kane's private room the walls went down into the earth. When he reached the stables he entered the one which sheltered his horse, closed the door behind him and made a hasty examination of the building, but found nothing which made him suspect a secret exit. He came to the opinion that the boards went down to the earth below Kane's quarters for the purpose of not allowing anyone to crawl under his rooms. In a few minutes he led his horse outside, mounted and rode around to the front of the gambling-hall, where he dismounted and went in for a drink, scowling slightly at the vigilant and militant Mr. Thorpe, who returned the look with interest.

"Got a cayuse?" he asked the bartender.

The other shook his head. "No, why?"

"Thought mebby you'd like to ride along with me. That one of mine will be better for a little exercise. What's east of here?"

"Sand hills, dried lakes, an' th' desert."

"Then I'll go west," grinned Bill. "But mebby it's th' same?"

"It ain't bad over that way; but why don't you ride south? There's real good country down in them valleys."

"Ain't that where th' T & C is?"

The bartender nodded.

"West is good enough for me. Better get a cayuse an' come along."

"Can't do it, an' I ain't set a saddle in two years. I'd be a cripple if I stuck to you. Why don't you hunt up that Nelson feller? He ain't got nothin' to do."

"Just left him. Don't reckon he'd care to go. Huh!" he muttered, looking at the clock. "I reckon I'll eat first, an' ride after."

Shortly after dinner Johnny strolled in and nodded to the bartender, who immediately called to Bill Long.

"Here's Nelson now; mebby he'll go with you," he said.

"Go where?" asked Johnny, pausing.

"Ridin'."

"What for?"

"Exercise. He wants to take th' devilishness out of his horse. You got one, too, ain't you?"

"Shore have," answered Johnny. "An' she's gettin' mean, too. It ain't a bad idea. Where are you goin', Long?"

"Anywhere, everywhere, or nowhere," answered Bill carelessly. "I'm aiming to ride him to a frazzle, an' I got to cut down his feed more."

"All right, if you says so," agreed Johnny, joining the group.

Red Thompson rode up to the door and came in. "Hey, anybody that's goin' down th' trail wants to ride easy. That T & C gang are so suspicious that they're insultin'. Got four men ridin' along their wire, with rifles across their pommels. Looks like they was goin' on th' prod."

Thorpe silently withdrew, to reappear in a few minutes and resume his watch.

Bill arose and nodded to Johnny as he went out. "Ready, Nelson?" he asked.

In a few minutes they met in front of the gambling-hall, and the SV foreman's black caused admiring and covetous looks to show on the faces of the idle group.

"Foller th' trail leadin' to Lukins' ranch, over west," suggested Fisher. "It's better than cross-country. You'll strike it half a mile above."

Long nodded and led the way, both animals prancing and bucking mildly to work off some of their accumulated energy. Reaching the cross trail they swung along it at a distance-eating lope.

"Tell me about everything" suggested Johnny. "How'd you come to ride south?"

"Kid," said Hopalong, "you got th' best cayuse ever raised in Montanny. That Englishman was shore right: it pays to cross 'em with thoroughbreds." Moodily silent for a moment, he slowly continued. "Kid, I've lost Mary, an' William, Junior. Fever took 'em in four days, an' never even touched me! I'm all alone. Either you move up north, or I stay with you till I die.

An' if I do that I'll miss Red an' th' others like th' devil. I'm goin' to have a good look at that Bar-H, that you chased them thieves off of. Montanny is too far north, an' I'm feelin' th' winters too hard. An' it's gettin' settled too fast, an' bein' ploughed up more every year. But all of this can wait: what's goin' on down here that I don't know?"

Johnny told him and when he had finished and listened to what his friend knew they spent the rest of the time discussing the situation from every angle and arranged a few simple signals, resurrected from the past, to serve in the press of any sudden need. They met two punchers riding in from Lukins' ranch, exchanged nods and then turned south into the cattle trail, crossed a crescent arroyo and turned again, when below the town, under the suspicious eyes of a Question-Mark sentry hidden in a thicket. Following the main trail north they entered the town and parted at Quayle's.

The evening passed uneventfully in Kane's and when the group began to break up Bill Long went up to his room. Gradually man after man deserted the gambling hall, until only Johnny and the head bartender were left, and after half an hour's dragging conversation the dispenser of liquids yawned and nodded decisively.

"Nelson, I'm goin' to lock up after you. See you tomorrow."

"Most sensible words said tonight," replied Johnny, and he stepped out, the door closing behind him. The lights went out, one by one, with a tardiness due to their height from the floor, and he stood quietly for a moment, scrutinizing the sky and enjoying the refreshing coolness.

Moving out into the middle of the street he sauntered toward the dark hotel, every sense alert as a previous experience came back to him. Suddenly a barely audible sound, like the cracking of a toe joint, caused him to leap aside. An indistinct figure plunged past him, so close that he felt the wind of it. His gun roared while he was in the air and when he alighted he was crouched, facing the rear, where another figure blundered into the second shot and dropped. Swiftly padding feet came nearer and he slipped further to the side, letting the sound pass with out hindrance. Moving softly forward he turned and crept along the wall of a building, smiling grimly at the low Spanish curses behind him on the street Again the kitchen door served him well and the deeper blackness of the interior silently engulfed him.

Up at Kane's, Red Thompson, who was awake and waiting until the building should be wrapped in sleep, heard the shots and crept to the window. He could see nothing, but he heard whispers and heavy, slow and shuffling steps, which drew steadily nearer. The Mexican tongue was no puzzle to Red, whose years largely had been spent in a country where it was constantly used and his fears, instantly aroused, were soon followed by a savage grin.

"That Nelson, he is a devil," floated up to him, the words a low growl.

"Again he got away. I will not face the Big Boss. It is the second failure, and with Anton dead, an' Juan's arm broken, I shall leave this town. Put him here, at the door. May God forgive his sins! Adios!"

"Wait, Sanchez!" called a companion. "We will all go, even Juan, for he'd better ride than remain. There will be trouble."

"What's all th' hellabaloo?" came Thorpe's truculent voice in English from the corner of the building, where he stood, clad only in boots and underwear, a six-shooter in his upraised hand. At the sudden soft scurrying of feet he started forward, and then checked himself.

"If them Greasers bungled it this time, may th' Lord help 'em. They'll shore get a-plenty. I wouldn't be " he stopped and stared at the door, and then moved closer to it. "By G-d, they got him!" he whispered, and bent down, his hand passing over the indistinct figure. "Huh! I take it all back," he muttered in disgust. "That's a Greaser, by feel an' smell. They made more of a mess of it this time than they did before. Well, you ain't no fit ornament for th' front door. Might as well move you myself," and, grumbling, he grabbed hold of the collar and dragged the unresisting bulk around to the rear, where he carelessly dropped it and went back into the building. Soon two Mexicans, rubbing sleepy eyes, emerged with shovel and spade, that the dawn should find nothing more than a carefully hidden grave.

Red waited a little longer and then, knowing better than to go on his feet along the old floor of the hall, inched slowly over it on his stomach, careful to let each board take his weight gradually. Reaching the second door on his left he slowly pushed it open, chuckling with pride at his friend's forethought in oiling the one squeaking hinge. Closing it gently he scratched on the floor twice and then went on again toward the answering scratch. An hour passed in the softest of whispering and when he at last entered his own room again and carefully stood up, the darkness hid a rare smile on his tanned and leathery face, which an exultant thought had lighted.

"Th' Old Days: They're comin' back again!" he gloated. "Me, an' Hoppy, an' the Kid! Glory be!" and the smile persisted until he awakened at dawn, when it moved from the wrinkled face to the secrecy of his heart,

Chapter IX
Ways of Serving Notice

If Sandy Bend had been seized with a local spasm when the senior member of the T & C had learned of the robbery of the Mesquite bank, it now was having a very creditable fit. The little printing-shop was the scene of bustling activities and soon a small bundle of handbills was on its way to the office of the cattle king. McCullough, drive-boss par excellence and one of the surviving frontiersmen who not only had made history in several localities, but had helped to wear the ruts in the old Santa Fe Trail until the creeping roadbed of the railroad had put the trail with other interesting relics of the past, was rudely torn from his seven-up game with his cronies by one of the several couriers who lathered horses at the snapping behest of the senior partner. He hastened to the office, rumbled across the outer room and pushed open the door of the holy of holies without even the semblance of a knock. He was blunt, direct, and no respecter of persons.

"Hello, Charley!" he grunted. "What's loose now?"

"Hell's loose!" snapped Twitchell. "Ridley's been murdered by one of Kane's gang. Shot in th' back —head near blowed off. There's only four men up there now, an' they may be dead by this time. Take as many men as you need an' go up there we just bought a herd of SV cows, if there's any left. But I want th' man that killed Ridley. That's first. I want th' man who robbed th' bank that's second. An' I want Pecos Kane that's first, second, an' third. D n it! I growed up with Tom Ridley!"

"I'll take twenty men an' bring you th' whole gang but some of 'em will shore spoil before we can get 'em here, this kind of weather. Do I burn that end of th' town?"

"You'll burn nothin'," retorted Twitchell. "You'll not risk a man until you have to. You'll stay on th' ranch an' watch th' cattle. I've lost one good man now, an' I'm spendin' money before I risk losin' any more. There's a bundle of handbills. When they've been digested by that bunch of assassins you can sit in th' bunkhouse an' have yore game delivered to you, all tied up, an' tagged."

"Orders is orders," growled McCullough; "but some are damned fool orders. If you want somebody to set on th' front porch an' whittle, why'n h--l are you cuttin' me out of th' herd for th' job?"

"I'm cuttin' you out because I want my best man out there!" retorted the senior member heatedly. "You may find it lively settin',-an' have to do yore whittlin' with rifles an' six-guns. Look out that somebody don't whittle you at eight hundred while yo're settin' on th' front porch! You talk like you think yo're goin' to a prayer meetin'!"

"I'm hopin' they come that close," said McCullough, picking up the package of bills. "So Tom's gone, huh? Charley, there ain't many of us left no more. Remember how you an' Ridley an' me used to go off trappin' them winters, hundreds of miles into th' mountains, with only what we could easy carry on our backs? That was livin'."

"You get out of here, you old fraud!" roared Twitchell. "Ain't I got enough to bother me now? Take care of yoreself, Mac; an' my way's worth tryin', an' tryin' good. If it don't work, then we'll have to try yore way."

"All right; I'll give it a fair ride, Charley; but it will be time wasted," replied the trail-boss. "In that case I'm takin' a dozen men. We relay at th' Squaw Creek corrals, an' again at Sweetwater Bottoms. Send a wagon after us you'll know what we'll need. You send a new boss to th' Sweetwater, for I'm pickin' up Waffles. He's one of th' best men you got, an' he's been picketed at that twobits station long enough."

"Good luck, Mac. Take who you want. Yo're th' boss. Any play you make will be backed to th' limit by th' T&C."

When McCullough got outside he found a crowd of men which the hard-riding couriers had sent in from all parts of the town. They shouted questions and got terse answers as he picked his dozen, the twelve best out of a crowd of good men, all known to him in person and by deeds. The lucky dozen smiled exultantly at the scowling unfortunates and dashed up the street in a bunch after their grizzled pacemaker. One of the last, glancing be hind him, saw a stern- faced, sorrowful man in a black store suit standing in the office door looking wistfully after them; and the rider, gifted with understanding, raised his hand to his hat brim and faced around.

"Th' old man's sorry he's boss," he confided to his nearest companion.

"An' there's plenty up in Mesquite that will be th' same," came the reply.

Despite his years McCullough held his lead without crowding from the rear, for he was of the hard-riding breed and toughened to the work. When the first relay was obtained at Squaw Creek that evening there were several who felt the strain more than the leader. A hasty supper and they were gone again, pounding into the gathering dusk of the northwest. All night they rode along a fair trail, strung out behind a man who kept to it with uncanny certainty. Dawn found them changing mounts in Sweetwater Bottoms, but without the snap displayed at the Squaw. Waffles, one-time foreman of the O-Bar-O, needed all his habitual repression to keep from favoring them with a war dance when he heard his luck. Impatiently waiting for the surprised but enthusiastic cook to prepare their breakfasts, they made short work of the meal when it appeared and rolled on again, silent, grim, heavy-lidded, but cheerful. They gladly would do more than that for McCullough, Twitchell and Tom Ridley. The second evening found them riding up to the buildings of the Question-Mark, guns across their pommels, and they were thankfully received.

Mesquite awakened the next morning to a surprise, for handbills were scattered on its few streets and had been pushed under doors, one of them under the front door of Kane's gambling-hall. When Johnny came down to breakfast the proprietor handed him the sheet, pointing to its flaming headline.

"Read that, me bye!" cried Quayle.

Johnny obeyed:

$2,500.00 REWARD!

For Information Leading to the Capture and Conviction of the Murderer of Tom Ridley

STRICTLY CONFIDENTIAL

TWITCHELL & CARPENTER, Sandy Bend

JOHN McCULLOUGH, Gen'l. Supt., Mesquite

He thoughtlessly shoved it into his pocket and shrugged his shoulders. "That man Twitchell thinks a lot of his money," he said. "But, if it's his way, it's his way. I'm glad to say it ain't mine."

Quayle looked at him from under heavy brows and smiled faintly. "Mac's here, hisself," he said. "They've raised th' ante, an' if I was as young as you I'd have a try at th' game. An', me bye, it isn't only th' money; 'tis a duty, an' a pleasure. Go in an' eat, now, before that wild Mick av a cook scalps ye."

Hoofbeats pounded up the street from the south and a Mexican galloped past towards Kane's, followed on foot by several idlers.

"There ye go!" savagely growled the proprietor; "an' I hope ye saw a-plenty, ye Greaser dog!"

After a hurried breakfast Johnny went up to Kane's and found an air of tension and suspicion. Men were going in and out of the door through the partition and the half-friendly smiles which he had received the night before were everywhere missing. Feeling the chill of his reception did not blunt his powers of observation, for he saw that both Red Thompson and Bill Long, being unaccredited strangers, drew an occasional suspicious glance. The former was seated in a chair at the lower end of the bar, his back to the wall and only a step from the diningroom door. Bill Long was leaning against the upper end of the counter, where it turned at right angles to meet the wall behind it. At Bill's back and only two steps away was the front door. His chin was in his hand and his elbow rested on the bar, where he appeared to be moodily studying the floor behind the counter, but in reality his keen, narrowed eyes were watching Thorpe and the loopholes in the checkerboard. From his position he caught the light on them at just the right angle to see the backing plates. He let Johnny go past him without more than a casual glance and nod.

Thorpe moved forward, cleaving a straight path through the restless crowd and stopped in front of the newcomer. "Nelson," he said, tartly; "th' boss wants to see you, pronto!" As he spoke he let his swinging hand rest against the butt of his gun.

Johnny took plenty of time for his answer, his mind working at top speed. If Kane had caused inquiries to be made around Gunsight concerning him he knew that the report hardly would please any man who was against law and order; and he knew that Kane had had plenty of time to make the inquiries. The thinly veiled hostility and suspicions on the faces around him settled that question in his mind. He slouched sidewise until he had Thorpe in a better position between him and the partition.

"You shore made a mistake," he drawled. "Th' boss never even heard of me."

"I said pronto!" snapped Thorpe.

"Well, as long as yo're so pressin'," came the slow, acquiescent reply, "you can go to h--l!"

Thorpe's gun got halfway out, and stopped as a heavy Colt jabbed into his stomach with a force which knocked the breath out of him and doubled him up. Johnny's other gun, deftly balanced between his palm and the thumb on its hammer, freezing the expressions as it had found them on the faces of the crowd. "Stick up yore han's! All of you! You, in the chair! "he roared. "Stick 'em up!" and Red lost no time in making up for his delinquency. Bill Long, being out of the angry man's sight, raised his only halfway.

"I was welcome enough last night," snapped Johnny; "but somethin's wrong today. If Kane wants to see me, he can send somebody that can talk without insultin' me. An' as for this sick cow, I'm warnin' him fair that I shoot at th' first move, his move or anybody else's. Stand up, you!" he shouted; "an' foiler me outside. Keep close, an' plumb in front of me. I'll turn you loose when I get to cover. Come on!"

As he backed toward the door, Thorpe following, Bill Long, seeing that Johnny was master of the situation, got his hands all the way up, but the motion was observed and Johnny's gun left Thorpe long enough to swing aside and cover the tardy one. "You keep 'em there!" he gritted. "You can rest 'em later!" and he cautiously backed against the door, moved along it the few inches necessary to gain the opening, and felt his way to the street. "Don't you gamble, Thorpe!" he warned. "Stick closer!"

Being furthest from the front door and soonest out of Johnny's sight, Red Thompson let his hands fall to his hips and cautiously peered over the top of the bar, ready to cover the crowd until Bill Long could drop his upraised hands.

Bill was unfortunate, since he would have to be the last man to assume a more natural position; but he was growing tired and suddenly flung himself sidewise beyond the door opening. As he left the bar there came a heavy report from the street and the bullet, striking the edge of the counter where he had stood, glanced upward and entered the ceiling, a generous cloud of dust moving slowly downward.

"He's a mad dog," muttered Bill, shrinking against the wall. "An' he can shoot like h--l! I reckon he's itchin' to get me on sight, now. Somebody look out an' see where he is. But what'n blazes is it all about, anyhow?"

The chief bartender's head reappeared further down, the counter. "You fool!" he yelled. "Why didn't you let me know what you was goin' to do? Don't you never think of nobody but yourself? That parted my hair!"

Fisher swore disgustedly. "Look out, yourself, Long, if yo're curious! But why didn't you get him?" he demanded. "You was behind him!"

"I wasn't neither behind him; I was on th' side!" retorted Bill. "He was watchin' me out of th' corner of his eye, like th' damned rattler he is! I could see it plain, I tell you!"

"You can see lots of things when yo're scared stiff, can't you?" sneered a voice in the crowd.

"I wasn't scared," defended Bill. "But I wasn't takin' no chances for th' glory of it. He never done nothin' to me, an' I ain't on Kane's payroll yet."

"An' you ain't goin' to be, I reckon," laughed another.

Fisher's face proclaimed that he had solved whatever problem there might be in Bill's lack of action. "Ain't had a chance to get it from him yet, huh?" he asked. Sneering, he gave a warning as he turned away. "An' don't you try for it, neither. If he won't come back here no more, I can get him playin' somewhere else."

Red arose fully and stretched, hearing a slight grating hoise at a loophole in the partition behind him, where the slide dropped into place. "I'm dry; bone dry," he announced. "I never was so dry before. All in favor of a drink, step up. I'm payin' for this round."

All were in favor of it, and the bartender moved slowly behind the counter toward the front door, his head bent over far to the right. "Don't see him; but we better wait till Thorpe comes back. Great guns! Did you see it!" he marveled.

"I can see it better now than I could then," said Red, leaning against the bar. "Come on, boys; he's done gone. This means you, too, Long; 'though I ain't sayin' you hardly earned it. If he saw you before he backed up, I says he's got eyes in his ears. Why, cuss it, he was lookin' plumb at me all th' time. You got too hefty an imagination, Long."

Out in the street Johnny, backing swiftly from the building, saw Bill Long's sudden leap and fired, for moral effect, at the place vacated. Yanking his captive's gun from its holster, he was about to toss it aside when his fingers gripped the telltale butt and a colder look gleamed in his eyes. Slipping his right-hand gun into its holster he gripped the captured weapon affectionately, and then hazarded a quick glance around him. Someone was riding rapidly down the trail from the north, and a second sidewise glance told him that it was Idaho.

"Faster, you!" he growled to the doorkeeper. "Keep a-comin' keep a-comin'. One false move an' Kane'll need another sentry. You may be able to make Bill Long climb up a wall, but I ain't in his class."

Idaho, who was riding in to appease his burning curiosity, felt its flames lick instantly higher as he saw his friend back swiftly from Kane's front door, with Thorpe apparently hooked on the sight of the six-gun. Drawing rein instantly in his astonishment, he at once loosened them and whirled into the scanty and scrawny vegetation on the far side of the trail. Going at a dead run he sent the wiry little pony over piles of cans, around cacti and other larger obstructions until he reached the rear of Red Frank's, facing on the next street. Here he pulled up and drew the Winchester from its scabbard, feeling that Johnny was capable of taking care of Kane's if not interfered with from behind.

Johnny, reaching the rear of the building which he had sought the night before, leaped back and to one side as he came to the end of the wall, glanced along the rear end and then curtly ordered Thorpe back to his friends.

"There'll be more to this," snarled Thorpe, white from anger, his face working. His courage was not of the fineness necessary to let him yield to the mad impulse which surged over him and urged him to throw himself, hands, feet and teeth, in a blind and hopeless attack upon the certain death which balanced itself in the gun in Johnny's hand. His blazing eyes fixed full on his enemy's, he let discretion be his tutor and slowly, grudgingly stepped back, his dragging feet moving only inches at each shuffle, while their owner, poised and tense and ready to take advantage of any slip on Johnny's part, backed toward the sandy street and the scene of his discomfiture. At last reaching the front of the building he paused, stood slowly erect and then wheeled about and strode toward Kane's. At the door he glanced once more at his waiting adversary and then plunged into the room, striding straight for the partition door without a single sidewise glance.

Idaho's voice broke the spell. "I thought he was goin' to risk it," he muttered, a deep sigh of relief following the words. "He was near loco, but he just about had enough sense left to save his worthless life. You would 'a' bio wed him apart at that distance."

"I'd 'a' smashed his pointed jaw!" growled Johnny. "I ain't shootin' nobody that don't reach for a gun. An' if I'd had any sense I'd 'a' chucked th' guns to you an' let him have his beatin'. Next time, I will. Fine sort of a dog he is, tellin' me what I'm goin' to do, an' when I'm goin' to do it!"

"Wait till pay day, when I'll have more money," chuckled Idaho. "I can easy get three to two around here. He's th' champeen rough-an'-tumble fighter for near a hundred miles, but I'm sayin' any man with th' everlastin' nerve to pull Kit Thorpe out from his own kennel an' pack ain't got sense enough to know when he's licked. An' that bein' so, I'm bettin' on yore condition to win. He's gettin' fat an' shortwinded from doin' nothin'. Besides, I'm one of them fools that allus bets on a friend." He laughed as certain memories passed before him. "I've done had a treat come on, an' let me treat you. How many was in there when you pulled him out? An' why didn't th' partition work like it allus did before?"

"Because th' man that worked it was out in front," answered Johnny. "Things went too fast for anybody else to get behind it." A sudden grin slipped to his face. "Hey, I got one of my pet guns back! He was wearin' it. I knowed it as soon as my fingers closed around th' butt, for I shaped it to fit my hand several years ago. Did you see th' handbills? Twitchell's put up another reward, this one for Ridley; an' McCullough is down on th' Question-Mark. Things ought to step fast, now."

Chapter X
Twice in the Same Place

Thorpe reappeared through the partition door armed anew with the mate to the gun he had lost, too enraged to notice that it was better suited to a left than to a right hand. An ordinary man hardly would have noticed it, but a gunman of his years and experience should have sensed the ill-fitting grip at once. He glared over the room, suspiciously eager to catch some unfortunate indulging in a grin, for he had been so shamed and humiliated that it was almost necessary to his future safety that he redeem himself and put his shattered reputation back on its pedestal of fear. There were no grins, for however much any of his acquaintances might have enjoyed his discomfiture they had no lessened respect for his ability with either six-guns or fists; and there was a restlessness in the crowd, for no man knew what was coming.

Fisher conveyed the collective opinion and broke the tension. "Any man would 'a' been fooled," he said to the head bartender, but loud enough for all to hear it. His voice indicated vexation at the success of so shabby a trick. "When he answered Thorpe I shore thought he was goin' prompt an' peaceful why, he even started! Nobody reckoned he was aimin' to make a gunplay. How could they? An' I'm sayin' that it's cussed lucky for him that Thorpe didn't!"

"Anybody can be fooled th' first time," replied the man of liquor. He looked over at the partition door and nodded. "Come over an' have a drink, Thorpe, an' forget it. I got money that says there ain't no man alive can beat you on th' draw. He tricked you, actin' that way."

"He's th' first man on earth ever shoved a gun into me like that," growled Thorpe, slowly moving forward. "An' he's th' last! Seein' as there's some here that mebby ain't shore about it, I'll show 'em that I was tricked!" He stopped in front of Bill Long and regarded that surprised individual with a look as malevolent as it was sincere. "Any squaw dog can tote two guns," he said, his still raging anger putting a keener edge to the words. "When he does he tells everybody that he's shore bad. If he ain't, that's his fault. I tote one an' yo're not goin' to swagger around these parts with any more than I got. Which one are you goin' to throw away?"

Bill blinked at him with owlish stupidity. "What you say?" he asked, as though doubting the reliability of his ears.

"Oh," sneered Thorpe, his rage climbing anew; "you didn't hear me th' first time, huh? Well, you want to be listenin' this time! I asked, which gun are you goin' to throw away, you card-skinnin' four-flush?"

"Why," faltered Bill, doing his very best to play the part he had chosen. "I I dunno I ain't goin' to to throw any of 'em away. What you mean?"

"Throw one away!" snapped Thorpe, his animal cunning telling him that the obeyance of the order might possibly be accepted by the crowd as grounds for justification, if any should be needed.

Bill changed subtly as he reflected that the crowd had excused Thorpe's humiliation because he had been tricked, and determined that no such excuse should be used again. He looked the enraged man in the eyes and a contemptuous smile crept around his thin lips. "Thorpe," he drawled, "if yo're lookin' for props to hold up yore reputation, you got th' wrong timber. Better look for a sick cow, or "

The crowd gasped as it realized that its friend's fingers were again relaxing from the butt of his half-drawn gun and that three pounds of steel, concentrated on the small circumference of the barrel of a six-gun had been jabbed into the pit of his stomach with such speed that they had not seen it, and with such force that the victim of the blow was sick, racked with pain and scarcely able to stand, momentarily paralyzed by the second assault on the abused stomach, which caved, quivered, and retched from the impact. Again he had failed, this time after cold, calm warning; again the astonished crowd froze in ridiculous postures, with ludicrous expressions graven on their faces, their automatic arms leaping skyward as they gaped stupidly, unbelievingly at the second gun. Before they could collect their numbed senses the master of the situation had backed swiftly against the wall near the front door, thereby blasting the budding hopes of the bartender, whose wits and power of movement, re turning at equal pace, were well ahead of those of his friends. It also saved the man of liquor from being dropped behind his own bar by the gun of the alert Mr. Thompson, who felt relieved when the crisis had passed without calling forth any effort on his part which would couple him with the capable Mr. Long.

"Climb that wall!" said Bill Long, his voice vibrating with the sudden outpouring of accumulated repression. "I'm lookin' for a chance to kill you, so I ain't askin' you to throw away no gun. This is between you an' me anybody takin' cards will drop cold. You got it comin', an' comin' fair. Climb that wall!"

Thorpe, gasping and agonized, fought off the sickness which had held him rigid and stared open-eyed, openmouthed at glinting ferocity in the narrowed eyes of the two-gun man.

"Climb that wall!" came the order, this time almost a whisper, but sharp and cutting as the edge of a knife, and there was a certainty in the voice and eyes which was not to be disregarded. Thorpe straightened up a little, turned slowly and slowly made his way through the opening crowd to the wall, and leaned against it. He had no thought of using the gun at his hip, no idea of resistance, for the spirit of the bully within him had been utterly crushed. He was a broken man, groping for bearings in the fog of the shifting readjustments going on in his soul.

"Climb!" said Bill Long's voice like the cracking of a bull- whacker's whip, and Thorpe mechanically obeyed, his finger-nails and boot toes scraping over the smooth boards in senseless effort. He had not yet had time to realize what he had lost, to feel the worthlessness which would be his to the end of his days.

The two-gun man nodded. "I told you boys I was a imitator," he said, smiling; "an' I am. I imitated him in his play to kill me. I imitated that SV foreman, an' now I'm imitatin' Thorpe again. It's his own idea, climbin' walls."

Fisher, watching the still-climbing Thorpe, was using his nimble wits for a way out of a situation which easily might turn into anything, from a joke to a sudden shambles. He now had no doubts about the real quality of Bill Long, and he secretly congratulated himself that he had not yielded to certain temptations he had felt. Besides, his arms were growing heavy and numb. There came to his mind the further thought that this two-gun, card-playing wizard would be a very good partner for a tour of the country, a tour which should be lucrative and safe enough to satisfy anyone.

"Huh," he laughed. "We're imitatin', too; only we're imitatin' ourselves, an' we're gettin' tired of holdin' 'em up. I'm sayin', fair an' square, that I ain't aimin' to draw no cards in any game that is two-handed. I reckon th' rest of th' boys feel th' same as I do. How 'bout it, boys?"

Affirmation came slowly or explosively, according to the individual natures, and the two-gun man was confident enough in his ability to judge character to accept the words. He slowly dropped his guns back in the holsters and smiled broadly. Even the lower class of men is capable of feeling a real liking, when it is based on audacious courage, for anyone who deserves it; and he knew that the now shifting crowd had been caught in the momentum of such a feeling. There was also another consideration to which more than one man present gave grave heed: They scarcely had quit marveling at the wizardy of one two-gun man when the second had appeared and made them marvel anew.

"All right, boys," he said. "Thorpe, you can quit climbin', seein' that you ain't gettin' nowhere. Come over here an' gimme that gun. I'm still imitatin'. This ain't been no lucky day for you, an' just to show you that you can make it unluckier," he said as he took the Colt, "I'm goin' to impress somethin' on yore mind." He threw the barrel up and carelessly emptied the weapon into the checkerboard partition with a rapidity which left nothing to be desired. The distance was nearly sixty feet. "Reckon you can cover 'em all with th' palm of one hand," he remarked as he shifted the empty gun to his left hand, where he thought it would fit better. He looked at it and turned it over. Three small dots, driven into the side of the frame, made him repress a smile. His own guns had two, while Red Thompson's lone Colt had four. He opened the flange and shoved the gun down behind the backstrap of his trousers, where a left-handed man often finds it convenient to carry a weapon, since the butt points that way. Letting his coat fall back into place he walked slowly to the door and out onto the street, the conversation in the room buzzing high after he left.

He next appeared in Quayle's, where he grinned at Idaho, Quayle, Johnny, and Ed Doane.

"I just made Thorpe climb th' wall," he said. "He looked like a pinned toad. Do you ever like to split up a pair of aces, Nelson?"

Johnny considered a moment and then slowly shook his head.

"Neither do I," replied the newcomer. His left hand went slowly around under his coat and brought out the captured Colt. "An' I ain't goin' to begin doin' it now. Here," and he handed the weapon to Johnny.

Johnny took it mechanically and then quickly turned it over and glanced at the frame. Weighing it judicially he looked up. "Th' feel an' balance of this Colt just suits me," he said. "Want to sell it?"

"I don't hardly own it enough to sell it," answered Bill; "but I reckon I can give it away, seein' that Thorpe set th' fashion. I'm warnin' you that he might want it back. But you should 'a' seen him a-climbin' that wall!" and he burst into laughter.

"I'll gamble," grinned Johnny. "I'll get you a new one for it."

"No, you won't," replied Bill, still laughing. "I got more'n th' value of a wore-out six-gun watchin' yore show up there. Besides, if it was better'n mine I would 'a' kept it myself. I ain't expectin' you'll be there, tonight," he finished.

"Suits me right here," replied Johnny. "Much obliged for th' gun." He looked at Idaho and grinned. "I aim to clean out this sage-hen at Californy Jack, tonight."

"Which same you might do," admitted Idaho, slowly looking at the Colt in his friend's hand; "for you shore are a fool for luck."

Chapter XI
A Job Well Done

Pecos Kane looked up at the sound of shooting and signaled for the doorkeeper. Getting no response he pulled another cord and waited impatiently for the man who answered it.

"What was that shooting, and who did it?" demanded the boss. He cut the wordy recital short. "Tell Bill Trask to assume Thorpe's duties and send Thorpe to me."

Thorpe soon appeared, slowly closed the door behind him and faced the boss, who studied him for a silent interval, the object of the keen scrutiny squirming at the close of it.

"You are no longer suited for my doortender," said Kane's hard voice. "Report to the dining-room, or kitchen, or leave the hotel entirely. But first find Corwin and send him to me. That is all."

Thorpe gulped and shuffled out and in a few minutes the sheriff appeared.

"Sit down, Corwin," said Kane, pleasantly. "Trask has Thorpe's job now. Wait a moment until I think something out," and he sat back in his chair, his eyes closing. In a few moments he opened them and leaned forward. "I have come to a decision regarding some strangers in this town. I have reason to believe that Long and Thompson know each other a great deal better than they pretend. I want to know more about Nelson, so you will send a good man up to his country to get me a report on him. Do it as soon as you leave me, and tell him to waste no time. That clear?"

Corwin nodded.

"Very well," continued the boss. "I want you to arrest both Long and Thompson before tomorrow, and throw them into jail. Since Long's exhibition today it will be well to go about it in a manner calculated to avoid bloodshed. There is no use of throwing men away by sending them against such gunplay. You are to arrest them without a shot being fired on either side. It is only a matter of figuring it out, and I will give you this much to start on: Whatever suspicions may have been aroused in their minds about their welcome here not being cordial must be removed. Because of that there should be no ill-advised speed in carrying out the arrests. They could be shot down from behind, but I want them alive; and it suits my purpose better if they are taken right here in this building. They are worth money, and a great deal more than money to me, to you, and to all of us. Twitchell and Carpenter are very powerful and they must be placated if it can be done in such a way as not to jeopardize us. I think it may be done in a way which will strengthen us. You follow me closely?"

The sheriff nodded again.

"All right," said Kane. "Now then, tell me where each of the three men, Nelson, Long, and Thompson, were on the occasions of the robbery of the bank and the death of Ridley. Think carefully."

Corwin gazed at the floor thoughtfully. "When th' bank was robbed Nelson was playin' cards with Idaho Norton in Quayle's saloon. Quayle an' Doane were in there with 'em. Long an' Thompson were here, upstairs, asleep."

"Very good, so far," commented Kane; "go on."

"When Ridley was shot Nelson was with Idaho Norton in Quayle's hotel, for both of them rustled into th' street an' carried him indoors. Thompson was in th' front room, here, an' Long come in soon after the shot was fired."

"Excellent. Which way did he come?"

"Through th' front door."

"Before that?" demanded the boss impatiently.

"I don't know."

"Why don't you?" blazed Kane. "Have I got to do all th' thinking for this crowd of dumb-heads?"

"Why, why should I know?" Corwin asked in surprise.

"If you don't know the answer to your own question it is only wasting my time to tell it to you. Now, listen: You are to send four men in to me but not Mexicans, for the testimony of Mexicans in this country is not taken any too seriously by juries. The four are not all to come the same way nor at the same time. The dumbheads I have around me necessitate that each be instructed separate and apart from the others, else they wouldn't know, or keep separate their own part. Is this plain?"

"Yes," answered the arm of the law.

"Very well. Now you will go out and arrange to arrest and jail those two men. And after you have arranged it you will do it. Not a shot is to be fired. When they are in jail report to me. That is all."

Corwin departed and did not scratch his head until the door closed after him, and then he showed great signs of perplexity. As he went up the next corridor he caught sight of a friend leaning against the back of the partition, and just beyond was Bill Trask at his new post. He beckoned to them both.

"Sandy, you are to report to th' boss, right away," ordered the sheriff. "He wants four white men, an' yo're near white. Trask, send in three more white men, one at a time, after Woods comes out. An' let me impress this on yore mind: It is strict orders that you ain't to fire a shot tonight, when somethin' happens that's goin' to happen; you, nor nobody else. Got that good?"

"What do you mean?" asked the sentry, grinning.

"Good G-d!" snorted the sheriff. "Do I have to do all th' thinkin' for this crowd of dumb-heads?"

"Yo're a parrot," retorted Trask. "I know that by heart. You don't have to. You don't even do yore own. You may go!"

Corwin grunted and joined the crowd in the big room and when Bill Long wandered in and settled down to watch a game the sheriff in due time found a seat at his side. His conversation was natural, not too steady and not too friendly and neither did he tarry too long, for when he thought that he had remained long enough he wandered up to the bar, joked with the chief dispenser, and mixed with the crowd. After awhile he went out and strolled over to the jail, where a dozen men were waiting for him. His lecture to them was painfully simple, in the simplest words of his simple vocabulary, and when he at last returned to the gambling-hall he was certain that his pupils were letter-perfect.

Meanwhile Kane had been busy and when the first of the four appeared the clear-thinking boss drove straight to his point. He looked intently at the caller and asked: "Where were you on the night of the storm, at the time the bank was robbed?"

"Upstairs playin' cards with Harry."

"Do you know where Long and Thompson were at that time?"

"Shore; they was upstairs."

"I am going to surprise you," said Kane, smiling, and he did, for he told his listener where he had been on that night, what he had seen, and what he had found in the morning in front of the door of Bill Long's door. He did it so well that the listener began to believe that it was so, and said as much.

"That's just what you must believe," exclaimed Kane. "Go over it again and again. Picture it, with natural details, over and over again. Live every minute, every step of it. If you forget anything about it come to me and I'll refresh your memory. I'll do so anyway, when the time comes. You may go."

The second and third man came, learned their lessons and departed. The fourth, a grade higher in intelligence, was given a more difficult task and before he was dismissed Kane went to a safe, took out a bundle of large bills and handed two of them to his visitor, who nodded, pocketed them and departed. He was to plant them, find them again and return them so that the latter part of the operation would be clear in his memory.

Supper was over and the big room crowded. Jokes and laughter sounded over the quiet curses of the losers. Bill Long, straddling a chair, with his arms crossed on its back, watched a game and exchanged banter with the players during the deals. Red Thompson, playing in an other game not far away, was winning slowly but consistently. Somebody started a night-herding song and others joined in, making the ceiling ring. Busy bartenders were endeavoring to supply the demand. The song roared through the first verse and the second, and in the middle of the following chorus, at the first word of the second line there was a sudden, concerted movement, and chaos reigned.

Unexpectedly attacked by half a dozen men each Bill and Red fought valiantly but vainly. In Bill's group two men had been told off to go for his guns, one to each weapon, and they had dived head-first at the signal. Red's single gun had been obtained in the same way. Stamping feet, curses, grunts, groans, the soft sound of fist on flesh, the scraping of squirming masses of men going this way and that, the heavy breathing and other sounds of conflict filled the dusty, smoky air. Chairs crashed, tables toppled and were wrecked by the surging groups and then, suddenly, the turmoil ceased and the two bound, battered, and exhausted men swayed dizzily in the hands of their captors, their chests rising and falling convulsively beneath their ragged shirts as they gulped the foul air.

Two men rocked on the floor, slobbering over cracked shins, another lay face down across the wreck of a chair, his gory face torn from mouth to cheekbone; another held a limp and dangling arm, cursing with monotonous regularity; a fifth, blood pouring from his torn scalp and blinding him, groped aimlessly around the room.

Corwin glanced around, shook his head and looked at his two prisoners in frank admiration. "You fellers shore can lick h--l out of th' man that invented fightin'!"

Bill Long glared at him. "I didn't see you no where near!" he panted. "Turn us loose an' we'll clean out th' place. We was two-thirds licked before we -knew it was comin'."

"Don't waste yore breath" snarled Red. "There's a few I'm aimin' to kill when I get th' chance!"

"What's th' meanin' of this surprise party?" asked Bill Long.

"It means that you an' Thompson are under arrest for robbin' th' bank; an' you for th' murder of Ridley," answered the peace officer, frowning at the ripple of laughter which arose. A pock-marked Mexican, whose forehead bore a crescent-shaped scar, seemed to be unduly hilarious and vastly relieved about something.

Thorpe came swiftly across the room toward Bill Long, snarled a curse, and struck with vicious energy at the bruised face. Bill rolled his head and the blow missed. Before the assailant could recover his balance and strike again a brawny, red-haired giant, whose one good eye glared over a battered nose, lunged swiftly forward and knocked Thorpe backwards over a smashed chair and overturned table. The prostrate man groped and half arose, to look dazedly into the giant's gun and hear the holder of it give angry warning.

"Any more of that an' I'll blow you apart!" roared the giant. "An' that goes for any other skunk in th' room. Bear-baitin' is barred." He looked at Corwin. "You've got 'em now get 'em out of here an' into jail, before I has to kill somebody!"

Corwin called to his men and with the prisoners in the middle the little procession started for the old adobe jail on the next street, the pleased sheriff bringing up the rear, his Colt swinging in his hand. When the prisoners had been locked up behind its thick walls he sighed with relief, posted two guards, front and rear, and went back to report to Kane that a good job had been well done.

The boss nodded and bestowed one of his rare compliments. "That was well handled, Sheriff," he said. "I am sorry your work is not yet finished. A zealous peace officer like you should be proud enough of such a capture as to be anxious to inform those most interested. Also," he smiled, "you naturally would be anxious to put in a claim for the reward. Therefore you should go right down to McCullough and lay the entire matter before him, as I shall now instruct you," and the instructions were as brief as thoroughness would allow. "Is that clear?" asked the boss at the end of the lesson.

"It ain't only clear," enthused Corwin; "but it's giltedged; I'm on my way, now!"

"Report to me before morning," said Kane.

Hurrying from the room and the building the sheriff saddled his horse and rode briskly down the trail. Not far from town he began to whistle and he kept it up purposely as a notification of peaceful and honorable intentions, until the sharp challenge of a hidden sentry checked both it and his horse.

"Sheriff Corwin," he answered. "What you holdin' me up for?"

A man stepped out of the cover at the edge of the trail. "Got a match?" he pleasantly asked, the rifle hanging from the crook of his arm, both himself and the weapon hidden from the sheriff by the darkness. "Where you goin' so late? Thought everybody was asleep but me."

Corwin handed him the match. "Just ridin' down to see McCullough. Got important business with him, an' reckoned it shouldn't wait 'til mornin'."

The sentry rolled a cigarette and lit it with the borrowed match in such a way that the sheriff's face was well lighted for the moment, but he did not look up. "That's good," he said. "Reckon I'll go along with you. No use hangin' 'round up here, an' I'm shore sleepy. Wait till I get my cayuse," and he disappeared, soon returning in the saddle. His quiet friend in the brush settled back to resume the watch and to speculate on how long it would take his companion to return.

McCullough, half undressed, balanced himself as he heard approaching voices, growled profanely and put the freed leg in the trousers. He was ready for company when one of the night shift stuck his head in at the door.

"Sheriff Corwin wants to see you," said the puncher. "His business is so delicate it might die before mornin'."

"All right," grumbled the trail-boss. "If you get out of his way mebby he can come in."

Corwin stood in the vacated door, smiling, but too wise to offer his hand to the blunt, grim host. "Got good news," he said, "for you, me, an' th' T & C."

"Ya-as?" drawled McCullough, peering out beneath his bushy, gray eyebrows. "Pecos Kane shoot hisself?"

"We got th' fellers that robbed th' bank an' shot Ridley," said the sheriff.

"The h--l you say!" exclaimed McCullough. "Come in an' set down. Who are they? How'd you get 'em?"

"That reward stick?" asked Corwin anxiously.

"Tighter'n a tick to a cow!" emphatically replied the trail-boss. "Who are they?"

"I got a piece of paper here," said the sheriff, proving his words. He stepped inside and placed it on the table. "Read it over an' sign it. Then I'll fill in th' blanks with th' names of th' men. If they're guilty, I'm protected; if I've made a mistake, then there's no harm done."

McCullough slowly read it aloud:

" 'Sheriff Corwin was the first man to tell me that and robbed the Mesqtiite bank, and that killed Tom Ridley. He will produce the prisoners, with the witnesses and other proof in Sandy Bend upon demand. If they are found guilty of the crime named the rewards belong to him.' "

The trail-boss considered it thoughtfully. "It looks fair; but there's one thing I don't like, Sheriff," he said, putting his finger on the objectionable words and looking up. "I don't like 'Sandy Bend.' I'm takin' no chances with them fellers. I'll just scratch that out, an' write in, 'to me' How 'bout it?"

"They've got to have a fair trial," replied Corwin. "I'm standin' for no lynchin'. I can't do it."

"Yo're shore right they're goin' to have a fair trial!" retorted the trail-boss. "Twitchell ain't just lookin' for two men he wants th' ones that robbed th' bank an' killed Ridley. You don't suppose he's payin' five thousan' out of his pocket for somebody that ain't guilty, do you? Why, they're goin' to have such a fair trial that you'll need all th' evidence you can get to convict 'em. Lynch 'em?" He laughed sarcastically. "They won't even be jailed in Sandy Bend, where they shore would be lynched. You take 'em to Sandy Bend an' you'll be lynched out of yore reward. You know how it reads."

Corwin scratched his head and a slow grin spread over his face. "Cuss it, I never saw it that way," he admitted. "I guess yo're shoutin' gospel, Mac; but, cuss it, it ain't reg'lar." "

"You know me; an' I know you," replied the trail-boss, smiling. "There's lots of little things done that ain't exactly reg'lar; but they're plumb sensible. Suppose I change this here paper like I said, an' sign it. Then you write in th' names an' let me read 'em. Then you let me know what proof you got, an' bring down th' prisoners, an' I'll sign a receipt for 'em."

"Yes!" exclaimed Corwin. "I'll deputize you, an' give 'em into yore custody, with orders to take 'em to Sandy Bend, or any other jail which you think best. That makes it more reg'lar, don't it?" he smiled.

McCullough laughed heartily and slapped his thigh. "That's shore more reg'lar. I'm beginnin' to learn why, they elected you sheriff. All right, then; I'm signin' my name." He took pen and ink from a shelf, made the change in the paper, sprawled his heavy-handed signature across the bottom and handed the pen to Corwin. "Now, d--n it: Who are they?"

The sheriff carefully filled in the three blanks, McCullough peering over his shoulder and noticing that the form had been made out by another hand.

"There," said Corwin. "I'm spendin' that five thou sand right now."

" 'Bill Long' 'Red Thompson' 'Bill Long' again," growled the trail-boss. "Never heard of 'em. Live around here?"

Corwin shook his head. "No."

"All right," grunted McCullough. "Now, then; what proof you got? You'll never spend a cent of it if you ain't got 'em cold."

Corwin sat on the edge of the table, handed a cigar to his host and lit his own. "I got a man who was in th' north stable, behind Kane's, when th' shot that killed Ridley was fired from th' other stable. He was feedin' his hoss an' looked out through a crack, seem' Long sneak out of th' other buildin', Sharp's in hand, an' rustle for cover around to th' gamblin'-hall. Another man was standin' in th' kitchen, gazin' out of th' winder, an' saw Long turn th' corner of th' north stable an' dash for th' hotel buildin'. He says he laughed because Long's slight limp made him sort of bob sideways. An' we know why Long done it, but we're holdin' that back. That's for th' killin'.

"Now for th' robbery: I got th' man that saw Long an' Thompson sneak out of th' front door of th' dinin'room hall into that roarin' sand storm between eleven an' twelve o'clock on th' night of th' robbery. He says he remembers it plain because he was plumb surprised to see sane men do a fool thing like that. He didn't say nothin' to 'em because if they wanted to commit suicide it was their own business. Besides, they was strangers to him. After awhile he went up to bed, but couldn't sleep because of th' storm makin' such a racket. Kane's upstairs rocked a little that night. I know, because I was up there, tryin' to sleep."

"Go on," said the trail-boss, eagerly and impatiently, his squinting eyes not leaving the sheriff's face.

"Well, quite some time later he heard th' door next to his'n open cautious, but a draft caught it an' slammed it shut. Then Bill Long's voice said, angry an' sharp: 'What th' hell you doin', Red? Tellin' creation about it?' In th' mornin', th' cook, who gets up ahead of every body else, of course, was goin' along th' hall toward th' stairs an' he kicks somethin' close to Long's door. It rustles an' he gropes for it, curious-like, an' took it down stairs with him for a look at it, where it wasn't so dark. It was a strip of paper that th' bank puts around packages of bills, an' there was some figgers on it. He chucks it in a corner, where it fell down behind some stuff that had been there a long time, an' don't think no more about it till he hears about th' bank bein' robbed. Then he fishes it out an' brings it to me. I knowed what it was, first glance."

"Any more?" urged McCullough. "It's good; but, you got any more?"

"I shore have. What you think I'm sheriff for? I got two of th' bills, an' their numbers tally with th' bank's numbers of th' missin' money. You can compare 'em with yore own list later. I sent a deputy to their rooms as soon as I had 'em in jail, an' he found th' bills sewed up in their saddle pads. Reckon they was keepin' one apiece in case they needed money quick. An' when th' sand was swept off th' step in front of that hall door, a gold piece was picked up out of it."

"When were you told about all this by these fellers?" demanded the trail-boss.

"As soon as th' robbery was known, an' as soon as th' shootin' of Ridley was known!"

"When did you arrest them?"

"Last night; an' it was shore one big job. They can fight like a passel of cougars. Don't take no chances with 'em, Mac."

"Why did you wait till last night?" demanded McCullough. "Wasn't you scared they'd get away?"

"No. I had 'em trailed every place they went. They wasn't either of 'em out of our sight for a minute; an' when they slept there was men watchin' th' stairs an' their winders. You see, Kane lost a lot of money in that robbery, bein' a director; an' I was hopin' they'd try to sneak off to where they cached it an' give us a chance to locate it. They was too wise. I got more witnesses, too; but they're Greasers, an' I ain't puttin' no stock in 'em. A Greaser'd lie his own mother into her grave for ten dollars; anyhow, most juries down here think so, so it's all th' same."

"Yes; lyin' for pay is shore a Greaser trick," said McCullough, nodding. "Well, I reckon it's only a case of waitin' for th' reward, Sheriff. Tell you what I wish you'd do: Gimme everythin' they own when you send 'em down to me, or when I come up for 'em, whichever suits you best. Everythin' has got to be collected now before it gets lost, an' it's got to be ready for court in case it's needed."

"All right; I'll get back what I can use, after th' trial," replied Corwin. "I'll throw their saddles on their cayuses, an' let 'em ride 'em down. How soon do you want 'em? Right away?"

"First thing in th' mornin'!" snapped McCullough. "Th' sooner th' better. I'll send up some of th' boys to give you a hand with 'em, or I'll take 'em off yore hands entirely at th' jail. Which suits you?"

"Send up a couple of yore men, if you want to. It'll look better in town if I deliver 'em to you here. Why, you ain't smoked yore cigar!"

McCullough looked at him and then at his own hand, staring at the crushed mass of tobacco in it. "Shucks!" he grunted, apologetically, and forthwith lied a little him self. "Funny how a man forgets when he's excited. I bet that cigar thought it was in a vise my hand's tired from squeezin'."

"Sorry I ain't got another, Mac," said Corwin, grinning, as he paused in the door. "I'll be lookin' for yore boys early. Adios."

"Adios," replied McCullough from the door, listening to the dying hoof beats going rapidly toward town. Then he shut the door, hurled the remains of the cigar on the floor and stepped on them. "He's got 'em, huh? An' strangers, too! He's got 'em too d——d pat for me. It takes a good man to plaster a lie on me an' make it stick an' he ain't no good, at all. He was sweatin' before he got through!" Again the trousers came off, all the way this time, and the lamp was turned down. As he settled into his bunk he growled again. "Well, I'll have a look at 'em, anyhow, an' send 'em down for Twitchell to look at," and in another moment he was asleep.

Chapter XII
Friends on the Outside

While events were working out smoothly for the arrest of the two men in Kane's gambling-hall, four friends were passing a quiet evening in Quayle's barroom, but the quiet was not to endure.

With lagging interest in the game Idaho picked up his cards, ruffled them and listened. "Reckon that's singin'," he said in response to the noise floating down from the gambling-hall. "Sounds more like a bunch of cows bawlin' for their calves. Kane's comin' to life later'n usual. Wonder if Thorpe's joinin' in?" he asked, and burst out laughing. "Next to our hard-workin' sheriff there ain't nobody in town that I'd rather see eat dirt than him. Wish I could 'a' seen him a-climbin' that wall!"

"Anybody that works for Kane eats dirt," commented Quayle. "They has to. He'll learn how to eat it, too, th' blackguard."

"There goes somethin'" said Ed Doane as the distant roaring ceased abruptly. "Reckon Thorpe's makin' an other try at th' wall." He laughed softly. "They're startin' a fandango, by th' sound of it."

"'Tis nothin' to th' noise av a good Irish reel," deprecated the proprietor.

"I'm claimin' low this hand," grunted Idaho. "Look out for yore jack."

Johnny smiled, played and soon a new deal was begun.

"Th' dance is over, too," said Doane, mopping off the bar for the third time in ten minutes. "Must 'a' been a short one."

"Some of them hombres will dance shorter than that, an' harder," grunted Idaho, "th' next time they pay its a visit. They didn't get many head th' last time, an' I'm sayin' they'll get none at all th' next time. Where they take 'em to is more'n we can guess: th' tracks just die. Not bein' able to track 'em, we're aimin' to stop it at th' beginnin'. You fellers wait, an' you'll see."

Quayle grunted expressively. "I been waitin' too long now. Wonder why nobody ever set fire to Kane's. 'Twould be a fine sight."

"You'll mebby see that, too, one of these nights," growled the puncher.

"Then pick out wan when th' wind is blowin' up th' street," chuckled Quayle. "This buildin' is so dry it itches to burn. I'm surprised it ain't happened long ago, with that Mick in th' kitchen raisin' th' divvil with th' stove. If I didn't have a place av me own I'd be tempted to do it meself."

The bartender laughed shortly. "If McCullough hap pens to think of it I reckon it'll be done." He shook out the bar cloth and bunched it again. "Funny he ain't cut loose yet. That ain't like him, at all."

"Waitin' for th' rewards to start workin', I reckon," said Johnny.

Idaho scraped up the cards, shaped them into a sheersided deck and pushed it aside. "I'm tired of this game; it's too even. Reckon I'll go up an' take a look at Kane's." He arose and sauntered out, paused, and looked up the street. "Cussed if they ain't havin' a pe-rade," he called. "This ain't th' Fourth of July, is it? I'm goin' up an' sidle around for a closer look. Be back soon."

Johnny was vaguely perturbed. The sudden cessation of the song bothered him, and the uproar which instantly followed it only served to increase his uneasiness. Ordinarily he would not have been affected, but the day's events might have led to almost anything. Had a shot been fired he swiftly would have investigated, but the lack of all shooting quieted his unfounded suspicions. Idaho's remark about the parade renewed them and after a short, silent argument with himself he arose, went to the door and looked up the street, seeing the faint, yellow patch on the sand where Kane's lamps shown through the open door and struggled against the surrounding darkness, and hearing the faint rumble of voices above which rang out frequent laughter. He grimly told himself that there would be no laughter in Kane's if his two friends had come to any harm, and there would have been plenty of shooting.

"Anythin' to see?" asked Quayle, poking his head out of the door.

"No," answered Johnny, turning to reenter the building. "Just feelin' their oats, I reckon."

"'Tis feelin' their ropes they should be doin'," replied Quayle, stepping back to let his guest pass through. "An' 'twould be fine humor to swing 'em from their own. Hist!" he warned, listening to the immoderate laughter which came rapidly nearer. "Here's Idaho; he'll know it all."

Idaho popped in and in joyous abandon threw his sombrero against the ceiling. "Funniest thing you ever heard!" he panted. "Corwin's arrested that Bill Long an' Red Thompson. Took a full dozen to do it, an' half of 'em are cripples now. Th' pe-rade I saw was Corwin an' a bunch escortin' 'em over to th' jail. Ain't we got a rip-snortin' fool for a sheriff?" His levity died swiftly, to give way to slowly rising anger. "With this country fair crowded with crooks he can't find nobody to throw in jail except two friendless strangers! D n his hide, I got a notion to pry 'em out and turn 'em loose before mornin', just to make things right, an' take some of th' swellin' out of his flat head. It's a cussed shame."

The low-pulled brim of Johnny's sombrero hid the glint in his eyes and the narrowed lids. He relaxed and sat carelessly on the edge of a table, one leg swinging easily to and fro as conjecture after conjecture rioted through his mind.

"They must 'a' stepped on Kane's toes," said Ed, vigorously wiping off the backbar.

Idaho scooped up his hat and flung it on the table at Johnny's side. "You'd never guess it, Ed. Even th' rest of th' gang was laughin' about it, all but th' cripples. I been waitin' for them rewards to start workin,' but I never reckoned they'd work out like this. Long an' Thompson are holdin' th' sack. They're scapegoats for th' whole cussed gang. Corwin took 'em in for robbin' th' bank, an' gettin' Ridley!"

Ed Doane dropped the bar cloth and stared at the speaker and a red tide crept slowly up his throat and spread across his face. Johnny slid from the table and disappeared in the direction of his room. He came down again with the two extra Colts in his hands, slipped through the kitchen and ran toward the jail. Quayle's mouth slowly closed and then let out an explosive curse. The bartender brought his fist down on the bar with a smash.

"Scapegoats? Yo're right! It's a cold deck an' you bet Kane never would 'a' dealt from it if he wasn't dead shore he could make th' play stick. Every man in th' pack will swear accordin' to orders, an' who can swear th' other way? It'll be a strange jury, down in Sandy Bend, every man jack of it a friend of Ridley an' th' T & C. Well, I'm a peaceable man, but this is too much. I never saw them fellers before in my life; but on th' day when Corwin starts south with 'em I'll be peaceable no longer an' I've got friends! There's no tellin' who'll be next if he makes this stick. Who's with me?"

"/ am," said Quayle; "an' _I_ got friends."

"Me, too," cried Idaho. "There's a dozen hickory knots out on th' ranch that hate Corwin near as much as I do. They'll be with us, mebby even Lukins, hisself. Hey! Where'd Nelson go?" he excitedly demanded. "Mebby he's out playin' a lone hand!" and he darted for the kitchen.

Johnny, hidden in the darkness not far from the jail, was waiting. The escort, judging from the talk and the glowing ends of cigarettes, was bunched near the front of the building, little dreaming how close they stood to a man who held four Colts and was fighting down a rage which urged their use. At last, thoroughly master of itself, Johnny's mind turned to craftiness rather than to blind action and formulated a sketchy plan. But while the plan was being carried through he would not allow his two old friends to be entirely helpless. Slipping off his boots he crept up behind the jail and with his kerchief lowered the two extra guns through the window, softly calling attention to them, which redoubled the prisoners' efforts to untie each other. Satisfied now that they were in no immediate danger he slipped back to his boots, put them on and waited to see what would happen, and to listen further.

"There ain't no use watchin' th' jail," said a voice, louder than the rest. "They're tied up proper, an' nobody ever got out of it before."

"Just th' same, you an' Harry will watch it," said Corwin. "Winder an' door. I ain't takin' no chances with this pair."

A thickening on the dark ground moved forward slowly and a low voice called Johnny's name. He replied cautiously and soon Idaho crawled to his side, whispering questions.

"Go back where there ain't no chance of anybody hearin' us, or stumblin' over us," said Johnny. "When that gang leaves there won't be so much noise, an' then they may hear us."

At last reaching an old wagon they stood up and leaned against it, and Johnny unburdened his heart to a man he knew he could trust.

"Idaho," he said, quietly, "them fellers are th' best friends I ever had. They cussed near raised me, an' they risked their lives more'n once to save mine. 'Most everythin' I know I got from them, an' they ain't goin' to stay in that mud hut till mornin', not if I die for it. They come down here to help me, an' I'm goin' to get 'em out. Did you ever hear of th' old Bar-20, over in th' Pecos Valley?"

"I shore did," answered Idaho. "Why?"

"I was near raised on it Bill Long is Hopalong Cassidy, an' Red Thompson is Red Connors, th' whitest men that ever set a saddle. Rob a bank, an' shoot a man from behind! Did Bill Long act like a man that had to shoot in th' back when he made Thorpe climb his own wall, with his own crowd lookin' on? Most of their lives has been spent fightin' Kane's kind; an' no breed of pups can hold 'em while I'm drawin' my breath. It's only how to do it th' best way that's botherin' me. I've slipped 'em a pair of guns, so I got a little time to think. Why, cuss it: Hoppy knows th' skunk that got Ridley! An' before we're through we'll know who robbed th' bank, an' hand 'em over to Mac. That's what's keepin' th' three of us here!"

"Bless my gran'mother's old gray cat!" breathed Idaho. "No wonder they pulled th' string! I'm sayin' Kane's got hard ridin' ahead. Say, can I tell th' boys at th' ranch?"

"Tell 'em nothin' that you wouldn't know except for me tellin' you," replied Johnny. "I know they're good boys; but they might let it slip. Me an' Hoppy an' Red are aimin' for them rewards an' we're goin' to get 'em both."

"It's a plumb lovely night," muttered Idaho. "Nicest night I think I ever saw. I don't want no rewards, but I just got to get my itchin' paws into what's goin' on around this town. An' it's a lovely town. Nicest town I think I ever was in. That 'dobe shack ain't what it once was. I know, because, not bein' friendly with th' sheriff, an' not bein' able to look all directions at once, I figgered I might be in it, myself, some day. So I've looked it over good, inside an' out. Th' walls are crumbly, an' th' bars in th' window are old. There's a waggin tongue in Pete Jarvis' freight waggin that's near twelve foot long, an' a-plenty thick. Ash, I think it is; that or oak. Either's good enough. If it was shoved between th' bars an' then pushed sideways that jail wouldn't be a jail no more. If Pete ain't taken th' waggin to bed with him, bein' so proud of it, we can crack that little hazelnut. I'm goin' back an' see how many are still hangin' around."

"I'm goin' back to th' hotel, so I'll be seen there," said Johnny.

"I'll do th' same, later," replied his friend as they separated.

Quayle was getting rid of some of his accumulated anger, which reflection had caused to soar up near the danger point. "Tom Ridley wasn't killed by no strangers!" he growled, banging the table with his fist. "I can name th' man that done it by callin' th' roll av Kane's litter; an' I'll be namin' th' bank robbers in th' same breath." He looked around as Johnny entered the room. "An' what did ye find, lad?"

"Idaho was right. They've got 'em in th' jail."

"An' if I was as young a man as you," said the proprietor, "they wouldn't kape 'em there. As ut is I'm timpted to go up an' bust in th' dommed door, before th' sheriff comes back from his ride. Tom Ridley's murderer? Bah!"

"Back from his ride?" questioned Johnny, quickly and eagerly.

"Shure. He just wint down th' trail. Tellin' Mac, I don't doubt that he's got th' men Twitchell wants. I was lookin' around when he wint past. This is th' time, lad. I'll help ye by settin' fire to Red Frank's corral if th' jail's watched. It'll take their attention. Or I'll lug me rifle up an' cover ye while ye work." He arose and went into the office for the weapon, Johnny following him. "There she is full to th' ind. An' I know her purty ways."

"Tim," said Johnny's low voice over his shoulder. "Yo're white, clean through. I don't need yore help, anyhow, not right now. An' because you are white I'm goin' to tell you somethin' that'll please you, an' give me one more good friend in this rotten town. Bill Long an' Red Thompson are friends of mine. They did not rob th' bank, nor shoot Ridley; but Bill knows who did shoot Ridley. He saw him climbin' out of Kane's south stable while th' smoke was still comin' from th' gun that shot yore friend. I can put my hand on th' coyote in five minutes. Th' three of us are stayin' here to get that man, th' man who robbed th' bank, an' Pecos Kane. I'm tellin' you this because I may need a good friend in Mesquite before we're through."

Quayle had wheeled and gripped his shoulder with convulsive force. "Ah!" he breathed. "Come on, lad; point him out! Point him out for Tim Quayle, like th' good lad ye are!"

"Do you want him so bad that yo're willin' to let th' real killer get away?" asked Johnny. "You only have to wait an' we'll get both."

"What d'ye mean?"

"You don't believe he shot Ridley without bein' told to do it, do you?"

"Kane told him; I know it as plain as I know my name."

"Knowin' ain't provin' it, an' provin' it is what we got to do."

"Tis th' curse av th' Irish, jumpin' first an' thinkin' after," growled Quayle. "Go wan!"

"Yo're friends with McCullough," said Johnny. "Mac knows a little; an' I'm near certain he's heard of Hopalong Cassidy an' Red Connors, of th' Bar-20. Don't forget th' names: Hopalong Cassidy an' Red Connors, of th' old Bar-20 in th' Pecos Valley. Buck Peters was foreman. I want you to go down an' pay him a friendly visit, and tell him this," and Quayle listened intently to the message.

"Bye," chuckled the proprietor, "ye leave Mac to me. We been friends for years, an' Tom Ridley was th' friend of us both. But, lad, ye may die; an' Bill Long may die life is uncertain anny where, an' more so in Mesquite, these days. If yer a friend av Tim Quayle, slip me th' name av th' man that murdered Ridley. I promise ye to kape han's off an' I want no reward. But it fair sickens me to think his name may be lost. Tom was like a brother."

"If you knew th' man you couldn't hold back," replied Johnny. "Here: I'll tell Idaho, an' Ed Doane. If Bill an' I go under they'll give you his description. I don't know his name."

"Th' offer is a good wan; but Tim Quayle never broke his word to anny man an' there's nothin' on earth or in hiven I want so much as to know who murdered Tom Ridley. I pass ye my word with th' sign av th' cross, on th' witness of th' Holy Virgin, an' on th' mem'ry av Tom Ridley I'll stay me hand accordin' to me promise."

Johnny looked deeply into the faded blue eyes through the tears which filmed them. He gripped the proprietor's hand and leaned closer. "A Greaser with a pock-marked face, an' a crescent-shaped scar over his right eye. He is about my height an' drags one foot slightly when he walks."

"Aye, from th' ball an' chain!" muttered Quayle. "I know th' scut! Thank ye, lad: I can sleep better nights. An' I can wait as no Irishman ever waited before. Annythin' Tim Quayle has is yourn; yourn an' yore friends. I'll see Mac tomorrow. Good night." He cuddled the rifle and went toward the stairs, but as he put his foot on the first step he stopped, turned, and went to a chair in a corner. "I'm forgettin'," he said, simply. "Ye may need me," and he leaned back against the wall, closing his eyes, an expression of peace on his wrinkled face.

Chapter XIII

Idaho slipped out of the darkness of the kitchen and appeared in the door. "All right, Nelson," he called. "There's two on guard an' th' rest have left. They ain't takin' their job any too serious, neither. Just one apiece," "he chuckled.

Johnny looked at the proprietor. "Got any rope, Tim?" he asked.

"Plenty," answered Quayle, arising hastily and leading the way toward the kitchen. Supplying their need he stood in the door and peered into the darkness after them. "Good luck, byes," he muttered.

Pete Jarvis was proud of his new sixteen-foot freighter and he must have turned in his sleep when two figures, masked to the eyes by handkerchiefs, stole into his yard and went off with the heavy wagon tongue. They carried it up to the old wagon near the jail, where they put it down, removed their boots, and went on without it, reaching the rear wall of the jail without incident, where they crouched, one at each corner, and smiled at the conversation going on.

"I'm hopin' for a look at yore faces," said Red's voice, "to see what they looked like before I get through with 'em, if I ever get my chance. Come in, an' be sociable."

"Yo're doin' a lot of talkin' now, you red-headed coyote," came the jeering reply. "But how are you goin' to talk to th' judge?"

"Bring some clean straw in th' mornin'," said Bill Long, "or we'll bust yore necks. Manure's all right for Greasers, an' you, but we're white men. Hear me chirp, you mangy pups?"

"It's good enough for you!" snapped a guard. "I was goin' to get you some, but now you can rot, for all I care!"

Johnny backed under the window, raised up and pressed his face against the rusty bars. "It's th' Kid," he whispered. "Are you untied yet?"

The soft answer pleased him and he went back to his corner of the wall, where he grudged every passing minute. He had decided to wait no longer, but to risk the noise of a shot if the unsuspecting guards could get a gun out quickly enough, and he was about to tell Idaho of the change in the plans when the words of a guard checked him.

"Guess I'll walk around again," said one of them, arising slowly. "Gettin' cramped, an' sleepy, settin' here."

"You spit in that window again an' I'll bust yore neck!" said Red's angry voice, whereupon Johnny found a new pleasure in doing his duty.

"You ain't bustin' nobody, or nothin'," jeered the guard, "'less it's th' rope yo're goin' to drop on." He yawned and stretched and sauntered along the side of the building, turned the corner and then raised his hands with a jerk as a Colt pushed into his stomach and a hard voice whispered terse instructions, which he instantly obeyed. "You fellers ain't so bad, at that," he said, with only a slight change in his voice; "but yo're shore playin' in hard luck."

"Keep yore sympathy to yoreself!" angrily retorted Bill Long.

Idaho, having unbuckled the gun-belt and laid it gently on the ground, swiftly pulled the victim's arms down be hind his back and tied the crossed wrists. Johnny now got busy with ropes for his feet, and a gag, and they soon laid him close to the base of the wall, and crept toward the front of the building, one to each wall. Johnny tensed himself as Idaho sauntered around the other corner.

"Makin' up with 'em?" asked the guard, ironically. "You don't want to let 'em throw a scare into you. They'll never harm nobody no more." He lazily arose to stretch his legs on a turn around the building. "You listen to what I'm goin' to tell 'em," he said. Then he squawked and went down with Johnny on his back, Idaho's dive coming a second later. A blow on his head caused him to lose any impertinent interest which he might have had in subsequent events and soon he, too, lay along the base of the rear wall, bound, gagged, and helpless.

"I near could feel th' jar of that in here," said Red's cheerful voice. "I'm hopin' it was th' coyote that spit through th' window. What's next?" he asked, on his feet and pulling at bars. He received no answer and commented upon that fact frankly and profusely.

"Shut yore face," growled Bill, working at his side. "He's hatchin' somethin' under his hat."

"Somethin' hatchin' all over me," grunted Red, stirring restlessly. "I'm a heap surprised this old mud hut ain't walkin' off some'ers."

Bill squirmed. ",You ain't got no call to put on no airs," he retorted. "Mine's been hatched a long time. I wouldn't let a dog lay on straw as rotten as that stuff. Oh!" he gloated. "Somebody's shore goin' to pay for this little party!"

"Wish th' sheriff would open that outside door about now," chuckled Red, balancing his six-chambered gift "I'd make him pop-eyed."

Hurrying feet, booted now, came rapidly nearer and soon the square-cornered end of a seasoned wagon tongue scraped on the adobe window ledge. Bill Long grabbed it and drew it between two of the bars.

"Go toward th' south," he said. "That's th' boy! Listen to 'em scrape!" he exulted. "Go ahead she's startin'. I can feel th' 'dobe crackin' between th' bars. Come back an' take th' next you'll have a little better swing because it's further from th' edge of th' window. Go ahead! It's bendin' an' pullin' out at both ends. Go on! Whoop! There goes th' 'dobe. Come back to th' middle an' use that pry as a batterin'-ram on this bar. Steady; we'll do th' guidin'. All ready? Then let her go! Fine! Try again. That's th' stuff she's gone! Take th' next Ready? Let her go! There goes more 'dobe, on this side. Once more: Ready? Let her go! Good enough: Here we come."

"Wait," said Johnny. "We'll pass one of these fellers in to you. If we leave 'em both together they'll mebby roll together an' untie each other."

"Like we did," chuckled Red.

"Give us th' first one you got," said Bill. "He's th' one that spit through th' window. I want him to lay on this straw, too. He's tied, an' can't scratch."

The guard was raised to the window, pushed and pulled through it and carelessly dumped on Red's bed, after which it did not take long for the two prisoners to gain their freedom.

"Good Kid!" said Bill, gripping his friend's hand. "An' you, too, whoever you are!"

"Don't mention no names," whispered Idaho. "We couldn't find no ear plugs," he chuckled, shaking hands with Red. "I'm too well known in this town. What'll we do with this coyote? Let him lay here?"

"No," answered Johnny. "He might roll over to Red Frank's an' get help. Picket him to a bush or cactus. Here, gimme a hand with him. I reckon he's come to, by th' way he's bracin' hisself. Little faster time's flyin'. All right, put him down." Johnny busied himself with the last piece of rope and stood up. "Come on Kane's stables, next."

As they crossed the street above the gambling-house, where in reality it was a trail, Bill Long took a hand in the evening's plans.

"Red," he said, "you go an' get our cayuses. Bring 'em right here, where we are now, an' wait for us. Idaho, you an' Johnny come with me an' stand under th' window of my room to take th' things I let down, an' free th' rope from 'em. I'm cussed shore we ain't goin' to leave all of our traps behind, not unless they been stole."

"I like yore cussed nerve!" chuckled Idaho. "Don't blame you, though. I'm ready."

"His nerve's just plain gall!" snapped Red, turning to Hopalong. "Think yo're sendin' me off to get a couple of cayuses, while yo're runnin' that risk in there? Get th' cayuses yoreself; I'll get th' fixin's!"

"Don't waste time like this!" growled Johnny. "Do as yo're told, you red-headed wart! Corwin will shore go to th' jail before he turns in. Come on, Hoppy."

"That name sounds good again," chuckled Hopalong, giving Red a shove toward the stables. "Get them cayuses, Carrot-Top!"

Red obeyed, but took it out in talking to himself as he went along, and as he entered the north stable he stepped on something large and soft, which instantly went into action. Red dropped to his knees and clinched, getting both wrists in his hands. Being in a hurry, and afraid of any outcry, he could not indulge in niceties, so he brought one knee up and planted it forcefully in his enemy's stomach, threw his weight on it and jumped up and down. Sliding his hands down the wrists, one at a time, he found the knife and took it from the relaxing fingers. Then he felt for the victim's jaw with one hand and hit it with the other. Arising, he hummed a tune and soon led out the two horses.

"Don't like to leave th' others for them fellers to use," he growled, and forthwith decided not to leave them. He drove them out of both stables, mounted his own, led Hopalong's, and slowly herded the other dozen ahead of him over the soft sand and away. When he finally reached the agreed-upon meeting place he reflected with pleasure that anyone wishing to use those horses for the purpose of pursuit, or any other purpose, would first have to find, and then catch them. They were going strong when he had last heard them.

Idaho had stopped under the window pointed out to him, and his two companions, leaving their boots in his tender care, were swallowed up in the darkness. They opened the squeaking front door, cautiously climbed the squeaking stairs and fairly oozed over the floor of the upper hall, which wanted to squeak, and did so a very little. Hopalong slowly opened the door of his room, thankful that he had oiled its one musical hinge, and felt cautiously over the bed. It was empty, and his sigh of relief was audible. And he was further relieved when his groping hand found his possessions where he had left them. He was stooping to loosen the coil of rope at the pommel of his saddle when he heard a sleepy, inquiring voice and a soft thud, and anxiously slipped to the door.

"Kid!" he whispered. "Kid!"

"Shut yore fool face," replied the object of his solicitude, striking a match for one quick glance around. The room was strange to him, since he never had been in it be fore, and he had to get his bearings. The inert man on the bed did not get a second glance, for the sound and weight of the blow had reassured Johnny. There were two saddles, two rifles, two of everything, which was distressing under the circumstances.

Hopalong had just lowered his own saddle to the waiting Idaho when the catlike Johnny entered the room with a saddle and a rifle. He placed them on the bed, where they would make no noise, and departed, catlike. Soon returning he placed another saddle and rifle on the bed and departed once more.

Hopalong, having sent down both of Johnny's first offerings, felt over the bed for the rest of Red's belongings, if there were any more, and became profanely indignant as his hand caressed another rifle and then bumped against another saddle.

"What'n hell is he doin'?" he demanded. "My G-d! There's more'n a dozen rooms on this floor, an' men in all of 'em! Hey, Kid!" he whispered as breathing sounded suddenly close to him.

"What?" asked Johnny, holding two slicker rolls, a sombrero, a pair of boots, and a suit of clothes. Two belts with their six-guns were slung around his neck, but the darkness mercifully hid the sight from his friend.

"D n it! We ain't movin this hotel," said Hopalong with biting sarcasm. "It don't belong to us, you know. !An' what was that whack I heard when you first went in?"

"Somebody jumped Red's bed, an' wanted to know some fool thing, or somethin', an' I had to quiet him. An' what'n blazes are you kickin' about? I've moved twice as much as you have, more'n twice as far. Grab holt of some of this stuff an' send it down to Idaho. He'll think you've went to sleep."

"You locoed tumble-bug!" said Hopalong. "Aimin' to send down th' bed, with th' feller in it, too?"

A door creaked suddenly and they froze.

"Quit yore d——d noise an' go to sleep!" growled a sleepy, truculent voice, and the door creaked shut again.

After a short wait in silence Hopalong put out an inquiring hand. "Come on," he whispered. "What you got there?"

Johnny told him, and Hopalong dropped the articles out of the window, all but the hat, boots, and clothes. "Don't you know Red's wearin' his clothes, boots an' hat, you chump?" he said, gratis. "Leave them things here an' f oiler me," and he started for the head of the stairs.

They were halfway down when they heard a horse gal loping toward the hotel. It was coming from the direction of the jail and they nudged each other.

Sheriff Corwin, feeling like he was master of all he surveyed, had ridden to the jail before going to report to Kane for the purpose of cautioning the guards not to relax their vigil. Not being able to see them in the darkness meant nothing to him, for they should have challenged him, and had not. He swept up to the door, angrily calling them by name and, receiving no reply, dismounted in hot haste, shook the door and then went hurriedly around the building to feel of the bars. One sweep of his hand was enough and as he wheeled he tripped over the wagon tongue and fell sprawling, his gun flying out of his hand. Groping around he found it, jammed it back into the holster, darted back to his horse and dashed off at top speed for Kane's to spread the alarm and collect a posse.

There never had been any need for caution in opening the hotel door and his present frame of mind would not have heeded it if there had been. Flinging it back he dashed through and opened his mouth to emit a bellow calculated almost to raise the dead. The intended shout turned to a choking gasp as two lean, strong hands gripped his throat, and then his mental sky was filled with lightning as a gun-butt fell on his head. His limp body was carried out and dropped at the feet of the cheerful Idaho, who helped tear up portions of the sheriff's clothing for his friends to use on the officer's hands, feet, and mouth.

"Every time I hit a head I shore gloat," growled Johnny, his thoughts flashing back to his first night in town.

"Couldn't you send him down, too?" Idaho asked of Hopalong. "An' how many saddles do you an' Red use generally?"

"He wasn't up there," answered Hopalong. "We run into him as we was comin' out."

Johnny's match flashed up and out in one swift movement. "Corwin!" he exulted. "An' I'm glad it was me that hit him!"

Idaho rolled over on the ground and made strange noises. Sitting up he gasped: "Didn't I say it was a lovely night? Holy mavericks!"

"You fellers aim to claim squatter sovereignty?" whispered Red from the darkness. "If I'd 'a' knowed it I'd 'a' tied up somethin' I left layin' loose."

"We got to get a rustle on," said Hopalong. "Some cusses come to right quick. That gent in Red's bed is due to ask a lot of questions at th' top of his voice. Come on grab this stuff, pronto!"

"I left another in th' stable that's goin' to do some yellin' purty soon," said Red. "Reckon he's a Greaser."

They picked up the things and went off to find the horses and as they dropped the equipment Red felt for his saddle. "Hey! Where's mine?" he demanded.

"Here, at my feet," said Johnny.

Red passed his hand over it and swore heartily. "This ain't it, you blunderin' jackass! Why didn't you get mine?" he growled.

"Feel of this one," grunted Johnny, kicking the other saddle.

Red did so. "That's it. Who's th' other belong to?"

"I don't know," answered Johnny, growing peeved. "Yo're cussed particular, you are! Here's two rifles, two six-guns, an' two belts. Take 'em with you an' pick out yore own when it gets light. I don't want 'em."

Red finished cinching up and slipped a hand over the rifles. He dropped one of them into its scabbard. "Got mine. Chuck th' other away."

"Take it along an' chuck it in th' crick," said Idaho. "Now you fellers listen: If you ride up th' middle of Big Crick till you come to that rocky ground west of our place you can leave th' water there, an' yore trail will be lost. It runs southwest an' northeast for miles, an' is plenty wide an' wild. If you need any thin' ride in to our place any night after dark. I'll post th' boys."

"We ain't got a bit of grub," growled Red. "Well, it ain't th' first time," he added, cheerfully.

"We're not goin' up Big Crick," said Hopalong, decisively. "We're ridin' like we wanted to get plumb out of this country, which is just what Bill Long an' Red Thompson would do. When fur enough away we're circlin' back east of town, on th' edge of th' desert, where nobody will hardly think we'd go. They'll suspect that hard ground over yore way before they will th' desert. Where'll we meet you, Kid, if there's any thin' to be told; an' when?"

Johnny considered and appealed to Idaho, whose knowledge of the country qualified him to speak. In a few moments the place had been chosen and well described, and the two horsemen pulled their mounts around and faced northward.

"Get a-goin'," growled Johnny. "Anybody'd reckon you thought a night was a week long."

"Don't like to leave you two boys alone in this town, after tonight's plays," said Hopalong, uneasily. "Nobody is dumb enough to figger that we didn't have outside help. Keep yore eyes open!"

"Pull out!" snapped Johnny. "It'll be light in two hours more!"

"So-long, you piruts," softly called Idaho. "Yessir," he muttered, joyously; "it's been one plumb lovely night!"

Not long after the noise of galloping had died in the north a Mexican staggered from the stable, groping in the darkness as he made his erratic way toward the front of the gambling-hall, his dazed wits returning slowly. Leaning against the wall of the building for a short rest, he went on again, both hands gripping his jaw. Too dazed to be aware of the disappearance of the horses and attentive only to his own woes, he blundered against the bound and gagged sheriff, went down, crawled a few yards and then, arising again to his feet, groped around the corner of the building and sat down against it to collect his bewildering thoughts.

Upstairs in the room Red had used, the restless figure on the bed moved more and more, finally sitting up, moaning softly. Then, stiffening as memory brought some thing back to him, he groped about for matches, blundering against the walls and the scanty furniture, and called forth profane language from the room adjoining, whose occupant, again disturbed, arose and yanked open his door.

"What you think yo're doin', raisin' all this racket?" he demanded.

"Somebody near busted my head," moaned the other. "I been robbed!" he shouted as the lack of impedimenta at last sank into his mind.

"Say!" exclaimed his visitor, remembering an earlier nocturnal disturbance. "Wait here till I get some matches!"

He returned with a lighted lamp, instead, which revealed the truth, and its bearer swiftly led the way into the second room down the hall. A pair of boots which should not have been there and the absence of the equipment which should have been there confirmed their fears. The man with the lamp held it out of the window and swore under his breath as a bound figure below him gurgled and writhed.

"Looks like Corwin!" he muttered, and hastened down to make sure, taking no time to dress. The swearing Mexican received no attention until the sheriff staggered back with the investigator, and then the vague tale was listened to.

A bellowing voice awakened the sleepers in the big building and an impromptu conference of irate men, mostly undressed, was held in the hall. Sandy Woods returned from the stables, reporting them bare of horses; the investigator from the jail came back with the angry guards, one of whom was too shaky to walk with directness. Others came from a visit to Red Frank's corral, leading half a dozen borrowed horses, and, a hasty, cold breakfast eaten, the posse, led by a sick, vindictive sheriff, pounded northward along a plain trail.

Those who were not able to go along stood and peered through the paling darkness and two deputies left to take up positions in the front and rear of Quayle's hotel where they could see without being seen, while a third man crept into the stable to look for a Tincup horse. Had he been content with looking he would have been more fortunate, but thinking that the master would have no further use for the animal, he decided to take it for himself, trusting that possession would give him a better claim when the new ownership was finally decided by Kane. Reassured by the earliness of the hour and by the presence of the hidden deputy, he went ahead with his plans.

Pepper's flattened ears meant nothing to the exultant thief, for it had been his experience that all horses flattened their ears whenever he approached them, especially if they had reason to know him; so, with a wary eye on the trim, black hoofs, he slipped along the stable wall to gain her head. He had just untied the rope and started back with the end of it in his hand when there was a sud den, sidewise, curving swerve of the silky black body, a grunt of surprise and pain from the thief, pinned against the wall by the impact, and then, curving back again and wheeling almost as though on a pivot, Pepper's teeth crunched flesh and bone and the sickened thief, by a miracle escaping the outflung front hoofs, staggered outside the stable and fell as the whizzing hind feet took the half-open door from its flimsy hinges. Rolling around the corner, the thief crawled under a wagon and sank down unconscious, his crushed shoulder staining darkly through his torn shirt.

The watching deputy arose to go to his friend's assistance, but looked up and stopped as a growled question came from Ed Doane's window.

"Jim's hurt," he explained to the face behind the rifle. "Went in to see if his cayuse had wandered in there, an' th' black near killed him. Gimme a hand with him, will you?"

Quayle had nearly fallen off the chair he had spent the night on when the crash and the scream of the enraged horse awakened him. He ran to the kitchen door, rifle in hand, and looked out, hearing the deputy's words.

"I'll give ye a hand," he said; "but more cheerful if it's to dig a grave. Mother av G-d!" he breathed as he reached the wagon. "I'm thinkin' it's a priest ye want, an' there's none within twinty miles." He looked around at the forming crowd. "Get a plank," he ordered, "an' get Doc Sharpe."

Ed Doane, followed by Johnny and Idaho, ran from the kitchen and joined the group. One glance and Johnny went into the stable, calling as he entered. Patting the quivering nozzle of the black he looked at the rope and came out again.

"That man-killer has got to be shot," said the deputy to Ed Doane.

"I'll kill th' man that tries it," came a quiet reply, and "the deputy wheeled to look into a pair of frosty blue eyes. "Th' knot I tie in halter ropes don't come loose, for Pep per will untie any common knot an' go off huntin' for me. It was untied. If you want to back up a hoss thief, an' mebby prove yore part in it, say that again."

"Yo're plumb mistaken, Nelson," said the deputy. "Jim was huntin' his own cayuse, which Long an' Thompson stampeded out of th' stable last night. He was goin' over th' town first before he went out to look for it on th' plain."

"That's good!" sneered Johnny. "Long an' Thomp son are in jail. I'm standin' to what th' knot showed. Do you still reckon Pepper's got to be shot?"

"They broke out an' got away," retorted the deputy; "an' they shore as h--l had outside help." He looked knowingly into Johnny's eyes. "Nobody that belongs to this town would 'a' done it."

"That's a lie," said Quayle, his rifle swinging up carelessly. "I belong to this town, an' I'd 'a' done it, mesilf, if I'd thought av it. Seein' that I didn't, I'm cussed glad that somewan had better wits than me own."

"I was aimin' to do it," said Idaho, smiling. "I was goin' out to get th' boys, an' bust th' jail tonight. I was holdin' back a little, though, because I was scared th' boys might get a little rough an' lynch a few deputies. They're on set triggers these days."

The cook started to roll up his sleeves. "I'll lick th' daylight out av anny man that goes to harm that horse, or me name's not Murphy," he declared, spitting. "I feed her near every mornin', an' she's gintle as a baby lamb. But she's got a keen nose for blackguards!"

Dr. Sharpe arrived, gave his orders and followed the bearers of the improvised stretcher toward his house. As the crowd started to break up Johnny looked coldly at the deputy. "You heard me," he said. "Pass th' word along. An' if she don't kill th' next one, *I* will!"

North of town the posse reached Big Creek and exulted as it saw the plain prints going on from the further bank. Corwin, sitting his saddle with a false ease, stifled a moan at every rise and fall, his head seeming about to split under the pulsing hammer blows. When he caught sight of the trail leading from the creek he nodded dully and spoke to his nearest companion.

"Leavin' th' country by th' straightest way," he growled. "It'll mebby be a long chase, damn 'em!"

"They ain't got much of a start," came the hopeful reply. "We ought to catch sight of 'em from th' top of th' divide beyond Sand Creek. It's fair level plain for miles north of that. Their cayuses ain't no better than ourn, an' some of ourn will run theirs off their feet."

Sand Creek came into sight before noon and when it was reached there were no tracks on the further side. The posse was prepared for this and split without hesitation, Corwin leading half of it west along the bank and the other half going east. Five minutes later an exclamation caused the sheriff to pull up and look where one of his men was pointing. A rifle barrel projected a scant two inches from the water and the man who rode over to it laughed as he leaned down from the saddle.

"It lit on a ridge of gravel an' didn't slide down quite fur enough," he called. "An' it shore is busted proper."

"Bring it here," ordered Corwin. He took it, examined it and handed it to the next man, whose head ached as much as his own and who would not have been along except that his wish for revenge over-rode his good sense.

"That yourn?" asked the sheriff.

The owner of the broken weapon growled. "They've plumb ruined it. It's one more score they'll pay. Come on!" and he whirled westward. Corwin drew his Colt and fired into the air three times at counted intervals, and galloped after his companions when faint, answering shots sounded from the east.

"They're makin' for that rocky stretch," he muttered; "an' if they get there in time they're purty safe."

Not long after he had rejoined his friends the second part of the posse whirled along the bank, following the trail of the first, eager to overtake it and learn what had been discovered.

Well to the east Hopalong and Red rode at the best pace possible in the water of the creek, now and then turning in the saddle to look searchingly behind them. Fol lowing the great bend of the stream they went more and more to the south and when the shadows were long they rode around a ridge and drew rein. Red dismounted and climbed it, peering over its rocky backbone for minutes. Returning to his companion he grinned cheerfully.

"No coyotes in sight," he said. "Some went west, I reckon, an' found that busted rifle where we planted it. No coyotes, at all; but there's a black bear down in that little strip of timber."

"I can eat near all of it, myself," chuckled Hopalong. "Let's camp where we drop it. A dry wood fire won't show up strong till dark. Come on!"

Chapter XIV
The Staked Plain

Pecos Kane sat behind his old desk in the inner room and listened to the reports of the night's activities, his anger steadily mounting until ghostly flames seemed to be licking their thin tongues back in his eyes. The jail guards had come and departed, speaking simply and truthfully, suggesting various reasons to excuse the laxity of their watch. The Mexican told with painful effort about the loss of the horses, growing steadily more incoherent from the condition of his jaw and from his own rising rage. Men came, and went out again on various duties, one of them closely interrogating the owner of the freight wagon, whose anger had died swiftly by the recovery of the great tongue, which was none the worse for its usage except for certain indentations of no moment. A friend of Quayle and hostile to Kane and for what Kane stood for, the wagon owner allowed his replies to be short, and yet express a proper indignation, which did not exist, about the whole affair. When again alone in the sanctity of his home he allowed himself the luxury of low-voiced laughter and determined to put his crowbar where any needy individual of the future could readily find it.

Bill Trask, because of his short-gun expertness temporarily relieved of guarding the partition door, led three companions toward Quayle's hotel, his face and the faces of the others tense and determined. Two went around to the stable, via Red Frank's and the rear street and one of them stopped near it while the other slipped along the kitchen wall and crouched at the edge of the kitchen door. The third man went silently into the hotel office as Trask sauntered carelessly into the barroom and nodded at its inmates.

"Them fellers shore raised hell," he announced to Ed Doane as he motioned for a drink.

"They did," replied Doane, spinning a glass after the sliding bottle, after which he flung the coin into the old cigar box and assiduously polished the bar, wondering why Trask patronized him instead of Kane's.

"They shore had nerve," persisted the newcomer, looking at Johnny.

"They shore did," acquiesced the man at the table, who then returned to his idle occupation of trying to decipher the pattern of the faded-out wall paper. Wall paper was a rarity in the town and deserved some attention.

"Them guards was plumb careless," said Kane's hired man. Not knowing to whom he was speaking there was no reply, and he tried again, addressing the bartender.

"They was careless," replied Doane, without interest.

Johnny was alert now, the persistent remarks awakening suspicion in his mind, and a slight sound from the wall at his back caused him to push his chair from the table and assume a more relaxed posture. His glance at the lower and nearer corner of the window let him memorize its exact position and he waited, expectant, for whatever might happen. The surprise and capture of his two friends had worked, but that had been the first time; there would be no second, he told himself, especially as far as he was concerned.

"Is th' boss in?" asked the visitor.

"Th' boss ain't in," answered Ed Doane as Johnny glanced at the front door, the front window and the door of the office, which the bartender noticed. "Too dusty," said Doane, going around the bar to the front wall and closing the window.

"When will he be in?"

"Dunno," grunted the bartender, once more in his accustomed place.

"I got to see him."

"I handle things when he ain't here," said Doane. "See me," he suggested, looking through the door leading to the office, where he fancied he had heard a creak.

"Got to see him, an' pronto," replied the visitor. "He made some remarks this mornin' about gettin' them fellers out. We know it was done by somebody on th' outside, an' we got a purty good idea of who it was since Quayle shot off his mouth. He's been gettin' too swelled up lately. If he don't come in purty quick I'm aimin' to 'dig him out, myself."

Johnny was waiting for him to utter the cue word and knew that there would be a slight change in facial expression, enunciation, or body posture just before it came. He was not swallowing the suggestions that it was Quayle who was wanted.

"You shore picked out a real job to handle all alone," said Doane, not letting his attention wander from the hotel office. "Any dog can dig out a badger, but that's only th' beginnin'," he said pleasantly, his hand on the gun which always lay under the bar. He expected a retort to his insult, and when none came it put a keener edge to his growing suspicions.

"I'm diggin' him out, just th' same," said Trask. "There's law in this town, an' everybody's on one side or th' other. Bein' a deputy it's my job to see about them that's on th' other side. Gettin' arrested men out of jail is serious an' I got to ask questions about it. Of course, Quayle don't allus say what he means we none of us do. We all like to have our jokes; but I got to do my duty, even if it's only askin' questions. Is he out, or layin' " low?"

"He's out," grunted Doane, "but he'll be back any; minute, I reckon."

"All right; I'll wait," said Trask, carelessly, but he tensed himself. "How's business?" and at the words he flashed into action.

A chair crashed and a figure leaped back from it, two guns belching at its hips. The face and hand which popped up into the rear window disappeared again as the smoking Colt swung past the opening and across Johnny's body to send its second through the office doorway, and curses answered both shots. Trask, bent over, held his right arm with his left hand, his gun against the wall near the front door. The first shot of Johnny's righthand Colt had torn it from Trask's hand as it left the holster and the second had rendered the arm useless for the moment. A shot from the corner of the stable sang through the window and barely missed its mark as Johnny leaned forward, but his instant reply ended all danger from that point.

"Trask," he said, "I'm leavin' town. I ain't got a chance among buildin's again' pot-shooters. I'm leavin' ' but th' Lord help Kane an' his gang when I come back. You can tell him I'm comin' a-shootin'. An' you can tell him this: I'm goin' to get him, Pecos Kane, if I has to pull him out of his hell-hole like I pulled Thorpe. Go ahead of me to th' stable I'll blow you apart if any pot-shooter tries at me. G'wan!"

Trask obeyed, the gun against his spine too eloquent a persuader to be ignored. He knew that there were no pot-shooters yet, and he was glad of it, for if there had been one, and his captor was killed, the relaxation of the tense thumb holding back the hammer of a gun whose trigger was tied back would fire the weapon. The man who held it would fire one shot after his own death, how ever instantaneous it might be.

Passing through the kitchen Johnny picked up his saddle and ordered his captive to carry the rifle and slicker roll. They disappeared into the stable and when they came out again Johnny ordered Trask into the saddle, mounted behind him and rode for the arroyo which lay not far from the hotel. At last away from the buildings he made Trask dismount, climbed over the cantle and settled himself in the vacated saddle.

"I'm goin' down to offer myself to McCullough," he said. "You can tell Kane that, too. They'll need men down there, an' I'll be th' maddest man they got. An' th' next time me an' you have any gun talk, I'm shootin' to kill. Adios!"

He left the cursing deputy and went straight for the trail, where the rising wind played with the dust, and along it until stopped by a voice in a barranca.

"I'm puttin' 'em up," he called. "My name's Nelson an' I'm mad clean through. Get a rustle on; I want to see Mac."

"Go ahead, Bar-20," drawled the voice. "I wasn't dead shore. There's a good friend of yourn down there."

"Quayle?" asked Johnny.

"There's another: Waffles, of th' O-Bar-O," came the reply, and a verse of a nearly forgotten song arose on the breeze.

I've swum th' Colorado where she runs down dost to hell, I've braced th' faro layouts in Cheyenne;

I've fought for muddy water with a howlin' bunch of Sioux, An' swallered hot tamales, an' cayenne.

"There's more, but I've done forgot most of it," apolo gized the singer.

Johnny laughed with delight. "Why, that's Lefty Allen's old song. Here's th' second verse:"
I've rid a pitchin' broncho till th' sky was underneath,
I've tackled every desert in th' land;
I've sampled Four-X whisky till I couldn't hardly see,
An' dallied with th' quicksands of th' Grande.

"That's shore O-Bar-O. Lefty made it up hisself, an' that boy could sing it. It all comes back to me now," he called it 'Th' Insult.' Why here, you!" he chuckled. "I said I was mad an' in a hurry. I ain't mad no more, but I am in a hurry. See you tonight, mebby. So-long."

Riding on again he soon reached the Question-Mark bunkhouse and dismounted as a puncher turned the corner of the house. They grinned at each other, these good, old-time friends.

"You son-of-a-gun!" chuckled Johnny, holding out his hand.

"You son-of-a-gun!" echoed Waffles, gripping it, and so they stood, silent, exchanging grins. It had been a long time since they last had seen each other.

McCullough loomed up in the doorway and grinned at them both.

"Hear yo're married," said Waffles.

"Shore!" bragged Johnny.

"It ain't spoiled you, yet. How's Hoppy an' Red?"

"Fine, now they're out of jail."

Waffles threw his head back and laughed heartily. "I near laughed till I busted when Quayle told us who they was. Hoppy an' Red in jail! It was funny!"

"Hello, Nelson," said McCullough. "What are you doin' down here?"

"Had to leave town; too many corners, an' too much cover. I'm lookin' for a job, if it don't cut me out of th' rewards."

"She's yourn."

"Wait a minute," said Johnny. "I can't take it. I got to be free to do what I want; but I'll hang out here for awhile."

"You've got th' job instanter," said the appreciative trail-boss smiling broadly. "It's steady work of bossin' yoreself. I've heard of yore work, up Gunsight way. Feed yet? Then come on."

"Shore will. Where's Quayle?"

"Rode back, roundabout; him not courtin' bein' seen; but I reckon everybody in town knows he's been here. He swears by you."

Despite Idaho's boasts to the contrary his ranch again had nocturnal visitors, and there was no lead-flying welcome accorded them. Having spied out the distribution of Lukins' riders the visitors chose a locality free from guards and with the coming of night drifted a sizable herd of Diamond L cattle across an outlying section of the range and with practiced art and uncanny instinct drove the compacted herd onto and over the rocky plateau, where the chief of the raiders obtained a speed with the cattle which always bordered upon a panicky flight, but never quite reached it. All that night they rumbled over the rocky stretch and as dawn brightened the eastern sky the running herd passed down a gentle slope, picked up the waiting caviya and not long thereafter moved over the hard bottom of a steep-walled ravine which could have been called a canyon without unduly stretching the meaning of the word.

The chief of the raiding party cared nothing for the fatness of the animals, or other conditions which might operate against the possibilities of a lucrative sale. There later would be time for improving their condition, plenty of time in a valley rich with grass. All he cared for now was to put miles speedily behind him, and this he was accomplishing like the master cattleman he was. After a mid-day breathing space they went on again, alternately walking and running, and well into the second night, stop ping at a water-hole known only to a few men other than these. Some miles north of this water-hole was another, and very much smaller one, being only a few feet across, and there also was a difference between the waters of the two. The larger was of a nature to be expected in such a locality, but much better than most such holes, for the water was only slightly alkaline and the cattle drank it eagerly. The other was sweet and pure and cold, but rather than to cover the distance to it and back again, it was ignored by all but one man, for the other stayed with the herd. There was grass around both; not enough to feed a herd thoroughly, but enough to keep it busy hunting over the scanty growth. With more than characteristic thought these holes had been named in a manner to couple and yet to keep them separate, and to Kane's drive crew they were known as "Sweet "and "Bitter."

Again on the trail before the sun had risen above the horizon, the herd was sent forth on another day's hard drive, which carried it, with the constantly growing tail herd of stragglers, far into the following night, despite all dumb remonstrances. No mercy was shown to it, but only a canny urging, and if no mercy was shown the cattle none was accepted by the drivers, who rode and worked, swore and panted on wiry ponies which, despite frequent changing, began to show the marks of their efforts under the pitiless sun and through the yielding sands. Both cattle and horses had about reached their limits when the late afternoon of the next day brought them to a rocky ledge sticking up out of the desert's floor, which now was hard and stony; and upon turning the south end of the ridge an emerald valley suddenly lay before their eyes, from whence the scent of water had put a new spirit into cattle and horses for the last few miles; and now it nearly caused a fatal stampede at the entrance to the narrow ledge which slanted down the steep, rock walls.

To a stranger such a sight would have awakened amazed incredulity, and strong suspicion that his sanity had been undermined by the heat-cursed, horror-laden desert miles; or he might have sneered wisely at so palpable a mirage, scorned to be tricked by it in any attempt to prove it otherwise and staggered on with contemptuous curses. But Miguel and the men he so autocratically bossed knew it to be no vision, no trick of air or mind, and sighed with relief when it finally lay before them. While they all knew it was there and had visited it before, none of them, except Miguel, had ever learned the way, try as they might, for until the high ledge of rock, hidden on the west by a great, upslanting billow of sand, came into sight there were no landmarks to show them the way. Each new journey across the simmering, shimmering plateau found fears in every heart but the guide's that he would lose his way. That their fears may be justified and to show them blame less in everything but their lack of confidence in him, it may be well to have a better understanding of this desert and what it meant; and to show why men should hold as preposterous any claim that a cattle herd could safely cross it. Some went even further and said no man, mounted or not, could make that journey, and confessed to themselves a superstitious fear and horror for it and everything pertaining to it.

Before the deep ruts had been cut in the old Santa Fe Trail in that year of excessive rains; before the first wheel had rolled over the prairie soil to prove that wagons could safely make the long and tiresome trip; before even the first pack trains of heavily laden mules plodded to or from the Missouri frontier, and even before the peltloaded mules of the great fur companies crossed Kansas soil to the trading posts of the East, Mexican hunters rode from the valley of Taos and Santa Fe to procure their winter meat from the vast brown herds of buffalo migrating over their curious, crescent-shaped course to and from the regions of the Arkansas, Canadian, and Cimarron. They dried the strips of succulent meat in the sun or over fires, the fuel for the latter having been supplied by the buffalo themselves on previous migrations; they stripped the hides from the prostrate bodies and cured them, and trafficked with the bands of Indians which followed the herds as persistently as did the great, gray wolves. Of these ciboleros, swarthy-skinned hunters of Mexico, some more hardy and courageous than their fellows, or by avarice turned trader, ventured further afield and were not balked by the high, beetling cliffs which bordered a great, forbidding plateau lying along and below the capricious Cimarron, in places a river of hide-and-seek in the sands, wet one day and dry the next.

From the mesa-like northern edge, along the warning arroyos of the Cimarron, where erosion, Nature's patient sculptor, carved miracles of artistry in the towering clays, shales, and sandstones, to the great sand hills billowing along its far-flung other edges, this barren waste of dreary sand and grisly alkali was a vast, simmering playground for dancing heat waves and fantastic mirage, and its treacherous pools of nauseous, alkaline waters shrunk daily from their encrusted edges and gleamed malignantly under a glowering, molten sun. Arroyos, level plain, shifting sand, and imponderable dust, with a scrawny, scanty, hopeless vegetation which the whimsical winds buried and then dug up again, this high desert plateau lay like a thing of death, cursing and accursed. It sloped imperceptibly southward, its dusty soil gradually breaking into billowy ridges constantly more marked and with deeper troughs, by insensible gradations becoming low sand hills, ever growing more separate and higher until at last they were beaten down and strewn broadcast by more persistent winds, and limited by the firmer soils which were blessed with more frequent rains to coax forth a thin cover of protecting, anchoring vegetation.

To the west they intruded nearly to the Rio Pecos, a stream which in almost any other part of the country would have been regarded as insignificant, but here was given greatness because its liquid treasure was beyond price and because it was permanent, though timid.

Of the first of the Mexicans to push out over this great desolation perhaps none returned, except by happy chance, to tell of its tortures and of the few serviceable waterholes leagues apart, the permanency of which none could foretell. But return some eventually did, and perhaps deprecated the miseries suffered, in view of the saving in miles; but their experience had been such as to impel them to drive a line of stakes along the happily chosen course to mark in this manner the way from each more trustworthy water-hole to the next, be they reservoirs or furtive streams which bubbled up and crept along to die not far from their hopeful springs, sucked up by palpitant air and swallowed by greedy sands, their burial places marked by a shroud of encrusted salts. In the winter and spring an occasional rain filled hollows, ofttimes coming as a cloudburst and making a brave showing as it tumultuously deepened some arroyo and roared valiantly down it toward swift effacement The trail was staked, if not by the swarthy traders, then by their red-skinned brothers, and from this line of stakes the tableland derived its name, and became known to men as the Lano Estacada, or Staked Plain.

Of this accursed desert no one man had full knowledge, nor thirsted for it if it were to be had only through his own efforts. There were great stretches unknown to any man, and there were other regions known to men who had not brought their knowledge out again; and what knowledge there was of its south-central portions was not to be found in men with white skins, but in certain marauding redmen fitted by survival to cope with problems such as it presented, and to live despite them. One other class knew something of its mysteries, for among the Mexicans there were some who had learned by bitter pilgrimages, but mostly from the mouths of men long dead who had passed the knowledge down successive generations, each increment a little larger when it left than when it came, who had a more comprehensive, embracing knowledge of the baking tableland; and these few, because what they knew could best be used in furtive, secretive pursuits bearing a swift penalty for those caught in them, hugged that knowledge closely and kept it to themselves. A man who has that which another badly needs can drive shrewd bargains. 'And of the few Mexicans who were enriched by the possession of this knowledge, those who knew most about it had mixed blood flowing through their veins, for the vast grisly plateau had been a short cut and place of refuge for marauding bands of Apaches, Utes, and Comanches while civilization crawled wonderingly in swaddling clothes.

Of the knowing few Pecos Kane owned two, owned them body and soul, and to make his title firmer than even proof of murder could assure, he threw golden sops to the wise ones' avarice and allowed them seats in the sun and privileges denied to their fellows. One of them, by name Miguel, a small part Spaniard and the rest Mescalero Apache, was a privileged man, for he knew not only the main trails across the plain but certain devious ways twisting in from the edges, one of which wandered for accursed miles, first across rock, then over sand and again over rock and unexpectedly turned a high, sharp ridge to look upon his Valle de Sorprendido, deep and green, whose crystal spring wandered musically along its gravelly bed from the graying western end of the canyon-like ravine to sink silently into the thirsty sands to the east and be seen no more. Manuel, also, knew this way.

Surprise Valley was no terminal, but a place for tonguelolling, wild-eyed cattle to pause and rest, drink and eat before the fearful journey called anew. No need for corral, fence, or herders here to keep them from straying, but an urgent need for pressing riders to throw the herd back on the trail again, to start the dumbly protesting animals on the thirty-six-hour drive to the next unfailing water, against the instinct which bade them stay. A valley of delight it was, a jewel, verdant and peaceful, forced by man to serve a vicious purpose; but as if in punishment for its perversion the glistening sand hills crept slowly nearer, each receding tide of their slow advance encroaching more and more each year until now the valley had shrunk by half and a stealthy grayness crept insiduously into its velvety freshness like the mark of sin across a harlot's cheek.

Near the fenced-in spring was an adobe building, deserted except when a drive crew sought its shelter, and it served principally as a storehouse should a place of refuge suddenly be needed. It lay not far from the sloping banks of detritus which now ran halfway up the sheer, smooth stone walls enclosing the valley. Across from it on the southern side of the depressed pasture a broad trail slanted up the rock cliffs to the desert above. The cabin, the trail, and the valley itself long ago would have been obliterated by sand but for the miles of rocks, large and small, which lay around it like a great, flat collar. Should some terrific sand storm sweep over it with a momentum great enough to bridge the rocky floor the valley would cease to be; and smaller storms raging far out on the encircling desert carried their sands farther and farther across the stubborn rock, until now its outer edge was closer by miles. Already each rushing wind retained sand enough to drop it into the valley and powder everything.

The pock-marked guide, disdaining the precarious labors of getting the herd down the ledge with no fatalities among the maddened beasts, lolled in his saddle on the brink of the precipice and watched the struggle on the plain behind him, where hard-riding, loudly yelling herders were dashing across the front of the weaving, shifting, stubborn mass of tortured animals, letting them through the frantic restraining barrier in small groups, which constantly grew larger. Here and there a more determined animal slipped through and galloped to the descending ledge, head down and tail up. The cracking of revolvers fired across the noses of the front rank grew steadily and Miguel deemed it safer to leave the brim of the cliff. It was possible that the maddened herd might break through the desperate riders and plunge to its destruction. Had the trail been a few hours longer nothing could have held them.

"Give a hand here!" shouted the trail-boss as the guide rode complacently out of danger. "Ride in there an' help split 'em!"

"I weel be needed w'en we leeve again," replied Miguel. "To run a reesk eet ees foolish. I tol' you to stop 'em a mile away an' spleet 'em there. Eet ees no beesness of Miguel's, theese. You deed not wan' to tak' the time? Then tak' w'at you call the consequence."

Eventually the last of the herd which mercifully was composed of stragglers whose lack of strength made them more tractable, were successfully led to the ledge and stumbled down it to join their brothers standing or lying in the little brook as if to appease their thirst by absorption before drinking deeply. The frantic, angry bawling of an hour ago was heard no more, for now a contented lowing sounded along the stream, where the quiet animals often waited half an hour before attempting to drink. They stood thus for hours, reluctant to leave even to graze and after leaving, left the grass and returned time after time to drink. There were a few half-blinded animals among the weaklings, but water, grass, and rest would restore their sight. Here they would stay until fit for the second and lesser ordeal, and the others in turn.

The weary riders, turning their mounts loose to join the rest of the horse herd, piled their saddles against the wall of the hut and waited for the cook to call them to fill their tin plates and cups. One of them, more energetic and perhaps hungrier than the rest, unpacked the load of firewood from a spiritless horse and carried it to the hut

The perspiring Thorpe looked his thanks and went on with his labors and in due time a well-fed, lazy group sprawled near the hut, swapping tales or smoking in satisfied silence. At the other side of the building Miguel sat with those of his own kind, boasting of his desert achievements and in reply to a sneering remark from the other group he showed his teeth in a mocking smile, raised his eyebrows until the crescent scar reached his sombrero and shrugged his shoulders.

"Eet ees not good to say sooch theengs to Miguel," he complacently observed. "Eef he should get ver' angree an' leeve een the night eet would be ver' onluckie for Greengos. Quien sabe?"

"He got you there, Jud," growled a low voice. "He shore hurts me worse'n a blister, but I'm totin' my grudge silent."

"Huh," muttered another thoughtfully. "A man can travel fast without no cattle to set th' pace. He shore can 'leeve' an' be damned, for all I care. An' I'm sayin' that if he does there'll be a d d dead Greaser in Mesquite right soon after I get back. Th' place for him to ' leeve ' us is at Three Ponds for then we shore would be in one bad fix."

"I ain't shore I'd try to get away," said Sandy Woods slowly. "There's good grass an' water here, no herdin', no strayin', nobody to bother a feller. A man can live a long time on one steer out here, jerkin' th' meat. Th' herd would grow, an' when it came time to turn 'em into money he'd only have to drive plumb west. It wouldn't be like tryin' to find a little place like this. Just aim at th' sunset an' keep goin'."

"How long would this valley feed a herd like th' one here now?" ironically demanded the trail-boss. "You can tell th' difference in th' grass plain at th' end of a week. Yo're full of loco weed."

"Eef you say sooch things to me I may leeve in the night," chuckled the other. "Wish they'd stampeded an' knocked him over th' eege! One of these days some of us may be quittin' Kane, an' then there'll be one struttin' half-breed less in Mesquite. Tell you one thing: I won't make this drive many more times before I know th' way as well as he does; an' from here on we could stake it out."

Soft, derisive laughter replied to him and the trail-boss thoughtfully repacked his pipe. "It ain't in you," he said. "You got to be born with it."

"You holdin' that a white man ain't got as much brains as a mongrel with nobody knows how many different kinds of blood in him?" indignantly demanded Sandy.

"'He's got generations behind him, like a setter or a pointer, an' it ain't a question of brains. It's instinct, an' th' lower down yore stock runs th' better it'll be. There ain't no human brains can equal an animal's in things like that. I doubt if you could leave here an' get off this desert, plumb west or not. You got a big target, for it's all around you behind th' horizon; but I don't think you'd live till you hit it at th' right place. Don't forget that th' horizon moves with you. If there wasn't no tracks showin' you th' way you'd die out on this fryin' pan."

"An' th' wind'll wipe them out before mornin'," said one of the others.

The doubter laughed outright. "Wait till we come back. I'll give you a chance to back up yore convictions. Don't forget that I ain't sayin' that I'd try it afoot I'd ride an' give th' horse it's head. There ain't nothin' to be gained arguin' about it now. An' I'm free to admit that I'm cussed glad to be settin' here lookin' out instead of out there some'ers try in' to get here to look in. Gimme a match, Jud."

The trail-boss snorted. "Now yo're takin' my end," he asserted. "If you ride a cayuse an' give it its head it ain't a white man's brains that yo're dependin' on. That ain't yore argument, a-tall. I'll bet you, cayuse or no cayuse, you can't leave Three Ponds an' make it. A cayuse has to drink once in awhile or he'll drop under you an' you'll lose yore instinct-compass."

"I'll take that when we start back," retorted Sandy, "if you'll give me a fair number of canteens. I'm figgerin' on outfittin' right."

"Take all you want at Cimarron corrals," rejoined the trail-boss. "After we leave there I'm bettin' no body will part with any of theirs." He looked keenly at the boaster and took no further part in the conversation, his mind busy with a new problem; the grudge he already had

Chapter XV
Discoveries

Hopalong and Red liked their camp and were pleased that they could stay in it another day and night. They jerked the bear meat in the sun and smoke and took a much-needed bath in the creek, where the gentle application of sand freed them from the unwelcome guests which the jail had given them. Clothing washed and inspected quickly dried in the sun and wind. Neither of them had anything on but a sombrero and the effect was somewhat startling. Red picked up his saddle pad to fling it over a rock for a sun bath and was about to let go of it when he looked closer.

"Hey, did you rip open this pad?" he asked, eying his friend speculatively.

Hopalong added his armful of fuel to the pile near the fire and eyed his friend. "For a growed man you shore do ask some childish questions," he retorted. "Of course I did. I allus rip open saddle pads. All my life I been rippin' open every saddle pad I saw. Many a time I got mad when I found a folded blanket instead of a pad. I've got up nights an' gone wanderin' around looking for pads to rip open. You look like you had sense, but looks shore is deceivin'. Why'n blazes would I rip open yore saddle pad? I reckon it's plumb wore out an' just nat'rally come apart. You've had it since Adam made th' sun stand still."

"You must've listened to some sky pilot with yore feet!" retorted Red. "Adam didn't make th' sun stand still. That was Moses, so they'd have longer light for to hunt for him in. An' you needn't get steamed up, neither. Somebody ripped this pad, with a knife, too. Seein' that it was in th' same camp all night with you, I nat'rally asked. I'm shore *I* didn't do it. Then who did?" He swaggered off to get his friend's pad and picked it up. "Of course you wouldn't rip yore own. That--" he held it closer to his eyes and stared at it. "Cussed if you didn't, though! It's ripped just like mine. I reckon you'll be startin' on th' saddles, next!"

Hopalong's amusement at the ripping of his companion's pad faded out as he grabbed his own and looked at it. "Well, I'm cussed!" he muttered. "It shore was ripped, all right. It never come apart by itself. Both of 'em, huh?" He pondered as he turned the pad over and over.

"They didn't play no favorites, anyhow," growled Red. "Wonder what they thought they'd find? Jewels?"

Hopalong pushed back his hat and gently scratched a scalp somewhat tender from the sand treatment. "Things like that don't just happen," he said, reflectively. "There's allus a reason for things." He grew thoughtful again and studied the pad. "Mebby they wasn't lookin' for anythin'," he muttered, suspiciously.

Red snorted. "Just doin' it for practice, mebby?" he asked, sarcastically. "Not havin' nothin' else to do, somebody went up to our rooms an' amused themselves by rippin' open our pads. You got a head like a calf, only it's a hull lot smaller."

"We was accused of robbin' th' bank, Reddie," said Hopalong in patient explanation. "They knowed we didn't do it so they must 'a' wanted us to be blamed for it. Th' best proof they could have, not seein' us do it, was to plant somethin' to be found on us. This is past yore ABC eddication, but I'll try to hammer it into you. If it makes you dizzy, hold up yore hand. What does a bank have that everybody wants? Money! Why do people rob banks? To get money, you sage-hen! What would bank robbers have after they robbed a bank? Money, you locoed cow! Now, Reddie, there's two kinds of money. One is hard, an' th' other is soft like yore head. Th' soft has pretty pictures on it an' smells powerful. It also has numbers. Th' numbers are different, Reddie, on each bill. Some banks keep a list of th' numbers of the biggest bills. Reckon I better wait an' let you rest up."

"Too bad they got us out of jail both of us," said Red. "I should 'a' stayed behind. It wouldn't 'a' been half as bad as hangin' 'round with you."

"Now," continued his companion, looking into the pad, "if some of them numbered bills was found on us they'd have us, wouldn't they? We wasn't supposed to have no friends. An' where would a couple of robbers be likely to carry dangerous money? On their hats? No, Reddie; not on their hats. In their pockets, where they might get dragged out at th' wrong time? Mebby; but not hardly. Saddle pads, says th' little boy in th' rear of the room. Right you are, sonny. Saddle pads, Reddie, is a real good place. While you go all over it again so you can get th' drift of it I'll put on some clothes. I'm near baked."

"It started some time ago," said Red innocently.

"What did?"

"Th' bakin'. You didn't get that hat on quick enough," his friend jeered. "I've heard of people eatin' cooked calves' brains, but they'd get little nourishment an' only a moldy flavor out of yourn. An' you'd shore look better with all yore clothes on. I can see th' places where you've stopped washin' yore hands, feet, an' neck all these years."

Hopalong mumbled something and slid into his under wear. "Gee!" he exulted. "These clean clothes shore do feel good!"

"You'd nat'rally notice it a whole lot more than I would," said Red, following suit. As his head came into sight again he let his eyes wander along the eastern and southeastern horizon. "You know, them bluffs off yonder remind me a hull lot of parts of th' Staked Plain," he observed. "We hadn't ought to be very far away from it, down here."

"They're its edge," grunted Hopalong, rearranging the strips of meat over the fire. Both became silent, going back in their memories to the events of years before, when the Staked Plain had been very real and threatening to them.

At daylight the following morning they arose and not much later were riding slowly southward and as near the creek as the nature of its banks would allow. When the noon sun blazed down on them they found the creek dwindling rapidly and, glancing ahead down the sandy valley they could make out the dark, moist place where the last of it disappeared in the sands. They watered their horses, drank their fill and went on again toward the place where they were to meet Johnny, riding on a curving course which led them closer and closer to the forbidding hills. In mid-afternoon they came to a salt pond and instead of arguing about the matter with their thirsty mounts, let them go up to it and smell it. The animals turned away and went on again without protest. A little later Red squinted eastward and nodded in answer to his own unspoken question.

"Shore it is," he muttered.

Hopalong followed his gaze and grunted. "Shore." He regarded the distant bulk thoughtfully. "Strikes me no sane cow ever would go out there, unless it was drove. It's our business to look into everythin'. Comin'?"

"I shore am. Nobody can buffalo me an' chuck me into jail without a comeback. I'm lookin' for things to fatten it."

"It can't get too fat for me," replied his friend. "Helpin' th' Kid get his money back was enough to set me after some of that reward money; but when I sized up Kane an' his gang it promised to be a pleasure; now, after that jailin', it's a yelpin' joy. If there's no other way I'm aimin' to ride into Mesquite an' smoke up with both guns."

As they neared the carcass Red glanced at his cheerful friend. "Head's swelled up like a keg," he said. "Struck by a rattler."

"Reckon so; but cows dead from snakebite ain't common."

They pulled up and looked at it at close range.

"Shot," grunted Hopalong.

"Then somebody was out here with it," said Red swinging down. "He was tender-hearted, he was. Gimme a hand. We'll turn it over an' look at th' brand."

Hopalong complied, and then they looked at each other and back to the carcass, where a large piece of hide had been neatly trimmed around and skinned off.

"Didn't dare let it wander, an' they plugged it after it got struck," said Red.

"Careful, they was," commented his companion. "They was too careful. If they'd let it wander it wouldn't 'a' told nothin', 'specially if it wandered toward home. But shootin' it, an' then doin' this I reckon our come back is takin' on weight"

"It shore is," emphatically said Red. "Cuss this hard ground! It don't tell nothin'. They went north or south an' not long ago, neither. Which way are you ridin'?"

Hopalong considered. "If they went either way they'd be seen. I got a feelin' they went right across. Greasers an' Injuns know that desert, an' there's both kinds workin' 1 for Kane. It allus has been a shore-thing way for 'em. Remember what Idaho said?"

"It can't be done," said Red.

"Slippery Trendly an' Deacon Rankin did it."

"But they only crossed one corner," argued Red.

"McLeod's Texans did it!"

"They didn't cross much more'n a corner," retorted Red. "An' look what it did to 'em!"

"It's a straight drive for them valleys along th' Cimarron," mused Hopalong. "Nobody to see 'em come or go, good grass to fatten 'em up after they got there, an' plenty of time for blottin' th' brands. I'll bet Kane's got men that knows how to get 'em over. There's waterholes if you only know where to look, an' how to head for 'em; an' some of these half-breeds down here know all of that. If they went north or south on a course far enough east to keep many folks from seein' 'ehi they'd find it near as dry. Well, we better go down an' meet th' Kid before we do anythin' else. We got our bearin's an' can find th' way back again. What you say?"

Red mounted and led the way. "If I'm goin' to ride around out here I'm goin' to have plenty of water, an' that means canteens. I'm near chokin' for a drink; an' this cayuse is gettin' mean. Come on."

"We might pick up some tracks if we hunt right now," said Hopalong. "If we wait longer this wind'll blot 'em out. I ain't thirsty," he lied. "You go down an' meet th' Kid an' I'll look around east of here. We can't gamble with this: if I find tracks they'll save us a lot of ridin' an' guessin'. Go ahead."

"If you stay I stay," growled Red.

"Listen, you chump," retorted Hopalong. "It's only a few hours more if I stay out here than if I go with you. Get canteens an' supplies. Th' Kid can bring us more tomorrow. I'm backin' my guess: get a-goin'.'"

Red saw the wisdom of the suggestion and wheeled, riding at good speed to the southwest while his friend went eastward, his eyes searching the desert plain. It was night when Red returned, picking his way with a plainsman's instinct to the carcass of the cow, and he softly replied to a low call which came from behind a billow of sand.

Hopalong arose. "You made good time," he said.

"Reckon so," replied Red, riding toward him. "I only got two canteens an' not much grub. Th' Kid'll be ready; for us tomorrow. What about yore cayuse?"

"Don't worry," chuckled Hopalong. "It's th' cayuses that's been botherin' me most. They're all right now. I found a little hole with cold, sweet water, an' there's grass around it for th' cayuses. There ain't much, but enough for these two goats. Th' water-hole ain't more'n three feet across an' a foot deep, but it fills up good an' has wet quite a spot around it. An' Red, I found somethin' else!"

"Good; what is it?"

"There's clay around it an' a thin layer of sand over th' clay," replied Hopalong. "I found th' prints of a cayuse an' a man, an' they was fresh not more'n twenty- four hours old if I'm any judge. I cast around on widenin' circles, but couldn't pick up th' trail any distance from th' hole. Th' wind that's been blowin' all day wiped 'em out; but it didn't wipe out much at th' edge of th' water. I could even make it out where he knelt to drink. There you are: a dead cow, with th' brand skinned off; tracks of a man an' a cayuse at that water-hole; no herd tracks, no other cayuse tracks just them two, an' our suspicions. What you think?"

Red chuckled. "I think we're gettin' somewhere, cussed slow an' I don't know where; but I'm playin' up that skinned cow. If it was all skinned I'd say a hide hunter might 'a' done it, an' that he made th' tracks you saw; but it wasn't. You should 'a' looked better near th' carcass instead of huntin' up th' water-hole. You might 'a' seen th' tracks of a herd, or what th' wind left of 'em, 'though I reckon they drove that cow off quite a ways before they dropped it."

"Did you cross any herd tracks after you left me?" asked Hopalong.

"No; why?"

"An' we didn't cross any before you left," said Hopalong. "If there's been any to see runnin' east an' west we'd 'a' found 'em. That was all hard ground; an' there was th' wind. There wasn't none to find."

"Huh!" snorted Red, and after a moment's thought he looked up. "Mebby that feller found th' cow all swelled up with snakebite, away off from water as he thought, an' just put an end to its misery?"

"Then why did he cut out th' brand?" snapped Hopalong.

"What are you askin' me for?" demanded Red, truculently. "How'd I know? You shore can ask some !d n fool questions!"

"Yo're half-baked," growled his companion. "I will be, too, before I get any answer to what I'm askin' myself. I'm aimin' to squat behind a rise north of that water-hole an' wait for my answer if it takes a month. I can get a good view from up there."

Red, whose hatred for deserts was whole-hearted, looked through the darkness in disgust at his friend. "You've picked out a fine job for us!" he retorted. "If yo're right an' they did drive a herd across to th' other side it'll shore be a wait. Be more'n a week, an' mebby two."

"They've got to drive hard between waters," replied Hopalong. "They'll waste no time; an' they won't waste time comin' back again, when they won't have th' cows to hold 'em down. There's one thing shore: They won't be back tomorrow or th' next day, an' we both can ride down an' see th' Kid, an' mebby McCullough. It's too good a lead to throw away. But before we meet Johnny we're goin' to have a better look around, 'specially south an' east."

"All right," agreed Red. "How'd you come to find th' hole?"

"Rode up on a ridge an' saw somethin' green, an' knowin' it wasn't you I went for it," answered his friend. "If it had been made for us it couldn't be better. With water, an' grass enough for night grazin', an a good ridge to look from, it's a fine place for us. We'll take turns at it, for it won't feed two cayuses steady. Th' off man can ride west to grass, mebby back to our camp, an' by takin' shifts at it we can mebby save most of th' grass at th' hole."

"An' mebby get spotted while we're ridin' back an' forth?"

"Th' ridge will take care of that, an' I reckon when it peters out there'll be others to hide us. I'm dead set on this: I'm so set that I'll stick it out all alone rather than pass it by. I tell you I got a feelin'"

"I ain't quittin'," growled Red; "I ain't got sense enough to quit. Desert or no desert I'm aimin' to do my little gilt-edged damndest; but I'm admittin' I'll be plumb happy when it's my time off. We'll get supplies an' more canteens from th' Kid tomorrow, an' be fixed so we can foller any other lead that sticks up its head. I shore can stand more than ridin' over a desert if it'll give us any thin' on them fellers."

"Here we are," grunted his companion, swinging from the saddle. "Finest, coldest water you ever drunk. I'm puttin' double hobbles on my cayuse tonight, just to make shore."

"Me, too," said Red, dismounting.

In the morning they rode up for a look along the ledge, found that it would answer their requirements and then went southeast, curving further into the desert, and it was not long before Red's roving glance caught something which aroused his interest and he silently rode off to investigate, his companion going slowly ahead. When he returned it was by another way and he rode with his eager eyes searching the desert beneath and ahead of him. Reaching his friend, who had stopped and also was scanning the desert floor with great intentness, he nodded in quiet satisfaction.

"Think you see 'em, too?" he smilingly inquired. "They're so faint they can't hardly be seen, not till you look ahead, an' then it's only th' difference between this strip of sand that we're on an' th' rest of th' desert. It's a cattle trail, Hoppy; I just found another water-hole, a big one. Th' bank was crowded with hoof marks, cattle an' cayuses. Looks like they come from th' west, bearin' a little north. Th' only reason we didn't see 'em when we rode down was because they was on hard ground. That shore explains th' dead cow."

"An' in a few hours more," said his companion, "this powdery dust will blot 'em out. If they was clearer I'd risk follerin' them, even if we only had a canteen apiece.

We can ride as far between waters as they can drive a herd, an' a whole lot farther. It's only fearin' that th' trail will disappear that holds me back."

"We don't have to risk it yet," said Red, grimly. "We've found out where they cut in an' how they start across; an' all we got to do is to lay low up there an' wait for 'em to come back, or start another herd across, to learn who they are."

"If we wait for their next drive we can foiler 'em on a fresh, plain trail, an' be a lot better prepared," supplemented Hopalong. "I reckon we're shore goin' to fatten our comeback!"

"It's pickin' up fast," gloated his friend. "All we got to do is watch that big water-hole' an' we got 'em. There ain't so many water-holes out on this skillet that they can drive any way they like. We'll camp at th' little one, of course, but we can lay closer to th' big one nights."

"An' from th' ridge up yonder th' man on day watch can see for miles."

"Yes; an' fry, an' broil, an' sizzle, an' melt!" muttered Red. "D n'em!"

Hopalong had wheeled and was leading the way into the southwest as straight as he could go for the meeting with Johnny, and Red pushed up past him and bore a little more to the west. They had seen all they needed to see for the day, and they had made up their minds.

At last after a long, hot ride they reached the bluffs marking the side of the plateau and soon were winding down a steep-walled arroyo which led to the plain below, and the country began to change with such insensible gradations that they hardly noticed it. Sage and greasewood became more plentiful and after an hour had passed an occasional low bush was to be seen and the ground sloped more and more in front of them. A low fringe of greenery lay along the distant bottom, where Sand Creek or some other hidden stream came close to the top of the soil, later to issue forth and become the stream into which the Question-Mark's creek later emptied. They crossed this and breasted an opposing slope, followed around the base of a low ridge of hills and at last stopped under a clump of live-oak and cotton woods in the extreme east end of the Question-Mark valley.

While the two friends were riding toward the little clump of trees west of the Question-Mark ranch visitors rode slowly up to the door of the ranchhouse and one of them dismounted. The shield he wore on his open vest shone in the sun with nickel brightness, but his face was anything but bright. The job which had been cut out for him was not to his liking and had destroyed his peace of mind, and the peace of mind of the two deputies, who needed no reflection upon their subordinate positions to keep them in the sheriff's rear. What little assurance they might have started with received a jolt soon after they had left town, when a gruff and unmistakably unfriendly voice had asked, with inconsiderate harshness and profanity, their intended destination and their business. At last allowed to pass on after quite some humiliation from the hidden sentries, they now were entering upon the dangerous part of their mission.

Corwin stepped up to the door and knocked, a formality which he never dispensed with on the Question-Mark. Other visitors usually walked right in and found a chair or sat on the table, but it never should be said to Corwin's discredit that an officer of the law was rude and ignorant in such a well-known and long-established form of etiquette. So Sheriff Corwin knocked.

"Come in!" impatiently bawled a loud and rude voice.

The sheriff obeyed and looked around the door casing. "Ah, hello, Mac," he said in cheery greeting.

"Mac who?" roared the man at the table.

"McCullough," said the man at the door, correcting himself. "How are you?"

"Yo're one full-blooded d--n fool of a sheriff," sneered the trail-boss. "Where's them two prisoners I been waitin' for?"

"They got away. Somebody helped 'em bust th' jail. I sent word back to you by yore own men."

"Shore, I got, it; I know that. That's no excuse a-tall!" retorted the trail-boss. "I went an' sent word down to Twitchell on th' jump that his fool way worked an' that I was goin' to send him th' men he wanted. Then you let 'em bust out of jail! Fine sort of a fool you made of me! Where's yore reward now, that you was spendin' so fast? An' what'll Twitchell say, an' do? He wants th' bank robbers, not excuses; an' more'n all he wanted th' man that shot Ridley. It ain't only a question of pertectin' th' men workin' for him, but it's personal, too. Ridley was an old friend of his'n an' he'll raise h--l till he gets th' man that killed him. What about it? What have you done since they got away?"

"We trailed 'em, but they lost us," growled Corwin. "Reckon they got up on that hard ground an' then lit out, jumpin' th' country as fast as they could. Kane had it on 'em, cold an' proper but I had my doubts, somehow. I ain't quittin'; I'm watchin' an' layin' back, an' I'm figgerin' on deliverin' th' man that got Ridley."

"(You mean Long an' Thompson are innocent?" demanded McCullough with a throaty growl. "Yo're sayin' it yoreself! What was you tryin' to run on me, then?"

"They must 'a' robbed th' bank," replied the sheriff; "but I got my own ideas about who killed yore friend. This is between us. I'm waitin' till I get th' proof; an' after I get it, an' th' man, I'll mebby have to leave th' country between sunset an' dawn. I ain't no dog, an' I'm gettin' riled."

"Then it was Kane who cold-decked them two fellers?" demanded McCullough.

"I ain't sayin' a word, now," replied the sheriff. "Not yet, I ain't, but I'm aimin' to get th' killer. Where's that Nelson?"

"What you want with him?" asked the trail-boss. "Reckon he done it?"

"No; he didn't," answered Corwin. "He only helped them fellers out of jail, an' I'm goin' to take him in."

"What?" shouted McCullough, and then burst out laughing. "I'm repeatin' what I said about you bein' full-blooded! Say, if you can turn that trick I won't raise a hand not till he's in jail; an' then I'll get him out cussed quick. He's workin' for me, an' he didn't do no crime, gettin' a couple of innocent men out of that mud hut; an', besides, I don't know that he did get 'em out. Go after him, Corwin; go right out after him." He glanced out of the window again and chuckled. "I see you brought some of yore official fam'bly along.

Shucks! That ain't no way to do, three agin' one. An' I heard you was a bad hombre with a short gun!"

"It ain't no question of how bad I am!" retorted the sheriff. "We want him alive."

"Oh, I see; aim to scare him, bein' three to one. All right; go ahead but there ain't goin' to be no pot-shootin'. Tell yore fam'bly that. I mean it, an' I cut in sudden th' minute any of it starts."

"There won't be no pot-shootin'," growled the sheriff, and to make sure that there wouldn't be any he stepped out and gave explicit instructions to his companions before going toward the smaller corral. When part way there he heard whistling, wheeled in his tracks and went back to the bunkhouse, hugging the wall as he slipped along it, his gun raised and ready for action.

Johnny turned the corner, caught sight of the two deputies, who held his suspicious attention, and had gone too far to leap back when he saw Corwin flattened against the wall and the sheriff's gun covering him. Presumably safe on a friendly ranch, he had given no thought to any imminent danger, and now he stood and stared at the unexpected menace, the whistling almost dying on his pursed lips.

"Nelson!" snapped the sheriff, "yo're under arrest for helpin' in that jail delivery. I'll shoot at th' first hostile move! Put up yore hands an' turn 'round!"

Johnny glanced from him to the deputies and thought swiftly. Three to one, and he was covered. He leaned against the wall and laughed until he was limp. When he regained control of himself he blinked at the sheriff and drew a long breath, which nearly caused Corwin to pull the trigger; but the sheriff found it to be a false alarm.

"What th' devil makes you think *I* was mixed up in that?" he asked, laughing again. He drew another long breath with unexpected suddenness, and again the nervous sheriff and the two deputies nearly pulled trigger; and again it was a false alarm.

"I've done my thinkin'!" snapped Corwin. "Watch him, boys!" he said out of the corner of his mouth. "An' if you wasn't mixed up in it you won't come to no harm."

"No; not in a decent town," rejoined Johnny, leaning against the wall again, where Corwin's body somewhat sheltered him from the deputies. The sheriff tensed again at the movement. "But Mesquite's plumb full of liars," drawled Johnny, "trained by Kane. How do I know I'll get a square deal?"

"You'll get it! Put 'em up!" snapped Corwin, raising his gun to give the command emphasis, and it now pointed at the other's head.

"Long an' Thompson "began Johnny, and like a flash he twisted sidewise and jerked his head out of the line of fire, the bullet passing his ear and the powder scorching his hair. As he twisted he slipped in close, his left hand flashing to Corwin's gun-wrist and the right, across his body, tore the weapon from its owner's hand. The movement had been done so quickly that the sheriff did not realize what had occurred until he found himself disarmed and pressing against his own weapon, which was jammed into his groin. Johnny's left-hand gun had leaped into the surprised deputies' sight at the sheriff's hip and they lost no time in letting their own guns drop to the ground in instant answer to the snapped command. Corwin's momentary surprise died out nearly as quickly as it was born and, scorning the menace of the muzzle of his own gun, he grabbed Johnny. As he shifted his foot Johnny's leg slipped behind it and a sudden heave turned the sheriff over it, almost end over end, and he struck the ground with a resounding thump. Johnny sprang back, one gun on the sheriff, the other on the deputies.

"Get off them cayuses," he ordered and the two men slowly complied. "Go over near th' corral, an' stay there." In a moment he gave all his attention to the slowly arising officer.

"All this was unnecessary," he said. "You put us all in danger of bein' killed. Don't you never again try to take me in till you know why yo're doin' it! My head might 'a' been blowed off, an' all for nothin'! You don't know who busted that jail, judgin' by yore fool actions, an' you cussed well know it. You got plenty of gall, comin' down here an' throwin' a gun on me, for that! I'm sayin', frank, that whoever done that trick did th' right thing; but that ain't sayin' that *I* did it. Hope I didn't hurt you, Corwin; but I had to act sudden when you grabbed me."

"Don't you do no worryin' on my account!" snapped the sheriff.

"I ain't blamin' you for doin' yore duty, if you was doin' it honest," said Johnny; "but you ain't got no business jumpin' before yo're shore. I ain't holdin' th' sack for nobody, Corwin; Kane or nobody else. Now then: you can tell what proof you got that it was me that busted th' jail."

Corwin was watching the smiling face and the accusing eyes and he saw no enmity in either. "Then who did?" he demanded.

Johnny shrugged his shoulders. "Quien sdbef" he asked. "There's a lot of people down here that would have more reason to do a thing like that, even for strangers, than *I* would. You ain't loved very much, from what I've heard. I don't want any more enemies than I got; but I'm tellin' you, flat, that I ain't goin' back with you; an' neither would you, if you was in my place, in a strange town. Here," he said, letting the hammer down and tossing the gun at the sheriff's feet, "take your gun. I'm glad you ain't hurt; an' I'm cussed glad *I* ain't. But somebody's shore goin' to be th' next time you pull a gun on me on a guess. You want to be dead shore, Corwin. We've had enough of this. Did you get any trace of them two?"

The sheriff watched his opponent's gun go back into its holster and slowly picked up his own. "No; I ain't," he admitted, and considered a moment as he sheathed the weapon with great care. "I ain't got nothin' flat agin' you," he said; "but I still think you had a hand in it. That's a good trick you worked, Nelson; I'm rememberin' it. All right; th' next time I come for you I'll have it cold; an' I'm shore expectin' to come for you, an' Idaho, too."

"That's fair enough," replied Johnny, smiling; "but I don't see why you want to drag Idaho in it for. He didn't have no more to do with it than *I* did."

"I'm believin' that, too," retorted the sheriff; "since you put it just that way. I haven't heard you say that you didn't do it. Before I go I want to ask you a question: Where was you th' night th' Diamond L lost them cows?"

"Right here with Mac an' th' boys."

"He was," said McCullough. "Yo're ridin' wide of th' trail, Cor win."

"Mebby," grunted the sheriff. "There's two trails. I mebby am plumb off of one of 'em, as long as you know he was down here that night; but I'm ridin' right down th' middle of th' other. When did you meet Long an' Thompson first?" he asked, wheeling suddenly and facing Johnny.

"Thinkin' what you do about me," replied Johnny, "I'd be a fool to tell you anythin', no matter what. So, as long as yo're ridin' down th' middle you'll have to read th' signs yoreself.

Some of 'em must be plumb faint, th' way yo're guessin', an' castin' 'round. Get any news about them rustlers?"

"What's th' use of makin' trouble for yoreself by bein' stubborn?" asked McCullough. He looked at Corwin. "Sheriff, I know for shore that he never knowed any Bill Long or Red Thompson until after he come to Mesquite. What news did you get about th' rustlers?"

"Huh!" muttered Corwin, searching the face of the trail-boss, whose reputation for veracity was unquestioned. "I ain't got any news about 'em. Once they got on th' hard stretch they could go for miles an' not leave no trail. I'm figgerin' on spendin' quite some time north of where Lukins' boys quit an' turned back. There's three cows missin' that are marked so different from any I've ever seen that I'll know 'em in a herd of ten thousan' head; an' when they're cut out for me to look at there's some marks on horns an' hoofs that'll prove whose cows they are. I'm takin' a couple of his boys with me when I go, to make shore. Of course, I don't know that we'll ever see 'em, at all. Well," he said, turning toward his horse, "reckon I'll be goin'." He waved to the deputies, who approached, picked up their guns under Johnny's alert and suspicious scrutiny, and mounted. "As for you, Nelson, next time I'll be dead shore; an' I'll mebby shoot first, on a gamble, an' talk afterward. So-long."

Watching the three arms of the law ride away and out of sight, Johnny swung around and faced the grinning trail-boss. "You told th' truth, Mac; but I wonder if Corwin heard it like I did?"

McCullough shrugged his shoulders. "Who cares? I'm thankin' you for an interestin' lesson in how to beat th' drop; but I reckon I'm gettin' too old to be quick enough to use it. I reckon Waffles has been tellin' th' truth about yore Bar-20 outfit. Where you goin' now?"

"Off to see a couple of better men from that same outfit," grinned Johnny.

He went on with his preparations and soon rode Pepper toward a gap in the southern chain of hills, leading a loaded pack horse behind him. Emerging on the other side of the pass he followed the chain westward and in due time rounded the last hill and headed for the little clump of trees where he saw his two friends waiting. They waved to him and he replied, chuckling with pleasure.

Red looked critically at the pack animal. "Huh! From th' looks of that cayuse I reckon he figgers we're goin' to be gone some months, like a prospector holin' up for th' winter."

"He never underplays a hand," grunted Hopalong, a warm light coming into his eyes. "Desert or no desert, it's shore good to be with him again. He never should 'a' left Montanny,"

Johnny soon joined them, dismounted, picketed the pack horse, pushed back his sombrero and rolled a cigarette, grinning cheerfully. "If you want any more can teens you can have th' pair on my cayuse," he said. "Find anythin'?"

They told him and he nodded in quiet satisfaction. "You shore ain't been asleep," he chuckled. "You've just about found out somethin' that's been puzzlin' a lot of folks down here for some years. I wonder how close they ever come to them water-holes when they was scoutin' around? But mebby they never scouted over that way much everybody was bankin' on 'em stayin' on th' hard stretch over Lukins' way, instead of crossin' it so close to town. You'd never thought of lookin' for 'em over east if you hadn't remembered Slippery Trendly, now would you?"

"We wasn't lookin' for nothin' nor nobody except you," admitted Hopalong. "But when Red saw a dead cow is far out on th' desert as it was, we just had to take a look at it. An' when we saw it had been shot we couldn't do nothin' else but look for th' brand. That bein' cut out made us plumb suspicious. One thing just nat'rally led to th' next, as th' mule said when its tail was pulled."

"What you bet that missin' brand wasn't a Diamond "w?" Johnny asked.

"Ain't that th' ranch Idaho works for?" queried Red.

Johnny nodded. "They raided Lukins th' night of th' day you an' Hoppy left town. That outfit put in two days ridin' along th' hard ground, half of 'em up an' half of 'em down. They lost over a hundred head."

His friends exchanged looks, each trying to visualize the all but obliterated trail, and both nodded.

"Mebby it was a Diamond L," said Hopalong, and he explained their plans to some length.

"That's goin' to win if you can stick it out," said Johnny. "McCullough's steamin' a little, but he's still carryin' out Twitchell's wishes; an' I been arguin' with him, too, to give you fellers a chance. Hey!" he ex claimed, grinning. "I allus knowed I'd get a bad name for hangin' out with you two coyotes; an' I done got it. I'm suspected strong of bein' a criminal, like you fellers, an' I'll mebby be an outlaw, too. Sheriff Corwin just said so, an' he ought to know if anybody does. He arrested me for helpin' to get you fellers out of jail, but he didn't say how he aimed to keep me in it, busted like it is."

"How'd you get away?" asked Red. "Wouldn't you go with him?"

"Mebby he didn't have th' rest of th' dozen," suggested Hopalong.

"Oh, he wasn't real shore about it really bein' me he wanted, so he turned me loose," replied Johnny. "Any how, I couldn't 'a' gone with him: I had to get this stuff out to you fellers. An' besides, I knowed if I got in that 'dobe hut you wouldn't have th' nerve to bust me out again."

"I'm honin' to bust Corwin's 'dobe head," growled Red.

"There's four canteens an' plenty of grub, with Mac's compliments," said Johnny, waving at the pack horse. "When am I to meet you again?"

Hopalong considered a moment. "There's too much ridin', comin' down here unless we has to," he said. "Tell you what: We'll find a hill, or a ridge up on th' plateau where a fire can be lit that won't show to nobody north of them hills you just come around. Take that white patch up yonder: we can see it plain for miles. You ride up to it every day about two hours after sun-up; an' every night just after dark. If you see smoke puffs in daylight, or a winkin' fire at night, ride toward that split bluff be hind us. We'll meet you there. If you get news for us, do th' same thing on th' other slope, so it can't be seen from across this valley. As long as it can be seen on a line with th' split bluff we won't miss it."

Johnny scratched his head. "Strings of six puffs or six winks means trouble: come a-latherin'," he suggested. "Strings of three means news, an' take yore time. Better have a signal for grub an' supplies: it'll mebby save ridin'. Say groups of two an' five, alternate?"

Hopalong nodded and repeated the signals to make certain that he had them right. "Two an' five, alternate, for supplies; strings of six, come a-runnin'; strings of three, news, an' take our time. Couple of hours after sun-up an' just after dark. All right, Kid."

"Mac's got an old spyglass. Want it, if I can get it?" asked Johnny.

"Shore!" grunted Red.

"Bring it next time you come," said Hopalong.

"All right. Where you goin' now?"

"Up on Sand Creek, where we're camped," answered Red. "We got a couple of days before we move out on th' fryin' pan, an' we're aimin' to make th' most of it"

"Wait till I get th' glass, an' I'll go along," suggested Johnny, eagerly.

"Get a rustle on an' take this pack animal back with you," smiled Hopalong as Johnny started without it. "We'll empty out th' canteens, an' we can tote th' sup plies without it."

Chapter XVI
A Vigil Rewarded

The days passed quietly for the two watchers after Johnny had gone back to the Question-Mark, the hours dragging in monotonous succession. In the Sand Creek camp time passed pleasantly enough, but out on the great, up-slanting billow of sand north of Sweet Spring, devoid of shelter from the blazing sun and from the reflected glare of the gray-white desert around it, was another matter. Prone on his stomach lay Hopalong on the northward slope, his face barely level with the crest of the ridge. Down in the hollow behind him was his horse, picketed and hobbled as well, and at his side on his blanket to keep the cutting sand and clogging dust from barrels and actions lay his rifle and his six-guns, so hot that their metal parts could not be touched without a grimace of discomfort coming to his face. The telescope at intervals swung around the shimmering horizon, magnifying the dancing heat waves until the distortion of their wavering, streaming currents at times rendered the view chaotic and baffling. Strange sights were to be seen in the air and knowing what they were he watched them as his only source of amusement. A tree-bordered lake appeared, its waters sparkling, arose into the air, became vague and slowly dissolved from view, calling from him caustic comment. Inverted mountains reached down from the heavens, standing on snow-covered tops, writhed more and more from their outer edges and melted down from the up-flung bases, slowly fading from view. They were followed by a silvery, winding river, certain features which caused him to think that he recognized it and while he studied it a herd of cattle upside down, and greatly magnified, pushed through into sight as the river scene faded away. Another hour passed and then a steepwalled, green valley inverted itself before his gaze. He could make out a hut and a few trees and then as mounted men began to ride up its slanting bluff trail his attention became riveted on it and he reached for the hot telescope. One look through the instrument made him grunt with disgust, for the figures danced and shrunk and expanded, weaved and became like shadows, through which he looked as though through a rare, discolored vapor. He was mildly excited and tried in vain to search his visual image of the sight for the faces of the men; but it was in vain, and he opened his eyes as the image faded and then closed them again to better search the memory picture. This, too, availed him nothing and he realized that he had not really seen the faces. He was perplexed and vexed, for there was something familiar about some of those riders. About to move for a look around through the telescope, he yielded to a humorous warning and lay quiet for awhile. Was it possible that the mirage had been double-acting, and had revealed each to the other?

"Mebby they won't put as much stock in theirs as I did in mine," he said, and slowly picked up the telescope for a final look all around the horizon before Red should relieve him. East, south, west he looked and saw nothing, Swinging it toward the Sand Creek camp he grunted in satisfaction as a figure very much like Red wavered and danced as it emerged over a ridge of sand. Further north he swung it and slowly swept the northern horizon. Swearing suddenly he stopped its slow progress and brought it back searchingly over ground it had just covered. Rigid he held it and looked with unbelieving eyes.

"Mirage?" he growled, questioningly. "It's too solid for that I'm goin' up to see."

Getting his horse he gingerly slipped the hot rifle into its scabbard, hastily dropped the six-guns into their holsters and, mounting, rode to meet his nearing friend.

"Cooked?" queried Red, grinning. "You shore didn't lose no time gettin' started after you saw me! Ain't it h lout here?"

"H--l is right," answered Hopalong, handing over the telescope. "But we got cayuses, full canteens, an' know where we are. Swing that blisterin' tube over yonder," pointing, "an' tell me what you see?"

Red obeyed and the moving glass suddenly stopped and swung back a little. After long scrutiny he raised his head and gazed steadily over the rigid tube as though along a rifle barrel. "I see him, now, without it," he said. "A-foot, he is, staggerin' every-which way. Comin'?"

His companion replied by pushing into the lead and setting a stiff pace through the soft sand and alkali dust. As they drew near they both shivered at the sight which steadily was being better revealed.

The figure of a man. and scarcely more than figure, stumbled crazily across the sand, hatless, his bare feet covered with dust which had become pasty with the blood exuding through the deepening clefts in the skin and flesh. Progress on such feet would have made him mad from pain if he had not already become so from other causes. His trousers were ripped and frayed to the swollen, dustplastered knees, the crimson fissures running up and down his swollen legs. Shirt he had none, save the strip which hung stiff and crimson from his belt. His upper body was a thing of horror, swollen, matted with crusts of dried blood, from beneath which more oozed out to in turn coagulate. His burning eyes peered through slits in the puffed face and his tongue, blackened and purplish, stuck out of his mouth.

"G-d!" muttered Red, glancing awesomely at the tense face of his companion.

"He's gone," said Hopalong, softly. "Nothing can save him. It would be a mercy "but he checked the words, searching Red's acquiescent eyes.

"Can't do it," said Red. "Can you?"

Hopalong drew in a deep breath and shook his head. "We got to try th' other first," he said. "It's wrong but there's nothin' else. We ain't doctors, an' there may be a fightin' chance. Hobble th' cayuses. We'll both tackle him one alone might have to be too rough, for he'll mebby fight."

"He's down," said Red as he swung from his saddle. "Lookin' right at us, too, an' don't see us."

The figure groveled in the sand, digging with blundering fingers worn to the bone by previous digging, and choked sounds came from the swollen throat. Red talked to himself as he hobbled his horse and pushed down the picket pin.

"Lost his cayuse, somehow, or went crazy an' chased it away. Used up his last water an' then threw away everythin' he had. Tore off his shirt because th' neck band got too tight, an' th' cloth stuck to th' blood clots an' pulled at 'em. I've seen others, but they warn't none of 'em as bad as him," growled Red more to himself than to his companion.

Hopalong pushed home his own picket pin and stood up. "Comin'?" he asked, starting slowly for the groveling, digging thing on the sand.

They stepped up to him and lifted the unfortunate from the ground. Dazed and without understanding, the pitiful object of their assistance suddenly snarled and reached its bleeding fingers for Red's throat, and for the next few minutes two rational, strong men had as hard a fight on their hands as they ever had experienced; and when it was over and the enraged unfortunate became docile from exhaustion they were covered with blood. Letting a few drops of water trickle down the side of the protruding tongue, which they forced to one side when the drops were stopped by it, they worked over the dying man as long as they dared in the sun and then, carrying him to Hopalong's horse they put him across the saddle, lashing him securely, and covered him with a doubled blanket to cheat the leering sun.

"Go ahead to th' water-hole," said Hopalong, straightening up from tying the last knot. "I'll take him to camp an' do what I can. There won't be no trouble handlin' him, tied like he is. Got to try to save him--'though I hope somebody puts a bullet through my head if I ever get like him."

"Bein' crazy, he mebby ain't feelin' it as much as he might," replied Red. "Seems to me he's the one they called Sandy Woods; but he's so plumb changed I ain't shore."

Hopalong thought of the last mirage he had seen, was about to speak of it, but abruptly changed his mind. He conveyed his warning in another way. "Keep a-lookin' sharp, Red," he said. "Th' poor devil shore was one of them rustlers; an' they mebby ain't far behind him. It's gettin' nearer an' nearer th' time they ought to come back. I'll stay with him in camp an' let th' Kid's signal go, if he makes one. This feller ain't got long to live, I'm figgerin'."

"It's a wonder he lived this long," said Red, riding off to take up the vigil.

Hopalong swung his belts and guns over the pommel of the saddle to lighten him, drank sparingly from a canteen and started on foot for the camp, leading his dispirited horse. After a walk through the hot, yielding sand which became a punishment during the last mile he sighed with relief as he stopped the horse on the bank of Sand Creek and tenderly placed its burden on the ground in the shade of a tree. More water, in judicious quantities, and at increasingly frequent intervals brought no apparent relief to the sufferer, and in mid-afternoon Sandy Woods lost all need of earthly care. Kane's thieving trail-boss had won his bet.

Hopalong looked down at the body freed of its suffering and slowly shook his head. "Th' other way would've been th' best," he said. "I knowed it; Red knowed it yet, both plumb shore, an' knowin' it was better, we just couldn't do it. A man's trainin' is a funny thing."

He looked around the little depression and walked toward a patch of sand lying near a mass of stones which had rolled down the slope; and before the evening shadows had reached across the little creek, a heaped-up pile of rocks marked the place of rest of one more weary traveler. At the head, lying on the ground, was a cross made of stones. Why he had placed it there Hopalong could hardly have told, but something within him had stirred through the sleep of busy and heedless years, and he had unthinkingly obeyed it.

He looked up at the sun and found it was time to go on watch again. He had been given no opportunity to sleep, but did not complain, carelessly accepting it as one of the breaks in the game. When he reached his friend, ready to go on duty again, Red looked up at him and scrutinized his face.

"Lots of sleep you must 'a' got," said Red. "How's our patient?"

"Gettin' all th' sleep there is," came the reply. "We was right both ways."

"Spread yore blanket here," said Red. "I'm stickin' to th' job till you have a snooze. Anyhow, somethin' tells me that two won't be more'n we need out here at night, from now on."

"It's my trick," replied Hopalong, decisively. "Spread yore own blanket."

"Him turnin' up like he did was an accident," retorted Red, "an' accidents are shared between us both. Anyhow, I ain't sleepy an' th' next few hours are pleasant. Get some sleep, you chump!"

"Well, as long as we're both handy, it don't make much difference," replied Hopalong, spreading the blanket. "We can spell each other any time we need to. Hope th' Kid ain't tryin' to signal nothin'."

"We got more to signal than he has," growled Red. "Shut up, now; an' go to sleep," and his companion, blessed by one of the prized acquirements of the plains man, promptly obeyed; but it seemed to him that he scarcely had dozed off when he felt his friend's thrusting hand, and he opened his eyes in the darkness, staring up at the blazing stars, in surprise.

"Yes?" whispered Hopalong, without moving or making any other sound, again true to his training.

His companion's whisper, a whisper by force of habit rather than for any good reason, reached him: "Turn over, an' look over th' ridge."

Hopalong obeyed, threw off the blanket which Red had spread over him when the chill of the desert night descended, and became all eyes as he saw the faint glow of a distant fire, which rapidly grew and became brighter. "It's them, down at th' other water-hole," he said, arising and feeling to see if his Colts had slid out of their holsters while he slept. "I'm goin' down for a better look," and he glanced at the northern sky just above the horizon, memorized a group of stars and disappeared noiselessly into the night.

Nearing the larger water-hole he went more slowly and finished by wriggling up to the crest of a sand billow, his head behind a lone sage bush, and his eyelids closed to a thin crack, lest the light of the fire should reflect from his eyes and reveal him to some keen, roving glance.

The grease wood fire blazed under a pair of skillets, while a coffeepot imitated the Tower of Pisa on the glowing coals at one edge. Around it, reclining on the powdery clay, or squatting in the more characteristic attitude of men of the saddle, were a half-dozen of Kane's pets, Miguel and his cronies well to one side. The hidden watcher knew them all by sight and saw several men who had helped the sheriff trick him and Red. In the darkness behind the group he heard their horses moving about as they grazed.

"Do you reckon he made it, Miguel?" asked the trailboss, apropos of the conversation around the fire.

Miguel turned his face to the light, the scar over his eye glistening against the duller skin around it. "I say no," he drawled. "He change hees horrse at the corrals, no? The-e horrse he took was born at the-e Cimarron corral an' foaled eet's firrst colt there. I would not lak' sooch a horrse eef I did not know my way. But, quien sabe?' '

The trail-boss looked at him searchingly, wondering how much the half-breed knew about Sandy's reasons for making the change. Kane would not allow fighting in the ranks, and grudges live long in some men. Besides, to lose the bet was to lose his share of the drive profits to a man he secretly hated, and this did not suit the trailboss.

Miguel smiled grimly into the cold, searching eyes and shrugged his shoulders, his soft laugh turning the cold stare into something warmer. "Eef he deed, then eet ees ver' good," he said; "eef he deed not, then eet hees own fault. But he should not change hees horrse."

"We'll know tomorrow night, anyhow," said a voice well back from the fire. "Get a rustle on you, Thorpe," it growled. "You move around like an old woman."

"Ain't no walls to climb," said another, laughing.

The red- faced cook did not raise his head or retort, but in his memory another name was deeply carved, to replace the one he was certain would be erased when they reached Mesquite. Sandy Woods' dislike for the horse given to him at the corrals had been overcome by the smooth words of the unforgiving cook, who also had a score to pay.

"When do we rustle next?" asked a squatting figure. "We been layin' low too long, an' my pile has done faded; I wasn't lucky, like you, Trask, an' the sheriff," he said, looking at the trail-boss. "Next time a bank is busted / aim to be in on it. You fellers can't hog all th' good things."

"Don't do no good to talk about it," snapped the trailboss. "Kane names them he wants. Trask an' me was robbed of half of our share I ain't forgettin' it, neither. An' as for th' next raid, that's settled. As long as all of us are in it, you might as well know. We're cleanin' up on McCullough's west range, an' there won't be much of a wait." Neither the speaker, his companions, nor the man behind the sage brush knew that Kane already had changed his mind, and because of Lukins' activity had decided to raid McCullough's east range.

"How soon?" demanded the questioner.

"Some night this week, I reckon," came the answer. "If we get a good bunch we'll sit back an' take things easy for awhile. Too many drives may cut a trail that'll show, an' we can't risk that"

"Too bad we have to drive west an' north before we hit for the plain," said Jud Hill. "Takes two days more, that way."

The trail-boss smiled. "I know a way that would suit you, Jud," he said. "So does Miguel but we've been savin' it till th' old route gets too risky. It joins th' regular trail right here. Well, at last th' cook has really cooked pass it this way, Thorpe. I'm eatin' fast an' I'm turnin' in faster. Th' more we beat th' sun gettin' away from here, th' less it'll beat on us. We're leavin' an hour ahead of it."

Not waiting until the camp should become silent, when any noise he might make would be more likely to be heard, Hopalong crept away while the rustlers ate and returned to his friend, who waited under a certain group of stars.

Red cocked his head at the soft sound, his Colt swinging to cover it, when he heard his name called in his friend's voice, and he replied.

Hopalong sat down on the blanket and related what he had seen and heard without comment from his listener until the end of the narrative.

"Huh!" said Red. "You learned a-plenty. An' I'm glad they reached that water-hole after dark, an' are goin' to go on again before it gets light. They missed our tracks. I call that luck," he said in great satisfaction. "We wasn't doin' much guessin'. That's shore their drive trail, an' th' best thing about it is that it's th' bottom of th' Y. They've got two ways of leavin' th' ranges without showin' tracks, but they both come together down yonder. I reckon mebby we'll have a piece to speak when they come this way again. Coin' to tell McCullough what's bein' hatched?"

"We ought to," answered his companion, slowly. "We'll tell th' Kid an' leave it to him. They must be purty shore of themselves to rustle Question-Mark cattle at this time. If th' Kid tells Mac, an' they try it, Mesquite shore is goin' to be a busy little town. I think I know his breed."

"They ain't takin' much of a chance, at that, if they try it," said Red. "They don't know that we know anythin' about it an' that McCullough will know it, if th' Kid tells him. Mebby they rigger that by springin' it right now when th' feelin' is so strong agin' 'em, that it would make folks think they didn't do it, because they oughten't to oh, pshaw! You know what I'm gettin' at!"

"Shore," grunted Hopalong. He was silent a moment and then stirred. "We ain't got no reason to stay out here for a day or two. Let's pull out an' go down where we can signal th' Kid after sun-up. We'll ride well to th' east past their camp. What wind is stirrin' is comin' from th' other way, an' there's no use makin' any fresh tracks in front of 'em."

An hour or so after daylight a small fire sent a column of smoke straight up, the explanation of its smoking qualities suggested by the canteen lying near it. Hopalong and Red slid a blanket over the fire and drew it suddenly aside, performing this operation three times in succession before letting the column mount unmolested for brief intervals. In the west, above and behind a bare spot on a ridge of hills an answering column climbed upward, and then a series of triple puffs took its place. Scattering the fire over the ground the two friends absent-mindedly kicked sand over the embers, and suddenly grinned at each other at the foolishness of their precautions.

When they reached the little grove they found Johnny waiting for them, his horse well loaded with more pro visions. As they transferred the supplies to their own mounts they told him what had occurred and he decided that McCullough should be informed of the forthcoming raid, whether or not it would in any way jeopardize the winning of the rewards.

"It's a toss-up whether Mac will wait for them to run it off," he said, "when I tell him. He's gettin' more riled every minute, but he seemed to calm down a little after Corwin visited him. Somethin' sort of pulls him back when he gets to climbin' onto his hind legs, an' he ends up by leanin' agin' th' wall an' swearin'. I'm not tellin' him nothin' about anythin' but th' raid. You aimin' to go back to that water-hole?"

Hopalong shook his head. "No, sir," he answered. "There ain't no reason to till th' raid happens. We're campin' on Sand Creek till you signal that it's been run off. Time enough then for us to watch on that cussed griddle."

"Have special signal for that?" suggested Red. "Say two, two an' three, repeated. Mebby won't have time to hear what th' news is. When you get our answer don't bother ridin' down here to tell us anythin' we'll be makin' tracks pronto."

Johnny nodded. "Two, two an' three is O. K. I'll be ridin' back to tell Mac there's goin' to be a party on his west range some night soon. I'm bettin' it'll be a bloody party, too. Say," he exclaimed, pulling up, "Lukins an 5 Idaho was down last night. They're mad as h--l, an' they're throwin' a cordon of riders plumb across th' hard stretch every night. Lukins an' Mac are joinin' forces, an' from now on th' two ranches are workin' together as one. With us scoutin' around east of town somethin' shore ought to drop." He pressed Pepper's sleek sides and started back to the sheltering hills.

"Somethin's goin' to drop," growled Red, the memory of the jailing burning strongly within him. "Don't for get, Kid two, two an' three."

Johnny turned in his saddle, waved a hand and kept on going. Rounding the westernmost hill he rode steadily until opposite the white patch of sand on the northern slope and then, dismounting, collected firewood, and built it up on the dead ashes of his signal fire, ready for the match. Going on again he rode steadily until he reached the place in the arroyo which lay directly behind the ranchhouse.

McCullough returned from a ride over the range to find his cheerful friend smoking some of his tobacco.

"Want a job, Nelson?" asked the trail-boss, swinging from the saddle with an easy agility belying his age and weight.

Johnny smiled at him. "A'nythin', that don't take me away from th' ranch too far or too long. Call it."

"One of th' boys, ridin' south of th' hills on a fool's errand, this mornin', thought he saw smoke signals back of White Face," said McCullough. "He says he reckons he's loco. I ain't goin' that far. Think you could find out any thin' about 'em?"

Johnny considered, and chuckled. "Huh!" he snorted. "He's plumb late. *I* saw them before he did, an' know all about 'em. You stuck a couple of jabs into me about bein' lazy, an' likin' to set around all day doin' nothin'. Any chump can wear out cayuses ridin' around discoverin' things, but th' wise man is th' feller that can set around all day, lazy an' no-account, an' figger things out. I don't have to go prowlin' around to find out things. I just set in th' shade of th' house, roll cigarettes an' hold pow wows with my medicine bag. [You'd be surprised if you knowed what I got in that bag, an' what I can get out of it. You shore would."

McCullough looked at him with an expression which tried to express so many uncomplimentary things at once that the composite was almost neutral; at least, it was somewhat blank.

"Ye-ah?" he drawled, his inflection in no way suggesting anything to Johnny's credit.

"Ye-ah," repeated the medicine man somewhat belligerently.

"Oh," said the trail-boss, eyeing his victim speculatively. "You know all about 'em, huh?"

"Everythin'," placidly replied Johnny, rolling another cigarette.

"I wish to heaven you'd quit smokin' them cussed things around here," said McCullough plaintively. "Yo're growed up now, purty near; an' you ain't no Greaser. I'll buy you a pipe if you'll promise to smoke it."

"Pipes, judgin' from yourn," sweetly replied Johnny, calmly lighting the cigarette, "are dangerous, unless a man hangs around th' house all th' time. When I used to go off scoutin', I allus wished th' other fellers smoked pipes, corncob pipes, like Mister McCullough carries around. Why, cuss it, I could smell 'em out, if they did. It would 'a' saved me a lot of crawlin' an' worryin'. I knowed you was comin' back ten minutes before I saw you. Now, you can't blame a skunk he was born that way, an' he's got good reasons for keepin' on th' way he was born. But a human, goin' out of his way, to smell like some I knows of," he broke off, shrugging his shoulders expressively.

McCullough slowly produced the corncob, blew through the stem with unnecessary violence, gravely filled and lit it, his eyes twinkling. "Takes a man, I reckon, to enjoy it's aromer," he observed. "Goin' back to yore medicine bag, let's see what you can get out of it," he challenged.

Johnny drew out his buckskin tobacco pouch, placed it on the floor, covered it with his sombrero and chanted softly, his eyes fixed on the hat. "I smell a trail-boss an' his pipe. They went to th' bend of th' crick, an' they says to Pete Holbrook, who rides that section, that he ought to ride on th' other side of th' crick after dark." He was repeating information which he had chanced to overhear near the small corral the night before; when he had passed unobserved in the darkness.

McCullough favored the hat with a glance of surprise and. Johnny with a keen, prolonged stare.

K Pete, he said that wouldn't do no good unless he went far enough north to leave his section unprotected. He borrowed a chew of tobacco before th' man an' th' pipe went away an' let th' air get pure again." The medicine man knew Pete's thrifty nature by experience.

"Yo're shore a good guesser," grunted McCullough. "What about them smoke signals, that you know all about?"

Johnny readjusted the hat a hair's breadth, passed his hands over it and closed his eyes. "I see smoke signals," he chanted. "There's palefaces in 'em, ridin' cautious at night over a hard plain. They're driftin' cows into a herd. Th' herd is growin' fast, an' it drifts toward th' hard ground. Now it's goin' faster. Th' brands are Diamond L. I see more smoke signals an' more ridin' in th' dark. Another herd, bigger this time, is runnin' hard over that same plain. Th' brands are SV, vented; an' plain Question-Mark. It seems near within a week an' it's on yore west range." He opened his eyes, kicked the hat across the room and pocketed the tobacco pouch.

"Mac," he said, gravely. "That's a shore-enough prophecy. Leavin' out all jokin', it's true. Hoppy an' Red told me, a little while ago, that they overheard some of Kane's gang talkin'. They're goin' to raid you like I said. Th' smoke signals was me answerin' theirs. They say Sandy Woods is dead. They ought to know because they buried him. They know three of th' men that robbed th' bank an' they've knowed ever since Ridley was shot, who killed him. They've seen Kane's drive trail crew an' they know a whole lot that I ain't goin' to tell you now; mebby I'll not tell you till we get th' rewards; but if it'll make you feel any better, I'm saying' that we're goin' to get them rewards right soon. When Kane raids you he springs th' trap that'll clear a lot of vermin off this range."

"How much of all that do you mean?" demanded the trail-boss, his odorous pipe out and reeking more than ever. He was looking into his companion's eyes with a searching, appraising directness which many men would have found uncomfortable.

"All of it," complacently answered the medicine man, rolling a new cigarette. "There's only one thing I'm doubtful about, 'though it was what Hoppy overheard, so I gave it to you that way. They said yore west range. If Kane learns how th' Diamond L riders are spread out, an' I'm bettin' he knew it near as soon as Lukins did, he'll be a fool to drive that way. If it was me, I'd split my outfit an' put half of 'em on th' east end! but I'm a gambler."

McCullough considered the matter. "They'll leave a plain trail if they raid th' east section," he muttered; "an' th' desert'll hold 'em to a narrow strip north or south. There's water up th' north way, but there's people scattered all around, an' they're nat'rally near th' water. South, there's less water, an' more people th' further they go. They might tackle th' desert, but Lukins an' me figger they go west from th' hard ground. I ain't agin' gamblin', but I don't gamble with anythin' *I* don't own. If yore friends heard them coyotes say 'west,' I'm playin' my cards accordin' to their case-rack. I may call it wrong, I may get a split, or I may win but I'm backin' th' case-keepers, 'specially when they're keepin' th' rack for me. West it is an' west is where h--l will pop when they pay their visit. An' lemme tell you this, Nelson: Win, lose, or split on th' raid, if it comes off within a week, I'll be dead shore who's behind it, an' there's a cyclone due in Mesquite right soon after. Twitchell had his chance. His game's no good I'm playin' th' cards I've drawn in my own way when they show their hand in this raid. I'm bein' cold-decked by Corwin but I'll warm it a-plenty. You hang around an' see th' fire works!"

Johnny stretched, relaxed, and grinned. "I'm aimin' to touch some off, myself," he replied, "an' I reckon Hoppy an' Red will send up a couple of rockets on their own account. Rockets?" He grinned. "No; not rockets there's allus burned sticks comin' down from rockets. Besides, they're too smooth an' easy. Reckon they'll touch off some pinwheels. Whizzin', tail-chasin' pinwheels; or mebby nigger-chasers. Most likely they'll be nigger-chasers, th' way some folks'll be steppin' lively to get out of th' way. Don't you bank on this bein' yore, celebration you'll only own th' lot an' make th' noise. Th' grand display, th' glorious finish is Bar-20. Just plain, old-fashioned Bar-20. Gee, Mac, it makes me a kid again!"

"It's got an easy job, then!" snorted the trail-boss.

Chapter XVII
A Well-Planned Raid

On night shift again Pete Holbrook reached the end of his beat, waited until his fellow-watcher on the east bulked suddenly out of the darkness, exchanged a few words with him and turned back under the starfilled sky, his horse having no difficulty in avoiding obstructions, but picking its way with ease around scattered thickets, grass-tufted hummocks, and across shallow ravines and hollows. Objects close at hand were discernible to eyes accustomed to the darkness and Pete's range of vision attained the enviable limits enjoyed by those who live out-of-doors and look over long distances. An occasional patch of sand moved slowly into his circumscribed horizon as he rode on; vague, squatting bulks gradually revealed their vegetative nature and an occasional more regular bulk told him where a cow was lying. These latter more often were catalogued by his ears before his eyes defined them and from the contentment in the sounds he nodded in satisfaction. Soon he felt the gentle rise which swept up to the breeze-caressed ridge which projected northward and forced the little creek to follow it for nearly a mile before the rocky obstruction could be passed.

There had been a time when the ridge had forced the creek again as far out of its course, but on quiet nights a fanciful listener could hear the petulant grumblings of the stream and its constant boast. Placid and slow above the ridge, the waters narrowed and deepened when they reached the insolent bulk as in concentrating for the never-ending assault. They had cut through softer resistance along the edges and now gnawed noisily at the stone itself. Narrower grew the stream and deeper, the pools clear and with clean rock bottoms and sides where the hurrying water, now free from the last vestige of color imposed by the banks further up, became crystal in the light of day. Hurrying from pool to pool, singing around bowlders it ran faster and faster as if eager for the final attempt against its bulky enemy, and hissed and growled as it sped along the abrupt rock face. Loath to leave the fight, it followed tenaciously along the other side of the ridge and at last gave up the struggle to turn sharply south again and flow placidly down the valley on a continuation of the line it had followed above.

This forced detour made the U-Bend, so called by Question-Mark riders, and the sloping ground of the ridge was as much a favorite with the cattle as were its bordering pools with the men. Here could be felt every vagrant breeze, and while the grass was scantier than that found on the more level pastures round about, and cropped closer, the cattle turned toward it when darkness came. It was the best bed-ground on the ranch.

The grunting, cud-chewing, or blowing blots grew more numerous as Holbrook went on and when he had reached the crest of the ridge his horse began to pick its way more and more to avoid them, the rider chanting a mournful lay and then followed it with a song which, had it been rightfully expurged, would have had little left to sing about. Like another serenade it had been composed in a barroom, but the barroom atmosphere was strongly in evidence. It suddenly ceased.

Holbrook stopped the song and his horse at the same instant and his roving glances roved no more, but settled into a fixed stare which drew upon itself his earnest concentration, as if the darkness could better be pierced by an act of will.

"Did I, or didn't I?" he growled, and looked around to see if his eyes would show him other lights. Deciding that they were normal he focussed them again in the direction of the sight which had stopped the song. "Bronch, I shore saw it," he muttered. "It was plain as it was short." He glanced down at the horse, saw its ears thrust rigidly forward and nodded his head emphatically. "An' so did you, or I'm a liar!"

He was no liar, for a second flash appeared, and it acted on him like a spur. The horse obeyed the sudden order and leaped forward, careening on its erratic course as it avoided swiftly appearing obstacles.

"Seems to me like it was further west th' last time," muttered Holbrook. "What th' devil it is, I don't know; but I'm goin' to show th' fambly curiosity. Can't be Kane's coyotes folks don't usually show lights when they're stealin' cows. An' it's on Charley's section, but we'll have a look anyhow. Cuss th' wind."

The light proved to be of will-o'-the-wisp nature, but he pursued doggedly and after a time he heard sounds which suggested that he was not alone on the range. He drew his six-gun in case his welcome should take that course and swung a little to the left to investigate the sounds.

"Must be Charley," he soliloquized, but raised the Colt to a better position. One would have thought Charley to be no friend of his. The Colt went up a little higher, the horse stopped suddenly and its rider gave the night's hailing signal, so well imitated that it might easily have fooled the little animal to whom Nature had given it. It came back like a double echo and soon Charley bulked out of the dark.

"You follerin' that, too?" he asked, entirely reassured now that his eyes were all right, for he had had the same doubts as his friend.

"Yes; what you reckon it is?"

"Dunno," growled Charley. "Thought mebby it was some fool puncher lightin' a cigarette. It wasn't very bright, an' it didn't last long."

"Reckon you called it," replied Holbrook. "Well, th' only animal that lights them is humans; an' no human workin' for this ranch is lightin' cigarettes at night, these nights. Bein' a strange human where strange humans shouldn't ought to be, I'm plumb curious. All of which means I'm goin' to have a closer look."

"I'm with you," said Charley. "We better stick to gether or we'll mebby get to shootin' each other; an' I'm frank in sayin' I'm shootin' quick tonight, an' by ear. There ain't no honest human ridin' around out here, day or night, that don't belong here; an' them that does be long ain't over there, lightin' cigarettes nor nothin' else. That lightnin' bug don't belong, but he may stay here. Look! There she is again this side of where I saw it last!"

"Same place," contradicted Holbrook, pushing on.

"Same place yore hat!"

"Bet you five it is."

"Yo're on; make it ten?"

"It is. Shut yore face an' Keep goin'. Somethin's happenin' over there."

Minute after minute passed and then they swore in the same breath.

"It's south!" exulted Charley. "You lose."

"He crossed in front of us, cuss him," said Holbrook.

As he spoke an answering light flashed where the first ones had been seen and Holbrook grunted with satisfaction. "You lose; there's two of 'em. We was bettin' on th' other."

"They're signalin', an' there's mebby more'n two. What's th' difference? Come on, Pete! We'll bust up this little party before it starts. But what are they lightin' lights for if they're rustlin'? An' if they ain't rustlin' what'n blazes are they doin'?"

"Head over a little," said his companion, forcing his horse against his friend's. "We'll ride between th' flashes first, an' if there's a herd bein' collected we'll mebby hit it. Don't ask no questions; just shoot an' jump yore cay use sideways."

South of them another puncher was riding at reckless speed along the chord of a great arc and although his section lay beyond Holbrook's, he was now even with them. When they changed their course they drew closer to him and some minutes later, stopping for a moment's silence so they could listen for sounds of the enemy, they heard his faint, far-off signal and answered it. He announced his arrival with a curse and a question and the answer did not answer much. They went on together, eager and alert.

"Heard you drummin' down th' ridge you know that rocky ground rolls 'em out," the new-comer explained. "Knowed somethin' was wrong th' way you was poundin', an' follered on a gamble till I saw th' lights. Reckon Walt ain't far behind me. I'm tellin' you so you'll signal before you shoot. He's loose out here somewhere."

When the light came again it was much further west and the answering flash was north. The three pulled up and looked at each other.

"There ain't no cayuse livin' can cover ground like that second feller," growled Holbrook. "He was plumb south only a few minutes ago, an' now will you look where he is!"

"Mebby they're ghostes, Bob," suggested Charley, who harbored a tingling belief in things supernatural.

"'Ghostes'!" chuckled Holbrook. "Ghosts, you means! Th' same as ' posts! ' Th' ' es ' is silent, like in 'cows.' I never believed in 'em; but I shore don't claim to know it all. There's plenty of things *I* don't under stand an' this is shore one of 'em. My hair's gettin' stiff!"

"Yo're a couple of old wimmin!" snorted Bob. "There's only one kind of a ghost that'll slow me up . that's th' kind that packs hardware. Seein' as they ain't supposed to tote guns, I'm goin' for that coyote west of here. He don't swap ends so fast. Mebby I can turn him into a real ghost. Look out where you shoot. So-long!"

"We'll assay his jumpin' friend," called Charley.

Again the flashes showed, one to the south, the other to the north, and while the punchers marveled, the third appeared in the southwest.

"One apiece!" shouted Holbrook. "I'll take th' last. Go to 'em!" and drumming hoofbeats rolled into silence in three directions.

Soon spitting flashes in the north were answered in kind, the reports announcing six-guns in action; in the west a thinner tongue of flame and a different kind of report was answered by rapid bursts of fire and the jarring crashes of a Colt. Far to the south three stabbing flashes went upward, Walt's signal that he was coming. From beyond the U-Bend, far to the east, the triple signal came twice, flat and low. Beyond them a yellow glow sprang from the black void and marked the ranchhouse, where six sleeping men piled from their bunks and, finishing their dressing as they ran, chased the cursing trail-boss to the saddled, waiting horses, their tingling blood in an instant sweeping the cobwebs of sleep from their conjecturing brains. There was a creaking of leather, a soft, musical jingling of metal and a sudden thunderous rolling of hoof-beats as seven bunched horses leaped at breakneck speed into the darkness, the tight-lipped riders eager, grim, and tense.

Through a bushy arroyo leading to Mesquite three Mexicans rode as rapidly as they dared, laughing and carrying on a jerky, exultant conversation. A mile be hind them came a fourth, his horse running like a frightened jack rabbit as it avoided the obstructions which seemed to leap at them. A bandage around the rider's head perhaps accounted for his sullenness. The four were racing to get to Red Frank's, and safety. Out on the plain the fifth, and as Fate willed it, the only one of the group openly allied to Kane, lay under his dead horse, his career of thieving and murder at an end. Close to him was a dead Question-Mark horse, and the wounded rider, wounded again by his sudden pitch from the saddle as the horse dropped under him, lay huddled on the ground. Slowly recovering his senses he stirred, groped and sat up, his strained, good arm throbbing as he shakily drew his Colt, reloaded it and fired into the air twice, and then twice more. A burst of firing answered him and he smiled grimly and settled back as the low rumbling grew rapidly louder. It threatened to pass by him, but his single shot caused a quick turn and soon his friends drew up and stopped.

"Who is it?" demanded McCullough, dismounting at his side.

"Holbrook," came the answer, shaky and faint. "They got me twice, an' my cayuse, too. Reckon I busted my leg when he went down I shore sailed a-plenty afore I lit."

"You got one!" called an exultant voice. A match flared and in a moment the cheerful dis-coverer called again. "Sanchez, that Greaser monte dealer of Kane's. Plumb through th' mouth an' neck, Pete! I call that shootin', with th' dark an' all "his voice trailed off in profane envy of the accomplishment.

But Pete, hardy soul that he was, had fainted, a fractured leg, the impact from his flying fall and three bullet holes excuse enough for any man.

The flaring of the match brought a distant report and a bullet whined above the discoverer's head. Someone hurriedly fired into the air and a little later the group heard hoofbeats, which stopped abruptly when still some distance away. A signal reassured the cautious rider and soon Walt joined the group, Bob and Charley coming up later. Two of the men started back to the ranchhouse with Holbrook, the rest of the group riding off to search the plain for the two riders who had not put in an appearance, and to see what devilment they might discover. Both of the missing men were found on the remote part of the western range, one plodding stolidly toward the ranchhouse, his saddle and equipment on his shoulders; the other lay pinned under his dead horse, not much the worse, as it luckily happened, for his experience.

While the outfit concentrated on the western part of the ranch, events of another concentra-tion were working smoothly and swiftly east of the ranchhouse, where mounted men, now free from interference, thanks to their Mexican friends, rode unerringly in the darkness, and drifted cattle into a herd with a certainty and dispatch born of long experience. Steadily the restless nucleus grew in size and numbers, the few riders who held it together chanting in low tones to keep the nervous cattle within bounds. The efficiency of these night raiders merited praise, nefarious as their occupation was, and the director of the harmonious efforts showed an uncanny understanding of the cattle, the men, and the whole affair which belongs to genius. Not a step was taken in uncertainty, not an effort wasted. Speed was obtained which in less experienced hands would have resulted in panic and a stampede. Steadily the circle of riders grew shorter and shorter; steadily, surprisingly, the shadowy herd grew, and as it grew, became more and more compact. Further down the creek a second and smaller herd was built up at the same time and with nearly the same smoothness, and waited for the larger aggregate to drift down upon it and swallow it up. The augmented trail herd kept going faster and faster, the guarding and directing riders in their alloted places and, crossing the creek, it swung northeast at a steadily increasing pace. The cattle had fed heavily and drunk their fill and to this could be ascribed the evenness of their tempers. Almost without realizing it they passed from the Question-Mark range and streamed across the guarding hills, flowing rapidly along the northern side. Gradually their speed was in creased and they accepted it obediently, and with a docility which in itself was a compliment to the brains of the trailboss. Compacted within the close cordon of the alert riders it maintained a speed on the very edge of panic, but went no further. Shortly before dawn two hardriding rustlers pounded up from the rear, reported all clear, and fell back again, to renew their watch far back on the trail. For three hours the herd had crossed hard ground and as it passed over a high, dividing ridge and down the eastern slope the trail-boss sighed with relief, for now dawn held no terrors for him. He had passed the eastern horizon of any keen-eyed watchers of the pillaged range. On went cattle and riders, and the paling dawn saw them following the hard bottom of a valley which led to others ahead, and kept them from dangerous sky lines. When the last hard-floored valley lay behind and sloping hollows of sand lay ahead, the trail-boss dropped back, uncorked his canteen of black coffee tempered with brandy, and drank long and deep. It was interpreted by his men to mean that the danger zone had been left in the rear, and they smilingly followed his example, and then leisurely t and more critically looked over the herd to see what they had gained. The entire SV trail herd was there, a large number of Question-Mark cattle and a score or more miscellaneous brands, which Ridley from time to time had purchased at bargain prices from needy owners. The trail-boss grinned broadly and waved his hand. It was a raid which would go down the annals of rustler history and challenge strongly for first honors. At noon the waiting caviya was picked up, and Miguel and his three friends added four more riders to the ranks. He took his place well ahead of the hurrying cattle, and remained there until the first, and seldom visited, water-hole was reached, where a short rest was taken. Then he led the way again, abruptly changing the direction of the herd's course and, following depressions in the desert floor, struck for Bitter Spring, which would be reached in the early morning hours. By now the raid was a successful, accomplished fact, according to all experience, and the matter of speed was now decided purely upon the questions of water and food, which, however, did not let it diminish much.

The trail-boss dropped back to his segundo and smiled. "Old Twitchell's got somethin' to put up a holler over now."

The other grinned expansively. "He'll mebby ante up another reward he shore is fond of 'em."

Back on the Question-Mark a sleepy rider jogged along the creek, idly looking here and there. Suddenly he stiffened in the saddle, looked searchingly along the banks of the little stream, glanced over a strangely deserted range and ripped out an oath as he wheeled to race back to the ranchhouse. His vociferous arrival caused a flurry, out of which emerged Johnny Nelson, who ran to the corral, caught and saddled his restive black, and scorning such a thing as a signal fire, especially when he feared that he could not start it within the limits of the time specified, raced across the valley, climbed the hills at a more sedate pace, dropped down the further slopes like a stone, and raced on again for the little camp on Sand Creek.

Chapter XVIII
The Trail-Boss Tries His Way

McCullough watched the racing horseman for a moment, a gleam of envious appreciation in his eyes at the beautiful action of the black horse, nodded in understanding of the rider's journey and wheeled abruptly to give terse orders.

Charley swung into the saddle and started in a cloud of dust for the Diamond L, to carry important news to Lukins and his outfit; two men sullenly received their orders to stay behind for the protection of the ranch and the care of Pete Holbrook, their feelings in no way relieved by the remark of the trail-boss, prophesying that Kane and his gang would be too busy in town to disturb the serenity of the Question-Mark. The rest of the outfit, procuring certain necessaries for the visit to Kane's head quarters, climbed into their saddles and followed their grim and taciturn leader over the shortest way to town.

Far back on the west end of the northern chain of hills a Mexican collapsed his telescope, hazarded a long-range shot at the hard-riding Charley and, mounting in haste, sped to carry disturbing news to his employer. The courier looked around as the singing lead raised a puff of dust in front of him, snarled in the direction from whence he thought it had come and, having no time for personal grievances, leaned forward and quirted the horse to greater speed. Whirring across the Diamond L range Charley caused another Mexican, watching from a ridge overlooking the ranch buildings, to run to the waiting horse and mount it, after which he delayed his departure until he saw the Diamond L outfit string out into a race for town, whereupon he set a pace which promised to hold him his generous lead.

In Mesquite a Mexican quirted a lathered horse for a final burst of speed up the quiet street, flung himself through Kane's front door, shouted a warning as he scrambled to his feet and dashed through the partition door to make his report direct to his boss. As he bolted out of sight behind the partition, other men popped from the building like weasel-pursued rabbits from a warren and scurried over the town to spread the alarm to those who were most vitally concerned by it. Two streams forthwith flowed over their trails, the first and larger heading for Kane's; the other, composed entirely of Mexicans, flowed toward Red Frank's, which had been allotted the role of outlying redoubt, to help keep harmless the broken ground between it and Kane's front wall, and was now being put in shape to withstand a siege.

Around Kane's was the noisy activity of a beehive. Hurrying men pulled thick planks from the piles under the floor and hauled them, on the jump, to windows and doors, feeding them into eager hands inside the building. Numbers of empty sacks grew amazingly bulky from the efforts of sand shovelers and were carried, shoulder high, in an unending line into the building. Great shutters were unfastened and swung away from the outer walls, their cobwebbed loopholes soon to play their ordained parts. A feverish squad emptied the stables of horses and food, taking both into the dining-room, and returned, posthaste, to remove doors and certain planks which turned the stables into sieves of small use to an attacking force, even if they were won. That the need for haste was pressing was proved by the sound of a handbell on the roof, where a selected group of riflemen lay behind the double-planked parapet to give warning, and exhibitions of long-range shooting. The shovelers hurled their tools through open windows, the plank carriers shoved the last board into the building and leaped to the shutters, slamming them shut as they hastened along the side of the building, and poured hastily through the front door, which now was protected by a great, outer door of planks, mortised, bolted, and braced in workman-like manner. From the roof sounded two heavy reports, and grim iron tubes slid into loopholes along the walls. The bartenders carried boxes of ammunition and spare weapons, leaving their offerings below every oblong hole. To threaten Kane was one thing; to carry it to a successful end, another.

Puffs of gray-white smoke broke unexpectedly from points around the building, to thin out as they spread and drifted into oblivion. The cracking of rifles and the echo-awakening, jarring reports of heavy six-guns, were punctuated at intervals by the booming roar of old-time buffalo guns, of caliber prodigious. Punchers, guns in their hands, made the rounds of the town, going from building to building to pick up any of Kane's men who might have loitered, or who planned to hide out and open fire from the rear. Their efforts were not entirely wasted, for although Kane's brood had flocked to its nest, there were certain of the town's inhabitants who were neither flesh nor fish and might become one or the other as expediency urged. These doubtful ones were weeded out, disarmed, and escorted to their horses with stern injunctions as to the speed of their departure and their continued absence. Some of the neutrals, seeing that the mastery of the town at present lay with the ranchmen, trimmed their sails for this wind and numbered themselves with the offense in spirit if not in deeds. Of these human pendulums Quayle had a fair mental list and the owners of certain names were well watched.

The first day passed in perfecting plans, assigning men to strategic stations, several of these vantage-points remaining tenantless during the daylight hours because of the alertness and straight shooting of the squad on Kane's roof, who speedily made themselves obnoxious to the attackers. The owner of the freight wagon, remembering a smooth-bore iron cannon of more than an inch caliber, a relic of the prairie caravans which had followed the old Santa Fe and other trails a generation past, exulted as he dragged it from its obscurity and spent a busy hour scaling the rust from bore and touch-hole. Here was the key to the situation, he boasted, and rammed home a generous charge of rifle powder. To find a suitable missile was another question, but he solved it by falling upon bar-lead with ax and hammer. Wheeled into position, its rusty length protruding beyond the corner of an adobe building, it was sighted by spasmodic glances, an occupation not without danger, for which blame could be given to the argus-eyed riflemen on the roof of the target. Consternation seized the defenders, who had not allowed for artillery, and they awaited its thundering debut with palpitant interest.

The discoverer and groom of the relic was unanimously elected gunner, not a dissenting voice denying his right to the honor, a right which he failed either to mention or press. The powder heaped over the touch-hole was jarred off by the impact of a Sharp's bullet and to replace it required a kitchen spoon fastened to a stick, which was an alluring if small target to the anxious aerial riflemen. At last heaped up again, the gunner declined methods in vogue for the firing of such ancient muzzle-loaders and used a bundle of kerosene-soaked paper swinging by a wire from the end of the spoon. A few practice swings were held to be fitting preliminaries to an event of such importance, and then the nervous cannoneer, screwing his courage to the sticking-point, swept the blazing mass across the scaly breach and shrunk behind the sheltering corner. He escaped thunderous destruction by an eyelash, for what he afterward found was a third of the doughty weapon whizzed past his corner, taking a large chunk of sun-dried brick with it. From the besiegers arose guffaws; from the defenders, howls of derision; and from the owner of the adobe hut, imprecation and denouncement in fluent Spanish. The wall of his habitation closest to the fieldpiece justified all he said and even all he thought.

"You should ought 'a run it under Kane's before you touched her off," bawled a hilarious voice from cover. "Got another?" he demanded. "Tie it together an' try again."

The cannoneer without a job affected gaiety, drew inspiration from the taunts and hastened home to fashion bombs out of anything he could which would answer his purpose, finally deciding upon a tomato can and baling wire, and soon had a task to occupy the flaming fires of his genius.

Red Frank's, being the weaker of the two defenses and only point-blank range from the old adobe jail whose walls, poor as they were, could be relied upon to stop bullets, formed the favorite point of attack while the offense settled down into better-ordered channels. Idaho and others of his exuberent youth decided that it was their "pudding" and favored it with attentions which were as barren of results as they were full of enthusiasm. Discovering that their bullets passed entirely through the frame second-story and whirred, slobbered, and screamed into the air, they wasted ammunition lavishly, ignorant that for three feet above the second-story floor the walls were reinforced with double planking of hard wood, each layer two inches thick. They might turn the upper two-thirds of walls into a bird cage and do no one any material damage. And so passed the first day, McCullough's efforts unavailing in face of the careless enthusiasm of his men, caused by the novelty of the situation; and not until one man had died and several others received serious wounds did the larking punchers come fully to realize that the game was deadly, and due to become more so.

Chapter XIX
A Desert Secret

While McCullough argued and swore and waited for sanity to return to his frisking men, three punchers lay on the desert sands north of Sweet Spring, and baked. The telescope occasionally swept the southern horizon and went back between the folds of the blanket, which also hid the guns from the rays of the molten sun. The situation and most of the possible variations had been gone over from every angle and a course of action yet had to be agreed upon. Knowing that a fight in town was imminent, each feared he would miss it and that the reward would be lost to them. From their knowledge of deserts in general they did not wish to assume the labors of driving a herd back across it, even if they were able to capture it; but neither did they wish to let it get entirely away and be lost to McCullough. And so they continued to discuss the problem, jerkily and without enthusiasm, writhing under the sun like frogs on a gridiron. The afternoon dragged into evening and with the coming of twilight came quick relief from the heat, soon to be fol lowed by a cold undreamed of by the inexperienced. The stars appeared swiftly and blazed with glittering brilliance through the chill air and the three watchers sought their blanket rolls for relief.

Hopalong unrolled from his covering and arose. "Dark enough, now," he said. "I'm goin' down to th' other water-hole to wait for 'em. May learn somethin' worth while." He rolled his rifle in the blanket to protect it from sand and stretched gratefully.

"I'm goin' with you," said Johnny, covering his own rifle.

"I reckon I'll have to lay up here an' hold th' sack, like a fool," growled Red, who longed for action, even if it were no more than a tramp through the sand.

"You shore called it, Reddie," chuckled Johnny. "Somebody has got to stay with th' cayuses; an' I don't know anybody as reliable as you. Don't forget, an' build a camp fire while we're gone," and with this parting insult Johnny melted into the darkness after his leader and plodded silently behind him until Hopalong stopped and muttered a command.

"We're not far away now," he said. "Reckon we oughtn't get too close till they come to th' hole an' get settled down. Some of 'em may have to ride far an' wide if th' herd's ornery, an' run onto us. We've got th' trumps, an' they're worth twice as much if they don't know we got 'em. They shoot off their mouths regardless out here."

Johnny grunted his acquiescence and squatted comfort ably on his haunches, the tips of the fingers of one hand in the sand. "Never felt more like smokin' than I do now," he chuckled. "Got any chewin'?"

His friend passed over the desired article and Johnny worried off a generous mouthful. "It's got too many stems in it; but bein' th' first chew I've had since I got married I ain't kickin'," he complacently remarked. "Margaret says it sticks to me for hours."

Hopalong grunted. "Gettin' to be real lady-like, ain't you?" he jeered. "Put perfumery on yore shirt bosom?"

"I would if she wanted me to," retorted his companion. "I don't just know what I wouldn't do if she wanted me to."

Hopalong snorted. "That so?" he demanded, pugnaciously. "Reckon she might like to know what yo're doin' down here, how much longer you aim to stay, an' if yo're still alive an' other little foolish things like that. Let me tell you, Kid, you don't know how big a woman fills up yore life till you've lost her."

"I can imagine what it would be without her," said Johnny, slowly and reverently, his heart aching for his friend's loss. "She knows all about it; nearly all, anyhow. I've writ to her every third day, when I could, an' some times oftener. She may be worryin', but I'm bettin' every cent I'll ever have that she ain't doin' no cryin'! There ain't many wimmen like her, even in this kind of country."

"Then she's shore got Red an' me figgered for a fine pair of liars," murmured Hopalong; "but just th' same I'm feelin' warmer toward you than I have for a week," he announced. "When did you tell her all about this scrambled mess?"

"When I found that I couldn't tell how much longer I'd have to stay here," confessed Johnny. "I couldn't write letters an' lie good enough to fool her; an' I had to write letters, didn't I?"

"I'll take everythin' back, Kid," said his companion, grinning in the dark.

Johnny grunted and the silence began again, a silence which endured for several hours, such a silence that can exist between two real friends and be full of under standing. It endured between them and was not even broken by the distant, dim flare of a match, nor when low sounds floated up to them and gradually grew into the clicking and rattle of horns against horns, and the low rumble of many hurrying hoofs hoofs hurrying toward the water which bovine nostrils had long since scented. The rumble grew rapidly as the thirst-tortured herd stampeded for Bitter Spring. A revolver flashed here and there on the edges of the animated avalanche and then a sweet silence came to the desert, soon to be tune fully and pleasantly broken by the soft lowing of cattle leg deep in the saving water.

Let th' air blow in up-on m-e-e,

Let me see th' mid-night s-k-y;

Stand back, Sisters, from a-round m-e-e:

God, it i-s s-o-o h-a-r-d to d-i-e, wailed a cracked voice, the owner relieving his feelings. "Thorpe, if you don't wrastle a hot snack damned quick, I'll eat yore ears!"

"Give him anythin' to stop that yowlin'," bellowed another. "Can't he learn nothin' but ' Th' Dyin' Nun '? Thank heaven he never learned no more of it. A sick calf ain't no cheerfuller than him."

"You'll have to eat lively, boys," sang out the trail-boss. "Everythin' is on th' move in an hour. If yo're in such a cussed hurry, Jud, get some wood for him. Take it from that lame pack horse. Reckon we'll have to shoot him if he don't get better in a hurry."

Up to my knees in mud I go

An' water to my middle;

Whenever firewood's to be got

I'm Cookie's sec-ond fid-die, chanted Jud, splashing out to where the lame pack horse conducted an experiment in saturation. "Hot, cussed hot," he enlightened the cheerful, but tired group on the bank. "Hot an' oozy. Hello, hoss," he greeted, slapping the shrinking shoulder. "You heard what th' boss said about you? Pick up, Ol' Timer; pick up or you'll get shot. What? Don't blame you a bit, not a cussed bit. I'd ruther be shot, too, than tote wood over this part of h--l. Oh, well; life's plumb funny. You'll fry if you do, an' you'll die if you don't. What's th' difference, anyhow, Ol' Timer?"

"Hey, Jud," called a voice. "Got a new bunkie?"

"I could have worse than a cayuse," replied Jud. "A cussed sight worse."

"There's mocassins, rattlers, copperheads, tarantulas, an' scorpions in that pond! "warned another.

"You done forgot Gila monsters, tigers an' an' Injuns," retorted Jud. "Now comes a job. With both arms full of slippin', criss-crossin' firewood, th' rest slidin' from th' pack, I got to hang on to what I got, put th' rest back like it ought to go an' make every thin' tight. Come out here, some damned fool, an' gimme a hand. Better move lively only got four arms an' six hands.

"There!" he exploded. "There goes th' shootin'-match off th' hoss. Th' wind'll blow 'em ashore an' we can pick up th' whole caboodle."

"Wind?" jeered the snake-enumerator. "Where's th' wind? Yo're a fool!"

"On th' bank, where yo're settin', you thick-headed ass!" yelled Jud. "You got so cussed much to say, suppose you muddy yore lily-white pants an' do somethin' besides bray!"

"Did you spill any of 'em, Jud?" anxiously asked a voice. "I heard a splash."

Jud's reply was such that the trail-boss snapped a warning which checked some of the conversation, and promised his help. "Wait for me, Jud; I'm comin'," he said.

"Why don't you send that white-washed idol?" asked Jud. "I'll show him who's th' fool; an' what a splash sounds like!"

Hopalong nudged his companion and they crept for ward, feeling before them for anything which might make a sound if stepped on. A vibrant whirl made them spring back and go around the warning snake, and soon they reached the little, sandy ridge which had sheltered Hopalong on his other visit.

"I'm glad you hung on to what you had, Jud," came Thorpe's thankful voice as his match caught the sun baked wood and sent a tiny flame licking upward among the shavings whittled by his knife. "What you do you allus do right. It's dry as a bone."

"An' so am I," grunted the horse wrangler. "Who's got their canteen?"

"He's askin' for a canteen, with th' whole pond in front of him!" laughed a squatting rustler. "Here; take mine."

The fire grew quickly and a coffeepot, staunch friend of weary travelers, was placed in the flame, no one caring what it looked like or how hot the handle got. Time passed swiftly in talking of the raid and in consuming the light, hurried meal and soon the wrangler argued to his charges from the bank, and then waded in for his own horse, after which the matter was much simplified. He had them bunched, the next change of horses had been cut out by the men and they were ready to resume the drive when a distant voice hailed them. Soon a lathered horse glistened in the outer circle of light, and the hardriding courier dashed up to the fire.

"They've hit th' town, boys!" he shouted. "Th f Question-Mark an' th' Diamond L have joined hands agin' us. Their friends in town are backin' 'em. Kane says to drive this herd hell-to-leather to th' valley, leave it there an' burn th' trail back. Where's Hugh Roberts?"

"Here," answered the trail-boss, stepping forward. "Hello, Vic."

"Got strict orders from th' boss," said Vic, leaning over and whispering in the ear of the trail-boss.

Roberts stiffened and swore angrily. "Is that all he says for us to do?" he sneered. "I got a notion to tell him to go to h--l!"

Eager questions assailed him from the pressing group and he pushed himself free. "He says we are to take Quayle's hotel, their headquarters, from th' rear at dawn of th' day we get back an' hold it! That's all!"

An angry chorus greeted the announcement and the shouting courier had a hard time to make himself heard, "That's wins for us!" he yelled. "You get their leaders, you split 'em in two an' Kane'll turn his boys loose to hit 'em during th' confusion. He's got a wise head, I'm shoutin'. Red Frank's gang smashes from th' west end, an' they'll never know what happened. We'll have 'em split three ways, leaderless, not knowin' what's happened. It'll be a stampede an' a slaughter. Cuss it, I'll be with you! That shows what I think of it!"

"Throw th' herd back on th' trail," ordered the boss. "We'll drive hard, an' turn th' rest of it over in our minds as we go. So we can have yore valuable assistance yo're goin' with us. Get a fresh cayuse from th' caviya. I say, yo're goin' with us, savvy?"

Covered by the noise of the renewed drive Hopalong and Johnny wriggled back until they could with safety arise to their feet, when they hastened back to Red and tersely reported what they had learned. Red's reply was instant.

"One of us has got to learn where that herd is kept; th' others light out for McCullough. Th' herd trailer can go to town when he gets it located. We can't lose them cattle, now."

"Right!" said Hopalong. "I'm puttin' cartridges in my hand. Th' worst guesser goes after th' herd. Odd or even. Red, you first," and he placed his clenched fist in Red's hand.

"Even," said Red, and then he opened the fist, felt of the cylinders and chuckled. There were two.

Hopalong fumbled at his belt and placed his fist in Johnny's hand. "Call it, Kid," he said.

"Even," said Johnny, carelessly. He felt the closed hand slowly open and cast his fingers over its palm, rinding two cartridges, and he grunted. "Better take th' extra canteens, Hoppy; an' that spyglass. It'll mebby come in handy. Want Pepper?"

"Just 'cause she's a good cayuse for you don't say that she is for me," chuckled the loser. "She knows you; I'm a stranger," and he led the way to the picketed and hobbled horses. In a few minutes he swung into the saddle, the telescope under his arm, cheerily said his good-byes and melted into the darkness, bound further into the desert, where or how far he did not know. Passing the southern water-hole he drew two cartridges from his belt, placed one in the palm of his right hand and held the other between his fingers. Slowly opening the clenched fist he relaxed the fingers and the second cartridge dropped onto its mate with a little click. There was no need to cough now and hide that slight, metallic noise, so he grinned instead and slowly pushed them back into the vacant loops.

"Fine job, lettin' th' Kid go out on this skillet," he snorted, indignant at the thought. "Me, now it don't matter a whole lot what happens to me these days; but th' Kid's got a wife, an' a darned fine one, too. Go on, you lazy cow yo're work's just startin'."

It was not long before he caught the noise of the harddriven herd well off to his right and he followed by sound until dawn threatened. Then, slowing his horse, he rode off at an angle and hunted for low places in the desert floor, where he went along a course parallel to that followed by the herd. Persistently keeping from sky lines, although added miles of twisting detours was the price, and keeping so far from his quarry that he barely could pick out the small, dark mass with the aid of the glass, he feared no discovery. So he rode hour after weary hour under the pitiless sun, stopping only once to turn his sombrero into a bucket, from which his horse eagerly drank the contents of one huge canteen, its two gallons of water filling the hat several times.

"Got to go easy with it for awhile, bronch," he told it. "Water can't be so terrible far ahead, judgin' from that herd pushin' boldlike across this strip of h--l but cows can go a long time without it when they has to; an' out here they shore has to. I'm not cheatin' you there's four for you an' one for me, an' we won't change it."

Mile upon burning mile passed in endless procession as they plodded through hard sand, soft sand, powdery dust, and over stretches of rocky floor blasted smooth and slippery by the cutting sands driven against it by every wind for centuries. An occasional polished bowlder loomed up, its coat of "desert-varnish "glistening brown under the pale, molten sun. He knew what the varnish was, how it had been drawn from the rock and the mineral contents left behind on the surface as its moisture evaporated into the air. An occasional "side-winder," diminutive when compared to the rattlesnakes of other localities, slid curiously across the sand, its beady, glittering eyes cold and vicious as it watched this strange invader of its desert fastness.

Warned at last by the fading light after what had seemed an eternity of glare, he gave the dejected horse another canteen of water and then urged it into brisker pace, to be within earshot of the fleeing herd when darkness should make safe a nearer approach.

With the coming of twilight came a falling of temperature and when the afterglow bathed the desert with magic light and then faded as swiftly as though a great curtain had been dropped the creeping chill took bold, sudden possession of the desert air to a degree unbelievable. So passed the night, weary hour after cold, weary hour; but the change was priceless to man and beast. The magic metamorphosis emphasized the many-sided nature of the desert, at one time a blazing, glaring thing of sinister aspect and death-dealing heat; at another cold, almost freezing, its considerable altitude being good reason for the night's penetrating chill. The expanse of dim gray carpet, broken by occasional dark blots where the scrawny, scattered vegetation arose from the sands, stretched away into the veiling dark, allowing keen eyes to distinguish objects at surprising distances. Overhead blazed the brilliant stars, blazed as only stars in desert heavens can, seeming magnified and brought nearer by the dry, clear air. His eyes at last free from the blinding glare of quivering air and glittering crystals of salts in the sand; his dry, parched, burning skin free from the baking heat, which sucked moisture from the pores before perspiration could form on the surface; he sucked in great gulps of the vitalizing, cold air and found the night so refreshing, so restful as to almost compensate for the loss of sleep.

The increased pace of his mount at last brought reward, for there now came from ahead and from the right the low, confused noise of hurrying cattle, as continuous, unobtrusive, and restful as the soft roar of distant surf. So passed the dark hours, and then a warning, silver glow on the eastern horizon caused him to pull up and find a sandy depression, there to wait until the proper distance was put behind it by the thirsty herd, still reeling off the miles as though it were immune to fatigue. The silver band widened swiftly, changed to warmer tints, became suffused with crimson and cast long, thin, vague, warning shadows from sage bush and greasewood and then a molten, quivering orb pushed up over the prostrate horizon and bathed the shrinking sands with its light.

The cold, heavy-lidded rider glowered at it and removed the blanket which had been wrapped around him, rolling it tightly with stiff fingers and fumblingly made it secure in the straps behind the cantle of his saddle.

"There it is again, bronch," he growled. "We'll soon wonder if th' cold was all a dream."

He stood up in the stirrups and peered cautiously over the bank of the depression, making out the herd with unaided eyes.

"They can't go on another day," he muttered. "This ain't just dry trail it's a chunk out of hell. They can't stand much more of it without goin' blind, an' that's th' beginnin' of th' end on a place like this. I'm bettin' they get to water by noon an' then we got to wait till th' coast is clear." He shook the canteen he had allotted himself and growled again. "About a quart, an' I could drink a gallon! All right, bronch; get a-goin'," and on they plodded, keeping to the hollows and again avoiding all elevations, to face the torments of another murderous day. Again the accursed hours dragged, again the horse had a canteen of water, a sop which hardly dulled the edge of its raging thirst. Earth, air, and sky quivered, writhed and danced under the jelly-like sun and the few, soft night noises of the desert were heard no more. The leveled telescope kept the herd in sight as mile followed mile across the scorched and scorching sand.

The sun had passed the meridian only half an hour when the sweeping spyglass revealed no herd, but only a distant ridge of rock, like a tiny island on a stilled sea.

"It shore is time," muttered the rider, dismounting. "Seein' as how we're nearly there, I reckon you can have th' last canteen. You shore deserve it, you game old plodder. An' I'm shore glad them rustlin' snakes have their orders to get back pronto; but it would just be our luck if that bull-headed trail-boss held a powwow in that valley of theirs. His name's Roberts, bronch; Hugh Roberts, it is. We'll remember his name an' face if he makes us stay out here till night. You an' me have got to get to that water before another sunrise if all th' thieves in th' country are campin' on it we got to, that's all."

An hour passed and then the busy telescope showed a diminutive something moving out past the far end of the distant ridge. Despite the dancing of the heat-distorted image on the object-glass the grim watcher knew it for what it was. Another and another followed it and soon the moving spots strung out against the horizon like a crawling line of grotesque, fantastic insects, silhouetted against the sky.

"There they go back to Mesquite to capture Quayle's hotel an' win th' fight," sneered Hopalong. "I could tell 'em somethin' that would send them th' other way but we'll let 'em ride with Fate; an' get to that water as quick as yore weary legs can take us. Th' herd is there, bronch; all alone, waitin' for us. It's our herd now, if we want it, which we don't. Huh! Mebby they left a guard! All right, then; he's got a big job on his hands. Come on; get a-goin'!"

Swinging more and more to the south he soon forsook the windings of the hollows and struck boldly for the eastern end of the valley, and when he reached it he hobbled and picketed the horse, frantic with the heavy scent of water in its crimson, flaring nostrils, and went ahead on foot, the hot Sharp's in his hands full cocked and poised for instant action. Crawling to the edge of the valley he inched forward on his stomach and peered over the rim. An exclamation of surprise and incredulity died in his throat as the valley lay under his eyes, for it was the valley he had seen in the mirage only a few days before.

The stolen herd filled the small creek, standing like statues, soaking in the life-giving fluid and nosing it gently. One or two, moving restlessly, blundered against those nearest them and the watcher knew that they had gone blind. The sharpest scrutiny failed to discover any guard, and he knew that his uncertain count of the kaleidoscopic riders had been correct. Hastening back to the restless horse he soon found that it had in reserve a strength which sent it flashing to the trail's edge and down the dangerous ledge at reckless speed. At last in the creek it, too, stood as though dazed and nosed the water a little before drinking.

Hopalong swung into the stream, removed saddle and bridle and then splashed across to the hut, dumping his load, canteens, and all against the front wall. To make assurance doubly sure he scouted hurriedly down one side of the little valley, crossed the creek and went back along the other wall.

Thorpe's carefully stacked firewood provided fuel for a cunningly built-up fire; one of Thorpe's discarded tomato cans, washed and filled in the spring near the hut's walls sizzled and sputtered in the blazing fire and soon boiled madly. Picking it out of the blaze with the aid of two longer sticks the hungry cook set it to one side, threw in a double handful of Thorpe's coffee, covered it with another washed can and then placed Thorpe's extra frying pan on the coals, filling it with some of Thorpe's bacon. A large can of Thorpe's beans landed close to the fire and rolled a few feet, and the cheerful explorer emerged from the hut with a sack of sour-dough biscuits which the careless Thorpe had forgotten.

"Bless Thorpe," chuckled Hopalong. "I'll never make him climb no more walls. I wouldn't 'a' made him climb that one, mebby, if I'd knowed about this."

Looking around as a matter of caution, his glance embracing the stolid herd and his own horse grazing with the jaded animals left behind by the rustlers, he fell to work turning the bacon and soon feasted until he could eat no more. Rolling a cigarette he inhaled a few puffs and then, picking up telescope and rifle, he grunted his lazy way up the steep trail and mounted the ridge, sweeping the western horizon first with the glass and then completed the circle. Satisfied and drowsy he returned to the valley, spread his folded blanket behind the hut, placed the saddle on one end of it for a pillow and lay down to fall asleep in an instant.

When he awakened he stretched out the kinks and looked around in the dim light. He felt unaccountably cold and he looked at the blanket which he had pulled over him some time during his sleep, wondering why he had felt the need for it during the daylight hours in such a place as this.

"Well, I'll cook me some more bacon before it gets dark, an' then set up with a nice little fire, with a 'dobe wall at my back. It'll be a treat just to set an' smoke an' plan, th' night chill licked by th' fire an' my happy stomach full of bacon, beans, an' biscuits an' coffee, cans an' cans of coffee."

It suddenly came to him that the light was growing stronger instead of weaker, that it was not the afterglow, and that the chill was dying instead of increasing. Shocked by a sudden suspicion he glanced into the eastern sky and stared stupidly, surprised that he had not noticed it before.

"I was so dumb with sleep that I didn't savvy east from west," he muttered. "It's daylight, 'stead of evenin' I've slept all afternoon an' night! Well, I don't see how that changes th' eatin' part, anyhow. No wonder I pulled th' blanket over me, an' no wonder I was stiff."

With the coming of the sun a disagreeable journey loomed nearer and nearer but, as he told the horse when cinching the saddle on its back, the return trip would not be one of uncertainty; nor would they be held down to such a slow pace by any clumsy herd. A further thought hastened his movements: there was a big fight going on in Mesquite, and his two friends were in it without him. Looking around he saw that he had cleaned up and effaced all signs of his visit and, filling the canteens and fastening them into place, he mounted and rode up the steep slope, turned his back to the threatening sun and loped westward along a plain and straight trail, a grim smile on his face.

Chapter XX

The Redoubt Falls

After Hopalong had ridden off on his desert trailing, Johnny and Red rode to the Question-Mark, reaching it a little after daylight and were promptly challenged when near the smaller corral. The sharp voice changed to a friendly tone when the sentry had a better look at the pair.

"Thought you'd be up with th' circus," said the Question-Mark puncher.

"On our way now," replied Johnny. "Come down here to learn what was happenin'. Meet Red Connors, an old friend of Waffles."

"Howd'y," grunted the puncher, looking at Red with a keener interest. "You fellers are lucky we got to stay here an' miss it all. Walt come down last night an' said Kane's goin' to be a hard nut to crack. He's fixed up like a fort."

"Reckon we'll take a look at it," said Johnny, wheeling.

"Hey! If you want to find Mac, he's hangin' out at Quayle's."

Johnny waved his thanks and rode on with his cheerful companion. In due time they heard the distant firing and not much later rode up to Quayle's back door and went in. McCullough was raging at the effectiveness of the sharpshooters on Kane's roof who had succeeded in keep-ing the fight at long range and who dominated certain strategic positions which the trail-boss earnestly desired to make use of; all of which made him irritable and unusually gruff.

"Where you been?" he demanded as Johnny entered.

"Locatin' a missin' herd of yore cattle," retorted Johnny, nettled by the tone. "They're waitin' for you when you get time to go after 'em. Now we'll locate them sharpshooters. Anythin' else you can't do, let us know. Come on, Red," and he went out again, his grinning friend at his heels. At the door Red checked him.

"Looks like a long-range job, Kid. My gun's all right for closer work, but I ought to have a Sharp's for this game."

Johnny wheeled and went back. "Gimme a Sharp's," he demanded.

"Take Wilson's they got him yesterday," growled the trail-boss, pointing.

Johnny took the gun and the cartridge belt hanging on it, joined Red and led the way to a place he had in mind. Reaching the selected spot, an adobe hut on the remote outskirts of the sprawled town, he stopped. "This is good enough for me," he grunted, "except th' range is too cussed long. Well, we'll try it from here, anyhow."

"I'm goin' to th' next shack," replied Red, moving on. "We'll use our old follow-shootin' an' make 'em sick. Ready? I'm goin' to cross th' open." At his friend's affirmative grunt Red leaned over and dashed for the other adobe. A bullet whined in front of him, barely heard above the roar of Johnny's rifle. He settled down, adjusted the sights and proceeded to prove title to his widely known reputation on other ranges of being the best rifle-shot of many square miles. "Make a hit, Kid?" he called. "It's mebby further than you figger."

"It is," answered Johnny. "Like old times, huh? Lord help 'em when you get started! Are you all set? I'm ready to draw 'em."

"Wind gentle, from th' east," mumbled Red. "Dirty gun got to shoot higher. All right," he called, nestling the heavy stock.

Johnny pushed his rifle around the corner of the building, aimed quickly and fired. A hatted head arose above Kane's roof and a puff of smoke spurted into the air above it as Red's Sharp's roared. The hat flew back ward and the head ducked down again, its owner surprised by the luck of the shot.

Johnny laughed outright. "For a trial shot I'm admittin' that was a whizzer. I ain't no slouch with a Sharp's but how th' devil you can make one behave like you do is a puzzle to me."

"I'm still starin'," said a humorous, envious voice behind them and they looked around to see Waffles hugging the end of the building. "If I can get over on Red's right I'll help make targets for him."

"Walk right over to that other shack," called Johnny. "Yo're safe as if you was home in yore bunk. Cover him, Red."

Waffles' mind flashed back into the past and what it presented to him greatly reassured him, but to walk was tempting Providence; he ran across the open and again Red's rifle roared.

"Got him!" yelled Johnny, staring at the body lying over the distant parapet. It was swiftly pulled back out of sight. The rest of Johnny's words were profanely eulogistic.

"Shut yore face," growled Red. "It was plumb luck."

"Shore it was," laughed his friend in joyous irony; "but yo're allus makin' 'em. That's what counts."

Waffles, having gained the shelter he coveted, looked around. "Heads was plentiful up there yesterday. There was allus one or two bobbin' up. I'm bettin' they'll be scarcer today."

"They'll be scarcer tomorrow, when we are behind them other shacks," replied Red. "They're easy three hundred paces nearer, an' that's a lot sometimes."

"An' twice as much to them," rejoined Johnny. "Th' nearer you get th' more you make it even terms. You stay where you are me an' Waffles'll go out there tonight."

When the afternoon dragged to an end Red had another sharpshooter to his credit, and the dominating group on the roof were much less dominant. They cursed the long-range genius who shot hats off of heads, clipped ears, and had killed two men. The shooting, with a rest and plenty of time to aim, would have been creditable enough; but to hit a bobbing head meant quick handling. They were properly indignant, for it was a toss-up with Death to show enough of their heads to sight a slanting rifle. One of their number, whose mangled ear was bound up with a generous amount of bandage, savagely hammered the chisel with which he was cutting a loophole through four inches of seasoned wood, vowing vengeance on the man who had ruined his looks.

The light failing for close shooting, the three friends left their positions and went to the hotel for a late supper, Red receiving envious, grinning looks as he entered the dining-room. Idaho promptly forsook his bosom friends and went over to finish his meal at the table of the new comers.

"We got Red Frank's place plumb full of holes you can see daylight through th' second floor," he announced; "but it don't seem to do no good. If I could get close enough to use a bomb I got, we might clean 'em up."

"Crawl up in th' dark," suggested Waffles.

"Can't; they spread flour all around th' place, an' th' minute a man crosses it he shows up plain. Two of us found out all about that!"

"Go through or over th' buildin's this side of th' place," said Johnny, visualizing the street. "They lead up close to Red Frank's."

Idaho stared, and slapped his thigh in enthusiastic endorsement. "I reckon you called it!" he gloated. "Wait till I tell th' boys," and he hastened back to his friends. Judging from the sudden noise coming from the table, his friends were of the same opinion and, bolting the rest of the meal, they hastened away to forthwith try the plan.

McCullough entered the dining-room and strode straight to Johnny. "Did I hear you say you know where my cattle are?" he asked, sitting down.

Johnny nodded, chewed hurriedly and replied. "I didn't finish it. *I* don't know where they are, but Hopalong is trailin' 'em, an' he'll know when he comes back. Pay us them rewards now, instead of later, an' I'll do some high an' mighty guessin' about yore head an' bet you th' rewards that I guess right."

The trail-boss laughed. "You've shore got plenty o nerve," he retorted. "When this fight is over there won't be no rewards paid. We got th' whole gang in them two buildin's, an' we got 'em good. You've had yore trouble for nothin', Nelson."

"How 'bout th' gang that are with th' herd?" asked Johnny, a note of anger edging his words.

McCullough shrugged his shoulders. "I ain't worryin' about them they'll never come back to Mesquite."

"That so?" queried Johnny, sarcastically. "I ought to keep my mouth shut, th' way yo're talkin', but I hate to see good men killed. I'll bet you they'll come back just at dawn, some time in th' next five days. An' I'll bet you they'll sneak up on this hotel an' raise th' devil, while Kane starts a bunch from his place and Red Frank's, to help 'em. Th' minute they start shootin' in here their friends '11 sortie out an' carry th' fight to you. Want to bet on it?"

McCullough regarded the speaker through narrowed lids. "How do you figger that?" he demanded suspiciously. "You gettin' that out of yore medicine bag, too?" and then he eagerly drank in every word of the explanation. After a moment's thought he looked around the room and then back to the smiling Johnny. "Much obliged, Nelson. I'm beginnin' to see that I owe you fellers somethin', after all. If them fellers we want were loose an' you got 'em, then of course th' reward would stand; but you can't win it very well when we've got 'em corraled. Who-all is in that bunch with th' herd?"

Johnny smiled but shook his head.

"Didn't you say you knowed who killed Ridley?" persisted the trail-boss.

"I know him, an' how he did it. Hopalong saw him while his gun was smokin', but didn't know what he had shot at till later."

"Why didn't you tell me, an' earn that reward right away?"

"That's only half of th' rewards," replied Johnny. "There's money up for th' fellers that robbed th' bank. If we got Ridley's murderer th' others might 'a' smelled out what we was after. You see, I was robbed of more than eleven hundred dollars th' first night I was in town. Th' money belonged to th' ranch. Th' only chance I had of gettin' it back was to make th' rewards big enough to stand three splits that would be large enough to cover it. An' I'm still goin' to do that, Mac. Pay it now an' we'll stick with you till you get th' men an' yore herd. Of course, yo're going to get th' herd, anyhow, as far as we are concerned. I ain't holdin' that over yore head; I'm only tryin' to show you why I can't be open an' free with you."

"I couldn't pay th' rewards now even if I wanted to," said the trail-boss.

"I know that, an' I didn't think you would. I was only showin' you how things are with us."

McCullough nodded, placed a hand on the speaker's shoulder and arose, turning to Red. "Connors," he said, "yo're a howlin' wonder with a Sharp's. Much obliged for holdin' down that roof. If you can clean 'em up there this fight'll go on a cussed sight faster. Th' cover on th' north side of Kane's is so poor that we can't do much out there, but we can do a little better when them sharp shooters are driven down. From what I know of you two, yore friend Cassidy is shore able to trail that herd. I've quit worryin' about everythin' but th' fight here in town. An' lemme make a long speech a little longer: If you fellers can earn them rewards I won't waste no time in payin' up; but there ain't a chance for you. We got 'em under our guns."

"Who was right about where that raid on you was goin' to take place?" asked Johnny. "You was purty shore about that, too, wasn't you?"

The trail-boss smiled and shook his head. "Yo're a good guesser," he admitted, and went out to consult with Lukins.

The next day found the line a little tighter around the stronghold, thanks to Red's shooting, which increased in accuracy after he had decided to use closer cover and cut three hundred paces out of the range. Better positions had been gained by the attackers during the night, some of the more daring men now being not far from pointblank range, which enabled them to make the use of Kane's loopholes hazardous. To the north another rifle man lay in a hollow of the sandy plain, but too far away to do much damage. The north parapet of the building was hidden from Red by the one on the south and the aerial marksmen made free use of it.

Red Frank's place was in jeopardy, for Idaho and his enthusiastic companions were in the building next on the south, separated from the Mexican's house by less than twenty feet. There was an open window facing the gambling-house and Idaho, chancing quick glances through it, noticed that one of the heavy, board shutters of a window of the upper floor sagged out a little from the top. Signaling the men behind the jail to increase their fire, he coiled his rope and cast it through the window. It struck the upper edge of the shutter, dropped behind it and grew swiftly taut. Two of his companions added their strength to his, while the other two covered them by pouring a heavy revolver fire at the two threatening loopholes. The shutter creaked, twisted, and then slowly gave way, finally breaking the lower hinge and sailing over against the other house to a cheer from the jail. Heavy firing came through the uncovered window, the bullets passing through the opposing wall and driving the Diamond L men to other shelter. Here they waited until it died down and then, picking up the bomb made by the owner of the new freight wagon, Idaho lit the jumpy, uncertain fuse, waited as long as he dared and hurled it across the intervening space and through the shutterless window as the opening was being boarded up. There was a roar, jets of smoke spurt from windows and holes and the wild cursing of injured men rang out loudly. A tongue of flame leaped through a trapdoor on the roof and grew rapidly brighter. At intervals the smoke pouring up be came suddenly heavy and thick, but cleared quickly be tween the onslaughts of the water buckets. Fire now crept through the side of the frame structure and mounted rapidly, and such a hail of lead poured through the smokespurting, upper loopholes that it became impossible for the buckets to be properly used. It was only a matter of time before the blazing roof and floor would fall on the defenders in the adobe- walled structure below, and through a loophole Red Frank suddenly shoved out a soiled towel fastened on the end of a rifle barrel.

"Come ahead, with yore hands up! "shouted a stentorian voice from the jail. "Quit firin', boys; they're surrenderin'." Almost on the tail of his words a hurrying line of choking Mexicans, bearing their wounded, streamed from the front door. They were promptly and proudly escorted by the hilarious attackers to safe quarters on the southern outskirts of the town.

Chapter XXI
All Wrapped Up

McCullough and Lukins drew men from the cordon around the gambling-hall until the line was thinned and stretched as much as prudence allowed, covering only the more strategic positions, while the men taken from it were placed in an ambuscade at the rear of Quayle's hotel. Both leaders would have preferred to have placed their reception committee nearer the outskirts of the rambling town but, not knowing from which direction the attack would come and not being able to spare men enough for outposts around the town, they were forced to concentrate at the object of the attack. When night fell and darkness hid the movement they set the trap, gave strict orders for no one to approach the rear of the hotel during the dark hours, and waited expectantly.

The first night passed in quiet and the following day found the cordonreen forced until it contained its original numbers. By nightfall of the second day Red, Johnny, and Waffles had cleared the parapet and made it useless during daylight, and as the moon increased in size and brightness the parapet steadily became a more perilous position at night for the defenders. All three marksmen, now ensconced within three hundred yards of the gambling-house and out of the line of sight of every lower loophole, had the range worked out to a foot. Red and Waffles had discarded their borrowed Sharp's and were now using their own familiar Winchesters, and it was certain death to any man who tried to shoot from Kane's roof on any side but the north one.

Evening came and with it came a hair-brained attempt by Idaho and his irrepressibles to capture and use the stables. Despite McCullough's orders to the contrary the group of young-sters, elated by their success against Red Frank's, made the attempt as soon as darkness fell; and learned with cost that the stables were stacked decks. One man was killed and all the others wounded, most of them so badly as to remove them from the role of combatants; but one dogged, persistent, and vindictive unit of the foolish attack managed to set fire to the sun-dried structures before crawling away.

The baked wood burned like tinder and became a mass of flames almost in an instant, and for a few minutes it looked as though they would take the gambling-hall with them. It was a narrow squeak and missed only because of a slight shift of the wind. The scattered line of punchers to the north of the building, not expecting the sudden conflagration, had crawled nearer to the gambling-hall in the encroaching darkness, only to find themselves suddenly revealed to their enemies by the towering sheets of flame. They got off with minor injuries only because the north side of the building was not well manned and be cause the stables were holding the attention of most of the besieged. When the flames died down almost as swiftly as they had grown, the smouldering ashes gave a longer and less obstructed view to the guards of Kane's east wall and rendered useless certain positions cherished by McCullough.

The trail-boss, seething with anger, stamped up to Lukins and roared his demands, with the result that Idaho and the less injured of his companions were sent to take the places of cooler heads in the ambush party and were ordered to stay in Quayle's stable until after the expected attack.

In Quayle's kitchen four men waited through the drag ging hours, breaking the silence by occasional whispers as they watched the faintly lighted open spaces and the walls of certain buildings newly powdered with flour so as to serve as backgrounds and to silhouette any man passing in front of them. Only the north walls had been dusted and there was nothing to reveal their freshly acquired whiteness to unsuspecting strangers coming up from the south. In the stable Idaho and his restless friends grumbled in low tones and cursed their inactivity. Three men at the darkened office windows, and two more on the floor above watched silently. Outside an occasional shot called forth distant comment, and laughter arose here and there along the alert line.

On the east end of the line a Diamond L puncher, stretched out on his stomach in a little depression he had scooped in the sand during the darker hours of the second night, stuck the end of his little finger in a bullet hole in his canteen and rimmed the hole abstractedly, the water soaking his clothes making him squirm.

"Cuss his hide," he growled. "Now I got to stay thirsty." He slid a hand down his body and lifted the dinging clothing from the small of his back. "If it was only as cold as that when I drink it, I wouldn't grumble. An' I wasn't thirsty till he spilled it," he added in petulant afterthought.

To his right two friends crouched behind the aged ruins of an adobe house, paired off because one of them shot left-handed, which fitted each to his own corner. "Got any chewin'?" asked Righthand. "Chuck it over. Seems to me that they "he set his teeth into the tobacco, tore off a generous quantity and tossed the plug back to its owner "ain't answerin' as strong as they was this after noon."

"No?" grunted Lefthand, brushing sand from the plug. He shoved it back into a pocket and reflected a moment. "It was good shootin' while th' stable burned." Another pause, and then: "Did you hear Billy yell when them fools started th' fire?"

Righthand laughed, stiffened, fired, and pumped the lever of the gun. "I'm gettin' so I can put every one through that loophole. Hear him squawk?" He dropped to his knees to rest his back, and chuckled. "Shore did. Billy, he was boastin' how near he could crawl to them stables. I reckon he done crawled too close. Lukins ought to send them kids home."

In a sloping, shallow arroyo to their right Walt and Bob of the Question-Mark lay side by side. Behind them two shots roared in quick succession. Walt lazily turned his head from the direction of the sounds and peeped over the edge of the bank.

"I reckon some coyote took a look over th' edge of th' roof," he remarked.

"Uh-huh," replied Bob without interest and without relaxing his vigil.

"I don't lay out here one little minute after Connors leaves that 'dobe," said Walt. He spat noisily and turned the cud. "I'm savin' shootin' like his is a gift. I'm some shot, myself, but h--l"

"You'd shore a thought so," replied Bob, grinning as he reviewed something, "if you'd seen that sharpshooter flop over th' edge of th' roof th' other day. I'd guess it was close to fifteen hundred." He changed his position, grunted in complacent satisfaction and continued. "Some folks can't see a man's forehead at that distance, let alone hit it. Of course, th' sky was behind it."

"Which made it plainer, but harder to figger right," observed Walt. "Waffles says Connors can drive a dime into a plank with th' first, an' push it through with th' second, as far away as he can see th' dime. When it's too far away to be seen, he puts it in th' middle of a black circle, an' aims for th' middle of th' circle. But I put plenty of salt on th' tails of his stories."

"Which holds 'em down," grunted Bob. "Who's that over there, movin' around that shack?"

Walt looked and cogitated. "Charley was there when I came out," he answered. "Cussed fool showin' hisself like that." He swore at a thin pencil of flame which stabbed out from a loophole, and fired. "Told you so!" he growled. "Charley is down!"

Both fired at the loophole and hazarded a quick look at the foolish unfortunate, who had dragged himself behind a hummock of sand. Rapid firing broke out behind them and, sensing what it meant, they joined in. A crouched figure darted from a building, sprinted to the hummock, swung the wounded man on its back, and staggered and zigzagged to cover.

"That was Waffles," said Walt, reloading the magazine of his rifle. "It's a cussed shame to make a man take chances like that by bein' a fool."

Behind the building Waffles lowered his burden to the ground, ripped off the wet shirt and became busy. He fastened the end of the bandage and stood up. "Fools are lucky sometimes," he growled; "an' I says you are lucky to only have a smashed collar bone. You try a fool trick like that again an' I'll bust yore head. Ain't you got no sense?"

"Don't you go to put on no airs, Waffles," said Red Connors. "I can tell a few things on you. I know you."

Johnny chuckled. "Tread easy," he warned. "We both know you."

"Go to h--l!" grunted the ex- foreman of the O-Bar-O, grinning. "Fine pair of sage-hens you are to tell tales on me! I got you thro wed and hog-tied before you even start." He wheeled at a noise behind him, and glared at the wounded man. "Where'n h--l are you goin'?" he demanded, truculently.

"Without admittin' yore right to ask fool questions," groaned Charley, still moving, "I'll say I'm goin' to join th' ambush party at Quayle's, an' relieve somebody else." He gritted his teeth and stood erect. "I can use a Colt, can't I?" he demanded.

"Yo're so shaky you can't hit a house," retorted Waffles.

"Which I ain't aimin' to do," rejoined the white-faced man. "You'll show more sense if you'll tie my left arm like it ought to be, instead of standin' with yore mouth open. You'll shore catch a cold if you don't shut it purty soon."

"You stubborn fool!" growled Waffles, but he fixed the arm to its owner's satisfaction.

"If he gets smart, Charley," suggested Johnny, "pull his nose. He allus was an old woman, anyhow."

With the coming of midnight the cordon became doubled in numbers as growling men rubbed the sleep from their eyes and took up positions for the meeting of Kane's sortie in case the hotel was attacked by his expected drive outfit.

The hours dragged on, the silence of the night infrequently broken by bits of querulous cursing by some wounded puncher, an occasional taunt from besieger or besieged and sporadic bursts of firing which served more for notifications of defiance and watchfulness than for any grimmer purpose. Patches of clouds now and then drifted before the moon and sailed slowly on. Nature's denizens of the dark were in active swing and filled the night with their soft orchestration. The besiegers, paired for night work, which let one man doze while his companion watched, hummed, grumbled, or snored; in the gamblinghall fortress weary men slept beside the loopholes, the disheartened for a few hours relieved of their fears or carrying them across the borderland of sleep to make their slumbers restless and broken, while scowling, disheartened sentries kept a keener watch, alert for the rush hourly expected.

South of town a group of horsemen pulled up, dismounted, tied their mounts to convenient brush and slipped like shadows toward the nearest house, approaching it round-about and with animal wariness. From house to house, corral to corral, cover to cover they crept, spread out in a fan-shaped line, silent, grim, vindictive and desperate. Not a shadow passed unsearched and unused, not a bowlder or thicket was above suspicion nor below being utilized. Nearer and nearer they worked their way, eyes straining, ears tuned for every sound, high-strung with nerves quivering, keyed to swift reflex and instant decision. The scattered, infrequent firing grew steadily nearer, every flat report was searched for secret meanings and the sharp squeak of a gyrating bat overhead sent every man flat to the earth. The last in the group became cannily slower as opportunity offered and soon managed to be so far behind that his quick, furtive desertion was un-noticed in the tenseness of conjecture as to what lay immediately ahead.

Kane's trail-boss slanted his watch under the moon's rays and gave a low, natural signal, whereupon to right and left a man detached himself and left the waiting group. Minutes passed, their passing marked on nervous foreheads by the thin trickle of cold sweat. Any instant might a challenge, a shot, a volley ring out on any side; hostile eyes might be watching every movement, hostile guns waiting for the right moment, like ravenous hounds in leash. The scouts returned as silently as they had departed and breathed their reassuring words in Roberts' ear. The town lay unsuspecting, every waking eye bent on the bulking gambling-hall. Not a hidden outpost, not a pacing sentry to watch the harmless rear. To the right showed the roof of a two-story building, bulking above the low, thick roofs of scattered, helter-skelter adobes, in any one of which Death might be poised.

Again the slow advance, and breathed maledictions on the head of any unfortunate who trod carelessly or let his swinging six-gun click against buckle or button. Roberts, peering around the end of an adobe wall, held his elbows from his sides, and progress ceased while a softly whistling figure strode across the street and became lost to sight. This was the jumping-off place, the edge of a black precipice of fate, unknown as to depth or what lay below. The savage, thankful elation which had possessed every man at his success in making this border line of life and death faded swiftly as his mind projected itself into the unknown on the other side of the house. Roberts knew what might follow if hesitation were allowed here, and that the conjecturing minds might have scant time to waver he nerved himself and snapped his fingers, leaping around the corner for Quayle's kitchen door, his men piling after him, still silent and much more tense, yet tortured to shout and to shoot. Ten steps more and the goal would have been reached, but even as the leaping group exulted there came a shredded sheet of flame and the deafening crash of spurting six-guns worked at top speed at point-blank range. The charging line crumpled in mid-stride, plunged headlong to the silvered sands and rolled or flopped or lay instantly still. At the head of his men the rustler trail-boss offered a target beyond the waiting punchers' fondest hopes, yet he bounded on unscathed, flashed around the hotel corner, turned again, doubling back behind the smoke-filled stable and scurried like a panic-stricken rabbit for the brush-filled arroyo, while hot and savage hunters searched the street for him until a hail of lead from Kane's drove them to any shelter which might serve.

When the sheltering arroyo led him from his chosen course Roberts forsook it and ran with undiminished speed toward where the horses waited. At last he reached them and as he stretched out his arm his last measure of energy left him and he plunged forward, rolling across the sand. But a will like his was not to be baffled and in a few moments he stirred, crawled forward, clawed him self into a saddle, jerked loose the restraining rope and rode for safety, hunched over and but half conscious. Gradually his pounding heart caught up with the demand, his burning lungs and spasmodic breathing became more normal, his head steadied and became a little clearer and he looked around to find out just where he was. When sure of his location he turned the horse's head toward, Bitter Spring, and beyond it, to follow the tracks he knew were still there to the only safe place left for him in all the country.

He seemed to have been riding for days when he caught sight of something moving over a ridge far ahead of him and he closed his eyes in hope that the momentary rest would clear his vision. After awhile he saw it push up over another low ridge and he knew it to be a horseman riding in the same direction as himself. Again he closed his eyes and unmercifully quirted the tired and unwilling horse into a pace it could not hold for long. Another look ahead showed him that the horseman was a Mexican, which meant that he was hardly a foe even if not a friend.

And he sneered as he thought how little it mattered whether the Mexican was an enemy or not, for one enemy ahead and a Greaser at that was greatly to be preferred to those who might be following him. Soon he frowned in slowly dawning recognition. It was Miguel and he had obtained quite a start. Conjecturing about how he had managed to be so far in the lead stirred up again the vague suspicions which had been intruding themselves upon him while he had been unable to think clearly; but he was thinking clearly now, he told himself, and his eyes glinted the sudden anger.

He thought he now knew why the town had been entered so easily, why they had been allowed to penetrate unopposed to its center. It was plain enough why they had been permitted to get within a few feet of Quayle's back door, and then be stopped with a volley at a murderously short range. As he reviewed it he almost was stunned by the thought of his own escape and he tried to puzzle it out. It might be that every waiting puncher thought that others were covering him and in this he was right. The compact group behind him had drawn every eye. It had been one of those freakish tricks of fate which might not occur again in a hundred fights; and it turned cold, practical Hugh Roberts into a slave of superstition.

On the way to town he had sneered when Miguel had pointed out a chaparral cock which raced with them for several miles and claimed that it was an omen of good luck; but from this time on no "roadrunner" ever would hear the angry whine of his bullets. Thinking of Miguel brought him back to his suspicions and he looked at the distant rider with an expression on his face which would have caused chills to race up and down the Mexican's back, could he have seen them. Miguel, unhurt, riding leisurely back to the herd, with a head-start great enough to be in itself incriminating. And then the Mexican turned in his saddle and looked back, and Roberts let his horse fall into a saner pace.

The effect upon Miguel was galvanic. He reined in, flung himself off on the far side of his horse and cautiously slid the rifle from its scabbard while he pretended to be tightening the cinch. His swarthy face became a pasty yellow and then resumed its natural color, a little darker, perhaps, by the sudden inrush of blood. After what he had done in town Hugh Roberts would be on his trail for only one thing. Miguel's racing imagination and his sudden feeling of guilt for his deliberate, planned desertion found a sufficient reason for the pursuing horse man. Sliding the rifle under his arm he waited until the man came nearer, where a hit would be less of a gamble. The Mexican knew what had happened, for he had delayed until he heard that crashing volley, and knew it to be a volley. Knowing this he knew what it meant and had fled for Surprise Valley and the big herd waiting there. That Roberts should have escaped was a puzzle and he wrestled with it while the range was steadily shortened, and the more he wrestled the more undecided he be came. Finally he slipped the gun back, mounted, and waited for the other to come up. He had a plausible answer for every question.

Roberts slowed to a walk and searched the Mexican's eyes as he pulled up at his side. "How'd you get out here so far ahead of me?" he demanded, his eyes cold and threatening.

Miguel shrugged his shoulders, but did not take his hand from his belt. "Ah, eet ees a miracle," he breathed. "The good Virgin, she watch over Miguel. An' paisano, the roadrunner deed I not tell you eet was good luck? An' you, too, was saved! How deed eet happen, that you are save?"

"They none of them looked at me, I reckon," replied Roberts. "They got everybody but me an' you. How is it that yo're out here, so far ahead of me?"

"Jus' before the firs' shootin' the what you call volley I stoomble as I try not to step on Thorpe. I go down the volley, eet come I roll away they do not see me an' here I am, like you, save."

"Is that so?" snapped Roberts.

"Eet ees jus' so, so much as eet ees that somewan tell we are comin' to Quayle's," answered Miguel. "For why they do not see us, in the town, when we come in? For why that volley, lak one shot? Sometheeng there ees that Miguel he don' understan'. An' theese, please: Why ees there no sortie wen we come in? We was on the ver' minute eet ees so?"

"Right on th' dot!" snarled Roberts, his thoughts racing along other trails. "Huh!" he growled. "Our shares of th' herd money comes to quite a sizable pile, mebby that's it. Take th' shares of all of us, an' it's more'n half. Well, I don't know, an' I ain't carin' a whole lot now. Think we can swing that herd, Miguel, an' split all th' money, even shares?"

The Mexican showed his teeth in a sudden, expansive smile. "For why not? Theese hor-rses are ver' tired; but the others they are res' now. We can wait at Bitter Spring tonight, an' go on tomorrow. There ees no hurry now."

"We don't hang out at Bitter Spring all night," contradicted Roberts flatly. "We'll water 'em an' breath 'em a spell, an' push right on. Th' further I get away from Mesquite th' better I'm goin' to like it. Come on, let's get goin'."

"There ees no hurry from Bitter Spring," murmured the Mexican. "They ees only one who know beyond; an' Manuel, he ees weeth Kane."

"I don't care a d--n!" growled his companion, stubbornly. "I'm not layin' around Bitter Spring any longer than I has to."

Neither believed the other's story, but neither cared, only each determined to be alert when the drive across the desert was completed. Before that there was hardly need to let their mutual suspicions have full play. Each was necessary to the success of the drive but after? That would be another matter. Fate was again kind to them both, for as they hurried east Hopalong Cassidy hastened west along his favorite trail, the rolling sand between hiding them from him.

Back in the town the elated ambushers buried the bodies, marveled at the escape of Roberts and drifted away to take places on the firing line, which soon showed increased activity. Here and there a more daring puncher took chances, some regretting it and others gaining better positions. Red, Johnny, and Waffles attended strictly to the roof, which now had been abandoned on all sides but the north, where lack of cover prohibited McCullough's men from getting close enough to do any considerable damage. The few punchers lying far off on the north were there principally to stop a sortie or an attempt at escape. As the day passed the defenders' fire grew a little less and the Question-Mark foreman was content to wait it out rather than risk unnecessary casualties in pushing the fighting any more briskly.

Evening came, and with it came Hopalong, tired, hungry, thirsty, and hot, which did not add sweetness to his disposition. Eager to get the men he wanted and to return for the herd, he listened impatiently to his friends' account of the fight, his mind busy on his own account. When the tale had been told and McCullough's changing attitude touched upon he shoved his hat back on his head, spread his feet and ripped out an oath.

"!" he growled. "All these men, all this time, to clean up a shack like that?"

"Mac's playin' safe it's only a matter of time, now," apologized Waffles, glaring at his two companions, who already had worn his nerves ragged by the same kind of remarks.

"Hell!" snorted Hopalong impatiently. "We'll all grow whiskers at this rate, before it's over!" He turned to Johnny and regarded him speculatively. "Kid, let Red an' Waffles handle that roof an' come along with me. I'm goin' to start things movin'."

"You'll find Mac plumb set on goin' easy," warned Waffles.

"Th' hell with Mac, an' Lukins, an' you, an' everybody else," retorted Hopalong. "We're not workin' for nobody but ourselves. All I got to do is keep my mouth shut an' Mac loses a plumb fine herd. Let me hear him talk to me! Come on, Kid."

Johnny deserted his companions as though they were lepers and showed his delight in every swaggering movement. A whining bullet over his head sent his fingers to his nose in contemptuous reply, but nevertheless he went on more carefully thereafter. As they reached the rear of a deserted adobe Hopalong pulled him to a stop.

"I'm tired of this blasted country, an' you ought to be, for you've got a wife that's havin' dull days an' sleepless nights. I'm goin' to touch somethin' off that'll put an end to this fool quiltin' party, an' let us get our money an' go home. By that I'm meanin' th' SV, for it's goin' to be home for me. Besides, it's our best chance of gettin' them rewards. So he's aimin' on cuttin' us out of 'em, huh? All right; I'm goin' to Quayle's, an' while I'm holdin' their interest you fill a canteen with kerosene an' smuggle it into th' stable."

"What you goin' to do?" demanded his companion with poorly repressed eagerness.

"I'm goin' to set fire to that gamblin'-joint an' drive 'em out, that's what!"

"Th' moon won't let you," objected Johnny, but as he looked up at the drifting clouds he hesitated and qualified his remark. "You'll have times when it won't be so light, but it'll be too light for that."

"When I start for th' hotel gamblin'-joint I go agin' th' northeast corner, where there ain't but one loophole that covers that angle. I got it figgered out. When I start, you an' Red won't be loafin' back there where I found you, target-practicin' at th' roof."

Reaching the hotel they found a self-satisfied group complacently discussing the fight. Quayle looked up at their entry, sprang to his feet and heartily shook hands with both.

"Welcome to Mesquite, Cassidy," he beamed. "Tis different now than whin ye left, an' it won't be long be fore honest men have their say-so in this town,"

"Couple of weeks, I reckon, th' way things are driftin'," replied Hopalong, smiling as Johnny left the office to invade the kitchen, where Murphy gave a grinning welcome and looked curiously at the huge canteen held out to him.

"Couple of days," corrected Quayle.

McCullough arose and shook hands with the new comer. "Hear you been trailin' my herd," he said. "Locate 'em?"

"They're hobbled, and' waitin' for yore boys to drive 'em home. Wish you'd tell yore outfit an' th' others not to shoot at th' feller that heads for Kane's northeast corner tonight, but to cut loose at th' loopholes instead. I'm honin' to get back home, an' so I'm aimin' to bust up this little party tonight. To do that I got to get close."

"That's plumb reckless," replied the trail-boss. "We got this all wrapped up now, an' it'll tie its own knots in a day or two. What's th' use of takin' a chance like that?"

"To show that bunch just who they throwed in jail! Somebody else might feel like tryin' it some day, an' I'm aimin' to make that ' some day ' a long way off."

"Can't say I'm blamin' you for that. Whereabouts did you leave th' herd?"

"Where nobody but me an' my friends, on this side of th' fence, knows about," answered Hopalong. "I'll tell you when I see you! again ain't got time now." He nodded to the others, went out the way he had come in and walked off with Johnny, who carried the innocent canteen instead of putting it into the stable.

As they started for the place where Hopalong had left his horse, not daring to ride it into town, they chose a short-cut and after a few minutes' brisk walking Hopalong pointed to a bunch of horses tied to some bushes.

"Th' fellers that owned them played safer than I did," he said, "leavin' 'em out here. I reckon they're all Question-Mark. "

Johnny put a hand on his friend's arm and stopped him. "I got a better guess," he said. "I know where all their cayuses are. Hoppy, that rustlin' drive crew must 'a' come in this way. What you bet?"

"I ain't bettin'," grunted his companion, starting toward the little herd, "I'm lookin'. I don't hanker to lose that cayuse of mine, an' they'll mebby get th' hoss I ride after I start for their buildin' tonight. He's so mean I sort of cotton to him. An' he's got some thoroughbred blood in his carcass, judgin' from what Arch said. In a case like this it's only fair to use theirs. Be sides, they're fresh; mine ain't."

Johnny pushed ahead, stopped at the tethered group and laughed. "Good thing you didn't bet," he called over his shoulder.

Hopalong untied a wicked-looking animal. "He looks like he'd buffi 1 th' ground over a short distance, an' that's what I'm interested in. I'm goin' down an' turn mine loose. If things break like I figger they will there's no tellin' when I'll see him again, an' I don't want him to starve tied up to a tree. He's so thirsty about now that he'll head for McCullough's crick on a bee line."

Johnny nodded, considered a moment and went toward the tie ropes. "Shore, an' not stray far from that grass, neither." He released the horses except the one he mounted and then rode up so close to his friend that their knees rubbed. "No tellin' when anybody will be comin' this way or when they'll get a drink. You look like you been hit by an idea. That's so rare, suppose you uncork it?"

"It's one I've been turnin' over," replied his friend, "an' it looks th' same on both sides, too."

"Turn it over for me an' lemme look."

"Kid, I'm lookin' for somethin' to happen that shore will bother Mr. McCullough a whole lot if he happens to think of it. When that buildin' starts burnin' it's shore goin' to burn fast They can't fight th' fire like they should with them punchers pourin' lead into them lighted loopholes. Once it starts nothin' can stop it; an' I'm tellin' you it's shore goin' to start right. Th' south side is goin' first. They know there's only a few men watchin' th' north side, an' them few are layin' too far back. It won't take a man like Kane very long to learn that he's got to jump, an' jump quick; an' when he does he'll jump right. Right for him an' right for us. He can't do nothin' else. You said they got their cayuses in there with 'em?"

Johnny nodded. "So I was told. I'm seem' yore drift, Hoppy; an' when Kane an' his friends jump me an' Red shore will have jammed guns an' not be able to shoot at 'em."

"Marriage ain't spoiled yore head," chuckled his com panion. "Kane havin' us jailed that way riled me; an' McCullough tryin' to slip out of payin' them rewards has riled me some more. I'm washin' one hand with th' other. Do you think you an' Red could get yore cayuses an' an extra one for me, in case they get this one, around west somewhere back of where yo're goin'?"

"How'll this one do for you?" asked his companion, slapping the horse he was on.

"Plenty good enough."

"Then he'll be there, ready to foller th' jumpers," laughed Johnny.

"Good for you, Kid. You shore have got th' drift. Now, seem' that I may get into trouble an' be too late to go after 'em when they jump, you listen close while I tell you where to ride, an' all about it," and the description of the desert trail and the valley was as meaty as it was terse. He told his friend where to take the horses and where to look for him before the night's work began, and then went back to Kane and his men. "They're bound to head for that valley. There ain't no place else for 'em to go. I'll bet they've had that figgered for a refuge ever since they learned about it."

Johnny laughed contentedly. "An' Mac tellin' me that he's got 'em all tied up an' ain't aimin' to pay no rewards! But," he said, becoming instantly grave, "there's one thin' I don't like. I'm admittin' it's yore scheme, but we ought to draw lots to see who's goin' to use that kerosene. After all, yo're down here to help me out of a hole. Dig up some more cartridges, you maverick!"

"Don't you reckon I got brains enough to run it off? " demanded his friend.

"An' some to spare," replied Johnny; "but I ain't no idjut, myself. Here; call yore choice," and he reached for his belt.

"Yo're slow, Kid," chuckled Hopalong, holding out his hand. "Call it yourself."

Johnny hesitated, pushed back the cartridges and placed his hand on those of his friend. "You went at that like you was pullin' a gun: an' I can't say nothin' that means anythin' faster. Why th' hurry?"

"Habit, I reckon," gravely replied his friend. "Savin' time, mebby; I dunno why, you chump!"

"It's a good habit; an' I'm shore you saved considerable time, which same I'm aimin' to waste," replied Johnny. He thought swiftly. Last time he had called "even," and lost. He was certain that Hopalong wanted the task. How would his friend figure? The natural impulse of a slow-witted man would be to change the number. Hopalong was not slow-witted; on the contrary so far from slow-witted that he very likely would be suspicious of the next step in reasoning and go a step further, which would take him back to the act of the slow-witted, for he knew that the cogitating man in front of him was no simpleton. Odd or even: a simple choice; but in this instance it was a battle of keen wits. Johnny raised his own hand and looked down at his friend's, the upper one clasping and covering the lower; and then into the night-hidden eyes, which were squinting between narrowed lids to make their reading hopeless. Being something of a gambler Johnny had the gambler's way of figuring, and this endorsed the other line of reasoning: he believed the chances were not in favor of a repetition.

"Cuss yore grinnin' face," he growled. "I said ' even ' last time, an' was wrong. Now I'm say in' ' odd.' Open up!"

Hopalong opened the closed hands and his squinting eyes at the same instant and laughed heartily. "Kid, I cussed near raised you, an' I know yore ways. Mebby it ain't fair, but you was tryin' hard to outguess me. There they are pair of aces. Count 'em, sonny; count 'em."

"Count 'em yourself," growled Johnny; "if you can count that far!" He peered into the laughing eyes and thrust out his jaw. "You know my ways, do you? Well, when we get back to th' SV, me an' you are goin' in to Dave's, get a big stack of two-bit pieces an' go at it. I'll cussed soon show you how much you know my ways! G'wan! Get out of here before I get rough!"

"He's too old to spank," mused Hopalong, kneeing the horse, "an' too young to fight with reckon I'll have to pull my stakes an' move along." Chuckling, he looked around. "Ain't forgot nothin' about tonight, have you, child?"

"No!" thundered Johnny. "But for two-bits I would!" Hopalong's laugh came back to him and sent a smile over his face. "There ain't many like you, you old son-of-a-gun!" he muttered, and wheeled to return to the town and to Red.

His departing friend grinned at the horse. "Bronch." he said, confidently, "he shore had me again. I'm gettin' so cheatin's second nature; an' worse'n that, I'm cheatin' my best friends, an' likin' it. Yessir, likin' it! Ain't you ashamed of me? You nod that ugly head of yourn again an' I'll knock it off you! G'wan: This ain't no funeral yet!"

Chapter XXII
The Bonfire

Johnny rode up to the hotel, got a Winchester and ammunition for it from the stack of guns in the kitchen and then went to the stable for Red's horse and Pepper. As he led them out he stopped to answer a pertinent question from the upper window of the hotel and rode off again, leading the extra mounts.

Ed Doane lowered the rifle and scratched his head. "Coin' for a moonlight ride," he repeated in disgust as he drew back from the window. "Cussed if punchers ain't gettin' more locoed every day. Moonlight ride! Shore go out an' look at th' scenery. Looks different in th' moonlight bah! To me a pancake looks like a pancake by kerosene, daylight, wood fire or or moonlight. I suppose th' moonlight'll get into 'em an' they'll be singin' love-songs an' harmonizin'; but thank th' Lord I don't have to go along!" He glanced around at a sudden thap! grinned in the darkness at the double planking on that side wall and sat down again. "Shoot!" he growled. "Shoot twice! Shoot an' be damned! Waste 'em! Reckon th' moonlight's got into you, you cow-stealin', murderin' pup." Filling his pipe he packed and lit it, blew several clouds through nose and mouth and scratched his head again. "Coin' for a moonlight ride, huh? Well, mebby you are, Johnny, my lad; but Ed Doane's bettin' there's more'n a ride in it. You didn't go for no moonlight rides before that missin' friend of yourn turned up; an' then, right away, you ride up on one hoss, collect two more an' go gallivantin' off under th' moon. I'm guessin' close. Eddie Doane, I'll bet you a tenspot them three grizzlies are out for to put their ropes on them rewards. An' I hope they collect, cussed if I don't. That Scotch trail-boss is puttin' on too many airs for me an' he's rilin' Nelson slow but shore. Go get it, Bar-20: I'm bettin' on you."

There came steps to his door. "Ar-re ye there, Ed? " called a voice.

"Shore; come in, Murphy."

The door opened and closed as the cook entered. "Have ye a pipeful? Mine's all gone."

"Help yourself," answered Doane, tossing the sack. "There it is, by yore County Cork feet."

"I have ut," grunted Murphy. "An' who was th' lad ye was talkin' to from th' windy just now?"

"Nelson. He's goin' ridin' in th' moonlight. Must aim to go far, for he's got three horses."

"Has he, now?" Murphy puffed in quiet satisfaction for a moment. "He's a good la-ad, Ed. Goin' ridin', is he? Well, ridin' is fine for them as likes it. But I'm wonderin' what he's doin' with th' kerosene I gave him?"

"Kerosene? When?"

"Whin he come in with his friend Cassidy an' a fine bye that man is, too. Shure: a hull canteen av it. Two gallons. He says for me to kape it quiet: as if I'd be tellin'! Quayle would have me scalp if he knowed it givin' away his ile like that. Now where ye goin' so fast?"

"For a walk, under th' moonlight!" answered Doane. "Yo're goin', too an' we're goin' with our mouths shut. Not a word about th' hosses or th' kerosene. You remember what Cassidy said about goin' agin' Kane's northeast corner? Come on an' see th' bonfire!"

"Shure, an' who's fool enough to have anny bonfires now?"

"Murphy, I said with our mouths shut. Come on, up near th' jail!"

The cook scratched his head and favored his companion with a sidewise glance, which revealed nothing because of the darkness of the room. "Th' jail?" he muttered. "He's crazy, he is. Th' jail won't make no bonfire. It's mud. But as long as he has th' 'baccy, I'll go wid him. Whist!" he exclaimed as another thap! sounded on the wall. "An' what's that?"

"This room's haunted," explained Ed.

"Lead th' way, thin; or let me," said Murphy in great haste. "I'll watch yore mud bonfire."

After leaving the hotel Johnny kept it between himself and Kane's building, rode to the arroyo which Roberts had found so useful and followed it until out of sight of anyone in town. When he left it he turned east, crossed the main trail and dismounted east of the place where he and Red had kept watch on the gambling-house roof. Working his way on foot to his sharpshooting friends he lay down at Red's side and commented casually on several subjects, finally nudging the Bar-20 rifleman.

"I'm growin' tired of this spot an' this game," he grumbled. "They know where we are now, an' that roof's plumb tame."

Red stirred restlessly. "You must 'a' read my mind," he observed. "You've had a spell off stay here while I take a rest."

"Stay nothin'!" retorted Johnny. "This ain't our fight, anyhow."

"Somebody's got to stay," objected Red.

"Let Waffles, then," rejoined Johnny. "You don't care if we look around?"

"I'd just as soon stay here as go any place else," said the ex- foreman of the O-Bar-O. "Where you fellers aimin' to go?"

"Over west to cover Hoppy," answered Johnny, remembering that this much was generally known. "He aims to make a dash for th' hotel, an' he's so stubborn nobody can stop him. He says th' fight's been goin' on too long; an' you know how he can use six-guns. To use 'em right he'll have to get plumb close."

"Cussed fool!" snorted Red, arising to his knees. "How can he end it by makin' a dash, an' usin' his short guns? Mebby he's aimin' to put his rope on it an' pull it over, shootin' as they pop out from under!" he sarcastically suggested.

"Mebby; better ask him," replied Johnny. "I did. Mebby you can get it out of him. When he wants to keep his mouth shut, he shore can keep it shut tight. There's no use wastin' our breath on it. He's got some fool scheme in his head an' he's set solid. All we can do is to try to save his fool skin. Waffles can hold down this place till we come back. Come on, Red."

Red grumbled and stretched. "All right. See you later mebby, Waffles."

Johnny turned. "Don't forget an' shoot at th' feller runnin' for th' east end of th' buildin'," he warned.

"Mac sent th' word along a couple of hours ago," re plied Waffles, settling down in the place vacated by Red to resume the watch on the hotel roof, which was fairly well revealed at times by the moon. He seemed to be turning something over in his mind, but finally shrugged his shoulders and gave his attention to the roof. "They've got somethin' better'n six-guns at close range," he muttered. "Well, a man owes his friends somethin', so I'm holdin' my tongue."

Reaching the horses Johnny and his companion mounted and rode northward, leading the spare mount.

"What's he up to?" demanded Red.

"Coin' to set fire to th' shack," answered Johnny, and he forthwith explained the whole affair.

"Huh!" grunted Red. "There ain't no doubt in my mind that it'll work if he can get there an' get th' fire started." He was silent for a moment and then pulled his hat more firmly down on his head. "If he don't get there, I'll give it a whirl. Anyhow, I'd have to leave cover to get to him if he went down so it ain't much worse goin' th' rest of th' way. An' I'm tellin' you this: That lone loophole is shore goin' to be bad medicine for any body try in' to use it after he starts. I'll put 'em through it so fast they'll be crowdin' each other."

"An' while yo're reloadin' I'll keep 'em goin'," said Johnny, patting his borrowed Winchester. "They'll shore think somebody's squirtin' 'em out of a hose."

Some time later he stopped his horse and peered around in the faint light.

Red stopped, also. "This th' place?"

"Looks like it we ought to get some sign of Hoppy purty soon. Anyhow, we'll wait awhile. Glad that moon ain't very bright."

"An' cussed glad for th' clouds," added Red. "Clouds like them ain't th' rule in this part of the country." He leaned over and looked down at the sand. "Tracks, Kid," he said. "Follow 'em?"

"No," answered his companion slowly. "I'm bettin' they're Hoppy's. Stay with th' cayuses I'm goin' to look around," and as he dismounted they heard a hail. Red swung to the ground as their friend appeared.

"You made good time," said Hopalong, advancing. "I been off lookin' things over. We can leave th' cayuses in a little hollow about long rifle-shot from th' buildin'. From there you two can get real close by travelin' on yore bellies from bush to bush. Th' cover's no good in day light, but on a night like this, by waitin' for th' clouds, it'll be plenty good enough."

"How close did you get?" asked Johnny.

"Close enough to send every shot through that loop hole, if I wanted to."

"Did they see you? Did you draw a shot?"

"No. They ain't watchin' that loophole very close. Ain't had no reason to since th' stables burned. There ain't nobody been layin' off in this direction. Th' cover wasn't good enough to risk it, with only a blank wall to watch, an' with them fellers on th' roof to shoot down. Red couldn't cover th' north part of it from where he was. I been wonderin' if I ought to use a cay use at all."

"There's argument agin' usin' one," mused Johnny.

"Th' noise, an' a bigger object to catch attention," re marked Red. "If you walked th' cayuse to soften its steps, it still looms up purty big; an' if you cut loose an' dash in, th' noise shore will bring a shot. Me an' th' Kid would have to start shootin' early an' keep it up a long while an' we're near certain to leave gaps in th' string."

"What moonlight there is shines on this end of th' buildin'," observed Johnny. "That loop-hole show up plain?" he asked.

"You can't see nothin' else," chuckled Hopalong. "It's so black it fair hollers."

Red drew the Winchester from its sheath and turned the front sight on its pivot, which then showed a thin white line. He never had regretted having it made, for since it had been put on he had not suffered the annoyance of losing sight of it against a dark target in poor light. "Bein' bull-headed," he remarked, "you chumps has to guess; but little Reddie ain't doin' none of it. I told you long ago to have one put on."

"Shut up!" growled Johnny, turning his own Win chester over in his hands.

"I reckon I'm travelin' flat on my stomach," said Hopalong, slinging the big canteen over his head. "I'll go with you till we has to stop, let you get set an' then make a run for it. Seein' that th' Kid has got a repeater, too, you'll be able to keep lead flyin' most of th' time I'm in th' open if you don't pull too fast; an' when you run out of cartridges I'll start with my Colts. I'll be close enough, then, to use 'em right. When you see that I'm under th' buildin' go back quite a ways so th' fire won't show you xip too plain, an' watch th' roof. I'll start a fire under that loophole before I leave, an' that'll spoil their view through it; an' I ain't leavin' before I've fixed things so them fellers will have so much to do they won't have much time for sharpshootin'. That buildin' will burn like a pine knot"

"Then yo're comin' back th' way you go in?" asked Red.

"Shore," answered Hopalong. "Everythin' plain?"

"Watch me," ordered Red, his hand rising and falling. J 'If we space our shots like this we ought to be able to reload while th' other is emptyin' his gun. Is it too slow?"

"No," said Johnny, considering.

"No," said the man with the canteen, watching closely. "It'll take that long to throw a gun into th' loophole an' line it up, in this light."

"Not bein' used to a repeater like Red is," suggested Johnny, "I'd better shoot th' second string that'll give us three of 'em before it's my time to reload. Red can slide 'em in as fast as I can shoot 'ern out, timin' 'em like that."

"You can put 'em through that hole as good as I can," said Red. "It's near point-blank shootin'. You do th' shootin' an' I'll take care of loadin' both guns. We can't make no blunders, with Hoppy out there runnin' for his life."

"That's why I ought to do th' runnin'," growled Johnny. "I can make three feet to his two."

"It's all settled," said Hopalong, decisively. "I got th' kerosene, an' I'm keepin' it. Come on. No more talkin'."

They followed him over the course he had picked out and with a caution which steadily increased as they advanced until at length they went ahead only when the crescent moon was obscured by drifting clouds. Ahead loomed the two-story gambling-hall, its windowless rear wall of bleached lumber leaden in the faint light. An occasional finger of fire stabbed from its south wall to be answered by fainter stabs from the open, the reports flat and echoless. A distant voice sang a fragment of song and a softened laugh replied to a ribald jest. A horse neighed and out of the north came quaveringly the faint howl of a moon-worshiping coyote.

The three friends, face down on the sand, now each behind a squat bush, wriggled forward silently but swiftly, and gained new and nearer cover. Again a cloud passed before the moon and again they wriggled forward, their eyes fixed on the top of the roof ahead, two of them heading for the same bush and the other for a shallow gully. The pair met and settled themselves to their satisfaction, heads close together as they consulted about the proper setting of the rear sights. One of them knelt, the rifle at his shoulder reaching out over the top of the bush, his companion sitting cross-legged at his side, a pile of dull brass cartridges in the sombrero on the ground be tween his knees to keep the grease on the bullets free from sand.

The kneeling man bent his head and let his cheek press against the stock of the heavy weapon, whispered a single word and waited. Twice there came the squeak of a frightened rat from his companion and instantly from the right came an answering squeak as the figure of a man leaped up from the gully and sprinted for the lead-colored wall, the heavy, jarring crash of a Winchester roaring from the bush, to be repeated at close intervals which were as regular as the swing of a pendulum. A round, dark object popped up over the flat roof line and the cross-legged man on the ground threw a gun to his shoulder and fired, almost in one motion. The head dropped from sight as the marksman slid another cartridge into the magazine and waited, ready to shoot again or to ex change weapons with his kneeling friend.

The runner leaped on at top speed, but he automatically counted the reports behind him and a smile flashed over his face when the count told him that the second rifle was being used. He would have known it in no other way, for the spacing of the shots had not varied. Again the count told of the second change and a moment later an other extra report confirmed his belief that the roof was being closely watched by his friends. A muffled shout came from the building and a spurt of fire flashed from the loophole, but toward the sky and he fancied he heard the sound of a falling body. Far to his left jets of flame winked along a straggling line, the reports at times bunched until they sounded like a short tattoo, while be hind him the regular crashing of an unceasing Winchester grew steadily more distant and flatter.

His breath was coming in gulps now for he had set himself a pace out of keeping with the habits of years and the treacherous sand made running a punishment. During the last hundred feet it was indeed well for him that Johnny shot fast and true, that the five-hundred grain bullets which now sang over his aching head were going straight to the mark. He suddenly, vaguely realized that he heard wrangling voices and then he threw himself down onto the sand and rolled and clawed under the building, safe for the time.

Gradually the jumble of footsteps over his head impressed themselves upon him and he mechanically drew a Colt as he raised his head from the earth. Suddenly the roaring steps all went one way, which instantly aroused his suspicions, and he crawled hurriedly to the black darkness of a pile of sand near the bottom of the south wall, which he reached as the steps ceased. No longer silhouetted against the faint light of the open ground around the building, a light which was bright by contrast with the darkness under the floor, he placed the canteen on the ground and felt for chips and odds and ends of wood with one hand while the other held a ready gun.

There came the sharp, plaintive squeaking of seldom-used hinges, which continued for nearly a minute and then a few unclassified noises. They were followed by the head of a brave man, plainly silhouetted against the open sand. It turned slowly this way and that and then became still.

"See anythin'?" came a hoarse whisper through the open trap.

There was no reply from the hanging head, but if thoughts could have killed, the curious whisperer would have astonished St. Peter by his jack-in-the-box appearance before the Gates.

"If he did, we'd know by now, you fool," whispered another, who instantly would have furnished St. Peter with another shock.

"He'd more likely feel somethin', rather than see it," snickered a third, who thereupon had a thrashing coming his way, but did not know it as yet.

The head popped back into the darkness above it, the trapdoor fell with a bang, and sudden stamping was followed by the fall of a heavy body. Furious, high-pitched cursing roared in the room above until lost in a bedlam of stamping feet and shouting voices.

"He ought to kill them three fools," growled Hopalong, indignant for the moment; and then he shook with silent laughter. Wiping his eyes, he fell to gathering more wood for his fire, careless as to noise in view of the free-for-all going on over his head. Removing the plug from the canteen he poured part of the oil over the piled-up wood, on posts, along beams and then, saturating his neckerchief, he rubbed it over the floor boards. Wriggling around the pile of sand he wet the outer wall as far up as his arm would reach, soaked two more posts and another pile of shavings and chips and then, corking the nearly empty vessel, he felt for a match with his left hand, which was comparatively free from the kerosene, struck it on his heel and touched it here and there, and a rattling volley from the besiegers answered the flaming signal. Backing under the floor he touched the other pile and wriggled to the wall directly under the loophole. Again and again the canteen soaked the kerchief and the kerchief spread the oil, again a pile of shavings leaned against a wetted post, and another match leaped from a mere spot of fire into a climbing sheet of flame, which swept up over the loop hole and made it useless. As he turned to watch the now well-lighted trapdoor, there came from the east, barely audible above the sudden roaring of the flame, the reports of the rifles of his two friends, the irregular timing of the shots leading him to think that they were shooting at animated targets, perhaps on the roof.

The trapdoor went up swiftly and he fired at the head of a man who looked through it. The toppling body was grabbed and pulled back and the door fell with a slam which shook the building. Hopalong's position was now too hot for comfort and getting more dangerous every second and with a final glance at the closed trapdoor he scrambled from under the building, slapped sparks from his neck and shoulders and sprinted toward his waiting, anxious friends, where a rifle automatically began the timed firing again, although there now was no need for it. Slowing as he left the building further and further behind he soon dropped into a walk and the rifle grew silent.

"Here we are," called Johnny's cheery voice. "I'm admittin' you did a good job!"

"An' *I'm* sayin' you did a good one," replied Hopalong. "Them shots came as reg'lar as th' tickin' of a clock."

"Quite some slower," said Red. "That gang can't stay in there much longer. Notice how Mac's firin' has died down?"

"They're waitin' for 'em to come out an' surrender," chuckled Hopalong. "Keep a sharp watch an' you'll see 'em come out an' make a run for it."

"Better get back to th' cayuses, an' be ready to foller," suggested Red.

"No," said Johnny. "Let 'em get a good start If we stop 'em here Mac may get a chance to cut in."

"An' we'll mebby have to kill some of th' men we want alive," said Hopalong. "Let 'em get to that valley an' think they're safe. We can catch 'em asleep th' first night"

The gambling-hall was a towering mass of flames on the south and east walls and they were eating rapidly along the other two sides. Suddenly a hurrying line of men emerged from the north door of the doomed structure, carrying wounded companions to places of safety from the flames. Dumping these unfortunates on the ground, the line charged back into the building again and soon appeared leading blind-folded horses, which bit and kicked and struggled, and turned the line into a fighting turmoil. The few shots coming from the front of the building increased suddenly as McCullough led a running group of his men to cover the north wall. A few horses and a man or two dropped under the leaden hail, the ac curacy of which suffered severely from the shortness of breath of the marksmen. The group expanded, grew close at one place and with quirts rising and falling, dashed from the building, pressing closely upon the four leaders, and became rapidly smaller before the steadying rifles of its enemies took much heavier toll. Before it had passed beyond the space lighted by the great fire only four men remained mounted, and these were swiftly swallowed up by the dim light on the outer plain.

McCullough and most of his constantly growing force left cover and charged toward the building to make certain that no more of their enemies escaped, while the rest of his men hurried back to get horses and form a pursuing party.

Chapter XXXIII
Surprise Valley

Hopalong turned and crawled away from the lurid scene, his friends following him closely. As soon as they dared they arose to their feet and jogged toward where their horses waited, and soon rode slowly northeastward, heading on a roundabout course for Sweet Spring.

"Take it easy," cautioned Hopalong. "We don't want to get ahead of 'em yet. If my eyes are any good th' four that got away are Kane, Corwin, Trask, an' a Greaser. What you say?"

Reaching the arid valley through which Sand Creek would have flowed had it not been swallowed up by the sands, they drew on their knowledge of it and crossed on hard ground, riding at a walk and cutting northeastward so as to be well above the course of the fleeing four, after which they turned to the southeast and approached the spring from the north. Reaching the place of their former vigil they dismounted, picketed the horses in the sandy hollow and lay down behind the crest of the ridge. Half an hour passed and then Johnny's roving eyes caught sight of a small group of horsemen as it popped up over a rise in the desert floor. A moment later and the group strung out in single file to round a cactus chaparral and revealed four horsemen, riding hard. The fugitives raced up to Bitter Spring, tarried a few moments, and went on again, slowly growing smaller and smaller, and then a great slope of sand hid them from sight.

Hopalong grunted and arose, scanning their back trail. "They've been so long gettin' out here that I'm bettin' they did a god job hidin' their trail. I can see Mac an' his gang ridin' circles an' gettin' madder every minute. Well, we can go on, now. By goin' th' way I went before we won't be seen."

"How long will it take us?" asked Red, brushing sand from his clothes as he stood up.

"Followin' th' pace they're settin' we ought to be there tonight," answered Hopalong. "Give th' cayuses all they can drink. If them fellers hold us off out there we'll have to run big risks gettin' our water from that crick. Well, let's get started."

The hot, monotonous ride over the desert need not be detailed. They simply followed the tracks made by Hopalong on his previous visit and paid scanty attention to the main trail south of them, contenting themselves by keeping to the lowest levels mile after burning mile. It was evening when they stopped where their guide had stopped before and after waiting for nightfall they went on again in the moonlight, circling as Hopalong had circled and when they stopped again it was to dismount where he had dismounted behind a ridge. They picketed and hobbled the weary, thirsty horses and went ahead on foot. Following instructions Red left them and circled to the south to scout around the great ridge of rock before taking up his position at the head of the slanting trail from the valley. His companions kept on and soon crawled to the rim of the valley, removed their sombreros and peered cautiously over the edge. The faint glow of the fire behind the adobe hut in the west end of the sink shone in the shadows of the great rock walls and reflected its light from bowlders and brush. Below them cattle and the horses of the caviya grazed over the well-cropped pasture and a strip of silver told where the little creek wandered toward its effacement. Moving back from the rim they went on again, looking over from time to time and eventually reached the point nearly over the fire, where they could hear part of the conversation going on around it, when the voices raised above the ordinary tones.

"You haven't a word to say!" declared Kane, his out stretched hand leveled at Trask, the once- favored deputy sheriff. "If it wasn't for your personal spite, and your d d avarice, we wouldn't be in this mess tonight! You had no orders to do that."

Trask's reply was inaudible, but Corwin's voice reached them.

"I told him to let Nelson alone," said the sheriff. "He was dead set to get square for him cuttin' into th' argument with Idaho. But as far as avarice is concerned, you got yore part of th' eleven hundred."

"Might as well, seeing that the hand had been played!" retorted Kane. "What's more, I'm going to keep it. Any body here think he's big enough to get any part of it?"

"Nobody here wants it," said Roberts. "Th' boys I had with me, an' Miguel, an' myself have reasons to turn this camp fire into a slaughter, but we're sinkin' our grievances because this ain't no time to air 'em. I'm votin' for less squabblin'. We ain't out of this yet, an' we got four hundred head to get across th' desert. Time enough, later, to start fightin'. I'm goin' off to turn in where there ain't so much fool noise. I've near slept on my feet an' in th' saddle. Fight an' be damned!" and he strode from the fire, keen eyes above watching his progress and where it ended.

The hum around the fire suffered no diminution by his departure, but the words were not audible to the listeners above. Soon Corwin angrily arose and left the circle, his blankets under his arm. His course also was marked. Then the two Mexicans went off, and the eager watchers chuckled softly as they saw the precious pair take lariats from the saddles of two picketed horses and slip noiselessly toward the feeding caviya. Roping fresh mounts, and the pick of the lot, they made the ropes fast and went back to the other horses. Soon they returned with their riding equipment and blankets, saddled the fresh mounts and, spreading the blankets a few feet beyond the radius of the picket ropes, they rolled up and soon were asleep.

"Sensitive to danger as hounds," muttered Johnny.

"Cunnin' as coyotes," growled Hopalong, glancing at the clear-cut, rocky rim across the valley, where Red by this time lay ensconced. "I hope he remembers to drop their cayuses first Miguel's worth more to us alive."

"An' easier to take back," whispered Johnny. "We want 'em all alive an' we'd never get 'em that way if they wasn't so played out. They'll sleep like they are dead luck is with us."

Down at the dying camp fire Kane, his back to the hut, talked with Trask in tones which seemed more friendly, but the deputy was in no way lulled by the change. He sensed a flaming animosity in the fallen boss, who blamed him for the wreck of his plans and the organization. Muttering a careless good night, Trask picked up his blankets and went off, leaving the bitter man alone with his bitterness.

Tired to the marrow of his bones, so sleepy that to remain awake was a torture, the boss dared not sleep. In the company of five men who were no longer loyal, whose greed exceeded his own, and each of whom nursed a real or fancied grudge against him and who searched into the past, into the days of his contemptuous treatment of them for fuel and yet more fuel to feed the fires of their resentment, he dared not close his eyes. On his person was a modest fortune compacted by the size of the bills and so well distributed that unknowing eyes would not suspect its presence; but these men knew that he would not leave his wealth behind him, to be perhaps salvaged from a hot and warped safe in the smoking ruins of his gambling-house.

He stirred and gazed at the glowing embers and an up-shooting tongue of flame lighted up the small space so vividly that its portent shocked through to his dulled brain and sent him to his feet with the speed and silence of a frightened cat. He was too plain a target and too defenseless in the lighted open, and like a ghost he crept away into the darker shadows under the great stone cliff, to pace to and fro in an agonizing struggle against sleep. Back and forth he strode, his course at times erratic as his enemy gained a momentary victory; but his indomitable will shook him free again and again; and such a will it was that when sleep finally mastered him it did not master his legs, for he kept walking in a circular course like a blind horse at a ginny.

When he had leaped to his feet and left the hut the watchers above kept him in sight and after the first few moments of his pacing they worked back from the valley's rim and slipped eastward.

"Here's th' best place," said Hopalong, turning toward the rim again. They looked over and down a furrow in the rock wall. "We'll need two ropes. It'll take one, nearly, to reach from here to that knob of rock an' go around it. Red's got a new hemp rope bring that, too. If he squawks about us cuttin' it, I'll buy him a new one. Got to have tie ropes."

Johnny hastened away and when he returned he threw Red's lariat on the ground, and joined the other two. Fastening one end around the knob of rock he dropped the other over the wall and shook it until he could see that it reached the steep pile of detritus. Picking up the hemp rope he was about to drop it, too, when caution told him it would make less noise if carried down. Slinging it over his shoulder he crept to the edge, slid over, grasped the rope and let himself down. Seeing he was down his companion was about to follow when Johnny's whisper checked him.

"Canteens better fill 'em while it's easy."

Hopalong drew his head back and disappeared and it was not much of a wait before the rope was jerking up the wall and returned with a canteen. To send down more than one at a time would be to risk them banging together. When they all were down Johnny took them and slipped among the bowlders, Hopalong watching his progress. For caution's sake the water carrier took two trips from the creek and sent them up again one at a time. Soon his friend slid down, glanced around, took the hemp rope and cut it into suitable lengths, giving half of the pieces to Johnny and then without a word started for the west end of the valley, treading carefully, Johnny at his heels.

Roberts, sleeping the sleep of the exhausted, awoke in a panic, a great weight on his legs, arms, and body, and a pair of sinewy thumbs pressing into his throat. His struggles were as brief as they were violent and when they ceased Hopalong arose from the quiet legs and re leased the limp arms while his companion released the throat hold and took his knees from the prostrate chest. In a few minutes a quiet figure lay under the side of a rock, its mouth gagged with a soiled neckerchief and the new hemp rope gleaming from ankles, knees, and wrists.

Corwin, his open mouth sonorously announcing the quality of his fatigue, lay peacefully on his back, tightly rolled up in his blankets. Two faint shadows fell across him and then as Johnny landed on his chest and sunk the capable thumbs deep into the bronzed throat on each side of the windpipe, Hopalong dropped onto the blanketswathed legs and gripped the encumbered arms. This task was easy and in a few minutes the sheriff, wrapped in his own blankets like a mummy, also wore a gag and several pieces of new hemp rope, two strands of which passed around his body to keep the blanket rolled.

The two punchers carried him between two bowlders, chuckled as they put him down and stood up to grin at each other. The blanket-rolled figure amused them and Johnny could not help but wish Idaho was there to enjoy the sight He moved over against his companion and whispered.

"Shore," answered Hopalong, smiling. "Go ahead. It's only fair. He knocked you on th' head. I'll go up an' spot Kane. Did it strike you that he must have a lot of money on him to be so h--l-bent to stay awake? I don't like him pacin' back an' forth like that. It may mean a lot of trouble for us; an' them Greasers are too nervous to suit me. When yo're through with Trask slip off an' watch them Mexicans. Don't pay no attention to me no matter what happens. Stick close to them two. I'll give you a hand with 'em as soon as I can get back. If you have to shoot, don't kill 'em," and the speaker went cautiously toward the hut.

Johnny removed his boots and, carrying them, went toward the place where he had seen the deputy bed down; but when he reached the spot Trask was not there. Thanking his ever-working bump of caution for his silent and slow approach he drew back from the little opening among the rocks and tackled the problem in savage haste. There was no time to be lost, for Hopalong was not aware that any of the gang was roaming around and might not be as cautious as he knew how to be. Why had Trask forsaken his bed-ground, and when? Where had he gone and what was he doing? Cursing under his breath Johnny wriggled toward the creek where he could get a good view of the horses. Besides the two picketed near the sleeping Mexicans none were saddled nor appeared to be doing anything but grazing. Going back again Johnny searched among the bowlders in frantic haste and then decided that there was only one thing to do, and that was to head for the hut and get within sight of his friend. Furious because of the time he had lost he started for the new point and finally reached the hut. If Trask was inside he had to know it and he crept along the wall, pausing only to put his ear against it, turned the corner and leaped silently through the door, his arms going out like those of a swimmer. The hut was empty. Relieved for the moment he slipped out again and started to go toward Kane.

"I'll bet a month's pay "he muttered and then stopped, his mind racing along the trail pointed out by the word. Pay! That was money. Money? As Hopalong had said, Kane must have plenty of it on him money? Like a flash a possible solution sprang into his mind. Kane's money! Trask was a thief, and what would a thief do if he suspected that the life savings of a man like Kane might easily be stolen? And especially when he had been so angered by the possessor of the wealth?

"I got to move pronto!" he growled. "I'm no friend of Kane's but I ain't goin' to have him killed not by a coyote like Trask, anyhow. We got to have him alive, too. An' Hoppy?" His reflections were such that by the time he came in sight of Kane his feelings were a cross between a mad mountain lion and an active volcano. He stopped again and looked, his mind slowly forsaking rage in favor of suspicion. Kane was walking around in a circle, his eyes closed; his feet were rising and falling mechanically and with an exaggerated motion.

"War dancin'?" thought Johnny. "What would he do that for? He ain't no Injun. I'm sayin' he's loco. Kane loco? Like hell! Fellers like him don't get loco. Makin' medicine? I just said he ain't no Injun. Prancin' around in th' moonlight, liftin' his feet like they had ropes to 'em to jerk 'em. An' with his eyes close shut! I'm gettin' a headache an' I'm settin' tight till I get th' hang of this walkin' Willy. Mebby he thinks he's workin' a charm; but if he is he ain't goin' to run it on me!"

He pressed closer against the bowler which sheltered him and searched the surroundings again, slowly, painstakingly. Then there came a low rustling sound, as though a body were being dragged across dried grass. It was to his left and not far away. If it is possible to endow one sense with the total strength of all the others, then his ears were so endowed. Whether or not they were strengthened to an unusual degree they nevertheless heard the rubbing of soft leather on the bowlder he lay against, and he held his breath as he reversed his grip on the Colt.

"Hoppy, or Trask?" he wondered, glad that his head did not project beyond the rock. A quick glance at the milling Kane showed no change in that person's antics and he felt certain that he had not been detected by the boss. He froze tighter if it is possible to improve on perfection, for his ears caught a renewal of the sounds. Then his eyes detected a slow movement and focussed on a shadowy hand which fairly seemed to ooze out beyond the rock. When he discerned a ring on one of the fingers he knew it was not Hopalong, for his friend wore no ring. That being so, it only could be Trask who was creeping along the other side of the rock. Johnny glanced again at the peripatetic gang leader and back to the creeping hand, and wondered how high in the air its owner would jump if it were suddenly grabbed. Then he men tally cursed himself, for his independent imagination threatened to make him laugh. He could feel the tickle of mirth slyly pervading him and he bit his lip with an earnestness which cut short the mirth. The hand stopped and the heel of it went down tightly against the earth as though bearing a gradual strain. Johnny was reassured again, for Trask never would be stalking Kane if he had the slightest suspicion that enemies, or strangers, were in the valley, and he hazarded another glance at Kane.

The mechanical walker was drawing near the rock again and in a few steps more would turn his back to it and start away. By this time Johnny had solved the riddle, for although such a thing was beyond any experience of his, his wild guess began to be accepted by him: Kane was walking in his sleep. Where was Hopalong? He hoped his friend would not try to capture the boss until he, himself, had taken care of Trask. This must be his first duty, and knowing what Trask would do very shortly he prepared to do it.

He got into position to act, moving only when the slight sound of Kane's footfalls would cover the barely audible noise of his own movements. Kane's rounding course brought him nearer and then several things happened at once. The owner of the hand leaped from behind the rock and as his head popped out into sight a Colt struck it, and then Johnny started for Kane; but as he reached his feet something hurtled out of the shadows to his right and bore the boss to the ground. Then came the sound of another gun-butt meeting another head and the swiftly moving figure seemed to rebound from the boss and sail toward Johnny, who had started to meet it. He swerved suddenly and muttered one word, just as Hopalong swerved from his own course. They both had turned in the same direction and came together with a force which nearly knocked them out. Holding to each other to keep their feet, they recovered their breath and without a word separated at a run, Hopalong going to Kane and Johnny to Trask. Less dazed by the collision than his friend was, Johnny finished his work first and then helped Hopalong carry Kane to the shelter of the rock.

"Good thing you forgot what I said about watchin' them Greasers," grunted Hopalong. "It's them next, if "his words were cut short by two quick shots, which reverberated throughout the valley, and without another word he followed his running companion, and scorned cover for the first few hundred yards.

When they got close to the trail they saw two bulks on it, which the moonlight showed to be prostrate horses.

"Where are they, Red?" shouted Johnny. "They're th' only ones free!"

"Down near you somewhere," answered the man above, and his words were proved true by a bullet which hummed past Johnny's ear. He dropped to his stomach and began to wriggle toward the flash of the gun, Hopalong already on the way.

Cut off from escape up the trail the two Mexicans tried to work toward the hut, from which they could put up a good fight; but their enemies had guessed their purpose and strove to drive them off at a tangent.

Red, watching from the top of the cliff, noticed that the occasional gun flashes were moving steadily northwestward and believed it safe to leave his position and take an active hand in the events below. After their experience on the up-slanting trail the Mexicans would hardly attempt it again, even though they managed to get back to the foot of it, which seemed very improbable. The thought became action and the trail guard started to wriggle down the declivity, keeping close to the bottom of the wall, where the shadows were darkest. Because of the necessity for not being seen his progress was slow and quite some time elapsed before he reached the bottom and obtained cover among the scattered rocks. The infrequent reports were further away now, and they seemed to be getting further eastward. This meant that they were nearer to the hut, and his decision was made in a flash. The hut must not be won by the fugitives, and he arose and ran for it, bent over and risking safety for speed. After what seemed to be a long time he reached the little cleared space among the rocks, bounded across it, and leaped into the black interior of the hut. Wheeling, he leaned against the rear wall to recover his breath, watching the open door, a grim smile on his face. While keeping his weary watch up on the rim he had craved action, and congratulated himself that he now was a great deal nearer to it than he was before.

Meanwhile the two fugitives, not stomaching a real stand against the men whom they had seen exhibit their abilities in Kane's gambling-hall, had managed to work on a circular course until they were northwest of the hut and not far from it. This they were enabled to do because they were not held to a slow and cautious advance by enemies ahead of them, as were the old Bar-20 pair. They were moving toward the hut, not far from the north wall of the valley, when they blundered upon Trask. In a moment he was released and began a frantic search for his gun, which he found among the rocks not far away. Losing no time he hurried off to release the man he would have robbed, glad to have his assistance. Kane went into action like a spring released and began a hot search for his Colt. When he found it, the cylinder was missing and suspicious noises not far away from him forced him to abandon the search and seek better cover, armed only with a deadly and efficient steel club.

Hopalong and Johnny, guided entirely by hearing, fol lowed the infrequent low sounds in front of them, thinking that they were made by the Mexicans, and drew steadily away from the hut. The Mexicans, motionless in their cover, exulted as their scheme worked out and finally went on again with no one to oppose them. Reaching the last of the rocky cover they arose and ran across the open, leaped into the hut and turned, chuckling, to close the door, leaving Trask to his fate.

Warned by instinct they faced about as Red leaped. Miguel dropped under a clubbed gun, but Manuel, writhing sidewise, raised his Colt only to have it wrenched from his hand by his shifty opponent. Clinching, he drew a knife and strove desperately to use it as he wrestled with his sinewy enemy. At last he managed to force the tip of it against Red's side, barely cutting the flesh; and turned Red into a raging fury. With one hand around Manuel's neck and the other gripping the wrist of the knife-hand, Red smashed his head again and again into the Mexican's face, his knee pressing against the knifeman's stomach.

Suddenly releasing his neck hold Red twisted, got the knife-arm under his armpit, gripped the elbow with his other hand and exerted his strength in a twisting heave. The Mexican screamed with pain, sobbed as Red's knee smashed into his stomach and dropped senseless, his arm broken and useless. Red dropped with him and hastily bound him as well as possible in the poor light from the partly opened door.

He had just finished the knot in the neckerchief when a soft, swift rustling appraised him of danger and he moved just in time. Miguel's knife passed through his vest and shirt and pinned him to the hard-packed floor. Before either could make another move the door crashed back against the wall and Kane hurtled into the hut, landing feet first on the wriggling Mexican. He put the knife user out of the fight and pitched sprawling. His exclamation of surprise told Red that he was no friend and now, free from the pinning knife, Red pounced on the scrambling boss.

The other struggles of the crowded night paled into in significance when compared to this one. Red's superior strength and weight was offset by the fatigue of previous efforts, and Kane's catlike speed. They rolled from one wall to another, pounding and strangling, Kane as innocent of the ethics of civilized combat as a maddened bob cat, and he began to fight in much the same way, using his finger-nails and teeth as fast as he could find a place for them. Red wanted excitement and was getting it. Torn and bleeding from nails and teeth, his blows lacking power because of the closeness of the target and his own fatigue, Red shed his veneer of civilization and fought like a gorilla.

Planting his useful and well-trained knee in the pit of his adversary's stomach, he gripped the lean throat with both hands and hammered Kane's head ceaselessly against the hard earth floor, while his thumbs sank deeply on each side of the gang leader's windpipe. Too enraged to sense the weakening opposition, he choked and hammered until Kane was limp and, writhing from his victim's body, he knelt, grabbed Kane in his brawny arms, staggered to his feet and with one last surge of energy, hurled him across the hut. Kane struck the wall and dropped like a bag of meal, his fighting over for the rest of the night.

Red stumbled over the Mexicans, fell, picked himself up, and reeled outside, fighting for breath, his vision blurred and kaleidoscopic, staring directly at two men among the rocks but seeing nothing. "Come one, come all damned you!" he gasped.

Trask, thrice wounded, hunted, desperate, fleeing from a man who seemed to be the devil himself with a six-gun, froze instantly as Red appeared. Enraged by this unexpected enemy and sudden opposition where he fondly expected to find none, Trask threw caution to the winds and raised the muzzle of the Colt. As he pulled the trigger a soaring bulk landed on his shoulders, knocking the exploding weapon from his hand and sending him sprawling. Snarling like an animal he twisted around, wriggled from under and grabbed Johnny's other Colt from its holster. Before he could use it Johnny's knee pinned it and the hand holding it to the ground. A clubbed six-gun did the rest and Johnny, calling to Red to watch Trask, hurried away to see if Roberts and Corwin were loose. The latter was helpless in the blanket, but Roberts had freed his feet and was doing well with the knots on his wrists when Johnny's appearance and growled command put an end to his efforts. He put the rope back on the kicking feet and arose as Hopalong limped up.

"Phew!" exclaimed Johnny. "This has been a reg'lar night! Here, you stay with Corwin while I tote this coyote to th' hut." He got Roberts onto his back and staggered away, soon returning for the sheriff.

Dawn found six bound men in varying physical condition sitting with their backs to the hut, their wounds crudely dressed and their bounds readjusted and calculated to stay fixed. Kane was vindictive, his eyes snapping, and he seethed with futile energy, notwithstanding the mauling he had received. His lean face, puffed, discolored and wolfishly cruel, worked with a steadily mounting rage, which found vent at intervals in scathing vituperative comments about Trask, whom he still blamed for the predicament in which he found himself. Corwin, sullen and fearful, kept silent, his fingers picking nervously at the buckle and strap on the back of his vest. Roberts was angry and defiant and sneered at his erstwhile boss, sending occasional verbal shafts into him in justification of Trask. The two Mexicans had sunk into the black depths of despair and acted as though they were stunned. Trask, a bitter sneer on his face, glared unflinchingly at the storming boss and showed his teeth in grim, ironical smiles.

"Th' crossbreed shows th' cur dog when th' wolf is licked," he sneered in reply to a particularly vicious attack of Kane's. "What you blamin' me for? You took yore share of Nelson's money, an' took it eager. You heard me!" he snarled. "I don't care who knows it I got it, an' you took yore part of it. It was all right then, wasn't it? An' you didn't know it was his you let him make a fool of you an' wouldn't listen to me. But as long as you got yourn you didn't care a whole lot who lost it. Serves you right."

"Shut up!" muttered Roberts.

"Shut up nothin'," jeered Trask. "Think I'm goin' to swing to save a mad dog like him? Look at him! Look at th' dog breakin' through th' wolf! Wolf! Huh! Coyote would be more like it. Don't talk to me!" He looked at the camp fire and at the man busy over it. "I can eat some of that, Nelson," he said.

Johnny nodded and went on with the cooking.

Sounds of horses clattering down the steep trail suddenly were heard and not much later Red rode up on a horse he had captured from the rustlers' caviya and dismounted near the fire. His face was a sight, but the grin which tried to struggle through the bruises was sincere. He dropped two saddles to the ground, the saddles belonging to the Mexicans, which he had stopped to strip from the dead horses on the trail up the wall.

"Our cayuses went loco near th' crick," he said. "I left Hoppy to take off th' saddles an' let 'em soak themselves," referring to the three animals they had left up on the desert the evening before. "I'm all ready to eat, Kid. How's it shapin' up?"

"Grab yore holt," grunted Johnny. He stood up to rest his back. "Mebby it would be more polite to feed our guests first," he grinned.

Red looked at the line-up. "We'll have to feed 'em, I reckon. I ain't aimin' to untie no hands. Who's first?"

"Don't play no favorites," answered Johnny. "Go up an' down th' line an' give 'em all a chance." He faced the prisoners. ",You fellers like yore coffee smokin'?" Only two men answered, Roberts and Trask, and they did not like it smoking hot. "Let it cool a little, Red; no use scaldin' anybody."

The prisoners had all been fed when Hopalong appeared on another horse from the rustlers' caviya and swung down. "Smells good, Kid! an' looks good," he said. "I got all th' saddles on fresh cayuses, waitin' all but these here. We'll lead our own cayuses. That Pepper-hoss of yourn acts lonesome. She ain't lookin' at th' grass, at all." He sat down, arose part way and felt in his hip pocket, bringing out the cylinder of a six-gun. Glancing at Kane, to whom it belonged, he tossed it into the brush and resumed his seat.

Johnny's face broke into a smile and he whistled shrilly. Quick hoof beats replied and Pepper, her neck arched, stepped daintily across the little level patch of ground and nosed her master.

"Ha!" grunted Trask. "That's a hoss!" A malignant grin spread over his face and he turned his head to look at Kane. "Kane, how much money, that money you got on you now, would you give to be on that black back, up on th' edge of th' valley? All of it, I bet!"

"Shut up!" snapped Roberts, angrily.

"Go to h--l," sneered Trask, and he laughed nastily. "You wait till I speak my little piece before you tell me to shut up! No dog is goin' to ride me to a frazzle, blamin' me for this wind-up, without me havin' somethin' to say about it!" He looked at Red. "What was them two shots I heard, up there on top? They was th' first fired last night."

"That was me droppin' th' Greasers' cayuses from under 'em on th' ledge," Red answered. "They was pullin' stakes for th' desert."

"Leavin' us to do th' dancin', huh?" snapped Trask. "All right; I know another little piece to speak. Where you fellers takin' us?"

Red shrugged his shoulders and went off to get horses for the crowd.

A straggling line of mounted men climbed the cliff trail, the horses of the inner six fastened by lariats to each other, and three saddleless animals brought up the rear. They pushed up against the sky line in successive bumps and started westward across the desert.

Chapter XXIV
Squared Up All Around

Mesquite, still humming from the tension of the past week felt its excitement grow as Bill Trask, bound securely and guarded by Hopalong, rode down the street and stopped in front of Quayle's, where the noise made by the gathering crowd brought Idaho to the door.

"Hey!" he shouted over his shoulder. "Look at this!" Then he ran out and helped Hopalong with the prisoner.

Quayle, Lukins, Waffles, McCullough, and Ed Doane fell back from the door and let the newcomers enter, Idaho slamming it shut in the face of the crowd. Then Ed Doane had his hands full as the crowd surged into the bar room.

"Upstairs!" said Hopalong, steering the prisoner ahead of him. In a few minutes they all were in Johnny's old room, where Trask, his ropes eased, began a talk which held the interest of his auditors. At its conclusion McCullough nodded and turned to Hopalong.

"All this may be true," he said; "but what does it all amount to without th' fellers he names? If you'd kept out of th' fight an' hadn't set fire to that buildin' we would 'a' got every one of them he names. Gimme Kane an' th' others an' better proof than his story an' you got a claim to that reward that's double sewed."

Hopalong seemed contrite and downcast. He looked around the group and let his eyes return to those of the trail-boss. "I reckon so," he growled. "But have you got th' numbers of th' missin' bills?" he asked, skeptically.

"Yes, I have; an' a lot of good it'll do me, now!" snapped McCullough. "We was countin' on them for th' real proof, but that fool play of yourn threw 'em into th' discard! What'n h--l made you set that place afire?"

Hopalong shrugged his shoulders. "I dunno," he muttered. "Waz you aimin' to find th' missin' bills on them fellers?" he asked. "Would that 'a' satisfied you?"

"Of course!" snorted the trail-boss. "An' with Trask, here, turnin' agin' 'em like he has it would be more than enough. Any fool knows that!"

Hopalong arose. "I'm glad to hear you come right out an' say that, for that's what I wanted to know. I've been bothered a heap about what you might ask in th' line of proof. You shore relieve my mind, Mac. If you fellors will straddle leather we'll ride out where Kane an' th' others Trask named are waitin' for visitors. I don't reckon they none of them got away from Johnny an' Red."

"What are you talkin' about?" demanded McCullough, his mouth open from surprise.

"I mean we've got Kane, Roberts, Corwin, Miguel, an' another Greaser all tied up, waitin' to turn 'em over to you an' collect them rewards. As long as we know just what you want, an' can give it to you, I don't see no use of waitin'. I'm invitin' Lukins an' th' rest along to see th' finish. What you goin' to do with Trask?"

McCullough was looking at him through squinting eyes, his face a more ruddy color. Glancing around the group he let his eyes rest on Trask. Shrugging his shoulders he faced Hopalong. "Take him south, I reckon, with th' others. If he talks before a jury like he's talked up here I reckon he won't be sorry for it." He walked to a window and looked down into the street. "Hey!" He called. "Walt, get a couple of th' boys an' come up here right away. We got somebody for you to stay with," and in a few minutes he and the others left Walt and his companions to guard and protect the prisoner.

The sun was at the meridian when Hopalong led his companions into the Sand Creek camp and dismounted in front of Red, who was watching the [missing].

"Where's th' Kid?" he asked curiously.

"Don't you do any worryin'" answered. He lowered ms voice and put his mouth close to his friend's ear. "Th' Greaser on th' end is goin' to pieces. Pound him hard an' he'll show his cards."

The information was conveyed to McCullough, who stood looking at the downcast group. He strode over to Miguel, grabbed his shoulders and jerked him to his feet. Running his hands into the Mexican's pockets he brought out a roll of bills. Swiftly running through them he drew out a bill, compared it with a slip which he produced from his own pocket, whirled the bound man around and glared into the frightened eyes.

"Where'd you get this?" he shouted, shaking his captive.

"Kane geeve eet to me--he owe me money," answered the Mexican.

"What for?" demanded McCullough, shaking him again.

"I lend heem eet."

"You loaned him money?" roared the trail-boss. "That's likely! Why did he give it to you?"

Miguel shrugged his shoulders and did not answer. McCullough jerked him half around and pointed to Hopalong. "This man here saw you sneakin' from Kane's south stable with a smokin' Sharp's in yore hand after you shot Ridley. Trask says you did it. Is this all Kane gave you for that killin'?"

"I could no help," protested Miguel, squirming in the trail-boss' grip. "Wen Kane he say do theese or that theeng, I mus' do eet. I no want to but I mus'."

McCullough whirled around and faced Corwin. "That story you told me down in th' bunkhouse that night about how Bill Long shot Ridley is near word for word what Bill says about th' Greaser, an' Trask's story backs him up. How did you come to know so much about it? Come on, you coyote; spit it out! Who told you what to say?"

Corwin's silence angered him and he showed his teeth.

"There's a lynchin' waitin' for you in town, Corwin, if you don't stop it by speakin' up. Who told you that?"

Corwin looked away. "Miguel," he muttered. "I told you I was hopin' to get th' real one."

"He lie! I never say to heem one word!" shouted the Mexican. "He lie! Kane, he was the only one who know like that--beside me!"

"Stand up, Sheriff!" snapped McCullough. He searched the sullen prisoner and found two rolls of bills. Going quickly over them he removed and grouped certain of them, and then compared them with his list. "There's five here that tally with th' bank's numbers." he said, looking up. "Where'd you get 'em?"

"Won 'em at faro-bank."

"Won five five-hundred-dollar bills at faro, when everybody knows yo're a two-bit gambler?" shouted the trail-boss. "I'm no damned fool! Don't you forget what I said about th' lynchin', Corwin. I'm all that stands between you an' it. Where'd you get 'em? Like Trask said?"

Corwin's hunted look flashed despairingly around the group. "No," he said. "Kane gave 'em to me, to get changed into smaller bills!"

"Reckon Kane must 'a' robbed that bank all by hisself," sneered McCullough. "I never knowed he had diamond drills an' could bust safes. Didn't you go along to protect an' keep an eye on that eastern safe-blower that Kane had come to do th' job? Pronto! Didn't you?"

"I had to," growled Corwin, in a voice so low that the answer was lost to all but the man to whom he was talking.

McCullough gave him a contemptuous shove and wheeled to question Roberts. "Get up," he ordered, and searched the rustler trail-boss. "By G-d!" he exclaimed when he saw the size of the roll. "You coyotes was makin' money fast! There's near three thousand here! Let's see how they compare with my list." In a few moments he nodded. "How'd you get these five hundred-dollar bills? Kane give 'em to you, too?"

"No, Kane didn't give 'em to me!" snapped Roberts in angry contempt. "I earned 'em as my share of th' bank robbery, along with Corwin, th' white-livered snake! Kane didn't give in to either of us." He glared at the one-time sheriff. "I'm sayin' plain that if I ever get a chance I'm aimin' to shoot this skunk, along with Trask. You hear me?"

"If you ain't got a gun, hunt me up an' I'll lend you one," offered Idaho.

"Shut up!" snapped McCullough, glaring at the puncher. Whirling he pushed Roberts away. "It'll be a long time before you shoot anybody or anythin'. Now, then," he said, stepping up in front of Kane: "Get up!"

Kane arose slowly, his eyes burning with rage. He submitted to the exploring fingers of the trail-boss and maintained a contemptuous silence as his shirt was whipped right out of his trousers and the two money belts removed from around his waist.

McCullough opened the belts and his eyes at the same time. Neatly folded bunches of greenbacks followed each other in swift succession from the pockets of the belts and, scattering as they were tossed into a pile, made quite an imposing sight. Staring eyes regarded them and more than one observer's mouth gaped widely.

"Seven thousand," announced McCullough, reaching for another handful. "I'm sayin' you wasn't leavin' nothin' behind." He looked up again after a moment. "Eighteen thousand five hundred," he growled and picked up another handful. "Holy mavericks!" he breathed as the last bill was counted and placed on the new pile. "Forty-nine thousand eight hundred and seventy! You was takin' chances, totin' all that with this gang of thieves! Fifty thousand dollars, U. S.!"

Handing his written list to Quayle, he selected the five-hundred-dollar bills and called off the numbers laboriously, Quayle as laboriously hunting through the list. It took considerable time before they were checked off and put to one side, and then he looked up.

"There's still a-plenty of them bills missin'," he announced. "Where did they get to?"

Hopalong stepped forward and drew a roll from his pocket. "Here's what I found on Sandy Woods when he died in this camp," he said, offering it to the astonished trail-boss.

McCullough took it, opened and counted it and called the numbers off to the excited holder of the list.

"They're all on th' list th' Lord be praised!" said Quayle.

"Where'd Sandy Woods come in this?" demanded' McCullough, looking around from face to face.

Roberts sneered. "Huh! He was th' man that took th' safe-blower out of th' country. He didn't have no hand in th' bank job. I'm glad th' skunk died, an' I'm glad it was me that planned his finish. He shore must 'a' held up that feller. How much is there, in th' bank's bills?"

"Five thousand," answered the trail-boss.

"He got it all, cuss him!" snorted Roberts.

McCullough looked at Kane. "I never hoped to meet you like this," he said. "I ain't goin' to ask you no questions--you can talk in court, an' explain how you came to have so many of th' registered bills; an' there's other little things you can tell about, if somebody don't tell it all first." He turned to Hopalong. "We'll be takin' these fellers to th' ranch now."

"Better take th' reward money out of that bundle," replied Hopalong, nodding at the money in the hands of the trail-boss. "We've dealt 'em like you asked, an' gave you th' cards you want. Our part is finished."

McCullough looked from him to the prisoners and then at his friends. "How can I hand it to you?" he asked. "Where's Nelson? He's settin' in this."

"He'll show up after th' money's paid," said Red innocently as he arose.

McCullough hesitated and looked around again. As he did so Idaho carelessly walked over to Red, smoothing out a cigarette paper, and took hold of a paper tag hanging out of Red's pocket and pulled it. Carelessly rolling a cigarette he shoved the tobacco sack back where he had found it, but he did not leave Red's side. Blowing a lungful of smoke into the air he smiled at McCullough.

"Shucks, Mac," he said. "You shouldn't ought to have no trouble findin' them rewards in that unholy wad. An' mebby you could find Nelson's missin' eleven hundred on Trask, if you looked real hard. I like a man that goes through with his play."

"I'm not lookin' for no eleven hundred at all!" snapped McCullough. "An' I ain't shore that they've earned th' reward, burnin' that buildin' like they did! They let these fellers get away, first!"

"I just handed you th' money I found on Sandy Woods," said Hopalong. "That's like givin' it to you to pay us with. H--l! You act like you hated to make good Twitchell's bargain. Well, of course, you don't have to take this bunch, nor th' money, neither; but I'm sayin' they don't go separate. Suits us, Mac we'll keep th' whole show money an' all, if you say so."

"Fine chance you got!" retorted the trail-boss, bridling. "They're here an' I'm takin' 'em, with th' money."

"There ain't nobody takin' nothin'," rejoined Hopalong calmly, "until th' bargain's finished. Don't rile Johnny, off there in th' brush; he's plumb touchy." His drawling voice changed swiftly. "Come on--a bargain's a bargain. Five thousand, now!"

"Mac!" said Quayle's accusing voice.

The trail-boss looked at the money in his hand and slowly counted out the reward amount, careful not to include any of the registered bills. "Here," he said, handing them to Hopalong. "You give us a hand gettin' 'em to th' ranch?"

"If three of us could catch 'em, an' bring 'em here," said Hopalong, coldly, "I reckon you got enough help to take 'em th' rest of th' way if you steer clear of town."

"Don't worry, Mac," said Idaho, cheerfully. "I'll go along with you."

The trail-boss growled in his throat and began, with Lukins, Waffles, and Quayle, to get the prisoners on the horses. This soon was accomplished and he headed them south, Lukins on the other side, Quayle and Waffles and Idaho bringing up the rear.

"Better come to town for a celebration," called the proprietor, disappointment in his voice. "Ye can leave at dawn."

Johnny shook his head. "There's a celebration waitin' at th' ranch," he shouted, and turned to find his two companions mounted and his black horse waiting impatiently for him. Mounting, he wheeled to face northward, but checked the horse and turned to look back in answer to a faint hail from Idaho, and grinned at the insulting gesture of the distant puncher.

He replied in kind, chuckled, and dashed forward to overtake his moving friends.

"Home!" he exulted. "Home an' Peggy!"

Tex

At sight of a rattler his gun leaped into crashing life

[Page 314]

Chapter I
The Trail Calls

Memory's curtain rises and shows a scene softened by time and blurred by forgetfulness, yet the details slowly emerge like the stars at twilight. There appears a rain-washed, wind-swept

706

range in Montana, a great pasture level in the center, but rising on its sides like a vast, shallow saucer, with here and there a crack of more somber hue where a ravine, or sluggish stream, lead toward the distant river. Green underfoot, deep blue overhead, with a lavender and purple rim under a horizon made ragged and sharp by the not too distant mountains and foothills. An occasional deep blue gash in the rim's darker tones marks where some pass or canyon cuts through the encircling barriers. A closer inspection would reveal a half-dozen earthy hollows, the rutting holes of the once numerous buffalo which paused here on their periodic migrations. In the foreground a white ranchhouse and its flanking red buildings, framed by the gray of corral walls, nestles on the southern slope of a rise and basks in the sunlight. From it three faint trails grow more and more divergent, leading off to Everywhere. Scattered over the vast, green pastures are the grazing units of a great herd, placid and content, moving slowly and jerkily, like spilled water down a gentle, dusty slope. But in the total movement there is one thread with definite directness, even though it constantly turns from side to side in avoiding the grazing cattle. This, as being different and indicating purpose, takes our instant attention.

A rider slowly makes his way among the cattle, by force of habit observing everything without being fully conscious of it. His chaps of soft leather, worn more because of earlier associations than from any urgent need on this northern range, have the look of long service and the comfort coming from such. His hat is a dark gray sombrero, worn in a manner suggesting a cavalier of old. Over an open vest are the careless folds of a blue kerchief, and at his right hip rubs a holster with its waiting, deadly tenant. A nearer approach reveals him to be a man in middle life, lean, scrupulously neat, clean shaven, with lines of deep humor graven about his eyes and mouth, softening a habitual expression which otherwise would have been forbiddingly hard and cynical.

His roving glances reach the purple horizon and are arrested by the cerulean blue of a pass, and he checks his horse with a gesture hopelessly inadequate to express the restlessness, the annoying uncertainty of his mood, a mood fed unceasingly by an inborn yearning to wander, regardless of any aim or other condition. Here is a prospect about him which he knows cannot be improved upon; here are duties light enough practically to make him master of his time, yet heavy enough to be purposeful; his days are spent in the soothing solitudes of clean, refreshing surroundings; his evenings with men who give him perfect fellowship, wordless respect, and repressed friendship, speaking when the mood urges, or silent in that rare, all-explaining silence of strong men in perfect accord. His wants are few and automatically supplied: yet for weeks the longing to leave it all daily had grown stronger--to leave it for what? Certainly for worse; yet leave it he must.

He sat and pondered, retrospective, critical. The activities of his earlier days passed before him, with no hypocritical hiding or blunting of motives. They revealed few redeeming features, for he carelessly had followed the easy trails through the deceptive lowlands of morality, and among men and women worse even than himself in overt acts and shameless planning, yet better because they did not have his intelligence or moral standards. But he slowly rose above them as a diver rises above treacherous, lower currents, and the reason was plain to those who knew him well. First he had a courage sparkling like a jewel, unhesitant, forthright, precipitate; next he had a rare mixture of humor and cynicism which better revealed to him things in their right proportions and values; and last, but hardly least by any means, an intelligence of high order, buttressed by facts, clarified by systematic study, and edged by training. In his youth he had aimed at the practice of medicine, but gave too much attention to more imaginative targets and found, when too late, that he had hit nothing. His fondness for drinking, gambling at cards, and other weedy sowings resulted from, rather than caused, the poor aim. Certain unforgivable episodes, unforgivable because of their notoriety more than because of the things themselves, brewed a paternal tempest, upon which he had turned a scornful back, followed Horace Greeley's famous advice, and sought the healing and the sanctuary of the unasking West.

In his new surroundings he soon made a name for himself, in both meanings, and quickly dominated those whose companionship he either craved or needed. An inherent propensity for sleight of hand provided him an easy living at cards; and his deftness and certainty with a six-gun gave him a pleasing security. However, all things have an end. There came a time when he nearly had reached the lowest depths of moral submersion when he met and fought a character as strong as his own, but in few other ways resembling him; and from that time on he swam on the surface. It would be foolish to say that the depths ceased to lure him, for they did, and at times so powerfully that he scarcely could resist them. For this he had to thank to no small degree one of the bitterest experiences of his life: his disastrous marriage. Giving blind love and unquestioning loyalty, he had lost both by the unclean evidence unexpectedly presented to his eyes. In that crisis, after the first madness, his actions had been worthy of a nature softer than his own and he had gone, by devious ways, back to his West and started anew with a burning cynicism. But for the steadying influence of his one-time enemy, and the danger and the interest in the task which Hopalong Cassidy had set before him, the domestic tragedy certainly would have sent him plunging down to his former level or below it.

Time passed and finally brought him news of the tragic death of his faithless wife, and he found that it did not touch him. He had felt neither pity, sorrow, nor relief. It is doubtful if he ever had given a thought to the question of his freedom, for with his mental attitude it meant nothing at all to him. He had put among his belongings the letter from his former employer, who had known all about the affair and the names and addresses of several of his western friends, telling him that he was free; and hardly gave it a second thought.

Turning from his careless scrutiny of the distant pass he rode on again and soon became aware of the sound of hoofbeats rapidly nearing him. As he looked up a rider topped a rise, descried him, and waved a sombrero. The newcomer dashed recklessly down the slope and drew rein sharply at his side, a cheerful grin wreathing his homely, honest face. Pete was slow-witted, but his sterling qualities masked this defect even in the eyes of a man as sharp as his companion, who felt for him a strong, warm friendship.

"Hello, Tex!" said the newcomer. "What's eatin' you? You shore look glum."

Tex thought if it was plain enough for Pete Wilson to notice it, it must be plain, indeed. "Mental worms an' moral cancer, Pete," replied the cynic, smiling in spite of himself at the cogitation started in his friend by the words.

"Whatever that means," replied Pete, cautiously. "However, if it's what I reckon it is, there's just two cures." Pete was dogmatic by nature. "An' that's likker, or a new range."

"Somethin's th' matter with you today, Pete," rejoined Tex. "Yo're as quick as a reflex." He studied a moment, and added: "An' yo're dead right, too."

"There ain't no reflection needed," retorted Pete; "an' there ain't nothin' th' matter with me a-tall. I'm tellin' you common sense; but it's shore a devil of a choice. If it's likker, then you lose; if it's driftin' off som'ers, then we lose. Tell you what: Go down to Twin River an' clean 'em out at stud, if you can find anybody that ain't played you before," he suggested hopefully. "Mebby there's a stranger in town. You'll shore feel a whole lot better, then." He grinned suddenly. "You might find a travelin' man: they're so cussed smart they don't think anybody can learn 'em anythin'. Go ahead--try it!"

Tex laughed. "Where you goin'?" he abruptly demanded. He could not afford to have any temptations thrown in his way just then.

"Over Cyclone way, for Buck. Comin' along?"

Tex slowly shook his head. "I'm goin' th' other way. Wonder why we haven't got word from Hoppy or Red or Johnny?" he asked, and the question acted like alum in muddy water, clearing away his doubts and waverings, which swiftly precipitated and left the clear fluid of decision.

"Huh!" snorted Pete in frank disgust. "You wait till any of them fellers write an' there'll be a white stone over yore head with nice letterin' on it to tell lies forever. You know 'em. Comin' along with me?" he asked, wheeling, and was answered by an almost imperceptible shake of his friend's head.

"I'll shake hands with you, Pete," said Tex, holding out his deft but sinewy hand. "In case I don't see you again," he explained in answer to his friend's look of surprise. "I'm mebby driftin' before you get back."

"Cuss it!" exploded Pete. "I'm allus talkin' too blamed much. Now I've gone an' done it!"

"You've only hastened it a little," assured Tex, gripping the outstretched hand spasmodically. "Cheer up; I don't aim to stay away forever!" He spurred his mount and shot away up the incline, Pete looking after him and slowly shaking his head.

When the restless puncher stopped again it was at the kitchen door of the white ranchhouse. As he swung from the saddle something stung him where his trousers were tight and he stopped his own jump to grab the horse, which had been stung in turn. A snicker and a quick rustle sounded under the summer kitchen and Tex took the coiled rope from his saddle, deftly unfastening the restraining knot. The rustling sounded again, frantic and sustained, followed by a half-defiant, half-supplicating jeer.

"You can't do it, under here!" said Pickles, reloading the bean-shooter from a bulging cheek. "I can shoot yore liver out before you can whirl it!" Pickles was quite a big boy now, but threatened never to grow dignified; and besides, he had been badly spoiled by everybody on the ranch.

"Whirling livers never appealed to me," rejoined Tex, putting the rope back. "Never," he affirmed decidedly; "but I'm goin' to whirl yourn some of these days, an' you with it!"

"Those he loves, he annoys," said a low, sweet voice, its timbre stimulating the puncher like a draught of wine. His sombrero sweeping off as he turned, he bowed to the French Rose, wife of the big-hearted half-owner of the ranch. If only he had chosen a woman like this one!

"I seem to remember him annoyin' Dave Owens, at near half a mile, with Hoppy's Sharps," he slowly replied. "Nobody ever told me that he loved Dave a whole lot." At the momentary cloud the name brought to her face he shook his head and growled to himself. "I'm a fool, ma'am, these days," he apologized; "but it strikes me that you ought to smile at that name--it shore played its unwilling part in giving you a good husband; an' Buck a mighty fine wife. Where is Buck?"

"Inside the house, walking rings around the table--he seems so, so--" she shrugged her shoulders hopelessly and stepped aside to let Tex enter.

"I don't know what he seems," muttered Tex as he passed in; "but I know what he is--an' that's just a plain, ornery fool." He shook his head at such behavior by any man who was loved by the French Rose.

Buck stopped his pacing and regarded him curiously, motioning toward an easy chair.

"Standin's good enough for me, for I'm itchin' with th' same disease that you imagine is stalkin' you," said Tex, looking at his old friend with level, disapproving gaze. "It don't matter with me, but it's plain criminal with you. I'm free to go; yo're not. An' I'm tellin' you frank that if I had th' picket stake that's holdin' you, all h--l couldn't tempt me. Yo're a plain, d--d fool--an' you know it!"

Buck leaned back against the edge of the table and thoughtfully regarded his companion. "It ain't so much that, as it is Hoppy, an' Red, an' Johnny," he replied, spreading out his hands in an eloquent gesture. "They could write, anyhow, couldn't they?" he demanded.

"Shore," affirmed Tex, grinning. "How long ago was it that you answered their last letters?" He leaned back and laughed outright at the guilty expression on his friend's face. "I thought so! Strong on words, but cussed poor on example."

"I reckon yo're right," muttered Buck. "But that south range shore calls me strong, Tex."

" 'Whither thou goest, I go' was said by a woman," retorted Tex. " 'Yore people are my people; yore God, my God.' I'm sayin' it works both ways. You ought to go down on yore knees for what's come to you. An' you will, one of these days. Think of Hoppy's loss--an' you'll do it before mornin'. But I didn't come in to preach common sense to a lunatic--I come to get my time, an' to say good-bye."

Buck nodded. Vaguely disturbed by some unnamed, intermittent fever, he had been quick to read the symptoms of restlessness in another, especially in one who had been as close to him as Tex had been. He went over to an old desk, slowly opened a drawer and took out a roll of bills and a memorandum.

"Here," he said, holding both out. "Far as I know it's th' same as when you gave it to me. Ought to be seven hundred, even. Count it, to make shore." While Tex took it and shoved it into his pocket uncounted and crumpled the memorandum, Buck also was reaching into a pocket, and counted off several bills from the roll it gave up. These he gravely handed to his companion, smiling to hide the ache of losing another friend.

"I shore haven't earned it all," mused Tex, looking down at the wages in his hand. "I reckon I'm doin' this ranch a favor by leavin', for there ain't no real job up here no more for any man as expensive as I am. You got th' whole country eatin' out of yore hand, an' th' first thing you know th' cows will catch th' habit an' brand an' count 'emselves to save you th' trouble of doin' it."

"You'll be doin' us a bigger favor when you come back, one of these days," grinned Buck. "You shore did yore share in trainin' it to eat out of my hand. For a while it looked like it would eat th' hand--an' it would 'a', too. Aimin' to ride down?"

Tex's eyes twinkled. "How'd you come to figger I'm goin' down?"

Buck smiled.

"No, reckon not," said Tex. "Ridin' as far's th' railroad. I'll leave my cayuse with Smith. When one of th' boys goes down that way he can get it. I'll pay Smith for a month's care." Reading the unspoken question in his friend's eyes, he carelessly answered it. "Don't know where I'm goin'. Reckon I'll get down to th' SV before I stop. That'd be natural, with Red an' Hoppy stayin' with Johnny."

"They might need you, too," suggested Buck, hopefully. If he couldn't be with his distant friends himself, he at least wished as many of them to be together as was possible.

"I'm copperin' that," grunted Tex. His eyes shone momentarily. "Yo're forgettin' that our best three are together. Lord help any misguided fools that prod 'em sharp. Well, I'm dead shore to drift back ag'in some day; but as you say, those south ranges shore do pull a feller's heart." He looked shrewdly at his friend and his face beamed from a sudden thought. "We're a pair of fools," he laughed. "You ain't got th' wander itch! You don't want to go jack-rabbitin' all over th' country, like me! All you want is that southwest country, with yore wife an yore friends on th' same ranch; down in th' cactus country, where th' winters ain't what they are up here. I'm afraid my brain's atrophied, not havin' been used since Dave Owens rolled down from his ambush with Hoppy's slugs in him for ballast."

Buck looked at him with eager, hopeful intentness and his sigh was one of great relief and thankfulness. He need not be ashamed of that longing, now vague and nameless no longer. His head snapped back and he stood erect, and his voice thrilled with pride. Tex had put his finger on the trouble, as Tex always did. "I've been as blind as a rattler in August!" he exclaimed.

"Not takin' th' time to qualify that blind-rattler-in-August phrase, I admits yo're right," beamed Tex. He arose, shoved out his hand for the quick, tight grasp of his friend and wheeled to leave, stopping short as he found himself face to face with Rose Peters. "A happy omen!" he cried. "Th' first thing I see at th' beginnin' of my journey is a rose."

She smiled at both of them as she blocked the door, and the quick catch in her voice did not escape Tex Ewalt.

"I was but in the other room," she said, her face alight. "I could not but hear, for you both speak loud. I am so glad, M'sieu Tex--that now I know why my man is so--so restless. Ruth, she said what I think, always. We are sorry that you mus' go--but we know you will not forget your friends, and will come back again some day."

Buck put his arm around his wife's shoulders and smiled. "An' if he brings th' other boys back with him, we'll find room for 'em all, eh Rose?" He looked at his friend. "We're shore goin' to miss you, Tex. Good luck. We'll expect you when we see you."

Tex bowed to Rose and backed into the curious Pickles, whom he lightly spanked as a fitting farewell; and soon the noise of his departure drummed softer and softer into the south.

Chapter II

Refreshed Memories

The dusty, grimy, almost paintless accommodation train, composed of engine, combination smoking-baggage car, and one day coach, rumbled and rattled, jerked and swayed over the uneven roadbed, the clicking at the rail joints sensible both to tactual and auditory nerves, and calling attention to the disrepair into which the whole line had fallen. In the smoking compartment of the baggage car sat Tex Ewalt, sincerely wishing that he had followed his first promptings and chosen the saddle in preference to this swifter method of traveling.

All day he had suffered heat, dust, cinders, and smoke after a night of the same. It had been bad enough on the main line, but after leaving the junction conditions had grown steadily worse. All day he had crossed a yellow gray desolation, flat and unending, under a dirty blue sky and a dust-filled air shimmering with heat waves. He had peered at a drab, distant horizon which seemed hardly to change as it crept eastward past him, at all times barely more than a thin circle about as interesting and colorful as a bleached hoop from some old, weather-beaten barrel. Wherever he had looked, it had been to see sun-burned grass and clouds of imponderable dust, the latter sucked up by the train and sent whirling into every crack and crevice; occasional white spots darting rearward he knew to be the grim, limy skulls of herbiverous animals; arrow-like trails cut deep into the drought-cursed earth, and not too frequently a double line of straggling, dispirited willows, cottonwoods, and box elders, marked the course of some prairie creek, whose characteristic, steep earth banks, often undermined, now enclosed sun-dried mud, curling like heated scales, with here and there pools of noisome water hidden under scabs of scum. Mile after mile of this had dulled him, familiar as he had once been with the sight, and he sat apathetic, dispirited and glum, too miserable to accept the pressing invitation of a traveling cardsharp to sit into a game of draw poker. Gradually the mild, long swells of the prairie had grown shorter, sharper, and higher; gradually the soil had become rockier and the creek beds deeper below the rims of their banks. The track wound more and more as it twisted and turned among the hills, and for some hours he had noticed a constant rising, which now became more and more apparent as the top of the watershed drew nearer.

He dozed fitfully at times and once the sharper had roused him by touching his shoulder to ask him again to take cards in a game. To this invitation Tex had opened his eyes, looked up at the smiling poker devotee and made a slight motion, dozing off again as the surprised gambler moved away from one he now knew to be of the same calling as himself. Towns had followed each other at increasingly long intervals, insensibly changing in their aspect, and the horizon steadily had been narrowing. Here and there along the dried beds of the creeks were rude cabins and shacks, each not far from an abandoned sluice and cradle. Between the hills the pastures grew smaller and smaller, their sides more precipitous, but as they shrunk, the number of cattle on them seemed to increase. Rough buildings of wood or stone began to replace the low sod dugouts of a few hours ago, and he knew that he was rapidly nearing his destination.

Suddenly a ribbon-like scar on the horizon caught his eye. It ran obliquely from a north-eastern point of his vista southwesterly across the pastures, hills, and valleys, like a lone spoke in some great wheel, of which the horizon was both felloe and tire. At this he sat up with a show of interest. Judging from its direction, and from what he remembered of it at this section of its length, it would cross the track some miles farther on. He nodded swiftly at this old-time friend of his cattle-driving days--he had been a fool not to have remembered it and the cow-town not far ahead, but the names of all the mushroom towns he had been in during his career in the West had not remained in his memory. Years rolled backward in a flash. He could see the distant, plodding caravans of homesteaders, or the long, disciplined trains of the freighters, winding over the hills and across the flats, their white canvas wagon covers flashing against the sky, the old, dirty covers emphasizing the newness and whiteness of their numerous patches. But on this nearing trail, winding into the southwest there had been a different migration. He almost could see the spread-out herd moving deliberately forward, the idling riders, the point and swing men, and the plodding, bumping chuck wagon with its bumptious cook. This trail, a few hundred yards wide, beaten by countless hoofs, had deepened and deepened as the wind carried away the dust, and if left to itself would be discernible after the passing of many years.

The name of the town ahead and on this old trail brought a smile to his lips, a smile that was pleasantly reminiscent; but with the name of the town came nearly forgotten names of men, and the smile changed into one that was not pleasant to look upon. There was Williams, Gus Williams, often referred to as "Muttonhead." He had been a bully, a sure-thing gambler, herd trimmer, and cattle thief in a small way, but he had been only a petty pilferer of hoofed property, for his streak of caution was well developed. Tex had not seen him, or heard of him, for twenty years, never since he had shot a gun out of Williams' hand and beat him up in a corner of his own saloon.

The rapidly enlarging ribbon drew nearer and more distinct, and soon it crossed the track and ran into the south. He remembered the wide, curving bend it took here: there had been a stampede one rainy night when he was off trick and rolled up in his blanket under the chuck wagon. They had reason to suspect that the cattle were sent off in their mad flight through the dark by human agency. Two days had been spent in combing the rough plain and in rounding up the scattered herd, and there had been a sizable number lost.

A deeper tone leaped into the dull roar of the train and told of a gully passing under the track. It ran off at a slight angle, the dried bed showing more numerous signs of human labors and habitations, and when the train came to a bumping, screeching stop at a ramshackle one-room station he knew that he was at the end of his ride and within three stations from the end of the line, which here turned sharply toward the northwest, baffled by the treacherous sands of the river, whose bank it paralleled for sixty miles. Had he gone on in the train he would have come no closer to his objective and would have to face a harder country for man and horse. Gunsight, where his three friends were located, lay about a hundred miles southwest of the bend in the track; but because of the sharp bend it lay farther from the station beyond. From where he now was, the riding would not be unpleasant and the ford across the river was shallower, the greater width of the stream offset by a more sluggish current. This ford was treacherous in high water and not passable after sudden rises for a day or two, because the force of the swollen current stirred up the unstable sands of the bottom. As a veteran of the old cattle trails he knew what a disturbed river bottom often meant.

The wheezing exhaust and the complaining panting of the all but discarded engine added dismal sounds to a dismal view. He stiffly descended the steps, a bulging gunny sack over his shoulder and a rolled blanket and a sheathed rifle fully utilized his other arm and hand. Dropping his burdens to the ground he paused to look around him.

It was just a frontier town, ugly, patched, sprawling, barely existent, and an eyesore even to the uncritical; and cursed further by Kansas politics which at this time were not as stalwart as they once had been, reminding one of the mediocre sons of famous fathers. In place of the old daring there now were trickery and subtle meannesses; in place of hot hatreds were now smoldering grudges; where once old-time politicians "shot it out" in the middle of the street, there now were furtive crawlings and treacherous shots from the dark. Like all towns it had a name--it will suffice if we know it as Windsor. Being neither in the mining country nor on the cattle range, and being in an out-of-the-way position even on the merging strip between the two, it undoubtedly would have died a natural death except for the fortuitous chance which had led the branch-line railroad to reach its site. The shifting cattle drives and a short-lived townsite speculation had been the causes for the rails coming; then the drives stopped at nearer terminals and the speculation blew up--but the rails remained. This once flamboyantly heralded "artery of commerce" swiftly had atrophied and now was hardly more than a capillary, and its diurnal pulsation was just sufficient to keep the town about one degree above coma.

Tex sneered openly, luxuriously, aggressively, and for all the world to see. He promised himself that he would not remain here very long. Before him lay the squalid dirt street with its cans and rubbish, the bloated body of a dog near the platform, a dead cat farther along.

There were several two-story frame buildings, evidently built while the townsite game was on. The rest were one-story shacks, and he remembered most of them.

He picked up his belongings and sauntered into the station to wait until the agent had finished his business with the train crew, and that did not take long.

The agent stepped into the dusty, dirty room, coughed, nodded, and passed into his partitioned office. In a moment he was out again, looked closely at the puncher and decided to risk a smile and a word: "Is there anything I can do for you?" he hazarded.

Tex put his sombrero beside him on the bench and wiped his forehead with a sleeve. He saw that his companion was slight, not too healthy, and appeared to be friendly and intelligent; but in his eyes lay the shadow of fear.

"Mebby you can tell me th' best place to eat an' sleep; an' th' best place to buy a horse," he replied.

"Williams' hotel is the best in town, and I'd ask him about the horse. You might do better if you didn't say I recommended him to you."

"Not if you don't want me to," responded Tex, smiling sardonically for some inexplicable reason. "Reckon he'd eat you because yo're sendin' him trade? Don't worry; I won't say you told me."

"So far as I am concerned it don't matter. It's you I'm thinking about."

Tex stretched, crossed his legs, and smiled. "In that case I'll use my own judgment," he replied. "Been workin' for th' railroad very long?"

"Little too long, I'm afraid," answered the agent, coughing again, "but I've been out here only two months." He hesitated, looked a little self-conscious, and continued. "It's my lungs, you know. I got a transfer for my health. If I can stick it out here I have hopes of slowly improving, and perhaps of getting entirely well."

"If you can stick it out? Meanin' yo're findin' it too monotonous an' lonely?" queried Tex.

The agent laughed shortly, the look of fear again coming into his eyes. "Anything but the first; and so far as being lonely is concerned, I find that my sister is company enough."

Tex cogitated and recrossed his legs. "From what I have already seen of this town I'd gamble she is; but a man's allus a little better off if he can herd with his own sex once in a while. So it ain't monotonous? Have many trains a day?" he asked, knowing from his perusal of the time-table that there were but two.

"One in and one out. You passed the other on the siding at Willow, if you've come from beyond there."

"Reckon I remember it. Much business here to keep you busy?"

"Not enough to tire even a--lunger!" He said the word bitterly and defiantly.

"That's a word I never liked," said Tex. "It's too cussed brutal. Some people derive a great deal of satisfaction in calling a spade a spade, and that is quite proper so far as spades are concerned; but why go further? A man can't allus help a thing like tuberculosis--especially if he's makin' a livin' for two. Yo're not very high up here, but I reckon th' air's right. It's th' winter that's goin' to count ag'in' you. You got to watch that. You might do better across th' west boundary. Any doctor in town?"

"There's a man who calls himself a doctor. His favorite prescription is whiskey."

"Yeah? For his patients?"

"For his patients and himself, too."

"Huh," grunted the puncher. He cleared his throat. "I once read about yore trouble--in a dictionary," he explained, grinning. "It said milk an' aigs, among other things; open air, both capitalized, day an' night; plenty of sleep, no worryin', an' no excitement. Have many heavy boxes to rustle?"

"No," answered the agent, looking curiously at his companion. "I had plenty of milk and eggs, but the milk is getting scarce and the eggs are falling off. I--" he stopped abruptly, shrugging his shoulders. "D--n it, man! It isn't so much for myself!"

"No," said Tex, slowly arising. "A man usually feels that way about it. I'm goin' up to th' hotel. May drop around to see you tomorrow if I'm in town."

"I'll be mighty glad to see you; but there's no use for you to make enemies," replied the agent, leading the way outside. He stopped and took hold of a trunk, to roll it into the building.

"Han's off," said Tex, smiling and pushing him aside. "You forgot what th' dictionary said. Of course this wouldn't kill you, but I'm stiff from ridin' in yore palatial trains, mile after weary mile." Rolling the trunk through the door and against the wall, he picked up his belongings, gravely saluted and went on his way whistling cheerily.

The agent looked after him wistfully, shook his head and retired into his coop.

Tex rambled down the street and entered Williams' hotel, held a brief conversation with the clerk, took up his key, and followed instructions. The second door on the right-hand side, upstairs, let him into a small room which contained a chair, bed, and washstand. There was a rag rug before the bed, and this touch of high life and affluence received from him a grave and dignified bow. "Charmed, I'm sure," he said, and went over to the window to view the roofs of the shacks below it. He sniffed and decided that somewhere near there was a stable. Putting his belongings in a corner, he took out his shaving kit and went to work with it, after which he walked downstairs, bought a drink and treated its dispenser to a cigar, which he knew later would be replaced and the money taken instead.

"Hot," said Tex as though he had made a discovery. "An' close," he added in an effort not to overlook anything.

"Very," replied the bartender. This made the twenty-third time he had said that word in reply to this undoubted statement of fact since morning. He did not know that his companion had used it because it was colorless and would stamp him, sub-consciously, as being no different from the common human herd in town. "Hottest summer since last year," said the bartender, also for the twenty-third time. He grinned expectantly.

Tex turned the remark over in his mind and laughed suddenly, explosively. "That's a good un! Cussed if it didn't nearly get past me! 'Hottest summer since last year!' Ha-ha-ha! Cuss it, it is good!" He was on the proper track to make a friend of the second man he had met. "Have another cigar," he urged. Good-will and admiration shone on his face. "Gosh! Have to spring that un on th' boys! Ha-ha-ha!"

"Better spring it before fall--it might not last through th' winter, though some'r tougher'n others," rejoined the bartender, his grin threatening to inconvenience his ears.

Tex choked and coughed up some of the liquor, the tears starting from his eyes. He had meant it for an imitation choke, but misjudged. Coughing and laughing at once he hung onto the bar by his elbows and writhed from side to side. "Gosh! You oughter--warn a fel--ler!" he reproved. "How'd'y think of 'em like that?"

"Come easy, somehow," chuckled the pleased dispenser of liquor. "Stayin' in town long?" he asked.

"Cussed if I know," frankly answered Tex. He became candid and confidential. "Expectin' a letter, an' I can't leave till it comes. Where's th' post office? Yeah? Guess I can find it, then. Reckon I'll drift along an' see if there's anythin' come in for me. See you tonight."

Crossing the street he sauntered along it until he came to the building which sheltered the post office, and he stopped, regarded the sign over its door with open approval, and then gravely salaamed.

"'Williams's Mecca,'" he read. "Sign painters are usually generous with their esses. Wonder why? Must be a secret sign of th' guild. Why are monument works usually called 'monumental'? Huh: Wonder if it is th' same Williams? If it is, where did he ever hear of 'Mecca'?" It was a refreshing change from the names so common to stores in towns of this kind and size. "An' cussed if it ain't appropriate, too!" he muttered. "In a place like this what could more deserve that name than the general store and post office, unless it be the saloons, hotels, and gambling houses?" He started for the door, eager to see whom he would meet.

A burly, dark-visaged individual looked up at his entry. He would have been amazed had he known that a score of years had slipped from him and that he was a callow, furtive-eyed man in his early twenties, cringing in a corner with his present visitor standing contemptuously over him and daring him to get up again.

Tex's face remained unchanged, except for a foolish smile which crept over it as he gave greeting. "Though I ain't goin' to pray, I shore am turnin' my face to th' birthplace of th' Prophet," he said. "Yeah, I'm even enterin' its sacred portals." He watched closely for any signs of recognition in the other, but failed to detect any; and he was not surprised.

The heavy face stared at him and a tentative smile tried to change it. The attempt was abortive and the expression shifted to one of alert suspicion, shaded by one of pugnacity. He was not accustomed to levity at his expense. "What you talkin' about?" he slowly asked.

"Why, th' faith of all true believers: *There is but one God, and Mohammed is his Prophet* . May th' blessin's of Allah be on thee. Incidentally I'm askin' if there's a letter for th' pilgrim, Tex Jones?" He cast a careless glance at a cold-eyed individual who lounged in the shadow of a corner, and instantly classified him. Besides the low-slung holster, the man had the face of a cool, paid killer. Tex's interest in him was not to be correctly judged by the careless glance he gave him.

"Then why in h--l didn't you say so in th' first place, 'stead of wastin' my valuable time?" growled the proprietor, reluctantly shuffling toward the mail rack in a corner. He wet his thumb generously, not caring about the color given to it by the tobacco in his mouth, and clumsily ran through the modest packet of mail. Shaking his head he turned. "There ain't nothin'," he grunted.

"It is Allah's will," muttered Tex in pious resignation. He would have fallen over had there been anything for him.

"Look here, stranger," ominously remarked the proprietor, "if yo're aimin' to be smart at my expense, look out it don't become yourn. Just what's th' meanin' of all these fool remarks?"

"Why, yore emporium is named 'Mecca,' ain't it?" asked Tex innocently, but realizing that he somehow had got on the wrong trail.

"What's that got to do with it?" demanded Williams, who could talk as mean as he cared to while the quiet, cold man sat in the corner.

"Everythin'. Ain't you th' proprietor, like th' barkeep of th' hotel said? Ain't you Mr. Williams?"

"I am."

Tex scratched his head, frankly puzzled. "Well," he said, "Mohammed came out of Mecca to startle th' world, an'—-"

"He didn't do nothin' of th' kind!" interrupted the proprietor. "Mecca was out of Prophet, by Mohammed; an' a cussed good hoss she was, too. Though she didn't startle no world, she was my filly, an' plenty good enough for this part of th' country. Of course, mebby back from where you came from, mebby she wouldn't have amounted to much," he sneered. "Now, if you got any more smart-Aleck remarks to make, you'll be wise if you save 'em till you get outside."

Tex burst out laughing. "It's all my mistake, Mr. Williams. I thought you named yore store after a poem I read once, that's all. No offense on my part, sir. Are you th' Mr. Williams that keeps th' ho-tel?"

"I am: what about it?"

"I'm puttin' up there," answered Tex. "If a letter comes for me, would you mind puttin' it in yore pocket an' bringin' it over when you go there? It'll save me from botherin' you every day. Yore friend at th' station said I'd find you right obligin'. An' he knows a good ho-tel when he sees it. He sent me there."

"That scut!" bellowed Williams, his face growing red. "You'll come after yore own mail, my man; an' you'll do it polite. There ain't no mail here for you. Good day!"

"I'm patient an' I can wait. I didn't hardly expect to get any letter so quick, anyhow. After th' recent experience of reasonin' right from th' wrong premises, however, I'll not be a heap surprised if I get a letter on tomorrow's train. Thank you kindly, sir. I bid you good day."

"An' mind you don't call that cussed agent no friend of mine, th' job stealer!"

"Whatever you say; but, don't forget to bring over that letter when it comes," sweetly replied Tex, and he carefully slammed the door as he went out. Going down the street he grinned expansively and snapped his fingers because of a strange elation.

"Th' old thief!" he muttered. "Heavier, more ill tempered, and downright autocratic--an' how he has prospered! Regular, solid citizen, the bulwark of the commonwealth. An' cussed if he ain't got himself a bodyguard; a regular, no-mistake gunman with as mean an eye as any I ever saw. Of course, his brains have improved with the years, for they couldn't go the other way and keep him out of an asylum. 'Muttonhead' Williams! All right: once a sheep, always a sheep. I'm going to enjoy my stay in Windsor. Good Lord!" he exclaimed as a sudden fancy hit him. "Wouldn't it be funny if the old fool has been working hard and saving hard all these years for his old enemy, Tex Ewalt? He always was crazy to play poker, and I got a notion to make it come true. Gosh, if a man ever was tempted, I'm tempted now! Muttonhead Williams, allus stuck on his poker playing. Get behind me, Satan!"

Chapter III
Tempted Anew

A hand bell, ringing thin and clamorous somewhere below caused Tex to gather up the cards with which for two hours he had been assiduously practicing shuffling, cutting, and dealing. Putting them away he washed his face and hands in the tin basin, combed his hair without slicking it with water, and went down to supper.

He paused momentarily in the doorway to size up the dining-room. The long table was crowded by all sorts and conditions of men. Miners down on their luck and near the end of their resources because of the long drought which had dried up the streams and put an end to placer mining operations, rubbed elbows with more fortunate men of their own calling, who had longer purses. Two cowpunchers from a distant ranch sat next to two cavalrymen on a prized leave from the iron discipline of a remote frontier post, both types dangerous because free from the restraint which had held them down for so long a time. A local tin-horn gambler and the traveling card-sharp were elbow to elbow, and several other men, evidently belonging to the town, nearly filled both sides of the table.

At the head sat Gus Williams, most influential citizen and boss of the town, and he made no attempt to hide his importance. Next to him on the left was a lean, hard-looking, shifty-eyed man who seemed to shine in reflected light, and who showed a deference to the big man which he evidently expected to receive, in turn, from the others. If it was true that there was only one boss, it was also true that he had only one nephew. To the right of the boss was the cold-eyed person whose seat in the general store was well back in the corner. No one moved or spoke except under his critical observance. His cocksure confidence irritated Tex, who was strongly tempted to try the effect of a hot potato against a cold eye. He thought of his friend Johnny Nelson and grinned at how that young man's temper would steam up under such an insolent stare. Moving forward under the gunman's close scrutiny Tex dropped into the only vacant chair, one near the nephew, and fell to eating, his vocal chords idle, but his optic and auditory apparatus making up for it. The conversation, jerky and broken at first, grew more coherent and increased as the appetites of the hungry men yielded to the bolted food. The protracted drought was referred to in grunts, growls, monosyllables, sentences, and profane speeches. It was discussed, rediscussed, and popped up at odd moments for new discussion.

"Never saw it so bad since th' railroad came," said a miner.

"Never saw it so bad since th' first trail herd ended here," affirmed the nephew.

" *I* never saw it so dry, for so long a spell, since th' first trail herd *passed* here," said the uncle, his remark the strongest by coming last; but he was not to enjoy that advantage for long.

"Hum!" said a cattleman, apologetically clearing his throat. "I never saw it as dry as it is now since I located out here."

The miner frowned, the nephew scowled, and the uncle snorted. The last named looked around belligerently and smote the table with his fist. "I remember, howsomever, that I did see it near as dry, that year I strayed from th' Santa Fe Trail, huntin' buffalers for th' caravan. We passed right through this section an' circled back. I come to remember it because when we crossed th' Walnut I jumped right over it, dry-shod. Them was th' days when men was men, or soon wasn't nothin' a-tall."

"I reckon they wasn't th' kind that would play off sick so they could get another man's job away from him, anyhow," growled the nephew, introducing his pet grievance. "I run that station a cussed sight better than it's bein' run now; an' anybody's likely to make mistakes once in a while."

"A few dollars, one way or another, ain't bustin' no railroad," asserted the uncle. "It was only th' excuse they was a-waitin' for."

"Nobody can tell me no good about no railroad," said the freighter, his fond memory resurrecting a certain lucrative wagon haul which had vanished with the advent of the first train over the line.

"Hosses are good enough for me," said Tex, looking around. "Which remark reminds me that a rider afoot is a helpless hombre. Bein' a rider, without no cayuse, I'm a little anxious to get me a good one. Anybody know where I can do it reasonable?"

All eyes turned to the head of the table, where Williams was washing down his last mouthful of food with a gulp of hot, watery coffee. He cleared his throat and peered closely, but pleasantly, at the stranger. "Why, it's Mr. Jones," he said. "I reckon I have such a hoss, Mr. Jones. Mebby it ain't any too well broken, but that hadn't oughter bother a rider."

Tex grinned. "If that's all that's th' matter with it I reckon it'll suit me; but I can tell better after I ride it, an' learn th' price."

"Want it tonight?" frowned Williams.

"No; I ain't in no hurry. Tomorrow'll be plenty of time, when you ain't got nothin' else to do but show it. Speakin' of railroads like we was, I reckon they ain't done nothin' very much for this town. While I'm new to these parts, I'm betting Windsor was a whole lot better when th' drive trail was alive an' kickin'."

Williams nodded emphatically. "I've seen these plains an' valleys thick with cattle," he said, regretfully. "There was a time when I could see th' dust clouds rollin' up from th' south an' away in th' north, both at once, day after day. This town was a-hummin' every day an' night. Money come easy an' went th' same way. Men dropped in here, lookin' like tramps, almost, who could write good checks for thousands of dollars. Th' buyers bought whole herds on th' seller's say-so, without even seein' a hoof, an' sold 'em ag'in th' same way. Money flowed like water, an' fair-sized fortunes was won an' lost at a single sittin'. I've seen th' faro-bank busted three days hand-runnin'–but, of course, that was very unusual. Mostly it was th' other way 'round. All one summer an' fall it was like that. Then th' winter come, an' that was th' end of it so fur's Windsor was concerned. Th' Kiowa Arroyo branch line was pushed further an' further southwest until th' weather stopped it; but it went on ag'in as soon as spring let it. By th' time th' first herds crossed th' state line, headin' for here, that line of rails was ready for 'em, an' not another big herd went past this town. Of course, there was big herds drivin' north, just th' same, bound for th' Yellowstone region on government contract, an' some was bein' sent out to stock ranges in th' West, but they followed a new trail found by Chisholm, or old McCullough. I've heard lately that Mac is workin' for Twitchell an' Carpenter. But if you'd seen this town then you shore wouldn't know it now. D--n th' railroads, says I!"

Tex frowned honestly at the thought of the passing of this once great cattle trail, for the memories of those old trails lay snug and warm in the hearts of the men who have followed them in the saddle. He looked up at Williams, a congratulatory look on his face. "Well, that shore was hard; but not as hard, I reckon, as if you had been a cattleman, an' follered it. It sort of hurts an old-time cowman to think of them trails."

"That's where yo're wrong," spoke up the nephew. "He is a cattleman. Th' GW brand is known all over th' state, an' beyond. It was knowed by every puncher that followed that old trail."

"There wasn't no such brand in them days," corrected Williams. He did not think it necessary to say that the GW mark was just starting then, far back in the hills and well removed from the trail; that it grew much faster by the addition of fully grown cattle than it did by natural increase; or that a view of the original brands on the full-grown cattle would have been a matter of great and burning interest to almost every drive boss who followed a herd along the trail. Later on, when he threw his herd up for a count, the drive boss was likely to have re-added his tally sheet and asked heaven and earth what had happened to him. "Well, them days has gone; but when they went this town come blamed near goin' with 'em. It shore ain't what it once was."

Tex thought that it was just as well, since the town was mean enough and vicious enough as it was; he remembered vividly its high-water period; but he nodded his head.

"It ain't hardly fair to judge it after such a long dry spell," he said. "Th' whole country, south an' west of th' Missouri is fair burnin' up. Th' Big Muddy herself was a-showin' all her bars."

"That's th' curse of this part of Kansas," said the nephew. "That an' job jumpers."

"Yes?" asked Tex. "How's that?"

"Station agent a friend of yourn?"

It became evident to Tex that the uncle and the nephew had been discussing him. Gus Williams was the only man to whom he had mentioned the agent. He shook his head. "Never saw him before I stepped off th' train today," he answered, looking vexed about something. "We up an' had some words, an' I told him I reckoned he might find healthier towns further west, across th' line. I'm a mild man, gents: but I allus speak my mind."

"An' you gave him some cussed good advice," replied the nephew warmly. "This ain't no place for any man as plays off sick an' does low-down tricks to turn another man out of a job. If it wasn't for his sister I'd 'a' buffaloed him *pronto* . Which reminds me, stranger," he warned with an ugly leer. "She's a rip-snortin' fe-male--but I shore saw her first. I'm just tellin' you so you won't get any notions that way. I'm fencin' that range."

"Don't you worry, Hen," consoled a friend. "Yo're able to run herd on her, balky as she is, an' when th' time's ripe you'll put yore brand on her. So fur's th' job's concerned, yore uncle'll get it back for you when he gets ready to move. We ought to ride that Saunders feller out of town, *I* say!"

"There's plenty of time for that," said Williams, as he turned to address another diner. "John, show Mr. Jones that gray when he gits around tomorrow. Aimin' to stay in town long, Mr. Jones?"

Tex shrugged his shoulders. "Got to wait for a letter--don't know what to do; but I shore could be in worse places than this here hotel, so I ain't worryin' a lot. Bein' a stranger, though, I reckon time'll drag a little evenin's."

Various kinds of smiles replied to this, and Williams laughed outright. "I reckon you understand th' innercent game of draw?" he chuckled.

Tex froze: "Sometimes I think I do," he said, and laughed to hide his struggle against the pressure of the old temptation. He fairly burned to turn his poker craft against this blowhard's invitation, to wipe from that self-complacent face its look of omniscience. "An' then, sometimes I reckon I don't," he continued; "but I'm admittin' she's plumb fascinatin'. From th' pious expressions around me I reckon mebby I've shocked somebody."

Williams led in the laughter that followed, his bull voice roaring through the room. "You'd better buy that hoss before you assist in th' evenin's worship," he cried in boisterous good humor, "for I'm sayin' a puncher ain't nowhere near in th' prospector's class when it comes to walkin'; though I reckon th' boys will play you for th' hoss, at that, an' you'd be no better off in th' end.

My remarks as how this town has slid back didn't have nothin' to do with our poker playin', Mr. Jones. If you feel like settin' in ag'in' a Kansas cyclone, you can't say I didn't warn you."

Tex wondered what the crowd would say if he should lean over and pull a royal flush out of Williams' ear, or a full-house from the nephew's nose. They might be surprised if they found out that the cold-eyed gunman at Williams' elbow carried a handful of Colt cartridges in his tight-shut mouth. He had no rabbits to lift out of hats, but that trick was threadbare from being overworked, anyhow. He waved both hands, a smart-Aleck grin sweeping across his face. "I've rode cayuses, punched cows, an' played draw from Texas to Montanny, an' near back ag'in. So far I ain't throwed, rolled under, or cleaned out; an' I'm allus willin' to be agreeable. Where you gents lead I'll foller, like a hungry calf after its ma." His voice had grown loud and boastful and he joined the swiftly forming card group with a swagger as it settled around the table in the barroom, his bovine conceit hiding the silent struggle going on within him.

Tex of the old days was fighting Tex of the new. The smug complacency of the local boss stirred up the desire to break him to his last cent, to make a fool of him in the way others had been broken and made ridiculous; but the new Tex won: As usual he would play Hopalong's game--which was as his opponents played, straight or crooked, as they showed the way. He had no real wish for large winnings, for if he made his expenses as he went along he would be satisfied, and he could do that from his knowledge of psychology, a knowledge gained outside of classrooms. He now had no reputation to defend or maintain, for Tex Jones was not Tex Ewalt, famed throughout the cow-country. The new name meant nothing. But how pleasant it would be to repeat history in this town, so far as Williams was concerned!

He always had claimed that he could learn a man's real nature more quickly in a game of poker than in any other way in the same length of time, and he did not mean some one more prominent trait, but the man's nature as a whole; and now he set himself to study his new acquaintances against some future need. The game itself would not engross him to the exclusion of all else, for while he was Tex Jones externally, it would be Tex Ewalt who played the hands, the Tex Ewalt who as a youth had discovered an uncanny ability in sleight of hand and whose freshman and sophomore years had given so much time to developing and perfecting the eye-baffling art that every study had suffered heavily in consequence; the Tex Ewalt who had found that his ability was peculiarly adaptive to cards, and who had given all his attention to that connection when once he had started to travel along the line of least resistance. So well had he succeeded that seasoned gamblers from the Mexican line north to Canada had been forced to admit his mastery.

Before the end of the second deal he had learned the rest of the nephew's more prominent characteristics, but had not bothered to retaliate for the cheating. On the third deal he was forced to out-cheat a miner to keep even with the game. Before the evening's play was over he had renewed his knowledge of Gus Williams, and now knew him as well as that loud-voiced individual knew himself; and he had not incurred the enmity of the boss, because while Tex had won from the others he had lost to him. While not yielding to the temptations rampant in him, he had compromised and left Williams in a ripe condition for a future skinning. At the end of the play only he and Williams had won.

As the others pushed back their chairs to leave the table, Williams ignored them and looked at Tex. "You an' me seem to be th' best," he said loudly. "So there won't be no doubt about it, let's settle it between us."

Tex raised a belated hand too late to hide his yawn, blinked sleepily, and squinted at the clock. "I'm surprised it's so late," he said. "It takes a lot out of a man to play ag'in' this crowd. My head's fair achin'. What you say if we let it go till tomorrow night? I been travelin' for three days an' nights an' ain't slept much. You'd take it away from me before I could wake up."

Williams laughed sarcastically. "You shore been crossin' a lot of sand since you left th' Big Muddy, but I don't reckon none of it got inter yore system." He paused to let the words sink in, and for a reply, and none being forthcoming he laughed nastily as he arose. "Texas is a sandy state, too. Reckon you was named before anybody knowed very much about you."

Tex paled, fought himself to a standstill and shrugged his shoulders. Out of the corner of his eye he saw Bud Haines, the cold-eyed bodyguard, become suddenly more alert.

"Windsor's got a h--l of a way of welcomin' strangers," he said. "You'll have a different kind of a kick to make tomorrow night, for you'll be eatin' sand. I play poker when I feel like it: just now I don't feel like it. I'll say good night."

"Ha-ha-ha!" shouted Williams. "He don't feel like it, boys! Ha-ha-ha!"

Tex stopped, turned swiftly, pulled out a roll of bills that was a credit to his country and slammed it on the table, reaching for the scattered deck. "Mebby you feel like puttin' up seven hundred dollars ag'in' mine, one cut, th' highest card, to take both piles? Ha-ha-ha!" he mimicked. "Here's action if that's what yo're lookin' for!"

Williams' face turned a deep red and he cursed under his breath. "That's a baby game: I said poker!" he retorted, making no effort to get nearer to the table.

"That's mebby why I picked it," snapped Tex, stuffing the roll back into his pocked. "You can wait till tomorrow night for poker." Turning his back on the wrathful Williams and the open-mouthed audience, he yawned again, muttered something to express his adieus, and clomped heavily and slowly up the stairs, his body shaking with repressed laughter; and when he fell asleep a few minutes later there was a placid smile on his clean-shaven face.

Chapter IV
A Crowded Day

After a late breakfast about noon Tex got the gunny sack, threw it over his shoulder and went to the Mecca, nodding to the proprietor in a spirit of good-will and cheerfulness. Bud Haines did not appear to be about.

"I come in to see about that cayuse," he said. "Where'll I find it?"

"Go down to th' stable an' see John," growled Williams. "You'll find it next to Carney's saloon, across th' street. Got rested up yet?" The question was not pleasantly asked.

Tex threw the sack over the other shoulder, hunched it to a more comfortable position, and grinned sheepishly. "Purty near, I reckon; anyhow, I got over my grouch. I was shore peevish last night; but th' railroad's to blame for that. They say they are necessary, an' great blessin's; but I ain't so shore about it. Outside of my personal grudge ag'in' 'em, I'm sore because they've shore played th' devil with th' range. Cut it all up--an' there ain't no more pickin' along th' old trails no more, like there once was. I don't reckon punchers has got any reason to love 'em a whole lot."

Williams flashed him a keen look and slowly nodded. "Yo're right: look at what they've done to this town. We ain't seen no real money since they came."

Tex shifted the sack again. "Everybody had money in them days," he growled. "If a feller went busted along th' trails he allus could pick up a few dollars, if he had a good cayuse an' a little nerve. Why, among them hills--but that ain't concernin' us no more, I reckon." He shook his head sadly. "What's gone is gone. Reckon I'll go look at that cayuse. You ain't got no letter for me yet, have you?"

"Le's see--Johnson?" puzzled the storekeeper, scratching his unshaven chin.

"No; Jones," prompted Tex innocently, hiding his smile.

"Oh, shore!" said his companion, slowly shaking his head. "There ain't nothin' for you so far."

Tex did not think that remarkable not only because there never would be anything for him, but also because there had been no mail since he had asked the day before; but he grunted pessimistically, shifted the sack again, and turned to the door. "See you later," he said, going out.

He easily found the stable, grinned at the bleached, weather-beaten "Williams" painted over the door and going into the smelly, cigar-box office, dumped the sack against the wall and nodded to John Graves. "Come down to look at that cayuse Williams spoke about last night," he said, drawing a sleeve across his wet forehead.

"Shore; come along with me," said Graves, arising and passing out into the main part of the building, Tex at his heels. "Here he is, Mr. Jones--as fine a piece of hossflesh as a man ever straddled. Got brains, youth, an' ginger. Sound as a dollar. Cost you eighty, even. You'll go far before you'll find a better bargain."

Tex looked at the teeth, passed a hypnotic hand down each leg in turn as he talked to the gray in a soothing voice. Children, horses, and dogs liked him at first look. He frankly admired the animal from a distance, but sadly shook his head.

"Fine cayuse, an' a fair price," he admitted; "but I'm dead set ag'in' grays. Had two of 'em once, one right after th' other--an' come near to dyin' on 'em both. If I didn't get killed, they did, anyhow. It's sort of set me ag'in' grays. Now, there's a roan that strikes me as a hoss I'd consider ownin'. Of course, he ain't as good as th' gray, but he suits me better." He walked over to the magnificent animal, which was far and away superior to the gray, and talked to it in a low, caressing voice as he made a quick examination. "Yes, this cayuse suits me if th' price is right. If we can agree on that I'll lead him down th' street an' see how he steps out. Ain't got nothin' else to do, anyhow."

Graves frowned and slowly shook his head. "Rather not part with that one--an' he's a two-hundred-dollar animal, anyhow. It's a sort of pet of th' boss--he's rid it since it was near old enough to walk. That gray's th' best I've got for sale, unless, mebby, it might be that sorrel over there. Now, there's a mighty good hoss, come to think of it."

Tex glanced at the beautiful line of the roan's back and thought of the massive weight of Williams, and of the sway-back bay standing saddled in front of his store. He shook his head. "Two hundred's too high for me, friend," he replied. "As I said, I don't like grays, an' that sorrel has shore got a mean eye. It ain't spirit that's showin', but just plumb treachery. If you got off him out on th' range he'd head for home an' leave you to hoof it after him. I got an even hundred for th' roan. Say th' word an' we trade."

Graves waved his arms and enumerated the roan's good points as only a horse dealer can. The discussion was long and to no result. Tex added twenty-five dollars to the hundred he had offered and the whole thing was gone over again, but to no avail. He picked up the sack, slung it onto his back, and turned to leave.

"I'm shore surprised at th' prices for cayuses in this part of th' country," he said. "Mebby I can make a dicker with somebody else. Of course, I'm admittin' that th' roan ain't got a sand crack like th' sorrel, or a spavin like th' gray--but that's too much money for a saddle hoss for a puncher out of a job. See you tonight, mebby."

Graves waved his arms again. "I'm tellin' you that you won't find no hoss in town like that roan--why, th' color of that animal is worth half th' price. Just look at it!"

"All of which I admits," replied Tex; "but, you see, I'm buyin' me a hoss to ride, not to put on th' parlor table for to admire. Comin' right down to cases, any hoss but a gray, that's sound, an' not too old, is good enough for any puncher. You should 'a' seen some that I've rode, an' been proud of!"

"Seein' that yo're a lover of good hossflesh, I'll take a chance of Gus gettin' peeved, an' let you have th' roan for one-ninety. That's as low as I can drop. Can't shave off another dollar."

"It's too rich for Tex Jones," grumbled the puncher. "See you tonight," and the sack bobbed toward the door just as a sudden brawl sounded in the street. Tex took two quick steps and glanced.

A miner and a cowpuncher were rolling in the dust, biting, hitting, gouging, and wrestling and, as Tex looked he saw the puncher's gun slip out of its open-top sheath. The fighting pair rolled away from it and someone in the closely following crowd picked it up to save it for its owner. The puncher, pounds lighter than his brawny antagonist, rapidly was getting the worst of the rough-and-tumble in which the other's superior weight and strength had full opportunity to make itself felt. Suddenly the miner, thrown from his victim by a tremendous effort, leaped to his feet, snarling like a beast, and knicked at the puncher's head. The heavy, hob-nailed boot crashed sickeningly home and as the writhing man went suddenly limp, the victor aimed another kick at his unconscious enemy. His foot swung back, but it never reached its mark. A forty-pound saddle in a sack shot through the air with all of a strong man's strength behind it and, catching the miner balanced on one foot, it knocked him sprawling through ten feet of dust and débris. Following the sack came Tex, his eyes blazing.

The miner groped in the dust, slowly sat up, moving his head from side to side as he got his bearings. At once his eyes cleared and his hand streaked to the knife in his belt as he half arose. Tex leaped aside as the heavy weapon cut through the air to sink into a near-by wall, where it quivered. The thrower was on his feet now, his face working with rage, and he sprang forward, both arms circling before him. Tex swiftly gripped one outstretched wrist, turned sharply as he pushed his shoulder under the armpit and suddenly bent forward, facing away from his antagonist. The miner left the ground on the surging heave of the puncher's shoulder, shot up into the air, turned over once as Tex, not wishing him to break his neck, pulled down hard on the imprisoned arm, and landed feet first against the wall, squarely under the knife. Bouncing up with remarkable vitality, the miner wrenched at the wicked weapon above him and then cursed as the steel, leaving its point embedded in the wood, flew out of his hand.

Tex shoved the smoking Colt back into his holster and peered through the acrid, gray fog. "If you don't know when yo're licked, you better take my word for it," he warned. "Seein' as how yo're a rubber ball, I'll make shore th' third time!"

A snarl replied and the miner leaped for him, the hairy hands not so far extended this time. Tex broke ground with two swift steps and then, unexpectedly slipping to one side and forward in two perfectly timed motions, swung a rigid, bent arm as the charging miner went blunderingly past. The bony fist landed fair above the belt buckle and it was nearly half an hour later before the prospector knew where he was, and then he was too sick to care much.

Tex turned and faced the crowd with insolent slowness. His glance passed from face to face, finding some friendliness, much surprise, and a few frank scowls. He stepped up to the man who had retrieved the puncher's gun and, ignoring the crowd altogether, took the weapon from the reluctant fingers which held it and went back to the front of the stable, where Graves had succeeded in bringing the prostrate puncher back to consciousness. Tex ran his fingers over the wobbly man's head and face, grunted, nodded, and smiled.

"Bad bruise, but nothin' is busted. Why there ain't I'm shore *I* don't know. I figgered you was a goner. Here, take yore gun, an' let us help you into th' stable."

Once on his feet the puncher pushed free from the sustaining hands and staggered to a box just inside the door, where he carefully seated himself, drew the Colt, and rested it on his knees, his blurred, throbbing eyes watching the street.

Tex grinned. "You can put that up ag'in--he's had all he can digest for a little while. Punchin' for Williams?"

"I'm ridin' for Curtis: C Bar. Over northeast, a couple of hours out. I'm keepin' th' gun where it is: th' miners run this town. Where do you fit in? One of th' GW gang?"

"Nope; I'm all of th' Tex Jones outfit. Stranger here, but shore gettin' acquainted rapid. Got any good cayuses for sale out at yore place? Our mutual friend, here, wants th' Treasury for th' only good animal he's got. Bein' a stranger is a handicap."

Graves leaned forward. "That hoss is worth--" he began in great earnestness.

"--not one red cent to me, now," interrupted Tex, smiling. "Come to think of it, I ain't goin' to buy no hoss, a-tall. I've changed my mind."

"We got th' usual run out on th' ranch," said the injured man. "You know 'em, I reckon. Poor on looks, mean as all h--l, with hearts crowded with sand. I'll be leavin' in half an hour if th' miners don't interfere--borry a cayuse an' ride out with me."

"Nope," replied Tex. "I ain't goin' to buy, a-tall, as I just said." He turned. "Good luck to you, friend. Barrin' th' soreness, an' yore looks yo're all right," and he went out, picked up the bulging sack, and passed down the street. Leaving the sack with the bartender in the hotel he went on to the station and smiled at the agent, who was joking with a red-headed Irishman.

"Hello; here he is now," exclaimed the boss of the depot. "Friend, shake hands with Tim Murphy. Tim, this is Mr.–Mr.—-"

"Jones," supplied Tex. "Tex Jones, of Montanny, Texas, an' New York."

"Pleased to meet you, Mr. Geography," grinned Murphy. "Th' lad here was a-tellin' me ye gave him a friendly word an' some good advice. From that I was knowin' ye didn't belong around here. I'll shake yer hand if ye don't mind. Th' sack wint like an arrow, th' wrestlin' trick couldn't be bate, I never saw a nicer shot, an' th' finish does ye proud. Ye fair tickled me when ye wint for th' soft spot. 'Tis a rare sight in street fights, an' in th' ring, too, for that matter. Welcome to Windsor!"

Tex laughed heartily and gripped the hairy fist. He liked the feel of the great, calloused hand, and the look on the smiling, tanned face, from which twinkled a pair of blue eyes alight with humor, honesty, and courage. "But did you ever see a man come back as quick as he did?" he asked.

"'Twas surprisin' for a bully," admitted Murphy, grudgingly.

"That's where yo're wrong: he's no bully," contradicted Tex. "He's a brute, all right, savage as th' devil, an' foul in his fightin'–but he ain't any coward. It fair stuck out of his eyes."

"Trust me to miss anything like that," growled the agent; "and trust Tim not to," he added.

"Hist, now!" warned Murphy, motioning with his thumb held close to his vest. "Here comes th' lass. An' what do ye be thinkin' av th' town now, Mr. Jones?"

"Just what you do," laughed Tex, turning slowly.

"An' how are ye this day, miss?" asked Murphy, his hat in his hand and his red face beaming.

"Very well, indeed, Tim," replied the girl. She glanced at Tex as she turned to her brother, holding out the lunch basket. "Jerry, I couldn't get any decent eggs--and they had no milk for me." There was a poorly hidden note of distress in her voice, and a faint look of anxiety momentarily clouded her face. Neither was lost to the observant puncher.

Tex liked her instantly. Her voice was full and sweet, of resonant timbre--a voice one would not easily tire of. Her figure was slender, and yet full and rounded, promising a wiry strength and great vitality. The sunbonnet she wore hid most of the chestnut-brown hair, but set off the face within it with a bewitching art. Altogether she made a very pretty picture.

"It doesn't matter, Jane," smiled her brother, quick to sense her worry. He pinched the full lips with caressing playfulness. "I'm getting stronger every day, and food isn't as critical a subject as it once was. The credit is all yours--Jane, meet Mr. Jones. I was speaking about him last night."

Tex bowed gravely. "How do you do?" he murmured. "Conscientious care is more than half of the battle. The credit he gave you appears to be well deserved."

Jane Saunders, accustomed to embarrassed self-consciousness or stammering volubility, smiled faintly as she acknowledged the introduction. The man was as impersonal and as sure of himself as any she ever had met. She looked him fairly in the eyes.

"How did you come to advise my brother to go farther west?" she asked, but while her voice was casual, her look challenged him.

"It was given upon certain conditions of the weather this winter, Miss--I do not believe I caught the name."

"No fault of yours," she laughed. "Jerry always ignores it in his introductions. It is Jane Saunders. Then it was only in the nature of a physician's advice?" she persisted, her eyes searching his soul for the truth.

Tex nodded. "My knowledge of his complaint is very sketchy; but like all amateurs I paraded what little I had. I thought that perhaps the winters out here might not be as dry as they are farther west. No doubt it was entirely uncalled for. We will hope so, anyway."

"Are you a physician, Mr. Jones?"

"No, indeed; although I went part way through the course. What little time I had left from more interesting activities, I gave to study."

"Ye was speakin' about th' aigs an' milk, miss," said Murphy, his face alight with eager anticipation. He chuckled. "Ye needn't be askin' no more favors av Williams' black heart. I've a little somethin' to show ye all, if ye'll step down th' track a bit. An' Costigan is goin' to get him a cow. Th' missus said th' word, an' divvil a bit Mike can wiggle out av it. Ye'll have first call on th' milk, so I hear. Mr. Jones, if ye'll be kind enough to escort Jerry, I'll lead th' march with th' lass."

"Oh, well," sighed Tex, gravely offering his arm to the station agent, "I suppose it *is* yore party; but I'm admittin' yo're not overlookin' Number One. Lead on, MacDuff." He caught her quick glance at the abrupt change in his language, and smiled to himself. It never paid to be too well understood by a woman.

"Th' Irish are noted for bein' judges av good whiskey, fine hosses, an' fair wimmin," retorted Murphy. "I'll take no chances of any pearls bein' cast careless."

"I notice you put th' wimmin last," countered Tex. "Grunt, Jerry! Quick, man! Before Miss Saunders looks around!"

"He said pearly, Mr. Jones," said Jane, laughingly. "I'm afraid he intended it all to be plural."

"It was wrongly written in th' first place," complained Tex. "Tim has an uncanny instinct; he only met me about ten minutes ago."

"Ten is a-plenty, sometimes," chuckled Murphy. "But I'll own to havin' a previous sight av ye. Wait now: here we are."

They stopped in front of the toolhouse and watched Murphy walk along one of the two ties spanning the drainage ditch at the edge of the roadbed. He unlocked the doors and flung them wide open as a clamorous cackling broke out in the building. On one end of a hand car was a crate of chickens and leaning against it were several bundles of long stakes. A pile of new lumber could be seen in the back of the shed, while a fat spool of wire rested near the stakes.

Murphy turned, his face red with delight at his surprise. "There ye are, miss," he cried proudly. "A round dozen av them, with their lord an' master. I couldn't let that Mike Costigan go puttin' on his airs over his boss, so now there'll be aigs for aignoggs that I'll have a claim to. For safe-keepin' we'll build th' coop in yore back yard where it will be right handy for ye. Ye can now tell Williams to kape his aigs. If he don't understand yer soft language, I'll be tellin' him in a way he can't mistook."

"You angel!" whispered Jane, tears in her eyes. She was not misled by his remarks about eggnoggs. "Oh, Tim--you shouldn't have done it! Why didn't *I* think of it? And how is it that Mrs. Costigan suddenly needs a cow? If I've heard her aright, she has stalwart, old-fashioned ideas, bless her, about nursing children. And I never knew she was partial to eggnoggs. Jerry, what shall we do to them?"

Jerry blew his nose with energy. "For a cent I'd lick Murphy right now, and Mike immediately afterward," he laughed, sizing up the huge bulk of bone, sinew, and toil-hardened muscle of the section-boss. "Tim, you and your boys are the one redeeming feature of this country. And you redeem it fully. How long have you been plotting this?"

"G'wan with ye, th' pair av ye!" chuckled the section-boss, his face flaming. "If Casey hadn't stopped th' train down by this shed yesterday we couldn't 'a' surprised ye. Ye never saw a consignment handled quicker or more gintly."

"And I was wondering why he did it," confessed Jerry. "The brakeman said he was trying his brakes. Tim, you should be ashamed of yourself!"

"An' I've been that, many a time," retorted Murphy. He turned to Tex. "I'll be leavin' it to ye, Mr. Jones, if a man hasn't certain rights after bein' nursed for three weeks by a brown-haired angel, an' knowin' that th' same angel nursed Mrs. Costigan an' th' twins whin they was all down with th' measles. Patient an' unselfish, she was, with never a cross word, day or night--an' always with a smile on her pretty face, like th' sun on Lake Killarney."

Tex looked gravely and judicially at Jane Saunders. "You haven't a word to say, Miss Saunders. The verdict of the court is for the defendant. Case dismissed, without costs of either party against the other." He turned to the section-boss. "When are we buildin' that coop, Murphy?" he asked.

"Tomorrow, Tex," answered the Irishman. "We'll be after runnin' th' darlin's up there right away, an' come back for th' lumber an' wire. That'll give us an early start. Th' sidin' will let us ride 'em near halfway an' save a lot of flounderin' in th' sand."

"We'd better come back for th' darlin's after th' coop is ready for 'em," said Tex, grinning. "If I know coyotes as well as I reckon I do, th' harem will be a lot safer in this here shed; an' I'm glad it's got a board floor, too. Lend a hand here an' we'll change th' cargo on this meek steed. *Gently, brother, gently pray* . Now for th' lumber." He burst into a chant: " *I once was a bloody pirate bold, an' I sailed on th' Spanish Main, yo-ho! Th' treasure chests were full of gold, which gave us all a pain you know.* " He glanced at one of his hands and grimaced. "Blast th' splinters. An' would you look at that corn? Blessed if th' man hasn't got enough to feed another Custer expedition! Murphy, you certainly do grow on one!"

Murphy paused with a huge armful of lumber, and looked suspicious. "On one what?" he demanded.

"Prickly pear plant, I reckon, in lieu of anything else; or on a mesquite tree, perhaps, for you shore do know beans when th' pod's open. *An' it stopped--short--never to go again, when th' old--man--died,* " hummed Tex. "All aboard. Clang-clang! Clang-clang! I can still hear that bell in my sleep. Yo're th' engineer, Murphy; I'll act in an advisory capacity, at th' same time pushing hard on my very own handle. Ladies first! Miss Saunders, if you please! That's right, for you might as well ride in state. Up you go. From your elevated position you may scan the country roundabout and give us warning of the approach of redskins. *A Book of Verses underneath the Bough, a Jug of Wine, a Loaf of Bread* —and fried eggs-- *Oh, Wilderness were Paradise enow!* "

"I see no redskins, Advisory Capacity," called Jane, who thoroughly was enjoying herself; "but hither rides a horseman on a horse."

Tex looked up and saw a recklessly riding puncher coming toward them. He slyly exchanged grins with Murphy and kept on pushing.

The rider, smiling as well as a swollen face and throbbing temples would permit, slid to a stand, removed his sombrero and bowed.

"My name's Tom Watkins," he said. "I just come down to tell you, friend, that I've learned what you done for me, awhile back. I'm-—"

Tex interrupted him. "You just came down in time, Thomas, to drop yore useful rope over that bobbin' handle an' head west at a plain, unornamental walk. High-heeled boots was never made for pushin' han' cars over ties an' rocks. An' I suspect Murphy of stealin' a ride every time my head goes down."

"Then I'd be cheatin' myself," retorted Murphy, looking upon the newcomer with strong favor. "Th' car would be after stoppin' every time I rode, like th' little boat with th' big whistle." He turned to the agent. "Jerry, there's no tellin' how fast this car will be goin', for I misdoubt that animal's intentions. Suppose ye run along an' throw th' switch for us. Hadn't ye better get down, miss?"

"Not for the world, Tim!"

The disfigured puncher grinned even wider, dropped his rope over the handle with practiced art and wheeled his horse. "What'll I do when I git to th' end of th' rails?" he asked, mischievous deviltry, unabashed by what had befallen him, shining in his eyes, and there was an eager curiosity revealed by his voice.

"What'll he do, Murphy?" demanded Tex.

"He'll stop, blast him!" emphatically answered the section-boss.

"You'll stop, Thomas," said Tex. "As Hamlet said: 'Go on, I'll follow thee!'"

"But he's not nearly a ghost yet," objected Jane. Her cheeks were flushed, her eyes sparkling from the fun she was having. Many days had passed since she had had so good a time. It was a treat to get away from the ever-lasting "Yes, ma'am" and "No, ma'am" which had been the formula for conversation with everyone to whom she had talked except her brother and Murphy.

"No, ma'am," said the puncher. "Not yet."

Jane shuddered and grimaced at Tex as the rider turned away. "That's all I've heard since I've been out here," she softly called down to him.

"Yes, ma'am," he replied, not daring to look up. The procession wended onward to the edification of sundry stray dogs, and Costigan's goats, tethered near the toolshed, promptly went into consultation as to what measures to pursue, apparently deciding upon a defensive course of action if the worst came to pass.

The end of the rails reached, the engineer of the motive power stopped, sized up the ground roundabout and then looked hopefully at his companions. "Reckon we can manage th' haul. Totin' them boards afoot shore will be tirin'. Where we drivin' to?"

Jerry pointed out the little house, but shook his head. "We can't make it."

"Cowboy," said Tex, "that ain't no plowhorse. When she feels th' drag of this vehicle in th' sand she'll display her frank an' candid thoughts about it."

"Then blindfold her," suggested Tom Watkins. "She won't know it ain't a steer she's fastened to. You fellers can git behind an' push, too."

"' *Sic transit gloria mundi,* '" murmured Jane, preparing to descend to earth.

"' *Sic transit* ' glorious Monday," repeated Tex, stepping to assist her. "Only it ain't Monday. Take my honest hand, lady, and jump." He turned and looked at the grinning engineer. "Now, you cactus-eatin' burro, try yore handkerchief. If *our* idea works, all right; if yore idea don't work, it's Murphy's fault. Commence!"

"I'm thinkin' it would work better if th' car was off th' track," caustically commented Murphy. "I misdoubt if we can climb that buffer; th' flanges on these wheels are deep an' strong an' I'm shore we can't pull th' rails over. If th' engineer will lend a hand here we mebby can clear th' track without unloadin'. I'll take th' off side; ye byes take th' other, which makes it even, for it is a well-known fact that one Irish section-boss is worth two punchers. Are ye ready, now?"

"I've heard they can run faster than two cowpunchers," retorted Tex. "For the ashes of your fathers, *lift* ! Try it again--now. Inch her over--that's the way. Now then, *lift* ! Once more--*lift* ! Phew! All right: proceed, cowboy," he grunted.

"Hold yer horses!" shouted Murphy. "What's th' good av a section-boss that can't lay a track?" he demanded, taking up a two-by-four, Tex following his lead. The car was lifted onto the timbers and the procession went on again. "Will they spread, now?" queried Murphy doubtfully, watching them closely. He had just decided they would not when they did. After numerous troubles the little house was reached, the lumber unloaded, and the car sent back without rails.

"Goin' to make any more hauls?" asked the horseman.

"We are not," said Tex with emphasis. "We could 'a' toted this stuff over in half th' time. *Tempus* fidgets, an' I'm catchin' it. Yore ideas are plumb fine till they're put in practice."

" *My* ideas?" queried the disfigured rider, his rising eyebrows pushing wrinkles onto his forehead. "Didn't you tell me to chuck my rope over that bobbin' handle?"

"Do you allus have to do what yo're told?" retorted Tex. "Answer me that! Do you?"

The rider looked down at Jane, who was nearly convulsed, and sighed with deep regret, and because her presence forbade the only appropriate retort, he shook his head sorrowfully and turned to haul the car back to the track.

"Hey!" called Tex. "Sling them spools of barb wire across yore saddle. We might as well get more of that stuff while we have yore good-natured assistance. Just chuck it on any place an' bring it here."

"You just can't chuck a spool of wire on a saddle any place," retorted the puncher. "Was you speakin' about ideas?"

"An' while yer about it," said Murphy, "ye might bring back a spade, th' saws, three hammers, that box av nails, an' them staples. Th' staples are in a little keg--th' one without th' handle.

I've a mind to start buildin' today. What do ye say, Tex? Good for ye: yer a man after me own heart."

Despite his aches and bruises the puncher's feet left the stirrups and slowly went up until he stood with his shoulder on the saddle. He waved his legs three times and resumed the correct posture for riding. Words were hopelessly inadequate. He looked at Jane, who was shrieking and pointing at the ground under the horse. Thomas craned his neck and looked down. He thereupon dismounted and picked up one Colt's .45, one pocket-knife, one watch which now needed expert attention, various coins, a plug of tobacco, and three horseshoe nails. Murphy stared at him, spat disgustedly, and attacked the pile of lumber.

After the puncher's return the work went on rapidly, and when the roof of the coop was finished, the three perspiring workmen stepped back to admire it.

"We've got to slat them windows," said Tex, thinking of coyotes.

"An' we got thirteen nests to build," said Thomas Watkins.

"Th' saints be praised!" ejaculated Murphy, staring incredulously at the battle-scarred recruit. "Mebby there'll be a coincidence about twelve layin' all at once, but there won't be no thirteenth on th' job. Mebby yer thinkin' th' Sultan will nest down alongside them to set them a good example? Six boxes will be a-plenty, Tommy, my lad."

Tommy tilted his sombrero to scratch his head. "Well, if you reckon there won't be no stampedin', mebby six will be enough, 'though I'd hate to think of 'em milling frantic for their turn on th' nests. An' while we're speakin' of calamities, I'm sayin' good chickens will fly over th' fence you fellers aim to build. Six feet ain't high enough, nohow."

"We clip their wings, Tommy," enlightened Tex.

"We clip one wing close up," corrected Murphy. "That lifts 'em on one side an' flops 'em around in a circle. I can easy see you ain't no *hen puncher* ."

"Th' principle is sound in theory an' proved by practice," said Tex. "Just like when you saw off th' laigs on one side of a steer. That allus keeps 'em from jumpin' fences."

"Too cussed bad you stopped that miner," growled Watkins. "I'd 'a' been a whole lot better off dead."

"We're sorry, too," retorted Murphy. "Now, then; we got a four-sided fence to build, three posts to a side. That's a dozen holes to dig."

"Tell you what," suggested Tommy, winking at Tex. "You can handle a spade all around us, one Irish section-boss bein' worth two punchers. Besides we only got one spade for th' three of us. You dig th' north an' south sides while me an' Tex start on nests an' put up th' roosts. Then we'll dig th' east an' west sides while yo're settin' yore posts an' tampin' 'em."

"An I'll have mine set while you fellers git ready to start on yer roosts," boasted Murphy, grabbing the spade and starting to work. Jane Saunders, who had come up unobserved, suddenly stuffed her handkerchief in her mouth and fled back to the house.

There ensued great hammering and frantic dirt throwing. Tex and his companion were hampered by mirth and were only building the last nest when Murphy stuck his head in the door.

"Ye wouldn't last in no gang av mine!" he jeered. "I got me holes dug an' th' posts set. Set 'em single-handed an' they're true as a plumb line."

"All right, Murphy," said Tommy without looking up. "Run along an' do th' other two while we're finishin' up. It's gettin' late."

"Tryin' to lay it onto me, eh?" demanded Murphy. "You an' yer two post holes! Ye must think--" he stopped short, thought a moment, and then slyly glanced out at the unfinished sides of the enclosure. "Hivin save us!" he muttered and slipped out without another word.

Tommy wiped his eyes and leaned against the wall for support. "Four sides," he babbled. "Three to a side: that's a dozen holes to dig! He will make smart remarks about my thirteen nests, will he?"

"Figures don't lie, an' logic is logic," laughed Tex. "Reckon we can't finish th' fence today; but it don't make no difference, anyhow. Them chickens are as safe in th' toolshed as they'd be up here. Did you close th' doors when you left?" he demanded anxiously.

"Yes; too many hungry, stray dogs around. I'd liked to 'a' gone to th' finish with you boys, but I got to get back to th' ranch. Climb up behind me an' I'll let you off at th' hotel."

"I'll wait for Murphy," replied Tex. "He'll mebby need help about somethin'. I'm cussed glad to know you, Watkins; an' I've shore had a circus today."

"You pulled me out of a bad hole, Tex; an' you shore as shootin' dug one for yoreself. This town's run by th' miners, a lot of hoof-poundin' grubs, with pack mules for pardners. There's been feelin's between us an' them walkin' fools," here he voiced the riders' contempt for men who walked, "for a long time. Yo're a puncher, an' you shore come out flat an' took sides today. Tell you what--either you come out to th' ranch with me, or I'll stay here in town with you. Come along: we'll find you a good cayuse, an' not rob you, neither."

"Can't do it, Tommy," replied Tex, warming to his new acquaintance. "I got my eye on a roan beauty an' I'm goin' to own him by tomorrow. He won't cost me a red cent. So far's danger is concerned, I ain't in none that my tongue or my six-gun can't get me out of. But I'll ride out an' pay yore outfit a visit after I get th' roan."

"That's th' third best cayuse in this section," replied Tommy. "Williams owns all three of 'em, too. There ain't nothin' on th' ranch that can touch any of 'em." He paused and looked closely at his companion. "You heard any war-talk ag'in' th' agent?"

"Only a rumblin', far off," answered Tex. "Th' dust ain't plain yet, so I can't tell how it's headin'. What do you know about it?"

"Not half as much as Murphy, I bet," replied Watkins. "You ask him. It's a cussed shame for a man to be hounded by a pack of dogs. Well, I'm off. Remember that you got friends on th' C Bar when you need 'em, which you shore as shootin' will. We'll come a-runnin'." He shook hands and went out, Tex loafing after him as far as the door. "Tim, I reckon you an' Tex can manage to get along without me now, so I'll drift along. I'm due at th' ranch."

"Whose?" asked Murphy carelessly, trying a post to see if it was well set.

"Julius Caesar Curtis: Judy, for short," answered Watkins, holding out his hand. "You can leave th' other four posts for me to set when I come in again," he grinned.

"For a bye's-sized chew av tobaccy I'd skin ye," chuckled Tim, shaking the hand heartily. "Much obliged, Thomas, me son. Come in an' see us when ye can. There's so few decent men in this part av th' country that ye'll be welcome as th' flowers av spring."

Tommy swung into the saddle, raised his hat to the woman who appeared in the kitchen door, and whirled around to leave.

"Mr. Watkins!" called Jane, running toward the little group. "You are not going to leave without your supper? Your place is set and Jerry is pouring the coffee."

Tommy Watkins flushed, swallowed his Adam's apple, looked blankly at Tex and Tim, stammered gibberish, and managed to convey the impression that the salvation of the ranch and its outfit depended on his immediate departure. His mute appeal for moral support was coldly received by his fellow-builders.

"I do not wish to be rude, Mr. Watkins," smiled Jane, "and I would not wish to turn you from your duty: but I shall be a little disappointed if you won't allow me to show my poor appreciation of what you have done for us. But I will not press you: if not tonight, then some other time?"

The savior of the C Bar flushed deeper, received scowling looks from his late bosom companions, who knew a liar when they heard one, and he ducked his head quickly. "Yes, ma'am," he blurted eagerly. "I'd admire to stay, but Curtis shore is dependin' on me to git back. If you'll excuse me, ma'am--I--so--by," and he was whirling away in a cloud of dust, his sombrero held out at arm's length.

Murphy looked gravely at Tex and flushed slightly. "He has an important job, miss," he said.

Tex looked gravely at Murphy and did not flush. "A great weight for shoulders so young," he lied, suspecting, however, that Tommy might have acquired, during the course of the day, a very great weight, indeed. He had observed his glances at Jane.

She smiled inscrutably and turned to look at the coop, clapping her hands in delight. "Isn't it fine, and new, and piney!" she exclaimed, sniffing the tangy odor. "And it looks so strong--I must peek in for a moment."

There was not much room to spare when they all had entered, a fact which Tex easily explained.

"You see, Miss Saunders," he said, waving his hands, "it is to serve only as a nesting place and a shelter from predatory animals. During the day your flock will roam about the enclosure outside; but at twilight, without fail, it must be confined securely in this coop. No self-respecting coyote will be restrained for five minutes by the wire--he either will force himself between the strands, or dig under; and there are any number of those thieves around this town. They cannot be trapped or baffled--they will outwait or outwit any watcher. The only thing that will stop them is something physically impregnable.

"Tim and I intend to weave slats and laths between the lower strands of wire, running them vertically up from the ground, in which their lower ends will be driven. They will offer some protection, but their chief value will be to keep the chickens from getting outside. No coyote will be bothered by them for very long, and in order to save yourself the labor of filling up the tunnels they surely will dig if they can get in in no other way, I'd advise you to leave the fence gate wide open every night.

"We lay this floor for that reason. No matter what they are able to do, they can't get into the coop. I'll wager that you will find tunnels running under it before long. Don't fail to close this building before nightfall, and your flock will be safe."

"Amen," said Murphy. "They're cunnin' divvils, coyotes are!"

"I don't know how to thank you," said Jane, impulsively putting her hands on the arms of her companions. "Think what it will mean to Jerry--a dozen fresh eggs a day!"

Murphy chuckled. "Four a day will be doin' good, an' not that many for awhile. I'll get ye some grit, an' make a batch av whitewash."

"Hey!" called a voice. "Everything's getting cold!"

"There's Jerry, playing domestic tyrant," laughed Jane. "Isn't it remarkable what a difference it makes to the cook? He thinks nothing of making me wait. Come on--you can tell me all about chicken raising after supper." She cast a furtive glance at Tex, and past him at the twilight-softened range beyond, where Tommy Watkins somewhere rode to save his ranch and outfit.

Chapter V
A Trimmer Trimmed

About ten o'clock that night Murphy and Tex neared the station and stopped short at the former's sudden ejaculation.

"Th' switch is open," he said. "Not that anythin' serious might happen, unless th' engineer went blind; but either av them would have plenty to say about it. Trust 'em for that. An' tomorrow is Overton's trick east-bound. He's worse than Casey. Wait here a bit," and the section-boss went over, threw the switch, and returned.

Soon they stopped again at the station to say good night to each other. Murphy seemed a little constrained and worried and soon gave the reason for it.

"Tex," he said in a low voice, "yer takin' sides with th' weakest party, an' yer takin' 'em fast an' open. Right now yer bein' weighed an' discussed, an' to no profit to yerself. I can see that yer a man that will go his own way--but if th' hotel gets unpleasant an' tirin', yer more than welcome in my shanty. 'Tis only an old box car off its wheels, but there's a bunk in it for ye any time ye want to use it. Tread easy now, an' keep yer two eyes open; an' while I'm willin' to back ye up, I daren't do it unless it's a matter av life an' death. I'm Irish, an' so is Costigan. There's a strong feelin' out here ag'in' us--an' when a mob starts not even wimmin an' childer are safe. Costigan has both, an' there's th' lass, as well. I've urged Mike to send his family back along th' line somewhere, but his wife says *no* . She's foolish, no doubt, but I say, God bless such wimmin."

"She's not foolish," replied Tex with conviction. "She's wise, riskin' herself mebby, on a long chance. While she stays here Costigan will use a lot of discretion--if she goes, he might air his opinions too much, or get drunk and leave her a widow. I'll do what I can to stave off trouble, even to eatin' a little dirt; but, Tim, I'd like nothing better than to send for a few friends an' let things take their natural course. Every time I look at that nephew I fair itch to strangle him. It can't be possible that Miss Saunders gives him any encouragement? I'm much obliged about yore offer. I'd take it up right now except that it would cause a lot of talk an' thinkin'. Here, you better hand me two dollars for my day's work--there ain't no use lyin' about anythin' if th' truth will serve. I'll return it th' next time I see you."

"Th' lass won't look at that scut. He follers her around like a dog," Murphy growled, and then a grin came to his face as he dug into his pocket. "Here. Yer overpaid, but I should 'a' dickered with ye before I let ye go to work."

"Thanks, boss," chuckled Tex. "You'll need me tomorrow, for th' wire stringin'?"

"Yer fired!" answered Murphy, his voice rising and changing in timbre. "Yer a loafin', windy, clumsy, bunglin' no-account. By rights that ought to make ye mad. Does it?"

Tex could not fail to read the answer he was expected to make, for it lay in the section-boss' tones; and he thought that he had seen something move around the corner of the station. He stepped on the toe of one of his companion's boots to acknowledge the warning.

"Am I?" he demanded, angrily. "Yo're so d--d used to bossin' Irish loafers that you don't know a good man when you see one. You don't have to fire me, you Mick! I'm quittin', an' you can go to h--l!"

Murphy's arm stopped in mid-air as Tex's gun leaped from its sheath.

"You checked it just in time," snapped Tex. "Any more of that an' I'll blow you wide open. Turn around an' hoof it to yore sty!"

Murphy, strangling a chuckle, backed warily away. "If ye was as handy with tools as ye are with that d--d gun--" he growled. "'Tis lucky for ye that ye have it!"

"This is my tool," retorted Tex. "Shut up an' get out before you make me use it. Fire me, hey? You got one ---- ---- gall!"

He stood staring after the shuffling Irishman, muttering savagely to himself, until the section-boss had been swallowed up by the darkness. Then he turned, slammed the gun back into its holster and stamped toward the hotel; but he stopped in the nearest saloon to give the eavesdropper, if there had been one, a chance to get to the hotel before him.

The bar was deserted, but half a dozen prospectors were seated at the tables, and they greeted his entrance with scowls. The two cavalrymen present glanced at him in disinterested, momentary curiosity and resumed their maudlin conversation. Some shavetail's ears must have been burning out at their post.

Tex stormed up to the bar and slammed two silver dollars on it. "Take this dirty money an' give th' boys cigars for it," he growled. "Me, I'm not smokin' any of 'em. Fire me, huh? I'd like to see th' section-boss that fires me! 'Overpaid,' he says, an' me workin' like a dog! 'I don't need ye tomorry,' he says: I cussed soon told him what he needed, but he didn't wait for it. Fire me?" he sneered. "Like h--l!"

The cavalrymen grinned sympathetically and nodded their thanks for the cigars, which they had no little difficulty in lighting. The other men in the room took their gifts silently, two of them abruptly pushing them across the table, away from them.

"There'll be others that'll mebby git what they're needin'," said a rasping, unsteady voice from a corner table. "'Specially if he sticks his nose in where it ain't wanted."

Tex casually turned and nodded innocently. "My sentiments exactly," he agreed, waiting to receive unequivocal notification that it was he for whom the warning was meant. A little stupidity was often a useful thing.

"Nobody asked you for yore sentiments," retorted the prospector. "Strangers can't come into this town an' carry things with a high hand. Next time, Jake will kill you."

Tex looked surprised and then his eyes glinted. "That bein' a little job he can start 'most any time," he retorted. "When a man fights worse'n a dog he makes me mad; an' he fought like a cur. I'd do it ag'in. He got what he was needin', that's all."

The miner glowered at him. "An' he's got friends, Jake has," he asserted.

"Tell him that he'll need 'em--all of 'em," sneered Tex. "Our little session was plumb personal, but I'll let in his friends. Th' gate's wide open. They don't have to dig in under th' fence, or sit on their haunches outside an' howl. An' let me tell you somethin' for yore personal benefit--I've swallered all I aim to swaller tonight. I'm peaceable an' not lookin' for no trouble--you hold yore yap till I get through talkin'--but I ain't dodgin' none. Somehow I seem to be out of step in this town; but I'm whistlin' that I'm cussed particular about who sets me right. I ain't got no grudges ag'in' nobody; I'm tryin' to act accordin' to my lights, but I ain't apologizin' to nobody for them lights. Anybody objectin'?"

"Fair enough," said one of the cavalrymen. "I like his frank ways."

"That rides for me, too," endorsed his companion, aggressively.

"Shut up, you!" cried the bartender.

"For two bits--" pugnaciously began a miner, but he was cut short.

"An' you, too!" barked the man behind the counter, a gun magically appearing over the edge of the bar. "This has gone far enough! Stranger, you spoke yore piece fair. Tom," he said, looking at the angry miner, "you got nothin' more to say: yo're all through. If you think you has, then go outside an' shout it there. Th' subject is closed. What'll you-all have?"

Tex tarried after the round had been drunk but he did not order one on his own account, feeling that it would be a mistake under the circumstances. It might be regarded as a sign of weakness, and was almost certain to cause trouble. Turning his back on the sullen miner he talked casually with the bartender and the cavalrymen, and then one of the miners cleared his throat and spoke.

"Did you have a run-in with th' big Irishman?" he asked.

Tex leaned carelessly against the bar, grinned and frankly recounted the affair, and before he had finished the narrative, answering grins appeared here and there among his audience. The sputter of a sulphur match caught his eye as his late adversary slowly reached for and lit the cigar he had pushed from him a few minutes earlier, but Tex did not immediately glance that way. When he had finished the story he looked around the room, noticed that all were smoking and he nodded slightly in friendly understanding. A little later he said good night, smiled pleasantly at the once sullen prospector, and went carelessly out into the night. The buzz of comment following his departure was not unfavorable to him.

When he entered the hotel barroom all eyes turned to him, and he noticed a grim smile on Williams' face and that the evil countenance of the nephew was aquiver with suspicion. Walking over, he stepped close to the table, watching the play, and from where he could keep tabs on Bud Haines' every move. During the new deal Williams leaned back, stretched, and glanced up.

"Had yore supper?" he carelessly asked.

Tex nodded. "Shore: reg'lar home-cooked feed. It went good for a change. I reckon I shore earned it, too." He drew out a sack of tobacco, filled a cigarette paper and held the sack in his teeth while he rolled himself a smoke. "What's paid around here for a good, half-day's work?" he mumbled between his teeth.

"What kind of work?" judicially asked Williams.

Tex removed the sack, moistened the cigarette and held it unlighted while he answered. "Freightin' on foot, carpenterin', diggin', an' doin' what I was told to do."

"Dollar to a dollar four bits," replied Williams. "What you doin'? Hirin' out?"

"I was; but I ain't no more," replied Tex, lighting up. He exhaled a lungful of smoke and dragged up a chair. "I asked two dollars, an' there was an argument. That's all."

The hands lay where they had been dealt, Williams having let his own lay, and the players were idly listening until he should pick it up.

"What's it all about?" asked Williams. "You talk like a dish of hash."

The eager nephew squirmed closer to the table and his assumed look of indifference was a heavy failure.

Tex laughed, leaned back, and with humorous verbal pigments painted a rapidly changing picture to the best of his by no means poor ability. He took them up to the digging of the post holes, and then leaned forward. "Murphy said we'd build a four-sided fence, three posts to th' side, makin twelve in all. That suited us, an' as there was only one spade, we told him to go ahead an' dig his holes while we worked on th' nest boxes. He was to do th' north an' th' south sides, which he said was fair." The speaker paused a moment, leaning back in his chair, his eyelids nearly closed. Between their narrowed openings he looked swiftly around. The card players grinned in expectation of some joke about to appear, Williams looked suspicious and puzzled, but the bartender's eyes popped open and he choked back a sudden burst of laughter. Tex drew in a long breath, pushed back into his chair and glanced around at the players. "I was honest an' fair enough to say th' diggin' wasn't evenly divided, us bein' two an' him only one. What do you boys say?"

"What's it all amount to anyhow?" snarled the nephew. "Who cares if it was or not? What did you think of th' gal?" he demanded.

Tex breathed deeply, relaxed, and gravely considered his boots. "Well, if I was aimin' to start a kindergarten I might have took more notice cf her--an' you, too, bub. Can't you do yore own lookin'?" he plaintively demanded. "Anyhow, I was warned fair, wasn't I? Huh! When you get to be my age an' have had my experience with this fool world you won't be takin' no more interest in 'em than I do. Beggin' yore pardon for interruptin' th' previous conversation we was holdin'. I'll perceed from where I was." He looked back at the card players. "We was debatin' th' fairness of th' offer to dig them holes. What you boys say?"

The man nearest to him pursed his lips and cogitated. The subject was no more frivolous than the majority of subjects which had furnished bones of contention many a night. Most barroom arguments start on even less. "I reckon it was, him bein' more used to diggin'."

His partner leaned forward. "What did he say about it, at first?"

"He was shore satisfied," answered Tex as the bartender, turning his back on the room, shook with the ague.

The last questioner bobbed his head decisively. "Then it shore was fair."

Williams nodded slowly, for his opinions were not lightly given. "I'd say it was. What about it?"

"Oh, nothin' much," growled Tex. "I reckon he changed his mind later on." He looked over at the gambler leaning against the wall, the same gambler he had seen on the train. At this notice Denver Jim, sensing possible bets, straightened up, winked, and made a sign which among his class was a notification that he had declared himself in for half the winnings of a game. Tex shook his head slightly and frowned, as if deeply puzzled over Murphy's conduct. The gambler repeated the sign and moved forward.

Tex did some quick thinking. He could not afford to be linked to a tin-horn and he did not intend to make any money out of his joke. Whatever he won in this town he would win at cards, and win it alone. His second signal of refusal was backed up by his hand dropping carelessly and resting on the butt of his gun. The gambler scowled, barely nodded his acquiescence and went to the bar for a drink. Bud Haines glanced up from the weekly paper he was reading, saw nothing to hold his interest, and returned to his reading.

Tex went on with his story, telling about the supper and his scene with Murphy at the station, repeating the latter word for word as nearly as he could from the time when he had detected the approach of the eavesdropper. From the constantly repeated looks of satisfaction on Williams' face he knew that the local boss had been given a detailed account of the incident, and that he was checking it up, step by step. Briefly sketching his trouble in the saloon, Tex threw the cigarette butt at a distant box cuspidor and stretched. "An' here I am," he finished.

Williams picked up his hand, glancing absent-mindedly at the cards. "Yes," he grunted, "here you are." Putting the cards back on the table he carelessly pushed them from him, squaring the edges with zealous care. "You come near not bein' here, though," he said, his level look steady and accusing. "Whatever made you jump on Jake that way?" he demanded coldly.

"Shucks! Here it comes again!" said Tex. He looked suspicious and defiant. "I did it to stop a murder, an' a lynchin'," he answered shortly.

"Very fine!" muttered Williams. "You was a little mite overanxious--there wouldn't 'a' been no lynchin' of Jake; but there might 'a' been one, just th' same. I had to do some real talkin' to stop it. It ain't wise for strangers to act sudden in a frontier town--'specially in this town. That's somethin' you hadn't ought to forget, Mr. Jones."

"If I get yore meanin' plain, yo're intendin' me to think I was in danger of bein' lynched?"

"You shore was."

"Then yo're admittin' that this town of Windsor will lynch a man because he keeps a murder from bein' committed, by lickin' th' man who tried to do it?"

"Exactly. Jake has lots of friends."

"He's plumb welcome to 'em, an' I reckon, if he's that kind of a man, he shore needs 'em bad. But from what I saw of Jake he ain't that kind of a man. I'm a friend of his'n, too. I'm so much a friend of Jake's that if he treads on my toes I'll save him from facin' th' trials an' hardships that come with old age. His existence is precarious, anyhow. He's allus just one step ahead of poverty an' grub stakes. Life for Jake is just one placer disappointment after another. He allus has to figger on a hard winter. Then he has to dodge sickness an' saddles, wrestlin' tricks, boxin' tricks, an' fast gunplay. But Jake is th' kind of a man that does his own fightin' for hisself. Yo're plumb mistaken about him."

"Mebby I am," admitted Williams. "I didn't know you was acquainted with anybody around here, 'specially th' C Bar outfit."

"I wasn't," replied Tex. "It ain't my nature to be distant an' disdainful, however." He grinned. "I get acquainted fast."

"You acted prompt in helpin' that Watkins," accused Williams.

"I shore had to, or he'd 'a' quit bein' Watkins," retorted Tex. "You look here: We'll be savin' a lot of time if we come right down to cases. I saw a big man tryin' to kick th' head off another man, a smaller one, that was down. I stopped him from doin' it without hurtin' him serious. If it'd been th' other way 'round I'd done th' same thing. As it stands, it's between Jake an' me. We'll let it stay that way until th' lynchin' party starts out. Then anybody will be plumb welcome to cut in an' stop it. Excuse me for interferin' with yore game--but th' fault ain't mine. Talkin' is dry work--bartender, set 'em up for all hands. Who's winnin'?"

Williams picked up his cards again, looked at them, puckered his lips and glanced around at his companions. He cleared his throat and looked back at Tex. "I reckon I was, a little. Want to sit in? After all, Jake's troubles are his own: we got enough without 'em."

Tex looked at the table and the players, shrugged his shoulders and answered carelessly. "Don't feel like playin' very much--ate too much supper, I reckon. Later on, when I ain't so heavy with grub, mebby I'll take cards. I'd rather play ag'in' fewer hands, tonight, anyhow."

Williams looked up and sneered. "Think you got a better chance, that way?"

"I get sort of confused when there's so many playin'," confessed Tex; "but I shore can beat th' man that invented th' game, playin' it two-handed. I used to play for hosses, two-hand. Allus had luck, somehow, playin' for them. Why, once I owned six cayuses at one time, that I'd won."

"That so? You like that gray: how much will you put up ag'in' him?"

"I wouldn't play for no gray hoss--they're plumb unlucky with me. I ain't superstitious, but I shore don't like gray hosses."

"Got anythin' ag'in' sorrels?" Williams asked with deep sarcasm.

"Nothin' much; but I'm shore stuck on blacks an roans. I call them hosses!" Tex grinned at the crowd and looked back at Williams. "Yes, sir; I shore do."

"How much will you put up ag'in' a good roan, then?"

"Ain't got much money," evaded Tex, backing away.

"Got two hundred dollars?"

"Not for no cayuse. Besides, I don't know th' hoss yo're meanin'."

"That roan you saw today," replied Williams. "John said you liked him a lot. I'll play you one hand, th' roan, ag'in' two hundred."

Tex glanced furtively at the front door and then at the stairway. "Let it go till tomorrow night," he mumbled.

"Yo're a great talker, ain't you?" sneered Williams. "I'll put up th' roan ag'in' a hundred an' fifty. One hand, just me an' you."

"Well, mebby," replied Tex. "Better make her th' best two out of three. I might have bad luck th' first hand."

Williams' disgust was obvious and a snicker ran through the room. "I wouldn't play that long for a miserable sum like that ag'in' a stranger. One hand, draw poker, my roan ag'in' yore one-fifty. Put up, or shut up!"

"All right," reluctantly acquiesced Tex. "We allus used to make it two out of three up my way; but I may be lucky. After you get through--I ain't in no hurry."

Williams laughed contemptuously: "You shore don't have to say so!" He smiled at his grinning companions and resumed his play.

Tex dropped into the seat next to the sneering nephew, from where he could watch the gun-fighter. Bud's expression duplicated that of his boss and he paid but little attention to the wordy fool who was timid about playing poker for a horse.

"Hot, ain't it?" said Tex pleasantly. "Hot, an' close."

"Some folks find it so; reckon mebby it is," answered the nephew. "What did you people talk about at supper?" he asked.

"Hens," answered Tex, grinning. "She's got a dozen. You'd think they was rubies, she's that stuck up about 'em. Kind of high-toned, ain't she?"

The nephew laughed sneeringly. "She'll lose that," he promised. "I don't aim to be put off much longer."

"Mebby yo're callin' too steady," suggested Tex. "Sometimes that gives 'em th' idea they own a man. You don't want to let 'em feel too shore of you."

Henry Williams shifted a little. "No," he replied; "I ain't callin' too often. In fact, I ain't done no callin' at all, yet. I've sort of run acrost her on th' right-of-way, an' watched her a little. I get a little bit scary, somehow--just can't explain it. But I aim to call at th' house, for I'm shore gettin' tired of ridin' wide."

"Ain't they smart, though?" chuckled Tex; "holdin' back an' actin' skittish. I cured a gal of that, once; but I don't reckon you can do it. It takes a lot of nerve an' will-power. You feel like playin' show-downs, two-bits a game?"

"Make it a dollar, an' I will. How'd you cure that one of yourn?"

"Dollar's purty steep," objected Tex. "Make it a half." He leaned back and laughed reminiscently. "I worked a system on her. Lemme deal first?"

"Suit yourself. Turn 'em face up--it'll save time. What did you do?"

"Made her think I didn't care a snap about her. Want to cut? Well, I didn't know--some don't want to," he explained. "Saves time, that's all. Reckon it's yore pot on that queen. Deal 'em up."

"How'd you do it? snub her?"

"Gosh, no! Don't you ever do that: it makes 'em mad. Just let 'em alone--sort of look at 'em without seein' 'em real well. You dassn't make 'em mad! You win ag'in. Yo're lucky at this game: want to quit?"

"Give you a chance to get it back," sneered the nephew. "Think it would work with her?"

"Don't know: she got any other beaux?"

"I've seen to that. She ain't. Take th' money an' push over yore cards. Do you think it will work with her?" Henry persisted.

"Gosh, sonny: don't you ask me that! No man knows very much about wimmin', an' me less than most men. It's a gamble. She's got to jump one way or th' other, ain't she? How was you figgerin' to win?"

"Just go get her, that's all. She'll tame down after awhile."

"But you allus can do that, can't you? Now, if it was me I'd try to get her to come of her own accord, for things would be sweeter right at th' very start. But, then, I'm a gambler, allus willin' to run a risk. A man's got to foller his own nature. I got you beat ag'in: this shore is a nice game."

"Too weak," objected the nephew. "Dollar a hand would suit me better. My eights win this. Want to boost her?"

Tex reflected covetously. "Well, I might go high as a dollar, but not no more."

"Dollar it is, then. What's yore opinion of that gal?"

"Shucks," laughed Tex. "She's nice enough, I reckon; but she ain't my style. Yore uncle's game is bustin' up an' he's lookin' at me. See you later. You win ag'in, but I allus have bad luck doublin' th' stakes, 'though I ain't what you might call superstitious. See you later."

Tex arose and went over to the other table, raked in the cards, squared them to feel if they had been trimmed, thought they had been, and pushed them out for the cut, watching closely to see how the face cards had been shaved. Williams turned the pack, announced that high dealt, grasped the sides of the pack and turned a queen. Tex also grasped the sides of the pack remaining and also turned a queen. He clumsily dropped the deck, growled something and bunched it again, shoving it toward his companion in such a way that Williams would have to show a deliberate preference for the side grip. This he did and Tex followed his lead. The ends of the face cards and aces had been trimmed and the sides of the rest of the deck had been treated the same way. Because of this the sides of the face cards stuck out from the deck and the ends of the spot cards projected. Yet so carefully had it been done that it was not noticeable. Williams cut again, turning another queen. Tex cut a king and picked up the pack. As he shuffled he was careful not to show any of his characteristic motions, for although his opponent had forgotten his face in the score of years behind their former meeting, it might take but very little to start his memory backtracking.

"My money ag'in' th' roan," said the dealer, pushing out the cards for the cut. "Hundred an' fifty," he explained.

Williams cut deep and nodded. "This one game decides it: a discard, a draw, an' a showdown. Right?"

"Right," grunted Tex, swiftly dropping the cards before them. Williams picked up his hand, but gave no sign of his disappointment. There was not a face card in it. He made his selection, discarded, and called for three cards. Tex had discarded two. Williams wanted no face cards on the draw, since he held a pair of nines. One more nine would give him a fair hand, and another would just about win for him. He drew a black queen and a pair of red jacks.

"Well," he said, "ready to show?"

Tex grunted again, glanced at Bud Haines, and lay down three queens, a nine, and a jack. "What you got?" he anxiously asked.

"An empty box stall, I reckon," growled his adversary, spreading his hand. He pushed back without another word to Tex, looked at his stableman and spoke gruffly. "John, give that roan to Mr. Jones when he calls for it. He's to keep it somewhere else. I'm turnin' in. Good night, all."

Chapter VI

Friendly Interest

Freshly shaven, his boots well rubbed, and his clothes as free from dust as possible, Tex sauntered down the street after breakfast the next morning and stepped into the stable. John Graves met him, nodded, and led the way to the roan's stall.

"You got a fine hoss, Mr. Jones," he said, opening the gate.

"Yes, I have; an' you've taken good care of him. His coat couldn't be better. I like a man that looks after a hoss."

"I ain't sayin' nothin' about nobody, but I'm glad to see him change owners," said Graves, glancing around. "Rub yore hand on his flank. I got th' coat so it hides 'em real well."

Tex stroked the white nose, rubbed the neck and shoulders, and slowly passed his hand over the flank. The scars were easily found. He wheeled and looked at the stableman. "Who in h--l did that, an' why?" he demanded.

"That ain't for me to say, an' sayin' wouldn't do no good; but I'm plumb glad he's in other hands. Just because a hoss fights back when he's bein' abused ain't no reason to cut him to pieces. An' a big man can kick hard when he's mad."

Tex held a lump of sugar to the sensitive, velvety lips before replying. "Yes, he can," he admitted. "Anybody in town that'll treat this hoss right, an' give him a stall?"

"Better see Jim Carney in his saloon. He's a good, reliable man an' likes hosses. He'll take good care of Oh My."

Tex stared at him. "Of what?"

"Oh My," replied the stableman. "Th' rest of th' name is Cayenne."

"'Suffer little children!'" exclaimed Tex. "Who named him that, an why?"

"I reckon Williams did, because he's peppery an' red."

"Good heavens!" ejaculated Tex. He thought a moment. "Huh! Prophet! Mecca! Mohammed!" he muttered. Suddenly seeing a great light, he flipped his sombrero into the air, caught and balanced it on his nose when it came down, sidestepped, and as it fell, punched it across the stable. Turning gravely he shook hands with the surprised stableman, slapped him on the shoulder and burst out laughing. "Where'n blazes did he dig 'em up? He don't know what one of them names means; *There was the Veil through which I might not see* . Come, John: *Oh, many a Cup of this forbidden Wine must drown the memory of that insolence!* Wait till I get my hat: *Better be jocund with the fruitful Grape than sadden after none, or bitter, Fruit.* "

Carney gave them a nonchalant welcome and displayed little interest in them until Graves told him about the horse.

"Th' roan, eh?" exclaimed the saloonkeeper. "I'll shore find a place for it, but I'm afraid it'll miss th' beatin's. There's a closet built across one corner of th' stable: I'll give you a key to it, Mr. Jones. It'll be handy for yore trappin's."

After a few rounds Tex went out, mounted bareback and, leaving Graves in front of the stable, rode to the hotel to get his saddle. Soon thereafter he dismounted at the station and smiled at the agent.

"'Richard is himself again,'" he chuckled, affectionately patting Omar. "An' I still have my kingdom."

"He looks fit for a king to ride," replied Jerry.

"He'd honor a king. How's th' hen ranch comin' along? Got th' fence up yet?"

"Yes; Murphy just finished it. That looks like Williams' roan."

"It was. I won it at poker. I could feel in my fingers that I was goin' to be lucky. Hello!" he exclaimed, looking at a box across the track. On it were painted irregular, concentric circles. "Looks like it might be a target."

Jerry laughed. "It is; and so far, unhit."

Tex glanced at the other's low-hung belt and gun. "Have you shot at it yet?"

Jerry nodded.

"From where?"

"Right here."

"Great mavericks!" said Tex. "Here: let's see how fast you can get that gun out, an' empty it at that box. I got a reason for it."

At the succession of reports the toolshed door flew open and a huge Irishman, rifle in hand, popped into sight. Seeing Tex he grunted and slowly went back again.

Tex looked from the box to the marksman, shook his head, silently unbuckled the belt from its owner's waist, took the empty gun from the agent's hand, and tossed the outfit on a near-by box.

"Don't you carry it, Jerry," he said. "Load it up an' leave it home. Popular feelin', even in this town, frowns at th' shootin' of an unarmed man. It's somethin' that's hard to explain away."

"But then I'll be defenseless!" expostulated Jerry, "It's some protection."

"You were defenseless before I took it from you," said Tex.

"But it is some protection," Jerry reiterated.

Tex shook his head. "It's a screaming invitation for a killin', that's what it is. Here: That's you," pointing to the target. "You got somethin' I want plumb bad. You try to stop me from gettin' it, an' I won't listen to you. I force th' hand an' you make a move that I can claim was hostile. Yo're armed, ain't you? I might even slap yore face. Then this happens."

The spurting smoke enveloped them both, the stabs of flame and the sharp reports coming with unbelievable rapidity. Stepping from the gray fog, Tex pointed. The box was split and turned part way around. The inner two circles showed six holes.

"I did it in self-defense. What chance did you have?" demanded the puncher.

"Great guns! What shooting!" marveled Jerry, his mouth open.

"That's good shootin'," admitted Tex. "Better, mebby, than most men in this town can do, quite a lot better than th' average. There's plenty of men who can't do as good. Th' draw was more'n fair, too; better than most gun-toters; but I know two men that would 'a' killed me before I jerked loose from th' leather. I wasn't showin' off: I was answerin' yore remark about a gun bein' some protection to you. While we're speakin' about guns, can Miss Saunders use one? Bein' a woman I hardly thought so, unless Hennery has taught her."

"Henry!" growled Jerry. "Why would he teach her?"

"Why a young woman like her would be right popular, out here, or anywhere else," replied Tex. "House full of admirers, an' others taggin' along. I reckoned Hennery might have showed her how to shoot."

"The devil had a better chance," retorted Jerry. "If Henry ever calls at our house she'll scald him. She thinks about as little of Henry as she does of a snake."

"I'm admirin' Miss Saunders more every day," said Tex. "Havin' disposed of th' interpolation, we'll get at th' main subject. As I was sayin', bein' a woman, she's not likely to be shot at. But I'm sorry yore Colt is so big: she couldn't drag a gun like that around with her. Besides, th' caliber needn't be so big."

"I got a short-barreled .38 home," said Jerry. He looked a little worried. "What makes you talk like that?"

"Bein' a gunman, I reckon; an' my ornery, suspicious nature," answered Tex. "Bein' a poker player for years, readin' faces is a hobby with me. I've read some in this town that I don't like. 'Taint nothin' to put a finger on, but I'm so cussed suspicious of every male biped of th' genus homo that I allus look for th' worst. Anyhow, it wouldn't be no crime if Miss Saunders knew how to use that snub-nosed .38, would it? Sort of give her a sense of security. Then, if Murphy or our adolescent Watkins took her out ridin' an showed her how to get th' most out of its limited possibilities, it ought to relieve yore mind."

"I don't know of anyone better qualified to get the most out of a gun than yourself," replied Jerry. "If it ain't asking too much," he hastily added.

"Havin' a brand-new, Cayenne pepper cayuse to learn about, an' show off," laughed Tex, "it wouldn't set on me like a calamity. Shall I bring a horse for Miss Saunders, or saddle up her own?"

"She hasn't any; but——"

"—me no buts," interrupted Tex. "I'll now pay my respects to yore sister, with yore permission, an' invite her to ride out with me, tomorrow, an' view th' lovely brown hills an' dusty flats, where every prospect pleases, an' only man is vile. Procrastination never was a sin of mine: it's th' one I overlooked. We'll likely go far enough from town so there won't be no panicky fears of a hostile raid. Does Miss Saunders favor any particular hoss?"

"No, and she can ride, so you won't have to get one that's nearly dead."

Tex laughed. "All right; but when she gets it, it won't be as ornery as it might be. How is it that nobody but Murphy paid any attention to our shootin'?"

"They're used to it by this time."

"Well, so-long," and Tex swung into the saddle and rode off.

Jane showed her pleasure at his visit and smilingly accepted his invitation to go riding. They examined the coop and yard, talked of numerous things and after awhile Tex turned to leave, but stopped and grinned.

"Bring your six-gun, Miss Saunders, and we'll have a match," he said. "The great western target, the ubiquitous tin can, is sure to be plentiful, despite the killing drought."

"My gun?" she laughed. "I have no gun. Do you think that I go around with a gun?"

He tapped his forehead significantly. "I'm so used to carrying one that I forgot. Shucks, that's too bad. Well, if we overtake any wild cans you can use mine, although a smaller gun would be more pleasant for you. Too bad you haven't a short-barreled gun--a .32, for instance. Shooting is really great sport. Then I'm to call at two o'clock?"

"If there was some place where we could enjoy a lunch," she murmured. "We could leave earlier and get back earlier."

"There is sure to be," assured Tex, smiling. "Say ten o'clock, then?"

"That will be much better. I'll have everything ready when you come. Is there anything in the eating line which you particularly fancy?"

Tex fanned himself with the sombrero, a happy expression on his face. "Yes, there is," he admitted. "Mallard duck stuffed with Chesapeake oysters. Plenty of cold, crisp, tender celery, and any really good brand of dry champagne. I'll enjoy anything you prepare, and I'll have a round-up appetite."

"I'll try to give you a change from hotel food," she laughed as he swung into the saddle.

She watched him ride away and walked slowly back to the house. Then her face brightened a little as she thought of the revolver in Jerry's room. Jerry had said it was a .38.

The station agent answered the hail and went out to the edge of the platform.

"All fixed?" he asked.

Tex nodded. "You get her to bring that gun. I paved the way for it, but you know her better than I do, and how to persuade her without making her frightened. What's it shoot: longs, or shorts? That's good; shorts are O.K. Is Murphy in th' toolshed?"

"He's married to it," smiled Jerry.

"If you see him, tell him I'm goin' to call on him late tonight. If his light's *out* I'll know he's home. Any fool would know it if it was lit. Well, so-long."

Jerry looked after him and shook his head, a peculiar, baffled, friendly light in his eyes. "I don't know when you are most serious: when you are serious, or when, you are joking. Was your warning about my gun just a general one, or did it have a special meaning? And about Jane learning to shoot? What do you know, how much do you know, and why are you bothering about us? The Heathen Chinee was simple beside you, Tex Jones."

He coughed and turned to enter the station, but stopped in his tracks as a possible solution came to him. "I wonder, now," he cogitated, and fell into the vernacular. "She's a fine girl, sis is; but headstrong. Cuss it, if it ain't one thing it's another. I don't even know his name is Jones, or how many wives he may have. Oh, well: I'll have to wait and see how it heads."

Tex rode slowly down the street, very well satisfied with himself. He had warned the agent, owned a fine horse that cost him nothing, and was going riding on the morrow with a very interesting and pretty young woman. Suddenly he took cognizance of a thought which had been trying to get his attention for quite some time: Where was Jake and what was he doing?

"I'm gettin' careless," he reproved himself. "I ain't seen my little playmate since I paralyzed his nerve system. He didn't act like a man who would go into retirement with a thing like that tagged to him. I reckon he's plannin' a comeback: but a man like him usually acts quicker. All right, Jake: you take plenty of time an' work it out well. An' that's shore good advice."

There came a sudden yelping from the other side of a near-by building, so high-pitched, continuous, and full of agony that something moved along his spine. He reacted to the misery in the sound without giving it any thought, and when he turned the corner of the store and saw a chained dog being beaten by one of the town's ne'er-do-wells his hand of its own volition loosened the coiled rope at the saddle and swung it twice around his head. The soft lariat leaped through the air like a striking snake, and as it dropped over its victim, the roan instantly obeyed its training.

Jerked off his feet, his arms imprisoned at his sides, the dog beater slid, rolled, and bumped along the ground, at first too startled to protest. Then his voice arose in a stream of blasphemous inquiry, finishing with a petition. Tex rode along without a backward glance, deeply engrossed by some interesting problem and nearly had reached Carney's saloon before he became conscious of his surroundings. A miner, cursing, leaped to the roan's head and checked her, shouting profanely at the rider.

Tex checked the horse, looked curiously down at the protestor and then, sensing the burden of the other's remarks and becoming aware of the maledictions behind him, turned languidly in the saddle and looked back in time to see a dust-covered figure stagger to its feet and throw off the slackened rope.

"Hey!" shouted Tex indignantly. "What you doin' with my rope? Think it's worth th' price of a few drinks, eh? You drop it, *pronto* ! An' as for you, my Christian friend," he said to the man at the roan's head, "if you ever grab my cayuse like that again me an' you are shore goin' to have an impolite little party all to ourselves. Drop that hackamore."

"You was killin' that man!" yelled the miner, loosening his hold and showing fight.

"Well, what of it?" demanded Tex. "Any man that chains up a dog an' then beats it like he was, ain't got no right to live. If I don't kill him, somebody else will. What you raisin' all th' hellabaloo about?"

"I reckon you ain't far from wrong," said the other, by this time fully aware of the identity of the dog beater. "I'm nat'rally for law an' order. Whiskey Jim ain't no good, I'm admittin'!"

"If yo're for law an' order you must be lonesome associatin' all by yoreself in this squaw town," replied Tex, grinning, but not for one moment losing sight of Whiskey Jim, who at that moment was stooping to pick up a stone lying against the corner of a building. Tex sent a shot over his head and the incident was closed. "What do you do for company?"

"I ain't hankerin' for none," answered the miner, smiling grimly. "I only come in for supplies, an' don't stay long. You a stranger here?"

"That's unkind; but, seein' as how I ain't as much a stranger now as I was when I come, I won't hold it ag'in' you. Mebby I am gettin' to look like I belonged here." He laughed. "I don't know very many, but everybody knows me. They point with pride when they see me comin'; an' cock their guns behind their backs with their other hand. Where you located, friend?"

"Second fork on Buffaler Crick, th' first crick west of town. Quickest way is to foller th' track. Be glad to see you any time. Mine's th' shack above Jake's."

"I envy you," replied Tex. "See much of our mutual friend?"

"Only when he wants to borry somethin'," grinned the other. "I see you got th' pick of Williams' animals under yore saddle."

"I was lucky pickin', I admits," beamed Tex. "Nice feller, Williams."

"For them as likes him. Well, friend, I'm mushin' on. Name's Blascom."

"Tex Jones is my *nom du guerre* ," replied Tex. "Th' north is a better country than this for minin'. How'd you ever come to leave it?"

Blascom looked at him questioningly. "Yes, reckon it is; but how'd you know I come from there?"

"They don't mush nowhere else that I know of," chuckled Tex. He coiled the dusty lariat, shook it, and brushed his chaps where it had touched, waved his farewell; and went on to Carney's, where he dismounted and went in.

"Just met Whiskey Jim," he said across the bar.

"I congratulate you."

"Who's he livin' on?"

"Th' whole town," answered Carney. "He used to hang around here, seein' what he could steal, but I kicked his pants around his neckband an' he ain't favorin' me no more. Reckon he belongs to Williams."

"Then he must do somethin' for his keep," suggested Tex. "Our friend Gustavus Adolphus ain't no philanthropist, I'm bettin'.'"

"No; Gus is a Republican," replied Carney. "Whiskey Jim used to ride for him, an' mebby Gus is scared not to look after him a little."

Tex nodded. "Good reason; good, plain, practical, common-sense reason. Now, Carney--I want a good hoss for a lady, an' I'll have a little ride on it before I turn it over. Want it tomorrow mornin' at eight o'clock."

"Miss Saunders won't thank you much for tirin' it out."

"You couldn't help guessin' right th' first time," accused Tex. "There ain't no other ladies that I've seen or heard about. What th' lady don't know won't hurt her pride or spoil her appetite. Cuss it, man; I ain't aimin' to kill th' beast!"

"I reckon you know what yo're goin' to do with th' hoss," replied Carney, thoughtfully; "but I wonder do you know what yo're doin', goin' ridin' with that little lady?"

Tex regarded him with level gaze. "Meanin'?" he coldly demanded.

"Meanin' that claim is staked, th' notices posted, an' trespassers warned off; which is a d--d shame!"

"Hearsay ain't no good. I ain't been formally notified in writin'," replied Tex. "Until I am, I act natural; an' after I am, twice as natural, bein' mean by nature an' disposition. All of which reminds me that this is a remarkable town, an' that there's a re-markable man in it."

His companion studied him for a moment. "You should keep yore hat on when yo're ridin' around in th' sun. Th' only remarkable thing about this town is that it's still alive. Th' only remarkable man in it has been buried these last twenty years, up yonder on Boot Hill."

"I'm joinin' issue with you on that," replied Tex. "Th' sense of loyalty an' affection of this town for its leadin' citizen is a great an' beautiful thing for these degenerate, money-mad days. Parenthetically, I wonder if there was ever a time when th' days were anythin' else? Why, everybody is his friend! There's Jake, an' th' nephew, Whiskey Jim, Tim Murphy, Jerry Saunders, John Graves, Blascom, you, an' me. I don't know any more at this writin'. An' that leadin' citizen, a man of culture, wealth, and discernment, is our most esteemed Mr. Gus Williams. Hear! Hear!"

"There's some names you can scratch, Carney among 'em," growled the saloonkeeper, spitting in violent disgust. "Yore touchin' paregoric near makes me weep. an' I'm hard-shelled, like a clam. Two-thirds of th' people here do what he says, because he either scares or fools 'em. Th' rest dassn't lynch him because they ain't strong enough. Wealth? Shore. He got most of it when th' trail was in full swing. His brands, an' he had a-plenty, were copied from some on th' south ranges near th' old trail. A herd comin' up, grazin' wide, or passin' through that scrub an' hill country would near certain pick up a few local head on th' way, cattle bein' gregarious. Whiskey Jim was th' local herd trimmer. He'd throw up a herd, claim any of th' stray brands as belongin' around here. He had th' authority an' th' drawin's of them brands. If it was a herd of Horseshoe an' Circle Dots he claimed every other brand with them that was found this side of th' Cimarron. You know th' rules. He got 'em. Then there was stampedes, an' cattle run off at night. One time it got so bad that there was talk of a third Texan Expedition to clean it up. Only this one would 'a' been for a different purpose than th' other two."

"You better keep off th' Texas Expedition," said Tex. "That was a covered invasion for th' freedom of th' pore, robbed, browbeaten New Mexicans; an' it come to a terrible end."

"Not th' one I'm referrin' to," retorted Carney, his face set and determined. "Th' second one--that plundered caravans on th' old Santa Fe. I called this other one th' third only because of th' number of men who would have been in it, an' because it was a Texas idea. But we'll not quarrel. I had a good friend in th' second, avengin' th' first."

"I won't quarrel about Texas," said Tex. "Not bein' a Texan, my withers are unwrung. What did Williams do in th' face of that threat?"

"Drifted his herds off before snow flew, to a distant winter range an' let th' trail herds alone."

"That story ain't unusual," observed Tex. "He's a strange man. Picks queer names for his hosses. I never heard such names. Take my roan, now: his name is Oh My Cayenne. That's a devil of a name for anythin', let alone a hoss. Where'd he ever git it?"

Carney laughed. "I'm agreein' with you, but he didn't name th' roan. That hoss was named by Windy Barrett, when he was blind drunk. Windy was a peculiar cuss; allus spoutin' poetry an' such nonsense. Read books while he was line ridin'. Well, he woke up one mornin' after a spree in Williams' stable. As he turned his head to see where he was, th' roan, then a colt, poked its nose over th' stall an' nuzzled him. One of th' boys was just goin' in th' stable an' saw th' whole thing. Windy pushes th' hoss away an' says, sadlike: 'Yo're dead wrong, Oh My Cayenne; it don't banish th' sorrers with its whirlwind sword.' Th' boys thought it was such a good joke they let th' name stick."

Tex looked dubious. "Mebby they thought so, but I'm not admittin' that I do; an' it's no joke for any cayuse to have a name like that. There goes Bud Haines, ridin' out of town: he ain't earnin' his pay. Well, reckon I'll drift up an' see Williams. I allus like to be sociable. So-long."

Chapter VII
Weights and Measures

The proprietor of the general store glanced out of the window as the roan stopped before his door, and he frankly frowned at Tex's entry.

"Ain't no letters come for no Joneses," he said brusquely.

"Hope springs eternal," replied Tex. He sauntered up to the counter and was about to turn and lean against it when his roving glance passed along a line of wide-necked bottles. They looked strangely familiar and he glanced at them again. A label caught his eye. "Chloral Hydrate" he read silently. He looked at Williams and chuckled. "I don't claim to be no Injun, but just th' same I got a lot of patience when it comes to waitin'. Looks like I'm goin' to need it, far as that letter is concerned." He looked along the walls of the store. "You shore carry a big stock for a town like this, Mr. Williams," he complimented, his eyes again viewing the line of bottles with a sweeping glance. "Strychnine," he read to himself, nodding with understanding. "Shore, for wolves an' coyotes. Quinine, Aloes, Capsicum, Laudanum--quite a collection for a general store. Takes me back a good many years." Aloud he said. "I was admirin' that there pipe, an' I've got to have it; but that ain't what I'm lookin' so hard for." Again he searched shelves, up and down, left and right, and shook his head. "Don't see 'em," he complained. His mind flashed back to one word, and his medical training prompted him. "Chloral hydrate--safe in the right hands and very efficient. Ought to be tasteless in the vile whiskey they sell out here. You never can tell, an' I might need every aid." He shook his head again, and again spoke aloud. "Too bad, cuss it."

"If you wasn't so cussed secret about it I might be able to help you find what yo're lookin' for," growled Williams. "Bein' th' proprietor I know a couple of things that are in this store. Yore article might be among 'em."

"I'm loco," admitted Tex. "What I want is some center-fire .38 shorts. Couple of boxes will be enough."

Williams flashed a look at the walnut handle of the heavy Colt at his customer's thigh. He could see that it was no .38. Suspicion prompted him and he wondered if his companion was a two-gun man, with only one of them being openly worn. Such a combination was not a rarity. A gun in a shoulder holster or a derringer on an elastic up a sleeve might well use such a cartridge. This would be well to speak to Bud Haines about.

"You would 'a' saved yore valuable time, an' mine, if you'd said so when you first come in," ironically replied Williams. "Got plenty of .45's, quite some .44's, less .41's, and a few .38's in th' long cat'ridges. I ain't got no .38 shorts, nor .32's, nor .22's, nor no putty for putty blowers. Folks around these diggin's as totes guns mostly wants 'em man-size."

"I reckon so," agreed Tex pleasantly. "Don't blame 'em. Failin' in th' other qualifications they'd naturally do th' best they could to make up for them they lacked. I'm shore sorry you ain't got 'em because my rifle cat'ridges are runnin' low. That's what comes of havin' to buy a gun that don't eat regulation food. It was th' only one he had, an' I had to take it quick, bein' pressed hard at th' time. Time, tide, an' posses wait for no man. Yo're dead shore you ain't got 'em, huh?"

"Well, lemme see," cogitated the proprietor, scratching his head. "I did have some--they sent me some shorts by mistake an' I never took th' time to send 'em back. You wait till I look."

"Then you've got 'em now," said Tex. "You never could sell 'em in these diggin's, where folks as totes guns mostly wants 'em man-size. I'll wait till you see." He idly watched the scowling proprietor as he went behind the counter and dropped to one knee, his back to his customer. As he started to pull boxes from against the wall Tex silently sat on the counter as if better to watch him.

Williams was talking more to himself than to Tex, intent on trying to remember what he had done with the shorts, and save himself a protracted search. "Kept 'em with th' rest of th' cat'ridges till I got mad from nearly allus takin' 'em down for longs. I think mebby I put 'em about here."

Tex leaned swiftly backward, his hand leaping to one of the wide-mouthed bottles on the shelf. "They shore are a nuisance," he said in deep sympathy.

"I allus have more or less trouble gettin' 'em," he admitted, his hands working silently and swiftly with the cork. "Didn't hardly hope to get 'em here," he confessed as he swung back and replaced the depleted bottle. He assumed an erect position again, one hand resting in a coat pocket. "Shore sorry to put you to all this trouble," he apologized; "but if you got 'em you are lucky to git rid of 'em, in this town."

Williams turned his head, saw his customer perilously balanced on the edge of the counter, and watching him with great interest. "I can find 'em if they're here, Mr. Jones," he growled. "You might strain yore back, leanin' that way--yep, here they are, four boxes of 'em. Only want two?"

"Reckon I better take all I can git my han's on," answered Tex. "No tellin' where I can git any more, they're that scarce."

"Yore rifle looks purty big an' heavy for these," observed Williams, craning his neck in vain to catch a glimpse of it. It lay on the other side of the horse. "Yes, it's one of them *sängerbund* , or shootin'-fest guns," replied Tex. "Made for German target clubs, back in th' East. Got fine sights, an' is heavy so it won't tremble none. Two triggers, one settin' th' other for hair-trigger pullin'. Cost me fifty-odd. Don't bother to tie 'em up; they carry easier if they ain't all in one pocket. Don't forget that pipe."

Williams did some laborious figuring. "I see yo're gettin' acquainted fast," he remarked, pushing the change across the counter. "Them Saunders are real interestin'."

"Oh, so-so," grunted Tex. "Tenderfeet allus are. But I reckon she'll make yore nepphey a good wife. Seems to be real sensible, an' she shore can cook!"

"Hennery is a fortunate boy," replied Williams complacently, so complacently that Tex itched to punch him. "He'll make her a good husban', bein' nat'rally domestic an' affectionate. An' he's so sot on it that I'm near as much interested in their courtship as they are. I shore would send anybody to dance in h--l as interfered with it. Gettin' cooler out?"

"Warmer out, an' in," answered Tex. "Well, they ought to be real happy, bein' young an' both near th' same age. I'm sayin' age is more important than most folks admit. Me an' you, now, would be makin' a terrible mistake if *we* married a woman as young as she is. We got too much sense. An' I'm free to admit that I'm rope shy--don't like hobbles of any kind, a-tall. I'm a maverick, an' aim to stay so. When is th' weddin' comin' off?"

"Purty soon, I reckon," replied Williams, his voice pleasanter than it had been since Tex had appeared in town. "She's nat'rally a little skittish, an' Hennery is sort of shy. Young folks usually are. He was tellin' me you gave him some good advice."

Tex laughed and shrugged his shoulders. "Don't know how good it is," he replied. "An' it wasn't no advice. I just sort of mentioned to him somethin' I found worked real well; but what works with one woman ain't got no call to get stuck on itself--th' odds ain't in favor of its repeatin'. If it was me, howsomever, I'd shore try it a whirl. It can't do no harm that I can see."

"He's goin' to back it a little," responded Williams, "till he sees how it goes."

"A little ain't no good, a-tall," replied Tex. "It might not show any results for awhile, an' then work fast an' sudden. Well, see you later mebby. This cayuse of mine needs some exercise. So-long."

Williams followed him to the door, hoping for a glimpse of the German shooting-club rifle, but Tex mounted and rode away without turning that side of the horse toward the store.

His next stop was the hotel, where he had a few sandwiches put up for him and then he left town, heading for Buffalo Creek. He had no particular object in choosing that direction, the main thing being to get out of town and to stay out of sight until after dark. As he rode he cogitated:

"Chloral hydrate. Twenty to thirty grains is the dose soporific. Yes; that's right. In a hydrous crystal of this nature that would just about fill--what?" He rode on, oblivious to his surroundings, trying to picture the size of a container that would hold the required weight of crystals. "In our rough-and-ready weights a silver half-dime was twenty grains; a three-cent piece was forty grains, and I think my three-cent silver piece of '51 weighed ten grains. But not havin' any of 'em now, all that does me no good. Shucks--there's plenty of miners' scales in this country. Bet Blascom has one that'll help me out: an' a grain is a grain, all th' way through." He hitched up his heavily loaded belt and as his hand came into contact with the ends of the cartridges he chuckled and slapped the horse in congratulation.

"Omar, we're gettin' close. Bet a .45 shell will hold the dose. However, not wantin' to kill nobody, we'd better make shore. Yo're a willin' cayuse, an' I like yore gait: suppose you let it out a little? We got business ahead."

When he came to the dried bed of a creek he followed it at a distance and had not gone far before he espied the first fork. On the north side of the gully was a miserable hut. "That must be Jake's: we'll detour so he won't see us." Twenty minutes later he came to the second fork and a second hut, not much better than the first. A familiar figure was just emerging from it, and soon Tex rode down the steep bank and hailed.

The prospector looked up and waved, turning to face his visitor. "Glad to see you," he called. "Hope Whiskey Jim ain't run you out of town."

"He might if he kept close to me, up wind," laughed Tex. "Busy doin' nothin'?"

"Busy as a hibernatin' bear. Git off an' come in th' house, where th' sun ain't so hot. An' I reckon yo're thirsty."

Tex accepted the invitation and found a box to sit on. The interior of the shack was not out of keeping with the exterior, and it was none too clean. His roving glances saw and passed the gold scales, two metal cups hanging by three threads each from a slender, double-taper bar. Beside it was a tin box which he guessed contained weights.

"Washin' out lots of gold, Blascom?" asked Tex, smiling.

"Can't even wash my face without totin' water, or goin' up to th' sump. Th' crick's like it is out there for as far up as I've been. If it wasn't for a sump I've dug in a sandy place in its bed I'd had no water at all." He reached into his pocket and produced several bits of gold, none of them much larger than a grain of wheat. "Found these when I was gettin' water just now. That sump's goin' to go deeper right quick, 'though I'm scared I'll lose my water."

"What'll they weigh?" asked Tex curiously, handing them back.

"About a pennyweight, I reckon," replied Blascom.

Tex shook his head. "Not them. You've got too trustin' a nature. Yo're too hopeful: but I reckon that's what makes miners."

Blascom arose, dropped the flecks into a scale pan and dug around in the tin box. There was a metallic clink and the two pans slowly sought the same level. "Couple of grains under," he announced. "About twenty-two, I'd say. That's close figgerin', close enough for a guess."

"Cussed good," complimented Tex as the prospector put back the weights and dumped the gold out into his hand. "I ain't never dug out no hunks of gold an' I'm curious. If you aim to put that sump down farther I'm just itchin' to give you a hand. Come on--what you say?"

"You'd be a mess, sloppin' around with me," laughed Blascom. He shook his head. "Better set down an' watch me, lendin' yore valuable advice; or stay here an' keep out of th' sun."

"I can do that in town."

Blascom considered, looking dubiously at his guest's clothes. "Here," he said, finally. "You can help me more by carryin' water an' fillin' up everythin' in here that'll hold it. After I get through wrastlin' with a pan in that sump th' water won't be fit to drink before mornin'. That suit you?"

"Good enough," declared Tex, arising and picking up the buckets. "Come on: reveal yore gold mine. I'm a first-class claim jumper. You had yore dinner yet?"

Blascom shook his head, picked up a shovel and his gold pan and led the way. "That can wait. It ain't often I have any free help forced on me an' I'd be a sucker to let an empty belly cut in."

"I can cook, too," said Tex. "After I fill th' hut with water I'll get you a meal that'll make you glad yo're livin'; but you got to come after it to eat it; an' when I yell, you come a-runnin'. If you don't I'll eat it myself."

The sump lay about a hundred yards up the creek bed, around a bend which was covered with a thin growth of sickly willows and box elders. It was a hole about two feet square, the sandy sides held up by a cribwork of sticks, pieces of boxes, and barrel staves. Blascom dipped both pails in and started back with them.

"Wait a minute," objected Tex, reaching for them. "Thought you was goin' after nuggets while I toted th' water?"

"I thought so, too," answered Blascom, "till I had sense enough to think that I couldn't go rammin' around in there with my shovel until after th' water was saved. You can carry 'em th' next trip. Sit down an' do th' gruntin' for me, this time. A dozen buckets will empty her, almost."

Tex shrugged his shoulders and obeyed, rolled a cigarette, and then plucked a .45 from its belt loop. Wiping off the grease, he placed his thumb against the lead and pushed, turning the cartridge slowly as he worked. When he heard Blascom's heavy, careless tread nearing the bend he slipped the loosened cartridge into his vest pocket and lazily arose.

"There ain't nothin' else to fill but these here buckets," said the prospector as he appeared. Filling them again he passed them to Tex and reached for the shovel and the gold pan. "There's beans you can warm up, an' some bacon. There's also some sour-doughs. Make a good pot of coffee an' yell when yo're ready. I'm surprised at th' way this hole's fillin' up, but I ain't mindin' that. As long as I dump it close by it's bound to get back again."

Tex picked up the buckets and departed clumsily, his high-heeled boots not aiding his progress. Reaching the house he set down his load and wheeled swiftly toward the swaying balance. The pennyweight disk slid into one pan as his other hand brought from his pocket a generous quantity of the whitish, translucent crystals. Sniffing them, he smiled grimly and then nodded as the biting odor gripped his nostrils. He let them drop slowly into the other pan and when the balance was struck he added one more crystal and put the rest back into his pocket. Glancing around the hut he saw a torn, discarded pamphlet in a corner and he removed some of the inner sheets. When he had finished weighing and wrapping he had a dozen little packages of more than twenty-four, and less than thirty, grains. Wiping out the little tray he replaced the weight, drank deeply from a bucket and then started a fire in the home-made rock-and-clay stove. While it caught he went out, picked up some clean pebbles and returned to the scales, soon selecting the pebble that weighed the same as his powders. He might have use for it sometime in the future. Taking another piece of paper he emptied into it the rest of the crystals from his pocket and, sorting out pieces of thickened lint and bits of tobacco, wrapped the chloral up securely. Then he got busy with the meal and when the coffee was ready he went to the door and shouted the old bunkhouse classic: "Come an' get it!"

Blascom soon appeared, his clothing wet and sandy, and in his hand were several rice grains of gold with quite some dust. "Looks fair to me," he said. "I can't hardly tell what I'm doin', th' sump fills up so fast, an' th' sand is washed in with th' water, fillin' it up from th' bottom as fast as I can dig it out an' pan it. I can't understand where all that water comes from. I know there's cussed little of it further down th' crick bed. When she dried up I nat'rally wanted a sump nearer th' hut, but I couldn't get one nearer than I have. Must be a spring somewhere under it." He sniffed cheerfully. "That coffee shore smells good," he declared, going out to wash his hands.

The meal was eaten rapidly, without much talking, but when it was finished Blascom packed his pipe and passed the pouch to his companion. "New pipe?" he asked. "Then wet yore finger an' rub it around in th' bowl before you light her. You don't want a job cookin', do you? I never drunk better coffee."

The new pipe going well, Tex leaned back and smiled. "I'll cook th' supper if you want. I ain't anxious to get back to town before dark. An' I'll put on them old clothes over there an' help you at th' sump th' rest of th' day. Let's get goin'."

"All right; it's a two-man job with that water comin' in so fast," answered the prospector. "We'll not do any pannin'–just get th' sand out an' dump it up on th' bank, out of th' way of high water. I can pan it any time. You see, this dry spell is due to end 'most any time, an' when it does it'll be a reg'lar cloud-burst. That'll mean no more placerin' near th' sump. Ever see these creek beds after a cloud-burst? They're full from bank to bank an' runnin' like bullets."

Tex nodded and looked steadily out of the door, his mind going back some years and vividly presenting an arroyo and the great, sheer wall of water which swept down it on the day when he and his then enemy, Hopalong Cassidy, were fighting it out in the brush. His eyes glowed as the details returned to him and went past in orderly array. From that sudden and unexpected danger, and the impulsive chivalry of the man who had had him at the mercy of an inspired six-gun, had come his redemption.

"Yes," he said slowly. "I've seen 'em. They're deadly when they catch a man unawares." He drew a deep breath and returned to the main subject. "Why don't you hire somebody, Jake for instance, an' clean up that sump as quick as you can?"

"An' have a knife in my back?" exclaimed Blascom, "or be killed in my sleep? I don't know much about Jake, but what little I do know about him, th' less he, or any of th' fellers in town know about that sump, th' better I'll like it. There ain't one I'd trust, an' most of 'em are busted an' plumb desperate. I've been pannin' a lot better than fair day's wages out here, but I'm doin' without everythin' that I can because I dassn't look so prosperous. Let me show much dust in town an' I'd be raided an' jumped th' same night. They're like a pack of starvin' coyotes. I don't even keep my dust in this shack. I cache it outside at night."

"Suppose you was to buy things in town with coin or bills, lettin' on that it is yore bedrock reserve that yo're livin' on," suggested Tex. "That ought to help some."

"But I ain't got 'em," objected Blascom. "Got nothin' but raw gold."

Tex laughed and dug down into his pocket. "That's easy solved. Here," he said, bringing up a handful of double eagles. "Gold weighs as much in one shape as it does in another--even less, bulk for bulk, without th' alloy. I'll change with you if you want." Then he drew back his hand and grinned quizzically. "It's allus well to think of th' little things. It might be better if we didn't swap. You fellers ain't likely to have a currency reserve: more likely to have it just as you dug it out. That right?"

Blascom nodded. "Yes; 'though I knowed a feller that allus carried big bills in place of gold when he could get 'em, an' when he wasn't broke. They weighed a lot less. Raw gold would be better, out here."

"All right; how'd you like to drop into th' hotel about eleven tonight an' win heavy from me in a two-hand game of draw? Say as much as we can fix up? How much you want to change? Couple of hundred?" He chuckled. "We can fix it either way: raw gold or currency."

"Make it raw gold, then; better yet, mix it," said Blascom, arising, his face wrinkled with pleasure. He nodded swiftly. "Be back in a minute," and he went out. When he returned he went into a corner where he could not be seen by anyone passing the hut and took several sacks from his pocket. It did not take him long to weigh their contents and, calling his visitor over to verify the weights and the cleanness of the gold, he put the odd gold back into a sack and handed the other to his companion.

"Two hundred even," he said. "Keep yore money till I take it away from you tonight. Much obliged to you, Jones."

"How do you know I'll be there?" asked Tex, smiling. "I got th' gold an' a cussed good cayuse. With such a good start it'll be easy."

Blascom chuckled and shrugged his shoulders. "Yore little game with Whiskey Jim an' your soiree with Jake tell me different," he answered. "I've rubbed elbows with all sorts of men for forty-odd years--ever since I was a boy of sixteen. A man's got to back his best judgment: an' I'm backin' mine. If I wasn't shore about you do you reckon I'd be tellin' you anythin' about that sump? Now then: what you say about settin' here an' takin' things easy for th' rest of th' day? I don't want you to get all mucked up."

Tex arose, took the boxes of .38 shorts out of his pockets and lay them on a shelf. He put the heavy little sacks in their places and turned. "It'll do me good; an' I might learn somethin' useful," he said. "A man can't never learn too much. Come on; we'll tackle that sump." As he changed his clothes for those of his host the latter's words of confidence in him set him thinking. To his mind came scenes of long ago. "Deacon" Rankin, "Slippery" Trendley, "Slim" Travennes, and others of that savage, murderous, vulture class returned on his mental canvas. Of the worst class in the great West they had stood in the first rank; and at one time he had stood with them, shoulder to shoulder, had deliberately chosen them for his friends and companions, and in many of their villainies he had played his minor parts. He stirred into renewed activity and dressed rapidly. Changing the gold sacks into the clothes he now wore and putting on his host's extra pair of boots, he stepped toward the door and then thought of Jake, who reminded him somewhat of his former friends, lacking only their intelligence. He turned and swept up his gun and belt, buckling it around him as he left the shack to help his new friend.

Chapter VIII
After Dark

Murphy's blocked-up box car was dark and showed no signs of life, making only a blacker spot in the night. To any prowler who might have investigated its externals, the raised shades and the closed door would have left him undecided as to whether or not its tenant was within; but the closed windows on such a night as this would have suggested that he was not, for the baked earth radiated heat and the walls of the modest habitation were still warm to the touch. Inside the closed car the heat must have been well-nigh intolerable.

The silence was natural and unbroken. The brilliant stars seemed rather to accentuate the darkness than to relieve it. An occasional breath of heated air furtively rustled the tufts of drought-killed grass, but brought no relief to man or beast; but somewhere along the branch line a stronger wind was blowing, if the humming of the telegraph wires meant anything. In the west gleamed a single glowing eye of yellow-white, where the switch light told that the line was open. To the right of it blotches of more diffused and weaker radiance outlined the windows and doors of the straggling buildings facing the right-of-way. An occasional burst of laughter or a snatch of riotous song came from them, mercifully tempered and mellowed by the distance. From the east arose the long-drawn vocal atrocity of some mournful coyote who could not wait for the rising of the crescent moon to give him his cue. Infrequent metallic complaints told of the contraction of the heat-stretched rails.

In the south appeared a swaying thickening of the darkness, an elongated concentration of black opacity. Gradually it took on a more definite outline as its upper parts more and more became silhouetted against a sky of slightly different tone and intensity. First a moving cone, then a saucer-like rim, followed slowly by a sudden contraction and a further widening. Hat, head, and shoulders loomed up vaguely, followed by the longer bulkiness of the body.

This apparition moved slowly and silently toward the rectangular blot at the edge of the right-of-way, advancing in a manner suggesting questionable motives, and it paused frequently to peer into the surrounding void, and to listen. After several of these cautious waits it reached the old car, against whose side it stood out a little more distinctly by contrast. The gently rolling tattoo of finger nails on wood could scarcely be heard a dozen feet away and ceased before critical analysis would be able to classify it. Half a minute passed and it rolled out again, a little louder and more imperative. Another wait, and then came a flat clack as a tossed pebble bounced from the wall at the waiter's side. Its effect was magical. The figure wheeled, crouched, and a hand spasmodically leaped hip high, a soft, dull gleam tipping it. While one might slowly count ten its rigid posture was maintained and then a rustling not far from the door drew its instant attention.

"What ye want?" demanded a low, curious voice. "If it's Murphy, he's sleepin' out, this night av h--l."

The figure at the door relaxed, grew instantly taller and thinner and a chuckle answered the query of the section-boss. "Don't blame you," it softly said, and moved quietly toward the owner of the car.

"To yer left," corrected the Irishman. "Who's wantin' Murphy at this time av night, an' for what?"

"Yore fellow-conspirator," answered Tex, sinking down on the blanket of his companion. "Didn't Jerry tell you to expect me?"

"Yes, he did; but I wasn't shore it was you," replied Murphy. "So I acted natural. Th' house is past endurin' with th' winders an' door closed; an' not knowin' what ye might have to talk about I naturally distrusted th' walls. This whole town has ears. Out here in th' open a man will have more trouble fillin' his ear with other people's business. How are ye?"

"Hot, an' close," chuckled Tex. "Also curious an' lonesome." He crossed his legs tailor fashion, and then seemed to weigh something in his mind, for after a moment he changed and lay on his stomach and elbows. "I don't stick up so plain, this way," he explained.

"I hear ye trimmed old Frowsyhead at poker," said Murphy, "an' won a good hoss. Beats all how a man wants to smoke when he shouldn't. Have a chew?"

"I'll own to that vice in a limited degree and under certain conditions," admitted Tex, taking the huge plug. "An' I'll confess that to my way of thinkin' it's th' only way to get th' full flavor of th' leaf; but I ain't sayin' it's th' neatest."

"'Tis fine trainin' for th' eye," replied Murphy, the twinkle in his own hidden by the night.

"An' develops amazin' judgment of distance," supplemented Tex, chuckling. "There's some I'd like to try it on--Hennery Williams, for instance."

"Aye," growled Murphy in hearty accord. "He'll be lucky if he ain't hit by somethin' solider than tobaccy juice. I fair itch to twist his skinny neck."

"A most praiseworthy longing," rejoined Tex, a sudden sharpness in his voice. "How long has he been deservin' such a reward?"

"Since *she* first came here," growled his companion. "That was why I wanted Mike Costigan to get his family out av th' way, for I'm tellin' ye flat, Costigans or no Costigans, that little miss will be a widder on her weddin' day, if it gets that far. Th' d--d blackguard! I've kept me hand hid, for 'tis a true sayin' that forewarned is forearmed. They'll have no reason to watch me close, an' then it'll be too late. Call it murder if ye will, but I'll be proud av it."

"Hardly murder," murmured Tex. "Not even homicide, which is a combination of Latin words meanin' th' killin' of a human bein'. To flatter th' noble Hennery a little, I'd go so far as to admit it might reach th' dignity of vermicide. An' no honest man should find fault with th' killin' of a worm. Th' Costigans should be persuaded to move."

"Ye try it," grunted Murphy sententiously. "Can ye dodge quick?"

"Nobody ever justly accused me of tryin' to dodge a woman," said Tex. "There must be a way to get around her determination."

"Yes?" queried Murphy, the inflection of the monosyllable leaving nothing to be learned but the harrowing details.

"Coax her to go to Willow," persisted Tex.

"She don't like th' town."

"Yore inference is shore misleadin'," commented Tex. "I'd take it from that that she does like Windsor."

"Divvil a bit; but she stays where Mike is."

"Then you've got to shift Mike. There's not enough work here for a good man like Costigan," suggested Tex.

"Yer like a dog chasin' his tail. Costigan stays where th' lass an' her brother are."

"Huh! Damon an' Pythias was only a dual combination," muttered the puncher. "Cussed if there ain't somethin' in th' world, after all, that justifies Nature's labors."

"An'," went on Murphy as though he had not been interrupted, "th' lass sticks to her brother, an' he stays where he's put. He's not strong an' he has a livin' to make for two. Ye can take yer change out av that, Mr. Tex Jones."

Tex grunted pessimistically. "Well, anyhow," he said, brightening a little, "mebby Miss Saunders won't be pestered for a little while by Hennery--an' then we'll see what we see. I'm unlucky these days: I'm allus with th' under dog," and he went on to tell his companion of his suggestions to the nephew.

"'Tis proud av ye I am," responded Murphy. "May th' saints be praised for th' rest she'll be gettin'. We can all av us breathe deep for a little while; an' meanwhile I'll be tryin' my strength with Lefferts, th' boss at th' Junction. I've hated to leave town even that long, but now I can make th' run; 'though I know it will do no good. Ye'll be stayin' in town tomorry?"

"Why, no; I'm goin' ridin' with Miss Saunders," and Tex explained that, to his companion's admiration and delight.

"It'll be a pleasure for her to be able to leave th' house without bein' tagged after by that scut," said the section-boss. "Yer a bye with a head. An' I see where ye not only get th' suspicions av that Tommy lad, but run afoul of that Henry an' his precious uncle. Haven't ye been warned yet?" The gleam of hope in his eyes was hidden by the darkness. "Ye'll mebby have trouble with th' last two--an' if ye do, keep an eye on Bud Haines. Ye'll do well to watch him, anyhow. Why don't ye slip out quiet-like, straight southwest from her house? Less chance av bein' seen; but a mighty slim one. They've eyes all over town."

"We are shore to be seen," quietly responded Tex. "If we sneak out it will justify their suspicions. I don't want to do that. I'm aimin' to ride plumb down th' main street, through th' middle of town, an' pay Tommy a little visit out at his ranch. *There is no shuffling, there th' action lies in his true nature* . Like Caesar's wife, you know. An', by th' way, Tim: we have some friends in town, an' I'm addin' an ally from Buffalo Crick. Time works for us." He paused and then asked, curiously: "Who is our friend Bud Haines, an' what does he do for a livin'? I've my suspicions, but I'd rather be shore."

Murphy swore softly under his breath. "He used to ride for Williams till he earned a reputation as a first-class gunman; but now he follows old Frowsyhead around like a shadder. Cold blooded, like th' rattlesnake he is; a natural-born killer. They say he's chain lightnin' on th' draw."

"I've heard that said of better men than him; some of them now dead," said Tex. "Must be a pleasant sort of a chap." He cogitated a bit. "An' how long has he been playin' shadow to friend Williams? Since I come to town, or before?" he asked as casually as he could, but tensely awaited the answer.

"Couple av years," answered Murphy; "an' mebby longer." He tried to peer through the darkness. "Was ye thinkin' ye made th' job for him?"

"Well, hardly," replied Tex. "I'm naturally conceited, suspicious, and allus lookin' out for myself. Th' thought just happened to hit me."

Their conversation began to ramble to subjects foreign to Windsor and its inhabitants, and after a little while Tex arose to leave. He melted out of sight into the night and half an hour later rode into town from the west, along the railroad, and soon stopped before the hotel.

The customary poker game was in full swing and he nodded to the players, received a civil greeting from Gus Williams, and after a short, polite pause at the table, wandered over to the bar, where Blascom leaned in black despondency.

"How'd'y," said Tex affably. "Fine night, but hot, an' close."

"Fine, h--l!" growled Blascom, sullenly looking up. "Not meanin' you no offense, stranger," he hastily added. "I'm grouchy tonight," he explained.

"Why, what's th' trouble?" asked Tex after swift scrutiny of the other's countenance. "Barkeep, give us two drinks, over yonder," and he led his companion to the table. "No luck?"

Blascom growled an oath. "None at all. My stake's run out, all but this last bag," and he slammed it viciously onto the table. "Th' claim's showin' nothin'." He scowled at the bag and then, avarice in his eyes and desperation in his voice, he looked up into the face opposite him. "This is next to no good: I'll double it, or lose it. What you say to a two-hand game?"

Tex looked a little suspicious. "I don't usually play for that much, rightaway, ag'in' strangers." He looked around the room and flushed slightly at the knowing smiles and sarcastic grins. "Oh, I don't care," he asserted, swaggering a little. "Come on; I'll go you. Deck of cards, friend," he called to the dispenser of drinks, and almost at the words they were sailing through the air toward his hands. "You've got as much chance as I have; an' if I don't win it, somebody else will. Draw, I reckon?" he asked nervously. "All right; low deals," and the game was on.

Blascom won the first hand, Tex the second. For the better part of an hour it was an up-and-down affair, the ups for Tex not enough to offset the downs. Finally, with a big pot at stake he pressed the betting on the theory that his opponent was bluffing. Suddenly becoming doubtful, he let a palpable fear master him, refused to see the raise, and slammed his hand down on the table with a curse. Blascom laughed, grandiloquently spread a four-card flush under his adversary's nose, and raked in his winnings.

"Shuffle 'em up." chuckled the prospector. "Things are lookin' better."

Glancing from the worthless hand into Blascom's exultant face Tex kicked the chair from in under him, arose and went to the bar where he gulped his drink, glanced sullenly around the room, and strode angrily to the stairs to go to his room. Wide and mocking grins followed him until he was hidden from sight, the expressions on the faces of Williams and his nephew transcending the others.

The prospector gleefully pocketed the money and dust, sighed with relief and swaggered over to the other table, one thumb hooked in an armhole of his vest. He stopped near Williams and beamed at the players, patting his pocket, but saying nothing until the hand had been played and the cards were being scooped up for a new deal.

"Williams," he said, laughing, "my supplies are cussed low, but now that I can pay for what I want I'm comin' in tomorrow mornin' an' carry off 'most all yore grub."

The storekeeper had glanced meaningly at one of the players and now he lazily looked up, his face trying to express pleasure and congratulation. The man he had glanced at arose, yawned and stretched, mumbled something about being tired and out of luck and pushed back his chair. As he slouched away from the table he turned the chair invitingly and nodded to Blascom.

"Take my place; I'm goin' to turn in soon," he said.

"Why, shore," endorsed Williams. "Set in for a hand or two, Blascom. It's early yet, too early to head for yore cabin. This game's been draggin' all evenin'; mebby it'll move faster if a new man sets in." Waiting a moment for an answer and none being forthcoming, he leaned back and stretched his arms. "How you makin' out on th' crick--bad?"

"Couldn't be much worse," answered the prospector, his face becoming grave. "I can't do much without water, an' th' only water I got is a sump for drinkin' an' cookin' purposes. You know that I ain't th' one to put up no holler as long as I'm gettin' day wages out of it; but when I can't make enough to pay my way, then I can't help gettin' a little mite blue."

"We all have our trials," replied Williams. He waved his hand toward the vacant chair. "Better set in for a little while. You've had good luck tonight: give it its head while it's runnin' yore way. Besides, a little fun an' company will shore cheer you up. You ain't got no reason to be hot-footin' off to yore cabin so early in th' evenin'."

The prospector smilingly shook his head. "I ain't needin' no cheerin' now," he asserted, again slapping the pocket. "I got a little stake that'll let me stick it out till we get rain. I got too much faith in that claim to clear out an' leave it; but now I got still more faith in my luck. It broke for me tonight an' I'm bettin' it's th' turnin' point; an' if a man ain't willin' to meet a turn of good luck at sunrise, with a smile, he shore don't deserve it. At sunup I'll be in that crick bed with a shovel in my hand, ready to go to work. I've been busted before; more'n once; but I don't seem to get used to it, at all. Well, good luck, everybody, an' good night," and he turned and strode briskly toward the door and disappeared into the darkness.

Williams looked disappointed and cautiously pushed the substitute deck farther back in its little slot under the table. Looking around, he beckoned to the unselfish player and motioned for him to resume his seat. The lamb having departed, the regular friendly game for small stakes would now go on again.

"You fellers heard what I said about sand, th' very first night that Jones feller showed up," remarked Williams, chuckling. "I'm sayin' it ag'in: he figgered Blascom was bluffin', played that way until th' stakes got high an' then got scared out an' quit. Quit cold without even feedin' in a few more dollars to see th' hand. Left th' table in a rage just because he lost a hundred or two. I was watchin' him as much as I could, an' I could see he was gettin' madder an' madder, nervouser an' nervouser all th' time; an' when a man gets like that he can't play poker good enough to keep warm in h--l. He ain't no poker player; an' as soon as I can buffalo him into a good, stiff game, I'll show you he ain't!"

He paused and looked around knowingly. "He didn't win that roan. I just sorta loaned it to him. Might have to bait him ag'in, too; but before he leaves this town I'll git it back, with all he's got to-boot. There ain't no call for nobody to start yappin' around about what I'm sayin'," he warned.

"I was a-wonderin' about him winnin' that hoss," said the unselfish player as he resumed his seat and drew up to the table. A broad grin spread itself across his face. "Prod him sharp, Gus: we'll get him playin' ag'in' th' gang, some night, an' win him naked."

The subject of their conversation was upstairs behind his closed door. He had taken off his coat and vest and was seated facing the washstand, from which he had removed the basin and pitcher. On the bench was a pile of 45's, their bullets greaseless, and he was working assiduously at the slug of another cartridge, his thumb pressing this way and that, and from time to time he turned the shell for assaults on the other side. It was hard on the thumb, but no other way would do, for no other way that he could take advantage of would leave the soft lead entirely free from telltale marks.

Time passed, but still he labored, changing thumbs at intervals. At last, all the leads removed and each one standing against its own shell, he emptied the powder from the brass containers and made a little paper package of it. Going to his coat and taking out the packets of chloral, he put the powder package in their place and returned with them to the bench.

The translucent crystals were of all sizes, some of them too large to be economically contained by the shells, which he had cleaned of powder marks. These crystals were larger only in two dimensions, for in thickness they were practically the same as the others. Doubtful whether the shells would hold a full dose and permit the leads to be replaced, he felt some anxiety as he placed the chloral in the folds of a clean kerchief and began crushing them by the steady pressure of the butt of his Colt. This was slower than pounding, but the latter was too noisy a process under present conditions. Dumping the reduced crystals into a shell lined with paper against possible chemical action on the brass, he gently tapped the outside of the container and watched the granules settle until there was room for the lead. He did not dare tamp it for fear it would not easily empty when inverted. Pushing home the bullet he up-ended the cartridge and tapped it again to loosen the contents. Shaking it close to his ear, he smiled grimly. The dose was loose enough to fall out readily, large enough to insure its proper effect, and the granules of a size small enough to dissolve quickly. When he had filled and reloaded the last shell he chuckled as he made a slight notch on the rim of each, for they would bear close inspection by weight, sight, and sound, and it was necessary that he mark them to keep from fooling himself.

He put them back into the pocket of the coat and grinned. "As I remember the action of chloral hydrate somebody may lose consciousness and muscular power and sensibility. Their expanding pupils as they wake up will expand under sore and inflamed eyelids. They'll sleep tight and not be worth very much for an hour or two after they do awaken. And these men gulp their whiskey without waiting to taste it, and it is so vile that they'll never suspect an alien flavor, 'specially if it's not too strong. Gentlemen, I bid you all good night: and may you sleep well and soundly."

Chapter IX
A Pleasant Excursion

After an early breakfast, early for him these days, Tex went down the street toward Carney's. As he passed Williams' stable he heard hammering, and paused to glance in at the door to see what his friend, Graves, was doing.

The stableman looked up and turned halfway around at the hail. "Hello!" he mumbled through a mouthful of nails. Removing them he nodded at the door. "Tryin' to fasten that lock so it'll do some good. It must 'a' been forced off more'n once, judgin' by th' split wood, which is so old that it ain't much good, anyhow. Th' nails sink into it like it was putty."

Tex was about to suggest the sawing out of the poorest part of the plank and the in-letting of a new piece in its place, but some subconscious warning bade him hold his peace.

"Much ado about nothin', Graves," he said, smiling ironically. "Hoss stealin' is a bigger risk in these parts than it is a profit; an' anyhow, th' slightest noise will wake you up, sleepin' like you do right next to th' door." He examined the wood. "Huh; them splits were made when th' wood was tough--it wouldn't split as dead as it is now: th' nails would just pull out. So you see it was done years ago. Hoss stealin' has gone out of style since then. All you want is a catch to hold it shut ag'in' th' wind." He winced suddenly and held a hand gently against his jaw. "That's all it wants."

"Reckon yo're right," agreed the stableman, glancing curiously at his companion's hand. "What's th' matter? Toothache?"

Tex growled a profane malediction and nodded. "Reckon I'll have to go around an' see th' doc, an' get some laudanum."

"An' pay that thief three prices!" expostulated Graves indignantly. "Chances are he's so drunk he'll give you strychnine instead. Why don't you go up to Williams' store? He's got th' laudanum, an' knows how to fix it up for toothaches an' earaches, I reckon."

"Williams?" queried Tex in moderate surprise. "What you talkin' about? He ain't runnin' no drug-store! What's he doin' with drugs an' such stuff?"

Graves laughed and contemplated the lock with strong disapproval. "No, it ain't no drug-store," he replied. "But th' doc drinks so hard he ain't got no money left to carry a full line of drugs, so Williams carries 'em for him, an' sells him stuff as he needs it. Besides, he allus did sell strychnine to th' ranchers, for coyotes an' wolves--though I ain't never heard it said that any wolves was ever poisoned. Sometimes they do get a coyote--but not no wolves. They've been hunted so hard they just about know as much as th' hunters." He stepped forward and felt of the wood around the lock. "I reckon yo're right," he admitted; "though while I ain't nat'rally a sound sleeper, it would take quite some racket to wake me up if I'd had a couple of drinks before goin' to bed, which I generally do have. I'll just let her stay like she is."

Tex looked at the lock and at the bolt receptacle on the door jamb. The lock was fastened securely for most people, seeing that the pressure from being pushed inward would not work against it very much; but the receptacle, the keystone of the door's defense, was nailed to even poorer wood than the lock itself and he saw at once that any real strain would force it loose.

"Shore; good enough," he said. "Have an eye-opener?"

Graves accepted with alacrity and in a moment they were smiling across Carney's bar at the good-natured proprietor.

"That hoss ready?" asked Tex when the conversation lulled.

"In th' stall next to th' roan," answered Carney. "Th' stable boys went to Europe last night an' won't be back till tomorrow; but I reckon you can saddle her yoreself."

"I'd rather do it myself," replied Tex.

"Labor of love?" queried Carney, grinning.

"Measure of precaution," retorted Tex, a slight frown on his face.

Carney nodded endorsement. "Can't take too much," he rejoined. "That goes for every kind, too. Nice gal, she is--though a little mite stuck up. I reckon she--—"

"Nice day," interrupted Tex, looking straight into the eyes of the proprietor; "though it's hot, an' close," he added slowly.

"It is that," muttered Carney. "As I was sayin', you'll find both hosses ready for saddles," he vouchsafed with slight confusion.

"Much obliged," answered Tex with a smile, turning toward the rear door. "See you boys later," he said, going out. In a few minutes they saw him ride past on a nettlesome black which put down its white feet as though spurning contact with the earth.

"Whitefoot shore glistens," observed Graves.

"She ought to," replied Carney. He mopped off the bar and looked up. "Beats all how them fellers ride," he observed. "They sit a saddle like they'd growed there. An'," he cogitated, "beats all how touchy some of 'em are. I can't figger him, a-tall," whereupon ensued an exhaustive critique of cowpunchers, their manners, and dispositions.

Meanwhile the particular cowpuncher who had started the discussion was riding briskly northeastward along the trail which he knew led to the C Bar, and after he had put a few miles behind him he took a package from his pocket and sowed black powder along the edge of the trail. After a short while he turned and rode back again.

Jane Saunders answered the knock and smiled at the self-possessed puncher who faced her, hat in hand. "Come in a moment," she invited, stepping aside. "This coffee is hardly cool enough to be put into the bottles, but it won't be long before it is. I am so glad you have brought Whitefoot. I have ridden her before."

"She's quite a horse," he replied. "Gaited as easy as any I ever rode."

She flashed him a suspicious glance. "Then you've ridden her? When, and what for?"

"I thought it would do no harm to learn her disposition," he answered carelessly. "She hasn't been out of the stable for two weeks. We had a nice five-mile ride, and she took it with plenty of spirit. She's a good hoss."

After awhile Jane filled two bottles with coffee and placed them with the lunch on the table. Tex took down a blackened tin pail from a hook over the stove and, picking up the bottles and the lunch, went out to his horse, followed by Jane, who had at the last moment buckled on a cartridge belt and the .38 Colt.

Tex looked at them and cogitated. "That'll be quite heavy and annoying, bobbing up and down at every step," he observed. "Why not leave the belt behind and let me slip the gun into my pocket?"

"But I should get accustomed to it," she protested.

"Intend to wear it steadily?"

"No; hardly that," she laughed.

"Then there's no reason to get accustomed to it," he replied. "Surprise is a great factor, because what is known can be guarded against. Will you allow me to advise you in a matter of this kind?"

"Jerry says I couldn't have a better adviser," she replied. She regarded him with level gaze. "Of course, Mr. Jones; but I want to carry it: you have too much without taking it. Frankly, I'm amused by your suggestion that I learn to use it, by Jerry's earnestness that I do learn, and by Tim's fear that I will not. Let us start out by being frank: Why do you think it necessary that I do?"

"Necessary?" asked Tex. "Why, I am not claiming that it is necessary; but I do know that it is a very pleasant diversion. Miss Saunders, there is a great deal said and written about the chivalry of western men. I won't say that most of it, or even nearly all of it is not deserved, for I believe that it is; but I will say that there are men who have no idea of chivalry, honesty, or even decency. You find them wherever men are, be it any point of the compass, or in any stratum of society. The West has some of them, even if less than its proportionate share; and this town of Windsor was not overlooked in their distribution. I know of no particular reason why you should learn the use of a revolver; but we are dealing with generalities. They suffice. With the odds a hundred to one that you never will have need to call upon knowledge of firearms, why refuse that knowledge when it is so easily acquired; and when the acquirement not only will be a pleasure but will lead to further pleasures? Shooting calls for that coordination of nerves and muscles which make all sports sport. And let me say, further, that the feeling of confidence, of security, which comes from the proper handling of a six-shooter is well worth what little effort has been expended to learn its use. Later I hope you will make use of my rifle--after I reduce the powder charges a little--but the short gun should come first. And I would much prefer that you carry it yourself, and make its carrying a habit rather than an exception."

"You are a very difficult man to argue against successfully, Mr. Jones," she said smiling. "I believe, quite the hardest I ever have met."

She took off the belt, slipped the gun inside her waist and hung the belt on a branch of a small tree beside her.

Tex dismounted, took the belt and carried it into the house and, returning, lifted her into the saddle, which she wisely sat astride. Swinging onto the roan he led the way toward town. She was about to speak of the direction when she decided to keep silent, and, glancing sidewise at him, smiled to herself at his easy assurance and rather liked his open defiance of the townspeople. She had no illusions as to what effect their ride together might have in certain minds, and she allowed her feelings, if not her thoughts, to choose her words.

"What a relief it is to have a day's freedom," she exulted, patting the black.

Tex nodded understandingly. "Yes," he said. "Being cooped up and hedged around does get tiresome, I suspect. Well," he laughed, "the fences are all down today. We ride where we listeth and let no man say us nay."

She looked at him smilingly. "Do you know that you are something of an enigma? I'm curious to know what's going on in your head," she daringly declared. "You just said the fences are all down, you know."

He laughed and glanced down the main street, into which they at that moment turned, and a certain grimness came to his face, which she did not miss. "Why allow yourself to be disappointed?" he asked. "Illusions have their worth; and a mystery solved loses its interest. As a matter of fact, the less that is known of what goes on in my head, the better for my reputation for wisdom and common sense. It reminds me of the mouse in the cave."

"Yes?"

"Yes. It was such a big cave and such a little mouse," he explained. "And except for the little mouse the cave was empty."

"I admire your humility; it is refreshing, especially in this country; but I fear it is a very great illusion. Like the other illusions to which you just referred, has it its worth?"

"Confession is good for the soul, and always has worth."

While he spoke he saw a lounger before the hotel come to startled life and hurry inside. Down the street three conversing miners stopped their words to stare open-mouthed at the two riders nonchalantly jogging their way. The door of the hotel became jammed and curious, surprised faces peered from its dirty windows, among them the angry countenance of Henry Williams.

The ordeal of proceeding naturally and carelessly down that street under such frank scrutiny would have tried the balance of any poise, and Jane, flushing and trying to ignore the stares, flashed a searching glance at her companion and felt a quick admiration for him. She could imagine Tommy under these conditions. For all she could detect, her companion might have been riding across the uninhabited plains with no observing eyes within a day's ride of him. Swaying rhythmically to the motion of his horse, relaxed, unconcerned, and natural, he talked with ease and smoothness; and unknowingly made an impression on her which time never would efface.

"That simile of the mouse in the cave," he was saying, "naturally sets up a train of thought--all thought being an unbroken, closely connected, although not necessarily manifest to us, concatenation--and leads to the ass in the lion's skin, being helped materially by the great number of asses in sight, despite the scarcity of even the skins of the nobler beasts. The dual combination does not end there, however; there are jackals in lobos' hides, and vultures posing as eagles. Even the lowly skunk has found a braver skin and bids for a reputation sweeter to bear than the one earned by his own striking peculiarity. For such a one there is nothing so disconcerting as a six-gun appearing from a place where no six-gun should be--and it loses none of its potency even if the bore be small and the charge light. Have you ever had the opportunity to study animals at close range, Miss Saunders?"

His companion, bent over the saddle horn in her mirth, gasped that she never had enjoyed such an opportunity, especially before today, whereupon he continued.

"The ass in the lion's skin was all right and got along famously until he brayed," he explained; "but the skunk fools no one for one instant, not even himself. He can't even fool Oh My, here," and he slapped the glossy neck of the roan.

"Who?" demanded Jane, her face red from laughter.

"Oh My; my horse," he answered. "He was named by one Windy Barrett, when that person awakened from a stupor acquired by pouring libations to Bacchus. The rest of the name is Cayenne."

"Why, that's an exclamation, not a name--Oh!" Jane went off into another fit of laughter. " *Omar Khayyam* ! Isn't that rich! Whatever did you do when you heard it?

"I led Graves to the tavern door agape," answered Tex, grinning.

By this time they had swung into the trail leading to the C Bar and the miles rolled swiftly behind them. Suddenly Tex touched his companion's arm, both reining in abruptly. Squarely in the middle of the trail was a rattlesnake, huge for the prairie, and it coiled swiftly, the triangular head erect and the tail whirring.

"Ugh!" exclaimed Jane, a wave of revulsion sweeping over her. "What a monster! Can you shoot it from here?"

Tex nodded. "Yes, but while I usually do, I rather dislike the job. He's a snake all right, man's hereditary enemy since the world was young, and the hatred for him comes to us naturally. Sinister, repellant, and all that, that chap is as square as any enemy in the wild, and he is coolly business-like. He hasn't a friend outside his own species, and even in that is to be found one of his chief enemies. There he lies, for all to see, his gauntlet thrown, whirring his determination to defend himself, and to depart if given a chance. Look at those coils, their grace and power, not an ungainly movement the whole length of him. Look at his markings--from the freshness of his skin and its vivid coloration I'd say he has very recently parted with his old skin, and the parasites which infected it. You shed your skin in vain, Old-Timer--you'll not enjoy it long," and his hand dropped to the holster. A flash and a roar, a rolling burst of smoke, and the defiant head jerked sidewise, hanging by a few shreds of muscle to the writhing coils. "'Dead for a ducat, dead!'" quoted Tex, leading the way past his victim.

A little farther on he pointed to a track along the side of the trail.

"Dog or wolf," he said. "They're identical except for directness. A dog's track wavers, a wolf's does not. From the fact that it follows the trail I'd say that was a dog; but it may puzzle us before we lose it. He was a big animal, though, and if a wolf he's a lobo, the gray buffalo wolf, cunning as Satan and brave as Hector. And what a killer! No carrion for him, no meat killed by anyone but himself, and usually he's shy about returning to that. He creates havoc on a cattle range. Poison he sneers at, and it takes mighty shrewd trapping to catch him. To avoid the scent of man is his leading maxim. Before the snow comes he is safe--afterwards his troubles begin if a tracer crosses his trail."

"Why I thought he was a big coyote," said Jane. "You make him out to be quite a remarkable animal."

"And justly," responded her companion. "Coyote? They shouldn't be mentioned together in the same breath. The buffalo gray is a king--the coyote a crawling scavenger, with wits in place of courage. The difference in the natures is indicated graphically by the way they hold their tails. The coyote's droops at a sharp angle, but the lobo's is held straight out. A single wolf is more expensive to ranchers now than he once was, because he has been hunted so hard with traps and poison that he now has learned not to eat dead animals, and in some cases even to ignore his own kill after once he has left it. I've heard of several wolves, each of which have been blamed for the killing of sixty cows in a year, and their score might have run quite some higher. Have you been watching this track? I'd say it's wolf--and as direct as an arrow. And there is the great western target--tomato, from the color of it. Suppose you try your hand at it?"

Jane produced the pistol and listened intelligently (and how rare a gift that is!) to all her companion had to tell her. When the pistol was emptied the can was still untouched. Laughing, Tex dismounted, and drew a long rectangle in the sand, with the can in the median line and to one end.

"The ground laying flat instead of standing up like a man," he explained, "I had to figure on your line of vision. If the upper half of a man's body were placed on the line nearer you, his head would just about intercept your view of the farther line. Now your third and sixth shots, having struck inside the four lines, would have hit a man at that distance. I'd say you hit his stomach with the third shot, and his right shoulder with the other. The can is of no moment, for cans are not dangerous; but when I show you how to reload, I want you to aim at the can, as if it were the buckle of a belt. You take to that Colt like a duck takes to water--and before you get home today you'll surprise yourself. Now, to eject the empties and to reload--and by the way, Miss Saunders, if I were you, carrying that gun as you must carry it, I'd leave one cartridge out, and let the hammer rest on the empty chamber."

The lesson went on, his pupil slowly becoming enthused and finding that it truly was a sport. When she had made four out of five in the marked-off space she was greatly elated and would have continued shooting after she was tired, but her tutor refused to let her.

"That is enough for now," he laughed. "On our way back you may try a few more rounds if you wish. No use to tire yourself, especially after such a creditable showing. In these few minutes you graduated out of the defenseless-woman class, and may God help anybody who discounts your defense. You see, the main thing is not the shooting, but the freedom from fear of weapons and knowing how to use them. There is nothing mysterious about a Colt--it won't blow up, or shoot behind. Whatever timidity you may have had about handling one has been overcome, and in a few minutes you have learned to hold it right and to shoot it. The bare threat of a gun held in capable hands is in most cases enough. Now, if you please, I'll try my left hand at the can. I wear only one gun, but it may be necessary to wear two--and while my left hand has been trained to shoot well, this is a good opportunity to exercise it."

Filling the can with sand and dirt to weigh it against rolling, he stepped back twenty paces, tossed his own Colt into his left hand, dropped the butt to his hip and sent six shots at the crimson target. Stepping from the smoke cloud he advanced and examined the can. One bullet had clipped its upper edge, another had grazed one side, while the other four were grouped in the sand within a radius only; a little larger than that of the target.

"That wouldn't do for two of my friends," he laughed, "but it's good enough for me. Not a shot would have missed the target I had in mind. Had I shot as quickly as I could, I might have missed the target altogether, but close enough for practical purposes. On the other hand, had I taken a little more time, the score would be better."

Jane's mouth still was open in delighted surprise. "Do you mean to tell me that anyone can do better than that, from the hip, without sighting at all?" she demanded incredulously.

"Oh, yes," he replied, reloading the weapon. "Quite some few, notably those two friends of whom I spoke. You see I am satisfied in attaining practical perfection in my left hand, knowing that my other is skilled to a higher degree; but my friends must spend their time and cartridges painting the lily. Either Johnny or Hopalong would feel quite chagrined if at least five hadn't cut into the can. You should see them shooting against each other, breaking matches to get the exact measurements and arguing as if a fortune depended on it. Why, Miss Saunders, either of them could walk into Williams' hotel on a busy night, give warning, and empty two guns in less than ten seconds, every shot hitting a man. They have faced greater odds than that, both of them."

"You mean that one man could defeat a crowd like that?"

"Exactly; but they would not have to fire a shot," he said, smiling. "You see, such a man would only have to throw down on the crowd to hold them in check, if they know he will go through with his play. It isn't unlike an arch. The keystone in this case is the fear of certain death to the man who leads. The first man in the crowd to make a play would die. To some people martyrdom has a morbidly pleasant appeal as an abstract proposition; but in a concrete state, where the suffering is not vicarious, it really has few devotees. And here is a psychological fact: every man in the front rank of such a crowd is fully convinced that he has been selected for the target if the rush starts. Hopalong and Johnny would go through with their play if their hand was forced, and they are the kind of men whose expressions assure that they will. It is a great comfort to have them with you if you must enter a hostile town. It's a gift, like the gift of keener, swifter reflexes."

"It seems so impossible," commented Jane. "Won't you please try your other hand at a can? Somehow I felt that the snake was killed by accident more than skill. It seemed absurd, the offhand way you did it."

"This really is no test," he responded, filling another can and stepping back as he shifted the weapon to the right hand. "There is not the tenseness which a great stake causes; but, on the other hand, there is not the high-tension signals to the muscles. Watch closely," and the jarring crashes sounded like a loud ripping. One hole through the picture of a perfect tomato, two just above it, two lower down, and the sixth on the upper edge of the can gave mute testimony that he shot well.

She fairly squealed with delight and clapped her hands in spontaneous enthusiasm. "Wonderful! Wonderful! Oh, if I ever could shoot like that! I don't believe those friends can even equal it, and I don't care how good they are." Her face beamed. "But that must have taken a great deal of practice."

"Years of it," he replied, "coupled to a natural aptitude. While the accuracy is good enough, that is of secondary consideration. Had only one bullet struck the target, or grazed it, the other five would not have been necessary. The speed of the draw is the great thing. Any man used to shooting a revolver can hit that mark once in six--but he is far from a real gunman if he can't beat ninety-nine men out of a hundred in firing the first shot. That is what counts with a gun-fighter. His target is almost any place between the belt and the shoulders. If he strikes there and does not kill his man he will have time for a second shot if it is needed. My left hand is as deadly as my right against a living target so far as accuracy is concerned; but pit it against my right and it would be hopelessly lost, dead before it could get the gun out of the holster. And Hopalong Cassidy twice gave me lessons in the fine art of drawing--once in an exhibition and the second time in what would have been mortal combat if he had not allowed his heart to guide his head. I did not in the least merit his mercy. I had lived a wild, careless life, Miss Saunders; but it changed from that day."

"Jerry told me why you made him give up wearing his revolver," she said, thoughtfully. "I did not fully appreciate his words; but the graphic exposition lacks nothing to be convincing. Was your interest in his welfare another of your generalities?"

Her companion laughed. "Jerry is a very likable chap, Miss Saunders. Knowing that some feeling against him existed, and not knowing into what it might develop, I only followed the promptings of caution. He is a gentleman and a man infinitely finer grained than the rest of the inhabitants of Windsor. He is honorable and he lacks insight into the common motives which impel many men to perform acts he would not countenance. I have knocked about the West for twenty years, seeing it at its best and at its worst--and you simply cannot conceive what that worst is. I have met many Gus Williamses and Jakes and Bud Haineses and Henry Williamses. They are almost a distinct variation of the human species; they are a recognized and classified type. I knew them all as soon as I saw them. Bud Haines is a natural killer. He'd kill a man at a nod from the man who hired him. Gus Williams hires him, knowing that. Henry, the nephew, is foul, a sneak, and a coward. I'd rather see a sister of mine in her grave than married to him. But he is Gus Williams' nephew, the second power in town and must not be overlooked; and he never will know how close to death he has been these last few days. It fairly has breathed in his face. But we've had enough of this: not far ahead is a fairly good place for our lunch, unless you would prefer to go on to the C Bar."

"Why have you mentioned the nephew to me?" demanded Jane, her cheeks flushed and a fear in her eyes.

"Did I single him out?" asked Tex in surprise. "Why, I only mentioned him, along with the others, while giving examples of a detestable type and to explain why Jerry should not go about armed. I hope I have not frightened you, Miss Saunders?"

"You have not frightened me," she answered. "I have been frightened for a long time. We are so helpless! Things which bother me, I dare not speak to him about them, for he only would get into trouble and to no avail. He cannot pick and choose; and I must stand by him, no matter where he goes, or what he does. Is there mercy in heaven, is there justice in God, that we should be so circumscribed, forced by ills hard enough in themselves to bear, into still greater ills? Jerry's lungs would be tragedy enough for us to bear; but when I look around at times and see--do you believe in God, Mr. Jones?"

"What I may or may not believe in is no aid to you, Miss Saunders," replied Tex, amazed at his reaction to her distress. It was all he could do to keep from taking her in his arms. It was a lucky thing for Henry Williams that he finally abandoned the idea of following them. "If you have been taught to believe in a Divine Power, then don't you turn away from it. To say there is no God is to be as dogmatic as to say there is; for every reasoning being must admit a First

Cause. It is only when we characterize it, and attempt to give It attributes that differences of opinions arise. I am not going to enter into any discussion with you on subjects of this nature, Miss Saunders. Nor am I going to tell you what my convictions are. They do not concern us. If you have any religious belief, cling to it: this is when it should begin paying dividends."

"Have you read Kant?"

"Yes; and Spencer tears him apart."

"You are familiar with Spencer?"

"As I am with my own name. To my way of thinking his is the greatest mind humanity ever produced--but, with your permission, we will change the subject."

"Not just yet, please," she said. "You admire his logical reasoning?"

"I refuse to answer," he smiled. "Here, let me give you an example of logical reasoning, Miss Saunders. Here are two coins," he said, digging two double eagles out of his pocket, "which, along with thousands of others, we will say, were struck from one die. You and I would say that they are identical, especially after the most thorough and minute examination failed to disclose any differences. I hardly believe that any man, no matter how much he may be aided by instruments of precision, can take two freshly minted coins from the same die and find any difference. But what does pure logic say?"

"Certainly not that there is any difference?" she challenged in frank surprise.

He chuckled. "That is just what it claims, and here is the reasoning: No one will deny that the die wears out with use, which is the same as saying that the impressions change it. To deny that they do is to say that it does not wear out, which is absurd. Therefore each impression, being a part of the total impressions, must have done its share in the changing. And each impression, having changed it, must be different from those preceding and following it. Now, if the die changes, as we have just proved that it does, so must the coins struck off from it, for to say otherwise is to claim that effects are not produced by causes, and that a changed die will not make changed coins. Therefore, there are no two coins absolutely alike, never have been, and never can be, even at the moment they leave the die. Put them into circulation and the hypothetical differences rapidly increase, since no two of the coins can possibly receive the same treatment in their travelings. There you have it, in pure logic: but does it get you any place? On the strength of it, would you persist in denying that these coins are dissimilar? Are they so practically? And it is from practical logic that we draw the deductions by which we think and move and live. So you take my word that it will be better for you to cling to whatever faith you may have. If it is not practical enough for you, I'll look after that end for you; and between your faith and the cunning of my gun-hand I'll warrant that your brother will come to no harm. Shall we lunch at the C Bar, or in that little clump of burned and sickly timber on the bank of that dried-up creek?"

"I'm really too hungry to postpone the lunch," she said, smiling; "besides I want to watch you in camp, and to listen to you. It seems to me that you have too keen a brain to be spending your life where it all is wasted."

"Your compliment is disposed of by the fact that I am what I am," he responded. "The return compliment of not being able to be in a better place, under present conditions, is so obvious that I'll not spoil its effect by saying it. Anyhow, a fair vocabulary and a veneer of knowledge are not the measures of wisdom, but rather a disguising coat. To come right down to elementals, I heartily agree with you about the lunch. I'll be better company after the inner man has been properly attended to, for food always leavens my cynicism. Did I hear you ask why I do not eat continually?"

The clump of browned trees reached, it took but little time to unpack the lunch and start a cunningly built fire of twigs and broken branches, over which the coffee quickly heated. Depressing as the surroundings were, barren and sun-baked as far as eye could see, the bed of the creek dried and cracked and curling, this scene was destined to live long in the memory of Tex Ewalt. The food, better cooked and far more daintily prepared than any he could recall, tasted doubly good in the presence of his intelligent, good-looking companion. The subjects of their interested discussions were wide in range and neither very long maintained a certain restraint which had characterized their earlier conversations. She led him to talk of the West as it was, as he had seen it, and as he hoped it would become; a skillful question starting him off anew, and her intelligent comments keeping him at his best. So absorbed were they that even he failed to hear the step of a horse and did not know of its presence until an eager, if timid, hail stopped him short.

"Gosh, you people look cheerful," called Tommy Watkins, gazing at Jane with his heart in his eyes.

"Sorry I can't say the same about your looks," chuckled Tex, his quick glance noting the boyishness of their visitor, his youthful freshness and the rebellious admiration in his unblinking eyes. Tex took himself in hand and crushed the feeling of jealousy which tingled in him and threatened to show itself in words, looks, and actions. He looked inquiringly at his companion and at her slight nod, he beckoned to the youth. "Come over here an' make it three-handed, cowboy," he called. "We'll salvage what we can of th' lunch an' feed it to you. Did you find the ranch there, when you got home th' other night?"

Tommy rode up and gravely dismounted. "Yes, it was there. They said you hadn't been around so far as they knew, so I had my hasty ride for nothin'. How'd'y do, ma'am?" he asked, his hat going under his arm.

"Very well, indeed," replied Jane, smiling and fixing a place for him at her other side. "I'm sorry you did not come while there was more to eat, although I'll confess that I am not apologizing for my share of the havoc. It has been a long time since I have enjoyed a meal as I have this lunch. Sit here, Mr. Watkins--I am glad that there is some coffee left."

"That's what I get for being thrifty and thinking of the future," laughed Tex. "It's like the men who work hard and save all their lives, so that someone else can spend for them. Here you go, Thomas: look out--it's still hot."

"Thank you, ma'am," said Tommy, flushing and embarrassed, as he dropped onto the spot indicated. "I ain't a bit hungry, though."

"You will be after the first bite," assured Tex. "The cups have been used, and there's no water for washing them. That's excuse enough for any man to drink out of the pail, and I envy you there, Tommy Watkins. Cattle gettin' along all right in spite of the drought? Expect to have a big gain this round-up? They ought to bring top-notch prices if they're in good shape."

Steered easily into familiar channels of conversation, Tommy got on well, so well that his embarrassment gradually disappeared and he was nearly his natural self; but he did envy his friend's ability to think coherently and to talk with fluent ease on any subject mentioned. Jane Saunders learned more about cows, cattle, steers, calves, cows, cattle, riding, roping, round-ups, branding, cows, calves, horses, cattle, and other ranch subjects than she thought existed to be learned. And she shot a glance of grateful appreciation at Tex Jones for the way in which he put their guest on his feet and kept him there through several vocal flounderings. It was so tactfully done that Tommy did not realize it.

Gradually Tex worked out of the conversation and studied his companions. He saw clean youth entertaining clean youth; a bubbling mirth free from suspicion or irony; an absence of cynicism, and an unbounding faith in the future. He hid his smile at how Tommy was led to talk of himself and of his ambitions. They looked to be about the same age, Tommy perhaps a few years her senior; and when she looked at Tommy there was friendliness in her eyes; and when Tommy looked at her there was a great deal more in his.

The keen, but apparently careless, observer silently and fairly reviewed the years that had passed since he had been at Tommy's age; the lack of illusions, the cold, cynical practicality of his thoughts and actions; the laws, both civil and moral, which he contemptuously had shattered. He could not remember the time when he had had Tommy's faith in men, nor his enthusiasm. Tommy was looking forward to a life of clean, hard work, and actually with a fierce eagerness. Never had such a thing been an impelling motive in the life of Tex Ewalt. Instead he had planned shrewdly and consistently how to avoid working for a living, and when it was solved, then how to live higher and higher with the least additional effort. And he now admitted that if he had the chance to live that period over again, under the same circumstances, he would repeat his course in the major things. He felt neither regret nor remorse at the contrast--he had lived as it pleased him, and the Tex Ewalt of today had no censure for the Tex Ewalt of yesterday. But he was fair, at all events; and to draw true deductions from accepted facts was an art not to be perverted because expediency might beckon. After all, he did not try to fool himself; and he was no hypocritical whiner. Being fair, he calmly realized that he was the unfitting unit of this triangle, that he did not belong there. But there would be time enough for such cogitation later on.

"Shore," Tommy was dogmatically asserting. "Th' rattler gets all cramped up an' tired, an' there is an instant when he can't turn fast enough to keep his nasty little eyes on th' other, that's racin' around him like a flash. That's th' end of th' rattler. Th' kingsnake darts in, grabs th' rattler behind th' head, an' after a great thrashin' around, kills him dead. *Ain't* that so, Mr. Jones?"

Tex lazily turned his head and looked at the doubting auditor and then at the anxious Tommy. He gravely nodded. "Yes that's th' end. That's the enemy within the snake's own species which I mentioned back on the trail, Miss Saunders."

The look of doubt faded from her face and a nebulous smile transformed it. She was certain of it now.

Tex flamed at what that change told him, tingling to his finger tips with a surging elation. He felt that he had but to speak three words to put her vague feelings into a coherent wonder of wonders; but to crystallize them into an everlasting passion by the alchemy of his avowal, or the touch of his lips. The lulled storm within him broke out anew and blazed fiercely. He arose, kicked an inoffensive tin can over the bed of the creek and spun it in mid-air by a vicious, eye-baffling shot from his Colt. Realizing how he had forgotten himself, and his resolutions, he, the cool, imperturbable Tex Ewalt, he recovered his poise and bowed, smilingly, to the surprised pair.

"That's shootin', Tex!" cried Tommy.

"It's more than that," smiled Tex. "It's notice that it's time to try that .38, Miss Saunders," he announced. "She is learning to use a gun, Tommy--I've been telling her how much fun it is. I'll call th' shots while you stand by her to answer questions. Suppose we have a more suitable target, this time. What can we use?"

Tommy grinned expansively. "Who's goin' to do th' shootin'?" he demanded.

"Miss Saunders," answered Tex. "Why?"

"Oh; all right then--here, prop up my hat," offered Tommy; "But not too all-fired close!" he warned.

"There's chivalry for you, Mr. Jones!" triumphantly exclaimed Jane, her eyes dancing.

"Think so?" queried Tex, grinning. "Huh!" He shook his head. "I'd say he is not paying you any compliment. Just for that I hope you shoot it to pieces."

He took the sombrero from Tommy's extended hand, went down and crossed the creek bed, and placed the hat against the opposite bank. Stepping off twenty paces he drew a line on the earth with the side of his boot sole and beckoned to the flushed markswoman.

"That hat is a pressing danger," he warned. "You've got to get it, or it'll get you. Don't be careless, and don't waste any sympathy on the grinning wretch who owns it."

"But I don't want to ruin it," she protested. "Surely something else will answer?"

"You go ahead an' ruin it, if you can," chuckled Tommy. "Don't *you* worry none-- *I* ain't!"

"I do believe it wasn't a compliment, or chivalry, at all," she laughed. "All right, Mr. Watkins: here goes for a new hat!" Slowly, deliberately, holding her arm as she had been instructed, she aimed and fired until the weapon was empty. The hat had a hole near one edge of the crown and another near the edge of the brim.

"Glory be!" exclaimed Tommy. "I'm votin' for a new target! Why that's plumb fine, Miss Saunders--if it ain't an accident!"

"Let's see if it was," suggested Tex, handing her another round of cartridges. "Here!" he exclaimed, glancing at Tommy. "Where you goin' so fast?"

"To collect th' ruins," retorted the puncher over his shoulder. " *You* got a hat, ain't you?"

"I have, and I'm keeping it right where it belongs," rejoined Tex. "I didn't suggest that it was any accident, did I?"

Chapter X
Speed and Guile

Tex and Tommy said their adieus, watched Jane enter the house, and then rode slowly toward the station where, after a few words with Jerry Saunders, Tommy went on alone, leaving Tex talking with the agent.

The C Bar puncher rode down the main street full of more kinds of emotion than he ever had known before, and among them was a strong feeling of his inability to gain Jane's attention while Tex Jones was around. Jealousy was working in the yeasty turbulence of his heart and mind. Taking off his perforated sombrero he gazed at it as though it were something sacred. There they were, two of them, made by her blessed bullets! Reverently pushing the ragged felt of their rims back into place, he patted the nearly closed holes and put the sombrero on his head again. There would be no new hat for Tommy Watkins, as she had laughingly said. No, sir! No, sir-e-e!

Opposite the hotel he became aware of his surroundings and suddenly decided that he needed a drink to steady himself, to shock himself into a more natural condition of mind. As he made the decision, he idly observed Bud Haines emerge from the door of the general store and start toward him on the peculiar, bow-legged, choppy stride he so much affected. And as Tommy swung off the horse and carelessly tossed the reins across the tie-rail he caught sight of Tex Jones waving to the agent and slowly wheeling the roan.

Tommy made his way through the card-table end of the room, noticing without giving any particular weight to the fact, that he was the cynosure of all eyes. Still strange to himself and very much occupied by his thoughts, he did not note whether there were six or two dozen men in the room; nor that their eager and low-voiced conversation abruptly ceased upon his entry, and that there was an air of expectancy which seemed to fill the room. He passed Henry Williams, who was seated at a small table, with a nod and rested his elbows on the bar. Silently a bottle and glass were placed before him, silently he poured out a drink and downed it mechanically. Then Henry spoke, his ratlike eyes for a moment not shifting.

"That's a fenced range," he said in a low, tense voice. "You keep off it!"

Tommy, not realizing that the words were intended for him, still rested his elbows on the bar, his back to the speaker and the rest of the room, buried in his abstractions. He neither saw nor heard the quiet, quick entry of Bud Haines through the front door, nor knew that the gunman stopped suddenly and leaned against the jamb. Neither he, nor anyone else, caught the quiet step nearing that same door from the street.

Henry Williams, finding his warning totally ignored, let his anger leap to rage.

"You!" he snarled. "I'm talking to you, Watkins!"

Tommy started and swung around, momentarily out of touch with his surroundings. The meanness in the voice, the deadly timbre of it, warned him subconsciously rather than acutely, and he stared at the speaker.

"What you say, Williams?" he asked, rapidly sensing the hostility in the air. "I was thinkin' of somethin'," he explained.

"I'm givin' you somethin' to think about!" retorted Henry, slowly arising and slowly leaning forward on the table. "You don't want to stop thinkin' about it, neither--unless you want to join th' dead uns on Boot Hill. I said that range is fenced-- *you keep off* !"

Tommy, alert as a coiled snake now, watched the angry man while he considered. A fenced range. He was to keep off. "I ain't gettin' th' drift of that," he said, slowly. "Any reason why you shouldn't talk so I'll know what yo're meanin'?"

"Yo're dumb as h--l, ain't you?" sneered Henry, his voice rising shrilly and the little, close-set eyes beginning to flame. "I wouldn't have nobody say you wasn't warned plain. I'm tellin' you for th' last time, to do yore courtin' somewhere else! I'm claimin' that Saunder gal. Keep away, that's all!"

Tommy went a little white around his stiffening lips. When his words came they sounded the spirit of the C Bar, but where they came from he did not know; perhaps he had heard them or read them somewhere. Certainly they did not by right belong to his direct method of conveying thought. He knew Henry Williams, his baseness, his petty villainies, his bestial nature. The picture of Jane, innocent and sweet, came to him and made a contrast which sickened him. Looking straight into Henry's eyes his voice rasped its insulting, deadly reply.

"It's bad enough for a coyote like me to admire a rose; but I'm d--d if any polecat's goin' to pluck it!"

Before the words were all spoken and before either of the disputants could move they heard the startling crash of a gun and instinctively glanced toward the sound. They saw Bud Haines, his smoking revolver forced slowly up behind his back, higher and higher, the gun wrist gripped in the sinewy fingers of Tex Jones, whose right hand held his own Colt at his hip, the deadly muzzle covering the two in front of the bar, without a tremble of its steely barrel. His gripping fingers kept on twisting, while one knee held the killer from writhing sidewise to escape the grip of the punishing bending of the imprisoned arm. Slowly the tortured muscles grew numb, slowly beads of perspiration stood out on the killer's forehead, and as his throbbing elbow neared the snapping point, he gasped, released his hold on the Colt and then went spinning across the room from the power of his captor's whirling shove. When he stopped he froze in his tracks, for Tex carelessly held two guns now, the captured weapon covering its owner.

"Phew!" sighed Tex, a grin slowly spreading across his red face. "That was close, that was! Reckon I done saved quite a mess in here." He glared at Tommy. "You get th' h--l out of here an' don't come back till you know how to act! Runnin' around like a mad dog, tryin' to kill men that never done you no harm! G'wan, or I'll let Hennery loose at you! I heard what you said, an' I wouldn't blame him if he blowed you wide open! G'wan! Shove that gun back where it belongs, an' git: *Pronto* ! You've gone an' got Bud an' me bad friends, I reckon, an' I can't hardly blame him, neither."

Henry's eyes were riveted on the menacing Colt, his hand frozen where it had stopped, a few inches above the butt of his own. Bud Haines leaned forward, balanced on the balls of his feet, but not daring to leap. The spectators were staring, open-mouthed, quite content to let things take their course without any impetus from them.

Tommy sullenly slid the gun back into its holster and walked toward the door, too angry to speak. Glaring at Tex he went out, mounted and rode toward the ranch; and it was half an hour later before he came to the realization that his life had been saved from a shot from the side, and by the time he had reached the ranchhouse he was grinning.

Tex flipped the captured gun into the air, caught it by the barrel, and tossed it, butt first, to the killer. "I shore am apologizin' to you, Bud," he said, "for cuttin' in that way--but I had to act sudden, an' rough."

As the weapon settled into its owner's hand it roared and leaped, the bullet cutting Tex's vest under the armpit. Before a second shot could follow from it Bud twisted sidewise and plunged face down on the floor.

Tensed like a panther about to spring, Tex peered through the thinning cloud of smoke rising from his hip, his attention on the others in the room. "Sorry," he said. "You saw it all. I gave him his gun, butt first, an' he shot at me with it. Clipped my vest under my left shoulder. I couldn't do nothin' else. I'm sayin' that doin' favors for strangers is risky business--but is anybody findin' any fault with this shootin'?" He glanced quickly from face to face and then nodded slightly. "It was plain self-defense. If I'd 'a' thought he was a-goin' to shoot I shore wouldn't 'a' chucked him his loaded gun. Reckon I'm a plain d--d fool!"

There were no replies to him. The tense faces stared at the man who had killed Bud Haines in a fight after the killer had shot first. While there were no accusations in their expressions, neither was there any friendliness. The killing had been justified. This seemed to be the collective opinion, for in no way could the facts be changed. Bud had been man-handled in a manner which to him had been an unbearable insult, the fight could be considered as of his adversary's starting, but the actual shooting was as the victor claimed; and it was the shooting which they were to judge.

Tex, feeling ruefully of the bullet-torn vest, shoved his gun into its sheath and went over to Henry's table. The nephew hardly had moved since the first shot.

"I got somethin' to talk to you about, Henry," said Tex in a low, confidential voice. "'Tain't for everybody's ears, neither; so sit down a minute. That fool Watkins came cuttin' in as we was ridin' back, or I might have more news."

Henry slowly followed his companion's movements and straddled his chair. He motioned to the bartender for drinks and then let his suspicious eyes wander over his companion's face. He had a vast respect for Tex Jones.

"I reckon he's been cured of cuttin' in," he growled, a momentary gleam showing. "That's a habit of yourn, too," he said. "An' it's a cussed bad one, here in Windsor."

Tex spread his hands in helpless resignation. "I know it. Ever since I've been in this town I been puttin' my worst foot forward. I'm allus bunglin' things; an' just when I was beginnin' to make a few friends, Bud had to go an' git blind mad an' spoil everythin'. I didn't have nothin' ag'in' Bud; but I reckon mebby I was a little mite rough."

"Oh, Bud be d--d!" coldly retorted Henry. "He had th' edge, an' lost. That's between him an' you. What I'm objectin' to, Jones, is th' way you spoiled my plans. Don't you never cut into my affairs like you did just now. I'm tellin' you fair. I'm admittin' yo're a prize-winnin' gun-thrower; but there's other ways in this town. Savvy?"

Tex shook his head apologetically and nodded. "You an' me ain't goin' to have no trouble, Hennery," he declared earnestly. "If you want that C Bar fool, go git him. It ain't none of my business. But I'm worryin' about what yore uncle's goin' to say about me shootin' Bud," he confessed with plain anxiety. "He's a big man, Williams is; an' me, shucks: I ain't nothin' a-tall."

"He'll take my say-so," assured Henry, "after he cools down. Now what you got to tell me?"

"It's about that Saunders gal," answered Tex. He hitched his chair a little nearer to the table. "You remember what I told you, couple of nights ago? Well, I got to thinkin' about it when I was near th' station yesterday, so I went in an' got friendly with her brother." He rubbed his chin and grinned reminiscently. "There was a box across th' track that he had been using for a target. I asked him what it was an' he told me, an' he said he couldn't hit it. I sort of egged him on, not believin' him; an' shore enough he couldn't--an', Hennery, it was near as big as a house! I cut loose an' made a sieve of it--you must 'a' heard th' shootin'? His eyes plumb stuck out, an' we got to talkin' shootin'. Finally he ups an' asks me can I show his sister how to throw a gun an', seein' my chance to learn somethin' about her, I said I shore could show anybody that wasn't scared to death of one, an' that had any sense. 'How much will you charge for th' lessons?' says he. I had a good chance to pick up some easy money, but that wasn't what I was playin' for. I just wanted to get sort of friendly with her, an' him, too. I says, 'Nothin'.' Well, we fixed it up, an' today we goes off practicin'--you should 'a' seen that lunch, Hennery! I'm cussed near envyin' you!" He laughed contentedly, leaned back, and rubbed his stomach.

"Well?" demanded Henry, grinning ruefully.

"Well," echoed Tex. "You know that sewin' an' crochetin' is a whole lot different from shootin' a .45; an' so does she, now. I reckon a .22 would 'most scare her to death. Did you ever shoot with yore eyes shut? You don't have to try: it can't be done, an' hit nothin'. Six-guns an' wimmin wasn't never made to mix; an' they shore don't. We ate up th' lunch an' started back ag'in, an' I was just gettin' set to swing th' conversation in yore direction, carelesslike, but real careful, an' see what I could find out for you, when cussed if that C Bar coyote didn't come dustin' up, an' I don't know any more than I did before. But I'm riskin' one thing, Hennery: I'm near shore she ain't got nothin' ag'in' you; an' on th' way out, when I refers to you she speaks up quicklike, with her nose turned up a little, an' says: 'Henry Williams? Why, he'll be a rich man some day, when his uncle dies. Ain't some folks born lucky, Mr. Jones?' Hennery, there ain't none of 'em that are overlookin' th' good old pesos, U.S. You keep right on like you are; an' save me a front seat at th' weddin'.'"

Henry sat back, buried in thought. He glanced at the huddled figure near the door and then looked quickly into his companion's bland eyes. "Her brother's dead set ag'in' it. He knows he done me a dirty trick, stealin' my job, an' like lots of folks, instead of hatin' hisself, he hates me. Human nature's funny that way. So he can't hit a box, hey?"

Tex chuckled and nodded. "He up an' says he's so plumb disgusted with hisself that he ain't never goin' to tote a gun again, not never. Seems to me yo're doin' a lot of foolish worryin' about losin' that job. That ain't no job to worry about. If I was Gus Williams' only relation, you wouldn't see me lookin' for no jobs! You shore got th' wrong idea, Hennery. What do you want to work for, anyhow?"

"Well," considered the nephew of the uncle who some day would die, "that is one way of lookin' at it; but, Tex, he did me out of it. That's what's rilin' me!"

Tex leaned back and laughed heartily. "Hennery, you make me laugh! If I got mad an' riled at every dog that barked at me I'd be plumb soured for life by this time. A man like you should be above holdin' grudges ag'in' fellers like Saunders. It ain't worth th' risk of spoilin' yore disposition. Let him have his dried-out bone: you would 'a' dropped it quick enough, anyhow. An' if it wasn't for him gettin' that two-by-nothin' old job you wouldn't never 'a' seen his sister, would you? Ever think about it like that? Well, what you think? Had I better try to go ridin' with her ag'in an' git her to talkin'? Or shall I set back an' only keep my eyes an' ears open?"

"What's interestin' you so much in this here affair?" questioned Henry, his glance resting for a moment on the face of his companion.

"Well, I ain't got that letter," confessed Tex, slyly; "an' what's more, I'm afraid I ain't goin' to get it, neither, th' coyote. He lets me come out here, near th' end of th' track, an' then lets me hold th' sack. Time's comin' when I'll be needin' a job; an' yo're aces-up with yore uncle." He grinned engagingly. "My cards is face up. I got to look out for myself."

Henry laughed softly. "You shore had me puzzled," he replied. "Well, we'll see what we see. I don't hardly know, yet, what kind of a job you ought to have. There's good jobs, an' poor jobs. An' while I think of it, Tex, you'd mebby better go ridin' with her ag'in. But don't you forget what I was sayin' about there bein' other ways than gun-throwin' in Windsor. I——"

The low hum of conversation about them ceased as abruptly as did Henry's words. He was looking at the door, and sensing danger, Tex pushed back quietly and followed his companion's gaze. Jake, under the influence of liquor, stood in the doorway, a gun in his upraised hand, staring with unbelieving eyes at the body of Bud Haines.

"Stop that fool!" whispered Tex. "I've done too much killin' today: an' he's drunk!"

Henry arose and walked quietly, swiftly toward the vengeful miner, who now turned and looked about the room. A spasm of rage shot through him and his hand chopped down, but Henry knocked it aside and the heavy bullet scored the wall. Two men near the door leaped forward at the nephew's call and after a short struggle, Jake was disarmed, pacified, and sent on his way again.

Tex dropped his gun back into the holster and went up to the nephew. "Much obliged, Hennery," he said. "I've been expectin' him most every minute an' I'm glad you handled it so good. Where's he been keepin' hisself, anyhow?"

"Out in his cabin, nursin' his grudge," answered Henry. "He's one of them kind. He's got it chalked up ag'in' you, Tex, an' it'll smolder an' smolder, no tellin' how long. Then it'll bust out ag'in, like it did just now. Keep out of his way--he's a good man, Jake is. He's a friend of mine."

"That's good enough for me," Tex assured him. "I ain't got no grudge ag'in' Jake. It's th' other way 'round. Reckon I'll put up my cayuse. See you later."

Chapter XI
Empty Honors

The dramatic death of Bud Haines created a ripple of excitement in Windsor which ran a notch higher than any killing of recent years. The late gunman posed as a gunman, swaggeringly, exultantly. Himself a contributor of victims to Boot Hill, his going there aroused a great deal more satisfaction than resentment. He was unmourned, but not unsung, and the question raised by his passing concerned the living more than the dead. How would his conqueror behave?

Bud was an out-and-out killer, cold, dispassionate, calculating; one whose gun was for hire and salary. He had no sympathy, no softer side to his nature, if his fellow-townsmen knew him right. The crooked mouth, grown into a lop-sided sneer, had been a danger signal to everyone who saw him, and through his up-to-then invincible gun Williams had passed his days in confidence, his nights in sleep. He had been taciturn, unsmiling, grim, and the few words he occasionally uttered were never cryptic. On the other hand Tex Jones was voluble, talked loosely and foolishly and had shown signs at poker that his courage was not what it should be to wrap the mantle of the fallen man about him and play his part; but had it been truly shown? Was his poker playing a true index to his whole nature? There was his brief, high-speed, complete mastery over Jake, himself a man bad enough to merit wholesome respect; there was the cool killing of Bud, and the nonchalant actions of the victor after the tragedy. He scarcely had given his victim a second look.

This question, as all questions do, provided argument. Gus Williams, sullen and morose at losing a valuable man in whose fidelity he could place full trust, and on whose prowess his own power largely rested, maintained that Tex Jones had pulled the trigger mechanically, and that it had been for him a lucky accident. His nephew took issue with him and paid his new companion full credit. The miners were about evenly divided, while Carney openly exulted and made the victory his principal topic of conversation. It helped him in another way, for there are some who blindly follow a champion, and the Windsor champion kept his horse and spent many of his spare hours at Carney's. John Graves sighed with relief at Bud's passing, due to an old score he had feared would be reopened, and he urged the appointment of Tex Jones for city marshal, a position hitherto unfilled in Windsor. Carney was for this heart and soul, and offered a marshal's office rent free. It was a lean-to adjoining his saloon.

The railroad element breathed easier now. Tim Murphy wanted to bet on the new man against anyone, at any style, and he glowed with pride as he realized that he, perhaps, was nearer to Tex Jones than any man in town. He had no trouble in persuading Costigan to look with warm favor on the successor to Bud Haines. Jerry Saunders, remembering a bit of gun practice, said he was not surprised and he exulted secretly. Tex Jones had been the first man outside of the railroad circle to give him a kind word and to show friendship; but he had little to say about it after the door of his home closed upon him.

Jerry's sister puzzled him. He saw traces of tears, strange moods came over her which swept her from gaiety to black despondency in the course of an hour or two, and no matter how he figured, he could not understand her. The story of how the affair had started and of Tommy Watkins' part in it made her moods more complex and unfathomable. Jane, he decided, was not only peculiar, but downright foolish. Bud Haines, being but a free member of Williams' own body, executing his wishes and the wishes of the detestable nephew, had been an evil whose potentiality could only be conjectured. He had been swept off the board and his conqueror was at heart very friendly to the Saunders family. They no longer were the most helpless people in town.

When Jerry had gone home on the day of the tragedy he had been full of the exploit, for Murphy and he had discussed it from every angle, and he had absorbed a great deal of the big Irishman's open delight.

Stunned at first, Jane flatly refused to talk about it, and had fled from the supper table to her room. Later on when he had cautiously broached the subject again, quoting the enthusiastic Murphy almost entirely, to show that his own opinions were well founded, she had listened to all he had to say, but had remained dumb. The evening was anything but pleasant and he had gone to bed in an unconcealed huff. She gave credit to Watkins but withheld it from Jones, who had earned it all. "D--n women, anyhow," had been his summing up.

The following morning he ate a silent breakfast and hurried to the station as he would flee to an oasis from the open desert. He found Tim waiting for him, eager to talk it all over again.

Hardly had the station been opened when Tex rode up, leaped from the magnificent roan, and sauntered to the door. His face was grave, his manner dignified and calm. "How'd'y, boys," he said in greeting.

"Proud I am this mornin'," beamed Murphy, his thick, huge hand closing over the lean, sinewy one of the gunman. "'Twas a fine job ye done, Tex, my boy; an' a fine way ye did it! Gave th' beast th' first shot! There's not another man could do it."

"There's plenty could," answered Tex. "I can name two, an' there's many more. I'm no gunman, understand: I'm just plain Tex Jones. But I didn't come here to hold any pow-pow--I'm wonderin' if you'd let me look in th' toolhouse--I might 'a' left it there when we loaded th' hand car."

"An' what's 'it'?" asked Murphy.

"My knife."

"Come along then," said the section-boss, swinging his keys and leading the way. They found no knife, but Murphy was given some information which he considered worth while. As they reached the station door again Tex burst out laughing.

"I know where it is! Cuss me for a fool, I left it in Carney's stable, stickin' in th' side of th' harness closet. Oh, well; there's no harm done." He turned to Jerry. "I wonder if Miss Saunders would like another bit of practice today?"

Jerry's face clouded. No matter how much he might admire Bud Haines' master in the late Bud's profession of gun-throwing, and no matter how much he might admire him for sundry other matters, nevertheless none of them qualified the new-found friend as an aspirant for his sister's hand. He did not wish to offend Tex, and certainly he did not want his enmity. To him came Jane's inexplicable behavior and in coming it brought an inspiration. Jane, he thought, could handle this matter far better than he could.

"She didn't seem to be feeling well this morning," he answered. "Still, I never guess right about her. If you feel like riding again, go up and ask her."

"I hear there's some talk about them makin' you marshal of this town," said Tim. "Don't you shelve it. This town needs a fair man in that job. It's been quiet of late, but ye can't allus tell. Wait till th' rains come an' start th' placerin' a-goin'. They'll have money to spend, then, an' trouble is shore to follow that. You take that job, Tex."

Jerry nodded eagerly, pointed to some bullet holes in the frame of one of the windows of the office and, grasping Tex by the arm, led him closer to the window. "See that bullet hole in there, just over the table an' below the calendar? The first shot startled me and made me drop my pen--I stooped to pick it up. When I sat up again there was a hole in the glass and under the calendar. When I stooped I saved my life. Just a drunken joke, a miner feeling his oats. One dead man a week was under the average. This town, under normal conditions, is a little bit out of h--l. Take that job, Jones: the town needs you."

Tex laughed. "You better wait till it's offered to me, Jerry. There's quite some people in this town that don't want any marshal. Gus Williams is the man to start it."

"He will," declared Tim. "Bud was his bodyguard, but he was more. Williams has a lot of property to be protected, an' now Bud is gone, th' saints be praised. He'll start it."

While they spoke, a miner was seen striding toward the station and soon joined them. "How'd'y," he said, carelessly, glancing coldly at Tim and Jerry. His eyes rested on Tex and glowed a little. "Th' boss wants to talk with you, Jones. Come a-runnin'."

"Come a-runnin'," rang in Tex's ears and it did not please him. If he was going to be the city marshal it would be well to start off right.

"Th' boss?" he asked nonplused.

"Shore; Gus--Gus Williams," rejoined the messenger crisply and with a little irritation. "You know who I mean. Git a move on."

"Mr. Jones' compliments to Mr. Williams," replied Tex with exaggerated formality, "an' say that Mr. Jones will call on him at Mr. Jones' convenience. Just at present I'm very busy--good day to you, sir."

The miner stood stock-still while he reviewed the surprising words.

Tex ignored him. "No," he said, "I ain't lookin' for no change in th' weather till th' moon changes," he explained to the two railroad men. "But, of course, you know th' old sayin': 'In times of drought all signs fail.' An' there never was a truer one. I wouldn't be surprised if it rained any day; an' when it comes it's goin' to rain hard. Still, I ain't exactly lookin' for it, barrin' the sayin', till th' moon changes. That's my prophecy, gents; you wait an' see if I ain't right. Well, I reckon I'll be amblin'. Good day."

They watched him walk to the roan, throw the reins over an arm, and lead it slowly down the street, followed by the conjecturing messenger. Tex Jones evidently was in no hurry, for he stopped in two places before entering the hotel, and in there he remained for a quarter of an hour. When premature congratulations were offered him he accepted them with becoming modesty and explained that he was not yet appointed.

Gus Williams looked up with some irritation when the door opened and admitted Tex into the store. The newcomer leaned against the counter, nodded to Gus and grinned at Henry. "Hear you want to see me about somethin'," he said, flickering dust from his boots with a softly snapping handkerchief.

"What made you shoot Bud Haines?" growled the proprietor, turning on the stepladder against the shelves.

Tex shook his head in befitting sorrow. "I shore didn't want to shoot Bud," he answered slowly. "Bud hadn't never done nothin' to me; but," he explained, wearily, "he just made me do it. I dassn't let him shoot twice, dast I?"

Williams growled something and replaced several articles of merchandise.

"Hennery says you had to do it," he grudgingly admitted. "I reckon mebby you did-- *but* , I don't see why you went at Bud like that, in th' first place."

"I aimed to stop a killin'," muttered Tex, contritely; "an', instead of doin' it, I went an' made one. I ain't none surprised," he said, sighing resignedly, "for I generally play in bad luck. Ever since I shot that black cat, up at Laramie, I've had bad luck--not that I'm what you might call superstitious," he quickly and defiantly explained.

"Well, a man can't allus help things like that," admitted Williams. "I had streaks of luck that looked like they never would peter out." He shifted several articles, leaned back to study their arrangement, and slowly continued. "You see, Bud had a job that ain't very common; an' men like Bud ain't very common, neither. He allus was plumb grateful because I saved his life once in a--stampede," he naively finished. "I got a lot of valuable property in this here town, and Windsor gets quite lively when th' placerin' is going good. I shore feel sort of lost without Bud." He wiped his dusty hands on his trousers and slowly climbed down. "Now, I remembered that Scrub Oak an' Willow both has peace officers, an' Windsor shore ain't taking a back seat from towns like them. Hennery was sayin' that folks here sort of been talkin' about a city marshal, an' mentionin' you for th' office. We ought to have our valuable property pertected, an' me, bein' the owner of most of th' valuable property here an' hereabouts, nat'rally leans to that idea; but, bein' th' biggest owner of valuable property, I sort of got to look the man over purty well before I appoint him. I got to have a good man, a man that'll pertect th' most property first. What you think about it?"

Tex removed his sombrero, turned it over slowly in his hands and stared at its dents. Punching them out and pushing in new ones, he gravely considered them. "Well," he drawled, "you see, if that letter comes--I don't know how long I'm goin' to stay in town; but if I did stay, I'd shore do my damndest to pertect property, an' you havin' the most of it, you'd nat'rally be pertected more'n others that had less."

Williams glanced swiftly at his nephew. "You still expectin' that letter, Jones?" he slyly demanded.

Tex hesitated and turned the hat over again. "Can't hardly say I am," he admitted, frowning at Henry. "But there's a sayin' that hope springs infernal--an' I reckon that's th' h--l of it; a man never knows when to quit waitin' for it to spring. Meanwhile I got to eat--an' I like a game of poker once in awhile. Here, tell you what--I'll take the job as long as I can hold it, if the pay is right. What you reckon the job's worth, in a lawless, desperate town like this, where no man's life or property is worth very much?"

Williams scowled. "This here town ain't lawless an' desperate," he denied. "There ain't a more peaceable town in Kansas!"

"Which same ain't payin' no compliments to Kansas towns, once the rains come," chuckled Tex. "I'm admirin' your humor, Mr. Williams--I ain't never heard dryer," he beamed in frank admiration. "But, wet or dry, there's allus them mean low-down cow-wrastlers comin' to town to likker up--an' them an' miners are as friendly as a badger and a dog. Let's name over them as would want the pertection of a marshal, an' then figger how much they'd sweeten the pot. Take Carney, now--he ought to be willin' to ante up han'some, his business bein' so healthy."

"Carney," sneered Williams in open contempt. "Huh! Here, gimme that pencil an' that old envelope!" He worked laboriously, revised the figures several times and then looked up. "I reckon two hundred a month ought to be enough. Scrub Oak pays that--Willow does likewise. You got your outfit. We furnish th' office, ammernition, an' pay extra expenses. That's th' best Windsor can do. Yore office will be next door to this store."

Tex looked questioningly at Henry, who nodded decisively, and carefully put the hat back on his head. "All right," he said. "When do I start in?"

"Right now," answered Williams, fumbling under the counter. "We ain't got no marshal's badge, but I got a sheriff's star somewhere around. He was killed up on Buffaler Crick last spring. Yep--here it is: this'll do for awhile. Lean over here, Marshal," he chuckled. "There: It ain't every marshal that's a sheriff, too." Smiling at Henry he said, jokingly, "Now let her rain!"

Tex nodded. "Let it come," he said. "Everybody that deserves it will have a slicker ag'in' th' rain. As marshal I'm playin' no favorites--there's no strings to a city marshal. My job's to keep th' peace of Windsor, an' let th' devil whistle." He smiled enigmatically, hitched up his belt, and then looked at Henry. "You know where Bud's belt an' gun are?"

Henry nodded. "Baldy's got 'em, behind th' bar. Want 'em?"

"Yes," answered Tex, slowly turning. "When it starts rainin', two guns will keep me on an even keel. My left hand feels empty-like. Reckon I'll go git Bud's outfit an' have th' harness-maker turn th' holster so it'll set right for th' left side; or mebby he's got a cavalry sheath, which won't need so much changin'."

"But you ought to have a rifle heavier than a .38 short," suggested Gus Williams. "That ain't no gun for this country."

Tex smiled. "For town use that's plenty heavy enough. But we won't argue about that because I ain't got it no more. I swapped with that section-boss, paying him fifteen dollars to-boot. To a thick Mick like him there ain't much difference between a .38 short and a .45-90. He can't use either one worth a cuss, anyhow. I'd say I was lucky stumblin' on him." He turned and walked toward the door, glanced up at the cloudless sky, and chuckled. "No signs of rain, yet. Oh, well; it'll come when it gets here. *Adios* ," and the slow steps of the walking roan grew softer down the street.

The harness-maker looked from the belt and holster to an up-ended box and waved at the latter. "Set down, Mr. Jones. 'Twon't take a minute, but you might as well set. Many a one I've turned. A new cut here, a new strap, an' a scallop out of th' top on th' other side so yore fingers'll close on th' butt first thing. Let's see th' other. Yep; deep cut down to th' guard. Now, if I put it back on th' belt at th' same place, it'll throw th' buckle around back--all right, then. They won't match each other, but that don't make no difference, I reckon. Ain't there been some talk of appointin' you city marshal?"

Tex nodded. "This star was th' only one they had," he explained.

"Well, you may be workin' both jobs afore long if Gus Williams has th' say-so," commented the harness-maker. "Funny, but I never work on a gun sheath but I think of th' one I made to order for Jack Slade after he got around ag'in from Old Jules' shotgun. Jack blamed it on his holster, an' it shore made him particular. That was back in Old Julesburg when I was a harness-apprentice there. Soon after that he was sent up to take charge of th' Rocky Ridge division of th' stage line, which was th' worst division of th' whole line. Holdups was a reg'lar thing. They soon stopped after he took charge. He was th' best man with a short gun I ever saw. I heard that he wore that holster to th' day th' vigilantes got him, up in Virginia City, Montanny. Now, Mr. Marshal, strap this on you an' see if th' gun comes out right. Sometimes they got to be shaped a little mite--ah, that looks all right. Reckon it'll do?"

With the newly acquired belt hanging over the old one, sloping loosely from the right hip across his body to a point below the left, the marshal went out, mounted the roan, and rode carelessly down to the toolshed, where he told Murphy of his appointment and of the fictitious swapping of rifles, and then went up to the station. As he neared it Jerry came out of the door, caught the flash of the sun on the nickel-plated star and turned, grinning, to await the coming of the new marshal.

"That looks mighty good to the station agent," Jerry laughed. "An' so you're wearin two guns instead of one? Gosh, that looks business-like!"

Tex reined in and grinned down at him. "Any time you feel urged to shoot up th' town, Mr. Agent, you'll find out that it is business-like. Better start by gettin' th' marshal first: it'll be a lot safer, that way."

"That's good advice, and I won't forget it," replied Jerry. "I'll notify the company of your appointment. That ought to make it feel good, and it might want to pay its share of your salary. I'm certainly wishing you luck."

"I may be needin' it," responded the marshal. "Reckon I'll go on to th' house an' show off my new bright an' shinin' star." He glanced down at the badge and grinned. "Seein' how you reads 'Sheriff' instead of 'Marshal' she'll mebby wonder what you are. So-long, Jerry!"

Reaching the little house, Tex swung gravely off Omar and proceeded to the door in mock dignity. Knocking heavily, he assumed a stern demeanor and waited. When the door opened he removed his sombrero, bowed, and grinned. "Behold the Law, Miss Saunders, in the person of the marshal of Windsor."

"I congratulate you, Marshal," she coldly replied. "Doubtless you may now take life with legal authority. It is too bad it comes a little late."

"I did not need legal authority, Miss Saunders, if I rightly interpret your remark," he rejoined. "The authority of Nature ever precedes and transcends it. Self-preservation is the first law. He fired, and I did not dare let him fire again."

"You provoked his attack!" she flashed. "He could do nothing else."

"That was because I preferred to risk his life than the certainty of him taking that of Tommy Watkins, who was being deliberately baited. Bud lost his rights when he drew his gun against an unsuspecting man. I am sorry if you look upon the unfortunate incident in any other light; but I am so sure of my position that I would repeat it today under the same conditions. Besides I am naturally prejudiced against assassins."

"Why did you give him his gun before he had time to master his anger?" she demanded, her eyes flashing.

"Because I wanted to show him how impersonal my interference was, and to help smooth over a tense situation. It was one of those high-tension moments when a false move might easily precipitate a shambles. There were a dozen armed men in the room, a ratio of ten to two. I followed my best judgment. I am not apologizing, Miss Saunders, even to you; I am merely explaining the situation as it existed. When Bud Haines drew his gun from the side to shoot a man who did not know of his danger, he broke our rules. I would have been justified in shooting him down at the move. Instead I tried to stop his shot and give him a way out of it." While he spoke his right hand had risen to his belt and now hung there by a crooked thumb, a position he was in the habit of assuming when he spoke earnestly.

She glanced down at it involuntarily, shuddered, and slowly closed the door.

"I am very sorry, Mr. Jones, but--" the closing of the door ended the conversation for both.

He studied the warped, weather-beaten panel and the white, china knob for a full minute, and then slowly replaced his hat and slowly walked back to his horse. Patting the silky neck he shook his head. "Omar, it's been comin' to me for twenty years--but it might have waited till I really deserved it. Come on--we'll go back to th' herd, where we belong."

Thoughtfully he rode away, his face older and sterner, its lines seemingly a little deeper.

Chapter XII
Closer Friendships

In the selection of the marshal's office Williams was overruled and rather than make a contest of it, since he could not deny the economy in using a building already erected, and knowing that his store was nearly as well protected, he gave his slow assent to Carney's offer; and soon the lean-to was cleared out, a table, some chairs, and a rough bunk put in it, the latter at the marshal's insistence. Over the door were two words, newly painted: CITY MARSHAL. The question of a jail came next, and was quickly solved by the addition to the lean-to of a room constructed of two-inch planks, walls, floor, and roof. Two pairs of new, shining handcuffs and a new badge, appropriately labeled, completed the civic improvements in the way of law and order. All prisoners guilty of major offenses were to be taken down to Willow and there tried; while minor offenders could sit in the jail until a suitable time had elapsed.

From his chair in the door of his office, Tex could keep watch of nearly all of the main street, and the trail leading in from the C Bar for half a mile. The end of his first week as peace officer found him in his favorite place, contentedly puffing on his pipe, despite the heat of the day. A few miners straggled past, grinning and exchanging shafts of heavy wit with the smiling officer. Blascom drifted into town a little later, learned of the appointment, and hurried down from the hotel to congratulate his new friend.

Tex reached behind him and pulled a chair outside the door. "Sit down, Blascom," he invited. "How's th' sump comin' along?"

Blascom glanced around before replying. "I'm sorry you ain't sheriff, as well," he replied. "I reckon I'm out of bounds, out there on Buffalo, an' I'm shore to be rushed if I'm figgerin' right on that crick. Anybody in th' new jail?"

"Not yet," smiled Tex. "Talk low an' nobody'll hear you. Strike somethin'?"

"I'll gamble on it. I'm so shore of it, I'm filin' a new claim: th' old one didn't quite cover it. You know where th' sump's located, of course; an' you remember how rapid it filled up with water every time I tried to bail it out?"

Tex nodded and waved carelessly at the C Bar trail as though discussing something far from placering. "Send th' location papers off through Jerry Saunders--tell him they're from me. Ever follow a trail herd day after day?" he asked.

"No; why?"

"Ever do anythin', out here, except minin'?"

"Shore; why?"

"What was it?"

"Freightin' from Atchison to Denver an' back: why?"

"Then yo're tellin' me about it now," prompted Tex, handing him a cleaning rod. "Trace th' old trail in th' sand an' keep referrin' to it while you talk. You don't know me good enough to talk long an' steady an' earnest. Here, gimme that rod--" and the marshal took it and drew a line. "This end is Atchison--from there you went up th' Little Blue, like this. Then, crossin' that divide south of th' Platte, you rolled down to that river near Hook's Station, an' follered it past Ft. Kearney, Plumb Crick, an' O'Fallon's Bluffs, an' so on. Here's Hook's Station, th' Fort, Plumb Crick, an' O'Fallon's--now you go on with it."

Blascom took the rod and finished the great curve. "As I was sayin', th' water in that sump kept me guessin'. I couldn't figger where it all come from. I had tried for sumps nearer to th' shack, of course, but got nothin'. Then I found water a-plenty when I dug *this* one." He jabbed at Ft. Kearney and waved his other arm. "I kept gettin' curiouser all th' time, an' yesterday, when th' idea hit me all of a sudden, I went back down th' crick bed twenty paces an' started diggin'. No water; an' yet, sixty feet up stream was more'n I could handle. I just sat down an' wrastled it out."

Tex leaned over and drew another line, one starting on the great curve. "Th' Salt Lake branch run up here, didn't it, Blascom? Th' ones th' troops used, near Old Julesburg, goin' out to lick th' Mormons?"

"How'd you come to know so much about that old trail?" demanded the miner. "It shore did--an' it was a bad section for stages. Well, I cut me a pinted stick an' after it got dark I went out an' jabbed it inter th' crick bed between th' wet sump an' th' last one I put down. About five feet below th' wet one I hit rock, not more'n six inches under th' sand, an' it sloped sharp, both ways, I'm tellin' you. Sort of a sharp hog-back, it is. Humans are blasted fools, Marshal: we can set right on top of a thing that's fair yellin' to be seen, an' not know it's there till somethin' knocks it inter our fool heads. Do you know what I got up there at that sump?"

Tex shook his head and grabbed the stick, a trace of vexation on his face. "You got it all wrong, Blascom," he declared loudly, drawing another line. "Th' old, original Oregon Trail never went up th' Rocky Ridge a-tall. It followed th' North Fork of th' Platte, all th' way to Ft. Laramie. It crossed th' river at Forty Islands, about twelve miles south of th' Fort. I crossed it there with a herd, myself. If you don't believe me, ask Hawkins--he was apprenticed to th' harness-maker at Old Julesburg, on th' South Fork."

"I got you there," laughed Blascom. "Th' Oregon Trail didn't cross at Forty Islands; but a lot of trail herds did. There was a waggin ferry at th' Fort that th' chuck waggins often used."

"It crossed either at Forty Islands or between 'em an' th' Fort," asserted Tex.

"Well, mebby yo're right, Marshal," admitted Blascom. He took the rod again. "That sump of mine is located in a rocky basin that's full of sand. Th' downstream side is that hog-back. That means that there's a thunderin' big, natural riffle in th' bed of th' crick, an' it's stopped and held th' sand till th' basin was full. Every freshet that comes along riles that sand up, lots of it bein' washed over th' riffle, an' carried along. More sand settles there as th' water quits rushin'; but here's th' pint." He jabbed at Denver and drew a line into the Gilpin County country, stopping at Central City. "Gold is heavy, an' it don't wash over riffles if it can settle down in front of 'em. While th' sand is soft from bein' disturbed by a strong current, it can settle. Ever since that crick has been a crick, gold has been settlin' in front of that riffle, droppin' down through th' sand till it hit th' rock bottom. Great Jehovah, Marshal--can you figger what I got?"

Tex roughly took the cleaning rod, traced a line in sudden vexation, slammed the rod on the floor behind him, and fanned his face with his hat.

"An' how long you been settin' on that?" he asked in weary hopelessness.

Blascom waved his arms and slumped back against the chair. "Three years," he confessed, and went off into a profane description of his intelligence that left nothing to imagination.

Tex laughed heartily. "If you was as bad as you just said I'd shore have to take you in. Cheer up, man: it's there, ain't it? You only have to git it out."

Blascom looked at him reproachfully. "Shore: that's all," he retorted with sarcasm. "Git it out before th' rain starts again, an' do it without Jake catchin' me at it! If he learns what I got, I'm in for no sweet dreams; an' if this starvin' bunch of gold hunters learn about it, I'll be swamped in th' rush! Good Lord, man! It'll take me a week to git th' water out, an' then there's th' sand!"

Tex stretched, caught sight of a rider bobbing along the C Bar trail and looked reflectively at Williams' Mecca. "You got to get some dynamite or blastin' powder. Dynamite's better. Put some sticks on th' down-stream side of that rock riffle an' wait till Jake comes into town. You crack that riffle open an' th' water will move out for you. Then you can dig down th' other face of it an' get to th' pocket a lot quicker." He laughed suddenly. "Do that blastin'. Then when Jake gets back to his shack, saunter over with a jug of whiskey an' forget to take it home with you. That'll give you a solid week for yore diggin' without him botherin' you."

"Good idea," said Blascom, arising. "I'll go over an' see if Williams has got any sticks. That's th' way to handle it, Marshal. You ever do any prospectin'?"

Tex pushed him back again. "No, I ain't; but I've been doin' a lot of thinkin' these days. Sit still. What does a miner want explosives for? To get gold, of course. Bein' a placer worker don't make no difference: th' connection is there, just th' same. It'll only make 'em that much more curious. You go buyin' any dynamite an' th' parade will start for yore place before night. I'd get it for you, only me not havin' no reason to buy th' stuff, it would be near as big a mistake as you buyin' it. *I* ain't got no call to want any dynamite. Sit still: you ain't in no hurry!" He leaned over and put his finger on the map in the sand. "They hit Ft. Hall about here," he explained. "We got to get somebody that ain't connected with you, gold diggin', or Buffalo Crick, that won't make no troublesome connections. They usually left their waggins at Ft. Hall an' went up this way. If this feller comin' down th' trail is young Watkins, an' I'm sayin' he is, we got th' way. I reckon he can buy dynamite for th' ranch. That'll be all right, but suppose somebody else from that outfit comes ridin' in an' gets pumped dry? Lean back, stick yore feet on th' Overland, an' don't look so cussed tense. Here: I got it! Th' railroad uses dynamite! I shore got it, Blascom. Tim Murphy can buy it as innocent as you can buy chewin' tobacco!"

"But I don't know him well enough!" expostulated Blascom. "Anyhow, what excuse can I give him?"

"None at all," said Tex. "Wait till yore feet are in th' stirrups before you spur a hoss! You don't have to know him. *I* know him, an' that's a-plenty. Here, you listen close to every word I say, an' act careless-like while yo're doin' it." The explicit directions were rich in details, but Blascom soaked them into his memory like water in a sponge. "Th' whole thing is gettin' to him nat'ral, an' then gettin' th' stuff from him afterward," Tex wound up. Thoughtful for a moment, he nodded in sudden decision. "Got it ag'in! It's near train time. You, bein' restless an' lonesome, hanker to watch it come in. Th' Lord knows nobody in towns like this ever needs any excuse to see a train come in. That's one of th' idle man's inalienable rights--an' it seldom weakens. An' now I know how yo're goin' to git it from him afterwards: you listen ag'in," and further directions came in rapid-fire order.

The rider was near enough now to dispel all doubts as to his identity. Blascom arose, gripped the marshal's hand and faced the Mecca.

"I'm goin' over to git a jug: much obliged, Marshal." He crossed the street diagonally and disappeared in the store.

The rider came nearer and nearer, a great dust cloud rolling behind him not much unlike the smoke of a moving locomotive. When even with Carney's he drew rein suddenly and in another moment had dismounted in front of the lazy Tex.

"I'll be cussed!" he exclaimed, staring from Tex to the sign over the door and then back at the new peace officer, cocking his head as he read the badge.

"Good for you!" he cried. "It's about time this dog's town had a white man to run it; an' they couldn't 'a' picked a better, neither!" His enthusiasm ebbed a little and he looked curiously and thoughtfully into the marshal's eyes. "How'd you come to get th' job?" he demanded.

Tex stuck his thumbs in the armholes of his vest and grinned. He knew the thought that had sobered his companion's face. "Pop'lar clamor, Thomas; 'an' all that sort of a thing,' as Whitby used to say. My great popularity an' my pleasin' nature an' disposition, not to mention my good looks an' winnin' ways, seem to have turned th' balance in my favor. But, outside of that I don't know why I got it. Carney thought I'd mebby bring him more trade; Williams mourned th' lack of anybody to give him adequate police protection, an' th' harness-maker mentions Jack Slade. He admires Jack Slade, an' says I remind him of that person by th' way I let him fix up my left-hand holster. That suits me because Slade was lynched."

"Then Williams really made th' play stick?" Tommy asked with poorly concealed suspicion.

"Williams pinned on my nickel-plated authority," said Tex. "Nobody else had one. He reckons I'm wearin' his colors; but, my Christian friend, th' only colors th' new marshal wears are his own. I'm to keep order in 'this dog's town,' as you put it, an' I'm goin' to do it. Miners, railroaders, storekeepers, cattlemen, an' ornery punchers please listen an' be enlightened. Th' badge is only a nickel-plate affair; but there ain't no nickel, nor rust, neither, on my Cyclopean twins. They're my real authority. Now, then, don't walk all over Blascom's Overland Trail, but set down in th' chair he just vacated. Tell me all about yoreself."

"Marshal," began Tommy in some embarrassment, "I didn't get th' hang of that little mix-up in th' hotel till I got quite some distance out of town. My head was whirlin' a little, an' I'm nat'rally stupid, anyhow. I just want to say that yo're wrong about them Colts bein' some kind of twins. Mebby they are durin' these peaceful days; but if things get crowded they'll turn into triplets, th' missin' brother bein' right here on my laig. Besides that, you got a craggy lot of deputies out on th' C Bar any time you need 'em. Don't stop me while I'm runnin' free! I'm sayin' I never saw a squarer, cleaner piece of shootin' than you showed us all in th' hotel th' other day. An'—you keep off th' trail while I'm comin' strong!—an' I've been somethin' of a fool about us an' that little lady. From now on I'm afoot where she's concerned, an' you know what us punchers amount to, afoot."

"I'm glad you said you was stupid," replied Tex. "It saves me from sayin' it, an' comin' from me it might sound sorta official." He glanced up the street and back to his companion. "Yo're not afoot, cowboy; yo're ridin' strong. I'm th' one that's afoot, an' I'll agree with you about a cowpunch amountin' to nothin' off his cayuse. Did you ever have a door slammed plumb in yore face, Tommy?"

Tommy wiped out Denver, Central City, Old Julesburg, and Ft. Kearney with one swing of his foot. "You--I--you *mean* that?"

The marshal nodded. "Every word of it. Outlawed steers should keep to th' draws an' brakes, Tommy. Besides, I'm over forty-five years old, an' I never was any parson. Keep right on ridin', Adolescence; an' I'm hopin' it's a plain, fair trail. Tommy, did you ever shoot a man?"

"Not yet I ain't; but I've come cussed near it. Seein' what's goin' on in this town, I has hopes."

"Don't yield to no temptations, Tommy; an' let yore hopes die," warned the marshal. "If there's any of that to be done, I'll do it. I reckon you'll shore have a easy trail."

"I--will--be--tee-totally--d--d!" said Tommy. He shook his head and leaned back against the front of the office. "Does she know all about it?"

"Everythin'; I owed myself that much," answered Tex, and then he helped to maintain a reflective, introspective, and emotional silence.

Blascom emerged from the Mecca with a two-gallon jug, empty from the way it jerked and swung. He looked at the silent pair leaning against the marshal's office, abruptly made up his mind, and strode over to them.

"You shore look sorrerful," he said.

"We've just been to a funeral," said Tex. "Th' corpse looked nat'ral, too."

"Sufferin' wildcats!" ejaculated Tommy in pretended dismay, his chair dropping to all fours. "Whiskey by th' jug! I'm plain shocked, but mighty glad to see you, Mr. Blascom." He turned to the marshal. "Here, Officer! Shake han's with Mr. Blascom, of Buffaler Crick. Give th' gentleman a cordial welcome."

Tex regarded the newcomer and his jug with languid interest. "Huh! I reckoned th' drought would shore end some day, but I figgered on rain. However, facts are facts. Pleased to meet you, sir!" He waved at Tommy. "Pass it to our friend first. It's dry work, settin' here, listenin' to me."

"It's like workin' in pay-dirt," retorted Blascom. He tapped the jug and it rang out hollowly. "I ain't give Baldy a chance at it, yet. Anyhow, a man's got to have some protection ag'in' snakes," he defended.

"A protection ag'in' snakes!" repeated Tex, thoughtfully. "Yes; he has."

"I'll pertect you ag'in' 'em as far as th' hotel," offered Tommy, arising and whistling to his horse, "seein' as yo're temporary defenseless. Come on, Blascom. See you later, Marshal," and he grabbed at the jug, missed it, and led the way, Tex smiling after the grinning pair.

Tommy's stride was swift and long for a puncher, due to his agitated frame of mind, and he suddenly slowed it to make an observation to his companion.

"Blascom, th' new marshal is shore quick on th' gun--this town ought to be right proud of him. I'm admittin' that he's a reg'lar he-man."

"He's a cussed sight quicker with his head," replied the miner, "an' that's shore sayin' a large an' bounteous plenty. If he don't play no favorites he's shore as h--l goin' to need friends, one of these days. I'm admittin' myself to that cat-e-gory: but it'll be my hard luck to be out on th' Buffaler when it starts."

Tommy nodded and spat emphatically. "I'll be a cat, an' gory, too," he affirmed. "Wild as a wildcat, an' gory as all h--l. That's me!" He glanced up quickly. "Talkin' ceases, for here we are." He tossed the reins over his pony's head and followed his companion into the hotel, where half a dozen men lounged dispiritedly.

Baldy grinned and lost no time in filling the jug, his efforts creating pleasant, anticipatory smackings among the dry onlookers, who from their previous unobserving weariness suddenly snapped into Argus-eyed interest. The alluring gurgle of the wicker-covered demijohn, the *slap-slap, plop-plop* of the leaping, amber stream, ebbing and flooding spasmodically up and down and around the greenish copper funnel, truly was liquid music to their ears, and the powerful odor of the rye diffused itself throughout the room, penetrated the stale tobacco smoke, and wrought positive reactions upon the olfactory nerves of the staring audience. It was scarce enough by the glass, these days, yet here was a reckless Croesus who was buying it by the gallon!

Blascom, smiling with quiet reserve, leaned against the bar to the right of the jug; Tommy, grave and forbidding, leaned against the bar to the left of the jug, both making short and humorous replies to the gift-compelling remarks of the erect crowd. The jug at last filled, Blascom pushed the cork in and slammed it home with a quick, disconcertingly forbidding gesture, which was as cruel as it was final. He paid for the liquor with one of the bills he had won from Tex, nodded briskly, and went out, Tommy bringing up the rear.

Reproachful, accusing eyes followed their exit, hoping against hope. A lounger nearest the bar, thirsty as Tantalus, shook his head in sorrowful condemnation.

"A man can be mean an' pe-nurious up to a certain, limit," he observed; "but past that it's plumb shameful."

An old man, his greasy, gray beard streaked with tobacco stains, nodded emphatically. "There *is* limits; an' I say that stoppin' before ye begin is shore beyond 'em!"

"Yo're dead right," spoke up a one-eyed tramp who honored himself with the title of prospector. "As for me, I never *did* think much of any man as guzzles it secret. Show me th' man that swizzles in public, an *I'll* show you a man as can be trusted. Two whole gallons of it! A whole, bloomin' jugful, at onct! Where'd he git all that money? I'm askin' you, *where'd* he git it? On Buffaler Crick?" His voice rose and cracked with avarice and suspicion.

"Naw!" growled the man in the far corner, slumping back against his chair. "He won it from that Tex Jones feller--th' new marshal--two hundred or more-- playin' poker. Th' same Tex Jones as shot Bud Haines. There ain't more'n day wages on Buffaler Crick. I know, 'cause I been lookin' around out there, quiet-like." He stiffened suddenly and sat up, excitement transforming him. "Boys, this here marshal has got money--I saw his wad when he an' Blascom was a-playin'.'"

"Yo're shore welcome to it," pessimistically rejoined the man nearest the bar, his vivid imagination picturing the amazing death of Bud Haines. "Yes, sir; yo're welcome to *all* of it. I don't want none, a-tall!"

The discoverer of the marshal's roll regarded the objector with deep scorn.

"That's you!" he retorted. "Allus goin' off half-cocked, an' yowlin' calamity! This here marshal likes poker, don't he? An' he can't play it, can he? Didn't Blascom clean him? He's scared to bluff, or call one, no matter how brave he is with a gun. Who's got any dust? Dig down deep, an' we'll pool it, lettin' Hank an' Sinful do th' playin' for us. Where's Hennery?" he demanded of the bartender.

Baldy mopped the bar and glanced at the ceiling. "Upstairs, sleepin' off a stem-winder. He got drinkin' to th' mem'ry of th' dead deceased last night--an' his mem'ry is long an' steady. He's too senti-mental, Hennery is, for a man as can't handle his likker good. If you fellers are goin' after th' marshal's pile, I'm recommendin' stud-hoss. He's nat'rally scared of poker, an' stud's so fast he won't have no time to start worryin'. Draw will give him too much time to think. Better try stud-hoss," he reiterated, unwittingly naming the form of poker at which the marshal excelled.

"Stud-hoss she is, then," agreed Sinful, licking his lips. "I like stud-hoss. We'll bait him tonight; an' we'll all have jugs of our own by mornin', since Buffaler Crick's settin' th' style."

The meeting forthwith went into executive session, depleted gold sacks slowly appearing.

Outside, Blascom offered the jug to his companion, who pushed it away, and shook his head in sudden panic.

"Don't want to smell like no saloon where I'm goin'," he hastily explained. "Now that yo're safe from snakes I'll be driftin' to my cayuse."

"All right, Watkins; I'll treat next time," and the miner, jug in hand, strode toward the station as Tommy mounted and wheeled to ride in the direction of the Saunders' home.

Blascom had timed his arrival to a nicety, for Murphy was on his way from the toolshed to the station to await the coming of the train, the smoke from which could be seen on the eastern horizon.

Blascom held up the jug invitingly and grinned. The section-boss came to an abrupt stop, saluted, and stepped on again with the bearing of a well-trained English soldier. "Hah!" he called. "'Tis better from a jug; an' 'twould be better yet if it had a little breath av th' peat fire in it; but 'tis well to be content with what we have. Thank ye: I'll drink yer health!" Handing the jug back to its owner Murphy wiped his lips with the back of his hand and seated himself on the bench at the prospector's side. "Have ye seen th' new marshal?" he asked, glancing from the distant smudge of smoke to his watch. "I hear he's fixed up in style."

"Yes; an' he gave me a message for you, if you'll lean over a little closer," replied Blascom, and, as Murphy obeyed his suggestion, he said what he had come for.

"It sounds like Tex," grunted Murphy. "All thought out careful. Have ye ever used stick explosive? It's treacherous stuff at any time above freezin', an' more so after this spell av hot weather. Ye have? Then there's no use av me tellin' ye to handle it gintly. If I was knowin' th' job ye have, I might help ye in th' number av sticks. But if yo're used to it, ye'll know. I'll get it after Number Three pulls out; an' after dark tonight ye'll find it where he said--but deal gintly with it, Mr. Blascom. I've seen it exploded by impact--it was a rifle ball fired into it--this kind av weather. Ye might even do better to load th' shots, this kind av weather, after th' sun goes down. Carry it as ye find it, without unpackin' th' box."

Blascom nodded. "If I leave th' jug for you to put away when you go down for th' box, would you mind puttin' it out tonight with th' dynamite? No use of me makin' two trips to my cabin, an' I don't want to tote it around till dark."

"I will that, an' be glad to. There she comes now, leavin' Whiterock Cut. Casey's late ag'in; but that's regular, an' not his fault, as I've told them time an' time ag'in. Th' grades are ag'in' him comin' west, an' with his leaky packin's an' worn cylinders it's a wonder he does as well as he has. 'Economy,' says th' super. 'No money for repairs that are not needed on this jerk-water line.' I wonder does he ever figger th' fuel wasted through them steam leaks? An' poor Casey gets th' blame--though divvil a bit he cares."

Number Three wheezed in, panted a moment, and coughed on again. Murphy took a package consigned to him, picked up the jug and went down the track toward the toolshed, Blascom wandering idly over to the Railroad Saloon to pass some of the time he had on his hands. In a little while the big Irishman, a small wooden box under his arm, sauntered carelessly down the street, nodded politely from a distance to the sleepy marshal and went into the Mecca.

"Good day, Mr. Williams," he said with stiff formality. "I'll be havin' six dynamite sticks if ye have them, with th' same number av three-minute fuses. Handle it gintly, if ye don't mind. Th' weather is aggravatin' to th' stuff, an' it's timpermental enough at best."

Williams glowered at him. "Don't you worry about me handlin' it gentle, because I ain't goin' to handle it at all. If you want any I'll give you th' key to th' powder-house an' wish you good luck. Th' sun beatin' down on that house, day after day, has got me plumb nervous. I wish you'd come for it all!" He shook his head. "I wouldn't let you even open th' door if it wasn't for gettin' that much more of it out of th' way."

"Is it ventilated well?" demanded Murphy, smiling a little.

"As well as it can be," sighed Williams. "You'll never catch me carryin' anythin' but powder over th' summer any more. I'm afraid a thunderclap will set it off every storm. What you got in that to pack it in?"

"Sawdust. While yo're cuttin' th' fuses I'll be gettin' th' stuff."

"You'll not come back for any fuses! Wait an' take em' with you! An' when you are through with th' powder-house, throw th' key close to th' back door: I don't want no man with six sticks of dynamite hangin' around this store today. Want a bill?"

Murphy nodded. "Two av them is th' rule av th' company. You can mark 'em paid an' take it out av this."

The receipted bills in his pocket, he threw the fuses over his shoulder, their wickedly shining copper caps carefully wrapped in a handkerchief, took up the bunch of keys and the box, and grinned. "If ye hear an explosion out back, ye needn't come out to gimme any help. I'm cleanin' up some bad cracked rocks hangin' from a cut west av town, over near Buffalo Crick. I'm tellin' ye th' last so ye won't think it's thunderclaps on their disturbin' way to town. But ye'll sleep through it, no doubt, an' never hear th' shot."

"Blastin' at night?" exclaimed Williams in incredulous surprise.

"I don't like th' sun shinin' on th' darlin's while I'm pokin' 'em in th' hot rocks, so I may load her an' shoot her after dark," replied Murphy. "I've a lot av respect for th' stuff, much as I've handled it. Good day, sir," and he left behind him a man who was nervous and jumpy until after the keys had tinkled on the ground near the rear door; indeed, such an impression had been made on him that he mentioned it, with profane criticisms and observations, at the table that night in the hotel.

The marshal moved his chair farther around in the shade and on his tanned face there crept a warm, rare smile. "'Lo, I will stand at thy right hand, and keep the bridge with thee!' Well said, Herminius! Yonder you go in spirit: Tim Murphy, you'd make complete any 'dauntless three'!"

The shadows were growing long when Tommy came into sight again, buried in thought as he rode slowly down the street. He stopped and swung to the ground in front of the lazy marshal.

"They shore do beat th' devil," he growled, throwing himself into the vacant chair and lapsing into silence.

Tex nodded understandingly. "They do," he indolently agreed, a smile flickering across his face. "Black is white an' red is green--they're the worst I've ever seen," he extemporized. "They're intuitive critters, son; an' don't you let anybody tell you that intuition hasn't any warrant for existing. It has. It's got more warrant than reason. It was flowering long before reason poked its first shoot out of the ground. Reason only runs back a few thousand generations, but intuition goes back to the first cell of nervous tissue--I might qualify that a bit and say before nervous tissue was structurally apart from the rest. Reason starts anew in every life, usually upon a little better foundation--often a poorer one. It is nursed and trained and cultivated an' when its possessor dies, it dies with him. Not so our venerable friend, intuition. He, or rather she, is cumulative. She is th' sum of all previous individuals in the life chain of th' last. She picks up an' stores away, growing a little each time--an' while she is vague, an' can be classified as a 'because,' or 'I don't know why,' she operates steady. Don't ask me what I know about it, for it has been a long time since I gave any study to things like this. I might guess an' say that it's th' physical changes in th' thought channels due to experience, or in th' structure of th' brain cells or th' quality of their tissues. Anyway, so far as practicability is concerned, you've summed up th' whole thing: 'They shore do beat th' devil'."

Tommy was looking at him, puzzled and intent; but puzzled intelligently. There is a difference.

"With me an' you, two opposites in thought result in th' cancellation of one of them. We don't say of th' same object: 'This is white, this is black,' at th' same time an' believe 'em both. Th' words themselves are intelligible; but th' conception ain't. We can't do it. One is chosen an' th' other dies. But I won't bet you that a woman cancels. She may not get a dirty white or a slate gray, but she gets a combination, all right. That's where intuition's family tree comes in. No matter how absurd its contentions may be they have force because of th' impetus coming from age. What did she get out th' colors for you?"

"Yo're th' easiest man to talk to that I ever met," said Tommy, wonderingly. "I don't know how you do it. Why, she got a bright red with a dull green cast--said you was justified, 'but a life's a life': an' then she cried!"

Over Tex's face came a light which only can be compared to the rising sun seen from some lofty peak, for in the radiance there were shadows.

Chapter XIII
Outcheating Cheaters

Gus Williams left the supper table, where he had held forth volubly upon the subject of dynamite, in his almost lecture to the other diners, some of whom knew more about it than he did, and walked ponderously toward the poker table for his usual evening's game. Seating himself at the place which by tacit consent had become his own, he idly shuffled and reshuffled the cards and finally began a slow and laborious game of solitaire to while away the time until his cronies should join him. This game had become a fixture of the establishment, played for low stakes but with great seriousness, and often ran into the morning hours.

The rest of the diners tarried inexplicably at the plate-littered table, engaged in a discussion of stud poker and of their respective abilities in playing it, and of winnings they had made and seen made. It slowly but surely grew acrimonious, as any such discussion is prone to among idle men who are very much in each other's company.

The new marshal sat a little apart from the eager disputants, taking no share in the wrangling. Finally Sinful, scorning a shouted ruling on a hypothetical question concerning the law of averages, turned suddenly and appealed to the marshal, whose smiling reply was not a confirmation of the appellant's claim.

Sinful glared at his disappointing umpire. "A lot you know about stud!" he retorted. "Bet you can't even play mumbly-peg!"

"That takes a certain amount of skill," rejoined Tex without heat. "In stud it's how th' cards fall."

Hank laughed sarcastically. "Averages don't count? We'll just start a little game an' I'll show you how easy stud-hoss is. Come on, boys: we'll give th' marshal a lesson. Clear away them dishes."

All but Sinful held back, saying that they had no money for gambling, but they were re-markably eager to watch the game.

Sinful snorted. "Huh! Two-hand is no good. I'm honin' for a little stud-hoss for a change. It's been nothin' but draw in this town. Reckon stud's too lively to suit most folks: takes nerve to ride a fast game. A man can have a-plenty of nerve one way, an' none a-tall another way. Fine bunch of paupers!"

Hank's disgust was as great. "Fine bunch of paupers," he repeated. "An' them as ain't busted is scared. You called th' turn, Sinful: it shore does take nerve--more'n mumbly-peg, anyhow. A three-hand game would move fast-- *too* fast for these coyotes."

"Don't you let th' old mosshead git off with that, Marshal!" cried a miner, "Wish *I* had some dust: I'd cussed soon show 'em!"

Tex was amused by the baiting. Hardly an eye had left him while the whole discussion was going on, even the two principals looking at him when they spoke to each other. He looked from one old reprobate to the other, and let his smile become a laugh as he moved up to the table, a motion which was received by the entire group with sighs of relief and satisfaction.

"I reckon it's my luck ag'in' yore skill," he said; "but I can't set back an' be insulted this way. I'm a public character, now, an' has got to uphold th' dignity of th' law. Get a-goin', you fellers."

Sinful and Hank, simultaneously slamming their gold bags on the table, reached for the cards at the same time and a new wrangle threatened.

"Cut for it," drawled Tex, smiling at the expectant, hopeful faces around the table. Williams' irritable, protesting cough was unheeded and, Hank dealing, the game got under way. Tex honorably could have shot both of his opponents in the first five minutes of play, but simply cheated in turn and held his own. At the end of an hour's excitement he was neither winner nor loser, and he shoved back from the table in simulated disgust. He scorned to take money so tragically needed, and he had determined to lose none of his own.

"This game's so plumb fast," he ironically observed, "that I ain't won or lost a dollar. You got my sportin' blood up, an' I ain't goin' to insult it by playin' all night for nothin'. I told you stud was only luck: That skill you was talkin' about ain't showed a-tall. If there's anybody here as wants a *real* game I'm honin' to hear his voice."

"Can you hear mine?" called Williams, glaring at the disappointed stud players and their friends. "There's a real game right here," he declared, pounding the table, "with real money an' real nerve! Besides, I got a hoss to win back, an' I want my revenge."

Tex turned to the group and laughed, playfully poking Sinful in the ribs. "Hear th' cry of th' lobo? He's lookin' for meat. Our friend Williams has been savin' his money for Tex Jones, an' I ain't got th' heart to refuse it. Bring yore community wealth an' set in, you an' Hank. Though if you can't play draw no better'n you play stud you ought to go home."

"I cut my teeth on draw," boasted Sinful. He turned and slapped his partner on the shoulder. "Come on, Hank!" he cried. "Th' lone wolf is howlin' from th' timber line an' his pelt's worth money. Let's go git it!"

They swept down on the impatient Williams, their silent partners bringing up the rear, and clamored for action. Tex lighting a freshly rolled cigarette, faced the local boss, Hank on his right and Sinful on his left, the eager onlookers settling behind their champions. The thin, worried faces of the miners appealed to the marshal, their obvious need arousing a feeling of pity in him; and then began a game which was as much a credit to Tex as any he ever had played. He rubbed the saliva-soaked end of his cigarette between finger and thumb and gave all his attention to the game.

Williams won on his own deal, cutting down the gold of the two miners. On Hank's deal he won again and the faces of the old prospectors began to tense. Tex dealt in turn and after a few rounds of betting Williams dropped out and the game resolved itself into a simulated fiercely fought duel between the miners, who really cared but little which of them won. Hank finally raked in the stakes. Sinful shuffled and Tex cut. Williams forced the betting but had to drop out, followed by Tex, and the dealer gleefully hauled in his winnings. Again Williams shuffled, his expression vaguely denoting worry. He made a sharp remark about one of the onlookers behind Tex and all eyes turned instinctively. The miner retorted with spirit and Williams suddenly smiled apologetically.

"My mistake, Goldpan," he admitted. "Let's forget it, an' let th' game proceed."

Tex deliberately had allowed his attention to be called from the game and when he picked up his cards he was mildly suspicious, for Williams' remark had been entirely uncalled for. He looked quickly for the nine of clubs or the six of hearts, finding that he had neither. He passed and sat back, smiling at the facial contortions of Hank and the blank immobility of Sinful's leathery countenance. Hank dropped out on the next round and after a little cautious betting Sinful called and threw down his hand. Williams spread his own and smiled. That smile was to cost him heavily, for in his club flush lay the nine spot, guiltless of the tobacco smudge which Tex had rubbed on its face in the first hand he had been dealt.

Tex wiped the tips of his sensitive fingers on his trousers and became voluble and humorous. As he picked up his cards, one by one as they dropped from Hank's swiftly moving hand, he first let his gaze linger a little on their backs, and his fingers slipped across the corners of each. Williams had cheated before with a trimmed deck and now the marshal grimly determined to teach him a lesson, and at the same time not arouse the suspicions of the boss against the new marshal. With the switching of the decks Williams had set a pace which would grow too fast for him. Marked cards suited Tex, especially if they had been marked by an opponent, who would have all the more confidence in them. After a few deals if he wouldn't know each card as well as a man like Williams, whose marking could not be much out of the ordinary, and certainly not very original, then he felt that he deserved to get the worst of the play. He once had played against a deck which had been marked by the engraver who designed the backs, and he had learned it in less than an hour. So now he prepared to enjoy himself and thereafter bet lightly when Williams dealt, but on each set of hands dealt by himself one of the prospectors always won, and with worthy cards. Worthy as were their hands they were only a shade better than those held by the proprietor of the hotel and the general store. One hand alone cost Williams over eighty dollars, three others were above the seventy-dollar mark and he was losing his temper, not only because of his losses, but also because he did not dare to cheat too much on his own deal. Tex's eyes twinkled at him and Tex's rambling words hid any ulterior motive in the keen scrutiny. Finally, driven by desperation, Williams threw caution to the winds and risked detection. He was clever enough to avoid grounds for open accusation, but both of the miners suddenly looked thoughtful and a moment later they exchanged significant glances. Thereafter no one bet heavily when Williams dealt.

The finish came when Tex had dealt and picked up his hand. Sinful stolidly regarded the cheery faces of three kings--spades, clubs, and hearts. Williams liked the looks of his two pairs, jacks up. Hank rolled his huge cud into the other cheek and tried to appear mournful at the sight of the queen, ten, eight, and five of hearts. Tex laid down his four-card spade straight and picked up the pack.

"Call 'em, boys," he said.

Sinful's two cards, gingerly lifted one at a time from the table, pleased him very much, although from all outward signs they might have been anything in the card line. They were the aces of diamonds and clubs. He sighed, squared the hand, and placed it face down on the table before him. Williams gulped when he added a third jack to his two pairs, and Hank nearly swallowed his tobacco at sight of the prayed-for, but unexpected, appearance of another heart. All eyes were on the dealer. He put down the deck and picked up his hand for another look at it. After a moment he put it down again, sadly shaking his head.

"Good enough as it is," he murmured. "I ain't havin' much luck, one way or th' other; an' I'm gettin' tired! of th' cussed game."

"Dealer pat?" sharply inquired Williams, suspicion glinting in his eyes.

"Pat, an' cussed near flat," grunted Tex. "Go on with her. I'll trail along with what I got, an' quit after this hand."

Notwithstanding the dealer's pat hand and his expression of resignation, the betting was sharp and swift. On the first round, being forty-odd dollars ahead, Tex saw the accumulated raises and had enough left out of his winnings to raise five dollars. He tossed it in and leaned back, watching each face in turn. Sinful was not to be bluffed by any pat hand at this stage of the play, no matter how craftily it was bet. He reflected that straights, flushes, and full houses could be held pat, as well as threes or two pairs, all of which he had beat. A straight flush or fours were the only hands he could lose to, and Williams had not dealt the cards. Pat hands were sometimes pat bluffs, more terrifying to novices than to old players. He saw the raise and shoved out another, growling: "Takes about twenty more to see this circus."

Williams hesitated, looking at the dealer's neat little stack of cards. He was convinced from the way Tex had acted that the pat hand was a bluff, for its owner had not been caught bluffing since the game started, which indicated that he had labored to establish the reputation of playing only intrinsic hands, which would give a later bluff a strong and false value. He saw and raised a dollar, hoping that someone would drop out. Hank disappointed him by staying in and boosting another dollar. They both were feeling their way along. Hank also believed the pat hand to be worthless; and worthless it was, for Tex tossed it from him, face down, and rammed his hands into his pockets.

Sinful heaved a sigh of relief, which was echoed by the others, squinted from his hand to the faces of the two remaining players, and grinned sardonically. "Bluffs are like crows; they live together in flocks. I never quit when she's comin' my way. Grab a good holt for another raise! She's ten higher, now."

With the disturbing pat hand out of it, which was all the more disturbing because it had belonged to the dealer, Williams gave more thought to the players on his left and right. He decided that Hank was the real danger and that Sinful's words were a despairing effort to win by the default of the others. He saw the raise and let it go as it was. Hank rolled the cud nervously and with a sudden, muttered curse, threw down his hand. A flush had no business showing pride and fight in this game, he decided. Sinful grinned at him across the table.

"Terbaccer makin' you sick, Hank?" he jeered. "I'm raisin' ten more, jest to keep th' corpse alive. He-he-he!"

There was now too much in the pot to give it up for ten dollars and Williams met the raise, swore, and called, "What you got, you devil from h--l?"

"I got quite a fambly," chuckled Sinful, laying down a pair of aces. "There's twin brothers," he said, looking up.

Williams snorted at the old man's pleasure in not showing his whole hand at once, and he tossed three jacks on the table. "Triplets in mine," he replied.

Sinful raised his eyebrows and regarded them accusingly. "Three jacks can tote quite some load if it's packed right," he said. "Th' rest of my fambly is three more brothers, an' they bust th' mules' backs. Ain't got th' extry jack, have you?"

Slamming the rest of the cards on the table Williams arose and without a word walked to the bar. Sinful's. cackles of joy were added to by his friends and they surrounded the table to help in the division of the spoils, in plain sight of all.

"Win or lose, Marshal?" demanded Sinful shrilly above the hubbub of voices.

"Lost a couple of dollars," bellowed Tex.

"Much obliged for 'em," rejoined Sinful. He looked at Hank, winked and said: "Marshal's been real kind to us, Hank," and Tex never was quite certain of the old man's meaning.

Williams looked around as Tex leaned against the bar. "How'd *you* come out?" he asked, his face showing his anger.

"I lost," answered Tex carelessly. "Not anythin' to speak of: a few dollars, I reckon. I told 'em two dollars, for they're swelled up with pride as things are. They must 'a' got into you real heavy."

Williams sneered. "Heavy for them, I reckon. I ain't limpin'. They got too cussed much luck."

"Luck?" muttered the marshal, gazing inquiringly at the glass of whiskey he had raised from the bar, as though it might tell him what he wanted to know. "I ain't so shore of that, Williams," he slowly said. "Them old sour-doughs get snowed in near every winter, up in th' hills; an' then they ain't got nothin' to do but eat, sleep, swap lies, an' play cards. Somethin' tells me there wasn't a whole lot of luck in it. I know I had all I could do to stay in th' saddle without pullin' leather--an' I ain't exactly cuttin' my teeth where poker is concerned. Listen to 'em, will you? Squabblin' like a lot of kids. I reckon they had this cooked up in grand style. They're all sharin' in th' winnin's, you'll notice." He paused in surprise as a dull roar faintly shook the room. "What's that?" he demanded sharply. "It can't be thunder!"

His companion shook his head. "No, it ain't; it's that Murphy blowin' up rock, like I was sayin' at supper. Hope he went up with it!" He laughed at a man who was just coming in, and who stopped dead in the door and listened to the rumble. "Yore shack's safe, Jake," he called. "Th' Mick's blastin' over past yore way. You remember what I've told you!" he warned.

Jake looked from the speaker to the careless, but inwardly alert, city marshal, scowled, shuffled over to a table, and called for a drink, thereafter entirely ignoring the peace officer.

Henry came in soon after and joined the two at the bar. "Yes, I'll have th' same. You two goin' ridin' ag'in, Marshal?" he asked.

Tex shrugged his shoulders. "It shore don't look like it. She mebby figgered me out. Anyhow, she slammed th' door plumb in my face." He frowned. "Somehow I don't get used to things like that. She could 'a' treated me like I wasn't no tramp, anyhow, couldn't she?"

Henry smiled maliciously, and felt relieved. "They're shore puzzlin'. I hear that coyote Watkins was out there this afternoon. There wasn't no door slammed in *his* face." His little eyes glinted. "I see where he's goin' to learn a lesson, an' learn it for keeps!"

"Oh, he got throwed, too," chuckled Tex, as if finding some balm in another's woe. "He stopped off on his way home an' told me about it. Got a busted heart, an' belly-achin' like a sick calf. That's what he is; an' it's calf love, as well. Shucks! When I was his age I fell in love with a different gal about every moon. Besides, he ain't got money, nor prospects: an' she knows it."

Henry took him by the arm and led him to a table in a far corner. "I been thinkin' I mebby ought to send her a present, or somethin'," he said, watching his companion's face. "You, havin' more experience with 'em, I figgered mebby you would help me out. *I* don't know what to get her."

"Weakenin' already," muttered the marshal, trying to hide a knowing, irritating smile. "Pullin' leather, an' ain't hardly begun to ride yet!"

"I ain't pullin' no leather!" retorted Henry, coloring. "I reckon a man's got a right to give a present to his gal!"

"Shore!" endorsed Tex heartily. "There ain't no question about it--when she comes right out an' admits that she is his gal. This Saunders woman ain't admittin' it, yet; an' if she figgers that yo're weakenin' on yore play of ignorin' her, then she'll just set back an' hold you off so th' presents won't stop comin'. This is a woman's game, an' she can beat a man, hands down an' blindfolded: an' they know it. I tell you, Hennery, a wild cayuse that throws its first rider ain't no deader set on stayin' wild than a woman is set on makin' a man go through his tricks for her if she finds he's performin' for her private amusement, an' payin' for th' privilege, besides. It ain't no laughin' matter for you, Hennery; but I can't hardly keep *from* laughin' when I think of you stayin' away to get her anxious, an' then sendin' her presents! It's yore own private affair, an' yo're runnin' it yore own way--but them's *my* ideas."

Henry stared into space, gravely puffing on a cold cigarette. His low, furrowed brow denoted intense mental concentration, and the scowl which grew deeper did not suggest that his conclusions were pleasant. The simile regarding the wild horse sounded like good logic to him, for he prided himself that he knew horses. Finally he looked anxiously at his deeply thinking companion.

"It sounds right, Marshal," he grudgingly admitted; "but it shore is hard advice to foller. I'm plumb anxious to buy her somethin' nice, somethin' she can't get in this part of th' country, an' somethin' she can wear an' know come from me." He paused in some embarrassment and tried to speak carelessly. "If you was goin' to get a woman like her some present--mind, I'm sayin' *if* --what would you get?"

Tex reflected gravely. "Candy don't mean nothin'," he cogitated, in a low, far-away voice. "Anybody she knew at all could give her candy. It don't mean nothin' special, a-tall." He did not appear to notice how his companion's face fell at the words. "Books are like candy--just common presents. A stranger almost could give 'em. Ridin' gloves is a little nearer--but Tommy, or me, could give them to her. Stockin's? Hum: I don't know. They're sort of informal, at that. 'Tain't everybody, however, could give 'em. Only just one man: get my idea?"

"I shore do, Marshal," beamed Henry. "You see, livin' out here all my life an' not 'sociatin' with wimmin--like her, anyhow--I didn't know hardly what would be th' correct thing. Wonder what color?"

Tex was somewhat aghast at his joke being taken so seriously. "Now, you look here, Hennery!" he said in a warning voice. "You promise me not to send her no stockin's till I says th' word." He had wanted to give Jane more reason to dislike the nephew, but hardly cared to have it go that far. "Stayin' away, are you? You make me plumb sick, you do! Stayin' away, h--l!"

A roar of laughter came from the celebrating miners and all eyes turned their way. Sinful and Hank were dancing to the music of a jew's-harp and the time set by stamping, hob-nailed boots. They parted, bowed, joined again, parted, courtesied and went on, hand in hand, turning and ducking, backing and filing, the dust flying and the perspiration streaming down. It seemed impossible that in these men lurked a bitter race hatred, or that hearts as warm and happy could be incubating the germs of cowardly murder. Not one of them, alone, would be guilty of such a thing; but the spirit of a mob is a remarkable and terrible thing, tearing aside civilization's training and veneer, and in a moment hurling men back thousands of years, back to the days when killing often was its own reward.

Chapter XIV
Tact and Courage

Things were going along smoothly for the new marshal until two of the C Bar punchers, accompanied by two men from a ranch farther from town, rode in to make a night of it. It chanced that the C Bar men had been with a herd some forty miles north of the ranch, where water and grass conditions were much better, and they had become friendly with the outfit of another herd which grazed on the western fringe of the same range. A month of this, days spent in the saddle on the same rounds, and nights spent at the chuck wagon with nothing to vary the monotony of the cycle, had given the men an edge to be bunted at the first opportunity; and their ideas of working off high-pressure energies did not take into consideration any such things as safety valves. Action they craved, action they had ridden in for, and action they would have. The swifter it started, the faster it moved, the better it would suit them. So, with an accumulation of energy, thirst, and money they tore into Windsor one noon at a dead run, whooping like savages, and proclaiming their freedom from restraint and their pride of class by a heavenward bombardment which frightened no one and did no harm.

It so chanced that when they passed the new marshal's office they were going so fast, and were so fully occupied in waking up the town, that the lettering over the door of the lean-to escaped their attention. And they were past, bunched in a compact group, and nearly hidden in dust before the mildly curious officer could get to the door. He watched them whirl up to the hotel, the stronghold and stamping ground of Williams and the miners and, dismounting with shrill yells, pause a moment to reload their empty guns, and then surge toward the door.

Tex rubbed his chin thoughtfully as he considered them. Carney's was the cowman's favorite drinking place, yet these four cheerful riders had not given it a second glance, judging from the way they had gone past it. This was no matter for congratulation, but bespoke, rather, a determination to show off where their efforts would create more interest. Who they were, or what they came in for, he neither knew nor cared. They were celebrating punchers from somewhere out on the range and they were going to hold their jamboree in the miners' chosen place of entertainment. A less experienced marshal, filled with zeal and conceit, might forthwith have buckled on his guns, and started for the scene of the festivities, to be on hand as a preventive, rather than a corrective, or punitive, force; and very probably would have hastened the very thing he sought to avoid. Tex hoped to take the edge from the class feeling, and determined to be openly linked with neither one side nor the other. His place was to be that of a neutral buffer and his justice must be impartial and above criticism. So, after turning back to buckle on the left-hand gun, he did not sally forth to blaze the glory of the law and precipitate a riot; he sat down patiently to await the course of events.

Williams poked his head out of the door of his store and looked anxiously down the street at the dismounting four. As they went into the hotel he hurried across to the marshal's office and stopped, panting, in the doorway.

"See 'em?" he asked excitedly. "Hear 'em?"

"What or who?" asked Tex, throwing one leg over the other.

"Them rowdy punchers!" exclaimed the storekeeper. "Nobody's safe! Go up an' take 'em in, quick!"

"What they do?" interestedly asked the marshal.

"Didn't you *see* an' *hear* ?" demanded Williams incredulously.

"I saw 'em ride past, an' I heard 'em shootin' in th' air; but what did they do so I can arrest 'em?"

"Ain't that enough? That, an' th' yellin', an' everythin'?"

"Sinful and his friends made more noise th' other night when they left town," replied the marshal. "I didn't arrest them. Hank was of a mind to see if it was true that a bullet only punches a little, thin-edged hole in a pane of glass an' don't smash it all to pieces. Bein' wobbly, he picked out yore winder, seein' they was th' biggest in town; but Sinful held him back, an' they had a scufflin' match an' made more noise than sixteen mournful coyotes. There bein' no pane smashed I didn't cut in. A man is only a growed-up boy, anyhow."

Williams looked at him in frank amazement. "But these here fellers are punchers!" he exploded.

"I shore could see that, even with th' dust," confessed the marshal. "That ain't no crime as I knows of."

"It ain't th' four to one that's holdin' you back, is it?" demanded Williams insinuatingly. "They're punchers, too: bad as h--l."

Tex languidly arose and removed the pair of guns and the belts, laying them gently on the floor. He pitched his sombrero on the bunk and faced his caller.

"Mebby I didn't understand you," he coldly suggested. "What was it you said?"

Williams raised both hands in quick protest, one foot fishing desperately behind him for the ground below the sill. "Nothin' to make you go on th' prod," he hastily explained.

"Listen to me, Williams," said the cool peace officer, his voice level and unemotional. "Anybody callin' me a coward wants to go into action fast, an' keep on goin' fast. That includes everybody from King Solomon right down to date. I'm responsible for th' peace in this town, an' when *anybody* starts smashin' it I'll go 'em a whirl. Yellin', ridin' fast, an' shootin' in th' air, 'specially by sober men, ain't smashin' nothin' in a town like this. I don't aim to run no nursery, nor even a kindergarden. I ain't makin' a fool out of myself an' turnin' th' law into a joke. Once let ridicule start an' h--l's pleasant by contrast. They ain't shootin' now. Th' first shot fired inside any buildin', or dangerously low, an' I inject myself an' my two guns. I can't make no arrests on a blind guess, mine nor yourn. You better go back to th' store an' keep th' vinegar from sourin' on its mother."

Williams' jaw dropped. This was not Tex Jones at all, at least it didn't sound like him. "As th' owner of th' most valuable property in town I want them coyotes stopped from ruinin' it. I——"

"When they show any signs of ruinin' *any* property I'll step in an' stop 'em," the marshal assured him. "I got my ears open, an' had my authority buckled on--which I'll now resume wearin'." He picked up a heavy belt and slung it around him, deftly catching the free end as it slapped against him. "We'll have law an' order, Williams--even if I have to fill some fool as full of holes as a prairie-dog town; but I ain't goin' out an' trample on a man's pride an' make him get killed defendin' it, unless I got good reason to. This is a long speech, but I'm goin' to make it longer so I can impress somethin' on yore mind. Bein' a busy merchant you've mebby never had time to think about it much; but me, bein' a marshal, I *got* to think of everythin' like that. This is one of 'em: When bad feelin's exist between two classes, helpin' one ag'in' th' other, without honest reasons, is only goin to make more bitterness. It can be held down only by impersonal justice. That's me. I don't give a d--n what a man is as long as he behaves hisself." Picking up the second belt he slung it around him the other way and buckled it behind him. As he shook them both to a more comfortable fit a yell rang out up near the hotel, followed by a shot. Grabbing his hat from the bunk he pushed Williams out of his way and dashed through the door, flinging over his shoulder: "I'm injectin' myself *now* ! You better go look to th' vinegar!"

He saw Whiskey Jim, the man whom he had caught beating the dog, in his blind terror run against the side of the harness-shop, recover from the impact and, stupefied by fear, frantically claw at the bleached boards. A spurt of dust almost under one of his feet made him claw more frantically. The hilarious puncher walked slowly toward him, raising the Colt for another shot. Behind him, laughing uproariously, stood his three friends, solidly blocking the hotel door.

"Hold that gun where it is!" shouted the marshal, dropping into a catlike stride. He was coming down the middle of the street, not more than forty paces, now, from the performing puncher.

The gun arm stiffened in air as the whiplike, authoritative phrase reached its possessor and, grinning exultantly, the puncher wheeled to get a good look at his next victim. He saw a grave-faced man of forty-odd years walking toward him, a bright star pinned to the open vest, two guns hanging low down on the swaying hips, the swinging hands brushing the walnut grips at every lithe, steady step.

"See what we got to play with!" exulted the surprised puncher, calling to his friends. "I want his badge: you can have th' rest!" His hand chopped down and a spurt of dust leaped from the ground at the marshal's side.

Disregarding it, the peace officer maintained his steady, swinging stride, his eyes fixed on those of the other, intently watching for a change in their playful expression. Another shot and the dust spurted close to his left foot. The hilarious laughter of the three in the doorway died out, and their friend in the street stood stock still, trying to figure out what he had better do next. The deliberate marshal was now only five paces away and at the puncher's indecision, plain to be seen in the eyes, he leaped forward, wrested the gun from the feebly resisting fingers, whirled the nonplussed man around and then kicked him his own length on the ground.

Ignoring the three men in the doorway, thereby tacitly admitting their squareness, the marshal calmly ejected the cartridges from the captured weapon and, as the angry and astonished puncher arose, handed it to him.

"It's empty," he said in a matter-of-fact voice. "Keep it that way till you leave town; an' when you come in again, intendin' to likker up an' raise h--l, either unload it or leave it with me, unless you promise to behave yoreself." He turned to Whiskey Jim, who appeared to be frozen into a statue. "Come over here, Jim," he commanded, and again turned to the puncher, who did not know whether to laugh or to curse. "I reckon Jim's th' only injured party. His feelin's has been trampled on to th' tune of about five dollars. Pay him before he takes it out of yore hide. He's a desperate bad man, Jim is!"

The three men in the door, who were nowhere near drunk yet, knew sparkling courage when they saw it, and they shouted with laughter at their crestfallen friend, who grudgingly was counting the fine into the eager hand of the aggrieved citizen.

"Hey, Walt!" burbled one of them, a beardless youth on one end of the line. "Still want to play with that badge?"

"If you do," jeered the man in the middle, laughing again, "better rustle, *pronto* , 'cause I'm buyin' its boss a drink."

Walt grinned expansively, shoved the money into Whiskey Jim's clutching fingers, took hold of the quiet marshal, and turned toward the hotel. "You come along with me, officer," he said. "I'll pertect you. That fool says he's buyin' you a drink--mebby he is, but I'm payin' for th' first one. Yo're about th' best he-man I've seen since I looked into a lookin'-glass. I'm obliged to you for not losin' yore valuable temper." He waved a hand at the unbelieving Jim, who doubted his reeling senses. Five whole dollars, all at once! Gosh, but the new marshal was a hummer. "Now don't you lay for me, Jim," laughed the puncher. "We're square, all 'round, ain't we?"

The cheerful three in the door grabbed the marshal of Windsor and hauled him in to the bar, where he pushed free and surveyed them.

"Four cheerful imbeciles," he murmured sadly. "Don't you reckon you better quit drinkin', or else empty them guns?"

"Now don't you be too hard on us, Marshal," chuckled the eldest. "We're so dry we rattles, an' th' dust, risin' out of our throats gets plumb into our eyes. Here," he said, dragging out his gun and gravely emptying it, "these are shore heavy. I'll carry 'em in my pocket for a change," and he made good his words. The others laughingly followed his. example, Tex's smile growing broader all the time.

"This ain't nothin' personal, boys," he said. "It's only that th' law has come to town. Knowin' you'll leave 'em empty till after you get out, I'll have one drink an' go about my business." He made no threats and his voice was friendly and pleasant; and it did not have to be otherwise. He had made four friends, and they knew that he would go through with any play he started. "Know Tommy Watkins?" he asked as he put down his glass.

"Shore!" answered Walt. "He's workin' with my outfit--C Bar. Ain't seen him for a month, him bein' off somewhere when we rode in for our pay. Marshal, shake hands with another C Bar rider--Wyatt Holmes. These two tramps is Double S punchers--Lefty Rowe, an' Luke Perkins. My name's Butler--Walt Butler. What's Tommy up an' done?" he finished somewhat anxiously.

"Glad to see you, boys," said Tex, heartily shaking hands all around. "My name's Tex Jones. Come in ag'in," he invited. "Oh," he said in answer to Walt's question, "Tommy ain't done nothin', yet. I was just wonderin'. Good boy, Tommy is. Sort of wild, I reckon, bein' young. Busy after th' gals. Most young fellers are hellers anyhow, or think they are. But he's a likable pup."

Walt laughed and the others grinned broadly. "You've shore figgered him wrong, Marshal. He's scairt of th' gals--won't have nothin' to do with 'em; an' I ain't never seen him nowhere near drunk; but" he hastily defended in loyalty to his absent friend, "he's all right, other ways. Yes, sir--barrin' them things, Tommy Watkins is a good man, an' I can lick any feller that says he ain't."

"Which won't be me," replied Tex, smiling. "I like him, first-rate. We been gettin' acquainted fast. Well, boys," he said, turning toward the door, "have a good time an' come in often. I like a little company from th' outside. It relieves th' monotony. So-long."

"You shore had th' monotony busted wide open today," chuckled Walt. "But Tommy's a good boy--whatever th' h--l he's been doin' since I saw him last." Watching the marshal until out of sight past the door he turned and regarded his companions. "I'm tellin' you calves there's a man who'd spit in th' devil's eye," he said. "We was playin' with giant powder like four fools. Here's to Tex Jones, Marshal of Windsor!"

Lefty, tenderly putting the glass on the bar, looked thoughtfully around the room and then at the partially stunned barkeep. "How's friend Bud takin' th' new marshal? Bud an' him shore will have an' interestin' Colt fandango some of these fine days."

Baldy sighed, wiped off the bar, and looked sorrowfully at the group. "Bud's planted on Boot Hill. They done had th' fandango, an' he did th' dancin'. My G--d, I can see it yet! It was like this--" and he left the bar, walked to the door, and painstakingly enacted the fight. When it was finished, he mopped his head and slowly returned to his accustomed place.

Wyatt Holmes reached out and gravely shook hands with his friends and finished by shaking his own. "You allus was a fool for luck, Walt," he said thoughtfully. "Giant powder?" he muttered piously. "Giant h--l! It was dynamite with th' fuse lit. Here," he demanded, wheeling on the startled Baldy. "I *need* this drink! Set 'em up!"

Walt shook his head. "Now, what th' devil has Tommy done?" he growled.

Baldy, remembering Tommy's share in the altercation, maintained a discreet silence.

Chapter XV
A Good Samaritan

Out on Buffalo Creek, Blascom, haggard, drawn, gaunt, and throbbing with an excitement which was slowly mastering him, scorning time to properly prepare and eat his food, drove himself like a madman. The creek bed at the old sump showed a huge, sloping-sided ditch from bank to bank, the upper side treacherous dry sand, the lower side a great, slanting ridge of rock, riven through in one place by the force of the dynamite, which had blown a great crater on the down-stream side of the natural riffle. In the bottom of the ditch a few inches of water lay, all that had saved him from fleeing from the claim because of thirst.

For year after weary year the miner had labored over the gold-bearing regions of the West, South, and North, beginning each period full of that abiding faith which clings so tenaciously to the gold-hunter and refuses to accept facts in any but an optimistic manner. A small stake here, day wages there, grubstakes, and hiring out, he had persistently, stubbornly pursued the will-o'-the-wisp and tracked down many a rainbow of hope, only to find the old disappointment. From laughing, hope-filled youth he had run the gauntlet of the years, through the sobered but still hopeful middle age, scorning thought of the twilight of life when he should be broken in strength and bitter in mind. Teeming, mushroom mining camps, frantic gold rushes, the majestic calm of cool canyons, and the punishing silences of almost unbearable desert wastes had found him an unquestioning worshiper, a trusting devotee of his goddess of gold. It was in his blood, it was woven into every fiber of his body, and he could no more cease his pursuit than he could stop the beating of his heart, or at least he could not cease while the goal remained unattained. Now, after all these years, he had won. He had proved that his quest had not been in vain.

Before the sun came up, even before dawn streaked the eastern sky, his meager, ill-cooked breakfast was bolted, and his morning scouting begun. First of all he slipped with coyote cunning down to the lower fork to see if Jake still kept his drunken stupor. The cold chimney of the miserable hut was the first eagerly sought-for sign, and every furtive visit awakened dread that a ribbon of smoke would meet his eye. A nearer approach made with the wariness of some hunted creature of the wild, let him sense the unnatural quiet of the little shack. A stealthy glance through a glassless opening, called a window, after the light made it possible, showed him morning after morning that his jug had not failed him. The unshaven, matted, unclean face of the stupefied man lay sometimes in a bunk, sometimes on the floor, and once the huge bulk was sprawled out inertly across the rough table amid a disarray of cracked, broken, and unwashed dishes. On the fifth morning the anxious prowler, fearing the lowered contents of the jug, had left a full bottle against the door of the hut and, slinking into the scanty cover, had run like a hunted thing back to the riven riffle and its unsightly ditch and crater.

Feverishly he worked, scorning food, unconscious of the glare of a molten sun rising to the zenith of its scorching heat. Shovel and bucket, trips without end from the ditch to a place above the steep bank where the carried sand grew rapidly higher and higher; panting, straining, frantic, worked Blascom. Foot by foot the ditch widened, foot by foot it lengthened, inch by inch it deepened, slide after sandy slide slipping to its bottom to be furiously, madly cursed by the prospector.

Then at last came the instant when the treasure was momentarily uncovered. Dropping the blunted, ragged-edged shovel, he plunged to all fours and thrust eager, avaricious fingers, bent like the talons of some bird of prey, into the storehouse of gold. Noiselessly responding to the jar and the impact of the groveling body, the great bank of sand had collapsed and slid down upon him, burying him without warning. The mass split and heaved, and the imprisoned miner, wild-eyed, sobbing for breath after his spasmodic exertions, burst through it and, raising quivering fists, cursed it and creation.

Hope had driven him remorselessly, but now that he had seen and felt the treasure, his efforts became those of a madman. More buckets of sand, jealous of each spilled handful, more punishing trips at a dogtrot, more frantic digging, and again he stared wildly at the pocket under his knees. Suddenly leaping erect, he cast anxious glances around him and a panicky fear gripped him and turned him into a wild beast. Yanking his coat from the rock riffle he spread it over the treasure and then, running low and swiftly, gun in hand, he scouted through the brush on both sides of the creek, and then bounded toward the lower fork. Approaching the hut on hands and knees, cruelly cut by rock and thorn, he studied the door and the open window. The bottle was where he had left it, the snores arose regularly, and once more he was reassured. Had there been signs of active life he would have murdered with the exultant zeal of a religious fanatic.

The day waned and passed. Night drew its curtains closer and closer, and yet Blascom labored, the treacherous sand turning him into a raving, frenzied fury. Higher and higher grew the sand pile on the bank, a monument to his mad avarice. With gold in lumps massed at the foot of that rock ridge, yet he must save the sand for its paltry yield in dust, pouring out his waning strength in a labor which, to save pence, might cost him pounds. At last he stumbled more and more, staggering this way and that, his tortured body all but asleep, forced on and on by his fevered mind, flogged by a stubborn will. Then came a heavier stumble, following a more unbalanced stagger and his numbed and vague protests did not suffice to get him back on his feet. When he awakened, the glaring sun shocked him by its nearness to the meridian, and the shock brought a momentary sanity; if he scorned the warning he would be lost--and another shadowy prompting of his subconscious mind was at last allowed to direct him. Calmly, but shakily, he weakly crawled and staggered toward his shack, from which came a thin streamer of smoke, climbing arrow-like into the quiet, heated air.

He stopped and stared at it in amazement, doubting his senses. Had he seen it the day before it would have enraged him to a blind, killing madness; but now, suspicious as he was, and deadly determined to protect his secret, the reaction of the high tension of the last six days made him momentarily apathetic. The abused body, the starved tissues and dulled nerves, now took possession of him and forced him, even though it was with gun in his hand, to approach the door of his squalid, disordered habitation erect and without hesitation. At the sound of his slowly dragging steps a well-known, friendly voice called out and a well-known, friendly face appeared at a window.

The marshal was nearly stunned by what he saw and then, surging into action, leaped through the door and caught his staggering friend.

The well-cooked, wholesome breakfast out of the way, a breakfast made possible only by the marshal's forethought in bringing supplies with him from town, he refused Blascom's request for a third cup of coffee and smilingly offered a glass of whiskey, over which he had made a few mysterious passes.

"Don't want none," objected the weary miner.

"But yo're goin' to overcome yore sudden temperance scruples an' drink it, for me," persuaded Tex. "A good shock will do you a lot of good--an' put new life into you. As you are you ain't worth a cuss."

The prospector held out his hand, smilingly obedient, and downed the fiery draught at a gulp. "Tastes funny," he observed, and then laughed. "Wonder I can taste it at all, after th' nightmare I've had since th' smoke of that blast rolled away. Where'd you think I was when you came?"

Tex chuckled and stretched. "I didn't know, but from th' glimpse I got of th' crick bed I was shore I wasn't goin' huntin' you, an' mebby get shot accidental. Did you find it, Blascom?"

"My G--d, yes!" came the explosive answer. "There's piles of it, all shapes an' sizes, layin' on a smooth rock floor. When that sand stops slidin' I can scoop it up with a shovel, like coal out of a bin. Half of it belongs to you, Jones: go look at it!"

"I don't want any of it," replied Tex with quiet, but unshakable, determination. "If you divide it, no matter how much there is, by th' number of years you've sweat an' slaved and starved, it won't be too much to pay you. You set here a little while an' I'll go on a scout in th' brush an' watch it till you come out. Better lay down a few minutes, say half an hour, an' give that grub a chance to put some life into you. I'll shake you if you fall asleep."

"Feel sleepy now," confessed the prospector, yawning and moving sluggishly toward his bunk. "Seein' as how yo're here, I'll just take a few winks--don't know when I'll get another chance. That sand shore is gallin' an' ornery as th' devil. Go up an' take a look at it--I'll foller in a little while."

Tex, closing the door behind him, slipped into the brush, where he made more than a usual amount of noise for Blascom's benefit, and as he worked up toward the ditch he chuckled to himself. There had been no need for a full dose, he reflected, and he was glad that he had not given one. Blascom's drink of whiskey had just enough chloral in it to deaden him and give his worn-out body the chance it sought; besides, he was not too certain of the effect of a full dose on a constitution as undermined as that of his friend.

The ditch, again slowly filling with sand, showed him nothing, and he stood debating whether he should disturb it for a look at the treasure, when he suddenly thought of Jake and the whiskey jug. He remembered that Jake had been almost senselessly drunk when he had left the hotel on the night of the blast and that he had not been seen by anyone since. It would do no harm to go down to the lower fork and see what there was to be seen. The thought became action, and he was on his way, down the middle of the creek bed, where the footing was a little more to his liking.

The hut appeared to be deserted and the bottle of whiskey outside the door brought a frown to his face, which deepened as a nearer approach showed him that the door was fastened shut by rope and wire on the outside, and that the snoring inmate virtually was a prisoner. There was a note in the snores that disturbed him and aroused his vague, half-forgotten professional knowledge. Hastening forward he pushed the bottle aside with an impatient foot and worked rapidly with the fastenings on the door. At last it opened, and gun in hand against any possible contingency, he entered the hovel and looked at its tenant, sprawled face down near the jumbled bunk. A touch of the drunken man's cheek, a tense counting of his pulse, sent Tex to his feet as though a shot had nicked him. Running back to Blascom's hut, where he had left his horse, he leaped into the saddle and sent Omar at top speed toward town.

His thundering knock on the doctor's door brought no response and, not daring to pause on the dictates of custom, he threw his shoulder against the flimsy barrier and went in on top of it. Scrambling to his feet, he dashed into the rear one of the two rooms and swore in sudden rage and disgust.

Doctor Horn lay on his back on a miserable cot and his appearance brought a vivid recollection to his tumultuous caller. Tex turned up a sleeve and nodded grimly at the tiny puncture marks and, with an oath, faced around and swept the room with a searching glance. It stopped and rested on a heavy volume on a shelf and in a moment he was hastily turning the pages. Finding what he sought he read avidly, closed the book, and hunted among the bottles in a shallow closet. Taking what he needed, he ran out, leaped into the saddle and loped south to mislead any curious observer, only turning west when hidden from sight of the town.

When night fell it found a weak and raving patient in the little hovel on the lower fork, roped in his bunk, and watched anxiously by the two-gun man at his side. The long dark hours dragged, but dawn found a battle won. Noon came and passed and then Tex, looking critically at his patient, felt he could safely leave him for a few minutes. Glimpsing the filled bottle of liquor at the door of the hut he grabbed it and hurled it against a rock.

Blascom was up and around when Tex reached the upper fork, dragging heavy feet by strangely dulled legs.

"Just in time to feed," he drawled. "Didn't sleep as long as I thought," he said dully, glancing at the sun patch on the floor. "Must be near two o'clock--an' I felt like I could sleep th' sun around."

Tex would not correct the mistake and nodded. "You must 'a' slept some last night," he suggested. "Looked like you had when I saw you from th' window this mornin'."

Blascom nodded heavily. "Near sixteen hours. I feel dead all over."

"A long sleep like that often makes a man feel that way," responded Tex. "Th' muscles are stubborn an' th' eyes get a little touchy, too," he added.

They ate the poorly cooked dinner and leaned back for a smoke, Blascom allowing himself to lose the time because he felt so inert.

"Have any visits from friend Jake?" carelessly asked the marshal.

Blascom laughed. "Not one. You see, Jake come home that night about as drunk as a man can get an' walk at all. I planted th' jug, a full bottle of gin, an' near half a quart of brandy in his cabin where he'd shore see it. He's been petrified for a week steady. To make shore I put another bottle of whiskey ag'in' his door."

Tex nodded. "I busted that, just now. You come near killin' him. I just about got him through. Don't give him no more. I sat up all last night with him, draggin' him back from th' Divide, an' only left him a little while ago. Get yore gold out quick an' you don't have no call to want him drunk. Cache it, an' then spend a week takin' things easy. You wasn't far behind Jake when I saw you."

Blascom was staring at him in vast surprise. "I never thought good likker would hurt an animal like him!"

"I didn't say it was good likker," rejoined Tex. "Even good likker will do it when drunk by th' barrel; an' there's no good likker in Windsor, if I'm any judge. Well," he said, arising and taking up his hat, "I'll drift along for another look at Jake an' then head for town. Seein' as how you got him that way, through my suggestion, I'll admit, you better look in at him once in awhile an' see he has what he needs. Take some of yore water with you: his stinks."

Chapter XVI
Buffalo Creek in the Spotlight

What instinct it is and how it operates, that leads vultures from over the horizon to a dying animal, has never been satisfactorily explained to a lot of people; no more than the instinct which led Sinful and Hank to go prowling around Buffalo Creek when by all rights they should have been hanging around their own camp or loafing in the hotel; but prowl they did, their cunning old eyes missing nothing, certainly nothing so new and shining and high as the sand heap above the creek bank.

Sinful saw it first and he nudged his companion, whose cud nearly choked him before he could cough it back where it belonged.

"Glory!" he choked. "Jest look at it! Come on, Sinful: we got to inwestigate. Nobody's diggin' all that out an' totin' it up there for th' fun of it. But why's he luggin' it so far?"

Sinful snorted scornfully. "Too busy totin' to pan it," he snapped. "Rain's due 'most any time an' he's workin' to beat it. I don't have to inwestigate it--anybody that's workin' like that knows what he's doin'; an' I ain't never heard it said that Blascom's any fool. If he didn't know it was rich, he wouldn't be workin' so hard in th' sun."

"Well, mebby," doubted Hank, always a cold blanket in regard to his companion's contentions. "Looks like he ain't got no water for pannin', like everybody else. He ain't lazy like you, an' instead of wastin' his time around th' hotel like us he's totin' sand so he can work while th' crick's floodin'. When th' floodin' comes everybody else'll have to set down an' watch it till it gets low enough. Me an' you would be doin' somethin' if we follered his example. Where you goin'?" he demanded as his sneering companion walked away.

Sinful flashed a pitying glance over his shoulder. "To git a handful of that sand an' prove you ain't got no sense, that's where. You keep yore eye open for Blascom while I raid his sand pile. Here's a can," he said, stooping to pick it up. "It'll mebby tell us somethin' when we gits it to some water. If you see him a-comin' out, throw a pebble at me. 'Twon't take me long, once I git my boots off."

Hank obeyed and scouted toward the hut, finally stopping when he could see its door. Watching it a few minutes he saw Blascom pass the opening, and after another few minutes, the watcher slipped away, hastening toward the sand pile. Reaching it, he saw no signs of his partner and backed into the brush to await developments. He no sooner had stopped behind a patch of scrub oak than he caught sight of Sinful carefully picking his way across the stony ground in his socks, one hand carrying the can, the other a pair of boots. On his leathery face was an expression of vast surprise and pious awe. He seemed almost stunned, but he was not so lost to his surroundings that he ignored a bounding, clicking pebble which passed across his path. Clutching can and boots in a firmer grip, he sprinted with praiseworthy speed and agility toward the somewhat distant railroad track. In his wake sped Hank, an unholy grin wreathing his face at the goatlike progress of his old friend over the rocky ground. To Sinful's ears the sound of those clattering boots spelled a determined pursuit and urged him to better efforts. At last, winded, a cramp in his side and his feet so tender and bruised that he preferred to fight rather than go any farther in his socks, he dropped the boots, drew his gun, and wheeled. At sight of Hank's well-known and inelegant figure a look of relief flashed over his face, swiftly followed by a frown of deep and palpitant suspicion.

"What you mean, chasin' me like that?" he shouted.

"Gosh!" panted Hank as he drew near. "That was shore close! An' for an old man yo're a runnin' fool. Jack rabbits an' coyotes can cover ground, but they can't stack up ag'in' you. Did you see him?"

Sinful, one boot on and the other balanced in his hand, looked up. "No, I didn't; did you?" he demanded, suspicion burning in his old eyes.

"Shore," answered Hank, lying with a facile ease due to much practice. "He suddenly busted out of th' door with a rifle in his hands an' headed for his sand pile. I dusted lively, heaved th' pebble; an' here we are." He cast an apprehensive glance behind him and then sharply admonished his friend. "Hustle, you! Yo're settin' there like there ain't no mad miner projectin' around in th' brush with a Winchester! Think I want to git shot?"

"I reckon mebby you ought to," retorted Sinful, struggling erect and trying each tender foot in turn. "Stone bruises, cuts, an' stickers, an' all because you git in a panic!" he growled. "Come on, you old fool: there's a pool of water in th' crick, t'other side of th' railroad bridge. Yo're too smart, you are. Mebby yore eyes'll pop out when you see what's in this here can. Great guns, what a sight I've seen!"

Panning gold in a tomato can might be difficult for a novice, but Sinful's cunning old hands did the work speedily and well. After repeated refillings and mystic gyrations he carefully poured out the last of the water and peered eagerly into the can, bumping his head solidly against his companion's, for Hank was as eagerly curious.

Sinful placed it reverently on the creek bank and looked at his staring friend.

"An' only a canful," he muttered in awe.

"Glory!" breathed Hank, and looked again to make sure. "Nothin' but dust--but Good Lord!" He packed a vile pipe with viler tobacco, lit it, and arose. "No wonder he grabbed his gun an' dusted for his sand pile! Come on, Sinful: we got a long walk ahead of us, some quick packin' to do, an' a long walk back ag'in. If we only could get a couple of mules, we'd load 'em with three-hundred pounds apiece an' go down th' crick a day's journey. It'd be worth it."

Sinful looked scornfully at his worrying companion and slowly arose. "No day's journey for me, mules or no mules," he declared, spitting emphatically. "I ain't shore it would be worth it, considerin' th' time an' th' trouble; but it's worth pannin' right where it is. I've jumped claims before in my life an' I ain't too old to jump another. When I looked over that bank an' saw that wallopin' big rock a-stickin' up in th' crick bed, from bank to bank; an' th' ditch he's put down on th' upstream side, I purty near knew what th' sand pile would show. I'm bettin' he's got *bushels* of gold at th' foot of that riffle. If his location don't run up that far, an' mebby it don't, we got somethin' to keep us busy. An' if it does, we've mebby got more to keep us busy. Come on, you wall-eyed ijut: we got to be gittin' back to camp. Great Jerus'lam!"

The marshal of Windsor, riding slowly toward town south of the railroad track after a long detour to mask his trail, saw two scarecrows bumping along the ties, bobbing up and down jerkily as they tried to stretch their stride to cover two ties and repeatedly fell back to one. They were well to the northeast of him and to his left, but he thought they looked familiar and he pushed more to the south to remain hidden from them while he rode ahead. When he finally had reached a point south of the station he turned and rode toward it, timing his arrival to coincide with theirs.

Sinful grinned up at the smiling rider, his missing teeth only making more prominent the few brown fangs he had left. Two dribbles of tobacco juice had dried at each corner of his mouth and reached downward across his chin, giving him an appearance somewhat striking. He mopped the perspiration from his face by a vigorous wipe of his soiled shirt sleeve and lifted each palpitating foot in turn.

"Been ridin' far?" he asked in idle curiosity and in great good humor, considering the aches in his body and the soreness of his feet.

"Oh, just around exercisin' Oh My," answered Tex. "I thought you two was located out on Antelope, west of town?"

"We are," replied Hank, ignoring his partner's furtive elbow. "Been gettin' sorta tired of it, though, not havin' nothin' to do but set around an' look at th' same things. Thought we'd take a look at th' Buffaler, south of th' track; but it ain't much better, though there is some water in th' pools. Anyhow, Antelope's kinda crowded. We may shift our camp. Jake's out on Buffaler som'er's, ain't he?"

Tex nodded and glanced at the can. "Been fishin'?"

"If we had enough bait to fill that can we'd 'a' ate it ourselves," chuckled Hank.

"Naw, there ain't no fish left now," said Sinful. "Hard-luck coffeepot, that's all it is. Good as anythin' else, an' shore plentiful. Punch a hole in each side of it an' shove in a piece of wire, an' she'll cook anythin' small. Ain't it hot?"

"Hot, an' close," replied the marshal. "Well, I reckon I'll be gettin' along. Feels like rain is due 'most any time, though I don't reckon we'll get any before th' moon changes. Still, you can't allus tell."

"Can't tell nothin' about it at all, this kind of weather," observed Hank, the can now against the other side of his body. "But one thing's shore--it's gettin' closer every day. So-long," and the grotesque couple went bobbing down the track toward their own camp.

Tex looked after them, humorously shaking his head. "'It's gettin' closer every day,'" he mimicked. "Shore it is. Pair of cunning old coyotes, an' entirely too frank about Buffalo Creek." Just then Sinful leaped into the air, cracked his sore heels together and struck his companion across the shoulders. This display of exuberance awakened a strong suspicion in the marshal. "I'll keep my eye on you two old codgers," he soliloquized, thoughtfully feeling of the handcuffs in his pocket. Wheeling abruptly he rode up to the station, where Jerry grinningly awaited him. "Let me know when those mossbacks go west, Jerry, if you see them," he requested. "They're too cussed innocent an' happy to suit me. How are things?"

Jerry shook his head. "I'll be cussed if I know. But I know one thing, and that is that I'm apologizing to you for the way Jane shut the door in your face. I don't know what's the matter with her lately."

"There's never any tellin' about wimmin," said Tex, smiling. "An' don't you ever apologize to anybody for anythin' she does. Wimmin see things from a different angle, an' they ain't got a man's defenses. A difference in structure is likely to be accompanied by differences in nature, in this case notably in the more delicate balance of th' nervous system. Their reactions are both more subtle an' more extreme. I wasn't insulted, but just folded my tents like th' Arabs, an' as silently stole away. Which I'm now goin' to repeat. See you later, mebby."

Jerry watched his visitor ride off and a puzzled frown crept over his face.

"Wish I knew more about you, Mr. Tex Jones," he muttered. "You're either as fine a human as I have seen, or the smoothest rascal: and I'm d--d if I can tell which."

The marshal rode to his office and sought the chair outside the door, his thoughts running back over recent events. Blascom's find and the physical condition of the man naturally brought to mind Jake's narrow escape. The latter bothered him, notwithstanding the certainty that Blascom would keep a good watch over the sick man. While he anxiously ran over his scant knowledge of Jake's illness and the remedies he had employed, he glanced up to see Doctor Horn nervously hurrying toward him. The doctor, in view of what he now knew of him, became a very interesting study for the marshal.

"Marshal!" cried the physician while yet a score of paces away, "somebody burst down my door during my absence and took some drugs which by their nature are not common out here and, consequently, hard to obtain. I am formally reporting it, sir."

"Doctor," replied Tex, "when a patient comes to you for help you naturally expect him to be frank and truthful. It is the same with a peace officer, who endeavors to cure not the ills of a single unit of society, but the ills of society as a whole. Here, as in your own field, a refractory or diseased unit may, and generally does, affect the body of which he is a part. So, as a social physician, I must ask of you that frankness so valuable to a medico. First, what drugs did you miss?"

"Your analogy, while clever, is sophistical and is entirely unwarranted," retorted the physician, taken somewhat aback by the words and attitude of a "cowhand," as he contemptuously characterized punchers. "Leaving it out of the argument, except to say, in passing, that your 'social physician' does not exercise a corrective influence, but rather a punitive one, I hardly see how the naming of the missing drugs will give any enlightenment to a layman. There still exists the forcible breaking into, and the unlawful entry of, my residence."

"For purposes of identification it might be well to know the drugs that were stolen; but I'll waive that. What time would you say this occurred?" asked Tex with professional interest.

"Some time yesterday," answered the physician.

"You certainly are not very specific, Doctor," commented Tex. "I'm afraid we must come closer to it than that. You say you were away at the time?"

"Yes: I did not return until quite late."

"In body or in spirit, Doctor Horn?"

"Sir, I do not understand you!" retorted the complainant, flushing slightly and gazing with great intensity into the marshal's eyes.

"There have been many others who did not understand me," replied Tex, calmly rolling and lighting a cigarette. "I'm mentioning that so you won't think you are an exotic variation of our large and interesting species. The study of man is the greatest of all, Doctor. The words were more of a joke than anything else. Have you ever suffered from hallucinations, Doctor? I've heard it said that too close confinement, too close an application to study, and too intimate relations with chemicals, volatile and otherwise, operate that way in these altitudes. Hothouse gardeners, for instance, notably those engaged in raising poppies, have slight touches of mental aberration. You are certain that your house was entered while you were away?"

The doctor, arms akimbo, was staring at this calm mind-reader as though in a trance, too stunned to be insulted.

Tex continued: "The value of the missing drugs and the damage to the door undoubtedly will be paid to you, Doctor, in a few days. In fact, I am so confident of that that I will pay you just damages now, taking your receipt in return. Do you agree with a great many people that a physician to the body has much the same high obligations as those belonging to a minister or a priest, who are physicians to the soul? That his work is of a humanitarian nature before it is a matter of remuneration; that he should hold himself fit and ready to answer calls of distress without regard to his own bodily comfort?"

Doctor Horn still stared at him, rallying his thoughts. He nodded assent as he groped.

"There are professional secrets, Doctor, which need not be divulged," continued Tex. "I understand that you have a horse?"

The physician nodded again.

"Then use it. I have reason to believe that a man named Jake, a miner, who is located on the first fork of Buffalo Creek, west of town, urgently needs your professional services. I understand that he has been brought back from death from alcoholic poisoning, but will be much safer if you look at him. Did you say you are going now? And by the way, before you start, let me say that the old idea of peace officers being corrective forces, in a punitive sense only, is rapidly becoming obsolete among the more intelligent and broader-minded men of that class. While punishment is undoubtedly needed as a warning to others, the cure's the thing, to paraphrase an old friend of mine. Is there any connection between the natures of the missing drugs and alcoholic poisoning, Doctor? But we are wasting time. This little problem can wait. Just now speed's the thing. Drop around again soon, Doctor: I always enjoy the companionship of an educated man," and the marshal, slowly arising, bowed and entered his little office, the door softly closing behind him.

Chapter XVII
The Rush

The marshal was leaving the hotel after breakfast the following morning when he saw Jerry walking briskly toward him from the station and he waited for the agent to come up.

"Those two old prospectors just passed the station, going west along the track," Jerry informed him. "From the way they were loaded down it looked as though they are moving their camp. And how men as old as they are can carry such packs is beyond my understanding."

"Thanks, Jerry," said the marshal. "Go back to th' station. I've got to take a ride. Trouble's brewin', I reckon."

Passing the hotel on his way to Carney's stable, Tex saw a running miner hurrying into it and in a moment an excited half-score of armed prospectors poured into the street, shouting and gesticulating. The little crowd picked up additions as it passed along the street and headed westward to strike the railroad at an angle. Some of them had partners with them and, when the tracks had been reached, quite a number turned and ran eastward toward their camps to pack up belongings and supplies.

"Mental telepathy?" murmured Tex, watching them in some surprise. "Hank and Sinful are too clever rascals to tell anybody anything of value that they might know. Huh! That's only a name, I guess, for subconscious weighing of facts subconsciously received: instinctive deductions from observations too vague to be definitely recognized. Instinct, I'm afraid you have more names than most people recognize. But it does beat the devil, at that! An animal does seemingly wonderful and impossible things because of the keenness of its scent, which passes our understanding; birds of prey have eyes nearly telescopic in power--but how the knowledge of this gold strike has spread about so quickly when everyone concerned in it naturally would be secretive, is too much for me. One thing is certain, however: it is known, and I have work to do, and quickly!"

Omar welcomed him and soon was stringing the miles out behind him as smoothly almost as running water. There was no need to urge the animal at its best speed, for it was doing two miles to the miners' one and easily would beat them to the scene of action.

When he reached the second fork, Blascom was not at the hut and, leading the roan into a brush-filled hollow, the marshal took his rifle from its scabbard and went up to the scene of the miner's operations. His hail was followed by a startled crouching on the prospector's part and a rifle barrel leaped up to the top of the ditch.

"Don't shoot: It's Jones," called the marshal, slowly emerging from his cover. "I come up to warn you that th' rush has started. Hank an' Sinful ought to get here in about half an hour, th' others a little behind them. I'm aimin' to be referee: th' kind of a referee I once saw at a turf prize fight: he had to jump in an' thrash both of th' principals--an' he did it, too. Get that bonanza cleaned out and cached yet?"

Blascom swore as he stood up again. "Yes: but nobody's goin' to git *this* without a fight! How th' devil did they find out I'd struck it rich?"

"Shore this claim is staked an' located?" demanded Tex.

"Yes; an' there's work enough done on it to make it stick. But how did they find out I'd struck it?"

"Don't know," answered the marshal. "You better climb out an' go off an' hide somewhere in th' brush from where yore rifle will cover th' cache. They're keen as hounds an' there's no use takin' chances of losin' th' greater to save th' less. I'll handle this end of it. If you hear a shot you better slip back an' look things over. Get a rustle on you--time's flyin'."

In a few minutes the creek bed and the little hut appeared to be deserted. Blascom lay on his stomach at a point from which he could see his cache and the ditch as well. After a short silence there came the sound of a snapping twig and a few minutes later Sinful's greedy eyes peered over the creek bank down at the big ditch. He slid a rifle over the edge and looked around eagerly. To his side crept Hank, who added his scrutiny to that of his partner. Sinful spoke out of one corner of his mouth as he gazed intently down the creek bed, where one corner of Blascom's hut could be seen through the scrawny timber on the little point. Hank nodded, crawled to the edge of the bank and was about to slip over it when a low warning from the brush at their side froze them both.

"Stay where you are," said a well-known voice, cold and unfriendly. "That claim's got one owner now, an' he ain't lookin' for no partners, a-tall. Better shove up yore hands an' face th' crick. You know me--an' so far you ain't seen me miss, yet."

Tex emerged from his cover, a Colt in one hand, a pair of shining handcuffs clinking from their short chains as they swung from the other. Snapping one over Sinful's wrist he curtly ordered Hank to his partner's side and linked the two together. Disarming them he unloaded the weapons, appropriated the cartridges, and searched them both to make certain they could do him no injury.

"Sit down," he said, "an' keep quiet. Th' real show is about to start. Who all did you chumps tell about this strike?"

Hank glared at Sinful, Sinful glared at Hank, and then both glared at their captor. "Nobody, so strike me blind!" snapped Sinful. "Hank ain't been out of my sight since we left here yesterday. Think we're fools?"

"Anything but that," grimly rejoined Tex. "Shut up, now: I want to listen. Any play you make that don't suit me will call for a gun butt bein' bent over yore heads. If I need you, I'll call: an' you come a-runnin'. Hear me?"

"We could come faster if we was loose from each other," whispered Sinful in bland innocence. "Couldn't we, Hank?"

"Can't come fast, a-tall, hooked up this way," said Hank earnestly.

"Shut up!" snapped the marshal in a low voice.

A winged grasshopper rasped up over the bank and rasped back again instantly. A few birds chirped and sang across the creek bed and chickadees flashed and darted in an endless search for food. Several birds shot suddenly into the air from the fringe of timber and brush on the farther bank halfway between the ditch and the cabin, quickly followed by vague movements along the ground. Then more than a half-score of men popped into sight and, leaping from the steep bank, landed in the bed of the creek and scurried to different points, fooled by the numerous sumps which Blascom had dug in his quest for water. None of them had the knowledge possessed by Hank and Sinful, and the weather conditions had been such that the ages of the various sumps could not be quickly determined. Each man, eager to grab a hole while there was one left to grab, and to become established, chose a mark and appropriated it without loss of time. No sooner had the scurrying crowd selected their grounds than the marshal, who had crept along the top of the high bank, jumped over it and held two guns on them, guns which they had good reason to respect.

"Han's up!" he roared. " *Pronto* an' high! You-all know me--don't gamble! I drop th' first man that makes a gunplay. *Hank! Sinful!* " he shouted. "Come a-runnin'!" Crouched, he faced the scowling crowd, his steady hands before his hips, his steady guns ready to prove his mastery. The handcuffed pair, squabbling as they came, shuffled up to him.

"You yank me any more an' I'll bust yore fool head!" growled Sinful to his bosom friend. "Just because yore laigs is longer is no reason for playin' kite with me! Knock-kneed old fool! Here we are, Marshal: what you want?"

"Hold yore han's close," ordered Tex, his left gun slipping into its sheath, his right becoming even more menacing. With the free hand he fished out the key, handed it to Hank and waited until he had made use of it. It went swiftly back into the pocket and the left hand again held a gun. "Slip around an' take their weapons!" he snapped. "Don't get between them an' me. Lively!"

"We ain't goin' to spoil yore aim, Marshal," Hank assured him with great fervor. "Come on, you bald-headed old buzzard--git them guns for th' marshal!" He gave his companion a shove forward. "He done us a good turn--an' one good turn deserves another. Come on!"

"Who you shovin'?" blazed Sinful, starting away.

"You ain't got no right, cuttin' in here!" shouted a red-faced, angry miner, his companions growling and cursing their hearty endorsements. "Yo're a town marshal, not a county sheriff! Turn them guns off us!"

"I got a wider range than marshal," rejoined Tex grimly and not for an instant relaxing his alertness. "Gus Williams said so when he 'pinted me; an', besides, I got th' very same authority out here as I have in town: twelve sections of th' Colt statutes as made an' pervided. Blascom has legally established his claim, drove his stakes, and done his work on it. When he comes he'll p'int out his boundaries. Hold still, you two! Git 'em all, Sinful; don't overlook nothin', Hank! No use turnin' this crick into a slaughter-pen."

"I ain't likely to overlook nothin'," replied Sinful, moving more rapidly, "though I'm shore bothered by these here cussed contraptions on my wrist. You'll notice Hank unlocked *his* end of 'em! D--d claim jumpers! A man's rights ain't safe no more these days. Hank an' me shore would 'a' planted some of this passel if they'd bothered us. How th' devil did they find out about it, *I* want to know?"

"What you reckon yo're goin' to do with us all?" sneered a wrathy prospector, his hands slowly coming down toward a harmless belt.

"I'll tell you that after I see Blascom," answered the marshal, firing a shot into the ground. He ordered Sinful and Hank to pile the weapons at his feet, locked them together again and ordered them to get closer to the rest of the miners. The shot brought Blascom as rapidly as he could get there with a due regard to caution. Obeying Tex's terse command he slid down the bank and went to him.

"Shore yore claim takes in th' ditch an' th' riffle?" asked Tex in a whisper.

"Th' new one does," answered Blascom. "I sent off th' papers with Jerry, like you said, th' day I got th' dynamite."

"Th' old one any good?"

"Not much; not much better'n day wages. 'Tain't no good without water; but neither is th' other, now."

"This crowd is fooled by yore old sumps," explained Tex hurriedly. "If we drive 'em off they'll be back ag'in, an' mebby add yore murder to th' rest of their crimes. I can't stay here day an' night; an' if I could, they'd get us both after dark, or at long range in daylight. You got to let 'em stay. By tomorrow there'll be twice as many. I'm scared some'll come slippin' up any minute an' turn th' tables on us. You let Sinful an' Hank divide a quarter of th' sand pannin' between 'em--they'll commit murder for half that, an' you've got to have partners in case of a rush. Besides, rain's due any day now, an' you need 'em to beat it."

"I hate like--" began Blascom stubbornly.

"We all has to do things we hate!" cut in his companion. "You can't do anythin' else. If you can, tell me quick!"

Blascom shook his head. He could do nothing else. He turned and faced the crowd, telling it to go ahead and stake out claims where each man had started to, on condition that there was to be no more jumping and that they join him in putting up a solid front against any newcomers other than partners. The scowls died out, heads nodded, and the hustle and bustle began again from where it had left off.

Tex called the Siamesed pair to him and they listened, with their eyes glowing, to Blascom's offer of limited partnership, Hank nearly swallowing his cud when asked if he was satisfied with the terms. Sinful smelled a rat and looked properly suspicious, his keen old mind racing along on the theory that no one ever gave away anything valuable. Suddenly he grinned so expansively that a generous stream of tobacco juice rolled down his sharp chin.

"Us three ag'in' that gang," he mused. "Huh! Fair enough, _I_ says. Hank an' me can lick 'em by ourselves. Can't we, Hank?"

"Shore!" promptly answered the other weather-beaten old rascal. "We shore kin, Sinful!"

Tex smiled at the cheerful old reprobates, bound closer together now than ever they had been before. "I ought to dump th' pair of you in th' new jail," he said, "though it shore wouldn't get no benefit from it. Yo're a pair of land pirates an' you both ought to be hung from th' yardarm of some cottonwood tree. Hold out yore hands till I turn you loose. You two youngsters want to keep th' bargain, or I _will_ hang you!"

"Glad to git shet of them cuffs," growled Sinful. "Hank takes sich long steps an' walks sideways, th' old fool. We'll play square, won't we, Hank? There; he said so, too. We allus has felt kind of friendly to Blascom, ain't we, Hank? Shore we has. An' he needs us to keep our eyes on them blasted claim jumpers. 'Sides, he's a friend of yourn, Marshal: an' we ain't forgettin' them few dollars we won from you t'other night-- _are_ we, Hank?" His shrewd old eyes baffled Tex's attempt to read just what he thought about the poker game.

"We ain't!" emphatically replied Hank, spitting copiously and vehemently. "We'll make these claim jumpers herd close to home; yes, sir, by glory!" He paused a moment and leaned nearer to his companion's ear. " _Won't_ we, Sinful?" he suddenly shouted.

"Who you yowlin' at that way?" blazed Sinful, and then his eyes popped wide open in frank surprise. "Cussed if th' doc ain't got th' fever, too!" he ejaculated. "Here he comes up th' crick! Beats all how news does spread! An', great Jerus'lam: if he ain't as sober as a watched Puritan!"

Nodding right and left Doctor Horn rode slowly among the busy claim jumpers and drew rein in front of Tex and his companions.

"How do you do, gentlemen?" he said, smiling. "I see you're quite busy, Marshal, which seems to be a habit of yours. I happened to have a patient out this way, down on the lower fork, and while I was in his vicinity I thought I would drop in and compliment Blascom for his care of Jake. While the efficient treatment he first received undoubtedly saved his life, Blascom's nursing comes in for well-earned praise. He is still a sick man, although out of danger. I hope you will disregard our former conversation, so far as my part of it is concerned, Marshal. Good day to you all," and wheeling, he rode up a break in the creek bank and slowly became lost to sight among the bowlders and timber.

Sinful had watched both men carefully while the doctor spoke, and now he covertly glanced at the marshal, who was gazing after the departing physician. Then he looked at Blascom, and from him to his own, disreputable partner.

"Come on, Hank," he said. "If any of these gold thieves start swappin' claims, we'll play 'em a smart tune for 'em to dance to. There's shore been a-plenty of lives saved on this crick plumb recent--our own, mebby, among 'em. An' who do you reckon yo're a-starin' at?"

"You, you pore ol' fool!" retorted Hank. He blew out a bleached cud, rammed in a fresh one, nodded at Blascom and the contemplative marshal, and followed his impatient partner toward their packs and guns.

Tex slowly turned and looked after them. "Hey, Sinful!" he called. "You still makin' coffee in old tin cans? If you are, you want to watch 'em close on account of sand gettin' in 'em!"

Sinful nudged his companion, stopped, scratched his head, and then grinned.

"Don't have to use 'em *now* . We got all our traps along, an' th' old coffeepot is with 'em, kivver an' all. Anyways, *we* don't mind a little sand once in awhile-- *do* we, Hank?"

"No, sir, by glory!" cried Hank. "Not no more, we don't, a-tall!"

Chapter XVIII
"Here Lies the Road to Rome!"

A few nights later Tex awakened to feel his little lean-to shaking until he feared it would collapse. A deafening roar on the roof made an inferno of noise, the great hailstones crashing and rolling. Flash after flash of vivid lightning seemed wrapped in the volleying crashes of the thunder. A sudden shift in the hurricane-like wind drove a white broadside against his front windows, both panes of glass seeming spontaneously to disintegrate. Another gust overturned a freight wagon in the road before the office and tore its tarpaulin cover from it as though it were tied on with strings, whisking it out of sight through the incessant lightning flashes like the instant passing of some huge ghost. The teamster, who saw no reason to pay for hotel beds while he had the wagon to sleep in, went rolling up the slatted framework and down again, bounced to his knees, and crawled frantically free, beaten by the streaking hail and buffeted by the shrieking wind. He was blown solidly against the lean-to, almost constantly in the marshal's sight because of the continuous illumination. Groping along the wall, he reached the shattered window and, desperate for shelter, promptly dived through it and rolled across the room.

Tex laughed, the sound of it lost to his own ears. "Yo're welcome, stranger!" he yelled. "But I'm sayin' yo're some precipitate! Better gimme a hand to stop up that window, or she'll blow out th' walls and lift off th' roof. Grab this table an' we'll up-end it ag'in th' openin'. I'll prop it with th' benches from th' jail. That's right. Ready? Up she goes."

After no mean struggle the window was closed enough to give protection against the raging wind, the two benches holding it securely. Then Tex struck a match and lit both of his lamps.

"We don't hardly need any light, but this is a lot steadier," he shouted, turning to look at his guest. His eyes opened wide and he stared unbelievingly. "Good Lord, man! You look like a slaughter-house! Here, lemme look you over!"

The teamster, cut, bruised, and streaked with blood, held up his hand in quick protest, shouting his reply. "'Taint nothin' but th' wallerin' I did when th' wagon turned over, an' th' beatin' from th' hail. I've seen it worse than this, friend. These stones are only big as hens' aigs, but I've seen 'em large as goose aigs, an' lost three yoke of oxen from 'em. I was freightin' in a load of supplies for a surveyin' party, down on th' old Dry Route, southwest of th' Caches. One ox was killed, his yokemate pounded' senseless, an' th' others couldn't stand th' strain an' lit out. I never saw 'em again. I was under th' wagon when they left, which didn't turn over till th' hail changed into rain, an' I wouldn't 'a' poked out my head for all th' oxen in th' country. This here's a little better than a fair prairie hail storm. Gosh," he said, grinning, as he glanced at the badge on his companion's vest. "I got plenty of nerve, all right, bustin' into th' marshal's office! Ain't got any likker, have you?"

Tex handed him a full bottle and packed his pipe. The deafening crashing of the hailstones grew less and less, a softer roar taking its place as the rain poured down in seemingly solid sheets. The great violence of the wind was gone and the lightning flashed farther and farther away.

"Feel better now," said the teamster, passing the bottle to his host and taking out his pipe. He accepted the marshal's sack of tobacco and leaned back, puffing contentedly. "Sounds a lot better, now. I'd ruther drowned than be beat to death, any time. There won't be a trail left tomorrow an' not a crick, ravine, or ditch fordable. Some of 'em with sand bottoms will be dangerous for three or four days. I once saw th' Pawnee rise so quick that it was fetlock deep when I started in, an' wagon-box deep before I could get across--an' a hull lot wider, too, I'm tellin' you. An' yet some fools still camp in dried crick beds!"

"That's just what I been thinkin' about," said the marshal, a look of worry on his face. "Out on Buffalo Crick there's near two dozen miners with claims staked out on th' dried bed. It shore would be terrible if this caught 'em asleep!"

"Don't you worry, Marshal," reassured his guest, laughingly. "Them fellers may have claims in a crick bed, but they don't sleep on 'em. They know too much!"

Tex related what a hail storm had done to a trail herd one night years before, and so they talked, reminiscence following reminiscence, until dawn broke, dull and watery, and they started for the hotel, to rout out the cook for hot coffee and an early breakfast.

All day it rained, but with none of the fury of the darker hours, and for the next ten days it continued intermittently. There was no special news from Buffalo Creek except that it had changed its bed in several places, and that two miners had been forced to swim for their lives. It was noteworthy, however, that the prospectors of the country roundabout began to spend dust with reckless carelessness. The hotel was well patronized during the day, and the nights were times of great hilarity. Drink flowed like water and old quarrels, fed by fresh fuel, added their share of turbulence to the new ones.

Sleeping late in the mornings, the marshal was on his feet until nearly every dawn, stopping brawls, deciding dangerous contentions, and once or twice resorting to stern measures. The little jail at one time was too full for further prisoners and had forced him to resort to fines, which brought his impartiality and honesty into question. He had been forced to wound two men and had been shot at from cover, all on one night. He grew more taciturn, grimmer, colder, wishing to avoid a killing, but fearing that it must come or the town would turn into a drunken riot. Then came the climax to the constantly growing lawlessness.

Busy in repairing washouts along the railroad and strengthening the three little bridges across the creeks of his section of track, Murphy and Costigan, reinforced by half a dozen other section-hands from points east, who had rolled into town on their own hand car, had scarcely seen the town for more than a week when they came in, late one Saturday afternoon. The extra hands were bedded at the toolshed and at Murphy's box car, and took their meals at Costigan's, whose thrifty wife was glad of the extra work for the little money it would bring her. Well knowing the feeling of the Middle West of that time against his race, the section-boss cautioned his crew to avoid the town as much as they could; but rough men are rough men, and wild blades are wild. Knowing the wisdom in the warning did not make it sit any easier on them, added to which was the chafing under the restraint and the galling sense of injustice.

Sunday morning found them quiet; but Sunday noon found them restless and resentful. The lively noise of the town called invitingly across the right-of-way and one of them, despite orders, departed to get a bottle of liquor. He drew hostile glances as he made his way to the bar in the saloon facing the station, but bought what he wanted and went out with it entirely unmolested. The news he brought back was pleasing and reassuring and discounted the weight of the section-boss' admonitions, and later, when the bottle had been tipped in vain and thirsts had only been encouraged by the sops given them, some wilder soul among the crowd arose and announced that he was going to paint the town. There was no argument, no holding back, and the half-dozen, laughing and singing, sallied forth to frolic or fight as Fate decreed.

The first saloon they entered served them and let them depart unharmed and without insult, raising their spirits and edging their determination to enjoy what pleasures the town might have for them. They were as good as any men in town, and they knew it, which was right and proper; but soon it did not satisfy them to know it: they must tell everyone they met. This, also, was right and proper, although hardly wise; but in the telling there swiftly crept a fighting tone, a fighting mood, a fighting look, and fighting words; yet they were behaving not one whit different from the way gangs of miners had behaved since the town was built. The difference was sharp and sufficient: The miners had been in the town of their friends; the section-gang was in the town of its enemies.

The half-dozen entered the hotel barroom, jostled and elbowed, jostling and elbowing in return, their tempers smoldering and ready to burst into flames. Calling for whiskey at the bar they drank it avidly and turned to look over the room, where all sorts and conditions of rough men and ready fighters were frowningly watching them. The frowns grew deeper, and here and there a gibe or veiled insult arose above the general noise. The gibes became more bitter, the insults less veiled, and finally a huge miner, belted and armed, stood up and shouted for silence. Sensing trouble the crowd obeyed him, waiting with savage eagerness to hear what he would say, to see what he would do.

"I'm goin' to tell you a story," he cried, and forthwith made good his promise. It was not a parlor story by any stretch of imagination, and it ended with St. Peter slamming shut the gates of heaven as he repeated one of the then popular slogans of the country along the roadbeds, "No Irish need apply." It was not couched in language that St. Peter would use, and suitable epithets of the teller's own gave added weight to the insult of the tale. Still swearing the miner sat down, an ugly leer on his face, while shouts, laughter, catcalls, and curses answered from every part of the room.

"Run 'em out of town!" came a shout, which swiftly became a universal demand.

The track-layer nearest the door, a burly, red-haired, red-faced fighting man, leaped swiftly to the miner's table, kicked the half-drawn gun from his hand, and went to the floor with him. "St. Peter will open no doors to th' like av ye!" he shouted. "I'm sendin' ye to h--l, instead!"

The bartender, fearing pistol work, whipped his own over the counter and yelled his warning and his demand for fair play. "I'll drop th' man that draws! Let 'em have it out, man to man!"

This suited the crowd as an appetizer for what was to follow, and chairs and tables crashed as it surged forward to better see the fight, the five section-hands, their broad backs against the bar, forming one side of the pushing, heaving ring, their faces set, their huge fists clenched, in spirit taking and giving the flailing blows of the rolling combatants, so intent, so lost in the struggle that consciousness of their own danger gradually faded from their minds. They had faith in their champion and were with him, heart and soul.

The miner could fight like the graduate he was of the merciless, ultra-brutal rough-and-tumble of the long frontier, biting, kneeing, gouging, throttling as opportunity offered, and he was rapidly gaining the advantage over his cleaner-fighting opponent until, breaking a throat hold, barely escaping the fingers thrust at his eyes and a wolflike snap of murderous jaws, the Irishman broke free, and staggered to his feet to make a fight which best suited him. Great gasps of relief broke from his tense friends, their low words of advice and encouragement coming from between set teeth.

"Steady, Mac, an' time 'em!" whispered his nearest friend. "He fights like a beast--lick him like th' man ye are. He's as open as a book!"

Panting, his breath whistling through his teeth, the miner scrambled to his feet, needlessly fearing a kick as he arose, and rushed, his great arms flaying before him as he tore in. Met by a straight left that caught him on the jaw a little wide of the point aimed at, he rocked back on his heels, his knees buckling, and his arms wildly waving to keep his balance. Before he could recover and set himself, a right flashed in against his chest and drove him back against the ring of men behind him. Gasping, he bent over and threw himself at his enemy's thighs, missing the hold by a hair. The Irishman retreated two swift steps and waited until his opponent had leaped up and then, feinting with his left at the swelling jaw, he swung his right shoulder behind a stiffening right arm and landed clean and squarely above the brass buckle of the cartridge belt. The crash shook the building, for the miner's feet came up as he was hurled backward and he struck the floor in a bunched heap.

The bruised and bleeding victor, filling his lungs with great gulps of foul air, started backing toward the bar to regain his breath among his friends, but he staggered sidewise on his course, coming too close to the first line of the aroused crowd and one of them leaped on him, the impact toppling him over, just as the five friends charged. Chaos reigned. Shouts, curses, the stamping of feet, bellows of rage and pain filled the dusty air with clamor as the crowd surged backward and forward, the storm center ever nearing the door. The valiant half-dozen, profiting by experience, resisted all efforts to separate them, keeping in a compact group, shoulder to shoulder, with their rapidly recovering champion in their middle. They had passed the end of the bar, which had been a sturdy bulwark against their complete encircling, and the crowd was pouring in to attack from that once-protected side when a hatless figure leaped through the deserted rear door, bounded onto the long bar without changing his stride, dashed along it and jumped, feet first straight at the heads bobbing nearest to the stout-hearted six. It was Costigan who, not finding Murphy, was acting on his own initiative and according to his lights. In his hand was a broken mattock handle and under its raining blows an opening rapidly grew in the crowd. Had he been given arm room, where his full strength could have been used, Boot Hill would have reaped a harvest. Audacity, that Audacity which is the fairest child of Courage, the total unexpectedness of his hurtling, spectacular attack won more for him and his friends than the deadly effectiveness of the hickory handle. The astonished crowd drew back in momentary confusion and Costigan, cursing at the top of his panting lungs, shoved the nearly exhausted handful through the door and into the street. As the last man staggered through and pitched to the ground, the club wielder leaped to the door, barring it with his body. He was about to tell the crowd what he thought of it when the situation changed again.

A hand clutched his shirt collar and yanked him back and he went striking with the club as he sprawled beside a battered friend. The change had been so sudden and the crowd just recovering from its surprise at Costigan's flaying attack that it looked like magic. One instant a red-shirted Irishman, his clothing torn into shreds, lovingly balancing his favorite weapon; the next, a calm, cold-faced, blue-shirted, leather-chapped gunman, bending eagerly forward behind the pair of out-thrust Colts, his thumbs holding back swift death in each hand.

"The devil!" growled a miner.

"Aye!" snapped Tex. "An' I'll find work for idle hands to do! *Why do you stop and turn away? Here lies th' road to Rome!*" he laughed, exultantly, sneeringly, insultingly; and never had they heard a laugh so deadly. It chilled where words might have inflamed. There was not a man who did not shrink instinctively, for before him stood a killer if ever he had seen one.

"I only got twelve handy--which dozen of you want to open th' way for th' rest?" asked the marshal. His quick eye caught a furtive movement in the crowd and the roar of his flaming Colt jarred the room. The offender-pitched forward before the paralyzed front line, rocking to and fro in his pain. "Th' next man dies!" snapped the marshal, his deadly intent fully revealed by his face.

The crowd gazed at impersonal Death, balanced in the two firm hands. They saw no hesitancy reflected between the narrowed lids of those calculating eyes, no qualifying expression on that granite face; and they were standing where Bud Haines had stood, facing the man he had faced. A restless surge set the mass milling, those behind pushing those in front, those in front frantically pushing back those behind. Tense and dangerous as the situation was, a verse of an immortal fighting poem leaped to the marshal's mind and a sneering smile flashed over his face. *Was none who would be foremost to lead such dire attack; but those behind cried "Forward!" And those before cried "Back!"* He seemed to tense even more, like some huge, deadly spider about to spring, and his clearly enunciated warning, low as it was spoken, reached the ears of every man in the room. "Go back to yore tables, like you was before."

The surge grew and spread, split following split, until the dragging rearguard sullenly followed its companions. The dynamic figure in the door slowly forsook its crouch, arising to full height. The left-hand gun grudgingly slid into its sheath, reluctantly followed by its more deadly mate. Casting a final, contemptuous look at the embarrassed crowd, each unit of it singled out in turn and silently challenged, the marshal shoved his hands into his pockets, turned his back on them with insolent deliberation and stepped to the street, where a bloody, battered group of seven had waited to back him up if it should be needed.

"Yer a man after me own--" began Costigan thickly between swollen lips, but he was cut short.

"That'll keep. Take these fellers back where they belong, an' *keep* 'em there," snapped Tex, the fighting fire still blazing in his soul. He watched them depart, proud of every one of them; and when they had reached the station he wheeled and went back into the hotel, had a slowly sipped drink, nodded to his acquaintances as though nothing out of the ordinary had occurred, and then sauntered out again without a backward glance, turning to go to the station.

When he reached the building he stopped and looked toward the toolshed where Murphy, just back from a run of inspection up the line, and Costigan, had turned the corner of the shed and stopped to renew their argument, which must have been warm and personal, judging from their motions. Finally Costigan, looking for all the world like a scarecrow, hitched up what remained of his trousers, squared his shoulders, and limped determinedly toward his little cottage, glancing neither to the right nor to the left. Murphy, hands on hips, gazed after him, nodded his head sharply, and was about to enter the shed when he caught sight of the motionless two-gun man. Snapping his fingers in sudden decision, he started toward his capable friend, his frame of mind plainly shown by the way his stride easily took two ties at once.

"God loves th' Irish, or 'twould be diggin' graves we'd now be doin'," he said. "An' me away! But they'll be mindin' their P's an' Q's after this. I was goin' to skin Costigan, but how could I after I learned what he did? It ain't th' first time he's tied my hands by th' quality av his fightin'. But 'twas well ye took cards, an' 'twas well ye played 'em, Tex."

"I have due respect for Costigan, but if he leaves th' railroad property he'll lose it quick," replied the marshal. "I turned that mob into a mop, but there's no tellin' what might happen one of these nights. Tim, I wish his family was out of town. It's no place for wimmin an' children these days, not with ten marshals. I can't be everywhere at once, an' I'm watchin' one house now more than I ought to."

"They're leavin' on tomorry's train east," said Murphy, breathing a sigh of relief. "I've Mike's word for it, an' if he can't get 'em to go without him, then he's goin' with 'em, superintendent or no superintendent! I'm sorry that it's my fault that ye had th' trouble, Tex; I should 'a' stayed close to them d--d fools."

"There's no harm done, Tim, as it turned out. It was comin' to a show-down, gettin' nearer an' nearer every day. Now that it's over th' town will be quiet for a day or two. I know of marshals who were paid from eight hundred to a thousand dollars a month--I'm admittin' that I've earned my hundred in just about five minutes today. For about fifteen seconds th' job was worth a hundred dollars a second--it was a close call."

"But look at th' honor av it," chuckled Murphy. "It's marshal av Windsor ye are, Tex--an' ye have yer Tower, as well!"

Tex laughed, glanced over the straggling town from Costigan's cottage to another at the other end of the street. "I'm not complainin'. I'm only contrastin' and showin' that Williams didn't pull any wool over my eyes when he offered me my princely salary. I agreed to it, and I'm paid enough, under th' circumstances."

"Aye," said Murphy, following his friend's glance, a sudden smile banishing his anxious frown. "Money ain't everythin'. Perhaps yo're not paid much now, Tex--but later, who can tell?"

Chapter XIX
A Lecture Wasted

That evening Tex had a caller in the person of Henry Williams, who seemed to be carrying quite a load of suspicion and responsibility. He nodded sourly, and nonchalantly seated himself on a chair at the other side of the door. His troubled mind was not hidden from the marshal, who could read surface indications of a psychological nature as well as any man in the West. No small part of his poker skill was built upon that ability. Should he lead his visitor by easy and natural stages to unburden himself; make a hearty, blunt opening, or make him blurt out his thoughts and go on the defensive at once? Having anything but respect and liking for the vicious nephew, he determined to make him as uncomfortable as possible. So he paid him the courtesy of a glance and resumed his apparently deep cogitations.

Henry waited for a few minutes, studying the ground and the front of his uncle's store and then coughed impatiently.

"'Tis that," responded Tex abstractedly; "but hot, an' close. I was thinkin'," he said, definitely.

Henry looked up inquiringly: "Yes?"

"Yes," said the marshal gravely. "I was." His tone repulsed any comment and he kept on thinking from where he had left off.

Henry shifted on the chair and recrossed his legs, one foot starting to swing gently to and fro. To put himself *en rapport* with his forbidding companion, he too, began thinking; or at least he simulated a thinker. The swinging foot stopped, jiggled up and down a few times, and began swinging more energetically. Soon he began drumming on the chair with the fingers of one hand. Presently he shifted his position again, recrossed his legs, grunted, and drummed alternately with the fingers of both hands. Then they drummed in unison, the nails of one set clicking with the rolling of the pads of the fingers of the other hand. Then he puckered his lips and began to whistle.

"Don't do that!" snapped Tex, and returned to his cogitations.

"What? Which?" asked Henry, starting.

"That!" exploded the marshal savagely and lapsed into intense concentration.

Henry's lips straightened and he looked down at the drumming fingers, and stopped them. Squirming on the chair, he uncrossed his legs and pushed them out before him, intently regarding the two rounded groves in the dust made by his high heels. Then he glanced covertly at his frowning companion, cleared his throat tentatively, and became quiet as the frown changed into a scowl.

The marshal thought that his visitor must have something important on his mind, something needing tact and velvety handling. Otherwise he would have become discouraged by this time and left. Was it about Jane? That would be the natural supposition, but he slowly abandoned it. Henry never had shown any timidity when speaking about her. It must be something concerning the riot in the hotel.

"I say it can't be nothin' else!" fiercely muttered the marshal, his chair dropping solidly to all fours as he rammed a fist into an open palm. "No, sir! It *can't!* " He glared at his companion. "What did you say?"

"Huh?" demanded Henry, his chair also dropping to all fours because of the impetus it had received from his sudden start. "What for?" he asked inanely.

"What for what?" growled Tex accusingly. "Who said: 'What for'?"

"I did: I just wanted to know," hastily explained Henry in frank amity.

"That's what you said!" retorted Tex, leaning tensely toward him; "but what did you mean?" he demanded.

"What you talkin' about?" queried Henry, truly and sincerely wondering.

"Don't you try to fool me!" warned Tex. "Don't pretend you don't know! An' let me tell you this. You are wrong, like th' ministers an' all th' rest of th' theologians. That's th' truest hypothesis man ever postulated. It proves itself, I tell you! From th' diffused, homogeneous, gaseous state, whirlin' because of molecular attraction, into a constantly more compact, matter state, constantly becomin' more heterogeneous as pressure varies an' causes a variable temperature of th' mass. Integration an' heterogeneity! From th' cold of th' diffused gases to th' terrific heat generated by their pressure toward th' common center of attraction. Can't you see it, man?"

Henry's mouth remained open and inarticulate.

"You won't answer, like all th' rest!" accused Tex. "An' what heat! One huge molten ball, changing th' force of th' planets nearest, shifting th' universal balance to new adjustments. 'Equilibrium!' demands Nature. An' so th' struggle goes on, ever tryin' to gain it, an' allus makin' new equilibriums necessary, like a dog chasin' a flea on th' end of his spine. Six days an' a breathin' space!" he jeered. "Six trillion years, more likely, an' no time for breathin' spaces! What you got to say to that, hey? Answer me this: What form of force does th' integration postulate? Centrifugal? Hah!" he cried. "You thought you had me there, didn't you? No, sir; not centrifugal--centripetal! Integration--centripetal! Gravity proves it. Centrifugal is th' destroyer, th' maker of satellites--not th' builder! Bah!" he grunted. "You can't disprove a word of it! Try it--just try it!"

Henry shook his head slowly, drew a deep breath and sought a more comfortable position. "These here chairs are hard, ain't they?" he remarked, feeling that he had to say something. Surely it was safe to say that.

Tex leaped to his feet and scowled down at him. "Evadin', are you?" he demanded. Then his voice changed and he placed a kindly hand on his companion's shoulder. "There ain't no use tryin' to refute it, Hennery," he said. "It can't be done--no, sir--it can't be done. Don't you ever argue with me again about this, Hennery--it only leads us nowhere. Was it Archimedes who said he could move th' earth if he only had some place to stand? He wasn't goin' to try to lift himself by his boot straps, was he, th' old fox? That's th' trouble, Hennery: after all is said we still got to find some place to stand." He glanced over Henry's head to see Doctor Horn smiling at him and he wondered how much of his heavy lecture the physician had heard. Had he expected an educated man to be an auditor he would have been more careful. "That was th' greatest hypothesis of all--the hypothesis of Laplace--it answered th' supposedly unanswerable. Science was no longer on th' defensive, Hennery," he summed up for the newcomer's benefit.

"Truly said!" beamed the doctor, getting a little excited. "In proof of its mechanical possibility Doctor Plateau demonstrated, with whirling water, that it was not a possibility, but a fact. The nebular hypothesis is more and more accepted as time goes on, by all thinking men who have no personal reasons strong enough to make them oppose it." He clapped the stunned Henry on the back. "Trot out your refutations and the marshal and I will knock them off their pins! Bring on your theologians, your special-creation adherents, and we'll pulverize them under the pestle of cold reason in the mortar of truth! But I never thought you were interested in such beautiful abstractions, Henry; I never dreamed that inductive and deductive reasoning, confined to purely scientific questions appealed to you. What needless loneliness I have suffered; what opportunities I have missed; what a dearth of intellectual exercise, and all because I took for granted that no one in this town was competent to discuss either side of such subjects. But he's got you with Laplace, Henry; got you hard and fast, if you hold to the tenets of special creation. Now that there are two of us against you, I'll warrant you a rough passage, my friend. 'Come, let's e'en at it!' We'll give you the floor, Henry--and here's where I really enjoy myself for the first time in three weary, dreary years. We'll rout your generalities with specific facts; we'll refute your ambiguities with precisions; we'll destroy your mythological conceptions with rational conceptions; your symbolical conceptions with actual conceptions; your foundation of faith by showing the genesis of that faith--couch your lance, but look to yourself, for you see before your ill-sorted array a Roman legion--short swords and a flexible line. Its centurions are geology, physics, chemistry, biology, astronomy, and mathematics. Nothing taken for granted there! No pious hopes, but solid facts, proved and re-proved. Come on, Henry--proceed to your Waterloo! Special creation indeed! Comparative anatomy, single-handed, will prove it false!"

"My G--d!" muttered Henry, forgetting his mission entirely. His head whirled, his feet were slipping so rapidly that he did not know where he was going. He stared, open-mouthed at Doctor Horn, dumbly at the marshal, got up, sat down, and then slumped back against his chair, helpless, hopeless, fearing the worst. Over his head hurled words he thought to be foreign, as his companions, having annihilated him, were performing evolutions and exercises of their verbal arms for the sheer joy of it. Finally, despairing of the lecture ever ending, he arose to escape, but was pushed back again by the excited, exultant doctor. Daylight faded, twilight passed, and it was not until darkness descended that the doctor, finding no opposition, but hearty accord instead, tired of the sound of his own voice and that of the marshal, and after profuse expressions of friendship and pleasure, departed, his head high, his shoulders squared, and his tread firm and militant.

Henry's sigh of relief sounded like the exhaust of an engine and he shifted again on the chair and tried to collect his scattered senses. Before he could get started the marshal sent him off on a new track, and his unspoken queries remained unspoken for another period.

"Seen Miss Saunders yet?" asked Tex, struggling hard to conceal his laughter.

Henry shook his head. "No; but I ain't goin' to wait much longer. I don't see no signs of her weakenin', an' that C Bar puncher is gittin' too cussed common around her house. For a peso I'd toss him in th' discard. I reckon yore way ain't no good with her, Marshal. I got to do somethin'--got to get some action."

"I know about how you feel," sympathized Tex. "I know how hard it is to set quiet an' wait in a thing like this, Hennery, even if action does lose th' game. Who was it you aimed to have perform th' ceremony?"

"Oh, there's a pilot down to Willow--one of them roamin' preachers that reckons he's found a place where he can stick. He'll come up here if th' pay's big enough, an' if I want any preacher. He'll only have to stay over one night to git a train back ag'in. Anyhow, if we has to wait a day or two it won't make much difference, as long as we're goin' to git hitched afterward."

Tex closed his eyes and waited to get a good hold on himself before replying. "He'll come for Gus, all right," he said. "Think you can hold out a few days more--just to see if my way will work? It'll be better, all around, if you do. Where was you aimin' to buy them presents for her?"

"Kansas City or St. Louie--reckon St. Louie will be better. Gus gets most of his supplies from there. You still thinkin' stockin's is th' proper idea?"

Tex cogitated a moment. "No; they're a little embarrassin': better try gloves. I'll find out th' size from her brother. Nice, long white gloves for th' weddin'--an' mebby a nice shawl to go with 'em--Cashmere, with a long fringe. They're better than stockin's. You send for 'em an' wait till they come before you go around. You shouldn't go empty-handed on a visit like that. An' you want th' minister with you when you go after her--you can leave him outside till he's needed. Folks'll talk, an' make trouble for you later. There's tight rules for weddin's; very tight rules. You don't want nobody pokin' their fingers at yore wife, Hennery. It'll shore mean a killin', some day."

"I ain't so cussed anxious to git married," growled Henry. "It's hard to git loose ag'in--but I reckon mebby I better go through with it."

"I--reckon--you--had," whispered Tex, his vision clouding for a moment. He grew strangely quiet, as though he had been mesmerized.

"A man can allus light out if he gits tired of it," reflected Henry complacently.

The marshal arose and paced up and down, thankful for the darkness, which hid the look of murder graven on his face. "Yes," he acquiesced; "a man--allus--can--do--that." This conversation was torturing him. Anything would be a relief, and he threw away the results of all his former talking. "What was on yore mind when you come down to see me today?"

"Oh!" exclaimed his companion a little nervously. "I plumb forgot all about it. You see," he hesitated, shifting again on the chair, "well, it's like this. Us boys admires th' way you handled things in th' hotel this afternoon, but somebody might 'a' been killed. 'Tain't fair to let a passel of Irish run this town--an' they started th' fight, anyhow. Th' big Mick kicked Jordan's gun out of his hand an' jumped on him. Then th' others piled in, an' th' show begun. We sort of been thinkin' that th' marshal ought to back up his town ag'in' them foreigners. Gus is mad about it--an' he's bad when he gits his back up. He thinks we ought to go down to th' railroad an' run them Micks out of town on some sharp rails, beatin' 'em up first so they won't come back. Th' boys kinda cotton to that idea. They're gettin' restless an' hard to hold. I thought I'd find out what side yo're on."

Tex stopped his pacing, alert as a panther. "I ain't on no side but law an' order," he slowly replied. "I told that section-gang to stay on th' right-of-way. They're leavin' town early tomorrow mornin', an' may not come back. A mob's a bad thing, Hennery: there's no tellin' where it'll stop. Most of 'em will be full of likker, an' a drunken mob likes bright fires. Let 'em fire one shack an' th' whole town will go: hotel, Mecca, an' all. It's yore best play to hold 'em down, or you an' yore uncle will shore lose a lot of money. Th' right-of-way is th' dead line: I'll hold it ag'in' either side as long as I can pull a trigger. You hold 'em back, Hennery; an' if you can't, don't you get out in th' front line--stay well behind!"

"Mob's do get excited," conceded Henry, thoughtfully. "Reckon I'll go see what Gus thinks about it. See you later."

Tex watched him walk away, silhouetted against the faintly illuminated store windows, and as the door slammed behind him the marshal shifted his heavy belts and went slowly up the street and into the hotel, where he received a cold welcome. Seeing that the room was fairly well crowded, accounting for most of the men in town and all of the afternoon crowd, he sat in a corner from where he could see both doors and everything going on.

In a few minutes Gus Williams and Henry entered and began mixing with the crowd, which steadily grew more quiet, but more sullen, like some wild beast held back from its prey. Henry sat at one table, surrounded by his closest friends, while his uncle held court at another. The nephew was drinking steadily and his glances at the quiet marshal became more and more suspicious. Around midnight, the temper of the crowd suiting him, Tex arose and went down the street toward his office, passed around it and circled back over the uneven plain, silently reaching the railroad near the box car.

Murphy quietly crept out of his bunk, gun in hand, and slipped to the door, pressing his ear against it. Again the drumming of the fingers sounded, but after what had occurred earlier in the day he wanted more than a tapping before he opened the door or betrayed his presence in the car. Soon he heard his name softly called and recognized the voice. As quietly as he could, he slid back the door and peered into the caller's face from behind a leveled gun.

"Don't let that go off," chuckled Tex, stepping inside. "Close th' door, Tim."

Murphy obeyed and felt his way to his visitor and they held a conversation which lasted for an hour. Tex's plans of action in certain contingencies were more than acceptable to the section-boss and he went over them until he was letter-perfect. To every question he gave an answer pleasing to the marshal and when the latter left to go up and guard the toolshed and its inmates he felt more genuine relief than he had known since he had become actively engaged in the town's activities. Things were rapidly approaching a crisis and the knowledge had filled him with dread; now let it come--he was ready to meet it.

Silently he chose a position against the railroad embankment close to the toolshed and here he remained until dawn. Murphy and Costigan passed him in the darkness on a nearly silent hand car, going west, but did not see him; and he did not know that they had returned until the sky paled. For some time he had heard a bustling in the building, and just as he was ready to leave he saw the section-gang roll out their own hand car and go rumbling up the line toward Scrub Oak.

Chapter XX
Plans Awry

For the next few days a tense equilibrium was maintained in the town, the marshal, grim, alert, and practically ostracized by nine-tenths of the population. He could feel the veiled hostility whenever he went up and down the street, and silence fell abruptly on groups of men conversing here and there whenever he was seen approaching. Hostile glances, sullen faces, shrugging shoulders greeted him on every side, and he felt more relieved than ever when he reviewed his arrangements with the section-boss.

Henry Williams was growing openly suspicious of him, impatiently awaiting the arrival of the presents from St. Louis, which he had ordered through Jerry's telegraph key, and he was drinking more and more and keeping more and more to himself, his only company being two men whom Tex had been watching since the death of Bud Haines. The marshal felt that with the coming of the presents trouble would begin, and he had asked Jerry to keep a watch for them, and let him know the moment they arrived. Fate tricked him here, for when they did come they were packed in a large consignment of goods for Gus Williams, and since he regularly was receiving shipments there was nothing to indicate to the station agent that Henry's gifts had passed through his hands.

Henry's suspicions of the marshal were cumulative rather than sudden. Never very confident about what Tex really thought and what he might do, certain vague memories of looks and of ambiguous words and actions recurred to the nephew. He was beginning to believe that the marshal would shoot him down like a dog if he pressed the issue as he intended to press it in regard to Jane Saunders, and he was determined that Tex should have no opportunity to go to her defense. Several methods of eliminating the disturbing marshal presented themselves to the coyote-cunning mind of the would-be lover. He could be shot from cover as he moved about in his flimsy office, or as he slept. He could walk into a rifle bullet as he opened his door some morning, or he could be decoyed up to Blascom's while Henry's plans went through. This last would taste sweeter in the public mouth than a coldly planned murder, but on the other hand the return of the marshal might end in cyclonic action. There was no doubt about Tex's feelings in regard to killing when he felt it to be necessary or justified. He would kill with no more compunction than a wolf would show. Then from the mutterings of rebellion and the sullen looks of discontent among the hotel habitues a plan leaped into the nephew's mind. It solved every objectionable feature of the other schemes; and Henry forthwith went to work.

The nephew was no occult mystery to a man like the marshal, who almost could see the mental wheels turning in any man like him. Tex was preparing for eventualities and part of the preparation was the buying of a pint flask of whiskey from Carney--a bottle locally regarded as pocket-size. When night fell he emptied into the liquor a carefully computed amount of chloral hydrate, recorked it, shook it well, and placed it among sundry odds and ends in a corner of the office, where it would be overlooked by any thirsty caller, whose glance was certain to notice the bottle of whiskey in plain sight on a shelf. Against the consciousness of sixteen men that innocent-looking flask would tip the scales to its own side with an emphasis; and the marshal not only knew the proper dose for horses but also how to shove it down their throats with practiced ease and swiftness. Buck Peters had paid him no mean compliment when he had said that Tex could dose a horse more expertly than any man he ever had known. Having put all of his weapons in order he marked time, awaiting the pleasure of the enemy.

He did not have long to wait. To be specific he waited two days more, which interval brought time around to the last day on the calendar for that month, the day which railroad regulations proclaimed to be the occasion for making out sundry and numerous reports, a job that kept many a station agent writing and figuring most of the night. Having sense and imagination, the agent at Windsor did what he could of this work from day to day and as a consequence saved himself from a long, high-tension job at the last minute; but he did not have imagination enough to know that a packing-case of formidable dimensions which he had received that noon from the west-bound train and later saw hauled to the Mecca, held the watched-for gifts that Henry Williams would eagerly present to Jane.

Contemptuous of any interference that Jerry might make in a physical sense, Henry nevertheless preferred to have him absent when he made his determined attempt. The brother doubtless would have great influence on Jane by his protests, and that would necessitate drastic measures which only would make the matter worse. If Jerry were detained by force, injured, or killed to keep him from the house it would cause a great deal of unpleasantness, from a domestic standpoint, to run through the years to come. There was only one night a month when the agent remained away from his house for any length of time, and this must be the night for the action to be carried through.

The mob was being slowly, but surely, inflamed by the nephew and his two friends, its anger directed against Murphy and Costigan since the section-gang had not returned to town. The section-boss and his friend came in every night while they worked along Buffalo Creek, and were careful not to give any excuse for a hostile demonstration against them. They were even less conspicuous because they walked in instead of rolling home on the hand car. But on this last night of the month the whole crew, rebelliously disobeying orders, came in on their crowded hand car, much to Henry's poorly concealed delight, and to Tex's rage. Murphy had promised otherwise.

Here was oil for the flames Henry had set burning! Here was success with a capital letter! The mob now would surely attack, divert Jerry's attention, and perhaps rid the town of its official nuisance. He would act on the marshal's kindly warning, for he would not be in the front rank of the mob; in fact, he would not be with the mob at all. He had other work to do.

The sudden look of joyous expectation, so poorly disguised, on Henry's face acted on Tex like the warning whirr of an angry rattlesnake and he quietly cleaned and oiled his guns, broke out a fresh box of cartridges, and dumped them into his right-hand pocket. The remaining chloral-filled shells he slipped in the pocket of his chaps. Shaking up the flask of whiskey to make certain of the crystals being dissolved and the drug evenly distributed throughout the fluid, he hid it again and, seating himself in his favorite place, awaited the opening number.

Darkness had just closed down when Tommy loped in from the ranch and stopped to say a few careless, friendly words, but he never uttered them, for the marshal's instructions were snapping forth before the C Bar rider could open his mouth.

"This is no time for pleasantries!" said Tex in a voice low and tense. "Turn around, ride back a way, circle around th' town an' leave yore cayuse a couple of hundred yards from Murphy's box car. Tell him trouble's brewin' an' to look sharp. Then you head for her house, actin' as cautious, an' go up to it on foot, an' as secretly as you know how. Lay low, outside. Don't show yourself at all--a man in th' dark will be worth five in th' light tonight. Stay there no matter what you hear in town. If she should see you, on yore life don't let her think there's any danger--on yore life, Tommy! Mebby there ain't, but there's no tellin' what drunken beast will remember that there's a woman close at hand. You stay there till daylight, or till I relieve you. Get-a-goin'--an' good luck!"

Tommy carried out his orders, gave Murphy the warning, and was gone again before the big Irishman, seething with rage at his crew's disobedience, could say more than a few words. Murphy had been forced to construct a plan of his own, and he wished to get word of it to the marshal's ears. Tommy having left so quickly, he could not send it. Convincing himself that it was not really necessary for the marshal to be told of it, and savagely pleased by the surprise in store for him and every man in town, the section-boss went ahead on his own initiative. Going to the toolshed he went in, frowning at the thoroughly cowed and humbled crew, blew out the lamps and with hearty curses ordered the gang to put their car on the rails and to start east for the next town.

"Roll her softly, by hand, till ye get out av th' hearin' av this hell-town, an' then board her, an' put yore weight on th' handles," he commanded. "An' don't ye come back till I send for ye. Costigan an' me are plannin' work for ourselves an' will not go with ye. Lively, now--an' no back talk. A lot depends on yer doin' as yer told. One more order disobeyed an' I'll brain th' pack av ye with a crowbar. Ye've raised h--l enough this night. Now git out av here, an' mind what I've told ye!"

The orders quickly obeyed and the car quietly placed on the rails, the gang went into the night as silently as bootless feet would take them, pushing the well-greased car ahead of them, and as gently as though it were loaded with nitro-glycerin. When far enough away not to be heard by anyone in town, they put on their boots, climbed aboard, and sent their conveyance along at an ordinary rate of speed. They hated to desert their two countrymen, and began to talk about it. Finally they made up their minds that Murphy's orders, in view of their recent disobedience, were to be followed, and with hearty accord they sent the car rolling on again, the greater part of the grades in their favor, toward the next town. The distance was nothing to become excited about with six husky men at the handles to pump off the miles.

Up at the station a single light burned in the little office where Jerry worked at his reports. Outside the building in the darkness Murphy lay on his stomach in a tuft of weeds, a rifle in his hand, and a Colt beside him on the ground. Within easy reach of his right hand lay a coatful of rocks culled from the road-bed, no mean weapons against figures silhouetted by the lamp-lighted windows of the buildings facing the right-of-way; and close to them were half a dozen dynamite cartridges, their wicked black fuses capped and inserted. Tim Murphy, like Napoleon, put his trust in heavy artillery.

Costigan was nowhere to be seen. Down the track lights shone under the cracks of the doors of the toolshed and the box-car habitation of the section-boss, and one curtained window of Costigan's rented cottage glowed dully against the night. Crickets shrilled and locusts fiddled, and there were no signs of impending danger.

In the hotel the tables were filled with lowly conversing miners in groups, each man leaning far forward, elbows on the table, his shoulders nearly touching those on either side. Gus Williams and his closest friends had pulled two tables together and made a group larger than the others. Henry and his two now inseparable companions were at a table near the back door, talking earnestly with Jake, who by this time had recovered from his recent sickness. The Buffalo Creek miner was quieter and more thoughtful than he had been before Blascom had nearly killed him, and his mind for several days had been the battle ground of a fiercely fought struggle between contending emotions, which still raged, but in a lesser intensity. He listened without comment to what was being said to him, swayed first one way and then another. His last glass of liquor was untasted, which was something of no moment to Henry's whiskey-dulled mind. Finally Jake nodded, tossed off the drink with a gesture of quick determination, hitched up his cartridge belt and, forgetting his sombrero on the floor, arose and slipped quietly out of the door. As he left, another man, peremptorily waved into the vacated chair, also listened to instructions and also slipped out through the rear door. He set his course toward the right-of-way, whereas Jake had gone in the other direction, toward Carney's saloon and the marshal's office.

The last man stopped when even with the line of shacks facing the railroad, noted the dully glowing shade in Costigan's house, the yellow strips of light around the rough board shutters of the box car, and the broader yellow band under the toolshed door. Satisfied by his inspection he slipped back the way he had come and made his report to Henry.

Jake crept with infinite caution toward the marshal's office, but when nearly to it he paused as the battle in his mind raged with a sudden burst of fury. The marshal had humbled him in sight of his friends and acquaintances and had boasted of worse to follow if his victim forced the issue; the marshal had saved his life in the little hut on the lower fork, laboring all night with him. Doctor Horn had said so, and Blascom, playing nurse at the marshal's request, had endorsed the doctor.

Ahead of him, plain to his sight, was the marshal's side window, its flimsy curtain tightly drawn; and silhouetted against it were the hatted head and the shoulders of the man he had been sent to kill. Again he crept forward, the Colt gripped tightly in his right hand. Foot by foot he advanced, but stopping more frequently to argue with himself. A few yards more and the mark could not be missed. He, himself, was safe from any answering fire. A heavy curse rumbled in his throat and he stopped again. He fought fair, as far as he knew the meaning of the term in its generally accepted definition among men of his kind. He never had knifed or shot a man from behind, and he was not going to do it now, especially a man who had no reason to save his sotted life, but who had done so without pausing. Jake arose, jammed the gun back into its holster and walked briskly to the door of the flimsy little office, which he found locked against him. He knocked and listened, but heard nothing. Again he knocked and listened and still there was no answer.

"Marshal!" he called in a rasping, loud whisper. "Marshal! Git away from that d--d window: th' next man won't be one that owes you for his life. I'm goin' back to Buffaler Crick. Look out for yoreself!" and he made good his words, striding off into the dark.

Back of the hotel, lying prone behind a pile of bleached and warped lumber, the marshal watched the rear door. He saw Jake leave, recognizing the man in the light of the opening door by certain peculiarities of carriage and manner. He smiled grimly when the man turned toward the north, and he waited for the sound of the shot which would drill the window, the shade, and the old shirt hanging on the back of a chair. He wondered if the rolled-up blanket, fastened to the broken broom handle, which made the head and held Carney's old sombrero, would fall with the impact. Then the door opened again and the second man hurried out, turning to the south. He came back shortly, left the door open behind him and with his return Henry's voice rang out in an impassioned harangue. The hotel was coming to life. The stamp of heavy boots grew more continuous; loud voices became louder and more numerous, and shouts arose above the babel. The protesting voice of Gus Williams was heard less and less, finally drowned completely in the vengeful roar. Sudden noises in the street told of angry men pouring out of the front door, simultaneously with the exodus through the rear door. Oaths, curses, threats, and explosive bursts of laughter arose. One leathern-lunged miner was drunkenly singing at the top of his voice, to the air of *John Brown's Body*, a paraphrase worded to suit the present situation.

The marshal leaped to his feet, secure against discovery in the darkness, and sprinted on a parallel course for an opening between the row of buildings facing the right-of-way. His sober-minded directness and his lightness of foot let him easily outstrip the more aimless, leisurely progress of the maudlin gang, which preferred to hold to a common front instead of stringing out. Drunk as they were, they were sober enough to realize, if only vaguely, that a two-gun sharpshooter by all odds would be waiting for the advance guard. In fact, their enthusiasm was largely imitation. Henry's mind had not been keen enough to take into consideration such a thing as anticlimax; he had not realized that the psychological moment had passed and that in the interval of the several days, while the once white-hot iron of vengeful purpose still was hot, it had cooled to a point where its heat was hardly more than superficial. The once deadly purpose of the mob was gone, thanks to Gus Williams' efforts, the ensuing arguments, and the wholesome respect for the marshal's courage and the speed and accuracy of his two guns. Instead of a destroying flood, contemptuous of all else but the destruction of its victims, the mob had degenerated into a body of devilish mischief-makers, terrible if aroused by the taste of blood, but harmless and hesitant if the taste were denied it.

Tex, sensing something of this feeling, darted through the alleyway between the two buildings he had in mind, dashed across the open space paralleling the right-of-way, crossed the tracks, and slipped behind the toolshed to be better hidden from sight. Its silence surprised him, but one glance through a knot hole showed the lighted interior to be innocent of inmates.

He forthwith sprinted to the box car and a warped crack in one of the barn-door shutters told him the same tale. A sudden grin came to his face: Murphy had done what he could to offset the return of his section-gang. He glanced at Costigan's house and its one lighted curtain, and at that instant he remembered that he had not noticed the gang's hand car in the toolshed. He brought the picture of its interior to his mind again and grunted with satisfaction. Its disappearance accounted for the disappearance of the gang.

The mob would now become a burlesque, having nothing upon which to act. Chuckling over the fiasco, he trotted toward the station to see that Jerry got away before the crowd discovered its impotence to commit murder as planned, and to stay on the west side of the main street in case the baffled units of the mob should head for Jerry's house. There was no longer any shouting or noise. He knew that it meant that the advance guard of rioters was cautiously scouting and approaching the lighted buildings with due regard to its own safety; and he reached the station platform before he saw the sudden flare of light on the ground before the toolshed which told of its doors being yanked open. Figures tumbled into the lighted patch and then milled for a moment before hurrying off to join their fellows on the way to attack the other two buildings.

"That you, Tex?" said a low voice close to him. "This is Murphy."

"Good!" exclaimed the marshal. "You've beat 'em, Tim. They're like dogs chasin' their tails; an' from th' beginnin' they didn't sound very business-like. But there's no tellin' what some of them may do, so you go up an' join Costigan while I take a look around Jerry's house. Where is he? His light's out."

"He went home when he heard th' yellin'," answered Murphy, "to git th' lass out av th' house an' to Costigan in case th' mob started that way. 'Tis lucky for them they didn't, an' pass within throwin' distance av me! 'Tis dynamite I'd 'a' fed 'em, with proper short fuses. Look out ye don't push that lighted cigar too close to th' darlin's!"

Tex stepped back as though he had been stung. "I'm half sorry they didn't give you a chance to use th' stuff," he growled. "Well, I reckon mobs will be out of style in Windsor by mornin'. This ain't no wolf-pack, runnin' bare-fanged to a kill, but a bunch of coyotes usin' coyote caution. We'll let Costigan stay where he is, just th' same. You better join him as soon as these fools go back to get drunker. Th' woman in this makes us play dead safe. I'll head up that way an' look things over. If I hear a blast I'll get back fast enough. Don't forget to throw 'em quick after you touch 'em to that cigar!"

"I'll count five an' let 'em go," chuckled Murphy. "I got 'em figgered close."

"Too close for me!" rejoined the marshal, moving off toward the Saunders' home.

"I'd like to stick one in Henry's pocket," said the Irishman, growling.

"D--n me for a fool!" snapped Tex, leaping into the darkness.

Chapter XXI
An Equal Guilt

Tommy Watkins, after delivering his message to Tim Murphy, hastened to the Saunders' home, where he carried out his orders, with but one exception; but the exception nullified all his efforts for a stealthy approach and a secret watch. The best cover he could find around the house was a little building near the back door in which firewood, kerosene, and odds and ends were kept. Despite the kindling and the darkness his entrance had been noiseless and he was paying himself hearty compliments upon the exploit when his head collided with a basket of clothespins which hung from a peg in the wall, and sent the basket and its contents clattering down on the kerosene can and a tin pan. He started back involuntarily and his spurred heels struck the side of a washtub which was nearly full of water, kept so against drying out and falling apart. Into this he sat with a promptness and abandon which would have filled the heart of any healthy small boy with ecstasies. Bounding out of the tub, he fell over the pile of kindling and from this instant his rage spared nothing in his way. Had he deliberately started out with the firm intention of arousing that part of Kansas he scarcely could have made a better job of it. While he cursed like a drunken sailor, and burned with rage and shame, the door was suddenly flung open and Jane, lamp in hand, stared at him in fright and determination, over the trembling muzzle of a short-barreled .38.

"Oh!" she exclaimed, the hand holding the gun now pressing against her breast. "Oh!" she repeated, and the lamp wobbled so that she tremblingly blew it out. For some moments she struggled to get back to normal, Tommy thankful that the lamp no longer revealed him in his present water-soaked condition. He felt that his flaming face would give light enough without any further aid.

He sidled out of the door, tongue-tied, crestfallen, miserable, and placed his back against the shed, intending to slip along it, and dash around the corner into the kindly oblivion of the black night.

"Wait!" she begged, sensing his intention. "Oh, my; how you frightened me! Whatever made you get into this shed, anyway? What were you trying to do?"

Here it was, right in his teeth. Tex fairly had hammered into him the warning not to frighten her--on his life he was to keep from her any thought of danger if she should see him. She had seen him, all right. She had seen entirely too much of him--and he was not to frighten her! Holy Moses! He was not to frighten her! He resolved that plenty of time should elapse before he allowed Tex Jones to see him. Not to frighten her--it was a wonder she had not died of fright.

"What on earth ever made you go in there?" she demanded, a little acerbity in her voice.

"Why, ma'am, I was hidin' from you," said the culprit. "Let me light th' lamp, ma'am, an' straighten things out in there. Everythin' slid that wasn't nailed fast. That tub, now: was you savin' th' water for anythin', ma'am? If you was I plumb spoiled it."

"No; it was only to keep the staves swelled tight--for heaven's sake, do you mean that you fell in it?" She reached out and grasped his coat, and suddenly collapsed against the building, shrieking with laughter. When she could speak she ordered him to feel for and pick up the lamp, and to lead the way into the house. "Go right into Jerry's room and change your clothes--I hope you can get his things on. But whatever made you go in there, anyway? What was it?"

"Like I done said, ma'am," he reiterated, flushing in the dark. "I was goin' to play a joke on Jerry when he came home--but I didn't aim to do no damage, ma'am, or scare you!" he earnestly assured her.

"Oh, but you were willing to scare Jerry!" she retorted.

"I don't reckon he'd 'a' been scared," he mumbled. "Here's th' lamp, ma'am, on th' step; I'll see Jerry at th' station. I'm fadin', now," and before she could utter a protest he had put down the lamp and disappeared around the house. But he did not go far. Wet clothes meant nothing to him, nothing at all in his present state of mind, and he intended to stay, and to keep his watch faithfully. And it was to his present flurried state of mind that he owed his more serious misadventure of the night, for he blundered around the second corner squarely into two figures hugging the wall and a descending gun butt filled his mental firmament with stars. He sagged to the ground without even a sigh and was quickly disarmed and bound. A soiled handkerchief was forced into his mouth and he was rolled against the wall, where he would be out of the way.

One of the two hirelings nudged the other as they stood up, putting his mouth close to his companions ear. "Hey, Ike!" he whispered. "This fool is wet as a drownded pup--wears a gun an' cowpunch clothes. He ain't the agent!"

"H--l, no!" responded Ike; "but he meant us no good, bein' here. We'll git th' agent, too. He'll be comin' soon, an' fast. Git over by th' path he uses."

Jane, somewhat vexed, had picked up the lamp and entered the house. The constantly repeated "ma'am" and the stammering explanations, which she put but little stock in, made her suddenly contrast this big, overgrown boy with a man she knew, and to Tommy's vast discredit. She had hit it: one was no more than an overgrown boy, coarse, unlearned, clumsy, embarrassed; the other, a grown man, cool, educated, masterful, unabashed. One was in his own way; the other, unobtrusive in manner but persistently haunting in his personality. She might not be able for good reasons to see Tex Jones in a room filled with people, but she could not fail to sense his presence. But the marshal was no longer to be thought of; he had taken a human life and was forever beyond the pale of her interest and affections. He had blood on his hands.

Suddenly she started and cast an apprehensive glance toward the window which faced the town. A low, chaotic roaring, indistinct in its blurred entirety, but fear impelling because of its timbre, came from the main street. A shot or two sounded flatly and the roaring rose and fell in queer, spasmodic bursts. Before she could move, a knock sounded on the door and, fearing bad news about her brother, she took a tight grip on herself and walked swiftly toward the summons, flinging the door wide open.

Henry Williams, a smirk on his face, bowed and entered, not waiting for an invitation. He forgot to remove his hat in his eagerness to place his packages on the table where she plainly could see them. Selecting the easiest chair, he seated himself on the edge of it, and tossed his sombrero against the wall.

"Nice evenin', ma'am," he said, flushing a little. "I was hopin' for more rain but don't reckon we'll git none for a spell. What we had has helped wonderful. You an' Jerry feelin' well?"

"It doesn't feel like rain, Mr. Williams," she replied, torn between fear and mirth at the presence of this unwelcome visitor. "Both my brother and myself are as well as we can expect to be. If you'll go to the station you'll find him there--this is report night and he may not be home until quite late."

"I ain't waitin' for Jerry," explained Henry, leering. "It's just as well if he is a little late. My call is shore personal, ma'am; personal between me an' you."

She was staring at him through eyes which were beginning to sparkle with vexation. She was now beginning to accept her first, intuitive warning.

"I am not aware that there is anything of a personal nature which concerns us both," she rejoined. "I believe you must be mistaken, Mr. Williams. If you will close the door behind you on your way out I will be duly grateful. Jerry is at the station." She stepped back to let him pass, but he ignored the hints.

There came an increase in the roaring from the direction of town and she started, casting an inquiring and appealing glance at her visitor.

"Th' boys are a little wild tonight," he said, smiling evilly. "They've got so much dust that they're bustin' loose to paint th' old town proper. There ain't nothin' to be scared about."

"But Jerry: my brother!" she exclaimed fearfully. "He's alone in the office!"

"No, he ain't ma'am," replied Henry with an air meant to reassure her. "I got four good boys, deputized by th' marshal, watchin' th' station in case some fool gets notions. Jones, hisself, is settin' on a bench outside, an' you know what *that* means. I allus look after my friends, ma'am." He smiled again. "'Specially them that are goin' to be real close to me. That's why I'm here--to look after you now--now, an' all th' time, now an' forever. Just see what I brought you--sent all th' way to St. Louie for 'em, an' shore got th' very best there was. Why," he chuckled, going to the table, and so engrossed in his packages that he did not see the look of revulsion on her face, a look rapidly turning to a burning shame and anger.

"These here gloves, now--they cost me six dollars. An' lookit this Cashmere shawl--you'd think I was lyin' if I told you what that cost. I told th' boys you'd show 'em off handsome an' proper. Put 'em on and let's see how they look on you." He held the gifts out, looking up at her, surprised by her silence, her lack of pleased exclamations, and paused, dumbfounded at her expression.

Mortification yielded place to shame and fear; shame and fear to anger with only a trace of fear, and then rage swept all else before it. The colors playing in her cheeks fled and left them white, her lips were thin as knife blades and her eyes blazed like crucibles of molten metal. She struck wildly at the presents, sending them across the room and raised her hand to strike him. Never in all her life had she been so furious.

"Why--what's th' matter?" he asked, not believing his senses. He put out a hand to pacify her. It touched her arm and turned her into a fury, her nails scoring it deeply as she struck it away.

"What's th' matter with you?" he demanded angrily, looking up from his bleeding hand. "Oh!" he sneered, his face working with anger. "That's it, huh? All right, d--n you! I'll cussed soon show you who's boss!" he gritted, moving slowly forward. "If you won't come willin'ly, you'll come unwillin'ly! Puttin' on airs like you was too good for me, huh? I'll bust yore spirit like you was a hoss!"

She flung a quivering arm toward the door, but he pressed forward and backed her into a corner, from where she struck at him again and again, and then felt his arms about her as he wrestled with her. Her strength amazed him and he broke loose to get a more punishing hold. "Ike!" he shouted. "George! Hurry up: she's worse'n a wildcat!"

Ike's head popped in through a window, George dashing through the door, and with them at his side Henry leaped for her. She clutched at her breast and crouched, as savage and desperate as any animal of the wild. He shouted something as he closed with her and then there came a muffled roar, a flash, and a cloud of smoke spurted from between them. Henry, his glazing eyes fixing their look of fear, amazement, and chagrin, spun around against his companions, his clutching hands dragging down their arms, and slid between them. For him the mob had been incited in vain.

His two friends, stupefied for an instant, gazed unbelievingly from Jane to Henry and back again, vaguely noticing that her horror and revulsion were unnerving her and that the short-barreled Colt in her hand was wobbling in ever-widening circles. Ike recovered his self-possession first and, reaching out swiftly, knocked the wavering weapon from her hand. Shouting savagely he leaped for her as a streak of flame stabbed in through the window he had entered by, the deafening roar filling the room. He stiffened convulsively, whirled halfway around and pitched headlong under the table, dead before he touched the floor. His companion's arms jerked upward with spasmodic speed.

"Keep 'em there! Sit down, Miss Saunders," came an even, unflurried voice from the window as the marshal, hatless and coatless, hoping that George would draw, crawled into the house behind a steady gun. "Good Lord!" he muttered, glancing over the room, his eyes passing the fallen .38 without betraying any recognition. "Steady!" he cried as Jane's knees buckled and she slid down the wall. "Keep 'em up!" he snarled at George as he swiftly disarmed him. "Face th' door!" As the frightened man obeyed, the marshal stepped quickly to a shelf on which stood a bottle of brandy and some glasses. He changed the gun to his left hand, snatched a cartridge from his chaps' pocket and, yanking out the lead with his teeth, emptied the shell into a glass. Quickly filling this and another he wheeled and thrust one out at the rigid prisoner. "Drink this," he ordered. "You shore need it; an' if you don't I'll blow you apart." George's stare of amazed incredulity changed to one of hope and relief and he downed the drink at a gulp. Tex slipped a pair of handcuffs over his wrists and ordered him to sit down. "Sit down in that big chair, an' close yore eyes. I got somethin' for you to do--relax!"

As he bent over Jane she stirred, opened her eyes, glanced at him, and then fixed them on the men on the floor, shuddering and shrinking from the sight; but she could not look away. "I killed him! I killed him!" she sobbed hysterically, over and over again.

"Drink this," ordered the marshal, forcing the glass between her lips. He nodded with quiet satisfaction. "Shore," he replied in an assumed matter-of-fact voice, as though it were an every-day occurrence. "Good job, too. I should have done it, myself, days ago." He held up the glass again. "Can you drink a little more of this, Miss Saunders? There are times when a little brandy is very useful." His low, even, unemotional tones were almost caressing, and she thankfully put herself in his capable hands. Slowly growing calmer she began to see things with a less blurred vision and the slow slumping of the sleepy man in the chair took her wondering attention.

"Why, is he--killed--too?" she asked shuddering.

"Oh, no; he's only half asleep," replied Tex, smiling. "Three more minutes an' he'll be sound asleep, for a dozen hours or more. Brandy has an hypnotic effect on some people, Miss Saunders, while it stimulates others. Will you please collect a small valise of your most valuable and indispensable possessions, all the money in the house, a good wrap of some kind, and allow me to escort you to Murphy and Costigan? You are leaving town, you know, never to return.”

“But I’ve killed a man, and you are an officer of the law! Do you mean--” she paused unbelievingly.

“You shot a mad skunk in plain self-defense,” he replied. “He has powerful friends and influence to avenge him. The jury would be packed and justice scorned. I’m marshal no longer, Miss Saunders. I accepted the appointment on the definite understanding that I would be marshal only as long as I could. The term has automatically come to an end. So far as this town is concerned I’m a rabid outlaw.” He tore the badge from his vest and threw it on the table. “Ah! George is sleeping more soundly than he ever slept before. There’s no need of gagging him, for he’ll give no alarm. Please fill that satchel, Miss Saunders--time presses.”

“You are a good friend, Mr. Jones; and I have wronged you,” she said, her words barely audible. “My hands are as bloody as yours--and I scorned you for taking life! Take me away from here--please--please!”

“As fast as I can,” replied Tex, soothingly. “You help me by filling a satchel and getting your wrap. Put your mind on your possessions, please; think what you wish to take with you, and then get them. Money? Jewels? Miscellaneous valuables, intrinsic or sentimental? Documents? Apparel? Please--you must aid me all you can if I’m to aid you. We have no time to lose!”

“But my brother--he is safe?”

“Waiting outside, tied, and gagged. I couldn’t stop to free him,” Tex answered. “Watkins, likewise. They laid their plans well, but the mob was a misfire and didn’t keep me as busy as they counted on. Will you obey me, Miss Saunders, or must we leave bare-handed? I’ll give you just three minutes by that clock--then we go.”

A pious, shocked exclamation came from the window where Murphy stared suddenly into a magic gun before he was recognized. “Holy Mother!” he whispered, and then: “I found Tommy--where is Jerry?”

“Don’t you ever do that again!” snapped Tex, a little white showing in his face. “I don’t know how I kept th’ hammer up! You look around by that clump of scrub oak, where the path goes around the big bowlder. I nearly fell over him. Take them both with you--we’ll follow close. Any signs of anyone coming from town?”

“Not yet--but ye needn’t stay here all night! Hurry, miss, or there’ll be a slaughter that’ll shake this country!”

As Jane obeyed, Tex walked over, drew up one of George’s eyelids and smiled grimly. Then he placed a hand on each of the figures on the floor and nodded, a sneer flickering over his face. In a moment Jane, still a little unsteady, returned and found the ex-marshal pinning the nickeled badge on the lapel of Henry’s coat, and while it meant nothing to her then in her agitated state of mind its significance came to her later. When that badge was found she would be freed of blame for Henry’s death. Opening the door Tex blew out the light and led the way. They hurried over the uneven, hard ground and soon reached the railroad, where a hand car, with Murphy, Costigan, and Tommy at the handles, waited to run them over a trail where no tracks would tell any tales.

“Head for Scrub Oak, an’ stop outside th’ town till Jerry’s party gets away,” ordered Tex. ”Th’ grades are mostly against you an’ all of you came from th’ east, where Mike’s family went. They’ll figger you went th’ same way, if they think of th’ hand car at all. It ain’t likely they will, because I’m aimin’ to give them something plain to read, when they’re *able* to read it. Got money? Got enough to buy three good cayuses with saddles, grub, an’ everythin’ you need? Good! Tommy, when you get to town, go in alone, get three outfits, an’ take Miss Saunders an’ Jerry to Gunsight as fast as they can travel. When you get there, ask for Nelson, an’ tell him Tex Ewalt says to hold off h--l an’ high water before givin’ up these two. I’ll join you there as soon as I can. Here, listen close,” and he gave a description of Gunsight’s location sufficient for a rider of the plains. “Off with you, now--let her roll gently near Buffalo Crick--she’ll rumble deep crossin’ that bridge an’ Jake may be at home. So-long--get a-goin’!”

"But you?" cried Jane. "Where are you going? Surely not back into that town!" The distress and anxiety brought a smile to the ex-marshal's lips. "You must come with us! You must! You must!" she insisted almost hysterically. "You can't fight the whole town!"

"I'm bettin' he can," growled Murphy. "Here, Tex! Better take a couple av these little fire-crackers! Count five an' let 'em go; but *you* better count sorta fast."

"No, thanks, Tim," laughed Tex. "I can't go with you, Miss Saunders. I've got a pack of coyotes to make fools of--see you at th' SV in four or five days. Don't you worry--it was clean self-defense. He brought it on himself. All right, Tim: get a-goin'!"

He listened to the sounds of the cautiously propelled car, the clicks of the rail joints growing softer and softer. When they had died out, he walked swiftly back to the house, where he got his hat and coat and then went on to town. Going to where the roan patiently waited for him he led it to John Graves' stable and reconnoitered the building. John was not at home on this night of excitement.

Tex forced the door, and quietly saddled the sorrel and the gray, threw a sack of corn across the latter and, leading them forth, led the three animals back of a deserted building and then went toward the hotel.

Chapter XXII
The False Trail and the True

The maudlin crowd was ugly and did not accept the marshal's appearance with any enthusiasm. While he had not opposed them he had warned and sent away their hoped-for victims. Frank scowls met him wherever he looked. He stopped at the table where Gus Williams and a dozen cronies, the bolder men of the town, were drinking and arguing.

"Blascom's cussed sick," he announced. "Sick as a dog. I rode out to spend th' night with him, knowin' that when that coyote section-boss sent his pack out of town there wouldn't be no reason for me to stay here an' make myself unpopular. I got a good job in this town, an' I've got a right to have friends here. Anyhow, I told Murphy that if his men came back they'd have to do their own fightin'. Reckon that's why he sent 'em along. Him an' Costigan follered 'em on th' other hand car." He glanced over the room. "Where's Hennery?" he asked. "I heard he wanted to see me."

Williams roused himself and looked up through bloodshot eyes. "Th' fool's gone courtin', I reckon; an' on a night like this, when I needed him. Don't know when he'll git back. He mus' be enjoyin' hisself, anyhow."

John Graves chuckled and endorsed the sentiment.

Tex nodded. "I reckon mebby he is, his star bein' bright tonight. Much excitement in town after I left? Station agent make any trouble?"

"A lot of chances he'd 'a' had to make any of us any trouble," sneered a miner. "I reckon he cut an' run right quick. We've been figgerin' he's better off in some other town. Been thinkin' of chasin' him out. Any objections from th' marshal of Windsor?"

"Not a cussed one," answered Tex. "He's a trouble-maker, stayin' here. Chuck him on th' train tomorrow an' send him back East, where he come from. An' his sister, too, if you want."

Williams shook his head. "Not her," he said. "Henry'll never let her git away from him. He's aimin' to take care of her; an' he shore can handle her, *he* can."

"I reckon he can," agreed Tex. "I just come in to get th' doc to go out an' look at Blascom. Since he's struck it rich he's been feedin' like a fool. Them as live by canned grub, dies by canned grub, says I; an' he's close to doin' it. I got a bottle of whiskey for him, but I reckon gin will be better for his stummick. Yes, a lot better. Hey, Baldy!" he shouted. "Put me out a bottle of gin an' set up th' drinks for all hands. We'll drink to a better understandin' an' to Hennery an' his bride." He pulled the pint flask from his pocket and winked at his companions. "I got a little somethin' extra, here. Th' smoke of Scotch fires is in it. Might as well use it up," and he quickly filled the glasses on the table, discovering when too late that he had none left for himself. "Oh, well; whiskey is whiskey, to me. I'll take some of Baldy's with th' boys," and he swaggered over to the bar, tossing a gold piece on the counter.

"Where's yore badge, Marshal?" asked Baldy, curiously.

Tex quickly felt of his coat lapel and then of his vest. "Cuss it!" he growled. "I knowed I'd lose that star--th' pin was a little short to go far enough in th' socket. Oh, well," he laughed, holding up his glass, "everyone knows me now; an' they'll know me better as time goes on. Here's to Hennery!" he shouted. "Drink her standin'!"

The toast drunk to roaring jests, he took the gin and went back to Williams. "Goin' after th' doc," he remarked. "Lost my badge, too; but lemme say that anybody found wearin' it shore will have bad luck. See you all tomorrow. He's sick as a pup, Blascom is. Good night, an' sleep tight, as th' sayin' is!" he shouted laughingly and nodding at the crowd he wheeled and went out. Once secure from observation of any curious inhabitants of the town, he ran to the horses, mounted, and rode up to the Saunders' house, a home no longer. Entering it he quickly collected a bag of provisions and then, milling the horses before the door to start a plain trail, he cantered toward the station, where he crossed the tracks and struck south for the old cattle trail.

All night he rode hard, sitting the sorrel to keep his own horse fresh, and at dawn, giving them a ration of corn each, he ate a cold and hurried breakfast and soon was on his way again. During the forenoon he let the sorrel go, riding the gray with the depleted corn sack tied to the pommel. Several hours later he threw the still further depleted sack on the roan, changed horses again and turned the gray loose. After nightfall he came within sight of the lights of a small town and, waiting until the hour was quite late, rode through it casually to lose the tracks of his horse among the countless prints on its streets. He left it along a well-traveled trail leading westward, one which would take him, eventually, to Rawlins.

In the town of Gunsight, Dave Green was polishing glasses behind his bar when a dusty, but smiling, stranger rode up to the door and called out. Grumbling, Dave waddled forth to answer the summons.

"Which way to th' SV?" asked the stranger. "I'm lookin' for my friend Nelson."

"What is it--a house-raisin' or a christenin'?" asked Dave, grinning broadly. "Th' SV's gettin right pop'lar these days--as it ought to be." Dave cogitated a moment. This man said Nelson was a friend of his; but if not, there would be no harm done to anyone on the SV. Dave was quite certain of that, with Hopalong, Red, and the outfit at Johnny's back. Still, his curiosity was aroused. "Yore name Jones, or Ewalt?" he asked.

"Ewalt," replied Tex, grinning.

Dave left the door and gravely held out his hand. "Heard tell about you, long ago," he said. "We're good friends till you horn into a poker game that I'm settin' in. Heard about you this mornin', too. A tenderfoot, a cowpunch, an' a reg'lar picture in skirts stopped an' asked me what you did. Also wanted to know if I had seen Jones or Ewalt. You just foller that Juniper trail," and he gave a description tiresome, and needlessly detailed, to a man to whom compass points would have sufficed. "Jones comin', too? Don't know I ever heard of him."

"Jones is dead," said Tex with touching sorrow. "Th' pore ol' soul, we'll never see him more. He had buttons runnin' up his back, an' buttons down before."

"Too bad," replied Dave, but he was suspicious of the other's grief. He shook his head. "Life shore is uncertain. You tell Johnny if he's havin' a party that I ain't too fat to ride that far, not if I'm invited. I ain't much on dancin', but I'll do my best."

Tex nodded, thanked him for his information and went on, gradually becoming lost in introspective musings.

"Omar," he muttered, shaking his head sadly, "I ain't got no right. I'm hard-boiled, an' I've reached purty low levels th' last twenty years. There ain't no human meanness, no human weaknesses, hardly, that I ain't seen. My view of life is so cynical that it near scares me, now. I lost my illusions years ago, an' I'm allus lookin' for th' basest motives for a man's actions. Besides, I'm forty-odd years old--an' that's *too* old.

"Now you take Tommy Watkins. He's fresh, young, chock-a-block with illusions; trustin', ambitious, steady. He's clean, body an' mind. When he grows up, ten years from now, he'll be a purty fair sort of a young man. It shore does beat all, Omar."

A little farther along he drew a deep breath and patted the roan. "Omar, I've made up my mind: Youth should be for youth; illusions, for illusions; freshness, for freshness; innocence, for innocence. Her purity deserves better than my mildewed soul--if a man's got one." After a moment's silence he patted the horse again. "Omar, yore name brings somethin' back to me:

> *Ah Love! could you and I with Him conspire*
> *To grasp this sorry Scheme of Things entire,*
> *Would not we shatter it to bits--and then*
> *Remould it nearer to the Heart's Desire!*

Raising his head he saw a rattlesnake sunning itself on a rocky patch of ground near the trail and his gun leaped into crashing life. The snake writhed, trying in vain to coil. A second shot stretched it lifeless.

"There, d--n you!" shouted Tex, shaking his fist at the quivering body, "that's how I feel!" and, the burst of passion gone as quickly as it had come, he shook his head and rode on again, calm and determined. At last he came to the top of the last hill hiding the ranchhouse and drew rein as he looked down into the north branch of the SV valley. A boy was riding along the bottom of the slope and Tex hailed him.

"Hey, sonny!" shouted the ex-marshal. "I'm lookin' for Hopalong Cassidy. Know where he is?"

"He's at th' house!" replied the boy. "Yo're Tex Ewalt! Foller me, an' I'll beat you to him!"

"Bet yo're Charley!" responded Tex. "Yo're shore goin' to ride some, cowboy, if you aim to beat me!" and a race was on.

There came a flurry of movement at the ranchhouse door and three men ran to their saddled horses. A sudden cloud of dust rolled up and the three, bunched leg to leg, raced toward the galloping newcomer. Heedless of Charley's vexatious appeal they shot past him and kept on while he swung his pony around and saw them sweep up to the slowing roan and surround him and his rider. More soberly, after a hilarious welcome, the four, with Charley endeavoring to wedge into shifting openings not half large enough for his pony, they rode up to the ranchhouse, where Jerry had run out to meet them, Margaret Nelson at his heels. As soon as he could Tex asked for Jane and learned that she was resting.

"She has been under a very heavy strain, Mr. Ewalt," Margaret told him. "She asked that you see her as soon as you came; but she is sleeping, now, and it will be better for her if you wait. Her remorse is as great as her horror and fatigue."

"I suppose so," replied Tex. "That's the woman of it. She shot a beast in plain self-defense and now she's remorseful. Shucks--it's all my fault. I should have done it, myself, days before."

"I didn't say just what I think is causing her remorse," replied Margaret, smiling enigmatically; "but that is something a man should find out for himself," and, turning quickly, she entered the house.

Tex stared after her and then around the circle of happy, grinning faces. An answering smile crept to his own, a smile wistful, but shaded with pain.

The next few days were busy ones from a conversational standpoint, for there was a great deal to talk about. Tex learned the history of the SV's rejuvenation, and his friends eagerly listened to the news he brought from Montana, and to the messages he brought from their friends; while Jane, much better because of the rest she had had, sat by the cheerful group, smiling at the perfect accord between its units and rapidly changing her ideas of western men. Here she saw friendships which seemed to be founded on the eternal rock, unshakable, unquestioning. She found it almost impossible to believe that these thin-lipped, yet kindly and smiling men, whose trick of looking out through narrowed lids at first made her wonder, each had killed again and again, as Margaret had told her. To her they were gravely kind, courteous, and deferential, accepting her without question, their manner a soothing assurance as to her safety. Jerry and Tommy were unquestionably accepted and made part of the happy circle--they were friends of Tex Ewalt, whom she now knew by his right name. Johnny's boyish enthusiasm and mischievous smile made it hard for her to believe that he, single-handed, had overcome the odds against him and cleared this range of its undesirable inhabitants. Margaret's proud account of his deeds rang true, and Jane knew that they were true.

There they all sat on the front porch, telling anecdotes on each other which amazed Jane, speaking of remarkable exploits in matter-of-fact voices. She learned of Tex's part in the saving of Buck Peter's ranch, and gradually pieced together the story of his activities in Windsor. Prodded by Tex, at last Johnny and Hopalong gave a grudging exhibition of revolver shooting which made her catch her breath. Tex Ewalt had been right: these two cheerful men could ride into Windsor and wipe it from the map; and she no longer feared the appearance of any of Williams' friends. If they could find and follow the trail, let them!

Tex was the quietest man in the party, and she was pleased because he spoke only in the vernacular. She had not heard him deviate from it for one instant. He had no wish to "show off" at the expense of his roughly speaking friends. Tommy's garrulity, considering how little he really had to say, sounded like the prattle of a child among grown-ups; but he was a good, well-meaning boy. Daily he spoke of getting work on the Double X, where Lin Sherwood could use another rider; but he had made no attempt to go, preferring to stay where she was and to follow her about at every opportunity.

Then came the afternoon when Johnny volunteered to show his guests about the ranch and they had set out, Tex remaining behind. Jane had felt a restraint at the thought of how close she and the ex-marshal would be thrown together on this ranch, but soon found it to be groundless. Deferential, reserved, friendly, he had not obtruded, and apparently had not noticed Tommy's attentions. They rode off, Jerry with their host, Tommy at the side of Jane. When down in the main valley Johnny had turned off to look at the fenced-in quicksands, Jerry going with him to see the now harmless death trap, and Tommy remained behind with her; and when they returned they found a flushed Jane and a despondent Tommy. The following morning when she sat down to a late breakfast with Mr. Arnold, Johnny's father-in-law, she learned quite casually that Tommy had gone to the Double X and that the rest of the men, her brother included, had ridden up to the north wire to make some repairs. Arnold explained about the difficulty of keeping the posts up along the bottom of the ravine where he had suffered his broken leg, and he told her of the fondness of the cattle for the wilderness of brush and of the difficult task of running a round-up on that part of the ranch.

"Let me throw a saddle on yore horse, Miss Saunders," he suggested. "It will make a pleasant ride for you; an' you can take 'em up some lunch if you like. They've got a bigger task than they think, for th' ravine floor is solid rock. I'll send Charley with you--he's on th' rampage because he overslept and I wouldn't let him go up and bother them. But he might as well go."

She thought for a moment, and then turned a grave and pitiful face to him.

"I feel that I can ask you anything, Mr. Arnold; and I'm so upset."

"You certainly can, Miss Saunders," he replied, abandoning the vernacular in response to her way of speaking.

She hurriedly told him of the killing of Henry Williams, of the blood on her hands, but avoided the real appeal, the question she must find her own answer to. He heard her through, and, arising, placed a fatherly hand on her shoulder.

"Jane," he said, slowly shaking his head. "Environment, circumstances, change all things. There's not a man on this ranch that doesn't feel proud of what he knows about you. A woman has as much right, and often a greater need, to defend herself, as a man has. Don't you worry about that beast; and don't you worry about anyone coming down here after you. We can muster forty fighting men, if we need them, purely on Johnny's say-so. We're all proud of you. Now I'll saddle your horse while Peggy puts up the lunch. You and Charley can easily carry it between you. There's no place down here where you can't safely go; but please keep in the saddle while you're on the range. These cattle are dangerous to anyone afoot."

While the simple preparations were being made she heard Charley's exultant whoops and soon she rode with him toward the upper end of the small valley, listening to his worshiping chatter about his heroes. Now he had a new one, the man who could pull poker hands out of a fellow's nose, eyes, and ears.

"He'd 'a' got that Hennery feller, too," he averred, "only you beat him out. Gee, Miss Saunders! Wish I'd 'a' been there! I ain't never shot nobody yet--but you just wait, that's all! I heard Tex say he'd 'a' shot up th' whole d--d town if they'd tried to bother you--an' Hoppy said he could 'a' done it, *easy* ! Hoppy knows, too. Why don't you like Tex, Miss Saunders? I think he's aces-up!"

"Why, I do, Charley. Whatever made you ask me that?"

"Well, if you do, Tex don't think so," he grumbled. "You know that pile of rock, up on th' hill where th' Gunsight trail winds like a letter S?"

She nodded. She could see it plainly from her window.

"Well, I was layin' up there, keepin' watch for that Williams' gang, an' he never even reckoned anybody was near him!" he boasted. "Takes a good man to find me when I don't want him to, I tell you. Injuns can't, an' they're cussed cute, Hoppy says."

"Who was it who didn't see you?"

"Tex," chuckled the boy. "He come walkin' along like there wasn't nobody around, an' he sorta slammed hisself down on th' rock next to th' top one. You an' Tommy an' Jerry was ridin' back from th' main valley. We could just see you, me an' him, only he didn't know *I* was there. After awhile we could see plain. Jerry rode off to look at somethin', an kinda fell back, leavin' you an' Tommy goin' on without him. I was watchin' Tex, because he had a funny look on his face. He just looked steady, an' when he saw you two ridin' along together, he threw out his arms an' said somethin' about bein' like Jerry. Somethin' about falling back an' seein' you an' Tommy ridin' through life together--as if anybody would ride as long as that! Tell you what: These grown-ups say some cussed foolish things. There was tears in his eyes--him, a grown-up, gun-fightin' son-of-a-gun! Huh! An' they used to tease me when *I* cried! What you think about that?" He looked eagerly at her for the answer and then snorted in frank disgust. "Cuss it--an' yo're snifflin', too! I'll be a son-of-a-gun!"

"You mustn't tell anyone about it, Charley!" she pleaded. "They won't understand!"

"I won't," he promised. "Don't blame you for bein' ashamed. Tex would 'a' been, too, if he knowed I saw him. Then mebby he wouldn't go up there every night an' watch yore window till the light goes out, an' I wouldn't have nobody to trail. Reckon he's scared that Williams gang will trail you down here? Huh! With him settin' up there, me roamin' loose, an' with Johnny, Hoppy, an' Red in th' house, I shore wish they would come a-pokin' their noses around here! I tell you, things'd shore pop. If Tex could clean out their whole town all alone, they'd shore have a pleasant time down here ag'in' him an' his friends! Gee!"

After supper the nightly gathering on the porch passed a pleasant hour or two and then dwindled as its members retired, the two women and Charley going first. Jerry followed soon afterward and not much later Red and Hopalong left to go to the bunkhouse, where they now were berthed. Arnold soon went into the house, to the room which Tex stubbornly had refused to occupy, the latter preferring the bunkhouse with his old friends. After a cigarette or two Johnny said good night and left his companion alone. Tex arose, paced restlessly to and fro across the yard and, wheeling abruptly, went toward the corral. He had not been gone very long when Charley, noiselessly crawling out of the window of the room he shared with his father, froze in his tracks as he heard a noise beyond the summer kitchen. He had Red's Winchester, which he had taken from the gun rack in the dining-room, and he scouted cautiously toward the suspicious sounds. The moonlight let him see plainly, and he drew back behind the corner of the building as Jane rode away, leaving the light burning brightly in her room.

Charley frankly was puzzled. "Somethin's goin' on," he cogitated. "I was goin' to stalk Tex--now I dunno. Shucks! He can look out for hisself, but she might get lost. Reckon I'll foller her." He suited action to the words and soon was riding after her, keeping out of her sight with a woodcraft worthy of his elders.

She led him along the Gunsight trail, closer and closer to the S it made up the rocky hill, and because of the view commanded by the rocky pile on the summit, he had to dismount, picket his horse, and proceed on foot, working from cover to cover, often on hands and knees.

Tex had taken his time, buried in thought, oblivious to everything outside of himself. He followed the well-marked trail instinctively and soon reached the top of the hill, where he sat quietly in the saddle for a few minutes. Finally, shaking his head, he dismounted and listlessly walked to the place of his nightly vigil. Seating himself on the top-most bowlder he gazed steadily at the yellow light of the distant window and, like many men of his class, given to solitude, he argued his problem aloud. It seemed that often he could think more clearly that way.

This could not go on. Tomorrow he would start back to Montana, and he soon arose to return to the SV, to spend his last night there. As he went back to his horse another verse came to his mind, a verse of finality, and one fitting the present situation. He laughed bitterly and flung out his arms:

> *And when like her, O Sákí, you shall pass*
> *Among the Guests Star-scatter'd on the Grass,*
> *And in your blissful errand reach the spot*
> *Where I made One--turn down an empty Glass!*

Suddenly he stiffened, his hands leaping instinctively to his guns. Then he let them fall to his sides and stared unbelievingly: "Miss Saunders!" he exclaimed in amazement. "Why--what are you--?" and ceased, tongue-tied.

"You are--going away?" she asked, her voice breaking, speaking so low he barely could hear her words.

"Tomorrow."

She hung her head for a moment and then turned a wistful, anxious face up to him. "I--I heard what you have been saying. O Tex--I--I am going with you!"

Footnotes

1. The boy and girl history of David Jones (Black Jack) and his sister, Veia (called Jill) was well known to some of the old timers who went to Montana in the first gold rush and stayed there. It was difficult to get them to tell it and one was sorry to have heard it, if successful.